PRAISE FOR
ASTOR PLACE VINTAGE

"This utterly engrossing novel gives us a portrait of one of the most fascinating cities in the world where long after the book has ended you will walk the streets in your mind."

—Stephanie Cowell, author of *Claude & Camille*

"A novel bound to be next summer's guilty pleasure! I love Amanda and Olive and how we come to understand what links them despite the passage of time. I love what Lehmann has done with the 1907 city—how real it is."

—Beverly Swerling, author of *City of Promise*

"A splendid banquet of fashion, style, and both old and contemporary New York City, couched in a riveting story. A feast not to be missed!"

—Lynn Cullen, author of *The Creation of Eve*

"Anyone who loves vintage clothing, feels the pull of nostalgia, and has a taste for retro will be utterly transported by this wise and wonderful novel. A mesmerizing story about two women separated by a century but united by a quest for independence, a talent for business, and the challenges of being a woman that arise in every era."

—Pamela Redmond, author of *The Possibility of You*

Stephanie Lehmann

A TOUCHSTONE BOOK

Published by Simon & Schuster

New York London Toronto Sydney New Delhi

Touchstone
A Division of Simon & Schuster, Inc.
1230 Avenue of the Americas
New York, NY 10020

First Touchstone trade paperback edition June 2013

Designed by Ruth Lee-Mui

Manufactured in the United States of America

1 3 5 7 9 10 8 6 4 2

Library of Congress Cataloging-in-Publication Data
Lehmann, Stephanie.
Astor Place Vintage / Stephanie Lehmann.
p. cm.
"A Touchstone Book."
1. Women—Fiction. 2. Vintage clothing—Fiction. 3. Diaries—Fiction. 4. Manhattan (New York, N.Y.)—Fiction. I. Title.
PS3612.E355 A88 2013
813'.6 2012031168

ISBN 978-1-4516-8205-2
ISBN 978-1-4516-8206-9 (ebook)

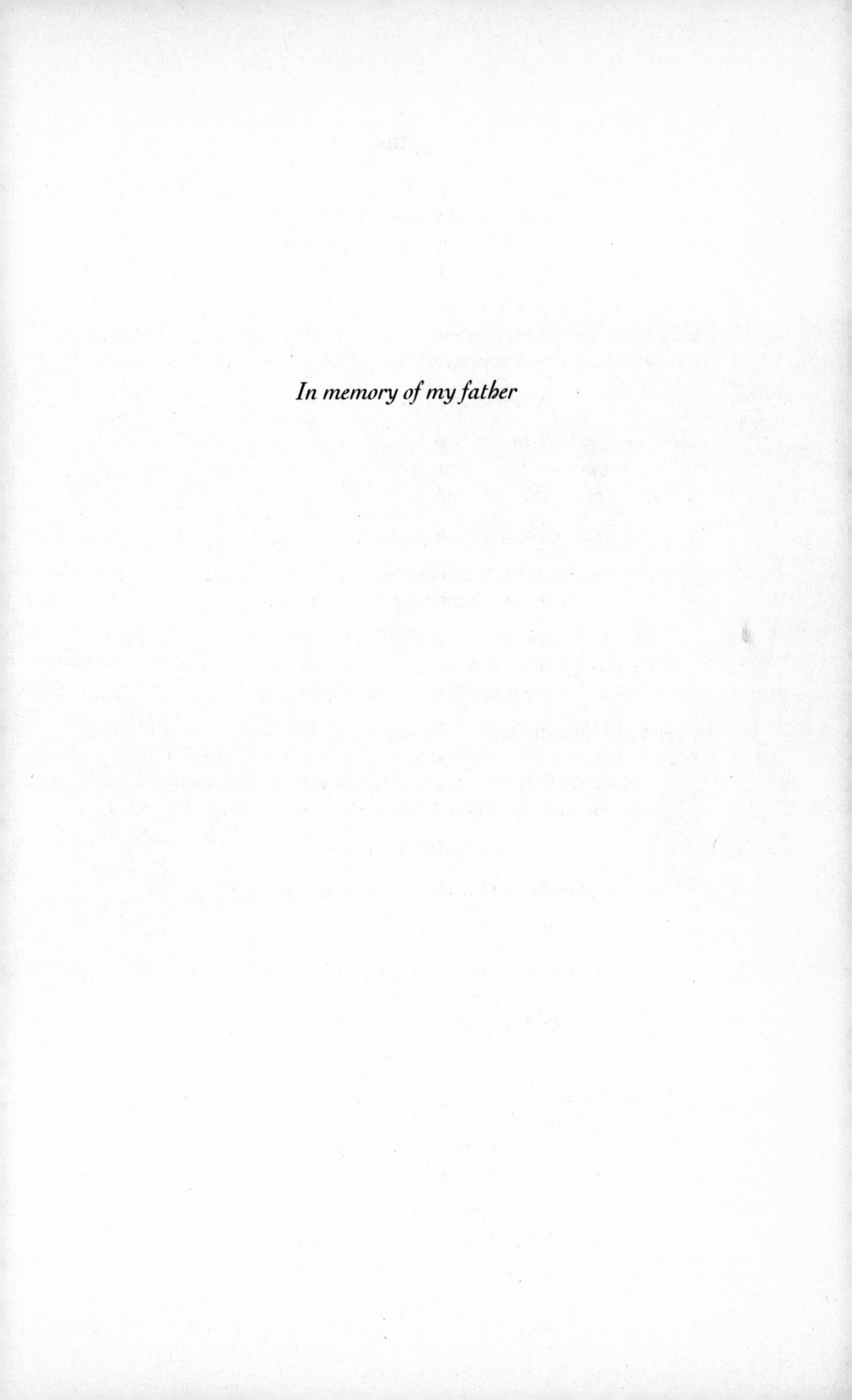

In memory of my father

Taxi stand on Madison Square, 1900

TUESDAY

JUNE 12, 2007

AMANDA

MY APPOINTMENT WAS in an apartment building called Stewart House—a white brick high-rise on Tenth Street, near Broadway, built in the sixties. I'd walked past it many times but had never been inside. The corner balconies, circular driveway, and chandeliered lobby made my tenement, just a few blocks away, seem downright prehistoric, though my rent was modern enough.

Fifteen floors up, at the end of a long hallway decorated with framed impressionist posters from museum exhibitions, a barefoot man wearing jeans and a T-shirt stood at the door. I guessed he was in his early forties, clinging to his twenties. Or maybe I was projecting. It happened to be my birthday, and I wasn't too thrilled about turning thirty-nine.

"I'm here to see Jane Kelly," I said. "She called about some clothes."

"Come on in."

He gave me a look-over as I stepped inside. I couldn't tell if he liked what he saw. Whatever. I found him attractive enough but not my type. Black hair, tan, a beard. I didn't go for men with facial hair—too scratchy.

He led me into a tidy living room furnished with Danish teak furniture, an amoeba-shaped coffee table, and a curved-back chair that might have been an original Eames. Furniture dealers would be salivating, but I wasn't there for the tables and chairs. In the corner, a tiny woman with sparse wispy gray hair sat hunched over a desk, staring into a computer screen.

"Grandma? Someone here about clothes."

Funny to hear a grown man calling someone Grandma. On the other hand, with a grandparent as old as this lady, he could be a member of AARP. Did he live with her? Maybe he was a good guy taking care of his aging relative—or maybe he was just a freeloader.

"The secondhand shop?" she asked, still staring at the screen.

I preferred "vintage clothing store" but let it go. "Amanda Rosenbloom from Astor Place Vintage. You asked me to come by?"

"He was going to call the Salvation Army," she said while scrolling down the front page of NYTimes.com. "Can you believe it?"

Grandson gave me a thumbs-up and left the room. The old woman didn't turn around. I peered out the set of triple windows. They faced north, so no direct sunlight warmed the room, but the high floor offered a spectacular view of Union Square, the Flatiron, the Empire State Building . . .

"Nice view," I said. She still didn't turn around. I stepped forward and cleared my throat. She clicked onto the obituary page. Maybe her hearing was bad. I stepped closer and spoke louder. "Would you like to show me what you have?"

"I don't see how a business like that can make it." She clicked on a headline about the death of "Mr. Wizard" from a TV science show back in the fifties. "How many old clothes can a person sell in a day?"

I let silence answer that one. She finally turned and peered at

me through her glasses. Then she rose, her freckled, bony hand gripping the top of the chair for support. So frail. Too skinny. Not long for this world. I couldn't help but think of skeletons.

"I'm getting rid of it all," she said, reaching for a metal cane leaning against the desk. "Cancer. Nothing they can do. So it goes."

"I'm sorry." Unfortunately, in my line of work, part of the territory is relieving clients of their possessions when the end is near.

"Not a tragedy. Not at my age. Ninety-eight," she announced with pride. "Though I was hoping," she added bitterly, "to make it to a hundred."

Mrs. Kelly's point of view certainly helped put my own age problem into perspective.

"I'll show you what I have," she said. "Some are designer dresses. A Rudi Gernreich. You know how rare those are? The Salvation Army!"

"I'll need to sort through and see what has resale value." I set my hobo bag on the coffee table. "Then we can agree on a price." Taking baby steps to match her pace, I followed Mrs. Kelly out of the room. "I noticed this building is named Stewart House. Is that for the old department store?"

"The A. T. Stewart department store stood right here. Of course, by the time I was born, they were out of business and Wanamaker's had moved in."

"But Wanamaker's was across the street." I was sure of this. The subway station on Astor Place had an exit that used to go directly into the store. Now it led into a Kmart.

"They added that building later," she said. "This was the original."

"Really." I was miffed at myself for getting that wrong. "I didn't realize there were two buildings." I was a compulsive Googler, and my favorite search subject was Manhattan history, especially accounts of what used to be where.

"They called it the Iron Palace. Burned down in the fifties. A beautiful landmark gone, just like that."

I pictured the flames shooting into the sky right where we stood. "And now hardly anyone knows Wanamaker's existed, much less A. T. Stewart."

"Why should they?" She slid the two folding doors of her closet apart. A wide expanse of clothing hung neatly on wood hangers. "Set aside anything that might fetch a good price. Then we'll talk." She hobbled back to the living room.

An odd aspect of my work: "vintage clothing" is a euphemism for "clothing worn by people who are probably dead." Unlike other antiques, clothing had actually draped on a human being—clung to the skin, absorbed the sweat, and warmed the body. I tended to forget those ghostly associations while looking at potential merchandise; the excitement of the hunt took over as I searched through piece after piece, hoping to discover something precious and extraordinary.

Jane Kelly had been a snazzy dresser in her time. It was hard to imagine her shrunken frame filling out the assortment of fashions on the rack. I set aside some casual forties and fifties day dresses that would sell. A great collection of sixties cocktail dresses suggested that Jane's income had grown in tandem with an expanding social life.

The Rudi Gernreich was fantastic: a mod floor-length A-line knit dress in mint condition. The upper bodice had a low scoop neck with a tiny checkerboard pattern of black squares on a purple background. From the empire waist to the knee, the same pattern was blown up to larger size. From the knee to the hem was a reverse pattern of purple squares on a black background. Very mod, very op art. Could easily go for five or six hundred dollars.

A sexy hourglass dress looked like it might fit me, and the royal blue would go great with my pale skin and black hair. I decided to give it to myself as a present—assuming Mrs. Kelly and I agreed on a deal. It would be perfect for my birthday dinner. White peep-toe heels, crimson lipstick, and matching nail polish would complete the look.

After going through everything and making my selections, I came up with a number and hoped it would sound high. If she insisted, I'd go up to thirteen hundred for the lot. I took a few stacks of clothing into the living room. Mrs. Kelly sat on the sofa with her eyes closed and her mouth open. Unsure how to rouse her, I proceeded as if she were awake. "I'd be willing to pay you a thousand."

Her eyes flicked open. "For which piece?"

"All of it," I said, suppressing a smile.

"Are you crazy?"

"I'm in business." I crossed my arms.

"Two thousand," she said.

"Twelve hundred, but that's as high as I can go."

She pulled a sixties shift from the pile. Really cute, with a mod black-and-white flower-power design and an unfortunate stain on the bust that I hoped to get out.

"You don't want this. It used to be my favorite dress. I was at a party laughing at some stupid joke and spilled red wine . . . never forgave myself."

"I could take a shot at cleaning it."

"If you want to waste your time." She tossed it to me. "For eighteen hundred, I'll throw in the trunk." She nodded toward an old flat-top steamer trunk. It had a few scratches and age wear, but with some olive oil and lemon juice, it would shine up just fine. Still, I had no space to put that clunky thing, and nobody used them anymore.

"There's clothing inside," she said. "Things that go back a long time. We're talking Edwardian. On second thought, nineteen hundred for everything."

Amazing how the urge to bargain could be so strong, even when facing the grave. "May I look inside?"

"Go ahead." She leaned her head back on the sofa and closed her eyes again.

Kneeling on the parquet wood floor, I removed a stack of *New Yorker* magazines and lifted the top. A whiff of dust shot up my nostrils with the familiar cocktail of mothballs and mold. A removable top shelf was crammed with buttons, lengths of ribbon and lace, white silk gloves, and a faded but darling striped parasol.

The main part of the chest was packed tight. Someone smart, presumably Mrs. Kelly, had stored the clothing inside pillowcases—a good way to protect it. Inside one, I found some white cotton nightgowns. The next one had some petticoats and camisoles. Another held a surprise treasure: a matching fur stole and muff. The plush stole was about a yard long, with a fox head and two feet on one end, the tail and two feet on the other. Black vacant glass eyes stared back at me; small white fangs seemed poised to bite. A label on the stole said C.G. GUNTHER'S SONS FIFTH AVENUE NEW YORK. The label made it worth more. I snuggled my hands inside the muff. Something hard pressed against my knuckle.

Strange.

I looked inside. The black satin lining had been torn at the seam and sewn closed with uneven stitches. Had someone hidden something inside? A wad of cash, perhaps?

I sneaked a look at Mrs. Kelly. She snored lightly with her mouth hanging open. Did I dare investigate? I crept silently across the room to retrieve my hobo bag. The big brown leather bag originally belonged to my mother. She bought it back in the seventies on one of our excursions to Altman's department store. Decades later, I rescued it from the top shelf of her closet. Now the soft and slouchy bag went with me everywhere, and so did the sewing kit I kept inside.

Sitting cross-legged on the floor by the trunk, I dug out the old Schrafft's candy tin that held my sewing supplies. I used the seam ripper to remove enough of the stitching so I could pull out the object hidden inside: a black leather-bound book.

Inside the front cover, the name Olive Westcott had been written in neat cursive script. I turned the page and realized it was a journal. Why had it been sewn inside the muff?

A feeling of déjà vu came over me, as if I'd done this before, right here in this room. I shook it off and read the first entry.

September 18, 1907

I've had this journal for ages. Father gave it to me when I turned twelve and I never bothered to use it. Now that I'm twenty I finally have something to write about. As of today I'm an official New Yorker! Father is managing the Woolworth's on 34th Street and we've just moved in to an apartment-hotel on the corner of 29th Street and Madison Avenue. It's awfully grand and up-to-date: long-distance telephone, electricity, hot and cold running water, steam heat, and—luxury of luxuries—daily maid service. I can't wait for my future to begin!

I wanted to read more. The adventures of a young woman arriving in Manhattan never got old for me. I could ask Mrs. Kelly to let me borrow it, but what if she refused? Did she even know it was there? It would be simpler to just take it and return it later, no harm done.

After checking to make sure Mrs. Kelly was still sleeping, I slipped the journal into my hobo bag—totally impulsive and dishonorable and not like me at all, as if I'd momentarily been possessed.

Turning back to the trunk, I continued to sort through. Everything appeared to have been laundered before being stored and was in good shape; no moisture or creepy-crawlies had compromised the condition. A white lace tea gown might sell; some women liked using those as wedding gowns. Otherwise, hardly any of it would appeal to my customers. The long skirts were heavy and cumbersome. The white puffy shirtwaists did nothing to flatter a woman's shape. Inside the last pillowcase, I found the prettiest item: a gorgeous green satin dress with a purple sash. I held it up to admire.

"That's in perfect condition," Mrs. Kelly said, almost giving me a heart attack. Her piercing voice gave no clue that she'd been asleep.

"Not really," I replied. "The material is extremely fragile, and these perspiration stains under the arms will never come out."

"You could put that on right now and go to dinner at the Plaza."

"If the Plaza wasn't closed for renovations because it's being turned into condos."

"The world is going downhill fast," she said with a crooked smile. "I'm lucky to be getting out now."

I sighed in sympathy—and to prepare her for my verdict. Clothing from before the twenties was more often for display than for wearing. It was almost cruel to traumatize the delicate fabric and trimmings by inserting a body. I'd be nervous letting customers try it on. "I don't generally carry stock this old. As much as I love clothing from this period, I don't get the sort of customers who would buy it."

I preferred dealing with clothes from the thirties to the sixties, and only pieces I really loved. I had a special attraction to minidresses, go-go boots, and black capris. Funny how styles from your own parents' day tend to call out with that seductive aura of nostalgia. Fashions that evolved after the sixties never impressed me like clothes from earlier decades could. The seventies were practically ruined by polyester. That material would probably survive along with the cockroaches after the human race got wiped out by global warming or the next ice age, whichever came first.

"Just give me two thousand for everything," Mrs. Kelly said, "and we'll call it a day."

We were back at two thousand? "No, sorry."

"Are you telling me these lovely garments aren't worth as much even though they're older?"

"They're worth something—sometimes quite a bit. They just don't move well. Look, here's what we could do. I'll take the other clothes for twelve hundred, and I'll take the things from the trunk on consignment. If they sell, we'll split it. The trunk itself you can keep. I don't have room for it."

"What's the split?"

"Sixty/forty."

"Sixty for me?"

I smiled. "For me." On that, I would not budge.

"Fine, take it," she said, as if everything had turned into garbage. "I don't want to see any of it again."

"Before I go, I'll make up an itemized list of the consignment pieces, and I'll need you to sign my standard agreement on the terms."

"Go ahead." She aimed a remote at the television. "Do what you need to do."

While she watched *The View,* I wrote out an inventory of all the Edwardian clothes from the trunk. After that was done, I handed her the list, along with a copy of my agreement and a pen. She put on her glasses and read every word of the agreement before signing it. She didn't bother to check the list.

"I can take a few things with me," I told her, "but would it be possible for you to have the rest delivered to my shop?"

"I'll have my grandson bring everything else."

"That would be great," I said, taking care not to reveal the journal as I opened my hobo bag. I placed the hourglass dress, stained A-line, stole, and muff at the top. "When he comes, I'll give him a check for the rest. Here's a card with all my contact information."

"I know where you are," she said, waving a hand in dismissal.

"Okay, then." I started out of the room. Clearly, she wasn't going to say good-bye, so I added for my own sense of closure, "Nice meeting you."

There was no sign of the grandson, so I tried opening the front door, but it was locked. I turned the deadbolt, but the door still didn't open. The grandson reappeared. "I'll get that."

"That's okay. I've got it." I turned the bottom lock, but the door refused to open.

He turned the deadbolt back to its original position. The door opened. "There you go."

"Thanks," I said, wishing he'd let me do it, though I knew he was just being polite.

"Take it easy," he said.

I nodded. "You, too."

As I walked down the hallway, past the impressionist posters to the elevator, he shut the door behind me.

OLIVE

"ANYTHING INTERESTING IN the news?" I asked, spreading a thin layer of butter on my roll.

"Not much," my father said from behind the paper. "The tone at the stock exchange seems more cheerful. Lots of talk about recovery."

I dabbed a bit of marmalade on top of the butter. "We've heard that before." Just two weeks earlier, Father and I had moved to Manhattan from Cold Spring, a town about two hours north of the city by train. My favorite part of living in our brand-new apartment-hotel was breakfast delivered every morning on a dumbwaiter. Boiled egg, bread basket, pot of coffee, butter, marmalade, copy of the *Sun*, and a bud vase with sprigs of fresh flowers; no effort required beyond carrying the tray to your table.

"At any rate," Father said, closing the paper, "the market closed firm."

"Let's hope it's a trend."

"Don't you worry, Olive, those bears will be shaken out soon."

Like so many others, he'd lost a chunk of money in the market that past March. I didn't know exactly how much. Father rarely divulged details about his investments, but I had utter confidence in his expertise. He'd always been perfectly responsible when it came to our finances. As a Woolworth's manager, he earned about ten thousand dollars a year, more than enough for us to live comfortably, and we had no reason to worry about future prospects. With everyone worried about the economy, it was an excellent time to be in the business of selling cheap goods. The Woolworth empire was doing better than ever.

"Do you have any special plans for today?" my father asked. "Or just taking inventory again?"

That's how he referred to my frequent visits to the department stores. I could spend hours analyzing stock and comparing prices. "As a matter of fact," I said in my most efficient-sounding voice, "I do have more merchandise to inspect."

"You really ought to treat yourself to a new gown for the dinner next month."

"That's very generous, Father dear, but I already have some perfectly lovely dresses."

Frank Woolworth was planning to throw a party in his Fifth Avenue mansion with Father as a guest of honor. It would give him an excellent opportunity to socialize with the New York executives. But Father seemed more eager for me to mingle with any eligible bachelors who might be in attendance. Though I had nothing against the idea of meeting someone who would sweep me off my feet, past experience suggested that I'd remain planted on the ground. I'd never been in love and wondered if any man would inspire such feelings.

Truth be told, I'd never been the inspiration for any boys from Cold Spring to fall in love, either. Perhaps I was too tall—or doomed by an urge to prove myself the more intelligent one instead of flirting pleasantly, as I was supposed to.

"I don't mean to badger, Olive, but you're such a pretty girl, and it would seem you don't want anyone to notice."

"You only think I'm pretty because I'm your daughter," I said with a pout.

"That's ridiculous. You're far too modest. And a new wardrobe is the best way to build up confidence. Take some enjoyment in your new status as a young lady in New York."

He couldn't let go of the idea of my becoming a fashionably decked-out ingenue. I preferred the simplicity of a skirt and waist. Comfort was more important to me than appearance. I didn't bother with a corset. No point trussing myself up with laces and bones, especially considering my figure, which resembled—or so I'd been told—the proverbial beanpole.

"You're very sweet," I replied, "but I don't need a shopping spree to feel better about myself."

"Thank goodness all my customers don't feel the way you do. In fact, I'd better finish getting dressed, or I'll be late."

Father hurried off to his bedroom. I poured myself another cup of coffee. Growing up around the Woolworth's that Father managed had undoubtedly taken some of the thrill out of shopping for me. Over the years, on weekends or after school, I often volunteered to fill in if the store was busy or a girl was out sick. I liked the sense of purpose it gave me and, I suppose, a feeling of superiority over the customers, who seemed so vulnerable as they scoured the aisles for bargains and cheap treasures.

I much preferred the practicality of working in the store to academics. After I graduated from high school, Father convinced me to spend a year at Miss Hall's, a finishing school in Lenox, Massachusetts, where I suffered through ladylike classes in deportment, art history, and the proper way to set a table. By the end of my stay, I'd learned one lesson particularly well: I had no talent for the domestic arts. I returned home secure in the knowledge that I was far more likely to succeed in managing a business than a household.

Now I wanted to learn more about the mind of a customer. What made an object so desirable that someone couldn't feel content without it? Why did a purchase lose its allure so quickly after being bought? Did people repeat this ritual compulsively in spite of the short-lived satisfaction—or because of it?

Father returned while buttoning his cuffs. I armed myself at the door with his fedora and coat. I couldn't help feeling proud of him—fit, trim, and handsome at forty-two, with thick wavy brown hair and a healthy complexion. Though I did so want to please him, I would never manage to conform to his idea of what a young lady ought to be. Indeed, he'd be unhappy to know that I was more intent on taking up a career than finding a husband.

"I worry about you spending so much time alone," he said, shrugging on his coat. "It's a shame we don't have family here anymore. I mean to track down some old friends, to see if they might introduce you to some young people."

"So you've promised," I said with affection, handing him his hat. He grew up in Greenwich Village but hadn't kept up with his old acquaintances since moving away over twenty years ago. "Please don't fret about me. You know how thrilled I am to be here."

"Perhaps it's not everything you imagined," he said, peering into the mirror by the door to smooth his mustache.

"I've barely had a chance to find out."

"At any rate," he said, giving me a kiss on the forehead, "if I'm not too late tonight, we'll go someplace nice for dinner."

"That sounds grand."

After closing the door, I sat back down and turned to the "Female—Help Wanted" section. Skimming down the listings, I vacillated between optimism and hopelessness. Father was not completely off the mark about my solitude. Despite the thousands of people surrounding me, I was beginning to feel rather isolated.

I didn't see social engagements as the solution. Once I set my career into motion, that problem would take care of itself.

Unfortunately, the classifieds were proving as daunting as a love life. There were ads for shopgirls among the listings of stenographers, factory workers, and telephone operators, but my sights were set higher than a position behind a counter. I hoped to become a buyer for one of the department stores. From reading Father's subscription to *Dry Goods Weekly,* I knew that many store buyers were women, and within professions open to females, they earned the highest salaries. Although I didn't presume to be qualified to step right into such a job, surely someone would be seeking an assistant. Yet I hadn't come across one single listing for an assistant buyer since I'd begun the search.

Finally, that morning, my eyes landed on an advertisement that I could almost hear shouting directly at me. *Seeking assistant buyer, shirtwaist department, apply Macy's department store.*

I pictured myself meeting with a salesman from Chicago showing me shirtwaists for next season. After we were done, I'd speak with the copywriter about new advertisements for the circular. Then I'd find out if I could go on the next buying trip to Europe.

Of course, I couldn't do any of that until I snapped out of my dream world and got the darn job. I went to run my bath. As water gushed out of the shiny nickel-plated spout, I thought of our horrible bathroom back in Cold Spring. The ancient tin-lined tub was encased in a wood box that reminded me of a coffin, and the linoleum floor looked dirty no matter how vigorously it was scrubbed. Now I could enjoy soaking in a sparkling clean porcelain tub. The white tile walls gleamed, the water heated almost instantly, and a full-length plate-glass mirror was built in to the door.

Actually, I could've done without the mirror. It had always been easy to avoid looking at my body naked, and now I kept catching glimpses of myself. I'd never felt comfortable unclothed and had no memory of anyone seeing me that way, either. Even my doctor had always let me wear a petticoat and camisole if I had to be examined. By the same token, I'd never seen another person naked. If not for museums, I'd have no idea what lurked under a man's union suit.

While luxuriating in the warm water, I debated over what to wear for my interview and decided on a smart navy blue dress that had a matching bolero jacket trimmed with a white band of lace. Thanks to Miss Hall's, I knew how to look refined when I needed to. The interviewer would see a tall young lady, handsome if not beautiful, with good taste and breeding.

By the time I finished dressing and was ready to go, my confidence had been replaced by a bad case of nerves. I hastened to my bureau, where I kept a journal hidden inside a muff that used to belong to my mother.

October 2, 1907

I'm finally going to my first interview. Must not doubt myself. Why the deuce wouldn't they hire me? I'm more than qualified—that shall be obvious. I simply need to stay calm and stop being a ninny.

The elevator took me down to the marble-floored lobby of the Mansfield. The red-haired doorman wished me a good morning. "Cab, miss?"

"No thank you."

I never asked for one, yet he posed the same question every time I stepped outside. Perhaps he disapproved of a young woman walking about the city by herself—or perhaps I imagined his disapproval because I wasn't used to such freedom. At any rate, it was ridiculous to worry over the doorman's opinion.

As I passed the Madison Square Garden, banners for the

horse show flapped in the wind. I probably should've brought an umbrella. Rain clouds blocked every bit of sun. I continued past an imposing church on the corner and remembered that Aunt Ida's letter still needed a response. She'd asked which church Father and I had decided to attend. My pious aunt, Father's younger sister, had come to live with us after my mother's death. I couldn't admit to Aunt Ida that we hadn't bothered going to services since moving to the city.

Up ahead, the steel framework of the Metropolitan Tower rose to the sky in its odd, half-built magnificence, set to become the tallest building in the world. The construction site blocked the sidewalk with piles of marble and steel, so I crossed the street and cut through Madison Square Park.

I heard the woman shouting before I saw her. Was she in trouble? Following the voice, I realized someone was making a speech. I found a lady standing up on a rostrum before a small gathering of people. She wore a white tailored suit and a hat with sweeping yellow plumes. Behind her, a yellow banner said: VOTES FOR WOMEN.

"I implore you not to silence the voices of your loving wives and mothers!"

I looked around at the crowd, nearly all men, and wondered if her words touched them.

"Don't deny your daughters the basic right every citizen of this nation deserves."

One young man standing near me threw an apple core that whizzed past the woman's head. She ignored it and kept on.

"Nothing shall change unless you join the fight! The future is in your hands!"

It didn't seem right that only men could give women the chance to vote. Why should our future be in their hands?

She raised a clenched fist in the air to conclude, "Give women the power to vote!"

A few in the crowd jeered, but most applauded politely. As

everyone dispersed, I continued to Broadway, exhilarated to be living in the middle of everything. Father liked to complain that the city had gone downhill since his boyhood, but I thought our neighborhood was as lovely as any Parisian boulevard. Not that I'd ever been to Paris, but Miss Hall had taken our class to the art gallery in Pittsfield to see the French impressionists. My dear best friend, Daisy, used to rhapsodize over the beauty of those paintings. She had a talent for drawing and longed to become an accomplished artist.

Daisy. If only she could be with me now. We'd been inseparable at Miss Hall's. There was great symmetry to our friendship: She was short, I was tall; she was creative, I was practical; she had a widowed mother, and I had a widowed father. Both of us fostered ideals about female equality, inspired by writers like Charlotte Perkins Gilman and Harriet Martineau. We'd planned to become independent women together. That would require convincing our parents to let us share an apartment in New York. We'd reject the tyranny of marriage and put all our energy into pursuing careers. She'd become a great artist while I succeeded as a businesswoman.

On the other side of the park, I came to a stop in order to prepare myself for crossing the street. Horns blared, bells rang, and whips cracked at the intersection where Fifth Avenue crisscrossed with Broadway in front of the Flatiron. When a lull in traffic finally came, I stepped off the curb. To my right, taking advantage of the same lull, a rubberneck wagon loaded with sightseers pulled out of its parking space. I sprang back as the driver braked to a stop. The guide sitting up top with the tourists shouted into his megaphone. "Go on, now, miss, make it lively!" I wasn't sure if he was being courteous or wanted to see if I'd make it across alive.

Charging into the street, I clamped my hat to my head while dodging a pushcart coming from the left, a delivery truck from the right, and a clump of horse manure down below. After triumphantly reaching the other side, I surged forward with my fellow pedestrians up Broadway. I had to walk quickly to keep up with those around me.

As it turned out, after we graduated from Miss Hall's, Daisy spent the summer touring Europe with her mother. When summer was almost over, I received an apologetic letter from her telling me that our plan to live in New York would have to be delayed. She had the opportunity to study art in London for a year at the prestigious Royal Academy. I was delighted for her and miserable for myself. That year had already passed, yet Daisy continued to live in London without any more apologies. Our scheme of sharing an apartment in New York had been a nice fantasy while it lasted.

I was fast approaching Thirty-fourth Street. Knowing Father's Woolworth's was nearby, I couldn't help myself from a furtive search for his face in the crowd, even though I knew running into him was highly unlikely. After crossing the wide thoroughfare, I joined a stream of women funneling into the double doors of Macy's. A pink-cheeked man stood behind the information booth. I asked him to direct me to the employment department.

"Take the moving staircase to the fifth floor," he said. "Walk to the very back of the store and go through the green door."

I thanked him and strode directly toward the escalator, but the sound of a tenor singing a popular tune tempted me to take a detour. I followed his voice to the sheet music counter, where a handsome young man in a black tuxedo sang while playing the piano.

Come away with me, Lucille, in my merry Oldsmobile . . .

Father would appreciate that song; he'd been the first person in Cold Spring to own an automobile. The very week our blacksmith installed a gasoline pump, Father dashed up to Poughkeepsie and bought a Runabout. The machine still sat under the porte cochere back at our house. I knew it had been hard for him to leave his favorite toy behind.

Down the road of life we'll fly, automobubbling, you and I . . .

Two women standing next to me didn't let the music disrupt their conversation. I couldn't stop myself from listening in.

"My husband is in a frightful state over the stock market," said one. She wore a picture hat weighed down with artificial fruits. "He keeps threatening we'll move to the suburbs if it doesn't go up soon."

To the church we'll swiftly steal, then our wedding bells will peal . . .

"Would you go?" asked the other, who wore an egret-plumed toque.

"I'd kill myself first."

Their hats bobbed up and down in agreement.

You can go far as you like with me in my merry Oldsmobile . . .

I would've liked to stay and admire the handsome singer, but the morning was slipping past; I forced myself to walk directly to the moving staircase and began my journey to the fifth floor.

3

AMANDA

AFTER LEAVING MRS. Kelly, I had time to kill before my next appointment. My birthday gift from my best friend, Molly, was an appointment to see a hypnotist, which hopefully would help me get over my sleep problem. I was skeptical, but she was a big fan of this guy—a legitimate MD who helped her quit smoking. God knows, lecturing Molly on how smoking would give her cancer, wrinkles, and a voice like Popeye had never done any good, so maybe there was something to it. At the very least it might be entertaining.

His office was a few blocks away, on MacDougal Street across from Washington Square Park. I strolled down Fifth Avenue, glad to be out on a warm, not too humid Tuesday afternoon. This was the second day of what counted as my "weekend." Saturdays and Sundays were the busy times in my shop. I decided to relax in the park and take another look at that journal. An empty bench had a good view of the Washington Square Arch. Just as I opened up the journal, a stroller-pushing mom sat down next to me. She beamed with pride over her baby, so I offered my admiration. "What a cutie. How old?"

"She's six months."

The baby's mouth widened into a charming toothless smile. "She's adorable." So adorable that it hurt. I didn't need reminding as I clung to my thirties that I'd yet to reproduce. For no apparent reason, the baby's smile turned into a grimace, and she began wailing like a banshee.

"It's time for her nap," the mom said miserably, "but she refuses to sleep."

I offered her a look of sympathy; at least I was free to escape. Checking my cell phone as if a pressing appointment demanded my presence, I put the journal back in my bag and wished them a good day.

Dr. Markoff's office was in a prewar building on the corner. The doorman nodded me through, and I entered the waiting room ready to explain to the receptionist that I was early. There wasn't anyone to greet me, though, only the whooshing sound of a white noise generator. Settling in on a green twill sofa, I yawned. If only I could bottle the drowsiness that plagued me during the day so I could use it at bedtime.

I opened the journal and forgot to be tired while reading about Olive Westcott and her ambition to be a department store buyer. I'd once considered that career myself. When I was growing up, Manhattan department stores were still considered an attractive destination. Tourists included the New York City flagship stores in their sightseeing, along with Broadway shows, restaurants, and museums. Suburban malls had no glamour, no history, no character. As nationwide chains they'd lost their soul.

Macy's, Altman's, Lord & Taylor, Bloomingdale's . . . As a little kid, I'd loved going with my mom. The scent of perfume when I walked in; all those pretty women, so sophisticated, behind the makeup counters; bright lights, shiny mirrors, and glimmering cases of jewelry. Festive—like a holiday year-round. In the girls' department, Mom would let me try on dress after dress. I marvel now at her patience. Would I be so tolerant with my own daughter? Would I have the chance to find out?

By my teen years, shopping with Mom had morphed into a classic power struggle, but I went to department stores with friends or, even better, by myself. By the time I was in my twenties, even the city stores had lost their pizzazz, as if no one could remember why they'd been worth visiting.

The sound of a man clearing his throat brought me back to the waiting room. "Miss Rosenbloom?"

"That's me."

I'd expected someone younger, wearing perhaps a black jacket over a black turtleneck and sporting a little pointy beard. Turned out Dr. Markoff was about seventy years old—tall and gaunt, with gray hair and age spots. He wore a dark suit, a white button-down shirt, and to my delight, a red bow tie. As he motioned me into his office, I gave a cheerful hello and smiled as if I didn't have a care in the world.

At first glance, his office looked elegantly conventional, with a blue and red Oriental rug, a couch, and a Chippendale claw-foot desk. I noticed an old phrenology chart on the wall. It showed a human head with the brain divided into different areas that supposedly determined particular character traits.

We sat opposite each other in two easy chairs: his big and leather, mine not so big, microfiber, in need of reupholstering. Two bookends on the shelf behind him were in the shape of a human head divided down the middle.

"So," he said, "how can I help you?"

"I've been having trouble sleeping."

"Insomnia?"

I didn't like that word. It made my problem seem more like an illness. "Well, it's just that for months, I've been staying up until four or five in the morning, and then during the day, I'm constantly tired."

"Yes, insomnia. I imagine you've already tried the usual remedies?"

"Nothing works. My friend Molly, who referred me, said you helped her quit smoking. Maybe I should try a different kind of sleeping pill. I tried Ambien for a while, but then it stopped working."

"Sleeping pills can be addictive. I'd recommend them only as a quick fix for the short term. But hypnosis can be helpful, especially when the problem is related to obsessive, negative ruminations. Do you feel open to trying?"

"I don't know. Maybe I should ruminate obsessively about it for a week." I grinned so he'd know I was joking.

He gave me an obligatory smile. "It's important for the subject to be ready to make a change and believe that change is possible. It would help if I could get a sense of what's on your mind. Can you identify any problems or important decisions that might be keeping you up at night?"

I'd gone over the situation a million times with my ex-therapist and didn't feel like exposing myself to this stranger, but clearly, I'd need to spill some ugly secrets. "Well," I began, "I'm having an affair. With a married man. We've been together six years. I've been trying to break up with him, on and off, for the past five. Therapy was supposed to help me figure out why I can't."

"It didn't?"

"Not really." I'd analyzed every angle in therapy so often that even I'd gotten sick of talking about it. That didn't lead me to take action, only to avoid the subject in sessions, which made me feel uncomfortable, which made me put an end to it. Therapy, not the affair. At least Jeff spent money on me instead of charging an hourly fee. "It helped me understand, but understanding didn't help me do anything about it."

"And what did you come to understand?"

"Basically, I stay up getting angry with myself for wasting the prime years of my life in a relationship with a married man I'm attracted to for being unavailable, like my father, who made me feel unlovable because he abandoned me and my mom for another woman, blah blah blah." Dr. Markoff and I stared at each other for a bit. I crossed my legs. "What do you think of Xanax?"

"As I said, the mental dilemma won't be resolved unless you get to the underlying problem. Perhaps you'd like to give me a general sense of your parents' marriage?"

"Right." I crossed my legs the other way. "So my mother found out my father was having an affair the summer before I started high school. Since our apartment was small and the yelling was loud I knew all about it. I took sides with Mom and felt rejected along with her."

"It must've been quite upsetting for you," he said, looking straight into my eyes with a serious expression.

I nodded and continued, dodging his obvious attempt to empathize so I'd break down in tears. "He moved out. They got a divorce. The end."

"You were about to begin high school . . . where?"

"La Guardia."

"The public school? With the theater program?"

"And dance, music, art . . . That's where I met Jeff. He came from a wealthy family but was sick of private schools. Plus, they had a really good art program. That's how we met, in a painting class."

"And what was your relationship like?"

"Really good. We started going out junior year. I lost my virginity with him, went to prom with him. It lasted two years."

"And then?"

"After high school, he went off to RISD to study architecture. I stayed in the city and went to FIT for business and fashion. The separation was sad but not horrible. I mean, we were young; it wasn't like we were going to get married. Occasionally, we'd meet up for coffee when he was in the city. We lost touch after a while, but a friend of mine spotted his wedding announcement in *The New York Times*. His fiancée was a descendent of J. P. Morgan. They were getting married at the Pierre Hotel. Later, I heard he lived up in Westchester and was designing houses for rich people. I guess he was slumming with me back in high school."

"And how did you reunite?"

"About six years ago, I was managing a vintage clothing store down on Mott Street. Jeff read an article in *New York* magazine that quoted me on the best places to shop in SoHo. He came to the store under the pretense of buying a present for his wife. Then he asked me out to dinner."

"And?"

"We've been seeing each other ever since," I said, punctuating the statement with closure. I didn't want to go into the dismal details.

"What about your father?" Dr. Markoff asked.

"He lives in Costa Rica. In a yurt."

"A yurt?"

"Uh-huh." I refrained from rolling my eyes.

"I can see this isn't easy for you to talk about, so thank you for sharing those details. Do you have any questions for me?"

"What if you hypnotize me and I never come out? Or my mind goes somewhere really upsetting?"

"Hypnosis merely puts you into a more receptive state. While your mind is open, I try to help you focus on the fears and anxieties that are holding you back. If you don't like where your thoughts are going, or you don't want to be in the trance anymore, you can always decide to come out. It's not like I'd be in control of your brain."

I nodded so he'd think I was reassured.

"But," he added, "you really do need to be open for this to work."

I wanted to be open. At the very least, I wanted to come through for Molly. We'd known each since we both went to FIT. Now she had her own store a few blocks away from mine—a teensy-tiny shop selling vintage buttons.

Besides, Dr. Markoff wore a bow tie. Bow ties never should've gone out of fashion. "I'd like to try."

Dr. Markoff nodded toward the couch.

I lay down, adjusted my skirt around my legs, and faced the ceiling. It surprised me, how vulnerable I felt to be splayed out in front of him.

"I'll tape our session," he said, "so you can take it with you to play at home when you're going to sleep. It might help put you in a relaxed state of mind. Before we begin, I'd like you to think of a place where you feel very comfortable and content."

"My apartment?"

"Somewhere you go to escape, to get away from your usual routine. It could be a beach, the woods, a mountain . . ."

"Nature makes me nervous."

"A place of worship."

"I'm not religious."

"Anywhere that helps take your mind off your troubles."

"That would be looking for clothes."

"A store? That's fine. Which one?"

He went for that? I was half joking. I rarely shopped for new clothes. So much stuff was overpriced or too generic. And as much as I liked thrift stores, they tended not to smell very good. I'd been thinking more of the hunt for merchandise to sell, not to buy.

"Somewhere that makes you feel secure," he said.

I could hear the impatience in his voice. Obviously, this part of the procedure wasn't supposed to be such a challenge. I could say a department store, but that applied more to how I remembered them than the way they were now. The store that appealed to me most no longer existed. “I’m thinking of Altman’s department store, except they aren’t in business anymore.”

“That’s fine. It exists in your mind, in your memory, and that’s all we need; that’s all we really want. Shall we start?”

OLIVE

WHILE RIDING THE moving staircase up to the second floor, I found myself behind a little girl pleading with her mother to buy a doll. The mother said the girl had enough dolls. The girl began to cry with all her might. I couldn't imagine having the patience to be a parent. As an only child, I'd never even held an infant in my arms.

Some of my girlfriends back in Cold Spring were already mothers; when they went on about their babies' alleged accomplishments, I could barely manage to pretend interest. I'd never quite fit in with the girls in my town and often used to doubt myself for being too odd.

When I met Daisy and we became good chums, I decided the girls from Cold Spring were too conventional, and I ceased caring if I was odd. That attitude was fine while living at Miss Hall's, but after returning home, I found it harder than ever to socialize with my old friends.

Mostly, I divided my time between helping Aunt Ida with the

chores and sitting on the porch swing staring into the trees. As the summer passed, a sense of melancholy came over me. My aunt already had her routines well established; trying to make use of me was probably more of a nuisance than anything else. Whereas she seemed to derive deep satisfaction from her efforts to clean and sanitize, I felt only futility and ineffectiveness, as if the act of trying to wipe out every germ that lived inside our house was gradually making me disappear. I decided to ask Father for a regular paying job at the store.

If I'd been a son, hiring me on as his assistant manager would've been a natural development. Since I was his daughter, he wouldn't even consider allowing me to "debase" myself by working for an hourly wage.

"Stop your crying!" the mother in front of me yelled. "Or I shall take you straight home!"

The little girl raged even louder. Luckily, when we reached the second floor, they stepped off and veered toward the shoe salon, and I could journey to the third floor in relative peace and quiet.

Father's attitude was not unlike that of his employer, Frank Woolworth, who believed the proper place for women was in the home, despite the fact that he employed hundreds of countergirls. To carry out his philosophy, he never promoted his female workers, and he paid a low fixed wage. This was for their benefit, so to speak, so the job would be seen as a temporary condition before marriage. This stance certainly benefited Mr. Woolworth, seeing as lots of the countergirls stayed in their positions for years without a raise.

With no employment other than housework, I felt utterly useless by the time my birthday came around in August. The anniversary of my birth had always been a dubious event, since it was also the anniversary of my mother's death. But I found that year particularly distressing. I turned nineteen, and my mother died at nineteen. Nothing could point up more keenly how unfairly short her life had been: finished and done at the same age I now had the privilege of frittering away. She never should've given up her existence for mine. If only we could go back in time and trade places.

Arriving on the third floor, I joined a cluster of women stuck behind an elderly lady who stood before the next flight of rising stairs as if working up the courage to hop on an amusement park ride. I came up beside her and offered my arm. "Would you like to step on with me?"

She hooked a fragile hand in the crook of my elbow and gave me a most grateful look. "Thank you, dearie."

We stepped forward together as if in a dance. Standing beside her, I couldn't help but feel tenderly for my frail partner. "Everything moves faster nowadays, doesn't it?"

"Dreadful how it's changed since I was a girl."

"I can imagine," I said without bothering to champion the merits of progress. "I think it's grand that you venture out despite the challenges."

"What would you have me do instead?" she asked. "Sit in my room all day?"

By the end of that summer, all I wanted to do was stay in my room. Sometimes I didn't want to get out of bed. Since I didn't know what to do with myself, I couldn't see the point in doing anything. Nothing seemed worth the effort. Everything was a waste of time. My appetite disappeared, and my naturally thin figure became gaunt. Out of nowhere, I'd tear up and cry.

Aunt Ida finally called in the family doctor. He prescribed bed rest, leeches, and when he noticed the stack of *Dry Goods Weekly* on my nightstand, the banishment of all reading materials.

"Here we are," the old woman said as the moving staircase reached the fourth floor. We stepped off together, she let go of my arm, and we wished each other a good day. As she wandered off to the gourmet food section, I continued on to the fifth floor.

The memory of that doctor's advice had the power to infuriate me still. In a sense, he did help restore me. My anger toward him fueled a healthy surge of energy that no amount of bed rest could have achieved. I refused his leeches, insisted the magazines stay where they were, and got myself out of bed. His ridiculous Victorian ideas reminded me that my sense of worthlessness was a reasonable response to a society bent on limiting the sphere of women.

That very day I presented Father with an ultimatum: Give me a regular job at the store, or I'd ask for employment in every shop on Main Street, and my first inquiry would be with his chief rival, Mr. Gottlieb, owner of the general store across the street.

Father compromised by giving me an official position behind the counter, but to ensure that my womanhood wasn't tainted, he made it clear to my coworkers and our acquaintances that I was doing it simply to amuse myself. Despite the lack of pay, my mood improved. Yet I wondered if I was doomed to spend the rest of my life in Cold Spring.

At last, I'd reached the fifth floor. I stepped off the moving staircase with the triumph of a mountain climber reaching the summit. My heart raced as I found the green door to the employment office.

Turning the knob, I entered a hallway where a young woman instructed me to stand at the end of a line to receive an employment application from a receptionist, who then directed me to enter a room where I found about a dozen women filling out their cards. I noticed with dismay that I'd overdressed. Almost all my competitors wore simple skirts and waists.

After finishing my application, I was ushered to yet another room, where I was surprised to find rows of benches crowded with even more applicants. Others hovered in the back, wondering where to go. My heart sank. Were all these women here for my job?

An energetic woman with gray hair stood up front, telling the girls to sit in the order of their application numbers. "Please pay attention! We need your cooperation. Who has number twenty-nine? Please sit here."

I had number seventy-five.

I berated myself for failing to bring a magazine and fought off the urge to leave. My path to this moment had been too tortuous for me to give up now.

The financial panic swept the country after I'd been working at Father's store for about six months, almost a year after I graduated from Miss Hall's. Many fortunes were lost in the stock market, and businesses went under. But the Woolworth chain weathered the crisis without trouble, reporting in the June newsletter that eight more stores were slated to open in 1907. It was another announcement in the issue that had particular interest for me. A new manager was needed at the Thirty-fourth Street location in New York City, known as the "mother store," the biggest one of all. Wasting no time, I encouraged Father to apply, reassuring him that I'd love to live in New York City. To bolster my case, I reminded him that moving to Manhattan would greatly improve my chances for marriage. I didn't mention anything having to do with department store buyers or high salaries for women.

Father admitted that he'd already seen the listing and was tempted. The move would mean a substantial raise in salary, and since the corporation's home offices were in Manhattan, it could very well give him entrée into Woolworth's inner circle.

Despite his interest, a considerable obstacle remained. Aunt Ida considered Manhattan a den of vice to avoid at all costs; she wouldn't take a day trip to the city, much less move there. The woman had uprooted her life to take care of us. How could we leave her alone in Cold Spring?

As fate would have it, the financial crisis provided a solution. Margaret, a neighbor and dear friend of Aunt Ida's, had kept most of her savings in the stock market. The crash wiped her out, and she had to sell her house for income. Since people were strapped and banks were nervous to lend, she didn't get nearly what it was worth—or had been worth. Aunt Ida proposed that Margaret move into one of our extra bedrooms.

Father and I welcomed her into the household. She was a plump, sweet-natured woman who baked the best pies in the world. Of course, it didn't escape me for a moment that her presence would enable our move to New York. It wasn't until the end of summer that we officially knew Father had been appointed manager of the Thirty-fourth Street store.

"Number seventy-five? Seventy-five!"

I snapped to attention as my number was called. An assistant directed me to my interviewer's office. A thickset woman who appeared to be about forty sat behind a large wood desk covered with neat piles of cards. Her nameplate said MISS LILLIAN HAPGOOD.

"Olive Westcott?"

"How do you do?"

Without bothering to introduce herself, she told me to sit on the chair across from her desk. I folded my hands together as she read my card; by the time she looked up, my grip was tight enough to strangle a cat.

"And your letter of reference?" she asked.

"I'm sorry, I didn't bring one."

Miss Hapgood raised her thick eyebrows. "Why not?"

"I practically grew up in a store. My father manages the Woolworth's on Thirty-fourth Street, and before that, he managed the one up in Cold Spring. I've been working behind the counter since I can remember. You can be sure I know all about the dry goods business."

"How much were you paid?"

"I wasn't."

"So you don't have any actual work experience."

"I've got lots of work experience; I just wasn't paid for it."

She smiled with tight lips. "We're looking for girls with paid experience."

I tried to keep the irritation from my voice. "Even though my father didn't pay me, I had the same responsibilities as the other countergirls. We could telephone him," I said, though he might tell her to send me straight home. "I'm sure my father would be happy to speak with you."

"That's not necessary. We need to see a written reference from a previous employer showing you're an experienced salesgirl."

"Oh, but I'm not here for a sales position. I'm here for the job as assistant buyer."

"Even more to the point. If you want to become an assistant buyer, you'll have to start as a countergirl. How could we put you in charge of our salesgirls if you've never even worked?"

I felt my cheeks get hot. "I'm sure I could learn anything I need to know in a flash."

"Then learn it. And come back. With a letter of reference." She put my card on a pile. "Thank you for coming in."

I took my leave with all the dignity I could muster. This was the limit. To be dismissed so out of hand! Exiting past the other applicants, I strained to keep the tears from sneaking out until I'd made it through the green door. Tears! How mortifying. I refused to be so easily broken and wiped them off quickly. It wasn't as though I needed the money. To think she didn't see me as qualified for the lowly position of salesgirl!

I found my way to the ladies' lounge, a lair of femininity decorated with pink-and-white-striped wallpaper, magenta drapes, and plush pink carpeting. Women clustered in front of a brightly lit mirror while freshening up and redoing their hair; puffs and curls lay scattered on the counter. At least the other ladies hadn't a hint of the humiliation I'd just suffered. After splashing some water on my face, I eked out a place in front of the glass so I could fix my sagging Psyche knot.

The woman next to me powdered her face while telling her companion about an article in the morning paper. "They say Harry Thaw is getting his meals catered by the Astor House restaurant while he's locked up in the Tombs! Can you believe it?"

"Next thing you know, they'll hire an orchestra for him."

People couldn't get enough of the dreadful scandal surrounding Stanford White's murder. I had no sympathy for the deranged Mr. Thaw, who'd shot the famous architect dead.

"If they let me sit on that jury," the woman next to me replied, "I'd put him away for good."

"It would be grand to see Evelyn Nesbit on the stand, if only to see what she'll wear."

I left the lounge and took the moving staircase down. On the fourth floor, a heavenly scent lured me to investigate the gourmet food section, where a small crowd watched a young woman sautéing mushrooms in a chafing dish. "Chafing dish cookery," she proclaimed, "is the ideal way to solve the problem of small kitchens in New York apartments."

Still smarting from rejection, I had no intention of buying a chafing dish, though it was a clever idea. The Mansfield apartments didn't have kitchens—a detail my aunt found unbelievable. Father would be delighted if I made him dinner now and then.

When the mushrooms finished cooking in the buttery sauce, the young woman spread them on a tray, stuck a toothpick in each one, and invited us to try a sample. My fellow spectators descended on the mushrooms like soldiers starving on the front lines. I stepped in and took one before they disappeared. It tasted delicious. Still, I turned away without buying one. Even the prospect of pleasing Father with a home-cooked meal couldn't compete with my wounded pride.

AMANDA

THE BUTTON CLICKED as Dr. Markoff turned on a cassette recorder. Did they still manufacture those?

I want you to stare at the ceiling.

His ceiling was much higher than mine. I bet the walls were thicker, too.

Keep your eyes focused on the flat white surface and try not to blink.

This was exciting. I was good at not blinking. Maybe I was good at being hypnotized.

You very much want to blink, but I want you to resist that urge.

I blinked.

Your lids feel so heavy, the temptation to close them is too great. So now you can close your eyes if you like.

Relief.

Now I want you to focus on your body by relaxing each part. The soles of your feet . . . your calves . . . your thighs . . .

He went slowly, lingering on every part. I relaxed. This was nice. I just wanted to lie there listening to his rhythmical, soothing, monotonous voice.

We're going to let your unconscious hear what it needs to hear while you think about your relationships with other people.

Well, that wasn't going to relax me. I didn't want to think about Jeff or why I couldn't give him up.

Life is not always a straight line. You take detours and go backward and forward and sideways.

It wasn't like I'd been pining away for Jeff after we lost touch. He was the one who came to me at the store on Mott Street.

It's impossible to know everything from the beginning.

I sold him a white alligator bag. Then he asked me to dinner.

We need to live in order to learn about ourselves, and the world and other people.

By the time we were on dessert, he'd confessed that his marriage was a failure.

We wouldn't grow if we didn't make mistakes.

We began to see each other regularly, just as friends, though his wife didn't know.

So it doesn't make sense to blame yourself for living your life.

One night, when I was hopeless about finding anyone I wanted to be with more than him, we made love.

We can't tell the future.

I told myself we'd have our fling, and then I'd move on to that serious relationship I couldn't seem to find anyway.

We don't know how we'll affect the people we cross paths with.

Months passed and then a year. Jeff talked about leaving his wife but couldn't bring himself to do it. His two sons needed him. His wife would never agree to a divorce. They both came from money, and fighting over a settlement would get ugly.

You've faced many challenges before, and you can face new ones.

I'd suffered through my parents' divorce, so I understood the difficulties—minus the coming-from-money part. I hated the woman my father left us for. Did I want to become the other woman? Give his kids a reason to hate me?

Not by making something happen but by allowing it to happen.

It took me a year to tell my mother about my affair. It took her two years to stop telling me it was wrong every chance she got. Eventually, we learned to avoid the subject.

Because you're strong, you're independent.

I knew I was behaving dishonorably. Still, I couldn't give Jeff up, just hovered like a shoplifter waiting for the right moment to pocket the loot.

You're able to open up to new ways of thinking.

Molly had a theory: Since he was my first love and my first sexual relationship, all my intense reactions to him were physiologically imprinted on my brain. Now it was chemical, like an addiction.

Even though it's frightening to you.

After a while I realized he'd never leave her. We began to fight a lot, make up, fight. He said he wanted to marry me, but it was impossible.

It's scary to let him go.

I told him it was over.

It's scary to feel alone again.

I deleted his number off my phone. Accepted congratulations from my friends. Joined Match.com, JDate, and Chemistry. Tried speed dating, wine-tasting mixers, cooking-for-singles workshops.

But in the end . . .

I missed Jeff.

We are all alone.

He called one day during that horrible week between Christmas and New Year's. Said he was miserable without me. Had to end his marriage. Wanted to see me.

And opening up to new challenges may lead to the feelings of purpose and intimacy that you desire so much.

Much as it annoyed me, my heart filled with hope. He picked me up in a limo and took me to Le Bernardin, the most expensive seafood restaurant in New York City. I wore a black tulle strapless cocktail dress with embroidered dots and velvet trim.

So rather than feel ashamed for your past, you should feel proud of every experience you've had.

He told me he'd decided to divorce his wife. He would do it after his younger son went to college.

Because to be alive is to be engaged, take chances and live in the present . . .

His younger son was in the second grade. If I still wanted him when the time came, we'd be together.

Opening up to new challenges that will make you feel more vital and alive.

We ended up at my place, having the greatest sex ever. Started seeing each other as if we'd never broken up. I put his number back on speed dial.

So now I'd like you to go to that place where you feel strong and secure.

When I told my friends we were together again, they didn't want to hear about it.

The place of wisdom.

I felt like an idiot.

The department store.

I wasn't getting any younger. Soon no man would want me. I'd be dead stock.

Wandering up and down the aisles, looking at dresses . . . shoes . . . handbags. Everything you could ever want.

Dr. Markoff was really trying to make this department store concept work.

It's a wonderful place, isn't it? So many tempting things, but also wisdom.

It wasn't gonna work.

Somewhere in Altman's, there's a department of wisdom where you can find everything you need to know.

If only. Right behind the shoe department, past the escalator . . .

When you visit this place, you'll achieve a sense of calm that will allow you to fall into a deep, restful sleep.

Don't bet on it.

I'm going to stop talking now. You can take as much time as you need to let your mind wander wherever it needs to go.

This was idiotic. I didn't even like department stores anymore. I should've picked something else, like my mother's backyard. Why didn't I think of that before?

But no, actually. Altman's probably was the right choice. Elegant but not snobby, it was the place where I went for peace and quiet. I could escape from the sound of my parents fighting in the next room and transport myself back to a more innocent time, or just wander around when I wanted to be alone but not lonely. The bulk of their customers were secretaries from the Empire State Building across the street, or little old ladies who wore hats and gloves and rubbers over their shoes. Those ladies had shopped there for years and loved being served by gray-haired saleswomen who knew their names. I found it all tremendously reassuring.

The clothing selection wasn't the best, and almost everything they sold could be found cheaper somewhere else, but the atmosphere was all on the house. Even the ladies' room was more luxurious than our living room. Red velvet chairs, ornate gold-framed mirrors, marble drinking fountains with a spout in the shape of a dragon's head. Not exactly a home away from home; more like a mansion away from home.

The highlight of any visit—whether alone or with my mom—was the Charleston Gardens Restaurant on the top floor. One side of the room had an actual re-creation of a Southern plantation facade, complete with white columns, shuttered windows, and lit lamps. Trees painted on the walls made it feel like a pretend outdoor garden. Grandmotherly waitresses wheeled around carts of tea sandwiches, and they had the best peach pie for dessert.

In the nineties, when they announced Altman's was closing for good, I couldn't believe it. Hadn't the store existed forever? Wouldn't it stay until the end of time? Now it remained only in my imagination, or should I say the collective imagination of those old enough to remember.

So.

Dr. Markoff's voice jolted me out of my thoughts.

Now I'm going to count from ten to one. When I reach one, you will open your eyes. Ten, nine, eight, seven, five, four, three, two . . .

I didn't want to move. Didn't want to open my eyes. No wisdom had been found. It hadn't worked.

When he reached "one," I forced my eyes open. Had I been in a trance? I wasn't sure. Maybe I was still in it, but no. This felt like regular, everyday, sucky reality.

"How do you feel?"

"Fine."

"Do you want to tell me what came into your mind?"

Red carpets. Dragons. Pie. "I don't think so."

"That's fine," he said neutrally. "It's up to you."

But I knew: I'd disappointed him. Failed at my trance. Couldn't be hypnotized.

He removed the cassette from the recorder. "Here's the tape. I suggest you listen to it in the evening before you go to bed. Train yourself to focus on that positive place of wisdom. Eventually, you won't need the tape; you'll be able to go there all on your own, and falling asleep won't be so hard anymore."

I sat on the edge of the couch. "Is it a matter of suggestion? The power of suggestion? Isn't that what hypnosis is all about?"

"You already know the answers," he said in his kind, deep voice. "It's a matter of allowing yourself to hear them."

That sounded all nice and reasonable, but I didn't know the answers, so how could I hear them? I thanked him and showed myself out.

OLIVE

WHEN I STEPPED outside, the sky looked ominous with gray storm clouds. The stuffy heat inside the store had made me forget about the weather. A man on the corner hawked cheap umbrellas, but I didn't stop to buy one. Instead, I bustled through the crowds on the sidewalk. At first, the sprinkles felt refreshing on my face, but then they turned into raindrops that rapidly turned into a downpour. Dashing under the marquee of a small shoddy theater, I tried to ignore the barker yelling through a megaphone. "Come on in, ladies and gents, and witness the powers of Lola Cotton, the most amazing mentalist in the world! Next show in five minutes!"

I had no interest in seeing a ridiculous mentalist.

"Ladies without escorts welcome!"

The rain came down in torrents. The box office queue grew longer.

"Only five cents admission!"

Lightning struck. I bolted to secure a ticket before they sold out.

Inside the lobby, a young boy handed out paper and pencils. "Ask Miss Cotton any question, any question at all, and she'll give you the answer!"

"Can she predict the future?" asked a bald man with a white beard.

"You bet," the boy said.

I watched the man write something on his paper and seal it inside an envelope. The boy placed the envelope inside a cigar box.

"Do you have a question for Miss Cotton?" the boy asked me.

The offer tempted me, but only to prove Lola Cotton wrong. I had no real wish to embarrass her—or myself—so I declined politely and entered the theater.

The small auditorium smelled like mold, and the pianist yawned while playing ragtime, but at least it was warm and dry. I sat on a hard wood seat in the last row. Soon every seat was filled. By the time a skeleton-thin man in a bone-white suit appeared onstage, I was ready to be entertained. "Thank you for coming to witness the amazing powers of my daughter, Lola Cotton."

The audience applauded as Lola came onstage and stood next to him. She wore a simple white tea dress. Younger than I would've expected, fifteen or so, she had a lovely, serene face.

"You may be skeptical of my powers," she said, as though reading my mind, except that most likely was what everyone was thinking. "I would be, too, if I didn't know them to be real and genuine."

"I ask everyone to send out your best thoughts," her father said. "You must keep your mind open so her guides will be willing to communicate."

The boy came onstage and held out the cigar box. Lola reached inside for one of the envelopes. With posture as straight as the long braid that hung down her back, she held it up to her forehead with her eyes closed. "I'm getting the name Horace," she said. Then she peered into the audience. "Is a man named Horace in the room?"

A heavy gentleman in the fifth row stood up. "That's me."

"You ask if your fiancée truly loves you," Lola said. "Indeed she does, but you must marry her soon. She won't wait much longer."

Lola's father asked the man if his question had been answered.

"I suppose you'd have to ask my fiancée," he said with a chuckle, "since she's sitting right next to me."

The audience murmured, utterly ready to be taken in.

"I always said I'd be married by the time I turned twenty," she said, patting her tinted yellow hair. "Well, I'm turning thirty next week."

The audience laughed.

"Well then," the man said, "why don't we get married on your birthday?"

"Sounds jolly good to me!" she said.

The audience applauded with delight. My own mental powers told me these subjects were actors planted in the audience.

After Lola answered a few more questions from the envelopes, her father tied a black blindfold around her head. "Lola will now demonstrate her powers of magnetism. Her guides will draw her attention toward those among you who have departed loved ones sending strong messages."

A few moments of silence passed before Lola asked, "Will a young woman wearing a navy blue dress please stand?"

Certainly not me. I waited to see who would rise.

"She's wearing a gold locket around her neck," Lola said. "Heart-shaped. And I believe there's a star?"

My face turned red. I looked down at my locket. Gold, heart-shaped, with a star engraved on the front. The woman sitting next to me stared with such urgency that she practically levitated me with her gaze. I rose and held up my locket for all to see. The audience applauded.

Lola wasn't done. "Inside the locket is a photograph."

"Is this true?" the father asked.

"Yes," I admitted.

"Someone who looks very much like you," she said.

My heart was beating fast, but I refused to be taken in or give anything away.

"Your mother?" she asked.

Still I said nothing, though my cheeks burned.

"Her spirit is here with us," Lola continued. "She wants you to know . . . you must not feel guilty. She forgives you."

I couldn't resist asking. "For what?"

"She says . . . she says she loves you more than life itself."

I fought to swallow, despite a huge lump that had formed in my throat. Was she saying I shouldn't feel guilty for my mother's death? No one would blame an innocent baby, but it couldn't be denied that I'd been instrumental to ending her life. I couldn't possibly pose the question aloud—couldn't believe she'd fooled me into caring.

Lola Cotton moved on to her next victim. After a few moments, I opened the locket and looked at the photograph of my mother. Her straight hair was pulled up in a tight bun. Short sausage bangs fringed her forehead. Dark eyes stared straight ahead. I always thought she looked terribly sad, as if she'd known her life would be cut short. My aunt said we had the same chestnut hair, fair skin, and deep brown eyes. But I knew she was prettier, petite and delicate, whereas I had my father's tall frame and long limbs.

The rain had stopped. As I walked down the block, everything seemed somehow different, as though all the stores had changed their window displays during the performance. At the corner, I checked the street sign and realized I'd been going in the wrong direction. I laughed at myself. That performance had made me daft. Walking back the other way, I recognized people from the audience. Some of them stared curiously at me. At least Lola took my mind off that ghastly job interview. If only she could also find me employment as a buyer. And, while she was at it, bring my mother back to life.

October 2, 1907

One advantage to searching for a job in secrecy is that I don't have to tell Father about that horrid interview. But can I hope to find one without asking him to write me a reference?

After the waiter set down our oyster soup, I asked Father the question I posed every night at dinner. "And how was business today?"

"Not as good as I'd like."

The decor in the Mansfield dining room was nothing exciting: white tablecloths, green drapes, and paintings of various species of birds. But the prices were easy to swallow, and nothing could beat the convenience. "When the train station opens, I wager sales will boom."

I'd seen the construction site of the Pennsylvania Station—eight square blocks that used to be crowded with tenements, now a colossal dirt pit.

"If it ever opens," he said. "And how was your day?"

Between sips of salty broth, I told him all about Lola Cotton. "I must say, she spooked me a bit. How did she even know I was wearing the locket?"

"Didn't you say that boy spoke to you in the lobby? He probably saw it."

"Of course," I said with relief. "He must've told her." Why hadn't I thought of that? Because I wanted to believe, like the rest of the audience? "Still, the way she said Mother loved me more than life itself. Those exact words. 'More than life.' As if she knew what happened."

"You're giving her too much credit. Imposing your meaning on her words."

"I suppose. Every daughter feels guilty about something when it comes to her mother."

"And what mother doesn't love her daughter unconditionally?"

I gave my father a satisfied smile. But while sipping the last few spoonfuls of soup, I couldn't help thinking that my mother never had a chance to love me unconditionally. After all, she gave birth to me on the dining room table; soon after that, she was dead. I'd never asked for details—had always been afraid to know. Now that marriage and childbearing hovered in the air, I felt more curiosity than fear. I really ought to know. And it wouldn't require a mentalist to tell me. The man who knew sat right across the table. I was on the verge of posing my question when he announced they'd be using a new type of straw for the soda water fountain.

"The paper is saturated with paraffin wax," he said. "One straw will last through an entire drink."

"Sounds brilliant."

The busboy swept away our bowls as the waiter arrived with our entrées. My mouth watered as I inhaled the steaming chicken croquettes: deep-fried, cork-shaped mounds of chicken, mushroom, and cream. While he ate his steak with gusto, Father went on to complain about the aggravations of installing a soda water fountain in the store. The moment to ask had passed. I'd broach the subject of my birth later.

That evening, after changing into my wrapper, I joined Father in the parlor. He sat on his overstuffed chair, reading the latest issue of *The Horseless Age*. I curled up on the sofa with the evening paper and noticed a headline about Niagara Falls. My parents had gone there on their honeymoon. Evidently, another one of those daredevils had tried to ride over the falls in a barrel. The article described how a crowd looked on as an assistant closed the lid over his head. Two men hauled the barrel into the river and let him float away. They all watched as it slipped over the edge and plunged to the waters below, disappearing into the thick sprays of mist. Some men ran to fish him out. After opening the lid, they found him inside—dead. The poor man.

"The doorman recommended a garage," my father said.

I looked up from the paper. "Is it close by?"

"Second Avenue. I think I'll bring the car down."

"I'm glad you two will be reunited," I teased.

"According to this article, John Jacob Astor has twenty-two motorcars in his stable, and owning fewer than four is poverty."

"Then we must be quite poor indeed."

Father went to his desk to take a cigar from the box. He'd smoked the same brand since I could remember. On the top of the cigar box was the picture of a beautiful woman with long dark hair whispering into the ear of another beautiful woman with long dark hair. I'd always wondered what she was whispering.

"I have a question, Father."

"Only one?" he said, lighting the cigar.

"What happened when I was born?"

"That nonsense with the mentalist still troubling you?"

"No, I'm just interested to know."

The tip of his cigar smoldered with an orange glow. "Don't you worry about that, my little Olive." He blew a ring of smoke toward the ceiling.

"I want to hear the details. You don't have to coddle me."

"There are no details of any importance. She had a long, difficult labor. Lost a lot of blood. The doctor did what he could."

"You must remember more about what went wrong."

He sat back down and stared at me with a grave expression. "It wasn't your fault. Nature is flawed. She made the ultimate sacrifice in what is an all too common tragedy. And it won't do you any good to dwell on it." With that, he returned to his magazine.

If there was more to know, he wasn't going to tell me. I turned back to Niagara Falls. An illustration pictured the barrel falling. I wondered what the man thought about as he rode down. Was it a thrilling journey that ended abruptly before he knew his life was over? Or did he realize his mistake right away and plummet to his death full of regret? Everyone said the power of Niagara Falls was mesmerizing. I couldn't imagine tempting death like that. Life was precarious enough.

AMANDA

MY CELL PHONE rang just after I left Dr. Markoff's office. Caller ID flashed Jeff's name. "Hi there," I said.

"How's the birthday girl?"

"I went to the hypnotist and let him put me in a trance!" A man walking past looked at me and laughed. Did I just yell that? "I don't think it did anything, though," I said, lowering my voice.

"Maybe you're in a trance and you don't know it."

"Because I'm walking down the street naked?"

He laughed. "No, that sounds like the same old you."

"Very funny." But it was the same old me: answering his call, pretending to be cool with everything.

"So everything is set for tonight," he said.

Except I could snap out of this. Tell him I was done. What did Dr. Markoff say? *You know the answers.* "Great." *You just have to allow yourself to hear them.* "I can't wait."

"Eight o'clock. I'll text you the restaurant. Happy birthday."

We hung up. It was really bright out, so I put on my sunglasses while waiting for his text. Before it came, I got one from Molly.

Happy birthday! How was Dr. M? Can't wait to hear. xoxo Molly

I considered calling her but decided to wait until I got home. Since she'd paid for the session, I wanted to sound upbeat. I'd pull that off better after having a chance to chill out. Maybe, if the hypnosis actually worked, I'd be able to deliver a glorious success story in the morning.

Jeff's text came a minute later with the name of the restaurant. Eleven Madison Park—one of the hardest reservations to get in the city. Across from Madison Square Park, it was on the ground floor of a gorgeous art deco skyscraper that connected to the Metropolitan Tower.

Jeff and I shared a love for the city and its history. As an architect, he was compulsive about pointing out landmarks and architectural details, and I'd become somewhat of an expert myself. He was also a major contributor to my collection of books about Manhattan. Some were vintage, some not, but almost all were out of print. I had oral histories, biographies, photographic collections, guides for tourists from various decades, and history books written when Canal Street really was a canal. I could pass hours of slow stretches in the store flipping through them—the more photographs, the better.

Continuing down Washington Place, I approached an important city landmark: the building where the Triangle Shirtwaist fire took place. Since the fire was contained on the top few floors, the building survived. A plaque on the corner reminded me which year it happened: 1911. Olive was probably transfixed by the catastrophe, along with the rest of the city. Sometimes, walking by, I couldn't help imagining the horrible scene. I'd read about the bolts of fabric igniting into flames. Girls jumping out the windows. Dead bodies on the sidewalk right there, right under my feet. Historians called it the worst workplace disaster in New York City until the planes hit the World Trade Center.

Now the building was owned by NYU. Students probably didn't even know what happened up on those top floors almost a hundred years ago. I wondered if they ever felt haunted in their classrooms. Not that I believed in ghosts. I just liked to think about how we occupied the same spaces as people from the past.

My own family history made me feel tangentially connected to that disaster. My grandmother liked telling me about the day her mother arrived in America. As she was leaving Ellis Island, my great-grandmother was approached by a contractor who took her straight to a factory, before she even had a place to live, and put her to work. It happened to be a glove factory on Mercer Street, where she met her future husband, so fate allowed for my eventual existence.

I turned down Broadway to Fourth Street; a red light brought me to a standstill at the thoroughfare of Bowery where Greenwich Village officially morphed into the East Village. It felt particularly hot on that corner under the glaring sun; no cars came, so I crossed. Olive may never have ventured down to my territory. Back then, middle-class women avoided going south of Eighth Street. The Lower East Side stayed pretty seedy all the way into the fifties, when beatniks began to make it cool. In the sixties, people started referring to the area north of Houston Street as the East Village, and real estate agents latched on to the name to associate it with the romantic and quaint Greenwich Village. The Bowery now boasted a glitzy new art museum and luxury condos so expensive that foreigners had to buy them.

I reached my street, one of the nicer tree-lined blocks in the neighborhood. My store, Astor Place Vintage, occupied the ground floor of the building where I lived. Not that it was on Astor

Place—that was a couple of blocks north—but I figured the association with John Jacob Astor, Manhattan's first multimillionaire, couldn't hurt.

Lots of small businesses kept my humble street vibrant: a food co-op, a custom-made lingerie shop, hair salons, a cutesy coffeehouse with room for five tables, and a couple of off-off-Broadway theaters. When the used record store occupying the street-front retail space in my building closed down in 2002, I decided to go for it. I'd learned enough, managing the store on Mott Street, to run my own business, so why not be my own boss for a change? Rents in the East Village had plunged after the World Trade Center disaster, which made it possible to negotiate a five-year lease with a reasonable rent. The federal government coughed up a small business loan that helped get me up and running.

After a year in business, I found myself operating at a loss while taking a lower salary than I had while managing the Mott Street store. Then my accountant told me the store was in danger of going under. Neither of my parents had money to spare. Jeff offered to supplement my income with a monthly check that basically covered my overhead. Saving the store was worth compromising my dignity; I took him up on it.

By the second year, my reputation in the neighborhood had been established. I switched to new wholesalers who gave me a better deal buying bulk items; beefed up my website, AstorPlaceVintage.com; and began selling online through eBay. My accountant said I could give myself a small raise. Jeff insisted on continuing his support, and I didn't object. It felt good to have some security, and I'd pay him back with interest eventually.

My third year in business, I started therapy, which my health insurance didn't cover, so I continued to accept Jeff's monthly check. The irony that I might not need therapy if I could extricate myself from my married lover was not lost on me.

The past year, business grew so much that my QuickBooks

spreadsheet told me I could get by without the expensive accountant I didn't need now that I'd mastered QuickBooks. I still kept accepting Jeff's monthly checks. It had become more about emotional security than financial. I liked the idea that he wanted to take care of me. I liked being taken care of. Even if he did have a wife.

Sometimes the arrangement did make me feel like a whore.

On the other hand, the sign hanging in front of my store made me swell with pride: ASTOR PLACE VINTAGE in white lettering set against a royal blue background. And I *would* go through with cutting myself off from Jeff—financially and emotionally. I was on the verge of taking action. Soon. I really was.

After unlocking the front door of my building, I opened my mailbox in the entrance hall and pulled out a few letters. Then I checked the table outside the super's office in the rear, where the mailman left packages. Jackpot! Happy birthday to me. Three boxes: one from my mother, one from my father, and a seriously heavy one from Alabama that had to be my impulsive eBay buy from a few weeks back. I took two trips getting everything up the stairs and piled the packages on the hall floor to unlock the door.

As usual, my place was horribly cluttered. Too much secondhand furniture, flea market collectibles, sewing paraphernalia, bags of clothing waiting to be altered for the store. I turned on the air conditioner and wondered how people survived hot summers without one. To think that a hundred years ago, an entire family probably sweltered away in this little studio apartment. I'd read about immigrants at the turn of the century, visited the Tenement Museum on Orchard Street, and seen photographs of the Lower East Side by Lewis Hine and Jacob Riis. Fathers hunched over sewing machines, mothers and children making artificial flowers, boarders sleeping on the floor, more bodies huddled on the fire escape. I'd never even been on my fire escape; the window gates were too hard to open, and it would probably collapse if anyone stood on it.

I plunked down on my green camelback sofa with my laptop and checked e-mail. A couple of eBay auctions I'd posted had ended with respectable bids. I really needed to step up my store's online presence, but the impersonal online selling world was a drag. Plus, I hated the drudgery of photographing clothes, getting all the precise measurements, and coming up with pithy descriptions.

Karin and Patricia, two old friends I'd known since middle school, had both sent birthday wishes. Karin had suggested getting together for dinner on Saturday at the Greenwich Grill, a sushi place in Tribeca. Patricia had responded with another option, a new place on Fourteenth Street called Home Cooking. The fried chicken and buttermilk biscuits were supposed to be amazing, she said.

It sounded great, but to protest the audacity of calling a restaurant "home cooking," I voted for sushi. Then I opened an e-mail from my mom.

> Hi sweetheart, thinking of the moment I first looked at your darling face that beautiful day you came into this world. Did you get my present? I couldn't resist. Love you, xo, Mom

My mom used to work in PR for the Metropolitan Museum of Art, one of those New York City jobs that offer an attractive setting and interesting coworkers in exchange for a salary that keeps you on the edge of financial ruin. Retired now, she lived up in Woodstock in a cottage my parents had bought when I was a baby, for escapes from the city. Like me, Mom wasn't much of a country person. She felt comfortable there despite all the nature—partially because it was filled with disaffected ex–New Yorkers and had good restaurants, and also because of the plethora of yard sales and flea markets.

When I was a kid, we'd have the best time driving around to find bargains. She taught me to fearlessly ask sellers if that was their best price, pretend I had only a certain amount in my pocket, and assume a forlorn expression before asking: will that do? When we accumulated too much stuff, we'd hold our own yard sale.

My father loved Woodstock because the spiritually enlightened hippie town indulged his fascination with transcendental meditation, yoga, and adultery. An affair with the woman who taught his Reiki class broke up their marriage. After a few months of fighting with my mother, he moved to an ashram in Northern California with his girlfriend. When the official divorce came a couple of years later, Mom got the Woodstock house in the settlement.

Done with e-mails, I turned to my letters and noticed that something had come from the managing agent of my building—probably about my lease coming up for renewal. I set it aside; he'd already warned me about the 6 percent rent hike. No hurry to look at the numbers in black and white, especially with packages waiting to be opened.

Since I knew what was inside, I opened my eBay package first, ordaining the extravagant purchase as a birthday present to myself. Removing the bubble wrap, I admired my new set of Homer Laughlin Kitchen Kraft dishware from the forties. The pattern of red tulips and blue pansies sprouting from flowerpots was so cheerful and adorable! I shouldn't have; the last thing I needed was dinnerware for eight. My Formica dinette seated four, and my sewing machine occupied half the surface. But maybe one day, if I ever married and moved to a larger apartment, I'd make use of it.

Next I unwrapped my mother's present, another head vase, most likely. Over the years she'd given me half a dozen of these vases in the shape of a head with a hole on top for stems. Some people collected baby heads, clown heads, Madonna heads . . . They were popular in the forties and fifties. Mine were all heads of attractive women wearing some variation of accoutrements, such as a faux pearl necklace, dangling earrings, a pillbox hat. My mother always wrote a pun on the card. *It's good to get aHEAD . . . Two HEADS are better than one . . .*

I opened the box: a head vase. I smiled while shaking my head at my new head. She wore a powder-blue hat with a large yellow bow on the side of the floppy brim. Her chin rested on a white-gloved hand. The card said, *Have a happy birthday, but don't lose your HEAD.*

Time to open my father's present. His Reiki instructor was ancient history; he now lived in a Costa Rican ecovillage community of about forty people. They grew their own food, bathed in waterfalls, and were devoted to taking care of the planet for future generations. Fine, but couldn't he have been around a little more to take care of me, his own future generation? I opened the box to find a bracelet made with pink and green stones. I read the printed enclosure.

> Wearing this jewelry clears the energy center to restore optimism, dissolve grudges, and revive hope. For best results, wear for ten days.

Ten days? I wouldn't wear it for an hour. Did he really think that after all these years, he'd convert me into a Zen zombie? He'd written a note on a plain white card made from 100 percent post-consumer waste.

> *Dear Amanda,*
>
> *The fourth chakra affirmation evokes clarity of the heart. The rose quartz heals emotional wounds. Jade is the stone of wisdom. The stones have been energized to increase their healing properties. FYI, it's okay to take it off at night.*

Why don't you come down to visit? It's beautiful and amazing here. You really should come. Have a beautiful birthday. I miss you, love, your dad.

Costa Rica probably was amazing, but I had no desire to fly to the other side of the equator and ride in some rented Jeep down unpaved roads to a tiny village between mountain ranges. If he truly missed me, he could come here.

I set the head vase on my maple bureau. Later I'd take her down to the store so she could sit with the others I kept behind the register. They made good conversation pieces. I put the chakra bracelet around the neck of the head vase. Maybe it could help her.

I'd just turned to clean up the wrappings from my presents when I heard something behind me; it sounded like a woman sobbing. I turned back—not that I expected to see anyone. The head vase stared at me with an eerie grin. Strange. Sometimes I got street noise, but the window was closed. Must've been a neighbor, or else I'd imagined it.

As I folded up the bubble wrap to use later, I thought of calling my mom to thank her, but she'd ask how I was celebrating, and I didn't want to admit to spending my birthday with Jeff. Instead, I went to my laptop and replied to her e-mail:

Hi Mom,

Thanks so much for the vase. I love her floppy hat with the bow! I'm thinking of HEADing up there Sunday night for a visit. I really, really need to sit out in the garden and get some sun. Does that work for you? Let me know. Love and kisses, your daughter

Bolstered by that accomplishment, I decided to go ahead and e-mail my thanks to Molly, too.

> Hey there, I had my session with Dr. Markoff and have now been officially hypnotized. It's amazing, but after leaving his office, I had absolutely no temptation to smoke! Seriously, he was really great and I can't wait to see if it helps me sleep. Thank you so much for setting that up! XOXO Amanda

Now that I was on a roll, I decided to e-mail my dad, too. Resisting the temptation to say I'd love to visit him down in Costa Rica if it didn't Costa so Mucha, I wrote a nice, polite e-mail and hit "send" with relief.

Time to try on the hourglass dress. I opened my hobo bag, pulled out the stash from Mrs. Kelly, and held up the gorgeous blue dress. So Marilyn. Jeff would love how sexy I'd look. If it fit. It had to fit. Please fit.

It didn't fit. Too damn tight, especially the bust . . . and my belly . . . and my hips. I struggled to pull it off, almost ripping a seam in the process. Jeez. I hoped this was just bloat. My period was late. At least a week, maybe two. I couldn't be pregnant. Jeff and I always used a condom.

Though if I *was* pregnant, that would be kind of exciting. Inconvenient, but at my age . . . No. Had to be stress messing with my cycle, that's all.

I opened my closet. What to wear, what to wear. Had to look great, preferably in something Jeff had never seen. My clothing was packed in there so tightly that it probably could've stayed suspended in midair without hangers. In the dark shadows to the rear of the closet, a place I considered synonymous to the back of my mind, hung a dress I'd been meaning to alter: a forties black taffeta with gold rickrack around the hem. The sweetheart neckline showed just the right amount of cleavage. The only problem was the waist was too loose. A couple darts would do the trick, and I'd been meaning to put them in. I had a few hours before I needed to leave for the restaurant. Today was the day.

After putting the dress on inside out, I pinned the darts. Then I pulled the dress back up over my head, careful not to stab myself with the pins.

My worries receded as I leaned over my reliable old Singer, cupped the metal wheel to position the needle, and pressed down on the foot pedal. It was my grandmother who taught me to sew. First a pillowcase, then an apron, then a dress using a Simplicity pattern we bought at my local Woolworth's on Twenty-third Street—God rest its soul. I remembered the joy of shopping there for supplies. Choosing a pattern from one of the big catalogs; picking out a fabric; finding the exact color of thread and zipper to match. Then we'd go home, spread our supplies out in the living room, and get to work. I loved to whiz down seams like a race car driver gunning for the finish line. Transforming a flat piece of fabric into a three-dimensional finished outfit seemed like magic.

After finishing the second dart, I tried on the dress in front of my closet door mirror. Now it fit perfectly. It needed pressing, but ironing taffeta was not a good idea. I'd steam it out later while taking a shower. I was about to pull it off when inspiration hit: A diamond necklace Jeff bought me might be just the thing to go with it.

I took out a shoe box from behind my cleaning supplies on the top shelf of the cabinet over the sink. That was the safest hiding place I'd come up with for my half dozen or so pieces of upscale jewelry, all presents from Jeff over the past few years. I rarely had the opportunity to wear them, and a while back I'd asked him to stop giving me more. For one thing, I liked picking out my own jewelry. For another, it made me feel like a prototypically "bought and paid for" woman. But he said it made him happy, and he went right on doing it.

I selected the necklace I had in mind—a yellow-gold choker with clusters of diamonds set between each link—and checked myself out in the mirror. It looked brazenly expensive, but it did go beautifully with the neckline of my dress. Just as I was undoing the clasp, I caught a glimpse of something in motion behind me: a dark blur. I spun around.

Nothing. Obviously, my brain was short-circuiting from lack of sleep. I put the necklace on my bureau and returned the shoe box to its hiding place above the sink.

OLIVE

AS THE HORSE clip-clopped past Madison Square, I gawked like a tourist. The city seemed even more dazzling at night, with brilliant arc lights lining the avenue and crowds hunting for entertainment. Diners packed the Café Martin, Anna Held performed to sold-out crowds, and audiences lined up at Proctor's to see moving pictures and vaudeville.

"I remember when this was a lovely, quiet residential neighborhood," my father said.

"And dull as doornails, no doubt."

"What's exciting about stone towers replacing quaint old houses?"

"You're the limit, Father. People come from all over to see the sights."

"I heard they're closing down the Fifth Avenue Hotel. It used to be one of the most fashionable addresses in the city. Now they can't fill their rooms—too old-fashioned for you thrillseekers."

"Well, I like having lots of people around me. Cold Spring is too quiet. Everyone shuts themselves away in their houses." Sometimes I used to imagine that everyone else on earth had died and left me alone.

"People can be lonely in the city, too," Father said. "I'm glad we're getting out tonight."

"So am I." The manager of the Woolworth's on Fourteenth Street had invited us to meet for coffee and dessert at what he claimed was the best Italian café in the city. "It was terribly sweet of this man to think of us."

"I think Mr. Pierce is in need of company, too. He lost his wife last year."

I nodded, thinking that he and Father had something in common. I wished Mr. Pierce had a daughter for me. After a month in the city, I still didn't have anyone I could call a friend. As for my employment search, I didn't dare go to another interview without a reference, and I couldn't bring myself to raise the unpleasant subject with my father.

Veering down Broadway, we passed the brightly lit store windows of Brooks Brothers, Lord & Taylor, and Arnold Constable's. At Union Square we crossed Fourteenth Street, farther downtown than I'd been yet. "One day I'd like to go all the way down to the seaport," I said.

"No need for you to go any farther than this, Olive."

"The Jewish quarter, Little Italy, Chinatown . . . it all sounds so exotic, and I'm sure it's perfectly safe in the daytime."

"Decent young woman don't wander around the slums."

I pressed my lips together. He'd been poisoned by a stew of recent newspaper stories about white slavery. They'd have us believe that every woman who took a walk by herself ended up in a house of ill repute.

"There's St. Mark's," Father said as we passed an old church. "Beautiful, isn't it? A hundred years old. Now here it is, surrounded by all these blasted tenements. Did you know Peter

Stuyvesant's farm once stood here? Can you imagine all this as green fields instead of concrete?"

"Why not go even further back, to the Indians? They must've been horrified to see men razing forests for their farms. And a hundred years from now, I wager New Yorkers will feel sentimental over the very tenements you're complaining about."

"Hard to imagine, but I suppose you might be right. The old always yields to the new—that's life." He patted my hand. "You're too smart for your own good, young lady."

I basked in his praise, such as it was, until we turned onto First Avenue, a wide shabby street, gritty from neglect, with El tracks running overhead. "I didn't think the El ran down First Avenue."

"This is the Second Avenue El. It only runs on First Avenue as far as Twenty-third Street; then it turns over to Second Avenue and goes clear up to the Bronx."

The driver pulled over on Eleventh Street, and Father took out his wallet. The Bronx was yet another part of New York I couldn't imagine. Stepping down from the carriage, I promised myself that one day I'd know all the ins and outs of the city.

Father took my arm as we walked down the street. Tenements lined both sides of the block, with the neighborhood shops on the ground floor and apartments above. An assortment of foreign-looking people passed by. A dark-skinned young man wore the oddest cone-shaped fur hat. A scrawny old woman wore wooden clogs and hunched under a yellow shawl. We reached a storefront with CAFFE PUGLIESE stenciled on the plate glass. A waif in a tattered sweater sat on the sidewalk by the door.

"Can you help me, ma'am, please?" She reached out with an open palm. "Just a penny for a piece of bread . . ."

Such sad eyes. Gaunt face. I buried my hands inside my muff, wishing I'd brought some coins. Father pretended not to notice her while opening the door. And then we entered yet another world. This one was warm, cheerful, and brightly lit, with a wonderful scent in the air.

"Is that licorice?" I took in a deep breath to make it linger in my nose.

"Anise."

A long wood counter displayed trays of pastries. Tarts piled with glistening fruit, cakes slathered with buttercream flowers, rows of rainbow-colored cookies . . . So much rich food for us, while that hungry waif would be grateful for just one bite. A dark-haired woman behind the counter welcomed us with a *buona sera,* took our coats, and directed us to the back, where the scent of anise faded to the less alluring odor of tobacco. Lots of men and very few women sat drinking coffee and reading the evening papers. Lively strains of Italian and English bounced off the tile walls.

"Someone appears to be with him," Father said, leading me to a table.

I looked eagerly to see the fourth person; it wasn't a daughter. Father introduced me to his manager friend Howard Pierce, who in turn introduced his son. "Ralph came by just before I was leaving, so I invited him along."

"How do you do?" he said, bowing slightly.

As I returned the greeting, I wondered if this had been a matchmaking scheme set up by the two fathers.

Sitting across from Ralph Pierce, I supposed most women would find him attractive. He had a clean-shaven face, boyish features, and dark brown hair. A waiter wearing a white ankle-length apron came to the table, and the older Mr. Pierce ordered for all of us, using the Italian names. Then he took up my father's current favorite subject. "Marble counters, porcelain syrup tanks, copper sink . . . Just keeping those soda fountains clean will be a nightmare."

"Not to mention," my father added, "the bother of keeping the syrups stocked and the water carbonated. Frank Woolworth can't leave well enough alone."

I sat up straight. "But he's right." All three men looked at me with surprise. "Men have their bars and saloons. Where can women sit by themselves for a quick refreshment without being conspicuous? A soda water fountain."

"No one wants to deny women their ice cream soda," my father said. "But let them get it somewhere else."

"That's right," Howard Pierce chimed in. "We're in the business of selling dry goods."

"If the sodas draw in more customers," I replied, "you'll be selling more dry goods."

Ralph Pierce chuckled. "I think she won that argument."

"And she's prettier than any of us," his father added.

I refrained from rolling my eyes at the patronizing comment.

A waiter arrived with our drinks and called me a *bella donna* while pouring steamed milk into my coffee. It seemed to be my night for compliments, but after the waiter set down our desserts, I couldn't compete. Rum baba cake, canoli, biscotti, and something called sfogliatelle, with crisp thin layers of buttery dough, sweet cheese filling, and chunks of candied orange. "I've never tasted anything so delicious," I said after savoring my first bite.

My father took a bite of rum cake before asking Ralph Pierce if he was in retail.

"I haven't time for all those nickels and dimes," he answered. "My line is advertising."

His father scowled while cutting the tube-shaped canoli into four pieces. "Advertising is a dead-end field. Woolworth doesn't spend a dime on it, and business is better than ever."

"How many men are in your company?" my father asked.

I feared Ralph Pierce would think Father was interviewing him as a potential son-in-law, so I tried to appear captivated by my piece of cannoli, which wasn't difficult. The deep-fried dough filled with cream, bits of chocolate, and candied cherries tasted scrumptious.

"Just four of us," Ralph said. "The stenographer, the office boy, an account man who brings in the work, and then I'm on the creative side. We just opened a big account for a new brand of soap. I'm writing the copy for it now."

"In hard times like this," his father grumbled, "the first thing any firm cuts from its budget is advertising. That business with the copper stocks is going to drive the market down, don't you think, Westcott?"

"The copper situation won't matter," my father said. "Something of that sort only affects the people directly involved."

Howard Pierce shook his head. "I predict there'll be a domino effect."

"Nonsense," Father said. "The market has found its bottom. We're poised for a recovery, you'll see."

The older men continued to argue about the market, so I tried to hold up my end of the conversation with Ralph Pierce. "It sounds as if your father wishes you'd take a job with Woolworth."

"You noticed," he said with a grim smile. "He refuses to accept that I'm not interested in retail."

"Tell me, how on earth does one think up anything interesting to say about soap?"

"That's the challenge. Anyway, you can't make something interest you that doesn't."

"I feel the same way about marriage," I couldn't resist saying.

He looked at me with surprise. "And why is that?"

"For one thing, I plan on having a career." As the words tumbled out, I wondered why I couldn't keep my mouth shut. At least Father was too involved in his conversation with Mr. Pierce to hear.

"Don't tell me you want to be an actress."

I laughed. "I'd pity the audience."

"A teacher?"

"I'd pity the students."

"I give up. Who wouldn't you pity?"

"My customers. I want to be a buyer in a department store."

He looked as though I'd announced plans to come down with a disease. "Why?"

"You don't think a woman ought to work?" I asked coyly.

"If there's a genuine need, they should be allowed. Certainly, teaching is an honorable profession. But the department stores are known to be a breeding ground of immorality. It would be a mistake to expose yourself to the lower-class women employed in those places."

"My goodness. You make department stores sound positively evil."

"I only know what I've read and heard. It's one thing to shop in a store, Miss Westcott. Quite another to work in one."

I wanted to tell him he was a pompous fool but took a sip of coffee instead.

"I wouldn't allow my future wife to work in such a place," he went on. "Not that it would be an issue. The woman I marry shall put family first."

"Then I won't be the woman you marry." I smiled pleasantly, but Ralph Pierce was regarding me with alarm, as if he'd just proposed and I'd turned him down. I changed the subject. "Have I ever seen any of your advertisements, Mr. Pierce?"

"Probably, if you read the ladies' magazines."

"I try not to. They're filled with such drivel, don't you think?"

"I'm told some women find the articles useful."

"If you want to know twenty ways to cook a chicken."

By his expression, I guessed he would like to know.

Our fathers had moved on to speculating about a rumor that Woolworth planned to build an office building taller than the

Metropolitan Tower. I changed the subject once more, resolving to sound agreeable.

"We've only just moved to the city. I think it's grand. The skyscrapers. All the people . . ." Now I sounded like a simpleton. "Did you have the good fortune to be born here?"

"As a matter of fact, I did, in a brownstone on Eighteenth Street."

"Then I'm sure you must know all the most interesting places."

He went on to hold forth on the city sights I must see. Meanwhile, I stuffed myself with pastry. When the waiter asked if we wanted anything else, everyone agreed we'd eaten more than enough. Thank goodness I wasn't wearing a corset; if I had been, every hook surely would've burst open.

October 19, 1907

Why is it that when I try to be charming and clever with men, I end up being arrogant and insufferable? Perhaps because they always seem to think that they're the whole show, and that makes me want to let them know they aren't. I can't seem to remember that I'm supposed to encourage them to feel superior. Will I ever meet a man whose arrogance doesn't rouse me to take him down a peg or two?

AMANDA

SITTING DOWN WITH a snack of whole wheat fig bars and green tea, I read about Olive's horrible job interview. When she mentioned everyone's obsession with Stanford White's murder, I remembered it had something to do with a love triangle. I had a vague memory of reading about it in one of my books, with a big photograph of the beautiful woman at the center of the scandal.

I went to the bookshelf and scanned the spines. *Valentine's Manual of Old New York*, *Crusades and Crinolines*, *King's Views of New York*, *Manhattan Manners*, *The History of Macy's*. Then I came across my old set of Time-Life books called *This Fabulous Century* and knew that was where I'd seen it. I got the complete series of eight books at a flea market when I was around ten years old, and they played a big part in launching my fascination with the past. *This Fabulous Century* only went up to the seventies, the decade it was published. In the first volume, 1870 to 1900 was covered. Each of the next seven decades got a full book to itself. I used to pore over every word and stare at the glossy photographs with laser-like eyes, trying to take in every detail and see beyond the edges to find answers to questions I couldn't quite put into words.

It was such a revelation to see that before I was born, people looked different. Their hairstyles, makeup, and clothes kept changing. I learned about style and how to pinpoint which time period a piece of clothing came from. I never could decide which decade was my favorite: the slender, empire waist silks of the teens; the unstructured flapper dresses of the twenties; the movie star–inspired cuts of the thirties; the shoulder-padded forties; the busty, hip-flaunting fifties; the mod Jackie O sixties; the bright bell-bottomed seventies . . . And then there was Olive's era, different from all the others because it was under the sway of the century that came before.

I took her volume from the shelf and flipped through the thick glossy pages. Incredible how the images still occupied a place in my head. A crowd celebrating a transcontinental auto tour waved their straw hats. A futuristic drawing of Manhattan in 1999 was not too far off the mark. The actress Anna Held reclined awkwardly with a corseted eighteen-inch waist. God, I remembered being mesmerized by her freakish hourglass figure and wondering how she could breathe. Then there was Teddy Roosevelt, wearing a monocle and leather boots, sitting for a portrait with his wife and six kids.

Women hid their legs under long dresses and wouldn't dream of wearing pants. Cars began to edge out horses, electricity replaced gaslight, moving pictures killed vaudeville. At the center of it all was New York City—my city. On the Upper East Side, beaux arts mansions went up on dirt lots previously home to squatters and farms. Fifty blocks to the south, developers tore down old wood houses to cram immigrants into cheaply made tenements like mine.

Finally, in a chapter called "The Very Rich," Evelyn Nesbit's beautiful portrait occupied an entire page. Lush full lips. Dark languid eyes. Long hair piled up in a romantically demure Gibson Girl coiffure. Her expression struck me as impossible to read. Seductive? Belligerent? Passive?

On the opposite page were small photos of the two wealthy men responsible for getting her into this chapter. Her husband, Harry Thaw, was clean-shaven and youthful, with deep-set eyes almost lost in the dark shadows of his brows. Her ex-lover, Stanford White, had an absurdly thick bushy mustache drooping over his mouth and appeared to have enjoyed too many big, fattening meals. A leading architect at the turn of the century, White worked on Fifth Avenue mansions for the Astors and the Vanderbilts, as well as the Washington Square Arch that I'd been sitting next to that morning. He was also known to be a womanizer.

The book gave a recap of the scandal. Nesbit became White's girlfriend back when she was a sixteen-year-old chorus girl in a Broadway show. That lasted a couple of years, and then he moved on to other girls. Nesbit began seeing the wealthy Harry Thaw, who was obsessively in love with her and desperate to marry, even after she confessed that White had taken her virginity.

They married in 1905, when Nesbit was twenty, but Thaw became tortured over the fact that White had "ruined" his wife. Then Thaw perceived that White was still making advances toward Nesbit. Her honor needed to be defended.

One summer night in 1906, Stanford White sat in the audience of a musical show on the roof garden of the Madison Square Garden. Thaw walked right up to him, pulled out a revolver, and shot him point-blank. The first trial ended with a hung jury. In 1907, all of New York City was anticipating the second trial.

My Time-Life book didn't mention the irony that Stanford White had designed the building where he died. Not the monstrously huge, round Madison Square Garden that now existed on top of Penn Station. It was then actually located on Madison Square, right up the block from where I'd be eating dinner tonight.

I returned the book to the shelf. Then I took my black dress with me to the bathroom to steam out on a hanger during my shower. Welcoming the soothing warmth of water on my skin, I slathered apricot-scented soap all over. It was ridiculous how my skin stayed so white even after a summer's worth of sun. At least Jeff didn't care for tans. He said he loved the transparency of my skin, how the blue veins showed beneath the surface.

After washing my hair, I ran the razor over every inch of both legs with the hope that he'd be taking a well-traveled journey of soft kisses that began at my toes and passed my calf and thigh before arriving at the ultimate destination. While giving myself a final rinse, I wondered, not for the first time, whether Jeff's wife knew about me. I generally avoided asking about her; it helped make their marriage less real. But in one of our few conversations about their marriage, he claimed she had no idea about the affair. Of course, he could've been lying to me. After all, he was lying to her. Six years was a long time to keep such a big secret.

What if she found out about me and flew into a jealous rage? Maybe she'd show up at the restaurant tonight and blow my brains out. Would Jeff's handsome photograph get the full-page treatment while I was relegated to an unflattering cameo?

The Stanford White scandal was obviously overstimulating my imagination. Time to get out of the shower and towel off. I checked my alarm clock, a rare old digital with a square yellow Bakelite frame: five-thirty P.M. I'd been trying not to nap in the daytime, but tonight I'd be staying up late with Jeff, so I had no need to deprive myself of a little snooze. I burrowed naked under my down quilt and shivered inside the cozy cocoon.

Just as I turned onto my stomach, I heard someone humming a tune. It sounded like it was coming from a few feet away. I looked up and was startled to see a woman wearing an ankle-length navy blue dress with a matching short jacket. She stood in front of my bureau mirror, adjusting the tilt of a wide-brimmed hat.

"Hello?" I whispered. I couldn't see her face. "Olive?"

She took no notice of me and walked out the door.

"Wait!" I wanted to go, too. I threw off my covers, grabbed my hobo bag, and ran after her.

The click of her heels echoed in the hall as she went down the stairs. "Olive!" I screamed, but she didn't slow down, and I heard the front door slam shut. Rushing to catch up, I caught a glimpse of her turning the corner. How did she walk so fast? I ran down the street; a man leered at me and laughed. I looked down and realized I was naked. I'd forgotten to put on my clothes! Jesus, I'd never done that before.

I took off like a sprinter in a race—I needed to get inside, somewhere, anywhere. Finally, I made it to Jeff's building. I pulled on the door to the lobby, but it was locked. It was never locked! I peered through the glass and saw that it had been totally redone since the last time I was there. New Ethan Allen–type furniture, as if it were someone's living room. Then I realized this was Jeff's house up in Katonah. His wife was coming toward the door. She wore a green dress with ruffles around the collar, and here I was, naked. The door opened, and she aimed a gun straight at me! I tried to scream but could manage only a pitiful warbling sound that took so much effort . . .

I woke up. I lay there staring at the ceiling. How bizarre. I checked the clock. Six-twenty? The dream seemed to last only a minute, but almost an hour had passed. I felt more exhausted than when I lay down.

At least I'd gotten the day out of the way. I threw off the covers. No more worries allowed, no thinking about jealous wives or ending the affair. It was time to celebrate the birth of me.

OLIVE

"YOU'RE SURE YOU'LL be all right?" my father asked. We stood near the entrance to the train platform at the Grand Central Station.

"I'll be fine." He was leaving for Cold Spring to fetch his motorcar and would be back the next day.

"I've left some extra cash in the leather box on my bureau," he said. "Just in case."

"I won't need it, Father, but thank you."

"I don't feel right leaving you unattended in the city."

"Don't be silly. I'm not a child anymore."

"Indeed. You're becoming quite an independent young lady. I'm not ready for you to be all grown up. Pretty soon you'll be the one taking care of me."

"Goodness, now I think you've aged me a bit too quickly."

We beamed at each other with affection. He gave me a kiss on the cheek and turned to walk away. A melancholy swept over me. At the last moment he turned to wave; I waved back as if perfectly cheerful. Leaving the station, I tried to shake off my gloom. Hadn't I been looking forward to the novelty of being on my own?

My plan was to see a fashion show at the Siegel-Cooper department store on Eighteenth Street. I boarded a trolley in front of the big new public library on Forty-second Street and forgot to be gloomy over Father while riding down Fifth Avenue, observing the many new places of business replacing the old mansions of the rich, who seemed to be constantly moving farther uptown. At Thirty-fourth Street, we passed Altman's, an elegant department store that I found rather dull. Then came an enclave of exclusive shops that catered to wealthy shoppers from around the world. It was fine entertainment to observe the posh establishments and the fashionably dressed clientele who could afford the prices.

When the trolley reached my stop on Eighteenth Street, I hopped off to walk over one block to the less exclusive realm of Sixth Avenue. Back in the eighties, this area was known as the Ladies' Mile because of the profusion of grand emporiums that served the wealthy. But fine ladies no longer pulled up in victorias driven by white-breeched grooms or promenaded down the avenue in their elegant gowns. These days, if well-heeled New Yorkers braved Sixth Avenue, they had to contend with the multitudes who poured in from all the boroughs on trolleys, buses, and the El trains that rumbled overhead on monstrous steel tracks.

The Siegel-Cooper department store occupied an entire square block. I'd explored it a few times but had only begun to find my way around. The store went all out to make the bargain-hunting middle class feel, if only for the day, like aristocracy. In the atrium, customers relaxed on settees and chairs by a pool of water hedged with tropical flowers and ferns. At the pool's center, a fountain with four arching sprays of water flanked a female statue holding a globe with an electric star lit up inside. A grand staircase led to the mezzanine, where specialty shops sold men's furnishings and copies of the latest Paris fashions.

Resisting the temptations of a soda water fountain, I pressed on to the main floor. The store bustled like a miniature city, luring people to shop between visits to a post office, a library, a tearoom, a beauty salon, and even an art gallery. I had ten minutes to spare, but nothing could sway me from the fashion show.

The auditorium was crowded, and most of the female audience wore massive headgear. I made sure to find an empty seat with an unobstructed view and settled in, grateful to have a chance to relax. The orchestra played a dreamy waltz. I closed my eyes and imagined a man who resembled Ralph Pierce. He apologized for being so old-fashioned. Would I please forgive him and dance? I supposed I would. He put his arms around me. I felt his breath on my skin as he whispered in my ear that I was not merely pretty, I was beautiful, and marvelously clever, too. If only I hadn't made such a fuss about wanting to work. I looked up into his eyes and pouted. Could he love a woman with a career? I had my answer when he leaned over and kissed me hard on the lips and—

The music stopped. I opened my eyes. Thank goodness no one could read my ridiculous mind.

A goateed man wearing a black suit accented with a red ascot stood behind a podium at the side of the stage. The curtain rose to reveal a backdrop with the painted silhouette of a cityscape. "New York, London, Paris . . . the vogue of the tailored suit has swept the major cities." A procession of young women paraded across the stage.

"Mannish in cut and material, our first suit features a semi-fitted coat of hip length. You'll note the skirt has wide fold trimmings that add a touch of novelty."

I stared at the beautiful models, wondering how they dared welcome strangers to purposely stare at them.

"The ensemble on our next model features a long cutaway jacket of thirty-six inches. Tweeds in tan and brown tones as well as stripes and checks shall be very popular this season."

I didn't own a suit; Father said they made a woman look too masculine. But these days it was essential attire for a career woman.

"All the tailored suits shown here today are available in ladies' ready-to-wear. Our customers shall find them exactly the same as the ones made by the custom shops."

They did look as good as tailor-made—at least from a distance. I would try one on later, perhaps after lunch. I was already feeling hunger pangs, so as the fashion show moved on to footwear, I sneaked out and took a lift to the restaurant on the top floor.

The maître d' led me to the "women only" side. Sunlight gleamed on the white tile floors through a glass skylight ceiling. The orchestra played a polka. I wasn't used to eating alone in public but tried to appear blasé as I took off my gloves and read the menu card. A plump waitress in a gingham apron and cap waddled up to take my order. "What'll it be, dearie?"

"Sardine sandwich and a lemonade, please."

I watched her return to the kitchen. While waiting for my food, I listened in on two women sitting behind me.

"I don't give a rap what Roosevelt says about race suicide. I'm only having two children—that's my limit."

"You ask me," her companion replied with a laugh, "one is more than enough."

"You'll change your mind when you meet the right man."

"Perhaps, as long as I have a chance to enjoy being married first."

"Same here. I'm putting it off as long as I can."

How would she do that? Keep her husband from having relations with her? Or did she know some other way? If so, what was it? Alas, they stood up to go before I could hear any more. As they passed my table, I noticed both women wore tweed suits.

The waitress brought my sandwich. It tasted delicious, and

I took tiny bites to make it last. My lack of sexual knowledge made me feel at such a disadvantage. The world seemed divided between those who knew and those who didn't. Aunt Ida undoubtedly belonged to the group who didn't, and she'd never been disposed to broach the subject. I'd warrant she'd never been kissed. If so, that meant we shared this condition; now *that* was a wretched thought. The most forthcoming she'd ever been was a warning about the honeymoon night. I could hear her voice in my head: "The first time is painful, and there will be blood."

My girlfriends had only giggled over details they'd picked up in romance novels. Those now married were too discreet or embarrassed, or perhaps they lacked the intimacy with me to divulge any details.

Presumably, Daisy had been as ignorant on the subject as I. In any case, since we'd amused ourselves over a mutual disdain for men as inferior beings, expressing any interest or curiosity would've betrayed our bond.

As for Father, I'd sooner take a job in a bordello than ask him for the facts.

The Cold Spring library carried no books on the subject—a thorough search of the shelves had confirmed that. But I knew such books existed. For years I'd noticed certain titles in the medical section of the Montgomery Ward catalog. One was titled *Confidential Talks with Young Women.* How I would've loved someone to talk with confidentially! I never dared order it. If Father or Aunt Ida happened to open the package first, I would've died.

"Anything else you need, dearie? Piece of pie?"

Yes, I wanted to tell her, *I'd like to have a confidential talk.* "No, thank you," I said, "that will be all."

After paying my check, I went directly to look at the suits. A salesgirl tried to help me find a skirt that was long enough to reach my ankles, paired with a jacket that wasn't too loose. It took some patience, but I finally found a smart green-and-tan-checked plaid that fit.

"It was made for you," the salesgirl said.

Father would not be pleased to find out I'd bought a suit instead of a pretty gown. But I would be forgiven—after suffering through his teasing that I looked like a suffragette. "I'll take it," I said.

AMANDA

I YELLED TO the cabdriver through the plastic partition, "Can you slow down?" Not because he was driving recklessly—which he was—but to avoid arriving early. I didn't want to sit alone waiting for Jeff.

The driver acquiesced. I still felt nervous. I should've waited ten more minutes before leaving the apartment but had been too revved up to start the evening. My face-to-face encounters with Jeff, even casual ones that didn't fall on my birthday, had a tendency to assume overblown importance. The fact that I'd taken extra care to look great only made it worse. Seeing him always involved planning when and where, secrecy, an underlayer of guilt—impossible to get together with any spontaneity. Even though I'd known Jeff half my life, I could still feel shy with him, like a fan meeting a celebrity for the first time.

At five minutes past eight, the driver turned onto Twenty-fourth Street and pulled up to the restaurant entrance just off the park. Too bad it wasn't five minutes later, but with any luck, he'd be there.

The maître d' delivered the unfortunate news that I was the first of my party to arrive. Would I like to be seated? I followed him through the large deco dining room. The tiles on the floor were laid in a gold zigzag. He led me to a table underneath huge windows facing Madison Avenue and the park. Olive must've walked down that sidewalk all the time. Too bad I hadn't thought of a stroll around the neighborhood before coming in. I got only a glimpse of the park foliage before the maître d' pulled out the table so I could slide onto the leather bench facing in. He left me there with two menus and a severe case of self-consciousness.

Placing my cell phone on the white tablecloth, I checked out the other diners. People wore business suits, evening wear, jeans, T-shirts. It was impossible to guess anyone's wealth by what they wore these days. My necklace would throw anyone off.

At a quarter past eight, a black-vested waiter asked if I'd like to order a drink. "I'll wait, thanks." I opened the menu. A three-course prix fixe dinner cost a hundred and fifteen dollars. My mouth watered as I read the selections: gnocchi with goat cheese ricotta, artichoke, olives, and bacon; poached Nova Scotia lobster that cost twenty dollars extra; bouillabaisse with bass, octopus, prawns, and chorizo. Where was he? *Relax.* Call him? No, he'd think I was waiting nervously. I stared at the menu if only to appear occupied. Twenty past eight. He could've called to warn me he'd be late. I shouldn't have worn the necklace—the last thing I wanted now was to draw attention to myself. My phone rang. Jeff.

"I'm sorry," he said.

"You're late."

"I had an emergency."

"What happened?"

"My wife," he said. "Denise." He rarely mentioned her, but when he did, he added her name as a qualifier, as if I didn't know.

"She was slicing an onion and cut a tendon. I had to rush her to the hospital. Would've phoned but couldn't get a moment alone. You're at the restaurant?"

"Yes."

"I'm sorry."

"It's fine."

"I can't get away. She's in the operating room."

"That sucks. I'm sorry."

"No," he said. "I'm sorry to disappoint you."

"Stop saying you're sorry."

"Sorry."

I frowned at the phone in silence.

"That was a joke," he said.

"I know."

"Sort of," he said.

"I know." Tears stung my eyes. I attempted a cheery tone. "I might as well"—did he notice my voice wavering?—"go home." And spend my birthday alone in my room, feeling like a stupid idiot.

"You sure you're okay?"

"Of course."

"I'll call you later tonight."

I said nothing, afraid a sob would come out instead of a sentence.

"Amanda? You okay?"

"I'm fine. I'm hanging up now."

"I love you," he said. "You know that, right?"

I sighed loudly enough for him to hear; a sigh was safer than a word.

"Happy birthday."

"Thanks."

I ended the call and gathered strength for my next challenge: getting out of the restaurant with my dignity intact. Taking a deep breath, I pushed the table away and followed the zigzag back out through the dining room, muttered an apology to the maitre d', and pushed open the door to the street. I thought of taking that walk around the neighborhood, but no, too dressed up, too hard to blend in. I needed to be alone so I could wallow in my self-pity in private. A cab turned the corner. I jumped in, slammed the door, and sank down in my seat as if paparazzi wanted a picture.

Leaving Madison Square behind, I cradled my cell phone in my palm and considered options. Call Molly? She was my only friend who still had the patience to hear about Jeff, and she was probably waiting to hear the details on Dr. Markoff. But it would be so humiliating to confess Jeff's latest snub, and, at this point, wasn't I getting what I deserved?

I could call some other friend and pretend to be happy. *Hey, it's my birthday, and I somehow forgot to make plans, wanna do something?* Maybe I'd buy a bottle of wine at Astor Wines and get drunk. Swing by Pinisi Bakery and gorge on red velvet cupcakes. Or put an end to the day before it got any worse. Go straight home and hit the sack. Except I felt wide awake. Too bad I took that nap. If Dr. Markoff had doled out a prescription for sleeping pills, I'd be all set; instead, I had a ridiculous hypnosis tape. Like that was gonna do anything.

Another option? Call Jeff and tell him it was over.

God, I was such a fool. My tears finally spilled. I opened the window and let the air hit my face and the street noise cover my sobs. Home sounded lonely and depressing, but where else could I go?

I took a few calming breaths so I could speak to the driver in a steady voice. "Excuse me?" I sat forward. "Can you let me out at Astor Place instead?"

He nodded and I sat back. Whether I called Jeff to end it or chickened out, a good bottle of zinfandel would only help.

12

OLIVE

EVERYTHING WAS GOING swimmingly, though it did feel odd to eat breakfast in the quiet apartment without Father sitting across from me, and the morning paper was filled with bad news. It didn't help that my monthly had come and cramps seemed to be pummeling me from inside.

I moaned softly and rocked back and forth while reading about the copper scandal. Father's prediction that no serious repercussions would result had proved wrong. The Knickerbocker Trust Company was in trouble, and some other banks, rousing fears they would fail. Thank goodness Father didn't do business with any of them. But the stock market had sunk to new lows, and J. P. Morgan had been summoned from a vacation in Europe to solve the crisis. Everyone seemed to think he would sort it all out.

I sent the breakfast dishes down in the dumbwaiter and decided to take a bath. Perhaps soaking in the tub would ease my pains. While removing my belt and unpinning the sanitary pad,

I tried not to breathe in the sour odor of my blood. Then I made good use of that depressing newspaper by wrapping the soiled pad inside. Hoping not to be seen, I scurried down the hallway and tossed it in the chute. An ingenious invention, that garbage chute—something even Aunt Ida might appreciate. She used to burn our sanitary pads in the fireplace so they wouldn't stink up the house.

While undressing for the bath, I caught a look at myself in the mirror and, as usual, looked away. I couldn't fathom overcoming my modesty to do whatever it was husbands and wives did alone together in bed. What a relief it was to stretch out in the tub and let the warm water envelop my skin. Perhaps proper women kept their nightgowns on during the sex act.

If only I knew exactly what the sex act was.

All I did know was the man's private part went inside the woman's opening to insert the seed. I'd learned that ghastly piece of information from one of Father's countergirls when I was a young girl. Her name was Tessie, and sometimes, if it was slow in the store, I'd get her talking about all sorts of things. Tessie was not the prettiest girl—stout, with reddish hair and freckles. But she did have a lovely deep voice, and I enjoyed listening to her talk about growing up on a prairie in Montana. She considered no subject out of bounds. Once she even told me about helping her mother give birth.

"You see, I had to. Papa was away, and there was a beastly snowstorm."

"Wasn't it scary?"

"Mama knew the routine—she already had three of us."

"Did you actually see it come out of her?"

"Sure, I caught him with my own hands, slippery little devil. Almost dropped him on the floor."

I didn't understand why she'd need to catch it. "Don't mothers give birth lying down?"

Tessie shrugged. "If they do, no one ever told Mama; she made it up as she went along. Stand, sit, squat . . . the only thing she didn't do was stay still."

"Wasn't it dreadful seeing her in all that pain?"

"By the fourth one, she said the opening was all stretched out like a rubber band." Tessie laughed and then leaned toward me, lowering her voice. "She told me it was like having a crap."

I flushed at the vulgar word. "I don't believe you."

"Just squat and . . . you know . . . out it comes."

Father cut my education short by firing her a few weeks later. He told me she talked too much behind the counter. I suspected her true crime wasn't the quantity of words so much as her free use of them. I tried convincing him it was my fault for peppering her with questions, but he refused to reconsider.

Now here I was, twenty years old and still as ignorant about my body as a virgin could be.

After finishing with my bath, instead of immediately wrapping myself in a towel, I decided to look at my naked body in the mirror. Perhaps having the apartment to myself gave me the courage.

I stood before the glass and forced myself to take inventory: long torso, slim hips, small breasts, and that disconcerting triangular patch of hair. Even though I hadn't the most curvaceous figure, there was no denying that the person reflected back was a grown woman.

October 25, 1907

Today I'm going to Wanamaker's. They're said to have the largest selection of books anywhere. I should like to see if they have some sort of medical book about female physiology. Since the store is off the beaten path, I'll have the advantage of feeling anonymous if I do gather my courage to actually buy such a book.

It was astonishing how the red-haired doorman always seemed to be at his post; one would think he slept there at night standing up.

"Taxi, miss?"

"Yes, please." I'd often wished he weren't there to observe my comings and goings, but his presence was proving to be a comfort during Father's absence.

I waited under the awning as he flagged down a motor taxi. It wasn't only because of the distance that I was treating myself to a ride; my sanitary pads had an annoying tendency to slip and chafe when I walked. I supposed other women experienced the same problem, though I'd never discussed the embarrassing issue with anyone, not even Daisy.

"Where to?" the doorman asked as a taxi pulled up.

"Wanamaker's, please."

He opened the door for me and spoke to the driver. "Take the young lady to Wanamaker's."

I thanked him as he swung the door shut. Aunt Ida would say the city was spoiling me even more than I already was. And I would have to agree.

Organ music played in the background as I entered the main floor. I looked up and let my mouth hang open like a child full of wonder as my gaze followed the progression of balconies that rose to a domed skylighted rotunda. The glistening glass cabinets and wide aisles festooned with colored lights tempted me to wander about the bustling main floor. I marched to the store directory, saw that the book department was up on the eighth floor, and took a lift straight there.

A diligent search through the piles of books in the health section began to seem fruitless until one promising title caught my eye: *The Four Epochs of Woman's Life: A Study in Hygiene.* The author was Anna Galbraith, MD. A woman! After making sure no one observed me, I scanned the table of contents. "Puberty," "Anatomy of the Generative Organs," "Menstruation," "Marriage"—all worthy topics—but when I saw the chapter titled "Sexual Instinct in Women," my heart fluttered with the thrill of victory. I'd struck gold.

The salesgirl didn't appear to notice the title, and I breathed easier as she wrapped it in brown paper. After paying with cash so no name would be associated with the purchase, I left the store as swiftly as I could manage, afraid some floorwalker would stop me. I felt certain I must look as guilty as a shoplifter.

The occasion of reading my book called for opening a box of chocolates Father had bought me from Maillard's. After telephoning down to the concierge for a pot of orange pekoe, I changed my pad and put on my wrapper and a pair of slippers. Soon the tea arrived on the dumbwaiter, and I settled onto the sofa to educate myself.

CHAPTER 1

PUBERTY

Sexual Changes; Ages of Puberty; Physical Changes at Puberty; First Onset of Menstruation; Psychic Changes at Puberty

I looked up at the empty room. Who was I trying to fool? I flipped straight to the most important chapter.

CHAPTER 8

SEXUAL INSTINCT IN WOMEN

Sexual Instinct in Women; Excessive Coitus; Causes of Sexual Excitability

Dr. Galbraith categorized women into three classes: those with little or no sex feeling, those with strong passion, and the majority—a moderate appetite. At first I put myself into the "having little sex feeling" category, but that would have me in the same boat as Aunt Ida, so I settled on the middle category. At least the doctor said that most women experienced sexual appetite, and she didn't bother preaching that it indicated a deficient character.

I popped a chocolate into my mouth, sipped my tea, and read on. The next paragraph had a surprise. When women experienced sexual excitement, it caused a congestion of blood in the genital organs. When the congestion peaked, there was a reflex movement called "orgasm." I'd never heard that word. It was equivalent, she said, to the male orgasm that occurred when men ejected the seed of the baby. *In the woman this consists of a movement of the tubes and uterus, and it causes a suction that draws the spermatozoa up into its interior, resulting in pregnancy.* I wasn't sure I wanted to experience such a thing. It reminded me of bathwater being sucked down the drain. She went on to say that if the man and woman experienced the orgasm simultaneously, a baby was likely to be conceived.

I paused to digest all this fascinating information while eating another chocolate and washing it down with some tea. I continued on, hoping for a description of what led up to that strange orgasm reflex.

The doctor said that too frequent activity in the uterus could cause inflammation of the genitals, warts, tumors, and cancer. She suggested ways to curb sexual excitement: gymnastics, cold baths, and the avoidance of alcohol. If all else failed, she said, use sheer willpower. I didn't drink alcohol, so that wasn't a concern, but the only thing I hated more than gymnastics was a cold bath. My willpower would have to do.

The chapter ended there. I turned the page.

CHAPTER 9

STERILITY

The Prevention of Conception and the Limitation of Offspring; The Crime of Abortion; Infidelity in Women

How had we arrived at sterility? I flipped ahead to the following chapter. Maternity? I didn't need to read about that. I turned back to the chapter on sexual instinct and skimmed through it again with disbelief. Dr. Galbraith had devoted the bulk of her attention to ways of avoiding sex, yet offered so few details on what occurred during it! Could it be there wasn't anything else to know? Perhaps the woman needed only to lie there while the man took care of his needs. If so, I wished she'd taken the trouble to explain that. I finished off my tea and closed the box of chocolates. I felt exhausted. Even my bed seemed too far away. I stretched out on the sofa, closed my eyes and drifted off to sleep . . .

A knock on the door woke me up. I had no idea what time it was. Could it be the delivery of my suit from Siegel-Cooper? Probably Father, too lazy to fish out his latchkey.

But it wasn't Father or my suit. A messenger boy handed over a yellow envelope addressed to me. A telegram. I handed the boy a few coins with my thanks. Then I shut the door and ripped open the envelope.

Your father is dead STOP Automobile accident STOP Please come home STOP I'm sorry STOP Aunt Ida

The room tilted. I sank onto the sofa and tried, as if anyone were observing me, to appear calm.

This couldn't be.

I looked at the yellow paper again. Your father is dead STOP Your father is dead STOP Your father is dead STOP Your father is dead

No. Must not think, must not feel. Someone had made a dreadful mistake.

Rising from the sofa, I walked in circles around the room. My body was going to burst through my skin.

I read it again. Dead STOP Dead STOP Dead! I crumpled the paper in my fist and let it drop to the floor. Then I wiped my tears, went to my room, and sat on the edge of my bed. He'd arrive at any moment, hungry for dinner after so many hours on the road.

I went to his bedroom as if I'd find him there. The maid had straightened up. His bed was made. His life was over. I lay down on the flat, neat cover and curled into a ball while moaning softly. *Don't let it be true. Don't let him be gone* . . . My father, the only person in the world who truly loved me. I couldn't bear it. How did it happen? I had to know. Now.

I went to the telephone and picked up the receiver. The ache in my heart cut off my breath. My lungs craved air, and I couldn't speak. Setting the receiver back down, I forced myself to take in a few breaths. Then I asked the hotel operator to put me through and waited for Central to make the connection.

Aunt Ida, never comfortable using the telephone, spoke loudly. "Who is this?"

"Olive." I gripped the cold metal handle as if it kept me tethered to the world.

"I would've telephoned," she said. "I'm sorry, I couldn't bring myself to. I've been sitting here waiting. It didn't seem right to speak of such a thing over the wires."

"It's true?"

"Yes."

"Are you sure?" My throat choked up.

"I'm sorry, dear. So sorry."

"How?" I held my breath as if about to go underwater.

"That machine," she said. "Brakes failed. Didn't get more than five miles from the house. They say he went careening down a hill and was thrown. Landed on his head, and—" Her voice caught. "He died instantly."

I could only whimper.

"I'm sorry," she repeated, "so sorry. I'm arranging everything, of course. The funeral. Don't worry about that."

"Yes," I whispered.

"What is that? I can't hear. You're upset, of course. You must come home immediately."

"Now?"

"You mustn't be alone at a time like this."

"No."

"What? You'll have to speak louder."

"Yes. The train. I'll come."

We rang off. Everything had changed too quickly. Father was supposed to return from Cold Spring; now I was supposed to go there? Pack, change my pad, remember to bring extras, go to the station, where we'd just said good-bye without knowing it was forever. I didn't want to go. I couldn't move. I had no choice. *The Four Epochs of Woman's Life* sat on the side table. I needed a good place to hide it. Then I remembered: It didn't matter. I had no father to hide it from.

13

AMANDA

I LOCKED THE door to my apartment and secured the deadbolt. This had to be my worst birthday ever. The room was silent. Too silent, like a graveyard at midnight. I waited to see if a madman would leap out from the shadows wielding a butcher knife. No one leaped. The head vase, wearing the chakra bracelet, stared at me with a superior expression, as if she knew I'd been stood up by my married lover.

Okay, I had to get out of this mood.

First order of business: Open the wine and let it breathe. Then I changed into leggings and a T-shirt. After spooning some hummus into a bowl and getting out a bag of pita chips, I poured myself a glass of wine and nestled into the sofa to see what was happening with Olive. I was reading along happily, enjoying my little meal, when I read that her father was dead.

Dead?

Jesus. Usually, when you read someone's diary—not that I made a habit of it—you start out hoping for all sorts of personal details and get shopping lists and train schedules instead. Not death. God, poor Olive, to suddenly find herself so alone in the world.

I stared at the vintage travel poster on my wall of a glamorous couple riding in a carriage in Central Park. The idea of my parents' death had always been unimaginable. I wanted to believe they'd never succumb to the laws of nature everyone else had to live by. Me, too, if possible. When either of them did die, I'd probably turn into a dysfunctional blubbering baby. I'd have no husband to anchor me, no kids to make me feel needed. I did have Molly, but she was married and starting her own family. There was my larger circle of friends, but really, people could be so flaky. I couldn't be Jeff's first priority, as this evening had made so painfully clear.

Here I was, scared to give him up because I'd be more alone. But that would be only temporary, theoretically; in time I'd be open to bonding with someone else. So staying with him made it more likely that I'd end up alone.

Maybe now was a good time to call him. Was it wrong to break up with a man when his wife was at the emergency room? What would Amy Vanderbilt say? I Googled "cut tendons" on my laptop to see how serious the injury was. A medical site explained how it would be sewn back up and the patient might have to wear a splint. That was bad, but not exactly life-threatening. Maybe Jeff was already home.

Maybe I'd wait until tomorrow.

I opened the journal but couldn't read. Again I sensed that eerie quietness. The furniture seemed to be standing extra still, as if pretending not to have moved when I wasn't looking.

I turned on the TV to fill the room with noise and stared like an idiot at some dumb sitcom while sipping my wine. It was very strange to be so spooked in my apartment. I was not a superstitious person and didn't believe in ghosts or any other affiliates of the supernatural world, so what was the deal? Maybe

Dr. Markoff's trance had taken control of my brain. Except didn't he say I was the one in control?

I decided to turn off the TV and do something productive, like get that stain out of Jane Kelly's dress. Bringing clothing back to life had a way of bringing me back to life, too. Then I'd call Jeff and tell him this was it; I needed to move on. My birthday gift to myself: freedom.

Leaning over the bathroom sink, I scrubbed the stain with a mixture of hydrogen peroxide and Dawn. Gradually, the blotch began to fade. I'd give it a wash and see how it looked after drying. Then I'd give it another wash and attack it with a bleach pen if necessary. After wiping the sink clean, I filled it with cold water, added a smidgen of Ivory Snow, and swished it around. Submerging the dress, I pushed down on the bubbles of cloth and wondered for the zillionth time why it was so damn hard for me to move beyond Jeff. I liked Molly's chemical imprint theory, since the scientific angle took some of the responsibility off me, but it was no excuse; I had to stop giving in to this urge to recapture the past. Even my business required a preoccupation with reviving history. Was my entire life ruled by nostalgia?

I pulled out the stopper. Then I hung the dress over the tub and sprayed it with the shower attachment to rinse out the soap. Abbie Hoffman, the rebel from the sixties, once said that nostalgia is a mild form of depression. It did have the potential to bring me down and make me long for something that couldn't be captured. But it could also make me feel a part of something bigger. The past doesn't just go away; it lingers on. You can actually touch and see the remains, and to the extent that these souvenirs survive, the past is present. You can't say that for the future. It's not here in any form. It can't be; it hasn't arrived yet. Once it does arrive, it's the present, but only fleetingly before it's the past. You can never hold the future in your hands.

I opened the bathroom window to get a breeze. Then I hung

the dress to dry on the shower curtain rod and imagined it thanking me for bringing it back to life. The past continued on in our clothes, photographs, knickknacks, music, film, the written word—if we made sure to take care of it. The stuff, that is, not the people. I wasn't into taking care of ghosts.

Except it would seem I was having an affair with one: the ghost of Jeff's past. Didn't I deserve a real human being instead of lavishing my feelings on a phantom who existed more in my imagination than in my life?

I reached for my cell phone. Time to break up with the ghost. I called his number and waited for him to pick up. This time I was gonna do it for real.

His voice mail answered. After a moment's hesitation, I hung up. No point in leaving a message. He'd see it was me and call back.

I sat down on my sofa, took a deep breath, and let it out. Then I reached for my laptop and stared at the computer screen. I tried to think of where to go online, as though the solutions to my problems could be found in cyberspace if I just knew the right place to look.

JDate?

I had an account from past forays into online dating. I logged on and scrolled down a column of men. Romancer007. Live4today. ClinicallySane1. Needlenahaystack. TheComebackYid.

Oy.

The shrill ring of my cell phone made me jump. Jeff. "Hello?"

"Did you call?" he asked.

"Yes. How's your wife?"

"She's out of surgery. They said it went fine."

"That must be a relief." I clicked on the profile of a fairly attractive man with dark hair, gray sideburns, black T-shirt.

"I'm just waiting for her to come out of the anesthesia," he said. "Then I'll take her home."

"Uh-huh." He called himself NativeNewYawker. Claimed to be forty-two.

"I still feel terrible about your birthday."

"Don't worry. I'm a big girl."

"Maybe I could still see you tomorrow."

"You know . . ." I swallowed. "I don't think that's a good idea."

"The doctor said her thumb might be sore, that's all."

"Still . . ." NativeNewYawker, unlike some of his competition, looked straight at the camera and smiled.

"I'd already told her I'd be away on business," he said, "so I could spend the night with you. She's expecting me to go. We talked about it in the cab on the way to the hospital."

"No. You should be home with her."

"Amanda, you're angry, I know, and you have a right to be, but please let me make it up to you. And I want to give you your birthday present."

I wanted to say his damn present wouldn't make up for my stolen youth. Instead, I glared at the computer screen. NativeNewYawker's face had small, even features. I read somewhere that people were attracted to symmetry.

"Let's meet for breakfast. We can spend the morning together."

Having sex? Forget it. "No."

"Name a time and a place and I'll be there, I promise."

"Nowhere," I said. "Never."

"Amanda, come on. Please don't do this, please?"

"It's over, Jeff. I can't do this anymore." We both knew I'd said those exact words before. Why should he believe me now?

"Listen, why don't you get a good night's sleep and we'll talk tomorrow, okay?"

"No. This is it. And if you care about me and my welfare, you'll do me a favor: Don't come to my apartment or my store. Don't call, text, e-mail, or contact me in any form that technology has or will make possible in the future. Good-bye."

"I love you, Amanda."

I hung up. Closed JDate. Turned off my laptop and put it back on the desk. That's when I noticed the unopened letter from the managing agent of my building. Might as well face the music. As expected, it was about the renewal of the lease for my retail space. Not as expected, the landlord had chosen not to renew, which meant that I had a month to close down the shop and vacate the premises.

What the hell?

This had to be a mistake. Typos. Sent to the wrong person. The managing agent, a smarmy guy named Chuck Grabowski, had definitely told me he'd be renewing at a 6 percent hike. I'd call in the morning and clear it up. All I could do now was go to bed and put this day behind me.

OLIVE

I WOKE UP confused. What was I doing back in my old bedroom?

Then I remembered.

At least today wasn't yesterday. The funeral, the graveyard, dirt on the coffin. People in our house, childhood friends. Looks of pity bombarding me from every direction.

"Olive?" Aunt Ida knocked on the door.

"Yes?"

She poked her head in. "Some of your friends have come to call."

"What time is it?"

"Almost noon. I don't know how you can sleep so late. I'll tell them to wait—"

"No, please. Ask them to come back in a few hours, will you?"

"Fine, but you'd better get out of bed or you'll never get to sleep tonight."

I fell back asleep. Later, the smell of apples and cinnamon woke me. I dressed and went down to the kitchen, where Margaret was rolling out dough for pies.

"Like some apple cake?" she asked.

"Please, it smells wonderful." The day before, I thought my appetite would never return. Now my mouth was watering.

"I was hoping it might tempt you out of bed," she said, cutting me a slice with her pink chubby hands. "Your apple trees were so generous this year. I've been trying out every recipe with apples that I can find."

"You've such a talent for baking."

"Oh, honey, it's only a matter of scooping and stirring. If you like, I'll teach you my recipes anytime."

My aunt entered the room with a bouquet of roses. "Good luck getting Olive anywhere closer to the stove than she is. Goodness, so many flowers, and I've nowhere to put them."

"Aren't those beautiful," Margaret said, wiping her hands on a towel. "I think I'll go upstairs and freshen up."

I was sorry to be left alone with my aunt.

"I thought the funeral was lovely," she said, trying to fit the bulky bouquet inside a lemonade pitcher. Tall and thin, my aunt wore her light brown hair coiled like a crown—an unflattering hairstyle that never varied.

"Thank you for arranging everything," I said.

"You don't have to thank me for that." She abruptly let go of the flowers and pulled a handkerchief from her pocket. "I still can't believe my dear Charles is gone," she said, pressing the cloth against her eyes.

"It must be devastating to lose your big brother." She'd always looked older than Father, even though she was a year younger. Now my aunt almost looked elderly. On her forehead were lines of wrinkles I'd never seen. Dark purple bags sagged under her blue eyes.

"I'll be fine." She tucked the handkerchief back into her pocket. "At least we can take comfort knowing he's in a better place. You're the one I'm worried about, so close to him, and he did like to indulge you. At times like this, I feel grateful to have my faith to keep me strong. You have been going to church since moving to New York, I hope?"

"There was a very nice one just up the block," I said, evading the question and knowing full well I hadn't fooled her.

As a devout Christian, my aunt would've done more to enforce her beliefs in our household if Father had let her. He was the sort who'd pray if there was a pressing need; the rest of the time, he couldn't be bothered. He liked to say it was up to an individual to behave morally rather than act a certain way to please God. I found this more reasonable than my aunt's fanatic views.

"Life doesn't stop," she said, continuing to fuss with the flowers so all the roses would splay out. "One must go on. Why did you turn away your friends? They came to give you comfort."

"They gave me their sympathy at the funeral. Today they'll just want to tell me how lovely it is to be married, so I must hurry up and find a husband before no one wants me."

"Perhaps you could stand to hear some of their advice."

I pushed away the last of my apple cake and tried to think of how I could excuse myself.

"Have you arranged anything with the Mansfield?" she asked. "You'll need to have everything sent up from the city."

"I haven't begun to think about that."

"What is there to think about?"

"I'll telephone the manager and sort things out later. I'd like to go down to the store. I've not been there yet."

"Might be hard," she said. "So many memories."

"That's all right." I took my dish to the sink. "I like those memories."

• • •

The countergirls greeted me solemnly and gave their condolences as I wandered up and down the aisles. I smiled at everyone with resilience and fooled nobody.

The very scent of dusty air and wood polish brought back the past. My childhood fantasyland of cherrywood counters, glass showcases, and mirrored walls made me feel close to Father. Yet the knowledge that my past was gone forever made me want to cry, and the strain of holding back tears brought on a throbbing headache. "It's terribly good to see everyone," I said to the head cashier. "Thank you for being so kind." The bell on the door tinkled as I left.

Strolling up Main Street, I saw a group of children laughing and jumping on the back step of Mr. Barrow's ice wagon. As the old horse plodded forward, Mr. Barrow kept snapping his whip back toward the kids, but that only made them laugh louder. I'd done the very same as a girl.

A rush of nostalgia for the town made my heart ache. I passed the dressmaker's shop, the Presbyterian church where I'd gone to Sunday School, the town library. Turning the corner, I walked down the road to my house. Painted yellow with green trim, our handsome Queen Anne presented the very picture of an idyllic home. I followed the stone path to the wraparound porch, sat down on the creaky old swinging bench, and stared into the branches of the elm trees. Aunt Ida was right. Of course I'd move back to Cold Spring. This town was peaceful and lovely. New York was chaotic and impossible. I had no ties there—had even been gently uninvited from Mr. Woolworth's party by an executive who came from the city for Father's funeral. And without a reference, it seemed I couldn't even get a job as a salesgirl.

That adventure was over. The past month in Manhattan would condense into memories of a brief and exciting time—the high point of my life. Most people would say I was lucky to have the security of a comfortable home; they'd think me spoiled for wanting more from life.

I forced myself to go inside and telephone the Mansfield. After I explained my situation to the manager, Mr. Redstone, he expressed his condolences. Then he asked when I could remove our belongings.

"Not before the end of October. Some business matters will keep me here a few more days."

"That presents a problem, Miss Westcott. I need to ready the apartment for new tenants."

"It is possible I might be staying on there," I said. Even though it was unlikely, I couldn't give up on the idea entirely.

"I'm sorry, but since you're no longer accompanied by your father, we can't offer you accommodations. The Mansfield doesn't allow single women."

"I didn't realize that."

"In any event," he added, "you'll owe for the month of November, seeing as we need fourteen days' notice to cancel the lease."

"Excuse me, Mr. Redstone. You're saying I must pay rent for next month even though you won't allow me to live there?"

"Those are the conditions of the lease." He took advantage of my stunned silence to end the call. "Let me say, Miss Westcott, that I'm so sorry for your loss. If there's any way I can be of help, please do let me know."

After replacing the receiver on the hook, I couldn't think of what to do, so I went up to my room, and sat on the edge of my bed. I didn't belong in this girlish room, decorated with pink-and-white-striped wallpaper, white lace curtains, and a yellow chenille bedspread. I didn't belong in New York, either.

I didn't belong anywhere.

"Olive!" Aunt Ida called for me from the parlor. "I need your help!"

I went back downstairs. At least someone needed me for something.

"It's time to beat the rug," she said while vigorously sweeping the old maroon carpet. Her valiant effort only kicked the dust up into new locations.

This was my least favorite chore, but anything was better than sinking into melancholy. We moved the furniture aside and lugged the rug to the clothesline in the backyard. Exposed to the light of day, the maroon wool carpet took on a magenta hue. Aunt Ida smacked it over and over with a bamboo cane. Clouds of dust billowed into the air. I turned toward the bare apple trees and the vegetable patch where my aunt planted beets, leeks, lettuce, tomatoes . . . all dormant now. The long winter lay ahead. Somehow we'd have to get through it.

When Aunt Ida had to stop for a coughing fit, I stepped forward. "My turn."

She handed me the cane. "I spoke to old Jimmy about your father."

"Good." Jimmy, a local stonemason, specialized in carving gravestones.

"He said he's busy and can't get to it for another few weeks."

I waited for the dust to settle. "There's a trade that will never run out of customers."

"The old man is worth waiting for. He did a lovely job with your mother's gravestone."

Positioning myself in front of the rug, I gripped the bamboo cane with both hands and swung. A cloud of dust exploded into my face. I stepped back to get a breath of clean air. The question came out as if I were making a casual inquiry. "What happened when I was born?"

"What do you mean?"

"Exactly what happened during the birth that made my mother bleed to death?"

She squinted with uncertainty. "Do you really want to know?"

"Yes, I do." I spoke with confidence and kept my face dispassionate so she wouldn't spare the details.

"Your mother's pelvis," she said, "was too small. You were stuck in the birth canal. Your mother, poor dear, was in labor for over two days."

"And how did I finally . . . get out?" My voice quivered. I hoped she didn't notice.

"The doctor tried forceps, but they didn't work. She was getting weaker and weaker, so finally, he made cuts to widen the opening. Soon after that, she went into shock. Bled to death. He managed to save you. Of course, it wasn't your fault; he had to do it, or the both of you would've died."

Even as I nodded, I thought it surely was my fault. If she'd never gotten pregnant, or if I'd been smaller . . . "I wonder why our bodies aren't better designed to give birth."

"Eve's curse."

"You don't honestly believe that, do you?"

"Women have to suffer for her sins."

"Doesn't God want babies to have their mothers?"

"It's not for you to question the Lord's ways, young lady."

Her sharp tone silenced me but not my doubts. How could I *not* question His ways? Did the Lord intend for me to bring about the death of my mother? Was the Lord punishing me for something? I felt an old familiar feeling, an unpleasant one, almost a physical revulsion to myself. As if something must be horribly, intrinsically wrong with me—something that was there before I was even born. My aunt had a way of stirring it up.

Positioning myself in front of the rug, I whacked as hard as I could. Any temptation to move back to Cold Spring must be resisted. I whacked the rug again. I'd go mad. I whacked, and whacked, and whacked. Perhaps this wasn't the worst chore in the world.

"The will was written many years ago," Mr. Beringer explained while cleaning his spectacles with a handkerchief.

Aunt Ida and I sat side by side across from the lawyer. The will sat on his desk. I didn't expect a large inheritance; just enough to provide a comfortable and secure future.

"Charles had meant to make some changes," he said, putting on his spectacles, "but he didn't get around to it before his untimely death."

Mr. Beringer read the passage that stated my aunt was the sole beneficiary of the estate. As my legal guardian, she was to care for my financial needs with "generosity and discretion." Upon her death, the remaining assets would pass to me.

"As it should be," my aunt said.

I kept my mouth shut. Aunt Ida had never been ill a day in her life and might very well outlive me. I didn't doubt her love and knew she wanted what was best for her niece, but we were bound to disagree on what that was.

"As you know," Mr. Beringer said, removing his spectacles, "Charles was sophisticated about the stock market and did a lot of trading over the years. Though he did enjoy taking some risks, he usually made out well. After all, the market was climbing to new highs the past ten years; it was nearly impossible to lose money even if you tried." At that point he gave us a look of pity that made my stomach turn. "As you can imagine, hardly anyone has been immune from the recent developments in the market. I'm afraid your father was no exception."

"He told me he was doing well," I said. "That we needn't worry." Or had he said the worst was over? That he hoped the worst was over?

"Perhaps. But as you must be aware, the situation with United Copper has led to the collapse of the Knickerbocker Trust. The repercussions are just now being felt."

"Yes," I said quietly. The other day, in the taxi to Grand Central Station, I saw it with my own eyes: a line of people stretching all the way down the block, frantically waiting to withdraw their money from a bank. At the doors, an angry crowd was pushing and yelling as policemen tried to break up the brawl. I could hear Father saying they shouldn't panic—it only made everything worse.

Did he panic?

"But Father didn't have any money with those banks," I said.

"No, but I've been in touch with his broker. Evidently, Charles was holding a great deal of stocks on margin. He thought the market would turn around and didn't want to sell at the bottom. He refused to get out. So he had to sell bonds to meet the margin calls. But the market sank lower and lower, and he still wouldn't get out."

I nodded, but in my mind, my head shook side to side.

"By the day of the accident," Mr. Beringer continued, "he had nothing left to sell. One can't help but wonder what was going through his mind while he was on the road . . ." The lawyer slumped for a moment of reflection before delivering the next blow. "I'm sorry to have to tell you he couldn't cover the margin calls."

"I don't understand what you're talking about," my aunt said in a burst of fury. "Just tell us what the estate is worth!"

"The holdings of the estate," he said, "have been exhausted."

I must've heard him wrong. That couldn't be. "Gone . . . completely?"

He drew a handkerchief from his waistcoat pocket. I thought he might shed a tear, but he used it to clean his spectacles again. "As a matter of fact, the estate currently owes money to the bank . . . and the brokerage house."

"This is absurd." Aunt Ida sat erect. "Charles would never let this happen. You've made a mistake."

"I know this is dreadfully upsetting, Miss Westcott. But you have to understand, Wall Street has just suffered its worst losses since 1893." Replacing his spectacles, Mr. Beringer opened a thick file of documents and rifled through. "Union Pacific,

General Electric, Western Union, Standard Oil . . . down, down, down, and we're not talking a little. Some of these over a hundred percent. It's bad all over. I'm hurting, too, everyone is."

A lump in my chest seemed to smolder and expand. I stared down at my black wool skirt as he continued. "No one could've predicted this, but when you buy on margin, you take that risk."

"What about the house?" Aunt Ida asked.

"That's the good news. You have the house to sell. That should take care of most of the debt."

"Sell the house?" my aunt practically screamed. "Where are you suggesting we live?"

"Or," he said, "it can be used as collateral to borrow. But the banks can't be generous right now with their rates, and you have no income to repay a loan."

Father was dead, and we were in debt. Worse than broke. There had to be a way out.

"I don't see that you have any other options," Mr. Beringer went on, "apart from selling anything else you own of value, and of course . . ." He paused to examine his nails, which allowed him to avoid looking at us while making another suggestion. "You might want to consider employment of some sort."

"We've heard enough for now." Aunt Ida stood. "And I have some errands to run."

"Wait," I said, unsure what I wanted to say, knowing only that I couldn't leave his office like this.

Mr. Beringer waited for me to speak. "Do you have a question?"

I gripped the armrests of my chair. "Something must've been overlooked." Father had told me he left money in his leather box, and I knew it couldn't be much, but there had to be something, somewhere. "What about cash? The bank account? Is there nothing at all?"

"You wouldn't be able to withdraw money from his New York

accounts. Those are in his name only, and the assets automatically go to the estate. However . . ."

I looked at him with hope. He cleared his throat and turned toward my aunt, who stood behind her chair. "I shouldn't say this, but you and Charles had a joint account at the bank here in town. You might want to go there directly to withdraw the balance before the assets are frozen."

Money! My spirits rose. But how much?

"As soon as I file these papers with the state," he continued, "that money will be held in escrow and used to pay off creditors. I believe you have approximately thirty dollars."

That was all? Just as quickly, my spirits sank.

"We'll go there now, thank you," my aunt said, already on her way to the door.

I made myself stand but kept staring at the will on the desk. Father must've known all of this when he began that drive back to New York.

"I'm sorry to have to break such unpleasant news," Mr. Beringer was saying, "before you've had a chance to recover from the shock of this dreadful tragedy."

"Olive? Are you coming?"

I crossed the room as though approaching my own execution. At the door, Mr. Beringer bowed his head and bid us a solemn farewell. "We shall all miss Charles very much. And of course . . ." He cleared his throat. "Under the circumstances, I'm willing to defer my fees until a more convenient time to settle the bill."

Aunt Ida and I went straight to the bank to withdraw the balance—thirty-seven dollars and sixty-four cents, to be exact. She gave me five dollar-bill. "You'll need cash to go down to the city to pack up that apartment."

"Thank you." She stacked the rest of the bills into a neat pile, slid them inside an envelope, tucked the envelope inside her purse, and snapped her purse shut. I couldn't admit to owing the Mansfield eighty dollars. That envelope held her entire fortune.

November 3, 1907

Since I never knew my mother, I never felt her absence, like I do with Father. My ears keep expecting to hear his voice. My eyes keep expecting him to come into view. How is it possible that a person can simply disappear off the face of the earth? I must get back to Manhattan and see for myself that he isn't there, either.

The black marble clock on the mantel ticked as we ate dinner, just us women.

"I do have some money in my savings account," Margaret said, taking a slice of corned beef from the platter. "I wish it were more, but under the circumstances, every bit helps."

"That's very kind." Aunt Ida passed me a bowl of peas. "But you need to live on that, and we can't accept."

"We're all in this together," Margaret said. "And if you have to sell the house . . ."

"We aren't selling the house." Aunt Ida took a piece of meat. "It's out of the question."

"We may not have a choice," I said, handing Margaret the peas and taking the platter of meat from my aunt.

"The girl's right, Ida. I didn't want to give up my house."

"We'll think of something. To begin with, we'll start selling things."

"The furniture?" I never did like the black walnut table with its fussy bow legs or the matching black walnut cabinets and cupboards.

"Better to start small," my aunt said. "We don't need the entire town knowing we're pinching. There's some jewelry from my mother. I could take it to a dealer in Poughkeepsie."

"Selling things can help only in the short term," I said, cutting a piece of meat. "I, for one, will take Mr. Beringer's suggestion and find a job."

"I imagine they'll take you on at Woolworth's," my aunt said.

"For three dollars a week?"

"You used to work there for nothing."

I clenched my jaw. "That job is a dead end."

"It might feel degrading at first, but we have to be practical."

Margaret wisely ate her meal in silence, staying out of the conversation.

"It makes much more sense for me to work in a department store. At least I could work my way up."

"Luckey, Platt?" she asked, referring to the department store in Poughkeepsie.

"There's much more opportunity in New York."

"You can't live in that vile city by yourself!"

I tried to keep the trembling out of my voice. "Lots of girls go to New York to make a living. I daresay some of them have less brains than I do."

"It's not your brain I'm worried about. Those stores are full of men just waiting for a chance to prey on a woman's weakness."

"I should hope you'd have more faith in me."

"You'll be especially vulnerable, my dear. After a lifetime of getting everything you want? How will you feel, standing on the other side of a counter day after day, selling things you can no longer afford?"

"I'll feel that I'm working toward a respectable career—one that has the potential to pay quite well, I might add. Even if you disapprove of women working outside the home, I should think that under the circumstances, you'd welcome my ambition."

"You're talking nonsense! You'll have no place to live, no

contacts, no money to establish yourself. Instead of running off to the city, you should take some time to rest and pull yourself together."

"I don't need rest—I need to keep busy."

"So keep busy here, where you have friends and family. Before too long, I'm sure you'll find some nice young man to marry. What do you find so dreadful about that?"

My eyes flashed back and forth between the two older women as I fought the temptation to pose the same question. "I'm sorry you don't agree with me, Aunt Ida, but my mind is made up. I'm moving back to New York."

"Your father would never allow you to go there by yourself. As your guardian, I strictly forbid it!"

"As my guardian, the only way you can stop me is to withhold money." I looked at Father's empty chair on the opposite side of the table. "Regrettably, there is none to withhold."

The next day, when I came downstairs with my suitcase, Aunt Ida was dusting out the chimney of a lamp. "You're making a mistake," she said without looking up. "You don't realize the state you're in. Pale. Thinner than ever. Your eyes are bloodshot. Do you even know anyone in that city who might help you?"

The only person I could think of was Ralph Pierce, though I couldn't bear the idea of him pitying me because of my change in circumstances. "Don't worry. I'll be fine."

"I know you think I'm hopelessly old-fashioned," she said while trimming the wick, "but I raised you the only way I knew how. I've never wanted anything but to make a good home for you and Charles."

"And you did that, and I'm awfully grateful, truly I am. I didn't mean to be unkind last night. I'm terribly sorry if I was rude."

"I know you loathe the idea of living here, but as long as we have this house, the door shall be open should you wish to return."

"It's not that, Aunt Ida; I simply don't belong here. I never have, for some reason, and I need to be somewhere I fit in."

She filled the reservoir with oil. "Well, I hope you find what you want."

"Thank you. I'll be sure to write as soon as I have news."

After replacing the chimney, she set the lamp aside and stood up. "Good-bye, then."

I stepped forward, managed to place a dry peck on her hollow, sagging cheek, and softly said, "I love you." A twinge of vulnerability drove my gaze toward the floor.

She mumbled something that included the word "love" and told me to take care of myself. I thought she might offer to walk me to the train station and felt relieved when she didn't. At least our leave-taking was done.

AMANDA

I TOOK ONE of Jeff's white button-down shirts out of my bureau. Even the tiniest stain prompted him to toss them out, so I tried to rescue the ones I could, to use as pajamas. It did seem wrong to encase myself in his shirt right after telling him we were through, but it was an incredibly soft Brooks Brothers Egyptian-cotton dress shirt that retailed for almost two hundred dollars. I loved how the oversize shoulders and sleeves made me feel petite.

After brushing and flossing, I dug my old boom box out of the closet with satisfaction. Sometimes what people would call "hoarding" turns out to be "saving something for the day you might just need it." I set it up on my nightstand and replaced Michael Jackson's *Thriller* with Dr. Markoff. Then I lay down in the dark, stared up at the ceiling, and waited to be lulled by that reassuring voice.

I want you to stare at the ceiling.

Cracks all over the place. I needed to call the super and get him to paint.

Keep your eyes focused on the flat white surface and try not to blink.

The wind blew through my open window.

You very much want to blink, but I want you to resist that urge.

I should close it, but that would involve getting out of bed.

Your lids feel so heavy, the temptation to close them is too great. So now you can close your eyes if you like.

Poor Olive. Would she stay in New York on her own?

Now I want you to focus on your body by relaxing each part.

She needed to find someone to comfort her.

The soles of your feet . . .

Caress her.

Your calves . . .

She needed to be touched.

Your thighs . . .

So did I.

We're going to let your unconscious hear what it wants to hear . . .

By a real person.

. . . while you think about yourself and your relationships with other people.

Not a ghost.

Life is not always a straight line.

What's that noise?

You take detours and go backward and forward and sideways.

A woman . . . moaning.

It's impossible to know everything from the beginning.

Maybe my neighbor got lucky.

We need to live in order to learn about ourselves and the world and other people.

But was it ecstasy . . . or pain?

We wouldn't grow if we didn't make mistakes.

She could be having really good sex . . .

So it doesn't make sense to blame yourself for living your life.

Or getting murdered.

We can't tell the future.

I turned off the tape and listened, but the noise was gone. That was weird. Maybe it had been on the tape? It didn't make sense.

This hypnosis business clearly wasn't working; I'd have to get to sleep on my own. So I fluffed up my pillow, closed my eyes, and hoped for the best. After spending twenty minutes mentally rearranging the display in my store window, I opened my eyes, feeling wide awake, and realized it was going to be another long night.

Might as well get some work done. After replacing Dr. Markoff with Michael Jackson, I got out my sewing box and a pile of clothes I'd bought at a recent estate sale. Then I settled in on the couch to do some alterations.

A simple cosmetic repair can often rescue a piece of clothing from being tossed or ignored or unappreciated. Hooks, eyes, snaps, buttons. Sometimes all that needs fixing is the closures. A forties white rayon top with red piping on the sleeve cuffs was missing two buttons; since I couldn't match the remaining ones, I removed them all. Then I whipstitched the buttonholes closed and covered them with deliciously glossy red casein buttons from my stash. When that was done, I added snaps underneath to do the actual fastening. Voilà. My version was better than the original.

Next up was a caramel-colored leather coat from the sixties—nice but not too exciting, and the collar and cuffs were worn and blemished. I remembered two fur sleeves left over from an old raccoon coat that would contrast nicely with the leather. Using the leather collar and cuffs as pattern pieces, I cut the fur and sewed it on. Now I had a glamorous fur-trimmed coat worth double the price.

As I held up the coat to admire my handiwork, a sudden loud bang scared me half to death. Not a gunshot, just the bathroom door. A gust of wind must've blown it shut. I opened it and froze with terror. Someone—!

No one. Just Jane Kelly's shift dress hanging over the bathtub, swaying ever so gently in the breeze from the still-open bathroom window. I was freaking myself out over nothing.

I closed the window, then the door; while I was at it, I checked inside my closet to make sure the ax murderer wasn't lurking in there and, just to cover all the bases, got down on my hands and knees to look under the bed. Nothing there but lots of dust balls and a crumpled piece of paper. I reached for it. Foil, actually. A condom wrapper from one of my nights with Jeff.

I got back up and sat on the edge of the bed. While smoothing out the empty packet on my thigh, I noticed the expiration date. My eyes widened. That date came and went six months ago.

I opened my nightstand drawer to check the box. All the condoms had the same expiration date. That meant Jeff and I had been using no-good condoms for months!

Oh my god. And my period was still MIA. I got dressed to go back outside. I didn't care that it was one in the morning. I needed a pregnancy test. Now.

Venturing under fluorescent lights that could illuminate a ball field, I searched up and down the drugstore aisles past the vast assortment of cosmetics, snack foods pretending to be dietary, and lotions preying on fear of wrinkles. The pregnancy tests turned up right between the Tampax and Trojans. One brand claimed to give results five days before your first period. *Ninety-nine percent accuracy. One easy step. Digital technology.* I decided to go for it. I grabbed a package of tampons for good luck and—why not—some lubricated Trojans, making sure to check the expiration date first.

Placing my purchases on the counter, I tried to project a casual nonchalance, as if splurging in the Genital Care aisle were something I did all the time. After the cashier scanned the bar code on the pregnancy test, she glanced at me with a friendly smile and wished me good luck. As she bagged my items, I wondered which result she considered the lucky one.

When I got back to my apartment, I ripped open the box with fumbling fingers and unfolded the instructions. My hands shook as I read the tiny print. *Place the tip in urine stream for five seconds. Results in three minutes.*

My heart raced as I sat on the toilet. My hand trembled while I did my best to aim the pee. Departing the bathroom, I held the stick in front of me like a lit candle threatening to go out. My Westclox said 1:45 A.M. I turned on the TV and continued to hold the stick. As the disembodied humans jabbered away on the screen, I told myself that the condom had probably been perfectly good; they put those dates there so people would dump them to buy new ones.

1:46 A.M.

Except I'd missed a period. Had bloated breasts. The truth was obvious. I didn't need a test to tell me. I was pregnant. A woman knows!

1:46 A.M.

Oh god, how could I go through with an abortion? I couldn't. This would probably be my last chance to get pregnant. A baby would change the entire equation. Jeff would see that I was the one who needed him, so maybe he'd actually leave his wife. Wow. This could be the best mistake that ever happened to me.

Still 1:46 A.M. Was that clock broken?

But maybe he'd think I was trying to trick him into marriage. I could just hear Jeff: "You gave me an expired condom? Are you insane?"

This did resemble a hackneyed soap-opera plot with me as the scheming, jealous diva using pregnancy to force a man to commit.

Maybe I *was* trying to trap him into marriage. How long had those condoms been there? For all I knew, they were bad when I bought them; I never thought to check. My carelessness could've been part of an unconscious plan to get him to leave his wife. My ex-therapist would've had a field day. But aren't the stores supposed to keep an eye on things like expiration dates?

I looked at the clock. 1:48 A.M. How did that happen? The results were in. Time to look at the objective, nonjudgmental stick. The future was now.

Not pregnant.

Oh.

Okay. Not pregnant.

Damn.

Except that was good. I should be relieved. Right?

I threw the stick in the garbage.

Just my luck.

OLIVE

I OPENED THE door of the apartment, half expecting to see Father sitting in his overstuffed chair, reading the paper. The maid had cleaned up, and everything looked spotless, almost like the day we moved in.

The Four Epochs of Woman's Life still sat on the end table next to the box of chocolates. I blushed, imagining the maid seeing the book. Perhaps she sat down to read it and learned all about the orgasm. Or perhaps she knew all about that and laughed at the ignorance of the girl who'd left it there.

The first order of business was to go straight to Father's bedroom for the money in his leather box. He'd owned that box since I could remember. I used to adore sifting through when I was little, knowing its contents rarely changed. Cuff links, collar buttons, scarf pins, an extra pocket watch. A leather fob I once gave him, with a metal charm of a baseball player. And now, to my relief, a twenty-dollar bill. My inheritance, so to speak. I sent up thanks to my father, returned to the living room, and put the money in my purse.

Many dreadful tasks lay ahead. Packing would be unpleasant enough. Even worse, I had to speak to the manager and find a way around paying the November rent. It was all too overwhelming. My eyes settled on Father's cigar box and the picture of the one beautiful woman whispering to the other. Remembering his enjoyment over that simple pleasure made my eyes fill with tears.

A rapping on the door forced me to pull myself together. Peering through the peephole, I saw a man with a handlebar mustache. "Who is it?"

"Mr. Redstone," he said, "the manager."

I gritted my teeth and opened the door.

"I don't mean to disturb you," he said. "The doorman told me you'd arrived. I'll have the porter bring your trunks up from the storage room. Is there anything else I can do?"

"I need to ship some things back to Cold Spring."

"Just call down to the lobby when you're ready. The porter will help you with a cab. By the way, in case you've not made other arrangements, I decided you can stay here tonight. If someone complains, I'll explain that I'm bending the rules out of decency." He puffed up his chest as though I should think he was a hero.

"Thank you."

"Now then." He cleared his throat. "There is the matter of the November rent. As I mentioned on the telephone, we require payment in advance."

"Mr. Redstone, since I can't stay on here, I'm still very much hoping you might waive the November rent."

"Yes, I'm very sorry about that, but as I explained, we rent on a month-to-month basis, and you're well beyond the required fourteen days' notice required."

"But my father died after the fourteen-day period had elapsed."

"I know this must seem insensitive, Miss Westcott, but as it is, we're almost a week into November. Since you've not vacated the premises, you're legally responsible for the rent."

My blood boiled, but I kept my tone steady. "I'm not allowed to live here anymore. And my father is no longer among the living. Under these circumstances, do you honestly think it's fair to charge either of us for living here?"

"I'm terribly sorry, but I have to answer to the owners of the building. It's not within my authority to allow our tenants to stay here free of charge."

"You must carry out your duty to your employers. That's your first priority, of course. But my father's death has brought about an overwhelming financial hardship."

"I'm sorry to hear that, Miss Westcott."

"The truth is, I haven't any funds available, and I'm hoping for your compassion. I'll do my best to empty the apartment as soon as possible."

"Perhaps you have some family members who can help you out?"

Father once told me that if you wanted something, you needed to ask at least three times. After the third request, the opponent's willpower often crumbles. "Sadly, I don't. I'm on my own now, Mr. Redstone, and I don't know how I'm going to make do. Wouldn't you please reconsider? I'd be most grateful." I appealed to him with my most helpless expression. My heart pounded so hard, I thought he must be able to see my chest throb.

"Well . . ."

His first sign of wavering. If I suggested a compromise, he might relent with his pride intact. "Would you allow me to pay you twenty dollars in cash right now? I could manage that much, though just barely. And perhaps you'd be willing to leave it at that?"

He leaned forward and lowered his voice. "I suppose we could manage some such arrangement. It would have to be off the record, though."

"Yes," I said, my voice soft and hushed. "Off the record, of course." I retrieved the precious twenty-dollar bill from my purse and handed it to him.

"So," he said, slipping the bill in his waistcoat pocket, "we'll consider the balance paid."

"Thank you," I said with gravity.

"As agreed, you'll vacate the premises in twenty-four hours."

"I don't suppose, since twenty dollars covers the week—"

"I'm already bending the rules for you, Miss Westcott."

"Very well. Tomorrow."

After he left, I turned the lock and leaned against the door to steady myself. Reaching under my collar, I pulled out my locket and rubbed the smooth gold with my thumb; the familiar indentation of the star somehow gave me reassurance. I'd need all the strength I could muster to endure the next few days.

Soon the porter arrived with the two steamer trunks. He also had a box from Siegel-Cooper, delivered while I was gone. My tailored suit. Father would never have the chance to tease me for being a suffragette. I reached into my purse once more and handed the porter a tip. Judging from his expression, it should've been more.

After he left, I dragged Father's trunk to the doorway of his bedroom. I would ship his things back to Aunt Ida. She could sort through it all and sell off what she wished.

I opened the top drawer of his bureau. Inside were neat rows of silk four-in-hand ties, bow ties, Windsor ties. It seemed too intimate to handle the clothing that had touched his body. And too cruel, as if I'd be folding him up and putting him away. Of course, it wasn't him and there was no use putting it off. The only way to end the ordeal was to suffer through it.

I worked my way through the collars and cuffs, suspenders and hose, and freshly laundered button-down shirts. Dead people had no privacy. My own belongings would be left behind one day. If I never had children, who would take care of my things? Next

I tackled his closet. Dress suits, dinner jackets, shoes . . . Then I opened the drawers of his desk. I couldn't bear to look at the papers, receipts, and ledgers—anything with his handwriting—so it all went straight into the trunk.

After that was done, it seemed like a good time to stop for lunch. Eating in the Mansfield sounded dreadful. I'd find a nearby restaurant.

On my way out, the red-haired doorman spoke in a confidential whisper. "Just wanted to say I'm sorry 'bout your father, miss. And if I can be of any help . . ."

"That's very kind, thank you."

I ended up at Child's restaurant on Twenty-third Street. The chain had spread through the city like weeds—or dandelions, depending on whom you asked. Other women sat at tables by themselves, so at least I didn't have to feel self-conscious. After ordering a plate of hash and eggs, I watched the people passing by on the other side of the plate-glass window. I perceived them all as lucky, protected by their circles of friends and family while going about their routines, blasé about living in the city. Would I ever become one of them?

When I returned to the Mansfield, the doorman sidled up to me again. "I wanted to mention, it happens I know someone who's got a shop for cast-off clothes. If you're interested, I can arrange for her to come by. I don't mean to interfere, but she can take some of those extras off your hands."

"That won't be necessary. I'll be shipping my father's things up to Cold Spring."

"Thought you might have some extras of your own, too."

The forced, offhand expression on his face made me realize that he knew I was financially ruined. The staff undoubtedly gossiped with zest about the tenants.

"I don't think so, but thank you for mentioning it."

"She pays cash," he added, "on the spot."

I continued on to the elevator. The idea of selling off Father's fine furnishings made me cringe. Almost all our clothes were tailor-made. Some secondhand shop woman couldn't possibly offer anywhere near a fair price.

As soon as I was back in the room I called the shipping company. When the man told me the estimated shipping costs, I repeated the staggering sum out loud, thanked him very much, and rang off. It made no sense to pay good money to ship Father's belongings only to burden Aunt Ida with disposing of them.

I telephoned down to the lobby and asked to speak with the doorman. A minute later, he was on the other end of the line. "You want me to send for Matilda?"

"I realized it probably would be more convenient."

A hefty woman with a big square face, Matilda held up each item for inspection. "I'll give you a total at the end—take it or leave it." As she worked her way through Father's clothes, I began to pack my own trunk. The desire to purge myself of everything and start fresh took hold of me. Even my favorite frocks seemed like a burden from the past.

Except I'd be foolish to give up my lovely clothes.

Or was it foolish to hold on to them when I needed the cash?

"I think I'd like to sell some of my own clothing, too," I announced.

"Just make up yer mind," she said. "I ain't got all day."

I kept only necessities: two skirts, three shirtwaists, three day dresses, two nightgowns, underclothing, wrapper, my new tweed suit, a pair of oxfords, high button boots, pumps, slippers, wool coat, summer coat, fur stole, muff, gloves, and two—no, three—of my finer dresses. I managed to fit two hats inside my biggest hatbox; the third I would wear.

After looking through everything, Matilda announced an amount. I'd hoped for more and countered with a higher sum.

"You wanna bargain with me?" Her voice boomed with incredulousness. "A poor old woman? I got a family to feed! You rich people always tryin' to cheat people like me. I gotta make a living too. You think someone else'll do better, then I'll be on my way."

"No," I said, "it's fine. I'll take what you offered." So much for my earlier finessing of Mr. Redstone.

Despite her victory, Matilda didn't soften one bit. "Look at this heap a clothes," she said, as if I were forcing her to take more than she wanted. "I can't carry all that myself. I'll have to come back tonight with my boy." She started out the door.

"Do you know what time you'll be returning?"

"I said tonight, didn't I?"

After she left, I buried my face in one of father's wool jackets and tried to find comfort in the scent of tobacco and aftershave. A clever business that Matilda had—taking advantage of the disadvantage of others.

November 4, 1907

I'm tempted not to let that woman back up. I could simply tell the doorman to send her away. But no, I shan't change my mind. I can't afford to be sentimental. Not now, when the only true asset I have is my freedom. Things do have a way of taking possession of people . . . if one lets them.

I went back to my packing, filling the shelf of my trunk with toiletry articles, sewing supplies, a mosaic box in which I kept trinkets and hatpins. Too bad I'd never gone in for jewelry, or I might've had something to pawn. My heart locket, the only piece I cared about, hung securely around my neck.

Matilda eventually returned with a glum-faced brawny son. He didn't say a word while helping her bundle up the clothes in paper wrapping. When they were done, she peeled my money off a wad of bills. Matilda might be poor, but compared to me, she was flush. I wondered how much time would pass before anyone handed me money again.

"By the way," I asked, "do you know of a respectable place where I could get a room? I need a place to stay right away."

"Can't say I do."

Her son spoke up for the first time. "What about Mrs. Craven?"

"You stupid?" she said. "This lady don't wanna joint like that."

He hung his head.

"Perhaps you could tell me where it is, just in case." I felt bad for him and wanted to show my appreciation. She told me an address over on First Avenue. I wrote it down and thanked him for mentioning it.

After they took everything away, I noticed Father's cigar box on his desk. I lifted the top; a whiff of tobacco went up my nose. Neat rows of cigars nestled inside. He'd never forgive me for throwing them down the garbage chute. I stuffed the box inside my already jam-packed trunk.

Finally, I'd finished my horrid tasks and could escape to bed. I washed up quickly, looking forward to lying down and freeing my mind from this new dreadful reality. Snuggling under the blanket, I thought surely I'd fall right off to sleep.

A half hour later, wide awake, I stared up at the ceiling. I couldn't stop thinking about Father's cigar box. It was foolish to take them with me. They'd make all my clothes smell of tobacco, and the sight of them would only make me sad. Missing Father hurt enough; I shouldn't suffer over missing his belongings, too.

I threw off the blanket, got out of bed, put on my wrapper, and took the cigar box from my trunk. I couldn't help staring at the two women with their secret. Perhaps it wouldn't be so awful to throw out the cigars and keep the box.

I removed the cigars from the box and shook out the remaining bits of tobacco. Then I went back to my trunk, pulled out the shabby little wicker basket that held my sewing supplies, and transferred all of its contents into the cigar box. Now that the basket was empty, I filled it with the cigars. For my final act of the day, I padded barefoot down the hallway to the garbage chute. After dropping the wicker basket inside, I waited for the faint, dull thud that let me know it hit bottom.

Astor Place where Eighth Street and Lafayette Street converge, 1892

Wanamaker's Department Store postcard of
original building and newer extension

Siegel-Cooper department store

Sightseeing tourists, circa 1904

WEDNESDAY
JUNE 13, 2007

17

AMANDA

ANOTHER LOUSY NIGHT'S sleep. Most of it was spent perusing the entire inventory of vintage fabrics on Etsy while entertaining an absurdly impractical idea of buying up yardage and starting a sideline business, sewing and selling my own line of clothes. Maybe in my next lifetime.

At around seven in the morning, I got up for some breakfast and read more of Olive's journal. It seemed like her life was falling apart in sync with mine. Then I went back to bed. I slept for a couple more hours and then woke up for a second breakfast. I still had a few hours before opening the store at one o'clock. Pretty much all the East Village slept until noon, so there was no point in opening any earlier, which was a good thing. Having my mornings free went a long way toward maintaining my sanity.

I needed to call Chuck to straighten out the lease, but I wouldn't be able to sound professional in my pajamas, so I tried to decide on what to wear. Either I'd gained some weight, or absolutely every piece of clothing I owned had shrunk. I voted for the latter.

Nevertheless, I resorted to my fat jeans. Searching for a cute top, I came across a Mexican peasant blouse with colorful birds embroidered down the front. It had come in a batch of ethnic tops from a wholesaler, and I'd been meaning to deal with a small cigarette burn near the hem before adding it to inventory. One advantage to the used clothing business: You could wear your stock without compromising the condition. After slipping on a white tank top, I dabbed at the cigarette burn with a bleach pen and then blotted it with a wet towel before laying it out to dry. If the stain still showed after the bleach dried, I'd camouflage it by turning the hem up a notch.

With that done, I was ready to call Chuck and find out my fate. I took a deep breath and dialed the number. As it rang, I geared up to be aggressive but not alienating. As it continued to ring, I tried to decide how detailed my voice mail should be. Then he picked up.

"Yeah, this is Chuck."

In a clear and calm voice, I explained my confusion over the letter. "I assume it's a mistake, since that's not what we last discussed."

"Right, uh, yeah," he said. "That was my understanding at the time. However, I'm sure you know nothing is official until it's in writing."

I did know. "So what are you saying?"

"It's not a mistake."

"I don't understand. I've been a good tenant. I've built up my business. I pay my rent on time."

"Rents have gone way up since you signed your lease. That's a destination neighborhood for restaurants and bars these days, and I've got clients willing to pay top dollar."

"Then I'd like to speak with the landlord." On my lease, the landlord was identified as Stella Realty Corporation, with no address or phone.

"That won't be possible."

"Considering I both live and work in the building, I think I deserve some consideration. What if I'm able to match what the others are willing to pay?"

"I doubt that."

So did I, but I continued, "Would you please give me the landlord's contact information?"

"No disrespect, but the landlord hires me so he doesn't have to deal with these problems. Look, you've been getting a good deal for that location, be thankful for that. Now it's over, and you have to be flexible. Reasonably priced rentals can be had if you're willing to move farther east."

"How far, Williamsburg?"

"You don't have to cross the river," he said, ignoring my sarcasm. "Prices are still reasonable on the other side of Avenue B."

"Moving is expensive and time-consuming, and I'm bound to lose customers. The disruption could easily destroy my business."

"It's hard to keep a small business going, even in good times. Let me know if you want to look at some properties. I might be able to help you out."

I refrained from thanking him for nothing and hung up.

My current retail space—five hundred square feet for eighteen hundred a month—had pretty much fallen into my lap. This time I'd have to start my search on good old Craigslist. Skimming down the listings, I saw that most places had square footage way too large for my needs. Hardly anything was under a thousand square feet. One place on First Avenue asked seven thousand for five hundred square feet. Another broker asked twenty-five hundred for six hundred square feet plus a basement, but that was way over on Avenue C. As feared, I'd have to pay more for less.

A new space would need renovations. That would cost. Movers would cost. I'd have to come up with a deposit on top of the rent. Start all over grooming customers.

I went through my alternatives. Give up the business; start a recycled-T-shirt shop in my father's ecovillage; go back to managing someone else's store; become a shopgirl at Macy's; crawl back to Jeff and beg for more help.

No. I shouldn't even think that thought.

Back to the listings. One got me all excited—a jewelry maker looking to share six hundred square feet for a thousand a month in an ideal location on Ninth Street and Second Avenue. That could be a solution—presuming she wasn't insane—and sharing could bring in more foot traffic. I clicked on the link and saw the ad was for a space on the third floor. Darn.

But that gave me an idea. Molly didn't open her button shop until one o'clock, so there was a chance I could get her to meet for coffee. I called her cell.

"Hey," she said. "Happy day after your birthday."

"Thanks! And thanks again for my session with Dr. Markoff. Do you have time to get together this morning? We need to catch up. Also, I'm having a little crisis I need to discuss."

"I gather your birthday dinner didn't go well?"

"It didn't even happen, but don't worry, this crisis has nothing to do with Jeff. I'd really like to run something by you."

"Okay. Where should we meet?"

"Remember De Robertis?" We used to go to that café all the time, back in our FIT days.

"Of course! I haven't been there in years."

"Me, neither. I always forget it's there."

"Me, too. Let's do it. See you there in half an hour?"

"Perfect."

We hung up, and I took a look at the peasant blouse. Victory. The bleach had dried, pretty much, and the cigarette burn was history.

On my way out, I grabbed the journal and stuffed it in my hobo bag. After seeing Molly, I'd probably go straight to the store. Maybe I'd want to read between customers. Or maybe not. I really couldn't take much more bad news.

OLIVE

DURING BREAKFAST, I studied the listings for rooms advertised in the paper. Some specified gentlemen or couples only. It didn't appear to be the custom to announce the rent. I hoped to stay in familiar territory but had no idea if that would be possible. The Martha Washington Hotel allowed women only, but they undoubtedly charged more than I ought to spend. The Seville, an elegant beaux arts hotel that stood kitty-corner to the Mansfield, would also be too expensive. I had no choice but to walk around to the addresses in the paper. After finishing breakfast I opened the Siegel-Cooper box. At least I could look smart in my new suit.

I soon discovered that the Mansfield's stance on renting to women was the norm. Smart-looking or not, I couldn't get anyone to consider me without a personal reference; anyone who would, offered a room too squalid to bear.

It occurred to me that I ought to ask for a reference from someone at Woolworth's—perhaps the executive who appeared at my father's funeral. Returning to the Mansfield, I telephoned the business office and asked to speak with him. Before long, I was pleading my case and trying to keep the desperation out of my voice.

The man told me he couldn't write a letter of reference for anyone who hadn't been an employee. "And," he added, "though we've met briefly, I can't squarely say I know you personally. Not that I doubt your character."

"But my father gave so many years of service to Mr. Woolworth. And your help would make all the difference."

"It's nothing against you. Just Mr. Woolworth's policy, that's all."

I thanked him and rang off. Damn Woolworth and his policies.

Then I remembered the Fifth Avenue Hotel. Didn't Father say they couldn't fill their rooms? The friendly woman who answered the telephone said they did indeed have a vacancy. When I gave my name to reserve it, she asked if I traveled alone. "We can't accommodate unescorted women, you see, 'specially on such short notice. We're a high-class hotel and have to be careful."

"I should hope so," I said, employing my haughtiest tone. "I'll be with my husband, Charles Westcott."

"Surely. Then we're all set, Mrs. Westcott."

The red-haired doorman helped load my belongings into a cab and wished me good luck. I thanked him for his help and pressed a coin into his hand. Less than five minutes later, the cab pulled up to the Fifth Avenue Hotel, a few blocks away, and the porter began to unload my bags. A red carpet led to a short man with wiry gray hair. His thin lips disappeared under his gray wiry mustache. "May I help you?"

"I have a reservation under the name of Charles Westcott."

"You're Mrs. Westcott?"

"Yes."

"Excellent. Welcome to the Fifth Avenue Hotel. I'll be happy to check you in when Mr. Westcott arrives."

"Thank you, but I'd prefer going directly to my room."

"I'm sorry, but I wouldn't be able to give you the room until your husband arrives."

"That might not be for a few hours."

"Perhaps you'd like to have a refreshment in the tearoom. Or do some shopping? Some of the stores are open late, and we can hold your luggage behind the desk. I'm sure you understand. It's for your own protection, too."

"Please, it's possible that my husband won't be arriving until tomorrow, and I'm horribly exhausted and nearly . . ." My voice choked with frustration. I couldn't believe my earnest request might be denied simply because I was a woman alone.

"I'm sorry," he said without sorrow. "There are many more hotels in this city. I have no doubt you'll be able to find a suitable one. You might try the Martha Washington."

Obviously, my ruse had failed. "Certainly you can see I'm a perfectly respectable woman. Perhaps you might call the Hotel Mansfield, where I've been staying with my father. He just passed away, you see. The manager would be happy to vouch for me."

"Then perhaps you should go back there for the night."

My cheeks flamed as I followed the red carpet back through the lobby. The doorman signaled for the porter to bring my luggage back to the curb. "Could you please call me a cab?" I asked.

"Sorry, miss, I'm only here to serve our—"

"Never mind." I stepped off the curb and hailed one myself. While the driver loaded my baggage, I wondered if the last train had already left for Cold Spring. I might end up spending the night on a bench in the station.

There was one last possibility. Reaching into my handbag, I found the paper with the place Matilda's son had suggested. I gave the cabdriver the address on First Avenue and prayed it wouldn't be too dreadful.

An El train thundered past as I rang the doorbell of a redbrick tenement. Little did I know just a few weeks ago, while gorging on pastries at the Caffe Pugliese, that I'd soon be desperate for a room just seven blocks up the same avenue. A dour matron answered the door. "What d'ya want?"

"Mrs. Craven? I was hoping you might have a room available."

"Mighty late to be lookin', ain't it?"

"I'm sorry. Matilda gave me your address. I'm looking for a room." Matilda, my only reference.

Mrs. Craven agreed to show me her "last" room. I stepped into the parlor with dismay. Cobwebs draped the corners of the mud-yellow walls, and plaster dangled in peels from the ceilings. I tried not to breathe in the moldy smell as she went behind a desk to select a latchkey from a locked drawer.

"Six dollars a week," she said, leading me up the staircase, "in advance."

I prayed the cab wouldn't disappear with all my worldly belongings. "Would it be possible to pay by the day?"

"What sorta place you think this is?"

"I only ask because I'm unsure of my plans. A week is fine."

I followed her down a wood-slat hallway that sloped sideways, like a shipwreck. "Water closet down the hall," she said, stopping in front of a room and inserting the key. It faced the street and the El tracks.

"Do you have something facing the back, by any chance?"

"Told you." She pushed the door open. "Last room. Yer lucky to get this."

The furnishings consisted of a cot, a tiny table with one chair, a narrow dresser and washstand, a small coal stove for heat, and a kerosene lamp for light. On the wall, a calendar with an illustration of a white puppy with black spots would shoulder the burden of cheering me up. Two flimsy gauze curtains provided the only privacy. I could practically reach out and touch the train tracks outside the window. But with my trunk down in the cab and nowhere else to go, I didn't feel inclined to haggle. "This will be fine, thank you."

I paid Mrs. Craven six dollars and went downstairs to pay the driver, who demanded an extra ten cents when I asked him to carry my trunk upstairs.

Left alone in the room, I didn't know what to do. I didn't want to touch anything, especially the bed, and couldn't bring myself to unpack. I needed to use the water closet—there was no way around that—so I decided to get it over with. I went down the hall and locked the door. While relieving myself, I tried not to breathe and covered my eyes so I could pretend filth didn't surround me. Someone tried the door.

"Just a minute!" Thank god I had locked it.

Soon enough there was banging again. "What'ya doin in there," a man's voice growled, "a number two?"

A Sears catalog hung from a nail in the wall. I tore out a page. Before using it, I noticed an illustration of a black revolver that cost $4.95. It came with a pearl handle for a dollar extra. The buyer could return it after three months if not pleased. You could buy it, shoot someone, and return it for a refund. Unless you killed yourself. No refund then.

After pulling the chain, I watched the water swirl sluggishly until, eventually, thank goodness, it went down. I avoided making eye contact with the man waiting. What had become of my life?

Even though it was already getting dark, I decided to venture outside to find something to eat. I searched for a restaurant along First Avenue, but every place was too seedy for a woman alone. I thought of the Caffe Pugliese but knew I wouldn't be happy gorging on sfogliatelle in that smoke-filled room. Turning onto Fourteenth Street, I passed cheap shops and penny arcades. Dozens of homeless men lined up in front of a bakery for day-old bread. When a Child's appeared on the corner of Third Avenue, I sped toward the entrance with relief. The brightly lit restaurant appeared almost identical to the one up on Twenty-third. Stepping inside, I felt the comfort of a familiar place.

The waitress led me to a table in the back. I ordered a chicken pot pie. To my surprise, it tasted excellent. Either the cook had great skill or I was simply ravenous. Unfortunately, before I was done, a man sat down at the next table and tried to engage me in conversation. I gave him every reason to believe I was deaf and dumb, but he persisted. I abandoned any hope of enjoying my meal and finished quickly. While leaving the restaurant, I avoided looking toward him. On the sidewalk, I glanced over my shoulder to make sure he hadn't followed.

Night had fallen. Fourteenth Street now crawled with a rougher crowd, seeking entertainment in the dance halls and nickelodeons. On the corner, two women stood in front of the glow of a shopwindow. "Lost your way, dearie?" one of them said as I turned up Second Avenue.

Rushing past a group of men loitering and laughing in front of a saloon, I continued straight through Stuyvesant Park and then regretted it. The darkness threatened to swallow me up. Footsteps came from behind, and I glanced back over my shoulder. A stranger followed.

"How do ya do?" he asked.

I picked up my pace, but that brought me farther inside the park, where the arc light on the corner didn't reach at all.

"Like to get a drink, miss?"

I kept going, searching ahead for Seventeenth Street. Why had I been so foolish to come this way? I'd almost made it when the man came up beside me, matching my strides. "Miss. I asked a question. Ya got a customer. How much?"

Did all men assume women out alone at night were for sale?

Well, why shouldn't they? After all, I'd never been out by myself at night before.

He put his hand on my arm. I shook it off.

He grabbed my wrist. "Hey, girlie, what you—"

"Leave me alone!" With my free hand, I pulled out my hatpin. I'd stab him with it—plunge it right into his eyeball.

He grinned. "You think yer gonna hurt me with that?"

I drew my hand back, but he smacked my fist. The hatpin flew to the ground. I jerked my wrist free as he laughed and spit at my face. "Dirty piece of trash."

As he walked off, I wiped my cheek with my sleeve. I would've scoured off my own skin if I could.

"Miss?"

Another one!

"Hungry, miss, I'm hungry."

I rushed up to the sidewalk, crossed the street, and turned east to walk the long block toward First Avenue, but he'd leeched on to me.

"A nickel's all I ask."

I couldn't give him money; I might be a beggar myself soon enough.

"Please, miss? I won't bother you or nuthin'. Just want a cupacoffee."

When I turned up First Avenue, he stopped following, yelling out an obscenity. Finally, I reached my block and the scant comfort of Mrs. Craven's front door.

November 5, 1907

The city used to tempt me with the promise of rescuing me from my past. Now Cold Spring tempts me with rescuing me from my future. My old bedroom sounds grand at the moment. Perhaps I'm completely misguided and ought to be doing everything I can to help Aunt Ida keep the house. I suppose that would mean forgetting my ambitions and marrying some man for his money. That would give Father a good laugh.

Exhaustion allowed me to let my skin touch the sheets without cringing. God only knew how long ago they'd been washed. A train sped past. My window offered a direct view of the passengers whizzing by. Some people sat slumped over, fast asleep in their seats. I wondered if their bedrooms were quieter than mine.

A newsboy sold the morning papers in front of the entrance to the El. I bought one and took it to breakfast at the coffee shop down the street. After ordering eggs and toast, I turned straight to the employment section and skimmed down the listings. Factory workers, laundresses, household servants . . . not one single advertisement for a shopgirl. The day loomed before me. I couldn't even hope for an arrogant employment manager to turn me away for lacking a reference.

I finished my greasy egg and lingered over a second cup of coffee with no idea where to go or what to do. When the waitress asked for the third time if I'd be needing anything else, I paid my bill and left to walk aimlessly up the avenue. Ahead of me, a mother held hands with her little girl. When they turned west on Twenty-third Street, I followed. How lovely that must feel to have your child's small hand tucked within your own; how reassuring to feel your mother's firm grip. My life could've been so different! Why did I have to be so unlucky?

The mother and daughter kept walking past the Eden Musee, the dime museum famous for its wax figures and a chamber of horrors. I stopped to look at a wax ticket taker by the entrance and considered going in. It would be a silly waste of time, but at least I could forget about myself for a while. A deep male voice interrupted my thoughts. "Welcome."

It sounded like Father.

"Allow me to tell your fortune."

A fortune-telling machine stood by the box office. Inside a glass booth was the bust of a dark-skinned man wearing a gold turban. I walked toward him.

"Welcome," he repeated, sweeping his mechanical hand over a crystal ball. "Allow me to tell your fortune."

Feeling sheepish, I inserted a penny.

"Thank you," the mannequin said. "Your fortune will be arriving soon."

I waited for the machine to enlighten me. A small white card slid out from a slot into a metal holder: *The future is in your hands.*

I scowled at the useless statement and was about to put the card back in the holder to save the next person a penny. His black eyes did seem to be staring at me, though, so I slipped it into my bag. My future seemed to be, if anything, completely out of my hands. I couldn't think of how to make use of my afternoon, much less my life.

Then I thought of a place I could go. The reading room in Altman's was lovely and peaceful, with comfortable easy chairs and free newspapers and magazines. Perhaps the chance to feel human again would help me come up with some sort of plan. I proceeded up Fifth Avenue to Thirty-fourth Street, relieved to at least appear as if I had purpose.

Entering Altman's, I appreciated the sedate atmosphere, which previously had struck me as dull. I took the elevator directly to the eighth floor and entered the reading room, just as I recalled, with thick red carpeting, mahogany wainscoting, and large windows letting in lots of light. The loudest sound was that of the occasional page being turned. Unfortunately, the easy chairs were all occupied; I had to settle for a seat at one of the writing desks.

The store provided customers with complimentary stationery, so I set a sheet in front of me and attempted to write Aunt Ida a letter. My pen hovered over the paper. I couldn't bring myself to deface the blank page with an account of my miserable time thus far. The stationery was really quite nice, with the store's logo and address engraved at the top. I imagined telling my aunt I was writing to her from my desk at Altman's, where I'd just been hired as a secretary. Anything would be better than the truth.

A woman sitting near me began to gather her things. Seeing my chance for an easy chair, I decided my letter writing could wait. I tucked a sheet of stationery into a complimentary envelope and was slipping it into my bag when I noticed the card from the mechanical gypsy. *The future is in your hands.* I was about to toss it in the trash when I noticed the advertisement printed on the flip side. *Siegel-Cooper department store. Real satisfaction by good merchandise, fair dealing and prompt service.* I turned the card over again. *The future is in your hands.*

An idea came to me. Could I get away with it? I hated to be dishonest, but I hated the desperation of my situation even more. I took an extra sheet of paper and envelope, put them in my bag, and left the reading room as another woman sat down to relax in the empty easy chair.

From the store, I hurried back to Mrs. Craven's, stopping only to make a telephone call from a drugstore on First Avenue. I rang Altman's and asked for the name of the employment manager.

"Thomas Porter. Would you like me to put you through?"

"Yes, please."

As she made the connection, I hung up. Then I went up to my room and sat down at the tiny table. In my neatest handwriting, on the Altman's stationery, I composed a highly flattering letter for my services as a counter girl in the notions department the previous year. Clenching my jaw, I signed Thomas Porter's name.

The man at the information booth in Siegel-Cooper directed me to a lift in the back that would take me to the employment department on the third floor. A receptionist had me fill out an employment card and then directed me to the anteroom of another office, where I was pleased to see only two other women waiting. Since no position had been advertised, perhaps the competition wouldn't be so brutal. Such a huge store, employing literally thousands of people—positions had to open up all the time. Barely ten minutes had passed when a bearded, heavyset man with steel-gray eyes called me into his office. As he read over my application and letter of reference, I stared at a photograph of his grim wife and six children on the desk.

"Live with your parents?" he asked.

"My parents have both passed away."

"Married?"

"No."

"And how," he asked, "do you intend to manage on your own? Most of our girls live with their parents—or find other means of support."

Were those cold eyes leering at me? "I assure you, I'll need no other means of support." Not that I had any idea how I should manage. Find someplace even worse than where I lived now? "My aunt is letting me stay with her, so I shan't have to worry about paying rent." It wasn't exactly a lie; if this didn't go well, I'd probably be back in Cold Spring soon enough.

He scowled while giving my reference a look-over. Perhaps he was friends with Thomas Porter. Everyone in the business probably knew one another. He could tell the signature had been forged, knew the stationery was from the reading room, would accuse me of fraud and call store security.

"Sorry," he said, handing back the letter. "You wouldn't be suitable."

"Are you sure? I can't tell you how much I need this job, sir."

"Your need is irrelevant. My concern is the store's needs, and the only position open right now is for a girl experienced in toiletries."

"As a matter of fact," I said, practically leaping from my chair, "I know all about selling toiletries from before I was at Altman's. My father managed a Woolworth's, and I helped all the time after school and on weekends. One of my favorite sections was toiletries. I studied the labels more than my schoolbooks."

"That's well and good," he said, "but I—"

"Soap, for instance. Different brands of soap are made from a variety of ingredients: oil, glycerin, tallow, tar . . . It's not that one type is better than another. It depends on your skin. Is it oily, dry, both? Even that can change depending on the weather, so you have to switch over as needed. There are so many effective products available these days that no woman needs to suffer with skin problems as long as she—"

"Stop!" He put the palm of his hand up between us. "I've heard enough. The position pays seven dollars per week. Are you available tomorrow?"

Seven dollars? I tried not to show my dismay and didn't dare ask for more. "I'm available right now if you need me."

"Tomorrow will do. You'll need to supply your own black skirt and a white shirtwaist. Just as you have on now would be acceptable, as long as it's nothing showy. Your job is to sell, not to be noticed. Take care not to use the customer entrance on Sixth Avenue, please. Employees use the side doors on Eighteenth Street. Don't forget to punch in. Eight o'clock sharp. You'll be fined a nickel for every ten minutes you're late. Tell the guard it's your first day, and he'll assign you a number and a locker. You'll report to the classroom for your training in the morning, and in the afternoon you'll work the floor."

"Thank you so much," I said. "You won't regret it." I rose from my chair, prepared to shake his hand, but he was already dipping a pen in his silver inkwell. As I made my way out to the street, I wasn't sure whether to smile with triumph or break down in tears.

19

AMANDA

ON THE WAY to De Robertis, I passed through Astor Place—or Disastor Place, as I'd come to call it. Rampant building had uglified the historic intersection where Eighth Street, Lafayette, and Fourth Avenue came together. A towering glass high-rise condominium dwarfed Cooper Union. Starbucks dueled with Dunkin' Donuts. Yet another NYU dorm had sprung up. Couldn't they see that the past should be preserved? My blood pressure spiked when I passed an empty lot I hadn't noticed before. That meant another tenement had been razed to the ground. Some high-rise or chain store was moving in. Why the hell wasn't this area landmarked? The East Village was being destroyed.

Olive would say I was being too sentimental. Maybe she'd be right. New York was constantly changing and growing, and if there was no modern architecture, what buildings would represent this generation in a hundred years? Still, we had to make sure at least some of the past was preserved, too.

When I reached First Avenue, I took it in with fresh eyes. I'd never realized that an El train had run along this stretch. I couldn't help but look for the Italian café where Olive met Ralph, as if an old bakery could've escaped my attention all these years. The Pugliese didn't magically appear on the block, but I did notice a new Pilates studio and resolved to look up their schedule online.

An orgasmic display of assorted wedding cakes filled the windows of De Robertis. Happy man-and-wife figurines stood atop three- and four-tiered masterpieces. I opened the door, and it hit me: the heavenly scent of anise. I inhaled deeply through my nose to get the full effect.

A sign on the wall proudly proclaimed that De Robertis had been there since 1904. Another sign announced they now had Wi-Fi. The young guy working behind the counter wore an Abercrombie T-shirt and a puka-shell necklace. He stared up at another recent modification to the decor: a flat-screen TV.

After feasting my eyes on the glass showcases crammed with rows of desserts, I walked back to see if Molly had arrived. She wasn't there, so I inspected some photographs on the wall commemorating De Robertis's past. I'd seen them before—the display had been there so long, it qualified to be photographed for posterity as well. The family matriarch and patriarch were prominently positioned at the top in separate portraits: a beautiful dark-haired woman and a handsome, clean-shaven man. Underneath were shots of the store interior. I checked the old against the new, as I was inclined to do. Same tile floor with a star design in the center; same tile walls with a border of blue and gold mosaic; same pressed-tin ceiling; same cut-glass doors in the back. The bottom photograph featured a group of five mustached waiters in long white aprons, standing in front of the store's plate-glass window. The awning said CAFFE PUGLIESE.

Pugliese?

I spun around and blurted out my surprise to the guy behind the counter. "Pugliese?"

After a moment he wrenched his face from a tennis match. "'Scuse me?"

"Did this used to be the Caffe Pugliese?"

"Yeah, my great-grandfather Paolo named it after his hometown in Italy. When Grandpa took over, he changed the name to De Robertis."

"Wow. Thanks."

"No problem," he said, his gaze already aimed back at the screen.

So this was the same place. Had I known that somewhere in my head? Not that it was such a big deal. After all, I'd suggested De Robertis because it reminded me of Olive's café. I pictured her sitting in the crowded, smoke-filled dining room, happy to be with her father, gorging on pastries, flirting with Ralph—or trying to.

I hoped the pastries hadn't gone downhill since my last visit, which could've been maybe ten years ago. The decor was pretty much the same as I remembered, but shabbier. Only one other patron, a young woman typing on a laptop, sat in the dining room. I turned back to the photographs and stared into the eyes of a waiter. Was he the one who called Olive a *bella donna*?

"Sorry I'm late!"

I turned around to the welcome sight of Molly. She wore an olive-green jersey dress with small fan-shaped mother-of-pearl buttons that she'd sewn on around the collar. Her golden-brown hair was pulled up into a bun. "You aren't late. I just walked fast."

"That top is great," she said as we hugged. "Where'd you get it?"

"Those new wholesalers I'm using." We took a table, and I nodded at her bracelet. "One of your creations?"

"Yeah, I'm currently obsessed with clear Lucite buttons from the fifties."

She held it out for me to take a closer look. Each of the square chunky buttons was translucent, with a decoration inside. "How did they get the designs embedded inside the Lucite?"

"There are different techniques. Some have carvings in the back that are painted and laminated. Some have metal inlays, some have pearl. This one has a real tiny flower inside. I was reading how they made buttons out of Lucite after World War II, from the leftover stands they used to mount guns on. It's bulletproof."

"Wow, that could come in handy. It's gorgeous. And I love your neckline, with the little fans."

"Thanks."

Molly had always been obsessed with vintage buttons. She started out selling them online and once floated the idea of partnering up on a shop, but I wasn't into it at the time. When her grandmother died and left her some money, Molly did it on her own and hired a handsome guy to handle the business end; it worked out so well, he became her manager and eventually her husband.

"So tell me." Molly sat up straight with anticipation. "How did it go with Dr. Markoff?"

"He was great, but I flunked. I hardly slept last night."

"Darn. Maybe you need to go back a few times for it to work."

"Maybe," I said, trying to sound like I believed it.

The great-grandson arrived with menus. "Can I get you ladies something to drink?" he asked. "Latte, espresso, cappuccino . . ."

"I'll have a latte."

"Same," Molly said. "And I'll have an almond horn."

"I'll have a sfogliatelle."

We handed him our menus. As he walked away, I rubbed my tired eyes and groaned.

"Okay," Molly said, "so you haven't slept, and you're in a crisis?"

"I just got an official notice from my landlord. I'm being evicted."

"You're kidding. From your apartment?"

"No, my retail space."

"I thought they were renewing."

"So he told me, but yesterday I got this letter, and now I have a month to get out."

"Wow. I'm so sorry. And you had a good deal there, right?"

"I don't know if I'll be able to find anything I can afford."

"It won't be easy."

"But I had this idea. I know you're going crazy in that tiny space." Molly's shop was so narrow that backpacks and pregnant bellies often led to dirty looks and gridlock. "I was wondering if you'd consider sharing a space with me. I bet we could find something big enough that would end up being less than we're paying now, and it would probably be good for both our sales to join forces."

"You know, that would be really tempting, and I wish I could help you out."

"But?"

"I can't make any changes to the business right now. I'm sorry."

"It's okay," I said, surprised by how disappointed I felt. "I knew it wasn't likely, but I had to ask."

"Of course," she said. "If I hear of anything, I'll let you know."

Great-grandson De Robertis arrived with our coffees, pastries, and two glasses of water. "I'm leaving the check," he said, "but feel free to stay as long as you like."

Considering the empty tables, his largesse didn't really impress, but I appreciated the sentiment. "Thanks."

We drank our coffee and sampled our pastries. The reason for the empty tables became clear. De Robertis had compromised on quality. The crust was too hard, and the filling tasted heavy with flour, light on ricotta, with only trace amounts of candied orange. When Molly sliced off a piece of almond horn, her knife hit the plate with an explosion of crumbs and almond slices.

"Either your knife is dull, or that pastry is stale."

She took a bite. "It's the pastry."

"Sorry."

"Don't apologize. I'm glad we came here, if only for old times' sake. I actually have some news of my own. Scott and I finally made the big decision, which is part of why I can't make any changes."

I knew what she was referring to. After years of growing their business, which did well, they'd turned their attention to growing a baby, which hadn't gone well at all. They'd given up on in vitro fertilization and were considering adoption or having another woman's egg implanted. "So what's the call?"

"I found this organization with an amazing website. It has pictures of all these kids waiting for someone to adopt them. You can narrow it down by age and sex and state, and then you click on a picture, and there's a profile describing the child's background and personality."

"Amazing. But can you trust them?"

"I know it sounds smarmy, but I've checked it out, and they're legit. And we'll be super-careful about who we pick."

"Of course you will. And I bet those kids really need homes. So that's exciting. I hope it works out."

"Thanks."

"Which reminds me: I had an exciting false alarm last night. My period is late, and I took a pregnancy test, but no bambino."

"Your periods have been screwy all year, right?"

"Sort of. It's just that I used to be regular as the rent, so when it's a little off, I notice."

"Hasn't it been more than a little off?"

"There was that month I kept expecting it to come and it didn't, and then it lasted, like, ten days the next month." I didn't mention the other month, when I only spotted.

"Look, I'm not a doctor, obviously, but this could be perimenopause."

"Come off it, I'm too young for that."

"Actually, you'd fall on the early end of the curve for normal—nothing diagnostically significant. You might want to have your FSH levels checked. You could be running low on viable eggs."

Molly had seen so many specialists and doctors, she was ready to become one herself. "You're saying the eggs I have left are drying up?"

"Don't panic. It wouldn't mean you aren't fertile. I'm just saying your body might be transitioning into the early stages of menopause, so if you do want a kid, you might think about sooner rather than later. You know the statistics, right? On average, by the time she's forty, a woman's chance of getting pregnant is five percent."

"Really? That bad?"

"I don't mean to freak you out," she went on, "but you know what I've been going through. And you're a businesswoman. You understand how important it is to plan ahead."

"One would think so. Hey, maybe I should have my eggs frozen."

"You could."

"I was being sarcastic."

"You know what you should really do?" Molly sat forward with excitement. "Have them fertilize some eggs and then freeze the embryos. They have a much better chance of surviving implantation than just eggs. At this moment in history, that's your best bet."

"Okay, and who would supply the sperm? Not that I'm taking this seriously."

"I'm not suggesting it should be Jeff, if that's what you're thinking. They've got tons of sperm donors, and you can do searches to get exactly what you want."

"I don't know. Is it right to force my egg to have a one-night stand with a stranger's sperm?"

"Very funny. Listen, five years ago they didn't have this technology or I would've done it. Anyway, if you do want to look into in vitro, there's a website that has donor profiles. If you register with them, you can search through the listings."

"You mean like Match.com?"

"Uh-huh. You can fix your egg up with the perfect sperm for that one-night stand."

"Great. All of a sudden my life seems to be going down the tubes—no pun intended."

"Maybe your real estate problem is a sign that your life is meant to change directions."

"You mean the declaring-bankruptcy-and-going-on-welfare direction?" I rubbed my temples. I didn't have a headache but should've.

"You could move in with your mom up in Woodstock. She'd help with the baby. That sounds kind of nice, doesn't it?"

"In a nervous-breakdown sort of way." Clearly, her judgment had been clouded by hormones stimulated by those photos of adoptive kids.

"I'm sorry, sweetie." She reached across the table and gave my wrist a reassuring squeeze. "Just ignore me. I've been so preoccupied with my whole baby drama, and it's probably the last thing you want to be thinking about now."

"I know you're just trying to be helpful. Anyway, we should probably get going. Almost time to open."

"I wish there was something I could do to help."

"It helps just to talk about it," I said, though I pretty much felt worse than when I walked in.

OLIVE

"DO NOT STAND in groups. Do not chew gum or tobacco. Do not eat, read books, or sew behind the counter."

An efficient middle-aged woman named Mrs. Underhill taught the class of ten new female employees. She wore a severe black dress, a gold watch pinned to her bosom, a tight bun on the back of her neck, and a permanent frown.

"Do not be out of your place. Do not be late. Do not make noise in the elevators. Do not talk across the aisle or in loud voices. Do not keep your hat, coat, or umbrella where you are working. Do not gossip. Any questions?"

After barely a glance at our faces, Mrs. Underhill launched into instructions on filling out sales checks, holds, deliveries, and returns. The clock ticked forward as she gave painstaking care to elaborate on every way in which a mistake could be made. "Now," Mrs. Underhill concluded, "we'll go look at the tube room so you can see how the money is processed."

We took the employee elevator down to the basement. As a

customer, I'd often wondered what was on the other end of the pneumatic tube, so I was quite curious while following Mrs. Underhill through a vaultlike door into a windowless room. The machinery made a dreadfully loud noise. Mrs. Underhill yelled to be heard. "You may feel superior to these workers! But they are the store's most important employees!"

A row of twenty or so women sat behind a counter that ran along the receiving end of tubes lining the wall like organ pipes. Metal capsules continually shot out from the tube openings onto the counter. Each girl would open a capsule, remove the money and the sales ticket, put the correct change in the tube, and send it back. My heart broke for them, stuck in this horrid room all day, doing their dull, repetitive task.

"If the money isn't handled correctly, there won't be profit; if there's no profit, there's no store; if there's no store," she concluded, "none of you would have jobs!"

After we left the tube room, Mrs. Underhill dismissed us for lunch. She advised us to use the female employee's cafeteria. "They serve quick, wholesome meals for a nominal charge. It's imperative to give yourself time to relax and eat a nutritious meal so you can keep up your strength."

Waiters rushed to serve the hundreds of workers passing through in the forty-five minutes allowed for breaks. The sound of female chatter echoed noisily off the walls. I sat with the other new girls and listened to them raving about some picture shows they'd seen. Some spoke with foreign accents; all used lower-class slang. By the time the waiter arrived with our plates of macaroni and cheese, buttered beets, and rhubarb pie, the break was nearly over, and I had to gobble down my food. Lunch might have provided some nutrition, but attending a riot would've been equally relaxing.

Back in the classroom, Miss Underhill issued each of us a

brown leather-bound sales book. I gripped it tightly on the way to the toiletries department while talking myself out of feeling shame over my lowly position. Unlike the day of my first job interview at Macy's, I couldn't afford to fall back on my pride.

A handsome woman stood by the toiletries counter, waiting to greet me. "Here you are. I'm Miss Cohen, the buyer for this section." She wore a dark brown tailored suit the same color as her dark brown hair and eyes. I guessed she was in her late thirties.

My heart beat faster. I did want to impress her. "How do you do?"

"Welcome to the toiletries department."

She moved aside so I could take my place behind the counter. I crossed over, making sure to appear as though I felt perfectly at ease.

"We're quite busy here on the ground floor," Miss Cohen was saying. "This department is different from any other. You need to know what product is best suited for a particular condition, almost like a doctor treating a patient, so it's imperative that you take some time to learn the stock."

"We're the experts,'" I said with a nod. "We give free advice, which makes the customer more inclined to buy our product."

"Exactly." By her raised eyebrows, I could see she was favorably impressed.

"Thank you so much for the chance to work here. I intend to do my very best."

"Sadie will answer any questions you might have," she said, nodding to a young woman behind my counter. "I suggest you watch her today and begin helping customers tomorrow. Now, if you'll excuse me, I must get to a sales meeting."

After Miss Cohen left, I turned to my coworker. Small and slim, she had a pale heart-shaped face framed by thick auburn ringlets swept up into a massive bun. At first glance, an indentation on her chin looked like a dimple; then I realized it was a pockmark. I gave her a friendly smile and held out my hand. "Olive Westcott. How do you do?"

"Sadie Bernstein." She gave my hand an obligatory shake and eyed me with suspicion. "Ever work in a store before?"

"Yes, but I'm sure I have loads yet to learn."

"I'll say."

"Miss Cohen seems nice."

"Don't expect her to become your friend."

"Of course, I didn't mean—"

"If we don't sell what she buys, it makes her look bad, and if she looks bad, you'll be the first to go."

"How long have you worked here?"

"The question is when *didn't* I."

Sadie left my side to fix her hair in the glass before going to help a customer. I began to familiarize myself with the products. Bleaches to remove freckles, scented soaps done up in fancy packages, treatments for facial eruptions, and depilatories for facial hair removal. I examined every box and bottle label—read about the ingredients and what they claimed to do. When Sadie helped customers, I listened in, but she didn't come alive until the girl handing out candy samples came by. "What's in the basket today?" she asked.

"Peanut brittle," the girl said as Sadie sneaked a piece into her pocket. "No sooner do I fill it up than it goes empty again."

She was quite lovely, with olive skin, black eyes, and lustrous black hair piled into a low, loose bun. The accent—a mixture of downtown, uptown, European—added an exotic flavor to her elegant beauty. I kept a smile on my face, unsure if she noticed me.

"Honestly," she went on, "the richer they are, the more they like to bag the free stuff. Say, are you working with someone new, Sadie? Why don't you introduce us?"

"She just started," Sadie said, as if that was all anyone needed to know.

"Olive Westcott," I said. "How do you do?" I forced myself not to stare at her high cheekbones, perfectly arched eyebrows, and full red lips.

"Angelina Spinelli. Here's the store's official welcome gift." She sneaked a piece of brittle across the counter and then looked past me. "Uh-oh. McGillicutty's giving me the evil eye. Gotta go."

"McGillicutty?" I asked.

"Floorwalker," Sadie said.

"He likes to come off like a bear," Angelina added, "but he's a sweetheart. See you next time around."

I watched her offer Mr. McGillicutty a piece of peanut brittle. He shook his head with disapproval, then snatched a piece from her hand as she was about to take it away. She laughed and walked off as he popped it in his mouth.

"Sure is slow today," Sadie said, leaning on the glass counter.

"If it picks up, perhaps I could start helping customers?"

"Miss Cohen said you should watch, and I don't want no trouble. Here, this should keep you busy." She handed me a stack of chamois and told me to roll up each one and tie it with a ribbon.

Before long, a matron wearing a fur jacket with a matching muff came to the counter. She kept asking Sadie to show her different brands of toilet water. Some other customers arrived, and I had to avoid their glares as they waited for Sadie's attention. Finally, a young woman interrupted them with a question about shampoo. That was when I noticed, out of the corner of my eye, a bottle of honeysuckle toilet water moving from the counter to the inside of the woman's fur muff. Was this truly taking place? On my first day? I considered pretending not to notice—it would make for such an embarrassing scene—but Mr. McGillicutty was patrolling nearby, so I motioned him to the other end of the counter and kept my voice low. "I believe you'll find something that belongs to the store inside that woman's muff."

"Are you sure?" he whispered back.

I nodded solemnly. Then I watched with palpitating heart as Mr. McGillicutty confronted the matron.

"I assure you," she said, "you're quite mistaken."

Mr. McGillicutty suggested the woman go with him to his office. "We can resolve the issue and send you on your way."

The woman protested until she realized spectators had gathered to enjoy the show. Mr. McGillicutty motioned for me to come along. I followed them to his office, praying I hadn't imagined her crime. In his office, I held my breath as he reached inside the muff. When he pulled out the bottle of toilet water, the poor woman fell to crying. My relief turned to pity.

"Please don't tell my husband," she pleaded. "He works for the mayor! It would be such an embarrassment. I promise not to do it ever again."

I wished I'd just let her take it.

"Seeing as you're a regular customer," Mr. McGillicutty said, "we'll let it go. But if we catch you again, I won't be so nice."

He gave back the muff. The woman signed a confession and left.

That was it? Now I didn't feel so bad.

"Do you honestly think that was her first time?" I asked as Mr. McGillicutty added her name to the store list of people to watch.

He snorted. "She'll be at it again soon enough. Classic case of kleptomania. Doesn't need what she steals—simply can't help herself."

Back at the counter, I told Sadie all about it. "It was ghastly. She cried and begged him to let her off. He called her a classic case of kleptomania."

"The wealthy ones are all kleptomaniacs. The poor ones are just thieves."

"He did let her off easy."

"They always let the rich ones go. The others get thrown in jail."

"That's awful."

"Even worse, if you get pinched and don't happen to notice, and the store detective nabs 'em? They blame you. Last month I had to pay for a bar of soap someone swiped. Ten cents outta my pocket."

I shook my head. "That's not fair."

"Last week I was back from lunch ten minutes late. Five cents off my paycheck. They don't give a fig about us, not with ten more waiting to take your place."

"Meanwhile, they don't pay enough for a girl to live." I hoped I might gain her trust by commiserating.

"That's why we got our friends," she replied.

"You mean a gentleman friend?" I didn't want Aunt Ida to be right.

Sadie laughed. "Sure, we all got at least one. How else can a girl make ends meet?"

At closing time, I staggered down to the cloakroom and jostled my way through the sea of salesgirls. My head spun, my feet ached, and my back longed for a mattress. Even so, I preferred the liveliness of the store to Mrs. Craven's. Reaching my locker, I was pleased to see Angelina. It turned out her locker was right across from mine.

"Made it through your first day?" she asked, tucking strands of that lustrous black hair into a blue felt mushroom hat with a fur-trimmed brim.

"My feet are killing me. If only I didn't have to walk home."

"Try shoe inserts," she said. "And a hot salty foot bath every night."

"Sounds grand." Too bad my room had no hot water.

"Which way you going?" She watched me adjust my white beaver boater, one of the few nice things I hadn't sold to Matilda.

"First Avenue. But I'm desperate to move. The El runs right past my window, and I'm not getting a wink of sleep."

"You should ask Sadie about her place. It's a boardinghouse for working girls; someone's always moving in or out."

"Thanks awfully, I will." Girls as pretty as she was usually put on airs, but Angelina seemed especially friendly. "Where do you live?"

"Downtown. Too far to walk after being on my feet all day—too close for the train. Every day I torture myself over paying my nickel or hoofing it."

We took turns dipping our cards into the time clock. When she called out a good night to the guard, I followed her example. His eyes stayed fastened on her. I couldn't blame him.

"I've got to run along," she said as we exited onto Eighteenth Street. "Dinner date. See you tomorrow!"

"See you tomorrow!" As she rushed off, I wondered if Angelina had a gentleman friend, too.

November 7, 1907

I'm exhausted but can't sleep. Actually stood behind the counter today and pretended to be a salesgirl. What would Father think? In a few hours I'll be back behind the counter again. I daresay it won't feel like pretend.

"You look beat," Sadie said as we removed the velvet covers from the glass showcases.

"The El train is driving me mad. I've got to find someplace else to live. Angelina thought your boardinghouse might have room."

"My place? It ain't exactly the Waldorf. The landlady watches over you like a prison guard, and everyone knows your business."

"What does she charge?"

"Six dollars a week includes breakfast, dinner, and the worst coffee you ever had."

"That's the same as I'm paying, and I don't get board."

Mr. McGillicutty passed by on the way to signaling the doorman to let people in.

"Where is it?" I asked.

"Fourteenth Street between First and Second."

That was only a few blocks from Mrs. Craven's. I could still walk to work. My hopes lifted as though it were indeed the Waldorf. "Do you think she has a vacancy?"

"Sure, the warden's always got room for one more inmate."

"I'd be terribly grateful if you spoke with her. I'd move in Sunday if I could."

"I'll tell 'er about you tonight." Sadie turned to help a woman peering through the glass. "May I help you?"

Moments later, another woman approached the counter. My first real customer.

"I need a shampoo, but my scalp is terribly dry."

I showed her an expensive soap made with olive oil and suggested she use it at least once a week.

"Every week? If I shampoo that often, my scalp gets worse."

"Not with this. The olive oil has special moisturizing effects. The more often you use it, the healthier your scalp shall be." I looked her square in the face with confidence.

"I suppose I might as well try it."

I wrote up my first sales ticket and put it inside a capsule along with the money. As I fed the capsule into the tube, I glanced over at Sadie, who smiled at me. The suction whisked it away.

While Sadie went on her lunch break, I handled the counter on my own. Miss Cohen came by to observe and gave a nod of approval before leaving. My relief was tempered by extreme hunger and a longing to sit. If only I could take the elevator up to the restaurant and enjoy a sardine sandwich along with a cold glass of lemonade.

When Sadie returned, I asked if there was anyplace to eat other than the cafeteria.

"I usually grab a bite at that dairy restaurant across the street."

"Is there someplace quiet? I've never spoken to so many people in one morning, and I'm crazy for a moment's peace."

"The employee lounge has comfy chairs. Did you pack a lunch?"

"No."

"Then you'll have to buy something outside and bring it back."

"Where's the closest place?"

"Same as I told you, the dairy restaurant down the street."

Picturing that comfortable chair in the lounge, I rushed to my locker for my hat; I'd have to hurry for those few minutes of peace. At least I'd get some fresh air. I crossed the street and found the dairy place, with its cheap basic menu painted on the plate-glass front.

With the dexterity of a magician performing a trick, the man behind the counter assembled a deviled egg sandwich, tomato slices, and a pickle. I paid and was on my way to the door when someone called out my name. I turned and spotted Angelina sitting at a table with three others, two of them men. "Come join us!" she said, waving me over.

Darn. I'd have to stay and make conversation or risk offending her. I walked over with a smile on my face. One of the men pulled a chair over from the next table. "For the new girl," he said gallantly. He was quite good-looking—almost a male version of Angelina. Could he be her beau? They'd make a striking couple.

"My brother, Joe," Angelina said, as if reading my thoughts. "Sporting equipment, sixth floor. A big tease, so ignore him as much as possible."

"I see the resemblance," I said, pleased to know he wasn't her boyfriend and annoyed with myself for being pleased. He had the same gorgeous skin, dark eyes, and sensuous smile as his sister. But the fine head of curly black hair, a neatly trimmed mustache, and classic chiseled features made the difference between handsome and lovely. At any rate, I had no intention of falling for anyone at the store. Nothing should distract me from making a go of this chance.

Angelina introduced me to Lucy, a blond girl I recognized from the handkerchief counter, and a husky man with sideburns named Bill, who sold furniture on the fifth floor.

"Bill was just complaining about his wife," Lucy said.

"She thinks hard work is an insult," he explained. "Quit the minute we got married to have a kid. Now she just gripes about being stuck in the house all day."

"Who can blame her?" Angelina pushed away an empty bowl of soup. "You won't catch me sitting home with a crying baby."

"Won't catch you behind a counter, either," Joe said.

"Only because I'm miserable at sales." She turned to me. "My main job is modeling in the fashion shows, but that's not regular enough to keep me busy, so they have me handing out samples."

"You must be a natural at modeling," I said, wondering if I'd seen her in the fashion show that inspired me to buy my ready-made suit.

"The truth is," Joe proclaimed, "none of you gals have the instinct or the discipline to be crack salesmen."

Angelina smirked at her brother. "I'd like to see you selling petticoats."

Bill claimed he could sell more petticoats in a day than any woman. "The skill is the same no matter what the merchandise."

"And the skill is the same," I chimed in, "whether you're a man or a woman. But a man can never be a woman, and a woman customer feels more comfortable with us because we understand her."

"Which makes you better friends," Joe said, "not sellers. You ask me, women shouldn't be allowed behind a counter. Most of 'em are only out to catch some rich chump."

"And you?" I couldn't resist asking.

"Me?" He leaned over the table on his forearms toward me. "I'm not looking for some rich widow to take me to a show, if that's what you're asking."

I blushed dreadfully.

"Does that mean you're looking for a wife?" Lucy asked with a saucy smile.

"When I find the right lady." He continued to stare straight at me. At least I was still blushing from the previous comment, so he couldn't perceive me blushing all over again.

"What bosh," Angelina said. "Joe's a dyed-in-the-wool bachelor. He'll never tie the knot."

"I'm not surprised," I ventured to say. "He doesn't seem to like women much."

"You got it wrong—I like 'em too much. 'Specially the pretty ones, like you."

I shook my head and exchanged an amused look of disdain with Angelina.

Joe sat back in his chair. "She's too smart to fall for a rogue like me. *Che peccato*. A man could go far in the world with a fine lady at his side."

"Enough of this nonsense," Angelina said, pulling on Joe's collar. "I gotta get back, and so do you."

"So do I," said Bill, rising from the table.

Lucy stood up, too. "Same here."

Joe furrowed his eyebrows at me with exaggerated concern. "I hope you won't be lonely sitting here all by yourself."

"Don't worry, I'll be fine." In fact, the chance to eat my sandwich alone, as originally planned, was entirely welcome. God knows I'd never taste anything with Joe's eyes fixed on me.

• • •

By the time Friday came, I felt as though I'd been working at the store half my life.

"My skin is so dry," said a woman with a bedraggled bird of paradise on her hat. "Nothing seems to help."

"I have some excellent products to suit your needs." I reached for a box under the counter. "This cream is a superb moisturizer."

"The last cream I bought from my druggist had a very unpleasant smell."

I took the blue glass jar from the box. "This one is made with cucumbers. It has a lovely, fresh scent." I only had to finish today, and then it would be my precious day off.

"Can you open it?"

"I'm sorry, we're not allowed to." If all went to plan, I'd move into Sadie's boardinghouse.

"I don't know . . . cucumber? I know what it's like in a salad, but I can't imagine. Does it work as well as you say?"

"Oh, yes, it's like food for the skin. I use it myself before going to sleep," I assured her, as if I could afford it.

"If you could just allow me to try a bit on my skin . . ."

"I'm sorry, but the jar is sealed so that you know it's sanitary. Once it's open, we wouldn't feel right selling it to the next person."

"But if I try it at home, you couldn't resell it, either."

She had a point, and I truly wished I could oblige. "I'm sorry, madam, but that's the store policy. It's very well priced at twenty-five cents, and the store will be happy to give a refund if it doesn't suit you."

"I'll have to think about it," she said before walking off.

I was about to put the jar of lotion back in its box when I saw a familiar face in the crowd. Celia was a girl I knew from Miss Hall's. I'd always suspected her of feeling some jealousy over my friendship with Daisy. As she walked toward me, I realized she was accompanied by two other girls from Miss Hall's.

Standing up straight, I prepared to greet them with as much pride as I could muster. Celia stared straight at me—or through me—as they passed by.

"Chocolate-covered cherries." Angelina set her tray down on my counter. "Want one? I hate 'em. Why did I stay up so late last night? I'm practically sleepwalking down the aisles. You all right?"

"Yes. Or no. Excuse me, what were you saying?"

"You look like you've seen a ghost."

"I think I *am* the ghost. Some girls I know just walked past. I could've sworn one of them looked at me, but she didn't stop or say hello."

"People don't think of us as people. You're just the salesgirl, if you know what I mean. I'm just the girl who gives out samples. When I do a fashion show, I'm just a mannequin, no different from the mannequins in the window."

"I suppose."

I'd just placed the box of cucumber lotion under the counter when Celia hurried up to me. "Olive Westcott, I couldn't believe my eyes. I didn't mean to ignore you." She lowered her voice. "I didn't want to embarrass you in front of the other girls, you poor thing. So many people have suffered terribly because of that darn stock market."

"If I'm suffering, it's because my father passed away."

"Oh my, I'm so sorry. I didn't know." She leaned toward me while turning her back to Angelina. "It must be utterly humiliating, reduced to working alongside these lower-class girls. I promise not to tell a soul. I must run along, the girls are waiting by the lift. Don't worry, I'll make sure we walk down the other aisle on our way out."

Angelina glared at Celia as she rushed off. "That girl has a lot of nerve, talking to you like that!"

I tried to laugh it off. "I didn't realize just how pitiful I was until she told me."

"I've got half a mind to run and give her a swift kick in the rear."

Finished with her customer, Sadie came over and joined us. "What did I miss?"

"Just a rude customer," I said.

Angelina picked up her tray. "I don't know how you stand it in sales. People are so much nicer when you give things away."

"So's my boyfriend," Sadie said, "but that don't get me nowhere."

"Then maybe it's time you start making him pay," Angelina said with a wry grin before continuing down the aisle.

At closing time, I ran into Angelina down in the locker room. "Thanks for being discreet with Sadie about those girls."

"Nothing she enjoys more than someone else's suffering. You want to get a drink? I know a place with good cheap beer a few blocks down."

I almost told her I didn't drink beer, but what did it matter? I'd been so utterly lonely, and this beautiful, spirited girl wanted to spend time with me. "I'd love to, thanks."

As we walked down Eighteenth Street, I inhaled the sweet, fresh air. Angelina's skin had such a healthy glow; her coloring seemed immune to lack of sun. "Are you originally from Italy?"

"Sicily. Is my accent so obvious?"

"No, it's subtle, actually, and sounds nice."

"My parents came over when I was ten," she said as we stopped at the curb. "Now I'm twenty-two and still can't get rid of my accent!"

"I don't think you should."

A street cleaner passed in front of us. He managed to wink at Angelina while sweeping a pile of horse dung into his shovel and saying something in Italian that made her laugh.

"How about you?" she asked. "Are you from New York?"

"I was born in Cold Spring, about ninety minutes north by train. I just moved here . . . a few days ago." It felt that way, anyway. The Manhattan I knew with my father existed somewhere else.

"By yourself? Must be lonely as the moon." The policeman blew his whistle, and we crossed the street. "Don't worry, you'll make friends with the other girls at the store in no time."

"That would be nice." Though it didn't seem possible. Not because I felt superior, as Celia would assume. Most of the girls I'd met were immigrants, or their parents were, and our experiences growing up had been so very different. On the other hand, Angelina was different, and that only made me more curious to know her.

She led me to a typical sort of saloon I'd seen all over Manhattan but never would have dreamed of entering. I followed her in the women's entrance. White sand covered the cement floor. Beer ads plastered the walls. The smells of smoke and liquor infused the air. We collapsed across from each other at a sticky wood table near the back. Honky-tonk music drifted in from the doorway to the men's side. At the next table, a bone-thin woman with painted lips and rouged cheeks sat alone, smoking a cigarette. A burly waiter came by, and Angelina ordered each of us a beer. "I've never been in a place like this," I said.

"Mercy," she said, observing me while twirling a lock of hair around her finger. "You are a riddle."

"What do you mean?"

Her red lips curled into a good-natured smile. "Someone as classy as you should be shopping in a store, not working in one. Like that girl said, you're too good to be a salesgirl."

"On the contrary, I'm lucky to have a job."

She let that ringlet of hair unwind from her finger and leaned forward over the table. "You're in a bad way, aren't you . . . because you lost your papa?"

My eyes widened. "How did you know?"

"You said something to that girl. And I can see a sadness in your eyes. I'm sorry, I'm too nosy."

I hesitated over whether to tell her my story. I'd hate my hard times to become twaddle for salesgirl gossip. "You wouldn't tell the others at work, will you?"

"No one keeps a secret as well as Angelina Spinelli. Not that you should say anything if you don't want to."

The need to have someone know who I was and what I'd been through won out. Ignoring the glass mug the waiter set down in front of me, I began telling her about Father. As I spoke, Angelina looked at me in silence with those penetrating black eyes. Her sympathy made my feelings rise to the surface, and everything spilled out in a muddle—even the story of my financial ruin.

"Poor dearie," she said after I wound down. "That sure is the limit. Losing your papa and all your money at the same time."

I pressed my lips together. Had I told too much?

"Have some of your beer," she said.

"I don't really drink," I said.

"Now would be a good time to start."

I took a timid sip; the bitterness was hard to swallow. "I didn't mean to talk your ear off. I'm sure you've had your own troubles. I must sound terribly spoiled."

"Who says? Could be worse coming down after you've been up instead of being down without ever knowing what it was like on the other end. And I bet you were close to your papa."

"Yes." I gripped my handkerchief as if holding on for dear life. The ache in my forehead spread to my temples. My body tensed up as if clenching my bones would freeze up my feelings.

Reaching across the table, Angelina gently squeezed my arm. "You must miss him something awful."

My pride was no match for her compassion, and I melted into heaving sobs. "Please ignore me." The woman at the next table stared at us while exhaling a cloud of smoke. Pulling out a handkerchief, I hid my face while blowing my nose and tried to compose myself. "I wouldn't be carrying on like this if I wasn't so beat. I've not had a decent night's sleep all week."

"The El?"

I nodded miserably. "I'm meeting Sadie's landlady on Sunday."

"Don't worry. You'll be fine. Mrs. Almond is a grouch, but she treats the girls fairly and keeps the place clean."

"You lived there?"

"Back when I first started to work, after Papa kicked me out."

"He didn't want you working?"

"I was supposed to stay home and help Mama clean up after everyone else. I would've killed myself. With five brothers, I've done enough cleaning for a lifetime."

Five brothers! Were they all as handsome as Joe? "Are you the oldest?"

"I'm second to last. Joe's the baby, a year younger than me."

That made him a year older than me. "Too bad your father couldn't appreciate that you were earning money."

"Appreciate? He thinks I've gone to the devil. When I went to work, he stopped speaking to me and said I was good as dead. If I managed to send money home, he sent it back, as if I made it by walking the streets at night. Joe finally brought him around to see me in the store. Papa never saw anything so grand in his life, not even back in Italy. He forgave me enough to take my money. Of course, I didn't tell him about the fashion shows—that would've set him off all over again. He still won't talk to me, though."

"What work does he do?"

"Whatever he can get. Digging tunnels, paving the streets, laying sewers. You know the joke, right? He came to America thinking the streets were paved of gold. Turned out there wasn't any gold in the streets, and he was expected to pave 'em." She gave a hearty laugh.

I smiled along with her. "That was daring of you to move out against his wishes."

"Not really. They were leaving New York anyway. Papa's got a brother in San Francisco who owns a *ristorante* and wants to open another. He talked my parents into moving out there. My older brothers, too. They say the city is booming since the earthquake." She grinned. "Lots of streets to pave."

"You didn't want to go with them?"

"There was already talk about marrying me off to some cousin out there I never even met. *Dio non voglia*. Mama can't wait to see her brood married so she has a houseful of grandchildren. My parents think they're still in the old country. She doesn't speak any English and never got north of Broome Street. She hated New York."

"She must miss her hometown."

"Only because she's forgotten almost starving to death. Papa's no better. Thinks he's gonna make America more like Italy. Try to get 'em to understand it's the other way around."

"And what about Joe? Why didn't he go to San Francisco?"

"He had a sweetheart and his job at the store. But it turns out my brothers are making loads of money fishing the bay, so now he wants to go, too."

"What about the sweetheart?"

"She lasted about a month. Longer than the others. I hope you aren't planning on falling in love with him."

"Don't worry." I laughed. "Not a chance."

"He's got his eye on you."

"I'm sure we have nothing in common."

"You mean he's too common for you?"

"No." Perhaps he was, but I didn't want to sound snooty. "I meant we seem to disagree about most things, especially his views on women. I differ with most men on that score, which is probably why I've never had a beau. I've never even been in love. Sometimes I wonder if I ever will be."

"Don't worry, you will, and then you'll wish you weren't—especially if you take a fancy to a scoundrel like Joe."

"He is very handsome."

"Don't he know it. Joe's like all the Italian men—thinks he's God, and Mama lets him believe it. Meanwhile, I'm the family shame."

"Well, they're wrong, as I see it. I think you're splendid. Look at how you take care of yourself. It's impressive."

"You're taking care of yourself, too, so I guess you should be impressed with yourself."

I picked up my nearly full glass of beer. "To us both for being impressive."

Angelina clinked her nearly empty glass against mine. "*Salute*."

"*Salute*."

After finishing her beer, she set the glass down with triumph. "That was good." She looked at my glass. "I guess there's no point waiting for you to finish."

"We'd probably have to stay all night."

"Isn't it vile how the evening hours pass so quickly? Before you know it, it's time to go to bed, wake up, and there you are, back in the store again. Ready to go?"

I would've preferred to stay in that saloon all night with Angelina than go back to my dismal room. "Ready."

21

AMANDA

AFTER TURNING ON the lights, I took a quick look around the store to make sure everything was in order. The women's clothing, all organized by decade, hung on racks along one entire wall. On the opposite wall, racks were divided between men's clothing, sale items, some shoes, and a full-length mirror next to a tiny curtained-off dressing room. In the middle of the store were a few tables displaying purses, gloves, scarves, and sunglasses. My station was in the back, behind a counter with a glass showcase filled with costume jewelry and miscellaneous tchotchkes.

I started a CD of hits from the sixties. The Lovin' Spoonful's "Do You Believe in Magic?" filled the store. Once I got behind my counter, I was a prisoner until closing, at eight. My sales assistant, Bettina, did come in on weekends, and when I traveled to auctions and flea markets, she kept things running, but for the most part, the store opened and closed with me. Just as I began to set up my cash drawer, I got a text message from Jeff.

R u still upset about last night? Let's talk ok?

He thought this was just another kiss-and-make-up fight. Tempted to let it be just that, I considered how to respond while booting up the desktop computer I'd programmed to use as a register. I still hadn't typed a response when two customers walked in.

They turned out to be mother and daughter. Mom was visiting from out of town, ready to treat her daughter, an NYU student, to whatever she wanted. Daughter had a great figure and it was hard for anything to look bad. They kept me busy replacing clothes on hangers and making suggestions. It warmed my heart to see them having such a good time. Would I ever get to play mom? Daughter finally settled for a floral chantilly-lace flapper dress and an adorable pink polka-dot romper.

After they left, I returned to my phone and typed in my response.

U don't think I'm serious but I am. Pls don't contact me again. If I call or text or email figure moment of weakness and ignore for my sake OK? THX

Except we had to work out my debt. What should I say about that? Before I could figure it out, a customer came in, desperate to find a cocktail dress. I closed the phone again without sending the message.

"Special occasion?" I asked.

"Dinner with five girlfriends. We're reuniting after losing touch for ten years."

"Sounds like fun."

"Except they're all married with kids, and I just got a divorce, so I really don't want to look frumpy. I've been searching the department stores, hating everything. Then I remembered I could go vintage."

"Absolutely. Let me pull a few things from the rack that would be a good fit. I bet we can get those housewives feeling like the frumpy ones when they see you."

She did present a challenge: large hips, small waist, flabby arms. I selected a few dresses for her to consider. The first two didn't work, but I had high hopes for a black chiffon dress from the sixties with sheer sleeves and marabou fur on the cuffs.

"I love it!" She held out her arms. "The sleeves are so gorgeous, and they camouflage my fat. You're a genius. Thank you so much. Now I can actually look forward to tonight."

While she changed back into her street clothes, I returned the other dresses to the rack. This was why I liked my work. Selling online could never bring the same satisfaction.

After she left, I ordered a turkey sandwich from the deli and went back to that text.

> Also want to pay back the IOU. Will figure out payment schedule and begin mailing checks to your accountant after going over my books.

I resisted confessing my lease crisis and hit send. That would've been too much of a mixed message. He'd take it as a call for help, then he'd offer money, and I'd be sorely tempted to take it. Just as I took out Olive's journal, a woman in her fifties wearing a sixties shift came in and went straight to the sale rack.

"Can I help you find anything in particular?" I asked.

"No thanks, just looking."

I nodded with a friendly smile, recognizing her as one of my regular customers and the dress as one she'd bought from me. Letting her alone to enjoy the hunt, I began to read.

OLIVE

SADIE INTRODUCED ME to her landlady and then left me to fend for myself. Mrs. Almond was a rotund woman trying to hide a pitted complexion behind a thick layer of powder. She lost no time before casting doubt on my moral character and virtue.

"No visitors allowed in your room," she said with irritation, as if I'd just asked how late my beau could stay. "I run a respectable place."

At least I knew enough not to take it personally. "I don't expect to have company."

She narrowed her eyes with suspicion. "I lock the door promptly at ten."

"I plan to be asleep every evening by nine."

"Six dollars a week—includes your own room, breakfast, and dinner."

"That would be acceptable."

She raised her chin so I'd know who was boss. "If you're one week late, out you go."

"I'll be paying in advance."

"I got my own bills to pay," she said with a sniff. "None of you girls seem to understand that."

I took that as my acceptance and opened my pocketbook.

November 16, 1907

Week's wages	*$7.00*
Expenses:	
Board (includes breakfast and dinner)	*6.00*
Lunch, 7 days @ 10 cents	*.70*
Paper, 3 days @ 2 cents	*.06*
Stamps	*.04*
Bananas	*.10*
Witch hazel	*.10*
Chewing gum	*.06*
Laundry	*.18*
Collar	*.15*
TOTAL	*7.39*

I haven't even included anything for clothing, medicine, or entertainment. Before too long the money from Matilda will run out. What will happen to me then? So many people think it's degrading for women to work. They're living in the past. It's no longer a matter of should or shouldn't. According to Miss Underhill, Siegel-Cooper employs three thousand salespeople and 76 percent of them are female. The real issue is how to expect women from degrading themselves when employers don't pay them enough to live.

I lay on my narrow bed, staring at a cockroach on the peeling wallpaper. I'd traded the El train outside my window for a dark airshaft. My room was smaller—not even space for a table. The bureau drawers didn't open without a fight, and the scuffed floor was only partially obscured by the previous tenant's faded green rag rug. I threw a shoe at the cockroach. The shoe missed. The cockroach didn't budge. After staring at its waving tentacles, my eyes drooped shut and I enjoyed the most deliciously deep sleep of my life.

A clanging bell startled me awake. I'd been living at the boarding house for a week and couldn't get used to that loathsome sound first thing in the morning. Only the fear of missing out on breakfast roused me from bed. I dragged myself down to the ground-floor dining room and found an empty seat next to a teacher who was reading a stack of student essays. Sipping my weak coffee, I listened to a telephone girl across the table complain about her boss. A fresh slice of bread was ruined by margarine instead of butter. No jelly. Time to go.

Girls poured out the front doors on their way to work. Since we were so far east, most everyone headed west. Some walked, some rode the trolley, others ascended to the El, and others descended into the subway. I caught a glimpse of Sadie lined up for a trolley. Riding inside the crowded car didn't seem worth the nickel, so I fell into step with the others marching down Fourteenth Street. When I reached the employee entrance, clogged because of the time clocks, I found myself bumping elbows with Angelina's brother.

"*Buongiorno*, Miss Westcott."

"Good morning, Mr. Spinelli."

As we inched forward, I couldn't think of what else to say, too aware of him standing so close, towering over me with his tall, athletic build. We took our turns punching in. He tipped his hat and said "*Ciao*" before turning in to the men's locker room.

In the women's locker room, everyone jostled and pushed in a mad rush to reach their departments on time. After taking my place on the sales floor, I could breathe easy. I had my territory. The crowds bumped and swayed on the other side of the counter.

Staring into the commotion with glazed eyes that hadn't adjusted to being awake, I mused that my encounter with Joe Spinelli that morning had been my most pleasant one yet. The sight of him could make a girl truly appreciate the male version of our species—until he had something to say.

Sadie appeared next to me. "What the devil are you smiling about?"

I gave her an innocent look. "Nothing."

I straightened up and asked a customer if she needed help. While showing her a bottle of toilet water, I scolded myself for daydreaming about Joe Spinelli. If I hoped to get a raise, I'd need to impress Miss Cohen and stand out from the other girls. I resolved to speak with her that day about my idea.

Instead of going to lunch, I stopped by her office and asked if she had a minute to talk.

"Now is as good a time as any," she said, motioning toward the chair opposite her desk.

I launched into my theory that we should be offering samples of our creams and lotions. "I've missed out on sales when a customer was afraid to try something new. If we allow them to try it out in the store, like they already do in the grocery section and housewares, we're certain to sell more merchandise. All we have to do is keep one container open."

"Allow all sorts of people to stick their fingers into the cold cream?"

"That way they can see it, and touch it, and smell it. They won't have to worry about the bother of returning something they don't like, and we won't have as many returns on opened products."

"But it's not sanitary. At least when it comes to food, we can hand out individual portions."

"If they're getting something for free, they won't care about the germs—not most of them, anyway. And it's not as though we'd be forcing anyone. We'd simply be giving the opportunity."

"I suppose that's true."

"Once they stop in front of the counter to take that little bit, I'll have a chance to tell them how well it works. I wager they'll be more disposed to pay for it."

"I think you may be on to something. I'll discuss it with Mr. Vogel."

Mr. Vogel, a distinguished-looking man I'd seen on the floor a few times, was one of the vice presidents. "That would be grand," I said. "Thank you, Miss Cohen."

"Thank you, Miss Westcott."

I rushed to the cafeteria to get something in my stomach before returning to my counter. The meeting had gone so well, I didn't even regret missing out on lunch with the crowd down the street.

When a letter arrived from Aunt Ida, I tore open the envelope, anxious to hear the latest news on our financial affairs. I was thrilled to find she'd included a letter from Daisy. I hadn't heard from my friend in months. I decided to save it and read my aunt's letter first. She reported that the bank had agreed not to charge interest on the debt for a year, as long as she made a payment every month. She'd taken lodgers to bring in some income, and Margaret had an arrangement with the town grocer to sell her baked goods. She already had large orders for the holiday, and my aunt urged me to come home for Christmas to help out. My bedroom, however, was no longer available; I'd have to sleep on a cot in the study. It didn't sound like the most inviting way to spend my time off. I put her letter aside.

Daisy's letter was disappointingly brief, and what little she said

I didn't want to hear. First she apologized for being such a rotten letter writer. Then she told me that London continued to be heavenly. Even though her courses at the art school were finished, she and her mother had no plans to return and were considering spending a few weeks in Rome.

I couldn't bring myself to write back. She knew nothing about the changes in my life—not even that Father had died. How could I tell her the best I could look forward to was an extra day off for the Christmas holiday? Now even that bright spot didn't sound so merry. Still, I wrote Aunt Ida that I would come. After all, she was my only family, and I hadn't been back in Cold Spring since the funeral.

The Christmas rush arrived with a wallop, along with freezing temperatures. Customers shopped in a frenzy that made the past two months seem like naptime in the nursery. The stock market had begun to recover and appeared to be driving everyone wild to spend, as if splurging would ensure that hard times were gone for good. We stayed open until ten every night to oblige the armies of customers desperate to buy.

The long hours were not so accommodating for us salesgirls. I fought off a constant state of exhaustion and could only manage to perform mechanically, like that fortune-teller in the glass booth at the Eden Musee.

December 23, 1907

The store was scheduled to close at six o'clock, but last-minute shoppers refused to leave. Mr. McGillicutty had to call the police to force them out the doors! I took the trolley home, gobbled down some bread and cheese, and changed into my nightgown. Now I'm in bed, feeling just as excited as when I was a little girl, knowing I'd be waking up to presents. Except now my "present" is time off from work. Too bad I have to spend it in Cold Spring.

I never heard the morning bell ring. Every now and then I woke, only to fall back into a dream. Eventually, I dressed and went downstairs. A woman who worked in a hotel restaurant sat in the dining room, sipping a cup of tea. We wished each other a merry Christmas, and I joined her at the table with my breakfast.

"Looks chilly out there," I said, dreading my trip to Cold Spring.

"It's below freezing." She handed me the morning paper. "They say it might snow."

An article warned travelers to expect the worst. The never-ending construction at Grand Central meant late trains and beastly crowds. "I thought everyone would've left the city by now."

"I'd say we're lucky to be right here, comfy and warm, even if it does make for a dull holiday."

"And I think you've helped me come to a decision. Excuse me, I'll be right back."

I went to the telephone in the front hall. It would be best to get the conversation out of the way so I could enjoy my breakfast. A man answered—one of the boarders. It was odd to think of a stranger living in my house. I told him who I was and asked him to fetch Aunt Ida.

"She's cooking up a storm," he said. "Hold on."

I tried to calm my nerves while waiting. A minute later, the man returned. "Sorry, miss, couldn't pry her from the stove."

I silently cheered. "Do tell her how very sorry I am that I can't come. And wish her a merry Christmas for me, please."

"Surely will. Sorry you'll be missing out, though. You should smell the pies baking in the oven."

I thanked him and said to eat a slice for me.

December 25, 1907

My first Christmas without family. Missing Father more than I can say. If I didn't feel so content relaxing by myself, with no demands on my time, I'm sure I'd feel utterly miserable and lonely.

The last week of 1907, the store continued to be overrun. Customers swarmed back to return gifts and reap profits on end-of-year clearance sales. When closing time on New Year's Eve finally came, I laid the black velvet cover over the countertop with relief.

"Miss Westcott?"

I looked up, startled to find Mr. Vogel, the vice president, standing in front of me. He might have been handsome in his day, but thinning, graying hair and a paunch were taking their toll.

"Yes, sir."

His lips curled into a smile under a thick mustache waxed to curl up at the tips. "I wanted to say hello. I hear you're doing an excellent job."

"Thank you, Mr. Vogel."

"Miss Cohen speaks highly of you."

"She's taught me so much."

"I had the impression that you've been teaching her. Your idea about the samples was first-rate. We'll give it a go after the New Year. Keep up the good work," he said, moving on.

Down in the locker room, I considered telling Angelina my good news, but then I decided not to, in case it should sound like boasting. "I can't believe this year is finally over," I said instead.

"How'd you like to go up to Times Square to ring in the New Year?" she asked.

"In this cold? With all the crowds?" It sounded like torture disguised as a good time.

"But it's exciting, with all the throngs milling about. Then at midnight everyone goes mad, yelling out 'Happy New Year!' And since we're closed tomorrow, you can stay out late for once. Won't you come, please?" she said with a winsome pout.

I had to smile, flattered that she'd chosen to ask me out of everyone. "How can I say no?"

"It'll be jolly fun," she said. "I promise."

She proceeded to ask a bunch of other girls, too. I felt like a fool and almost backed out, but sitting alone in my room now sounded dreary. At the very least, it would be an adventure.

Our group of seven squeezed onto a trolley with barely enough room to stand. When it was time to get off on Forty-second Street, we traded our cramped, claustrophobic captivity for the freedom to dodge hordes of moving bodies. Restaurants overflowed with revelers, and lines of people queued up for shows. Weaving through the crowds, I wondered what everyone was really celebrating. Making it to another year alive? What was so wonderful about living, anyway?

"Isn't it silly," Angelina said, hooking her arm in mine, "how we live in the grandest city in the world but hardly ever leave our own neighborhood? I'll never forget the first time I walked north of Canal and didn't stop. Must've been around ten years old. I found myself on Sixth Avenue and turned in to a department store; thought I'd died and gone to heaven—until the floorwalker kicked me out. I must've looked a sight in my hand-me-downs. That's why I always take care to dress nice. If you look cheap, men'll treat you cheap."

As if to prove her point, we passed a woman standing by the stage door of a theater. There was no doubt about her profession. She wore a crimson dress trimmed with fur. She'd painted her lips as red as an American Beauty rose. Her peroxide-blond hair was swept up in a towering pompadour.

"I don't understand . . ." I let my voice trail off.

"Understand what?"

"How she makes sure she doesn't . . . get into trouble."

"You've never heard of a rubber bag?"

"Rubber bag?"

"If the fellow wears it, you're perfectly safe."

I nodded, though I couldn't imagine what it was or how it worked. "I wish it weren't all so mysterious."

"My mama never told me a thing, either. I guess she wanted me to have the same shock she had on her wedding night. You hungry? Let's round up the others for a bite to eat."

We turned in to the first cheap restaurant that had an empty table. As the other girls joked and flirted with some sailors sitting nearby, I wished I could ask Angelina exactly what had shocked her mother. Had Angelina already experienced that shock, too?

We prolonged our stay in the warm restaurant by ordering coffee and tea. New customers crowded the doorway, though, and before long our waiter gave us the evil eye, so we piled back out into the cold. Half a block down, the girls insisted on going into a brightly lit arcade. Though a sign said UNESCORTED LADIES WELCOME, I didn't find the place particularly inviting—perhaps because of the sign in back that said FOR MEN ONLY. It hung over a long row of automatic picture machines. In front of every machine stood a man—except in one case, a boy was propped up on a box. They undoubtedly were watching some sort of vulgar peep show.

I tried to ignore them and let the girls entertain me with their skittish pleasure at feeding nickels into slots for the privilege of receiving an electric shock, or listening to a scratchy phonograph record, or stepping on a scale to find out their weight. The bright lights and seedy atmosphere began to wear on me, though; when midnight finally approached, I was more than ready to move on.

The girls insisted on pushing through the crowd to get as close to the square as possible. The year 1908 blazed in huge electric lights way up on the tower of the Times Building. The newspaper had said it could be seen for miles. I wondered if my parents could see it from heaven. I wondered what they'd think of their daughter now.

At the stroke of midnight, everyone's eyes turned up to the illuminated ball on the Times tower. Shouts of "Happy New Year" and joyous singing filled the street. Angelina yelled a hearty "Happy New Year" at me. When I countered with my own "Happy New Year," she opened her arms and we hugged. Soon I was hollering along with everyone else. The hoopla continued for at least five minutes of what seemed like utter madness. Perhaps it wasn't so very awful to be alive.

Times Square, circa 1905

Sixth Avenue in front of Siegel-Cooper, circa 1903

Herald Square and the Sixth Avenue elevated train, circa 1910

THURSDAY
JUNE 14, 2007

AMANDA

WHEN THE SHOP door opened, I looked up from the journal, hoping it would be the delivery guy with my sandwich.

"I believe you're expecting these?" said Mrs. Kelly's grandson, lugging a couple of garbage bags.

"Oh yes, from Mrs. Kelly. You can set them on the floor back here, that's great."

"I'll be right back." He turned and dashed to a cab parked out front. I slid the journal into a drawer as he returned with two more bags.

"Thanks for bringing all that down," I said, trying to remember his name—or maybe I'd never been told.

"I'm glad to get rid of it." Seeming to remember this was a business transaction, he added, "She tells me some of it's worth a lot."

He wore khaki pants and a blue T-shirt with Nikes and a Yankee baseball cap. The look would be fine if he were in high school, but this guy was old enough to remember life without e-mail. No ring. Commitment issues? "There are some nice pieces. She has good taste," I said.

"Grandma used to work as a buyer in a department store."

"That explains it."

"Yeah." He checked his watch and peered out the door.

"So . . . do you live there with her?"

"No, no, god forbid. Santa Monica."

"Oh." So why the Yankee cap? "You like it out there?"

"It's pretty nice, other than the traffic. Those are interesting," he said, peering at the shelf behind me.

"They're head vases." I took one down and showed him the opening on top. "They were big in the forties and fifties. Highly collectible now." I needed to bring down my new one.

"I've never seen one before. They're great."

"Thanks. You know, I don't think I ever got your name."

"I'm sorry. Rob. Rob Kelly."

"Amanda Rosenbloom."

We nodded and smiled, but no one initiated a handshake. I got that feeling you get when you're a single woman and you're with a man who might also be single and you imagine he's imagining that you're desperate and would marry him tomorrow if he'd only say the word but why would he when he could have a twenty-year-old instead of a woman approaching forty. *Well,* I wanted to tell him, *I'm not desperate. I have a successful business—I think—and I like living alone and don't need to be in a relationship to feel like I have a right to exist.*

"You ever been out there?" he asked.

"Once. I don't like L.A. much, but Santa Monica was nice, with the beach."

"Yeah, the air quality is better." He looked toward the door again, and I wondered why he didn't just leave. Then I realized I needed to give him the check and he was probably trying not to be crass. "I owe you money," I said, my index finger in the air. "Hold on a sec."

I wrote out the check for twelve hundred dollars and handed it to him with regret. I never would've made this deal if I'd known about my lease. As he put the check in his wallet, the delivery guy arrived with my lunch. I expected Rob to make his exit, but he wandered up and down the store, giving the men's rack a cursory look. After I paid the delivery guy, Rob returned to my counter.

"I'm just here to help her get rid of things," he said. "Take care of some loose ends."

"That's nice of you." I took my turkey sandwich out of the bag.

"My older sister lives in New Jersey, and she helps out a lot more than I do, but she's a lawyer and has two little kids, so I wanted to do my share. Grandma's driving me a little crazy, actually. She's an ornery old woman."

I smiled but wasn't sure how to respond, especially since it occurred to me to mention the journal, but then he might say I had no business reading it and should give it back.

"So, I was wondering," he said, "maybe you could suggest a good place for dinner. The neighborhood's changed so much, I don't know where to go anymore."

"Dinner?" He didn't mean with me, did he? Of course not, so why was I blushing? "There are tons of places. What kind of food do you like?"

"Pretty much anything."

"There's a good tapas bar on Ninth Street. And a great vegetarian place on Second Avenue. Or if you're in the mood for comfort food, there's a new place near your grandmother's called Home Cooking that's supposed to be really good."

"I'm always in the mood for comfort food." He hesitated. "You wouldn't by any chance consider joining me?"

I had a moment of panic. Should I say yes? What about the

beard? The fact that he lived on the other side of the United States? Did I really need to follow my adulterous affair with a long-distance relationship? Not to presume he wanted anything other than company over dinner. And a one-night stand, perhaps. "That's so nice of you to ask, but I stay open till eight, and then I have some bookkeeping I really should get to."

"No need to explain. I know how it is. Running a business can eat up all your time if you let it."

"It really can."

"So I'll get going. And thanks again. My grandmother likes knowing her things will be appreciated."

"I'll be sure to place them in the finest of homes." If I didn't go out of business first.

The door shut behind him. I took a few bites of my sandwich before checking my phone. Jeff had responded.

I'm sorry I hurt you. I love you.

Tears welled up in my eyes. He didn't like the way things were any more than I did. But I couldn't give in. He'd just pull me back under his spell. Damn. I had to distract myself. I queued up Ella Fitzgerald singing "Bewitched, Bothered, and Bewildered" before turning to the computer. I Googled "perimenopause," not because I put stock in what Molly said but just for the hell of it. One site had a checklist.

Hot flashes. No.

Trouble sleeping. Yes.

Irregular periods. Sort of, okay, yes.

Weight gain. Unfortunately.

Mood swings. Doesn't everyone's?

Loss of libido. Only when my married lover missed my birthday.

Trouble lubricating. Same.

Feelings of dread, apprehension, anxiety, doom. Yes, because my best friend told me I was running out of eggs.

Irritability. Who wouldn't be?

Disorientation, mental confusion. Like getting spooked in my own apartment? Freaky dreams? Allowing a hypnotist to convince me I could find wisdom in a department store?

Maybe Molly was right: My eggs were numbered. I typed in "freezing embryo." A zillion links popped up. It seemed that if you wanted to fork over fifteen thousand dollars, you could easily find someone to refrigerate your offspring. Every site agreed on one thing: The chances for a healthy baby decreased significantly after the age of thirty-seven. Some places wouldn't take women thirty-eight and older because success rates dropped so much. Jesus. I wouldn't even make the cut.

Three teenage girls arrived in a whirl of giggles. I kept an eye out in case anyone was contemplating a five-finger discount. They complained to one another over the lack of prom dresses from the eighties, a category of clothing I particularly loathed.

"Can I help you?" I asked.

One of the girls turned to me. "Where are your clothes from the nineties?"

"I don't carry the nineties," I said, resisting the temptation to suggest the nearest Goodwill.

"Oh, too bad," she said.

After they left, I neatened up the mess they'd managed to make after twenty minutes in the store. Then I went back to Olive.

OLIVE

"I WANT TO buy perfume." A handsome man in a dark suit and fedora peered at the display of pastel boxes. "It's for a lady who . . . She's my sister."

I noticed his wedding band. "Do you know what kind of scent she likes?"

He pulled at his collar. "I'm afraid I have no idea."

I showed him a midpriced bottle of lavender perfume. After almost three months of working in the store, I was wise to all the married men buying perfume for their girlfriends. "This has a lovely, fresh fragrance."

"I want her to feel appreciated."

"Well, if you don't mind spending a little more . . ." I turned to the glass cabinet behind me and selected one of our most expensive scents. "Women are always pleased with the latest from Paris."

"Can it be gift-wrapped?"

"Certainly."

"And . . ." He scratched his left eyebrow. "Can you send it to the Knickerbocker Hotel?"

I kept my voice neutral. "Of course."

"It needs to be there by dinnertime."

"I'll make sure it reaches the hotel in time." Smiling pleasantly, I offered him a lilac card with the store initials and a matching envelope. He wrote something and sealed it up. Wishing I could lecture him on the error of his ways, I accepted his money and gave my thanks.

At lunch I walked briskly in the cold to the dairy restaurant and ordered oyster soup. Joe and Angelina, along with a large group from the store, were sitting at two tables pushed together. When I sat down, it came as no surprise that everyone was talking excitedly about the big news: Harry Thaw had been acquitted of murder and taken to the State Hospital for the Criminally Insane, an asylum that happened to be just north of Cold Spring. Over the next few weeks, doctors would be evaluating his mental condition for a diagnosis. I quietly sipped my soup as they debated the decision.

"Obviously, he's off his rocker," Joe maintained. "You don't need a parade of experts to figure that out. The point is, he killed the fellow and deserves to rot in jail."

"But you're wrong," said Lucy from the handkerchief counter. "The point is whether he planned it or not."

"He had a gun on him, didn't he?" countered a young man who demonstrated vacuums in housewares.

"But it was a crime of passion," insisted a girl who worked down in the tube room. "He was defending his wife's honor. You can't punish a man for being in love."

I couldn't resist joining in. "I don't see why feelings of passion should excuse the fact that he murdered another human being in cold blood."

Angelina jumped in right after me. "Maybe because you've never experienced real passion."

As I turned crimson, some of the others hooted with laughter, perhaps even Joe—I didn't want to know. Keeping my gaze down, I stirred my soup slowly, as if searching for a pearl in the broth.

"I'm sorry, Olive," Angelina said. "That slipped out."

I nodded and felt grateful when the vacuum demonstrator turned the conversation back to Harry Thaw. "They treated him to a feast at some hotel up in Fishkill before locking him up in the madhouse."

"He sure won't be enjoying his meals in there," Lucy said.

My own appetite seemed to have evaporated, but I forced myself to finish the soup. As Miss Underhill had said on my first day, it was important to keep up your strength.

Angelina walked with me back to the store. "I shouldn't have teased you back there. I'm sorry. Do you forgive me?"

I crossed my arms over my chest and hugged my jacket closed to keep out the chill. "Of course. I'm sure the others have already forgotten." At least I hoped so.

"You're a peach."

"Goodness, I'm sick of the winter, aren't you?" I still felt wounded but didn't want to dwell on the matter any longer.

"February is evil," she agreed. "You feel like winter will never end. And here I am, rehearsing the spring fashion show for next week."

"Spring is a nice thought."

"Hard to imagine going outside in those pongee dresses and cotton frocks. Anyway, thank goodness tomorrow is Sunday. Have any special plans for your day off?"

"I'd been hoping to go to the Electric Show at the Madison Square Garden. The employee association had free tickets, but when I went to pick one up, the social secretary said I was too late."

"That's too bad. Sounds like fun."

We entered the warmth of the store. I returned to my counter, wishing for something more to look forward to than sleeping late on my day off. The afternoon dragged. February was notoriously slow, and the weather didn't help. At closing time, I went down to my locker and found Angelina waiting for me. She held up two tickets. "Still like to go?"

"The Electric Show? You're pulling my leg! How did you get them?"

"That social secretary likes to hoard a few for herself in case she needs 'em. Sometimes it's a good idea to check again at the last minute."

"So that's the secret. I'd love to go." There was no one I'd rather spend the day with, even if everyone knew I'd never experienced passion.

On our way out, the guard warned us we'd better have umbrellas. Neither of us did. "You're in big trouble," he said. "Those clouds are about to burst!"

Angelina punched the time clock. "Wasn't the sky clear this morning?"

I punched out after her. "This morning seems like ages ago. Who can remember?"

As soon as we stepped outside, gusts of wind swirled our skirts. "He was right," Angelina said as we looked up at the sky. "It's gonna pour. I better take the subway."

"And the trolley for me." I mentally subtracted the fare from my week's budget. We walked side by side with our heads bent against the wind and our skirts billowing around our knees. With one hand, I clutched my skirt to keep it from blowing up; with the other, I clamped down my hat. By the time we reached the curb, raindrops were falling. A policeman signaled for us to cross, and we moved along with everyone else, forging a path between the fender of a delivery truck and a cabbie who was trying to keep his horse from charging.

On the other side of the street, carriages lined up in front of a theater. The doorman blocked the way, forcing a sea of pedestrians to wait as a woman wearing a diamond tiara and an ermine fur coat descended from a carriage. Someone behind us whispered that she was Mrs. Vanderbilt Whitney, but I didn't know whether to believe it. The rain came down harder and pelted the captive audience as a white-gloved man with the bearing of a prince escorted the woman under the awning. Finally, the regal pair disappeared into the brightly lit gilded lobby. The weather never touched them.

With the ermine coat safely inside, the doorman let everyone through. Angelina and I continued on. A gust of wind slapped a spray of rain in my face, and another squall took my beaver boater along with it.

"My hat!"

We watched it fly into the street, where a streetcar promptly ran over it. My hatpin dangled from my hair. I pulled it out, and we kept going. Just as we reached the corner, lightning struck and the storm let loose. We dashed through the downpour and took refuge under a narrow awning. I stood there, a wreck, my hair drooping.

"I should make a run for the trolley," I said as one approached.

"You'll never get on. It's packed."

"I might as well walk. I'm soaked anyway." At least I wouldn't have to wash out my waist that night.

"You'll catch your death. Why don't you come home with me? Then we can go together to the show tomorrow. The subway's right across the street."

I'd never ridden on the subway. "That's very kind, but I shouldn't impose."

"I wouldn't offer if I thought you would be."

"It's terribly sweet of you." I stared at the entrance to the subway. For years I'd read about the excavations on Fourth Avenue: dynamite explosions, cave-ins, injuries, deaths. Aunt Ida liked to say the devil lived down there. I wanted to see for myself. And, for that matter, have a glimpse of how Angelina lived. "You have your own apartment?"

"It's not much, but it's all mine."

"Well then, yes, thank you. I don't know why you bother being so kind to me."

She laughed. "It's purely selfish. I'm hoping some of your polish might rub off on me."

"If it doesn't turn to rust before I dry off, you're welcome to it."

We ran across the street and down the cement steps. After paying our nickels, we fed our tickets into the chopper and joined the others on the crowded platform. A train approached with a low rumble that gradually built into a horrendous shriek of metal. When the guard opened the doors, we had to push our way onto the already packed car.

Squeezed in on all sides while speeding through the tunnel, I stared at the only diversion my eyes could find—an advertisement picturing a large cigar. It had an absurd slogan underneath. *A man is known for the company he keeps. Men are in good company when they smoke our cigars.* I kept reading the slogan over and over, as if it would say something new the next time.

The train screeched to a stop at the Astor Place station, and we joined the exodus up to the street. The sky had darkened and the rain had stopped. Wet streets reflected the city lights. I took a deep breath and appreciated what a gift fresh air could be.

Knowing we were about to enter the streets of the East Side ghetto, I observed my surroundings with keen interest. Astor Place was only a few blocks south of the Shopping District, but as we walked south past the Cooper Union, I felt as if we were entering a foreign country. Along Bowery, pushcarts lit with gas torches lined the gutters. A mishmash of motor cars, trucks, and horses carved out paths between trolleys running on three sets of tracks.

The Third Avenue El roared past overhead. I'd never seen so much movement taking place in such a small area by so many human beings trying to get somewhere else.

We soon turned a corner onto a narrow side street of six-story walk-ups. Despite the absence of office buildings and tall apartment houses, I had the sensation of being closed in on all sides. Black metal fire escapes zigzagged up the front of drab, grimy tenements. Wet garbage sat in piles along the sidewalk. We stopped in front of a doorway next to a smoke shop, entered a dark hall, and marched single-file up steep stairs barely lit by a flickering gas jet. After jiggling her latchkey to turn the sticky lock, Angelina pushed open the door.

I followed her into the small apartment. "Sorry about the mess," she said, unpinning her soggy hat.

"I'm sure you don't need to apologize."

"I haven't the time to fix it up, so there it is."

I took in my surroundings: wide-plank wood floors, a low ceiling, only the most basic furnishings. A small coal stove and sink made do for a kitchen. An alcove in the back had a bed. A pink throw rug with a yellow border covered the center of the floor, and elaborately decorated hats hung on the walls. A light pink sheet on a clothesline separated off the back corner of the room.

"But you've made it lovely, really." I particularly liked the wallpaper of purple roses climbing a jade-green trellis.

As I shook my wet hair loose, she put a coin in the gas meter. I wondered how Angelina could afford an apartment all to herself. She hadn't ever mentioned any gentleman friend. I hoped there was another explanation.

"Sit down, take your shoes off. I'm getting out of these wet clothes. Let me find you a robe so you can change, too."

We took turns using the bathroom down the hall and changing behind the pink curtain, where she had layers of clothing piled on hooks. When she hung up my outfit to dry, she noticed I was missing a garment. "No corset?"

"I can't stand them," I said, twisting my hair into a knot and pinning it in place.

"And I feel naked without one."

"But how do you breathe?"

"Simple: I let more air out than I let in."

I laughed. "I've never understood why women are so willing to suffer for their looks."

"So you can enjoy it when your suffering is over," she said with a touch of wickedness. "I love letting a man undo me one hook at a time."

My face turned crimson. Angelina smiled with indulgence. "Sorry, didn't mean to shock you. Forgot you're still an innocent *bambina*. How about I make us some dinner and warm the place up. You like spaghetti?"

"I love macaroni and cheese." My mouth watered as she turned on the stove.

"I haven't any cheese . . . but I do have a can of tomatoes and some garlic."

"That would be grand." I'd been craving butter and cheese something awful but didn't let on. I'd never eaten spaghetti cooked with tomatoes.

Angelina put a pot of water on to boil. Then she chopped up some garlic and poured olive oil in a skillet. I'd always thought that kind of oil was only for salad dressing. When the oil was hot, she tossed in the garlic. As it sizzled, the aroma filled the room.

As she wrestled with a can opener and a tin of tomatoes, I took a closer look around. On her bureau was an untrimmed straw hat surrounded by all sorts of feathers, different-colored ribbons, wire, and glue. A tall stack of hatboxes took up a corner of the room. "Looks like you have a talent for hatmaking, too."

"And buying." She dumped the tomatoes into the pan. "It's easier on my pocketbook when I make copies of the ones in stores, but sometimes a girl just can't resist. So we'll let that simmer and put in the spaghetti."

She used noodles such as I'd never seen: thin sticks that were so long, they had to be broken in half to fit in the pot. By the time she served the bowls of spaghetti, I couldn't keep myself from gulping down the hot soupy meal.

"This is the most delicious food," I said, trying not to embarrass myself while slurping the slippery noodles into my mouth.

"Thanks, I make it all the time."

"Did your mother teach you to cook?"

"I guess you could say that."

"Must be nice to have your own place. Or do you get lonely?"

"Joe lives right next door." She nodded toward the wall.

"Right on the other side?" I ignored a small cockroach crawling up the wallpaper.

"You want me to invite him over?"

"Please don't."

"You sure?"

"Quite sure." I seemed to be amusing her. "I've often wondered what it would be like having a brother—or a sister, for that matter."

"Not missing much, dearie. Nothing Joe likes better than telling me how to live my life. The other four are just as cocky. But he got the best of the looks."

"Except for his sister," I said. "I bet men fall for you all the time."

"Now and then, I guess."

"Anyone now?"

"Well . . ." Her voice trailed off with uncertainty as she wrapped a tendril of hair around her finger.

"You don't have to answer. I'm sure it's none of my business."

"Let's just say I got my catch."

"That's good."

"A well-heeled one, at that."

"Even better."

She let the tendril loose. "How else could I have my own place?"

I did my best to appear blasé. "He pays your rent?"

"Oh, he's awfully generous."

"That's nice."

She arched her eyebrows. "Are you shocked?"

"No."

Now she drew her eyes into narrow slits, almost challenging me to disapprove. "You think it's wrong."

It didn't sit right, but I had no wish to insult her. "I think it's your decision to make. How did you meet him?"

"He saw me modeling in a fashion show at the store. When it was over, he asked me to dinner. You know where we went? The Café Martin. Can you imagine me sitting there with all those rich swells?"

A strange sensation came over me as Angelina described her visit to the restaurant I passed all the time while living at the Mansfield. How did I end up here, eating spaghetti with an Italian shopgirl who lived one step away from prostitution?

"Are you in love with him?" I asked.

"I like him well enough."

"So you don't hope to marry him."

"Oh, he's crazy to marry me. Loves to go on about how we should chuck everything and move to Paris so we can sit in cafés, meet artists, drink wine all afternoon . . ."

"Sounds romantic."

"For a few weeks; then I'd be dying to come home."

"You could go to the fashion shows and shop for clothes."

"When you put it that way, it's tempting." She rose to clear the table. "But I see him enough as it is."

Later that night, crowded next to Angelina in bed, I lay on my back with my arms at my sides, trying not to move an inch. I'd never shared a bed with anyone and didn't want to brush against her by mistake.

"What are you afraid of more than anything?" she asked.

I stared into the dark before answering. "Childbirth. My mother died giving birth to me. Her mother died giving birth to her."

"Mercy. So you may never have children?"

"I'd sooner ride in a barrel over Niagara Falls. What's your greatest fear?"

"Being penniless," she said. "Ending up in the poorhouse or on the street."

I wished I could honestly reassure her that could never happen. "Life is so terribly uncertain." As we lay there in silence, I cursed the world for being such a heartless, lopsided place. Why should comfort and pleasure come so easily to some while others had to demean themselves simply to get along? "Does your brother know about . . . your gentleman friend? Seems like it would be hard to keep it a secret if he lives right next door."

"My gentleman friend," she said with an edge of bitterness, "is the reason Joe lives next door. He was still living at home when I helped him get work at the store, and then he happened to find out. *Madonna mia,*" she said with a roll of her eyes. "Joe threatened to tell my parents and kill that man who turned me into a whore. So I talked my gent into pulling a few strings, and he got Joe the apartment next door so he could 'look after me.' "

"That satisfied Joe?"

"Oh, he was delighted, and you can be sure he doesn't care two cents about leading his girlfriends down the same path."

"Isn't it interesting how men adjust their opinion as to a woman's behavior depending on how it best suits their needs?"

"I'll say."

"It's utterly galling." Though I couldn't shake my own distaste over the idea of Angelina compromising herself for money.

At the same time, I was intensely curious to know exactly *how* she compromised herself. Did she allow this man to have his way with her completely? Did it feel good? Did it hurt? Had she ever experienced the orgasm? Exactly how much money did he give her?

I tried to reassure myself; one day I'd know what I needed to know. Meanwhile, I ought to count myself lucky to find someone so kind and refreshingly open. Daisy was more educated and refined, but Angelina was more worldly-wise. Before too long, the steady rhythm of her breathing lulled me to sleep.

"Would you mind terribly lending me a hat?" We were just about to leave for the Electric Show when I remembered the sight of my poor white beaver boater being squashed under the wheel of that trolley.

"Sorry," Angelina said with a mischievous glint in her eyes, "I have no extras."

I pouted. "Please?"

She pretended to take pity. "I suppose I could spare one for the day."

I scanned the assortment of hats scattered about the apartment. "How should I ever be able to choose?"

"May I suggest this one?" From the wall, she took a felt toque trimmed with a turquoise velvet bow. "Or . . ." She selected a wide-brimmed black beaver with long pink and green ribbon tails. "This?"

"They're both lovely. The toque has less chance of flying off my head . . ."

"But the brim on the beaver is better protection from the rain."

"And the ribbons are darling. You decide!"

"Why don't we each wear one and then switch at lunch."

"Perfect!"

"Now we'd better skedaddle or we'll never have time to see everything."

Following her out, I remembered Joe lived right next door. It was funny to think he might be only a few feet away. I let Angelina start down ahead of me and peeked back at his door. I didn't want her to see—she'd be sure to tease me for being sweet on him. The truth was, I found her much more interesting.

"Ladies and gentlemen, allow me to give you a glimpse into the future," said the pretty young woman who led our tour through the most popular exhibit on the floor: a replication of an entire modern apartment with everything powered by electricity. The attention to detail was exacting, down to bric-a-brac on the fireplace mantel, a bookshelf filled with classics, and a box of chocolates sadly wasted on phantom residents. I couldn't believe the sheer audaciousness of creating it all just for show.

The last room on the tour was the most impressive: a kitchen fitted out with all the latest gadgets. "Clothes can be washed, rinsed, dried, and ironed with ease," she said while opening and closing an electric laundry machine. Her voice sounded so automatic, I thought she might be a machine, too. "Temperatures can be set so low, it's possible to store your food for days." She opened the door to a refrigerator. "No need for an iceman anymore.

"Soon electricity will be the new servant," our guide concluded, "and even your servants will be able to afford it." Most of her audience chuckled at the notion. As we left the apartment, an automatic piano played "All She Gets from the Iceman Is Ice."

"The idea of living with all those machines sounds dreadful," Angelina said as we walked on. "People will never accept it."

"Do you really think so?"

"What could be more romantic than dinner by candlelight?"

"You wouldn't have to give that up. Simply turn down the lights after your meal is made, and imagine how much easier it will be to make it."

"Given the choice, I'd rather have servants do it for me."

"And perhaps one day you will."

We passed exhibits for curling irons, weight reducers, coffee percolators, and toasters. Women gaped at the new appliances with longing. Unlike Angelina, I suspected that people in the future would embrace all these new devices, and the department stores would need to make lots of space for them.

When we stopped to watch the demonstration of a waffle iron, the heavenly scent put us both in mind for lunch. After waiting for the chance to sample a piece of waffle, which was quite delicious, we walked toward the entrance to find the restaurant. "So you don't find it tempting?" I ventured to ask. "The idea of living in a house done up with all those gadgets to help you raise a family?"

"A house? In the suburbs? With scads of kids running about? Never. I'm a city girl, and if I ever do get hitched, I'm not having sons. Girls only. I always wished I could have a sister. When I think of what Mama went through, raising the pack of us! Of course we're Catholic, so there was hardly a time she wasn't pregnant or nursing. That's why I'm stopping at two."

"But how, if I may ask, would you put a limit on it?" I couldn't believe my boldness, and asking in public, no less.

"My gent makes sure that's taken care of."

"So he uses those rubber bags you mentioned?"

"No, he doesn't like 'em, so he sent me to his fancy doctor uptown, had me all checked out, and fit me up with a pessary."

"What's that?" It seemed I could have an intimate conversation surrounded by hundreds of people in New York City, while exchanges of importance had utterly eluded me in the quiet town of Cold Spring.

"Like a rubber but for a woman. Goes inside and blocks his seed."

"Sounds awfully uncomfortable."

"After it's in, you can't feel a thing. Anyway, it's a bother no matter how you manage—except the old-fashioned way, of course."

"What's that?"

"You're the limit!" she said with a laugh. "Make him withdraw before it's too late."

By "too late," I supposed she meant before the orgasm. Dr. Galbraith's book said both the man and the woman needed to have one for pregnancy to occur.

"And they say," she went on, "your chances are best during your monthly."

"Best to get pregnant?"

"Best *not* to."

"Are you sure?"

"Sure I'm sure—the doctor told me so."

"Thank you for being frank with me. Honestly, I feel like such a dunce when it comes to men and anything having to do with, well, you know."

"Sex?"

"Yes," I said shyly. "And you're so worldly."

She laughed. "My family would say wicked, not worldly. God knows, I'm well on my way to hell if everything the Church says is true."

"If you ask me, too many who preach religion are just trying to impose their own views on other people."

"I think so too," she said. "At least I hope so, seeing as I stopped going to confession. I got my fill of telling the priest what a sinner I am. Do you think that's awful?"

"Not at all. My aunt who raised me is a devout Christian. She never hesitated to make sweeping pronouncements about what is and isn't God's will. I have to say, I find it very suspicious when any mere mortal claims to know with certainty what God wants."

"That makes perfect sense, and I never could've put it so

well. You may not know much about men, Olive, but you sure are clever."

"Why, thank you," I said, feeling pleased as punch—until we reached the restaurant. "Oh, my." A terribly long line of customers stood waiting.

"This is mad."

"We could leave the Garden and find someplace nearby."

"I'm too beat. Let's stick it out."

"I bet the line will move fast," I said, observing the vast sea of tables.

I bet wrong. Having claimed their bits of real estate, the seated patrons seemed happy to remain settled for good. Nor did they appear to be moved by the hungry, tired, and outright hostile looks coming from those of us in line.

"I almost forgot," Angelina said after we'd been waiting awhile. She began to unpin her hat. Thus reminded, I did the same. We made our trade as people around us watched with perplexed faces. Then each of us made sure the other's hat and hair were in place.

"I have this crazy idea," she said after the exchange was accomplished.

"I hope you're going to tell me what it is."

"You must promise not to laugh."

"I give my word."

"Someday I want to own my own millinery shop. Someplace elegant, on Fifth Avenue, where I can sell my own designs to an exclusive clientele. Or to the less exclusive clientele on Sixth Avenue," she added with a modest smile. "Or even"—she laughed—"the Bowery, if I must. Of course it's just a pipe dream."

"Why do you say that?"

"I don't know a thing about owning a shop."

"You could learn."

She shook her head. "I'd be a dreadful businesswoman. My heart has a knack of ignoring my good sense."

"Even if you're selling your own creations?"

"Especially if I'm selling my own creations."

When we were finally seated, it took half a century for the waiter to take our order. After he scurried off, I feared we might never see him again. "I don't think owning your own shop has to be a dream," I said. "May I ask something that's none of my business?"

"Ask away. Then we'll see if I answer."

"How much does he pay you?"

She knew who I meant. Her eyes refused to meet mine. "Plenty."

"I can't even guess what that would be."

"Five, usually, after spending an evening together."

"May I ask how he gives it to you?"

"Cash."

"Yes, but how? Isn't it awkward?"

"He slips it in my purse when I'm in the bathroom, freshening up. And let me tell you," she said, finally looking me square in the face, "the chance to use that porcelain tub instead of a tin bucket makes *me* want to be the one to pay *him*. He keeps a room at the Plaza, you know, that new hotel that just opened up on Central Park."

"Does he really?" I took care to hide my disapproval so she could have the chance to impress me.

"Everything is so grand. The water closet flushes simply by pressing a little button, can you imagine?"

Her choice of detail made me smile. "That truly is a luxury."

"You should see the room, all done up with the most elegant furniture, a gorgeous marble fireplace, and it's up on the fourteenth floor. I can look out the window and see a glorious view: little people way down on the sidewalk; the traffic going by; horse cabs all lined up in front of the park; the mansions on Fifth Avenue . . ."

"It does sound lovely." The Plaza Hotel most certainly would have turned me away that night when I had nowhere to go.

"The best part is, we can telephone to the kitchen, day or night, for food. He lets me order anything I want off the menu, no matter how expensive, and a bellboy rolls a table on wheels right to our room."

"What fun," I said, remembering the pleasures of breakfast delivered on a dumbwaiter.

"If he ever does throw me over, I can't imagine going back to counting pennies."

"You must have a good amount saved."

"How much do you think?"

"I don't know." I took a wild guess. "Two hundred dollars?"

"If only! Closer to fifty." She confessed the number as if admitting a crime.

"That's a good sum."

"I should be saving more. Seems like there's always something to spend money on."

"True enough. Perhaps you ought to draw up some sort of plan."

"Of what sort?"

"For your business. So you'd know how much capital you'd need to get established."

"I wouldn't know where to begin."

"Let's pretend the rent would be twenty a month for any place decent. Plus the cost of coal and oil. And you'd need at least thirty a month for food and clothes and other necessaries."

"So much?"

"You can't scrimp on health or the way you look if you're going to run a business."

"I suppose."

"Multiply all that by twelve, and you'll have a general idea of how much would be required for a year. There are also onetime expenses like furnishings, and you'd need insurance . . . and let's not forget the cost of supplies so you could make your hats!"

"Mercy, I'm snowed under just thinking about it. You do have a mind for business, don't you."

"Mostly, it's common sense. But I suppose I picked up a few things from my father."

"More than a few things. Say, you know what? We should become partners."

"Partners?"

"It's brilliant! We'll open my hat shop together. I'll handle the artistic side, and you'll take charge of the business part."

"But I don't know anything about owning a shop."

"You know more than you think, and you've obviously got the smarts and good sense." She put her hand on my mine and squeezed. "Say you'll do it, won't you?"

"My goodness." I couldn't resist humoring her. "It does sound like an intriguing idea."

"Just imagine! We'll be our own bosses, do what we love most, and make tons of money so we can buy beautiful, expensive clothes and eat in all the swank restaurants."

"Listen to you, spending our profits before we've made any."

"See?" she said. "You're my perfect partner."

I blushed. I liked the idea of being important to her. In fact, the scheme was growing on me by the second. By the time the waiter brought our food, we were discussing how the shop ought to be decorated, and I no longer knew if I was simply humoring her or not.

AMANDA

AFTER CLOSING FOR the day, I took the two garbage bags full of Mrs. Kelly's Edwardian clothes up to my apartment. I'd spend an exciting evening sorting through to see what needed washing and mending. Except before doing any of that, I really needed to go over my accounts.

I glared at my laptop. Facing those numbers seemed incredibly depressing. How had my life turned into such a disaster?

Nothing to do but go across the street and have a stiff one. Carol would be on tonight. She'd worked as a bartender at Phebe's ever since I'd moved to the block. Carol gave me courage, and not just the liquid kind. She was surviving her fifth decade just fine—living with a longtime boyfriend, looking great, still pursuing an art career with zest. Life could continue on just fine after your first half century.

I took my favorite seat at the end of the bar, but where was Carol? Instead of her mop of red curls, a head of straight black hair on a young skinny body took my order. She had the de rigueur trendy piercings—tongue, nostril—and a butterfly tattoo on her wrist. When she set down my Jack Daniel's with Diet Coke and a bowl of peanuts, I asked about Carol.

"She had to take off for a couple days. Death in the family."

"I'm sorry to hear that. I've known Carol for years. Do you know who it was?"

"Her mom. Sucks, right?"

I nodded.

"Awesome top," she said.

"Thanks."

"My name is Hadley. Let me know if you need anything else."

Poor Carol. Poor me. Poor everybody. Mothers shouldn't die. It just shouldn't be allowed. I reminded myself to call my mom about going up to Woodstock on Sunday night. Then I downed a nice big sip of my drink. Goddamm it. Was I ever going to be a mother? Had I already blown my chance? Molly was right to freak me out. Suddenly, her idea of chucking it all and moving in with my mom to raise my baby appealed to me.

I could become a Woodstocky, tie-dyed hippie, natural-foods single mom. All I needed was the sperm. Forget the anonymous donors, though. I'd get Jeff to contribute. Didn't he owe me after using up my most fertile years? Bonus points: If I were raising his baby, I wouldn't have to feel obligated to settle my financial debt. After his kids were off to college, he'd come for me in Woodstock, ask for my hand in marriage, and whisk me back to the city.

I finished off my drink. Dizzy and a little buzzed but perfectly in charge of my facilities . . . faculties . . . whatever . . . maybe I should've gotten something to eat.

Hadley came by and asked if I wanted another.

"Okay."

I watched her mix the drink while I chomped on some peanuts. My new plan had me all excited. Only fear could stop me now. I should text him immediately, before changing my mind. As

Hadley set down my drink, I took out my cell phone and began typing.

Hi there. Nice casual opening. *I've been thinking. I'm not getting any younger.* Delete. *I've been thinking. I wasted my thirties on u. So u really do owe me.* Delete. *So I had this wild and crazy idea.* No. *Hi, how are ya? We have something very special. And circumstances have kept us from being able to be together. But I love you, and I want to have your child.* Oh my god, did I really just type that? Delete, delete, delete. It was absurd to be texting something important like this. At the very least, I had to be businesslike. It was business, after all. Didn't Molly say so? And no one gives away the important information until they have to. *I have an idea and need to discuss it with u.*

I stared at the screen. Sipped my drink. Went back and changed the "u" to "you." That was it. Sure, I could wait to send it in the morning, when I might be thinking more clearly, but then I might chicken out. Chicken out on my eggs, ha ha. Except maybe I didn't want to think clearly. I moved my finger to the send button.

No! Don't do it! Don't be a fool!

I moved my thumb to delete.

Don't be a coward! Move things forward! You aren't getting any younger!

Was this my mood swinging here? Was I experiencing the apprehension, anxiety, doom, and mental confusion of a perimenopausal thirty-nine-year-old? Screw that. I pressed send.

Damn. Why did I do that? Now it was gone . . . into the ether, cyberspace, wherever it went, impossible to retrieve. I texted him again.

PLS IGNOREPREVIOUS TXT. THX

Before I could convince myself that text was equally pitiful, I pressed send.

• • •

Back in my apartment, I put a package of frozen mac and cheese in the microwave and sat down in front of my laptop with the honorable intention of opening Quickbooks. The whiskey was in my system, though, and my level of concentration, not to mention motivation, was not conducive to getting anything done. I checked my e-mail.

My friend Karin had agreed to sushi in Tribeca. She added that we should seriously consider Home Cooking next time because *The New York Times* said they had the best pancakes in the world. After e-mailing back that I looked forward to my tuna roll, I clicked on the Home Cooking website. The decor was retro mid-century modern, so "in" these days. I was pretty sure Olive wrote about going to a Child's restaurant that used to be on the same corner—maybe in the very same building. To think I could've gone there with Rob Kelly instead of drunk-texting Jeff for his sperm.

I checked the time. Ten o'clock. I was too weary to be productive, but if I drank coffee, I'd be up all night.

The microwave bell rang. I got out the tray of mac and cheese, pulled off the plastic, and sat down for my scrumptious meal. Two bites later, I pushed it away with disgust. I needed *real* comfort food, and this wasn't making the cut. Why sit around getting depressed when I could go and enjoy the best pancakes in New York? I grabbed a black sweater and went out into the night.

26

OLIVE

THE SIEGEL-COOPER EMPLOYEE association had organized a trip to Coney Island for the first Sunday of spring. I'd never been, and when the day finally came, I bubbled with the same excitement I might have for a holiday abroad. We'd been warned that lots of the shows weren't scheduled to open until the summer, and rides that burned down the year before had yet to be replaced. Starved for the sun, none of us gave a hoot. I couldn't wait to breathe in the fresh air after suffering through the toughest winter of my life.

The journey itself was a diversion. Surrounded by my fellow employees, I had no fear of the subway, as I did that first time. Or at least not until someone mentioned we were traveling inside a metal tube underneath the East River. I sat prone until we reached Brooklyn, where the train ran aboveground and I could contentedly look out my window at the scenery. Our route passed endless rows of square brick houses, but the drabness of the dwellings was relieved by the variety of backyards. Some had toys scattered about; some had gardens; some were trimmed and orderly; some were ramshackle. I wondered if the residents thought about how their yards served as entertainment for the passing train riders.

Some of the girls sitting around me were trying to plan out which attractions were the highest priority, since there was never enough time to do everything. Sadie couldn't wait to ride the loop-the-loop. Angelina longed for the beach. A girl who worked in the tube room was set on the shooting galleries. And Helen, who worked in housewares, raved about an exhibit of "incubator babies."

"Is that part of the freak show?" Sadie asked.

"Goodness, no," Helen said. "Haven't you heard about it? A doctor rescued tiny babies that were born too soon and keeps them alive inside glass boxes that keep 'em warm. It's a genuine medical marvel!"

Having no interest in wasting time at Coney Island looking at babies, I turned back to the window. The landscape had become more suburban, with the occasional school, church, ball field, and train station surrounded by a cluster of shops. We stopped occasionally to let more people on; the aisle was packed by the time we reached the white dunes of the island.

When the train pulled up to Surf Avenue at the end of the line, everyone clamored to get outside. As I stood up, my hatpin fell to the floor and rolled away. I had to squat down to conduct my search. It ended up next to a piece of paper soiled with a footprint. The caption in bold letters caught my eye: THE WIFE'S FRIEND. Then the subtitle: HOW TO PREVENT CONCEPTION. I folded the flyer and stuffed it inside my jacket pocket.

Having exited the car, I stood still on the platform and let the sun bathe my face while breathing in the salty sea air. What good luck to come on such a lovely day. I pinned on my hat, adjusted the brim to shade my eyes, and went to join the others.

Those first impressions of nature evaporated as I descended

the stairs to the fairgrounds. Vendors shouted, people shrieked on rides, and a brass band in one direction competed with an orchestra in the other. Our group was immediately squabbling about where to go first and pulling in different directions. The majority seemed intent on visiting the incubator babies.

Angelina sidled up to me. "You don't want to see the *bambini,* do you?"

"Not in the least. Shall we walk to the beach?"

"*Perfetto.*" She hooked her arm in mine, and the two of us ambled off on our own. As we passed a camel chewing cud while waiting to be hired for a ride, I couldn't resist asking why Joe hadn't come.

"He finally gave notice and bought his train ticket to San Francisco. All he can think about is moving. I guess he'll be getting all the fresh air he wants soon enough."

"How exciting!" I said, taking care not to sound sorry to hear the news.

"He's been talking about it long enough."

"Oh, but you'll miss him."

"If you say so." She stopped in front of a blue tent decorated with gold stars. A wood sign said: ANNIE SMITH, WORLD-FAMOUS PSYCHIC! COMMUNICATE WITH THE SPIRIT WORLD! "I've never been to a psychic, have you?"

"Never," I said, but then I remembered Lola Cotton.

Next to the tent stood a woman, the sort they called an albino, with acutely pale skin and white hair and eyebrows. "Only a nickel," she said. "Money back if you're not satisfied."

"Let's give it a go." Angelina pulled me forward through the slit in the tent. Since I was mildly curious, I didn't bother to object. As my eyes adjusted to the dark, I made out a rotund woman sitting at a square table. One gold candle on the table cast an eerie glow.

"Welcome," she said. "I'm Annie Smith. Are you ready to contact the spirit of a loved one who's gone on to the next world?" She motioned to the empty folding chairs on either side of her. "We will begin."

Angelina and I sat across from each other. I thought a proper psychic ought to have an exotic accent—Spanish or Hungarian, perhaps—but this woman sounded thoroughly American. Two thick braids of dark red hair framed her round, pale face. She instructed us to place our palms on the table and close our eyes. "Think of the name of a loved one you'd like to contact. I'll do my best to summon their spirit, but keep in mind, sometimes we hear from someone if they have an urgent message or a strong need to visit us. Someone shy may not speak up. The spirits have their personalities."

In other words, she'd already given us her excuse if she failed.

I lay down my palms and closed my eyes but couldn't decide whether to summon my father or my mother. Then I reminded myself this was nonsense, so I purposely kept my mind as blank as I could. I heard Annie Smith taking deep rhythmical breaths punctuated by occasional light moans, and I couldn't resist opening my eyes enough to peek. Every time she exhaled, the candle flickered, on the brink of going out. Angelina sat with her eyes obediently closed.

"Concentrate!" Annie Smith yelled. "Concentrate on the spirits that surround us!"

She continued moaning while rolling her head in circles. Then the table began to jiggle back and forth. Suddenly, Angelina gasped. "Someone touched me!"

"Please announce your presence!" the psychic called out to the room.

Angelina sat ramrod-straight, her eyes still closed. "They squeezed my shoulder."

I couldn't believe she was taken in by this claptrap.

"If a spirit is here," the psychic implored, "please make yourself known!" Annie Smith began to retch and gag as though someone was choking her. Sticking out her tongue, she rolled back her eyes, and her head dropped forward. Then she began moaning and rolling her head in circles again. After doing that for a while she fell silent, raised her head slowly, and opened her eyes.

I quickly shut mine. Now she spoke in a deep, hoarse whisper. *"Please . . . listen to me."* There was silence, and I waited for what would come next. Then Annie Smith—or the spirit—yelled: "*Blood!*"

I had to peek again—not that I expected to see blood.

"*Everywhere!*" she screamed. "*Can't be helped!*"

"Why?" Angelina asked. "Why is there blood?"

"*Muh . . . muh . . . mother.*"

"Mother?" Angelina repeated. "You?"

"*Baby!*" she shouted.

"You're the baby's mother?" Angelina asked.

Her mother was alive. Was I supposed to think this was my mother? I wasn't going to be taken for a fool this time around.

"*Don't . . . be . . . afraaaaid!*" the psychic yelled.

Angelina still had her eyes squeezed shut. "Of what?"

"*The past!*"

"Don't be afraid," Angelina repeated, "of the past?"

"*Or you will regret . . . regret . . .* "

"What?" Angelina pressed, as if she really had to know.

"*The future!*"

Angelina shook her head. "I don't understand. Regret the future? Can you please explain?"

"*Blood!*" the psychic yelled. "*Everywhere! Can't be helped!*"

After that, the psychic's eyes rolled back in her head, and her chin dropped. A moment later, she lifted her head and opened her eyes. "The spirit," she announced in a perfectly calm voice, "has departed." Her regular Annie Smith voice had returned—notwithstanding a trace of annoyance, especially as she looked sideways at me. "They don't like their presence to be doubted."

"You can't regret the future," I said. "Or fear the past. It's backward." Under the table, my shin received a kick, but I doubted it was from a spirit.

"Sometimes," Annie Smith said, "it can take time to understand a spirit's message. I'm here every Saturday and Sunday if you should like to visit with them again." Then she bowed her head to each of us. "Good day."

We both thanked her, Angelina more sincerely than I could manage. Back outside the tent, we squinted from the sun. The albino woman held out a golden bowl, and we dropped our nickels in.

"I know you thought that was all hogwash," Angelina said as we continued toward the boardwalk, "but you could knock me over with a feather."

"People regret the past," I insisted, "not the future."

"Haven't you ever experienced something wholly fantastic that made no sense?"

"No." Lola Cotton flitted through my mind again. Then I remembered the mechanical gypsy. But I was not about to confer them with special powers. People liked to make sense out of nonsense to suit their needs. "At any rate, if there was a spirit in that tent, you were the one it was trying to reach, not me."

"How do you know?"

"I wasn't concentrating one bit. And you were the one who felt someone's touch."

"But didn't the spirit say she was a mother? My mother is alive."

"She said it was the *baby's* mother, which meant nothing."

"Did she?"

"You see, that's how they pull you in. Make it vague enough to apply to anyone."

"It's more than that," Angelina said with irritation.

We walked on in silence. I was trying to think of how to

smooth things out without saying I was wrong when a food pavilion came into view. Stopping to get a bite to eat seemed like a good idea.

"Shall we get something to eat?" Angelina asked.

"I was about to say the same thing."

"See?" She smiled. "I read your mind."

Her good mood seemed to be restored, so I forgot about apologizing. After buying hot dogs, crispettes, and sodas, we found an empty table and began to devour the salty food.

"Have you had any more thoughts about our millinery shop?" I asked. One of us raised the topic every now and then to keep the hope alive.

"I'm starting to wonder if it's such a good idea. After all, it would be a very big commitment and take lots of work. Not that I'm afraid of the work. But what if it failed? I'd lose everything."

"Sounds like you're regretting the future," I teased, hiding my disappointment behind a smile. Not that I'd been counting on that scheme. It was the fantasy that I didn't want to give up.

"I'm sorry," she said. "I don't mean to let you down."

"Not at all," I said, vaguely aware of trying to wound her pride. "I never really believed you'd save enough money to get it started."

"You didn't? Well, I'm sure I could."

"How much more have you put aside since the original fifty?"

She stared at me with a hurt expression. Having managed to wound her, I immediately felt the worse for it. "I'm sorry, I didn't mean—"

"Hey!" A shout from a familiar voice cut me off. "Where've you two been?" Sadie and some of the other girls from the store descended, pulling chairs up to our table and jabbering with excitement. Their favorite attraction had been the incubator babies.

"They were such precious little miracles," Helen from housewares said, clasping her hands to her chest. "Some of the poor darlings are orphans; I could take one home with me today."

"Then you better find a husband to take home, too," Sadie said.

"Mercy me," Angelina said. "Can you believe we still haven't seen the beach? I'm dying to lie out in the sun for a bit."

"That sounds grand." I hoped we might have a chance to patch things up, but the others decided to join us. Before we reached the boardwalk, the girl from the tube room convinced everyone to take a quick look at the Seven Wonders of the Ancient World. By the time we finished admiring the Hanging Gardens of Babylon, it was time to meet up with the rest of the group and return to the city. I never did reach the ocean.

That evening, in the privacy of my room, I pulled out the flyer I'd found on the train. The Woman's Friend turned out to be an advertisement for Vital Soluble Tablets to prevent pregnancy. The Vital Pharmaceutical Company claimed these pills were highly reliable and had no ill effects. They also sold a pessary, the device Angelina used, and suggested irrigating with a special Vital Quinine Solution afterward. The flyer said women could also use a sponge soaked in that solution, and all three methods were equally and reliably effective. However, they pointed out, the pill and pessary could be used without the husband's knowledge, and that made them better "friends." I smiled, thinking of all the husbands who'd object to their wives socializing with that type of friend.

The end of the advertisement noted that women were most likely to conceive during the monthly flow. Strange. Hadn't Angelina told me that was the *least* likely time to conceive?

I pulled out *The Four Epochs of Woman,* hidden at the bottom of my trunk, to see what Dr. Galbraith wrote on the subject. After all, as a medical doctor, she had the most trustworthy credentials.

She said it was a well-established fact that women were most likely to conceive on the days immediately before and immediately following menstruation. At that time, mucus that usually blocked the sperm's passage to the egg was washed out. She didn't mention the days during, but it seemed logical to assume she included those, too.

Perhaps I was mistaken about Angelina and had remembered the reverse of what she'd said. It was so hard to keep straight, even with the information right before me in black and white.

April 26, 1908

I spent the entire time at Coney with Angelina. We went to a psychic, and she fell for the whole act. I wonder why she soured on the hat store. Has she soured on me? I'm probably being silly. It's inevitable that we have our ups and downs. Daisy and I used to have our tiffs, too. Mercy, it's been ages since she's written. Has she forgotten about me? I think I had too much sun. My mind is spinning. Must go to sleep. Hope my dreams are sweet.

Joe Spinelli held me in his arms and kissed me so hard, I thought my lips would bleed, and yet I kissed him back just as hard. Our audience stood on the other side of the plate glass, their mouths gaping open in shock. Who cared if we were on display in the store window? Let them all watch! A fire alarm went off. Police sirens wailed. We kept on. Were they coming to arrest us? Let them!

My eyes opened to the clanging of the morning bell. What a ridiculous dream! Kissing Joe Spinelli in public was the last thing I wanted to do.

Miss Cohen appeared while I was straightening the shelves. "Shall we have a little stroll around the floor?"

"Yes, Miss Cohen."

Sadie observed my departure with curiosity. I had no reason to worry, but one never knew what to expect.

"Your sales record has been excellent," Miss Cohen said as we walked side by side down the aisle. "I've observed your dedication to the job and your instinct for customer service. The sample idea worked out splendidly. Clearly, you have a flair for retail."

"Thank you," I said, my heart racing with anticipation.

"I want to talk with you about beauty products. You may have noticed how the attitude toward them is shifting. Some still consider making up a sign of vulgarity, but I predict we'll soon be seeing perfectly respectable women on the streets with painted faces, and we shan't think anything of it."

Was she going to ask me to sell makeup? I never wore a speck, and I thought it looked cheap. "I sold rouge to a lady whose address is one of the best on Fifth Avenue."

"Exactly. Even Mr. Vogel has finally acknowledged the trend. So we've decided to move the lace counter down to the basement in order to make room for a line of cosmetics."

"That sounds like a brilliant idea."

"I'm glad you think so, because I'd like you to be in charge. Do you know of the Madame du Jardin Salon?"

"I've walked past it on Fifth Avenue."

"Then you know they carry the highest-quality products. We'll be devoting a counter specifically to her products. In addition to face creams, body lotions, and perfumes, they have a line of cosmetics: face powder, rouge, lip pencils, eyelash paint, kohl, even a colored polish for nails."

"Why, that's grand, Miss Cohen. It sounds like just the thing."

"I should mention you'll be expected to wear these products. A representative from Madame du Jardin shall teach you how to apply them correctly, and then you'll be able to teach the customer. I know you aren't in the habit of making up, but I assure you all these products promote a natural, healthy look. Will that present a problem for you?"

I'd have to stand there in public, looking like some kind of harlot. And teach other women to look like harlots. Aunt Ida would be horrified. Father would've forbidden it. But if this was necessary to please Miss Cohen, what choice did I have? "It sounds like this position will involve a lot more responsibility. Shall I be receiving a raise in pay?"

"Didn't I mention that? Of course. I'm prepared to pay you nine dollars a week. On top of that, you'll receive a three percent commission on your sales. It's a substantial raise, but you've been underutilized in the store, and I don't want to lose you to someone else. It also happens that you're exactly the sort of person Madame du Jardin requires in this position. It's vital to have someone of your character standing behind these products. Our customers will see that a more sporting look doesn't have to mean you're fast. I have the feeling that if we do this right, it will be quite a success."

Nine dollars a week—and a commission! "I suppose I could adjust to the idea of wearing makeup. But . . ." I hesitated, afraid to negotiate, yet aware this could be my only chance. I'd hate myself later if I didn't try. "I've heard commissions of seven percent are common in many departments." The ones that employed men.

"Certainly not to start with. I could speak with Mr. Vogel about raising it to five, but I seriously doubt he'd authorize more than that."

"I would accept five to begin with."

"Splendid. We'll arrange for someone to come next week to show you the products, and then, if all goes to plan, the counter will be open for business the following week. I must warn you, the other girls will be jealous, especially the ones who've been here longer. You have the polished manner they all want: poise, confidence, and refinement. Even the best actresses can't reproduce those qualities. People who know the difference can always spot a fake."

"Thank you, Miss Cohen. I do appreciate your faith in me."

"Look at this." Miss Cohen stopped abruptly in the wide central aisle of the dressmaking department. Salesgirls stood listlessly in front of shelves stacked with bolts of fabric. Hardly any customers occupied the stools along the counters. "The entire dressmaking department should be moved to another floor. Everything is shifting to ready-to-wear."

"It's true. Even wealthy women are giving up their tailors. It would make much more sense to use this location to sell toiletries."

"And that's my aim. With your help, I'll show those men upstairs that they need to stay ahead of the times, not behind them. Now, if you'll excuse me, I have a meeting in the sample room." With a swish of her skirts, Miss Cohen turned toward the moving staircase.

As soon as I returned to the counter, Sadie asked, "What's up?"

"Just a little talk about sales. She wants me to smile more to the customers."

"Did she say anything about me?"

"Not a word." Miss Cohen was right—the others would only resent my promotion. I might as well keep my mouth shut so I could enjoy the news before anyone else could spoil it.

It turned out my silence was for naught. Two days later, I stood next to Sadie, adding some figures in my sales book, when Angelina came by with a basket of taffy samples. "I heard something exciting," she said as Sadie took a piece of candy. "Someone's moving up in the world. They're putting in a counter especially for makeup, and Miss Westcott here's been asked to sell it. Got a raise, too."

"Has she," Sadie said, narrowing her eyes at me. "Doesn't that take the cake."

I blushed, completely unprepared. "Well . . ."

"And when was I gonna hear about this?" Sadie asked.

"Miss Cohen wanted me to keep it to myself," I said, glad to come up with any excuse.

Angelina pretended to be sorry. "Me and my big mouth. Guess I ruined her plan."

Sadie popped the taffy in her mouth. "It ain't fair. I been working here longer."

"Maybe you should complain to Miss Cohen," Angelina said.

"Fat lotta good that'll do."

I gave Angelina a puzzled look. It wasn't like her to make trouble between me and Sadie.

"Shucks," she said, "Mr. McGillicutty's on his way—better shake a leg."

"But wait," I said, realizing something else that was odd. "How did you find out?"

"Oh, you know how gossip spreads in this store." Walking off, Angelina looked back over her shoulder at me with exaggerated innocence. "Isn't it horrid?"

27

AMANDA

I SLOWED DOWN while passing the window of Home Cooking so I could check it out before going in. A man on the other side of the glass looked just like Rob Kelly. I froze. A woman walking behind me collided into my backside.

It *was* Rob Kelly.

The woman swore while detouring around me, so I didn't bother to apologize. Rob Kelly smiled and motioned for me to come in. I smiled back as if that were a great idea and headed for the door. Crap. Had I even looked in the mirror before going out? And why was he having dinner so late?

If this once was a Child's restaurant, nothing short of an architectural dig would provide any evidence. The interior had been renovated to the hilt with fake-wood "rec room" paneling and lava lamps. Rob sat on a maroon banquette for two. "What a funny coincidence," I said, standing next to him as if about to take his order.

"How'd you happen to be going by this time of night?"

Fate? Destiny? Dead spirits controlling every decision I made? "I was just on my way to buy groceries," I lied, in case he thought I was stalking him. "There's a great Whole Foods on Union Square."

"Good old New York," he said. "Where people go shopping day and night. Would you like to join me? I haven't ordered yet."

A large glossy menu splayed out in front of him tempted me with pictures of chicken in a basket and "just like mom's" pancakes topped with golden pats of butter and maple syrup dribbling down the sides. "Okay, that would be nice, thanks."

I settled in opposite him, and he turned the menu around for me. I was considering an "astro burger" but craving the pancakes when a waitress wearing a cotton-candy-pink shirtwaist dress came to take our order. Her size two figure made me rethink the pancakes. In a panic of indecision, I asked for the scrambled eggs and then caved with an order of biscuits and gravy. Rob went for steak and eggs.

"And how do you like it?" the waitress asked him. The glint in her eyes made me wonder if she was referring to the meat.

"Medium," Rob said.

"Hot and red in the middle," she said, "with a little pink surrounding the center?"

"Sounds good."

She whisked the menu away. I smiled politely at Rob. He asked how I got interested in vintage clothing, and I told him my mom was to blame. "She took me to flea markets when I was a kid and taught me how to scour thrift stores and attics and even the sidewalks, like when people put their trash out for the garbage trucks. I know it must sound crazy, but I've found great stuff that way."

"I believe it. Tomorrow morning I'm emptying out my grandmother's storage bin in the basement. It's like a tomb down there, and I'm sure most of its junk, but you never know; maybe I'll find a missing Picasso or two."

"If you see any more clothing, let me know."

"You'll be the first vintage clothing store owner I call."

"Thanks. So what kind of work are you in?"

"I own a bicycle shop. Sales and repair, near the beach."

"So you're in retail, too. I didn't realize." A bicycle store in Santa Monica? Near the beach? That sounded kind of cool. Maybe I *was* interested in him. "Is it doing well?"

"Really well. I'm thinking of opening another location."

"That's great. And you grew up in Santa Monica?"

"No, I'm from here. Grew up near Gramercy Park, and then after college, I had a place in the West Village."

"Oh." That explained the Yankees cap, but the West Village? And no ring? Now I wondered if he was gay.

"I miss New York," he said "but I shouldn't complain. Santa Monica is beautiful, the weather is great. I live in a 1930s bungalow near the beach."

"Do you? That sounds lovely." Why was I using the word "lovely"? I never used that word. "And what took you out to Santa Monica?"

"Kind of a long story . . ." He looked out the window and stroked his beard, evidently not in the mood to tell it.

"Speaking of long stories," I said, "something really interesting turned up when I was going through your grandmother's clothing. An old diary from 1907, and I've been reading it—I hope that's okay."

"As long as there's nothing about me in it," he joked.

"Don't worry, your reputation is safe."

Rob Kelly really wasn't bad-looking. If he shaved off that beard, he could actually be quite handsome. And Santa Monica wouldn't be the worst place to live. I'd love a cute deco bungalow near the beach. And there was a great market for vintage clothing out there. "It was written by a woman named Olive Westcott." It felt odd to say her name out loud, as if she were a stranger. "I'm guessing she was your great-grandmother. Do you recognize the name?"

"Can't say I do, but that doesn't mean anything. My grandmother doesn't talk much about her past. It's too bad, really. When she's gone, all her memories go with her."

"She's still here, though. You can keep trying."

"True. The cancer hasn't affected her thinking. She's pretty sharp for ninety-eight."

"She sure is." Mrs. Kelly had told me her age, but I'd forgotten she was that old. Subtracting her age from 2007, I came up with 1909. It didn't seem like Olive was about to get married and pregnant, but anything could happen. "I wonder if your grandmother is even aware this journal exists."

"Yeah, it's terrible how family history gets lost."

The waitress returned with our gigantic plates of food. "Need anything else here?"

"We're good," Rob said.

"No, thanks," I added, not that she was directing the question at me.

"Enjoy." The waitress winked at Rob before leaving. She sure didn't seem to think he was gay. Thank goodness restaurant etiquette precluded joining your customers at their tables.

I dug in. The eggs were soft and creamy—the biscuits light and buttery. Total comfort, except for the guilty conscience. "This is yummy," I said. "How's your steak?"

"It's done perfectly."

I was about to say I was glad I'd suggested the place. Then I remembered he'd invited me to come along and I'd turned him down. As we sat there eating, a gap in the conversation began to feel awkward. "So," I said, "about the journal . . . I was gonna mention . . . of course I want to return it, but I was hoping to finish it first, if that's okay with you."

"Sure, take your time. I don't know about my grandmother, but I'd definitely like to take a look at it. I bet my daughter would love to read it at some point, too."

Damn. "You have a daughter?" I would've preferred gay over married. I smiled and stopped eating so he could see I appreciated how wonderful it was that he had a child. I was sure his wife appreciated that he was asking women out to dinner while helping to sell off his dying grandmother's stuff. What an asshole. "What's her name?"

"Betsy."

"I love that name." Was I a magnet for married men? "How old?"

"Ten."

"That's the best age," I said, as if I knew.

"I'm a little afraid of what comes next."

"Oh, you'll be able to handle it. Or your wife will, anyway." Of course he was taken. And like an idiot, I was giving him a makeover and planning my entire future around him. Why wasn't he wearing a frickin' ring? I bet he was gay and his wife was just a beard. That would mean he had two beards.

"It's tough, because my wife actually died in a car accident a few years ago."

"Oh." I was a jerk. "I'm sorry." Thank god he couldn't read my callous, cruel, mean-spirited mind. "That must be hard on your daughter."

"She's doing pretty well, considering."

"It must be rough for you, too." I put down my fork and gave him a sympathetic look. At least he was available again. And not gay.

"I met my wife in California, and she has lots of family there, but I miss New York. I'm thinking about coming back, especially since it looks like I'll be inheriting my grandmother's apartment.

Along with my sister, of course, but she likes her split-level house with a pool in Jersey and has no interest in moving."

Not gay, runs a successful business, owner of prime real estate. "It's a nice apartment."

"I just don't know how well Betsy will adjust."

"Oh, you know how resilient kids are." That's what people said, anyway. "You mentioned growing up in Gramercy Park. Where did you go to high school?"

"Dalton."

"When did you graduate?"

"1984."

So he was two years older than I was. I dropped some names, and it turned out we knew a few of the same people. We finished the rest of the meal, trading high school memories. It was possible we saw Debbie Harry perform at CBGB on the same night. When we were done eating, he offered to walk me home.

"You're on my way, so I'll walk you home," I said.

He pulled out his wallet. "Then at least let me get the check."

"Don't be silly."

"I did ask you out to dinner earlier."

"And I said no. I should make amends and take you out."

"Now you're being silly." He flagged the waitress for the check.

"Thanks, that's very nice of you." I wanted to say I'd pay next time, but would there be one?

He opened the door for me, and we walked down Third Avenue. "How long will you be in the city?" I asked.

"I'm flying out tomorrow."

"So soon? What about your grandmother?"

"She has a really good live-in nurse, thank god, who just came back from vacation. And my sister checks in all the time. But I'll be here again soon enough. There's a lot that needs taking care of, and no telling how long Grandma will, you know . . ."

I nodded. "I bet your daughter misses you."

"That she does."

As we approached Jane Kelly's building, I wondered if he might try to kiss me good night. We stopped in front of the curved driveway and faced each other. I thanked him again for the eggs.

"You're welcome. And I guess you'll be in touch about those clothes."

"Yes, the ones on consignment. Absolutely." Suddenly, I was scared by the idea of him kissing me. Not that there was any reason to think he would.

"Well . . ." He leaned toward me ever so slightly. Was he going to? No, it was just a nod. "Good night."

"Good night."

We parted ways. Maybe the idea of a kiss scared him, too.

28

OLIVE

AFTER FEEDING A receipt into the tube, I looked up and nearly jumped out of my skin. Ralph Pierce, walking past, saw me the very moment I saw him. "Miss Westcott."

"Mr. Pierce."

His friendly smile faded as his eyebrows puckered with concern. "I heard about your father. I'm so sorry."

"Oh, yes . . . thank you."

"When my father told me what happened, I wanted to convey my sympathies. I contacted the Mansfield, but they said you'd moved and had no forwarding address."

"I'm sorry. Circumstances changed and . . ." I trailed off with awkwardness.

"Please don't apologize. I'm sure it's been devastating. He was so young, and I could see the two of you were very close."

"It has been hard."

His eyes swept over the counter. "I see you've followed through on your career plans. I'm impressed." His tone was kind, with a touch of amusement.

"I seem to remember you disapprove of this environment."

"Still. Lots of women wouldn't have the gumption to go to work."

"I had no choice."

"Yes. Well, I should probably let you get back to it."

"Yes," I agreed, though no customer waited for my attention.

"Miss Westcott . . ." He hesitated. "Perhaps you'd allow me to call on you in the next few days."

I imagined him in the dusty, dingy parlor of my boardinghouse. He wouldn't be so impressed with my gumption then. "I don't think that would be possible."

"Are you sure?"

"I'm terribly busy."

"How about Saturday evening? Could I persuade you to dine with me?"

"Thank you, that's very kind, but I have an engagement this Saturday." It happened to be true. The producers of a Broadway show had donated tickets to the store's employee association; once again Angelina had worked her magic with the social secretary.

"Perhaps the next Saturday?"

He was persistent. I wondered why. I couldn't have made a good impression that first time we met. Perhaps he felt sorry for me. "I wouldn't want you to be asking out of obligation."

"I think we got off on the wrong foot that evening we met. I would be grateful if you'd give it another go." He hung his head for a few moments and then looked back up at me uneasily. "To be perfectly honest, I'm going through a rough time of it. Nothing like what you've been through, but you see, I was recently engaged to a very nice girl from an excellent family—I've known her for years—and just last week I had a change of heart and called it off."

"Oh my . . ."

"A lot of people happen to think I'm worth less than dirt right now. So I'd be honored if you'd keep me company over a good meal. And," he added, "I'd wager your father would be pleased for you to keep a connection with Woolworth's, even if it is one step removed."

My resistance melted, and I consented. When he asked my address, I almost suggested meeting somewhere else. Then I decided there was no point in deceiving him. If he couldn't accept the truth of my situation, then why bother with him?

The moment after he left, Sadie appeared by my side. "Who was that handsome gent flirting with you?"

"He wasn't flirting. Just someone I used to know. He's taking me to dinner."

"See, you'll be married in no time, all your worries behind you."

"To him? Never. We don't even get along."

Sadie laughed. "Wait till he pays for your supper—you'll see how easy getting along can be."

Saturday night, Sadie and I arrived at the Empire Theatre on Broadway with the secret satisfaction of knowing everyone else had paid for admission while our tickets were free. Angelina was already waiting for us in the lobby. She looked stunning, if a bit showy, in a cobalt-blue dress with black lace trim. The cut emphasized her hourglass figure. Was it a gift from her gentleman friend? She'd made her gorgeous hat, a black boater adorned with two gracefully drooping ostrich plumes on a wide floppy brim.

Sadie was all gussied up in a pink ready-made dress trimmed with yellow ruffles along the hem and a matching sailor hat that sported a fat pink bow. It broke my heart to think how she'd scrimped and saved to buy the ensemble from a cheap shop on Fourteenth Street.

I wore the finest dress saved from my old wardrobe. This day marked my first chance to make use of the tailor-made green satin with a contrasting purple sash wrapped around the empire waist. Purple rosettes circled the crown of my matching green Pamela hat. It had been such a long time since I'd felt pretty.

As we entered the auditorium, I observed how the theater had been designed, like the department stores, to flatter the middle-class patrons' hunger for sumptuous upper-class surroundings. Plush velvet chairs and three tiers of boxes faced a vast stage. Carved golden cupids ornamented the ceiling, along with the largest chandelier I'd ever seen.

Our free admission included the privilege of sitting up in the second balcony. When Father used to take me to the theater, we always sat in the orchestra, preferably on the aisle, so he could stretch his long legs. Angelina took the seat between me and Sadie. I leaned forward to peer down at the orchestra section.

"Did you hear the latest?" Sadie said as we waited for the play to begin. "The Prince George Hotel threw Evelyn Nesbit out of her rooms. They said the other guests complained because she attracts too much attention."

"Still?" I asked with amazement. It had been at least two months since the trial.

Angelina fanned her face with the program. "The judge is supposed to decide on her annulment suit next week."

Sadie shook her head with disappointment. "I don't see why she'd want to give up Harry Thaw, even if he is crazy. That family's got a fortune."

"Thaw's mother probably forced her into it," said Angelina.

"You think they still love each other?" Sadie asked.

No one had an answer to that. The play began, and I soon forgot where I sat. A woman secretary, played by the famous Eleanor Robson, marries her rich employer, played by a chubby middle-aged actor I'd never heard of. She moves into his Fifth Avenue mansion and promptly falls in love with the handsome chauffeur. The dashing young actor who played him made most of the women in the audience fall in love, too.

After the show, we went to a low-priced restaurant that catered to the theater crowds. A hidden orchestra churned out show tunes loud enough to fill an auditorium, but the patrons seemed happy enough to scream over the noise to converse. The maître d' led us to a table in a back room for women only. The air was muggy with steam heat.

Angelina and Sadie swooned over the menu even more than the actor. My mouth watered at the idea of steak and potatoes, though I knew the modest prices meant mediocre food. After ordering, we didn't waste a moment before reaching into the bread basket.

"What did you think of the play?" I asked, spreading a thin layer of butter on my roll.

Angelina buttered her own piece of bread more generously. "The girl's big mistake was getting married. Up until then she had everything she wanted."

"Are you kidding?" Sadie tore her roll in half and dipped it directly in the butter pot. "If a rich man asks, I'll marry 'im in a second. I'm tired of playing the game."

I ate my roll slowly, savoring my first taste of real butter in weeks.

Angelina laughed. "You? Tired of good times? Going out?"

"I like having my boyfriends," Sadie admitted, "but every year I get older, the odds get worse. I'm ready to be a one-man girl and raise babies. I even told my stockbroker friend to stop coming by."

I finished swallowing before asking why.

She grinned. "I can't stand kissing a man without a mustache."

"Same here," Angelina said. "Feels like kissing a baby's bottom."

Though I still didn't know what a kiss on the lips felt like—with mustache or without—I smiled along in agreement.

"Men are animals," Sadie said, scooping more butter from the pot. "He wanted me, but not to get married. I didn't want him *except* to marry."

I thought of my father. He hadn't been an animal—or so I believed; it was entirely possible I carried around a childish, idealized memory of him. After all, he'd kept the collapse of our finances a secret. Who knew how many other secrets he'd hidden?

The waiter arrived with my ginger ale and their pitcher of beer. The three of us gulped down our cool beverages with relief.

"You ask me," Sadie said, pausing to belch quietly and pat her chest, "whoever wrote that play has a screw loose. Let that secretary live like us a week and see if she looks twice at any chauffeur."

"And show me any chauffeur half as handsome," Angelina added.

"Or a rich man who'd marry his secretary," I chimed in.

Angelina cupped her palms around her cold glass. "Marriage is always a bargain, and somebody's gotta get the wrong end."

"Fifth Avenue sounds like the right end to me." Sadie eyed me with obvious envy. "If only I could be refined, like you, then I'd attract the right sort."

"Does the right sort exist?" I asked. "It seems as if every man who comes to my counter buys perfume for some girl on the side. I hate to think I'm encouraging them to cheat on their wives."

"Why should you care?" Angelina said. "That'll happen whether you sell them perfume or not."

"But it's horrid being nice to those beasts."

"Men got their needs." Sadie wiped crumbs off the front of her dress. "Always have and always will."

I couldn't agree. "That wouldn't excuse them from running around with some tramp. What if their poor wives knew?"

"Wives know what they wanna know," Angelina replied before taking a long sip of beer.

"And if children are involved?" I asked. "Why must a child suffer because of the parents' mistakes?"

Angelina set her glass down. "If those wives stopped sleeping in separate bedrooms, you can bet that perfume wouldn't be going to those tramps."

I widened my eyes in amazement. "You're blaming the wife for the husband's behavior?"

"Sure," she said, giving me a sly look. "If she thinks she's too good to do it with him."

I turned red as Sadie laughed with complicity. "Why else you think they got so many bawdy houses up Seventh Avenue?"

"Ain't that the truth," Angelina agreed. They clinked glasses.

That was when it finally dawned on me: Angelina's gentleman friend . . . he was married. That was why she defended cheating husbands—and the women I'd just called tramps.

"Angelina, if I said anything offensive, I'm truly sorry. I didn't mean to, honestly."

She arched her eyebrows with disdain and said nothing.

"I didn't mean to insult you or say anything stupid."

"Why would I be insulted?"

"Well," I stumbled on, "I don't know, perhaps your gentleman friend might happen to be married."

"What if he is?"

Sadie flagged down the waiter as he was racing past. "Say, what's takin' our food so long?"

"The kitchen is backed up."

She held out the empty bread basket. "Then fill this up, will you?"

"I'd have to charge."

"Never mind," she said, letting him go. "Charge for bread? He's sure got nerve."

"I was speaking in general," I said, still trying to dig out of my hole. "I don't want you to feel judged. I wasn't thinking—"

"You *weren't* thinking," Angelina said.

"But you sure was judging," Sadie cut in. "You people take every chance you get to turn up your nose at people like us. Well, you know what? I didn't have no chance to go to any finishing school. I barely got a chance to *begin* school before my parents made me go in as a cash girl when I was ten years old."

"I'm sorry," I said inadequately.

Sadie turned to Angelina. "She don't think us girls should have no fun."

Angelina nodded. "Fun is only for rich folks, while we work ourselves to the bone."

"That's not what I meant."

"I know what you meant," Angelina said, her cheeks flushed with indignation. "You think I'm wicked. Sunk low as a woman can. Spit in God's eye and gone to the devil."

"No! You're getting me all wrong. I simply think there has to be another way."

"And which way is that?" Angelina said with a sneer.

"We're all ears," Sadie added.

"I'm not saying it's easy," I began. "We're intelligent women." They stared at me with feigned curiosity. "We can't spend all our energy on serving the needs of men. We need to work, and make money, and *earn* our independence."

"We work, all right," Angelina replied, unimpressed, "but how much can we earn?"

"Seven per," Sadie said. "Eight if we're lucky."

"It's possible to work your way up," I persisted. "If you stick with it. I'm hoping to become a buyer one day. They make an excellent salary, sometimes as much as the men."

"That's nice for a refined girl like you," Angelina said. "But girls like us don't get chances like that."

Wasn't she the one who changed her mind about our hat shop? "There's no guarantee I'll get the chance, either."

"Don't be coy." Angelina scowled at me. "Everyone knows you're Miss Cohen's pet."

"She thinks you're a peach," Sadie added. "A real jewel."

On that sour note, the waiter arrived with our plates. Angelina and Sadie attacked their food, exclaiming how everything tasted so delicious. I could barely swallow my gristly meat. While they continued to gorge and babble, I pretended to enjoy the wretched meal. It surprised me how much their hostility hurt. I never could've predicted the friendship of two shopgirls would mean so much. Even if I did put on airs, they were the ones barring me from the club.

After dinner we took the trolley downtown. All three of us looked out the windows in silence as if traveling alone. When the trolley reached Fourteenth Street, Sadie and I had to leap off, calling out hasty good-byes, so we could catch the cross-town. After hopping aboard, we grabbed our straps as the conductor clanged his bell and the motorman pulled out.

Sadie chattered on about how the theater wasn't half as jolly as a dance hall. "The other night some vulture picked the wrong girl to dance, and her boyfriend pulled a knife!"

"Good gracious. Then what happened?" At least she'd stopped going on about how beastly I was.

"By the time the cops hauled 'em off," she said merrily, "two tables and a chair was broken, the floor was splattered with blood, and they had to close the place down."

"Sounds ghastly."

"Only because I had to go home early. No matter how much my feet hurt from standing all day, I swear I could twirl all night."

I hadn't a chance to change the subject until we got off the trolley. "I feel awful about Angelina."

"You sure did put your foot in it."

"I must seem like a naive idiot."

"More like a swelled head. Wouldn't hurt to come down off that perch."

"And keep my mouth shut." Still, I couldn't resist trying to get more details. "I don't suppose you know who the man is?"

"All I know is he's loaded and just turned fifty-five."

"Fifty-five?" That was ancient. Older than Father. How could she stand letting him have his way with her?

"You was imagining Prince Charming?"

"No." Though I suppose I had been clinging to some such thought.

She returned to her favorite subject as we climbed the steps to the boardinghouse. "You ever been to a dance hall?"

"Can't say I have."

"You should come along next Saturday night. We're havin' a send-off for Joe. He's leaving the next day for San Francisco."

I followed her inside, wondering why Angelina hadn't mentioned the party. "I don't think so, but thanks for asking."

She shrugged. "It's your funeral."

Sadie joined some girls playing cards in the parlor. I retreated to my room. In any case, my dinner with Ralph Pierce was next Saturday, so I couldn't have joined them even if I'd wanted to.

May 23, 1908

Angelina hates me. I feel wretched.

A few days later I went to the dairy restaurant for lunch, hoping to make things right. When I sat down with my egg sandwich, Angelina gave me a nearly imperceptible nod. The news that Evelyn Nesbit decided to drop her annulment suit had everyone talking.

"Now she'll go after his fortune," Joe said.

"What d'ya mean?" asked a girl from the toy department. "She's already got it."

"She has to be appointed guardian," Joe explained. "You think the Thaw family is gonna let that happen? She only married him for his money—"

"In your opinion," Angelina cut in, "which is worth exactly nothing. The fact is, as long as he's stuck in that madhouse, she should have control of his money."

"His money is Mrs. Thaw's money," said the vacuum demonstrator. "And they've already promised to pay the younger Mrs. Thaw a thousand a month not to cause any trouble."

"Hah," Angelina replied, "and the older Mrs. Thaw will cut off her daughter-in-law as soon as she can."

Joe looked at his sister as if she were the one who belonged in the asylum. "You don't believe that tart actually cared for Thaw, do you? For god's sake, she used to be one of those Florodora girls, dancing around half naked on the stage!"

"Her feelings for Thaw don't matter," Angelina maintained. "She's his legal wife."

"Feelings don't matter?" he cried out. "I can't believe my ears. Weren't you always going on about how Thaw was innocent because he murdered for love? So why should that girl get his money if she never loved him?" That was when Joe turned to me. "Let's ask the only smart person here. What do you think?"

Since I planned to deliver my gracious apology to Angelina, and it appeared her opinion differed from mine, I shrugged and kept my mouth shut.

Joe leaned closer. "You agree with me, right?"

"I don't have an opinion on the subject," I said calmly, even as I wondered how he had the power to make my body feel just a bit more alive.

"Don't you have an opinion on everything?" Angelina asked.

"Even if I had, I wouldn't pretend to always be right."

"Go ahead and tell us," she said, "and we'll decide if you're wrong or right."

The limits of my diplomacy had been reached. I'd been insensitive, fine, but she reveling in her wrath. "It seems to me that a thousand dollars a month is more than enough compensation for what she's been through. And why insist on staying in a family who doesn't want you? She'd do best to take her monthly check and move on."

Angelina glowered. "Like a good little whore?"

Having silenced the table, she pushed back her chair and strutted out. How had this gotten so out of hand? I left the last bite of my sandwich, excused myself to the others, and caught up with her on the sidewalk. "Angelina, I wish we weren't having a row. I'm so sorry I offended you. Can't we be friends again?"

"I don't need friends who judge me."

"But I don't judge you. If anyone's to blame, it's your fellow. He's the one committing adultery."

"You think his wife is suffering? She gets the fancy house in the suburbs, the fur coats, the dinner parties."

The light changed. She dashed across the street. I scurried to keep up. She greeted the guard as we entered the building. "Then what about you?" I asked once we were safely past him. "You're the one I care about. How long can this last? He could drop you anytime. And then—"

"I'll be a used-up tramp?" she said, turning the head of a girl leaving the locker room.

"That's not what I . . . Don't you see how he's taking advantage of you?"

Angelina laughed. "What if I told you I had a swell time with him? And not just because of the fancy hotel and the restaurants. If you weren't such a prude—"

"I'm not a prude. I'm simply—"

"Better than the rest of us?"

"I didn't say that."

"You didn't have to."

Slamming her locker shut, she left me standing there like a fool. My temples throbbed. I considered dashing to the sick office for headache powder, but then I'd risk a fine for lateness. Hurrying out of the locker room, I nearly collided with Joe.

"Whoa, there, what's the trouble? My sister giving you a hard time?"

"I want to make peace but keep saying the wrong thing."

"Don't pay no mind to her. Angie's got a temper."

"Really? I've never been on the receiving end before."

"Flares up like fireworks and fizzles just as fast." He opened the door leading to the stairway to the first floor. "Coming Saturday night? You can celebrate seeing the last of me."

Our footsteps echoed in the empty staircase. "I'm sorry, I can't."

"Now you're saying the wrong thing to *me,*" he said, producing a gravely wounded expression.

"I'm sure you'll get over it by the end of the day," I teased, "or even by the end of our conversation."

"Did my sister turn you against me? Don't listen to her—I'm not such a rake as she makes me out."

"If you say so." I'd reached my exit to the floor.

"Listen, Olive, I mean it. You should come on Saturday."

"I don't dance." Learning to waltz and minuet at Miss Hall's didn't count, not in a dance hall.

"Go on, you're joshing me, right? You need to put on some glad rags and have some fun. The Majestic on Bowery, right around the corner from my place."

"Thanks, but honestly, I can't. I do hope you enjoy California."

As I reached for the door, he grabbed my hand and pulled me toward him. I stepped backward. He stepped forward, trapping me between his body and the wall.

"The day I first set eyes on you . . ."

He stood so close. I found it thrilling to have him tower over me, not something every man could do. My knees wobbled under my skirts.

" '*Bella ragazza,*' I said to myself. That girl is swell elegant. Worth staying around for."

I looked into his eyes. I couldn't make out if this was on the level.

"Won't you come?" he asked, looking squarely back at me.

I clenched my hand so it wouldn't reach up to brush a curl of black hair off his forehead. "I'm sorry. I really do have other plans."

"So break 'em." He leaned over me, one arm propped against the wall. As his face came toward mine, I had every chance to laugh, slap him, run away; instead, I froze—apart from the tremors coursing through my body. After all, it was about time I received my first kiss.

His lips pressed lightly against mine. I barely felt the scratch of his mustache before he pulled away. Nevertheless, my disappointment over the brevity of the kiss didn't keep me from ducking under his arm and darting for the exit.

"Don't be late," he said as the door closed behind me.

Did he mean to my counter—or the dance hall? Not that it mattered.

I took my place behind the counter and greeted Sadie with a surprisingly cheerful "good afternoon." A customer walked up and asked for something to remove blemishes. I reached for a brand currently on sale and smiled. My first kiss. Short but sweet. Finally, I'd gotten it. And my headache had gone away in the bargain.

29

AMANDA

DINNER WITH ROB left me too excited to even think of going to sleep, so I delved into the two bags of clothing I'd brought up from the store to examine them more closely for stains or rips. Settling into the couch, I aimed my lamp to get the best light and began to empty the pillowcases. I was pleased to see that only minor alterations would be needed. Anything with stains must not have been kept, because I didn't find a single one.

In the next bag I found the green satin dress with a purple sash that I'd admired at Mrs. Kelly's apartment. Olive had described a dress just like it in her journal. I'd been assuming everything from the trunk belonged to her; now I felt sure. Next I pulled out a nightgown, beautifully made, in perfect condition. It had a lace-trimmed neckline with a narrow pink ribbon woven though that tied in front. Teensy white buttons ran down the front. I decided to try it on, curious to see what I'd look like as a resurrected virgin.

Modeling it in front of the mirror, I felt soft and pretty. Sweet and innocent. Girlish. It thrilled me to know this very material had been on Olive's body and was now on mine. I decided to keep it on for the night. A classic bona fida nightgown might put me in a better mind-set to sleep than an ex-lover's reject button-down shirt.

After flicking off the lights, I snuggled into bed. Does anything feel better than going to sleep when you're tired? Moments after closing my eyes, I began to sink into luscious oblivion.

My cell phone jingled. My eyes opened. Oh god. Was that Jeff answering my drunk text after I told him not to? Yep.

> We really should talk. Tomorrow night. My place. Come over after you close, ok? I miss you. xoxo

His place, meaning his office—not his home up in Katonah. Before getting married, Jeff lived in an apartment on Thirtieth and Park Avenue. He held on to it and converted the living room into an office, keeping the rest as a pied-à-terre. It turned out to be a perfectly convenient place to have our little trysts.

Now I was wide awake. I got out of bed, sat down on the sofa, and stared at my phone. I didn't want to say yes to him and didn't want to say no, so I tossed the phone aside and turned on the TV. The only thing that appealed to me was *Top Hat,* a Fred Astaire movie I'd seen a couple of times before. Sitting cross-legged on the sofa, I watching Fred do a soft-shoe in Ginger's hotel room to help her fall asleep. Back in high school, Jeff and I went to old movies all the time. Silent-film festivals at Lincoln Center, film noir at the Thalia, independents at Theatre 80 on St. Marks . . . We were total snobs about rejecting all the new "garbage" churned out by Hollywood.

My education in fashion flourished with the help of Joan Crawford, Katharine Hepburn, Marilyn Monroe, Audrey Hepburn. If they'd taught American history in my high school using movies instead of textbooks, I would've aced the class. Fred Astaire moved so wonderfully; I didn't want to take my eyes away.

By the end of the dance, Ginger had dozed off. I decided to give that hypnosis tape another try. I turned off the TV, replaced Michael Jackson with Dr. Markoff, and lay down in bed.

I want you to stare at the ceiling.

If only Fred Astaire lived above me. He could do a soft-shoe every night to put me to sleep.

Keep your eyes focused on the flat white surface and try not to blink.

It didn't matter that Fred was too skinny and had a receding hairline. He danced like the best lover in the world.

You very much want to blink . . .

Jeff was a good lover.

. . . but I want you to resist that urge.

Was Rob?

Your lids feel so heavy, the temptation to close them is too great. So now you can close your eyes if you like.

Damn. There she was again. That moaning woman.

Now I want you to focus on your body by relaxing each part. The soles of your feet . . . your calves . . . your thighs . . .

Maybe I should call the police. But what if she was just having sex? That would be embarrassing.

We're going to let your unconscious hear . . .

Maybe it was on the tape.

. . . what it needs to hear while you think about your relationships with other people.

Maybe some woman had been moaning in the next room while Dr. Markoff hypnotized me.

Life is not always a straight line.

I sat up and turned Dr. Markoff off. The moaning continued. It was going to drive me crazy. I went to the bathroom to get a pair of earplugs from the medicine cabinet. When I came out, two women were in my room wearing long skirts and shirtwaists. Olive and Angelina?

"May I suggest this one?"

Olive was trying on hats.

"They're both lovely."

"Hello?" I said. "Can you hear me? How did you get it my apartment?"

"Why don't we each wear one and then switch at lunch."

Except it wasn't my apartment. It was Angelina's apartment, just as Olive had described it. A small coal stove and an iron sink. A bed back where my bed should've been, and the prettiest wallpaper I'd ever seen, with green trellises and purple roses.

"Now we'd better skedaddle or we'll never have time to see everything."

They walked out the door. I yelled, "Wait for me!" and ran to catch up, but the door wouldn't open. Though I yanked and pushed and pulled and turned the knob this way and that, it didn't budge, so I tried to scream for help, but my throat closed up, and I couldn't get it to make a sound, no matter how hard I tried. The effort of trying to scream finally woke me up.

I stared up at the ceiling. My heart pounded. My hands were balled into tight fists, as if I'd actually been pounding hysterically on the door. The sound of a man's voice made me sit up and look around.

So rather than feel ashamed for your past, you should feel proud of every experience you've had.

The tape. Dr. Markoff was still going. I must've dreamed I'd turned it off.

Because to be alive is to be engaged, take chances and live in the present.

I pushed the off button. At least the moaning had stopped. Maybe it really was on the tape. I'd check it in the morning, in the light of day. Not now.

I turned the TV back on. For all I'd been through—or imagined I'd been through—I'd missed hardly any of *Top Hat*. Fred was pretending to be a hansom cabdriver with Ginger as his passenger. I watched him drive her to the park. They danced together on the pavilion and fell in love.

I reached for my sewing box. While watching Ginger resist Fred's charms, I mended seams, replaced buttons, realigned a zipper. When *Top Hat* ended, *Shall We Dance* came on. It turned out to be a Fred Astaire/Ginger Rogers marathon. Next *Swing Time* started, and I watched Fred win over Ginger for the third time that night. I didn't end up falling asleep until after the opening credits of *Flying Down to Rio,* my least favorite Ginger and Fred collaboration. I woke up to Jimmy Stewart as a young Abe Lincoln. My Westclox said eight o'clock. I'd snoozed about three hours total. Thanks very much, Dr. Markoff, for one of the worst night's sleep of my life.

OLIVE

A CLUTCH OF girls gathered in the parlor and stared at Ralph Pierce while I pinned on my hat. He wore a dark blue suit with thin white stripes. I'd pressed my green satin gown into service again. Dressing was much simpler when one had nothing from which to choose.

Opening the door for me, he pretended not to hear one of the girls call him a "lady-killer." She offered up a smile that suggested she wouldn't mind being slain. I pretended not to notice his dismay at how far down in the world I'd come.

"You've not been square with me," he said, as we walked to the corner.

"What do you mean?"

"You've had a rough time of it, much more than you let on. You should've come to me for help."

"We barely know each other."

"Even so, considering the conditions you're living in."

"You'd be surprised what a person can get used to."

He stepped off the curb to flag a cab without thinking twice about it. Though he wasn't strikingly gorgeous, like Joe, Ralph Pierce cut a handsome figure, with his impeccable wool overcoat, leather gloves, and fur felt hat. I couldn't decide if I was disappointed or relieved that he didn't rouse the same trembling excitement.

I slid into the cab and straightened my skirts without letting on that this was a forbidden luxury. As we sped up the avenue, the world outside my window didn't seem quite so menacing or indifferent. A sense of security descended on me—something I hadn't truly felt since my father's death. "Sometimes I think my past was a dream," I said, leaning my head back against the seat. "I'm losing my memory of what it was like before and who I was."

He gave me a gentle smile. "Perhaps I can help you remember."

"You already have, Mr. Pierce."

"Please, won't you call me by my first name?"

"Only if you'll agree to call me by mine. Where are we going, by the way?"

"I was thinking the Café Martin."

"The Martin?"

"Is that all right?"

"It sounds grand. I've always wanted to go there."

Sadie's comment echoed in my mind. Ralph had already paid for the cab, and later, he'd pay for the meal, an expensive one at that. I resolved to ignore it and enjoy myself.

The maître d' pulled out the table so I could take my seat. When the waiter came by, Ralph proposed ordering a bottle of wine, but I declined. "Soda water is fine for me."

"Then I'll just have a glass, if you don't mind."

"Of course, go ahead." Peeling off my gloves, I took in the festive surroundings. Tall arched windows, colored bulbs strung around white columns, closely spaced tables. Lively chatter vibrated off the walls and nearly drowned out a string quartet playing on the balcony. Charles Dana Gibson was said to be a regular, and Ethel Barrymore, too, but I detected no famous faces in the crowd.

"They say Stanford White ate his last meal here," I said. "The poor man."

"Only the way he died," Ralph replied. "The man spent a fortune on food and women."

An attractive couple to our left sipped coffee. The man smoked a cigarette while insulting the actors in an "atrocious" play that had just received rave reviews on Broadway. The woman laughed with venom between sneaking puffs from a cigarette hidden behind her fan. Her face was heavily painted with rouge and lip pencil. The neckline of her maroon silk dress plunged. The spectacle of her was so entertaining, I decided not to spoil my fun by disapproving.

The waiter delivered our drinks. Then he turned to our neighbors and spoke to the man as if the woman didn't understand English. "We don't permit ladies to smoke in the restaurant. Would you please ask her to stop?"

"We were done anyway," the man replied. "You can bring us the check."

"Right away," the waiter said; indeed, he returned almost immediately with their bill. Then he turned to us, and Ralph told him we'd both decided on asparagus à la vinaigrette and broiled lobster.

As he left, the waiter gave the woman a dirty look. She continued to smoke, taking advantage of no longer having to hide it. I caught her eye and smiled to let her know that we were on the same side. She smiled back, and I felt pleased with the connection we'd made.

Looking across the table at Ralph Pierce, I decided to see what I could learn about his wedding fiasco. "I hope you won't be cross if I raise the subject," I began cautiously, "but I'm curious to know why you called off your wedding."

He took a sip of his white wine. "I'm not sure."

"But you must have given it a great deal of thought."

"It made no sense. My fiancée was sweet and pretty—the nicest girl you'd ever meet. We'd known each other since I can remember. She never wanted anything more than to marry me and raise a family together."

"You must feel terribly guilty."

"But I had to do it. As the day came closer, I realized it wouldn't have been right to go on fooling myself or her." He frowned down at the table. "Not that anyone believed I was doing her a favor."

"And in what way were you fooling yourself?" Honestly, a man had to be interrogated like a thief to get him to confess his feelings.

He took another sip of wine before venturing to speak. "Committing to a marriage with her seemed too boring and predictable—as if my entire life would be sewn up. I couldn't put aside this feeling that there was something more, something else out there to discover. Does that make any sense?"

"Perfectly."

Our neighbors relinquished their table while discussing plans to see a show at the Hippodrome. After they were gone, the waiter came to us and apologized. "I hope their rude behavior wasn't too much of a disturbance."

Ralph thanked him with a polite smile. After he left, I told Ralph it was the waiter who caused the disturbance.

"Why do you say that? He was just doing his job."

"But you do agree it isn't fair."

"What's not fair?"

I could hear Sadie telling me to keep my trap shut. It opened anyway. "If a man can smoke in a restaurant, why can't a woman?"

"I understand your point of view. But the sight of a woman smoking is rather unattractive, don't you think?"

"I imagine you simply aren't used to it." Even if he was going to pay, why shouldn't I express my opinion?

"I just don't think women are the same as men, and they shouldn't pretend to be."

"Of course they aren't the same, but does that mean they should have fewer rights? I'll have you know the Mansfield Hotel forced me to move out straightaway after Father died. They don't allow single women. The manager wouldn't even let me stay out the month."

"I'm sorry," he said, leaning forward over the table, "that's beastly unfair."

"Not that I could've paid the rent. We were absolutely ruined when Father died, so I was grateful to find this boardinghouse. It's really quite decent, you know. The landlady only takes working-women."

He regarded me with genuine sympathy. "It must've been quite an ordeal to get on your feet again."

"You can't imagine."

"But you must get out of that place, Olive. It's really not fit to live. The dirt, the germs, the lack of sanitation . . ."

"I've not been sick one day."

"That's fine. And no doubt your father would be proud of how you've managed all on your own. But I daresay he'd also want his daughter to have the best that life can offer. Don't you think he'd be horrified to see you living in such squalid conditions?"

"I should like to think he'd be horrified by how little I'm paid. You wouldn't believe what some of the girls do to survive."

"I would believe it. That's why I'm worried about you. Isn't there anywhere else you can go? Don't you have family in Cold Spring?"

"My aunt, but she's struggling, too. And there's no work for me there. Don't you see? I've already had a promotion, and another is sure to come. Eventually I'll become a buyer, just as I always planned."

"Perhaps. In the meanwhile, I hate to see you cast adrift like this."

"I'm not adrift." He couldn't even acknowledge my promotion, as if I were a child musing about a visit from the sugarplum fairy.

"I'm sure you believe that," he said, "but you don't have the perspective to judge. Not after having suffered the worst kind of upset and loss. All I'm suggesting is that you need to return to the standard of living that a young woman with your background deserves. If there's anything I can do to help . . ."

If I didn't know better, I would've thought he was asking me to be his mistress. "I don't see what you can possibly do."

"A loan, perhaps, so you can move to a reputable place with a higher class of people."

"I have no way of repaying a loan."

"But eventually, as you say, if your career advances . . ."

"I really don't care to go into debt only to find myself vulnerable to those who could take advantage of me."

"Please don't think me rude—I meant nothing improper, I assure you, but there must be something that can be done."

"Sadly, the world doesn't provide such guarantees. I know you're shocked by how low I've sunk, but I've managed to adjust, and I'm doing fine."

"I'd rather you didn't adjust. The sort of women surrounding you can be an evil influence. All it takes is one moment of weakness to put you over the edge."

"That's a mighty big assumption you're making about women who work for a living."

"But a safe assumption, don't you think? Those girls grew up in different home atmospheres than people like you and me. It's well known that they're more likely to resort to . . ." He trailed off.

"What?" I wanted him to say it.

"I'm sorry. We shouldn't be talking about such delicate matters."

"Men of every social class 'resort to' such 'delicate matters' all the time. Tell me, why is it considered normal for a man to desire a woman, but if a woman desires a man, she's evil?"

Ralph's cheeks turned red. "Do I really need to explain the dangers?"

"Oh posh," I said, as if I knew all about it, "there are ways around that. And don't these dangers apply to men also? It does take two, I believe."

Ralph stared at me, completely taken aback. Indeed, I myself was surprised that our conversation had degenerated this way, but I couldn't stop myself from going on. "At any rate, that's an utterly different issue from why a woman who desires a man is considered wicked."

"Listen to you. If I didn't know better, I'd fear it's too late."

"To save me from being a tramp?" I didn't give him a chance to answer. "Or from being narrow-minded, like most of society?" I tossed my napkin onto the table and began putting my gloves back on.

"What the deuce are you doing?"

"I'm sorry. I couldn't possibly have a pleasant meal with you now."

"Because you know there's truth to what I'm saying."

"Your truth, not mine."

"I've been insensitive. Please accept my apology. We can talk of anything else."

Every bone in my body wanted to stay at that table to enjoy the friendly meal we were supposed to have had. I rose. "Forgive me. I wish I could pretend everything is fine, but that doesn't seem to be in my nature, I don't know why. Please give my regards to your father."

I marched out of the restaurant and had to suffer the indignity of walking past him on the other side of the plate-glass window. I mustered a proud face while feeling like an utter fool and mourning my uneaten lobster.

My surroundings passed in a blur as I flew down the street with my mind racing. It seemed as if I agreed with Angelina's way of thinking while I was with Ralph, and I agreed with Ralph while I was with Angelina. Meanwhile he thought I was on the path to ruin, while she thought I was a prude. Sadie would surely think me a fool to repulse his offer, and perhaps my reaction had been too extreme. What if I'd just turned down a good man's well-meaning attempt to help fix the wrong that fate had done me?

And yet most men expected something in return when they offered financial help to a woman. The very solution he proposed would have forced me into a compromised position: beholden to him, dependent on his goodwill. And hadn't he broken off with his childhood sweetheart? For all I knew, Ralph Pierce was the worst kind of cad who walked the earth. And really, he had no right to patronize me. How dare he presume to speak for my father?

The blocks passed so quickly, it was like gliding over the sidewalks on a moving staircase. The boardinghouse appeared before me, and when I breezed in the door, one of the girls asked why I was back so soon. I swept past, giving some excuse about a headache, went to my room, shut the door, and collapsed onto the bed, expecting to have a good cry. The tears didn't come. I pulled out my journal. I had to think.

May 30, 1908

Who makes all these rules about how men and women are supposed to behave? God? It's the same sort of injustice that allows men to smoke in restaurants, rent hotel rooms without having their morals questioned, hold better-paying jobs and enjoy the right to vote! I don't think God is concerned with smoking in restaurants, but I do think men are. It seems to me they make these rules to suit themselves. And why should I live by rules that benefit the rule makers at my own expense? Angelina is right. Women must make their own rules. And I was wrong to shame her for making her own decisions about how to live. I must go talk with her. I must tell her I understand. She'll be at the dance hall tonight. The Majestic on Bowery, Joe said. Do I dare go alone?

Stanford White

Harry Thaw

Evelyn Nesbit

Flatiron Building, circa 1903

FRIDAY

JUNE 15, 2007

AMANDA

MY CUSTOMER TURNED to go and said, "Thanks, I love your stuff."

"Thank you," I said in my singsong voice as she left.

I needed to be prepared for that evening with Jeff. Without a game plan, the risk would be too high that I'd weaken, kiss, and make up.

Another customer walked in—scary-skinny, with long blond locks and huge square sunglasses that she didn't take off. When she lingered in front of the shoes, I asked if she needed help.

"No, thanks, just looking."

If only I didn't need his financial help. It wasn't fair. My business could very well be going under, yet I couldn't bring myself to ask him for more money. Not because he'd miss the cash one bit, but because it was too goddamn humiliating. Forget about whether Jeff truly loved me, was "there for me" and all that; the most important reason to be married was community property.

Gee, how did I become such a romantic?

"Those look great," I said. The woman had slipped on a pair of lime-green sling-back sandals. "How do they feel?"

"Good. I'm just not sure about the color."

"They're fun. Very seventies."

"Oh." She pouted. "I thought they were eighties."

"Late seventies," I said, wanting to tell her the seventies were cooler than the eighties any day. "That crinkly patent leather was really in then—and the clunky heel."

"I just don't know what they'd go with."

I resisted suggesting that she take off her sunglasses to appreciate them. "I could see them with yellow. Some darker blues. And they'd look great with anything white."

"True."

"They're in excellent condition."

"Considering how old they are."

She continued staring at them in the mirror, but I could tell she wasn't going to buy.

"Let me know if you have any questions."

I'd give him an ultimatum. We were over—unless he left his wife and married me. Not in five years but now.

My customer had her own shoes back on. "I'm gonna think about them. Thanks."

"Thank you," I said as she left.

Or I could forget about giving my ultimatum and just blow him off. Don't see him, delete him from my phone again, and get myself out of this mess.

I went to straighten up the shoes. The afternoon dragged. Browsers came and left without trying on. Meanwhile, I input as many eBay listings as I could. I was glad when three male German tourists walked in, looking for fifties-style Elvis blazers for downtown club hopping. I managed to match each of them with something snazzy and was especially pleased to find a home for a particularly outrageous gold lamé blazer with black velvet trim.

After they left, it was time to call it a day. I turned out the closed sign, pulled down the gate, and locked up.

Before heading to Jeff's, I needed to go upstairs to change. Part of me wanted to wear a sexy dress, but the mixed signal might confuse him or, worse yet, me. Better to give my ultimatum wearing something down-to-earth so he'd know I meant business about ending the affair. Though my outfit should also be attractive enough to entice him to call a divorce lawyer in case our negotiations went in that direction. I settled on slim black Laura Petrie capri pants, a green scoop-neck Marimekko top with a purple pinwheel print, and black leather ballet flats comfortable for walking. Jeff would subliminally see me as the perfect wife with a touch of sex appeal.

The streets were unusually quiet: light traffic, empty sidewalks, no ambulance sirens piercing the calm. It was as if New Yorkers had made a collective decision to stay home for the evening. Walking up Bowery, I tried picturing trolleys, horses, and motorcars, and the El tracks overhead. I imagined crowds of people out for a good time at theaters, restaurants, stores, and saloons. It wasn't easy. The dreary avenue reflected none of its former spirit.

Continuing up Fourth Avenue, I found where half the population was hanging out: Union Square. Vendors sold T-shirts, bad art, photos of the World Trade Center. I passed an entrance to the same subway station where Olive took her first underground ride with Angelina that rainy day so long ago. Some buildings from her era still stood, but it was easy to miss them among the mishmosh of high-end apartment towers that went up in the nineties and the big-box retail stores that came after.

Veering up Broadway, I reached the corner of the Flatiron. The triangular building with its terra-cotta facade really was extraordinary. The architect would despise the ugly seventies apartment building directly across the street. I couldn't imagine that the passage of time would ever bring character to that clunker.

I crossed over to Fifth Avenue and noticed a historical plaque on the side of an office tower. It said the present building went up in 1909, after the Fifth Avenue Hotel was demolished. Aha. So Olive's father had been right about the building's demise. If he were alive today, Charles Westcott would be horrified to see what the city had become. Even Olive might feel a tug of nostalgia for her old neighborhood.

Continuing on to the corner where the Café Martin used to be—now a bank—I couldn't resist turning back for another look at the Flatiron, directly south of me. From this vantage point, I faced the front of the building. People liked to say it was reminiscent of the prow of a boat, but I thought that was pushing it. Maybe the building fascinated people so much because it was just wrong. Unbalanced. Asymmetrical. Like a love triangle.

I turned east and cut through the park. Unlike Union Square, Madison Square Park offered a calm retreat from the city—not a vendor to be seen other than the Shake Shack. Jeff and I used to go there for burgers before it got trendy and attracted inexplicably long lines. I purposely kept myself from even glancing at Eleven Madison Park, the site of my aborted birthday celebration. Instead, I gawked up at the Metropolitan Tower. It had always been one of my favorites, more suggestive of an Italian campanile than an office building. Crossing the street, I passed the huge deco New York Life building. It stood right where Stanford White's Madison Square Garden used to be. I thought of Olive and Angelina wandering around the Electric Show. Some would agree with Angelina's distaste for the concept of electricity replacing servants. Some would say the human race had become servants to electricity.

A few minutes later, I reached Park Avenue. Approaching the entrance to Jeff's apartment, I flashed on my nightmare from the other day. I looked down to make sure I wasn't naked. The door to his building swung open without any problem, the lobby had no living room furniture, and a gun-toting wife did not wait to greet me. The security guard sat behind his desk, armed with a copy of the *Post,* as usual. He knew me by sight and always managed, despite his consummately professional poker face, to make me feel like a hooker. We nodded to each other, and I took the elevator to the penthouse.

I rang the buzzer. The door opened, and there was Jeff, with a sheepish grin. "Hi."

Damn. The man didn't age. "Hi." Tall and lean, with wavy brown hair, he still looked pretty much the same as the guy I dated in high school, except now he spent a fortune on clothes, designer labels like Tom Ford and Marc Jacobs. The wire-rimmed John Lennon glasses he'd worn straight through high school had been replaced by Oliver Peoples.

He stepped forward and held me in a tight embrace as if to squeeze out all my angst. I let him, even though he was the one causing the angst. Feeling his body against mine, I sensed myself softening. I had to get some control of the situation. This could not become just another kiss-and-make-up fight, goddammit; I wasn't going to let that happen.

I stepped backward, and when he released me, I didn't know how to look at him. I couldn't decide what expression to have on my face. Anger? Affection? Sorrow? Guilt?

"You okay?" he asked. "Your eyebrows are all knit together."

I relaxed my forehead and rubbed my eyes. "Just haven't been sleeping well."

"I'm sorry," he said, giving me a gentle kiss on the cheek and then the lips. "I hope you're hungry. I ordered some food."

I followed him to the table. "Wow, this looks great."

He'd already set our places and opened a bottle of wine. I recognized the assortment of six or seven round tins filled with pasta and side dishes. They came from an expensive Italian restaurant down the street. Each one probably cost at least twenty dollars—same as on the menu, but without the service and ambiance. He generally didn't bother with wines under fifty dollars.

As he poured me a glass of cabernet, I felt my willpower dissipating. Being face-to-face with the actual man was a lot different from being with fantasy Jeff, who was so much easier to confront and manage. I should've written myself a script. A list of points to be made and requirements to comply with. Instead, I wanted to avoid everything. Sperm, eggs, tendons, tears. The idea of telling him I was going bankrupt seemed not only humiliating but downright crass. "How's your wife?"

"She'll be fine, thanks for asking. I still feel horrible about the other night." He reached into his pocket and said, "Happy birthday" while placing my present on the table. "I hope you like it."

I stared at the small, instantly recognizable Tiffany-blue gift box.

He nudged it closer to me. "Aren't you going to open it?"

I pushed away the notion that I'd find an engagement ring inside. "Yes, I am." What I did find was a gold bangle bracelet with a heart as the centerpiece. The heart was embedded with a border of diamonds. "It's beautiful," I said, knowing it was expensive. Why couldn't he buy something vintage? "I'll put it on right now."

"Do you really like it?"

I held out my wrist while pretending to admire it. "Yes, I love it. Thank you." This made two birthday bracelets that weren't to my taste. He had to know I'd prefer something deco or nouveau over this, a high school girl's dream. We weren't in high school anymore, and it wasn't as if he had to impress me with Tiffany's. Still, I tried to be gracious. Unlike my father's chakra bracelet, at least Jeff's jewelry had resale value. If I hocked all the pieces he'd given me, I could afford my rent for a year—or at least begin to pay him back.

"Thanks again. It's so pretty."

"You're welcome. And I'm sorry again about the other night."

"I mean, really," I said, pretending to be offended, "how dare she end up in the emergency room on my birthday?"

"Inconsiderate of her," he said with a little smile, "wasn't it?"

"I can't help but wonder, though . . . if her accident really was a coincidence."

The smile went away. "You think she did it on purpose?"

"Well." I met his eyes. "Accidentally on purpose."

He shook his head. "No."

"Maybe she found out about us, and she's angry but can't confront you, and that's how it played out."

"Amanda, she was slicing an onion. It was an accident. You're the one who's upset, and I don't blame you, so please. Let me make it up to you, okay?"

He loaded my plate with food. I sipped my wine and tried to enjoy his good intentions. It was such a relief to be taken care of, to allow someone to pamper me and let immediate gratification compensate for all the vicissitudes of life. As we ate dinner, he talked about a Warhol exhibit at the Guggenheim and how postmodernism was dead and hyper-reality was in and nothing was authentic anymore. "Which is all good for you," he said.

"Me?"

"Your business. I know you think of yourself as an alternative to mainstream fashion, but I'm afraid you're trendier than ever."

"Yes," I said, "I suppose there's some truth to that." *But the landlord is evicting me, and I'll probably have to declare bankruptcy and won't have enough money to live on. I'm tired of degrading myself by borrowing money all the time. So I'm giving you an ultimatum: You have to get a divorce and marry me now, or I'm going to leave you, and I'm not kidding.* "I'll have to make sure to see that exhibit."

"You'll like it," he said, "you should."

"I should." But what I shouldn't be doing struck me as far more pertinent. Should not be thinking about how much I wanted to kiss him. Should not forgive him for standing me up again, then fall into his arms just because he was getting up from the table and pulling me to my feet and circling his arms around my waist.

"I missed you," he said, kissing my lips over and over.

I resisted, letting my arms hang by my sides. *Should* tell him he couldn't blow me off on my birthday and then expect me to come here, at his beck and call, for sex.

His soft, tender kisses turned into one long warm kiss.

Should tell him I was not going to do this anymore!

His gentle touch sapped my will. My hands sneaked around his waist. As we embraced, pressed flat up against each other, I kissed back, my body tingling and turning to mush.

He took my hand and led me to the bedroom.

"We shouldn't be doing this," I said, but my tone only told him we would.

So much for ultimatums.

We lay down on his bed—the one place in the world where I had his undivided attention. No phone calls, no family, no work, no electronics, just us. As we kissed again, his hands went to all the places he knew so well, fingers teasing me until I was dying for him. Soon I pressed against him. Wanted him inside me, right up against me, nothing in the way between us. He pulled my underwear down. I unzipped his pants. As he pulled them off, I unbuttoned my shirt and undid my bra.

"You're so beautiful," he said, observing my naked body as if discovering it for the first time.

He took a condom from the nightstand drawer. I considered telling him not to bother this time, to let nature take its course, but that would've required a force of will I couldn't summon. After the condom was in place, he took off his glasses—a moment I loved, when his face became vulnerable and soft. We rolled so that he lay on his back and I got on top. By the time he'd guided himself in, I barely felt him inside, couldn't perceive where he ended and I began. He moaned with pleasure beneath me as I moaned along because I was a bad girl, a very bad girl, but it felt so good. A girl needed to feel good or she'd feel worse than bad, she'd feel nothing. I felt like everything everywhere and didn't want it to ever end. Finally, I couldn't be stopped from exploding into a moment of pure delight that ended too quickly.

I rolled off him and lay on my back. My chest rose and fell with each breath. The bracelet pressed into my wrist. He cuddled up to me, nestled his face into my hair, and exhaled with satisfaction. My heartbeat slowed back down. My utter failure to assert myself sank in.

32

OLIVE

RAGTIME BLASTED FROM the half-basement of a saloon on Bowery. A handmade sign over the door let me know I'd found THE MAJESTIC. I went down the cement steps into a large dim room where dancing couples crowded the floor. Admission was free, but the hat check cost a nickel. The stifling smells of tobacco, alcohol, and sweat made me wish I didn't need to inhale.

I stood by the wall and observed the scene while trying to get my bearings. Angelina sat with a crowd from the store. Sadie danced past with the young man who demonstrated vacuums. I didn't see Joe, but he had to be somewhere. A waiter asked if I wanted a drink. "No. Wait. Yes." Everyone else used liquor to relax. "A whiskey, please."

Dancing couples whirled past. I gaped at a girl in a shimmering red satin skirt. The entire front of her body was grinding in a circular motion against her partner. How could she do that in full view of anyone who wanted to see? I turned away, as shocked as Ralph Pierce would've been at the idea of me seeing it. Now Angelina's seat was empty. I scanned the crowd for her, and my eyes snagged on a man staring back at me. He was short, unshaved, and wore ragged clothes. His smile revealed two missing front teeth. I pretended not to notice him and prayed he'd go leer at someone else.

The waiter handed me my glass of whiskey. I took a gulp of the sour, bitter drink. A tumbler of gasoline would've been as enjoyable. I made myself drink more. Unfortunately, the place didn't appear to serve food. I hadn't eaten since lunch and not much then. To think I could've had lobster! The leering man started toward me, so I navigated to the other side of the room. While standing in a dark corner, I downed the entire glass—hang the consequences. Sadie danced past again, laughing, her frizzy hair already coming loose. I'd never seen her so happy.

I skirted the room once more and found Angelina sitting at a table, talking with Joe. My stomach did its own dance at the sight of him. Angelina rose from her chair. A moment later, so did Joe, handsome in dark trousers and a waistcoat that showed off his broad shoulders. She gave him a sisterly kiss on the cheek, said something that made him laugh, and then made her way toward the door. I rushed across the room to head her off. "Angelina, wait!"

She turned and saw it was me. "I'm just leaving."

"I need to talk with you."

"Better make it quick, then." She stopped to get her things from the coat check. I inserted myself beside her.

"I've been an idiot," I said, frustrated that I had to appeal to her profile. "You were right, and I was awful to judge you. Won't you please accept my apology?"

"You want my forgiveness?" she said, looking straight ahead. "Fine."

"You mean it?"

"Sure," she said, watching the girl search through a clutter of hats and coats.

I wished I could cup my hand under Angelina's chin and turn her face toward me. "So we're friends again."

"I didn't say that."

"Then you've not forgiven me."

"We're too different, that's all."

If only we could be alone, somewhere quiet. "But we aren't so different, not really."

The girl finally returned with Angelina's hat and jacket. I followed her to the door, where she stopped to pin her hat.

"I realized something," I said, thinking I should've retrieved my own hat, since I had no reason to stay now that she was leaving. "All the ways they say we're supposed to behave, and these rules we're supposed to follow—they're impossible."

"I suppose that's true," she said. "Well, good night."

I followed her out the door. If I went back for my hat, I'd never catch up.

"They're not only impossible," I continued, "they're set up to keep us down, and then if we ignore them, we're told we're evil, and who has any right to judge someone when life can be so dreadfully hard?"

She stopped and finally turned toward me. "Please don't bother trying to make it right. It doesn't matter."

"But it does. Anything I said that hurt or insulted you was from ignorance. You once said you wanted to learn from me; the truth is, I'm the one who needs to learn from you."

She laughed sharply. "That's a joke."

"I'm serious."

"Pretty words, but I don't believe 'em."

"Why not?" I couldn't understand why she had to be so stubborn.

"If push came to shove, you'd be judging the next girl, same as ever."

"That's not true. People can change."

"So you say. Anyway, I gotta go." She took off down the street.

I caught up. "Why don't you believe me?"

"You'll never be able to understand a girl like me, not really. Even if you got it all worked out in your head, you won't feel it in your gut."

"You think I'm so insensitive?"

"Far as that goes, I'd say you're better than most."

"Then why?"

We'd reached the corner. A truck barreled past, and she was forced to stop. Light from the streetlamp hit her face and illuminated a sadness in her eyes. I wanted to give her a hug, to make her laugh. "Why?" I asked again.

She turned to face me. "Because." She crossed her arms over her chest. "You're too scared."

I stared into those dark eyes as if I'd be able to see into her brain. "Of what?"

She stared back. "Being a woman."

All I could do was stand there and blink as she turned away and crossed the street.

Remembering my hat, I returned to the Majestic. I didn't want to stay but felt too weak to walk home. I needed food. Spotting an empty chair by Sadie, I went straight to it and dropped onto the seat as if it were the last life raft off a sinking ship.

"What's wrong?" Sadie said. "Relax. You want a drink?"

"Have they nothing to eat here?"

"You think this is a restaurant?"

A young man I didn't recognize asked her to dance. She took a sip of her drink and then handed it to me. "Go ahead," she said as he pulled her to the floor, "finish it off."

I hesitated and then took a gulp. My throat burned with every swallow. Soon the room transformed into a blur. Red lips, rouged cheeks, warm bodies pressed together. With the music washing over me, my muscles pulsed with the urge to move. Why should I resist? The wish to dance was only human. Didn't I qualify?

Joe sat across the room with Bill from the furniture department. If I could see him, presumably he could see me, yet he hadn't asked me to dance. Obviously, his sweet talk and stairwell kiss meant nothing—the brute. On the other hand, he wasn't dancing with any other girl either. I started toward him, ignoring the wooziness in my head and the floor shifting sideways under my feet.

He smiled as I approached and seemed to be surprised. "So you came after all!"

Perhaps he hadn't noticed me before. I extended my hand toward his face. "Wanna dance?"

"You were drinking?"

"Just a little."

"A little too much," he said with a laugh, taking my hand nevertheless, and pulling me to an empty spot on the floor. The moment we faced each other, panic washed over me. I'd never moved my body by instinct alone—not even in the privacy of my bedroom, much less a roomful of people. But his arms went around me, and I had to move my limbs. Attempting to imitate the other women was useless. My body simply couldn't match the syncopations of the music. I shook my head and shuffled my feet back and forth and laughed at my own ineptness. "I can't!" I tried pulling him off the dance floor, but he wouldn't budge.

"Stop thinking," he yelled back, "and move!"

I was about to yell that I was moving—off the dance floor. But the room went dark. My initial relief at turning invisible was replaced by fear that something had gone wrong. I braced to get trampled in a rush for the door. Then I heard giggles and whispers and realized the lights had been extinguished on purpose. In a moment Joe's arms pulled me right up against him. My hands found the smooth silk on the back of his waistcoat. The music was calmer now, slower, but my heart raced as if I'd just run out the door. We swayed back and forth together. "*Sei così bella,*" he whispered in my ear. "*Così bella* . . ."

Of course he'd try seducing me with his Italian. It wasn't necessary. The nearness of his warm body was too tempting to resist and my curiosity too powerful to ignore. Enveloped in his arms, cloaked by darkness, I let his lips find mine and let them stay. His mustache felt like the silky fur of my old beaver hat, and I nearly laughed to think of it. Our lips melded with slippery warmth, and I wished I could swallow him up. Nothing had ever felt so luscious. I wanted it never to end.

His hands began to creep down into areas no one had ever touched. Could he tell I wore no corset? As he caressed and cradled my waist and hips, I could imagine I actually had curves. A voice in my head reminded me not to let him have his way. As Dr. Galbraith said, I needed willpower. Except with every passing moment, his way blurred into mine. He pressed hard against me and I pressed hard back, even with the shock of that bulge of his stroking the opening between my legs. If only we could squeeze through the weave of our clothes, or melt away the layers of fabric separating our skin. Shouldn't I have the chance to find out what everyone else seemed to know? I was sick of being innocent; being the innocent was being the fool. This man could show me everything far better than any book, and then I'd never see him again, and no one would ever have to know.

The lights came on. Squinting from the sudden brightness, I didn't know where to look, didn't want to see or be seen.

"Let's go," Joe said under his breath.

He took me by the hand and pulled me across the room. Once again I failed to retrieve my hat. We flew out the door and ran down the sidewalk as if leaving ourselves behind. Before the fresh air had a chance to clean my lungs, we reached the door to his building. I remembered entering this same hallway once before. Funny, I was missing my hat that time, too.

While climbing the stairs lit by a flickering gas jet, I counted the days since my last monthly. Fourteen days, two weeks, the middle of the cycle. According to Dr. Galbraith, I didn't have to worry. Not that I'd let it reach that point—the risk was too great, and I wasn't a fool. But it was nice to know, just in case.

He unlocked the door next to Angelina's, and I followed him in. From the glow of the streetlamp outside the window, I made out two trunks against the wall. His room was the mirror image of hers, except that it was nearly empty. Before I could say anything, his arms circled my waist and he pulled me close again.

"*Bella ragazza,*" he whispered in my ear. "*Stasera sei mia.*" His lips nuzzled my neck with little kisses. "*Tutta mio.*" He let go of me to pull off his boots. I sat on one of the trunks and unbuttoned my shoes while asking myself what I thought I was doing. Getting comfortable, that was all. He pulled off his vest and then his shirt, and I barely had a chance to admire the bulging muscles of his arms or the burly bronze chest that tapered down to his slim waist before he pulled me up from the trunk and into his arms for more kisses.

Once more I was lost in his embrace with my eyes clenched shut. The smoldering itch for his touch that had propelled me to this room almost instantly flamed back up. I couldn't stop wanting his lips and his body, and my skirts just got in the way. He pulled up my dress and my petticoat and ran his hands up and down and around everywhere he could reach. I'd never known I could open up so wide with such a wild craving to be filled. Except I had known, in my dreams; I just wouldn't let myself realize it while awake. Yes, she was right; I'd always been afraid.

I wasn't afraid now. Joe began to fumble with the buttons

down the front of my dress. I wondered if he had one of those rubber bags. I couldn't possibly mention such a thing, and not only because it was vulgar; I couldn't let him think I might let him continue to ravish me. And what if he didn't have one? Then I'd have to insist we stop at once, and I'd never know what happened next.

Too impatient for any more buttons, he pulled the dress up over my head. I felt utterly naked in my camisole, petticoat, and bloomers. If he was surprised that I wore no corset, he didn't show it. Pulling the combs and pins from my hair, I let my locks unravel down to my waist. At least they made a curtain around my body. He lifted the camisole over my head. I unbuttoned my petticoat and let it drop to the floor. Even as the release of my clothing allowed me to breathe more freely, a grip of terror constricted my lungs. Where was my willpower? I must put a stop to this now, or I'd never forgive myself. The only place to hide was under the covers on his bed, or what remained of his bed—a mattress on the floor.

"You're so beautiful," he said as I slipped under the blanket. I couldn't keep myself from watching as he took off his socks, pants, and then drawers. For the first time, I took in the sight of a living naked man.

So that was it.

He seemed proud to show me. I hadn't expected . . . the thing . . . to stick out like that or to be so large. How could it possibly fit inside a woman? It didn't seem possible. I envied his lack of shame for how it stuck out in such an undignified way. I felt embarrassed that he could glimpse my own tiny nipples while sliding under the blanket next to me.

He kissed my lips gently. Shivers tickled down my spine. I would stop him. In a moment. First I needed to visualize his hand as it rode up the slope of my hip and back down to my waist and then paused to cup my breast.

"*Come lo fai?*" he whispered in my ear. "How is your skin so soft?"

Not from the costly lotions that I sold but couldn't buy. I loved knowing he found my skin soft, my poor neglected skin, always denied the touch of anything other than clothing and soap and water. How sealed off from other people I'd been.

He leaned over me. I shifted from my side to my back. He threw the blanket aside and lowered himself right on top of me so that his legs enclosed mine. It felt so right to be flat up against another human being.

I shut my eyes. Felt the hard thing poking between my legs. He rubbed it against me, hot breath on my face, kisses wet, slobber on my chin, my cheeks, his tongue in my mouth—disgusting! I pulled my face away. Willpower. Maybe I still had some.

"We ought to stop," I whispered. "Before it's too late."

"Of course," he said, "don't worry, we will."

He nuzzled his nose into my hair and began to work himself within me. He'd misunderstood. I said nothing, my mixed feelings no match for his drive. He burrowed deeper into the tightness inside me, and then came the pumping in and out—tentative at first and then a deliberate rhythm. I sensed him getting ahead of me and wanted to tell him to stop, slow down, he was going too fast, leaving me behind, going too deep, yet I remained silent. It was all so strange and curious, and then it began to hurt. Aunt Ida's warning about my honeymoon night came back to me. *The first time is painful and there will be blood.* Of course, this wasn't my honeymoon. I'd never see him again in my life.

Red-hot pain silenced my thoughts. I moaned as he jabbed in and out against a barrier deep within until he broke through, and we merged as completely as two human beings could. He continued to thrust, but softer and yet softer, and I began to feel it again—that desire. Was he done? Now I didn't want it to end.

I groaned again, this time to encourage, and he continued moving around, starting to grunt and growl like some kind of wild savage. I had to stifle a laugh and felt rather proud that my skinny body could inspire such a performance—until it dawned on me that this had to be the orgasm, and it was going to be too late!

"Joe!" I said in a cross between a yell and a whisper. Just in time, it seemed, he withdrew and then pressed back against me, smearing wet stickiness on my belly while twitching in a paroxysm of ecstasy such as I'd never observed in my life. Surely a woman wouldn't do the same—I couldn't imagine. Finally, he collapsed, depleted, done. I lay under him, annoyed and relieved, our bodies stuck together, wet with sweat.

"Are you all right?" he whispered.

"I can't breathe very well with you on top of me."

He peeled himself off and settled on his back next to me. The air cooled his sticky discharge on my skin. A patch of wetness lingered underneath my thighs. We lay next to each other, completely still with exhaustion, until he broke the silence to pose the inevitable question: "Do you want to use the water closet?"

I knew I had to clean myself, but the idea of leaving the bed in all my nakedness was too horrid. If only I could curl up and go to sleep. "You go first."

I kept my eyes closed until hearing the door shut. Groping the floor, I found his shirt and, in short order, had it on, pleased at the way it billowed around me and swallowed me up.

When Joe returned, he asked again if I was all right.

I decided not to complain that he'd nearly neglected to withdraw. He handed me the key to the water closet, and I padded across the floor to the hall. Searching for the keyhole by the light of the blue-burning gas jet, I imagined Angelina's door opening to reveal me in her brother's shirt. At least she might be convinced that I'd changed.

I spent as little time there as possible and hurried back to the bed, where I promptly turned my back to Joe. He immediately put his arm around me. It felt remarkably cozy. I could stay exactly like this forever.

I was no longer a virgin.

I couldn't believe I'd allowed it to happen.

I couldn't believe I didn't regret it.

A man had desired me, and I'd desired him back.

Thank god he was leaving the next day.

I dreaded facing him in the morning.

At least for now I could sleep.

When I woke, Joe was already dressed and making coffee. If only I could've snapped my fingers to magically transport back to my own room. I closed my eyes as if that would make him go away, but no luck.

"Could you hand me my clothes?" I asked.

"*Buongiorno*."

"My clothes."

"Did you sleep well?"

"I would very much like my clothes."

They were just out of my reach on the floor. He handed them to me. "*Signorina*."

"Could you wait outside a moment?"

He bowed like a servant. "Of course."

As soon as he was gone, I began to dress and noticed dried smears of blood between my legs and, horror of horrors, on the bedsheet. I hid the stain under his blanket; nothing else to be done about it now. After buttoning up my dress with relief—one step closer to escape—I opened the door. "You can come back in."

"Thanks. Are you all right?"

"I just need to use the . . ."

I nodded toward the hall. He handed me the key and opened the door to the hall. Revisiting that dreadful little chamber, I took care of my needs as efficiently as possible so I could leave. Even the mirror over the sink didn't tempt me to linger over fixing my hair.

When I returned to the room, Joe was sitting on one of the trunks while drinking a tin mug of coffee.

"I ought to go," I said, searching the room for my combs, hairpins, and hat.

"So soon?"

I found the combs and pins on the floor by the mattress and remembered that my hat never made it out of the Majestic. "My head doesn't feel right. I'm not used to alcohol."

"The coffee should help," Joe said, nodding toward the other trunk, where he'd already set out a mug for me.

Perhaps there was no reason to hurry. After putting up my hair as best I could, I sat down on the other trunk. "Thank you."

"Sorry there's nothing to eat. I could run out for something."

"That's all right. My stomach feels strange." The hot liquid did help to clear my brain, which wasn't necessarily a good thing. "I can't believe this happened."

"Relax," he said. "We did what we did. It was good, right?"

"Depends on your definition."

"*Grande*. First-rate. Swell. At least I thought so. Maybe you, too? Just a little?" Joe waited with hope in his eyes, as if my opinion on the matter actually meant something to him. He was a handsome devil, no doubt about that. I managed a tiny smile. "So why beat yourself up about it?" he said.

"People saw us leave together."

"They don't know where we went."

"You'll tell Angelina."

"My lips are sealed."

"Do you promise? I would die if she found out."

"And she's the last person I'd tell. As for the others, I'm as good as gone."

"That's right," I said, mustering cheer so he wouldn't think I planned to suffer over his absence. "Today's the big day. You must be excited."

"I can't wait to be out on a boat in the San Francisco Bay." He leaned back as if already floating on the waves. "Much better than being cooped up in a store."

"Going to a new place," I said, "starting over . . . sounds grand. I wish I could go."

Now he leaned all the way forward, elbows on his knees. "You wanna?"

"Oh, but I couldn't. I just meant the idea of it sounded nice."

"Why don't you, then?"

"Your parents would be none too pleased."

He laughed. "Come! It'll be an adventure."

I used to imagine Joe as more grown up than me; now I could see he wasn't very mature. Or perhaps I'd caught up with him. "It's entirely impractical."

"I wasn't kidding about being crazy for you, Olive."

"That's sweet—"

"And I don't take it lightly, what we did. I know you're a high-class girl—too good for a fellow like me."

"Nonsense. But think about it. What would we do, tell everyone we're engaged? Married?"

"If that's what you want."

"Now you're being utterly ridiculous. This is the first genuine conversation we've ever had. I'm sure we'd wear on each other's nerves soon enough."

"Maybe I'd get on yours—not the other way around. '*Potrei quasi innamorami di te.*' "

"What does that mean?"

"Someday . . ."

He looked into my eyes, and I feared he might try to kiss me. I couldn't let it happen again. "I mustn't stay any longer." I rose, accidentally knocking my cup and sloshing coffee on the trunk. So much for an elegant departure. "I'm sorry."

"It's nothing." He pulled out a handkerchief to wipe the spill. "*Di niente*."

I went to find my shoes. After I'd buttoned them up and was ready to go, he walked me to the door. Clasping both my hands, he pressed his lips on my forehead and gave me a chaste kiss. "*Ciao.*"

"*Ciao.*"

In the hall, I passed Angelina's closed door. My footsteps echoed on the stairs like a hammer nailing a coffin shut.

Metropolitan Tower

Toiletries counter

East Side tenements circa 1900

SATURDAY
JUNE 16, 2007

AMANDA

JEFF'S VOICE WOKE me up. "I confirmed everything with the insurance people."

Wearing pants but no shirt, he spoke into his cell phone while looking out the window to the street. The clock on his nightstand said ten past eight.

"Everything is covered, even the ambulance."

I wondered who he was talking to. Was this about his wife? I kept my eyes closed while listening.

"Great, so that's all been taken care of."

I'd slept horribly. At least I didn't have any weird dreams—not that I remembered, at least.

"Okay, thanks for your help."

He hung up and dialed another number. I kept my eyes closed.

"So it's all arranged," he said into the phone. "I'll tell her tonight."

Tell who, his wife? I waited to hear what he'd say next.

"I'm hoping she'll be agreeable."

Maybe he was leaving her.

"It will be good for Denise. For all of us."

Maybe I didn't need to make an ultimatum; he'd been thinking along the same lines.

"The kids will understand it's for the best."

That's right. Who wanted to live with two parents who didn't love each other?

"At the very least, it'll give her a chance to relax."

Wait a second. Divorce was not relaxing.

"It seems to be a nice place," he said. "Expensive enough."

Vacation? He was making her take a trip somewhere? I opened my eyes. Now he faced the room and saw that I was awake.

"Listen, I'll call you later, I've gotta go." He put the phone into his pocket and came to sit on the edge of the bed. "Do you mind if I take a quick shower?"

"That's fine, go ahead."

"Make some coffee if you want," he said, stroking my hair. "There's some good bread, and that jam you like in the refrigerator."

"Thanks. Who were you talking to?"

"Just my father-in-law."

"Your wife is going somewhere?"

"Yeah, she might take a cruise with her parents."

"Oh really? Where to?"

"Barbados. I've never been, but it's supposed to be great."

His deliberately casual tone of voice convinced me he was lying, but I didn't press. "Sounds nice."

He took off his pants and threw them on the bed. "I'll be right out."

As soon as he shut the bathroom door, I got dressed. What a slut I was, or should I say tramp, falling into bed with Jeff when I needed to assert myself, and now what? I went to the window, leaned my forehead on the glass, and stared down at Park Avenue. No other city could boast having a cluster of twelve yellow cabs waiting at a red light. I thought of Angelina in her "gentleman friend's" room at the Plaza as she looked out the window at the horse cabs.

Jeff had taken his wife to the hospital in a cab. So what was he saying on the phone about insurance to cover an ambulance? The only explanation would be if she'd been taken to another hospital. If that was the case, her injury was more serious than he was letting on.

The shower was still running on the other side of the door. I'd never snooped around in his stuff. Now I wondered why I'd always been so honorable. My heart pounded as I reached into his pocket and pulled out the phone. The last outgoing call was to someone named Bob, presumably the father-in-law. The call before that had no name, but it was to a 203 area code. Connecticut. I wanted to dial it to see who would pick up, but not on his phone, so I dashed into the dining room to get mine, punched in the number, and returned his phone to the pants pocket. The shower was still on. I put the call through.

A woman answered. "Silver Hill."

"Silver Hill?"

"Yes, may I help you?"

"Hi, yes, I'm wondering, could you give me some information . . . about Silver Hill?"

"Admissions won't open until nine."

"Okay, I'll call back. Thanks."

I hung up and took a seat in front of his computer and turned it on. At this point I didn't care if Jeff caught me red-handed. While I waited for it to boot up, I looked at a framed photograph on his desk. It was of his two handsome boys and his wife—blond hair, dark roots, and a pretty enough face. She wasn't smiling.

As soon as I got the Internet connection, I Googled "Silver Hill Connecticut." The top listing was Silver Hill Hospital. I clicked on the site.

Restoring Mental Health Since 1931. A Psychiatric Hospital Distinguished by Eighty Years of Excellence.

Wow. Not exactly Barbados. I stared at Jeff's wife in the photograph. That woman didn't have an accident while slicing an onion. She had an accident . . . while slitting her wrist?

By the time Jeff emerged from the bathroom, I'd dressed, made coffee, and eaten a piece of toast. He leaned over and kissed the top of my head. Smelling slightly of lime, he glowed with clean-shaven innocence.

"We have to talk," I said.

"Now?" Jeff knew I wouldn't normally want to have a conversation before reading the morning paper.

"Now." I'd waited long enough.

"I need coffee." He got a mug from the cabinet.

"Your wife. She didn't really have an accident, did she."

"Amanda," he said, pouring the coffee, "we went over this already."

"You mean you lied about this already."

Without responding, he went to the refrigerator for milk.

"She isn't going on a vacation, is she, Jeff. Your wife is going to a mental hospital."

He silently poured the milk into his coffee as if mixing dangerous chemicals.

"She tried to kill herself, didn't she."

He didn't ask how I knew. No denial sprang from his lips. So it was true?

Leaning back against the counter, he sipped his coffee and stared at the floor. His face was hard. With anger? Resentment? I couldn't tell.

"Is it true?"

He looked up at the ceiling and sighed.

So it was true. "I don't understand," I said. "How could you have an affair when your wife is . . ." I didn't know how to put it, so I let my voice trail off. Crazy? Depressed? Suicidal?

He was done looking at the ceiling; now he looked at the floor again.

"Jeff! Speak! What happened? Did she find out about us? Is that why she tried to kill herself?"

He shook his head. "That's your imagination."

"What else do I have? You don't tell me anything about your marriage."

"You don't ask."

"I'm asking now."

"Okay." He came to the table but remained standing behind the chair opposite me. "Okay. You're right. She did try to kill herself."

"Oh my god."

"And I'm very upset about it, don't get me wrong. But it wasn't her first attempt. And it wasn't so bad that . . . Let's just say she wasn't close to dying. I was home. She knew I'd find her."

"She found out about us, right? And couldn't handle it. She needed to keep you home, get your attention."

"Our relationship has nothing to do with this, Amanda. She doesn't know about us. She has no way of knowing, believe me. The money for your business comes out of an account she has no access to. I use a separate phone to contact you, and she doesn't know it exists. She never comes into the city—it freaks her out."

"Maybe she hired a detective."

He shook his head. "She doesn't think about me. She thinks about herself."

"What do you mean? I don't understand."

He looked at me, hesitated, and then groaned so miserably that I thought remaining in a state of ignorance might have been better.

"She has a mental illness," he said. "She's bipolar."

"Bipolar? You mean, like, manic-depressive?"

He nodded. "She takes a cocktail of medications. The doctor is always trying different pills, special diets, even electric shock . . . nothing works. I keep my expectations low."

"Wow." Electric shock? Did they still use that? "God. It sounds hard, very hard. I'm sorry you've had to go through this, I really am. But I still don't understand. When you got married . . ." I didn't know how to put it. "Was she this way already?"

He let out a short, bitter laugh. "Back then, no. Maybe a little down sometimes, but nothing that seemed extreme. Everything changed after the kids were born. She had terrible postpartum depression. The first time around, she bounced back. The second time, she got more depressed than ever. She didn't want to get out of bed or leave the house. It went on for months."

"Did she see a shrink?"

"Yeah, she went to a psychiatrist." He sat down opposite me. Finally, he opened up about what he should've told me the very first time he came to see me at the store on Mott Street and took me out to dinner. "He gave her an antidepressant. That made her crazy. Too happy. Manic. All of a sudden she proclaims she's going to become an interior designer and starts going around to our friends, to people whose houses I designed, offering her services."

"Isn't that good, though?"

"She knows nothing about interior design. No training, no skills, no idea what she was doing or getting involved in. Once she got people interested, she started going to auctions, flying off to Europe on shopping sprees, randomly buying expensive furniture and art that piled up in some warehouse. Meanwhile, she kept missing appointments with clients. She couldn't face them, couldn't deal with it. The whole thing was a disaster. She got depressed again." He shook his head. "It's like I'm her caretaker, Amanda. She doesn't seem to conceive that I might have my own needs or my own feelings. She isn't curious about my life. Mostly, she likes . . . I don't know . . . sitting in bed and staring into space."

"I don't know what to think, Jeff. I sympathize, I really do. But I can't believe you kept this secret from me all this time." I *had* been carrying on with a ghost.

"I'm sorry," he said.

"I mean, didn't you *need* to talk about it?"

He shook his head. "I've got a therapist for that. And her family."

"Sure, but I mean didn't you want to talk about it with me?" I used to congratulate myself for being so good about not meddling in his relationship with his wife. Now I wondered if I'd just been selfish, completely missing signals that he was suffering and needed comfort.

"It felt good to be able to leave all that behind. It's horrible how it takes over everything. I was glad to keep us separate and unaffected by it."

"But we couldn't really be unaffected." Maybe I'd always sensed there was something about his marriage that I needed to leave alone. If I'd pushed him to reveal it, we wouldn't have been able to continue our relationship. Now it was out and couldn't be ignored.

"I try being patient with her," he went on. "I try to help every way I can. But after years of trying and getting nothing back and seeing no change, I started getting depressed, too. Then I found you again. I don't think I could've stayed married otherwise. At least when I'm with you, I can get away . . . forget about her for a while, have a life."

His words hit me hard. "Did you hear what you just said? You just said you can't stay married without me." I stood up and looked down on him from across the table. "What am I, some kind of marital aid? Why bother with couples counseling? Just go out and have an affair!"

"Come on, that's not what I meant."

"That's exactly what you meant. Jesus! I've been helping you keep your marriage together! As long as I stick around, you don't need to leave her. Meanwhile, I'm supposed to keep my life on hold." I pulled on the bracelet. The gold band dug into my skin like a handcuff. "I never knew that was the bargain here, Jeff, you know? And now . . . I'm afraid of waking up all alone in the world one day with no one who truly cares about me."

"I care. You know that. I love you, Amanda. And I'll always be here for you."

"But you aren't here for me, not really. She comes first. She has to. She needs you. And here you are, having an affair!"

"You don't know what it's like," he said, glaring straight at me. "You can't imagine! No one can if they haven't lived through it."

"I'm sure it's hard. And I feel horrible for you, I do. But still, this is wrong." I went to the window and looked out. I couldn't face him. My eyes teared up as it hit me in the gut. I knew. No one else had to tell me—not Molly, a therapist, a hypnotist, a psychic, or a mechanical gypsy. This was the end.

"You think I'm a bad person for cheating on her."

"No." I leaned my forehead against the glass as tears trickled down my cheek. "You're a good person, Jeff. That's not what I meant."

"I could've left a long time ago, but I stayed. I make sure she gets the care she needs."

"I understand that."

"The last thing I wanted was to hurt you. I'm sorry. I've tried to figure this out, but it seems to be an impossible situation, especially because I don't know what she might do if I leave her."

The truth was too horrible to say out loud. Kill herself. Or him. Or even, potentially, if she did find out about the affair, me.

"Yes," I said. "You've devoted yourself to her." I wiped the tears off my cheek and then turned around. "Her, not me. And you're there for your kids, which you need to be. Meanwhile, I may never have any kids because I've spent my late thirties hoping a man will leave his wife for me when that was never a real possibility."

He slumped in his chair and looked up at me. "I'm sorry. I'll say it a million times if it will do any good. I'm sorry!"

It didn't do any good. Not one bit. I pulled the bracelet off my wrist and set it on the table. "I can't accept this."

"Amanda, don't be ridiculous."

"I should go."

"I know you're in shock. I know this is a lot to absorb. You need to give it some time to sink in."

"Time isn't going to help." I went to the bedroom to find my shoes. He followed me in.

"You feel that way now," he said, "but at least the truth is out. That means we can talk about it and figure something out together. And we will work it out, I promise."

I slipped on my flats. "No, we won't." Now I knew ultimatums pertaining to me didn't matter. My needs didn't factor in here. "There isn't anything to work out, Jeff." Though that wasn't totally true. "Except the money I owe you."

"Don't worry about that."

"I'll pay it back somehow, I promise."

"The money doesn't matter," he said with annoyance. "Forget the money." He held out the bracelet. "Please take this. It's your birthday present. I want you to have it."

I shook my head. "I'm sorry." He looked so sad, like a little boy; it made me want to kiss him and make everything better. Instead, I forced my legs to walk away from him. "I've gotta go." I went back to the living room, grabbed my bag, and headed for the door.

Jeff, still barefoot, followed me down the hallway to the elevator. "I'll call you later."

"No. Please?"

"We can't all of a sudden just stop seeing each other."

"We aren't. It's taken me years to all of a sudden just stop seeing you."

I got on the elevator without giving him the chance to kiss me. We stood across from each other, two sad people in a situation that couldn't be fixed. I waited for the door to slide shut between us.

OLIVE

ON MY WAY home from Joe's, I stopped in a bakery for some fresh, warm rolls. While walking up the block, I promptly wolfed one down. A newsboy was selling papers on the corner. A headline caught my eye. THAW LOSES SUIT FOR RELEASE: COURT DECLARES PRISONER INSANE. I bought a copy to read in my room later.

The more distance I put between me and Joe, the more stupid I felt for my behavior, the more nervous I became over the consequences. What if my memory of the fertile period was wrong? I might've switched it around in my mind, just as I did when I was trying to remember what Angelina had told me. Or perhaps *she'd* switched it around. Or perhaps she'd been right and the information in my book was wrong. No, I could trust Dr. Galbraith. But now I couldn't remember if she'd said the woman was *most* fertile during her monthly or *least* fertile. My god. I might be pregnant this very moment. It would be disastrous. My entire life ruined. How could I be so careless? I hurried the rest of my way home.

As soon as I reached my room, I took *The Four Epochs of Woman's Life* from the bottom of my trunk and flipped through the pages. He'd pulled out just in time, the sticky residue on my belly proved it, but still . . .

Indeed, as I remembered, Dr. Galbraith said it was a well-established fact: The woman was most likely to conceive on the days immediately before and immediately after menstruation. How reassuring those words were. A well-established fact. I closed the book. My monthly had finished eight days ago. Everything should be fine.

I washed up and ate another roll while reading the newspaper. The judge who'd presided over Thaw's trial said he felt the verdict was correct. In his opinion, Thaw was paranoid and ought to remain in the asylum as long as he'd be a danger to society.

Angelina once said I didn't understand Harry Thaw because I'd never felt passion. Perhaps she'd been right. For the first time, I felt sorry for the man. I understood how passion could make you crazy. Joe's kisses had made me temporarily insane. My body had decided my actions instead of my head. Reason had flown out the window. Part of me wished I could tell Angelina what happened—perhaps she'd change her mind about me. But I could never admit it was her brother who'd seduced me.

I took myself out for a proper breakfast at the Child's on Fourteenth Street. Eating my eggs with hash, I remembered how bereft I felt the last time I'd been here, just after Father died. At least I felt like a part of the city now, no longer on the outside looking in. After finishing my meal, I decided to stroll by the Mansfield. Even though it wasn't far, my first home in New York seemed like a world away.

The same red-haired doorman who'd summoned Matilda stood in the doorway. He didn't notice me, or pretended not to, as I passed by and took a peek inside. The lobby looked the same as before, yet I was a completely different person. Or perhaps I was more myself than I'd ever been.

Turning down Fourth Avenue, I noticed the time on a street clock. Joe's train wouldn't be leaving for another hour. Instead of wandering aimlessly, I could be racing to the station to see him. Had I been a fool not to go with him? I smiled at the idea of being with him in San Francisco, living as the wife of a fisherman, giving birth to a brood of Italian babies, and learning how to cook spaghetti from his mother. Grand Central was only twenty blocks north. A fifteen-minute walk could lead to an entirely different future.

It didn't seem worth the effort. He'd throw me over soon enough, or I'd grow tired of him. His mother would never accept a girl who wasn't Italian, and his father would run me out of the state.

I entered the park. The steel frame of the Metropolitan Tower had grown taller, reaching almost its full height. The marble facade encased around twenty floors. The sleek skyscraper dwarfed the Madison Square Garden and made it look old-fashioned and quaint. The city was already leaving Stanford White behind.

Monday morning I passed by the lace counter. Workmen had dismantled the old counter and were replacing it with a new showcase designed specifically for the Madame du Jardin cosmetics. Mr. McGillicutty showed me how the interior was fitted out with special hidden reflector lights that were designed to draw the eye. "How clever," I said. "When do you think it will be ready?"

"I expect you'll be open for business by the end of the week," he said. "I believe someone is coming to familiarize you with the products on Wednesday. I don't know if this will be one of the most popular counters on the floor or one of the most criticized."

"You needn't worry, Mr. McGillicutty. I'll manage just fine."

The past week had thoroughly prepared me to be both popular and criticized.

"Have fun at the Majestic?" Sadie asked when I took my place behind our counter.

"It was fine."

"Looked like more than that."

"Not particularly." Did she know something? It was impossible.

"If you say so," she said.

So far I hadn't missed Joe one bit. Granted he'd been gone only one day. And I did find myself remembering how it felt to have those hands touching my skin, our bodies pressed together. At least I finally knew what made everyone else snicker, condemn, rhapsodize . . .

No. I had to forget. I turned to my first customer of the day. "May I help you?"

Mrs. Maytell, an attractive woman with a proper British accent, came to show me how to apply Madame du Jardin's cosmetics. We installed ourselves behind the beautiful new mahogany showcase and placed the entire line of makeup on the glass countertop. The pretty collection of tiny pale pink boxes decorated with yellow irises consisted of three shades each of powder, rouge, lip pencil, and eyebrow pencils. Before using one of the other girls as my guinea pig, she wanted me to have the customer experience. I perched on a tall stool at the end of the counter. She leaned over me, dabbing powder on my forehead and cheeks. I inhaled the scent of her lavender perfume.

"I have absolutely no experience when it comes to cosmetics," I confessed.

"You'll catch on soon enough. Once you start using these products, you'll feel naked without them." She went on to apply rouge to my cheek. "Using two fingertips, always blend upward to combat the effects of gravity."

I hoped she'd use it sparingly but didn't dare speak up. After all, she was the expert. Her gentle touch did feel soothing. The customers would likely enjoy the personal attention. "What are the ingredients?" I asked.

"Madame du Jardin insists on keeping that a highly guarded secret. If anyone wants to know, tell them she rescued the recipes from a locked cabinet that dates from before the French Revolution."

"She must be an interesting woman. Will I have the chance to meet her?"

"Oh, no. Madame is getting on in years and has become something of a recluse. She used to be a great beauty, but now she can't bear the idea of anyone seeing how she looks."

"How sad."

"Don't breathe a word," she said, lowering her voice, "but I heard she once tried to kill herself with arsenic. A wealthy woman like that! There now, we're all done." Mrs. Maytell stepped back to assess her work. "Lovely. Let me show you."

As she reached for a mirror, I held out hope that Mrs. Maytell had managed to add a new facet of beauty to my appearance. When she held up the glass to catch my reflection, all I saw was a woman trying too hard to prove she was a woman.

The morning my new counter opened for business, I arrived early to make sure everything was ready to go, especially my face. Trying to achieve the most natural look possible, I applied the products with a light touch. Miss Cohen arrived just as I put away my cosmetics box.

"Everything looks perfect," she said, "except you. Are you wearing the makeup?"

"Yes. I wanted to keep it subtle."

"But not invisible. You'll have to put on more."

"Yes, Miss Cohen." I retrieved my supplies. Miss Cohen stood there while I applied more lip pencil, rouge, and a dusting of powder.

"That's more like it."

I nodded and smiled and felt like a tart. Miss Cohen wished me luck as Mr. McGillicutty signaled the doormen to allow the waiting customers in. Moments later, I faced my first customer.

"I'm looking for powder that won't cake on my face."

Nature had blessed this young woman with a pink-cheeked, healthy complexion and smooth, unblemished skin. I wondered why she felt the need to cover it.

"Perhaps your skin is dry." I set a box on the counter. "I suggest applying a layer of Madame du Jardin's face cream under the powder. It has a lovely scent of geranium."

"I've tried using creams, but they never work."

"Just use a very small amount. After you've blended it completely, add a light dusting of the powder, and use a chamois to smooth it out." I put a pink chamois tied with a gold ribbon next to the box.

"I don't know . . . they make my face look too greasy."

"This one won't. I have a sample right here." I opened the jar, and she dipped the tip of her finger in. "The secret is to use a tiny amount. One jar can last an entire year. It works wonders—like food for the skin—and it prevents wrinkles, too."

"You don't say."

"For a limited time, if you buy the cream along with the powder, you'll receive a twenty-five-cent discount."

"Well then, I suppose I'd best get them both."

"Can I interest you in some of her cosmetics? The lip pencils come in three shades; the lightest one would work perfectly with your coloring."

"No, thank you, I think cosmetics are hideous."

"I used to think so too, but they're becoming quite popular.

Perhaps another time. Shall I include the chamois? It's only fifteen cents."

"Might as well."

All day women flocked to my counter. Many stopped short of buying the rouge and lip pencil, unsure if those had reached the showcase with God's approval, but they spared no expense at the altar for face creams and powders. It seemed Madame du Jardin had answered their prayers for youth and beauty. Too bad she felt too old and ugly to enjoy her success.

June 8, 1908

Eight days have passed since Joe's send-off. I haven't seen Angelina all week. She must be involved in preparations for the next fashion show. I suppose I'm feeling lonely. I ought to try harder to be sociable with the other girls at the house. Nowadays my only friend seems to be Sadie, and I don't like her so very much! I have some mending to do. Perhaps I'll take it downstairs, where the light is better.

I poked my head in the sitting room. A chorus girl who was out of a job pounded out a show tune on the piano while some other girls sang along, letting her brassy voice drown them out. In the sewing room, two machines droned away, as usual. The parlor was empty. I took a seat on the musty couch next to a kerosene lamp and set Father's cigar box with my sewing supplies on the side table. I desperately needed to fix a rip in the silk lining of my muff. My journal kept getting caught on the satin and ripping it further. In the past I'd always given my mending to a tailor or Aunt Ida. Sewing was not one of my talents; I'd never met a needle that didn't draw blood.

By some miracle, it took only about ten minutes to thread the needle. I tried making neat and tidy stitches, but they insisted on coming out in different lengths. Aunt Ida's voice echoed in my ears, telling me to slow down and be more careful.

The front door slammed shut. I looked up as Sadie flounced in. "I need a change," she said, plopping down next to me as I was about to stick the needle into the cloth. Instead, I pricked my finger, flinched with pain, and dropped the needle.

"A change?" I asked, pulling a handkerchief from my pocket to blot a small bead of glistening blood.

"I'm sick of the store. Maybe I'll quit."

"What would you do instead?"

"My father works at a shirtwaist factory. He can get me in the door there, with better pay than I'm pulling in now."

"Why don't you ask for a raise before making a change like that? Factory work can be terribly hard."

"Who gives a fig? Long as I get my nights free. And with Angelina gone, it sure ain't gonna be the same."

"Gone?"

"Didn't you hear? She quit."

"Why?"

"Got something better."

"Where?"

"I swore not to tell. Don't want the entire store gossiping. I gotta do something," she went on, "before I end up an old maid."

"Don't be silly," I said, looking around for the needle. "You're young and pretty, and if marriage is what you want, I'm sure you'll find someone."

"Sounds dandy, but I won't hold my breath."

The needle didn't appear, and I couldn't bear the idea of threading another, so I put my sewing things back in the cigar box. "Well, I must be getting to bed."

"So early?"

"I'm beat." I smiled warmly so she wouldn't feel snubbed.

"Maybe I will ask for that raise. Didn't you get a promotion when I been there three years already?"

"I'm sure you deserve one. And it never hurts to ask." Rising from the sofa, I heard my needle hit the floor with a ping. Pretending not to notice, I wished Sadie a good night.

June 15, 1908

Two weeks and one day have passed. No letter from Joe. Not that it would've gotten here by now. Not that he said he'd write or is even the sort who would. Meanwhile, no one at the store seems to know where Angelina is working. I don't know why I should care. She made it clear she doesn't care about me.

Trying to appear occupied, I wiped my counter even though it was already clean. Suddenly, a pair of elbows landed on the glass. "Wish me luck," Sadie said.

"Why?"

"This morning I decided you were right, so I marched myself up to Miss Cohen's office and popped the question."

"What did she say?"

"I got this song and dance about how she couldn't do nothing without Mr. Vogel's approval, so I gave her my notice."

"You quit? Sadie, why don't you wait for him to come back? It's only a matter of a couple weeks."

"That's what you think. He'll be gone for two months, cooling his heels in Paris!"

"Where did you hear that?"

"Where'd you think? Miss Cohen told me, that's who. Anyway, I've had enougha this place. I'll be getting a dollar more to start at the factory. For the first time in my life, I'll have spare change in my pocket. Before too long, my father says, I'll make forewoman, and then I'll be telling the others what to do."

"Well, if it turns out badly, I'm sure the store will welcome you back."

"You off your trolley? This place is a dead end." She gave me a chilly look. "For some of us, that is."

She left me to continue wiping the counter in pointless loops. Business was slow and getting slower. Any New Yorker who had the means would be leaving the city to escape the heat. I had my own precious vacation coming in August and couldn't wait. I planned to spend it by the ocean in New Jersey, where the store had vacation cottages for employees. Everyone said the place was perfectly lovely, and we could stay two weeks for free.

How strange to think both Sadie and Angelina would be gone.

Stranger still that Miss Cohen had told Sadie about Mr. Vogel's extended vacation yet hadn't mentioned it to me.

I stopped wiping as something else came to mind: the memory of Angelina teasing me over my promotion. The only people who could've known were Miss Cohen and Mr. Vogel.

Had Mr. Vogel told her? Could Mr. Vogel be her married man? That would explain her secrecy over his identity. She once told me her gentleman friend had begged her to go off to Paris. Perhaps she'd finally agreed and was there with him now. Maybe he'd left his wife for her and would never be coming back to the store. That could explain why she pushed me away. She thought I'd never forgive her for breaking up his marriage.

I returned to wiping my counter. Most likely I was indulging in imaginings that had no basis in reality. Even so, they made perfect sense.

June 26, 1908

I desperately need my monthly to come. Never before have I anticipated its arrival so eagerly. I won't truly have peace of mind until I see blood.

35

AMANDA

I'D BEEN GONE from Jeff's maybe five minutes when my cell phone rang. His name flashed on my caller ID. I winced but didn't pick up. A minute later, he texted. My fingers tingled to open the message, but I resisted. Instead, I focused my attention on Twenty-ninth Street and Madison and used all my mental powers to imagine the Mansfield. It stood right on this intersection.

A redbrick beaux arts building dominated the southwest corner. A plaque by the main entrance said it used to be the Hotel Seville. Olive had mentioned that was kitty-corner to the Mansfield, which meant . . . I turned around. My eager eyes landed on a towering, bland eighties high-rise. Worse yet, I saw the name they'd given it on the awning: the Ascot. Yes, an ascot could suggest culture and refinement, but what an idiot name for an apartment house. It rose up thirty floors and was probably filled with characterless cookie-cutter apartments.

One of the retail spaces on the Ascot's ground floor was a coffee shop. Maybe it occupied the same space as the old Mansfield dining room. It was only a quarter past nine in the morning, but I felt like I'd been up for hours. I needed sustenance; eggs and potatoes sounded just right. I went inside.

The place was pretty empty, and I got a table by the window. After giving my order to the waiter and dumping four creamers into my coffee, I pulled out the journal. My eyes grew wide as I read Olive's description of the tumultuous night that had led to making love in Joe's apartment. Wow. I couldn't believe she'd allowed it to happen. I felt proud of her, but it worried me that she had her facts about contraception all confused.

As a matter of fact, Mrs. Kelly had said she was ninety-eight years old. And the night with Joe happened on May 30, 1908. I closed the journal and got out a pen. Scribbling on a napkin, I worked it out, remembering to include the nine months of pregnancy and factor in that a person doesn't turn one until she's been alive for a year. My tabulations indicated that I'd probably just read about Jane Kelly's moment of creation.

The waiter arrived with my plate of eggs. The twin yellow yolks seemed to stare back at me as I considered the fact that Joe Spinelli was Jane Kelly's father. But he'd gone to live in San Francisco. Did Olive raise Jane all on her own? I preferred to think Joe came back and "made a decent woman out of her."

I stabbed a yolk with my fork; it bled out onto my plate. I did not want to dwell on the possibility that Olive hadn't survived the birth. I scarfed down my breakfast without even reading anything while I ate. After paying my check, I continued walking downtown. There was an important place that I needed to see. At Twenty-third Street, I turned west and walked to Sixth Avenue, where I tried once again to imagine the tracks of an El train encroached on the street. Still, the image wouldn't gel. A few blocks down, I arrived at my destination: the magnificent beaux arts building that once was Siegel-Cooper.

Glorious as any monument from ancient Rome, the massive

block-long building radiated magnificence despite the fact that Bed Bath & Beyond, T. J. Maxx, and Filene's Basement now shared the rent. Wreaths, columns, balconies, and lion heads along the cornice adorned the facade. Bronze columns and lanterns flanked the front doors. Olive, Sadie, and Angelina had used the employee entrance on Eighteenth Street, but still. Here it stood. I had to remind myself that I didn't actually know those women who worked there so many years ago.

Something up near the roof made my jaw drop. A crest, like a coat of arms, engraved with the letters S and C. Siegel-Cooper! I saw more of the same crests evenly spaced along the top. I'd never noticed them even though I'd walked by a zillion times. I couldn't help taking this discovery as a message to me personally. Who else in recent history had observed the inscription of the original owners up there? Who would care? I wanted to sit right down on the curb and sob. The past! Right here in our midst, and we were so utterly oblivious, going about our days worshiping the present, as if the generation of "now" was the only one that mattered.

I walked through the revolving door with a thrill, as though I'd find Olive on the main floor, standing behind a counter. The lobby was a joke. So modernized, so stark, so bright, so white. So completely removed from the original design. To the left, people poured into the Bed Bath & Beyond. On the right, they wheeled out shopping carts filled with housewares. In the center a set of escalators—or should I say moving staircases—led down to Filene's Basement. Some of the original support columns remained, and some gold trim lined the walls; otherwise, I saw no vestiges of the past. I had to leave. I didn't want the sterile place to obliterate the lovely interior that existed in my mind.

Back on the street, I resented the cacophony. A parked van vibrated with rap music; mustard from a hot dog cart spiced the air; street vendors hawked cheap socks and cell phone cases. The crowds submissively wore their regulation Gap clothing while hooked up to iPods and checking e-mail on BlackBerries. I yearned to replace it all with trolleys and carriages. The clip-clop of horseshoes on a cobblestone street. Women in skirt suits and picture hats. Men in bowlers and waistcoats.

Except Olive's era wasn't exactly utopia. Could I honestly say I wanted to live back then? Deal with men like Ralph Pierce assuming a woman was damaged goods just because she lived with women who worked? Thank god for all the freedom I took for granted. Olive risked breaking rules that I never had to bother with. Her very life straddled the transition from Victorian to Modern. She'd certainly embraced her era. It was about time I embraced mine.

Maybe I already was living my era. It would take someone looking back from the future to have the perspective to know. I might be the perfect example of a woman from the first decade of the new millennium: failing small business owner in a haze of nostalgia for a romanticized past while living in perpetual childless bachelorettehood in a society that encouraged people to replace human contacts with virtual ones.

I stopped at a red light. My cell phone rang. Jeff again. Suffering. How could I abandon him? Was I being a coldhearted bitch? What if no man ever wanted me again? No. I had to be hopeful. Think positive thoughts. You never knew who might come into your life. A bicyclist zoomed past, inches from my face. Rob Kelly? He was flying back to Santa Monica later today. If only I had some excuse to call him.

Maybe I did.

I headed to Washington Square Park so I could have some relative peace and quiet to make the call. The morning was heating up, but it was pleasant enough to sit outside. I returned to the bench with a good view of the arch that I'd sat on before my session with Dr. Markoff. Was that only five days ago? It seemed like a year.

Staring at my phone, I fought off the fear that Rob Kelly had no interest in seeing me, and I punched in Jane Kelly's number. Why did life seem to involve one humiliation after another? When she answered, I asked for Rob without identifying myself. She put the phone down with a clunkity-clunk. I began to think I'd been forgotten and was just about to hang up, relieved to at least have my dignity intact, when he said hello.

"Rob? Hi, it's Amanda."

"Hi," he said with surprise. "How ya doin'?"

"Good," I said, and then barreled ahead. "Remember you mentioned that storage bin in the basement you have to go through? I was thinking—I mean, maybe you've done it already, and I know you have to catch that plane—but if you haven't, maybe you'd like some help, because I'd like to take a look because I'm almost done reading the journal and I feel like I practically *know* these people, so if you wouldn't mind having some company going through that stuff . . ." I paused. Grimaced with exasperation. Could I have done a better job of sounding more convoluted?

"No," he said, "I haven't done it yet. And yes, I would like the company. Can you get here around eleven-thirty?"

"Yes. Sounds great."

"See you then."

I put away my phone and waited for my heart to stop racing. Then it dawned on me. Of course. Rob's gorgeous Mediterranean skin, his dark curly hair. He got that from handsome hunk Joe Spinelli.

I took out the journal but hesitated before opening it. I didn't want Olive to be pregnant; except I did, so she could have Jane; except I didn't want her to die; except if Jane didn't live, Rob wouldn't exist. I began to read. This time around, with any luck, no crying baby would arrive to share my bench.

OLIVE

"AS YOU KNOW," Miss Cohen said when I took the chair in front of her desk, "our sales have been quite impressive."

When she'd called me in to her office, I had no idea why, though I dared to think it would be good news. The employee newsletter had named me one of the top salesgirls for the month of June. Lacking any real friends to speak of made it easy for me to put everything into my work.

"The lip pencils," she continued, "are selling better than expected, and while the rouge hasn't caught on as much as we'd hoped, the face creams continue to perform splendidly."

"We'd sell even more Eternal Youth," I added, "if it weren't eternally running out of stock."

"I'll speak with our suppliers again." She nodded and wrote herself a note. "So." She set the pencil down. "The reason for this meeting. I've finally convinced management to move the dressmaking department upstairs. Cosmetics and toiletries will be taking its place."

"How exciting!"

"This means we'll be undergoing a major expansion and adding more merchandise. In addition to finding new brands of wrinkle creams, we'll begin selling nail enamels, hair dyes, and tonics. The upshot is that I'll be traveling to more trade shows, so I'll need someone here I can count on to keep track of sales, inventory, and pricing." She paused before getting to the point. "Would you be interested in a promotion to assistant buyer?"

I told myself to remain calm. "I would."

"It will mean a lot more work and responsibility."

"I understand."

"And staying late on occasion."

"That won't be a concern, Miss Cohen. I have no one to answer to but myself." If I weren't pregnant, that is. My monthly was due to come any day.

"Excellent. Then you'll now be on salary at five hundred dollars a year, but keep in mind, you shan't be receiving commissions anymore, and there won't be overtime."

I'd no longer have to punch a time clock anymore, either. "That sounds just fine." With my excitement over the new job title, I couldn't even think about trying to negotiate.

"We'll be hiring someone new to work behind the counter, so you'll have more time to order stock and work with the advertising department and the window dressers. I can't tell you what a relief it is to be able to rely on you, especially since Mr. Vogel insisted on taking such a long holiday. As you know, a great deal of his usual duties fell upon me."

"I'm sure that's been frustrating. I hope nothing is wrong with his health to keep him away from work so long."

"Oh, no, nothing like that." She hesitated. "I'm really not at liberty to discuss it."

"I heard . . ." I cleared my throat and spoke in a solemn tone. "There's a rumor that he's getting a divorce." In truth, I'd heard no such thing, but I hoped to encourage her to admit the truth, or to set the record straight, as the case may be. I raised my eyebrows and silently willed her to confide.

"Well," she said, lowering her voice, "you must promise to be discreet."

"Of course."

She rose to close the office door. Instead of returning to her chair, she perched directly in front of me on the edge of the desk. "Please promise me you won't repeat this to anyone."

"I shan't, I promise."

She leaned forward and kept her voice low. "One of our employees made a complaint that he got her into trouble."

"My goodness." Angelina? Could Mr. Vogel be her gentleman friend? It couldn't be; she'd taken precautions.

"He denied it, of course."

"Were there repercussions?"

"Let's just say that no action was taken against him."

"What about the woman?"

"Fired."

"Oh dear."

"Well, it's too bad she got herself into that mess. But she got her revenge by informing his wife."

"And then what happened?"

"He whisked his wife off to Europe. Then we got a telegram saying he wasn't coming back until the end of August."

"So his wife forgave him?"

"First-class hotels have a way of doing that."

"I should imagine."

"At any rate," Miss Cohen said, returning to her desk, "I have some work to finish up, and you probably want to get home. I'll make sure the new salary is reflected in your next paycheck. By the way, I know you were planning on going down to Long Branch next week."

"Yes." I prayed she wouldn't ask me to give up my vacation. "Do you need me here?"

She must've read my face. "I suppose I can get along without you. But I'll need your undivided attention when you get back."

"Don't worry about that, Miss Cohen. I'll be all yours. Thank you so much."

"You've earned it, Miss Westcott. Have a good evening."

Walking down Fifth Avenue, I tried to feel happy about my promotion, but the fear that I was carrying a child made any celebration impossible. And now there was the mystery of whether the woman in trouble was Angelina. How bizarre it would be if both of us were pregnant at the same time. Perhaps we'd reconcile and go through the ordeal together. The idea would've given me some measure of comfort if I hadn't been consumed by anxiety and dread.

That evening, while changing into my nightgown, I felt a cramp. *Please, God, let it be my monthly.* I lay in bed and waited to see if another would come. I fell asleep, still waiting.

In the morning, my eyes shot open with the horrid bell. Was that a cold wetness between my legs? I took a peek and saw a red blotch on my nightgown and another on the sheet. Blood! My heart sang. *Thank you, God, for not punishing me.* Pressing my thighs together to keep more from seeping out, I rose from bed and joyously collected my belt and sanitary napkin. I'd never given that darn bloody mess such a welcome in my life.

July 10, 1908

The only way to find out the truth about Angelina is to go knock on her door. I could call on her this weekend. But what if she snubs me again? I'll feel like a fool for having given her another chance to do so.

Sunday morning I sat in the parlor, reading the columns listing flats for rent in the newspaper. The page had a large advertisement for a new building on the upper West Side that boasted steam heat, hot water, a separate bedroom, and private bath. They even publicized the rent, which was surprisingly moderate and would be manageable, just barely, with my raise. It might be rather isolating to live all the way up there, but the subway would take me practically door-to-door. And how lovely it would be to have my own private bathroom! Hopefully, they wouldn't hold my being a single woman against me.

But first I needed to read the society page. While I was skimming the gossip column, a familiar name caught my eye.

> Mr. and Mrs. Fulton Winthrop of 107 East Sixty-fifth Street have sent out invitations for the wedding of their daughter, Vivian Winthrop, to Mr. Ralph Pierce. The ceremony shall take place at the St. Regis Hotel. In August the young couple, who were childhood sweethearts, will leave for a honeymoon in Niagara Falls, followed by a train tour out west.

He must've gone back to the girl he'd broken off with. A sense of failure came over me, as if our aborted evening had made him appreciate anew how much he loved his sweet and dutiful fiancée. Meanwhile, having willfully challenged his attitudes, I continued on alone. Were all women who tried to be treated as equals condemned to live solitary lives? Well, I didn't have to be alone. If only Daisy would come back from Europe. My last letter from her was from before Christmas, and I never did manage to write back. Perhaps that explained her silence.

I folded up the newspaper. Daisy was across the ocean; Angelina lived a fifteen-minute walk away. Angelina, who had extended a hand to me when I was at my lowest. I couldn't allow pride to stand between us now.

• • •

"This is a surprise." Angelina didn't look overjoyed to see me.

"I hope I'm not intruding."

We stood on opposite sides of the doorway. She didn't invite me in. It took all my willpower not to sneak a look at her belly. I held out the hat she lent me when we went to the Electric Show. "I came across your lovely hat, and I wanted to return it."

"You could've kept it," she said, but she accepted my offering.

"I was also hoping we might talk a bit, if you wouldn't mind?"

"About what?"

"I wanted to make sure you're all right."

She narrowed her eyes. "Why wouldn't I be?"

"I thought you might . . . I was worried . . ." I finally had to look down at her stomach, which appeared to bulge out under a silvery-blue kimono embroidered with cherry blossoms. "Won't you let me in so we can talk?"

Her cheeks colored ever so slightly. "If you dropped by to pity me . . ." She began to shut the door.

"Angelina, I'm here because I've missed you terribly. Please," I asked, aware this would be my third time asking, "may I come in?"

As she stared intently at my face, I wondered if Father's theory would work. Finally, she stood aside and allowed me inside. I took in the full view of her. When I'd last seen her almost two months ago, she'd managed to hide it. That wouldn't have been possible now.

"Do you want some tea?" she asked grudgingly.

"Please don't trouble yourself."

We sat across from each other at her small wood table. I cast a look about the apartment. The night I slept here seemed ages ago.

"I should've figured Sadie would tell you," she said.

I didn't confirm or deny it. "And Mr. Vogel is the father."

She nodded.

"And he doesn't admit the truth?"

"Didn't you hear? He left his wife to marry me. Soon as the baby's born, we're going to Paris for our honeymoon. Then he's gonna buy me a mansion on Fifth Avenue, and we're throwing ourselves a fancy ball so he can introduce me to all his friends."

I winced. "There must be some way to make that man pay."

"I tried. Looks like I'll be paying the price all by myself."

"And your family?"

"*Madonna mia!*" She went to fill the kettle with water. "You think I'm about to tell them? My mother would pretend I was dead. My father would kill me so she wouldn't have to pretend."

"Mr. Vogel is a rotten scoundrel for letting you go through this on your own."

"When I told him, he said I must've been with someone else, because we took precautions, but I wasn't, I swear."

"The brute. Of course he doesn't want the scandal. Or the responsibility."

She sat back down and looked at me with pleading eyes. "I thought I was safe. He sent me to his own doctor. You should've seen the gent's office—a fancy building on the Upper East Side with a grand marble lobby. I followed the instructions, kept my appointments, even made sure to rinse like he said. A lot of good it did me."

"There must be some way to prove it was Mr. Vogel," I said. "That doctor knows—"

"All he knows is who pays the bills. There isn't anything to do."

I pictured that gun in the Sears & Roebuck catalog. "We could buy a pistol and shoot him."

"It wouldn't solve anything."

"Sure would feel good."

"Would you do that for me?"

"I saw a nice one for sale with a pretty pearl handle."

"You'd need a pearl necklace to go with it."

"I'll steal one from the store."

"You'd never get away with it."

"I'll plead insanity. Harry Thaw got away with it."

"I'll be sure to visit you in the insane asylum."

We exchanged shy smiles; I knew our friendship had been repaired. Then she looked down at the mound straining against her robe. "Along with the baby."

Our smiles faded. The water had come to a boil. She got up to make the tea.

"Please." I rose from my chair. "Let me."

"I'm not a cripple," she replied.

I sat back down. "I guess you've been keeping this secret a long time."

"I suspected back when we went to Coney, but I didn't want to believe it."

"Even then?" No wonder she wasn't interested in those incubator babies.

"Then that psychic . . . remember her?"

"Do I ever. *'Don't regret the future,'*" I said ominously, "*'or fear the past!'*"

"It made perfect sense to me," Angelina said. "That's when I made myself accept it. I knew I had to go through with it or I'd never forgive myself."

"I couldn't be as brave as you."

"Is it brave when you've got no choice?" she asked while pouring us each a cup of tea.

I remembered saying something along the same line to Ralph Pierce. "I suppose we always have a choice; it's just that it might not be the choice we want. I'm sorry this happened. You don't deserve it."

"I'm sorry I was so horrid to you when you didn't deserve it."

"I said some stupid things."

"Who doesn't?"

"That night at the Majestic . . ."

"I was so ashamed. Thought I'd die if you knew."

"Of course. I understand." How easily I could've been in her position.

We were silent a few moments as we sipped our tea. Then I made myself bring him up. "Does Joe know?"

"God forbid. He'd squeal to my parents in a second. I'd have hell to pay for eternity. I'm just thankful they're on the other side of the country right now."

"You can't keep it a secret forever."

"Yes, I could. Or maybe I'll give it up."

At first I wasn't sure what she meant by that. "Could you bear to?"

"I might not have a choice. I've got a little money saved, as you know, but that'll run out soon enough."

"Angelina. You must let me help you."

"You aren't exactly rolling in dough."

"I did just get a raise," I said, taking care not to sound boastful. "Miss Cohen promoted me to assistant buyer."

"Why, that's grand," she said. "Congratulations."

"Thanks."

"I'm sure you'll need every penny."

"I'm not only talking about money. Who will help you when the baby comes?"

"I have a doctor."

"You need someone to be with you during confinement, and then at least the first few weeks." I didn't dare say it, but what if something should go wrong?

"I'll manage. My friends will help."

"Might I count as a friend?"

"Of course."

I had an idea. "Listen. I'm going to look at an apartment to rent on the upper West Side. Eighty-sixth Street and Broadway. It's a brand-new building—the roaches haven't even moved in yet. You ought to come live with me there."

"You don't know what you're saying."

"It's got a separate bedroom. And a private bathroom. With a tub!" If that didn't tempt her, nothing would.

"They'll never take two women. Especially one that's almost eight months pregnant."

"We'll tell them we're sisters. Your husband works overseas."

"They'd never take us for sisters."

"Sisters-in-law, then. Your husband is my brother."

She laughed. "You have learned to manage."

"Angelina. You went out of your way to be kind when I felt alone in the world. Let me return the favor."

"Thanks, but I'm not budging from this place. For one thing, the doctor delivering the baby lives down on Cherry Street. I don't want to be any farther away than this. Also, I don't pay any rent."

"Why not?"

"Mr. Vogel owns the building."

"Yes, of course." Now I remembered her telling me how her "gent" helped get Joe the apartment next door. "And he's letting you stay?"

"Maybe he's too guilty to put me on the street. Or he just hasn't gotten around to it."

"But he could any time. When he gets back from Paris."

"Maybe. Who knows? I never had a lease. The way I see it, he owes me, and this place doesn't begin to pay his debt."

"All right, then I'll just have to move in with you."

"Here? You've gone crazy."

"Only until the baby is born and you're back on your feet. I won't let you be alone at a time like this. After I've seen you through, then I'll move uptown."

"Don't be silly. I'll be fine. My mama gave birth to all six of us with no trouble."

"She had a husband, didn't she?"

"You think he was any help?"

"Angelina. If you can swallow your pride and live here on Mr. Vogel's dime, then you can swallow a bit more pride and let me look after you."

She drew her eyebrows together. Me and my big mouth. I'd managed to offend her again. Angelina picked up the hat I'd returned and held it out. "You might as well take this back," she said. "Because if you're hell-bent on moving in, I'll never be able to repay you for your kindness."

"That sounds fair to me." I took the hat.

July 13, 1908

My suspicions were right. Angelina is pregnant. Thank goodness I went to see her. Not only are we friends again, I've decided to move in with her—just until after the baby is born. That's not my real sacrifice, though. Now, instead of going on vacation to the seashore in New Jersey, I'll be up to my elbows in a bucket of soapy water, helping to clean her East Side tenement.

AMANDA

ANGELINA WAS THE pregnant one, not Olive? Jesus. Only a few more entries were left, but it was a quarter past eleven already, so I made myself put away the journal. I didn't want to be late meeting Rob; as it was, I'd need to hustle the five or six blocks to Mrs. Kelly's.

In a way, I was glad to have an excuse to stop reading. I needed a chance to process the news. This meant Angelina was Jane Kelly's mother. I was pretty sure the math worked out, even though the birth would happen a few months later than I'd figured for Olive. But then why did Jane Kelly have Olive's trunk?

It was getting hot out. My black capris were too heavy, and my top was soggy from sweat. I stopped to buy a bottle of water. Too bad I didn't have time to swing by the apartment and change.

Reaching the Stewart House, I entered the air-conditioned, gleaming lobby with relief. The doorman from my first visit called up to the apartment and told me I could take a seat. Perching on a white leather sofa, I realized it was highly unlikely that I'd get to the store by one o'clock. Luckily, it was Saturday and my assistant would be coming in. So I texted Bettina to let her know I was running late and she'd have to open without me. She texted back right away that it wouldn't be a problem. Good, one less thing to worry about.

I leaned back against the sofa and thought about how this building occupied the same footprint as the old Wanamaker's department store, where Olive bought the book by the misinformed woman doctor. The main floor would've existed all around me.

The elevator door opened, and Rob stepped off, holding a box of jumbo-sized Hefty bags. Today he wore a pair of jeans and wore them well. Angelina's great-grandson, not Joe's.

"I knew I'd tempt you back," he said as we went to the doorman for a key to the storage room.

"I have help in the store on Saturdays, so I don't need to be in till later."

"That's lucky. For me, at least."

The elevator took us down one flight to a dingy gray hallway. A steep metal staircase led to an even lower level where we passed a humongous boiler. Continuing along one more hallway, we reached a door marked STORAGE ROOM. Rob had to jiggle the key, but finally, it unlocked. After opening the door, he hooked the knob with a loop of rope nailed to the wall so it wouldn't slam shut. "Only the most sophisticated safety precautions down here," he said.

"I'm impressed."

He flicked on the lights, illuminating a dungeonlike windowless room filled with floor-to-ceiling cages separated by chain-link fencing. I followed him down a narrow passageway past one padlocked cage after another stocked with valuable belongings: hot-air popcorn poppers, disassembled exercise equipment, rusted file cabinets. Things people couldn't bring themselves to throw away but would never want; headaches destined to be dealt with by surviving members of the family.

We made a right turn and he stopped, checked a crumpled piece of paper with numbers on it, and announced we'd reached our destination. "My sister warned me about the mess," he said with a frown. Indeed, everything inside the cage appeared to be randomly crammed inside and stacked into jumbled piles.

"Over the years," he said, dialing the padlock combination, "Grandma's had her bring stuff down here." He pulled on the lock, but it didn't open. He tried the combination again. "This was not the way my sister wanted to spend her free time, which, as she's fond of reminding me, she doesn't have." He got the combination right and swung open the door.

Rob then proceeded to stand there, frozen with befuddlement over the task at hand. As one who lives for the thrill of scouring giant country flea markets and wholesale used-clothing warehouses, I stepped forward and took charge. "First we need to separate out the garbage from what might have value." I pulled a yogurt maker, a typewriter from the fifties, and three old wood tennis rackets into the aisle. Rob joined in, and we gradually worked our way through. He tried to make a case for taking a kitschy lampshade with reindeers on it back to Santa Monica. I talked him into keeping an old dial phone from the forties. Everything appeared to belong to his parents or Jane and her husband, a businessman who died before Rob was born. "Doesn't look like there's any clothing here," he said. "I completely understand if you want to go."

"Are you kidding? I love this. You never know what'll turn up next. Which reminds me—in the journal, I just read about an unexpected pregnancy that leads me to believe a woman named Angelina was Jane Kelly's mother, not Olive Westcott."

"Really? I don't recognize that name, either."

"I was hoping I'd be able to give you the journal today," I said, which wasn't quite true, "but I'm not done reading it yet."

"No hurry. I'll pick it up when I'm back in town."

"Great, thanks." I opened a box filled with one of the most

predictable stashes: *Life* magazines from the fifties and sixties. Was there a flea market in North America without a vendor trying to get rid of a stack? Another box held *Playbills* for Broadway shows from the fifties and sixties. Rob thought they were worthless, but I knew collectors who would buy them, so he set those aside.

We kept on weeding until the aisle got so cluttered with garbage bags that there was no room to navigate. Rob took as many bags as he could carry and staggered to the elevator. While he was gone, I battled my conscience. It was already a quarter past one, and I'd have to stop at home to change and shower before going to the store. I could do the responsible thing and leave right away, but then I'd have to say good-bye to Rob. And what if there was something buried here that had been Olive's that I wouldn't want to miss?

I continued to forage. Rob took up a couple more loads. Finally, the only stuff left in the cage was a cardboard box and two big rolled-up rugs leaning against the side.

"I'm sorry," Rob said. "This is looking like a bust for you."

"Believe it or not, I like doing this. Anyway, I never give up hope until every nook and cranny has been explored."

"I think we're down to about one nook and two crannies."

While Rob dragged out one of the rugs, I opened the last box. Inside, rusty old pots and pans mingled with Tupperware, an electric can opener, and a cheese grater. Darn. But when I looked up, I yelped with surprise. "Look at who was hiding behind the rugs!"

On the floor, partially obscured by the other rug, sat a big round black-and-white-striped hatbox. Maybe one of Angelina's creations was inside. I crouched down next to it and pulled off the lid.

No hat.

The stuff on top should've gone straight to a garbage pail. Take-out menus, used message pads, and envelopes of junk mail, like coupons for limo services and carpet cleaners. Rob's sister must've been particularly pressed for time that day. Underneath was a legal-size manila envelope. I opened it and found a treasure trove of ephemera: a booklet advertising French lessons in the Yersin Phono-Rhythmic Method; a receipt from Louis Goldzeiger & Son, Interior Decorators, dated 1914; a Hudson River steamboat timetable from 1919. Had they belonged to Olive? Angelina?

"Oh, jackpot, here you go." I handed Rob a baseball program from 1912. Maybe a husband had been the pack rat.

"Whoa. New York Giants versus. Boston Red Sox. World Series. This is worth, what do you think, a hundred bucks?"

"More than that. A lot more."

As he flipped through the program, I found something else in the envelope: a yellowed front page of *The New York Times* dated March 26, 1911. It had a horrific headline. 141 MEN AND GIRLS DIE IN WAIST FIRE: HIGH UP IN WASHINGTON SQUARE BUILDING; STREET STREWN WITH BODIES; PILES OF DEAD INSIDE. I stood up to get better light and read it more closely. Sad stories about the Triangle Shirtwaist fire and eyewitness accounts filled the page. At the bottom was a list of the dead. Someone had drawn a circle around one of them: Sadie Bernstein. It shocked me to see her name; she was real, not just some character imagined in my head. I stared at the photograph of the building with flames shooting out the windows of the top floors. What a horrible way to die. Poor Sadie.

"Anything interesting?" Rob asked, setting aside the baseball program.

"Interesting," I said, "but sad." I held up the clipping. "Triangle Fire. Mrs. Kelly's mother must've saved this."

"I've heard of that—it was terrible."

"Maybe your grandmother would like to look through this hatbox." There was still a lot piled inside.

"Nah, she's been very clear. Toss everything unless it might be worth something, and then sell it."

"Do you want to look through? There could be something else valuable in there."

"Like an envelope holding a million dollars in cash? I don't have the time. Why don't you take it? Would you mind?"

"I'd be happy to. And I promise to let you know if I find that million."

"I know you're good for it," he said with a grin.

"Thanks." I slid the papers back in the manila envelope. "I guess Mrs. Kelly isn't very sentimental."

"Nope, though she did choose your store to sell off her clothes. That was kind of sentimental."

"How so?"

"She lived in the tenement where you have your shop."

I crouched back down to close up the hatbox. "I'm sorry, what did you say?"

"My grandmother lived in the apartment over your store. She noticed your address, searching online for a consignment shop, and that's why she called you."

I jerked my head up and shot him a look of disbelief. The sudden movement made me wobble backward until my bottom landed on the cement floor. Good thing I was wearing pants. "Over my store? You're sure about that?"

"Yeah, one flight up, facing the street." He held out his hand.

I took it. "I live in that building." As he helped lift me to my feet, I felt hyper-aware of our palms pressed together. "And my apartment is right over the store."

"You're kidding. So you live in the same apartment she did."

"Uh-huh."

"Are you okay? You look like you've seen a ghost."

"I'm fine, just a little surprised." I decided not to mention anything about the strange vibes I'd felt in the apartment since I started reading Olive's journal. He already had to think I was too interested in his ancestors. "Anyway, you must be anxious to get ready for your flight. And I should get to my shop."

He checked his watch. "Yeah, my flight is at six o'clock."

I picked up the hatbox, finding it heftier than expected, and we took the elevator back to the lobby. Under the watchful eye of the doorman, Rob and I faced each other for a final good-bye.

"I'm glad we unearthed that baseball program," I said.

"If I sell it, you're getting a commission."

"That's okay, really."

"At least let me take you out to dinner next time I'm in town."

"That would be nice."

"I'll hold you to it."

"And I promise not to turn you down."

I didn't dare ask when he'd be back; instead, I told myself to play it cool and enjoy the fact that he'd made a date, sort of, for the future.

"Thanks for coming by and helping," he said, leaning forward a bit, like he might be thinking of kissing me.

"You're very welcome," I said, blushing like a gosh-darn virgin.

"So . . . until next time."

His face came toward mine. I tried to look casual, as if to say, *Of course you're going to kiss me.* The hatbox bulged between us as his lips pressed lightly against my cheek. His beard scratched my skin, and a chill went down my spine. Not because of any ghostly presence—just the real man standing in front of me.

OLIVE

July 24, 1908

A Jew with dangling sidelocks pulled us into his store. He showed us a cot and asked $1.85. Angelina talked him down to $1.50 including delivery. Afterward we picked up my belongings at Mrs. Almond's. By the time we returned, a boy stood waiting by the front door with my new bed. He helped us carry everything up, and we gave him an extra five cents. Now here I am, writing this while sitting on my cot next to the window, looking out at the tenements across the street.

My trunk served as footstool, desk, chiffonier, and closet. Despite the dingy quarters and my longing for a private bathroom, I felt surprisingly at home, especially after we washed the windows, scrubbed the floor, and wiped the pretty wallpaper clean. Aunt

Ida would've been proud of my burst of domesticity. As it was, she could only disapprove of my move to the ghetto when I wrote her my new address, noting it was temporary. I didn't mention my promotion, in case she should decide that my strange behavior warranted a visit to make sure I hadn't lost my mind.

My most ambitious effort was taking on the cockroaches. After consulting with a hardware store, I painted all the pipes, cracks, and entry points with turpentine. Then I set dishes of borax and sugar around the apartment. Every day we swept up a fresh supply of dead roaches and took great pleasure in burning them in the stove.

Another major nuisance was the stove. The ashes made a dreadful mess, and the fire needed constant tending. When I noticed a cart on Bowery piled high with secondhand kitchenware, I stopped to explore and found what I wanted. I didn't bother haggling with the old woman vendor and proudly carried home my purchase: a used chafing dish in perfectly good condition.

With Angelina's guidance, I made my first meal. First I sautéed some canned peas and onions in butter. Then I fried up some thin slices of beef. I made the sauce using cream, salt, pepper and, after simmering, stirred in an egg yolk. The simple meal tasted surprisingly good.

"Mercy!" Angelina said as we gobbled it down. "When I let you move in, I didn't know I'd be getting a housewife in the bargain."

"Neither did I." I felt proud of my modest domestic achievement, but my triumph was tinged with sadness; I'd never have the chance to please my father with a home-cooked meal.

July 27, 1908

I must force myself to read the description of childbirth in The Four Epochs. *The only account of labor I've ever heard was back when Tessie told me about helping her mother giving*

birth on the prairie. In her book, Dr. Galbraith describes three stages of delivery, but every time I start to read it, I can't bear the ghastly details and have to put it down.

A few nights later, I was back at the chafing dish while Angelina read aloud a letter from Joe. As I stirred in fresh tomatoes, the steamy scent of beef stew made my mouth water.

My Dearest and Only Sister,

They say everything was destroyed in the earthquake but you'd never know it. The Italians were the first to rebuild so now it's the best neighborhood in the city, and I'm not just talking through my hat. Everything is new and clean.

We live by the North Beach. Some people call it the Latin Quarter but Mama fancies she's in heaven or back in Italy—same thing. The sky is so blue and the mountains so brown you'd think you was living in a painting. You're a fool to stay in that sewer of a city. I don't miss New York one bit.

It would've been nice to think he missed me, if only a smidgen, but of course our night together had happened ages ago.

All Mama wants now is a pack of grandchildren. You know that cousin they tried to fix you up with? Mama made me take his sister to a show. She's got a big nose and yellow teeth. Ma che! *I met a girl who works the candy counter. Prettiest thing I ever saw. I'm planning on making her fall in love with me.*

"That boy hasn't changed," Angelina said.

"Mmmm." Adding salt to the stew, I tried to appear preoccupied with getting the flavor just right.

If you're wondering, I'm done with that actress. She turned out to be a tramp and anyway she cared too much about her career.

Angelina looked up from the letter. "Maybe I should've encouraged the two of you. You would've been a good influence on him."

"Or he would've been a bad one on me." I wasn't blushing, only flushed from steam rising from the stew.

"I always knew you were sweet on him."

"And I still say I wasn't! Is there more to the letter?"

They got a big department store downtown called the Emporium. You could get a job there easy. I feel sorry for you slaving away in the heat. Lots of men around to make an honest woman out of you. Say the word and I'll mail a train ticket.

Love,
Joe

I poured a cup of beer. "If things were different, would you ever move out there?"

"I don't like hills," Angelina said. "Or earthquakes."

"Me neither." I took a sip of the beer before adding it to the stew and wished everything could stay just like this forever.

August 4, 1908

Dreadfully hot. Sunday afternoon I don't plan on moving more than an inch all day. If Angelina's baby is smart, it won't be born until after this heat wave is over.

I sat at the table trying to read a pamphlet Angelina had brought home from her doctor. Sadie stretched out on my cot while Angelina lay on her bed. Most weekends, Sadie came by to complain about her new job, which she hated, and the young man who worked there named Harry Katzenberg, whom she loved. "This time I'll play my cards right," she said. "Before you know it, I'll be Mrs. Katzenberg."

"Good luck to Mr. Katzenberg," I said with a grin.

"And when I have my firstborn," she said, ignoring my comment, "you won't catch me coming near no doctor. Rosie is the best midwife on the East Side. Birthed over a thousand babies and ain't lost one yet."

Angelina laughed. "All those old ladies with their mustaches say that."

I'd still failed to read Dr. Galbraith's account of childbirth, and this pamphlet, with its detailed illustrations, scared me so much that I didn't want to open the cover. The ordeal of labor worried Angelina far less than it did me. She firmly believed her experience would be the same as her mother's, just as I feared sharing my own mother's fate.

"I'll stick with my Dr. Singer," Angelina went on. "A girl who works in the accounting office gave me his name. He's a nice young man and never bothers to make me feel like a hussy."

I couldn't decide how I'd give birth. It was easier to imagine exposing my private areas to a woman, but a doctor would know all the latest methods. Except I was delivered by a doctor, so perhaps a midwife was a safer bet.

"Well, I'm using Rosie," Sadie said. "She's got loads more experience than any wet-behind-the-ears doctor."

"Dr. Singer can give me chloroform for the pain," Angelina said. "And he can use forceps to help the baby out. Can your midwife do that?"

"If you have complications," Sadie said, "he'll send you to the hospital, where you'll probably catch an infection and die."

"If I die," Angelina said with a laugh, "I won't have to face my family with the truth."

"For pity's sake!" I interrupted. "Please don't say such beastly things! Can we change the subject?"

"You thought of a name yet?" Sadie asked.

"I'm considering Alice, if it's a girl."

"And for a boy?" she asked.

"You forget, I refuse to have a boy."

"I pity him if you do. Me, I like long names," Sadie said. "Elizabeth is my favorite for a girl. And for a son, I want Benjamin. What's your favorites, Olive?"

"I've not thought about it." I gave up on the pamphlet and set it aside. "I can't imagine having a child."

"What was your mother's name?" Angelina asked.

"Jane."

Sadie grimaced. "Plain Jane. If I were you, I'd pick something else."

"It's a perfectly good name," Angelina said. "Short and sweet."

Just as her life had been, I thought, reaching for my *Dry Goods Weekly,* though I'd already read all the interesting articles.

August 7, 1908

The baby is due to come any time. Just thinking about it makes my stomach clench with fear. Angelina, however, seems more tranquil than ever. We've been sleeping on the roof to escape the heat indoors. At first I wasn't sure about spending the night out-of-doors with other people about, but the fresh air is sweet, and now I prefer it. I do love whispering in the dark with Angelina lying right next to me and gazing up at the stars before dozing off. If only I needn't worry about what is to come! No matter what happens, I pray her life will be spared.

39

AMANDA

HUGGING THE HATBOX to my belly, I trudged up the stairs to my apartment. I hadn't dared peek into the store before coming up; I felt too dirty and disgusting to be seen. It was two-thirty already, but Bettina hadn't called, so I'd take a nice shower and have a bite to eat before going down.

The windows had been closed all night, and the apartment was stifling. I went straight to the air conditioner, turned it on full blast, and stripped off my soggy clothes on the way to the shower. Relief washed over me as I rinsed off the grimy sweat, Stewart House dust, and lovemaking stickiness that coated my skin. It would've been pleasant to dwell on Rob, but my thoughts kept returning to earlier in the morning and Jeff. I tried to wrap my mind around the fact that he was out of my life, as if he'd died, even though he was alive. I turned up the hot water and let myself have a good cry. Then I told myself to quit crying over the guy who'd been deceiving me the past six years. That led to wondering if my period had any intention of returning. The concept that "Aunt

Flo" might soon be out of my life, too, made me cry all over again, until I considered another possibility. That pregnancy test was only 99 percent accurate, which meant it was 1 percent inaccurate; maybe Aunt Flo was on a nine-month vacation. If that turned out to be the case, how would I tell Jeff that I was carrying his child after my pronouncement that we could never be together?

The hot water was starting to make me feel faint. I got out and wrapped myself in a towel. While combing my hair, I stared in the mirror. My pale complexion had a sallow tinge, with dark circles under bloodshot eyes. A pimple was emerging under my left nostril. I barely had the strength to run the comb through my hair, and my stomach was aching for nourishment. I pulled on an oversize T-shirt and stood in front of the refrigerator. Even though I was starving, nothing appealed to me, so I stood by the counter eating a few spoonfuls of almond butter and drank down a glass of apple juice. Then I called down to the store. Bettina picked up right away. "Astor Place Vintage."

"Hi, it's me. How's it going?"

"Pretty slow. I think the heat is keeping people away."

"Okay, then I might be another hour." Or two. I wanted to look in that hatbox before I went downstairs.

"That's fine."

The journal could wait. I wanted to put off saying good-bye to Olive.

"I mean, really," Bettina said, "if you need the whole afternoon, whatever . . ."

Once she said that, I realized how great it would be to unwind and relax, and there was no reason in the world to stress about it. "You know what? I'll plan on coming in around five or six, but give me a call if anything changes."

Thank god for Bettina. If I weren't going out of business, it would've been time to give her a raise.

I went straight to the hatbox and pulled out the top pile of junk mail and menus. They went straight to my garbage pail. I set aside the manila envelope. Underneath that, I found a stack of worthless white cotton handkerchiefs yellowed with age, a neatly folded linen tablecloth with a large stain, and under that, a cigar box. On the top of the box, a beautiful woman with long dark hair whispered into the ear of another.

My hand trembled as I lifted the lid, releasing the scent of tobacco, which had miraculously lingered after all those years. The remains of Olive's detested sewing supplies brought a smile to my face. I found a book of needles, a wad of lace, wooden spools of thread, and a set of French ivory buttons that I set aside for Molly. A hodgepodge of other stuff was in there, too: a dirty, possibly fossilized eraser, a pin in the shape of a yellow lollipop, and a small red velvet box that promised to hold something more valuable than the junk it had been squirreled away with.

Indeed, inside the box was a piece of gold jewelry. A heart locket, to be exact, with a star engraved on the front. Olive's locket. I opened it up, expecting to see the picture of her mother with the sad face fringed by sausage bangs. Instead, I found pictures of two young women, one on either side. They wore their bangs swept up in the pompadour style. The more beautiful one with dark hair—that had to be Angelina. And the other one, radiating confidence, would be Olive. They both smiled.

"Hello," I said.

Jane must've been pretty close to Olive if she kept her picture in there along with her own mother's. Olive must've been like an aunt to her. Or maybe it was more than that. After all, Jane had Olive's trunk, too. Did Angelina die in childbirth? Leave Jane to be raised by Olive? I pushed away that line of thought and closed the heart. Next time Rob was in town, I'd make sure to give it to him. For now I'd keep it safe by wearing it around my neck.

The idea of curling up in bed for a nap tempted me. But the risk was too high that I'd sleep away the rest of the afternoon, and then I'd never get to sleep that night. I set myself up on the couch to mend a forties dress with rips under both sleeves. I brought the boom box to the couch so I could have some music while mending. Michael Jackson would help keep me awake. A cup of tea sounded like a good idea, too.

I put water on to boil. Then I sat down with my sewing box and turned on the tape.

So now I'd like you to go to that place where you feel strong and secure.

Darn. I forgot Dr. Markoff was in there.

The place of wisdom. The department store.

The *Thriller* cassette was over on my nightstand.

Wandering up and down the aisles, looking at dresses . . . shoes . . . handbags. Everything you could ever want.

At that moment, the effort of crossing the room to get it seemed equal to walking from the Battery to the Bronx.

It's a wonderful place, isn't it? So many tempting things, but also wisdom.

Dr. Markoff's spiel was about to end, anyway. I'd get Michael when I made my tea. I threaded the needle; tried to, that is. My groggy eyes wouldn't focus.

Somewhere in Altman's, there's a department of wisdom where you can find everything you need to know.

Maybe it would be okay to put my head down for a second, until the water came to a boil.

When you visit this place, you'll achieve a sense of calm that will allow you to fall into a deep, restful sleep.

Except now my stomach was cramping in earnest. Maybe my period was going to make its appearance. I began to feel hot again, so I sat up and pulled off my T-shirt. But the sofa upholstery was too scratchy for my naked body, so I made the journey across the room and collapsed on my bed. Maybe this wasn't my period but a hot flash. Could you get them both at the same time? That wouldn't be fair, though I bet Aunt Ida would defend the double insult as another proviso of Eve's curse.

Suddenly, a man wearing a black suit and bowler burst into the room. "Sorry, I'm late. Got here fast as I could."

"Hey!" Embarrassed to be caught naked on my bed in the middle of the day, I scrambled to get under my sheet. "You can't just come in here." Maybe this was a dream.

"Please spread your legs. I need to examine you."

Definitely a dream. "Look, mister, if you don't get out of here, I'm waking up."

"You're the one who sent for me, miss. Your water broke."

"Sorry, you've got the wrong person."

"I don't think so." He gestured to the floor next to the bed. I leaned over. A puddle of water.

"I'm not even pregnant. I took the test. Unless," I said with a smirk, "I'm one of the lucky one percent."

He wasn't smiling. "You're afraid," he said, putting on a pair of rubber gloves, "and it's perfectly natural. But there's no use putting it off. You can't avoid the pain."

"No, you don't understand—"

"Just calm down and we'll get this baby out. Forceps won't do the job. We'll have to operate." He removed a knife from his satchel. It was huge, more like a sword or a machete.

"You're not using that on me."

"We have no choice. Now stop making this difficult. We're running out of time. Don't you want this baby?"

I looked down at my stomach. It was huge. Massive. My god, he was right. I *was* going to have a baby. My very own baby! A rush of elation washed over me. It wasn't too late!

The doctor checked the edge of the knife with his thumb. "Shall we begin? I want you to lie on your back, stare at the ceiling, and let yourself breathe. By the time I count to zero, you'll be asleep."

"But I'm already asleep."

"Ten, nine, eight . . ."

"It's not going to work."

He raised the knife. "Seven, six, five . . ."

I curled up my legs. "Don't do it! Please! I'm begging you!"

"Four, three, two . . ."

"Stop counting! Don't you see? I'm wide awake!"

"One!"

Just as he began to swing the knife down, I sprang from the bed with the sheet wrapped around me and ran for the door. Grabbing the handle, I turned the knob, but the deadbolt was locked. The doctor, walking toward me, peeled off his handlebar mustache and removed his bowler, revealing that he was a woman! Pretty and blond—she wasn't smiling. I knew it. Jeff's wife. She'd come to kill me.

"It's over," I yelled, backing up against the wall as she drew nearer. "I swear to god, it's over!"

Standing right in front of me, she raised the knife—except the knife had turned into a gun. She was going to shoot me point-blank, like Harry Thaw shot Stanford White! As the gun went off, I screamed at the top of my lungs. My scream turned into the whistle of the teakettle. I bolted upright on the bed.

Still naked, I looked around for my T-shirt. Jesus. What a nightmare.

I put the T-shirt back on, got up, and turned off the burner. As the whistle faded, I heard her. That woman moaning. Not again! It sounded like she was right outside my apartment. I unlocked the door and looked into the hall. Nobody. Maybe she was on the next floor up. I probably should've put on more clothes, but curiosity drove me to the stairs. When I reached the next floor, there was still no woman, but the moaning got louder. I kept going. The higher I went, the louder she got.

By the time I reached the fifth floor, the woman sounded like she was in pure agony. My heart raced, and I had to catch my breath before climbing the final staircase that led to the roof. Approaching the door, I kept my eye on the rusty gold knob. I grasped it and turned. The door swung open. The glare of the sun stung my eyes.

Before going any farther, I propped the door open with a brick. Taking a few steps, I regretted my lack of shoes; the gravelly surface cut into the bare soles of my feet. I didn't see anyone. The sound of a jackhammer drifted up from the street. The moaning was gone. I went farther, and then a little farther, and saw no one. The view sure was great, though, overlooking an expanse of neighboring rooftops and the Williamsburg Bridge off in the distance. I should've been making use of the roof all summer to sunbathe.

I turned to go back inside, stepping gingerly on the gravel. I'd come up here for nothing, like a fool, and now the moaning would continue to haunt me. At the doorway, I knelt to remove the brick. That was when I noticed something out of the corner of my eye. Someone was lying on a mattress over by the edge.

I straightened up and crept closer. It was a woman; she had one long braid of chestnut-brown hair. Her eyes were closed. Dead? No, her chest rose and fell with each breath. It had to be Olive, sleeping on the roof as she'd described in that journal entry. She looked peaceful and serene, not at all like someone who'd been moaning. Why was she sleeping up here all by herself?

A hot gust of wind blew against my bare legs. Something in my mind clicked. Jane Kelly once lived in my apartment. I bet she was born there, too. Maybe that was what I'd been hearing. Moans of pain. The pain of childbirth.

But where was Angelina? Was she giving birth now? A hundred years ago? Down in my apartment, all alone? Maybe the moans had lured me up here to get Olive.

I knelt and spoke with calm urgency so I wouldn't scare her. "Olive?" She didn't move. "Olive, you have to wake up." She didn't respond. "It's time," I said, but she didn't open her eyes or even move. I spoke more loudly. "Angelina needs you. She's giving birth." Still no reaction. I gave up on calm. "Olive! You've got to get downstairs!" I yelled. "Now! Right now! Now!"

Just as Olive's eyes finally opened, the sound of my own screams woke me up.

I was standing on the roof of my building. Alone. In my T-shirt.

What the hell? Jesus Christ. Something very strange was going on. And I bet it was Dr. Markoff's fault.

I flew down the stairs, intending to get right on the phone and give that man a piece of my mind. When I reached my floor, I charged through the open door of my apartment and came to a dead stop.

The room was completely empty: no furniture, no books, no mess. All my stuff gone. Stolen? The walls . . . I turned in every direction, gaping with disbelief. All four walls were covered with wallpaper. Purple roses climbing green trellises. I went to press my hand against the flat, cool surface. Angelina's wallpaper had been there all the time, surrounding me without my knowing it. And that meant Jane Kelly probably was born in this very room.

A whistling sound made me turn around. My water had to be boiling.

I opened my eyes. I was lying on the couch. One of my arms hung over the side, and my palm was flat on the wood floor. I must've dozed off during the end of Dr. Markoff's tape. But hadn't I moved to the bed? No, that was in the dream. The man in the bowler hat, too. And the gun. Sitting up, I saw that all my belongings were in their usual locations, along with the usual mess. Alas, no wallpaper. I didn't go up to the roof, either. All of it had been a dream. Damn.

The hiss of the kettle grew louder. I got off the couch to turn it off. Something wet, like a very long teardrop, trickled down my thigh. Dots of blood splattered on the floor. Finally. My period had arrived.

OLIVE

THE SUN'S GLARE pried my eyes open. I turned onto my stomach. Just a little more sleep. People around me woke up with loud yawns and muttered curses. A child cried. Somebody stepped on my braid and didn't bother to apologize. The roof door slammed shut every so often as someone left to start the day. I must've dozed off again, because I was having a strange dream about a woman yelling at me to wake up. When I opened my eyes no one was there, just the rhythmic sound of a jackhammer on the street.

I sat up and realized I was by myself on the roof. Everyone else had awakened and gone. Angelina, too, and she'd taken her bedding. What time was it? I quickly stood up and put my wrapper over the housedress I slept in on the roof. Undoubtedly, I'd be late for work. Ever since my vacation ended three weeks ago, I'd been working late almost every night, just as Miss Cohen had promised. I bundled up my mattress and sped down the stairs. She would simply have to understand.

I entered the apartment. Angelina lay on the bed, moaning in pain. Her flushed face was wet with tears and perspiration; her black hair splayed over the pillow in a matted mess.

"Angelina . . ."

Her eyes pleaded. "It's time."

"Now?"

"It's coming fast."

What a day to oversleep. "Why didn't you wake me?"

"I couldn't sleep, so I came inside. Still couldn't sleep but didn't want to go back up, then I couldn't. Olive, it's coming!"

"I'd better get help—"

"Don't leave!" she whimpered in pain.

"I'll call for the doctor and come right back."

"No . . . please . . ." Drawing her knees up, she planted her feet on the mattress, let her nightgown fall open, and moaned. The bedsheet was soaked. "There's no time!"

"Your water broke?"

"Yes! It's happening right now!"

I forced myself to look between her legs. My eyes widened as the sliver of a dark, hairy head bulged out. "I see it!" I tried to mask my horror with enthusiasm. "It's coming out!" But then it went back in, and she sobbed in distress.

"It keeps trying," she said, "but it can't. You have to help me!" She moaned miserably as that patch of hair poked out again and back in.

"Are you pushing?"

"I don't know!"

She didn't know if she was pushing? Should she? How could she not be, with its head poking out like that? God almighty, why hadn't I read the pamphlet from her doctor more carefully? "I'm getting help."

"Thirsty," she said.

"Of course. Water." I spotted a glass on the counter. A carving knife sat next to it. I cringed at the idea of having to use it. What if she was dying . . . like my mother . . . and that was the only way to save the baby? No. Never.

I gave Angelina's neck support so she could sip until she shoved the glass aside and groaned while writhing on the bed. "Help me! You've got to help me!"

"I'm going for help. I'll be back before you know it."

"Don't leave!"

"I'll be right back!"

No time to dress properly. I flew down the stairs and out the door to the tobacco store. "I need to use your telephone!" The row of old men sitting on a bench by the door stared at me in my wrapper as I yelled into the receiver. I had to repeat the number three times before the operator understood me. Thankfully, Dr. Singer answered immediately.

"Please hurry! Her water already broke! I saw the head!"

"I'll take a taxi right up."

"What should I do?"

"Boil some water. Stay calm. Try to keep her comfortable."

"But it's trying to come out!"

"That is the baby's objective, miss. Now don't worry. I'll be there straightaway."

I rang off and screamed at the old geezers as I ran out. "Does anyone know how to birth a baby?"

They stared at me as if I'd gone daft. As I ran back upstairs, Angelina's cries grew louder. Where were the women who lived in this building? Shouldn't they be bursting through the doors to help their neighbor?

"He's on his way!" I announced triumphantly as I ran into the room.

"It's too late!"

For a moment my spirits lifted as I thought the baby had been born.

"Please help me!" she screamed. "I can't bear it any longer!"

"Stay calm," I said, as much to myself as to her, as I lit the stove. "This is what we're going to do." I didn't know what to say. I was useless! He said to make her comfortable, but that would seem the most unlikely thing possible.

"Oh god, get it out of me, please!"

While I was filling the kettle with water, one idea occurred to me. "Stand up."

She rocked her head back and forth and fell to whimpering.

"Did you hear me? I think you ought to stand up."

"I can't."

"Yes, you can." I hoped Tessie had been square with me when she described how her mother gave birth.

"You aren't supposed to stand," Angelina said.

"The baby has to come down, not sideways. Like a waterfall. Let gravity help it."

She drew her knees up again and began to moan with pain from the contraction. I saw the hairy top of that head poke out and then disappear back inside, like before. When the contraction eased off, she whimpered, "I'm gonna die."

"No, you're not." I saw blood seeping out between her thighs.

"God have mercy . . ."

"Stand up!"

"I can't! *Non ce la posso fare.*"

"I'll help you!"

"How?"

I knelt, facing away from her, next to the bed. "Here, lean on my back."

Using me as a crutch, she hoisted herself to a seated position on the edge of the bed. Then I slowly rose, letting her lean on me all the way up. As soon as we were both standing, she came around in front of me, hugging me with her arms around my waist and resting her head on my chest. The bed was against the back of my knees. At least it would break my fall if I buckled under her weight. She pressed up against me, wet with sweat and blood. "There. Good. Is that better?" I asked.

She groaned in response. Now what? Where was that damn doctor? Continuing to moan, she rocked from side to side, and I rocked with her in a strange kind of dance. She was heavy, like deadweight. Supporting her took all my strength.

Her moaning stopped. Something shifted. She lifted her head, her face tensed up, and her fingers dug into my back so hard that I felt the edges of her nails straight through my wrapper. "It's starting again," she said, on the edge of hysteria. "I have to push."

"All right," I said, recalling something else Tessie had told me. "When you push, pretend you're using the toilet." Angelina didn't reply. "Pretend you're . . . you know . . ."

"What?"

"As if you're . . ." I heard Tessie's vulgar word "crap" in my mind but couldn't force myself to utter it. I settled on the phrase I'd heard that man use at Mrs. Craven's. "You know . . . as if you're having a number two." Whether Angelina had heard it before, the meaning was obvious enough.

"You've gone mad."

"I have it on the best authority."

The water began to boil. How would I turn it off? Another idea occurred to me. "And you ought to squat. That's supposed to help." Didn't Tessie say that? In any case, I couldn't hold her up much longer. "I'm going to help you down."

I lowered myself, and she came along for the ride, leaning on me until I was sitting on the edge of the bed and her head was cradled on my lap. Knees on the floor, thighs open wide, she groaned with what I hoped was some relief mixed in with the pain. "Ohhhhhhhh . . ."

Nice as it was to be sitting, I knew I was on the wrong end of where I needed to be to help. So I lifted her head from my lap and slid out from under her. By now the water was boiling furiously, so

I ran to turn off the flame. "When the next contraction comes, you ought to push . . . you know . . . like I said."

She rested her forehead on the mattress and splayed her arms on the bed for support. Her groaning turned into grunts. Actual grunting, like a pig or a hog or a sow.

"Good! That's good!" This seemed more promising. "Give the baby room . . . let gravity help her down!"

I hiked up her nightgown to get it out of the way. No time for prudery now—least of all my own. At any rate, she didn't appear to notice. The grunting got louder. Her face was convulsed and twisted in pure effort and agony, so red that she practically turned purple. I realized I had to stop gawking in case the baby should come out, so I knelt on the floor behind her. What happened next filled me with fascination and horror. The entire head of the baby popped out and hung down between her legs.

"It's out!" I yelled. "The head is out! Completely out!"

She sobbed with misery from the effort.

I cupped my hands underneath the dangling head. "The baby is coming!"

But it quickly became clear that the baby wasn't coming. It was stuck there with the head outside and the body inside. Angelina screamed as the pain got even worse.

My god. What now? Shoulders were wider than heads. How would she ever get it out? Should I pull on it? Reach inside? Try to turn it? I was afraid to, and my hands weren't sterilized, and what if I was only helping her to die? "Keep pushing, you're nearly done!" I said, praying I was right. "Keep pushing as hard as you can!"

She grunted and pushed. I couldn't believe she still had the strength. Blood seeped out around the head. Her skin must have been tearing, but the baby remained lodged in place.

She began to sob. The contraction must've eased off. She rested her cheek on the mattress. "I'm sorry," she said. "I can't do it. *Non ce la posso fare.*"

"You mustn't say that. You can't give up."

"I'm done for. Too weak. You must save the baby. Forget about me."

"Don't talk like this."

"Before the baby dies, too! Whatever you have to do, just let it be born."

"You're talking crazy."

"I'm sorry."

"Angelina." I began to cry. "Please . . ."

She opened her eyes wide but appeared not to see. "Promise you'll take care of my baby."

"I'll take care of both of you."

"Don't tell my family. I beg of you. They'll never accept it."

"Stop talking like this!"

"It's starting again." Her head lifted as the contraction wracked her body. "It hurts!" Her voice rose in a frenzied panic. "It hurts! I don't know what to do! What should I do!" She let out a full-throttled wail of pain.

"Push!" I yelled, hysterical myself. "Push as hard as you can! As if a ten-ton piece of crap is in there and you're gonna get that damn thing out no matter what!" The words tumbled out as if another being spoke through me.

From somewhere deep inside—or perhaps from the shock of hearing me be so vulgar—Angelina managed to quiet down and take a few breaths. Then she heaved in a mouthful of air as if about to swim to the bottom of the ocean, squeezed her entire face, gritted her teeth, and bore down so hard that I thought the veins in her neck would explode. That was when her body turned into something else: an extraordinary piece of equipment; a machine with the express purpose of using every ounce of strength to get that baby out. Angelina lifted her head, braced her forearms on the bed, and made a low guttural sound. I watched in silent wonder as one shoulder popped out and then the other. Realizing I needed to catch the little creature emerging from her body before it landed on the floor, I reached out just as it slithered out in a glistening, bloody mess and plopped into my waiting hands.

"It's out!" I yelled. "The baby! It's in my hands!"

Angelina let herself collapse over the side of the bed to catch her breath. I sat on the floor and held the slimy, shriveled, tiny human being attached to that pulsating red cord. Blood seeped through my fingers and onto the floor.

"Is it a girl?" Angelina asked.

"I'd say so."

"Thank god."

AMANDA

AFTER TURNING OFF the kettle, I stood there, flabbergasted. What an insane dream. It seemed to go on forever. Had I gone up to the roof and seen Olive? No, of course not, but it sure felt that way—as if I'd actually spoken with her and sent her down to this room to help Angelina.

It certainly could've been Angelina's apartment, and Jane Kelly might very well have been born in this room. Joe would've lived next door. Olive's cot would've been next to the window. Did she stare across the street at those very tenements? If I scraped off decades of paint on the wall, would I find Angelina's wallpaper?

Had I been the kind of person who believed in dead spirits, I would've thought some were floating around my apartment. Since I wasn't, I grabbed my cell phone and called Dr. Markoff. Much more likely, his little hypnosis trick had screwed with my brain.

His voice mail answered, so I left a message asking him to call back. Since it was Saturday, I wondered if he'd bother to return my call until Monday. I wanted answers now.

There was nothing to do but finish the journal. Right when I found my place, the phone rang, scaring the hell out of me, but it was just Dr. Markoff.

"Hi," I said, trying to sound calm and sane, "thanks for calling back. Something really strange is happening. I keep having these vivid dreams, unlike anything I've ever experienced, where the people seem to be real and I feel like I'm getting out of bed and talking to them, but then I wake up and realize I was dreaming. It's intense, almost like I'm hallucinating, and I'm wondering if the hypnosis has done something weird to my brain."

"How did you sleep last night?"

"Lousy—and the night before that was lousy too. After listening to your tape, I saw four Fred Astaire movies in a row. I can't remember the last good night's sleep I've had."

"That explains it. You've been short on sleep a long time. Your mind is playing tricks on you, but not from the hypnotic trance. You're probably suffering from sleep deprivation or REM behavior disorder."

"What?"

"A type of parasomnia. The lack of sleep can lead to nightmares, lucid dreams; it's as if your sleeping and waking worlds have collided. How do you feel right now?"

"Okay, I guess."

"See if you can stay up until the evening, and then I'd like you to take some medication to help you sleep tonight. Do you have the number of a pharmacy?"

I was finally getting some pills? "Yes," I said.

"I'll phone in a prescription for Klonopin. It's an anti-anxiety medication that should help you relax—it's often used off-label for sleep conditions like this."

Should a doctor I barely knew be prescribing me a sedative? Hadn't he warned me about their addictive qualities?

"I'm only prescribing three tablets," he continued. "Take one at night just before going to sleep."

Three pills? So much for my future stay in rehab. "Okay."

"If you're still experiencing symptoms, I want you to come see me on Monday. But my guess is that after having one good night's sleep, you'll be fine."

"I hope so. Thanks."

After we hung up, I went straight back to the journal. Nothing was going to stop me from finishing now.

OLIVE

"FOR GOD'S SAKE, where is Dr. Singer?" Angelina said, dragging herself to the bed.

I followed, holding the crying baby—still attached by the cord—and set it down gently next to her. "On his way, I suppose."

Utterly done in, I sank down to the floor, lay flat on my back, and stared up at the ceiling.

"Olive, aren't we supposed to cut the cord?"

I thought about that for a moment. It wasn't an appealing proposition. "I don't know."

"I think it said we should in that pamphlet."

I did not want to slice through that red pulsating thing—or get up off the floor, for that matter.

"Maybe it said you *shouldn't* cut it," she added. "I don't remember."

"Where is that pamphlet?"

"The last time I saw it, Sadie was on your cot paging through it while snickering over the illustrations."

I enjoyed one more moment on the floor and then forced myself to stand up. As I searched through a mess of papers that had accumulated on my trunk, someone pounded on the door. I opened it and Dr. Singer burst in. "Sorry!" he said, rushing across the room and rolling up his sleeves. "Got stuck in traffic and ended up running the rest of the way."

Angelina had said he was young, and I'd enjoyed imagining him as tall, dark, and handsome. As it was, the doctor stood at least a foot shorter than I did. He did have dark hair.

"Thank goodness you're here," I said, allowing only a subtle hint of sarcasm to color my voice.

"Too many people in this city," he said, rubbing his spectacles clean with a handkerchief. "Now what do we have here?" He finally noticed. "Oh. We have a baby. Well, congratulations. Seems most of my work has already been done. I'll just need to cut the cord and deliver the placenta."

Angelina nodded in agreement and stared up at him with a serene smile. One would think she'd just spent the past hour at a spa. I, on the other hand, felt ready for a sanitarium. "Can I be of any assistance, Doctor? I boiled some water, as you asked."

"Excellent," he said, opening his medical bag. "That's all I need. You did fine. More than you bargained for, I'm sure."

While Angelina suffered through his final ministrations, I set about my own toilet, rushing to the water closet and then ducking behind the pink sheet to shed my soggy, stained clothes. He was finishing up when I emerged in a fresh housedress.

"Everything looks as good as one can expect," he was telling Angelina. "Just as you predicted, your body was made for childbirth, like your mother. Did she have a history of delivering early?"

Angelina shrugged. "Early, late, right on time . . ."

"And have you chosen a name?"

"I'm thinking about the name Jane." She looked at me.

I hadn't expected this. "Angelina, are you sure?"

"If it's all right with you."

"Of course. That would be wonderful." I whispered my thanks.

"Some bleeding will continue for the next day or two," said Dr. Singer. "You'll need to rest as much as possible and let yourself heal. Have you any sanitary napkins?"

"Yes. Olive, could you? In my dresser, bottom drawer. In the back."

"Of course." I knelt in front of her bureau, moved aside a union suit and cotton vests, and found the pads and belt, along with something else she'd stashed away: a small cardboard box labeled RING PESSARY.

Dr. Singer was advising Angelina on how to nurse, so I took a look. Inside the box was an odd round object with a wire rim and a rubber pouch. There was also a piece of paper folded up inside with a doctor's name and address printed on top. *Ernest Litwack, MD, 100 Fifth Avenue, New York City.* He'd written instructions explaining how the wire ring folded so it could slide inside, then unfolded to lodge in place. Afterward she was to inject a mixture of water and carbolic acid with a syringe.

If only there were a way to use this as proof that Mr. Vogel was the father rather than proof for why he wasn't.

"As long as you nurse," Dr. Singer was saying, "your monthly won't return. But don't assume you can't get pregnant. Stranger things have happened."

Angelina winced. "Don't worry. That's the last activity I'll be interested in."

Indeed, the events of the morning had convinced me I'd be perfectly delighted to become a childless old maid.

I put away the pessary and delivered the belt and napkin to Angelina. She accepted them without enthusiasm. "Sure was nice to forget about these for a while."

Dr. Singer helped Angelina rise from the bed. "You're very

swollen. Don't be surprised if it takes a while to empty your bladder."

While he helped her down the hallway, I hoped the baby would stay asleep. I wanted to take advantage of the interlude to speak privately with Dr. Singer. When he returned, I apologized for being a terrible host and offered him some tea. "Please do sit down. You must be exhausted after racing all the way here."

"You're the one who did the brunt of the work," he said, taking a seat at the table. "Good thing she has you here to help."

I sat opposite him. "I'll be moving out soon, and I have to work very long hours, so she's hired a girl to come in. I don't know how long she'll be able to afford that, though. It's a shame, because the father of the baby is wealthy, but he refused to take responsibility. I wish there were a way to prove his paternity."

"Someday that may be possible. We have a lot to learn about the science of human reproduction."

"I have a question along those lines, if you don't mind my asking."

"Of course."

"I read in a book written by a medical doctor that women are most likely to conceive on the days just before and after their monthly. Angelina was told that's the *least* fertile time. Can you tell me which version is true?"

I never would've believed I could engage in such a frank discussion with a man, even a doctor, but after what I'd just witnessed, it seemed perfectly natural.

"Most scientists now agree that midcycle, fourteen days after menstruation commences, is the most likely time for conception to take place."

"The *most* likely. Not the least?"

"Correct."

"So my source was wrong." I stared out the window, thinking

how easily I could've been the pregnant one. I would've lost my job, suffered the humiliation of being judged, endured the agony of birth and the uncertainty of its outcome.

Though it was possible that Dr. Singer had it wrong and Dr. Galbraith was right.

"However," he added, "I should mention that you can't narrow it down so definitely. It's possible for the egg to become fertilized at any time of the month. The sperm can live up to a week in the woman."

"Is that so? I don't know why all this information can't be readily available to women."

"God knows it should be," he said, shaking his head. "Too many people believe withdrawal is a reliable way to prevent pregnancy. I should have a word about that with your friend."

"She knows all about that," I said, "and she did take precautions."

"I see. Condoms are usually fairly reliable, but there is no guarantee."

"She used something else." I retrieved the box from her drawer and handed it to him.

Upon opening it up, he shook his head. "For pity's sake."

"What's wrong?"

"This is useless. Completely ineffective."

"Are you sure? It was given to her by a doctor. His name is on that piece of paper."

Dr. Singer looked. "Ernest Litwack. I know that old coot. Someone ought to make him retire."

"He also gave her instructions for some sort of rinse." I pointed to the other piece of paper in the box.

He read it and sighed. "That rinse is more likely to cause inflammation than anything else."

"Really. How interesting."

"Unfortunately, there are many in my profession who never advanced their knowledge past what they learned in the previous century."

"This might actually be good news." As I mulled the ramifications, my heart almost beat out of my chest. "Dr. Singer, do you think . . . Is it possible to take legal action against a man who refuses to acknowledge he's a baby's father?"

"Yes, but the mother has to go before a judge and somehow prove the man is the father."

"You mean by having some sort of witness?"

"People who would vouch for her character. Also letters or documents, that sort of thing. Anything that might help to convince the judge."

"I imagine Dr. Litwack would loathe being involved in a scandal that might harm his reputation—especially one that occurred because he believes in an outmoded form of preventing conception. Do you agree?"

"He's on the board of trustees at the New York Polyclinic Medical School, so I would say that's a safe assumption." Dr. Singer caught on to my train of thought. "The entire process can be horribly embarrassing for everyone involved. That can make the option of settling quietly, out of court, a very attractive one."

"May I ask one more question, Dr. Singer?"

"Certainly."

"Do you know the name of a good lawyer . . . one who isn't too expensive?"

Dr. Singer thought a moment. "As a matter of fact, I do. And if it did become necessary, I'd be happy to testify that no doctor worth his salt would still be recommending the use of a pessary with a rinse of carbolic acid."

"Oh, Dr. Singer, if only you would, that would be grand." We were smiling at each other over the prospect of our coup when

Jane broke out into furious wails. I approached the bed along with Dr. Singer. Her small cheeks were bright pink, and the little mouth was twisted into a grimace as if protesting all the injustices of the world.

"Is something wrong?" I asked.

"She's thirsty. Go ahead, pick her up. I'll get some water."

"Me? Pick her up?" I stared at Jane as if she were a ticking bomb. "I don't know how."

"Nothing to it," he said, pouring some of the water I'd boiled earlier into one of the glass bottles Angelina had ready. "Just be sure to support the head."

I scooped her up very carefully, surprised by how light and flimsy she felt. The creature seemed to sense my lack of confidence and screamed louder.

Dr. Singer held out the bottle to me. I held out the baby to him. "Please, won't you?"

"Don't worry," he said, "holding a baby is a cinch compared to delivering one."

I could see he was enjoying my terror and would not indulge me. Shifting Jane to one arm, I took the bottle and poked the nipple into her mouth. As soon as she realized it was there, she latched on to the rubber. I watched in silence as she sucked for dear life.

September 18, 1908

Today is my one-year anniversary of moving to New York. Never could I have imagined what a tumultuous year it would be. I've been working harder than ever, and then Angelina still needs me, and I've become quite attached to Jane. Now that she's gained a few pounds, I do believe she's the prettiest baby I've ever seen. I haven't even begun to look for my own apartment.

Life ought to become a bit easier now, at least I hope so. Angelina hired a lawyer recommended by Dr. Singer. Dr. Litwack refused to involve himself in a trial, and Mr. Vogel decided to settle quickly. I would like to think some part of him wanted to do the right thing. Jane will be receiving a sum of money for monthly living expenses, and Mr. Vogel has added a codicil to his will granting her a portion of his real estate holdings. He insists it be kept secret until his death. Our lawyer has cautioned us that Mr. Vogel's other heirs might then contest the will.

Since my account in this journal would ring true, I decided to tell Angelina of its existence. The lawyer told me it could prove useful to help establish the legitimacy of Jane's connection to Mr. Vogel. Angelina was grateful to know about it and promised never to peek inside. I do cringe at the idea of anyone reading my words—especially her. She still doesn't know about my night with Joe. That's why I've decided to hide it away, safe and sound, in case it should be needed, but protected from curious eyes.

And so this is my last entry. I feel as though I ought to say good-bye. But who might I be saying good-bye to? I do wonder what someone from the future might think of us simpletons living at the turn of the century. Perhaps the day will come when women exist in the world as equals to men. If only I could be alive long enough to see it.

AMANDA

"FORGOT SOMETHING," I said, entering the now familiar lobby without slowing down. The doorman nodded to me without bothering to call up. The elevator doors slid open as if waiting for my return and took me straight to Jane Kelly's floor. I rang the doorbell. Rang again. A short woman in a white nurse's outfit opened the door, and I asked to speak with Mrs. Kelly.

"She's sleeping," the nurse said.

"Then is her grandson here?"

"Mr. Kelly? He just left for the airport."

"Oh, right." The reality of "Mr. Kelly's" absence hit me. Our promising relationship already seemed, in retrospect, to end up being a long-distance lack of relationship. "I should've called ahead, but I really do need to see her."

"Well . . . let me check."

The nurse didn't ask me in, but she did leave the door open. I took the liberty of following her to the living room. Mrs. Kelly sat on the couch with her eyes closed and her head tilted back.

"She's sleeping," I said with disappointment.

The nurse turned, surprised to find me right behind her. "Maybe you would like to leave a note?"

"I don't think so. I have a situation—"

Mrs. Kelly's voice cut me off. "What situation?"

I silently cheered. "Sorry if I woke you."

"I wasn't asleep," she said, though her eyes were still closed. "What situation?"

I took a step closer. "I have a problem, and I think you might be part of the solution. It's hard to explain." I paused, unsure where to begin. "You see, I found a journal among your things in the trunk."

Her eyes opened a crack. "You woke me for that?"

"It was sewn inside a fur muff. Did you know it was there?"

"Why, is it worth something?"

"Moneywise? Maybe a hundred dollars; that's not why I'm here. I've been reading it."

"If that's the reason you barged in—"

"Please, Mrs. Kelly. This could be very important."

"I think you should come back later," the nurse said. "Mrs. Kelly needs her rest."

"Weren't you going to make me something to eat?" Mrs. Kelly snapped.

As the nurse left the room, I gave her a nod of sympathy. Then I sat on the chair next to the couch. "So I'm guessing you never read the journal. It was written in 1907 and 1908."

Mrs. Kelly didn't react. Her mind seemed to be somewhere else. It was odd to think this was the same person whose birth I'd just read about in Olive's last entries. Loose skin sagged under her cheekbones and jaw. Red-rimmed, glassy eyes sank deep in the sockets. What was it like to look at yourself in the mirror every day and see you'd turned into an old lady? Not that it happened overnight, but still. I couldn't imagine getting used to it. "I'd been assuming the woman who wrote it was your mother. Olive Westcott. Then I realized she wasn't."

"Look, young lady, I'm not interested in going down memory lane."

My cell phone signaled a text. Bettina? Jeff? I didn't bother to look. "I'm sorry if I'm raising an uncomfortable subject. Trust me, there's a good reason why I need to talk with you. Do you know why the journal was sewn inside the muff?"

"I don't see how it's any of your business."

"Actually, it is my business. That's exactly why I need to talk to you, Mrs. Kelly. My business. Today your grandson told me you once lived in my building. At first it seemed like a pretty big coincidence."

"Why? I was searching online for a place to sell my clothes. When I saw the address, I chose your store."

"I know, Rob explained that, but what really surprised me was finding out you once lived in the apartment above the store. I suspect you were born there. Would I be right?"

She scowled with impatience. "Will you get to the damn point?"

That wasn't a denial, so I went on. "Maybe you don't realize I also happen to live there." That didn't get a response, either. "After reading the last entry of the journal, I found out the building was owned by a man named Mr. Vogel. That was when everything fell into place. Olive sewed the journal inside the muff, and no one was supposed to take it out unless there was a fight over Mr. Vogel's will. Since it was still inside the muff when I found it, I'm guessing the will was never contested. Mr. Vogel's daughter—you—stood to inherit some of his real estate. So I'm thinking he might have left my building to you. Would I be right?"

"Why does it matter?"

"You don't know?"

"I'm not a mind reader."

"But you do own the building."

"You should moonlight as a detective."

"So you're my landlord—lady."

"If you've come to complain about your apartment, you can forget about it. Take it to Chuck. That's why I hired him, so I wouldn't have tenants barging into my living room complaining. I got fed up dealing with you people decades ago. Roaches. Plumbing problems. Noisy neighbors. It's an old building! No one expected those tenements to last ten years, much less a hundred. You want new plumbing? Move to Trump Tower."

"That's not why I—"

"I don't care! Now I'm tired," she said, closing her eyes again. "Would you get my nurse? I need to lie down."

"I spoke with Chuck. He was no help. And if I have to give up that retail space, I could very well lose my business."

"So don't give it up."

"But I have to. You're evicting me! I have thirty days to get out."

"Didn't you pay your rent?"

"Of course I did. My rent is always on time for both the store and the apartment. I'm a great tenant. I've never complained about anything. And it's going to be impossible to find something in the same area for what I'm paying."

"Then you must not be paying enough."

"Mrs. Kelly, the East Village isn't SoHo or the West Village. I see empty storefronts around. Plus, I should mention, I won't be able to sell your things if I go out of business."

That announcement motivated her to look straight at me for the first time since I'd entered the room. That was when the shiny gold heart dangling from my neck caught her attention.

"What are you wearing?" She sat up straight as her frail little skeleton would allow and put on a thick pair of reading glasses.

"I found it. In a hatbox. In your storage room."

"I've been looking for that locket for years."

I undid the clasp and handed Mrs. Kelly the necklace. Her trembling fingers had some trouble opening the heart. I offered to help. She ignored me and eventually got it open. When Mrs. Kelly looked at the photographs, her eyes glistened, and I thought she might even shed a tear. "If you don't mind," she said in a gentle soft voice I didn't know she had, "this is something I'd like to keep."

"Of course," I said. "It's yours."

"Olive gave it to me. I used to bother her all the time because I wanted it for myself. She liked to tease me that I'd have to wait until she died." Jane Kelly smiled at the memory. "I didn't have to, though. She gave it to me as a wedding present, so I could wear it the day I married. She even replaced the picture of her own mother and put in the only picture she had of . . ."

She actually choked up. I waited to see if she would cry, but no tears emerged. One or two trickled down my cheek, though, sentimental fool that I am. I wiped them away and made myself press for more details while I had the chance. "Can you tell me how it was that Angelina . . . your mother . . . how she died?"

"Influenza. 1918."

"The epidemic. It must've been devastating. I'm sorry."

"What's it matter now? I'm almost dead myself!" She clicked the locket shut.

I leaned forward and spoke gently. "And I suppose your father . . . he didn't step forward? So Olive took care of you?"

She sighed as if answering me were a defeat. "I was ten. Olive was like a mother to me. Never had her own children."

"I imagine she was focused on her career."

"Oh, yes. She was a buyer at Lord and Taylor for years. Suits, coats, dresses, gowns . . ." Mrs. Kelly stared ahead while rubbing the smooth gold heart with her thumb. "I was always afraid of losing this locket, and then it disappeared. Never thought I'd see it again."

"I'm glad I found it," I said quietly.

Mrs. Kelly put the locket on the coffee table. Then she looked at me like she didn't know who I was. "What is it you want from me?"

"We were talking about the apartment. My eviction." The subject seemed so crass.

"I'm an old lady. An old lady shouldn't have to think about these things."

"I'm sorry."

She took off her glasses, rubbed her eyes, hesitated, put the glasses back on, and then said in a grudging tone: "Get me the phone."

I sprang up and looked around the room but didn't see one.

"Over there, on my desk."

While crossing the room I took in the view and saw the Flatiron standing there like an old friend. I grabbed the phone, a black push-button from the eighties with an extension cord that reached across the room, and placed it on the coffee table next to the necklace.

She punched in a number while muttering something about not being dead yet. Sitting back down on the edge of my seat, I tried to calm myself as the ringing continued. I feared the call would end up in voice mail. Then I heard a voice answer.

"Chuck?" she barked. "East Fourth Street. What's happening with that ground-floor retail space?"

I could hear him talking but couldn't make out what he said.

"Right . . . okay . . . and . . . ? I'm not so sure I like that idea. Because restaurants are a fire hazard, that's why. So who is it? What? Why? You're being greedy. Then why thirty days? Find someone!"

I heard Chuck arguing on the other end.

"Fine, so when you have someone, let me know. In the meantime, renew it for one year at seven percent. What? Look, Chuck, I have another call coming in, gotta go. Just handle it!" She slammed down the receiver. "If it's not one problem, it's another."

My heart pounded as I waited for her to tell me what I was pretty sure I'd heard.

"He wants you out," she said. "Thinks we can get considerably more, especially if we rent to a restaurant, and he's probably right. Lucky for you, he hasn't lined up another tenant yet. The economy isn't exactly roaring back to life, so why should I let the space go empty? I'm raising your rent seven percent and giving you another year."

"Thank you," I said. "You're saving my life, really. This is a huge relief."

She waved away my gratitude. "Lots of restaurants moving into the neighborhood, driving up the rents. A bar wouldn't be so bad . . . those college kids like to drink. You should open a bar."

"I don't know anything about running a bar."

"Times are always changing," she said. "You gotta keep up or you'll fall behind."

"You're right. It's true." What I really needed to do was get over my revulsion of polyester. Stock up on punk, grunge, one-piece jumpsuits, Joan Collins power dresses with oversize shoulder pads. Whether I liked that clothing or not, eighties fashions qualified as vintage for twenty-year-olds, and twenty-year-olds made up the biggest demographic in the neighborhood. I'd probably been fighting the truth because it made me feel old, as if my stubbornness would keep time from moving forward.

"And no promises for next year when that lease comes up, young lady. Don't think you'll be able to sweet-talk my grandson. His sister's a lawyer, and she'll be taking charge of this headache."

"I wouldn't think of asking any more favors." I'd been there, done that with Jeff. "I just want a fair deal. And a year gives me a fighting chance."

I'd put more pieces on eBay. Blog and tweet and get a damn Facebook page if it would help drive those online sales. And maybe I should look into Brooklyn. Stop being such a snob about it. Didn't Olive learn to adjust to her new circumstances?

"And while you're at it," Mrs. Kelly said, "make sure you get a good price on my clothes."

"I will, don't worry."

I wanted to hug her but didn't take her for the hugging type. I wanted to hug Angelina and Olive, too, but that wasn't going to happen. Maybe I'd at least get to hug Rob at some future date. After all, she'd noticed something going on between us—enough to think he'd be vulnerable to sweet talk.

"Oh, one other thing," I said, taking the journal from my hobo bag. "I was going to hand this over to Rob, but I think you'd find it really interesting."

"Please don't," she snapped as I was about to set it on the coffee table. "I'm trying to get rid of things, not take them back."

"But this is Olive's account of her first year in New York. There's a lot about Angelina, too, and how they became friends. I think you'd be fascinated—and it would warm your heart."

"Who ever gave you permission to read that, anyway?"

Our bonding time was obviously over. Time to make a gracious exit. "I should probably get to the store."

"One more thing."

"Yes?" I hoped she'd have something to tell me about Olive or Angelina. Like some gossip about Olive's love life, perhaps a trip to San Francisco to see Joe.

"Will you get that nurse in here?"

"Of course." I hadn't thought to ask if she ever met her Italian grandparents. And what about the hat shop? Did that ever happen? Maybe I'd be able to find out more another day. Or maybe those details would remain among the many mysteries of the past. I entered the kitchen, where the nurse was emptying a package of frozen peas into boiling water. "Mrs. Kelly needs you," I said.

She nodded. "In a minute."

I returned to the living room. "The nurse will be right here. I'm heading out, but I'll be in touch. Thanks again for extending the lease, I really appreciate it."

"You take my advice, young lady. Start thinking more about your future and stop dillydallying in the past."

"I'm sure you're right, Mrs. Kelly." Even so, after a moment of indecision, without saying anything, I set the journal on the coffee table next to the necklace. Mrs. Kelly murmured in protest, but this time she allowed it to remain. And I did notice her lean closer to look at the cover.

I let myself out. While waiting for the elevator, I checked my cell phone. That last text wasn't from Bettina or Jeff. It came from a number I didn't recognize.

Did you find that million dollars in the hatbox?

My heart did a flip-flop as I typed out my answer.

Something even better.

As I saved Rob's number to my contacts, I reminded myself to stop at the pharmacy on the way to the store, though I had a suspicion that my sleep problems might be over. Then I remembered my plans to see Karin and Patricia later that night. Maybe I'd tell them about Rob and the journal over sushi. They'd have fun giving me a hard time about falling for a guy who lived on the other side of the country.

The elevator came and I stepped on. As it descended, I thought how wonderful it would be if I reached the lobby to find it had turned into the ground floor of Wanamaker's. Aisles of mahogany counters, a grand double staircase leading to the mezzanine, eight flights of balconies leading to the glass-domed ceiling . . . Women in long skirts and picture hats would be browsing as organ music played in the background. I waited for the elevator to come to a stop. When the door slid open, I stepped out.

Acknowledgments

I'D LIKE TO acknowledge three "California Girls" for helping this New York novel come to life. First off, thanks to my motivating mom Minnette Lehmann, originally from Sacramento, for repeatedly helping me feel the manuscript was wonderful when I wasn't able to love it enough. Secondly, thanks to my steadfast agent Emma Sweeney, originally from San Diego, for helping me when my manuscript wasn't wonderful and I was loving it too much. Thirdly, thanks to my brilliant editor Heather Lazare, originally from Carmel, whose love for the manuscript helped me get it right where it needed to go. This writer, originally from San Francisco, doesn't know where this novel would be without their insight, enthusiasm, and thoughtful guidance.

And then there are all the other people who gave me insight, enthusiasm, and thoughtful guidance, each in his or her own way: Elizabeth Kandall, Karin Sibrava, Amanda Selwyn, Patricia Kelley, Bill and Elaine Koster, Ellen Twaddell, Julie Carpenter, Leah Pike, Richard Friedman, Marsha Levy Warren, Andres San Martin, Allison Dickens, Jennifer Quinlan, and Lucia della Paolera.

Finally, there is my brood. Thank you to David and Steve Kronovet for being there to hang out with when I wasn't writing, and for not being there when I was. And thanks to Madeleine Kronovet for being the quintessential New Yorker.

Photo Credits

Author's collection: postcards on pp. 135, 136, *top*.

Library of Congress, Prints & Photographs Division—Detroit Publishing Company Collection: p. vi (reproduction number: LC-D4-13619); p. 136, *bottom* (reproduction number: LC-D4-17555); p. 197 (reproduction number: LC-D4-10907 R); p. 198 (reproduction number: LC-D4-9145); p. 199 (reproduction number: LC-D419-51); p. 278, Harry Thaw, circa 1909 (reproduction number LC-DIG-ggbain-04038); Evelyn Nesbit, circa 1900 (Gertrude Kasebier, photographer, reproduction number: LC-DIG-ppmsca-12056); p. 279 (reproduction number: LC-D4-16462); p. 308 East Side tenements, between 1900 and 1910 (reproduction number: LC-DIG-det-4a18586). Library of Congress, Prints & Photographs Division—Bain Collection: p. 306 Metropolitan Tower, 1908 (reproduction number: LC-DIG-ggbain-01486); p. 396 Two women crossing a street, 1911 (reproduction number: LC-USZ62-123183).

Museum of the City of New York: toiletries counter, 1910, Byron Company: p. 307.

The New York Public Library; Astor, Lenox and Tilden Foundations; Milstein Division of United States History, Local History & Genealogy; Photographic Views of New York City; Ewing Galloway, photographer: p. 134.

TOUCHSTONE READING GROUP GUIDE

Astor Place Vintage

FOR DISCUSSION

1. When Amanda first visits Jane Kelly's apartment to assess her clothes, she ponders, "funny how styles from your own parents' day tend to call out with that seductive aura of nostalgia" (page 10). What era's styles appeal to you?

2. While Amanda is being hypnotized, her doctor asks her to think of a place that makes her feel "comfortable and content" (page 29), and she has some difficulty deciding on one. Why do you think it was such a challenge for her? What place would you choose?

3. Olive is both unable and unwilling to rely on financial aid from men—from her father or a potential husband—yet Amanda regularly accepts checks from her married lover, Jeff. Which of the two women seems more modern?

4. Amanda's fascination with history was originally inspired by her collection of Time-Life books called *This Fabulous Century*. She thinks, "I used to pore over every word and stare at the glossy photographs with laser-like eyes trying to take in every detail and see beyond the edges to find aswers to questions I couldn't quite put into words" (pages 74–75). Are there books in your life that have had a similar effect on you?

5. Do you think Olive's father's car accident was a true accident, or was it suicide? If Olive had not been forced to find work to support herself after his death, in what ways might her life have turned out differently?

6. A woman of Olive's socioeconomic background is expected to become a wife and mother; and the idea of working is considered base, and therefore shocking, to friends and family. As a store clerk she is offered low wages and few opportunities for advancement. Despite this, Olive pursues a career. How does this illustrate her character? How do Olive's ways of dealing with change compare to Amanda's? How are their challenges different?

7. Amanda continues to see Jeff even though she knows she shouldn't. Why do you think it's so hard for her to end the affair? Do you see this as a weakness in her character? Does the fact that she dated Jeff before he got married affect your opinion of their affair?

8. When Amanda finds out she is not pregnant, why do you thinks she seems disappointed? How does her pregnancy scare contrast with Olive's?

9. Psychic Lola Cotton seems to contact Olive's dead mother, telling Olive: " 'She wants you to know . . . you must not feel guilty. She forgives you' " (page 49). Olive views this with skepticism. Is she too focused on looking forward to deal with feelings about her mother's death?

10. Amanda wonders whether her whole life is "ruled by nostalgia." She thinks, "The past doesn't just go away; it lingers on. You can actually touch and see the remains, and to the extent that these souvenirs survive, the past is the present. You can't say that for the future. . . . You can never hold the future in your hands" (page 100). Do you agree? Does Amanda spend too much of her life looking back? Why is it so hard for her to leave Jeff? What finally convinces her to do it?

11. As a single woman in the early 1900s, Olive cannot stay alone at a hotel; there are women-only areas in restaurants and bars; the idea of her working is met with significant disapproval; and the Victorian attitudes about women's sexuality leave her ignorant and unprepared. At the end of the book she thinks, "Perhaps the day will come when women exist in the world as equals to men" (page 386). Do you think that day has come? If not, do you think it ever will?

12. The theme of change as constant and unstoppable is present throughout the novel. Is the past always worth leaving behind? Is newer always better? Is it possible to strike a balance between preserving what is worthy about the past while allowing for modern developments?

13. The author leaves the story open at the end, and we never know whether Jane Kelly reads the journal, whether Amanda starts a relationship with Rob, even whether Olive and Angelina ever open a hat shop. Why do you think the author chose to end her book this way? What do you think happens to the characters?

A CONVERSATION WITH STEPHANIE LEHMANN

You are visible online on your personal website and book websites and on Facebook and Twitter. Do you feel these outlets bring you closer to your readers?
Absolutely. I especially like how social media makes it possible for me to enhance the novel with additional material for readers who want to know more. When I was researching *Astor Place Vintage*, I got completely absorbed in early twentieth century New York City, but couldn't begin to use all I learned. There are so many great online resources, and it's great that I can use them to share historical details and photographs on my websites.

Do you ever meet your fans in person? If so, what is the most valuable or helpful aspect of being face-to-face?
I've done lots of readings and enjoy speaking to book clubs. Part of the thrill of getting published is knowing that people are going to engage in a world that I've been immersed in for years and felt passionate about creating. But reading is a solitary, anonymous act. As the author, I don't necessarily experience the fact that this story that is so near and dear to my heart has made an impression. Meeting people face-to-face can be a wonderful way to have a dialogue with readers.

***Astor Place Vintage* is your fifth novel. Does it get easier the more you write? Were there any new challenges this time?**
Every time I start a new novel, I feel like I have to learn how to write one all over again. Part of this is the mental intimidation. It's daunting to create a whole, big "something" from "nothing." The difficulty also comes from the fact that every novel is different and inevitably poses problems that are intrinsic to the world that's being created. I like to compare the process to doing a jigsaw puzzle while the final picture keeps changing as you're trying to find the pieces that fit together.

Astor Place Vintage posed particular challenges because of my decision to set it in two time periods with two main characters whose narratives resonate and come together in a meaningful way. After a few drafts, I realized that it's one thing setting out to do this and quite another to pulling it off. I began with an outline that became obsolete. It took a lot of trial and error to find my way to a story that fulfilled my intention. Almost every revision seemed to set off a domino effect of changes. Keeping track of the details could be mind-boggling. I like to tell people this novel counts as three books: Olive's story, Amanda's story, and the story of both of them melded together.

Each of your previous novels is set in the present, yet *Astor Place Vintage* explores the world of 1907 New York. What inspired you to include this historical aspect, and why did you select that time in particular?

The answer to this question seems to have taken on its own historical narrative, but here goes.

Hoping to find inspiration for a novel idea, I was browsing the shelves of my neighborhood library. A book by Bella Spewack called *Streets: A Memoir of the Lower East Side*, caught my eye. Bella was the name of my grandmother, who could've been Spewack's neighbor if she hadn't gone straight from Ellis Island to join her father in Sacramento. And I lived on the Lower East Side when I was an NYU student. At that time, my one-room walk-up apartment was considered a coveted piece of Manhattan real estate in the "cool and trendy" East Village. But still, it was pretty decrepit, with a low ceiling, tilting floor, no kitchen, no closet, no light, a tiny bathroom, and proverbial cockroaches that roamed, especially at night. I checked out the book.

Bella Spewack's memoir transported me back to the first two decades of the twentieth century in New York City. Having landed there, I didn't want to leave; I launched into a slew of similarly set memoirs and novels, including *81 Sheriff Street* by Gertrude Ford, *Out of the Shadow* by Rose Cohen, *Jews Without Money* by

Michael Gold, *Christ in Concrete* by Pietro Di Donato, *The Rise of David Levinsky* by Abraham Cahan, *Empty Pockets* by Rupert Hughes, *Susan Lennox: Her Fall and Rise* by David Graham Phillips, and *Bread Givers* by Anzia Yezierska.

The idea of writing a novel taking place in New York City in the early part of the twentieth century would seem to have chosen me. Except I still had no idea what that novel might be.

Next came a trip down to the Tenement Museum on Orchard Street. I went on their tour of apartments done up to look just as they had when people lived at that address between 1863 and 1935. I couldn't help but notice . . . these apartments were quite similar to my old East Village apartment. Wow. I'd lived in a place worthy of being a museum exhibit—an authentic tenement straight from history, still standing, still being used! Forgive me if I sound like I've had too much coffee, but in a way, New York is a living museum. Every street offers some historical revelation that you can only hope will survive the city's never-ending makeovers.

I still didn't know how to turn any of this into a novel. But I was more sensitized to the past that surrounded me and began to think differently about my current apartment, where I lived with my husband and two kids. The building went up in 1928. How many families had lived there over the years? I tried to picture people walking from room to room, or looking at themselves in the same built-in mirrors on my bathroom doors. Who slept in my bedroom? Did they have a bed against the same wall? I wished I could see the clothes that used to hang in my closets. What tragedies and celebrations took place in these rooms? Did anyone ever die in these rooms? Did anyone give birth?

The idea of writing a novel that takes place in two time periods took hold. Someone in the present would connect with someone in the past. But who were they? And what were their stories? And how did they connect? Should it take place on the Lower East Side? I still wasn't sure. One thing I did know: they'd both be women. I can't help being more interested in the experiences of living as a female. Still, no story idea came to mind.

Around this point a book I once borrowed from my mother, *Just Looking: Consumer Culture in Dreiser, Gissing, and Zola* by Rachel Bowlby, called out to me from my bookshelf. I'd tried reading it before, attracted by its fun subject of shopping, but had found it too academic. Now I tried again, and this time my interest was piqued by one of the novels she analyzes *The Ladies Paradise* by Émile Zola, which centered on people who work in a huge department store in 1860s Paris.

Department stores. I had fond memories of going downtown in San Francisco when I was a kid to shop at Macy's, the Emporium, City of Paris, and I. Magnin. As a matter of fact, I always thought those happy memories were part of why I was drawn to New York. Downtown San Francisco and the streets of Manhattan were both conducive to my favorite state of being: having lots of people around me with no obligation to speak with them.

I was intrigued enough with Zola's novel to bypass the library and actually purchase a copy. Before I was done reading *The Ladies Paradise*, I knew I wanted the historical sections of my novel to include the setting of a department store. Not the present time sections, though—department stores of today are so dull compared to shopping on the Internet. I love vintage clothes, though, so why not have my present-day character own a vintage clothing store? It made perfect sense. The modern character would romanticize the past, and the character from the past would aspire to be modern.

I still needed to know when my character from the past lived. Initially, I was attracted to the second decade of the 1900s because the style of dresses was so beautiful then—less corseted, with the empire waist in favor. But as my plot took shape, I realized it made sense to set the novel one decade earlier, during the financial panic of 1907. The fashions of that year didn't appeal to me as much, but I was mature enough to accept that what the characters wore couldn't be the decisive factor.

Finally, I was ready to start writing.

Your character Amanda has a love for vintage clothing. Do you share her passion? On your website you discuss hunts for "junktique." Is that more of a draw for you than clothing?

I love going to flea markets and thrift stores, and might be a hoarder. My first vintage obsession was 1930s kitchenware, inspired by a set of bowls inherited from my grandmother. Now, my dining room is filled with cabinets of dishware that will never be used for an actual meal, a collection of vintage paper napkins that shall never wipe a face, greeting cards never to be sent, and shelves of vintage books—most of which I've read. Because I like to sew, I also have stacks of vintage fabrics and jars full of vintage buttons that are waiting for me to stop writing and get crafty.

As for vintage clothes, one closet in my apartment is crammed with dresses from the forties, fifties, sixties, and seventies. They aren't for wearing, so I don't restrict myself to buying what fits. Most of them would make too much of a statement for me to feel comfortable in public. So it's not that I want to be looked at while wearing one of these dresses; I buy them because looking at them gives me pleasure. I might be attracted to the pattern of the fabric, the styling, some particular way the piece conjures a decade . . . or it might just be from an amused sense of "What was that designer thinking?" Also, they were all cheap. I only buy vintage when I'm getting a good deal.

You write about New York, both in the early 1900s and now, with the insight of a true New Yorker. As a native of San Francisco, what originally drew you to New York City? What keeps you there?

I was accepted into the graduate English programs at New York University and also the University of Washington. I'd visited New York a couple times before, hated it, and thought anyone who chose to live there had to be crazy. Seattle, on the other hand, I knew to be beautiful, clean, and filled with "slacker" types like me.

But everyone said that New York City was the place to go if I seriously wanted to "be a writer." I turned Seattle down.

My second semester at NYU, I began dating a guy who was in one of my writing workshops. He happened to be a native New Yorker, and our relationship made it easier for me to get used to the city. About a year later, I moved in with him. Eventually we got married. By then I'd fallen in love—with the city, that is. Sometimes I wonder . . . if I'd gone to school in Washington, would I have married a lumberjack, stayed in Seattle, and written novels set in the Pacific Northwest?

You are married with children, yet the two main characters in the book are single and childless, possibly not by choice for Amanda but in Olive's case, most decidedly. Each character expresses curiosity about motherhood. Did anything in your experience inform this aspect of the book?

I've always focused on aspects of sexuality that challenge my female main characters, so it was only natural for me to delve into how Olive and Amanda grapple, each in her own way, with the prospect of being childless.

This novel is about two businesswomen. They're passionate about their work, and they're conflicted about motherhood and marriage. But the *potential* to have a child is integral to every woman's existence. After all, a woman lives in a body that is equipped to give birth. She grows breasts that are designed to feed an infant, and bleeds out of her vagina for a few days every month from her teen years until menopause. This goes on whether she ever gets pregnant or not.

I think it's amazing how invisible the act of menstruation is in our society. By all appearances, it isn't happening. We've managed to keep blood and its stains underneath our clothing and out of sight. But blood is extremely, even unrelentingly, present in the daily life of a woman—much more than in a man's. This is why I wanted to include a realistic sense of the anticipation, arrival, and presence of blood for my characters.

You include elements of magical realism to enhance your story. Why did you decide to do this?

I don't lean toward mystical or supernatural ways of thinking, and I didn't originally intend to have those elements in the novel. As a matter of fact, in my original concept, the novel was primarily about Olive, and Amanda's story was much less important. I thought she'd mainly serve to bookend the story from the past. But Amanda's role gradually expanded until finally I reached the point of alternating every chapter between the two characters.

In the process of intertwining their stories, I needed to make sure their narratives had a consistent connection, so I began to play with heightening Amanda's sense of being haunted by Olive. Apart from adding some mystery, I think it works to bring the reader in more viscerally to Amanda's fascination with the past and her sense that Olive "speaks to her," or resonates, on an emotional level.

The blurring of reality and fantasy is something I do experience as a writer. Since I'm constantly visiting the make-believe world of the novel, the characters can take on a life of their own. So, for example, I occasionally walk up Sixth Avenue and stare at the building where Siegel-Cooper used to be—now primarily occupied by a Bed, Bath & Beyond. I've had to remind myself that Olive and Angelina never actually worked in that building, and, oh yes, they didn't exist.

The ending of *Astor Place Vintage* is left relatively open, with a few questions unanswered. Do you feel it is more authentic to not have the ending neatly tied together?

Yes, it's more authentic and more in keeping with the themes of the novel.

Amanda remembers staring at the pages of her Time-Life books, wishing she could see beyond the edges. She wants to know more about the people in the photographs and what they were thinking. Olive's journal gives her a chance to do this. But as Amanda reaches the last entries, she dreads finishing. This is partially because she's afraid of what she'll find out, but it's also because she doesn't want to say good-bye to Olive.

When she does finish, parts of Olive's story are unresolved, and Amanda goes to Jane Kelly, hoping for resolution. While she does tie up some loose ends, she also accepts that what's past is past and the entire story can never be known. I think it's important for the reader to experience that same sense of loss along with Amanda.

In earlier drafts, I experimented with giving Amanda more of a chance to question Jane Kelly about what happens to Olive and Angelina after the journal ends. I was never satisfied with these exchanges. Jane Kelly's answers didn't fool me: the author was obviously making arbitrary executive decisions about the fates of these two women.

I do think the important questions are answered enough to satisfy the reader.

Once the story lines of Amanda and Olive come together, and the dramatic action comes to a climax, the story needs to wind down and there's only so much more that can be told. Beyond that, one can guess, based on character, what will happen to a character, but supplying too much information feels false.

Are you currently working on a new project? Will you continue the story lines of Olive or Amanda in any future novels?

I'm working on another historical idea. It doesn't involve Olive or Amanda. But I do like to think about what other interesting items of clothing Amanda might come across, so you never know!

ENHANCE YOUR BOOK CLUB

1. On Stephanie Lehmann's website dedicated to the book, www.AstorPlaceVintage.com, you can find out more about the story, read Stephanie's blog about her passion for vintage clothing and collectables, and discover more about what it was like to live at the turn of the twentieth century. She has a growing collection of New York City historical photographs on www.VintageManhattan.com. Stephanie also has her own website, www.StephanieLehmann.com, where you can learn how she came to be an author and read about some of her thoughts on the process of writing. As a group you can contact her to ask questions or tell her about your discussion.

2. Vintage clothing and fashion are a central element in the book. Have members of your group bring (or better yet, wear) a vintage item of clothing that has special meaning to them. If they don't have clothing, substitute an object that kindles nostalgia. Have each member take turns explaining the importance of her or his contribution.

3. Have members of your group think of a department store, or any store they remember shopping in as a child. Is that store still there? What do you remember about shopping there? Share your stories with one another.

4. If you have access to an Italian bakery, order some pastries to enjoy at your meeting: cannoli, biscotti, rum baba, and especially sfogliatelle.

THE PROCESS OF LEGAL RESEARCH

THE PROCESS OF LEGAL RESEARCH

FOURTH EDITION

CHRISTINA L. KUNZ
Professor of Law

DEBORAH A. SCHMEDEMANN
Professor of Law

MATTHEW P. DOWNS
Professor of Law

ANN L. BATESON
Director of the Law Library
Associate Dean
Professor of Law

all of William Mitchell College of Law

LITTLE, BROWN AND COMPANY
Boston New York Toronto London

Library of Congress Catalog Card No. 96-75340

ISBN: 0-316-50732-6

Fourth Edition

MV-NY

Published simultaneously in Canada by Little, Brown & Company (Canada) Limited

Printed in the United States of America

This book is dedicated to the thousands of students of William Mitchell College of Law who have worked with and helped us to improve these materials during the past fifteen years

and

to the faculty, administration, and staff of William Mitchell College of Law, whose unwavering support for skills instruction has made this book possible.

SUMMARY OF CONTENTS

TABLE OF CONTENTS

7 LOCATE, READ, AND UPDATE PRIMARY AUTHORITY: STATUTES AND CONSTITUTIONS 175

Chapter 9. Administrative Materials

Chapter 10. Rules of Procedure

Chapter 11. Nonlegal Materials

Chapter 12. Developing an Integrated Research Strategy

PREFACE TO THE STUDENT

The book you are holding is the fourth edition of *The Process of Legal Research;* the first was published a decade ago, in 1986. During that decade, some things have changed; some remained the same.

The purpose and strategy of this book have remained the same. Our goals are to instruct you well in the process of legal research: to acquaint you with the sources and vocabulary of legal research, to show you how each source works, to give you a sense of how to combine them into a research process, to establish criteria for excellence in research, to show you how research contributes to the resolution of legal problems. Our teaching strategy is to engage you as fully as possible in actual research problems; this text describes the sources, shows you portions of sources you would use to research a typical client problem, and gives you many opportunities to research realistic client situations yourself.

Yet if you compared this text to its predecessors, you would notice some changes. Some of these changes reflect our attempts to improve the text's usefulness (through visual aids and a consistent streamlined organization, for example). Other changes reflect the evolution of the law; much of the law presented in the feature case did not exist when the first edition was published. Still other changes reflect the revolution in the technology of information; for example, this edition covers the Internet for the first time.

Over the past decade, the stature of lawyers and the public's regard for the legal system have changed as well, generally for the worse. Because this text assists you in learning one of the core skills lawyers employ on behalf of their clients, we hope you reflect on why it is a valuable skill to learn: how you can use research to assist a client with a problem and how you can contribute to the positive development of the law that future law students will come to research.

Christina L. Kunz
Deborah A. Schmedemann
Matthew P. Downs
Ann L. Bateson

March 1996

ACKNOWLEDGMENTS

First and foremost, we would like to recognize the work of our research assistants: Kristen Anderson, Courtney Candalino, Joann Holland, Paula Jensen, Kim Kozar, Darren Lederfine, Renee Michalow, Sjur Midness, Tom Min, Tom Newby, Stella Pagonis, Hassan Saffouri, Jodi Sharrow, Tim Stocking, and Jennifer Tichey. They worked hard, long, and diligently on the new research situations for this edition. We also would like to salute the work of our many research assistants on the previous editions. The perspectives and contributions of our research assistants have been invaluable in making this book more useful for our readers.

More so than other publications by law school faculty, this book draws on the talents and hard work of the College's professional librarians, Anne Abramson, Anne Anderson, Anna Cherry, Pat Dolan, Paul Healey, Betty Karweick, Phyllis Marion, and Paddy Satzer. They tracked down sources, answered our questions, and offered top-notch suggestions.

Professors Eric Janus, Neil Hamilton, and Russ Pannier graciously provided their substantive expertise. Professor Peter Erlinder and former Professor Clifford Greene, now in practice in Minneapolis, were our co-authors on portions of the earlier editions. Former Professor Kevin Millard, now in practice in Colorado, wrote the first draft of a chapter for the first edition of this book, breaking important new ground for his fellow authors.

We are grateful for the expertise of Cal Bonde, our word-processing wizard. She made sense of contorted and detailed revisions; she also constructed sophisticated exhibits from our mere sketches. Judy Holmes has provided valuable administrative support on this edition as well as two previous editions.

The College's faculty and administration have shown considerable interest and support for the project. The financial resources have been constant and unwavering since the day in the spring of 1981 when then-Associate Dean Melvin B. Goldberg gave his blessing to this project with the immortal words: "Of course, none of this is carved in stone. In fact, I take it that this proposal is barely written on paper." Former Dean James Hogg and current Dean Harry Haynsworth have continued that generous support.

This book has been blessed with talented professionals on the publisher's end of the phone. Lisa Wehrle, our editor on this edition, presided over the complex process of assembling the fourth edition; we thank her for her precision, consistency, and calmness. We also want to recognize the excellence of Heather Shaff's redesign and production work, Robert Norton's and Jennifer Bishop's considerable efforts in assembling the art packet, and Joan Horan's work on the copyright permissions for the art packet. The staff of the Boston University law library graciously let us borrow their sources for the photostatting process.

Nick Niemeyer, now head of sales in the law school book division, originally played a key role in bringing our manuscript to the attention of Little, Brown and Company and has since taken an active interest in the book's evolution and progress; we thank him for his keen insights into the market of legal education. Richard Heuser originally acquired the manuscript for this book; we have appreciated his attention, his enthusiasm, his good advice, and his genuine interest in this book. Carol McGeehan took over as the Law School Books Editor at Little, Brown at the outset of the third edition; she has proven to be a fast study and a source of countless good ideas. Her professional talents have enabled this book to continue to break new ground. Elizabeth Kenny has skillfully managed the administrative arm of this book for all four editions.

On a larger scale, we would like to thank the community of legal writing and research teachers who have encouraged us and enriched us over the years with their ideas about the pedagogy of legal skills instruction. The same measure of gratitude and recognition goes to our students, who remain our best source of insights about learning the process of legal research.

We especially thank our spouses, companions, families, and friends for their support and their interest in this project. Every three or four years, they, like us, have been called upon to endure long hours and high stress levels. We thank them from the bottom of our hearts.

We also would like to acknowledge those publishers who permitted us to reprint copyrighted material in this book.

Chapter 2: Identify Research Terms

Illustration 2-1: *The Plain Language Law Dictionary* 74 (Robert E. Rothenberg ed., 1981). Reprinted with permission of Penguin USA.

Reprinted with permission from *Black's Law Dictionary,* 6th ed., pp. 322-23, 325, copyright © 1990 by West Publishing Company. All rights reserved.

Reprinted with permission from *Oran's Dictionary of the Law,* 2nd ed., p. 100, copyright © 1991 by West Publishing Company. All rights reserved.

Burton, *Legal Thesaurus* 115 (2d ed. 1992). Reprinted with permission of Simon & Schuster.

Illustration 2-2: Reprinted with permission from *Ballentine's Law Dictionary,* copyright © by Lawyers Cooperative Publishing, a division of Thomson Information Services, Inc.

Reprinted with permission from *West's Legal Thesaurus/Dictionary: A Resource for the Writer and the Computer Researcher* by William Statsky, p. 273, copyright © 1985 by West Publishing Company. All rights reserved.
Reprinted with permission from *Black's Law Dictionary,* 6th ed., pp. 1471, 1612-13, copyright © 1990 by West Publishing Company.

Chapter 4: Locate, Read, and Update Secondary Sources

Illustration 4-1: Reprinted with permission of Lawyers Cooperative Publishing, a division of Thomson Information Services, Inc., copyright © 1992.
Illustration 4-2: Reprinted from C.J.S., vol. 30, p. 36, copyright © 1992, with permission from the West Publishing Company.
Illustration 4-3: Reprinted with permission of Lawyers Cooperative Publishing, a division of Thomson Information Services, Inc., copyright © 1995.
Illustration 4-4: Reprinted from C.J.S., vol. 30, p. 1, copyright © 1992, with permission from the West Publishing Company.
Illustration 4-5: Reprinted with permission of Lawyers Cooperative Publishing, a division of Thomson Information Services, Inc., copyright © 1992.
Illustration 4-6: Reprinted from C.J.S., vol. 30, p. 2, 1995 Supplement, copyright © 1994, with permission from the West Publishing Company.
Illustration 4-7: Reprinted from 60 *Tennessee Law Review* 905 (1993) by permission of the author, David Ezra, and the Tennessee Law Review Association, Inc.
Illustration 4-8: Copyright © 1996 Information Access Company. Reprinted from the *Current Law Index* ™ with permission.
Illustration 4-9: Copyright © 1996 Information Access Company. Reprinted from the *Current Law Index* ™ with permission.
Illustration 4-10: Reprinted with permission from *Current Law Index,* vol. 15, no. 6, p. 1092 (June 1994). Copyright © 1996 Information Access Company.
Illustration 4-11: *Index to Legal Periodicals & Books,* 1993-1994, p. 803. Copyright © 1993 by The H. W. Wilson Company. Material reproduced with permission of the publisher.
Illustration 4-12: Reprinted from *Shepard's* entry for the Murphy Article, *Shepard's Law Review Citations,* 1990-1995 Supp., at 376. Copyright © 1995 by Shepard's, a subsidiary of The McGraw-Hill Companies. Reproduced by permission. Further reproduction of any kind is strictly prohibited.
Illustration 4-13: Reprinted with permission of Lawyers Cooperative Publishing, a division of Thomson Information Services, Inc., copyright © 1984.
Illustration 4-14: Reprinted with permission of Lawyers Cooperative Publishing, a division of Thomson Information Services, Inc., copyright © 1995.
Illustration 4-15: Reprinted with permission of Lawyers Cooperative Publishing, a division of Thomson Information Services, Inc., copyright © 1993.
Illustration 4-16: *Shepard's* entries for 33 A.L.R. 4th 120 in *Shepard's Citations for Annotations* 1989-95 Supp., at 1011. Copyright © 1995 by Shepard's, a subsidiary of The McGraw-Hill Companies. Reproduced by permission. Further reproduction of any kind is strictly prohibited.
Illustration 4-17: Copyright © 1996 by Matthew Bender & Company, Inc.

Reprinted with permission from *Employment Discrimination* by Lex K. Larson. All rights reserved.

Illustration 4-19: Reprinted with permission from the Library of Congress, copyright © 1995.

Illustration 4-20: Copyright © 1981 by The American Law Institute. Reprinted with the permission of The American Law Institute.

Illustration 4-21: Copyright © 1990 by The American Law Institute. Reprinted with the permission of The American Law Institute.

Illustration 4-22: Copyright © 1994 by The American Law Institute. Reprinted with the permission of The American Law Institute.

Illustration 4-23: *Shepard's* entries for Restatement (Second) of Contracts § 2, in *Shepard's Restatement of the Law Citations* 288. Copyright © 1994 by Shepard's, a subsidiary of The McGraw-Hill Companies. Reproduced by permission. Further reproduction of any kind is strictly prohibited.

Illustration 4-24: Copyright © 1982 by The American Law Institute. Reprinted with the permission of The American Law Institute.

Chapter 6: Locate, Read, and Update Primary Authority: Case Law

Illustration 6-1: Reprinted from *1995 Judicial Staff Directory,* 501, with permission of Ann L. Brownson, copyright © 1995.

Illustration 6-2: Reprinted from *Lukoski v. Sandia Indian Management Co.,* 748 P. 2d 507-10 (N.M. 1988) with permission of the West Publishing Company.

Illustration 6-3: Digest Entries for Master and Servant, 4B N.M. Digest 14 (Supp. 1995). Reprinted with permission from the West Publishing Company.

Illustration 6-4: Descriptive Word Index Entries under Discharge of Servant, in 1 N.M. Digest 443 (1948). Reprinted with permission from the West Publishing Company.

Illustration 6-5: Outline of Master & Servant Topic, in 4B N.M. Digest 10-11 (1965). Reprinted with permission from the West Publishing Company.

Illustration 6-6: *Shepard's* entries for Lukowski v. Sandia Indian Management Co., 748 P. 2d 507, in 2 *Shepard's Pacific Reporter Citations* [Part 7] 649 (1994) & 399 (Supp. March 1995). Copyright © 1995 by Shepard's, a subsidiary of The McGraw-Hill Companies. Reproduced by permission. Further reproduction of any kind is strictly prohibited.

Illustration 6-7: Cover page from *Shepard's Pacific Reporter Citations,* (vol. 87 March 1995 Supp.). Copyright © 1995 by Shepard's, a subsidiary of The McGraw-Hill Companies. Reproduced by permission. Further reproduction of any kind is strictly prohibited.

Illustration 6-8: *Shepard's Abbreviations — Analysis,* in 2 *Shepard's Pacific Reporter Citations* [Part 7] xi-xii (1994). Copyright © 1994 by Shepard's, a subsidiary of The McGraw-Hill Companies. Reproduced by permission. Further reproduction of any kind is strictly prohibited.

Illustration 6-9: Citation List Resulting from Natural Language Search, NM-CS Database. Reprinted from WESTLAW, copyright © 1995, with permission from West Publishing Company.

Illustration 6-10: First page of *Lukowski v. Sandia Indian Management Co.*, NM-CS Database. Reprinted from WESTLAW, copyright © 1995, with permission from West Publishing Company.
Illustration 6-11: First page of *Steiber v. Journal Publishing Co.*, NM-CS Database. Reprinted from WESTLAW, copyright © 1995, with permission from West Publishing Company.
Illustration 6-12: Citation List Resulting from Key Number search, NM-CS Database. Reprinted from WESTLAW, copyright © 1995, with permission from West Publishing Company.
Illustration 6-13: WESTLAW *Shepard's* entry for *Lukowski v. Sandia Indian Management Co.* Reprinted from WESTLAW, copyright © 1995, with permission from West Publishing Company.
Illustration 6-14: WESTLAW QuickCite Screen for *Lukowski v. Sandia Indian Management Co.* Reprinted from WESTLAW, copyright © 1995, with permission from West Publishing Company.
Illustration 6-15: WESTLAW Insta-Cite Screen for *Lukowski v. Sandia Indian Management Co.* Reprinted from WESTLAW, copyright © 1995, with permission from West Publishing Company.

Chapter 7: Locate, Read, and Update Primary Authority: Statutes and Constitutions

Illustration 7-1: The statutes reprinted or quoted verbatim in the following pages are taken from the NEW MEXICO STATUTES ANNOTATED, Copyright © 1993, by The State of New Mexico and The Michie Company. All rights reserved.
Illustration 7-3: Reprinted with permission of Lawyers Cooperative Publishing, a division of Thomson Information Services, Inc., copyright © 1993.
Illustration 7-4: The statutes reprinted or quoted verbatim in the following pages are taken from the NEW MEXICO STATUTES ANNOTATED, Copyright © 1995, by The State of New Mexico and The Michie Company. All rights reserved.
Illustration 7-5: Popular Name Table, in [General Index U-Z] U.S.C.A. 848. Copyright © 1995, with permission of the West Publishing Company.
Illlustration 7-6: Reprinted with permission of Lawyers Cooperative Publishing, a division of Thomson Information Services, Inc., copyright © 1993.
Illustration 7-7: 42 U.S.C.A. § 12102, pp. 630-632. Copyright © 1995, with permission of the West Publishing Company.
Illustration 7-8: Reprinted with permission of Lawyers Cooperative Publishing, a division of Thomson Information Services, Inc., copyright © 1995.
Illustration 7-9: Table 3 — Amendments and Repeals, U.S.C.C.A.N. [11] (Supp. July, 1995) Reprinted with permission of the West Publishing Company.
Illustration 7-10: Copyright © 1995 by Shepard's, a subsidiary of The McGraw-Hill Companies. Reproduced by permission. Further reproduction of any kind is strictly prohibited.
Illustration 7-11: Copyright © 1995 by Shepard's, a subsidiary of The McGraw-Hill Companies. Reproduced by permission. Further reproduction of any kind is strictly prohibited.

Illustration 7-13: Copyright © 1995 by LEXIS-NEXIS. Reprinted with permission from LEXIS-NEXIS, a division of Reed Elsevier Inc. LEXIS® and NEXIS® are registered trademarks and FREESTYLE is a trademark of Reed Elsevier Properties Inc.

Illustration 7-14: Copyright © 1995 by LEXIS-NEXIS. Reprinted with permission from LEXIS-NEXIS, a division of Reed Elsevier Inc. LEXIS® and NEXIS® are registered trademarks and FREESTYLE is a trademark of Reed Elsevier Properties Inc.

Illustration 7-15: Model Employment Termination Act, § 1, 7A U.L.A. 71-72, 75-76 (Supp. 1995). Copyright © 1995 by the National Conference of Commissioners on Uniform State Laws. Reprinted with permission.

Illustration 7-16: Jurisdictions and Acts Table, in *Uniform Laws Annotated Directory of Uniform Acts and Codes: Tables-Index* 48 (West 1995). Copyright © 1995. Reprinted with permission of the West Publishing Company.

Illustration 7-17: Uniform Arbitration Act, 7 U.L.A. 1 (West Supp. 1995). Copyright © 1995. Reprinted with permission of the West Publishing Company.

Illustration 7-18: The statutes reprinted or quoted verbatim in the following pages are taken from the NEW MEXICO STATUTES ANNOTATED, Copyright © 1992, by The State of New Mexico and The Michie Company. All rights reserved.

Chapter 8: Locate, Read, and Update Primary Authority: Legislative Process Materials

Illustration 8-1: Reprinted from *Guide To Congress,* 4th edition, copyright © 1991 with permission of Congressional Quarterly.

Illustration 8-2: Reprinted with permission from The Legislative History of the Americans with Disabilities Act, "Ill. 8-2: Bill: S.933, the bill for ADA of 1990." Copyright © 1996 by LRP Publications, 747 Dresher Road, P.O. Box 980, Horsham, PA 19044-0980. All rights reserved. For more information on this or other products published by LRP Publications, please call (800)341-7874, ext. 274.

Illustration 8-4: Reprinted from U.S.C.C.A.N., copyright © 1990, with permission of the West Publishing Company.

Illustration 8-5: Reprinted from U.S.C.C.A.N., copyright © 1990, with permission of the West Publishing Company.

Illustration 8-7: Reprinted from U.S.C.C.A.N., copyright © 1990, with permission of the West Publishing Company.

Illustration 8-8: Reprinted from U.S.C.C.A.N., copyright © 1990, with permission of the West Publishing Company.

Illustration 8-9: Reprinted with permission of American Association of Law Libraries, Fred B. Rothman & Co., and Nancy P. Johnson, copyright © 1993.

Illustration 8-10: 42 U.S.C.A. § 12102, p. 630. Copyright © 1995, with permission of the West Publishing Company.

Illustration 8-11: Reprinted from U.S.C.C.A.N., copyright © 1990, with permission of the West Publishing Company.

Illustration 8-12: Copyright © 1990 by Congressional Information Service, Inc. (Bethesda, MD). All rights reserved. Reprinted with permission.
Illustration 8-13: Copyright © 1990 by Congressional Information Service, Inc. (Bethesda, MD). All rights reserved. Reprinted with permission.
Illustration 8-14: Copyright © by Congressional Information Service, Inc. (Bethesda, MD). All rights reserved. Reprinted with permission.
Illustration 8-15: Copyright © by Congressional Information Service, Inc. (Bethesda, MD). All rights reserved. Reprinted with permission.

Chapter 9: Locate, Read, and Update Primary Authority: Administrative Materials

Illustration 9-7: *Shepard's Code of Federal Regulations Citations* (Part 2, 1994). Copyright © 1994 by Shepard's, a subsidiary of The McGraw-Hill Companies. Reproduced by permission. Further reproduction of any kind is strictly prohibited.
Illustration 9-10: General Index in *Labor Relations Reporter, Master Index* (June 1995). Reprinted with permission from *Labor Relations Reporter.* Copyright by The Bureau of National Affairs, Inc. (800-372-1033)
Illustration 9-11: *Labor Relations Expediter* in *Labor Relations Reporter* (October 1988). Reprinted with permission from *Labor Relations Reporter.* Copyright by The Bureau of National Affairs, Inc. (800-372-1033)
Illustration 9-12: List of Major Expediter Chapters in *Labor Relations Expediter* in *Labor Relations Reporter.* Reprinted with permission from *Labor Relations Reporter.* Copyright by The Bureau of National Affairs, Inc. (800-372-1033)
Illustration 9-13: 29 C.F.R. § 103.2 as reprinted in Text of Laws and Regulations in *Labor Relations Expediter* in *Labor Relations Reporter* (August 1994). Reprinted with permission from *Labor Relations Reporter.* Copyright by The Bureau of National Affairs, Inc. (800-372-1033)
Illustration 9-14: N.M. statutory materials from *State Laws* (Minnesota to Wyoming) in *Labor Relations Reporter* (November 1994). Reprinted with permission from *Labor Relations Reporter.* Copyright by The Bureau of National Affairs, Inc. (800-372-1033)
Illustration 9-15: Labor Relations Outline of Classifications in *Master Index* in *Labor Relations Reporter.* Reprinted with permission from *Labor Relations Reporter.* Copyright by The Bureau of National Affairs, Inc. (800-372-1033)
Illustration 9-16: *Labor Relations Cumulative Digest and Index 1986-1990.* Reprinted with permission from *Labor Relations Reporter.* Copyright by The Bureau of National Affairs, Inc. (800-372-1033)
Illustration 9-17: *Labor Relations Cumulative Digest and Index* in *Master Index* in *Labor Relations Reporter* (September 1995). Reprinted with permission from *Labor Relations Reporter.* Copyright by The Bureau of National Affairs, Inc. (800-372-1033)
Illustration 9-18: *Meyer Industries, Inc.,* 123 L.R.R.M. 1137 (September

1987). Reprinted with permission from *Labor Relations Reference Manual.* Copyright by The Bureau of National Affairs, Inc. (800-372-1033)

Illustration 9-19: *Shepard's Labor Law Citations* (Part 10, 1995). Copyright © 1995 by Shepard's, a subsidiary of The McGraw-Hill Companies. Reproduced by permission. Further reproduction of any kind is strictly prohibited.

Chapter 10: Locate, Read, and Update Primary Authority: Rules of Procedure and Ethics

Illustration 10-1: Rule 4(h), in *Federal Civil Judicial Procedure and Rules* 20. Copyright © 1995, reprinted with permission of West Publishing Company.

Illustration 10-2: Rule 4(h) Comments of Advisory Committee, in *Federal Civil Judicial Procedure and Rules* 30. Copyright © 1995, reprinted with permission of West Publishing Company.

Illustration 10-3: Table of Contents, in *Federal Civil Judicial Procedure and Rules* vii. Copyright © 1995, reprinted with permission of West Publishing Company.

Illustration 10-4: Appendix of Forms, Form 1 — Summons, in *Federal Civil Judicial Procedure and Rules.* Copyright © 1995, reprinted with permission of West Publishing Company.

Illustration 10-5: 4A Wright & Miller, *Federal Practice and Procedure* §§ 1100-1101 (2d ed. 1987 & Supp.). Copyright © 1995, reprinted with permission of West Publishing Company.

Illustration 10-6: Reprinted with permission of Lawyers Cooperative Publishing, a division of Thomson Information Services Inc., copyright © 1991-93.

Illustration 10-7: Reprinted with permission of Lawyers Cooperative Publishing, a division of Thomson Information Services Inc., copyright © 1991-93.

Illustration 10-8: Reprinted with permission of Lawyers Cooperative Publishing, a division of Thomson Information Services Inc., copyright © 1995.

Illustration 10-9: Reprinted with permission of Lawyers Cooperative Publishing, a division of Thomson Information Services Inc., copyright © 1995.

Illustration 10-10: Document List Screen for Wright & Miller, *Federal Practice and Procedure* (2d ed. 1987). Copyright © 1987, reprinted with permission of West Publishing Company.

Illustration 10-11: Screen showing § 1100 from Wright & Miller *Federal Practice and Procedure* (2d ed. 1987). Copyright © 1996, reprinted with permission of West Publishing Company.

Illustration 10-12: The statutes reprinted or quoted verbatim in the following pages are taken from the NEW MEXICO STATUTES ANNOTATED, Copyright © 1992, by The State of New Mexico and The Michie Company. All rights reserved.

Illustration 10-13: Model Rules of Professional Conduct Rule 4.2 and Comments (1994). Reprinted by permission of the American Bar Association.

Illustration 10-14: *Annotated Code of Professional Responsibility* 277, 331 (1979). Reprinted with permission from the American Bar Foundation.

Illustration 10-15: The statutes reprinted or quoted verbatim in the following pages are taken from the NEW MEXICO STATUTES ANNOTATED, Copyright © 1995, by The State of New Mexico and The Michie Company. All rights reserved.

Illustration 10-16: ABA Comm. on Ethics and Professional Responsibility, Formal Op. 359 (1991). Reprinted by permission of the American Bar Association.

Illustration 10-17: Model Rules of Professional Conduct, Table A, at 118 (1994). Reprinted by permission of the American Bar Association.

Illustration 10-18: 2 Hazard & Hodes, *The Law of Lawyering: A Handbook on the Model Rules of Professional Conduct,* p. 737, Sec. 4.2:106. Published by Prentice Hall Law & Business, copyright © 1994, with permission from Aspen Law & Business.

Illustration 10-19: 16 *Shepard's Professional and Judicial Conduct Citations* [No. 1] 125 (Nov. 1995). Reproduced by permission of Shepard's, a subsidiary of The McGraw-Hill Companies. Further reproduction of any kind is strictly prohibited.

Illustration 10-20: Reprinted with permission from LEXIS-NEXIS, a division of Reed Elsevier Inc. LEXIS® and NEXIS® are registered trademarks and FREESTYLE is a trademark of Reed Elsevier Properties Inc.

Chapter 11: Incorporate Nonlegal Materials

Illustration 11-1: Fielding, *Smoking: Health Effects and Control,* 313 New Eng. J. Med. 491 (1985). Reprinted by permission of The New England Journal of Medicine, copyright © 1985.

Illustration 11-2: *Nicotine Addiction* as obtained through the Internet. Reprinted with permission from The American Heart Association.

Illustration 11-3: Reprinted with permission from LEXIS-NEXIS, a division of Reed Elsevier Inc. LEXIS® and NEXIS® are registered trademarks and FREESTYLE is a trademark of Reed Elsevier Properties Inc.

Illustration 11-4: Copyright © 1992 by The Roper Center for Public Opinion Research, University of Connecticut, Storrs. Reprinted by permission.

THE PROCESS OF LEGAL RESEARCH

1 INTRODUCTION

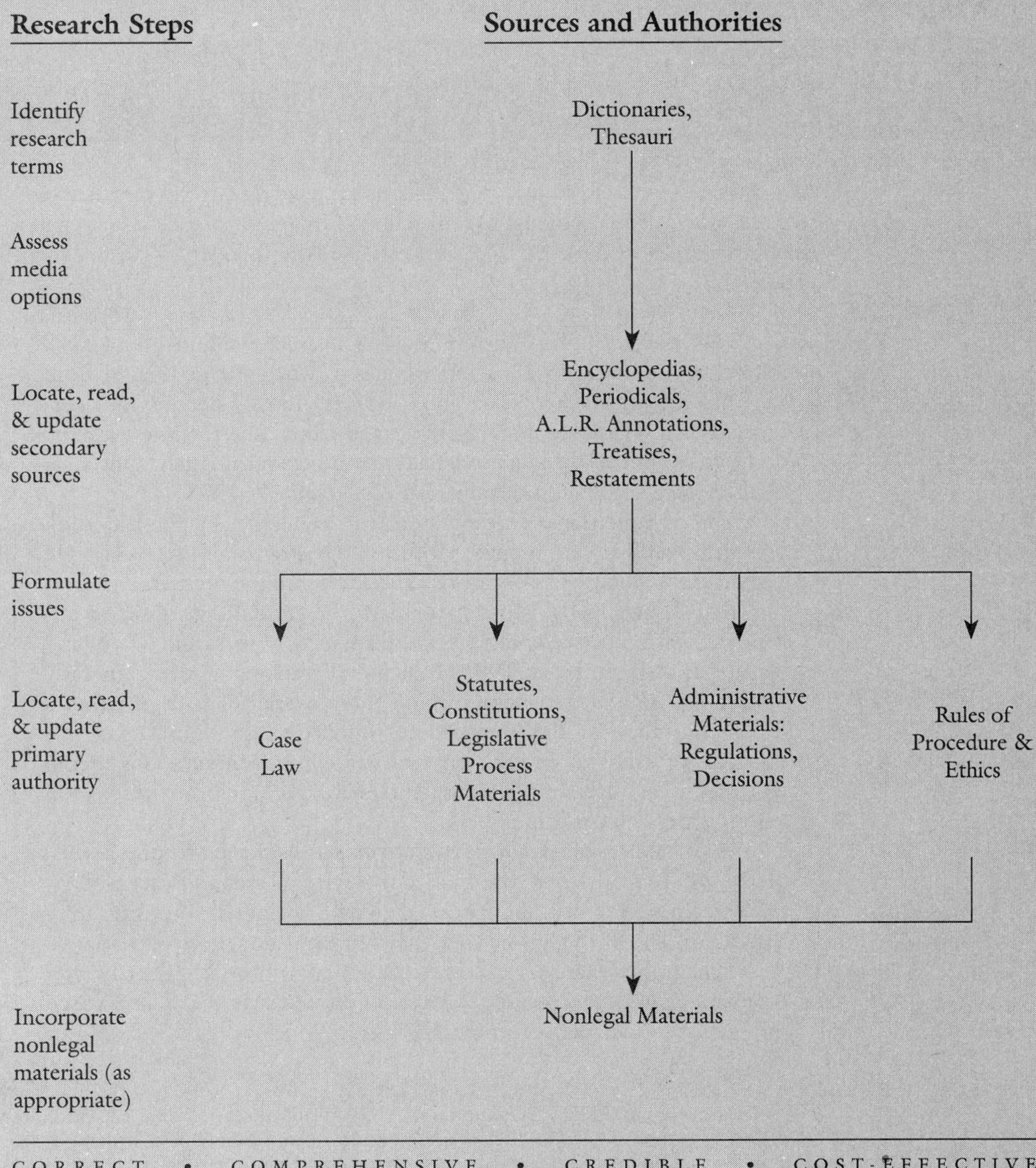

CORRECT • COMPREHENSIVE • CREDIBLE • COST-EFFECTIVE

Summary of Contents

A. The Canoga Case and the Role of Legal Research

As a lawyer or legal assistant,* you will conduct legal research as one of several steps in solving the problems of your clients. Imagine yourself a lawyer in a small firm in Taos, New Mexico, and consider the following fictional client problem:

> Your client, Emilia Canoga, began her career as a flutist for a small symphony orchestra in Taos, New Mexico, when she graduated from the Juilliard School five years ago. She has enjoyed her job and performed well. However, she has disagreed from time to time with the orchestra's general manager, especially over personnel issues. One such disagreement led to her termination on January 7, 1995.
>
> Throughout the preceding year, the general manager had been pressuring all smoking members of the orchestra to quit smoking. He argued that smoking is a health risk and increased the orchestra's health care costs substantially. More particularly, he argued that smoking impairs the wind capacity, and hence performance, of brass and woodwind players. In September of 1994, he banned smoking at work. In early December, he issued a memo asking these musicians to sign either a statement indicating that they did not smoke, whether on-duty or off-duty, or a pledge to embark on a no-smoking program. This memo was met with varying reactions and provoked significant discussion among the orchestra's members.
>
> In particular, Ms. Canoga, a smoker who had tried to quit several times, was perturbed by the manager's early efforts and incensed by the December memo. She returned it with a signed note indicating that she intended to sign neither the statement nor the pledge.
>
> The general manager called Ms. Canoga to his office shortly after receiving the note. A heated discussion ensued. Ms. Canoga accused the general manager of overstepping his bounds as an employer

*This text has several primary audiences: students in law schools, lawyers, students in legal assistant programs, and legal assistants. For ease of discussion, we generally refer to lawyers or law students; we trust that readers who plan to be or are legal assistants will read "legal assistant" where appropriate.

and intruding into her personal life. He told her she was fired for insubordination. Ms. Canoga angrily left his office.

Two days later, Ms. Canoga received her paycheck with a note stating that her employment was no longer needed by the orchestra. Ms. Canoga sought advice from a senior colleague about how to get her job back. He suggested that she exercise her right to plead her case before the board of directors, as stated in the orchestra's employee handbook. The handbook reads:

> It is the Orchestra's intent to resolve all employment disagreements amicably. If at any time, during your employment or thereafter, you are unable to resolve a disagreement by discussing the issue with management, you may bring the matter to the board. The board will make every effort to listen to both sides and facilitate a just solution.

Ms. Canoga wrote a letter to the board president requesting board consideration of her termination according to the handbook. About a week later, she received a letter stating that the board was aware of her situation, believed management had handled it appropriately, did not intend to revisit the topic, appreciated her contributions to the orchestra, and wished her well in her future endeavors.

In asking a lawyer for assistance, Ms. Canoga is seeking not just sympathy, but a resolution of her problem according to the law and within the legal system. The lawyer's role in bringing about that resolution is described well in the first rule of a widely adopted ethics code for lawyers: "A lawyer shall provide competent representation to a client. Competent representation requires the legal knowledge, skill, thoroughness and preparation reasonably necessary for the representation." Model Rules of Professional Conduct Rule 1.1 (1995).

In Ms. Canoga's case, as in any client representation, the lawyer employs various skills to solve the problem: listening to Ms. Canoga to determine the facts of her situation and her interests; investigating the facts through other sources; researching the law; analyzing the facts in light of applicable legal rules; identifying and assessing means of obtaining a resolution, such as negotiating with the orchestra's lawyer, mediating the case, working through a government agency, or pursuing civil litigation; advocating for Ms. Canoga in those processes, in writing and orally; and, along the way, helping Ms. Canoga to determine which actions should be taken on her behalf.

This text teaches you how lawyers acquire the legal knowledge necessary for competent client representation. It focuses on a critical skill lawyers employ on behalf of clients: legal research. As Ms. Canoga's advocate, you could not assess the strengths and weaknesses of her case against the orchestra if you did not know the law applicable to her situation; nor could you negotiate effectively with the orchestra's lawyer or argue her case convincingly before a tribunal without a firm understanding of the law. Similarly, if you served as an advocate for an employer association before a legislature or administrative agency contemplating new laws on employee privacy, you must be well informed about the current state of the law. Knowledge of the law also is critical to lawyers acting as advisors. For example, had the orchestra sought a lawyer's advice before adopting its no-smoking policy, that lawyer could be of service only if he or she knew the legal constraints on employers in such situations.

Furthermore, legal research is central to the ethical obligation that runs concurrent with client representation: service to the legal system. *See* Preamble to Model Rules of Professional Conduct (1995). As Ms. Canoga's advocate, you would ensure the proper functioning of the legal system as a peaceful mode of resolving disputes, and you would contribute to the rational development and application of the law if the dispute entered the court system and yielded a judicial decision. As the lawyer advising the orchestra, you would seek to secure the orchestra's compliance with applicable legal rules. In either setting, you could not fulfill these roles without a firm understanding of the applicable law.

Thus it is fitting and not surprising that incompetent legal research can have serious personal consequences for the lawyer. Failure to know the law may lead to disciplinary action. *See, e.g., People v. Yoakum,* 552 P.2d 291 (Colo. 1976); *Nebraska State Bar Ass'n v. Holscher,* 230 N.W.2d 75 (Neb. 1975). Inadequate research also may result in liability to the client for legal malpractice. For example, in *Smith v. Lewis,* 530 P.2d 621 (Cal. Sup. Ct. 1975), the court approved an award of $100,000 against a lawyer who had failed to apply principles of law commonly known to well informed attorneys and to discover principles readily accessible through standard research techniques. Furthermore, no attorney can afford to tarnish his or her professional reputation by becoming known for poor research.

B. Categories of Legal Research Materials

In researching Ms. Canoga's case as her lawyer, you would encounter a wide range of materials, as this text will demonstrate. Materials used in legal research are not all created equal; rather, the law is a strongly hierarchical field. This part describes that hierarchy, which is depicted in Exhibit 1.1 on page 5.

1. Primary Authority

"Primary authority"* constitutes the law. It is issued by a branch of the government acting in its lawmaking capacity. In basic terms, American law emanates from three types of government bodies: the legislature, the judiciary, and administrative agencies.

*This text uses the term "authority" to refer to the content of research materials, while "source" refers to the publication in which they are located.

Exhibit 1.1 Hierarchy of Legal Sources.

Primary Authority

Legislation
Judicial case law
Administrative regulations and decisions
Rules of procedure and ethics

Secondary Authority

Encyclopedias
Periodicals
A.L.R. annotations
Treatises
Restatements

Finding Tools

Digests
Citators
Other primary and secondary authorities

First, legislative bodies at the federal, state, and local levels create constitutions, statutes, charters, and ordinances. Constitutions and charters create the government and define the rights of citizens vis-à-vis the government. Statutes and ordinances regulate a wide range of behavior by individuals, private entities, and the government; legislation typically is written in broad, general terms. It is interpreted according to the legislature's intent, thus rendering the materials created during the legislative process of some importance.

Second, the federal and state judiciaries decide cases based on specific disputes that have arisen between two litigants (whether individuals or entities). In doing so, a court not only resolves the dispute for the litigants but also creates precedent. Precedent is the result, rule, and reasoning in a decided case to be followed in the resolution of future similar disputes.

Third, administrative agencies at the federal, state, and local levels generate law through two chief mechanisms. Agencies promulgate regulations, which resemble statutes in that they address a range of behavior and are stated in general terms. Agencies also issue decisions, which resemble judicial cases in that they simultaneously resolve specific disputes and stand as precedent for future disputes.

Any particular area of law is likely to be governed by some combination of legislative, judicial, and administrative agency law. Although it is possible that a legal problem will be governed solely by a statute or by a line of judicial opinions, it is more likely that a statute and case law will operate together. For example, the legislature may have passed a statute that the courts have interpreted in specific disputes. In a more complicated example, the legislature may have created an agency by statute, that agency may have promulgated a regulation and then applied it in a series of agency decisions, and the courts may then have reviewed the agency's actions in a series of judicial opinions.

In addition, all three branches also create rules governing the functioning of the legal system. Rules governing the operation of the court system are created by the legislature, courts, or jointly. The procedural rules promulgated by an agency govern litigation before the agency.

For any particular client's situation, some primary authority will be weightier than other primary authority. In most situations, the weightier primary authority is the mandatory (binding) authority emanating from the legislature, courts, or agency within the jurisdiction of the situation. The less weighty primary authority is the persuasive authority emanating from another jurisdiction.

For example, as you will see, the Canoga case is governed by the following forms of primary authority: statutes, judicial cases, regulations, and agency decisions at the federal level; a New Mexico state statute and New Mexico judicial cases; and rules governing litigation within the federal or New Mexico state courts (depending on where a suit might be brought).* All of these authorities are mandatory because they emanate from the federal or New Mexico governments, which have the power to regulate the Canoga situation. If there were less extensive mandatory authority, you might look to persuasive authority, such as judicial cases from neighboring states.

2. Secondary Authority

Secondary authority is defined by what it is not: It is not primary authority. Rather, it is created by individuals and nongovernmental bodies. Because most secondary authority comments on the law, it also is called "commentary." Some secondary authority represents the author's attempt to state what the law should be, and some of this secondary authority has proven influential with lawmakers.

You will find that some secondary sources resemble sources you have seen before in other fields, such as encyclopedias, treatises, and periodical articles. Some secondary sources have formats unique to the law, such as *American Law Reports* annotations and the Restatements.

Every secondary source has its particular place in legal research. For example, encyclopedias provide broad overviews, periodical articles provide

*The text does not present all authority pertinent to the Canoga case, although it presents major authorities on point.

arguments for law reform, *American Law Reports* annotations provide insight into rules that vary across jurisdictions, and the Restatements provide distilled rules of law that have been adopted in some jurisdictions.

3. Finding Tools

As you would no doubt guess, you will need assistance in locating pertinent materials in primary and secondary authorities. Finding tools help you to do so. Many authorities operate as finding tools for other authorities; for example, a court may refer in its opinion to another important case, or a treatise author may list cases from which he or she has drawn the legal rule under discussion. In addition, some materials used in legal research carry no authority themselves, but rather operate as finding tools for other authorities. Examples are case digests and *Shepard's Citations.* While these nonauthorities appear at the bottom of the hierarchy of legal materials, they are critical because they lead you to legal authority.

4. A Caveat about Media

The three categories of legal materials described above—primary authority, secondary authority, and finding tools—appear in various media. These media include paper, microforms, CD-ROMs, and online databases. While you must know how to research in all media, the more critical distinction for purposes of legal research is the type of authority, as described in this part, not the medium. The medium in which a source is published does not affect its place in the hierarchy of legal research sources.

C. The Process of Legal Research

As the previous part suggests, legal research materials are voluminous and complex. If your research is to be competent, you must use these materials well by researching strategically. Webster's defines "strategy" as "the art of devising or employing plans or stratagems toward a goal." *Merriam-Webster's Collegiate Dictionary* 1162 (10th ed. 1993). Your goal is research that meets the following criteria:

- *correct:* the law that governs your client's facts and that applies to the time the situation occurred;
- *comprehensive:* necessary mandatory primary authority, helpful persuasive primary authority, and useful secondary authority;
- *credible:* authority that carries weight because of its quality and the expertise of its authors;

- *cost-effective:* results that justify the efforts devoted to research, in light of the client's interests and available research options.

These criteria are further developed throughout this text.

To research strategically, you must have a plan or stratagem. For most research projects, your plan will proceed through the following stages:

- Identify research terms.
- Assess your media options.
- Locate, read, and update secondary sources to find background and primary authority references.
- Formulate issues for research in primary authority.
- Locate, read, and update primary authority (the law).
- Incorporate nonlegal materials (as appropriate).

You may wonder why secondary sources precede primary authority in this sequence, if primary is superior to secondary in the hierarchy. There are several reasons (developed further in Chapter 4): Secondary sources generally are more accessible when you know little about a topic. They provide references to and an overview of primary authority, permitting you to locate primary authority and fit it into a framework developed by an expert.

Your specific research plan will vary somewhat from project to project, of course, reflecting the difficulty of the topic, your knowledge of it, the time available, and other factors. For example, you will need to decide which of various similar commentary sources to consult, which media to employ for a source appearing in more than one medium, and how much persuasive authority (if any) to explore. As you make these judgments with skill, flexibility, and creativity, you will see that legal research is not a mechanical process, but rather an art in its own way.

Furthermore, although this list suggests that research is a tidy linear process, research actually is an untidy "linear-with-loops" process. The general course of most research projects tracks the steps set forth above—but with frequent backward loops along the way. For example, if your initial set of research terms yields no useful authority, you will need to return to the first stage to identify additional terms. As another example, you may encounter a reference to a promising article or treatise (secondary source) within a case (primary authority) and decide to return briefly to that secondary source to pursue that lead. As a final example, after you have completed your research in primary authority, you may find yourself quite puzzled about how to synthesize the primary authority and may seek additional assistance in secondary sources. These loops "backward" do not signify that your research has gone awry; they are standard events in legal research.

Finally, as noted already, the research process described in this book is only one of several related phases of legal representation. As with legal research, the broader process of legal representation is linear-with-loops. For example, you very often will return to legal research or exploration of the facts during the writing process when you realize that you are missing critical information.

D. The Organization of This Text

Not surprisingly, the organization of this text mirrors the sequence of research steps suggested in Part C, as follows:

- Identify research terms. Chapter 2.
- Assess your media options. Chapter 3.
- Locate, read, and update secondary sources to find background and primary authority references. Chapter 4.
- Formulate issues for research in primary authority. Chapter 5.
- Locate, read, and update primary authority (the law). Chapters 6-10.
- Incorporate nonlegal materials (as appropriate). Chapter 11.

This sequence also is presented at the beginning of each chapter in flowchart form. See page 1. At the same time, each chapter is designed to stand on its own; thus it also is possible to take the chapters "out of order."

Several chapters develop analytical processes key to successful research: Chapter 2 on developing research terms, Chapter 3 on assessing media, and Chapter 5 on developing research issues for primary research. These chapters, which are relatively short, aim to provide you with structured means of performing these three critical analytical steps.

For the most part, each of the remaining chapters covers a type of authority; stated another way, each covers a set of closely related research materials. For example, Chapter 4 covers secondary sources, and Chapter 6 covers case law sources. Each of these chapters follows a standard format reflecting the following questions: What is the source? Why would you research in it? How do you research in it? What else should you know? And how do you cite it? Two of these subtopics merit a word or two of explanation.

First, as to the "how do you research in it" discussion: The discussion generally leads off with research in paper media and then demonstrates an alternative, such as online or CD-ROM research. We have selected this order for several reasons. You are likely to understand a source or tool best if you first encounter it in paper media because its features and relationships to other sources are most apparent in paper. Despite today's many technological advances, for many materials, paper is still the most useful medium. Finally, during your time in law school or when you practice, you may not have access to other media, but you are likely to have paper media available for most materials.

It is important that you realize that this text does not demonstrate all non-paper media for all sources. Rather, we have selected an alternative medium or two for each source as follows:

Secondary sources (Chapter 4):	CD-ROM (for periodicals)
	online catalog (for treatises)
Case law (Chapter 6):	WESTLAW (online service)
Statutes (Chapter 7):	LEXIS (online service)
Legislative process (Chapter 8):	CD-ROM and LEXIS
Administrative materials (Chapter 9):	Internet (online service)
Rules of procedure (Chapter 10):	CD-ROM
Nonlegal materials (Chapter 11):	various

Because the various technologies operate similarly across sources, you can adapt what is said in one chapter to sources covered in another chapter. For example, if you wished to research cases in LEXIS, you could extrapolate from the LEXIS demonstration in the chapter on statutes. Furthermore, the information in the chapters listed above is intended to be supplemented by Chapter 3 on assessing media options and by the user information provided by the vendors of these rapidly evolving services.

Second, as to the "how do you cite it" discussion: Citation is the practice of providing the reader with a precise reference to a source. As you will see, legal citation is complicated and technical—but also manageable if you work through it in a systematic way. This text provides you with starting information on citation and refers you to the predominant manual on legal citation, *The Bluebook: A Uniform System of Citation* (15th ed. 1991).

Almost every chapter of this text is written in several modes: The text first describes its topic in general, abstract terms. This description is followed by a specific example—the Canoga case introduced at page 2. Several types of visuals also are interspersed throughout the text: flowcharts and exhibits, such as those at pages 1 and 5 in this chapter, and illustrations, or photocopies of legal research materials pertinent to the Canoga case, such as those on pages 47 and 48 in Chapter 4.

Furthermore, the problem sets at the end of the text present you with fairly straightforward client situations to research, using the materials and following the steps covered in the text. Working the problem sets will not make you an accomplished researcher; no single practice opportunity could do that for a skill as complicated as legal research. The problem sets do afford you the opportunity to put what you have learned into practice and to acquaint yourself with the sources available to you in the law library.

The final chapter, Chapter 12, is an epilogue. It is structured differently from the other chapters and does not explore the Canoga case. Rather it poses a new client situation to research and shows you how several law students researched that problem using the materials and steps described here. You will see that their research processes vary, yet resemble each other in important ways. Their common threads are important lessons to learn as you complete your study of legal research.

2 Identify Research Terms

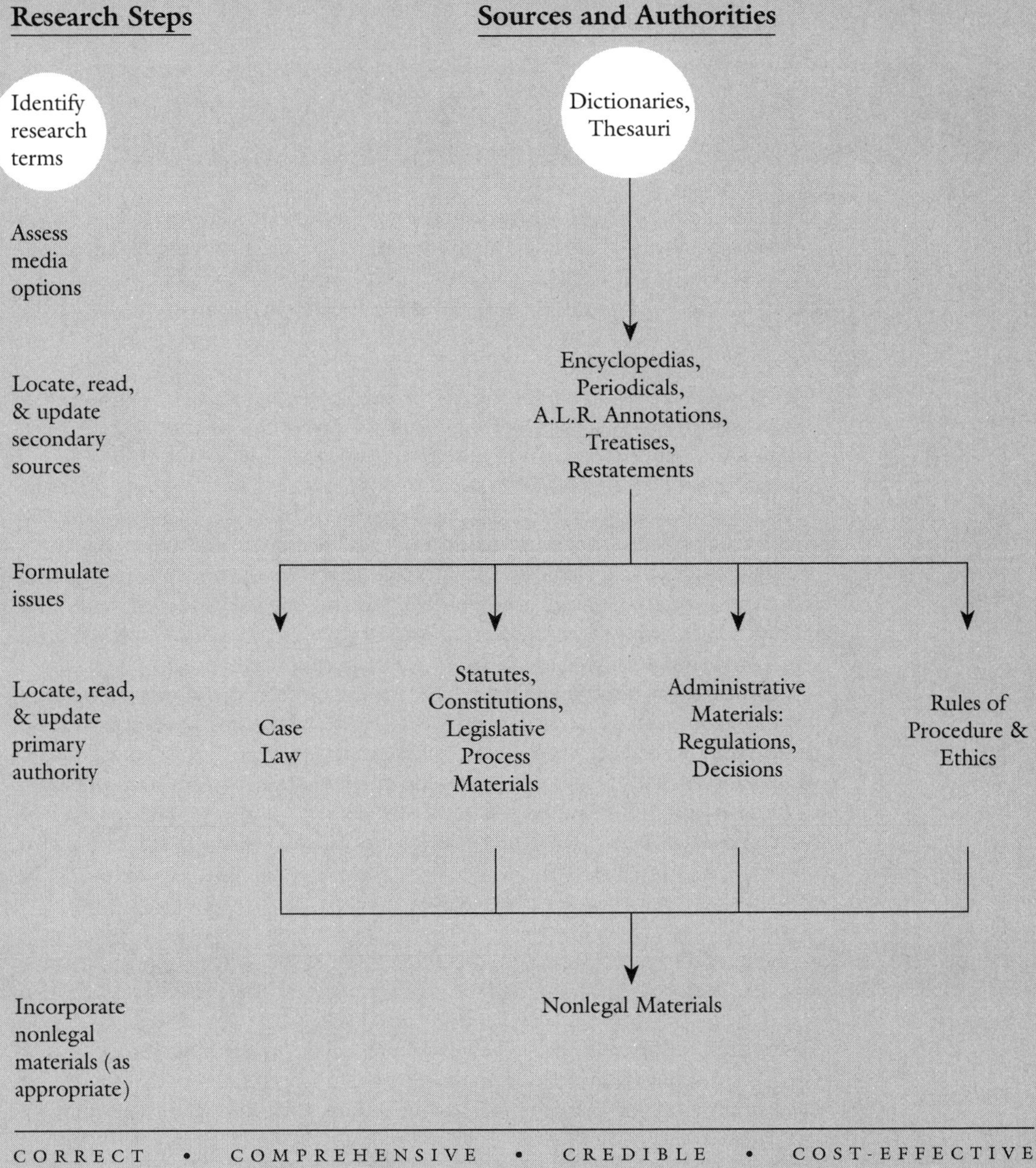

CORRECT • COMPREHENSIVE • CREDIBLE • COST-EFFECTIVE

Summary of Contents

A. Factual and Legal Concepts in the Law

Legal research begins as a search for words because the law finds expression in language. Some of the law's words describe the factual aspects of a situation, while others describe the legal consequences of the situation. Consider, for example, the following legal rule (which you will learn more about in Chapter 7):

> It is **unlawful** for an *employer to . . . require* as a condition of employment that any *employee . . . abstain from smoking during nonworking hours.* . . . Any employee **claiming to be aggrieved** by [such an] **unlawful action** . . . may bring a **civil suit** for **damages**. . . .

The factual aspects appear in italics; the legal consequences are in boldface.

Secondary authority also refers to factual and legal concepts in language that typically is quite similar to that used in the law itself. For example, the text and index of a treatise describing the rights of smoking employees will use words similar, if not identical, to those highlighted above.

Thus, your preliminary research task is to discern the words most likely used in legal sources pertaining to your client's situation. You then will use these words, or research terms, to locate pertinent sources and passages within those sources. This task is essentially the same whether you research in paper, CD-ROM, or online sources. Hence, time spent at the very beginning of the research process in carefully developing research terms is time very well spent.

B. Eight Categories of Concepts

To develop a thorough list of research terms, you must think through your client's situation from various angles. You should consider both factual and legal dimensions of the situation, to the extent your knowledge permits.

1. Five Fact Categories

At the beginning of the research process, you will know some facts of your client's situation. You may not know all of the facts, however, for a variety of reasons. For example, if you are litigating a case for a client, you may start with only the client's view of the case and research those facts, before learning the opponent's view. Or, if you are advising a client about a future transaction, some facts may not have occurred yet. Nonetheless, you should analyze carefully what you do know about what has occurred or is likely to occur.

To generate a thorough list of factual concepts and potential research terms, ask yourself the following five questions:

(1) *Who is involved?* The answer may be people or legal entities, such as a corporation or government body. Focus not on the exact identity of each participant, but rather on their roles and their relationships.
(2) *What is involved?* The answers may be physical items, intangible items, or activities.
(3) *When did (or will) the important events occur?* Focus not only on the precise date and time, but also on the sequence of events and the significance of their timing.
(4) *Where did (or will) the important events occur?* Again focus not only on the precise location, but also on the significance of the location.
(5) *Why did (or will) the participants act in this way?* Analyze their motives or states of mind.

Of course, not every factual concept you list will prove to be a useful research term. Yet a fact that may seem insignificant at the outset may prove pivotal in light of the pertinent legal rules. As you work through these categories, err on the side of including, rather than excluding, too much.

If you were researching the Canoga case (stated at pages 2-3 in Chapter 1), you might develop the following set of factual concepts based on these five questions:

(1) *Who:* musician, flutist, smoker, or employee; employer, orchestra, general manager, or board of directors
(2) *What:* employment, termination of employment, smoking, insubordination, denial of board review, employee manual, no-smoking policy, protest against that policy
(3) *When:* termination on January 7, 1995, five years after hire; smoking during nonwork hours
(4) *Where:* Taos, New Mexico; smoking away from the orchestra's premises
(5) *Why:* protest against policy for privacy reasons; termination for insubordination or refusal to cease smoking

As you will see, many of these factual aspects are indeed important in the law pertinent to the Canoga case.

2. Three Legal Categories

Your initial insight into the legal dimensions of your client's situation will depend on how much law you already know and how close the situation comes to an area you have studied or researched. When you are new to the law, you may have only vague ideas about legal research terms for most client situations. With time and experience, though, you may become so familiar with an area that you will know exactly which terms to use. Most lawyers in most situations have several good ideas about where to start.

To prompt yourself to think carefully about the legal dimensions of a client situation, consider the following categories:

(1) What is the *legal theory* applicable to this situation? That is, what is the legal basis for penalizing the wrongdoer and benefiting the wronged party or for excusing the wrongdoing?
(2) What *relief* has the wronged party sought through the legal system?
(3) What is the *procedural posture* of the case? That is, what is the stage of the case as it progresses through the legal system?

Note that all three of these legal categories (especially the third) rest on the assumption that there is a dispute in litigation. Sometimes your client's situation will not yet involve litigation; you may be providing advice about whether to litigate. Or there may not even be an existing dispute; you may be assessing how to structure a transaction to avoid future disputes. Nonetheless, as you consider the three legal categories in such situations, for ease of analysis, imagine that a dispute has indeed occurred and anticipate how it might be handled in litigation. Of course, in research situations where there is no actual litigation, the procedure category typically will be less important than the others.

If you were researching the Canoga case from the perspective of a relative novice with some awareness of employment relations, you might generate the following legal research terms:

(1) *Legal theory:* breach of contract, discrimination against smokers, violation of privacy rights
(2) *Relief sought:* money (damages), return to work (reinstatement), cleared work record
(3) *Procedure:* nothing specific at this point

As you will see, these concepts are indeed pertinent legal concepts in this situation.

3. Fact and Legal Categories Synthesized

In summary, as you consider the factual and legal dimensions of your client's situation, you should consider the following eight categories of concepts for possible research terms:

> *Factual:* who, what, when, where, why
> *Legal:* legal theory, relief sought, procedure

In the abstract, these eight categories seem entirely distinct; in practice, they are not. The line between law and fact is often blurry, as is the line between any two factual or two legal categories. Fortunately, it is not all that important to place a potential research term firmly in the proper category. It is instead important that you work through these categories so as to generate many possible concepts.

As you review your list of concepts, consider how they may relate to each other. For example, a legal theory may depend on the motivation of the wrongdoer (the factual "why" question). The relief available to a wronged party may depend on the relationship between the participants (the factual "who" question). Your research will reveal these relationships.

C. Related Terms

Many factual and legal concepts can be phrased various ways. To maximize your chances of matching the phrasing chosen by lawmakers, as well as legal scholars and editors, you should develop a set of related terms for each of your concepts. Related terms may be synonyms, words with the same approximate meaning as your initial term. Or they may be antonyms, words with the opposite meaning. Or they may be words with broader or narrower meanings than your initial term.

As you brainstorm about related terms, you may find one of two visual aids helpful. The first is a "ladder," in which the broadest term appears at the top and the narrowest term appears at the bottom. The second is a "wheel," in which the initial term appears on the hub and the various related terms appear on the spokes. You also may develop your own diagram, or you may want to draw links among your ladders and wheels.

In researching the Canoga case, for example, you might generate the following sets of related terms:

synonyms for employment: work, labor, service

a ladder of terms relating to termination of employment:
separation from employment
termination
involuntary termination, discharge, firing
discharge for insubordination, for violation of employer policy

a ladder of terms relating to the right to smoke:
privacy
right to engage in legal activities
right to smoke
right to smoke off-duty, away from employer premises

a wheel of terms related to contract:

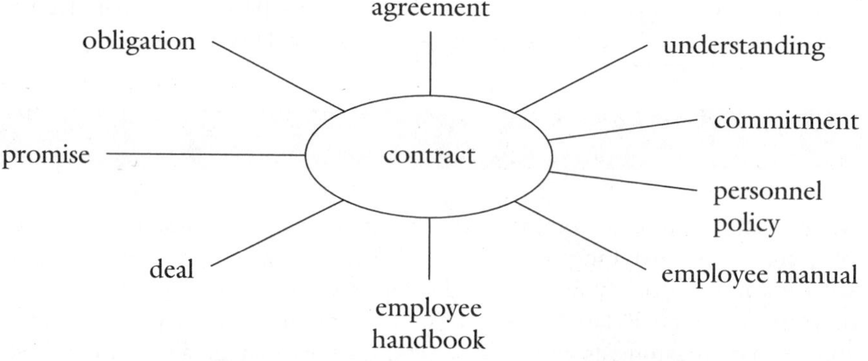

D. Legal Dictionaries and Thesauri

1. Why Are Legal Dictionaries and Thesauri Useful?

Use of dictionaries and thesauri can significantly aid your development of research terms. These sources may point you to terms you may not have thought of yourself. They also can help you understand the terms you have listed.

Because many terms have particular legal connotations that differ somewhat from their nonlegal connotations, the first dictionary you should use to define an unfamiliar term is a legal dictionary. Indeed, you may wish to look up your most important terms, even if they are familiar to you, to be sure that your understanding comports with legal usage. Of course, if your research involves a term defined outside of the law, you should use an appropriate nonlegal dictionary.

As you will soon see, some legal dictionaries contain references to primary or secondary authority from which the definitions were derived. To some extent, these dictionaries function as finding tools. However, this function is limited because the references are illustrative, not exhaustive, and do not necessarily present current law or the law in your jurisdiction. Dictionaries are unlikely to provide direct references to useful authority, but are likely to aid you in developing research terms to use with other research sources.

2. What Are Legal Dictionaries and Thesauri, and How Do You Use Them?

You will find quite an array of legal dictionaries and thesauri, each with its strengths and weaknesses. Exhibit 2.1 on page 18 presents an overview of dictionaries and thesauri that provide general coverage of legal vocabulary.

Dictionaries provide definitions of legal words and phrases and may include pronunciations, word derivations, and references to legal authorities. In general terms, there are three types of dictionaries:

(1) *Ballentine's* and *Black's* are substantial volumes, cover a very wide range of terms, and use terminology best suited to a reader with legal training. *Black's* also offers an abridged version.
(2) The dictionaries by Gifis, Hill and Hill, Oran, and Rothenberg define essential or basic legal terms with minimal use of legal jargon; they thus are well suited to readers with less legal training.
(3) The dictionaries by Gilmer, Radin, and Redden and Veron fall in between the two previous types.

As for thesauri, *West's Legal Thesaurus/Dictionary* contains definitions, synonyms, and antonyms. Burton's *Legal Thesaurus* contains synonyms, associated concepts, and some foreign words and phrases.

You may well develop a strong preference for one or two of these sources. On the other hand, it may be most efficient to use different sources for different tasks. For example, if you are simply seeking to generate a wider range of related terms, consult a thesaurus. If you are seeking a short working definition of a common legal term, consult one of the compact dictionaries. If you are seeking a more complete definition of a less common term, consult one of the full-size dictionaries.

As you work with dictionaries and thesauri, keep these tips in mind: First, many legal terms are actually phrases, containing more than one word, and thus can be alphabetized letter-by-letter or word-by-word. For instance, "contract remedy" would appear before "contractor" in word-by-word indexing, but the order would be reversed in letter-by-letter indexing. Be sure you know which method is used in the sources you consult so you do not miss a definition. Second, you are likely to discover new terms; be sure to look them up if they seem potentially significant. Third, keep track of where you located key definitions in case you need to cite them

Exhibit 2.1 General-Coverage Law Dictionaries and Thesauri.

Dictionaries	*Size*	*Primary Orientation*	*Pronunciation*	*Illustration of Term in Other Sources*
Ballentine's Law Dictionary (3d ed. 1969)	full-size	legal audience	yes (some)	yes
Black's Law Dictionary (6th ed. 1990)	full-size (also published in abridged edition)	legal audience	yes (some)	yes
Steven H. Gifis, *Law Dictionary* (3d ed. 1991)	pocket-size	legal novice	yes (some)	yes
Wesley Gilmer, Jr., *The Law Dictionary* (6th ed. 1986)	pocket-size	legal novice	yes (some)	yes
Gerald N. Hill & Kathleen Thompson Hill, *Real Life Dictionary of the Law* (1995)	intermediate	legal novice	yes (some)	no
Daniel Oran, *Oran's Dictionary of the Law* (2d ed. 1991)	pocket-size	both	yes (some)	no
Max Radin, *Radin Law Dictionary* (Lawrence G. Greene ed., 2d ed. 1970)	intermediate	legal audience	no	yes
Kenneth R. Redden & Enid L. Veron, *Modern Legal Glossary* (1980)	intermediate	legal audience	no	yes
The Plain-Language Law Dictionary (Robert E. Rothenberg ed., 1981)	pocket-size	legal novice	no	no
Thesauri				
William C. Burton, *Legal Thesaurus* (2d ed. 1992)	intermediate	both	no	no
William P. Statsky, *West's Legal Thesaurus/Dictionary: A Resource for the Writer and the Computer Researcher* (1985)	intermediate	both	only the emphasis syllable	no

(discussed below). Finally, if you use a dictionary that includes references to other legal authorities, you may use these references to locate illustrations of the definitions in the dictionary. However, a dictionary does not provide complete references to other authorities and thus should not be relied on as a finding tool.

In the Canoga case, for example, you might look up the term "contract" from the legal theory category. You would find it in virtually any dictionary or thesaurus, of course. Illustration 2-1 below and on page 20 presents pertinent excerpts from several sources: Rothenberg's concise definition, written in nonlegalistic language; Oran's somewhat more extensive definition; and an excerpt from *Black's* definition, which contains nearly forty subparts and runs for several pages. Note that the latter two sources provide references to other sources, such as the Restatement of Contracts (covered in Chapter 4), cases (covered in Chapter 6), and statutes (covered in Chapter 7). Illustration 2-1 also presents the beginning of the page-long contract entry in Burton's *Legal Thesaurus.* These entries provide useful additions to the list of research terms for the Canoga case: promise, obligation or duty, consideration, cer-

Illustration 2-1 Contract Entries from Dictionaries and Thesauri.

The Plain-Language Law Dictionary 74 (Robert E. Rothenberg ed., 1981).

Contract. An AGREEMENT between two or more people, one PARTY (or parties) agreeing to perform certain acts, the other party (or parties) agreeing to pay for or give other consideration for said performance. A contract places an OBLIGATION on one party to do something and an obligation upon the other party to reward the doer.

Daniel Oran, *Oran's Dictionary of the Law* 100 (2d ed. 1991).

Contract An agreement that affects or creates legal relationships between two or more persons. To be a *contract,* an agreement must involve: at least one promise, **consideration** (something of value promised or given), persons legally capable of making binding agreements, and a reasonable certainty about the meaning of the terms. A contract is called **bilateral** if both sides make promises (such as the promise to deliver a book on one side and a promise to pay for it on the other) or **unilateral** if the promises are on one side only. According to the **Uniform Commercial Code,** a contract is the "total legal obligation which results from the parties' agreement," and according to the Restatement of the Law of Contracts, it is "a promise or set of promises for the breach of which the law in some way recognizes a duty." For different types of contracts, such as **output, requirement,** etc., see those words.

Black's Law Dictionary 322-23, 325 (6th ed. 1990).

Contract. An agreement between two or more persons which creates an obligation to do or not to do a particular thing. As defined in Restatement, Second, Contracts § 3: "A contract is a promise or a set of promises for the breach of which the law gives a remedy, or the performance of which the law in some way recognizes as a duty." A legal relationship consisting of the rights and duties of the contracting parties; a promise or set of promises constituting an agreement between the parties that gives each a legal duty to the other and also the right to seek a remedy for the breach of those duties. Its essentials are competent parties, subject matter, a legal consideration, mutuality of agreement, and mutuality of obligation. Lamoureux v. Burrillville Racing Ass'n, 91 R.I. 94, 161 A.2d 213, 215.

Illustration 2-1 *(continued)*

Under U.C.C., term refers to total legal obligation which results from parties' agreement as affected by the Code. Section 1-201(11). As to sales, "contract" and "agreement" are limited to those relating to present or future sales of goods, and "contract for sale" includes both a present sale of goods and a contract to sell goods at a future time. U.C.C. § 2-106(1).

The writing which contains the agreement of parties, with the terms and conditions, and which serves as a proof of the obligation.

Contracts may be classified on several different methods, according to the element in them which is brought into prominence. The usual classifications are as follows: . . .

Express and implied. An express contract is an actual agreement of the parties, the terms of which are openly uttered or declared at the time of making it, being stated in distinct and explicit language, either orally or in writing.

An implied contract is one not created or evidenced by the explicit agreement of the parties, but inferred by the law, as a matter of reason and justice from their acts or conduct, the circumstances surrounding the transaction making it a reasonable, or even a necessary, assumption that a contract existed between them by tacit understanding. . . .

Unilateral and bilateral. A unilateral contract is one in which one party makes an express engagement or undertakes a performance, without receiving in return any express engagement or promise of performance from the other. Bilateral (or reciprocal) contracts are those by which the parties expressly enter into mutual engagements, such as sale or hire. Kling Bros. Engineering Works v. Whiting Corporation, 320 Ill.App. 630, 51 N.E.2d 1004, 1007. When the party to whom an engagement is made makes no express agreement on his part, the contract is called unilateral, even in cases where the law attaches certain obligations to his acceptance. Essence of a "unilateral contract" is that neither party is bound until the promisee accepts the offer by performing the proposed act. King v. Industrial Bank of Washington, D.C.App., 474 A.2d 151, 156. It consists of a promise for an act, the acceptance consisting of the performance of the act requested, rather than the promise to perform it. Antonucci v. Stevens Dodge, Inc., 73 Misc.2d 173, 340 N.Y.S.2d 979, 982. *Compare* Bilateral Contract.

William C. Burton, *Legal Thesaurus* 115 (2d ed. 1992).

CONTRACT, *noun* accord, accordance, agreement, arrangement, articles of agreement, assurance, avouchment, avowal, bargain, binding agreement, bond, charter, collective agreement, commitment, compact, compromise, concordat, *condicio, conductio,* confirmation, *conventio,* covenant, deal, embodied terms, engagement, *entente,* guarantee, instrument evidencing an agreement, ironclad agreement, legal document, mutual agreement, mutual pledge, mutual promise, mutual undertaking, negotiated agreement, obligation, pact, paction, *pactum,* pledge, pledged word, private understanding, promise, ratified agreement, set terms, settlement, stated terms, stipulation, terms for agreement, understanding, undertaking, warranty, written terms tainty of terms, and competent parties, express or implied, bilateral or unilateral, bargain covenant, guarantee.

You also might look up the terms "employee" and "employer" from the factual "who" category. These concepts appear in only a few of the dictionaries. Illustration 2-2 on pages 23 and 24 presents several pertinent definitions from *Ballentine's* dictionary and Statsky's thesaurus. Note that the former includes references to other sources, including encyclopedias such as *American Jurisprudence, Second Edition, American Law Reports* annotations (both covered in Chapter 4), cases, and statutes. These entries introduce some important terms: master and servant, employment at will (a hiring for an indefinite period). (As a bonus, the Statsky excerpt makes for mildly entertaining reading; note the last few lines of synonyms in the "employee" entry.)

You also might look up "termination of employment" from the factual "what" category. The definition provided in *Black's* is presented in Illustration 2-2, it refers to another potentially interesting new term—"wrongful discharge." If you looked it up in *Black's*, you would find the final definition that appears in Illustration 2-2. This definition indicates that wrongful discharge is a legal theory used by at-will employees to challenge discharges that violate antidiscrimination statutes, public policy, implied employment contracts, or implied covenants of good faith and fair dealing.

These illustrations are exactly that: illustrative. To prepare an even more complete set of research terms, you would look up additional terms from your original list. And you would look up any potentially significant terms gleaned from the dictionaries and thesauri.

3. What Else?

Legal Usage Texts. Two texts resemble dictionaries but go beyond providing definitions to address stylistic choices in legal writing. Bryan Garner's *A Dictionary of Modern Legal Usage* (2d ed. 1995) contains definitions of common legal terms along with notes on frequently misused or confused terms and short essays on points of grammar and style. Similarly, David Mellinkoff's *Mellinkoff's Dictionary of American Legal Usage* (1992) supplements definitions with the author's opinion about preferred usage and clear writing.

Specialized Dictionaries. If you experience difficulty finding your term in the dictionaries described above or need additional detail, you may wish to consult a specialized legal dictionary. They exist in many subjects, such as constitutional, international, and business law. There also are special-purpose dictionaries, such as *Bieber's Dictionary of Legal Abbreviations* (4th ed. 1993).

Other Media. Although you are most likely to use a dictionary or thesaurus in paper form, the following appeared in other media as of early 1996:

	Paper	CD-ROM	Computer-Assisted Research		Microform
			LEXIS	*WESTLAW*	
Ballentine's Law Dictionary	√				
Black's Law Dictionary	√			√	
Law Dictionary, Gifts	√				
The Law Dictionary, Gilmer	√				
Real Life Dictionary of the Law, Hill & Hill	√				
Oran's Dictionary of the Law	√				
Radin Law Dictionary	√				
Modern Legal Glossary, Redden & Veron	√				
The Plain-Language Law Dictionary, Rothenberg	√				
Legal Thesaurus, Burton	√				
West's Legal Thesaurus/Dictionary, Statsky	√				
Dictionary of Modern Legal Usage, Garner	√		√		
Mellinkoff's Dictionary of American Legal Usage	√				

4. How Do You Cite Dictionaries?

Citation to a legal dictionary is relatively rare; it is better to cite a primary authority providing a definition than to cite a dictionary. You may, however, cite a dictionary for a definition of a term that is undefined in the primary authority in your jurisdiction.

Rule 15 of *The Bluebook: A Uniform System of Citation* (15th ed. 1991) (*The Bluebook*) governs citation to dictionaries. The general sequence includes the author, title, pertinent page number, editor, edition and date; there may be an author or an editor, or both. The two most frequently cited dictionaries (*Ballentine's* and *Black's*) have special, shorter citation forms in Rule 15.7(a). For example, here are correct citations to several of the definitions presented in this chapter:

Ballentine's Law Dictionary 399 (3d ed. 1969).
Black's Law Dictionary 1471 (6th ed. 1990).
Daniel Oran, *Oran's Dictionary of the Law* 100 (2d ed. 1991).
The Plain-Language Law Dictionary 74 (Robert E. Rothenberg ed., 1981).

Illustration 2-2 Employment Entries from Dictionaries and Thesauri.

Ballentine's Law Dictionary 399-400 (3d ed. 1969).

employee. An expression more euphonious than "servant" but ordinarily meaning the same. 35 Am J1st M & S § 2. One who is in such a relation to another person that the latter may control the work of the former and direct the manner in which it shall be done. 35 Am J1st M & S § 2.

One is an "employee" for the purposes of Social Security and Unemployment Compensation where in rendering services for another he acts under the control and direction of the latter, not only as to the result to be accomplished, but as to the means and details by which the result is accomplished. United States v Silk, 331 US 704, 91 L Ed 1757, 67 S Ct 1463; Schwing v United States (CA3 Pa) 165 F2d 518, 1 ALR2d 548. Only persons who perform menial services, manual labor, or work which is subordinate in its nature, and immediately subject to the directions and orders of the superior, are within the contemplation of statutes imposing liability upon corporate stockholders for debts of the corporation owing to laborers, servants, "employees," etc. Anno: 104 ALR 765. In other contexts, the term has a broader meaning, for example, in exemption statutes, where, under the rule of liberal construction, persons engaged in positions requiring services far above those of a menial character, such as sales manager, auditor, comptroller, etc., are deemed "employees." 31 Am J2d Exemp § 20. An officer of a corporation may be an "employee" for the purposes of Social Security. 48 Am J1st Soc Sec § 16.

See **public employee; servant.** . . .

employer. One, formerly known as "master," who is in such relation to another person that he may control the work of that other person and direct the manner in which it is to be done. 35 Am Jlst M & S § 2. The person by and for whom an independent contractor is engaged. 27 Am J1st Ind Contr § 27.

The concept of the term in labor legislation is broader than the common law or usual statutory concept. Anno: 1 L Ed 2d 2078. As defined by the National Labor Relations Act, an employer includes any person acting as an agent of an employer, directly or indirectly. 29 USC § 152(2). Expressly excluded from the definition of "employer" in the National Labor Relations Act are the United States, any wholly owned government corporation, any federal reserve bank, or any state or political subdivision of a state; national banks are not excluded. 31 Am J Rev ed Lab § 185. . . .

employment at will. A hiring for an indefinite period of time. 35 Am J1st M & S § 19.

employment contract. A contract between employer and employee; a collective labor agreement.

See **collective labor agreement; contract of hire.**

William P. Statsky, *West's Legal Thesaurus/Dictionary: A Resource for the Writer and the Computer Researcher* 273 (1985).

Em*ploy*ee, *n.* A person in the service of another under an express or implied, oral or written contract of hire, in which the employer has the power and the right to control and direct the employee in the material details of how the work is to be performed (the employee

Illustration 2-2 (*continued*)

acted within the scope of her employment). Servant, salaried worker, agent, wage earner, laborer, jobholder, staff member, hand, apprentice, journeyman, retainer, hireling, lackey, messenger, attendant, subordinate, workman, artisan, mechanic, craftsman, workaholic, breadwinner, helper, aide, henchman, valet, underling, domestic, retainer, white-collar worker, proletarian, hustler, flunky, man Friday, personnel. See also assistant. *Ant.* Employer.
Em*ploy*er, *n.* One who employs the services of others for wages or other compensation, with the right and power to control and direct them in the material details of how the work is to be performed (the employer was liable for the tort of her employee). Master, proprietor, contractor, owner, principal, manager, director, boss, chief; company, business, organization. See also builder, entrepreneur, patron (2), backer. *Ant.* Employee.
Em*ploy*ment, *n.* The activity in which a person is engaged or is employed, usually on a day-to-day basis (employment as a paralegal). Occupation, job, profession, work, vocation, line, trade, activity, labor, craft, livelihood, service, business, calling, task, assignment, function, position, situation, industry, living, career, specialty, duty, post. See also domain, operation, application.

Black's Law Dictionary 1471, 1612-13 (6th ed. 1990).

Termination of employment. Within policies providing that insurance should cease immediately upon termination of employment, means a complete severance of relationship of employer and employee. Edwards v. Equitable Life Assur. Soc. of United States, 296 Ky. 448, 177 S.W.2d 574, 577, 578. *See also* Employment at will; Wrongful discharge. . . .
Wrongful discharge. An at-will employee's cause of action against his former employer, alleging that his discharge was in violation of state or federal anti-discrimination statutes (cf. 42 U.S.C.A. §§ 2000e to 2000e-17), public policy (Morris v. Hartford Courant Co., 200 Conn. 676, 513 A.2d 66, 68), an implied employment contract (Woolley v. Hoffman-LaRoche, Inc., 99 N.J. 284, 491 A.2d 1257), or an implied covenant of good faith and fair dealing (Cleary v. American Airlines, Inc., 111 Cal.App.3d 443, 168 Cal.Rptr. 722, 729). *See also* Employment at will; Whistle-blower Acts.

A note about typeface in *The Bluebook:* Because *The Bluebook* is written by the editors of four law reviews, its primary focus is how to cite within law review footnotes, with a secondary focus on citations in court documents and legal memoranda. Thus, the examples on the inside front cover and in the text of *The Bluebook* demonstrate the typefaces used in law review footnotes, including large and small capital letters and other typefaces not commonly available to students and practitioners.

Practitioners' Note P.1 (in the blue pages toward the front of *The Bluebook*) sets out the typeface rules for court documents and legal memoranda. Examples demonstrating these typefaces appear on the inside back cover and in Practitioners' Notes P.1 through P.7. The citations in this text follow the practitioner rules, with italics used where Note P.1 calls for italics or underlining.

Your selection of typefaces for your problem set answers will depend on your professor's instructions.

E. Concluding Points

Because the law and legal research sources consist of words describing the factual and legal aspects of a client's situation, the first step in legal research is to develop a set of research terms. To do this well, you first should consider your client's situation from various perspectives: As a factual matter, who did what when, where, and why? As a legal matter, what legal theory might be used to obtain what relief, and what are the procedural dimensions of the situation? Then you should generate related terms for the concepts you have identified, in the form of synonyms, antonyms, broader terms, and narrower terms. Legal dictionaries and thesauri help you understand your terms and generate a wide range of related terms.

On page 26 is a depiction of the research terms developed for the Canoga case through this process. As you will see, many of these terms will lead to pertinent legal authorities.

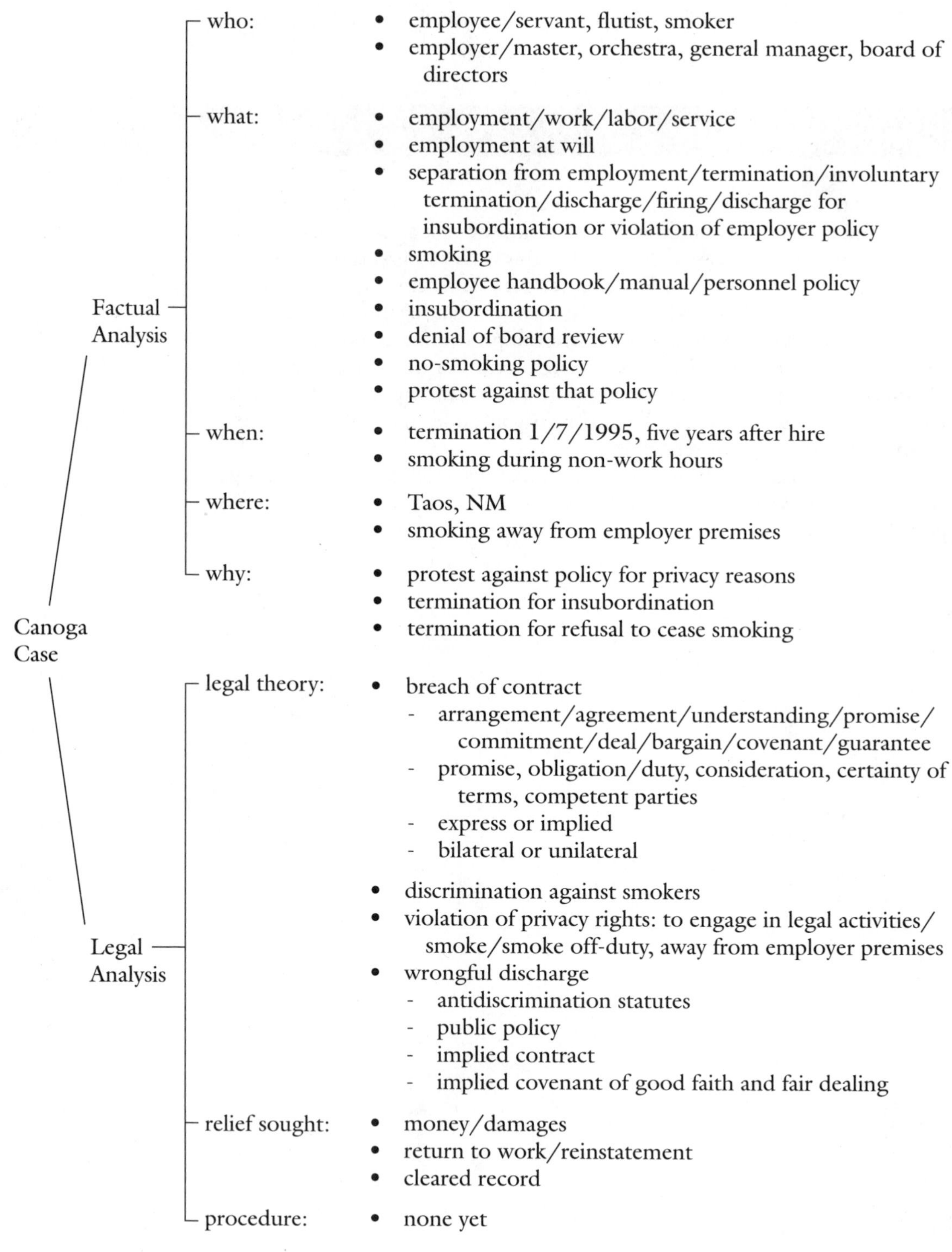
Canoga Case
Factual Analysis
who:
• employee/servant, flutist, smoker
• employer/master, orchestra, general manager, board of directors
what:
• employment/work/labor/service
• employment at will
• separation from employment/termination/involuntary termination/discharge/firing/discharge for insubordination or violation of employer policy
• smoking
• employee handbook/manual/personnel policy
• insubordination
• denial of board review
• no-smoking policy
• protest against that policy
when:
• termination 1/7/1995, five years after hire
• smoking during non-work hours
where:
• Taos, NM
• smoking away from employer premises
why:
• protest against policy for privacy reasons
• termination for insubordination
• termination for refusal to cease smoking
Legal Analysis
legal theory:
• breach of contract
- arrangement/agreement/understanding/promise/commitment/deal/bargain/covenant/guarantee
- promise, obligation/duty, consideration, certainty of terms, competent parties
- express or implied
- bilateral or unilateral
• discrimination against smokers
• violation of privacy rights: to engage in legal activities/smoke/smoke off-duty, away from employer premises
• wrongful discharge
- antidiscrimination statutes
- public policy
- implied contract
- implied covenant of good faith and fair dealing
relief sought:
• money/damages
• return to work/reinstatement
• cleared record
procedure:
• none yet

3 Assess Your Media Options

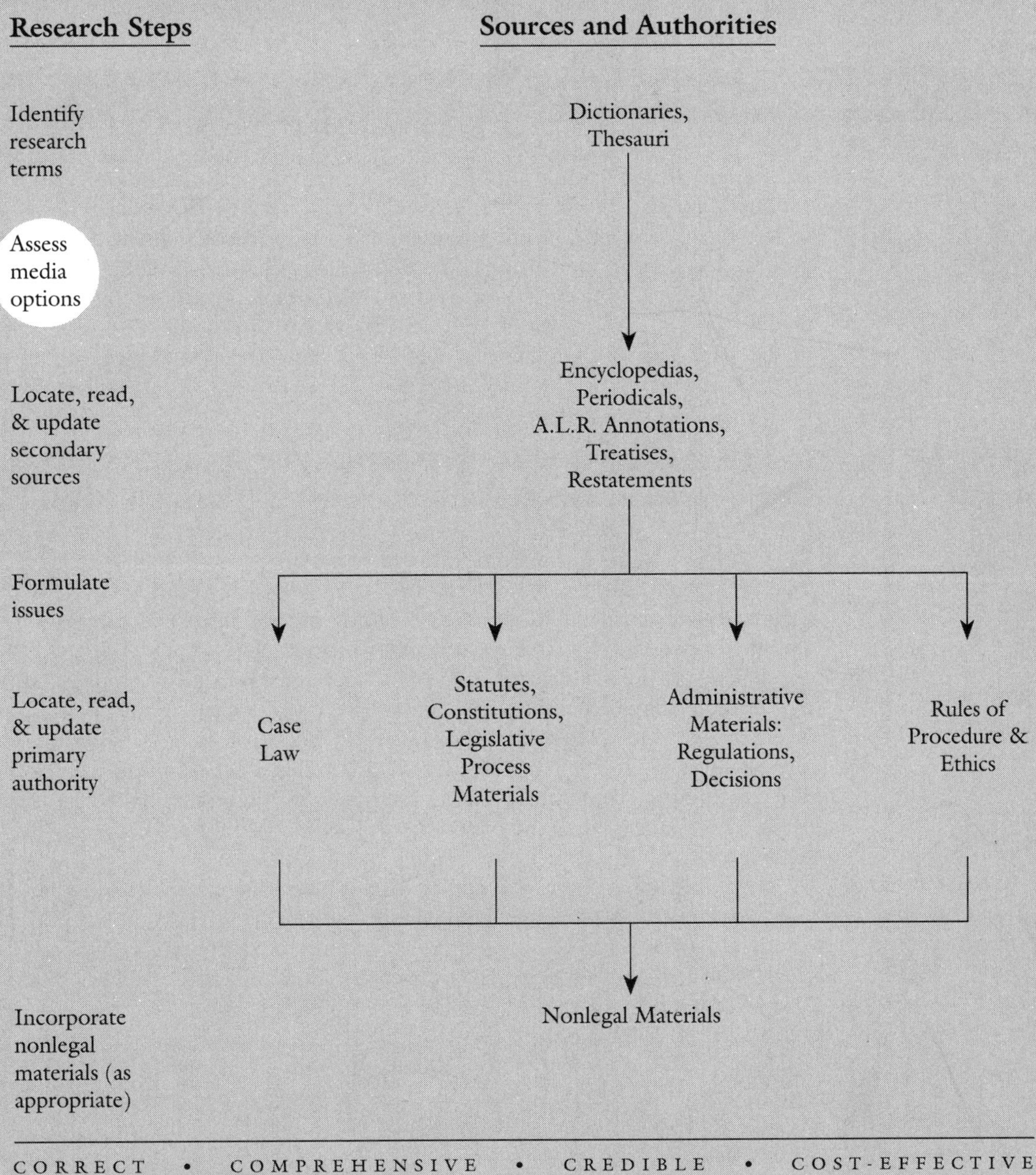

CORRECT • COMPREHENSIVE • CREDIBLE • COST-EFFECTIVE

Summary of Contents

A. Preliminary Points
B. What Are Your Media Options?
C. How Do You Research in the Various Media?
D. What Factors Do You Consider in Choosing among Media?
E. Concluding Points

A. Preliminary Points

In Chapter 2, you learned that factual and legal concepts can be phrased in various ways and that effective research often requires that you generate related terms for each concept. Similarly, the sources that you use to research your concepts are found in multiple media, and effective research requires that you pick wisely among those media. This chapter introduces you to your media options, explains the differences in research techniques among those media, and sets forth additional factors to consider in choosing among the media.

B. What Are Your Media Options?

Paper is the traditional medium for legal research, but it is only one of the available media. Others are microforms, online sources, and CD-ROMs. Online sources and CD-ROMs are becoming increasingly important as the amount of material available in these media increases.

Microforms include both microfilm and microfiche. Both consist of photographic film containing images that have been reduced in size, typically in a ratio of 24:1. Microfilm is available in both rolls and cartridges. A microfiche is a flat sheet of film, which resembles a note card. The major difference between microfilm and microfiche is that microfiche can be browsed randomly, while the pages on a roll of microfilm must be viewed in sequence.

Online databases are collections of text and graphics (and sometimes audio and video) in computer-readable form. "Online" means the information in a database is stored in a computer at a remote location. You typically reach the database via a personal computer, a modem, and a telephone line. The information you receive from the remote database is displayed on a terminal at your location.

CD-ROM stands for "compact disk, read only memory." A CD-ROM disk is a plastic disk that contains information stored in pits molded into the surface of the disk. A laser beam is used to read the information. A CD-ROM disk can hold many types of information, including text, graphics, audio, and video. A typical CD-ROM disk holds the equivalent of about 600,000 typed pages.

Each of these media has its advantages and disadvantages, and you will no doubt develop a preference for some media over others. Nevertheless, you should become adept at locating and using information in all of them for three reasons: the information you need may be published in only one medium; the information you need may be published in multiple media, but the medium you prefer may not be the one most conveniently or economically available to you; and you may prefer different media for different purposes.

Of course, within each of the categories of media, some products are better than others, and you must learn to evaluate the products themselves as well as the media.

C. How Do You Research in the Various Media?

To choose among media, you need a basic understanding of how to research in each of them. The following text covers paper and microform media, then online media, and finally CD-ROM as a medium.

1. Paper and Microforms

The methods of searching in paper and microform are relatively straightforward. You locate information in both in roughly the same way: by using an index, table of contents, or other finding aid supplied by the publisher; by using a reference obtained from some other source; or by browsing.

You will be most effective in using these paper and microform media—and comparing them to other media—if you understand how indexing works.

To prepare an index, the indexer first reads the text to be indexed and notes the concepts covered on each page. The indexer may select all or almost all of the concepts to index, or the indexer may select a more limited number. If the indexer does not index a concept, you will not be able to locate it through the index. In addition, many concepts can be expressed by more than one word or phrase and frequently are, even within the same text; nonetheless, the indexer must choose one word or phrase to represent a concept so that all entries relating to that concept will appear together in the index. The indexer may choose a term that is used in the text of a document or a different term. An indexer often works off of an established list of terms, which tells the indexer which of the synonyms, antonyms, or variant forms of a term to use and which cross-references to create. Thus, when you use an index, you benefit from—and are constrained by—the indexer's attempts to standardize vocabulary.

2. Online Sources

Online sources free you from reliance on an indexer by giving you other search options. These options may be in lieu of, or in addition to, your paper search options. Three online sources are of particular importance to legal research—LEXIS, WESTLAW, and the Internet.

a. LEXIS and WESTLAW

(1) Introduction

LEXIS and WESTLAW are the two major online legal research systems. Both contain a wide variety of primary and secondary legal research materials. Both also give you access to nonlegal materials through related systems—NEXIS on LEXIS and DIALOG on WESTLAW.

The materials in these systems are organized into searchable units that are called databases on WESTLAW and files on LEXIS. (The LEXIS files are subdivisions of its libraries, which are not searchable units.) This text uses the term "database" to refer to both WESTLAW databases and LEXIS files.

LEXIS and WESTLAW work in roughly the same way. Both systems allow you to retrieve documents by doing a full-text search of a database or by doing a citation search. A full-text search is one in which the computer attempts to match words that you specify against words in the database that you have selected to search. A citation search is one that allows you to retrieve the text of a document by entering its citation in the format required by the system. You need not specify the database to search.

To do a full-text search effectively, you must know (1) how to pick a database and (2) how to write a search.

(2) Selecting a Database

There are two simple methods for identifying databases and obtaining the code you must enter into the computer to reach a database. The first is to use a system's paper database directory. The second is to consult its online directory. An online directory typically is more up-to-date than its paper counterpart.

The appropriate database for your search will, of course, depend on the type of authority or source you wish to search and, if you are researching primary authority, on which jurisdiction's law governs your research situation. The same information may be available to you in more than one database on the same system. For example, you can search New Mexico's statutes by searching in a database that includes only New Mexico's statutes or by searching in a database that contains the statutes of all the states. To search LEXIS or WESTLAW cost-effectively, you should, as a general rule, begin your search in the smallest appropriate database because a smaller database may cost less to search than a larger one.

Once you have identified a potentially useful database, you should determine its scope of coverage. Scope of coverage refers to both the content of the material available online and the time span covered by the database. Some databases closely parallel a paper source while others contain information from various sources. A database that has the same name as a paper source may or may not cover the same time period and may or may not contain the same content for the time period covered. You may determine the scope of a database by using a paper directory or reference manual for the system. You also may obtain scope information online by using the GUIDE library on LEXIS or by entering a "scope" command on WESTLAW.

(3) Drafting a Search

After you have picked a database, you must design your search. Searches can be designed and evaluated in terms of two characteristics: recall and precision. Recall is the ratio of relevant documents retrieved to all the relevant documents in the database. It answers the question: Did you retrieve all or almost all of the relevant documents in the database? Precision is the ratio of relevant documents retrieved to all documents retrieved. It answers the question: Are most or all of the documents you retrieved relevant?

Recall and precision tend to vary inversely. Therefore, know which is more important to you. Do you want to find all or almost all relevant documents, or do you need to retrieve a few highly relevant documents? If you need high recall, you may be willing to tolerate (and pay for) low precision. That is, you may accept some irrelevant documents in order to get all relevant ones. On the other hand, if you do not need high recall, you probably do not want to wade through many irrelevant documents. You should design your search according to your needs.

Throughout the discussion that follows, brackets designate a computer search.

(a) Natural Language Searches

If you are primarily interested in finding a few highly relevant documents, you may do a "natural language" search of a database; that is, you may enter your search in plain English, just as you would write it or speak it. [May an employer fire an employee for smoking?] is an example of a natural language search. LEXIS refers to a natural language search as a Freestyle search; WESTLAW refers to a natural language search as a WIN (WESTLAW Is Natural) search.

When you do a natural language search, LEXIS and WESTLAW will display a limited number of documents that most closely match your search request, beginning with the most statistically relevant document.

A natural language search is particularly useful if you are (1) beginning research on a broad topic about which you know little; (2) researching a legal issue or concept that can be expressed in many different ways or that can be expressed only with very common words; (3) researching an issue that is likely to appear in many documents so that you want to see the most relevant documents first; or (4) having a difficult time formulating a Boolean search (see the next section). You also may wish to use a natural language search to supplement a Boolean search to ensure thorough results.

(b) Boolean Searches

Boolean searching is a more stylized use of research terms and connectors to give more precise direction to the system. You may do a Boolean search for (1) single-word alternatives, (2) a multiple-word concept, or (3) multiple concepts. You also may combine a Boolean search with a "field" search—that is, a search of a named part of a document.

(i) The Search for Single-Word Alternatives

Some concepts may be expressed more than one way—by a variety of single-word alternatives or by various forms of the same word. Your success in searching for the concept depends largely on how well you (1) recognize the alternatives that may be used to express it; (2) use root expanders and universal characters; and (3) recognize and apply a system's rules for plurals, possessives, and equivalent terms.

Alternative terms. Because LEXIS and WESTLAW perform searches by matching words rather than by searching concepts, you must consider all possible alternative terms for any concept you wish to search if you wish to retrieve all of the relevant documents. Alternative terms may include synonyms, antonyms, broader terms, narrower terms, and related terms.

For example, if you want to search for all cases that discuss employee manuals, you may need to use "manual" and "handbook" as search terms, and you will have to tell the computer that you wish to search for the terms as alternatives. The computer technique for joining terms that are intended as alternative terms is to use an "or" connector. The search [manual or handbook] tells LEXIS or WESTLAW to retrieve a document if it contains either or both of those terms.

Variant forms of the same word. You also must consider the variant forms of your alternative search terms. Variant forms for a noun include its related verb forms. For example, "dismissal" may be expressed as "dismissed." Variant forms for a verb include its different tenses and its related noun form. For example, "terminate" may be expressed as "terminates," "terminated," and "terminating," as well as by the related noun "termination."

Root expansion is a technique whereby you can search for different words that share the same root, without having to type each of those words. LEXIS and WESTLAW share two root expansion symbols: the exclamation point [!] and the asterisk [*].

The exclamation point is an unlimited root expander: It instructs the computer to search for all terms that begin with that root, whatever the lengths of the terms. For example, [terminat!] retrieves "terminate," "terminates," "terminated," "terminating," and "termination."

The asterisk is a limited root expander: one asterisk retrieves the root term and any term that is one letter longer than the root, two asterisks retrieves the root term and any term that is one or two letters longer, and so on. Use the limited root expander (or type your alternative search terms) whenever use of the unlimited root expander might retrieve too many irrelevant terms.

The asterisk may also be used within a word as a universal character to substitute for some other character. For example, [mari*uana] retrieves both "marihuana" and "marijuana." When typed within a word, each asterisk holds a place for one character. Therefore the search [judg*ment] will not retrieve the word "judgment."

Variant forms for a noun also include plurals and possessives. As to plurals, both LEXIS and WESTLAW automatically retrieve a regular plural when you enter the singular form of a word. A regular plural is a plural that ends in "s," "es," or "ies." WESTLAW also automatically retrieves many irregular plurals, such as women; on LEXIS, by contrast, you must enter both the singular and irregular plural forms as alternatives. LEXIS automatically retrieves the singular form of a regular plural when you enter the plural; WESTLAW does not.

As to possessives, LEXIS also retrieves the singular and plural possessive forms when you enter either the singular or plural form of a word that has a regular plural. However, if you search for a word that does not have a regular plural, entering the singular retrieves only the singular possessive, and entering the plural retrieves only the plural possessive. On WESTLAW, entering the singular form of a word automatically retrieves the singular and plural possessives. Entering the plural retrieves only the plural possessive. The main point to remember is that for both systems if you use the singular form of a word, you usually retrieve the singular, plural, and singular and plural possessive forms. Thus, your best strategy is usually to search for the singular form of a word.

(ii) The Search for Multiple-Word Concepts

Some concepts require multiple words. Multiple-word concepts include phrases, initialisms, and compound terms.

Americans with Disabilities Act is an example of a phrase. The systems diverge in their treatment of phrases. On LEXIS, you search for a phrase exactly as you would search for a single word. For example, to search for the phrase "Americans with Disabilities Act," just enter [americans with disabilities act]. On WESTLAW, you must enclose a phrase in quotation marks. Thus your search is ["americans with disabilities act"]. In the absence of quotation marks, WESTLAW is programmed to read a space between words as an "or" instruction. Thus, without quotation marks, WESTLAW would interpret the same search as [americans or with or disabilities or act].

Be very cautious about searching for a concept as a phrase. This approach works only if the concept is always written exactly the same way. "Americans with Disabilities Act" is a good phrase search. However, if you searched for "employee handbook" as a phrase, you would not retrieve documents that use an alternative expression, such as "company handbook."

Initialisms are strings of letters that are usually pronounced as letters. For example, the National Labor Relations Board (a federal agency regulating certain aspects of employer-employee relations) is often referred to simply as the N.L.R.B.

On WESTLAW, if you enter an initialism that contains periods but no spaces, WESTLAW retrieves the other forms of the initialism automatically. For example, if you enter [n.l.r.b.], WESTLAW retrieves documents containing "N.L.R.B.," "N. L. R. B.," "NLRB," or "N L R B." If you enter one of the other forms of the initialism, however, WESTLAW retrieves only the form you enter. Furthermore, if you enter the initialism, WESTLAW does not retrieve documents containing the form "National Labor Relations Board." To retrieve those documents, you would have to enter ["National Labor Relations Board"] as an alternative search term.

LEXIS does not have a preferred form that retrieves all equivalent initialisms automatically, but some initialisms have automatic equivalents on LEXIS. These are listed in various LEXIS reference and training materials. You will have to enter as alternatives the forms that are not listed as equivalent.

Some terms may be written as one word, multiple words, or a hyphenated word. "Good-will" is an example. On WESTLAW, if you enter the hyphenated form of a word, you retrieve all three forms. If you enter a different form, WESTLAW retrieves only the form you enter. LEXIS treats hyphens as spaces. Thus to LEXIS, [good-will] is the same as [good will]. To retrieve all three forms of the term on LEXIS, you would have to enter [goodwill or good will].

(iii) The Search for Multiple Concepts

Almost all searches combine two or more concepts. A good technique for identifying the concepts is to write your issue in sentence form; then underline the terms that might be useful search terms or concepts. Here is an issue related to, but broader than, the smoking issue in the Canoga case: May an *employer fire* an *employee* for *smoking*? (For simplicity, this statement of the issue focuses on smoking generally, regardless of location.) This issue contains three concepts: employer-employee, fire, and smoking.

Next, list alternative terms for each of the concepts; then apply the principles relating to root expansion and to plurals and possessives. You will come to the following terms:

employ!	fir***	smok!
	discharg!	
	dismiss!	
	terminat!	

Your next task is to join these concepts in a logical way. Online systems, including LEXIS and WESTLAW, generally share three Boolean connectors: "or," "and," and "not." (These connectors are called Boolean connectors because they are derived from Boolean logic.) Some systems, including LEXIS and WESTLAW, also have numerical and grammatical connectors.

Boolean connectors. The "or" connector tells the computer to retrieve a document if it contains *one or more* of the terms joined by the connector. Use the "or" connector if your terms are alternatives. On WESTLAW, you may use a space between words as an alternative to writing out the word "or." The terms in the middle column above are alternatives and should be joined by the "or" connector.

The "and" connector tells the computer to retrieve a document only if it contains *both* of the terms joined by the "and." You may use an ampersand (&) as an alternative to writing out the word "and." Because the "and" connector tells the computer to look for the terms anywhere within the document, it is a very broad connector. The words could be paragraphs or even pages apart.

The "not" connector tells the computer to *exclude* a document if it contains a specified term. On LEXIS, type "and not" for the "not" connector. On WESTLAW, type "but not" or the percent symbol (%). The "not" connector is risky to use because it excludes every document that contains both the terms you want and the terms you think you do not want.

Numerical connectors. In addition to the Boolean connectors, you also can use numerical connectors. On both LEXIS and WESTLAW, you can require that search terms appear *within a specified number of words* of each other by using "/n" or "w/n." The "n" can be any number of words from 1 to 255. For example, the search [employee w/3 manual] tells the computer to retrieve documents in which the word "employee" appears within three words of "manual." LEXIS includes only searchable words when counting words; it omits certain common words, which it calls "noise" words. WESTLAW counts all words. For a more precise numerical search, use the "pre/n" connector, for example pre/3, on either system (or "+n" on WESTLAW) if you want the term to the left to precede the term on the right.

There are at least two drawbacks to numerical connectors. First, sometimes terms will appear closer together or farther apart in a document than you anticipated. Second, because the numerical connectors do not recognize sentences and paragraphs, the search terms may be in unrelated sentences or paragraphs.

Grammatical connectors. In addition to Boolean and numerical connectors, you also can use grammatical connectors. On LEXIS and WESTLAW, you may require that your search terms appear in the same paragraph (by using the "/p" or "w/p" connector) or in the same sentence (by using the "/s" or "w/s" connector). In the search [discharg! /s smok!], the systems retrieve only documents that contain some form of the word "discharge" in the same sentence as some form of the word "smoke." On WESTLAW, you may use the "+s" connector to require that the term to the left of a connector precede the term to the right within the same sentence. Grammatical connectors are useful because they allow you to specify that the computer search for your terms in units that occur naturally in the English language.

Exhibit 3.1 on page 36 lists the LEXIS and WESTLAW connectors.

Sequence of connectors. Each system processes its connectors in a predetermined order as listed in Exhibit 3.1. As Exhibit 3.1 shows, both systems process a phrase first, "or" before the numerical connectors, the numerical connectors before the grammatical connectors, and the grammatical connectors before the "and" connector. Both systems also process a lower-numbered numerical connector before a higher-numbered connector, except that WESTLAW processes all "+n" connectors before any "/n" connectors.

You can override the normal order of processing (or protect yourself if you do not know it) by using parentheses. LEXIS and WESTLAW process connectors inside parentheses before connectors outside parentheses.

Exhibit 3.1 List of Connectors in the Order in Which LEXIS and WESTLAW Process Them.

LEXIS	*WESTLAW*
phrase	"phrase"
or	or, space
w/n, /n, pre/n, not w/n	+n, pre/n
w/s, /s	/n, w/n
not w/s	+s
w/p, /p	/s, w/s
not w/p	/p, w/p
and, &	and, &
and not	but not, %

Alternative methods of writing multiple-concept searches. You may search for all of the concepts in a multiple-concept search at the same time, but you should not always do so. The simplest search is sometimes best.

One strategy, which is useful if you think that combining all your concepts at once will retrieve too few documents, is to begin with the broadest concept or concepts and then add on narrower concepts to limit your search.

A second strategy is to search for the most specific (that is, concrete or well defined) concept first. If the number of documents you retrieve is small enough, you may never have to add the other concepts to the search. If you retrieve too many documents, you then can add other concepts, one at a time.

A third strategy is to search first for the concept that probably will retrieve the fewest documents. If you retrieve a small enough group of documents, you may not need to add the other concepts.

On the other hand, if your initial search retrieves too few documents and you want to increase your recall, try one of these techniques: add alternative terms; use broader search terms; delete a required term; use broader connectors; or search a broader or different database.

(iv) Sample Search for the Canoga Problem

Applying the principles described above to the Canoga problem yields the following search, which works on both systems:

employ! /p fir*** or discharg! or dismiss! or terminat! /p smok!

(v) Field Searches and Date Searches

Just as most books have a common format so that you expect to find certain information in certain locations, so too the documents in each database have a common structure with easily identifiable parts. These parts are called "segments" on LEXIS and "fields" on WESTLAW, and you may instruct the computer to retrieve only those documents that contain your search terms in the segments or fields you name. When you do so, you are likely to increase the ratio of relevant documents you retrieve. For example, the fields for a case include its title, its citation, the name of the judge who wrote the majority opinion, and the names of counsel. If you wish to find all cases in which a particular attorney served as counsel, you will be more efficient if you search for the attorney's name in the attorney field, rather than in the full text of the case.

Similarly, you may wish to limit your search to a particular time period. For example, you may want to update a paper source online. Again, LEXIS and WESTLAW allow you to do so by using a date search, and doing so is a cost-effective method of searching.

(c) Citation Searches

In addition to natural language and Boolean full-text searches, LEXIS and WESTLAW often allow you to quickly retrieve a document for which you have a citation if you enter the citation in the proper format for the system. Thus, these online systems serve as convenient tools for document retrieval. It may be cost-effective to use the system for this purpose if a document you need is not available to you in another medium.

b. The Internet

The Internet is an international network that connects thousands of other computer networks, including government, university, and business networks. It is an incredibly large source of both legal and nonlegal information, and it is growing very rapidly. The Internet serves a number of information functions: it allows you to talk to and learn from others through e-mail (electronic mail) and through discussion groups to which you can subscribe; it allows you to move documents between sites through its FTP (file transfer protocol) function; and it allows you to use computers in other locations through its telnet (or remote login) function. Most importantly, it allows you to do research and find information at thousands of Internet information servers.

You will most likely search the Internet using the World Wide Web (WWW), an information service that uses hypertext links to locate the information available on the Internet. (Hypertext links are embedded markers that allow you to move quickly from one online location or document to another.) You connect to the WWW using a Web browser, which is a software package that is installed on your computer. The most common Web browser is Netscape; others are Cello, Mosaic, and Lynx.

There are four ways to locate information on the Internet using the WWW. First, you may go directly to a known source by typing in its address. A typical WWW address, also called a Uniform Resource Locator, looks something like this: http://www.law.cornell.edu. You must key an address exactly as it is writtten; spacing, punctuation, and capitalization matter.

Second, you may use one of the search engines on the Web to do a word search or Boolean search to locate sources of information. Think of a search engine as a reference tool that takes your search terms and tells you which servers on the Internet may have relevant data. Infoseek is a commonly used search engine. Infoseek provides links to other search engines, such as Lycos and Web Crawler. You may find Infoseek by selecting the Net Search option on Netscape or by keying its address (http://home.netscape.com/home/internet-search.html).

Third, you may search some Internet sites by subject. The Yahoo site (http://www.yahoo.com) probably is the best known site organized by subject.

Fourth, you may search a paper or online Internet directory to find what you need. One of the best known directories is Erik Heels' *The Legal List: Internet Desk Reference: Law-Related Resources on the Internet and Elsewhere.* The online version is found at http://www.lcp.com/The-Legal-List/TLL-home.html.

Your WWW browser will let you use both web sites and gopher sites. While web sites use hypertext links, gopher sites use hierarchical menus that you must work your way through until you come to what you need. The concepts you learned for LEXIS and WESTLAW will help you search web sites, but do not assume that the search conventions that work on LEXIS and WESTLAW always work on the Internet. Each site is different; many contain their own online search instructions, which you should look for and follow.

The Internet has some similarities and some differences compared to LEXIS and WESTLAW. Like LEXIS and WESTLAW, it is an especially rich source of government information and current information. However, unlike LEXIS and WESTLAW, the Internet is not well organized. It has no comprehensive directory, no uniform editorial or quality control, no standardized search methodology, and no customer service to help you. Also, it does not contain many of the older documents that are available on LEXIS and WESTLAW. On the other hand, the Internet is the most cost-effective online alternative for some information.

3. CD-ROMs

Your first task in using a CD-ROM is to understand its scope of coverage. Typically, you will find a note regarding the scope of a CD-ROM on a preliminary screen, on a search screen, on a help screen, on another screen in response to selecting a scope command, in a directory listing, or in a paper user's guide.

The search options available to you on a CD-ROM will depend on the type of source or finding tool on the CD-ROM and on the software used to create it. Two common software packages are Premise and Folio Views. A CD-ROM index typically will offer you the capacity to do a subject-heading search and a Boolean full-text search, but the details of how you do the searches may vary greatly. A full-text CD-ROM may offer you the opportunity to search traditional tables of contents and indexes (if the source you are searching contains those features) and the ability to do full-text, field, and citation searches.

Various CD-ROMs offer the following useful features, which also are available on LEXIS and WESTLAW: hypertext links, the ability to download documents to a word processing program, and the capacity to search multiple sources at the same time. In addition, some CD-ROMs also offer an electronic notebook feature that allows you to copy information from a research session into a CD-ROM notebook and to add your own comments to the text. Also, some CD-ROMs offer the capacity to connect to and update your research on the online system of the same vendor.

The best way to become proficient at using a CD-ROM is to read its help screens, to read its paper user's guide, or to use its tutorial (if it has one).

D. What Factors Do You Consider in Choosing among Media?

As a student researcher, you will want to consider the following factors in deciding which of the available media to use.

(1) *Availability of information:* Does the medium include the source you need? Does it cover both historical and current information? For which dates?

(2) *Search options:* How do you locate information in the medium? May you do a natural language search? Boolean search? Citation search? Field search? Does the medium include indexes, tables of contents, or other finding aids?

(3) *Ease of use:* How easy is it to use the medium? Is the medium portable? Does it require the use of cumbersome or complex equipment? Does it require electricity or a modem? Does it take special training to use the medium? Can you browse the medium easily? Can you underline or highlight text? Does the medium provide links between various documents? Can you easily print, photocopy, or download material from the medium? Do you like the layout and style of the information in the medium? Is customer service support available for the medium?

(4) *Reliability:* How correct or reliable is the content likely to be? Does a known publisher exercise editorial and quality control?

(5) *Cost:* What are the costs of using the medium? Are the costs fixed or based on the amount of use? Although all the costs of a medium may not be relevant to you as a student, you should be aware that total costs for a medium include initial product costs, update costs, space costs, equipment costs, maintenance costs, and training costs. These costs will be important to you in law practice.

Exhibit 3.2 below and on page 41 compares some of the factors to consider in choosing among media.

Generally, if you wish to do background reading, a paper source is your best choice. If you wish to scan index listings for citations to useful articles, a CD-ROM index may be your best choice because it cumulates entries found in multiple paper indexes and allows you to search without incurring an online charge. If you need the most current information available, an online source often is your best choice. If you need to read an out-of-print document or a document that is hard to store in paper, such as a newspaper, your library may have the document only in microform.

Whichever your choice, it is critical to remember that the more important category is the type of authority you are researching, not its medium.

E. Concluding Points

With one exception, this text introduces you first to the paper medium for each of the legal sources it covers. It emphasizes the paper medium not because that medium is always the best medium to use, but because the paper medium is often the easiest to visualize and understand. Moreover, it often is the medium on which other versions of a source or finding tool are based. Thus, if you understand the paper version, you are more likely to understand and use well the same source or finding tool in other media.

Exhibit 3.2 Selected Factors to Consider in Choosing among Media.

Factors to Consider	*Paper*	*Microfilm Microfiche*	*CD-ROM*	*Online*
How do you locate information within the medium?	Must use the index, table of contents, and other finding aids provided by the publisher, or browse.	Must use the index, table of contents, and other finding aids provided by the publisher, or browse.	May use the finding aids provided by the publisher. You also may search for words you pick.	Usually must create your own search by identifying and combining relevant terms. Some systems allow natural language searches.
How easy is it to browse in this medium?	Easy to browse.	You may dislike browsing on a microform reader. Microfilm does not permit you to bypass pages. Quality of filming varies.	Varies with systems; some allow paging through documents. Some provide hypertext links.	You may be limited to browsing the documents retrieved by your search. You can view only one screen at a time. Hypertext links may facilitate browsing.

Exhibit 3.2 *(continued)*

Factors to Consider	*Paper*	*Microfilm Microfiche*	*CD-ROM*	*Online*
How easy is it to copy information from this medium?	Must make handwritten notes or photocopy relevant information.	If the microform machine does not have a printer, you must take notes. If it does, you may make copies; quality of copies varies.	You may be able to print information, download information to a computer disk, or both. Some systems allow you to add your own notes.	You may be able to print or download information to a computer disk.
How current is the information in this medium?	Information may be outdated by the time it is published. Some paper sources are updated; some are not. Frequency of updating varies.	Currency is not a strength of this medium. Microforms are often not updated.	Many disks are updated at regular intervals. The intervals vary, but often are monthly or quarterly. Some systems allow access to online updates.	Some information is updated on a "same day" basis. Other information is no more up-to-date than the information in a paper counterpart.
What special expertise is needed to use this medium?	Understanding of indexing is helpful.	Knowledge of how to locate microforms in your library and how to use microform equipment.	Knowledge of a system's hardware and software.	Knowledge of how to find computer databases, write computer searches, and browse results. Searching and browsing techniques vary somewhat among databases.
What is the primary cost of using this medium?	Your time.	Your time.	Your time, unless you use an online update.	Online time or subscription fees, in addition to your time.

In addition to introducing each resource in the paper medium, this text also illustrates the use of the resource in one of the technological media. Our goal is not to demonstrate all of the media in which you may use each resource, but to remind you that resources are available in multiple media and to show by concrete illustration some of the similarities, differences, advantages, and disadvantages of research in different media.

This text does not attempt to teach you all the details of how to use either LEXIS or WESTLAW because the vendors of both systems regularly publish thorough, up-to-date training materials for their systems. Nor does it attempt to teach you the details of how to use the Internet because those research techniques vary with the source you are searching. Rather, this text attempts to introduce you to the concepts you need to understand if you are to use those tools effectively.

4 Locate, Read, and Update Secondary Sources

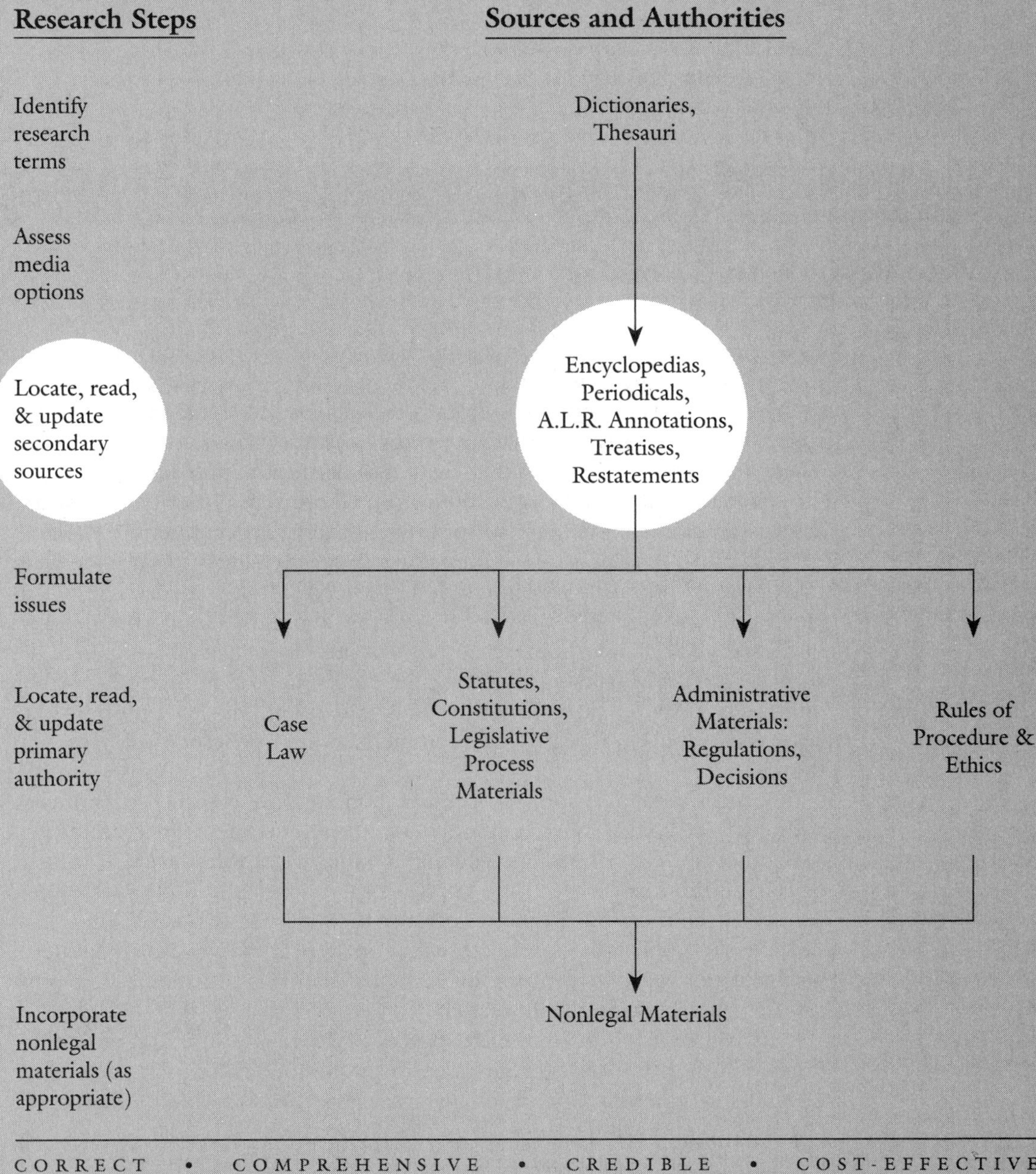

CORRECT • COMPREHENSIVE • CREDIBLE • COST-EFFECTIVE

Summary of Contents

A. Preliminary Points

1. Why Begin with Secondary Sources?

As you learned in Chapter 1, your ultimate goal in legal research is to discern the rule of law governing your client's situation. That rule derives from primary authority, whether cases, statutes, administrative materials, or court rules. Yet this text suggests that you start your research in secondary sources. There are several reasons for this seemingly circuitous approach.

First, secondary sources introduce you to primary authority. Secondary sources contain commentary on primary authority; they describe, explain, analyze, and, in some cases, critique and suggest changes in rules derived from primary authority. Although you are not reading the law itself when you read this commentary, you are reading about it. Good commentary synthesizes the major primary authorities into a framework prepared by an expert. This synthesis would be time-consuming, tedious, and possibly difficult to develop on your own. Thus you often will find grasping the law easier when you begin with commentary than when you begin with the law itself.

Second, secondary sources operate as finding tools to lead you to primary authority. Secondary source authors provide references to primary authority in support of their analyses, and you may use these references to locate leading primary authorities.

Third, compared to primary authority, secondary sources are fairly accessible. As you will fully appreciate with experience, it is easier to locate a pertinent portion of a treatise, for example, than it is to locate a pertinent case, if you are starting from scratch.

As you research in secondary sources as a means to the end of finding primary authority, evaluate your research by the four criteria for competent research introduced in Chapter 1: correct, comprehensive, credible, and cost-effective. As you will see throughout this chapter, each secondary source has its strengths and weaknesses. For most research projects, you will want to combine secondary sources so that your research is correct, comprehensive, and credible, and yet avoids excessive effort that undermines your cost-effectiveness.

As you read secondary sources, you should keep your client's situation in mind and extract information pertinent to it. That information is of various sorts. First, virtually all secondary sources state legal definitions, rules, and principles. You have already read about definitions and rules in Chapter 2. A legal principle, or policy, is broader than a legal rule; it expresses general goals of the law and the legal system. In addition, some secondary sources provide examples of legal outcomes in fairly specific situations, illustrating the definitions, rules, and principles. Second, you should note any critique of the current law and suggestions for reform, to the extent these points pertain to your client's case. Third, you should note the references to primary and other secondary authorities.

2. What Should Your Notes Include?

As you research in secondary sources, you should take careful notes. To some extent, taking notes in the context of legal research is not much different than taking notes for any research project. A good set of notes includes five components:

(1) the *research terms and modes of access* (for example, index) you used to locate pertinent information within the source;
(2) useful *pertinent information*, such as legal principles, rules, and definitions of legal concepts, along with where you located it (which volume, which page);
(3) a list of *references* to primary authority and other secondary sources;
(4) the means you used to *update* your research within the source (for example, supplement pamphlet); and
(5) the information needed to *cite* the source correctly.

Of course, you may want to photocopy long passages of pertinent material.

Your time is well spent in taking meticulous notes. Doing so reduces the likelihood of a return trip to the library to obtain a missing bit of information for a citation, to check whether you looked up a particular research term, or to verify that you updated the research. Needless to say, these return trips undermine the cost-effectiveness of your research.

3. How Is This Chapter Organized?

Parts B through F of this chapter each cover one of the major types of secondary sources. The sequence starts with sources that are analogous to nonlegal sources (such as encyclopedias and periodicals) and then moves into sources that are unique to the law (such as Restatements of the Law). Part G covers, in briefer form, several minor secondary sources. Part H synthesizes the information in the preceding parts and develops strategies for research that is correct, comprehensive, credible, and cost-effective.

Within each part, the text provides a general overview of how the source operates, followed by an illustration of the source's use in the research on the Canoga case. That case appears in Chapter 1 at pages 2-3; potentially useful research terms appear at page 16 of Chapter 2.

B. ENCYCLOPEDIAS

1. What Is an Encyclopedia?

Like nonlegal encyclopedias, legal encyclopedias cover a wide range of topics, present fairly general information, and order the topics alphabetically. The text is written by authors on the publisher's editorial staff, who generally are not well known experts.

Two encyclopedias cover American law, including state and federal law: *American Jurisprudence, Second Edition* (Am. Jur. 2d) and *Corpus Juris Secundum* (C.J.S.). Both are successors to older and now outdated encyclopedias, *American Jurisprudence* and *Corpus Juris.*

An encyclopedia is organized by topics, which are presented alphabetically. Some topics are quite narrow, others very broad. Within each topic, the discussion is organized by subtopics into sections, as dictated by the legal rules and principles involved. It is fairly common for the opening sections to cover the substantive legal rules, while the closing sections cover procedure and remedies. (In a general sense, these sections parallel legal theories, procedural posture, and relief sought, as discussed in Chapter 2.) Each section provides text discussing the topic as well as fairly extensive footnotes containing references to the authorities supporting the text.

Illustration 4-1 on page 47 is from Am. Jur. 2d's discussion of Wrongful Discharge, and Illustration 4-2 on page 48 is from C.J.S.'s discussion of the Employer-Employee Relationship. Both are pertinent to the Canoga case.

2. Why Are Encyclopedias Useful?

As secondary sources, encyclopedias describe the law and operate as finding tools for primary authority. They do not, however, critique the law or suggest legal reforms.

For the typical research project, encyclopedias are most useful at the very beginning of the research process. Because they cover such a wide range of topics, you very likely will find some pertinent material. That material will provide a broad overview of your topic, which can be skimmed fairly easily. Furthermore, it is easy to browse, that is, to move from subtopic to subtopic or from one topic to related topics within an encyclopedia. For these reasons, encyclopedias are useful in providing the "big picture."

Illustration 4-1 82 Am. Jur. 2d *Wrongful Discharge* § 96 (1992).

rules in the manual, and the courts increasingly recognize that employers have a like duty to abide by the promises they make.[40]

Practice guide: In one state it is provided by statute that a discharge is wrongful if the employer violates express provisions of its own personnel policy.[41]

Employee handbooks are viewed as one component or term of the employment agreement.[42] Unless an employee handbook or manual specifically negates any intention on the part of the employer to have it become a part of the employment contract,[43] a court may conclude from a review of the employee handbook that a question of fact is created regarding whether the handbook was intended[44] by the parties to impliedly express a term of the employment agreement.[45] Accordingly, where unilateral contracts are recognized, employment handbooks which contain provisions specifying progressive discharge procedures,[46] or specifying the grounds on which employees could be discharged,[47] or providing that discharge may be for cause only,[48] have been found binding on the employer, constituting a promise not to terminate the employee in violation of such provisions.[49]

40. Toussaint v. Blue Cross & Blue Shield, 408 Mich 579, 292 NW2d 880, 895 ("having announced the policy, presumably with a view to obtaining the benefit of improved employee attitudes and behavior and improved quality of the workforce, the employer may not treat its promise as illusory"); Lukoski v Sandia Indian Management Co., 106 NM 664, 748 P2d 507, 2 BNA IER Cas 1650; Thompson v St. Regis Paper Co., 102 Wash 2d 219, 685 P2d 1081, 1 BNA IER Cas 392, 116 BNA LRRM 3142, 105 CCH LC ¶55616 ("promises of specific treatment in specific situations found in an employee manual or handbook issued by the employer . . . may, in appropriate situations, obligate the employer to act in accord with those promises").

41. See Meech v Hillhaven West, Inc., 238 Mont 21, 776 P2d 488, 4 BNA IER Cas 737, 112 CCH LC ¶ 56073, upholding the constitutionality of the Montana Wrongful Discharge from Employment Act.

42. Lincoln v Sterling Drug, Inc. (DC Conn) 622 F Supp 66; Loffa Intel Corp. (App) 153 Ariz 539, 738 P2d 1146; Finley v Aetna Life & Casualty Co., 202 Conn 190, 520 A2d 208, 2 BNA IER Cas 942; Watson v Idaho Falls Consol. Hospitals, Inc., 111 Idaho 44, 720 P2d 632; Duldulao v St. Mary of Nazareth Hospital Center, 115 Ill 2d 482, 106 Ill Dec 8, 505 NE2d 314, 1 BNA IER Cas 1428; Small v Springs Industries, Inc., 292 SC 481, 357 SE2d 452, 2 BNA IER Cas 266, 106 CCH LC ¶55766, appeal after remand 300 SC 481, 388 SE2d 808, 5 BNA IER Cas 145, 115 CCH LC ¶56241.

The employment agreement is composed of written and verbal statements, custom, policy, past practice, industry practice, and any other fact which may define the terms of the contract. Shah v American Synthetic Rubber Corp. (Ky) 655 SW2d 489, 114 BNA LRRM 3343, 99CCH LC ¶55423.

43. As to manuals not constituting part of the employment contract, see § 97.

44. Generally, as to intent needed to form a contract, see § 88.

45. Metcalf v Intermountain Gas Co., 116 Idaho 622, 778 P2d 744, 4 BNA IER Cas 961, 113 CCH LC ¶ 56136.

See Lukoski v Sandia Indian Management Co., 106 NM 664, 748 P2d 507, 2 BNA IER Cas 1650, noting that the handbook did nothing to alert employees that it was subject to revocation or that employees should not rely on it.

46. § 117.

47. § 119.

48. § 120.

49. Towns v Emery Air Freight, Inc. (SD Ohio) 3 BNA IER Cas 911 (applying Ohio law);

Illustration 4-2 30 C.J.S. *Employer-Employee Relationship* § 21 (1992).

§ 21 EMPLOYER-EMPLOYEE 30 C.J.S.

C. CONTRACTS OF EMPLOYMENT

§ 21. In General

A contract of employment cannot arise without the consent of an alleged party thereto, and when a contract is made without a choice-of-law provision, the law of the state with the most significant relationship to the particular issue or transaction may be applied to resolve any disputes.

Library References

Master and Servant ⇐2.

The relation of master and servant arises out of contract, and a contract of employment usually involves the agreement of one party to render services or labor for the benefit of another, who in turn becomes obligated to pay a consideration therefor,[24] and the rights of an employer and an employee under an employment contract are correlative.[25]

A contract of employment cannot arise against the will or without the consent of an alleged party thereto,[26] and contracts of employment cannot be created by the subjective expectations of an employee.[27]

The parties to an employment agreement have the right to bargain for termination provisions.[28] An employee has the right to enter into a contract imposing restrictions on an employer's power to discharge an employee,[29] and a contract may include provisions preventing immediate discharge without cause.[30]

What law governs.

It has been held that a contract of employment is governed as to its construction and effect by the law with reference to which the parties in good faith intended to contract [31] unless application of that law would be an affront to the law or public policy of some state with more significant contact with the matter in dispute.[32]

When an employment contract is made without a choice-of-law provision, the law of the state with the most significant relationship to the particular substantive issue or transaction in a contract dispute,[33] the law of the state with which the facts are in most intimate contact,[34] or the law of the state having the greatest interest in the litigation [35] will be applied to resolve any issues.

A contract made without reference to the law of a particular place [36] may also be governed by the law of the place where the contract was made.[37] This is undoubtedly true in so far as the place where the contract is made is the same as

23. U.S.—Wardle v. Central States, Southeast and Southwest Areas Pension Fund, C.A.Ind., 627 F.2d 820, certiorari denied 101 S.Ct. 922, 449 U.S. 1112, 66 L.Ed.2d 841.

Torrence v. Chicago Tribune Co., Inc., D.C.Ill., 535 F.Supp. 743.

24. U.S.—Rickenbaker v. Layton, D.C.S.C., 59 F.Supp. 156.

La.—ODECO Oil & Gas Co. v. Nunez, App. 1 Cir., 532 So.2d 453, writ denied 535 So.2d 745.

N.H.—Swiezynski v. Civiello, 489 A.2d 634, 126 N.H. 142.

Contractual basis of relation see supra § 7.

25. Wash.—Blanchard v. Golden Age Brewing Co., 63 P.2d 397, 188 Wash. 396.

26. U.S.—Vaughan v. Warner, C.C.A.Pa., 157 F.2d 26.

La.—ODECO Oil & Gas Co. v. Nunez, App. 1 Cir., 532 So.2d 453, writ denied 535 So.2d 745.

N.M.—Jelso v. World Balloon Corp., App., 637 P.2d 846, 97 N.M. 164.

Pa.—Saldukas v. McKerns, 16 A.2d 30, 340 Pa. 113.

Wash.—Bradley v. S.L. Savidge, Inc., 152 P.2d 149, 21 Wash.2d 556.

Acquiescence

In order to establish contract, there must be at least implied acquiescence by employee in relationship.

Ill.—A.J. Johnson Paving Co. v. Industrial Commission, 412 N.E.2d 477, 45 Ill.Dec. 126, 82 Ill.2d 341.

27. Nev.—Vancheri v. GNLV Corp., 777 P.2d 366, 105 Nev. 417.

28. Iowa—Chard v. Iowa Machinery & Supply Co., Inc., App., 446 N.W.2d 81.

Me.—Libby v. Calais Regional Hosp., 554 A.2d 1181.

Wis.—Hale v. Stoughton Hosp. Ass'n, Inc., App., 376 N.W.2d 89, 126 Wis.2d 267.

Termination of employment relationship generally see infra § 35 et seq.

29. U.S.—Stack v. Allstate Ins. Co., D.C.Ind., 606 F.Supp. 472.

30. U.S.—Morris v. Chem-Lawn Corp., D.C.Mich., 541 F.Supp. 479.

Ohio—Williams v. State, Ohio Expositions Com'n, 518 N.E.2d 966, 34 Ohio App.3d 361, motion overruled 533 N.E.2d 786, 38 Ohio St.3d 717.

31. U.S.—Simpson v. Norwesco, Inc., C.A.S.D., 583 F.2d 1007.

N.C.—A.E.P. Industries, Inc. v. McClure, 302 S.E.2d 754, 308 N.C. 393.

What law governs contracts generally see C.J.S. Contracts § 12.

32. U.S.—Matter of Penn-Dixie Industries, Inc., Bkrtcy.N.Y., 22 B.R. 794.

33. U.S.—Gillespie v. Equitable Life Assur. Soc. of U.S., D.C.Del., 590 F.Supp. 1111.

34. Ind.—Eby v. York-Division, Borg-Warner, App. 4 Dist., 455 N.E.2d 623.

35. U.S.—Fallis v. Pendleton Woolen Mills, Inc., C.A.6(Ohio), 866 F.2d 209.

36. Mass.—Weiner v. Pictorial Paper Package Corp., 20 N.E.2d 458, 303 Mass. 123.

36

This big picture is correct in general terms. The text is likely to be correct as to general principles, but it will not precisely state the law of your jurisdiction. Because the scope of Am. Jur. 2d and C.J.S. is so broad, they do not provide much detail or explore the nuances of the law from state to state. Similarly, while you may well find a reference to a leading primary authority from your jurisdiction in Am. Jur. 2d or C.J.S., you should not expect to find exhaustive references. Encyclopedias are updated regularly, with the references typically more current than the text.

Because encyclopedias are not written by well recognized experts, they are not as credible as some of the other sources covered in this chapter. They are cited most frequently for broad, well established points.

3. How Do You Research in Encyclopedias?

Researching in an encyclopedia entails three steps: locating pertinent material, reading it, and updating it. This sequence is applicable, in fact, to all other research sources.

a. Locating Pertinent Material

There are two primary means of locating pertinent material in an encyclopedia: the index and the topic list. The index is located in multiple separate volumes, typically shelved at the end of the set. Am. Jur. 2d and C.J.S. both update their indexes annually; you should check the front cover or spine to be sure that you are using the index for the current year. Encyclopedia indexes are complex and detailed, with several levels of entries used for the largest topics. Hence you may need to spend significant time looking up alternative research terms, pursuing cross-references, and reading through the listings under a particular research term. You may identify more than one potentially pertinent topic by use of the index, as well as multiple specific sections within those pertinent topics.

The second primary means of locating pertinent material is through the topic list. Both Am. Jur. 2d and C.J.S. contain a list of their topics in alphabetical order, which you can skim for potentially pertinent topics. In Am. Jur. 2d this list appears as the Table of Abbreviations at the front of each index volume. In C.J.S. the topic list appears as the List of Titles in the beginning of each non-index volume as well as the Abbreviations of Titles in the index volumes. (C.J.S. uses the term "title" for topic.) While using the topic list tends to be quicker than using an index, it also yields only general information; you will not obtain information about specific sections within a topic from the topic list.

In the Canoga case, for example, if you began by looking up "employer and employee" in the Am. Jur. 2d index, you would see a cross-reference to "employment" and a further cross-reference to "master and servant." The "master and servant" entry runs over twenty pages and employs not only subentries but also sub-subentries. It points to quite a variety of sections within several topics, including Contracts, Job Discrimination, Master and Servant, and Wrongful Discharge. See Illustration 4-3 on page 50. If you

Illustration 4-3 Index, Am. Jur. 2d.

AMERICAN JURISPRUDENCE 2d

90 **For assistance using this Index, call 1-800-527-0430**

scanned the C.J.S. topic list, you would learn that C.J.S. contains the following potentially useful topics: Contracts, Employer-Employee Relationship, Labor Relations, and Right of Privacy.

Incidentally, if you began your research in Am. Jur. 2d with knowledge of a pertinent federal statute, regulation, court rule, or uniform act, you could consult the Table of Statutes, Rules, and Regulations Cited, which appears in its own volume. This table lists all Am. Jur. 2d topics and sections citing these authorities.

b. Reading the Pertinent Material

Once you have located a potentially useful topic, whether by the index or the topic list, you are ready to read the discussion of your subject. You should read the introductory material first. The introductory material may contain helpful references to other topics as well as other sources published by the same publisher. The outline at the beginning of each topic will show you the coverage and organization of the topic and permit you to discern the most pertinent sections. There may be both general and detailed topic outlines; you should work from the general to the specific. An alternative means of pinpointing pertinent sections is to consult the index for your topic appearing at the end of most topic volumes. You should use these tools to identify pertinent sections even if you have used the general index because they provide more detailed information than the general index provides.

Once you have located the most pertinent sections within your topic, read them carefully with two distinct but related purposes in mind: (1) to learn pertinent legal rules, principles, and definitions, and (2) to obtain references to other potentially pertinent authorities. Be sure that you take time to browse through related sections and glance at cross-reference topics to assure that your research is comprehensive.

In the Canoga case, Illustration 4-4 on page 52 shows the C.J.S. general topic outline for Employer-Employee Relationship; a quick scan reveals that sections 21-30 on contracts and sections 35-105 on termination are potentially pertinent. The introductory material to Am. Jur. 2d's Wrongful Discharge topic, Illustration 4-5 on page 53, establishes that the topic covers pertinent legal theories (such as at-will employment and implied contract), directs you to related topics elsewhere in Am. Jur. 2d, and points you toward several treatises. From the text in both encyclopedias, found in Illustrations 4-1 and 4-2 on pages 47 and 48, you would learn the same essential point: that the employer and employee may contract, through an employee handbook, for discharge procedures or limitations on the grounds for discharge. Furthermore, New Mexico cases (*Lukoski* and *Jelso*)—mandatory primary authority—are referred to in the footnotes in both sources.

c. Updating and Expanding Your Research

Because your research must be current, you must seek the most current information in the encyclopedia. For most topics, you will read the material in the main volume and then update that material by checking for new material in the pocket part. A pocket part is a set of pages inserted into a pocket, generally in the back of a bound volume; it is used to bring the bound volume up to date (or at least within a year or less of the present).

Illustration 4-4 Topic Outline, C.J.S.

CORPUS JURIS SECUNDUM

EMPLOYER-EMPLOYEE RELATIONSHIP

Analysis

See also General Index

1

The pocket part may provide additional text with supporting authorities or simply additional references.

In addition, Am. Jur. 2d provides the New Topic Service, a looseleaf binder containing topics too new to be located in the appropriate bound

Illustration 4-5 Introductory Material, Am. Jur. 2d.

WRONGFUL DISCHARGE

by

Irwin J. Schiffres, J.D.

Scope of topic: This article discusses modern developments which have modified the long-standing "at-will" doctrine under which the discharge of employees was permitted for any cause or no cause at all. It considers the development of theories on which discharged private sector employees—not protected by union contracts or civil service regulations—may base an action against their former employers. Actions for wrongful discharge have been permitted under a "public policy exception" which protects employees who are discharged for exercising legal rights, for refusing to commit illegal acts and for disclosing employer misconduct ("whistleblowing"). Such actions have also been permitted under an implied contract theory (based frequently on representations in employee manuals and handbooks), on the basis of a covenant of good faith and fair dealing, and under various traditional tort remedies, including interference with contractual relations, infliction of emotional distress, invasion of privacy, and fraud. Also discussed are defenses to such actions and the remedies available, including the recoverability of compensatory and punitive damages.

Federal aspects: This articles discusses the premptive effect of various federal statutes on a state common-law claim for wrongful termination. Among the statutes included are the National Labor Relations Act, the Labor-Management Relations Act, the Labor-Management Reporting Disclosure Act, the Railway Labor Act, ERISA, federal safety and environmental laws, and federal banking and lending laws. The rights of discharged employees generally under federal statutes are discussed in other articles, as indicated under "Treated elsewhere," infra. (See "Federal Legislation," infra, for USCS citations).

Treated elsewhere:

Rights of discharged employees who:

are covered by collective bargaining agreements, see 48 Am Jur 2d, Labor Relations §§ 920 et seq.

were employed by governmental agencies, see 15A Am Jur 2d, Civil Service §§ 52 et seq.

were discharged because of age, race, color, religion, sex, or national origin, see 45A, 45B Am Jur 2d, Job Discrimination §§ 873 et seq.

Discharge of employee in violation of ERISA, see 60A Am Jur 2d, Pensions and Retirement Funds

Discharge of employee hired for a definite term, see 53 Am Jur 2d, Master and Servant §§ 43-70

Discharge of employee by reason of the fact that his earnings have been subjected to garnishment, see 6 Am Jur 2d, Attachment and Garnishment § 176 (Supp)

Effect of discharge for cause on right to unemployment compensation, see 76 Am Jur 2d, Unemployment Compensation §§ 77 et seq.

Research References

Text References:

Modjeska, Employment Discrimination Law (LCP, 2d edition)

Pepe and Dunham, Avoiding and Defending Wrongful Discharge Claims (CBC)

Tobias, Litigating Wrongful Discharge Claims (CBC)

RIA Employment Discrimination Coordinator ¶¶ 101 et seq.

657

volume. It merits a brief check as you complete your research in Am. Jur. 2d.

In the Canoga case, the pocket parts of both Am. Jur. 2d and C.J.S. contain additional references. Illustration 4-6 on page 55 shows the C.J.S. pocket part, which provides additional text as well. The Am. Jur. 2d New Topic Service includes a topic on the Americans with Disabilities Act, which could be of interest.

In the Canoga case, encyclopedias have provided fairly typical information: general principles and references to two cases from your jurisdiction. The illustrations pertain to one legal theory (contract); similar information could be obtained on other theories. For more precise and extensive discussions of any theory, as well as critique of the law, you would consult other secondary sources. Of course, to fully understand the law, you must read the primary authorities.

4. What Else?

Tables of Abbreviations. Both encyclopedias provide tables of abbreviations, which can be useful if you do not recognize the abbreviation for a source that appears pertinent. The C.J.S. tables appear in the main topic volumes, while the Am. Jur. 2d tables appear in the pocket parts to the topic volumes.

Converting from the First to Second Series. If you know about a pertinent section from the original *American Jurisprudence* and wish to locate the corresponding material in Am. Jur. 2d, you should consult the Table of Parallel References at the beginning of the appropriate topic volume. Analogous information for *Corpus Juris* appears at the beginning of some topics in C.J.S.

Am. Jur. 2d Desk Book. This single volume includes a wide range of miscellaneous information, such as the structure and membership of federal government bodies, statistics on various aspects of life in America, selected international legal documents, and financial tables.

State Encyclopedias. In many states, a state encyclopedia covers the law of that state only. While much of the text above applies to state encyclopedias, there are some differences. For example, a state encyclopedia is, of course, very likely to contain references to mandatory primary authority. The encyclopedia may have greater credibility than Am. Jur. 2d or C.J.S. with the courts of that state.

Specialized Encyclopedias. In some areas of law, such as criminal and international law, specialized encyclopedias exist. They may resemble Am. Jur. 2d and C.J.S. in organization, but their scope is narrower.

Illustration 4-6 Pocket Part, C.J.S.

EMPLOYER—EMPLOYEE

30 CJS 2

46 U.S.C.A. Sec.	C.J.S. Sec.	Note
60	74	60
	80	14
	87	10
431 et seq.	69	84
441(a)	69	85

46 U.S.C.A.–Shipping

46 U.S.C.A. Sec.	C.J.S. Sec.	Note
688	75	11

46 U.S.C.A. Sec.

49 U.S.C.A.—Transportation

49 U.S.C.A. Sec.	C.J.S. Sec.	Note
20103 et seq.	69	84
20109(a)	69	85
40101 et seq.	69	82

49 Appendix U.S.C.A.—Transportation

49 Appendix U.S.C.A. Sec.	C.J.S. Sec.	Note
1301 et seq.	69	82

§ 4. Statutory Regulation in General

page 18

Criminal statutes.

Statutes which authorize the prosecution and imprisonment of employers for failure to pay wages due violates state constitutions which prohibit imprisonment for debt.[73.5]

73.5 Okl.—State ex rel. Moss v. Couch, Cr., 841 P.2d 1154.

75. Whistle-blower's statute
Fla.—Walsh v. Arrow Air, Inc., App. 3 Dist., 629 So.2d 144, quashed on oth. grds. 645 So.2d 422.

§ 6. Essentials of Relation in General

page 20

The courts have considered other different tests to determine employment status.[8.5]

8.5 "Agency test"
"Agency test" for determining employment status turns on alleged employer's right to control alleged employee.
U.S.—Nowlin v. Resolution Trust Corp., C.A.5(Tex.), 33 F.3d 498.

"Economic realities test"
"Economic realities test" for determining employment status turns on whether alleged employee, as matter of economic reality, is dependent on business to which he renders service.
U.S.—Nowlin v. Resolution Trust Corp., C.A.5(Tex.), 33 F.3d 498.

"Hybrid test"
"Hybrid test" for determining employment status focuses on extent of alleged employer's right to control means and manner of worker's performance.
U.S.—Nowlin v. Resolution Trust Corp., C.A.5(Tex.), 33 F.3d 498.

§ 9. Direction and Control

page 22

29. Ala.—Harris v. Food Equipment Specialist, Inc., 559 So.2d 1066.

§ 13. In General

page 27

9. Neb.—McKinstry v. Cass County, 424 N.W.2d 322, 228 Neb. 733, app. after remand 488 N.W.2d 552, 241 Neb. 444.

page 28

24. Neb.—McKinstry v. Cass County, 424 N.W.2d 322, 228 Neb. 733, app. after remand 488 N.W.2d 552, 241 Neb. 444.

§ 22. Forms, Requisites, and Validity in General

page 39

72. Mo.—Gross v. Diehl Specialties Intern., Inc., App., 776 S.W.2d 879, app. after remand 870 S.W.2d 246.

73. Consideration implied where contract implied
N.M.—Hartbarger v. Frank Paxton Co., 857 P.2d 776, 115 N.M. 665, cert. den. 114 S.Ct. 1068, 127 L.Ed.2d 387.

page 40

78. Contract containing nonsolicitation clause
Continued employment and compensation was consideration for employment contract which contained nonsolicitation clause.
Ala.—Corson v. Universal Door Systems, Inc., 596 So.2d 565.

A provision stating that employment may be terminated upon notice of either party as prescribed constitutes consideration sufficient to support an employment contract.[79.5]

79.5 Mo.—Sanfillippo v. Oehler, App.E.D., 869 S.W.2d 159, reh. and/or transfer den., transfer den.

page 42

25. Tenn.—Williams v. Maremont Corp., App., 776 S.W.2d 78, app. den.

§ 24. Construction and Operation in General

page 45

71. More than one meaning
Mo.—Enyeart v. Shelter Mut. Ins. Co., App., 693 S.W.2d 120, op. after remand 1989 WL 380448, affd. 784 S.W.2d 205.

page 47

86. Tenn.—Williams v. Maremont Corp., App., 776 S.W.2d 78, app. den.

§ 25. Personnel Handbooks or Manuals in General

98. Wis.—Bantz v. Montgomery Estates, Inc., App., 473 N.W.2d 506, 163 Wis.2d 973.

page 48

1. Ark.—Crain Industries, Inc. v. Cass, 810 S.W.2d 910, 305 Ark. 566.
Minn.—Hoemberg v. Watco Publishers, Inc., App., 343 N.W.2d 676, review den.

Implied contract
U.S.—Jackson v. Integra Inc., C.A.10(Okl.), 952 F.2d 1260, app. after remand 30 F.3d 141.

5. Colo.—Cronk v. Intermountain Rural Elec. Ass'n, App., 765 P.2d 619, cert. den., app. after remand 1992 WL 161811, cert. den.

10. Absence of specific disciplinary procedures
Ill.—Tolbert v. St. Francis Extended Care Center, 1 Dist., 545 N.E.2d 384, 136 Ill.Dec. 860, 189 Ill. App.3d 503, app. den. 550 N.E.2d 566, 140 Ill.Dec. 681, 129 Ill.2d 572.

11. Ill.—Lee v. Canuteson, 3 Dist., 573 N.E.2d 318, 157 Ill.Dec. 900, 214 Ill.App.3d 137, app. den. 580 N.E.2d 117, 162 Ill.Dec. 491, 141 Ill.2d 543.

page 49

15. Colo.—Cronk v. Intermountain Rural Elec. Ass'n, App., 765 P.2d 619, cert. den., app. after remand 1992 WL 161811, cert. den.

Provisions not generally known
Employee could not rely on statements in employer's policy manual that was distributed to supervisors only and not to employees to support claim that employer breached employment contract when it terminated him, where there was no evidence that provisions of manual were generally known.
Wash.—Hatfield v. Columbia Federal Sav. Bank, 790 P.2d 1258, 57 Wash.App. 876, app. after remand 846 P.2d 1380, 68 Wash.App. 817, review den. 856 P.2d 382, 121 Wash.2d 1030.

20. Contextual examination necessary
Language in employee handbook stating that handbook was for information only and was not employment contract did not automatically prevent handbook from becoming party of employment contract, but rather such language had to be examined in context with handbook as whole, where such language was located on last page of 52-page handbook, and there was nothing to distinguish that language from rest of text or highlight such language as being particularly important.
U.S.—Davis v. Connecticut General Life Ins. Co., M.D.Tenn., 743 F.Supp. 1273.

However, handbook representations are enforceable under certain circumstances despite the presence of a disclaimer.[20.5]

20.5 Ill.—Perman v. ArcVentures, Inc., 1 Dist., 554 N.E.2d 982, 143 Ill.Dec. 910, 196 Ill.App.3d 758.

Promissory estoppel shown
Employee is entitled to enforce representation in employee handbook, despite disclaimer of contract in handbook, if he can demonstrate that employer should have reasonably expected employee to consider representation as commitment from employer, employee reasonably relied upon representation to his detriment, and injustice can be avoided only by enforcement of representation.
Wyo.—McDonald v. Mobil Coal Producing, Inc., 789 P.2d 866, on reh. 820 P.2d 986.

§ 27. Commencement and Duration of Employment

page 52

54. U.S.—Sneed v. American Bank Stationary Co., Div. of ABS Corp., W.D.Va., 764 F.Supp. 65.

Other Media. As of early 1996, encyclopedias appeared in the following media:

	Paper	*CD-ROM*	*Computer-Assisted Research*		*Microform*
			LEXIS	*WESTLAW*	
Am. Jur. 2d	√	√			
C.J.S.	√				

5. How Do You Cite Encyclopedias?

A complete and proper citation consists of the volume, abbreviated name of the encyclopedia, topic name, section, and year, according to Rule 15.7(a) of *The Bluebook*. Note that you must include the year of the supplement if pertinent information appears there as well as in the main volume, according to Rule 3.2(c).

In the Canoga case, the proper citations to the excerpts in Illustrations 4-1 and 4-2, including a reference to the supplement for C.J.S. but not for Am. Jur. 2d, are:

82 Am. Jur. 2d *Wrongful Discharge* § 96 (1992).
30 C.J.S. *Employer-Employee Relationship* § 21 (1992 & Supp. 1994).

C. Legal Periodicals

1. What Is a Legal Periodical?

A legal periodical is a secondary source that provides commentary on a range of topics. Articles in legal periodicals are written by private authors and tend to be scholarly or theoretical. They not only describe the current state of the law but also explore underlying policies, critique current legal rules, and advocate new approaches.

The term "legal periodical" includes five different types of publications. The first and most common type is the law review or law journal. Most law reviews cover a wide range of legal topics. They typically carry the names of a particular law school; for example, *Pepperdine Law Review* or *Yale Law Journal.* The students of the school serve as the editors and editorial staff. They select articles from those submitted by legal scholars, judges, or practitioners; evaluate the ideas; verify the authority given for the ideas propounded; assure the accuracy of the citations; and edit the author's writing. Students also write some articles. Generally, a law review staff publishes a new volume annually in two to six separate issues.

Law reviews typically publish several types of articles in each issue. Long pieces with extensive citations written by practitioners, professors, or judges are called "articles." Shorter pieces written by non-students that have fewer footnotes and reflect the opinion or expertise of the author may be called "essays." On occasion, a law review will publish a feature article by a prominent author followed by short discussions of the feature article, usually labeled "commentaries." A "symposium issue" is an issue of the law review that is dedicated to one topic. Some issues contain "book reviews" of recently published treatises.

Student pieces are called "case notes" or "case comments" if they focus on a narrow topic or on a recent court or agency decision. The label "recent developments" is often used for a lengthy survey of an area of law cowritten by a group of students or faculty. A law review's table of contents generally classifies its contents by the categories described above. You must know which type of article you are reading to evaluate the credibility of the article and to cite it properly.

A second type of legal periodical is the special-interest legal periodical. These periodicals focus on a specific, well defined area of law. For example, the *Employee Relations Law Journal* and the *Labor Law Journal* focus on labor and employment law. Some special-interest periodicals, such as *Social Responsibility: Business, Journalism, Law, Medicine,* are interdisciplinary. Special-interest periodicals are edited and published by various organizations. Some are published by law schools and edited by student staffs or faculty, so they resemble general-scope law reviews. Others are published by an association of lawyers or by commercial publishers; they generally are called "journals" and may be less theoretical and more practitioner-oriented than those published by law schools.

The third type of legal periodical is the bar association journal, such as the *ABA Journal.* Many national, state, and local bar associations and other professional organizations of lawyers publish journals that contain articles on the law as well as news of interest to members. Typically, these articles are more practical than theoretical, and they focus on how to accomplish a particular legal task. The news in these journals can be of great value. For example, a bar journal may report on changes in court rules or publish opinions of a lawyers professional responsibility board.

Fourth, commercial legal newspapers are exactly what the name suggests. These newspapers are legal periodicals because they are issued "periodically" on a regular and frequent schedule. They typically report (in full text, summary, or news form) on new court decisions and other important changes in the law. They also often carry legal notices mandated by law, such as notices of incorporation of businesses or foreclosures of property, as well as feature stories about the persons, law firms, or new developments in the law. Some legal newspapers are national in coverage, such as the *National Law Journal;* others cover one city or state, such as the *Los Angeles Daily Journal.*

Fifth, commercial publishers and others publish newsletters on specific legal topics. These newsletters generally are short; are issued monthly, weekly, or even daily; and cover very recent developments. They provide information on new cases, statutes, and regulations, as well as on other legal and nonlegal developments.

In the Canoga case, Illustration 4-7 on pages 59-60 is a portion of an article on smoking in the workplace. It is from the *Tennessee Law Review,* which is a general-scope law review published by a student board of editors. As noted in the first footnote, the author is a practitioner.

2. Why Are Legal Periodicals Useful?

Periodical articles are good research materials because they describe, analyze, and comment on the law. A good periodical article, which is often quite comprehensive in the scope and accuracy of its research, provides background information on the legal issue you are researching. This background often includes extensive analysis that may assist you by synthesizing and explaining the rules and principles. Because of the extensive editing that each article typically undergoes, it is likely that the information contained in an article is correct. Some articles also may provide factual information or statistical data.

Within the text of the article and in the numerous footnotes, you can find a wealth of references to primary authority, such as cases and statutes. Occasionally, an article may even contain references to the primary authorities in each of the fifty states. Additionally, most articles contain references to other secondary sources, such as treatises and other periodical articles, and to nonlegal sources.

You may use the commentary found in legal periodicals to formulate a novel argument on behalf of your client. Because the function of legal periodicals is to present serious, creative legal thought, you may find original thoughts or arguments that propose legal reform. Indeed, in some circumstances, you will find a series of articles on the same subject, each presenting a different viewpoint and responding directly to other authors' viewpoints. Although periodicals are merely commentary sources, some articles have prompted changes in the law. Typically, these articles are written by established scholars or practitioners and reflect serious research and thought; few of the many articles written each year attain this status.

Because a law review article can be written and published in less time than other materials can be published, periodicals are a good source for a discussion of a new legal topic. However, periodical articles lose currency quickly because the references contained in an article are current only to the date on which the article was completed, which may be some time prior to the date of publication. Consequently, some of the existing references need to be updated (their current validity confirmed) with other sources, and new references to more recent primary authority need to be found.

Illustration 4-7

David B. Ezra, *"Get Off Your Butts": The Employer's Right to Regulate Employee Smoking*, 60 Tenn. L. Rev. 905, 905, 950 (1993).

"GET OFF YOUR BUTTS": THE EMPLOYER'S RIGHT TO REGULATE EMPLOYEE SMOKING

DAVID B. EZRA*

INTRODUCTION

Smokers in the workplace are the modern day lepers.[1] In order to smoke, many are exiled into cramped smokers' lounges or pushed outside into the cold by employer policies requiring a smoke-free workplace.[2] For others who smoke, the situation is even more grim because some employers simply refuse to hire smokers.[3] Smokers complain that this treatment is an unfair infringement upon their rights and some smokers have even formed groups to lobby for protection of their right to smoke.[4]

However, smokers are not the only people who are fired up over the

---

* Associate, Berger, Kahn, Shafton, Moss, Figler, Simon & Gladstone. B.A. 1987, California State University, Fullerton; J.D. 1990, University of Southern California. The views expressed herein are those of the author, and are not intended to reflect the views of Berger, Kahn, Shafton, Moss, Figler, Simon & Gladstone or its clients. The author would like to thank Valerie A. Smith, whose comments improved the Article throughout, and Paul Babbitt, for his valuable research assistance.

1. *See, e.g.*, Tim Falconer, *No Butts About It*, CANADIAN BUS., Feb. 1987, at 66; Elaine H. Fry, *Not Smoking in the Workplace: The Real Issue*, BUS. HORIZONS, Nov.-Dec. 1990, at 13; William S. Hubbartt, *Smoking at Work—An Emerging Office Issue*, ADMIN. MGMT., Feb. 1986, at 21.

2. *See* Nancy R. Gibbs, *All Fired Up Over Smoking: New Laws and Attitudes Spark a War*, TIME, Apr. 18, 1988, at 64.

3. *See, e.g.*, Andrew M. Kramer & Laurie F. Calder, *The Emergence of Employees' Privacy Rights: Smoking and the Workplace*, 8 LAB. LAW. 313, 322 (1992) ("[A]pproximately 6,000 United States companies now refuse to employ smokers."); Mark A. Rothstein, *Refusing to Employ Smokers: Good Public Health or Bad Public Policy?*, 62 NOTRE DAME L. REV. 940 (1987); Jimmy Goh, Comment, *"Smokers Need Not Apply": Challenging Employment Discrimination Against Smokers Under the Americans with Disabilities Act*, 39 KAN. L. REV. 817 (1991) ("[S]ome employers are taking the extreme measure of refusing to hire smokers—even if these individuals only smoke off duty.").

4. Many smokers say they would like to quit smoking if they could. Thus, some argue that smokers' rights groups are a product of the tobacco industry, not individual smokers. *See* Bruce Samuels & Stanton A. Glantz, *The Politics of Local Tobacco Control*, 266 JAMA 2110 (1991). While it may be true that the tobacco industry finances and organizes many smokers' rights groups, anyone who has witnessed the confrontations that take place in public when nonsmokers ask smokers to stop smoking can verify that there are many smokers who strongly believe in their right to smoke.

Illustration 4-7 *(continued)*

Civil Rights Act.[291] The Court acknowledged that 63% of persons in public methadone programs were black or Hispanic.[292] Nevertheless, the Court refused to find a violation of either Title VII or the Constitution.[293] Even though more than half of all persons disqualified were minorities, the Court found the statistical showing "weak."[294]

Because blacks currently are only slightly more likely to smoke than are whites, and because blacks are far less than half of all smokers, the link between blacks and smoking is substantially less certain than the weak minority-methadone link that the Supreme Court rejected in *Beazer*. As a result, it is very unlikely that employer policies which prohibit smoking will be found to unlawfully discriminate against minorities.[295]

D. Handicap and Disability—Addiction to Tobacco

Nonsmokers have had modest success arguing that sensitivity to tobacco smoke can amount to a handicap that warrants protection under federal law.[296] Therefore, it is not altogether unlikely that smokers will also advance this same argument, only in reverse based on their addiction to smoking.

Two basic federal laws protect the employment rights of disabled workers. These laws call on employers to take reasonable steps to accommodate the disabled persons, to the extent that such steps are consistent with job function and business needs.

The first law protecting disabled persons' employment rights is the Rehabilitation Act of 1973.[297] The Rehabilitation Act precludes discrimination based on a person's handicap in federal jobs and programs receiving federal funding.[298] The second law is the Americans with Disabilities Act of 1990 (ADA).[299] The ADA's reach is far broader than that of the Rehabilitation Act. The ADA applies to all employers with twenty-five or more employees.[300] Like the Rehabilitation Act, the ADA precludes

---

291. *Beazer*, 440 U.S. at 585; *see supra* note 283.

292. *Beazer*, 440 U.S. at 585.

293. *Id.* at 587.

294. *Id.* In addition, the Court in *Beazer* noted that the restriction on the hiring of persons in the methadone program was sufficiently job-related to rebut any inference of discrimination. *Id.* For the most part, employers will find it easy to establish that smoking restrictions are supported by valid business needs. *See* Hames, *supra* note 191, at 227-30.

295. *See, e.g.*, Moore v. Inmont Corp., 608 F. Supp. 919 (W.D.N.C. 1985) (upholding discharge of black employee who was observed smoking in a nonsmoking area against a charge that termination based on smoking was merely a pretext for racial discrimination).

296. *See supra* notes 150-62 and accompanying text.

297. 29 U.S.C. § 794 (1988).

298. *Id.*

299. 42 U.S.C. § 12101 (Supp. II 1990).

300. *Id.* § 12111(5)(a). Beginning in 1994, it will apply to all employers with fifteen

Periodicals do not cover every topic in the law, but rather those topics about which authors have chosen to write. Each article generally covers its subject in depth; indeed, you may find a lengthy article on a very narrow topic. On the other hand, the analysis in an article may be weak or one-sided, and without a thorough understanding of the topic you might have a difficult time discerning that defect.

3. How Do You Research in Legal Periodicals?

Researching in periodicals entails three steps: locating a pertinent article, reading and evaluating the article, and expanding your search by using *Shepard's Law Review Citations.*

a. Locating a Pertinent Article

Most often, to locate a legal periodical article you will use a system no different from that used for finding a periodical article in fields outside of law—an index. There are several major indexes to law reviews, legal journals, and legal newspapers; these indexes are published in various media. This chapter covers indexes available in CD-ROM, microform, and print services.

Indexes for legal periodicals are commercial products with differing features. Depending on the index, you may be able to search for articles by using a subject or author search or other search methods. Within a subject search, indexing vocabulary and cross-references also differ. The coverage of various indexes differs as to the number and type of periodicals indexed, as well as the years covered.

Furthermore, indexes have various "cumulation schedules"—that is, how often the updated materials are merged into the main body of the index, if they are at all. The cumulation schedule affects how many sets of update materials you must consult to fully update the index. For instance, if an index is updated quarterly but cumulated only on an annual basis, you might have to check as many as three or four sets of update materials in addition to the main body of the index. Still other kinds of indexes are "totally cumulative," which means that the entire index is replaced every time it is updated.

Some index features change from time to time as the index publishers modify their products to remain competitive. To keep up-to-date, read the instructions for the index you use, and do so regularly. These instructions may appear on the first few screens of a CD-ROM reader, in the user's manual, or in the first few pages of a printed volume.

(1) Using Non-Paper Periodical Indexes

Compared to traditional paper indexes, non-paper periodical indexes generally allow a wider range of search methods. They also are totally cumulative, so all entries on a topic appear in a single listing under a subject heading and its subheadings. Thus, you need not collect and search multiple volumes as with paper indexes. Of course, CD-ROM disks have limited capacity, and at some future date the capacity will be exceeded so that it may become necessary to search multiple disks. This section focuses on CD-ROM indexes because they quickly are becoming the preferred format.

LegalTrac and WILSONDISC are the two CD-ROM indexes for legal periodicals. *LegalTrac* is based on a paper index called the *Current Law Index* (discussed fully below), and it covers over 875 periodicals from 1980 forward; it covers English-language legal periodicals from the United States, Canada, the United Kingdom, Ireland, Australia, and New Zealand. All articles, case notes, and book reviews published in these periodicals are indexed. The legal periodical index available on WILSONDISC is based on a paper index called the *Index to Legal Periodicals and Books* (discussed fully below), which covers over 650 periodicals from 1908 forward, as well as some books. Your library's WILSONDISC subscription may also include some of the Wilson Company's 20 other indexes, such as the *Social Sciences Index* and the *Reader's Guide to Periodical Literature*. However, very short articles are not indexed. Thus, WILSONDISC covers a longer time frame, while covering fewer articles per year.

Because the features of the two legal periodical indexes are fairly similar, the following text will focus on *LegalTrac*, a CD-ROM index to which you likely will have access. You have two options for searching on *LegalTrac*: You may perform a subject-guide search, which focuses on finding appropriate subject headings, or you may perform a key-word search, which finds articles that contain your specific search terms in their title or subject heading. A key-word search also may be used to find specific articles by the author's name.

The subject-guide search is typically a broader search because it allows you to retrieve all indexed articles on a topic, even if the topic word does not appear within the title or text of the article. Although you are unlikely to know the exact subject heading used in the index, you may begin your research using any search terms familiar to you. If your search terms match a *LegalTrac* subject heading, *LegalTrac* presents a list of subjects with your search result highlighted. If there is no exact match, *LegalTrac* displays other related subject headings that may be useful.

In the Canoga case, for example, the term "employment" is too broad. Likewise, the search "employment and smoking" does not result in an exact match with a *LegalTrac* subject heading, but the system suggests an alternative subject heading, "smoking in the workplace." When you select that subject heading, *LegalTrac* displays the total number of records found under that subject heading; it also indicates how many subdivisions (subheadings) exist for that subject heading. Because there are many articles (forty-eight at the time this chapter was written) under the subject heading "smoking in the workplace," it is more efficient to narrow your search by examining the subdivisions. When you select the subdivisions entry on the screen, *LegalTrac* displays a list of the subdivisions and the number of records found under each subdivision. See Illustration 4-8 on page 63. Under the subdivision "laws, regulations, etc.," there are twenty-one records; several of the articles

Illustration 4-8 *LegalTrac* Screen.

```
=============================================================================
   InfoTrac EF   |                     LegalTrac                  Subject Guide
=================+-----------------------------------------------------------+
| Subdivisions of: Smoking in the Workplace                                  |
|                                                                            |
+---------------------------------------------------------------- Rec.'s -+
   - analysis                                                              9
   - bibliography                                                          1
   - environmental aspects                                                 1
   - health aspects                                                        3
   - laws, regulations, etc.                                              21
   - litigation                                                            8
   - management                                                            3
   - prevention                                                            1
   - research                                                              1
   - social aspects                                                        1
   - surveys                                                               1



=============================================================================
   Press Enter + to view       | Esc Return to subject list
   the citation(s) for the     |
   highlighted subject         |  F1 Help  F2 Start over  F3 Print  F4 Mark
```

appear to be worth reading, including an article by David B. Ezra, *"Get Off Your Butts": The Employer's Right to Regulate Employee Smoking,* published in the summer of 1993 *Tennessee Law Review.* See Illustration 4-7 on pages 59-60.

An alternative approach in *LegalTrac* is to do a key-word search. Recall that a key-word search retrieves articles that contain your research terms in the title, subject heading, or author's name. Your search may include the Boolean connectors ("and," "or," "not"). You also may use an asterisk to search for words with the same beginning letters but different ending letters; for instance, "employ*" will retrieve titles or subjects with the words "employment," "employer," "employee," "employ," "employed," and "employing." The asterisk is a truncating symbol that matches any number of characters.

In the Canoga case, for instance, using the key-word search "smoking and dismiss*" would yield only articles that contain "smoking" and a variant of "dismiss" in their titles. The Ezra article is not found when performing the key-word approach because the word root "dismiss*" does not appear in the title or subject heading for the article. Although the key-word approach is sometimes an efficient method for finding some highly relevant articles, it clearly is effective only if the title of the article describes the scope of the article. This is not the case when authors use clever or unconventional titles rather than descriptive ones.

Finally, when using either a subject-guide search or a key-word search, if your search retrieves too few or too many articles, it is possible to further narrow or expand the search by following the prompts on the bottom of the screen. To narrow your search, select the "narrow" option and limit your search by adding additional key words. Alternatively, it is possible to expand your search using the "explore" option; when you pick this option, *LegalTrac* automatically suggests subject headings or subheadings related to those already retrieved.

Once you have used *LegalTrac* to retrieve a list of articles, you need to scan the list and select articles that are appropriate for your research situation. A unique feature of *LegalTrac* assists you: *LegalTrac* will display abstracts of some articles. In Illustration 4-9 below, note the abstract available for the article written by Donald J. Petersen.

(2) Using Paper Periodical Indexes

The traditional medium for periodical indexes is paper. Most legal periodicals written in English are covered in two major paper indexes published in the United States, *Current Law Index* and *Index to Legal Periodicals and Books.* You also may consult several more specialized paper indexes from time to time.

Illustration 4-9 Citation List, *LegalTrac* Screen.

```
================================================================================
Database: LegalTrac
Subject:  Smoking in the Workplace
Subdivision:  laws, regulations, etc.
Holdings: * Indicates that Library subscribes to this journal
--------------------------------------------------------------------------------

        No smoking! The arbitration of smoking restricting policies. Donald
        J. Petersen. Dispute Resolution Journal, Jan 1995 50 n1 p44(7).
         -- Abstract Available --

        Workplace smoking in New Jersey: time for a change. Rebecca R.
        Smith. Seton Hall Law Review, Spring 1994 24 n2 p958-997.

        An assessment of the current legal climate concerning smoking in the
        workplace. (Symposium on Smokers' and Non-Smokers' Rights) John C.
        Fox. Saint Louis University Public Law Review, Wntr 1994 13 n2
        p591-634.

        "Get off your butts": the employer's right to regulate employee
        smoking. David B. Ezra. Tennessee Law Review, Summer 1993 60 n4
        p905-955.

        'Smokers need not apply': challenging employment discrimination
        against smokers under the Americans with Disabilities Act. Jimmy
        Goh. University of Kansas Law Review, Spring 1991 39 n3 p817-843.

        Smoking in the workplace: an annotated bibliography. Eugenie
        Tyburski and Herbert Abramson. Legal Reference Services Quarterly,
        Winter 1988 8 n3-4 p203-217.
```

Current Law Index (C.L.I.) has nearly the same coverage as *LegalTrac*, described above; however, *LegalTrac* indexes selected legal newspapers and contains abstracts of selected periodical articles, whereas C.L.I. does not. C.L.I. is published twelve times a year, with three issues serving as quarterly cumulations; the final issue is a hardbound annual cumulation. Consequently, often it is necessary to consult the cumulative volumes as well as the recent softbound issues to cover the entire time frame you are researching. For most projects, start with the most recent softbound issues and work back in time through the hardbound volumes until you find enough references. (Of course, if the articles on your topic probably appeared in a specific year or two, begin with the volumes covering that period.)

C.L.I. is comprised of four divisions. The most useful division in many cases is the subject division, which employs indexing headings developed by the Library of Congress. These headings also are used in most American libraries in their card and online catalogs. In selecting a subject heading, start with the most specific search terms possible. If the heading is divided by subheadings, scan the subheadings before reading the entries so that your research is well focused. To find additional subject headings for comprehensive research, review the cross-references found at the beginning or end of a topic. The articles under a subject heading are ordered by date of publication, with the most recent articles appearing first.

In the Canoga case, for example, you might start with "smoking." If you browsed for other related headings, you would find a heading for "smoking in the workplace." The Ezra article appears under this heading. See Illustration 4-10 on page 66.

C.L.I. also has separate divisions for a table of cases and a table of statutes. The table-of-cases division lists articles and case notes that contain substantial analysis of one or more cases; likewise, the table-of-statutes division lists articles that focus on a specific statute. These divisions are useful if you know the name of the case or statute related to your research situation and wish to locate commentary on that authority.

Finally, C.L.I. has an author/title division. You would use this division to locate articles by a particular author or title.

The second major print index, the *Index to Legal Periodicals and Books* (I.L.P.B.) was, until recently, called the *Index to Legal Periodicals*. It has nearly the same coverage as WILSONDISC, described above. In format, I.L.P.B. both resembles and diverges from C.L.I. It follows much the same publication and cumulation schedule as C.L.I.; however, I.L.P.B. contains a subject division that is merged with the author division. I.L.P.B. uses a system of headings, subheadings, and cross-references that are similar to C.L.I. but not necessarily the same. Some researchers perceive that the I.L.P.B. headings are more "legal," whereas C.L.I. uses subject headings that are closer to ordinary English. I.L.P.B. lists articles alphabetically by title, rather than by date of publication. It contains a table of cases and a table of statutes, as does C.L.I. It also contains a section of book reviews.

A useful feature of I.L.P.B. is the list of subject headings found at the beginning of recent hardbound volumes. You may be able to find additional search terms by scanning this list. I.L.P.B. also publishes a thesaurus that

Illustration 4-10 *Current Law Index.*

SMOKEFREE AREAS — **SUBJECT INDEX**

SMOKEFREE areas *see*
Nonsmoking areas

SMOKERS

Warning - smoking can seriously affect your job prospects. (United Kingdom)
IRS Employment Trends 3-4 Oct 15 '94

Experience with the cytological demonstration of smoker cells in the identification of disaster victims illustrated by the findings concerning the Lauda-Air airliner crash near Bangkok. by Christian Reiter and Daniele Risser
66 Forensic Science International 23-31 May 25 '94

Nonsmoking hiring policies: examining the status of smokers under Title I of the Americans with Disabilities Act of 1990. by Mark W. Pugsley
43 Duke Law Journal 1089-1114 March '94

Should the ill effects of environmental tobacco smoke exposure affect child-custody decisions? by Carolyn J. Wheatley *32 University of Louisville Journal of Family Law 115-132 Wnt[illegible]*

Parental smoking: a form of child abuse? by [illegible] Anderson *77 Marquette Law Review 360-384 Wnt[illegible]'94*

Whose life is it anyway - employer control of off-duty behavior. (Symposium on Smokers' and Non-Smokers' Rights) by Lewis L. Maltby and Bernard J. Dushman
13 Saint Louis University Public Law Review 645-659 Wntr '94

SMOKING

Promoting smokers' welfare with responsible taxation. (Tax Policy and the Social Agenda) by W. Kip Viscusi
47 National Tax Journal 547-558 Sept '94

Cigarette taxes to fund health care reform. (Tax Policy and the Social Agenda) by Jane G. Gravelle and Dennis Zimmerman *47 National Tax Journal 575-590 Sept '94*

The top ten ways to attack the tobacco industry and win the war against smoking. (Symposium on Smokers' and Non-Smokers' Rights) by Ahron Leichtman
13 Saint Louis University Public Law Review 729-747 W[illegible]

Workplace smoking in New Jersey: time for a change. by Rebecca R. Smith
24 Seton Hall Law Review 958-997 Spring '94

Risk management of passive smoking at work and at home. (Symposium on Smokers' and Non-Smokers' Rights) by James L. Repace
13 Saint Louis University Public Law Review 763-785 Wntr '94

An assessment of the current legal climate concerning smoking in the workplace. (Symposium on Smokers' and Non-Smokers' Rights) by John C. Fox
13 Saint Louis University Public Law Review 591-634 Wntr '94

Smoking in the workplace: developing a policy that works for your company. by L. Lynne Pulliam
19 Employee Relations Law Journal 279-286 Winter '93

Clearing the air: legal regulation of smoking at work. (United Kingdom) by Robert A. Watt
Journal of Business Law 585-590 Nov '93

'Get off your butts': the employer's right to regulate employee smoking. by David B. Ezra
60 Tennessee Law Review 905-955 Summer '93

Smoking and the sack. (dismissal of employees) (United Kingdom) by Robert A. Watt
143 New Law Journal 207(2) Feb 12 '93

SMOKING paraphernalia *see also*
Cigarette lighters

SMOLLA, Rodney A.

Some anxious thoughts about utopian dreams: a reply to Professor Smolla. (response to article by Rodney A. Smolla in this issue, p. 149) (A Free and Responsible Press) by Lillian R. BeVier
1993 University of Chicago Legal Forum 187-195 Annual '93

Proposal for a Substance Abuse Testing Act: the Report of the Task Force on the Drug-Free Workplace, Institute [illegible] comments by members

Drink driving - specimens for analysis - no warning given as to prosecution for failure to provide - admissibility of specimens where no warning given - admissibility where no prejudice caused - way in which such submissions should be dealt with. (United Kingdom) by Gavin Eynon and D.J. Birch
Criminal Law Review 968-970 Dec '93

Road traffic - section 8(2) of the RTA 1988 - option to provide a replacement specimen - whether failure to provide might lead to prosecution - whether duty to give statutory warning under section 7(7). (United Kingdom) by Gavin Eynon and D.J. Birch
Criminal Law Review 966-968 Dec '93

Can your eyes be used against you? The use of the horizontal gaze nystagmus test in the courtroom. (roadside sobriety test of eye movement) (Symposium on Scientific Evidence) by Stephanie E. Busloff
84 Journal of Criminal Law and Criminology 203-238 Spring '93

see also
Breath tests

SOBRIETY tests, Roadside *see*
Roadside sobriety tests

SOBRIQUETS *see*
Nicknames

SOCAGE *see*
Land tenure

SOCCER

Ancient legal ban on football in Scotland. by Gordon M. MacKay *Scots Law Times 282-283 August 26 '94*
see also
World Cup (Soccer)

SOCCER players

Summary of criminal prosecutions for football and rugby violence: culminating in custodial sentences. (United Kingdom) by Alistair M. Duff
Scots Law Times 281-282 August 26 '94

Civil actions and sporting injuries sustained by professional footballers. (Scotland) by Alistair M. Duff
Scots Law Times 175-178 May 27 '94

Civil actions and sporting injuries [illegible]

-Cases

Creating a constitutional right to be free from environmental tobacco smoke. (Case Note) Helling v. McKinney 113 S. Ct. 2475 (1993) by Louise E. Weiss
7 Tulane Environmental Law Journal 249-270 Winter '93

SMOKING and women *see also*
Women

SMOKING cessation programs

Utilization of hair analysis for therapeutic drug monitoring with a special reference to ofloxacin and to nicotine. (Special Issue: Hair Analysis as a Diagnostic Tool for Drugs of Abuse Investigation) by Toshihiko Uematsu *63 Forensic Science International 261-268 Dec 15 '93*

SMOKING in the workplace

Warning - smoking can seriously affect your job prospects. (United Kingdom)
IRS Employment Trends 3-4 Oct 15 '94

Where they smoke, they may get fired: an overview of significant workplace smoking issues. (Florida) by Deborah S. Crumbley and Gregory A. Hearing
68 Florida Bar Journal 108-111 Oct '94

How to handle indoor air quality problems. by Ian K. Portnoy and John O'Neill
10 The Practical Real Estate Lawyer 65-84 Sept '94

Legal aspects of passive smoking: an annotated bibliography. by Maria Okanska
86 Law Library Journal 445-501 Summer '94

1092

Bites and stings

SNAKEBITE *see*
Bites and stings

SNOW, Cora Georgiana

Utah's first women lawyers: Phoebe Wilson Couzins and Cora Georgiana Snow. by Steven L. Staker and Colleen Y. Staker *6 Utah Bar Journal 10-12 Dec '93*

SNOWMOBILES

Snowmobile fatalities. by Simon P. Avis
39 Journal of Forensic Sciences 1161-1167 Sept '94

SOBRIETY checkpoint breath testing *see*
Random breath testing

SOBRIETY checkpoint roadblocks *see*
Roadblocks (Police methods)

SOBRIETY checkpoints, Roadside *see*
Roadside sobriety tests

SOBRIETY tests

Drink driving: specimen procedure. (United Kingdom) by Christine Clayson
138 Solicitors Journal 1134(2) Nov 4 '94

Disqualification for failure to provide specimen. (United Kingdom) by J.A. Coutts
58 Journal of Criminal Law 227-229 August '94

Driver preference. (Drink Driving, part 1) (United Kingdom) by Jonathan S.W. Black
138 Solicitors Journal 200(2) March 4 '94

Trying to be reasonable about drunk driving: individualized suspicion and the Fourth Amendment. by Elizabeth F. Rubin
62 University of Cincinnati Law Review 1105-1133 Wntr '94

[illegible] social change. (Symposium: Constitutionalism in the Post-Cold War Era) by Laszlo Solyom
19 The Yale Journal of International Law 223-237 Wntr '94

Exponential change: today is already tomorrow. (Fourth Annual Comparative Health Law Conference, 'Medical Malpractice: A Comparative Analysis') by Jack R. London *3 Annals of Health Law 153-166 Annual '94*

Health care reform and the probabilities of change. (Health Care Symposium, part 2) by Raymond G. Davis
3 The Kansas Journal of Law & Public Policy 25-30 Winter '93

Alliances and coalitions: building associations for mutual benefit. by Jane Hardin
27 Clearinghouse Review 766-772 Nov '93

Law and social change. by Martha Minow
62 UMKC Law Review 171-183 Fall '93

The role of lawyers in social change. (International Association of Legal Sciences Symposium: The Social Role of Lawyers) (Panel Discussion)
25 Case Western Reserve Journal of International Law 137-168 Spring '93

America's counterrevolution - unlearned lessons. (The Fifty-Fourth Cleveland-Marshall Fund Lecture) by Nathaniel R. Jones
41 Cleveland State Law Review 205-213 Spring '93

Le protecteur du citoyen du Quebec comme agent de changement. (includes Engilsh translation) by Daniel Jacoby and Patrick Robardet
The Ombudsman Journal 99-125 Annual '93

---

provides terms that are narrower ("NT") or broader ("BT") than the term you have looked up, or that are related to it ("RT"). In the thesaurus, the most useful terms are marked with the designation "USE."

In the Canoga case, for example, if you searched for articles in the 1993-94 I.L.P. volume using the search term "smoking," you would find the Ezra article. See Illustration 4-11 on page 67. Whether you used *LegalTrac*, WILSONDISC, C.L.I., or I.L.P., research using periodical indexes would have led you to several articles on smoking rights of employees.

Illustration 4-11 *Index to Legal Periodicals.*

Smith, Vicki L.—*cont.*
Effects of the dynamite charge on the deliberations of deadlocked mock juries; by V. L. Smith, S. M. Kassin. 17 *Law & Hum. Behav.* 625-43 D '93
When prior knowledge and law collide: helping jurors use the law. 17 *Law & Hum. Behav.* 507-36 O '93
Smith, Victor
Can we rely on the Children Act? 137 *Solic. J.* 706-7 Jl 23 '93
A licence to sell counterfeit goods? 137 *Solic. J.* 822-3 Ag 20 '93
Smith, W. Mark
The implications of Mertens v. Hewitt Associates [113 S. Ct. 2063 (1993)] for future ERISA litigation; by S. H. Thomsen, W. M. Smith. 29 *Tort & Ins. L.J.* 129-40 Fall '93
Smith, W. Robert
Effective tax rates in the oil and gas industry: an empirical analysis of the effects of ERTA and TRA 86; by W. R. Smith, G. B. Manzon, Jr. 42 *Oil & Gas Tax Q.* 1-12 S '93
Smith, Walter L.
A tribute to John R. Brown; by A. R. Lee, W. L. Smith. 41 *La. B.J.* 117-22 Ag '93
Smith, William J.
Linguistic school boards in Quebec—a reform whose time has come: Reference Re Education Act of Québec (Bill 107) [[1993] 105 D.L.R.4th 266] 39 *McGill L.J.* 200-23 Mr '94
Smith, William T., III
Cipollone's [Cipollone v. Liggett Group, Inc., 112 S. Ct. 2608 (1992)] effect on FIFRA preemption; by W. T. Smith, III, K. M. Coonrod. 61 *UMKC L. Rev.* 489-502 Spr '93
Smog *See* Air pollution
Smoger, Gerson H.
Using experts wisely in toxic tort cases. 29 *Trial* 30-5 S '93
Smoke prevention *See* Air pollution
Smoking
Are you treating your employees like prisoners? Employers' liability for environmental tobacco smoke. C. W. Lewis, S. J. Bliss. 73 *Mich. B.J.* 416-22 My '94
Environmental tobacco smoke: cruel and unusual punishment? L. I. Ginestra, student author. 42 *U. Kan. L. Rev.* 169-99 Fall '93
Exposure to tobacco smoke is more than offensive, it is cruel and unusual punishment. J. S. Kinsler. 27 *Val. U. L. Rev.* 385-409 Spr '93
"Get off your butts": the employer's right to regulate employee smoking. D. B. Ezra. 60 *Tenn. L. Rev.* 905-55 Summ '93
Helling v. McKinney [113 S. Ct. 2475 (1993)]: creating a constitutional right to be free from environmental tobacco smoke. L. E. Weiss, student author. 7 *Tul. Envtl. L.J.* 249-70 Wint '93
Nonsmoking hiring policies: examining the status of smokers under Title I of the Americans with Disabilities Act of 1990. M. W. Pugsley, student author. 43 *Duke L.J.* 1089-114 Mr '94
Parental smoking: a form of child abuse? J. D. Anderson, student author. 77 *Marq. L. Rev.* 360-84 Wint '94
Second-hand smoke: the asbestos and benzene of the nineties. S. B. Ross, student author. 25 *Ariz. St. L.J.* 713-31 Fall '93
Should the ill effects of environmental tobacco smoke exposure affect child-custody decisions? C. J. Wheatley, student author. 32 *U. Louisville J. Fam. L.* 115-32 Wint '94
Smoking in the workplace: developing a policy that works for your company. L. L. Pulliam. 19 *Empl. Rel. L.J.* 279-86 Wint '93/'94
Smoking out the enemy: new developments in tobacco litigation. R. A. Daynard. 29 *Trial* 16-18+ N '93
Symposium on smokers' and non-smokers' rights. Sticks and stones can break my bones, but tobacco smoke can kill me: can we protect children from parents that smoke? D. B. Ezra; An assessment of the current legal climate concerning smoking in the workplace. J. C. Fox; Second-hand smoke and the ADA: ensuring access for persons with breathing and heart disorders. M. A. Gottlieb, R. A. Daynard, J. B. Lew; Whose life is it anyway—employer control of off-duty behavior. L. L. Maltby, B. J. Dushman; Environmental tobacco smoke as cruel and unusual punishment. C. F. Hitchcock; Smoking, the perception of risk, and the eighth amendment. E. Alexander, D. C. Fathi; Sensible application of stare decisis or a rewriting of the Constitution: an examination of Helling v. McKinney [113 S. Ct. 2475 (1993)]. J. S. Kinsler; The top ten ways to attack the tobacco industry and win the war against smoking. A. Leichtman; A policy for clean indoor air in Missouri: history and lessons learned. J. R. Davis, R. C. Brownson; Risk management of passive smoking at work and at home. J. L. Repace. 13 *St. Louis U. Pub. L. Rev.* 547-785 '94

See/See also the following book(s):
Smoking policy; law, politics, and culture; edited by Robert L. Rabin and Stephen D. Sugarman. Oxford Univ. Press 1993 243p

California
Passive cigarette smoke: an appropriate determinant in child custody decisions? M. K. Wedel. 1 *San Diego Just. J.* 403-13 Summ '93

France
Snuffing out a national symbol: what the United States can learn from France's new no-smoking law. J. A. Lerner, student author. 4 *Ind. Int'l & Comp. L. Rev.* 165-95 Fall '93

Missouri
A policy for clean indoor air in Missouri: history and lessons learned. J. R. Davis, R. C. Brownson. 13 *St. Louis U. Pub. L. Rev.* 749-62 '94

New Jersey
Workplace smoking in New Jersey: time for a change. R. R. Smith, student author. 24 *Seton Hall L. Rev.* 958-97 '93

United States
Snuffing out a national symbol: what the United States can learn from France's new no-smoking law. J. A. Lerner, student author. 4 *Ind. Int'l & Comp. L. Rev.* 165-95 Fall '93

Western Australia (Australia)
Tobacco Control Act 1990 (WA). N. Walker. 21 *U.W. Austl. L. Rev.* 391-8 D '91

Smoking policy; law, politics, and culture; edited by Robert L. Rabin and Stephen D. Sugarman. Oxford Univ. Press 1993 243p $35
ISBN 0-19-507231-6 LC 92-33045
Smolin, David M.
The free exercise clause, the Religious Freedom Restoration Act, and the right to active and passive euthanasia. 10 *Issues L. & Med.* 3-54 Summ '94
The jurisprudence of privacy in a splintered Supreme Court. 75 *Marq. L. Rev.* 975-1066 Summ '92
Smolka-Day, Maria
Selected current bibliography on foreign and comparative labor law; by M. Tarnawsky, M. Smolka-Day. 14 *Comp. Lab. L.J.* 518-28 Summ '93
Selected current bibliography on foreign and comparative labor law; by M. Tarnawsky, M. Smolka-Day. 15 *Comp. Lab. L.J.* 131-41 Fall '93
Selected current bibliography on foreign and comparative labor law; by M. Tarnawsky, M. Smolka-Day. 15 *Comp. Lab. L.J.* 292-302 Wint '94
Selected current bibliography on foreign and comparative labor law; by M. Tarnawsky, M. Smolka-Day. 15 *Comp. Lab. L.J.* 430-9 Spr '94
Smolla, Rodney A.
Report of the Coalition for a New America: platform section on communications policy. 1993 *U. Chi. Legal F.* 149-85 '93
Smyer, Michael A.
Autonomy, competence, and informed consent in long term care: legal and psychological perspectives; by W. M. Altman, P. A. Parmelee, M. A. Smyer. 37 *Vill. L. Rev.* 1671-704 '92
Smyth, Paul
Toward fully understood compliance: knowing enforcement mechanisms; by M. Mason, P. Smyth. 8 *Nat. Resources & Env't* 3-6+ Spr '94
Smyth, Shane
Service mark registrations in Ireland: a myth or a reality? 16 *Eur. Intell. Prop. Rev.* 167-9 Ap '94
Snarr, Steven W.
Deregulation of natural gas utilities: a proposal for legislative reform in state utility regulation. 11 *J. Energy Nat. Resources & Envtl. L.* 199-240 '91
Sneed, Don
A survey of the professional person as libel plaintiff: reexamination of the public figure doctrine; by H. W. Stonecipher, D. Sneed. 46 *Ark. L. Rev.* 303-32 '93
Sneed, William M.
Confronting reinsurers' rescission claims: some suggestions for cedents. 61 *Def. Couns. J.* 217-25 Ap '94

b. Reading and Evaluating the Article

When you read a periodical article, evaluate the important aspects of the article as a source of information or authority. In critiquing the article, you should consider the following:

Coverage: How much of the article is useful to your research topic? How much of your topic is covered by the article? Is the article general enough or specific enough for your needs?

Accuracy: Are the propositions in the article adequately supported by footnoted authorities? Do the supporting authorities accurately say what they are supposed to say? If an article contains incorrect citations and other errors, you should be suspicious that the article was researched and analyzed sloppily and should consider using another article.

Persuasiveness: If the article is espousing a new viewpoint or arguing for a change in the law (as many articles do), how well does the author convince you? Are the arguments logically ordered and well constructed? Or are there jumps in logic and faulty analogies? How have subsequent critics treated the article? (See the next section on Shepardizing.)

Reputation (author): How credible is the author of the article? Check the initial footnote of the article for the author's position, field of expertise, and experience. You also could check a periodical index to see whether the author has published other articles in the same area or check a library catalog for book publications. Another way to check an author's credentials is to look in *Who's Who in American Law* or the *A.A.L.S. Directory of Law Teachers.*

Reputation (periodical): How well regarded is the periodical? Look at the credentials of other authors in the same periodical. You also could Shepardize the periodical to see generally how often it is cited, locate a current ranking of legal periodicals in terms of the citability, or ask a librarian or professor about the reputation of that periodical.

In the Canoga case, the Ezra article appears in the sixtieth volume of a general-scope student-run law review of a well regarded law school. It is written by an associate (a non-partner) at a law firm; he published the article three years after he graduated from law school. An author search on the library catalog shows that he previously had published a student note on this topic and, a year after this article, he published an article on this topic in a major journal. Hence, this article has a fair amount of credibility because the author is developing considerable expertise on this topic.

The article provides background on two issues. The first issue relates to the rights of employees to be free of policies that interfere with their off-duty privacy rights. It reads in pertinent part: "The primary argument against such an extensive ban on employee smoking is that it is excessively intrusive. By extending beyond the work premises into the homes of employees, such a ban arguably invades the privacy of employees." David B. Ezra, *"Get Off Your Butts": The Employer's Right to Regulate Employee Smoking,* 60 Tenn. L. Rev. 905, 933 (1993). The second issue is that smokers may be protected on the grounds that they have a disability—an addiction to smoking. This argument is based on two major federal disability laws, the Rehabilitation Act of 1973 and the Americans with Disabilities Act of 1990 (ADA).

The Ezra article seems well supported. It summarizes the applicable provisions of the law and explains the law relevant to both of these points. It provides references to applicable primary authority, such as statutes and case law; it also refers you to secondary authority, including other legal periodical articles. The article seems to be worth relying on.

c. Expanding Your Research: *Shepard's Law Review Citations*

On occasion, you might find an article that addresses your issue directly and sets forth an important new idea. You may want to know whether the idea has been received favorably by courts or other legal scholars. *Shepard's Law Review Citations* enables you to expand your research by locating references to law review articles found in recent court decisions or in other law reviews. This research helps you determine the credibility of the article. You will encounter *Shepard's Citations* again in Chapter 6; the following is a brief description of how it expands the research capabilities of law reviews.

Shepard's Law Review Citations began publication in 1957 and now covers articles published in over 200 law reviews. *Shepard's* consists of hardbound volumes updated by one or more softbound or paper pamphlets. In using any set of *Shepard's,* you always should be sure to check all pertinent volumes. Look on the cover of the most recent pamphlet for the list of *Shepard's* volumes to collect to perform a comprehensive search.

The first step in using *Shepard's Citations* is to identify your "cited source." This is the source you look up in *Shepard's.* Under the entry for the cited source, you will find a list of "citing sources," that is, published court decisions and law review articles that refer to the cited article.

In the Canoga case, for instance, no other sources have cited the Ezra article as of fall 1995. However, if you had looked for other articles on smoking as a protected disability under the federal disabilities discrimination statute, you might have found Rosalie K. Murphy's article, *Reasonable Accommodation and Employment Discrimination under Title I of the Americans with Disabilities Act,* in volume 64 of the *Southern California Law Review,* starting at page 1607. Using this article as your "cited source," you would look up *Southern California Law Review,* volume 64, page 1607 in *Shepard's Law Review Citations* to determine whether this cited source has been referred to in other sources. See Illustration 4-12 on page 70. Note that the Murphy article has been cited in volume 40 of the *Buffalo Law Review,* at page 777. You could now look at the article in the *Buffalo Law Review* to update and expand the information you had previously gleaned from the *Southern California Law Review.*

Illustration 4-12

Shepard's Law Review Citations.

SOUTHERN CALIFORNIA LAW REVIEW

66CK303
62CUR603
63CUR328
60GW1691
66ILJ29
68ILJ866
69ILJ3
69ILJ106
77ILR741
89McL727
44MeL282
55MR37
70NCL1232
67NDL581
67NYL7
140PaL224
141PaL377
141PaL442
53PitL961
63SCL1723
63SCL1761
63SCL1811
63SCL1823
63SCL1844
65SCL2565
45StnL347
45StnL820
69TxL1659
27UCD613
80VaL488
45VLR537
29WML192
67WsL757
100YLJ410

—1597—
36AzL349
81CaL1283
77Cor1430
63CUR328
42DuLJ665
42EmJ65
81Geo2639
22GGU586
43HLJ872
104HLR472
20Hof301
66ILJ35
69ILJ106
89McL1830
50MdL975
75MnL1674
57MoL388
36NYF25
67NYL528
52OhLJ849
17ONU652
139PaL947
141PaL447
63SCL1757
63SCL1764
63SCL1806
63SCL1823
63SCL1844
66SCL1219
67SCL93
67SCL278
45StnL827
45StnL1362
45StnL2015
69TxL1639
27UCD614
77VaL1179
45VLR538
34W&M745
1991WLR932

67WsL773
100YLJ433

—1653—
62FR643
27Goz234
66ILJ35
77ILR666
42KLR590
89McL1870
141PaL442
63SCL1772
63SCL1812
63SCL1825
66TuL1121
69TxL1707
60UCR4
28VLP214
67WsL757
100YLJ410

—1671—
78Cor786
81Geo2630
106HLR1420
66ILJ32
51MdL43
67NYL61
54OhLJ1303
139PaL1041
63SCL1711
63SCL1756
63SCL1768
63SCL1816
63SCL1826
63SCL1845

—1699—
36AzL107
36AzL349
35BCR11
80CaL105
82CaL357
23CnL868
77Cor305
77Cor1398
93CR431
62CUR625
63CUR328
60FR624
81Geo2515
81Geo2639
82Geo193
61GW1756
43HLJ867
107HLR1181
66ILJ26
69ILJ106
69ILJ1012
1991IILR417
89McL755
72NCL1265
66NDL1251
67NDL647
54OhLJ1302
139PaL1041
141PaL37
141PaL454
142PaL1208
23Pcf1539
63SCL1600
63SCL1753
63SCL1764
63SCL1802
63SCL1812
63SCL1824

63SCL1843
65SCL1176
65SCL2576
45StnL1
45StnL349
45StnL416
45StnL811
45StnL1573
45StnL1895
69TxL1707
27UCD614
61UCR1295
45VLR538
67WsL757
67WsL773
100YLJ410
100YLJ1389
100YLJ1791

—1727—
81CaL518
42DuLJ666
67SCL257
45StnL852
45StnL1895

—1728—
66ILJ29
63SCL1807
63SCL1825
67SCL129
45VLR538
49W&L332
67WsL773
100YLJ427
100YLJ1587

—1747—
60FR2
54OhLJ1306

—1753—
72BUR103
66CK135
89McL758
74MqL345
45StnL2016

—1763—
39Buf787
1993BYU
[1229
81CaL1282
66CK123
40CM334
77Cor1403
1991DuL315
43EmJ3
43EmJ238
43FLR427
81Geo2484
81Geo2637
107HLR1228
21Hof1254
69ILJ118
1992IILR983
53OhLJ1304
142PaL550
63SCL1828
65SCL1179
65SCL2173
43StnL1189
45StnL23
67TLQ221
59TnL487
79VaL502

1993WLR721
67WsL771
100YLJ1357
100YLJ1517

—1783—
81Geo2244
54OhLJ1271
141PaL454
45StnL19
67TuL1026
72TxL254

—1797—
81Geo2639
45StnL1362
69TxL1719

—1811—
58ChL1038
77Cor306
42DuLJ841
81Geo2639
66ILJ29
69ILJ2
90McL2451
77MnL1073
54OhLJ1302
141PaL454
69TxL1708
67WsL757
100YLJ410

—1821—
46AkL204
62CUR603
42EmJ4
81Geo2636
66NDL1255
67NDL651
86NwL4
63SCL1650
45StnL1313
69TxL1644
79VaL508

—1843—
81Geo2639
54OhLJ1302

—1911—
67NYL528

Vol. 64

—1—
92CR1063
44HLJ640
25UCD63
44VLR224
101YLJ139

—51—
1991BYU799
92CR1118
30Wsb203

—105—
19JCU346
53OhLJ5
71OLR855

—235—
Utah
846P2d1268
869P2d935
Wis
162Wis2d836
470NW888
Wyo
820P2d115
58BR1252
105HLR617
71OLR848

—293—
958F2d396
D C
294ADC178
44AkL1088
41Buf618
1992IILR342
55OhLJ123

—363—
22Cum472
22Cum521
22Cum646
40EmJ502
28WFL900

—461—
29CFW160
96DLR211

—549—
60ChL54
66TuL804

—605—
96DLR211
52OhLJ1471

—685—
788FS1045
41DuLJ1046
50MdL360
52MdL337
76MnL69
68NDL325
71OLR613
69WsL140

—741—
52MdL406
47MiL310

—951—
67ILJ563
24Tol626

—1057—
49W&L1448

—1103—
69DJ394

—1143—
78MnL1536

—1187—
91CR1641
97DLR2
38SDR22

—1231—
36AzL324
43HLJ146
43HLJ1192
106HLR1244
68ILJ631
25LoyL100
91McL34
72NbL782
45StnL1991
25UCD46
69WsL596

—1261—
27LoyL586
67NYL1211
55PitL457
46RLR351
79VaL991
27WFL459

—1393—
967F2d654
D C
296ADC287
78Cor1030
79Cor126
93CR313
81Geo2649
23NML41
46RLR254
45VLR1575
17VtL656
35W&M309
102YLJ1078

—1607—
40Buf777

—1645—
41DeP746

Vol. 65

—1—
57Alb682

—11—
72OLR151
65SCL115
65SCL122
65SCL304
65SCL356
28SFR648

—121—
65SCL20

—205—
65SCL66
65SCL225
65SCL241

—241—
65SCL297

—255—
65SCL57
65SCL285
46StnL521

—293—
65SCL342
65SCL356
60TnL163

—341—
65SCL294
65SCL356
45StnL369
45StnL420
60TnL206

—355—
65SCL295

—373—
65SCL37

—383—
65SCL37

—411—
65SCL42
65SCL393

—423—
Pa
429PaS633
633A2d200
Tex
883SW365
36AzL477
65SCL214
32Wsb302

—445—
54PitL540
65SCL252
65SCL395

—461—
53LLR446

—503—
65SCL215
65SCL225
65SCL252

—529—
65SCL259

—565—
65SCL275
65SCL283

—597—
65SCL265
19WmM459

—623—
Calif
5C4th97
19CaR2d503
851P2d785
57Alb735
65SCL331
65SCL352
28SFR670
60TnL152

—683—
65SCL320
65SCL392
50W&L656

—705—
Ill
158Il2d178
198IlD409
632NE1020

—735—
93CR338
27GaL438
60GW1708
91McL608
45StnL633
70WQ1127

—781—
26CnL218
62UCR910

—845—
971F2d982
985F2d477
3F3d499
8F3d987
17F3d967
48BL8
61GW684
62GW5
71NCL427
72NCL1225
67NYL956
67SCL597
66TLQ454
70TxL1355
79VaL13
79VaL593

—1035—
24SeH629

—1171—
26AzSJ426
35BCR4
40CM334
78Cor581
81Geo2623
61GW648
45HLJ963
77MnL1174
45StnL814
72TxL260
1994UtLR
[696
79VaL1531

—1279—
73BUR2
1993BYU
[1270
43EmJ208
67SCL147
61UCR1241

—1283—
77Cor1254
81Geo290
81Geo2486
81Geo2636
106HLR544
37NYF149
67NYL549
65SCL1376

376

In the Canoga case, each of the legal periodical indexes provides citations to several pertinent law journals. Several of these articles are very well researched and provide extensive citations in their footnotes to cases, other legal periodical articles, and some treatises, most of which should be examined. As an additional step, you may use *Shepard's Law Review Citations* to Shepardize the major articles to search for articles that you might not have found in the periodical indexes.

4. What Else?

Specialty Print Indexes. Many other print indexes cover legal periodicals. Some, such as the *Index to Federal Tax Articles,* cover particular subject areas within law. The *Index to Periodical Articles Related to Law* (I.P.A.R.L.) indexes periodicals not covered in other major indexes; it includes social science, business, and technical journals as well as popular magazines, to the extent that their articles pertain to law.

Indexes to Foreign Journals. If your research pertains to the law of a particular foreign jurisdiction, you may wish to consult an index covering journals from that country, such as the *Index to Canadian Legal Periodical Literature* and *Legal Journals Index* (for British law). The *Index to Foreign Legal Periodicals* (I.F.L.P.) indexes over 500 legal periodicals and other sources covering international and comparative law and the law of countries other than the United States, United Kingdom, Canada, and Australia. When you are doing research on legal issues arising in the United States you should consider whether foreign periodicals may contain articles of significance to persons or businesses from the United States involved in transactions occurring in other countries.

Law Reviews—Specific Indexes. In addition to the comprehensive indexes discussed above, many law reviews periodically publish indexes to their own volumes. These indexes, which generally are bound along with the law review's issues, usually are organized by subject, title, and author. An index of this sort can be helpful in a specialty journal covering the subject area you are researching. It is indispensable in a periodical not covered by the other indexes discussed above.

Nonlegal Periodicals. Nonlegal periodicals often are of great interest to lawyers because many legal problems touch on fields such as health, medicine, business, psychology, management, and economics. The *Social Science Index* and even the massive *Readers' Guide to Periodical Literature* may be sources for information of value to lawyers. Chapter 11 covers research in nonlegal materials.

Other Media. Legal periodical indexes and the full text of articles are available in a variety of media. These are the media available early in 1996:

			Computer-Assisted Research		
	Paper	*CD-ROM*	*LEXIS*	*WESTLAW*	*Microform*
Legal Periodical Indexes					
Current Law Index	√	*LegalTrac*	*Legal Resource Index*	*Legal Resource Index*	
Index to Legal Periodicals and Books	√	WILSONDISC	√	√	
Index to Foreign Legal Periodicals	√	√			
Legal Journals Index	√				
Index to Canadian Legal Periodical Literature	√				
Shepard's Law Review Citations	√		√	√	
Full text of selected articles	√	√	√	√	√

5. How Do You Cite Legal Periodicals?

Rule 16 in *The Bluebook* governs citation to articles in legal periodicals. The standard citation consists of the author's name, the article title, the volume number of the law review, the abbreviation for the law review, the page number on which the article begins, the page number on which the cited material is located, and a parenthetical containing the date of publication. The name of the law review should be abbreviated according to Table T.13 (in the blue pages). If the law review does not use volume numbers, use the publication date as the volume number and delete the parenthetical date. The proper citation to the page of the Ezra article in Illustration 4-7 on pages 59-60 is:

David B. Ezra, *"Get Off Your Butts": The Employer's Right to Regulate Employee Smoking*, 60 Tenn. L. Rev. 905, 905, 950 (1993).

Citations to signed pieces written by students follow the same style but include a label, such as "Note" or "Comment," after the author's name. For example:

> Mark W. Pugsley, Note, *Nonsmoking Hiring Policies: Examining the Status of Smokers under Title I of the Americans with Disabilities Act of 1990,* 43 Duke L.J. 1089 (1994).

You should consult Rule 16 for additional special rules for citing book reviews, symposia, and other types of articles and for guidance on matters such as multiple authors and unsigned student work. Rule 16 also has a separate form for citing newspapers, newsletters, and other material paginated anew in each issue.

D. *American Law Reports* (A.L.R.)

1. What Is A.L.R.?

American Law Reports (A.L.R.) contains two kinds of resources: selected cases and "annotations." The case is a court opinion that the publisher has selected for illustrative purposes because it raises a significant legal issue. For research purposes, other commentary sources are better for finding case law; hence, the primary purpose for using A.L.R. is to find annotations. The annotations (or articles) address the issues raised by the illustrative cases.

A.L.R. is published by a commercial publishing house, Lawyers Cooperative Publishing, and the annotations are written by its staff attorneys or attorneys hired to write particular annotations. Most annotations focus on issues of current controversy, such as those in which courts in different jurisdictions have split (rendered incongruous decisions) or have advanced inconsistent theories. Other annotations focus on issues that are so factually sensitive that cases with differing facts result in different holdings.

Each A.L.R. annotation provides a brief analysis of a legal issue raised in a recent court decision, then collects and analyzes other cases in which courts have addressed the same issue. Thus, A.L.R. annotations cover many jurisdictions within the United States, citing to relevant authority in each of those jurisdictions.

A.L.R. is a large multivolume set that takes up many shelves in your law library. Since its earliest publication in 1919, A.L.R. has been published in multiple series. These series cover different dates and topics, as listed below:

Series	*Dates*	*Topics*
A.L.R.1st	1919-1948	State and federal
A.L.R.2d	1948-1965	State and federal
A.L.R.3d	1965-1969	State and federal

A.L.R.3d	1969-1980	State
A.L.R.4th	1980-1991	State
A.L.R.5th	1992 to date	State
A.L.R. Fed.	1969 to date	Federal

Note that until 1969, A.L.R. covered both state and federal topics. Since 1969, A.L.R. Fed. has covered federal topics, while A.L.R.3d, A.L.R.4th, and A.L.R.5th have covered state topics.

The annotations in each new series do not necessarily replace or update the annotations in a previous series, nor do they necessarily cover the same topics as the previous series. However, some early A.L.R. annotations have been superseded by more up-to-date annotations published in later series. Because many of the annotations in the first and second series have been superseded or become outdated, you are likely to use the later sets more frequently. Thus, this part focuses predominantly on the third, fourth, fifth, and federal A.L.R. series.

Six to nine A.L.R. volumes are issued each year for each current series, and each volume contains approximately twelve to fifteen annotations. The annotations contained in each A.L.R. volume typically cover a wide range of subjects, such as contracts, torts, criminal law, or employment law, but they are not organized in any special manner.

The format of annotations in A.L.R.3d and A.L.R.4th generally follows the format of the annotation in Illustration 4-13 on pages 75-78. Preceding each annotation is an illustrative case. Note the following features of the annotation:

- title
- Total Client-Service Library References (materials published by Lawyers Cooperative Publishing)
- table of contents
- index
- Table of Jurisdictions Represented
- text of the annotation (organized by section)
  - Introduction (including scope and related annotations)
  - Background, summary, and comment (sometimes including practice pointers)
  - body of the annotation

Annotations in A.L.R.5th follow a slightly different format than their predecessors. The illustrative cases appear at the end of the volume. The annotation itself contains some additional research features:

- prefatory statement (an abstract of the annotation, brief of the illustrative case, cross-reference to page of the illustrative case)
- Research Sources (materials published by other publishers, related tools)
- Jurisdictional Table of Cited Statutes and Cases (replacing the Table of Jurisdictions Represented)

Illustration 4-13

Theresa L. Kruk, Annotation, *Right to Discharge Allegedly "At-Will" Employee as Affected by Employer's Promulgation of Employment Policies as to Discharge,* 33 A.L.R.4th 120, 120-23 (1984).

ANNOTATION

RIGHT TO DISCHARGE ALLEGEDLY "AT-WILL" EMPLOYEE AS AFFECTED BY EMPLOYER'S PROMULGATION OF EMPLOYMENT POLICIES AS TO DISCHARGE

by

Theresa Ludwig Kruk, J.D.

TOTAL CLIENT-SERVICE LIBRARY® REFERENCES

53 Am Jur 2d, Master and Servant §§ 34, 43–70

Annotations: See the related matters listed in the annotation, infra.

7 Am Jur Legal Forms 2d, Employment Contracts §§ 99:111, 99:121, 99:146–99:147

7 Am Jur Proof of Facts 2d 1, Retaliatory Termination of Private Employment; 11 Am Jur Proof of Facts 2d 679, Reduction or Mitigation of Damages—Employment Contract; 29 Am Jur Proof of Facts 2d 335, Wrongful Discharge of At-Will Employee

US L Ed Digest, Master and Servant § 21

ALR Digests, Master and Servant § 51

L Ed Index to Annos, Contracts; Labor and Employment; Waiver or Estoppel

ALR Quick Index, Contracts; Discharge from Employment; Estoppel and Waiver; Manuals; Master and Servant; Restitution and Implied Contracts

Federal Quick Index, Contracts; Discharge from Employment; Labor and Employment; Manuals and Handbooks; Restitution and Implied Contracts; Waiver and Estoppel

Auto-Cite®: Any case citation herein can be checked for form, parallel references, later history, and annotation references through the Auto-Cite computer research system.

Consult POCKET PART in this volume for later cases

120

Illustration 4-13 *(continued)*

33 ALR4th EMPLOYMENT AT WILL—RESTRAINTS ON DISCHARGE
33 ALR4th 120

Right to discharge allegedly "at-will" employee as affected by employer's promulgation of employment policies as to discharge

---

INDEX

121

Illustration 4-13 *(continued)*

TABLE OF JURISDICTIONS REPRESENTED
Consult POCKET PART in this volume for later cases

---

§ 1. Introduction

[a] Scope

This annotation[1] collects the state and federal cases that consider whether an employer's promulgation of employment policies regarding the procedures and reasons for termination or discharge of employees[2] affects an employer's right to discharge an at-will employee at any time and for any or no reason.

This annotation includes only those cases in which an at-will employee relies upon the policy statements of his or her employer regarding termination or discharge and contends that his or her discharge was effectuated in a manner or for reasons contrary to the express general policy of the employer,[3] as opposed to personal assurances or representations by the employer, regardless of whether such policy was written or unwritten, and the employer defends against such a charge by asserting the at-will status of the employee.

[b] Related matters

Recovery for discharge from employment in retaliation for filing workers' compensation claim. 32 ALR4th 1221.

Modern status of rule that employer may discharge at-will employee for any reason. 12 ALR4th 544.

---

1. This annotation supersedes § 7 of 12 ALR4th 544.

2. For treatment of cases dealing with an at-will employee's right to severance pay as provided by an employer's general policy on severance, see 53 Am Jur 2d, Master and Servant § 81.

3. For a discussion of cases involving at-will employees who claim to have been hired as "permanent" employees or "for life," see generally 53 Am Jur 2d, Master and Servant §§ 20, 32–34. See also the annotation in 24 ALR3d 1412 entitled "Employer's misrepresentation as to prospect, or duration of, employment as actionable fraud."

Illustration 4-13 *(continued)*

Liability for discharging at-will employee for refusing to participate in, or for disclosing, unlawful or unethical acts of employer or coemployees. 9 ALR4th 329.

Right of corporation to discharge employee who asserts right as stockholder. 84 ALR3d 1107.

Reduction in rank or authority or change of duties as breach of employment contract. 63 ALR3d 539.

Employee's arbitrary dismissal as breach of employment contract terminable at will. 62 ALR3d 271.

Employer's termination of professional athlete's services as constituting breach of employment contract. 57 ALR3d 257.

Nature of alternative employment which employee must accept to minimize damages for wrongful discharge. 44 ALR3d 629.

Employer's misrepresentation as to prospect, or duration of, employment as actionable fraud. 24 ALR3d 1412.

Elements and measure of damages in action by schoolteacher for wrongful discharge. 22 ALR3d 1047.

Liability of federal government officer or employee for causing discharge or separation of subordinate. 5 ALR Fed 961.

§ 2. Background, summary, and comment

[a] Generally

The common-law rule regarding the termination of an at-will employment contract is that if the employment is not for a definite term, and if there is no contractual or statutory restriction on the right of discharge, an employer may lawfully discharge an employee whenever and for whatever cause, without incurring liability for wrongful discharge.[4] Few legal principles have been better settled than the at-will concept, whose roots date back to the 19th century laissez-faire policy of protecting freedom to contract. In recent years, however, there has been a growing trend toward a restricted application of this rule in order to comport with express and implied public policy, as well as statutory concerns. Some jurisdictions have been willing to depart from the traditional contract rule of terminability at will and to impose an implied contractual duty not to discharge an employee for reasons regarded as violative of public policy or to recognize the tortious nature of a discharge violative of public policy, whether such policy is expressly codified or implied.[5]

In keeping with this modern trend of judicial re-evaluation and legislative modification, a number of jurisdictions have held or recognized that under particular circumstances, the right of an employer to freely discharge at-will employees may be contractually restricted as a result of the promulgation of corporate employment policies specifying the proce-

4. Although the at-will rule is generally regarded as vesting in the employer absolute discretion to terminate employment, this "right" is actually a rule of contract construction rather than a right grounded in substantive law. Absent an express contractual provision specifying the term of employment, the duration depends upon the intention of the parties as determined from the circumstances of each case. It is still the general rule that an indefinite hiring, under circumstances that do not permit the implication of any fixed period of duration, is presumed to be terminable at the will of either party, with the burden on the party asserting a fixed period. 53 Am Jur 2d, Master and Servant §§ 27, 43.

5. See generally, the annotation in 12 ALR4th 544, for a discussion of the modern status of the at-will rule.

Until the fifth series, the Table of Jurisdictions Represented is arranged by jurisdiction and provides references to sections of the annotation that discuss cases from particular jurisdictions. Beginning with the fifth series, the Jurisdictional Table of Cited Statutes and Cases provides reference to statutes, regulations, rules, and constitutional provisions that are discussed in the annotation. Since 1993, tables in each A.L.R. Fed. annotation lists similar sources that are discussed in that annotation.

2. Why Is A.L.R. Useful?

A.L.R. is a helpful research tool because it describes, analyzes, and comments on current legal topics, sometimes before those issues are addressed comprehensively in other sources. Because they provide a good overview of a topic, A.L.R. annotations are most useful at the beginning of the research process.

A.L.R. annotations are valuable for collecting cases with similar fact patterns. In addition, each annotation contains descriptive commentary on how a specific legal issue has been addressed in jurisdictions throughout the United States that have published court decisions or enacted legislation on that issue. This commentary provides current information about the rules of law and the legal theories relied on by various courts.

The textual discussions of cases and other primary authorities are arranged under subtopics and by outcome within subtopics. The comparisons among the different lines of holdings and reasoning assist you in analyzing persuasive authority and in understanding where your jurisdiction stands in relation to other jurisdictions. Besides providing commentary, an A.L.R. annotation also gives references to primary and secondary sources. Those references are updated in annual pocket parts in most series.

However, A.L.R. has its limitations. Although the commentary in each A.L.R. annotation is quite comprehensive, it tends to be more descriptive than analytical. As a research tool for finding other sources, one of the major weaknesses of A.L.R. is that many of the earlier series limit their secondary sources references to legal materials published by Lawyers Cooperative Publishing. Furthermore, although an A.L.R. annotation may be a good resource for a brief overview of a current topic, because it is written typically by a staff lawyer, the research and writing may be accurate, but the writer is not a recognized scholar or expert in the area. Thus, the annotation likely will not carry great credibility before a judicial body.

3. How Do You Research in A.L.R.?

a. Locating Pertinent Annotations

The most efficient means to locate a pertinent A.L.R. annotation is to use the *ALR Index,* a multivolume set typically shelved at the end of the most recent A.L.R. series. The *ALR Index* encompasses the second, third, fourth, fifth, and federal series of A.L.R. You can access this index by using research terms you would use for any paper index.

For the Canoga case, the *ALR Index* entry "discharge from employment or office" lists eight annotations under the subentry "at-will employee"; one annotation addresses the "promulgation of policy, right to discharge allegedly at-will employee as affected by employer's promulgation of employment policies as to discharge" and may be pertinent to your research. This annotation is found in volume 33 of A.L.R.4th, beginning on page 120, and is shown in Illustration 4-13 on pages 75-78. After you have checked the index entries in the main volume, it is important to also check the pocket part (if any) for possible additional entries.

b. Reading the Annotation

Skim the prefatory statement (if there is one) and the Introduction to learn of the scope of the annotation and whether other annotations might be more helpful or might supplement your research. To locate pertinent portions of a lengthy annotation, you may wish to consult the annotation's table of contents, index, or Table of Jurisdictions Represented. In the text of the annotation, the jurisdictions of the cases are in bold print to assist you in scanning the annotation for cases from the jurisdiction of your research problem. Of course, you also would read the full opinions of the cases cited to determine their significance for your research problem.

Once you have read the annotation text, you may wish to consult the Total Client-Service Library References (TCSL) section (and the Research References section, if you are using the fifth series or the federal series after 1992). These sections contain cross-references to other secondary sources.

Finally, you may wish to read the illustrative case. It typically is a leading or early case that addresses the topic. Depending on the jurisdiction, it may be mandatory or persuasive authority for you.

For the Canoga case, many sections of the annotation at 33 A.L.R.4th 120 are valuable. The background section provides an overview of the employment-at-will doctrine and how courts throughout the United States generally have treated it. The index directs you to specific sections of the annotation (sections 3-5) for a discussion on employment manuals or handbooks; these annotation sections may address concerns raised by the Canoga case. Although the Table of Jurisdictions Represented often is helpful for locating a discussion of cases from a given jurisdiction, unfortunately for the Canoga research problem, New Mexico is not listed as a jurisdiction represented in the annotation. On the other hand, the illustrative case, *Weiner v. McGraw-Hill, Inc.,* decided by the New York Court of Appeals in 1982, is one of the leading cases on this topic. Because *Weiner* is a New York case, it is persuasive rather than mandatory authority for the Canoga case.

c. Updating and Expanding Your Research

The annotations in the third, fourth, fifth, and federal series are updated and expanded by annual pocket parts. After you find a useful annotation, consult the pocket part to that volume to see if the annotation has been supplemented or superseded. If the annotation has been supplemented, the pocket part may contain additional textual commentary and case references.

For the Canoga case, additional information concerning the sample annotation is contained in the pocket part. As shown in Illustration 4-14 on page 82, the pocket part includes a description of several additional, more current cases from throughout the United States. Most significant, the discussion includes two cases from New Mexico, *Lukoski v. Sandia Indian Management Co.* and *Kestenbaum v. Pennzoil Co.* These cases are mandatory authority and reflect the New Mexico court's view of whether employee handbooks are binding contracts.

An additional method for updating your research in A.L.R. is to use the Annotation History Table in the tables volume of the *ALR Index.* This table indicates whether the annotation you have been researching has been either superseded or supplemented. The sample annotation, 33 A.L.R.4th 120, has not been supplemented or superseded. See Illustration 4-15 on page 83.

You may bring your research up-to-the-minute by calling the Latest Case Service "hot line" for cases decided since the last supplement. The telephone number is listed on the front covers of the pocket parts for the third, fourth, fifth, and federal series.

As an additional step, you may check *Shepard's Citations for Annotations* to find additional cases or A.L.R. annotations that have cited your annotation. This step is a valuable way to assess the credibility of your annotation. For the Canoga case, the annotation found at 33 A.L.R.4th 120 is the cited annotation. Illustration 4-16 on page 84 shows that *Shepard's* lists seven cases and ten other annotations that have cited this annotation.

In the Canoga case, the *ALR Index* directs you to only a few annotations that are on point, yet those annotations provide a good overview of the major issues. The annotations and the supplements provide citations to several cases that appear to be pertinent, and the jurisdictional tables are especially valuable in directing you to recent New Mexico cases, the jurisdiction for the Canoga case. In each of the annotations, you could also scan the Total Client-Service Library References or Research Sources sections to find other research tools.

4. What Else?

The Digest Approach to Finding a Pertinent A.L.R. Annotation. In addition to the index approach, A.L.R. annotations can also be located by the digest approach, using those volumes marked "digest" on the spine (the complete title varies among series). A "digest" is a finding tool that organizes and synopsizes articles, cases, or other works under the topics to which they relate. The A.L.R. digests synopsize the cases and annotations in A.L.R. and organize them under broad alphabetical topics. The digests also contain citations to relevant annotations and other titles published by Lawyers Cooperative Publishing. A unified digest covers the third, fourth, fifth, and federal series. In the front of each digest volume is a listing of the topics used in the digests.

Illustration 4-14 Supplement, A.L.R. Annotation.

33 ALR4th 120–138 ALR4th

sentations as attractive alternative to collective bargaining, employer could not avoid its obligations on basis of semantic differences. Preston v Claridge Hotel & Casino, Ltd. (1989) 231 NJ Super 81, 555 A2d 12, 4 BNA IER Cas 493.

New Jersey law recognizes claim for breach of employer's stated termination policies. Boginis v Marriott Ownership Resorts (1994, ED Va) 855 F Supp 862, 9 BNA IER Cas 1024, 129 CCH LC ¶ 57784 (applying NJ law).

In wrongful discharge action against employer, substantial evidence supported finding that employee handbook modified employment relationship and created warning and suspension procedures which were not followed; termination procedures became amendment to employee's contract and personality, not severe offenses of insubordination or disobedience, caused employee's termination. Handbook characterized disciplinary policy regarding warnings, suspensions, and terminations as established procedure and language of handbook did nothing to alert employee that it was subject to revocation at any time or that employee should not rely on it. Lukoski v Sandia Indiana Management Co. (1988, NM) 748 P2d 507, 2 BNA IER Cas 1650. LC ¶ 55496, mod on other gnds 101 NJ 10, 1985 NJ 10, 499 A2d 515.

Evidence was sufficient to overcome presumption that employment contract was terminable at will and to support finding that implied employment provision for discharge only for good reason was in effect between employer and employee, where during initial employment negotiations, employee's immediate supervisor made clear that employment would be long term and permanent as long as employee did job, other supervisory employees stated employer released permanent employees for good reason, just cause, and where neither insurance benefits manual nor severance pay plan and policy manual addressed effect of without cause termination of employment. Kestenbaum v Pennzoil Co. (1988) 108 NM 20, 766 P2d 280, 4 BNA IER Cas 67, cert den (US) 104 L Ed 2d 1026, 4 BNA IER Cas 672.

Employee can rebut presumption of employment at will by establishing that employee was made aware of written policy of limitation on employer's right to discharge at time employment commenced, and in accepting employment, employee relied on termination only for cause limitation. For manual or other written policy to limit employer's right to terminate, it must contain express limitation. Preston v Champion Home Builders, Inc. (1992, 3d Dept) 187 App Div 2d 795, 589 NYS2d 940.

To sustain cause of action for breach of employment contract, employee must demonstrate that employment manual contained clear and express limitation that employee would not be terminated or disciplined except for cause, and that employee specifically relied on this language. Charyn v National Westminster Bank, U.S.A. (1994, 2d Dept) 204 App Div 2d 676, 612 NYS2d 432.

Where employee manual in substance states that employment will continue so long as work performance is satisfactory, and employee relies on that statement by resigning from his prior employment or passing up other offers of employment, employee who is later discharged without cause may have viable claim for wrongful discharge. Mulder v Donaldson, Lufkin & Jenrette (1994, Sup) 161 Misc 2d 698, 611 NYS2d 1019.

Presumption that, absent agreement establishing fixed duration, employment relationship is at will does not apply when employer had promulgated policies in personnel manual specifying procedures or grounds for termination; these procedures become part of employment contract and must be followed. Thus, job security policy stated in handbook contractually bound employer and did not amount to nonbinding general statements of policy and supervisory guidelines, where policy set forth very specific and detailed procedure for work force reduction in mandatory and unqualified terms. Further, severance pay provision was explicitly invoked and followed in case of discharged employee asserting cause of action for breach of contract in connection with reduction in force. Handbook's general language of qualification that stated "in the final analysis, specific judgment and discretion will govern," did not negate binding force of handbook's more specific provisions under state law. Mycak v Honeywell, Inc. (1992, CA2 NY) 953 F2d 798, 7 BNA IER Cas 117, 120 CCH LC ¶ 56780, (applying NY law).

Under New York law, at-will employee can have cause of action of breach of implied contract against employer where he or she is discharged in absence of circumstances or procedures specified in employer's handbook. Thus, terminated at-will executive of registered securities broker-dealer satisfied all elements of state cause of action for wrongful discharge alleging that employer's manual created implied contract of employment because it assured continued employment as long as employee did not transgress manual's provisions; that employer breached implied contract where it did not fire him for any stated ground contained in manual, but rather for no apparent or stated reason or cause, evidence indicated that no misconduct occurred before

For latest cases, call the toll free number appearing on the cover of this supplement.

Illustration 4-15 Annotation History Table, *ALR Index.*

ANNOTATION HISTORY TABLE

59 ALR3d 1205
§ 3 Superseded 16 ALR4th 1335

60 ALR3d 333
§ 10-14 Superseded 41 ALR4th 812
41 ALR4th 877

60 ALR3d 651
Superseded 73 ALR4th 1053

61 ALR3d 244
Superseded 85 ALR4th 284

61 ALR3d 264
Superseded 20 ALR4th 855

61 ALR3d 1041
Superseded 7 ALR5th 73

62 ALR3d 271
Superseded 12 ALR4th 544

63 ALR3d 979
Superseded 32 ALR4th 1221

64 ALR3d 246
Superseded 79 ALR4th 844

66 ALR3d 885
Superseded 1 ALR5th 817

69 ALR3d 528
Superseded 11 ALR4th 549

69 ALR3d 553
Superseded 54 ALR4th 112

69 ALR3d 713
§ 4-6 Superseded 61 ALR4th 1070
§ 10 Superseded 88 ALR4th 1266

75 ALR3d 493
Superseded 19 ALR4th 830

75 ALR3d 600
Superseded 17 ALR4th 1077

75 ALR3d 751
Superseded 77 ALR3d 1349

75 ALR3d 1000
Superseded 77 ALR3d 1363

76 ALR3d 1020
Superseded 39 ALR4th 556

79 ALR3d 237
Superseded 48 ALR4th 67

79 ALR3d 955
Superseded 41 ALR4th 111

80 ALR3d 1212
Superseded 61 ALR4th 1155

81 ALR3d 394
§ 4 Superseded 66 ALR4th 622

81 ALR3d 638
Superseded 87 ALR4th 1004

82 ALR3d 218
§ 3 Superseded 60 ALR4th 732

83 ALR3d 15
§ 9 Superseded 74 ALR4th 798

86 ALR3d 454
Superseded 52 ALR4th 853

88 ALR3d 182

33 ALR4th 983
34 ALR4th 761
35 ALR4th 1063

96 ALR3d 968
§ 4[a] Superseded 78 ALR4th 1028
§ 5 Superseded 5 ALR5th 550
5 ALR5th 788
6 ALR5th 1 § 6
6 ALR5th 69

97 ALR3d 338
Superseded 73 ALR4th 782

97 ALR3d 528
§ 10-13 Superseded 62 ALR4th 16

ALR4th

12 ALR4th 544
§ 7 Superseded 33 ALR4th 120
§ 16 Superseded 32 ALR4th 1221

31 ALR4th 389
Superseded 2 ALR5th 301
2 ALR5th 337

35 ALR4th 441
§ 17 Superseded 50 ALR4th 843

57 ALR4th 911
§ 3, 7[a] Superseded 98 ALR Fed 124

ALR Fed

1 ALR Fed 295
Superseded 105 ALR Fed 755

The terms used for the topic headings in the A.L.R. digests do not correspond with the *A.L.R. Index* headings. The A.L.R. digest topics are generally much broader than the index headings. These broad topics are divided into subtopics. The breadth of the topics and the lengthy listing of subtopics sometimes make the digest approach a difficult and inefficient research approach to A.L.R.

Table of Laws, Rules, and Regulations. If you already know a pertinent statute or regulation, an efficient approach to locating an annotation may be to use this table, which appears in the tables volume of the *ALR Index* and in the last A.L.R. Federal tables volume. This table lists annotations that cite particular federal statutes, federal administrative regulations, federal court

Illustration 4-16

Shepard's Citations for Annotations.

AMERICAN LAW REPORTS, 4th SERIES (Annotations)

Vol. 36

—828—
71A4513n

—840—
71A4557n

—909—
775SW537

—921—
28A5427n

—933—
21A5102n

—990—
851P2d1267
90A41137n
122ARF437n

—1177—
622A2d251
249CaR421
249CaR422
503NW54
570So2d759

—1196—
247CaR800
82A41040n
83A4690n
121ARF637n

—1221—
737FS1428
475NW633
506NW608
770P2d1373
821P2d21
843P2d599
10A5259n
11A5731n
12A5678n
16A5245n
17A517n
18A5607n
20A5357n
20A5684n
21A520n
99ARF778n
99ARF785n
100ARF671n
101ARF225n
101ARF381n
103ARF833n
104ARF566n
106ARF403n

Vol. 33

—14—
70A4603n
72A4233n
14A5720n

—47—
907F2d588
391SE369
579So2d1214
597So2d1005
766SW930
72A4302n
80A4191n

—82—
572A2d147
840P2d1039
374SE847
16A5284n
22A5499n

—120—
709FS1385
712FS1235
717FS1356
554A2d1183
773P2d1233
417SE914
431SE689
72A4500n
78A4184n
86A4312n
11A5731n
16A5245n
17A517n
18A5607n
19A5446n
21A519n
99ARF788n

—212—
564NE137
440NW896
785P2d251
85A4816n
19A548n

—301—
80A4551n
81A4877n
111ARF206n
115ARF583n

—368—
810P2d554
599So2d1379
199IlLR662
70A427n
78A4156n
14A555n

—404—
110LE690n

—429—
944F2d209
609NE1214
615NE173
632So2d979
16A5160n
93ARF137n
115ARF392n
119ARF595n

—506—
122ARF607n

—539—
80A4414n
112ARF156n
118ARF456n

—579—
882P2d834
70A41011n
81A417n
6A5619n
7A5152n
18A5484n
23A586n

—635—
627A2d192

—650—
82A41117n

—663—
423SE141
13A5129n

—767—
644A2d1003
20A525n

—790—
80Geo1957
6A5547n

—809—
567So2d574
28A5614n

—944—
71A4513n

—964—
81A4208n
115ARF472n

—983—
604NE692
610NE485
438NW642
459NW25
461NW240
474NW328
828P2d66
875P2d191
78CaL1029
19A5539n

—1017—
382SE74

—1062—
789P2d66
118ARF272n

—1166—
85A4346n
103ARF124n
107ARF761n

—1206—
4A5702n

Vol. 34

—13—
923F2d908
72A4424n
80A4670n
13A5847n

—63—
78A41108n
9A5591n

—95—
80A4974n
9A512n

—167—
878F2d244
15A510n
27A560n
93ARF316n

—191—
87A419n
7A5524n

—228—
398SE123
85A4345n
17A5185n
25A5790n

—293—
762FS889
563NE1281
597NE483
631NE1278
778P2d834
813SW674
20A526n

—328—
6F3d399
603A2d1208
476NW566
802P2d885
794SW143

—457—
118ARF628n

—547—
99ARF891n
114ARF494n

—609—
818P2d1070
441SE67
70A4136n
72A41151n
28A5139n
121ARF262n

—665—
70A4832n
16A5284n
27A5776n

—698—
552A2d1277

—761—
445NW830
776P2d126
776P2d131
412SE819

—778—
3A5255n
98ARF663n

—814—
17A5152n

—857—
13A5178n

—888—
645A2d485
111ARF559n
114ARF361n

—914—
800P2d971
8A5805n

—958—
521NW87
770P2d837
849P2d1213
870SW268
12A5678n
14A511n
26A5146n
102ARF578n

—1054—
78A41137n

—1121—
70A4503n

—1167—
439NW93
15A547n
18A523n

Vol. 35

—12—
858P2d109
89A4858
72A4283n

—61—
78A41033n
81A41103n
15A5713n
20A5560n

—225—
812FS360
7A5868n
7A5869n
119ARF209n

—272—
85A4345n
17A5185n
23A515n
25A5790n

—328—
85A4345n
17A5184n
23A515n
25A5789n

—364—
726FS1244

—390—
90A4865n
27A5728n

—441—
908F2d685
150FRD216
106LE730n
87A4150n
2A5458n
12A5258n
16A5135n
99ARF507n

—538—
810FS1535
106LE730n
87A4150n
2A5458n
6A5329n
9A5716n
14A5302n
16A5135n
99ARF507n

—626—
969F2d924
811SW305
882SW751

—663—
72A493n
9A512n

—691—
500NW67
811P2d909
565So2d1144
78A4184n

—731—
824SW130
80A41030n

—757—
94LE844n
82A41098n
3A5753n
23A5808n

—810—
149FRD613
78A4574n
78A4577n

—861—
915F2d1508
933F2d1383
462NW353
393SE66
78A4156n
83A41190n
84A41125n
4A5673n
14A555n

—872—
491NW216

—890—
773P2d935
399SE652
546So2d1168
550So2d593

—947—
616NE1093
22A5270n

—985—
88A4572n
88A4616n
88A4648n

—1002—
928F2d93
129FRD185
876SW821
85A4816n
88A41065n

—1031—
820P2d918
425SE217
11A5730n
16A5245n
17A517n
18A5607n
19A5446n
20A5684n
21A519n
99ARF779n
99ARF787n
100ARF671n
101ARF225n
101ARF381n
106ARF403n

—1063—
575A2d891
589A2d37
450NW457
376SE583
412SE819
599So2d1317
8A5264n
21A5305n

—1094—
443SE221

—1117—
380SE840
82A4241n
14A5201n
24A5784n

—1167—
80A4208n

—1237—
13A5575n

Vol. 36

—7—
864SW898

—117—
2A5291n
118ARF528n

—144—
783SW584
81A4425n

—212—
981F2d132
85A4288n
8A5482n

—395—
560A2d511
490NW303
80A411n
15A5662n
23A5188n

—419—
87A4808n
90A420n

—502—
408SE559
11A5278n

—588—
25A568n

—598—
64A4567s
17A5855n

—625—
22A5804n

—684—
84A4273n

—726—
845P2d576

—747—
25A568n

—769—
518NW178
819P2d267
113ARF530n

—807—
512NW786
85A4816n
19A548n

—824—
16A5558n
20A5251n

—907—
82A4241n
26A522n

—941—
84A4423n
5A5479n
5A5519n
7A5410n
7A5449n
10A5345n
10A5369n

—978—
81A41010n
82A4897n

—997—
596NE307
502NW835
829P2d664
569So2d1185
1A5784n
20A5560n

—1046—
267CaR416
490NW499
11A5840n

1011

rules, state statutes, uniform laws, model acts, Restatements, and codes of ethics. If you already know a citation to one of these kinds of sources, these tables are your fastest access method to an on-point A.L.R. annotation.

Features That Are Distinctive (or Unique) to Certain Series. Some features are distinctive to various A.L.R. series:

- A.L.R. and A.L.R.2d each has its own *Word Index* and *Quick Index.*
- The federal series has its own *A.L.R. Federal Quick Index.*
- There is one *A.L.R. Digest* each for the first and second series; the digest for the first series is called *Permanent A.L.R. Digest*; the digest for the second series is *A.L.R.2d Digest.*
- Most series are updated using pocket parts. However, A.L.R.2d annotations are updated by a separate set of volumes entitled *A.L.R.2d Later Case Service*; these volumes contain pocket parts. The annotations in the first series are supplemented by the *A.L.R. Blue Book of Supplemental Decisions,* which is a collection of hardbound volumes plus a softbound volume that is updated annually until it is replaced by the next hardbound volume.
- Online search queries and West Digest Key Numbers for the topics in the fourth series annotations are contained in the A.L.R.4th pocket parts and a separate volume so marked.

Other Media. As of early 1996, A.L.R. appeared in the following media:

			Computer-Assisted Research		
	Paper	*CD-ROM*	*LEXIS*	*WESTLAW*	*Microform*
A.L.R.	√				
A.L.R.2d	√		√		
A.L.R.3d	√	√	√		
A.L.R.4th	√	√	√		
A.L.R.5th	√	√	√		
A.L.R. Fed.	√	√			
Shepard's Citations for Annotations	√				

5. How Do You Cite A.L.R.?

Rule 16.5.5 in *The Bluebook* requires that you begin an A.L.R. citation with the author's full name, if available, followed by "Annotation." (In early A.L.R. volumes, the author's name never appeared. Later, initials appeared at the end of the annotation or, still later, at the beginning of the annotation. In recent volumes, the author's name appears at the beginning of the annotation.) Next comes the title of the annotation, volume, series, beginning page number and date, including a reference to the supplement as appropriate. The annotation in Illustration 4-13 on pages 75-78 would be cited as follows:

> Theresa L. Kruk, Annotation, *Right to Discharge Allegedly "At-Will" Employee as Affected by Employer's Promulgation of Employment Policies as to Discharge,* 33 A.L.R.4th 120, 120-23 (1982 & Supp. 1995).

E. Treatises

1. What Is a Treatise?

Put simply, a treatise is a comprehensive book on a particular subject. The subject may be a broad subject (such as contracts or employment law) or it may be a narrow subject (such as a single statute protecting disabled workers). The term "treatise" connotes a scholarly, systematic treatment of the subject covered.

Legal treatises are secondary sources, typically written by private authors, such as law professors and legal practitioners, although some are written by publishers' staffs. A treatise may consist of a single volume or multiple volumes. Treatises are published in hardbound, softbound, and looseleaf forms. A looseleaf treatise consists of separate pages held together by some type of binder; this format facilitates updating.

A treatise typically contains at least three parts: (1) scholarly text, with footnotes or endnotes containing supporting citations and tangential remarks; (2) finding aids, such as one or more tables of contents, an index, and other tables; and (3) miscellaneous features, such as a preface and appendices, which may include the text of important documents such as statutes. A treatise also may have a supplement.

The text in legal treatises often is organized by sections or paragraphs. In the Canoga case, for example, Illustration 4-17 on page 87 from Lex K. Larson's *Employment Discrimination* shows a treatise that is organized by section number.

2. Why Are Treatises Useful?

Treatises excel in the scholarly, comprehensive analysis of a discrete area of the law. This analysis can be especially useful to you when you begin researching and are still unfamiliar with the vocabulary, issues, subissues, arguments, and policies for your research problem. The arguments propounded

Illustration 4-17

3A Lex K. Larson, *Employment Discrimination*, § 108A.56 (2d ed. 1994).

The Report accompanying Senate Bill 933 offers additional guidance on the treatment of other insurance issues under the ADA. The Report states that employers can not completely deny health insurance coverage to a disabled individual due to the disability:

> For example, while it is permissible for an employer to offer insurance policies that limit coverage for certain procedures or treatments, *e.g.*, only a specified amount per year for mental health coverage, a person who has a mental health condition may not be denied coverage for other conditions such as for a broken leg or for heart surgery because of the existence of the mental health condition.[40]

The ADA calls for equal access to whatever health insurance coverage that the employer provides; it does not require that the employer provide greater coverage to the individual with a disability who may have a greater need. And, the ADA does not affect pre-existing condition clauses in insurance policies, so long as they are not used as subterfuge to evade the purposes behind the ADA.[41]

§ 108A.56—Restrictions on smoking

The ADA provides that nothing in the Act prevents a covered entity from prohibiting or imposing restrictions on smoking in places of employment.[42] This clause curiously appears under the heading "Relationship to Other Laws." The legislative history does not provide any clues about how this came to be or what it means: does it imply that only government-imposed restrictions such as anti-smoking ordinances are referred to? The breadth of the language and the purposes of the ADA militate against any such narrow construction, so that purely employer-imposed workplace smoking rules are no doubt legitimized as well.

[40] Senate Report at 29 § 108A.14 n.56 *supra*.

[41] *Id.* The Senate Report also suggests that it is permissible for an employer to offer insurance policies that limit coverage for certain procedures or treatments; for example, an annual limit on health coverage benefits. *Id.*

[42] ADA § 501(b), 42 U.S.C. § 12201(b).

in the treatise, while not primary authority, may be especially persuasive secondary authority because of the credibility of the author or the quality of the work.

Because updating practices for treatises vary, some will provide more current information than others. You typically will need to update the references to primary authority.

3. How Do You Research in Treatises?

Researching in a treatise entails four steps: (1) finding and selecting an appropriate treatise; (2) locating pertinent material within it; (3) reading the material; and (4) and updating it (if an update is available). All of the steps except the third require some explanation. (You will read a treatise much as you will read a periodical article.)

a. Finding a Treatise

To find an appropriate treatise, you need to know which area of law encompasses the problem you are researching. If initially you have trouble discerning the area of law, think about the names of the courses offered in law school, or ask a professor or a librarian for assistance.

Once you know the subject areas of your research, you may use any of these techniques to find treatises:

(1) Look in the library's catalog to find out what your library owns. Or, if you want a larger selection, consult other local, regional, or national cataloging systems.
(2) Find out the call number range of the subject matter and browse the relevant shelves. In addition, ask at the library reserve desk to see reserve treatises within that call number range.
(3) Ask a professor, librarian, legal practitioner, or colleague who is knowledgeable about the subject for a recommendation.
(4) Look at the front or back of a textbook for a list of treatises published by the publisher. Or look in the textbook for footnotes and bibliographies that cite treatises.

The first two search methods need some elaboration.

(1) Using the Library Catalog

Your library catalog may be in paper, on microfiche, or on an online computer database. All three media most likely will permit you to search for treatises by author, title, and subject. An online catalog may offer additional search options, including key-word searching.

As you learned in Part C of this chapter, a subject search is the broadest search, so it usually will retrieve the most titles. Searching by subject is not always as easy as you might think, however, because you often must use the exact subject heading used by the cataloger. Your initial choice may prove to be the relevant subject heading, or you may find a cross-reference to the correct subject heading. If not, you may use one of two other methods to find the subject heading. First, if you know of at least one source on point, locate that source in the catalog by means of its author or title. Then use the relevant subject headings listed for that source to find other sources.

In the Canoga case, Illustration 4-18 below shows you that if you knew of the Larson title when you began your research, you could use it to find the subject heading "Discrimination in employment—Law and legislation—United States." You could then use that subject heading to find additional sources.

The second method is to consult the multivolume set entitled *Library*

Illustration 4-18 Online Catalog (Facsimile).

CALL # KF3464.L374
LOCATIONS Reserve

AUTHOR Larson, Lex K.
TITLE Employment discrimination/by Lex K. Larson; practice forms by Lex K. Larson and Jonathan R. Harkavy.
EDITION 2nd ed.
IMPRINT New York: M. Bender, 1994--
1 > Reserve
LIB. HAS: 1994--
Latest received: December 1994 38
DESCRIPT v. (loose-leaf): forms; 26 cm.

NOTE Earlier ed. by: Arthur Larson.
Includes index.
SUBJECT Sex discrimination in employment--Law and legislation—United States.
Discrimination in employment--Law and legislation--United States.
ALT AUTHOR Harkavy, Jonathan R., 1943--
Larson, Arthur.
1 > Reserve
LIB. HAS:1994--
Latest received: December 1994 38

of Congress Subject Headings. These subject headings are the starting point for the creation of many library catalogs. They also offer you a shortcut to efficient use of a library catalog. Illustration 4-19 below shows you the page containing the entry "Discrimination in employment," which is relevant to the Canoga case. The entries printed in bold type are subject headings that may be used as search terms. The notations "BT" and "NT," which appear under the bold-faced headings, alert you to broader and narrower search terms. You may need to look up these broader and narrower search terms for your research to be comprehensive.

If you search an online catalog, pay close attention to the example screens

Illustration 4-19 *Library of Congress Subject Headings.*

Discrimination in employment
(Continued)
UF Bias, Job
Employment discrimination
Equal employment opportunity
Equal opportunity in employment
Fair employment practice
Job bias
Job discrimination
Race discrimination in employment
BT Employment (Economic theory)
RT Trade-unions—Minority membership
SA *subdivision* Employment *under names of racial or social groups, e.g.* Afro-Americans—Employment; Women—Employment
NT Affirmative action programs
Age discrimination in employment
Blacklisting, Labor
Equal pay for equal work
Reverse discrimination in employment
Sex discrimination in employment
— Law and legislation *(May Subd Geog)*
BT Labor laws and legislation
— United States
Discrimination in higher education
(May Subd Geog)
[LC212.4-LC212.43]
UF Discrimination in colleges and universities
Race discrimination in higher education
BT Education, Higher
Discrimination in housing *(May Subd Geog)*
UF Fair housing
Housing, Discrimination in
Open housing
Race discrimination in housing
Segregation in housing
BT Housing

Discrimination in mortgage loans
(May Subd Geog)
UF Race discrimination in mortgage loans
Red lining
Redlining
BT Mortgage loans
— Law and legislation *(May Subd Geog)*
Discrimination in municipal services
(May Subd Geog)
UF Race discrimination in municipal services
BT Municipal services
— Law and legislation *(May Subd Geog)*
Discrimination in public accommodations
(May Subd Geog)
UF Public accommodations, Discrimination in
Race discrimination in public accommodations
Segregation in public accommodations
NT Segregation in transportation
— Law and legislation *(May Subd Geog)*
Discrimination in sports *(May Subd Geog)*
UF Integration in sports
Race discrimination in sports
Racial integration in sports
Segregation in sports
[Former heading]
BT Sports
Discrimination in transportation
USE Segregation in transportation
Discrimination learning
BT Transfer of training
Discrimination theory (Statistics)
USE Discriminant analysis
Discriminators, Frequency
USE Frequency discriminators
Discs, Compact
USE Compact discs
Discs, Optical
USE Optical disks

and help screens. Be careful to correctly spell the title, the author's name, or the subject heading because a misspelled word may cause your search to be unsuccessful. Be careful, too, about your use of singulars and plurals because the two forms will not yield the same result. And remember to search in the right "part" of the catalog. You cannot find an author's name in the title or subject file, and so on.

In the Canoga case, Illustration 4-18 on page 89 shows the kind of bibliographic information found on a catalog "card" (be it paper, microfiche, or computerized). "Location" tells you the name of the collection in which that source is located (for instance, the reserve collection). "Call number" tells you the order in which the source in that collection is arranged.

(2) Browsing the Shelves

Most libraries use one of two call number systems: Library of Congress or Dewey decimal. Under the Library of Congress system, most American legal publications have a call number that begins with "KF." In the Dewey decimal system, American legal publications appear in classes 340-349.

A good research strategy for finding a treatise is to use the library catalog, a list posted in your library, or a table like Exhibit 4.1 on page 92 to ascertain the call numbers of the legal topic you are researching. You then can browse the shelves of books with those call numbers, looking for useful treatises.

(3) Recognizing a Treatise

As a researcher new to legal research, you may find it difficult to determine what is and what is not a treatise. The following tips may help:

(1) Do not expect the word "treatise" to appear in the title or the subject heading for the book.
(2) Sources with "cases and materials," "problems, text, and cases," "casebook," or similar words in the title or subject heading are probably casebooks, not treatises.
(3) Sources with titles or a publisher's name containing "Institute," "Seminar," or "Legal Education" are probably not treatises; they may be continuing legal education (CLE) materials. (Casebooks and CLEs are covered in Part G.)
(4) "Restatements" of the law, covered in Part F, are not treatises.

b. Locating Pertinent Information within a Treatise and Evaluating the Treatise

You may use either an index or a table of contents to locate information within a treatise. If you use the index approach, be sure to consult all indexes; a treatise may have both a main index and one or more updates to it.

It often is easier and more effective to find the relevant sections of a treatise by consulting its table of contents rather than its index. You can scan

Exhibit 4.1 Library of Congress Call Numbers in the KF Classification (Law of the United States).

Administrative Law KF 5401-5425
Antitrust KF 1631-1657
Banking KF 966-1032
Bankruptcy KF 1501-1548
Business Associations, generally KF 1355-1480
Children and Law KF 479, 540-550
Civil and Political Rights KF 4741-4788
Civil Procedure KF 8810-9075
Commercial Transactions KF 871-962
Conflict of Laws KF 410-418
Constitutional Law KF 4501-5130
Contracts, quasi-contracts KF 801-1244
Copyright KF 2986-3080
Corporations KF 1384-1480
Criminal Law KF 9201-9479
Criminal Procedure KF 9601-9797
Education Policy and Law KF 4101-4257
Employment Discrimination KF 3464-3469
Environmental Law KF 277.E5
Equity KF 398-400
Evidence
  In civil cases KF 8931-8969
  In criminal cases KF 9660-9677
Federal Courts KF 8700-8807
Immigration Law KF 4801-4848
Insurance Law KF 1146-1238
International Law JX 1-6731
Jurisprudence KF 379-382
Juvenile Criminal Law KF 9771-9827
Labor Law KF 3300-3580
Land-Use Planning KF 5691-5710
Legal History KF 350-374
The Legal Profession KF 297-334
Legal Research and Writing KF 240-251
Legislative Process KF 4945-4952
Local Government/Municipal Law KF 5300-5332
Marital Relations and Dissolution KF 501-553
Medical Legislation KF 3821-3829
Mental Health Law KF 3828-3829
Oil and Gas KF 1841-1870
Patents KF 3091-3192
Public Safety KF 3941-3977
Real Property KF 560-698
Regulation of Industry, Trade, and Commerce KF 1600-2940
Secured Transactions KF 1046-1062
Securities Regulations KF 1066-1083, KF 1428-1457
Social Legislation KF 3300-3771
Taxation KF 6271-6645
Torts KF 1246-1327
Trial Advocacy Principles/Tactics KF 8911-8925
Uniform State Laws KF 165
Water Resources KF 5551-5590
Wills and Trusts KF 726-780

a table of contents relatively quickly. This scan may jog your thinking about additional topics and vocabulary to consider. You also can see whether the author organizes the topic differently than you do. Thus, using a table of contents keeps you from being tripped up by your own limited view of the topic or by the indexing vocabulary.

Many treatises include both a summary table of contents and a detailed table of contents. A classic technique is to use the summary table of contents to locate the pertinent section in the detailed table of contents. A detailed table of contents may follow the summary table, or the relevant parts of a detailed table may appear at the beginning of the volumes or chapters to which they relate.

You may find more than one treatise on the same topic. Treatises vary in quality and in usefulness for a particular purpose. To decide which one is the best treatise for your needs, consider the following:

Coverage: Treatises on the same subject vary in the particular topics covered and in their level of detail. Pick one with the coverage and level of detail that best matches your needs. In an unfamiliar area of law, you first might examine a single-volume treatise to gain familiarity with the basics of the subject, then read a more detailed discussion in a multivolume treatise. In addition, some treatises are written for scholars, and some for practitioners. While all describe and synthesize the law, some also analyze it, criticize it, and promote changes in it. Your choice will depend on your needs.

Organization: Treatises are organized in a variety of ways, including chronologically, topically, by statute, and by type of transaction. They also vary in the number and quality of the special features (tables of contents, indexes, appendices, etc.) they provide. Pick one that works well for you.

Currency: If you are trying to learn about the current law on your subject, select a treatise that has been published or updated recently. For a bound treatise, check the copyright date of the volume you are using as well as the date of any updates, such as pocket parts or pamphlet supplements. If you are using a looseleaf treatise, check for dates on the individual pages or on any supplement filed in the binder. Because there always is a delay between the completion of the text and its publication, look too for any statements about the scope of coverage of the text. You often find these statements in the preface of a publication or on the cover of a supplement.

Accuracy: If your research is to be credible, the sources you are relying on must be accurate. If you pick up indications that a source contains errors (from incorrect footnotes or citations, outdated text, poor reviews, or otherwise), consider using another treatise.

Reputation (book): Some treatises develop a reputation for being the classics in their field; that is, the analysis in these treatises is considered particularly credible. To determine which titles are considered especially reputable: (1) look for a treatise that has been cited in a textbook or course syllabus; (2) pick a treatise that is kept on reserve; (3) pick a treatise cited by a court; (4) find a treatise that has been published in multiple editions; or (5) use a book review (published in a periodical) to help you judge the quality of a treatise.

Reputation (author): Look for a treatise by an author who is an expert in the field. Check the author's credentials as noted in the treatise or as noted in a reference book, such as *Who's Who in American Law* or *The AALS Directory of Law Teachers.* Check periodical indexes or library catalogs to see if the author has written extensively on the topic. Or use a treatise written by the author of a textbook.

Reputation (publisher): Some publishers focus on particular subjects. In addition, publishers differ in the quality of their editorial work and in the design of their publications. As you become a more experienced researcher, you will develop your own opinions about various publishers' quality, their reliability, and the usefulness of their products. For the time being, you may want to ask reference librarians and other experienced legal researchers for their opinions.

In the Canoga case, the source in Illustration 4-17 on page 87 is from a well known, multivolume, looseleaf treatise entitled *Employment Discrimination*, now in its second edition. The main volumes have been published recently, beginning in 1994, and they are updated regularly by a cumulative supplement. The first edition of the treatise was authored by Arthur Larson, a Duke University professor of law who was a former Secretary of Labor. The second is authored by Lex K. Larson, the president of Employment Law, Inc., who also lectures at the law school. The set is organized in part by major statutes, making it easy to find material on the Americans with Disabilities Act (ADA), a statute that you learned about while doing periodical research. Finally, the set is published by a reputable legal publisher.

The treatise excerpt in Illustration 4-17 alludes to a potentially important provision of the ADA, which apparently permits restrictions on smoking in the workplace.

c. Updating

Just like treatises in other subject areas, legal treatises are sometimes "updated" through the publication of new editions. You should check the library catalog to be certain that the edition you are using is the most current one in your library. To find out whether there is a new edition that your library does not have, check *Books in Print* or *Law Books & Serials in Print* or ask a librarian for help.

The individual editions of legal treatises often are updated too. Therefore, you should check the publication date of the main volume and determine whether the source has an update service covering changes in the law since the original publication date. Most multivolume treatises have update services, as do some single-volume treatises. Update services are organized by page, paragraph, or section to correspond to the page, paragraph, or section of the original volume. Updates come in several forms:

Pocket parts: These updates are pamphlets that slip into a pocket on an inside cover of a volume. Pocket parts usually are replaced annually. If a pocket part becomes too large, it may be replaced by a softbound supplement. Be sure to check the date of publication of the pocket part to guard against relying on one that is out-of-date.

Supplemental volumes: Some sources have separate volumes or softbound pamphlets updating the original volumes. These supplements usually are shelved next to the volumes they update. The library catalog may alert you to the existence of these supplements.

Looseleaf supplements: Sources bound in looseleaf binders may be updated with looseleaf supplements that are inserted periodically into the looseleaf volumes. These supplements often are printed on colored paper to distinguish them from the original material.

Looseleaf page replacements: Sources bound in looseleaf binders may be updated with replacement pages that arrive at regular intervals or on an "as needed" basis.

Update services often contain supplementary indexes and tables. The supplementary indexes add index entries to reflect the new contents and sometimes change index entries for the original text.

If a treatise has a supplement, you must check both the main volumes and any supplements to ensure that your research is comprehensive, correct, and as current as it can be through use of the treatise.

In the Canoga case, neither the main volumes of the Larson treatise nor the recent looseleaf supplements to them discussed the effect of the ADA on an employer's ability to regulate employees' smoking away from the workplace. Because the topic was not covered in this recently updated leading treatise, you might reasonably decide to check another leading employment treatise, a very current ADA treatise, or a legal periodical index. If you still don't find any commentary, you may wish to turn directly to case law research to see if any courts have addressed the issue yet. See Chapter 6. Case law often precedes commentary on a topic.

4. What Else?

Additional Techniques for Finding Treatises. You may use a book bibliography, such as *Law Books & Serials in Print,* or a periodical bibliography to find treatise titles. You also may find book bibliographies by doing a subject search in the library catalog under "Law—United States—Bibliography," "Law—Bibliography," or "[your specific subject]—Bibliography." Also, recall that the *Index to Legal Periodicals and Books* has begun indexing some treatises.

Hornbooks. "Hornbook" generally refers to a single-volume treatise that explains the basic principles of law in a particular field. Hornbooks often are written by a top scholar in a field and usually are designed with the needs of law students in mind. They can be an excellent place to begin your research on an unfamiliar topic.

Table of Primary Authorities. Treatises often have tables of primary authorities, which help you locate the text and footnotes within the treatise that discuss those authorities. The two most common tables are tables of cases and tables of statutes. These tables are useful only if you know the name of the case or the name or citation of the statute on point and the case or statute is cited in the treatise.

Other Media. Some treatises are available in microform, on CD-ROM, or on online research systems, as well as in print. Treatises in these media may not appear in your library's catalog. The number of treatises in these media is growing, so you may wish to check with a librarian to see if a treatise that interests you is available in one of these media.

5. How Do You Cite Treatises?

Rule 15 of *The Bluebook* covers all books. Unless the special citation forms in Rule 15.7 apply, the citation includes the volume number (if the treatise has more than one volume); the author's (or authors') full name (or names); the full main title of the book as it appears on the title page (not the cover); the page, section, or paragraph number (if only part of the volume is cited); and the edition (if other than the first) and year in parentheses. A subtitle is given only if it is particularly relevant. Rule 15.2. Here is a straightforward example from Illustration 4-17 on page 87:

> 3A Lex K. Larson, *Employment Discrimination* § 108A.56 (2d ed. 1994).

Rule 15.1.1 states that if there are more than two authors, the name of the first author is followed by "et al."

F. RESTATEMENTS

1. What Are Restatements?

The Restatements are a source unique to law. They differ from the other commentary sources in this chapter in five respects. First, the Restatements have a unique purpose: They seek to unify the common (case) law on a national basis. Second, they are written in rule form with explanations following. Third, they are written and revised through a deliberative process by more than one expert. Fourth, although they are not themselves primary authority, parts of the Restatements often are adopted by courts. When part of a Restatement is adopted by a court, the adopted language then becomes primary authority in the adopting jurisdiction. Fifth, Restatements are available only for a limited number of subjects: agency, conflict of laws, contracts, foreign relations law, judgments, property, restitution, security, torts, trusts, and unfair competition.

The Restatements are products of the theoretical conflicts that shaped twentieth-century American jurisprudence. The immense geographical and industrial growth of the United States in the mid-nineteenth century generated an increasing amount of litigation and case law. Legal scholars known as "the rationalists" were concerned about apparent inconsistencies in the flood of decisions, which left courts, attorneys, and citizens without a secure understanding of the law. The rationalists believed that the law consisted of immutable principles that could be reduced to a consistent, organized, and scientific system. They sought to impose this vision of consistency and order on the common law.

Legal "realists," on the other hand, concluded that laws were not derived from immutable laws of nature. They maintained that the common law often reflected the needs of particular litigants, the biases of judges, and the prevailing social ethic.

This philosophical challenge by the realists, coupled with a continuing development of seemingly contradictory case law, caused the rationalists to mobilize in the hope of enhancing the predictability and organization in American common law. In 1923, they helped organize the American Law Institute (ALI). Its objective was to reduce the complexity and uncertainty of American common law by reforming common law principles into one authoritative, rule-like source. The Restatements of the Law are the results of this effort.

The authors of the first series of Restatements set a lofty goal: to "restate" precisely the principles of the existing common law. By so doing, the drafters hoped to produce an "authority greater than that now accorded to any legal treatise, an authority more nearly on a par with that accorded the decisions of the courts." Report of the Committee on the Establishment of a Permanent Organization for the Improvement of the Law Proposing the Establishment of an American Law Institute (Feb. 23, 1923), *in The American Law Institute 50th Anniversary* 34 (2d ed. 1973).

In the first Restatement series, the drafters did not take into account "what the law ought to be . . . [if that] result had no judicial support or was a minority position." A. James Casner, *Restatement (Second) of Property as an Instrument of Law Reform,* 67 Iowa L. Rev. 87, 88 (1981). Thus the Restatement's codification of a majority rule had the potential of retarding the growth of a minority rule and inhibiting the natural (albeit infrequent) occurrence of judicial overturning of existing doctrines. *See id.* at 91. However, in 1966 the ALI changed its policies to allow choice of a minority position.

When the ALI decides to prepare a new Restatement, it appoints a "Reporter," who is an eminent scholar in the field. With the help of assistants, the Reporter prepares a draft of the Restatement. A committee of advisers who are experts in the field review and revise the draft. The revised draft then is reviewed by the ALI's Council—a group of fifty or so judges, attorneys, and professors—who may refer the draft back to the Reporter or who may approve a draft and submit it to the annual meeting of the ALI members. After ALI members have discussed and approved a draft, with or without changes, the draft is released to the public and to the legal profession for further debate. The drafts of the Restatements bear various names, such as "preliminary draft," "council draft," or "tentative draft," depending on the stage of development. Eventually a "proposed final draft" is submitted to the ALI Council and membership. If it is approved by the Council and then the ALI membership, it is published in final form.

The ALI has published Restatements in three series. The Restatements initially adopted between 1932 and 1942 are first-series Restatements; those initially adopted between 1957 and 1981 are second-series Restatements; and those initially adopted beginning in 1986 are third-series Restatements.

When the ALI wishes to make major changes in a particular Restatement, it publishes the Restatement in a new series. Thus some Restatements have been published in multiple series. See Exhibit 4.2 on page 99. New Restatement subjects may be covered for the first time in a second or third series without being covered in a previous series.

Each Restatement is organized by chapters. The chapters are divided into topics, which in turn are divided into numbered sections. Each section begins with a Restatement rule, which is printed in boldface.

A rule is followed by two kinds of explanation: comments and illustrations. The comments clarify the scope and meaning of the Restatement rule; they also may offer insights into the rationale for it. The illustrations use examples to further define the rule and the comments. Some examples are based on real cases.

For the second and third series, the illustrations may be followed by Reporter's Notes, which typically explain the history of the rule, note the cases that have discussed the issue, identify the primary authorities on which the text and illustrations are based, and provide other useful references to primary and secondary sources. For some subjects, the Reporter's Notes are in an appendix. See Exhibit 4.3 on pages 100-101.

Finally, appendices contain summaries and citations of cases that have interpreted each Restatement section.

In the Canoga case, Illustration 4-20 on pages 101-104 shows § 2 of the Restatement (Second) of Contracts. This section might help you determine if the employer's issuance of an employee handbook was a promise that could be the basis of a contract.

2. Why Are Restatements Useful?

The Restatements not only set forth majority common law rules or emerging or proposed rules the ALI believes preferable; they also clearly explain those rules and serve as a finding tool for cases that have interpreted them.

When no primary authority supports an argument, or when existing primary authority is adverse, a Restatement section may be used persuasively to suggest what the law should be. The prestige of the Reporters and advisers of the Restatements has made the Restatements unusually credible compared to other secondary sources. As of March 1, 1995, the Restatements had been cited by the courts 129,533 times. 1995 A.L.I. Ann. Rep. 19. Hence the Restatements are particularly useful as persuasive support for legal arguments that have not been addressed by the courts in a particular jurisdiction.

On the other hand, recall that Restatements are available only for a limited number of subjects. Also, the law may evolve away from a position adopted by the Restatements more rapidly than the Restatements can reflect that development. Further, some commentators believe the Restatements do not embody dispassionate and accurate recording of existing common law.

Exhibit 4.2 Restatement Finding Tools.

Subject	*Series & Dates of Adoption*	*Table of Contents*		*Index**	
		Location	*Coverage*	*Location*	*Coverage*
Agency	1st (1933)	front of each volume	Agency 1st	end of last volume	Agency 1st
	2d (1957)	front of each volume	Agency 2d	end of last topical volume	Agency 2d
Conflict of Laws	1st (1934)	front of volume	Conflicts 1st	end of volume	Conflicts 1st
	2d (1969, 1988)	front of each volume	Conflicts 2d	end of last topical volume	Conflicts 2d
Contracts	1st (1932)	front of each volume	Contracts 1st	end of last volume	Contracts 1st
	2d (1979)	front of each volume	Contracts 2d**	end of last topical volume	Contracts 2d
Foreign Relations	2d (1962, 1964, 1965)	front of each volume	Foreign Relations 2d	end of volume	Foreign Relations 2d
	3d (1986)	front of each topical volume	Foreign Relations 3d	end of last topical volume	Foreign Relations 3d
Judgments	1st (1942)	front of volume	Judgments 1st	end of volume	Judgments 1st
	2d (1980)	front of each volume	Judgments 2d**	end of last topical volume	Judgments 2d
Property	1st (1936, 1940, 1944)	front of each volume	only that volume, except that volumes I & II are merged	end of volumes II, III, IV & V	only that volume except that volumes I & II are merged
(Landlord & Tenant)	2d (1976)	front of each volume	L. & T. 2d	end of last topical volume	L. & T. 2d
(Donative Transfers)	2d (1981, 1984, 1987, 1990)	front of each volume	only that volume	end of each volume	only that volume
Restitution	1st (1936)	front of each volume	Restitution 1st	end of topical volume	Restitution 1st
Security	1st (1941)	front of volume	Security 1st	end of volume	Security 1st
Torts	1st (1934, 1938, 1939)	front of volume	only that volume	end of volume	only that volume
	2d (1963, 1964, 1976, 1977)	front of each volume	only that volume**	end of each topical volume	only that volume
Trusts	1st (1935)	front of each volume	Trusts 1st	end of last volume	Trusts 1st
	2d (1957)	front of each volume	Trusts 2d	end of last topical volume	Trusts 2d
(Prudent Investor Rule)	3d (1990)	front of volume	Trusts (P.I.R.) 3d	end of volume	Trusts (P.I.R.) 3d
Unfair Competition	3d (1993)	front of volume	Unfair Competition 3d	end of volume	Unfair Competition 3d

*A General Index covers all first series titles.

**Appendix volumes may contain tables of contents for both series.

Exhibit 4.3 Restatement Features.

Subject	*Series & Dates of Adoption*	*Reporter's Notes*	*Arrangements of Case Digests*	*References to A.L.R., West Topics & Key Numbers*	*Tables of Cases, Statutes*	*Conversion Tables*
Agency	1st (1933)	no	n/a	no	no	tent. drafts → 1st series
	2d (1957)	first appendix volume	by series	first appendix volume	no	none
Conflict of Laws	1st (1934)	no	n/a	no	no	tent. drafts → 1st series
	2d (1969, 1988)	after each section in topical volume	by series	first appendix volume	cases only, first appendix volume	1st ↔ 2d series tent. drafts ↔ 2d series
Contracts	1st (1932)	no	n/a	no	no	tent. drafts → 1st series
	2d (1979)	after each section in topical volume	by series	first appendix volume	end of last topical volume	tent. drafts ↔ 2d series
Foreign Relations	2d (1962, 1964, 1965)	after each section	by series w/in the supplement	no	cases only, end of volume	tent. draft → 2d series
	3d (1986)	after each section in topical volume	by series	end of last topical volume	end of last topical volume	3d → 2d series tent. drafts ↔ 3d series
Judgments	1st (1942)	no	n/a	no	no	tent. drafts → 1st series
	2d (1980)	after each section in topical volume	by series	first appendix volume	end of last topical volume	1st → 2d series tent. drafts ↔ 2d series
Property	1st (1936, 1940, 1944)	no	n/a	no	no	tent. draft → 1st series
(Landlord & Tenant)	2d (1976)	after each section in topical volume	n/a because 1st series did not cover landlord-tenant law	end of last topical volume	end of last topical volume	none
(Donative Transfers)	2d (1981, 1984, 1987, 1990)	after each section in topical volume	by series	each volume has own table	each volume has own table	1st ↔ 2d series (each volume has own tables)
Restitution	1st (1936)	no	n/a	no	no	tent. draft → 1st series
Security	1st (1941)	no	n/a	no	no	tent. drafts → 1st series
Torts	1st (1934, 1938, 1939)	no	n/a	no	no	tent. drafts → 1st series
	2d (1963, 1964, 1976, 1977)	first appendix volume	varies by section	first appendix volume	no	none
Trusts	1st (1935)	no	n/a	no	no	tent. drafts → 1st series
	2d (1957)	first appendix volume	by series	first appendix volume	cases only, first appendix volume	none

Exhibit 4.3 *(continued)*

Subject	*Series & Dates of Adoption*	*Reporter's Notes*	*Arrangements of Case Digests*	*References to A.L.R., West Topics & Key Numbers*	*Tables of Cases, Statutes*	*Conversion Tables*
(Prudent Investor Rule)	3d (1990)	after each section in topical volume	n/a	end of volume	end of volume	none
Unfair Competition	3d (1993)	after each section in topical volume	n/a	end of volume	end of volume	Restatement of Torts (1938) → Unfair Competition

Rather, they argue that the Restatements actually reflect compromises between the divergent views of the participants in the ALI drafting and approval process; these compromises may have been adopted to achieve consensus among the ALI members rather than to achieve the goals of the Restatement process. Consequently, as the legal realists would have predicted, the Restatements are at times inconsistent, vague, or ambiguous.

3. How Do You Research in the Restatements?

a. Locating a Relevant Section

To locate a relevant Restatement section, you must first determine which Restatement subject, if any, encompasses your research issue. Consult the list

Illustration 4-20 Restatement (Second) of Contracts § 2 cmts. A-D, illus. 1-2 (1979).

§ 2. Promise; Promisor; Promisee; Beneficiary

(1) A promise is a manifestation of intention to act or refrain from acting in a specified way, so made as to justify a promisee in understanding that a commitment has been made.

(2) The person manifesting the intention is the promisor.

See Appendix for Court Citations and Cross References

8

Illustration 4-20 *(continued)*

(3) The person to whom the manifestation is addressed is the promisee.

(4) Where performance will benefit a person other than the promisee, that person is a beneficiary.

Comment:

a. Acts and resulting relations. "Promise" as used in the Restatement of this Subject denotes the act of the promisor. If by virtue of other operative facts there is a legal duty to perform, the promise is a contract; but the word "promise" is not limited to acts having legal effect. Like "contract," however, the word "promise" is commonly and quite properly also used to refer to the complex of human relations which results from the promisor's words or acts of assurance, including the justified expectations of the promisee and any moral or legal duty which arises to make good the assurance by performance. The performance may be specified either in terms describing the action of the promisor or in terms of the result which that action or inaction is to bring about.

b. Manifestation of intention. Many contract disputes arise because different people attach different meanings to the same words and conduct. The phrase "manifestation of intention" adopts an external or objective standard for interpreting conduct; it means the external expression of intention as distinguished from undisclosed intention. A promisor manifests an intention if he believes or has reason to believe that the promisee will infer that intention from his words or conduct. Rules governing cases where the promisee could reasonably draw more than one inference as to the promisor's intention are stated in connection with the acceptance of offers (see §§ 19 and 20), and the scope of contractual obligations (see §§ 201, 219).

c. Promise of action by third person; guaranty. Words are often used which in terms promise action or inaction by a third person, or which promise a result obtainable only by such action. Such words are commonly understood as a promise of conduct by the promisor which will be sufficient to bring about the action or inaction or result, or to answer for harm caused by failure. An example is a guaranty that a third person will perform his promise. Such words constitute a promise as here defined only if they justify a promisee in an expectation of some action or inaction on the part of the promisor.

d. Promise of event beyond human control; warranty. Words which in terms promise that an event not within human control will occur may be interpreted to include a promise to answer for harm caused by the failure of the event to occur. An example is a warranty

See Appendix for Court Citations and Cross References

Illustration 4-20 *(continued)*

§ 2 **CONTRACTS, SECOND** Ch. 1

of an existing or past fact, such as a warranty that a horse is sound, or that a ship arrived in a foreign port some days previously. Such promises are often made when the parties are ignorant of the actual facts regarding which they bargain, and may be dealt with as if the warrantor could cause the fact to be as he asserted. It is then immaterial that the actual condition of affairs may be irrevocably fixed before the promise is made.

Words of warranty, like other conduct, must be interpreted in the light of the circumstances and the reasonable expectations of the parties. In an insurance contract, a "warranty" by the insured is usually not a promise at all; it may be merely a representation of fact, or, more commonly, the fact warranted is a condition of the insurer's duty to pay (see § 225(3)). In the sale of goods, on the other hand, a similar warranty normally also includes a promise to answer for damages (see Uniform Commercial Code § 2–715).

Illustrations:

1. A, the builder of a house, or the inventor of the material used in part of its construction, says to B, the owner of the house, "I warrant that this house will never burn down." This includes a promise to pay for harm if the house should burn down.

2. A, by a charter-party, undertakes that the "good ship Dove," having sailed from Marseilles a week ago for New York, shall take on a cargo for B on her arrival in New York. The statement of the quality of the ship and the statement of her time of sailing from Marseilles include promises to pay for harm if the statement is untrue.

of subjects in the first column of Exhibit 4.2 on page 99. Alternatively, use your library catalog to identify the subjects of the Restatements.

Next you must determine which series on that subject will be useful in your research. The various Restatement series and their dates of adoption are listed in Exhibit 4.2. As a general rule, begin in the newest series. Consider working backward and consulting an earlier series if you have questions about the derivation of the rule in the current series. If you are using the Restatements because you have a citation from another source to a particular section in a particular series, you may need to use only that series, although even then you may wish to check the newest series to understand the current trend.

Once you know the subject and series to use, you can locate an applicable Restatement section using either a table of contents or an index.

Illustration 4-20 *(continued)*

REPORTER'S NOTE

This Section substitutes the concept of a "manifestation of intention to act . . . " for the phrase used in former § 2(1): "an undertaking . . . that something shall happen. . . . " The older definition did not identify the essential characteristics of an undertaking. See Gardner, An Inquiry Into the Principles of Contracts, 46 Harv. L. Rev. 1, 5 (1932). The present definition of promise is based on 1 Corbin, Contracts § 13 (1963 & Supp. 1980). See also 1 id. § 15; 1 Williston, Contracts § 1A (3d ed. 1957). The definitions of "promisor," "promise" and "beneficiary" are new. Compare Gardner, Massachusetts Annotations, Restatement of Contracts, Chapter 6, at 64 (1935).

Comment a. See Coffman Industries, Inc. v. Gorman-Taber Co., 521 S.W.2d 763 (Mo. Ct. App. 1975); Farnsworth, The Past of Promise: An Historical Introduction to Contract, 69 Colum. L. Rev. 576 (1969).

Comment d. This Comment is based on former § 2(2). Illustrations 1 and 2 are based on Illustrations 2 and 3 to former § 2.

Comment e. See Pappas v. Bever, 219 N.W.2d 720 (Iowa 1974). Illustration 3 is based on Illustration 4 to former § 2.

See Appendix for Court Citations and Cross References

12

A table of contents is located in the front of most Restatement volumes. It usually encompasses the entire subject in that series. However, for a few subjects (indicated in Exhibit 4.2), the table of contents covers only topics found in that particular volume. Thus, for multivolume Restatement subjects, you occasionally will have to examine the table of contents in more than one volume to find the appropriate topic.

Most Restatement subjects have an index in the last topical (non-appendix) volume of the set. Exceptions are noted in Exhibit 4.2; these subjects have an index in the back of each volume indexing only sections located in that volume, so you occasionally will have to consult indexes in more than one volume.

A one-volume comprehensive index covers all of the first-series Restatements. The second and third series have no comprehensive index.

The relevant subject in the Canoga case is contracts, and the most useful series is the second series. A quick glance at the table of contents in the Restatement (Second) of Contracts reveals multiple sections worth checking. These include:

§ 1, Contract Defined;
§ 2, Promise; Promiser; Promisee; Beneficiary; and
§ 4, How a Promise May Be Made.

The index leads to the same sections. For example, it has an entry for "promise, defined."

b. Reading a Restatement Section

Once you have located a section number, look for that section first in a main volume, not an appendix volume or a supplement. Read the boldface Restatement rule carefully. Remember that many words were deliberated over by the ALI; some subtle meanings may escape you on the first several readings. Also read related Restatement sections so that you understand the context of the section you are researching. Related sections may include cross-referenced sections, sections in the vicinity of the section you are researching, and other sections that look promising in the Restatement index or table of contents.

Once you have read all of the pertinent Restatement rules (or after reading each rule), skim the comments and illustrations under the rule to locate those dealing with language or concepts that you need clarified. See Illustration 4-20 on pages 101-104. Read those comments and illustrations just as carefully as you read the rule.

Next, locate the Reporter's Note for each relevant second- or third-series section. Consult Exhibit 4.3 on pages 100-101 for the location of the Notes. The Notes may tell you if the Restatement rule represents a choice between conflicting positions and, if so, whether the Rule reflects the majority or minority position. They also may tell you if the Restatement rule covers an area that is not yet covered by statute or case law. In the Canoga case, Illustration 4-20 on page 104 shows the Reporter's Note for § 2.

If you decide to use more than one series, there are two ways you can find the equivalent section in another series on the same topic. Some Restatement subjects include tables that convert first-series sections to second-series sections and vice versa; these tables are noted in Exhibit 4.3. (Some tables even convert tentative draft sections to final sections.) In addition, the Reporter's Notes for second- and third-series sections usually indicate at the outset which prior series section was the predecessor for the subsequent-series section. In the Canoga case, the Reporter's Note tells you this section also was § 2 in the first series.

In reading the Restatements and applying their rules to your fact situation, you should keep these tips in mind. First, differences among jurisdictions are not reflected in the Restatement rules. The Restatements purport to set forth a unitary common law, not the common law of any particular jurisdiction. Your jurisdiction may not follow the Restatement rule.

Second, for your research to be credible, you should attempt to discern the status of the rule. A rule adopted by the Restatements may be a majority rule or a minority rule. It may be a rule that is the subject of increasing criticism, or it may be a rule which is becoming accepted by a growing number of jurisdictions.

Third, a court may adopt only portions of a Restatement section or may adopt the section but not the comments or the illustrations.

Fourth, the issuance of a second- or third-series of the Restatement does not repeal or otherwise affect an earlier version of a Restatement that has been adopted by a court or legislature.

c. Locating Sources Citing the Restatements

To maximize the credibility of your research in the Restatements, you will want to learn how courts, especially the courts in your jurisdiction, and scholars have responded to the various rules. You can locate sources that cite particular Restatement sections by using finding tools within and outside of the Restatements.

(1) Finding Tools within the Restatements

The Restatements contain summaries, or digests, of cases that have cited a particular Restatement rule, comment, or illustration. These digests include the holding and citation of the citing case and an abbreviated phrase that tells which portion of the Restatement was involved and how it was treated by the court. See Illustration 4-21 on page 107.

These digests usually are located in the appendix volumes of the most recent series for a subject. They cite sections from all series of a particular Restatement subject. The appendix volumes may be updated by pocket parts or cumulative supplements. (Occasionally the digests appear only in the pocket part of a current or earlier Restatement.)

In the first appendix volume for some subjects, each section contains separate headings for first-series case digests and second-series case digests (if any). In other appendix volumes, the first-series case digests appear at the front of the volume, followed by the second-series case digests, then the third-series case digests (if any). Consult Exhibit 4.3 on pages 100-101 for organizational differences among arrangements of case digests in appendix volumes.

The most recent citing cases can be found in *Interim Case Citations to the Restatements of the Law,* which updates all of the Restatements. See Illustration 4-22 on page 108. This finding tool does not contain digests.

In the Canoga case, Illustration 4-21 on page 107 shows the digests of several cases citing § 2 that have facts somewhat parallel to the Canoga case, although none from New Mexico. Illustration 4-22 on page 108 shows a page from the *Interim Case Citations*; the entry for § 2 shows two case citations, though again, neither are from New Mexico.

(2) Finding Tools Outside the Restatements

Shepard's Restatement of the Law Citations lists cases, annotations, and selected legal periodical articles and treatises that have cited each Restatement section, comment, and illustration. It usually is within a month of being current.

To use *Shepard's* effectively, you must locate the entry for the Restatement subject, series, and section you are researching. This entry is the "cited

Illustration 4-21 Appendix, Restatement (Second) of Contracts.

injustice can be avoided only by enforcement. Continental Air Lines, Inc. v. Keenan, 731 P.2d 708, 712.

Hawaii, 1986. Cit. in case cit. in sup. A federal court of appeals certified a question to this court as to whether an airline's employment manual constituted a contract enforceable by the employees. This court answered affirmatively that an employer is held to the policies set forth in an employment manual because it constitutes a promise. The court reasoned that announcing employment policies in a manual manifested an intent to abide by them, and that because employees could not selectively choose by which policies to abide, the employer should be similarly bound. Kinoshita v. Canadian Pacific Airlines, Ltd., 68 Hawaii 594, 724 P.2d 110, 117.

Mass.1986. Quot. in sup., cit. in sup. A driver injured in an automobile accident sued the other driver's insurance agent, alleging that the agent was negligent in failing to fulfill his preaccident promise to the insured to obtain optional liability coverage on his motor vehicle. The superior court granted the agent's motion for dismissal. The plaintiff's application for direct appellate review was granted, and this court reversed and remanded. The court held that, unlike an incidental beneficiary who was owed no duty and had no right to bring an action for breach of contract, the injured driver was an intended beneficiary of the alleged agreement for optional liability coverage between the insured and his agent, and was thus owed a duty by the insured's agent and entitled to bring an action for the agent's breach of contract. The court reasoned that the injured driver was an intended beneficiary because he was to receive the amount of his judgment against the insured, up to the limit of the optional insurance, as a result of the contract between the insured and the insurance agent. Flattery v. Gregory, 397 Mass. 143, 489 N.E.2d 1257, 1261.

Mass.App.1985. Quot. in sup. Prospective tenants brought an action against the building owner for disavowance of a lease. This court affirmed a judgment awarding the tenants compensatory and punitive damages. The court held that the owner's misrepresentations of the true situation were calculated to make the tenants conclude that only a bureaucratic formality remained to complete the lease and that such misrepresentations worked an estoppel in favor of the tenants. Greenstein v. Flatley, 19 Mass.App. 351, 474 N.E.2d 1130, 1134.

N.D.1986. Cit. in case quot. in sup. A discharged at-will employee sued her employer for wrongful termination on the ground that the employer did not follow the progressive discipline policy provisions of its employee handbook. The trial court granted summary judgment to the defendant. Affirming, this court held that the employer had clearly and conspicuously stated that the handbook was not to be construed as a contract. The court reasoned that the employer had not acted or refrained from acting in a specified way so as to justify an understanding that a commitment had been made. Bailey v. Perkins Restaurants, Inc., 398 N.W.2d 120, 122.

N.D.1987. Cit. in case quot. in disc. A charge nurse assigned to the position of in-service director of individual resident care plans sued her employer and immediate supervisor for breach of employment contract, after being relieved of her in-service director duties. This court affirmed the trial court's grant of summary judgment to the defendants, holding that the personnel policy handbook did not constitute an employment contract and that the disclaimer in the handbook's closing statement preserved the presumption that the plaintiff was an at-will employee. The court said that, although an employer may be bound when the employer makes a unilateral objective manifestation of intent, creating in the employee an expectation and in the employer an obligation of treatment, here the employer's disclaimer negated any such manifestation or creation. Eldridge v. Evan. Luth. Good Sam. Soc., 417 N.W.2d 797, 799.

Ohio App.1984. Cit. in case quot. in disc. Employees sued their former employer to recover severance benefits. On appeal of the lower court's grant of summary judgment in favor of the employer, this court held that the sale of the company by the former employer triggered the employees' rights to severance pay pursuant to their employee manual, and that the agree-

Abbreviations: cit.—cited; com.—comment; fol.—followed; quot.—quoted; sec.—section; subsec.—subsection; sup.—support.

Illustration 4-22 *Interim Case Citations to the Restatements of the Law.*

CONTRACTS 2d

Section 339

Me. 1993. United Air Lines v. Hewins Travel, 622 A.2d 1163, 1170. Cit. generally in sup., subsec. (1) cit. in case cit. in sup.

N.J.Super. 1993. J.L. Davis & Associates v. Heidler, 622 A.2d 923, 928. Cit. in case quot. in disc.

Pa.Super. 1992. Hanrahan v. Audubon Builders, Inc., 614 A.2d 748, 750-751. Quot. in case quot. in sup.

Section 341

D.Md. 1992. Jih v. Long & Foster Real Estate, Inc., 800 F. Supp. 312, 320. Cit. in disc. (Erron. cit. as §31 of the Second Restatement of the Law of Contracts.)

Section 357

D.Me. 1992. Combustion Engineering, Inc. v. Miller Hydro Group, 812 F. Supp. 260, 263. Cit. in ftn., com. (f) cit. in ftn.

Section 387

Colo. 1993. Weston Group v. A. B. Hirschfeld Press, 845 P.2d 1162, 1165. Cit. in case cit. in disc.

Section 391

Colo. 1993. Weston Group v. A. B. Hirschfeld Press, 845 P.2d 1162, 1164, 1167. Cit. and quot. in ftn. but not fol.

Section 394

Colo. 1993. Weston Group v. A. B. Hirschfeld Press, 845 P.2d 1162, 1165. Quot. in ftn.

Section 548

E.D.Wis. 1992. U.S. v. Van Engel, 809 F. Supp. 1360, 1376. Cit. in appendix to op.

Section 598

Ill.App. 1992. Kedzie & 103rd Currency Exchange v. Hodge, 601 N.E.2d 803, 809-810. Com. (a) cit. in diss. op.

Section 601

C.A.10, 1993. Castleglen, Inc. v. Resolution Trust Corp., 984 F.2d 1571, 1583. Illus. 1 quot. in sup.

CONTRACTS 2d

Section 1

Ohio App. 1992. Schlupe v. Ohio Dept. of Adm. Serv., 605 N.E.2d 987, 987, 989. Quot. in sup., cit. generally in headnote.

Section 2

E.D.Pa. 1992. F. Schumacher v. Silver Wallpaper & Paint, 810 F. Supp. 627, 635. Subsec. (1) cit. in disc.

Ala. 1992. Joe Cooper & Assoc. v. Central Life, 614 So.2d 982, 989. Com. (e) cit. in sup.

Section 3

C.A.1, 1993. McCullough v. F.D.I.C., 987 F.2d 870, 873. Com. (a) quot. in ftn.

Section 4

C.A.3, 1992. Aetna Cas. & Sur. Co. v. Duncan, 972

source." (You may, of course, wish to check the citations to your rule from more than one series of a Restatement.)

In the Canoga case, Illustration 4-23 on page 109 shows the *Shepard's* entry for § 2 of the Restatement (Second) of Contracts. The citations that follow are the citing sources. Case citations come first. They are arranged by the court that made the decision. Note that no New Mexico case is listed under § 2. Note also the separate sub-listings of sources that have cited specific comments or illustrations.

In most cases, the only information provided about the citing source is the citation. There is no explanation of the facts or holding of a case or of how the Restatement segment is used in it. Thus, the digests in the Re-

Illustration 4-23 *Shepard's Restatement of the Law Citations.*

CONTRACTS, SECOND

Sec. 1 et seq.
Cir. 6
825F2d958
Cir. 7
611FS950
Cir. 10
660FS506
RRR
598FS1580
Idaho
109Ida256
706P2d1367
Mass
16MaA81
448NE1316
Wyo
834P2d1132
74Cor447
5A4513n

Secs. 1 to 255
R I
113RI482
322A2d636

Sec. 1
Cir. 1
750FS33
Cir. 3
48BRW677
102BRW438
Cir. 6
959F2d615
Cir. 8
661FS1419
Cir. 9
899F2d784
15BRW194
Ariz
142Az576
148Az12
691P2d667
712P2d925
Calif
147CA3d110
148CA3d321
48CC676
195CaR12
195CaR[illegible]
Colo
722P2d1023
Conn
202Ct339
20CtA683
23CtA250
521A2d145
570A2d220
580A2d535
Fla
573So2d27
Ill
88IlA970
114IlA186
411NE94
448NE1023
Nebr
217Neb814
351NW416
Ohio
61OS3d369
30OA3d268
78OA3d630
507NE1164
605NE989
Pa
364PaS123
527A2d558
Vt
144Vt207
475A2d1077
Wash
101Wsh2d549
682P2d876
70CaL214
67Cor742
67Cor793
76Cor208
81CR111
89CR1487
89CR1549
70MnL165
78VaL1070
1985WLR1406
1990WLR346
1992WLR1804

Comment b
67Cor742

Comment c
Ore
310Ore65
793P2d322

Comment e
78VaL1070

Comment f
Mass
17MaA121
456NE772
55LCP(3)93

Comment g
Cir. 2
95BRW874

Sec. 2
Cir. DC
747FS80
Cir. 2
602F2d53
129FRD41
Cir. 3
810FS635
Cir. 4
773FS821
Cir. 7
931F2d1224
Cir. 11
804FS1545
Calif
155CA3d506
202CaR618
Colo
731P2d712
Haw
68Haw603
724P2d117
Mass
397Mas148
19MaA357
474NE1134
489NE1261
Mich
500NW108
Nebr
237Neb882
468NW359
N Y
61NY112
460NE1081
472NYS2d596
N C
101NCA4
398SE891
N D
398NW122
417NW799
488NW413
Ohio
20OA3d118
72OA3d557
484NE1373
595NE507
Pa
364PaS123
45DC3d571
527A2d558
Wash
101Wsh2d549
102Wsh2d230
105Wsh2d774
111Wsh2d613
56WAp897
682P2d876
685P2d1088
762P2d1145
786P2d313
Wyo
820P2d993
70CaL306
75CaL2000
52ChL932
67Cor794
86CR276
97HLR690
1985WLR501
1990WLR346
94YLJ1040
101YLJ140

Comment a
Mich
500NW108

Comment b
Cir. 1
809F2d945
Cir. 4
900F2d741
Cir. 8
613FS523
Ariz
147Az235
709P2d592
Mass
31MaA612
581NE1314
Utah
777P2d509
Wis
102Wis2d186
306NW658
86CR273
94YLJ1040

Comment c
97HLR692

Comment d
Cir. 2
602F2d53
97HLR692

Comment e
Cir. 2
95BRW874
Cir. 9
966F2d447

Comment f
Cir. 6
959F2d616

Sec. 3
Cir. DC
735F2d1427
745F2d1493
Cir. 1
39BRW60
Cir. 2
579FS1430
Cir. 5
5BRW33
Ariz
134Az563
658P2d216
Calif
147CA3d110
48CC676
195CaR12
Ill
96Il2d526
451NE861
Kan
232Kan699
659P2d831
N H
130NH741
547A2d268
Ohio
30OA3d268
507NE1164
Vt
144Vt209
475A2d1077
Wash
842P2d477
70CaL297
67Cor743
67Cor793
90McL445
70MnL197
1992WLR289

Comment a
484US91
98LE346
108SC401
56USLW4027
Cir. 1
987F2d873
Cir. 2
927F2d687
Cir. 10
697FS1163
Conn
202Ct338
521A2d145

Comment c
Cir. DC
735F2d1427
67Cor742
78VaL1070

Comment e
Cir. 2
95BRW874

Sec. 4
Cir. DC
641FS376
Cir. 1
581FS972
Cir. 2
530FS1133
Cir. 3
743F2d1025
972F2d526
Cir. 7
681FS526
724FS609
Cir. 9
649FS159
Ariz
142Az576
145Az114
148Az13
691P2d667
700P2d501
712P2d926
Calif
47C3d678
254CaR223
765P2d385
D C
608A2d127
Iowa
461NW855
N Y
90NYAD966
456NYS2d557
Ohio
15OA3d8
20OA3d118
484NE1373
Utah
818P2d1004
W Va
173WV427
317SE512
70CaL306
67Cor793
70MnL191

Comment a
Cir. 7
741F2d1515
Cir. 9
723FS426
Calif
47C3d678
254CaR223
765P2d385
Conn
202Ct337
215Ct349
521A2d144
576A2d157
Md
575A2d748
Mass
19MaA141
472NE1351
Nev
107Nev231
808P2d921
N J
111NJ77
543A2d39
Pa
137PaC528
586A2d1024
Utah
818P2d1004
67TxL126
94YLJ1015

Illustration 1
65TxL700

Comment b
Cir. 8
667F2d672
ClCt
17ClC798
Calif
214CA3d1584
263CaR408
Ill
110IlA642
443NE605
Ind
452NE1004
Iowa
314NW397

statements may be more efficient for finding pertinent cases than using *Shepard's* because they reduce the need to read every case cited. However, the digests are not nearly as current as the citations in *Shepard's,* and the digests do not cover the range of secondary sources included in *Shepard's.*

Finally, the last volume of the *ALR Index* has a table listing annotations that refer to various Restatement sections.

In the Canoga case, the Restatement appendix volumes, their supplements, and the *Interim Case Citations* provide a wealth of case citations, some of which seem pertinent. Your next step would be to read the cases. Likewise, *Shepard's* yielded a large collection of case citations but sorting them was difficult. You definitely would skim the cases from New Mexico, the jurisdiction of the Canoga case, if there were any. You also could select cases cited under the Restatement comments of most interest to you.

4. What Else?

Special Features of the Restatements. Some Restatements have these special features:

(1) tables of cases and statutes cited, from which you may be able to find a pertinent Restatement section by the name of a leading case or by the citation to a statute;
(2) citations to A.L.R. annotations that pertain to the topic of a particular Restatement section; and
(3) West topics and key numbers (see Chapter 6) that pertain to the topic of a particular Restatement section.

See Illustration 4-24 on page 112 for the latter two features, and see Exhibit 4.3 on pages 100-101 for a list of which Restatements have these features.

Work in Progress. Drafts of new Restatements are not listed in Exhibit 4.2. You can learn about work in progress on Restatements in the ALI's current *Annual Report,* the ALI's annual *Proceedings,* or in *The ALI Reporter,* the Institute's quarterly newsletter.

Restatement in the Courts. The 1944 Permanent Edition of *Restatement in the Courts* and its hardbound supplements list and summarize all cases citing all Restatements from 1932 to 1975. You need not use this set, though, because the digests in it have been incorporated into subsequently published appendix volumes or pocket parts.

Other Media. Although as a beginning researcher you are most likely to use the Restatements in paper form, they are available in these media as of early 1996:

			Computer-Assisted Research		
	Paper	*CD-ROM*	*LEXIS*	*WESTLAW*	*Microform*
Agency 1st	√				√
Agency 2d	√	√	√	√	√
Conflict of Laws 1st	√				√
Conflict of Laws 2d	√	√	√	√	√
Contracts 1st	√				√
Contracts 2d	√	√	√	√	√
Foreign Relations 2d	√				√
Foreign Relations 3d	√	√	√	√	√
Judgments 1st	√				√
Judgments 2d	√	√	√	√	√
Property 1st	√	√	√	√	√
Property 2d (Landlord and Tenant)	√	√	√	√	
Property 2d (Donative Transfers)	√	√	√	√	
Restitution 1st	√	√	√	√	√
Security 1st	√	√	√	√	√
Torts 1st	√				√
Torts 2d	√	√	√	√	
Trusts 1st	√				√
Trusts 2d	√	√	√	√	
Trusts 3d (Prudent Investor Rule)	√	√	√	√	
Unfair Competition 3d	√		√	√	

In addition, the A.L.I. Microfiche Publications set contains, among other documents, the drafts of many Restatements.

5. How Do You Cite Restatements?

Here are some examples of how to cite the Restatement section in Illustration 4-20 on pages 101-104. The year used is the year in which the Restatement was adopted or last amended.

Restatement (Second) of Contracts § 2 (1979).
Restatement (Second) of Contracts § 2 cmt. a (1979).

Illustration 4-24 Appendix, Restatement (Second) of Contracts.

to the dissent's view, it was the plaintiff contractor's duty to procure the permit, and, therefore, it was the plaintiff contractor who breached the contract. It is also possible to take the view, the dissent stated, that the non-existence of a proscription against front yard swimming pools was a condition precedent to the formation of a binding contract. The failure of this condition would have the effect of discharging the duties of performance of the parties. Contractor Industries v. Zerr, 241 Pa.Super. 92, 359 A.2d 803, 809.

Cross References to

1. **Digest System Key Numbers**

Contracts ⇐15, 187

§ 3. Agreement Defined; Bargain Defined

Or. 1977. Cit. in disc. in ftn. Section 3 of Tentative Drafts 1 through 7, Revised and Edited, which is now Section 3 of the Official Draft. Plaintiff-contractor brought suit, alleging an oral agreement that a business owned by the defendants would provide plaintiff with helicopter services for a construction job which plaintiff contracted to perform for the United States Forest Service. The trial court entered judgment awarding plaintiff damages. The Supreme Court affirmed, holding that it was not error to permit plaintiff's vice president to testify to his own sense of the state of negotiations where the jury was instructed that its conclusions depended upon an "objective test," and thus was not misled into treating his testimony as something more than evidence bearing on the behavior and perceptions of the parties to the negotiations. Kabil Developments Corp. v. Mignot, 279 Or. 151, 566 P.2d 505, 507.

Pa. 1973. Quot. in sup. Section 3 of Tentative Draft 1, which is now Section 3 of the Official Draft. The plaintiffs, former employees of defendant law firm, brought action against the firm to obtain files of clients who had personally retained plaintiffs, and for distribution of the assets of the firm under an alleged partnership agreement. On plaintiffs' appeal from a judgment for defendants, the court affirmed, and held that evidence of the use of a corporate form rather than a partnership supported conclusion of no partnership, no agreement whereby plaintiffs acquired a proprietary interest, nor conduct from which such agreement could be implied, and no misrepresentation by the attorney of the firm from which plaintiffs could claim detrimental reliance. Murphy v. Burke, 454 Pa. 391, 311 A.2d 904, 907.

Cross References to

1. **Digest System Key Numbers**

Contracts ⇐15, 25

2. **A.L.R. Annotation**

What constitutes a contract for sale under uniform commercial code § 2–314. 78 A.L.R.3d 696.

§ 4. How a Promise May Be Made

U.S.Ct.Cl. 1966. Cit. in sup. Section 5 of Tentative Draft 1, which is now Section 4 of the Official Draft. After performing certain land appraisal services for the United States Attorney, the plaintiff submitted a bid for additional work, which bid was approved by the Department but about which the U.S. Attorney said nothing to the plaintiff. The plaintiff proceeded to perform his services without explicit approval of the Attorney, although several of the latter's assistants communicated with the plaintiff as to the progress of his work. In an action to recover payment for the plaintiff's services, the court

See also cases under chapter and topic which include section under examination. See Vol. 3, p. 253 for Conversion Table showing the numbers of these sections in tentative draft.

Restatement (Second) of Contracts § 2 cmt. d, illus. 1 (1979).
Restatement (Second) of Contracts § 2 (Tent. Draft No. 1, 1964).

For additional detail, see Rule 12.8.5 of *The Bluebook.*

G. Other Secondary Sources

In addition to the major secondary sources described above, three other secondary sources merit mention: continuing legal education materials, pattern jury instructions, and casebooks.

CLE Materials. Many states require lawyers to take courses to continuously improve their skills. Presenters at continuing legal education (CLE) programs prepare written materials containing outlines, important cases and statutes, checklists, and sample documents. CLE materials can be useful for several reasons: they address practical aspects of a topic, they typically provide significant detail about a specific jurisdiction's law, and they may provide the first discussion of new developments.

You can locate CLE materials through the catalog, using a subject or key word search. (Note that an author search must use the name of the CLE organization and likely will yield many sources.) Or you may browse the shelves; CLE materials may be shelved in a separate section of your library. A CLE volume typically is organized by presentation; it may contain one or more tables of contents, but is unlikely to have an index. A CLE volume is not itself updated (although some programs are offered annually, so that more recent materials "update" the materials from previous programs). CLE materials are cited according to Rule 15 of *The Bluebook.*

Pattern Jury Instructions. At the end of a jury trial, the jury is instructed on the law applicable to the case. Often the instructions are drawn from a set of pattern jury instructions or jury instruction guide (JIG). JIGs typically are written by private authors (professors or lawyers), a group of judges, a bar association committee, or combination. An instruction states the rule in a form paralleling a Restatement section and typically is supplemented by notes stating the source of the instruction and discussing the pertinent cases and statutes. Thus JIGs can be useful not only when you are seeking sample instructions in a trial setting, but also in nonlitigation settings.

As with CLE materials, you can locate JIGs through a catalog or shelf-browsing. Most JIGs are accessible through tables of contents; indexes; and tables of cases, statutes, and rules. Many JIGs are updated with pocket parts or other supplements. JIGs are cited according to Rule 15 of *The Bluebook.*

Casebooks. Casebooks are law textbooks containing cases and supplementary materials, such as statutes, regulations, excerpts from articles and treatises, notes by the author, and problems. While a casebook may provide useful starting references, it is not designed as a reference tool.

Media. CLE materials and JIGs appeared in the following media as of early 1996:

	Paper	*CD-ROM*	*Computer-Assisted Research*		*Microform*
			LEXIS	*WESTLAW*	
CLE materials	√			√	
Pattern jury instructions	√	√			

H. Research Strategy for Secondary Sources

1. Setting Goals for Your Use of Secondary Sources

In Chapter 2, you started with the eight categories of factual and legal analysis, and your goal was to generate a research vocabulary by brainstorming initial terms, then finding related terms and legal definitions. Then you moved into secondary sources to obtain

(1) introductory commentary on primary authority, including a synthesized analytical framework of particular areas of law; and
(2) references to primary authority.

This final part of Chapter 4 compares and contrasts the various secondary sources discussed in this chapter.

2. Choosing Secondary Sources Suited to Your Research Project

All of the secondary sources covered in this chapter serve dual functions as both commentary sources and finding tools for secondary and primary sources. Hence, you do not need to use every source on every research project. But how do you know when to use which source? Your answer should pivot on which secondary source or combination of sources will make your research comprehensive, correct, and credible and yet avoid excessive effort that would undermine the cost-effectiveness of your research.

Before you choose among the secondary sources you have studied in this chapter, you need to assess the characteristics, strengths, and weaknesses of each secondary source. Fill in the chart on pages 116 and 117 to see more clearly the differences among these sources. Although the characteristics are grouped under the four research goals (cost-effectiveness, comprehensiveness, etc.), many of the characteristics have an impact on more than one research goal; for instance, accuracy and lack of bias relate to both correctness and credibility of research. While filling in the chart, you may notice some patterns as to the characteristics of these sources. Here are but a few:

A wider scope of coverage usually comes at the expense of detailed coverage. Encyclopedias try to cover the full range of legal topics in general terms, while A.L.R. annotations and legal periodical articles seek to give detailed coverage of the "hot spots" in law practice and legal scholarship. Treatises and Restatements usually fall somewhere in between these ends of the continuum.

The generality of an encyclopedia can be helpful at the outset of a research project when you need "big picture" information, but that generality is frustrating later on when you need more specificity. Conversely, the narrowness of an A.L.R. annotation or a legal periodical article may not be helpful at the outset of a research project; however, it may be of great assistance if your research has advanced to the stage where you are seeking the answer to a narrow, well defined question.

The collection of articles in legal periodicals and A.L.R. annotations do not present a comprehensive overview of the law, nor are the articles arranged in a logical order. However, they excel in devoting attention to current controversies. They both are published periodically rather than as a set, so they are better able to respond quickly to the changing profile of the law than are encyclopedias and other sources published as a complete set. Thus, legal periodicals and A.L.R. annotations often are the best sources on highly current topics. If you cannot find up-to-date coverage in a legal periodical, your research might be more cost-effective in an updated source. A.L.R. annotations, encyclopedias, and many treatises are updated annually with supplements, while legal periodicals are not.

Publications written by staff members are able to cover many legal topics. The publishers of encyclopedias and A.L.R. annotations can assign a particular topic to a staff member and be assured of coverage, while publishers of treatises and legal periodicals must look (or hope) for someone willing to write the needed book or article. However, the authors of treatises and legal periodicals (other than students) may have credentials that give them recognized expertise in their field of authorship.

Once you have filled in the chart, your first step in choosing among secondary sources is to evaluate what kind of research is demanded by a particular client's situation. Once you have made this evaluation, you can use your filled-in chart to choose which source or sources will best meet the needs of your client's situation. Some secondary sources serve admirably in some research settings but are not particularly useful in others.

Your second step is to decide on the order in which to use the chosen sources, so that you obtain the information in an order that is useful to you.

	Cost-Effectiveness			*Correctness*		
	Type of Organization (alphabetical, topical, serial)	*Range of Access Methods (index, table of contents, etc.)*	*Connections to Other Research Tools* (Shepard's, *etc.)*	*Accuracy, Lack of Bias*	*Attention to Current Topics*	*Updating Means & Frequency*
Encyclopedias						
Periodicals						
A.L.R. annotations						
Treatises						
Restatements						

For instance, if you are researching an unfamiliar topic, you probably will prefer to use general sources (for example, encyclopedias) before specific sources (for example, legal periodicals). If you are using a source that provides cites to other sources, you will want to use the citing source before the other sources. If the client's situation presents multiple issues that are dependent on each other, you first should research the issue upon which the other issues depend. Other factors also may influence the order in which you use the secondary sources.

By the time you have completed this text, you should begin to develop some preferences as to the more important factors differentiating secondary sources. The polishing of a research strategy, however, requires experience and encounters with a wide range of fact situations and research settings.

3. Setting Priorities and Selecting Leads within a Secondary Source

When you use an index or table of contents within a secondary source to find pertinent material, you may generate so many leads that you cannot (or should not) track down all of them. If you plow through a list of possible leads in no particular order, you may find yourself reading overlapping commentary as well as some not-so-useful commentary; this is not cost-effective research.

	Comprehensiveness				*Credibility*			
	Breadth of Topics Covered	*Depth of Coverage of Each Topic*	*Attention to Rules, Facts, & Principles*	*Description Only, or Critique Too*	*Reputation of Publisher(s) or Book*	*Reputation of Author(s)*	*Clarity, Persuasiveness*	*Other Strengths & Weaknesses*
Encyclopedias								
Periodicals								
A.L.R. annotations								
Treatises								
Restatements								

Rather than skimming all of these leads to determine their value, you first should rank them by how much promise they show. Give high priority to the leads with the Chapter 2 brainstorming terms in their titles and subject descriptions. If a particular lead appeared in more than one place, pursue that lead first. Pursue leads that are narrowly focused on your research topic before you pursue leads with a broader focus.

4. Assembling a Sample Research Strategy for the Canoga Case

To some extent, Ms. Canoga's case seems to pivot on a hot new argument: the employment rights of smokers. This topic is unlikely to be discussed yet in sources such as encyclopedias and treatises, but may be discussed in periodicals and A.L.R. annotations. Periodicals may be especially useful as a source of policy arguments in the event the law is still being formed or is currently adverse to Ms. Canoga's case. CLE materials may be worth a quick look for tips on theories evolving among practitioners.

Viewed more broadly, Ms. Canoga's case raises the issue of when an employer can terminate an employee. This aspect of employment law has been evolving rapidly during the past decade or so, somewhat unevenly from state to state. Thus, it is important to know about general trends and to obtain current information. An encyclopedia may provide general background, updated to within the last year. Even better would be a treatise on termination of employment, especially if it were updated or very recently published.

Although there is no Restatement on the law of employment relations, Ms. Canoga's case does seem to raise issues grounded in contract (the handbook) and tort (protection of her private life), both of which are covered by Restatements. Hence, it may be useful to consult those Restatements for general principles if the narrower and current sources described above are not sufficient.

5. When to Cite Secondary Sources

As you research, keep in mind which sources you eventually will be able to cite in the final written product embodying your research. All other sources are useful only because they lead to or explain citable sources.

Recall that primary authority has the force and effect of law. All other research sources are secondary sources, which in turn can be divided into commentary and finding tools. Keep in mind that none of these secondary sources are written under governmental authority.

You should cite primary authority—cases, statutes, rules of court, regulations—whenever possible. Moreover, you should never rely on secondary sources without investigating and reading the related primary authority. Reading the full text of primary authority gives you the full flavor of the law. It also allows you to detect ambiguities, misinterpretations, and perhaps even mistakes made by the commentator.

A secondary source may be cited if primary authority does not support the proposition. Secondary sources can be cited for some propositions that do not require primary authority citation, such as a statement on the number of jurisdictions adopting a certain rule of law. It also could be cited for its criticism or policy analysis of an established rule of law.

Never cite finding tools, such as *Shepard's, A.L.R. Digests,* library catalogs, and periodical indexes.

5 Formulate Issues

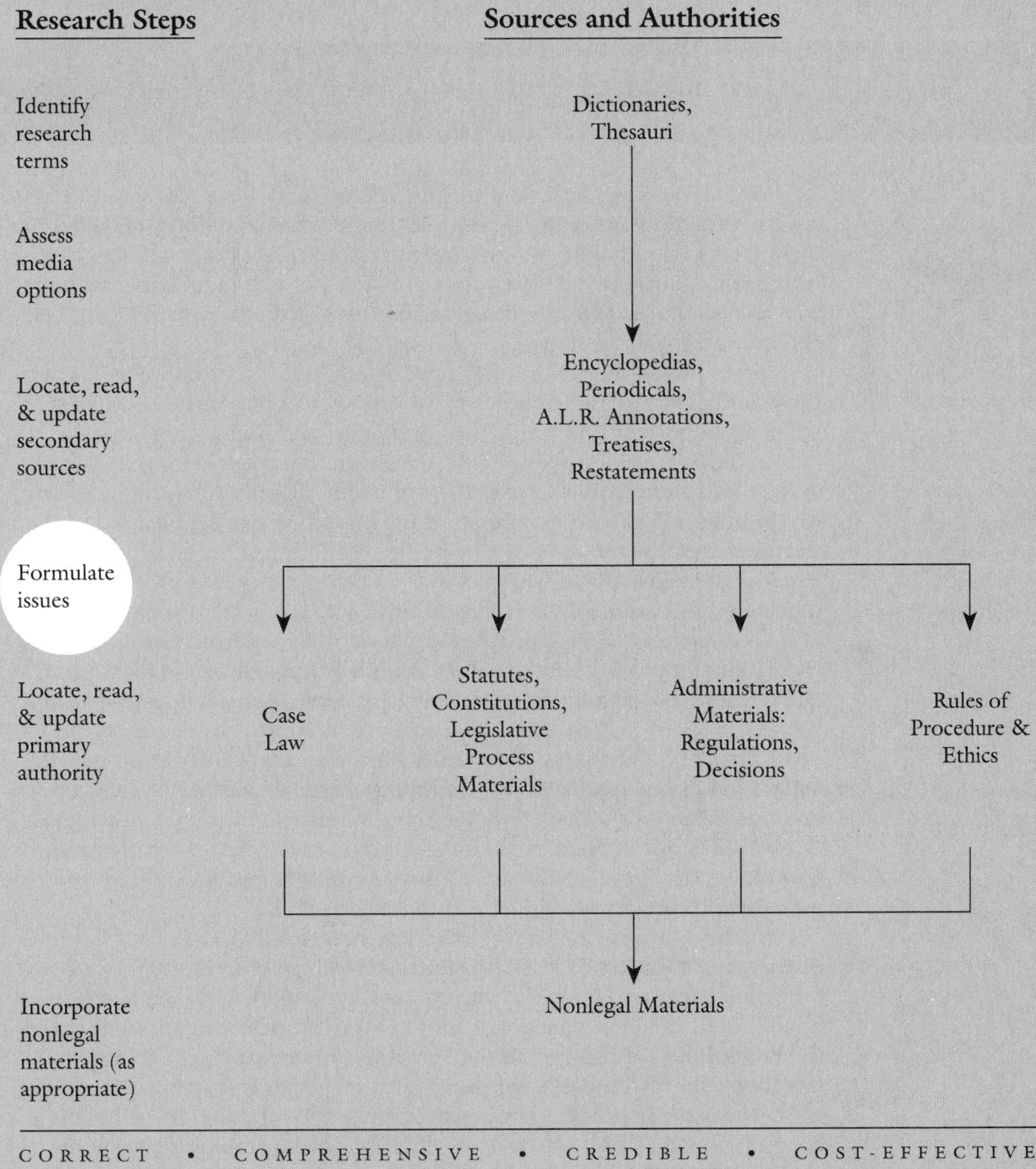

CORRECT • COMPREHENSIVE • CREDIBLE • COST-EFFECTIVE

Summary of Contents

A. Synthesizing the Results of Your Research in Secondary Sources
B. Formulating Issues
C. Turning to Research in Primary Authority
D. Calling It Quits

A. Synthesizing the Results of Your Research in Secondary Sources

As discussed in Chapter 4, your research in secondary sources should yield a wealth of information: legal principles, rules, and definitions; examples of these; perhaps critique of the current law; and references to potentially pertinent primary authority. Before you begin your research in primary authority, you first should synthesize this material into a cohesive framework. This process entails several steps.

First, discern the major legal topics appearing in your notes, and group the materials according to those topics (rather than by source). Legal topics are more important than the source of your information.

In the Canoga case, for example, the illustration material from encyclopedias, A.L.R. annotations, and the Restatement all pertain to contract; they would be grouped together. Some of the material from periodicals and the treatise material pertain to a federal statute prohibiting discrimination on the basis of disability, potentially nicotine addiction; they would be grouped together. The periodical also refers to privacy rights, a third topic.

Second, weave together the information obtained from various sources on the same topic by discerning how the major principle (or perhaps principles), rules, and definitions relate to each other. In general, principles are broader than rules, and rules incorporate definitions. Rules may relate to each other in various ways. Some rules form an analytical chain, so that the application of one (such as a rule on liability) leads to another (such as a rule on measurement of damages). Some rules are distinct from each other (such as two rules on different bases for liability). In presenting the framework you draw from your secondary research, consider two possible forms of presentation: the classic outline and the flowchart.

In the Canoga case, from what you have learned thus far, wrongful discharge is a cause of action available to at-will employees who have been terminated wrongly. "At-will employment" means that the employee was hired for an indefinite period of time. One type of wrongful discharge is the employer's violation of an implied employment contract. An employee handbook specifying discharge procedures or grounds may be such a contract—unless it specifically negates the employer's intention to be bound in contract. Another type of wrongful discharge is the employer's violation of nondiscrimination statutes. In particular, the Americans with Disabilities Act (ADA) protects disabled employees. To come within the ADA, the employer must have fifteen or more employees, and the employee must have an impairment substantially limiting a major life activity. That same statute seems to indicate that restrictions on smoking at the workplace are permissible. Finally, a ban on off-duty smoking may violate the right to privacy guaranteed by state law. This material appears in a flowchart in Exhibit 5.1 below.

Third, sort your references to primary authority according to your framework. You may wish to list only a few sources to start with; select the mandatory primary authority for your jurisdiction and the authorities appearing prominently in the secondary sources. The outline in Exhibit 5.2 on page 122 lists several major authorities drawn from the secondary sources illustrated in Chapter 4.

Note that the framework you develop from secondary sources must be tentative, precisely because it is based only on secondary authority. You still must locate and read primary authority. During that process the framework will evolve. As noted in Chapter 1, research is not strictly linear; you often will loop back to revise this framework.

Exhibit 5.1 Flowchart Synthesizing Secondary Source Research.

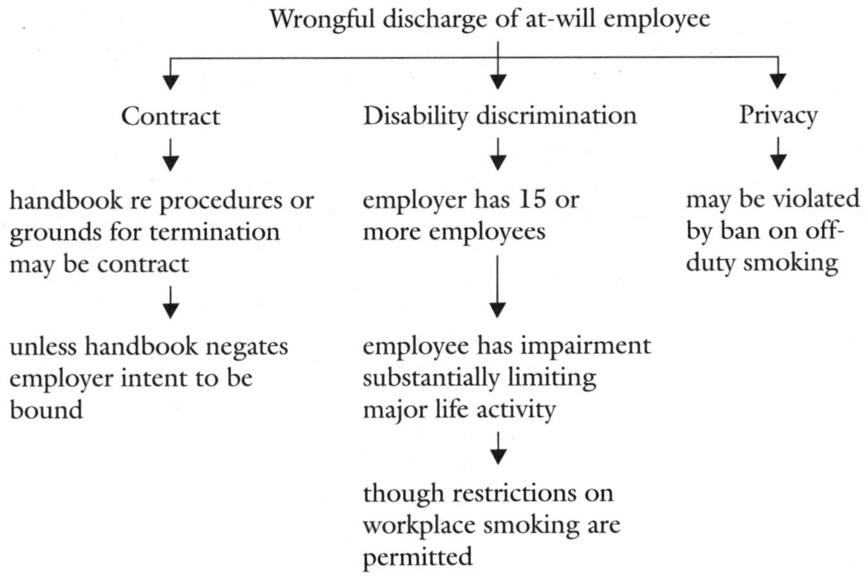

Exhibit 5.2 Outline Showing Law and Facts.

Wrongful discharge of at-will employee ("at will" means hired for indefinite period of time)

Law	Facts
I. Contract	
A. Employee handbook re procedures or grounds for termination may be contract	Handbook says disagreements go to board; board will try to listen and facilitate solution
B. Not so where handbook negates employer intention to be bound	No such language
Sources: *Lukoski*, 748 P.2d 507; *Kestenbaum*, 766 P.2d 280; *Jelso*, 637 P.2d 847	
II. Disability discrimination	
A. Employer has fifteen or more employees	Small orchestra (?)
B. Employee has impairment substantially limiting a major life activity	Nicotine addiction
C. Restrictions on workplace smoking are permissible	Sept. 94 ban goes to on-duty—Dec. 94 pledge goes to on- and off-duty smoking
Source: ADA, 42 U.S.C. § 12101 etc.	
III. Right to privacy	
May be violated by ban on off-duty smoking	Sept. 94 ban goes to on-duty—Dec. 94 pledge goes to on- and off-duty smoking program
Source: Check state law	

Note: The references to legal authorities in this exhibit are not in proper *Bluebook* form.

B. Formulating Issues

Once you have developed a tentative legal framework, you should formulate issues to pursue in primary authority. A legal issue is a question that connects the law to the facts of your client's situation. Developing legal issues is the core of the analytical process of legal research. Put simply, if you ask the right question, you probably will locate pertinent law; if you ask the wrong question, your research likely will falter.

To develop your legal issue, look carefully at the legal principles, rules, and definitions suggested by the secondary authority you read. This legal material will speak in more or less general terms about factual situations covered by the law. Your task is to identify the corresponding specific facts from your client's situation. As you work through this process, you may discover factual matters that the law focuses on that you had not emphasized in your initial consideration of your client's situation. You then will need to review the information you currently have or develop additional sources of information. If you cannot fill in the gap, you may need to make the most sensible assumption under the circumstances and proceed. Exhibit 5.2 above shows you how to integrate facts with the law in parallel outline form.

For some topics, a single issue will suffice, at least until you gain a greater understanding of the structure of the law within that topic and its relationship to your client's situation. For other topics, you may need to formulate more than one issue (because more than one rule applies to the client's situation) or sub-issue (because the applicable rule has multiple parts, known as elements, and more than one part is in doubt in your client's situation). Sub-issues help you to segment and focus your research.

In the Canoga case, your information about the contract and privacy topics is quite general (a basic rule as to contracts and a principle as to privacy). Using this process, you might draft fairly simple research issues as follows:

> Did the orchestra breach a contract with Ms. Canoga when its employee handbook stated that the board would listen to both sides of unresolved disputes, yet the board did not do so after Ms. Canoga was terminated? [This issue does not refer to the handbook's negation of the employer's intent to be bound, because the facts do not indicate that such language exists.]
>
> Did the orchestra violate the privacy rights of Ms. Canoga, a flutist, when it prohibited her from smoking off-duty?

Your information about the topic of disability discrimination is more detailed, including rules and definitions. You might develop an issue with sub-issues for the ADA topic:

> Did the orchestra illegally discriminate against Ms. Canoga, a smoker, on the grounds of disability protected by the ADA when it forbade her from smoking on- and off-duty?
>
> a. Is the orchestra covered by the ADA in light of the fifteen-employee threshold? [This issue requires further factual development. The most sensible working assumption is that the orchestra does have fifteen or more employees.]
> b. Is Ms. Canoga's condition as a smoker an impairment that substantially limits major life activities so as to be a protected disability?
> c. How does the ADA's provision on workplace smoking rules relate to the orchestra's on- and off-duty smoking bans?

C. Turning to Research in Primary Authority

As noted several times in this text, your ultimate goal is to locate mandatory primary authority on your topic. As you turn to that specific task, think carefully about what you have learned from your secondary source research about the nature of authority on your issues. Of course, you will want to verify this information through your own research in primary authority. You should ask yourself two fundamental questions.

First, do the secondary sources discuss cases, statutes or constitutions, administrative materials, or court rules? The research sources differ for these categories of primary authority. Many issues are governed by combinations of these types of primary authority. For example, once a legislature creates a statute, the courts interpret it in case law. As another example, agencies are created by statute, so that statutes and administrative regulations are linked.

Second, do the secondary sources suggest that the issue is a federal or state issue or both? Federal law appears in sources dedicated to federal law, while the laws of the fifty states appear in sources dedicated to the law of one or more states.

In the Canoga case, the secondary source research illustrated in Chapter 4 suggests that the contract issue is governed by state case law, here New Mexico; that a federal statute governs disability discrimination; and that state law on privacy may protect smokers.

D. Calling It Quits

Research in primary authority can be time-consuming, and it may seem that the law to be discovered is endless. Unfortunately, there is no clearly defined point at which you can be certain that your research is complete. Deciding when to stop researching is a matter of judgment based on several considerations. Research projects vary in the amount of authority to be located, the ease or difficulty of locating it, and the thoroughness needed to provide competent representation. On the latter point, you would need to research less extensively when your task is to counsel a client seeking preliminary advice on a possible transaction than when your task is to argue a case before a supreme court. Although cost-effectiveness is relative to the project, a few guidelines apply to most situations.

First, do not stop until you have updated every authority that you intend to use in analyzing your client's situation. Legal research is not correct unless you know the law current with your client's situation.

Second, do not keep searching simply because you have not yet located the legal authority that resolves your situation without ambiguity, tempting though it may be. Rarely is a solution to a legal situation free from ambiguity, given the vagaries of human behavior. A case identical to your client's is unlikely to have arisen before; the legislature or agency is unlikely to have anticipated exactly your client's situation in drafting a statute or regulation. Stated another way, do apply the law of diminishing returns. When your research is not yielding new rules or authorities, you most likely have accomplished comprehensive research. Your goal is comprehensive, not excessive, research.

Third, research only as truly necessary in persuasive primary authority. Exhaust the research possibilities in mandatory primary authority first; then discern where there may be gaps. Pursue only those gaps in persuasive primary authority. For example, research in persuasive primary authority is appropriate when your jurisdiction has addressed the basic legal rule involved in your case, but not a similar set of facts. It also is appropriate when your case involves a statute that has yet to be interpreted in your jurisdiction, yet other jurisdictions have interpreted similar statutes. It also is appropriate when your jurisdiction has yet to address your client's issue at all or when you seek a change in your jurisdiction's law. Your research will be more credible if you focus on mandatory primary authority and temper your reliance on persuasive primary authority.

Fourth, resolve any inconsistencies you have uncovered in your research to assure correctness. For example, if two secondary sources describe the effect of a statute in different terms, check them against the statute to determine the actual wording and effect.

Fifth, put your research to the tests of analysis and writing. Then check your analysis against that presented in the most credible and pertinent commentary you have read. Most of the time, weaknesses in your research will become apparent when you put pen to paper or hands to the keyboard to draft your own analysis of your client's situation.

6 LOCATE, READ, AND UPDATE PRIMARY AUTHORITY: CASE LAW

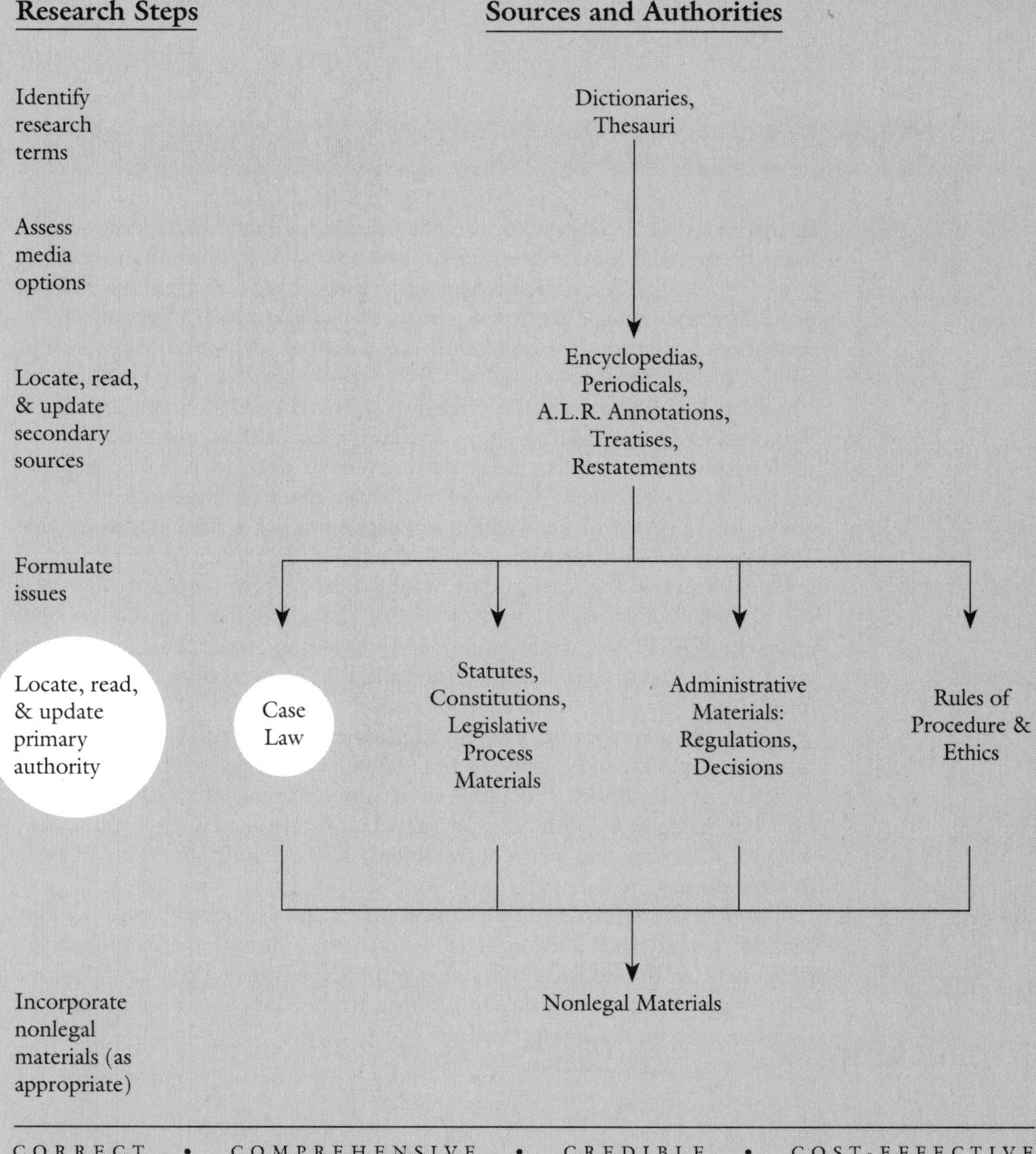

CORRECT • COMPREHENSIVE • CREDIBLE • COST-EFFECTIVE

Summary of Contents

A. Preliminary Points

In the American legal system, the law emanates from many sources at the federal, state, and local levels: decisions of courts; constitutions and statutes passed by legislatures; regulations and decisions issued by agencies; rules of procedure and practice created by courts and legislatures. This chapter is the first of four discussing research into the law itself, or primary authority; it focuses on the decisions of courts.

Parts B and C explain the centrality of case law research and the critical judgments lawyers make as they seek and select useful cases. Part D first shows you how to use the three-part system of case law research in paper sources: (1) case reporters, which contain the cases; (2) digests, which help you to locate pertinent cases within reporters; and (3) citators, which provide information about the authoritativeness of cases and lead you to additional cases. As you will see, case law research proceeds from digests to reporters to citators. Part D also illustrates one of the online alternatives to paper research: WESTLAW, a computer-assisted research service, which permits you to locate and update cases electronically. Part E covers some miscellaneous details, and Part F covers citation of cases.

This chapter continues to illustrate the research of the Canoga case (stated at pages 2-3 in Chapter 1). One of the issues suggested by the research in secondary authority presented in Chapter 4 is whether the orchestra breached its contract with Ms. Canoga when it terminated her employment without following the procedures stated in the handbook. This chapter focuses on that issue.

A note about terminology: The term "case" has several meanings for lawyers: a matter handled on behalf of a client, a dispute that is litigated in the courts, or the decision of a court resolving a litigated dispute. We have used "case" in the first sense in referring to the Canoga case. This chapter uses the term in all three senses.

B. WHAT IS A CASE?

Courts decide cases for two essential purposes. First, the decision provides a peaceful and principled resolution to a dispute the parties were unable to resolve otherwise. Second, as explained in more detail in Part C, the decision provides an example, or precedent, for participants in future similar situations; these participants use the case as a guideline in conducting their affairs or resolving their own disputes. Both purposes are served by the court's written explanation of the dispute before it, the outcome, and the reasoning behind the outcome.

1. How Does a Case Come to Be Decided?

Courts are reactive institutions. They resolve disputes brought to them by litigants; they do not seek out disputes or render legal opinions on issues unconnected to actual disputes. Furthermore, the lawyers for the litigants frame the issues for the court to address, bring the facts to the court's attention, and develop the arguments on both sides.

A dispute enters litigation when one side, the plaintiff, sues the other, the defendant; some cases involve more than two parties. The case is handled initially by a trial court, typically called a "district court." This court provides the forum for presentation of the facts to a jury or judge, determination of the facts in dispute, and application of the law to the facts, resulting in an initial resolution of the dispute. This process may take place through a trial, at which witnesses testify orally and documents and items are reviewed. Or it may take place through motion practice, in which the judge decides the case before trial. The basis of a motion varies from case to case. For example, the judge may dismiss the case very early on, with little development of the facts, if the plaintiff has sued on a theory without adequate legal support. Or it may be resolved by motion after extensive discovery (factual exploration conducted by the lawyers) when the judge decides that the facts are not essentially disputed and one side is entitled to win.

If the side losing in the trial court wishes to pursue the case, it may appeal. The side bringing the appeal is the appellant or petitioner, while the side defending against the appeal is the appellee or respondent. Appellate proceedings differ from trial court proceedings. The appellate court relies on the written transcript of the trial court proceedings and the written and oral arguments of the lawyers. Cases are decided by panels of three or more judges. The panel may be drawn from the court's membership, or the case may be heard by the entire court en banc.

There may be one or two tiers of appellate courts. In the typical two-tier structure, the judges of the intermediate court, typically called the "court of appeals," review the trial court's handling of the case for reversible errors. The justices of the highest court, typically titled the "supreme court," conduct a secondary review, but focus primarily on the development of legal doctrine.

Appeal to the intermediate court is as of right, while the supreme court generally affords discretionary review. In a simpler one-tier structure, the sole appeals court handles both appellate functions and reviews all appeals.

2. How Are Court Systems Structured?

The federal court system is a complex two-tier court system. The federal trial courts are called United States District Courts; each state has one to four district courts, each covering part or all of the state. The intermediate appellate courts are called United States Courts of Appeals; there are eleven numbered circuits, each covering several states, and the District of Columbia Circuit. See Illustration 6-1 below. The United States Supreme Court hears cases on discretionary review from the courts of appeals. Furthermore, specialized trial and appeals courts exist in such areas as bankruptcy and international trade.

The New Mexico state court system is somewhat simpler. The trial courts are called district courts. The single intermediate court is called the New

Illustration 6-1

Map of Federal Circuits, *1995 Judicial Staff Directory* 501 (Ann L. Brownson ed., 9th ed. 1994).

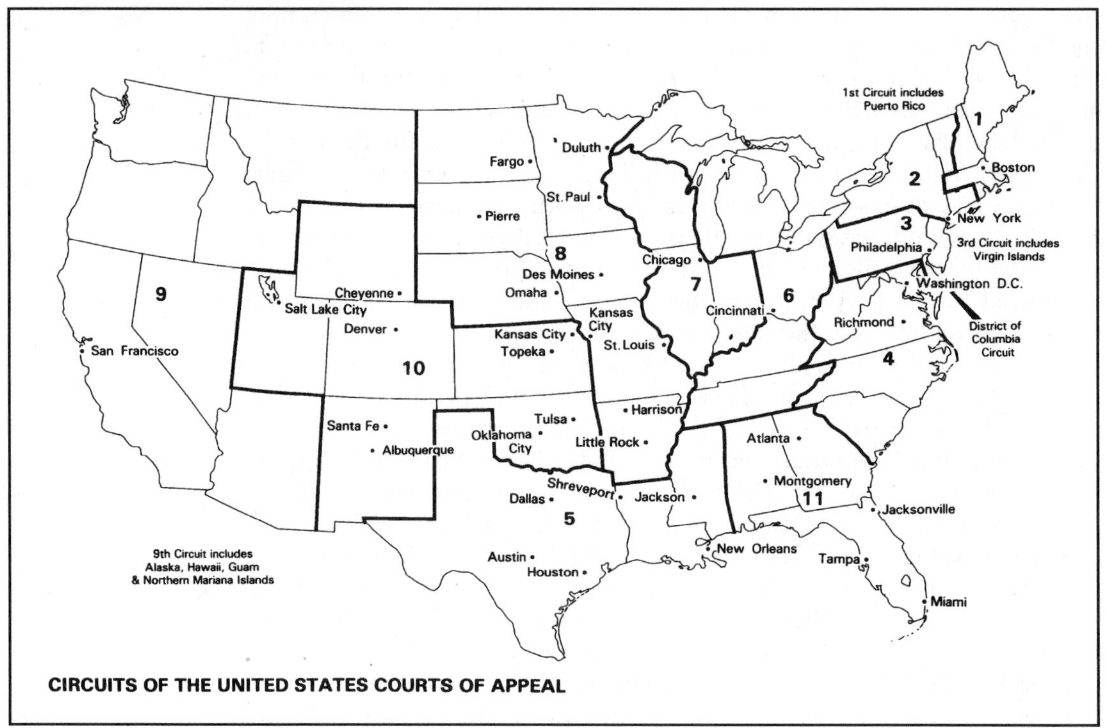

Mexico Court of Appeals, and it handles appeals from all district courts. The highest court is the New Mexico Supreme Court. New Mexico's system is typical for state courts.

Table 1.1 of *The Bluebook: A Uniform System of Citation* (15th ed. 1991) (*The Bluebook*) identifies the courts for all American jurisdictions.

3. What Does a Published Case Look Like?

Most published case decisions follow a fairly standard framework, depicted in the margins of Illustration 6-2 on pages 132-135, which shows the case of *Lukoski v. Sandia Indian Management Co.* The opening block includes the names of the parties and their positions in the litigation (item 2), the court deciding the case (item 4), the case's docket number (item 3), and the date of decision (item 5). The opening block also may contain a parallel citation (item 1); parallel citations are discussed in parts D and F.

Following the opening block are several brief paragraphs describing the main points in the case. There may be a synopsis, or brief summary, written by the court itself or the court's staff. The remaining material is written by the publisher's editorial staff. The publisher's editorial matter typically begins with a one-paragraph overview of the facts and outcome, also called a "synopsis" (item 6). Next are "headnote" paragraphs, each describing a discrete aspect of the case (item 7). You should not view any of these paragraphs as legal authority; the opinion itself is the legal authority. The lawyers handling the case appear next (item 8).

Of course, the largest portion of the published case is comprised of the court's opinion. Each opinion begins with the name of the judge or justice who wrote the opinion (item 9). ("Judge" refers to a jurist of a trial court or intermediate appellate court; high court jurists are "justices.") The text of the opinion (item 10) typically includes a summary of the facts of the case, the course of the litigation, the court's holding, and its reasoning. The holding is the legal outcome of the case; it may be understood in procedural terms (for example, the lower court's ruling is affirmed) and in substantive terms (for example, the defendant is liable on the facts of the case). The reasoning typically encompasses references to and discussion of legal authorities the court relied on, an analysis of how the legal rules from those authorities apply to the facts of the case, and perhaps an exploration of the public policies served by the chosen result.

The court also may opine about a situation not strictly before the court, as it elaborates on its resolution of the case before the court. This material is called "obiter dicta" (or "dictum" in the singular) and is not as authoritative as material bearing directly on the court's resolution of the case.

If the court consists of more than one judge, there is, of course, the potential for disagreement. If the disagreement is significant, either as to the resolution of the case or as to the best reasoning for the result, the case will yield multiple opinions. The opinion garnering more than half of the votes

Illustration 6-2 *Lukoski v. Sandia Indian Management Co.*, 748 P.2d 507, 507-10 (N.M. 1988).

LUKOSKI v. SANDIA INDIAN MANAGEMENT CO. N.M. 507
Cite as 748 P.2d 507 (N.M. 1988)

court's finding of damages, it is our opinion that an "as is" clause provides absolute protection to a seller such as Horizon only when the buyer and seller possess equal knowledge of the property. Here, while Lambert's knowledge of the property was equal to that of Horizon's insofar as most essentials of the contract were concerned, Lambert relied on Horizon for its knowledge of the total acreage in the property, and for such information as would have informed him about the realignment of Golf Course Road. Hence the trial court did not err in finding damages as to the realignment of Golf Course Road despite the "as is" clause. *See Archuleta v. Kopp,* 90 N.M. 273, 562 P.2d 834 (Ct.App.), *cert. dismissed,* 90 N.M. 636, 567 P.2d 485 (1977).

THE ISSUE OF THE ARROYO

[5] If as to the issue of the realignment of Golf Course Road and the total number of acres conveyed the parties were not in possession of equal knowledge, when the issue of the arroyo is raised, it is clear that Lambert did have knowledge of the property equal to that of Horizon. Indeed, it appears from the testimony of past officers of Horizon that Lambert's knowledge as to the arroyo may in some respects have been superior to that of Horizon. Lambert's principal argument against the terms of paragraph 6 of the contract insofar as it applies to the arroyo is that he talked to Horizon's legal counsel before signing the contract and was told that "natural drainageway" did not refer to the arroyo, but referred to a swale running north and south across the property.

Yet, the court found in its findings of fact that Lambert (1) "read and agreed to all the terms and conditions of the Contract," (2) "had personal knowledge of, and had inspected and investigated" the property before entering into the contract, (3) that George Lambert "is a knowledgeable and sophisticated real estate broker with 20 years of experience" and that he had available to him certain engineering drainage studies dealing with the problems of the arroyo, and (4) "[a]n Arroyo is a natural drainageway." We have no reason to dispute any of these findings since they are all supported by substantial evidence. "[T]he circumstances surrounding the Agreement, the import of that Agreement as a whole, and the undisputed parol evidence of the parties show that [Lambert's] right to acquire [Horizon's] interests was not conditioned upon . . ." [an interpretation of "natural drainageway" as a "swale".] *Schaefer v. Hinkle,* 93 N.M. 129, 131, 597 P.2d 314, 316 (1979); *see also Smith v. Price's Creameries,* 98 N.M. 541, 544, 650 P.2d 825, 828 (1982), which likewise involved the issue of a conflict between contractual language and alleged oral assurances modifying the contractual language.

The judgment of the trial court is affirmed.

IT IS SO ORDERED.

WALTERS and RANSOM, JJ., concur.

106 N.M. 664 — 1

Scott J.L. LUKOSKI, Plaintiff–Appellee,

v.

SANDIA INDIAN MANAGEMENT COMPANY, Defendant–Appellant. — 2

No. 16462. — 3

Supreme Court of New Mexico. — 4

Jan. 7, 1988. — 5

Former general manager brought action against former employer for wrongful discharge. The District Court, Bernalillo County, William W. Deaton, D.J., entered judgment in favor of manager. Employer appealed. The Supreme Court, Ransom, J., held that evidence established that employee handbook amended employment contract and that employer breached contract by failing to comply with warning and suspension procedures. — 6

Note: 1. Parallel citation
2. Parties
3. Docket number
4. Court
5. Date of decision
6. West synopsis

Illustration 6-2 *(continued)*

508 N. M. 748 PACIFIC REPORTER, 2d SERIES

Affirmed.

Stowers, J., dissented and filed opinion.

7a

7 **1. Trial ⚿392(1)**

Defendant waived specific findings of fact on issues on which it failed to tender requested findings. SCRA 1986, Rule 1–052, subd. B(1)(f).

7 **2. Master and Servant ⚿40(3)**

Evidence supported trial court's conclusions that termination procedures in employee handbook amended general manager's employment contract, that handbook created warning and suspension procedures which were not followed, and that personality, rather than insubordination, caused employment termination; handbook characterized disciplinary policy regarding warnings, suspensions, and terminations as established procedure; and handbook did not indicate that it was subject to revocation at any time or that employees should not rely on it.

---

8 Grammer & Grammer, David A. Grammer, III, Albuquerque, for defendant-appellant.

Turpen & Wolfe, Donald C. Turpen, Albuquerque, for plaintiff-appellee.

OPINION

9 RANSOM, Justice.

10 Scott J.L. Lukoski brought a wrongful discharge action against his employer, Sandia Indian Management Co. (SIMCO). Lukoski had been employed as general manager of the Sandia Pueblo bingo operation. In a bench trial, the court decided that SIMCO violated the termination procedures prescribed for "less serious" offenses by an employee handbook. For salary due on the remaining term of his one-year oral contract, Lukoski was awarded $18,629.05. We affirm.

The court found that, in October 1983, Lukoski and SIMCO entered into a one-year oral employment agreement under which Lukoski would provide services as the general manager of a bingo hall operation for a specified annual salary plus commission. There was no written agreement between the parties. In February 1984, SIMCO distributed to all employees an employee handbook and requested each to sign the last page as verification of receipt, acknowledgement of acceptance, and agreement to conform with the stated policies and procedures. After Lukoski signed the back page as requested, it was placed in his personnel file. The court concluded that:

> The parties amended the oral employment contract * * * when [SIMCO] proffered, and [Lukoski] signed, [the] Employee's Handbook containing new duties and obligations on the part of employee and employer over and above said oral contract, including Rules to be obeyed by [Lukoski] and a termination procedure to be followed by [SIMCO].

[1] Although we determine the above-quoted language is a finding of ultimate fact, rather than a conclusion of law, that is of no consequence. *See Hoskins v. Albuquerque Bus Co.*, 72 N.M. 217, 382 P.2d 700 (1963); *Wiggs v. City of Albuquerque*, 57 N.M. 770, 263 P.2d 963 (1953). SIMCO challenges this finding and for the first time on appeal raises two other issues. First, it claims that Lukoski, as general manager, was not the type of employee intended to be covered by the handbook. Distribution to all employees with request for signatures constituted evidence to the contrary, and resolution of any ambiguity regarding management personnel would have been a specific question of fact. *See Shaeffer v. Kelton*, 95 N.M. 182, 619 P.2d 1226 (1980). Second, SIMCO claims that any breach was not material because it neither went to the substance of the contract nor defeated the object of the parties. Materiality is likewise a specific question of fact. *See Bisio v. Madenwald (In re Estate of Bisio)*, 33 Or.App. 325, 576 P.2d 801 (1978). As the contract stood after amendment, it was not materiality, as argued by SIMCO, but rather severity of offense that was at issue under the termination procedures. In any event, by failing to tender requested findings, SIMCO waived specific

Note: 7. Headnotes
7a. Topic and key number
8. Names of counsel
9. Justice who wrote majority opinion
10. Majority opinion begins

Illustration 6-2 *(continued)*

findings on these fact issues. SCRA 1986, 1–052(B)(1)(f).

[2] There is substantial evidence supporting the court's findings of ultimate fact that the termination procedures became an amendment to Lukoski's contract, and that personality—not the severe offenses of insubordination or disobedience—was the cause for termination. He was terminated without warning or suspension for a cause not so severe as to constitute cause for immediate termination. His personality and interpersonal dealings were found by the court to create an atmosphere of fear and anxiety and bad morale among employees and managers.

Relying only on *Ellis v. El Paso Natural Gas Co.,* 754 F.2d 884 (10th Cir.1985), the thrust of SIMCO's appeal is that the language of the employee handbook is "too indefinite to constitute a contract" and lacks "contractual terms which might evidence the intent to form a contract." It maintains that the parties did not conduct themselves as if the employee handbook was to govern Lukoski or as if they expected it to form the basis of a contractual relationship. In support of its position, SIMCO refers to the disciplinary action, suspension, and warning provisions,[1] and argues that the language of the termination policy is ambiguous and contains no required policy for termination.

SIMCO's argument, however, overlooks the handbook's characterization of the disciplinary policy regarding warnings, suspensions and terminations as "an *established procedure* regarding suspension of problem employees and termination for those who cannot conform to Company Policy." (Emphasis added.) Moreover, the language of the handbook does nothing to alert an employee against placing reliance on any statement contained therein or against viewing such discipline and termination policy as only a unilateral expression of SIMCO's intention that is subject to revocation or change at any time, in any manner, at the pleasure of SIMCO. To the contrary, from the language of the handbook and the conduct of SIMCO in adopting the policy, it could properly be found that the policy was part of the employment agreement.

Whether an employee handbook has modified the employment relationship is a question of fact "to be discerned from the totality of the parties' statements and actions regarding the employment relationship." *Wagenseller v. Scottsdale Memorial Hosp.,* 147 Ariz. 370, 383, 710 P.2d 1025, 1038 (1985) (en banc).

> Evidence relevant to this factual decision includes the language used in the personnel manual as well as the employer's course of conduct and oral representations regarding it. We do not mean to imply that all personnel manual will become part of employment contracts. Employers are certainly free to issue no personnel manual at all or to issue a personnel manual that clearly and conspicuously tells their employees that the manual is not part of the employment contract and that their jobs are termina-

1. The referenced handbook provisions state:

OTHER DISCIPLINARY ACTION:
In order to protect the good employees [sic] jobs and Sandia Indian Bingo, there is an established procedure regarding suspension of problem employees and termination for those who can not conform to Company Policy. Suspensions without pay may be given to employees who violate company policies. There are violations which are so severe [including insubordination and disobedience] that immediate termination may be necessary....

SUSPENSIONS:
Suspension without pay may be given when the incident is not sufficiently serious to warrant discharge and/or the particular employee's overall value to the Company [is considered], if [in] the opinion of the Department Manager [the employee] warrants another chance. Minimum suspensions are (3) three days, maximum suspensions are (5) five days. No employee may be suspended more than once in a year; thereafter, if the incident would normally warrant suspension he/she must be discharged.

DISCIPLINARY WARNING:
Disciplinary warning slips will be issued where the offense is less serious and where corrective action may salvage an employee. More than one (1) disciplinary warning, whether for the same offense or not, may subject an employee to suspension or termination. Warning slips become a permanent part of an employee's personnel record.

Illustration 6-2 *(continued)*

510 N.M. 748 PACIFIC REPORTER, 2d SERIES

ble at the will of the employer with or without reason. Such actions * * * instill no reasonable expectations of job security and do not give employees any reason to rely on representations in the manual. However, if an employer does choose to issue a policy statement, in a manual or otherwise, and, by its language or by the employer's actions, encourages reliance thereon, the employer cannot be free to only selectively abide by it. Having announced a policy, the employer may not treat it as illusory.

Leikvold v. Valley View Community Hosp., 141 Ariz. 544, 548, 688 P.2d 170, 174 (1984). Here, substantial evidence supports the finding of the trial court that the employee handbook modified the employment relationship and created warning and suspension procedures which were not followed in this case.

Accordingly, based upon the foregoing, the judgment of the trial court is affirmed.

IT IS SO ORDERED.

SCARBOROUGH, C.J., SOSA, Senior Justice, and WALTERS, J., concur.

STOWERS, J., dissents.

11 STOWERS, Justice, dissenting.

I respectfully dissent from the majority's holding that SIMCO did not abide with the termination procedures.

Substantial evidence does support the findings of the trial court that the employee handbook modified the employment relationship and that Lukoski was terminated for just cause. The trial court erred, however, in concluding that SIMCO did not follow the proper termination procedures. To the contrary, SIMCO did not breach any of the provisions in the employee handbook when it discharged Lukoski without a warning and suspension. The handbook explicitly states that, "there are violations which are so severe that *immediate termination may be necessary.*" (Emphasis added).

Overwhelming evidence was presented at trial to show that Lukoski's violations of company policies were of the type to fall within the category of "so severe" that a warning and any suspension procedures were not required. *See State ex rel. Goodmans Office Furnishings, Inc. v. Page & Wirtz Constr. Co.*, 102 N.M. 22, 24, 690 P.2d 1016, 1018 (1984). Generally, this evidence indicated that Lukoski had an overall attitude problem towards his employees, other managers and representatives of the Sandia Pueblo to the extent that SIMCO was in jeopardy of losing its bingo contract with the Pueblo; moreover, he was abusive towards the accountants, argued or fought publicly with customers, the assistant bingo manager, the construction supervisor and an admittance clerk; Lukoski also failed to install proper security measures and verification methods, and hired unqualified personnel. Further, testimony indicated that on several occasions, Walker, Lukoski's supervisor, spoke to Lukoski about this attitude problem, and, in fact, interceded on Lukoski's behalf when the Sandia Pueblo desired to discharge Lukoski.

As enumerated in the handbook, Lukoski's violations included, "fighting on company property, refusal to obey reasonable orders of a supervisor, discourtesy to customers, and disobeying or ignoring established written or oral work rules or policies." These are, and I again quote from the handbook, "violations which are so severe that *immediate termination* may be necessary." (Emphasis added.) Therefore, the trial court was in error when it decided that SIMCO violated the termination procedures prescribed for "less serious" offenses in the handbook. Lukoski was not entitled to those termination procedures since his offenses were not of the "less serious" type. Under the circumstances in this case, the only process due Lukoski for the seriousness of his violations was immediate termination. Thus, there was no breach by SIMCO when it discharged him for just cause.

The judgment of the district court should be reversed and this case remanded for dismissal.

Note: 11. Dissenting opinion begins

is designated the majority opinion; this opinion resolves the case. A dissent expresses the view of judges or justices who would have reached a different result in the case. A concurrence expresses the view of judges or justices who favor the majority's result, but for different reasons. On fairly rare occasions, no opinion garners over half of the votes; the opinion garnering the largest number of votes is then deemed the plurality opinion and generally is the most influential.

Lukoski is a case you would certainly read if you were researching the Canoga case. In Illustration 6-2, note that *Lukoski* was decided by the New Mexico Supreme Court on January 7, 1988, and bore the docket number 16462. Scott Lukoski, the plaintiff, sued the Sandia Indian Management Company, the defendant. Sandia must have lost in the trial court because here before the Supreme Court it was the appellant, while Mr. Lukoski was the appellee.

In Illustration 6-2, all three paragraphs following the opening block were written by the publisher's staff. The first is the publisher's synopsis. The remaining two paragraphs are the headnotes, also written by the publisher.

In Illustration 6-2, the facts of the *Lukoski* case are scattered throughout the opinion. In simple terms, a manager was terminated for poor interpersonal dealings, yet the employer did not follow the suspension procedures for less serious misconduct that were outlined in its handbook (quoted in the footnote). In the trial court, the case was tried to the judge, without a jury (called a "bench trial"). The judge ruled in favor of the employee and awarded him money damages. The case then proceeded to the New Mexico Supreme Court because contract cases did not go to the court of appeals at that time. The supreme court affirmed the trial court's result. Again in simple terms, the supreme court determined that the handbook language about suspensions became part of the employment agreement and was enforceable as a contract. The manager's difficulty in interpersonal dealings should have been handled through the suspension process. In so ruling, the court relied on decisions from various state and federal courts and emphasized the precise wording of the handbook. There is no dictum.

In the illustration, one justice dissented from the majority opinion. Justice Stowers agreed that there was a contract requiring use of suspension procedures. But he would have ruled that the interpersonal problems were so severe as to permit immediate termination under the disciplinary procedures provision of the handbook.

The outcome and reasoning in the *Lukoski* case no doubt were of considerable interest to Mr. Lukoski and Sandia. The significance of *Lukoski* for the Canoga case is explored next.

C. Why Would You Research (Which) Cases?

The simple answer to the question posed above is that cases constitute the law in the American "common law" system. In the context of a particular research problem, not all cases are equal in importance. You should locate cases that are good law and, ideally, mandatory precedent. An important aspect of case law research is the assessment of the relative weights of the potentially useful cases you locate.

1. The Common Law, Stare Decisis, and Precedent

In a common law system, case law forms part of the law of the land. The operative principle in a common law system is "stare decisis et non quieta movere," which means "to adhere to precedent and not to unsettle things which are settled." According to stare decisis, a court should follow certain cases, or precedents, on the same legal topic. Hence, as you research the law applicable to a client's situation, you should take guidance from precedent. Even if you hope and reasonably anticipate that the situation will never come before a court, you should try to deduce how the court would handle the dispute.

Stare decisis has several chief advantages. Situations involving similar facts receive like treatment. Outcomes are based on legal principles, rather than the unconstrained biases of judges and juries. Because it is possible to predict the outcome of a case by looking to precedents, many cases can be settled. Furthermore, people can conform their future conduct to the law by looking to precedents.

Yet overly strict adherence to precedent would produce a static legal rule. While some areas of law benefit from stability, others do not. When social values change, or information improves, or new situations develop, the law must be able to evolve accordingly.

Fortunately the American legal system has several mechanisms for achieving change. A court may modify the common law by refining or modifying existing precedents. Or a court may distinguish those precedents and decide the case using a different rule. Or a court may overrule precedent in response to a significant need for change. Furthermore, as you will see in Chapter 7 on statutes, legislatures may enact statutes modifying the common law to a greater or lesser degree.

2. History and Treatment of the Case

Before you rely on a case, you first must determine that it is good law. The status of a case as good law is a function primarily of its subsequent history and secondarily of its treatment. Subsequent history is the product of later rulings in the same litigation, while treatment is the product of decisions rendered in other, later cases.

a. Subsequent History

Before you rely on a decision, you must know whether it has been reviewed by a higher court and, if so, what the outcome was. The higher court may affirm the lower court's decision, reverse the lower court's decision, or take intermediate action, such as modifying or reversing and remanding with instructions to the lower court to handle the case differently the second time. These later decisions in the same litigation constitute the original decision's subsequent history.

Obviously, your research is not complete until you have identified the subsequent history of any decision you intend to rely on. Then you must carefully read any decisions in your case's subsequent history to determine whether they adversely affect the outcome and reasoning you are planning to rely on. If they do, it is incorrect to rely on the original decision. On the other hand, if your case has been affirmed in a later decision by a higher court, the original decision has greater credibility. Ordinarily you will rely instead on the higher court's decision. The exception to this rule arises when the higher court does not expressly rule on a point that is covered by the lower court, important to your case, and consistent with the higher court's ruling.

Furthermore, if you intend to rely on a decision that is very recent and is not from the highest court, you should know whether an appeal is pending before a higher court. If so, you should monitor the case's progress and be prepared to adjust your analysis when the higher court rules.

For a simple example, consider the *Lukoski* case. As already noted, the New Mexico Court of Appeals did not review *Lukoski*. But assume that you had located a court of appeals decision in *Lukoski*. Assume further that the court of appeals reversed the trial court award in favor of Mr. Lukoski, while the supreme court ruled in favor of Mr. Lukoski. You would rely not on the court of appeals decision, but rather on the supreme court decision. As you will see in Part D, there is no subsequent history undermining the authoritativeness of *Lukoski*. Because the *Lukoski* case in Illustration 6-2 is a 1988 decision from New Mexico's highest court, you can assume no appeal is pending.

b. Treatment

Under stare decisis, a court typically refers to decisions rendered in earlier similar cases to support its reasoning in the current case. The court may follow an earlier decision, distinguish it, criticize it, modify it, or even overrule it. For any decided case, there may be several or even many such references in later cases. These references constitute the treatment of the earlier case.

Your research is not complete until you have discerned the treatment of the case you have located through your research. Your focus should be on its treatment by the courts in the same court system because those courts have the greatest power to enhance or undermine the case's credibility. You should be especially concerned with indications that the case has been overruled; it then is no longer good law. You also should be wary of relying on a case that has been criticized significantly or distinguished frequently. Furthermore, you should check for later legislation undermining the case through the methods discussed in Chapter 7.

For example, as you will learn in more detail in the next part, the *Lukoski* case has been cited seven times by the New Mexico state courts; it also has been cited a handful of times by other courts (the Tenth Circuit, California, and Washington). It has not been overruled by later New Mexico cases or criticized by any court. This record of favorable treatment indicates that *Lukoski* remains good law.

3. Mandatory versus Persuasive Precedent: Federalism, Jurisdiction, and Level of Court

While all cases constitute the law, as to a particular situation some constitute binding or mandatory precedent, while others merely have persuasive force. The distinction between mandatory and persuasive precedents is critical. Stare decisis operates as to mandatory precedents only. Persuasive precedents may influence a court, but they do not bind it. A court is most likely to rely on a persuasive precedent when its own case law does not cover the issue or is outdated in light of legal developments elsewhere. The distinction between mandatory and persuasive precedent is based on two main factors: jurisdiction and level of court.

a. Federalism and Jurisdiction

The American legal system is a federal system, that is, a collection of legal systems. A particular legal issue may be governed by federal law, or it may be governed by state law. Or it may be governed by both. A few issues are governed by local (municipal, county) law.

If the legal issue is governed by federal law, then mandatory precedents would emanate from the federal courts. If the legal issue is governed by state law, then mandatory precedents would emanate from the courts of the pertinent state. Other decisions would be persuasive precedent.

As is true of the term "case," the term "jurisdiction" has several common meanings in the law. It often is loosely used to refer to a legal system of a particular geographic region. In a more technical sense, "jurisdiction" is the power of a specific court to render and enforce a decision in a particular case. Generally, jurisdiction in this sense aligns with jurisdiction in the geographic sense. That is, the courts of a particular state have the power to render and enforce decisions arising under the law of that state, and federal courts have the power to render and enforce decisions arising under federal law and within their geographic regions.

However, in several common situations, that alignment is not present. For example, in diversity jurisdiction, a federal court has the power to decide cases arising under state law if the case involves citizens of different states and the amount in controversy exceeds $50,000. Similarly, under supplemental jurisdiction, a federal court has the power to decide a case arising in part under state law if the case also involves a federal claim. Congress has given state and federal courts concurrent jurisdiction over certain claims stated in federal law. The courts of one state may apply the law of a different state if a multistate contract identifies the second state's law as governing.

In these situations, the courts follow as mandatory precedent decisions from the courts whose law governs. For example, when operating in diversity or supplemental jurisdiction, a federal court will follow the law of the state that governs the claim and will seek to emulate the approach of that state's supreme court; the decisions of other federal courts are not as weighty.

Unfortunately, there are few broadly applicable principles to explain the distribution of legal topics among the three levels of government, and jurisdiction can be complex. As you begin your research into a new area, you should assume that federal, state, and local law are all potentially applicable, and you should be alert to jurisdictional possibilities. Your research in secondary sources will provide preliminary guidance on these matters. Of course, you should verify that information through your own research in primary authority.

In the Canoga case, the contract issue is a state law question (as is generally true of contract law). New Mexico would be the jurisdiction of the client's situation, and New Mexico state court decisions, such as *Lukoski,* would be mandatory precedent for a court deciding the Canoga case. The *Lukoski* court was itself bound by and cited earlier New Mexico cases—mandatory precedent—in its decision. Note that the *Lukoski* court also cited Oregon and Arizona cases—persuasive precedent—which is not surprising given how rapidly the law of employee handbooks was evolving at that time (the late 1980s).

The *Lukoski* decision alludes to an example of diversity jurisdiction. The majority referred to a federal case, *Ellis v. El Paso Natural Gas Co.* That case involved an employee's challenge to his termination under state law, yet it was heard in federal court under diversity jurisdiction. The federal court in *Ellis* relied on New Mexico Supreme Court cases.

b. Level of Court

An additional determinant of mandatory versus persuasive precedent is the level of the court issuing the decision. As noted above, all court structures have more than one level, with most having three and the rest having two. Stare decisis operates hierarchically. Any particular court is bound by decisions of higher courts within the same court system and must take its own decisions into account, but is not bound by decisions issued by lower courts. Hence, you would rely on a supreme court decision over that of an intermediate appeals court; similarly you would rely on an intermediate appeals court decision over that of a trial court.

For example, the decision in *Lukoski* binds the New Mexico Court of Appeals and the New Mexico trial courts; it also must be taken into account by the New Mexico Supreme Court in future cases. But a New Mexico Court of Appeals decision binds only the trial courts, not the supreme court. Similarly, a Tenth Circuit Court of Appeals decision binds the federal district courts within the Tenth Circuit (including the federal district court in New Mexico), but it does not bind the United States Supreme Court. Furthermore, because each federal circuit court has a geographic range covering only a part of the country (see Illustration 6-1 on page 130), a Tenth Circuit decision does not bind other federal circuit courts of appeals or district courts within other circuits.

4. Additional Factors

Your research may well yield multiple cases that are good law and mandatory precedent. In these situations, you should consider the following factors in selecting cases to emphasize.

First, the higher the degree of similarity between the facts and legal issues of your client's situation and those of the case you have located, the stronger your research. In some situations, you may find a case that is factually, but not legally, parallel to your case, or vice versa. Your goal is to obtain both types of parallelism, to the extent possible.

Second, the clearer and more convincing the reasoning of the case you have located, the stronger your research. A clear, well reasoned case is inherently more credible and will afford a stronger basis for predicting the outcome in your client's situation.

Third, the more recent the case you have located, the stronger your research, all else being equal. While some cases age well, many lose their force. Age by itself does not render a case bad law, but it may make it less credible than a newer case.

In the research of the Canoga case based on these factors, the *Lukoski* case would be a strong case to rely on. It is less than ten years old, and the reasoning is fairly straightforward. Furthermore, the facts of *Lukoski* and the Canoga situation are similar, and the issues are nearly identical. There is, of course, some difference, in that Mr. Lukoski alleged that his employer should have suspended him, whereas Ms. Canoga would argue that the employer must provide board review. This difference is nearly insignificant; rarely will you locate a case so closely on point.

On occasion, you may need to rely on persuasive precedent due to a dearth of mandatory precedent. You also may seek to rely on persuasive precedent when your mandatory precedent is dated or adverse to your client's interest and you wish to seek a change in the law. In selecting from possible persuasive precedents, you should consider the following factors, in addition to those stated above: which courts your jurisdiction's courts typically look to, which courts or cases are viewed as leaders in the subject matter, how geographically close the sister jurisdiction is to yours, how much the law of the sister jurisdiction tracks the law of your jurisdiction on related legal topics, and how closely the policies underlying the precedent mesh with your jurisdiction's policies. Your commentary research will help you to assess some of these factors.

In the *Lukoski* case, as already noted, the court relied heavily on a persuasive precedent from Arizona, *Wagenseller v. Scottsdale Memorial Hospital. Wagenseller* is a recent (1985) case from a nearby state. It involved fairly similar facts and the same legal issues as *Lukoski.* Based on its reasoning, it became a leading case in the developing area of employee's contract rights.

D. How Do You Research Cases?

Quite often, you will have found a reference to some pertinent cases from your research in secondary sources. However, your research in secondary sources is unlikely to yield all of the case law you should locate because the author of the periodical or treatise, for example, did not have your specific situation in mind and probably chose only illustrative cases to discuss. Thus you will need to research cases directly.

The traditional and still standard means of researching case law is through a set of linked paper sources: case reporters, digests, and citators. Exhibit 6.1 below shows the relationships among these sources. An alternative is to use an online service; this chapter demonstrates the use of WESTLAW, one of the two major online services for legal research. Whether you research in paper or online, you must accomplish two distinct tasks: locating the case and updating it.

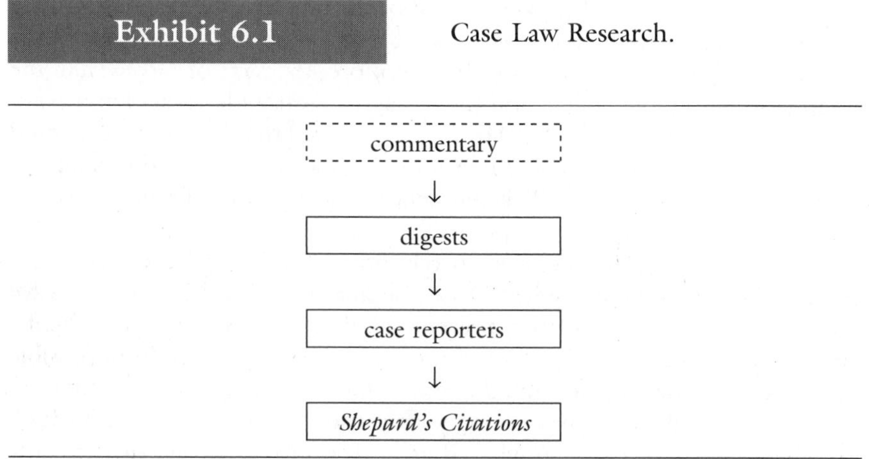

1. Researching in Paper: Reporters, Digests, and Citators

It takes several sources to research case law through paper sources. One source, the case reporter, actually contains the case. You must use a second source, the digest, to locate the case and a third source, the citator, to update the case. In selecting from the many reporters, digests, and citators available to you, you will focus on the jurisdiction of your client's situation.

a. Locating Case Law in Reporters through Digests

(1) Understanding Reporters

Cases are compiled into books called "case reporters." Each case reporter contains the decisions issued during a particular time period by a single court or a set of courts.

The most prominent reporters comprise the National Reporter System published by West Publishing Company. As synopsized in Exhibit 6.2 on page 144, West currently publishes reporters containing decisions of the federal courts as follows: *Supreme Court Reporter* for decisions of the United States Supreme Court, *Federal Reporter* for decisions of the various courts of appeals, and *Federal Supplement* for decisions of the various district courts. While all decisions of the Supreme Court are published, only some decisions of the lower federal courts, selected by the courts, appear in the West reporters.

West's reporter system also covers case law from state courts. West has divided the country into seven regions, each containing four to fifteen states and each served by one of the regional reporters. Exhibit 6.2 lists the regions and corresponding states. The regional reporters contain the decisions designated for publication by the covered states' appellate courts; some decisions may not be designated for publication by the courts. Decisions of lower courts typically are not published. Keep in mind that West's regions are not synonymous with jurisdiction; a case from a sister state within the same West region as your state is no more binding than a case from a sister state outside your state's West region. In recognition of the sheer volume of decisions issued in California, Illinois, and New York, West also publishes *California Reporter, Illinois Decisions,* and *New York Supplement.*

For most of the reporters described above, West has published more than one series. The first series of a reporter contains the oldest cases, while the second (or even third) series contains the newest. The volume numbers start again with a new series.

Most volumes of a reporter are hardbound books. However, the most recent decisions appear in softcover pamphlets called "advance sheets." West publishes advance sheets in order to release new cases more quickly than a hardbound publication schedule can accomplish. Once the hardbound book is prepared, it supersedes the softcover pamphlet.

Exhibit 6.2

West Reporters and Digests.

Cases from these courts	*appear in these reporters*	*and are digested in these digests*
Federal Courts		
Supreme Court	*Supreme Court Reporter*	*United States Supreme Court Digest*; *Federal Practice Digest*; older cases covered by *Modern Federal Practice Digest* and *Federal Digest*
courts of appeals for various circuits	*Federal Reporter* (currently in third series)	*Federal Practice Digest* (currently in fourth series); older cases covered by *Modern Federal Practice Digest* and *Federal Digest* (also separate digests for Fifth and Eleventh Circuits)
district courts	*Federal Supplement* since 1932; older cases in *Federal Reporter*	*Federal Practice Digest* (currently in fourth series); older cases covered by *Modern Federal Practice Digest* and *Federal Digest*
State Courts		
Connecticut Delaware District of Columbia Maine Maryland New Hampshire New Jersey Pennsylvania Rhode Island Vermont	*Atlantic Reporter* (currently in second series)	*Atlantic Digest*; state digests (except Delaware) (including federal cases from state)
Illinois Indiana Massachusetts New York Ohio	*North Eastern Reporter* (currently in second series); also *Illinois Decisions* and *New York Supplement* (currently in second series)	state digests (including federal cases from state)
Georgia North Carolina South Carolina Virginia West Virginia	*South Eastern Reporter* (currently in second series)	*South Eastern Digest*; state digests (Virginia and West Virginia are merged) (including federal cases from state)
Alabama Florida Louisiana Mississippi	*Southern Reporter* (currently in second series)	state digests (including federal cases from state)
Arkansas Kentucky Missouri Tennessee Texas	*South Western Reporter* (currently in second series)	state digests (including federal cases from state)

Exhibit 6.2 *(continued)*

Cases from these courts	*appear in these reporters*	*and are digested in these digests*
State Courts (continued)		
Iowa Michigan Minnesota Nebraska North Dakota South Dakota Wisconsin	*North Western Reporter* (currently in second series)	*North Western Digest*; state digests (North and South Dakota are merged) (including federal cases from state)
Alaska Arizona California Colorado Hawaii Idaho Kansas Montana Nevada New Mexico Oklahoma Oregon Utah Washington Wyoming	*Pacific Reporter* (currently in second series); also *California Reporter* (currently in second series)	*Pacific Digest*; state digests (except Nevada and Utah) (including federal cases from state)

All jurisdictions also are covered in the *Century Digests*, *Decennial Digests*, and *General Digests*.

As an example of the West reporter system, consider first the *Lukoski* case, Illustration 6-2 on pages 132-135. That case was decided by the New Mexico Supreme Court in 1988. It appears in volume 748 of the second series of the *Pacific Reporter* (starting at page 507). (West's Pacific region is quite expansive, stretching to include Kansas!) As a second example, consider the *Ellis* case referred to in *Lukoski*. As a 1985 decision of the federal Tenth Circuit, it appears in volume 754 of the second series of the *Federal Reporter* (starting at page 884).

While the West National Reporter System is the most expansive and best established set of reporters, it is not the exclusive source of cases published in paper. For example, *United States Supreme Court Reports, Lawyers' Edition*, published by Lawyers Cooperative Publishing, contains decisions of the United States Supreme Court.

Some case reporters are published by the government (or with its authorization) and thus are deemed official reporters. At the federal level, the United States Government Printing Office publishes *United States Reports*, containing decisions of the United States Supreme Court. Many states (including New Mexico) publish official reporters. As you will see in Part F, you may need to know about a case's publication in an official reporter in order to cite it properly. However, official reporters are not particularly useful in the research process because they may not be accompanied by digests and they typically are published on a slower schedule than West follows.

(2) Researching in Digests

(a) Understanding Digests

Cases are published in case reporters as they arrive at the publisher and clear the editorial process. For example, a volume of the *Supreme Court Reporter* (which may comprise several books) contains the decisions of the United States Supreme Court for a one-year period. Case reporters are organized chronologically, not topically. Hence you need some mechanism for locating pertinent cases within a reporter. The solution is a digest.

West's "key number digest" is the most highly developed legal digest. The main features of the West system are the headnotes, topics and key numbers, and digests.

For each case published in its reporters, West's editors write brief paragraphs describing the points of law. These paragraphs are called "headnotes" and appear before the opinion itself in the reporter. To enable you to locate the portion of the opinion giving rise to a headnote, West inserts small numbers in brackets within the opinion.

For an example, review Illustration 6-2 on pages 132-135. Two headnotes appear in the top left-hand column of page 508 (item 7). The text supporting the first headnote appears in the opinion (item 10) in the lower right-hand column of page 508, while the text supporting the second appears in the top left-hand column of page 509. (Note the corresponding bracketed numbers.)

Each headnote is then assigned to a topic and key number. West has divided the law into over 400 main topics. This list of topics appears near the front of digest volumes. Each topic is then divided into subtopics, which are assigned key numbers; some subtopics are divided into sub-subtopics. By this device, the headnotes from all cases published by West are fit into a broad outline of the law.

For example, the first headnote for the *Lukoski* case was assigned to the 388th topic, Trial, key number 392(1). The second headnote, which is more pertinent to the Canoga case, was assigned to the 255th topic, Master and Servant, key number 40(3).

The headnotes are then published in "digests." Digests are organized topically—that is, by topics and by key numbers within each topic. The headnotes appear under the assigned topics and key numbers. Each includes the case's citation.

For example, Illustration 6-3 on page 147 is a digest page listing cases pertaining to the Master and Servant topic, key number 40(3). Subtopic 40 is "evidence" of wrongful discharge, and sub-subtopic 3 is "in general." Note that the bracketed paragraph in Illustration 6-3 is identical to the second headnote for *Lukoski* and includes a citation to *Lukoski*.

Illustration 6-3 *New Mexico Digest.*

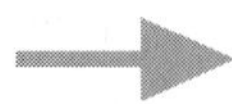

⚷40(3.1) MASTER & SERVANT 4B N M D—14

ployer and employee; personnel manual implied that employment would not be terminated except for a good reason and manual strictly controlled employer's and employee's conduct.—Newberry v. Allied Stores, Inc., 773 P.2d 1231, 108 N.M. 424.

Determination that employee was discharged without a good reason and in violation of implied contract between employer and employee that allowed termination only for cause was not supported by the evidence; evidence showed that employee was discharged for removing merchandise from store in which he worked without filling out the appropriate charge ticket, as was required under company policy.—Id.

Former employee failed to establish that his employer acted in bad faith in the manner and method used to terminate him, as was required for employee to collect punitive damages from employer in his breach of contract action.—Id.

N.M. 1988. Substantial evidence supported finding that employer did not act upon reasonable grounds in terminating employee, where employer's vice-president, before he fired the employee, only reviewed a summary of an investigation into allegations of sexual harassment, illegal conduct, and mismanagement by employee, which failed to differentiate between firsthand knowledge and rumor, which made no attempt to evaluate the credibility of persons interviewed, and which was not intended to stand alone.—Kestenbaum v. Pennzoil Co., 766 P.2d 280, 108 N.M. 20, certiorari denied 109 S.Ct. 3163, 490 U.S. 1109, 104 L.Ed.2d 1026.

N.M. 1988. Evidence supported trial court's conclusions that termination procedures in employee handbook amended general manager's employment contract, that handbook created warning and suspension procedures which were not followed, and that personality, rather than insubordination, caused employment termination; handbook characterized disciplinary policy regarding warnings, suspensions, and terminations as established procedure; and handbook did not indicate that it was subject to revocation at any time or that employees should not rely on it.—Lukoski v. Sandia Indian Management Co., 748 P.2d 507, 106 N.M. 664.

N.M. 1984. Evidence supported trial court's finding that former employee did not violate terms of his employment agreement and that he was a good employee thereby warranting conclusion that former employee's employment was terminated by former employer without good cause; therefore, former employee was not bound, as provided in the agreement, by the covenant not to compete contained in the employment agreement and was entitled to 30 days' termination pay.—Danzer v. Professional Insurors, Inc., 679 P.2d 1276, 101 N.M. 178.

N.M.App. 1983. In most instances, claim under judicially created tort action based on employee's discharge which contravenes some clear mandate of public policy will assert serious misconduct; thus, proof should be made by clear and convincing evidence.—Vigil v. Arzola, 699 P.2d 613, 102 N.M. 682, reversed in part 687 P.2d 1038, 101 N.M. 687.

N.M.App. 1972. In action alleging wrongful discharge from employment in connection with dispute as to duties employee was to perform under contract, finding that employee was employed as a manager, rather than as advisor and supervisor, was supported by substantial evidence.—Clem v. Bowman Lumber Co., 495 P.2d 1106, 83 N.M. 659.

⚷40(4). —— Retaliatory discharge.

C.A.10 (N.M.) 1987. Three-part analysis requiring plaintiff to establish prima facie case, requiring employer to show nondiscriminatory reason, and requiring plaintiff to prove discriminatory intent applies in retaliation cases. Age Discrimination in Employment Act of 1967, §§ 2 et seq., 15, 15(a), as amended, 29 U.S.C.A. §§ 621 et seq., 633a, 633a(a); Civil Rights Act of 1964, § 701 et seq., 42 U.S.C.A. § 2000e et seq.—Lujan v. Walters, 813 F.2d 1051.

District court's conclusion following full trial that employee failed to prove retaliation for filing age discrimination charge was adequate without addressing each step of three-step analysis for employment discrimination cases. Age Discrimination in Employment Act of 1967, §§ 2 et seq., 15, 15(a), as amended, 29 U.S.C.A. §§ 621 et seq., 633a, 633a(a); Civil Rights Act of 1964, § 701 et seq., 42 U.S.C.A. § 2000e et seq.—Id.

N.M. 1987. Employee must prove claim of retaliatory discharge by clear and convincing evidence.—Silva v. Albuquerque Assembly & Distribution Freeport Warehouse Corp., 738 P.2d 513, 106 N.M. 19.

⚷41(1). Measure in general.

N.M. 1990. When awarding damages to employee for breach of employment agreement, jury properly computed damages based on assumption that employee would have remained employed until her retirement 14 years later at age 65, where employer's policy was to provide continuing gainful employment for all qualified regular employees, and employment agreement qualified stipulation that employment could be terminated at any time. —McGinnis v. Honeywell, Inc., 791 P.2d 452, 110 N.M. 1.

N.M. 1987. Employee who established that employer breached employment contract by terminating employee could not recover damages for tort of retaliatory discharge.—Silva v. Albuquerque Assembly & Distribution Freeport Warehouse Corp., 738 P.2d 513, 106 N.M. 19.

N.M. 1985. Wrongfully discharged employee is generally entitled to damages in amount equal to amount due during remainder of term of wrongfully terminated contract, offset by any income which the employee has earned, or could earn, through the exercise of reasonable diligence, during the remainder of the contract period.—Board of Educ. of Alamogordo Public School Dist. No. 1 v. Jennings, 701 P.2d 361, 102 N.M. 762.

N.M.App. 1983. Without attempting to identify every conceivable element, damages in judicially created tort action based on employee's discharge which contravenes some clear mandate of public policy might include lost wages while unemployed, cost and inconvenience of searching for new job, moving costs for relocating, and possible punitive damages; discharged employee must mitigate his or her damages by securing other employment if not reinstated by defendant.—Vigil v. Arzola, 699 P.2d 613, 102 N.M. 682, reversed in part 687 P.2d 1038, 101 N.M. 687.

Actual pecuniary losses are more compatible with objectives of judicially created tort action based on employee's discharge which contravenes some clear mandate of public policy, and recovery of damages will be limited in order to prevent any chilling effect on employer's freedom in hiring; thus, emotional distress, traumatic neurosis, mental suffering, and similar damages of nonpecuniary nature will not be allowed.—Id.

N.M.App. 1975. Where contract for permanent employment provided that employees were subject to discharge only for cause but furnished no further consideration other than employment and payment of wages, award of one month's net wages for wrongful discharge of employees was not inadequate.—Garza v. United Child Care, Inc., 536 P.2d 1086, 88 N.M. 30.

⚷41(2). Elements of damage.

N.M. 1993. If employee proves retaliatory discharge claim by preponderance of evidence, he is entitled to recover damages for his pecuniary loss

(b) Using Digests

Using West's digest system entails several steps:

(1) selecting an appropriate digest and collecting the most current updates for that digest,
(2) identifying a pertinent topic (or topics) and key numbers, and
(3) perusing the headnotes.

The first step is selection of the appropriate digest. There is a rough correlation between West's reporters and its digests, as indicated in Exhibit 6.2 on pages 144-145. The two primary federal digests are (1) the *United States Supreme Court Digest* for the *Supreme Court Reporter* and (2) *Federal Practice Digest* covering the *Supreme Court Reporter,* the *Federal Reporter,* and the *Federal Supplement.* (There also are separate digests for the Fifth and Eleventh Circuits.) West publishes digests for the following regional reporters: Atlantic, North Western, Pacific, and South Eastern. West also publishes digests for all states except Delaware, Nevada, and Utah; some cover two states (such as Virginia and West Virginia). The state digests cover state court decisions published in the regional reporters as well as federal cases arising in or appealed from that state.

As is true of West reporters, many digests consist of more than one bound series, with the second or later series containing more recent information than the first; some later series incorporate the information from the prior series. Furthermore, the most recent bound digest typically is updated by a pocket part inserted into the back of the bound volume and by pamphlets that generally are shelved at the end of a set of digest volumes. Finally, for the most recent information in paper, you should consult the hardbound volumes and advance sheets for the pertinent reporter that have been published since the most recent digest material; each includes digest material for the cases it contains. In other words, if you were to work backward in time, on the premise that recent case law is most useful, you would consult:

- digest material in reporter advance sheets and recent hardbound volumes,
- digest pamphlets,
- digest pocket part,
- digest bound volumes (newest to oldest series).

West has compiled the information in its various federal, state, and regional digests into master—and hence voluminous—digests. These volumes are labeled *Century Digest, Decennial Digests,* or *General Digests* depending on the number of years covered. You are most likely to use recent *Decennial Digests,* which cover ten years (sometimes in two parts), or *General Digests,* which update the *Decennial Digests* and eventually are superseded by them. You generally would use these master digests only when you already have explored a narrower digest and have found nothing on point or need, for some other reason, to locate persuasive precedent.

If you were researching the Canoga case, seeking case law in New Mexico on a state law question, you would use the *New Mexico Digest* or *Pacific Digest*. In the former, you would locate not only state cases in the *Pacific Reporter*, but also pertinent federal cases. As of late summer 1995, to research in the state digest, which is still in its first series, you would consult a hard-bound volume, published in 1965; the 1995 annual pocket part, which includes Illustration 6-3; a July 1995 pamphlet, covering cases published through late April of 1995; and the digest materials in the reporter volumes and advance sheets that cover cases published from May to date.

Once you have selected your digest, the second step is to identify a pertinent topic (or topics) and pertinent key numbers. One method is to scan the list of topics near the front of digest volumes. Another method is to look up your research terms in the Descriptive Word Index, a separate volume or volumes accompanying your chosen digest, updated by pocket parts or pamphlets. The index may direct you not only to a useful topic, but also to potentially useful key numbers. You should look up various research terms and explore the cross-references thoroughly. A third method is to follow the lead of a case you may have located through your research in secondary sources; once you locate the case within a West reporter, you can identify a pertinent topic and key number by reading the headnotes at the outset of the case. An alternative to the third method is to look up your case in the Table of Cases volume for your digest; that table lists the topics and key numbers to which the case has been assigned.

After using any one of these methods to locate a useful topic, you should scan the general and detailed outlines at the outset of your topic within the digest volume. Doing so should enable you to locate a range of potentially pertinent subtopics or key numbers. Because some subtopics overlap, there rarely is only one useful subtopic.

In the Canoga case, a scan of the topic list would indicate that Master and Servant is a potentially useful topic. As an example of the Descriptive Word Index, if you looked up "employment" in the 1948 main volume of the *New Mexico Digest*, you would obtain a cross-reference to "master and servant" under "contracts of employment." That very long listing in turn would direct you to "Discharge of Servant," shown in Illustration 6-4 on page 150. In the 1995 pocket part to the Descriptive Word Index, you would find comparable information under the more modern term "labor and employment." Based on a scan of the detailed outline of the Master and Servant topic, a portion of which appears as Illustration 6-5 on page 151, you likely would pursue key numbers between 19 and 47, as they pertain to termination. The *Lukoski* case appears under key number 40(3); the *Ellis* case appears under key number 36.

The third step is to peruse the headnotes appearing under a pertinent key number. In a state digest, federal court cases appear before state cases. Decisions of the highest court appear before decisions of lower courts. Cases by the same court appear in reverse chronological order. You would use the descriptions in the headnotes to identify potentially pertinent cases.

The process just described enables you to locate potentially pertinent cases. It is not a substitute for reading the cases themselves. The headnote

Illustration 6-4 Descriptive Word Index, *New Mexico Digest.*

1 N Mex D—443 **DESCRIPTIVE-WORD INDEX** **Disclosure**

References are to Digest Topics and Key Numbers

DISCHARGE FROM INDEBTEDNESS, OBLIGATION OR LIABILITY (Cont'd)

SURETIES (Cont'd)
- Payment (Cont'd)
  - Estoppel or waiver as to unauthorized payment to principal. **Princ & S 129(5)**
  - Extension of time for. **Princ & S 103–108**
  - Unauthorized payment to principal. **Princ & S 117**
- Penalty, alteration as to. **Princ & S 101(4)**
- Performance—
  - Alteration as to time and place. **Princ & S 101(5)**
  - Extension of time for. **Princ & S 103–108**
- Promise by surety after release from liability. **Princ & S 130**
- Receiver's bonds. **Receivers 213**
- Release of—
  - Cosurety. **Princ & S 116**
  - Other securities. **Princ & S 115**
- Rescission of contract of principal. **Princ & S 119**
- Reservation by creditor of rights against surety in transaction with principal. **Princ & S 127**
- Satisfaction—
  - By—
    - Principal. **Princ & S 111–113**
    - Surety. **Princ & S 131**
  - Discharge of principal without satisfaction. **Princ & S 118**
- Securities, release of discharging surety. **Princ & S 115**
- Service of notice by surety to proceed against principal. **Princ & S 126(4)**
- Specifications for building, change in. **Princ & S 100(3)**
- Subsequent release or agreements. **Princ & S 89**
- Taking additional or new obligation as extension of time. **Princ & S 105(3)**
- Taking additional or substituted surety. **Princ & S 109**
- Time of—
  - Notice by surety to proceed against principal. **Princ & S 126(2)**
  - Performance, alteration of instrument. **Princ & S 101(5)**
- Trustees' bonds. **Trusts 382**
- Unauthorized payment to principal. **Princ & S 117**
- Waiver. **Princ & S 129**

TENDER as discharging liability, see this index **Tender**
TRUSTEE administering corporation being reorganized in bankruptcy. **Bankr 668**
WAR risk insurance, discharge of liability. **Army & N 76**
WILLS, CONDITIONS. **Wills 664**

DISCHARGE FROM MILITARY OR NAVAL SERVICE

ENLISTED MEN. **Army & N 22**
OFFICERS. **Army & N 11**
PREFERENTIAL APPOINTMENT, see this index **Officers**

DISCHARGE OF SERVANT

ACTS constituting discharge. **Mast & S 31**
BREACH of contract as ground. **Mast & S 30(2)**
COMMENCEMENT of suit for wrongful discharge before expiration of term. **Mast & S 41(3)**
COMPENSATION as affected by. **Mast & S 73(5, 7)**
CONDITIONS precedent to action for. **Mast & S 36**
CONDONATION of grounds for. **Mast & S 30(7)**
DAMAGES. **Mast & S 41, 42**

DISCHARGE OF SERVANT (Cont'd)

EVIDENCE in action for wrongful discharge. **Mast & S 40, 41(6)**
EXEMPLARY DAMAGES. **Mast & S 41(5)**
FEAR of discharge inducing compliance with commands or threats involving risks. **Mast & S 245(6)**
GROUNDS—
- For discharge. **Mast & S 30**
- Of action for discharge. **Mast & S 36**

INCOMPETENCY as ground of discharge. **Mast & S 30(3)**
INJUNCTION, United States courts. **Courts 262.7(14)**
INJURIES to servant by malicious procurement of discharge. **Mast & S 341**
INSUBORDINATION as ground for discharge. **Mast & S 30(5)**
INTEMPERANCE as ground for discharge. **Mast & S 30(6)**
LIMITATIONS of actions. **Mast & S 38**
MALICIOUS procurement of discharge. **Mast & S 341**
MISCONDUCT as ground for discharge. **Mast & S 30(4)**
NEGLECT of duty as ground of discharge. **Mast & S 30(3)**
NOMINAL or substantial damages for wrongful discharge. **Mast & S 41(4)**
OPERATION and effect of discharge of servant. **Mast & S 33½**
PLEADING in action for wrongful discharge. **Mast & S 39**
REDUCTION of damages for wrongful discharge, effect of other employment. **Mast & S 42**
RE-EMPLOYMENT, see this index **Re-employment**
REFUSAL to serve as ground for discharge of servant. **Mast & S 30(2)**
STATEMENT of cause for discharge. **Mast & S 32**
SUPERINTENDENT of asylum. **Asylums 7**
UNEMPLOYMENT COMPENSATION, ground for. **Mast & S 78.3(36)**
UNION ACTIVITIES. **Mast & S 15(14)**
- Evidence. **Mast & S 15(47–49, 58)**

WAIVER of right to discharge servant. **Mast & S 30(7)**

DISCIPLINE

JUDGES. **Judges 11**
MILITIA. **Militia 14**
PUPILS—
- Private schools and academies. **Schools 8**
- Public schools. **Schools 169**

SEAMEN. **Seamen 30**

DISCLAIMER

CONTEMPT, disclaimer of intention to commit. **Contempt 58(4)**
COSTS as affected by. **Costs 47**
EJECTMENT. **Eject 71**
EQUITY. **Equity 192**
ESTOPPEL on ground of. **Estop 71**
EXEMPTIONS. **Exemp 103**
GARNISHMENT PROCEEDINGS. **Garn 208**
PARTY, effect on competency as witness. **Witn 139(6)**
PATENTS, see this index **Patents**
PLEADING, setting aside fraudulent transfers. **Fraud Conv 266(3)**
QUIETING TITLE. **Quiet T 38**
TENANCY. **Land & Ten 16**
TITLE to property—
- **Exemp 103**
- **Quiet T 38**

TRESPASS TO TRY TITLE. **Tresp to T T 34, 47(2)**
TRUSTS—
- Limitations as affected by. **Lim of Act 103**

WRIT of entry. **Entry Writ of 17**

DISCLOSURE

AGENCY, signature of memorandum within statute of frauds. **Frds St of 116(9)**

Illustration 6-5

Topic Outline, *New Mexico Digest.*

MASTER & SERVANT

4B N Mex D—10

I. THE RELATION.

A. Creation and Existence.

⚷1. Nature and existence of relation in general.
2. Contracts of employment.
3. —— Express contracts.
(1). Requisites and validity.
(2). Construction and operation.

C. Termination and Discharge.

⚷19. Expiration of term.
20. Indefinite term.
21. Termination under provisions of contract.
22. Termination by mutual agreement.
23. Change in business of master.
24. Insolvency of master.
25. Disability of master.
26. Death of master.
27. Disability of servant.
28. Death of servant.
29. Abandonment of employment by servant.
30. Grounds for discharge.
(1). In general.
(2). Breach of contract or refusal to serve.
(3). Incompetency or neglect of duty.
(4). Misconduct.
(5). Disobedience and insubordination.
(6). Intoxication or intemperance.
(7). Waiver, condonation, and effect of reparation.
31. Acts constituting discharge.
33½. Operation and effect of discharge.
34. Actions for wrongful discharge.
35. —— Nature and form.
36. —— Grounds and conditions precedent.

4B N Mex D—11

MASTER & SERVANT

I. THE RELATION—Continued.

C. Termination and Discharge—Continued.

⚷37. —— Defenses.
38. —— Time to sue and limitations.
39. —— Pleading.
(1). In general.
(2). Issues, proof, and variance.
40. —— Evidence.
(1). Presumptions and burden of proof.
(2). Admissibility.
(3). Weight and sufficiency.
41. —— Damages in general.
(1). Measure in general.
(2). Elements of damage.
(3). Commencement of suit before expiration of term.
(4). Nominal or substantial damages.
(5). Exemplary damages.
(6). Evidence as to damages.
42. —— Other employment as ground for reduction of damages.
(1). In general.
(2). Nature of work and efforts to secure employment.
(3). Working for former employer or for himself.
43. —— Questions for jury.
44. —— Instructions.
45. —— Appeal and error.
46. —— Costs.
47. Re-employment after discharge.

may not reflect nuances of the case that are important to your client's situation, and, on rare occasions, the headnote may be in error. Headnotes are not law and may not be cited or quoted; you must cite to and quote the case itself.

As noted above, there are non-West case reporters. These reporters, such as *United States Supreme Court Reports, Lawyers' Edition,* also employ digest systems that may be similar to the West system.

b. Updating and Expanding Case Law through *Shepard's Citations*

After you have read a case and determined that it is pertinent, you must update it by tracking its subsequent history and treatment through use of a citator. A citator is a research tool that lists later sources that have cited earlier sources. A later source is a "citing source"; the earlier source (the one you have located and plan to rely on) is the "cited source." Illustration 6-6 below and on page 153 shows two sample pages from *Shepard's Citations.*

Shepard's Citations, published by Shepard's/McGraw-Hill, Inc., are the

Illustration 6-6 *Shepard's Pacific Reporter Citations* (1994 & Supp. 1995).

PACIFIC REPORTER, 2d SERIES Vol. 748

—483—
Barnes v Eighth Judicial District Court 1987
(103Nev679)
801P2d[1]1387
810P2d[8]1211

—488—
M & R Investment Company Inc. v Mandarino 1987
(103Nev711)
781P2d766
849P2d[4]315
853P2d106

—494—
Blanton v North Las Vegas

—507—
Lukoski v Sandia Indian Management Co. 1988
(106NM664)
766P2d[2]284
f 773P2d[2]1233
775P2d[2]247
777P2d[2]374
Cir. 10
856F2d[2]1476
j 856F2d1478
Wash
826P2d671

—511—
Graff v Glennen 1988
(106NM668)
853P2d723
Cir. 10
857F2d731
935F2d1171

—520—
Cunningham v Oklahoma 1987
755P2d[1]94
762P2d[1]957
764P2d[5]904
781P2d[5]330
813P2d531

—523—
Wood v Oklahoma 1987
792P2d[1]80
813P2d[1]531

—526—
Thompson v Oklahoma 1988
761P2d[5]862
f 786P2d[1]1253
805P2d688
827P2d1342

—538—
Oklahoma v Ebenhack 1985
787P2d[4]478
q 853P2d795

—542—
In the Matter of Ballot Title of Robert J. Wright's Initiative Petition 1988
(304Ore649)
752P2d[6]1218
767P2d[1]71
774P2d[1]1096
774P2d[2]1096
777P2d[6]409
781P2d[2]345
783P2d[6]1003
785P2d[7]1049
787P2d[1]487
787P2d[6]487

s 704P2d537
s 715P2d93
80A4937n

—555—
Oregon v Larsen 1988
(89OrA260)

—558—
Utah v Egbert 1987
f 746P2d[1]762
747P2d[2]1034
j 748P2d569
f 749P2d628
754P2d57
f 754P2d[2]58
j 754P2d60
754P2d667
f 758P2d[2]904
j 759P2d1157
f 760P2d[2]301
f 765P2d[2]1270
e 770P2d[2]996

—579—
Stewart v Coffman 1988
s 765P2d1277
763P2d[2]1213
767P2d[1]139
771P2d684
790P2d589
793P2d394
f 852P2d[1]1037

—582—
Wilburn v Interstate Electric 1988
s 765P2d1277
750P2d1229
751P2d257
751P2d261
755P2d[2]753
757P2d482
758P2d[2]929
763P2d816
765P2d9

Illustration 6-6 *(continued)*

PACIFIC REPORTER, 2d SERIES **Vol. 748**

d 861P2d[2]1310
Cir. 10
859FS512

—1347—

Cir. 9
41F3d[9]446

—1356—

862P2d[2]416
878P2d[1]242

—1380—

856P2d1388
863P2d1042
874P2d[3]735
877P2d546

—1386—

d 877P2d1066

Vol. 748

—10—

862P2d1232
862P2d1269
872P2d851
23ALR5308n

—24—

d 878P2d435
878P2d436
j 878P2d440
880P2d457
Utah
868P2d[5]1389

—176—

864P2d[1]1358

—178—

864P2d[2]1358

—181—

856P2d659
860P2d[1]957
861P2d439
861P2d[1]440
863P2d41
863P2d[1]58
e 869P2d[1]935
873P2d1132
875P2d587
Ala
623So2d397

—188—

871P2d[9]530

—194—

860P2d[1]1007

—307—

Case 2

j 882P2d347
24CaR2d523
27CaR2d30
27CaR2d381
33CaR2d630
j 34CaR2d689

—341—

873P2d[1]766
880P2d[4]764

—349—

Case 2

862P2d935

—365—

861P2d741
e 881P2d519
881P2d[1]520
883P2d[4]667
883P2d[8]691

—372—

861P2d[3]19
Calif
c 35CaR2d329

—381—

—473—

877P2d1012

—477—

856P2d[7]209

—488—

866P2d[2]283
867P2d[7]1130
881P2d644

—494—

a 57USLW4314

—507—

857P2d780
d 857P2d784
874P2d[1]1273
Calif
e 23CaR2d815

—512—

871P2d1345

—516—

874P2d[1]798

—523—

876P2d[1-]277

—597—

857P2d1088
d 857P2d[5]1089
884P2d925

—621—

875P2d709

—673—

860P2d1036
884P2d617

—686—

856P2d[7]715
Minn
512NW875

—695—

877P2d246

—704—

861P2d1097
866P2d738
Cir. 10
853FS389

—718—

f 856P2d444
870P2d1056

—826—

Nev
881P2d6

—833—

o 872P2d241
872P2d[2]245

—839—

Cir. 10
32F3d[7]1443

—851—

Cir. 10
859FS1406
So C
440SE370

—856—

Idaho
876P2d[2]146

—870—

879P2d[3]644

—875—

865P2d[1]221
f 872P2d[1]250
f 872P2d[2]250
874P2d[2]1182

most commonly used legal citators. *Shepard's* case citators serve four primary functions:

(1) They provide parallel citations to your cited case.
(2) They trace its history.
(3) They help you determine the treatment of the case by leading you to other cases that have cited it.
(4) They provide references to commentary sources that discuss the case.

Using *Shepard's* entails several steps. You must assemble the appropriate *Shepard's* titles and volumes, read the citation lists carefully, and update your results.

(1) Selecting the Appropriate Titles and Volumes

First, you must pick the appropriate *Shepard's* title or titles. Shepard's/McGraw-Hill publishes state, regional, and federal citators. If your research involves a state court case, you may use a state or regional citator, or both, to Shepardize it.

Shepard's/McGraw-Hill publishes a citator for each state, the District of Columbia, and Puerto Rico. As you would expect, one division of these state citators allows you to Shepardize a case by its official reporter citation, if it has one. As you might not expect, a second division of a state citator allows you to Shepardize a case by its regional reporter citation.

Both divisions of a state citator list citing cases from that state's courts and from federal courts. The state reporter division lists citing cases by their official reporter citations, while the regional reporter division lists them by their regional reporter citations. The state reporter division lists citations from additional sources, such as opinions of the state's attorney general, state bar publications, selected legal periodicals, and annotations in *American Law Reports.* Citations from those sources appear in the regional reporter division of the state citator if there is no corresponding official state reporter. See Exhibit 6.3 below to see these differences. Because the state reporter division of the citator includes more citing sources but the regional reporter division contains citations from a regional reporter that typically is published more frequently, you may wish to Shepardize your case in both divisions of a state citator.

In addition to publishing state citators, Shepard's/McGraw-Hill also publishes a citator for each of the regional reporters. Regional citators include citing cases from the courts of every state, not just from federal courts and the courts of the state in which the case arose. On the other hand, regional citators include citations from the *ABA Journal,* but they do not include

Exhibit 6.3 Major Citing Sources in Various *Shepard's Citations.*

Citing Sources	Pacific Reporter, Second Series, Citations	New Mexico Citations	
		Regional Division	*State Division*
United States Supreme Court reporters	√	√	√
Federal Reporter	√	√	√
Federal Supplement	√	√	√
Regional reporters	√	New Mexico cases from *Pacific Reporter*	
New Mexico Reports			√
ABA Journal	√		√
Selected law reviews			√
American Law Reports annotations	√		√

citations from other legal periodicals and attorney general opinions, which are found in state citators. Review Exhibit 6.3 on page 154 for a comparison.

A good strategy for Shepardizing state cases is to start with the appropriate *Shepard's* state citator, checking, if applicable, both the state reporter division and the regional reporter division to retrieve all mandatory case law authority from your state and possibly some commentary. Then expand your research to the appropriate *Shepard's* regional citator and search for persuasive authority. You also may wish to use a regional citator if your research has led you to a persuasive case because the regional reporter citator will tell you if that case has been cited by the courts of your state.

If your research involves a United States Supreme Court case, use *Shepard's United States Citations, Case Edition,* to determine the subsequent history and treatment of the case. This *Shepard's* lists citations to your cited case in later federal and state court opinions, plus a few other sources.

Similarly, if you are researching a case reported in the *Federal Reporter* (court of appeals cases) or *Federal Supplement* (district court cases), use the appropriate unit of *Shepard's Federal Citations* to Shepardize your case. *Shepard's Federal Citations* is divided into separate sets of bound volumes for each of these two reporters.

In addition, you also must be sure you have all the volumes needed for your research. To identify those volumes, find the most recent paper supplement for the title. The most recent supplement should generally be no more than a month old. Look at "What Your Library Should Contain" on the cover to determine what constitutes a complete set of *Shepard's* volumes for that title. See Illustration 6-7 on page 156. Select from that set only those volumes that include citations to the reporter volume and series in which your case is printed.

The example case, *Lukoski,* has both an official reporter citation (*New Mexico Reports*) and a regional reporter citation (*Pacific Reporter, Second Series*). See item 1 in Illustration 6-2 on page 132. Thus you may Shepardize it in *Shepard's New Mexico Citations* in either the official reporter division (*New Mexico Reports*) or the regional reporter division (*Pacific Reporter, Second Series*). If you Shepardize *Lukoski* in the official reporter division using its N.M. citation, the citing references from the state's cases will be from *New Mexico Reports*; however, if you Shepardize it in the regional reporter division using its P.2d citation, the citing references will be from the *Pacific Reporter, Second Series.* You also may Shepardize the *Lukoski* case in *Shepard's Pacific Reporter Citations.* The *Shepard's* entries for the *Lukoski* case in Illustration 6-6 on pages 152-153 are from the 1994 main volume of *Shepard's Pacific Reporter Citations* and its March 1995 supplement.

(2) Reading the Citation List

Once you have selected the appropriate *Shepard's* volumes, the initial task is to locate your cited case within those volumes. Turn to the appropriate division or divisions in each of the volumes you have selected; then locate the volume and page number that correspond to your citation. (One common mistake is to turn to the wrong division within a citator—to turn, for example,

Illustration 6-7 Cover Page, *Shepard's Pacific Reporter Citations.*

VOL. 87 MARCH, 1995 NO. 7

Shepard's Pacific Reporter Citations

ANNUAL CUMULATIVE SUPPLEMENT

(USPS 605410)

IMPORTANT NOTICE

Do not destroy the March, 1995 gold paper-covered Annual Cumulative Supplement until it is removed from the "What Your Library Should Contain" list on the front cover of any future supplement.

WHAT YOUR LIBRARY SHOULD CONTAIN

1994 Bound Volume, Vol. 1 (Parts 1-5)*
1994 Bound Volume, Vol. 2 (Parts 1-7)*
**Supplemented with:*
–*March, 1995 Annual Cumulative Supplement Vol. 87 No. 7*

DESTROY ALL OTHER ISSUES

SEE "THIS ISSUE INCLUDES" ON PAGE III

RECYCLE YOUR OUTDATED SUPPLEMENTS

When you receive new supplements and are instructed to destroy the outdated versions, please consider taking these paper products to a local recycling center to help conserve our nation's natural resources. Thank you.

to a first series division when your citation is to a second series case, or vice versa.)

Your next task is to read the citation list for your case carefully. Refer again to Illustration 6-6 on pages 152-153. *Shepard's* case citators first list parallel citations, if any, to your cited case in the official reporter, an unofficial reporter, or *American Law Reports,* as appropriate. Parallel citations are printed when they first become available and are not reprinted in subsequent volumes of *Shepard's.*

Shepard's next indicates the subsequent history of a cited case, if any, as well as published decisions in the case preceding the one you are Shepardizing. You can recognize a history citation because it includes one of *Shepard's* history abbreviations, explained at the beginning of any *Shepard's* volume. Be especially alert for the "r," "m," and "v" abbreviations. An "r" means the case has been reversed on appeal; "m" means it has been modified; and "v" means the decision has been vacated and no longer has precedential value. See Illustration 6-8 on page 158 for a list of history codes.

Next *Shepard's* lists citations to your cited case in later court decisions. The basic format includes the citing case's volume number, its reporter title (in abbreviated format), and the page on which you will find the reference to the cited case. You may clarify the title of any citing source by using the "Abbreviations—Reports" list that appears at the beginning of a *Shepard's* volume.

Shepard's provides three sets of clues as to which citing cases are most important to you. First, the citing sources in a *Shepard's* citator are grouped in a specified order. For example, in the regional citators, the first citations after the history citations are from the courts of the state that decided the cited case. The preliminary material in a hardbound *Shepard's* typically explains the order of citation used in that *Shepard's.*

Second, *Shepard's* alerts you to how some later decisions have treated your case through the use of treatment codes, which appear at the beginning of some citations. See Illustration 6-8 on page 158 for a list of the treatment codes. These codes tell you, for example, if a later case has explicitly overruled your case (noted by an "o"). Since the overruling may or may not relate to the issue you are researching, you must read the citing case to understand its impact on your case. Treatment codes also tell you if a citing case criticizes your case (noted by a "c"), questions it ("q"), explains it ("e"), follows it ("f"), or distinguishes it ("d").

If a citing case does not have a treatment code, it probably refers to the case being Shepardized in a less significant way. While you cannot be certain that this is true, if you want your research to be cost-effective, you typically will check citations without treatment codes only if the citations are mandatory precedents for your problem.

Third, the case you are Shepardizing may involve more than one issue, and you may not need to research all of them. To help you select the citing cases that discuss those points of law you are interested in researching, some *Shepard's* citing cases include references to the headnotes of the cited case. A raised number to the left of a page number corresponds to the headnote

Illustration 6-8

Abbreviations, *Shepard's Pacific Reporter Citations.*

ABBREVIATIONS—ANALYSIS

CASES

History of Case	
a (affirmed)	Same case affirmed on appeal to a higher level court.
cc (connected case)	The case is related to your case in some way in that it involves either the same parties or arises out of the same subject matter. However, it is not the same action on the merits.
D (dismissed)	An action which has been appealed from a lower court to a higher court has been discontinued without further hearing.
De (denied)	Review or rehearing denied.
GP (granted and citable)	Review granted and ordered published.
Gr (granted)	Review or hearing granted.
m (modified)	The lower court's decision is changed in some way, either during a rehearing or by action of a higher court. For example, if a court of appeals affirms a trial court decision in part and reverses it in part, that trial court decision is shown as modified by the court of appeals.
Np (not published)	Reporter of Decisions directed not to publish this opinion.
Op (original opinion)	Citation of original opinion.
r (reversed)	The lower court is reversed on appeal to a higher court.
RE (republished)	Reporter of Decisions directed to publish opinion previously ordered not published.
s (same case)	The case is the identical action to your case, although at a different stage of the proceedings. "Same case" refers to many different situations, including motions and opinions that preceded your case. It is important to read these cases if you need to know exactly what occured.
S (superseded)	A subsequent opinion has been substituted for your case.
v (vacated)	The opinion has been rendered void and is no longer of precedential value.
#	Citing references may be of questionable precedential value as review was granted by California Supreme Court or case was ordered not published.
US cert den	Certiorari has been denied by the U. S. Supreme Court.
US cert dis	Certiorari has been dismissed by the U. S. Supreme Court.
US reh den	Rehearing has been denied by the U. S. Supreme Court.
US reh dis	Rehearing has been dismissed by the U. S. Supreme Court.
US app pndg	Appeal pending before the U.S. Supreme Court
Treatment of Case	
c (criticized)	The court is disagreeing with the soundness of your decision, although the court may not have the jurisdiction or the authority to materially affect its precedential value.
d (distinguished)	The case is different from your case in significant aspects. It involves either a dissimilar fact situation or a different application of the law.
e (explained)	The court is interpreting your case in a significant way.
f (followed)	Your case is being relied upon as controlling or persuasive authority.
h (harmonized)	The cases differ in some way; however, the court finds a way to reconcile the differences.
j (dissenting opinion)	Your case is cited in the dissent of this opinion.
L (limited)	The court restricts the application of your opinion. The court usually finds that the reasoning of your opinion applies only in very specific instances.
o (overruled)	The court has determined that the reasoning in your case is no longer valid, either in part or in its entirety.
p (parallel)	This letter is usually found in older cases where your case was described as "on all fours" or "parallel" to the citing case. Your case is being relied upon as controlling or persuasive authority.
q (questioned)	The soundness of your case is at issue. For example, your decision may have been legislatively overruled, or its reasoning may have been overruled by an opposing line of authority.

number from the cited case and cited reporter that is discussed on that page of the citing case. In other words, if your cited source is reported in the *Pacific Reporter,* the headnote numbers from the case as printed in the *Pacific Reporter* are referred to in the citing sources. If your cited source is reported in *New Mexico Reports,* the headnote numbers from the case as printed in the *New Mexico Reports* are referred to in the citing sources. The headnotes in the two sources are not identical.

The last citations in a citation list are from secondary sources, such as legal periodicals, annotations in *American Law Reports,* and selected legal texts published by Shepard's/McGraw-Hill. In state citators, these citations may be preceded by citations from state attorney general's opinions.

In Illustration 6-6 on page 152, immediately after the case name and date, you will see in parentheses the parallel citation to the case in *New Mexico Reports.* The *Lukoski* case has no reported prior or subsequent history, but it has been cited in other cases. For example, *Lukoski* has been followed and distinguished by the courts of the state, cited in a dissenting opinion by the Tenth Circuit Court of Appeals, explained in a California case, and cited in a Washington case. Many of the citing cases involve the issue that was reflected in headnote two of *Lukoski,* as printed in the *Pacific Reporter, Second Series*— the issue relevant to your research. The citation list for *Lukoski* is relatively short. You could decide immediately not to check the case that deals with the issue reflected by headnote one, nor the citation from the Washington case. You would focus your research on those New Mexico cases dealing with headnote two, beginning with the case that clearly followed *Lukoski.* You also might check to see if the Tenth Circuit decisions involved cases from New Mexico and, if so, how the Tenth Circuit interpreted state law. Finally, because the California case "explained" *Lukoski,* you might choose to check its reasoning to see if the reasoning might be helpful for your case. The *Shepard's* entry in Illustration 6-6 for the *Lukoski* case does not include citations from secondary sources.

(3) Updating Paper *Shepard's*

Because there is a time lag between when a case is decided and when the citations in it are reflected in *Shepard's Citations,* you have not completed Shepardizing until you have updated every citation that is important to your research. *Shepard's* offers for a fee unlimited use of *Shepard's Daily Update,* a subscription service that allows you to update your *Shepard's* research for many jurisdictions by phone, fax, the Internet, and a Shopnet bulletin board. In addition, as discussed in the next section, you may update your *Shepard's* research online on LEXIS or WESTLAW.

(4) Using *Shepard's* Effectively

A *Shepard's* citation list is often very long and can appear overwhelming. It will seem less so if you keep these tips in mind. First, use *Shepard's* early in your research. Doing so may help you avoid spending too much time on a mandatory primary authority that has been reversed or overruled. It may lead you to a better authority than the one with which you began your research. It may also alert you to the number of citing sources available to you and thus help you plan your time.

Second, quickly check the history of any case in which you are interested to be sure it has not been reversed; then work from the newest supplement backward and from the bottom of a citation list to the top. That way you will be finding the newest citing sources first. Often the analysis in those sources will include a discussion of the important earlier sources, so if you fail to get to the earlier sources, you may have covered them anyway.

Third, use the headnote numbers and treatment codes to help you focus your research.

Fourth, adapt your *Shepard's* research to your research needs. If your earlier research in commentary has shown that the point of law you are researching is well settled, you may need to check only a few recent citations. You may not need to pursue cases without treatment or history codes if a current, trustworthy secondary source synthesizes the law well. On the other hand, if you are researching a developing or changing area in which the law differs among jurisdictions, you may need to explore a larger number of cases.

2. Researching Online: WESTLAW as an Example

Online legal research services, WESTLAW and LEXIS, also may be used to research case law. Online research affords several advantages over paper research: Some cases, namely very recent cases and ones deemed not for publication by the deciding court, are available online but not in paper. You can use research terms online that are not used by an indexer of a paper source; the best example is a factual term. The total cumulation of information online can make an online medium easier to use compared to several volumes of a paper source, such as *Shepard's Citations.*

On the other hand, you should not view online research as a perfect option. Some cases, chiefly older ones, are not available online. Because of the nature of the terms involved, some client situations are difficult to search online; the best example is a situation involving very common legal terms.

This section demonstrates several standard uses of online research for both locating and updating cases. The demonstration focuses on WESTLAW, although nearly all of the searches (except the key number search) could be done in similar fashion on LEXIS. It covers use of online services to locate and update case law and focuses on the proper selection of databases and search strategies.

a. Locating Case Law Online

(1) Selecting Databases

The first step in online research is to identify an appropriate database. For most projects involving case law research, you will have a choice of databases, each containing a collection of cases in full text. You can learn about these online databases by consulting the directory screens or a paper directory. In general, you should select the narrowest database containing the cases you wish to research because the cost is likelier to be lower than researching a wider database.

In the Canoga case, a good choice on WESTLAW would be NM-CS, which contains New Mexico Supreme Court cases since 1945 and New Mexico Court of Appeals cases since that court's inception in 1966. In general, West's state databases include cases published in bound West reporters and advance sheets as well as more recent cases and cases that will not be published there; a state database also may include selected trial court opinions. NM-CS-ALL is a broader database that also includes United States Supreme Court and Tenth Circuit cases as well as cases from the federal district court for New Mexico. The searches shown below were conducted in NM-CS.

(2) Writing and Running Searches

The second step is to write your search, edit it as necessary, and run it. You may choose a natural language search or a Boolean search using terms and connectors. You should consider whether you prefer to get all cases meeting the requirements of your search, which a Boolean search yields, or a selected set of probably pertinent cases, which a natural language search yields. Your research terms also should influence this choice. The more certain you are that certain words will appear in a certain pattern in pertinent cases, and the more distinctive these terms are, the more likely a Boolean search will work well. A natural language search is preferable when you are less certain of the terms themselves (the thesaurus can help you to expand your terms) or of their likely proximity to each other. Natural language also is preferable where the terms are very common legal terms. Finally, your choice also may be driven in part by personal preference.

In the Canoga case, natural language and Boolean searches worked out quite similarly. The natural language search [Can an employer fire an employee for smoking off-duty away from work without following the procedures in the employee handbook?] yielded twenty cases (WESTLAW's programmed number), displayed with those deemed most relevant at the beginning. The citation list is shown in Illustration 6-9 on page 162. For example, in the first case, *Hartbarger v. Frank Paxton Co.*, an employee fired for refusing to accept reduced commissions asserted breach of an implied contract derived from his employer's retirement policy, oral promises, and personnel practices. The third case is the *Lukoski* case, and Illustration 6-10 on page 163 shows the first screen you would see if you read that case online. If you explored this citation list further, you would note one case available only online at the time of this search (late August of 1995): *Steiber v. Journal Publishing Co.*, the seventeenth case, a New Mexico Court of Appeals decision dating to late May of 1995. Its first page is reprinted as Illustration 6-11 on page 163. If you used a locate search for [smoking], you would learn that none of the twenty cases contained that concept.

The WESTLAW thesaurus could have been used to develop the terms in the original search further. For example, the thesaurus listed the following

Illustration 6-9 Citation List, Natural Language Search, WESTLAW.

PAGE 1

CITATIONS LIST
Database: NM-CS

Search Result Documents: 20
=>LOCATE Documents: 0 of 20

1. Hartbarger v. Frank Paxton Co., 115 N.M. 665, 857 P.2d 776, 127 Lab.Cas. P 57,664, 8 IER Cases 1114 (N.M., Jun 14, 1993) (NO. 19,913)

2. Sanchez v. The New Mexican, 106 N.M. 76, 738 P.2d 1321, 109 Lab.Cas. P 55,918, 2 IER Cases 1427 (N.M., Jul 15, 1987) (NO. 16,362)

3. Lukoski v. Sandia Indian Management Co., 106 N.M. 664, 748 P.2d 507, 2 IER Cases 1650 (N.M., Jan 07, 1988) (NO. 16,462)

4. Newberry v. Allied Stores, Inc., 108 N.M. 424, 773 P.2d 1231, 4 IER Cases 562 (N.M., May 01, 1989) (NO. 17,712)

5. Kiedrowski v. Citizens Bank, 119 N.M. 572, 893 P.2d 468, 130 Lab.Cas. P 57,930, 10 IER Cases 840 (N.M.App., Feb 02, 1995) (NO. 15,644)

6. Shull v. New Mexico Potash Corp., 111 N.M. 132, 802 P.2d 641, 6 IER Cases 184 (N.M., Dec 04, 1990) (NO. 19,142)

7. Chavez v. Manville Products Corp., 108 N.M. 643, 777 P.2d 371, 58 USLW 2084, 122 Lab.Cas. P 56,927, 4 IER Cases 833 (N.M., Jul 05, 1989) (NO. 17,596)

8. Barber v. Los Alamos Beverage Corp., 65 N.M. 323, 337 P.2d 394 (N.M., Jan 23, 1959) (NO. 6203)

9. Kestenbaum v. Pennzoil Co., 108 N.M. 20, 766 P.2d 280, 4 IER Cases 67 (N.M., Nov 30, 1988) (NO. 16,965)

10. Otero v. New Mexico Employment Sec. Div., 109 N.M. 412, 785 P.2d 1031 (N.M., Jan 22, 1990) (NO. 18,560)

11. McGinnis v. Honeywell, Inc., 110 N.M. 1, 791 P.2d 452, 58 USLW 2707, 117 Lab.Cas. P 56,524, 5 IER Cases 564 (N.M., May 02, 1990) (NO. 18,103)

12. Wheatley v. County of Lincoln, 118 N.M. 745, 887 P.2d 281 (N.M., Nov 07, 1994) (NO. 21,178)

13. Paca v. K-Mart Corp., 108 N.M. 479, 775 P.2d 245, 4 IER Cases 727 (N.M., May 31, 1989) (NO. 17,983)

14. Brown v. Pot Creek Logging & Lumber Co., 73 N.M. 178, 386 P.2d 602 (N.M., Sep 16, 1963) (NO. 7037)

15. Narney v. Daniels, 115 N.M. 41, 846 P.2d 347 (N.M.App., Dec 18, 1992) (NO. 12,127)

16. Fautheree v. Insulation & Specialties, Inc., 67 N.M. 230, 354 P.2d 526 (N.M., Jun 15, 1960) (NO. 6640)

17. Tamar Stieber v. Journal Publishing Co., d/b/a Albuquerque Journal, --- P.2d ----, 1995 WL 490882 (N.M.App., May 31, 1995) (NO. 16,302)

18. Wilson v. Rowan Drilling Co., 55 N.M. 81, 227 P.2d 365 (N.M., Sep 16, 1950) (NO. 5244)

19. Boudar v. E.G. & G., Inc., 106 N.M. 279, 742 P.2d 491, 2 IER Cases 1420 (N.M., Aug 27, 1987) (NO. 16,167)

20. Velkovitz v. Penasco Independent School Dist., 96 N.M. 587, 633 P.2d 695 (N.M.App., May 08, 1980) (NO. 4386)

END OF CITATIONS LIST

Illustration 6-10

Lukoski, WESTLAW.

```
                                                                    PAGE   1

Citation              Rank(R)          Page(P)          Database        Mode
748 P.2d 507          R 3 OF 20        P 1 OF 12        NM-CS           P LOCATE
 2 IER Cases 1650
(Cite as: 106 N.M. 664,   748 P.2d 507)
                     Scott J.L. LUKOSKI, Plaintiff-Appellee,
                                        v.
             SANDIA INDIAN MANAGEMENT COMPANY, Defendant-Appellant.
                                   No. 16462.
                          Supreme Court of New Mexico.
                                  Jan. 7, 1988.
 Former general manager brought action against former employer for wrongful
discharge.  The District Court, Bernalillo County, William W. Deaton, D.J.,
entered judgment in favor of manager.  Employer appealed.  The Supreme Court,
Ransom, J., held that evidence established that employee handbook amended
employment contract and that employer breached contract by failing to comply
with warning and suspension procedures.
 Affirmed.
 Stowers, J., dissented and filed opinion.
                         Copr. (C) West 1995 No claim to orig. U.S. govt. works
```

Illustration 6-11

Steiber v. Journal Publishing Co., No. 16,302, 1995 WL 490882 (N.M. Ct. App. May 31, 1995).

```
                                                                    PAGE   1

Citation              Rank(R)          Page(P)          Database        Mode
--- P.2d ----         R 17 OF 20       P 1 OF 11        NM-CS           P LOCATE
(Cite as: 1995 WL 490882 (N.M.App.))

                      Tamar STEIBER, Plaintiff-Appellant,
                                        v.
     JOURNAL PUBLISHING CO., d/b/a Albuquerque Journal, Defendant-Appellee.
                                  No. 16,302.
                         Court of Appeals of New Mexico.
                                 May 31, 1995.
 Ray Twohig, Ray Twohig, P.C., Albuquerque, NM, for plaintiff-appellant.
 Jim M. Dines, Martin R. Esquivel, Dines, Wilson & Gross, P.C., Albuquerque,
NM, for defendant-appellee.
                                    OPINION

 PICKARD, Judge.
 *1 Plaintiff appeals from an order of the trial court granting Defendant
summary judgment on Plaintiff's claims for breach of implied contracts and for
intentional infliction of emotional distress.  The implied contracts were:  (1)
to promote Plaintiff;  and (2) not to discriminate against her.  Plaintiff
raises four issues in her brief in chief.  Because several of these issues are
closely related, we address them in the following manner.  First, we consider
                         Copr. (C) West 1995 No claim to orig. U.S. govt. works
```

synonyms for "employee handbook": company manual, employee manual, employment handbook, personnel manual, and handbook.

The Boolean search [employ! /p discharg! dismiss! terminat! /p handbook manual] yielded thirty-one cases. (In WESTLAW that search asks for cases with the following three terms in the same paragraph: (1) a word beginning with "employ" and ending with any number of additional letters, (2) a word beginning with "discharg" or "dismiss" or "terminat" and ending with any number of additional letters, (3) and "handbook" or "manual.") That Boolean search also yielded *Hartbarger, Lukoski* (ranked eighteenth), and *Steiber.* On the other hand, if you added in factual aspects to narrow the search, by adding terms such as [smok!] or [musician], you would have obtained no pertinent cases.

While the two search methods just described also can be used with LEXIS, a unique feature of WESTLAW for case law research is the key number search. Because WESTLAW databases contain cases as they are published by West in the National Reporter System, you can search for key numbers. This strategy is useful when you already know a pertinent key number from preliminary research in digests or from a pertinent case. A key number search permits you to do a single search in a cumulative database and to avoid working through various volumes of a paper digest. Furthermore, you may add additional terms to locate cases with both headnotes and words of your choice. However, you will not obtain references to unpublished or very recent cases through a key number search because they lack headnotes and key numbers.

In the Canoga case, a possible key number search is [255k40]: 255 refers to the topic of Master and Servant (the 255th topic on the West topic list), and 40 refers to the subtopic of evidence in actions for wrongful discharge. That search yielded thirteen cases, arrayed from newest to oldest. The citation list appears as Illustration 6-12 on page 165. The *Lukoski* case appears as the eighth case on that list. Because thirteen is not a large number of cases, you probably would not use a locate search to narrow it. In any event, if you added a factual dimension such as smoking or musician, you would obtain no pertinent cases.

Note that the three searches demonstrated here did not yield identical information because they sought slightly different information. For example, cases digested under a different key number than 255k40—or not digested at all—would not appear in the key number search, but they might appear in the natural language search or Boolean search.

A final method of using an online service to locate case law is to employ a find search. If you had a case name but no citation (or a misrecorded citation), or you had a citation but could not locate the reporter volume you needed, you could enter the information you did have and locate the case.

In the Canoga case, the search for a case by name would be run in NM-CS and would entail a field search, that is, a search of a particular segment of a document, here the title block of a case. The search would read [ti(lukoski)]. The search for a case by citation can be run without entering a specific database and would read [fi 748p2d507]. Both would yield the *Lukoski* case.

Illustration 6-12 Citation List, Key Number Search, WESTLAW.

```
                                                              PAGE   1

CITATIONS LIST                          Search Result Documents: 13
Database: NM-CS

    1.  Kiedrowski v. Citizens Bank, 119 N.M. 572, 893 P.2d 468,
        130 Lab.Cas.  P 57,930, 10 IER Cases 840 (N.M.App., Feb 02, 1995)
        (NO. 15,644)

    2.  Hartbarger v. Frank Paxton Co., 115 N.M. 665, 857 P.2d 776,
        127 Lab.Cas.  P 57,664, 8 IER Cases 1114 (N.M., Jun 14, 1993)
        (NO. 19,913)

    3.  Shull v. New Mexico Potash Corp., 111 N.M. 132, 802 P.2d 641,
        6 IER Cases 184 (N.M., Dec 04, 1990) (NO. 19,142)

    4.  McGinnis v. Honeywell, Inc., 110 N.M. 1, 791 P.2d 452, 58 USLW 2707,
        117 Lab.Cas.  P 56,524, 5 IER Cases 564 (N.M., May 02, 1990) (NO. 18,103)

    5.  Chavez v. Manville Products Corp., 108 N.M. 643, 777 P.2d 371,
        58 USLW 2084, 122 Lab.Cas.  P 56,927, 4 IER Cases 833
        (N.M., Jul 05, 1989) (NO. 17,596)

    6.  Newberry v. Allied Stores, Inc., 108 N.M. 424, 773 P.2d 1231,
        4 IER Cases 562 (N.M., May 01, 1989) (NO. 17,712)

    7.  Kestenbaum v. Pennzoil Co., 108 N.M. 20, 766 P.2d 280, 4 IER Cases 67
        (N.M., Nov 30, 1988) (NO. 16,965)

    8.  Lukoski v. Sandia Indian Management Co., 106 N.M. 664, 748 P.2d 507,
        2 IER Cases 1650 (N.M., Jan 07, 1988) (NO. 16,462)

    9.  Boudar v. E.G. & G., Inc., 106 N.M. 279, 742 P.2d 491, 2 IER Cases 1420
        (N.M., Aug 27, 1987) (NO. 16,167)

   10.  Silva v. Albuquerque Assembly & Distribution Freeport Warehouse Corp.,
        106 N.M. 19, 738 P.2d 513, 107 Lab.Cas.  P 55,835, 2 IER Cases 446
        (N.M., May 29, 1987) (NO. 16,323)

   11.  Danzer v. Professional Insurors, Inc., 101 N.M. 178, 679 P.2d 1276
        (N.M., Apr 10, 1984) (NO. 15,033)

   12.  Vigil v. Arzola, 102 N.M. 682, 699 P.2d 613, 2 IER Cases 377
        (N.M.App., Jul 05, 1983) (NO. 5921)

   13.  Clem v. Bowman Lumber Co., 83 N.M. 659, 495 P.2d 1106
        (N.M.App., Mar 24, 1972) (NO. 774)

END OF CITATIONS LIST

                    Copr. (C) West 1995 No claim to orig. U.S. govt. works
```

b. Updating and Expanding Case Law Online

You may update your case law research on WESTLAW or LEXIS by using *Shepard's* online or by using another citator that is unique to the system. Again, this demonstration focuses on WESTLAW.

(1) Searching *Shepard's Citations* Online

To use *Shepard's* on WESTLAW, you merely enter [sh] if you are viewing the case you want to Shepardize; if you are not viewing it, you add its citation. When you enter your search, WESTLAW searches all applicable online *Shepard's* titles and consolidates the citations from each into one document. The online *Shepard's* display generally contains the same information as the corresponding paper versions, but the information appears in a different format. See Illustration 6-13 below.

First, under the heading "Citations to," WESTLAW verifies the citation you entered as your search. WESTLAW then tells you that you may view coverage information for your *Shepard's* search result. That information in-

Illustration 6-13 *Shepard's* Entry, WESTLAW.

```
Shepard's              AUTHORIZED FOR EDUCATIONAL USE ONLY              PAGE    1
                                                    Date of Printing: JAN 15,96

                                  SHEPARD'S
 Citations to: 748 P.2d 507
               Lukoski v Sandia Indian Management Co. 1988

    Coverage:•View coverage information for this result
                                                                      Headnote
   ------Analysis------ -----------------Citation-----------------       No.
       Same Text         ( 106 N.M. 664)
                          766 P.2d 280, 284                               2
   F   Followed           773 P.2d 1231, 1233                             2
                          775 P.2d at 247                                 2
                          777 P.2d 371, 374                               2
                          857 P.2d 776, 780
   D   Distinguished      857 P.2d 776, 784
                          874 P.2d at 1273                                1
                          117 N.M. at 609                                 1

                            Cir. 10
                          856 F.2d 1473, 1476                             2
   J   Dissenting Opin    856 F.2d 1473, 1478

                            Calif
   E   Explained           23 Cal.Rptr.2d 810, 815

                            Wash
                          826 P.2d 664, 671

 Copyright (C) 1996 McGraw-Hill, Inc.; Copyright (C) 1996 West Publishing Co.
```

cludes the titles and volumes of the *Shepard's Citations* from which your search results were derived.

Most of the WESTLAW screen describes the citing documents in three columns, whose names and functions follow:

Analysis: Analysis includes the history or treatment code used by *Shepard's* to explain the relationship between the citing document and the cited case, as well as the meaning of the codes. The column indicates a parallel citation by the phrase "Same Text" and an *American Law Reports* or other annotation by "Anno."

Citation: The citations are the same as those in the paper *Shepard's,* and they appear in the same order, except that citations from various *Shepard's* titles and supplements are integrated. WESTLAW sometimes adds the first page of a citing document before the number of the page on which the citation to the cited case appears.

Headnote No.: This number is the number of the headnote in the cited case that reflects the issue being discussed by the citing case.

You could enter [sh 748p2d507] to Shepardize *Lukoski.* Look at Illustration 6-13 on page 166, the WESTLAW *Shepard's* screen for *Lukoski.*

WESTLAW allows you to limit your *Shepard's* display to only those citations with negative history and treatment codes; this is especially useful when a display has many pages. You also may use a locate command to restrict your *Shepard's* display to a specific history or treatment code, headnote number, publication, or court. For example, [loc 2] limits the display to cases citing headnote 2.

WESTLAW has two updating services for its online *Shepard's.* The first, *Shepard's* PreView, lists the newest citing cases as reported in West's National Reporter System advance sheets. These cases are listed without history or treatment codes or headnote numbers because they are too new to have them. To use *Shepard's* PreView, enter [sp] if you are viewing the case or a citator display for it; add its citation if you are not.

The second updating service, QuickCite, allows you to automatically search case law databases for citations to your case name and citation. This search is important because a citing case reference may be available in a full-text case database four to six weeks before it is available even in *Shepard's Preview.* To use QuickCite, enter [qc] if you are viewing a case or a citator display for it; add its citation if you are not. You may wish to use a date restrictor to focus the search on very recent cases. You will come to a screen like that shown in Illustration 6-14 on page 168, from which you may continue your search.

When this was written, *Shepard's* PreView did not contain any additional

Illustration 6-14 QuickCite Screen, WESTLAW.

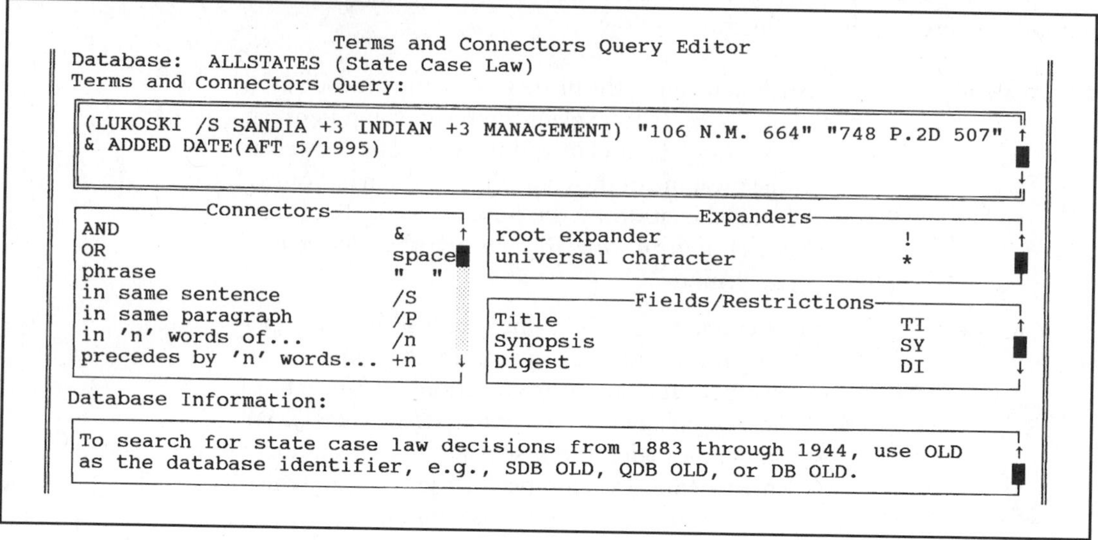

citations to *Lukoski.* A QuickCite search for *Lukoski* did not retrieve any additional citations either.

(2) Updating through Insta-Cite

WESTLAW has its own online citator called Insta-Cite. (The comparable LEXIS citator is Auto-Cite.) Insta-Cite can be used to

(1) verify a case citation;
(2) obtain parallel citations;
(3) determine the history of a case;
(4) determine negative treatment of a case; and
(5) obtain references to secondary sources, such as C.J.S., that cite your case.

To use Insta-Cite, enter [ic] if you are viewing your case or a citator display for it; add its citation if you are not viewing it.

Illustration 6-15 on page 169 is the Insta-Cite display for *Lukoski.* It gives only the case name, citations, court, date of decision, and docket number; it does not convey history, negative treatment, or secondary source cites because there are none.

Although Insta-Cite and online *Shepard's* serve some of the same functions, there are a number of differences between them. First, Insta-Cite is much more up-to-date. Second, Insta-Cite does not list every case that cites a case you are researching, as *Shepard's* does; it lists only cases that are part of the history of the cited case or that treat it negatively. Third, Insta-Cite

Illustration 6-15 Insta-Cite Screen, WESTLAW.

```
  File  Search  Browse  Services  Help            |(Press the Alt Key for Menu)
                                  INSTA-CITE                         Only Page
CITATION: 748 P.2d 507
=>    1  Lukoski v. Sandia Indian Management Co., 106 N.M. 664, 748 P.2d 507,
           2 IER Cases 1650 (N.M., Jan 07, 1988) (NO. 16,462)

      ▸ Shepard's  ▸ Shepard's PreView  ▸ QuickCite  ▸ Commands  ▸ SCOPE
(C) Copyright West Publishing Company 1995
```

does not indicate if a citing case relates to a particular headnote of a cited case, while *Shepard's* does. Fourth, Insta-Cite does not include citations from law reviews. Because Insta-Cite it is more current as well as more limited and focused than *Shepard's*, you may wish to begin your citation research in Insta-Cite. If you learn that your case has been reversed or overruled or that its precedential value has been substantially weakened, then you may avoid some unnecessary research. If not, proceed to *Shepard's* with its complete citation coverage.

c. Comparison to Paper Research

The searches demonstrated in this section reveal the standard advantages and disadvantages of online research to locate cases. The natural language and Boolean searches yielded a yet unpublished case, but no search yielded older (pre-1945) cases. Due to the generality and commonality of the research terms, the results of the online searches were no more precise than the results of paper research, although it was interesting and somewhat informative to learn that there are no cases regarding smoking (or musicians). Online research would be useful if you had fragmented information about a specific case you wished to find. Here, online research to locate cases is not significantly preferable to paper research, and online costs should be assessed carefully. Of course, if you use online research to locate cases, you still should read the published cases in paper.

The online *Shepard's* has several advantages over the print version. First, it allows you to search multiple citators at the same time, and it automatically searches the correct divisions of those citators. Second, it displays information from *Shepard's* main volumes and supplements in a single integrated list. Third, it is easier to read. Fourth, with *Shepard's* online, you can ask the computer to show you only citing documents that meet the criteria you specify; you can, in effect, create customized *Shepard's* lists. Fifth, through the retrieval function the online *Shepard's* provides links between the citations of the citing documents and the full text of those documents, making it fast and easy for you to scan citing documents for relevance. Finally, the online *Shepard's* may be updated conveniently online, using updating services not available in paper. Insta-Cite also provides the advantage of currency and a clear focus on the history and negative treatment of the case.

E. What Else?

Paper Sources of Very New Cases. At both the national and state levels, legal newspapers and newsletters provide copies of very recent cases, typically within a week of issuance by the court. For example, *The United States Law Week* and *United States Supreme Court Bulletin* publish decisions of the United States Supreme Court (as well as information on cases pending before the Court) on a weekly basis. Your state may have a similar source.

If you are aware of a pertinent new decision from a specific court, you may wish to contact the court itself to get the "slip opinion," that is, a copy of the decision the court releases to the parties as well as law publishers.

Specialized Reporters. This chapter focuses on reporters containing cases on a wide range of legal subjects. Specialized reporters contain cases on a single area of law. For example, as you will learn in Chapter 10 on research in procedure, West publishes *Federal Rules Decisions,* a reporter with cases pertaining only to federal civil or criminal procedure.

State Versions of Regional Reporters. You may have available to you a state-specific version of a regional reporter, that is, a volume containing only the cases from one of the states covered by a regional reporter, reprinted as they appear in the regional reporter. The advantage of such a reporter is its smaller size.

Updating of Key Numbers. As the law or legal vocabulary evolves, West occasionally changes key numbers. You often will find a translation table at the end of the outline of the revised topic.

***National Reporter Blue Book* and State Blue Books.** These sources contain tables of parallel citations, permitting you to look up a case by its official citation and locate the unofficial citation, and vice versa. Because parallel citation information also appears in *Shepard's Citators* and online, these sources are not often used.

Specialized *Shepard's*. *Shepard's* publishes a number of topical citators, such as *Shepard's Federal Tax Citations,* which contain case citations for cases on tax law topics. To find law review articles that have cited a federal case, use *Shepard's Federal Law Citations in Selected Law Reviews.* It lists citations to reported federal cases in approximately twenty major law reviews.

Other Media. As of early 1996, the sources discussed in this chapter appeared in the following media:

	Paper	CD-ROM	Computer-Assisted Research		Microform
			LEXIS	WESTLAW	
Digests					
United States Supreme Court Digest	√	***			
Federal Practice Digest	√	***			
Modern Federal Practice Digest	√				
Federal Digest	√				
Fifth and Eleventh Circuit digests	√	***			
Regional reporter digests	√				
State digests	√	√			
Reporters					
United States Reports	√	√	**		√
Supreme Court Reporter	√	√	**	√	√
United States Supreme Court Reports, Lawyers' Edition	√	√	**		√
Federal Reporter	√	√	**	√	√
Federal Supplement	√	√	**	√	√
Atlantic Reporter	√	*	**	√	√
North Eastern Reporter	√	*	**	√	√
North Western Reporter	√	*	**	√	√
Pacific Reporter	√	*	**	√	√
South Eastern Reporter	√	*	**	√	√
South Western Reporter	√	*	**	√	√
Southern Reporter	√	*	**	√	√
California Reporter	√	√	**	√	
Illinois Decisions	√	√	**		
New York Supplement	√	√	**	√	√
Citators					
Shepard's Citations	√	√	√	√	
Other citators	√	√	√	√	
Other Sources					
United States Law Week	√		√	√	
United States' Supreme Court Bulletin	√				
National Reporter Bluebook	√				

*State cases are available on CD-ROM for individual states rather than on a regional reporter basis.
**LEXIS covers federal and state cases, but its coverage is not tied to this reporter.
***As of this writing, West Publishing Co. is preparing a CD-ROM federal digest.

F. How Do You Cite Cases?

A proper citation to a case has three or four components, according to Rule 10 of *The Bluebook:*

1. the case name;
2. its location in one or more reporters;
3. a parenthetical containing information about the court (where needed) and date of decision; and
4. information about the authoritativeness of the case, where needed.

First, the case's name generally is derived by stating the names of the first listed party on each side. Rule 10.2 lists numerous fine points, such as deletion of the given name of an individual and handling of procedural phrases. Rule 10.2 calls for abbreviation of a few common words when the case's citation is woven into a regular sentence; when the citation instead appears in a citation sentence or clause, additional words are abbreviated according to Table T.6. The case's name is underlined or italicized.

Second, according to Rule 10.3 and Table T.1, for many cases, you need to provide only one reporter citation; for others, you will need to provide two, or parallel, citations. United States Supreme Court cases appearing in *United States Reports* are cited to that official reporter; if the case does not yet appear in the official reporter, you should cite to *Supreme Court Reporter, United States Supreme Court Reports, Lawyers' Edition,* or *United States Law Week.* Lower federal court decisions are cited to the applicable *Federal Reporter* or *Federal Supplement.* State cases are cited to the regional reporter. When the state has an official reporter and you are writing to a court of that state, the official reporter citation should precede the unofficial citation. All of these citation forms consist of the volume number, the abbreviation of the reporter and series as listed in Table T.1, and the page number on which the case first appears.

Some cases are not published in the reporters discussed in the preceding paragraph. Some appear in looseleafs, discussed in Chapter 9. Some appear in online databases. According to Rule 10.8, the citation form for online databases consists of the case's docket number and the WESTLAW or LEXIS identifier for the case (in addition to the case name as described above and court and date information described below). In the rare situation that you have a case available in none of these ways, consult Rule 10.8 for citation to slip opinions or Rule 16.4 for citation to a legal newspaper.

Third, according to Rule 10.4, the parenthetical following the reporter information may contain an abbreviation for the court deciding the case, listed in Table T.1. This abbreviation is necessary if the reporter citation itself does not reveal the court's identity. For example, a citation to *United States Reports* clearly identifies the court as the United States Supreme Court. But a citation to the *Federal Reporter* does not fully identify the court because various federal courts of appeals' decisions are published there. Similarly a citation to the *Pacific Reporter* does not identify the court; it may be any of fifteen states' courts. But if you also have provided a parallel citation to an official reporter containing the decisions of only one court, you need not identify the court further.

In any event, according to Rule 10.5, the parenthetical includes the date of decision: only the year for cases published in West and official reporters; month and day as well for cases cited to an online service, looseleaf service, slip opinion, or legal newspaper.

Fourth, in some situations, you must provide information about the authoritativeness of the cited case. According to Rule 10.7, if the case has a subsequent history, it must be cited (unless it is history on remand or denial of rehearing not relevant to the point for which the case is cited); similarly you must indicate any overruling of your case. If you cite a nonmajority opinion, you must so indicate with a parenthetical note, according to Rule 10.6. You also may indicate such matters as an en banc or per curiam decision with a parenthetical.

Here are illustrative citations to the cases featured and discussed in this chapter:

for reader other than New Mexico state court:	*Lukoski v. Sandia Indian Management Co.*, 748 P.2d 507 (N.M. 1988)
in document written to New Mexico state court:	*Lukoski v. Sandia Indian Management Co.*, 106 N.M. 664, 748 P.2d 507 (1988)
abbreviated for citation sentence:	*Lukoski v. Sandia Indian Mgmt. Co.* . . .
case's actual cite:	*Ellis v. El Paso Natural Gas Co.*, 754 F.2d 884 (10th Cir. 1985)
citation if review by U.S. Supreme Court had been sought and denied:	*Ellis v. El Paso Natural Gas Co.*, 754 F.2d 884 (10th Cir. 1985), *cert. denied,* 123 U.S. 456 (1986)
cited to WESTLAW:	*Steiber v. Journal Publishing Co.*, No. 16,302, 1995 WL 490882 (N.M. Ct. App. May 31, 1995)

G. Concluding Points

Because cases are primary authority, your research will not be correct, comprehensive, or credible unless you research the case law on your topic competently. As you research in case law, focus on cases from your jurisdiction (mandatory cases) that are good law. Turn to persuasive precedents only as needed to augment your mandatory authority. To research case law in a cost-effective manner, you must be proficient at both paper and online research.

Paper research in case law entails use of an interlocking system of digests, reporters, and *Shepard's Citations.* Digests provide headnotes of key points from cases organized by topics and then by key numbers. The headnotes include citations to cases, permitting you to locate cases within reporters. Once you have located a pertinent case and read it, you must Shepardize the case to learn whether it has been altered on appeal and how it has been treated in later cases. *Shepard's* also directs you to cases citing your case, that is, cases on the same topic.

An alternative to paper research is online research. To research cases effectively online, you must select a pertinent database and write a search (natural language, Boolean, or key number) to identify pertinent cases within your database. Some legal topics are more easily searched online than others. Case law research can be updated and expanded online through use of such functions as *Shepard's, Shepard's* PreView, QuickCite, and Insta-Cite.

In many situations, you may choose to research case law through a combination of paper and online methods. For example, you often will use online means to update a case located in a reporter through digests. Or you may read in paper form (a reporter) a case you have identified online. (On the other hand, it makes little sense to update in paper cases located online.)

This chapter has demonstrated these methods in the context of the Canoga case. They would lead you to a range of pertinent cases, including the featured case, *Lukoski,* as well as additional New Mexico and federal cases. While this chapter has highlighted *Lukoski,* you would, of course, read additional cases and then synthesize those you deem pertinent. This case law suggests that Ms. Canoga may have a viable contract claim. As Chapter 7 demonstrates, she may have a viable statutory claim as well.

7 Locate, Read, and Update Primary Authority: Statutes and Constitutions

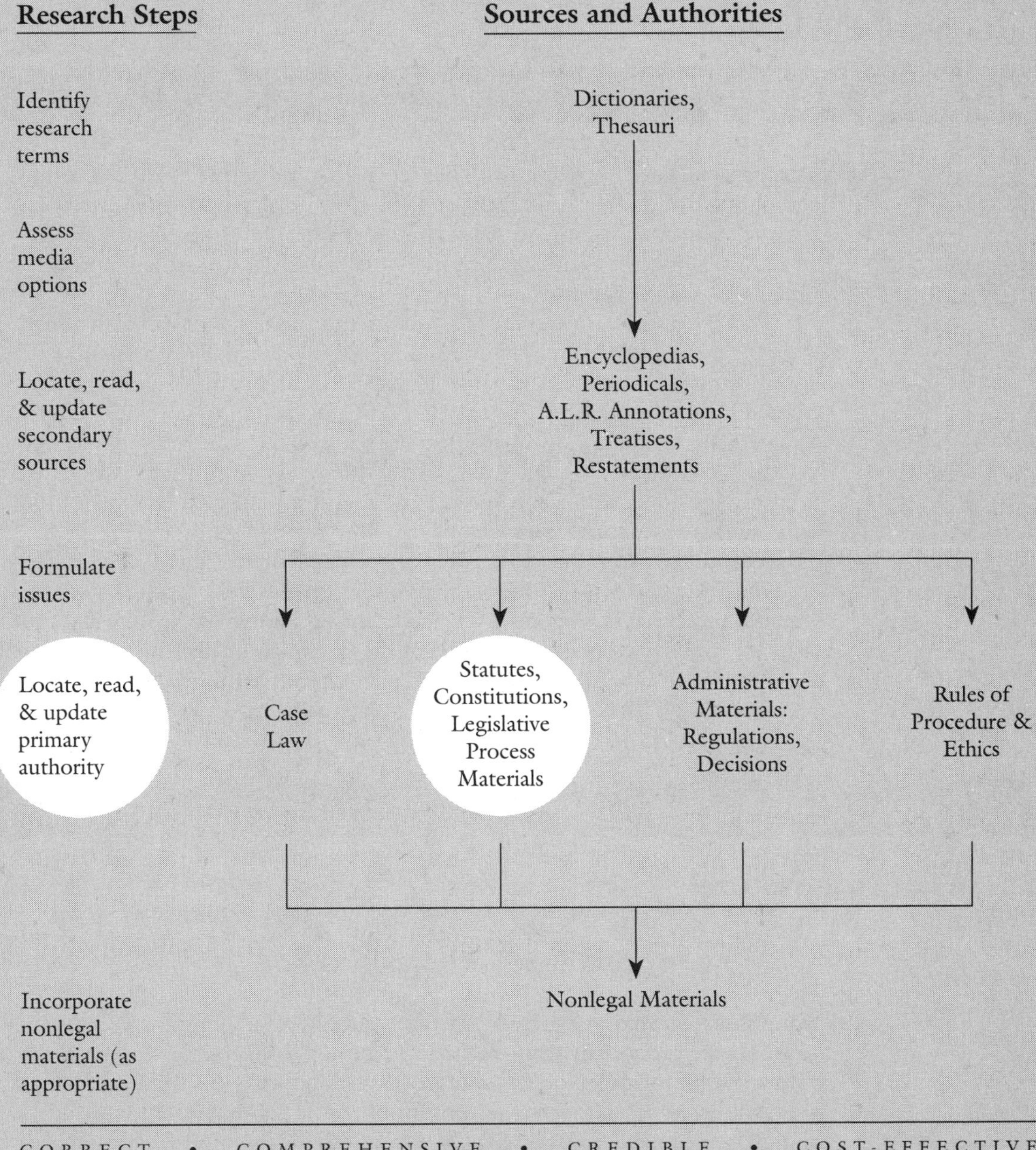

CORRECT • COMPREHENSIVE • CREDIBLE • COST-EFFECTIVE

Summary of Contents

A. Preliminary Points

Thus far, you have learned how to use secondary authority to help you locate and understand primary authority, and you have learned how to research one form of primary authority—case law. In this chapter, you will learn to research an additional body of primary authority—federal and state statutes, constitutions, and related materials.

Part B covers state and federal statutes and the different forms in which they are published, as well as the finding tools associated with statutes. It also illustrates an online alternative to paper research: LEXIS, a computer-assisted legal research (CALR) service. Part C focuses on uniform and model acts, which are drafted outside of the legislature and then later adopted by various legislatures. Part D covers state and federal constitutions. Constitutions are included in this chapter because they are published in some of the same sources as statutes, so many of the same research skills apply.

This chapter continues to illustrate the research of the Canoga case (stated at pages 2-3 in Chapter 1). One of the issues suggested by the secondary source research presented in Chapter 4 is whether the orchestra has the legal right to regulate employees' smoking outside of the workplace. This issue implicates the employee's right to privacy. A second issue pertains to discrimination based on a disability. This chapter focuses on these two issues.

B. Statutes

1. What Is a Statute?

a. How Are Statutes Developed?

Statutes are created in a state legislature or the federal Congress in a highly collaborative process involving legislators, the executive branch, and members of the public (both as lobbyists and as interested individuals). Legislatures are both proactive and reactive institutions. Although interested individuals and groups bring broad current concerns to the legislature, legislation also arises from the legislature's efforts to anticipate or respond to trends and evolving issues. The legislative process is open to all constituencies, so it inevitably is "political" in the sense that a government body is listening to the diverse interests of its constituencies and having to decide how to honor those interests.

Any of these parties generate the ideas in a "bill"—a new piece of proposed legislation. The bill itself must be introduced by a legislator. If it is successful, it typically passes through committee hearings, committee deliberations, full-chamber floor debate, and eventual votes in both houses of the legislature before it is sent to the executive (governor or president) for approval or veto. Of course, the bill may be amended or may perish at any of these steps. A detailed description of the legislative process appears in Chapter 8 on pages 232-237.

A statute may create new law, amend existing law, or repeal an existing law. To locate the correct law, you must discern which version of the law was in effect at the time of your fact situation. Statutes are presumed to be prospective, although they can be retroactive if that effect is clearly stated. The effective date of a statute is any date stated in the statute's effective-date provision or, if none, a default date set by a separate statute governing all legislation. For federal legislation, the default effective date is the date of the President's approval.

b. What Does a Statute Look Like?

Although statutory law on a topic may consist of a single section, many topics are governed by multiple related sections. A statute (or group of related statutes) generally begins with definitions, a statement of the purpose of the statute, and a delineation of the scope of the statute. Next come the operative provisions (the general rule, any exceptions to the rule, consequences of violations, and enforcement provisions). The closing sections often include a provision on how the statute is to be severed if part of it is invalid, as well as a provision on the statute's effective date. Each section and subsection is separately numbered, sometimes with gaps in the numbering sequence to accommodate later additions and to set off separate topics. However, some compact statutes do not contain all of these components. In other statutes, the components may be unlabeled or presented in a different order.

In the Canoga case, Illustration 7-1 on page 178 shows New Mexico's Employee Privacy Act, a six-section statute organized with definitions at the outset, the general rule in section three, and the consequences of section three in the remaining sections.

Illustration 7-2 on pages 179-180 shows portions of the federal Americans with Disabilities Act of 1990, a fifty-section statute broken into one preliminary unit and four topical subchapters (on employment, public services, public accommodations, and miscellaneous topics). Within each subchapter definitions generally come first, operative provisions make up most of the sections, and enforcement is toward the end.

Illustration 7-1

New Mexico Employee Privacy Act, N.M. Stat. Ann. §§ 50-11-1 to -6 (Michie 1993).

ARTICLE 11
Employee Privacy

50-11-1. Short title.

This act [50-11-1 to 50-11-6 NMSA 1978] may be cited as the "Employee Privacy Act".

History: Laws 1991, ch. 244, § 1.

50-11-2. Definitions.

As used in the Employee Privacy Act [50-11-1 to 50-11-6 NMSA 1978]:

A. "employee" means a person that performs a service for wages or other remuneration under a contract of hire, written or oral, express or implied, and includes a person employed by the state or a political subdivision of the state;

B. "employer" means a person that has one or more employees and includes an agent of an employer and the state or a political subdivision of the state; and

C. "person" means an individual, sole proprietorship, partnership, corporation, association or any other legal entity.

History: Laws 1991, ch. 244, § 2.

50-11-3. Employers; unlawful practices.

A. It is unlawful for an employer to:

(1) refuse to hire or to discharge any individual, or otherwise disadvantage any individual, with respect to compensation, terms, conditions or privileges of employment because the individual is a smoker or nonsmoker, provided that the individual complies with applicable laws or policies regulating smoking on the premises of the employer during working hours; or

(2) require as a condition of employment that any employee or applicant for employment abstain from smoking or using tobacco products during nonworking hours, provided the individual complies with applicable laws or policies regulating smoking on the premises of the employer during working hours.

B. The provisions of Subsection A of this section shall not be deemed to protect any activity that:

(1) materially threatens an employer's legitimate conflict of interest policy reasonably designed to protect the employer's trade secrets, proprietary information or other proprietary interests; or

(2) relates to a bona fide occupational requirement and is reasonably and rationally related to the employment activities and responsibilities of a particular employee or a particular group of employees, rather than to all employees of the employer.

History: Laws 1991, ch. 244, § 3.

50-11-4. Remedies.

Any employee claiming to be aggrieved by any unlawful action of an employer pursuant to Section 3 of the Employee Privacy Act [50-11-1 to 50-11-6 NMSA 1978] may bring a civil suit for damages in any district court of competent jurisdiction. The employee may be awarded all wages and benefits due up to and including the date of the judgment.

History: Laws 1991, ch. 244, § 4.

50-11-5. Court fees and costs.

In any civil suit arising from the Employee Privacy Act [50-11-1 to 50-11-6 NMSA 1978], the court shall award the prevailing party court costs and reasonable attorneys' fees.

History: Laws 1991, ch. 244, § 5.

50-11-6. Mitigation of damages.

Nothing in the Employee Privacy Act [50-11-1 to 50-11-6 NMSA 1978] shall be construed to relieve a person from the obligation to mitigate damages.

History: Laws 1991, ch. 244, § 6.

Illustration 7-2

Americans with Disabilities Act of 1990, 42 U.S.C. §§ 12101, 12102 (Supp. V 1993).

(2) After opportunity for public comment and consideration, as appropriate, of such comment, the Secretary shall publish the plan.

(3) In addition to describing the Secretary's intentions for administering this chapter, the plan shall include a comprehensive strategy for assisting the private sector—

(A) in commercializing the renewable energy and energy efficiency technologies developed under this chapter; and

(B) in meeting competition from foreign suppliers of products derived from renewable energy and energy efficiency technologies.

(4) The plan shall address the role of federally-assisted research, development, and demonstration in the achievement of applicable national policy goals of the National Energy Policy Plan required under section 7321 of this title and the plan developed under section 5905 of this title.

(5) In addition, the Plan [1] shall—

(A) contain a detailed assessment of program needs, objectives, and priorities for each of the programs authorized under section 12005 of this title;

(B) use a uniform prioritization methodology to facilitate cost-benefit analyses of proposals in various program areas;

(C) establish milestones for setting forth specific technology transfer activities under each program area;

(D) include annual and five-year cost estimates for individual programs under this chapter; and

(E) identify program areas for which funding levels have been changed from the previous year's Plan.[1]

(6) Within one year after October 24, 1992, the Secretary shall submit a revised management plan under this section to Congress. Thereafter, the Secretary shall submit a management plan every three years at the time of submittal of the President's annual budget submission to the Congress.

(c) Report on options

As part of the first report submitted under subsection (a) of this section, the Secretary shall submit to Congress a report analyzing options available to the Secretary under existing law to assist the private sector with the timely commercialization of wind, photovoltaic, solar thermal, biofuels, hydrogen, solar buildings, ocean, geothermal, low-head hydro, and energy storage renewable energy technologies and energy efficiency technologies through emphasis on development and demonstration assistance to specific technologies in the research, development, and demonstration programs of the Department of Energy that are near commercial application.

(Pub. L. 101-218, § 9, Dec. 11, 1989, 103 Stat. 1868; Pub. L. 102-486, title XII, § 1202(c), (d)(5), title XXIII, § 2303(b), Oct. 24, 1992, 106 Stat. 2959, 2960, 3093.)

[1] So in original. Probably should not be capitalized.

AMENDMENTS

1992—Subsec. (a). Pub. L. 102-486, § 1202(d)(5), substituted "and projects" for ", projects, and joint ventures".

Subsec. (b)(1). Pub. L. 102-486, § 1202(c)(1), inserted "three-year" before "management plan".

Subsec. (b)(4). Pub. L. 102-486, § 2303(b), inserted before period at end "and the plan developed under section 5905 of this title".

Subsec. (b)(5), (6). Pub. L. 102-486, § 1202(c)(2), added pars. (5) and (6) and struck out former par. (5) which read as follows: "The plan shall accompany the President's annual budget submission to the Congress."

SECTION REFERRED TO IN OTHER SECTIONS

This section is referred to in section 12003 of this title.

§ 12007. No antitrust immunity or defenses

Nothing in this chapter shall be deemed to convey to any person, partnership, corporation, or other entity immunity from civil or criminal liability under any antitrust law or to create defenses to actions under any antitrust law. As used in this section, "antitrust laws" means those Acts set forth in section 12 of title 15.

(Pub. L. 101-218, § 10, Dec. 11, 1989, 103 Stat. 1869.)

CHAPTER 126—EQUAL OPPORTUNITY FOR INDIVIDUALS WITH DISABILITIES

Illustration 7-2 *(continued)*

and, despite some improvements, such forms of discrimination against individuals with disabilities continue to be a serious and pervasive social problem;

(3) discrimination against individuals with disabilities persists in such critical areas as employment, housing, public accommodations, education, transportation, communication, recreation, institutionalization, health services, voting, and access to public services;

(4) unlike individuals who have experienced discrimination on the basis of race, color, sex, national origin, religion, or age, individuals who have experienced discrimination on the basis of disability have often had no legal recourse to redress such discrimination;

(5) individuals with disabilities continually encounter various forms of discrimination, including outright intentional exclusion, the discriminatory effects of architectural, transportation, and communication barriers, overprotective rules and policies, failure to make modifications to existing facilities and practices, exclusionary qualification standards and criteria, segregation, and relegation to lesser services, programs, activities, benefits, jobs, or other opportunities;

(6) census data, national polls, and other studies have documented that people with disabilities, as a group, occupy an inferior status in our society, and are severely disadvantaged socially, vocationally, economically, and educationally;

(7) individuals with disabilities are a discrete and insular minority who have been faced with restrictions and limitations, subjected to a history of purposeful unequal treatment, and relegated to a position of political powerlessness in our society, based on characteristics that are beyond the control of such individuals and resulting from stereotypic assumptions not truly indicative of the individual ability of such individuals to participate in, and contribute to, society;

(8) the Nation's proper goals regarding individuals with disabilities are to assure equality of opportunity, full participation, independent living, and economic self-sufficiency for such individuals; and

(9) the continuing existence of unfair and unnecessary discrimination and prejudice denies people with disabilities the opportunity to compete on an equal basis and to pursue those opportunities for which our free society is justifiably famous, and costs the United States billions of dollars in unnecessary expenses resulting from dependency and nonproductivity.

(b) Purpose

It is the purpose of this chapter—

(1) to provide a clear and comprehensive national mandate for the elimination of discrimination against individuals with disabilities;

(2) to provide clear, strong, consistent, enforceable standards addressing discrimination against individuals with disabilities;

(3) to ensure that the Federal Government plays a central role in enforcing the standards established in this chapter on behalf of individuals with disabilities; and

(4) to invoke the sweep of congressional authority, including the power to enforce the fourteenth amendment and to regulate commerce, in order to address the major areas of discrimination faced day-to-day by people with disabilities.

(Pub. L. 101-336, § 2, July 26, 1990, 104 Stat. 328.)

References in Text

This chapter, referred to in subsec. (b), was in the original "this Act", meaning Pub. L. 101-336, July 26, 1990, 104 Stat. 327, which is classified principally to this chapter. For complete classification of this Act to the Code, see Short Title note set out below and Tables.

Short Title

Section 1(a) of Pub. L. 101-336 provided that: "This Act [enacting this chapter and section 225 of Title 47, Telegraphs, Telephones, and Radiotelegraphs, amending section 706 of Title 29, Labor, and sections 152, 221, and 611 of Title 47, and enacting provisions set out as notes under sections 12111, 12131, 12141, 12161, and 12181 of this title] may be cited as the Americans with Disabilities Act of 1990'."

§ 12102. Definitions

As used in this chapter:

(1) Auxiliary aids and services

The term "auxiliary aids and services" includes—

(A) qualified interpreters or other effective methods of making aurally delivered materials available to individuals with hearing impairments;

(B) qualified readers, taped texts, or other effective methods of making visually delivered materials available to individuals with visual impairments;

(C) acquisition or modification of equipment or devices; and

(D) other similar services and actions.

(2) Disability

The term "disability" means, with respect to an individual—

(A) a physical or mental impairment that substantially limits one or more of the major life activities of such individual;

(B) a record of such an impairment; or

(C) being regarded as having such an impairment.

(3) State

The term "State" means each of the several States, the District of Columbia, the Commonwealth of Puerto Rico, Guam, American Samoa, the Virgin Islands, the Trust Territory of the Pacific Islands, and the Commonwealth of the Northern Mariana Islands.

(Pub. L. 101-336, § 3, July 26, 1990, 104 Stat. 329.)

Section Referred to in Other Sections

This section is referred to in sections 12211, 12581, 12594 of this title; title 20 sections 1141, 2471.

c. How Do Statutes Relate to Case Law?

Although cases and statutes are both primary authority, each is analyzed differently because they are developed differently. As discussed in Chapter 6, case law typically develops in a case-by-case fashion, and each case focuses on the situation that occurred before the case was brought. Decisions that evolve from this process serve as binding or persuasive precedent for future disputes involving similar situations. In contrast, statutory analysis focuses on the meaning of legal rules enacted by legislatures, not by judges. Statutes typically apply to situations that will arise in the future, so they usually are drafted to apply generally to broad categories of parties and situations.

Statutes bear various relationships to earlier common law. Some statutes codify, clarify, or supplement case law. Some statutes overturn the common law. Still other statutes create whole new areas of law not covered in case law. Because the constitution grants the legislative branch broad powers to create legal rules to govern society, statutes usually take precedence over case law that conflicts with statutory provisions.

In turn, statutes become the subject of discussion in case law. Under our system of government, the authority to govern is carefully balanced; the legislature enacts laws and courts interpret these laws in light of real cases in controversy. The legislature's exclusive authority to enact statutes is balanced by the court's authority to apply those statutes and other laws, to assess the constitutionality of the statutes, and to make common law rules.

2. Why Would You Research a Particular Statute?

Succinctly stated, you would research a statute because it is "the law." It is mandatory primary authority if it was validly enacted by the legislature in your jurisdiction. Courts in your jurisdiction then are compelled to interpret and apply the statute to the facts falling within its scope.

Often it may be unclear to you initially if a federal statute, a state statute, a local ordinance, or a combination may apply. Under our federal system, federal and state governments each have separate as well as overlapping rights to enact the law within constitutionally prescribed limits. For example, the federal government has authority to govern in areas that preserve its national sovereignty (such as the authority to negotiate international treaties or to coin money) or that have been expressly granted to it by the United States Constitution. State governments have authority to govern matters that are state concerns (or that have been delegated to the states by Congress). Furthermore, as provided by the United States Constitution, states also are empowered to govern in areas not expressly assigned to the federal government (such as providing a state educational system or maintaining a state police force).

The federal system is hierarchical in that federal law sometimes preempts state law on the same topic. In areas of potential federal authority,

Congress can dictate whether its laws pre-empt state laws or co-exist with them. If Congress is silent on whether its law is pre-emptive, then the courts must decide whether the federal law impliedly pre-empts the state law. This decision is based on the strength of the state interest and a determination whether the state law interferes with the overall federal regulatory scheme or the federal statute itself.

If you are uncertain which jurisdiction's statutes to research on a particular topic, begin with research in the federal statutes, followed by the statutes from your state, as well as local ordinances. Thereafter, you may seek out a statute from another jurisdiction when a similar statute from your jurisdiction is unclear or silent and needs interpretation. A statute from another jurisdiction and its interpreting cases may carry persuasive authority in your jurisdiction.

In the Canoga case, you would consult both federal and state statutes. Although there is no federal statute on the privacy topic, there is a pertinent state statute on employer regulation of employee smoking. As to disability discrimination, a federal statute exists and is illustrated here. That statute, the Americans with Disabilities Act, does not forbid overlapping statute statutes, and New Mexico has statutory provisions protecting disabled persons. This chapter does not illustrate the state provisions, however.

3. How Do You Research Statutes?

a. Understanding the Relationships among Statutory Sources

Statutes appear in several forms, some more useful for research purposes than others. This section provides an overview of those forms, while the next two sections show their uses in researching state and federal statutes.

A recently enabled law first appears in a "slip law"—that is, a copy of the individual statute as enacted. The slip law will carry the public law number (for federal statutes) or chapter number (typically used for state statutes) for the new law. These numbers reflect the session of the legislature in which the law was passed, as well as the order of passage during that session.

For example, the Americans with Disabilities Act, pertinent to the Canoga case, is Public Law Number (or Pub. L. No.) 101-336, which means that it was the 336th statute enacted by the 101st Congress. At the state level, New Mexico's Employee Privacy Act, relevant to the Canoga case, was enacted as the 244th chapter of laws from the 1991 New Mexico legislature.

Not long after the legislative session ends, the slip laws for the session are republished, in order of enactment, in one or more volumes. These volumes are called "session laws."

The next step is that the new law is "codified," that is, it is woven into the jurisdiction's "code." A code is a topically organized set of statutes currently in force. Thus if the new law amends an existing statute, the old language is displaced by the new language. If the new law covers new ground, it will be inserted near other laws on the same broad subject. A jurisdiction's code typically contains only public permanent laws, and not private laws (which relate to a very specific situation) or temporary laws (such as appropriations for government agencies).

As you would expect, the law is assigned numbers reflecting its place in the code. The numbering schemes for codes vary considerably. The federal code has fifty titles, which are subdivided into chapters and sections (although the chapter numbers are not necessary to find the section numbers). Some state statutes are similarly divided into titles or chapters and sections, while others use a single set of numbers, typically with decimals or other refinements.

Illustration 7-1 on page 178 shows New Mexico's six-section act on employee privacy that comprises article 11, which is part of title 50. Hence, the first section is numbered as section 50-11-1.

Illustration 7-2 on pages 179–180 shows a portion of the federal Americans with Disabilities Act, a large act, the core of which extends from section 12101 to section 12213 (although not every number is used in that range). The act comprises chapter 126, which is part of title 42. The first section is numbered as 42 U.S.C. § 12101.

Many jurisdictions have two codes. One is an "official code," published by the government; the other is an "unofficial code," published by a private publisher. Both use the same numbering scheme and should contain the same statutory language (subject to differences in updating). The significant difference is that most unofficial codes are annotated, while most official codes are not. An annotated code provides references to cases citing the statute and commentary discussing the statute. The names of codes vary, including "code," "revised statutes," "consolidated laws," "general laws," or "compiled laws."

Although there rarely is conflict among session laws, official codes, and unofficial codes, there is a hierarchy among them. From time to time, Congress will examine specific titles of the *United States Code* and re-enact those titles as "positive law." Once re-enacted, those titles are the law. Titles that have not been re-enacted as positive law are only prima facie evidence of the law, and any conflict between provisions in the code and the original act will be resolved by deferring to the act. In Illustration 7-3 on page 184, you will notice asterisks before some titles of the federal code. These asterisks indicate the titles that have been re-enacted as positive law.

Table T.1 of *The Bluebook* lists the statutory sources in paper media for American jurisdictions.

Your statutory research nearly always will begin in a code. The following discussion begins with how to research in state codes in paper media. It then moves to the more complicated federal codes (also in paper media), including how to use *Shepard's,* slip laws, and session laws. See Exhibit 7.1 on page 185. This section concludes with an example of online research using LEXIS.

Illustration 7-3 Titles List, *United States Code Service.*

TITLES OF UNITED STATES CODE

* 1. General Provisions
2. The Congress
* 3. The President
* 4. Flag and Seal, Seat of Government and the States
* 5. Government Organization and Employees; Appendix
†† 6. [Surety Bonds]
7. Agriculture
8. Aliens and Nationality
* 9. Arbitration
* 10. Armed Forces
* 11. Bankruptcy
12. Banks and Banking
* 13. Census
* 14. Coast Guard
15. Commerce and Trade
16. Conservation
* 17. Copyrights
* 18. Crimes and Criminal Procedure; Appendix
19. Customs Duties
20. Education
21. Food and Drugs
22. Foreign Relations and Intercourse
* 23. Highways
24. Hospitals and Asylums
25. Indians
26. Internal Revenue Code
27. Intoxicating Liquors
* 28. Judiciary and Judicial Procedure; Appendix
29. Labor
30. Mineral Lands and Mining
* 31. Money and Finance
* 32. National Guard
33. Navigation and Navigable Waters
† 34. [Navy]
* 35. Patents
36. Patriotic Societies and Observances
* 37. Pay and Allowances of the Uniformed Services
* 38. Veterans' Benefits
* 39. Postal Service
40. Public Buildings, Property, and Works
41. Public Contracts
42. The Public Health and Welfare [§§ 1395z-1399 are contained in this volume]
43. Public Lands
* 44. Public Printing and Documents
45. Railroads
* * * 46. Shipping; Appendix
47. Telegraphs, Telephones, and Radiotelegraphs
48. Territories and Insular Possessions
* * 49. Transportation; Appendix
50. War and National Defense; Appendix

* This title has been enacted as positive law. However, any Appendix to the title has not been enacted as law
* * Subtitles I, II and IV of this title have been enacted as positive law.
* * * Subtitles II and III of this title have been enacted as positive law.
† This title has been superseded by the enactment of Title 10 as positive law.
†† This title has been superseded by the enactment of Title 31 as positive law.
Titles of the United States Code which have been enacted into positive law are legal evidence of the general and permanent laws, while nonpositive law titles only establish prima facie the laws of the United States (1 USCS § 204(a)). Consult pocket part supplements for any subsequent changes to the list of Titles of the United States Code.

814-244 (1993)

b. Using State Codes in Paper Media

Your state code research usually will involve locating pertinent code material, reading that material, using an advance legislative service, and using a statutory citator.

Exhibit 7.1 Statutory Research in Paper Media.

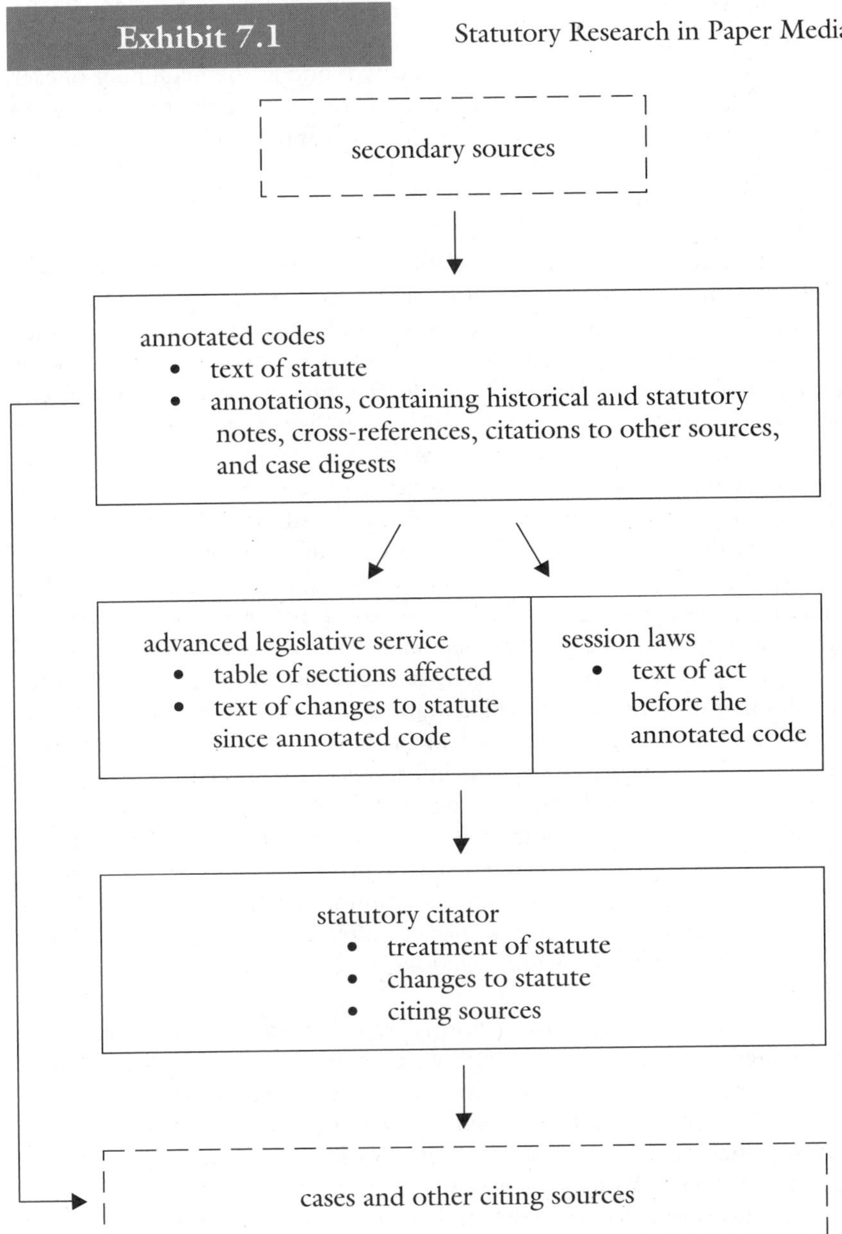

(1) Locating Pertinent Code Material

As with most legal sources, you may use several means to gain access to a state code. First, you may have a citation from a secondary source. Second, all state codes are accessible by the index approach; the index for a code typically is located in the code's opening or closing volumes. A third approach is to locate a pertinent title, article, or chapter by scanning the book spines or a list of titles, articles, or chapters (usually found at the beginning of each volume, if at all). You then scan the table of contents for the title, article, or chapter, looking for pertinent sections. A fourth approach is to use a popular name table, if any, to locate the statute by its popular name, if you have some idea what that might be.

In the Canoga case, to determine if there are state statutes that regulate the rights of employers to restrict smoking by employees when away from the place of employment, you would research in *New Mexico Statutes Annotated*, the annotated (and only) code for New Mexico. Although it is published by a private company (The Michie Company), the code is authorized by the state legislature as the official state code. To gain access to the code, you would first use the General Index, which is published as a separate volume. This index has a subject heading for "smoking-employee privacy act" with references to six code sections beginning at section 50-11-1. These six sections make up the Employee Privacy Act, shown in Illustration 7-1 on page 178.

The hardbound volumes of a code are updated various ways. You may find new statutory language, case annotations, and references to secondary sources in a pocket part filed at the back of the hardbound volume containing your statute; in a supplementary pamphlet, shelved after your hardbound volume (used when there are so many changes the pocket part has become too bulky); or in looseleaf pages filed in the supplement section of the binder containing your statute. These supplements in turn may be updated by pamphlets containing even more recent information for the entire code; these pamphlets typically are filed at the end of the entire code.

Take care to track recent legislative changes as well as new case annotations. The supplementing material may reprint amended sections of the statute and refer you to the hardbound volume for sections not amended. Or it may reprint the law as it was enacted, often by showing the old statute with crossed-out text showing deletions and underscored text showing additions.

In the Canoga case, *New Mexico Statutes Annotated* is a looseleaf code; it is updated by annual supplementary pages filed in the looseleaf volumes behind the tabs labeled "Supplement." More recent supplementation is published in the pamphlets called *Advance Annotation and Rules Service*. None of these supplements contained any changes in statutory text or any new annotations. This lack of legislative and published judicial activity reflects the fact that it takes time for a new law to become known to the public and then become the basis of a published case.

(2) Reading the Pertinent Code Material

If you are working with a multisection act, first read the title, any legislative findings, statement of purpose, or other introductory sections to obtain an overview of the intended effect of the statute. Then read any definitions included in the act so that you understand any particularized meanings of the statutory language. Also read any scope or applicability provision to determine the people, places, or situations regulated by the statute.

Next read all of the operative sections of the statute; these sections include the general rule and also may include any exceptions and the consequences or enforcement provisions. They tell you what conduct the statute requires or prohibits, as well as the remedies and procedures for obtaining compliance with the statute.

As you work on understanding the statute, focus on determining the version in force as of the date of your client's situation. First read the statutory history notes following pertinent sections to learn when the language you will be using was enacted. Then discern the effective date of each of the laws enacting the pertinent language. You may need to consult the session laws for the year of the law in question. If the session law does not include an effective-date provision, check the code for your jurisdiction to determine the default effective date in the jurisdiction. If the version of the statute governing your client's situation is not the one in the current code, you will need to locate and read the applicable version in the session laws.

Pay close attention to every word in a statute. Unlike cases, statutes do not contain dicta. You should assume that each word has a purpose and is potentially significant. If you encounter vague, ambiguous, or conflicting language, you may wish to locate rules of statutory construction. Some jurisdictions have statutory provisions that set forth rules for analyzing statutory language. *See, e.g.,* N.M. Stat. Ann. § 12-2-2 (1993). Other rules and methods of statutory construction can be found in Norman J. Singer, *Statutes and Statutory Construction* (C. Dallas Sands 5th ed., 1992 rev.).

After you have read the statute itself, examine the annotations to each pertinent section of the statute. Scan the case digests to see what topics have been litigated concerning this statute. Determine whether any of those cases and other research sources are ones you need to read.

New Mexico's Employee Privacy Act begins with the short title of the act, proceeds to a definitions section, followed by the general rule, and ends with remedies and damages sections. Section 50-11-3 limits the rights of employers to regulate smoker-employees' behavior when not at the workplace. The legislative history notes tell you that the statute was enacted in 1991 as chapter 244. It became effective ninety days after passage, on June 14, 1991, pursuant to the default-date provision in the New Mexico Constitution.

(3) Using an Advance Legislative Service

An advance legislative service is a series of pamphlets publishing new laws shortly after they are enacted. The text of these laws is set out in the service, typically in order of enactment. You can locate the pertinent new laws in the service by using either a subject index or a table listing new, amended, or repealed code sections.

In the Canoga case, you would search for more recent legislative activity by using the New Mexico *Advance Legislative Service,* an annual pamphlet. The easiest method to determine if any of the recent enactments affected the Employee Privacy Act is to search the Table of Changes in the back of the last volume of the *Service.* This table is organized by section number of the code, and it lists recent enactments contained in the *Service.* As indicated

Illustration 7-4 Table of Changes, *New Mexico Advance Legislative Service.*

2396 Table of Changes

NMSA	Action	Session Law Ch. No.	Session Law Sec. No.	Effective Date	ALS Page
47-8-48	Amended	195	23	7/1/95	1692
47-8-49	Amended	195	24	7/1/95	1693
48-3-5	Amended	195	25	7/1/95	1693
48-3-16	Amended	195	26	7/1/95	1693
48-8-4	Amended	78	1	6/16/95	693
48-8-6	Repealed	78	2	6/16/95	693
51-1-5	Amended	196	1	4/6/95	1695
53-19-3	Amended	213	1	6/16/95	2180
53-19-16	Amended	213	2	6/16/95	2181
53-19-17	Amended	213	3	6/16/95	2183
53-19-39	Amended	213	4	6/16/95	2185
53-19-45	Amended	213	5	6/16/95	2186
53-19-46	Amended	213	6	6/16/95	2188
53-19-59	Repealed and Reenacted	213	7	6/16/95	2190
53-19-60	Repealed and Reenacted	213	8	6/16/95	2191
53-19-61	Repealed and Reenacted	213	9	6/16/95	2193
53-19-62	Repealed and Reenacted	213	10	6/16/95	2195
53-19-62.1	Added	213	11	6/16/95	2197
53-19-62.2	Added	213	12	6/16/95	2199
53-19-62.3	Added	213	13	6/16/95	2201
53-19-63	Amended	213	14	6/16/95	2201
54-1-1	Amended	185	1	6/16/95	1534
54-1-2	Amended	185	2	6/16/95	1534
54-1-6	Amended	185	3	6/16/95	1535
54-1-15	Amended	185	4	6/16/95	1536
54-1-18	Amended	185	5	6/16/95	1537
54-1-34	Amended	185	6	6/16/95	1539
54-1-36	Amended	185	7	6/16/95	1539
54-1-40	Amended	185	8	6/16/95	1540
54-1-44	Added	185	9	6/16/95	1543
54-1-45	Added	185	10	6/16/95	1546
54-1-46	Added	185	11	6/16/95	1546

in Illustration 7-4 above, section 50-11-3 of the Employee Privacy Act has not undergone any amendment, addition, or repeal.

At the state level, session laws did not contain any material pertinent to the Canoga case.

(4) Using a Statutory Citator

Statutory research also can be updated and expanded by using statutory citators. However, at the state level, the citator did not contain any material pertinent to the Canoga case. Accordingly, discussion of statutory citators is deferred to the next section on federal statutory sources in paper media.

c. Using Federal Codes in Paper Media

As was true at the state level, your federal code research will involve locating pertinent code material, reading that material, using an advance legislative service, and using a statutory citator. It also may involve using session laws. See Exhibit 7.1 on page 185.

The federal code appears in three versions. The two unofficial versions are *United States Code Annotated* (U.S.C.A.), published by West Publishing Company, and *United States Code Service* (U.S.C.S.), published by Lawyers Cooperative Publishing. The official version is *United States Code* (U.S.C.), published by the United States government, albeit not promptly. These three versions contain the same statutory sections and use the same organizational scheme.

Yet these codes differ in two major respects. First, both unofficial codes, U.S.C.A. and U.S.C.S., are annotated; they supplement the text of the code with annotations of decisions that have applied or interpreted particular sections of the code, and with historical notes and references to other sources that interpret and analyze the code. The official code, U.S.C., is unannotated; it contains only the text of the code. Second, the unofficial codes are published and updated far more frequently than is the official code. Thus, you probably will use unofficial codes more often for your research.

(1) Locating Pertinent Code Material

Of course, you can easily find a statute in U.S.C.A., U.S.C.S., or U.S.C. if you already know the citation from another source. You also may find a statute by using any of these three research approaches:

(1) the index approach,
(2) the popular name approach, or
(3) the title outline approach.

U.S.C.A. and U.S.C.S. each have a multivolume General Index that is issued annually, so it is fairly current. The General Index covers the sections that existed when the annual index was published. In addition, each of the fifty titles in U.S.C.A. and U.S.C.S. has an individual title index, which usually is located in the last hardbound volume of the title. The title index is not updated and does not cover any material in supplements to those volumes. Hence, the General Index is often more current than the individual title indexes. U.S.C. has a multivolume General Index; unfortunately it is updated infrequently. The annual supplements to U.S.C. each include a noncumulative index.

If you already know the name of the statute you are seeking, a second approach is to use a Popular Names Table. Some, but not all, statutes have official or popular names for easy identification. "The Americans with Disabilities Act" is an example. The last volume of the softbound U.S.C.A. General Index contains a "Popular Name Table." See Illustration 7-5 on page 191. The U.S.C.S. "Tables" volumes include a table of Popular Names; it is supplemented in a softbound cumulative supplement. The U.S.C. tables volume (with the words "Popular Names" printed on its spine) contains a table entitled "Acts Cited by Popular Name," and each of the annual supplements also contains a Popular Name Table.

A third method for finding applicable sections within the federal code is to use the title outline approach. This approach involves moving from a list of titles (in the front of each code volume) to a list of chapters within a title, then to a list of sections within a chapter. In U.S.C.A. and U.S.C.S., the list of chapters for each title appears at the front of each volume for the title or at the beginning of a new title in mid-volume. In U.S.C., the list of chapters within titles follows the list of titles. The list of sections within a chapter is found at the beginning of each chapter. For an example of a list of titles in the federal code, see Illustration 7-3 on page 184. For an example of a list of chapters in U.S.C.S., see Illustration 7-6 on page 192.

The title outline approach seldom works well for a novice legal researcher because he or she does not yet know enough law to find the correct title or chapter. Thus, this research approach initially is less valuable than other approaches.

In the Canoga case, if you knew the popular name of the act but not its citation, the fastest way to find the Americans with Disabilities Act would be to check the popular names table in one of the federal codes. See Illustration 7-5 on page 191. As indicated, this act is found in title 42, beginning at section 12101. Of course, if you did not know the popular name, the General Index also would have led you to that portion of title 42. In U.S.C.A., the index entries "disabled persons and children" and "handicapped persons and children" both provide cross-references to "equal opportunity for individuals with disabilities," the entry for the ADA provisions.

U.S.C.A. and U.S.C.S. are supplemented more frequently and more promptly than U.S.C. is. Exhibit 7.2 on page 193 shows an updating checklist for each of the three federal codes.

To update U.S.C.A., you first would check the annual pocket part or pamphlet supplement. Then you would use the noncumulative "advance" pamphlets, which are issued about six times a year and cover the entire code. Organized by title and code section number, these pamphlets update both the text of the statute (if any changes have been made) and the annotations. At the end of each pamphlet is an update to the popular names table, a table showing where each new statute will be codified in U.S.C.A., and an index for the material in the pamphlet. At the end of the year, the final pamphlets are organized by public law number and contain those laws passed too late in the session to include in earlier pamphlets.

Illustration 7-5

Popular Name Table, General Index, *United States Code Annotated.*

POPULAR NAME TABLE

American-Mexican Treaty Act of 1950—Continued
Aug. 17, 1977, Pub. L. 95–105, Title V, § 514(c), 91 Stat. 862 (22 § 277d–3)
Oct. 28, 1991, Pub.L. 102–138, Title I, Part E, § 165, 105 Stat. 676 (22 § 277d–3)

American National Red Cross Acts
June 6, 1900, ch. 784, 31 Stat. 277
Jan. 5, 1905, ch. 23, 33 Stat. 599 (36 §§ 1, 1 note 2, 3, 5, 6, 8. See, also, 18 §§ 1, 706, 917)
June 23, 1910, ch. 372, 36 Stat. 604 (36 § 9. See, also, 18 §§ 1, 706, 917)
Dec. 10, 1912, ch. 1, § 1, 37 Stat. 647 (36 § 5)
Feb. 27, 1917, ch. 137, 39 Stat. 946 (36 § 6)
May 29, 1920, ch. 214, § 1, 41 Stat. 659 (36 § 7)
Mar. 3, 1921, ch. 131, § 1, 41 Stat. 1354 (36 § 5)
May 8, 1947, ch. 50, 61 Stat. 80 (36 §§ 1 note, 2, 3, 4a, 5, 9)
July 17, 1953, ch. 222, §§ 4, 5, 67 Stat. 178 (36 §§ 3, 6, 7)

American National Red Cross Headquarters Act
Feb. 7, 1930, ch. 42, §§ 1, 5, 46 Stat. 66 (36 § 13)

American Printing House for the Blind Amendments of 1988
Pub.L. 100–630, Title IV, Nov. 7, 1988, 102 Stat. 3316 (20 §§ 101 notes)

American Samoa Labor Standards Amendments of 1956
Aug. 8, 1956, ch. 1035, 70 Stat. 1118 (29 §§ 206, 213, 216)

American Society of International Law Headquarters Act
Pub. L. 86–208, Aug. 25, 1959, 73 Stat. 431 (36 § 344 note)

American Society of International Law Incorporation Act
Sept. 20, 1950, ch. 958, 64 Stat. 869 (36 §§ 341 to 352)

American Technology Preeminence Act of 1991
Pub.L. 102–245, Feb. 14, 1992, 106 Stat. 7 (15 §§ 271 note, 272, 278d, 278f note, 278g, 278g–1, 278k, 278l note, 278n, 278n note, 1453, 1453 note, 1454, 1536, 3701 notes, 3703, 3704, 3704b, 3704b–1, 3704b–2, 3710, 3710a, 3711a, 3716, 3717, 4603, 4603a, 4632; 42 §§ 6611 note, 6618, 6683)
Pub.L. 102–329, § 3, Aug. 3, 1992, 106 Stat. 848 (15 §§ 1453, 1453 note, 1454)

American Television and Radio Archives Act
Pub.L. 94–553, Title I, § 113, Oct. 19, 1976, 90 Stat. 2601 (2 § 170)

American University Incorporation Amendments Act of 1990
Pub.L. 101–480, Oct. 31, 1990, 104 Stat. 1160

American War Mothers Incorporation Act
Feb. 24, 1925, ch. 308, 43 Stat. 966 (36 §§ 91 to 104)
Sept. 26, 1942, ch. 563, 56 Stat. 758 (36 § 97)
June 26, 1953, ch. 152, 67 Stat. 81 (36 §§ 97, 98)
Apr. 2, 1974, Pub. L. 93–267, 88 Stat. 85 (36 § 97)

Americans with Disabilities Act of 1990
Pub.L. 101–336, July 26, 1990, 104 Stat. 327 (29 § 706; 42 §§ 12101, 12101 note, 12102, 12111, 12111 note, 12112 to 12117, 12131, 12131 note, 12132 to 12134, 12141, 12141 note, 12142 to 12150, 12161, 12161 note, 12162 to 12165, 12181, 12181 note, 12182 to 12189, 12201 to 12213; 47 §§ 152, 221, 225, 611)
Pub.L. 102–166, Title I, § 109(a), (b)(2), Title III, § 315, Nov. 21, 1991, 105 Stat. 1077, 1095 (42 §§ 12111, 12112, 12209)

Amnesty Acts (Removal of Disabilities under Fourteenth Amendment)
May 22, 1872, ch. 193, 17 Stat. 142
June 6, 1898, ch. 389, 30 Stat. 432

Amnesty Proclamations
Dec. 8, 1863, No. 11, 13 Stat. 737
May 29, 1865, No. 37, 13 Stat. 758
Dec. 25, 1868, No. 15, 15 Stat. 711

Amtrak Authorization and Development Act
Pub.L. 102–533, Oct. 27, 1992, 106 Stat. 3515 (45 §§ 431, 501 note, 502, 544, 546, 563, 601, 602, 650, 650b, 650c, 650d, 650e, 838, 856)
Pub.L. 103–429, § 8(17), Oct. 31, 1994, 108 Stat. 4391 (45 §§ 650d, 650e)

Illustration 7-6 List of Chapters, *United States Code Service.*

TABLE OF CONTENTS

TITLE 42—THE PUBLIC HEALTH AND WELFARE

[Sections 1395z—1399 of Chapter 7 are contained in this volume]

Chapter		Beginning Section
1.	The Public Health Service [Repealed or Omitted].	1
1A.	The Public Health Service Supplemental Provisions [Repealed]	71
2.	Sanitation and Quarantine	81
3.	Leprosy [Repealed]	121
3A.	Cancer [Repealed]	137
4.	Viruses, Serums, Toxins, Antitoxins [Repealed]	141
5.	Maternity and Infancy Welfare and Hygiene [Repealed]	161
6.	The Children's Bureau	191
6A.	The Public Health Service	201
7.	Social Security	301
7A.	Temporary Unemployment Compensation Program [Omitted]	1400
8.	Low Income Housing	1401
8A.	Slum Clearance, Urban Renewal, and Farm Housing	1441
8B.	Public Works or Facilities [Omitted]	1491
8C.	Open-Space Land [Omitted or Repealed]	1500
9.	Housing for Persons Engaged in National Defense	1501
10.	Federal Security Agency [Transferred or Omitted]	1601
11.	Compensation for Disability or Death to Persons Employed at Military, Air, and Naval Bases Outside the United States	1651
12.	Compensation for Injury, Death, or Detention of Employees of Contractors With the United States Outside the United States	1701
122.	Native Hawaiian Health Care	11701
123.	Drug Abuse Education and Prevention	11801
124.	Public and Assisted Housing Drug Elimination	11901
125.	Renewable Energy and Energy Efficiency Technology Competitiveness	12001
126.	Equal Opportunity for Individuals With Disabilities	12101
127.	Coordinated Services for Children, Youth, and Families	12301
128.	Hydrogen Research, Development, and Demonstration Program	12401
129.	National and Community Service	12501
130.	National Affordable Housing	12701
131.	Housing Opportunities for Persons with AIDS	12901
132.	Victims of Child Abuse	13001
133.	Pollution Prevention	13101
134.	Energy Policy	13201
135.	Residency and Service Requirements in Federally Assisted Housing	13601

In U.S.C.S., you first would check the annual pocket part or pamphlet supplement. Then you would use the *Cumulative Later Case and Statutory Service* (C.L.C.S.S.), which is published quarterly in softbound pamphlets. Like its U.S.C.A. counterpart, C.L.C.S.S. is organized by title and code

Exhibit 7.2 Updating Federal Codes.

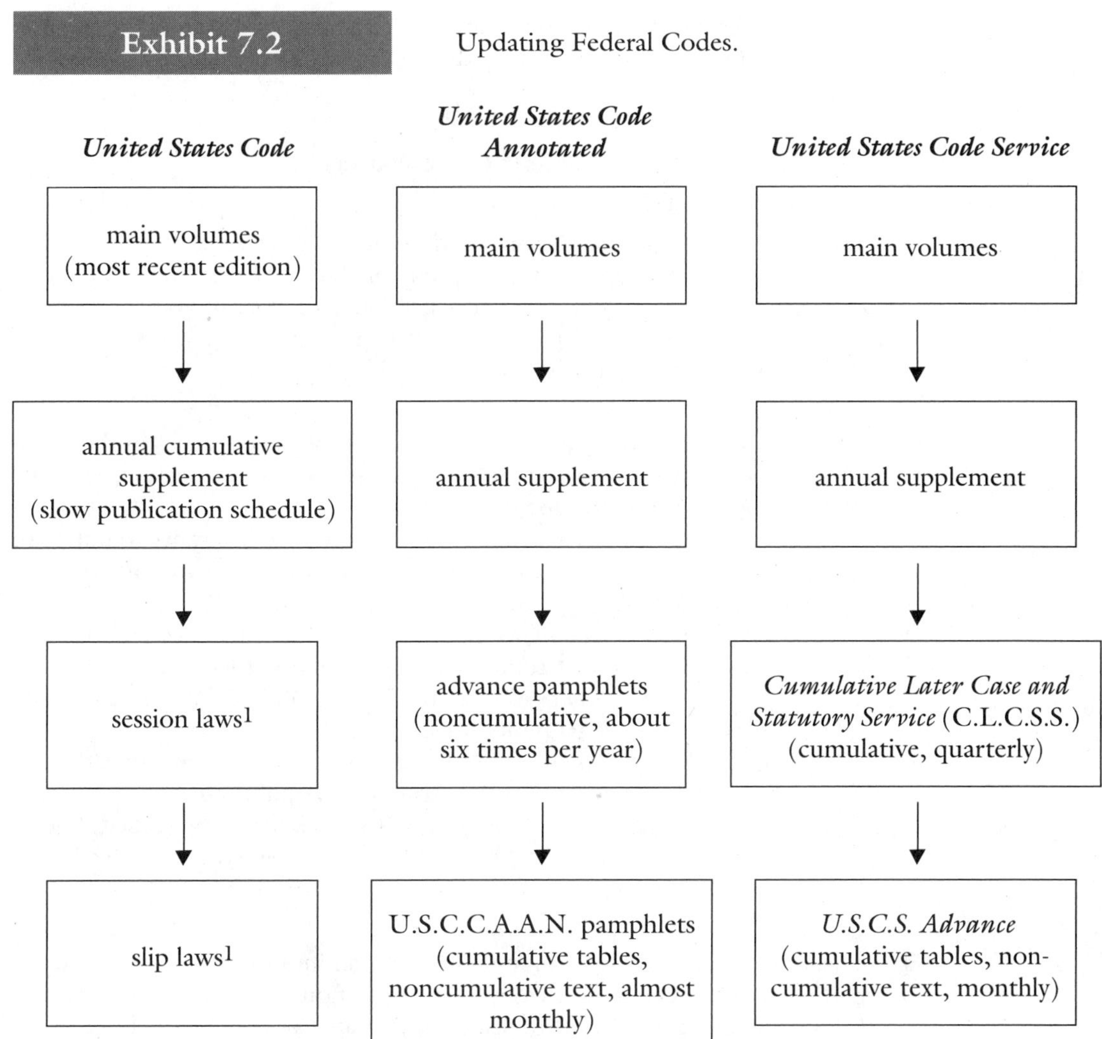

1. Alternatively, use a commercial source to update the cumulative supplement.

section number, updates both statutory text and annotations, contains a table showing where each statute will be codified, and contains updates to the popular name table and index.

A new edition of U.S.C. is published every six years. The edition is supplemented annually by multivolume hardbound cumulative supplements. The first annual supplement is entitled "Supplement I," the second one, "Supplement II," and so on. These designations are on the spine of each volume. Each annual set of supplements includes a cumulative index and tables. Thus to locate statutes enacted since the publication of the main volumes, you must use the index in the most recent cumulative supplement.

These supplements often are issued one or two years after a statute was enacted, so you will need to use other sources, described above, to update your research further.

(2) Reading the Pertinent Code Material

Once you have found a pertinent code section, read it carefully, as outlined at pages 186-187. At the end of a section, note the reference to each version of the law as it passed and to its location in *Statutes at Large* (the compilation of federal session laws, described at pages 202 and 204). If you are using an annotated code, pay particular attention to the annotations, which include the following types of information:

- historical and statutory notes, which explain references in the statutory text, summarize the statutory history of the section, and cite legislative history documents;
- cross-references to related statutes and administrative regulations (and, in U.S.C.S., "reverse cross-references" to statutes that cite that particular section);
- citations to pertinent secondary sources and other research tools:
  U.S.C.A.: West topics and key numbers, encyclopedia (C.J.S.), other West publications, WESTLAW searches, and legal periodicals;
  U.S.C.S.: A.L.R. annotations, encyclopedia (Am. Jur. 2d), and other Lawyers Cooperative publications;
- digests of cases that have addressed that code section (called "Notes of Decisions" in U.S.C.A. and "Interpretative Notes and Decisions" in U.S.C.S.).

The latter feature, the case digests, provides an important bridge between a particular code section and cases. See Illustrations 7-7 (U.S.C.A.) and 7-8 (U.S.C.S.) at pages 195-198. Case digests appear under numbered topic headings; a particular case may appear under several headings if it is applicable to several topics. The topic headings and their corresponding numbers are listed at the beginning of the case digest section.

Although West's goal in U.S.C.A. is to be comprehensive rather than selective in its coverage of relevant cases, U.S.C.A. does not cite every case that discusses a statutory section. On the other hand, U.S.C.S. aims to be selective, excluding annotations to cases its editors judge obsolete, insignificant, or repetitive.

In the Canoga case, you must determine whether an addiction to smoking is a disability protected by the ADA. The definitions section of the act, section 12102, defines the disabilities that the legislature intended to cover, and the subsequent annotations provide some understanding of the courts' interpretation of this provision. By examining the U.S.C.A. and U.S.C.S. annotations in Illustrations 7-7 and 7-8 on pages 195-198, you can determine that the courts have not yet rendered a decision on addiction to smoking. (You

Illustration 7-7 42 U.S.C.A. § 12102 (West 1995).

42 § 12101 OPPORTUNITY FOR THE DISABLED Ch. 126
Note 7

7. Schools and universities

University's blanket policy prohibiting assignment of roommates to students with disabilities who require personal attendant care unnecessarily separated students with disabilities from those without disabilities and, thus, struck at essence of Americans with Disabilities Act (ADA) and specifically violated statute's stated purpose to provide clear and comprehensive national mandate for elimination of discrimination against individuals with disabilities. Coleman v. Zatechka, D.Neb. 1993, 824 F.Supp. 1360.

§ 12102. Definitions

As used in this chapter:

(1) Auxiliary aids and services

The term "auxiliary aids and services" includes—

(A) qualified interpreters or other effective methods of making aurally delivered materials available to individuals with hearing impairments;

(B) qualified readers, taped texts, or other effective methods of making visually delivered materials available to individuals with visual impairments;

(C) acquisition or modification of equipment or devices; and

(D) other similar services and actions.

(2) Disability

The term "disability" means, with respect to an individual—

(A) a physical or mental impairment that substantially limits one or more of the major life activities of such individual;

(B) a record of such an impairment; or

(C) being regarded as having such an impairment.

(3) State

The term "State" means each of the several States, the District of Columbia, the Commonwealth of Puerto Rico, Guam, American Samoa, the Virgin Islands, the Trust Territory of the Pacific Islands, and the Commonwealth of the Northern Mariana Islands.

(Pub.L. 101–336, § 3, July 26, 1990, 104 Stat. 329.)

HISTORICAL AND STATUTORY NOTES

Revision Notes and Legislative Reports

1990 Acts. House Report No. 101–485(Parts I–IV), House Conference Report No. 101–596, and Statement by President, see 1990 U.S. Code Cong. and Adm. News, p. 267.

CROSS REFERENCES

Auxiliary aids and services as defined in this section for purposes of national service trust fund program, see 42 USCA § 12581.

630

Illustration 7-7 *(continued)*

"Disability" as having same meaning as under this section for purposes of higher education resources and student assistance, see 20 USCA § 1141.

"Individual with handicaps" as meaning any individual with any disability as defined in this section for purposes of vocational education, see 20 USCA § 2471.

LIBRARY REFERENCES

American Digest System

Prohibition against discrimination against handicapped persons generally; programs receiving federal assistance, see Civil Rights ⚷107(1 to 4), 126.

Encyclopedias

Prohibition against discrimination against handicapped persons generally; programs receiving federal assistance, see C.J.S. Civil Rights §§ 18, 20, 49 et seq.

Law Reviews

AIDS in the food industry. Rebecca Winterscheidt, 28 Ariz.Atty. 13 (Mar. 1992).

AIDS-related benefits equation: Costs times needs divided by applicable law. Peter D. Blanck, Clifford H. Schoenberg and James P. Tenney, 211 N.Y.L.J. 1 (Feb. 28, 1994).

Americans with Disabilities Act as it relates to AIDS in the workplace. Vimal K. Shah, 6 CBA Rec. 33 (Nov. 1992).

Americans with Disabilities Act "readily achievable" requirement for barrier removal: Proposal for the allocation of responsibility between landlord and tenant. 15 Cardozo L.Rev. 569 (1993).

An employer's guide to the Americans with Disabilities Act: From job qualifications to reasonable accommodations. Lawrence P. Postol and David D. Kadue, 24 J. Marshall L.Rev. 693 (1991).

Medical exams and inquiries under the Disabilities Act. Leo T. Crowley, 211 N.Y.L.J. 3 (June 30, 1994).

Mental disabilities in the workplace. Louis Pechman, 211 N.Y.L.J. 1 (March 2, 1994).

Nonconsensual HIV testing in the health care setting: The case for extending the occupational protections of California proposition 96 to health care workers. 26 Loy.L.A.L.Rev. 1251 (1993).

Reasonable accommodation under the Americans with Disabilities Act: The limitations of Rehabilitation Act precedent. Barbara A. Lee, 14 Berkeley J. of Empl. & Lab.L. 201 (1993).

WESTLAW ELECTRONIC RESEARCH

Civil rights cases: 78k[add key number].

See, also, WESTLAW guide following the Explanation pages of this volume.

NOTES OF DECISIONS

Illustration 7-7 *(continued)*

42 § 12102 **OPPORTUNITY FOR THE DISABLED Ch. 126**

Note 1

1. Auxillary aids and services

Even if Americans with Disabilities Act requires that auxiliary aids and sources for disabled person such as computer-assisted transcripts be made available to litigants, Act did not require admission of alleged statement regarding sexual abuse, made by 16–year-old autistic child through facilitated communication, with aid of facilitator and device such as letter board or typewriter, in neglect proceeding, absent showing that facilitated communication satisfied reliability and validity requirements of *Frye* test. Department of Social Services on Behalf of Jenny S v. Mark S, N.Y.Fam.Ct.1992, 593 N.Y.S.2d 142.

2. Disability—Generally

Employee's esphofical reflux, which was condition which prevented her from becoming pregnant naturally, was "physical or mental impairment," for purposes of determining whether condition was covered under ADA. Pacourek v. Inland Steel Co., Inc., N.D.Ill.1994, 858 F.Supp. 1393.

3. —— Mental impairments

Depression and other mental illnesses can qualify as disabilities for purposes of ADA. Stradley v. Lafourche Communications, Inc., E.D.La.1994, 869 F.Supp. 442.

Mental or nervous disorders are not "impairments," for purposes of Americans with Disabilities Act (ADA), unless they substantially limit one's ability to care for oneself, learn, work, go to school, see, hear, or walk. Clark v. Virginia Bd. of Bar Examiners, E.D.Va.1994, 861 F.Supp. 512.

Patient who was diagnosed with mental illness and was limited in major life activity in that her ability to work was limited by side effects of her medication was "disabled" within meaning of Americans with Disabilities Act (ADA). Dees v. Austin Travis County Mental Health and Mental Retardation, W.D.Tex.1994, 860 F.Supp. 1186.

4. —— Major life activity limited

Work-related injury preventing employee from performing his job as order selector in grocery warehouse was not substantial limitation in major life activity of working, as required for unlawful discharge claim under ADA, absent evidence showing significant restriction in ability to perform class of jobs or broad range of jobs in various classes; even assuming physicians' testimony and other evidence showed severe impairment of long duration, employee's evidence did not address his vocational training, accessible geographical area, or number and type of jobs demanding similar training from which he would also be disqualified. Bolton v. Scrivner, Inc., C.A.10 (Okla.) 1994, 36 F.3d 939, certiorari denied 115 S.Ct. 1104, 130 L.Ed.2d 1071.

Plaintiff who contended that his reduction-in-force layoff constituted disability discrimination did not establish that he was "disabled" within meaning of the ADA; plaintiff failed to produce any evidence that his alleged high blood pressure, unspecified angina, and coronary heart disease "substantially limited" one or more of the ADA's recognized "major life activities"; there were no medical reports substantiating plaintiff's claim as to his medical condition, or any objective affirmative evidence that provided some indication as to exactly how plaintiff was impaired. Aucutt v. Six Flags Over Mid-America, Inc., E.D.Mo.1994, 869 F.Supp. 736.

Former employee's knee injury was not "disability" within meaning of ADA, even assuming that knee injury impaired major life activities; injury was of relatively short duration, preventing employee from working for a few days in each of three months, employee's postinjury physical condition was nearly as good as it was prior to injury, and employee's inability to run briskly and climb stairs easily were not sufficient residual effects to constitute "disability." Blanton v. Winston Printing Co., M.D.N.C.1994, 868 F.Supp. 804.

Attorney, infected with Human Immunodeficiency Virus (HIV), had physical or mental impairment that substantially limited one of his major life activities, and thus had disability within meaning of ADA; attorney suffered from fever, skin disorder, and physiological disorder of hemic and lymphatic systems, and attorney was substantially limited in major life activity of procreation because of significant risk of transmitting HIV infection to partner or child. Doe v. Kohn Nast & Graf, P.C., E.D.Pa.1994, 862 F.Supp. 1310.

632

Illustration 7-8 42 U.S.C.S. § 12102 (Law. Co-op. Supp. 1995).

§ 12102. Definitions

As used in this Act:

(1) Auxiliary aids and services. The term "auxiliary aids and services" includes—

(A) qualified interpreters or other effective methods of making aurally delivered materials available to individuals with hearing impairments;

(B) qualified readers, taped texts, or other effective methods of making visually delivered materials available to individuals with visual impairments;

(C) acquisition or modification of equipment or devices; and

(D) other similar services and actions.

(2) Disability. The term "disability" means, with respect to an individual—

(A) a physical or mental impairment that substantially limits one or more of the major life activities of such individual;

(B) a record of such an impairment; or

(C) being regarded as having such an impairment.

42 USCS § 12102 PUBLIC HEALTH AND WELFARE

(3) State. The term "State" means each of the several States, the District of Columbia, the Commonwealth of Puerto Rico, Guam, American Samoa, the Virgin Islands, the Trust Territory of the Pacific Islands, and the Commonwealth of the Northern Mariana Islands.

(July 26, 1990, P. L. 101-336, § 3, 104 Stat. 329.)

HISTORY; ANCILLARY LAWS AND DIRECTIVES

References in text:

"This Act", referred to in this section, is Act July 26, 1990, P. L. 101-336, 104 Stat. 327, popularly referred to as the Americans with Disabilities Act of 1990, which appears generally as 42 USCS §§ 12101 et seq. For full classification, consult USCS Tables volumes.

RESEARCH GUIDE

Am Jur:

45A Am Jur 2d, Job Discrimination (1993) § 70.

Americans with Disabilities:

1 Am Disab, Programs, Services and Accommodations §§ 1:5, 10, 2:1–3, 7, 9, 14, 15, 23, 24, 3:1, 4, 11–13, 24, 52, 182, 302, 309, 4:1–5, 10, 45, 56, 67, 79.

Law Review Articles:

Teitelbaum, Accessibility of ATMs to handicapped persons. 45 Bus Law 1981.

DuYang, Women with disabilities in the work force: outlook for the 1990's. 13 Harv Women's L J 13.

Feldblum, The Americans With Disabilities Act definition of disability. 7 Lab Law 11 (Winter 1991).

INTERPRETIVE NOTES AND DECISIONS

Court will look to similarity between definition of "disability" in Rehabilitation Act, 29 USCS § 706, and Americans with Disabilities Act, 42 USCS § 12102, to determine that EEOC considers that insulin-dependent diabetic has disability per se under ADA. Chandler v City of Dallas (1993, CA5 Tex) 2 F3d 1385, 2 ADD 952, 2 AD Cas 1326, 62 CCH EPD ¶ 42584, reh, en banc, den (CA5 Tex) 9 F3d 105 and petition for certiorari filed (Jan 31, 1994).

In action alleging discriminatory discharge in violation of ADA (42 USCS §§ 12101 et seq.), trial court correctly applied case law interpreting Rehabilitation Act (29 USCS §§ 701 et seq.) and its implementing regulations to define major life activity for ADA purposes to rule that employee's inability to return to his particular job without some accommodation did not demonstrate substantial limitation in major life activity of working. Bolton v Scrivner, Inc. (1994, CA10 Okla) 36 F3d 939, 6 ADD 911, 65 BNA FEP Cas 1498, 3 AD Cas 1089.

In employment discrimination action against city under ADA (42 USCS §§ 12101 et seq.) brought by police officer who was being treated for depression, complaint's factual allegations that officer is capable of performing duties of full-fledged police officer affirmatively show that conclusory allegation that officer is "disabled" is unfounded. Thompson v City of Arlington (1993, ND Tex) 838 F Supp 1137, 4 ADD 296, 2 AD Cas 1756.

In determining whether individual has disability within meaning of ADA (42 USCS § 12102), it makes no difference whether major life function is affected directly by disability or indirectly by side effects of medication taken for medical or physical condition. Fehr v McLean Packaging Corp. (1994, ED Pa) 6 ADD 217, 3 AD Cas 798.

Although statute, in defining "disability," provides no express guidance as to whether HIV-infected person comes within ambit of Act, examination of regulations which interpret statute indicates that HIV-positive individual should be considered to have disability. Doe v Kohn Nast & Graf, P.C. (1994, ED Pa) 6 ADD 571, 3 AD Cas 879, motion to strike den, complaint dismd, in part (1994, ED Pa) 1994 US Dist LEXIS 13476.

Plaintiff does not qualify as disabled by reason of having record of impairment where record relied on by plaintiff was report detailing plaintiff's previous workers' compensation claims and settlements, but plaintiff presented no evidence that physical losses reflected in report historically limited his major life activities in substantial way. Flasza v TNT Holland Motor Express (1994, ND Ill) 6 ADD 939.

Plaintiff does not qualify as individual with disability as defined in statute by reason of being regarded as having such impairment where plaintiff presented no evidence that ... perceived him as having was

could reasonably be result of many other factors, such as stress, nervousness, cautiousness, and lack of motivation. Pazer v New York State Bd. of Law Examiners (1994, SD NY) 849 F Supp 284, 5 ADD 29, 3 AD Cas 360.

Fact that individual has diabetes and is dependent on insulin does not constitute per se disability under 42 USCS § 12102(2)(A), and EEOC interpretive guide provisions relating to diabetes (29 CFR Part 1630 Appx) will be rejected as contrary to § 12102(2)(A); however, in action by such individual charging food company, to which individual unsuccessfully applied for job, with employment discrimination on basis of disability in violation of ADA, food company's motion for summary judgment will be denied where individual has demonstrated genuine issues of material fact as to whether he (1) had record of impairment for purposes of § 12102(2)(B), given affidavits by individual and his doctor indicating that individual has been hospitalized more than once as result of his disease, and (2) had been regarded as having impairment for purposes of § 12102(2)(C), given conflicting accounts of his interview with company wherein fact that individual has diabetes surfaced in some disputed manner. Coghlan v H.J. Heinz Co. (1994, ND Tex) 851 F Supp 808, 5 ADD 69, 3 AD Cas 273, summary judgment gr, in part, summary judgment den, in part (ND Tex) 851 F Supp 815, 3 AD Cas 422.

Individual diagnosed with learning disability has disability within meaning of ADA (42 USCS § 12102). Pottgen v Missouri State High Sch. Activities Ass'n (1994, ED Mo) 857 F Supp 654, 6 ADD 756, 3 AD Cas 364, revd, remanded (1994, CA8 Mo) 1994 US App LEXIS 32275.

In determining whether plaintiff who suffers from migraine headaches is disabled, only issue is whether this impairment substantially limits one or more of plaintiff's major life activities, and frequency that plaintiff is forced to miss work due to his impairment is not determinative factor in finding that he is thus substantially limited. Dutton v Johnson County Bd. of County Comm'rs (1994, DC Kan) 859 F Supp 498, 6 ADD 151.

Individual with insulin-dependent diabetes has disability as defined by statute since it is undisputed that without medication he would be unable to perform major life activities, would suffer various physical symptoms, and could die. Sarsycki v United Parcel Serv. (1994, WD Okla) 862 F Supp 336, 6 ADD 1126, 3 AD Cas 1039.

Former state trooper who was terminated from employment because of her weight has failed to prove her claim of actual disability or handicap where she offered no evidence that she was substantially limited by her obesity, nor has she shown that her employer regarded her as incapable of performing ...

would, of course, research additional sections of this large statute, including the provisions on workplace smoking rules discussed below.)

(3) Using Advance Legislative Services

Both U.S.C.A. and U.S.C.S. are updated further by advance legislative services.

In U.S.C.A., you can update your research by using the *United States Code Congressional and Administrative News* (U.S.C.C.A.N.) pamphlets published by West. These softbound pamphlets are issued almost monthly, so they may bring you more up-to-date than the supplements to U.S.C.A. The U.S.C.C.A.N. pamphlets contain the text of new laws and amendments to laws, arranged in order of public law number. Table 3 lists, in code section order, U.S.C. titles and sections that have been changed by recently enacted legislation and gives a citation to the corresponding public law that makes the change. It also notes the location of that public law in U.S.C.C.A.N. See Illustration 7-9 on page 200. Because the tables in U.S.C.C.A.N. are cumulative, you need only check the table in the most recent issue. However, the text of each pamphlet is not cumulative, so you may be directed to an earlier U.S.C.C.A.N. pamphlet.

In U.S.C.S., the C.L.C.S.S. is further updated by *U.S.C.S. Advance,* a monthly compilation of the text of slip laws passed after the publication of the last C.L.C.S.S. You most likely will use *U.S.C.S. Advance* in one or both of the following ways: (1) by checking the table of "Code Sections Added, Amended, Repealed, or Otherwise Affected" to see if the statutory section you are researching has been changed recently or (2) by using the subject index. As with U.S.C.C.A.N., although the textual material in *U.S.C.S. Advance* is not cumulative, the tables and index are cumulative. Therefore, you need to consult the tables and index in only the most recent issue of *U.S.C.S. Advance.*

In the Canoga case, Illustration 7-9 on page 200 is from U.S.C.C.A.N. It shows that 42 U.S.C. § 12209 has been amended by Public Law No. 104-1 and that the text of the amendments appears on pages 8, 41, and 16 of U.S.C.C.A.N.

(4) Using a Statutory Citator

Shepard's United States Citations, statute edition, covers federal statutes; *Shepard's* state citators also include statute editions. These statutory citators assist you in performing the following functions in statutory research:

- tracking the amendment of a statute;
- locating citations to other sources that have discussed the statute you are researching; and
- quickly determining, by means of *Shepard's* abbreviations, the impact of some of the citing sources on the cited statute (such as an amendment or repeal).

The cited sources in the statute editions of *Shepard's Citations* include annotated and unannotated codes, session law sections that are not included

Illustration 7-9

Table 3—Amendments and Repeals, *United States Code Congressional and Administrative News.*

TABLE 3—AMENDMENTS AND REPEALS

U.S.Code and U.S.C.A.		1995–104th Cong.		109 Stat. at Large and 1995 Cong. News
Title	**Sec.**	**P.L.104–**	**Sec.**	**Page**
26 (Cont'd)				
	1033(j)	7	3(b)(1)	94
	1033(k)	7	3(b)(1)	94
	1033 nt	7	3(a)(2)	94
			3(b)(2)	95
	1071	7	2(a)	93
	1071 nt	7	2(d)	93
	1245(b)(5)	7	2(b)	93
	1250(d)(5)	7	2(b)	93
29	203(e)(2)(A)(iii)	1	203(d)(1)	10
	203(e)(2)(A)(iv)	1	203(d)(2)	10
	203(e)(2)(A)(v)	1	203(d)(3)	10
	203(e)(2)(A)(vi)	1	203(d)(3)	10
	633a(a)	1	201(c)(2)	8
	2611(4)(A)(ii)	1	202(c)(1)(A)	9
	2611(4)(A)(iii)	1	202(c)(1)(A)	9
	2611(4)(A)(iv)	1	202(c)(1)(A)	9
	2617(f)	1	202(c)(1)(B)	9
31	751 nt	1	504(c)(2)	41
	5302 nt	6	401 to 407	89 to 92
36	115	3	—	47
40	166b–7(e)	1	504(c)(1)	41
42	2000e–16(a)	1	201(c)(1)	8
	12209	1	201(c)(3)	8
			504(a)(2)	41
	12209(6)	1	210(g)	16
43	1606(h)(4)	10	1(a)	155
	1607(c)	10	1(b)	157
44	101 nt	13	1	163
	prec. 3501	13	2	163
	3501	13	2	163
	3501 nt	13	4	185
	3502	13	2	164
	3503	13	2	166
	3504	13	2	167
	3505	13	2	170
	3506	13	2	171
	3507	13	2	176
	3508	13	2	179
	3509	13	2	180
	3510	13	2	180
	3511	13	2	180
	3512	13	2	181
	3513	13	2	181
	3514	13	2	181
	3515	13	2	182
	3516	13	2	182
	3517	13	2	182
	3518	13	2	183
	3519	13	2	183
	3520	13	2	184

[11]

in codes, and local ordinances. Following each cited section are citing sources that may include subsequent legislative enactments, cases, attorney general opinions (for state statutes), legal periodicals, and annotations, including those in *American Law Reports* (A.L.R.).

Shepard's statutory citators are organized by code section numbers and reflect the jurisdiction's numbering scheme. See Illustration 7-10 on page 202. Citations to specific subsections of the statute follow citations to the statute as a whole. *Shepard's* statutory citators provide one- or two-letter abbreviations to indicate the effect of some of the citing sources on the cited statute. These abbreviations are explained in the beginning of each *Shepard's* volume. See Illustration 7-11 on page 203. The analysis abbreviations used in *Shepard's* statutory citators differ from those used in the case editions. Abbreviations to which you should pay particular attention include "A" (amended), "Ad" (added), "R" (repealed), "S" (superseded), "C" (constitutional), "U" (unconstitutional), and "Up" (unconstitutional in part).

As you learned earlier in this chapter, all of *Shepard's* functions also are met by the annotated codes. *Shepard's* may provide more citations than an annotated code, but its treatment abbreviations do not give you as much information as do the case digest paragraphs in the annotated codes. *Shepard's* may also provide more recent citations than those in an annotated code. Thus, you may wish to use both sources.

With regard to the Canoga case, Illustration 7-10 on page 202 shows the *Shepard's* entries for 42 U.S.C. § 12102. This section of the ADA has been cited in a handful of cases from the Tenth Circuit Court of Appeals (which encompasses New Mexico), as well as in many other federal cases. None of the citing case citations are preceded by abbreviations showing any special effect. There are no citations to secondary sources.

(5) Using Session Laws

The new laws initially published in advance legislative services eventually are published in a permanent hardbound form. These publications are called "session laws" and contain all laws enacted by a legislature in a particular session. Session law compilations are important research sources because they

- contain the exact text of the laws as enacted;
- contain all the laws enacted during a particular legislative session, including laws that are not codified;
- make it possible to track changes in a statute from year to year; and
- form a permanent historical record of the law, enabling you to find even those laws that have been repealed.

Although you will use session laws primarily in legislative history research (see Chapter 8), they are valuable in statutory research in two settings: (1) if the statute you are researching is not published in a code or (2) if you need to know which statutory language was in effect as of a particular date. The correct statute to use, if any, is the version effective at the time of the events that gave rise to your legal controversy. Although the code will contain

Illustration 7-10 *Shepard's United States Citations.*

TITLE 42 **UNITED STATES CODE '88 Ed.**

51F3d355
872FS1093
Cir. 4
35F3d131
862FS1491
874FS121
Cir. 5
851FS811
Cir. 6
843FS1166
846FS620
Cir. 7
Dk7 94-1884
44F3d541
835FS488
Cir. 8
815FS1259
824FS1373
Cir. 9
829FS1174
843FS1335
844FS589
Cir. 11
859FS1494
Subd. 2
Cir. 2
51F3d355
Cir. 6
846FS620
Cir. 9
829FS1174
844FS589
Subd. 4
Cir. 2
[illegible]
Cir. 9
844FS579
Cir. 11
859FS1494
§ 12102
et seq.
Cir. 11
868FS315
868FS316
874FS1301
§ 12102
Cir. 2
863FS146
Cir. 5
2F3d1391
Cir. 6
863FS488
Cir. 7
863FS665
Cir. 10
836FS787
Cir. 11
864FS1205
Subsec. 1
Subd. A
Cir. 5
Dk5 94-60499
Subd. B
Cir. 5
Dk5 94-60499

Subsec. 2
Cir. 1
859FS603
Cir. 2
808FS130
819FS293
860FS87
Cir. 3
860FS199
862FS1319
Cir. 4
Dk4 94-1585
824FS577
831FS1306
832FS1028
862FS1474
868FS807
871FS856
Cir. 5
Dk5 94-60499
838FS1152
851FS811
851FS818
869FS443
Cir. 6
843FS1181
846FS617
861FS617
Cir. 8
857FS662
866FS392
869FS744
Cir. 9
844FS585
Cir. 10
Dk10 94-6308
36F3d942
836FS787
859FS504
862FS339
868FS1262
Cir. 11
826FS1371
858FS1579
866FS1381
868FS316
868FS324
Subd. A
125LE281
113SC2651
Cir. 2
813FS220
849FS286
Cir. 5
851FS812
869FS443
Cir. 6
873FS78
Cir. 7
Dk7 94-1884
44F3d541
858FS1404
Cir. 10
36F3d942
Cir. 11
866FS1386

Subd. B
Cir. 5
851FS814
Subd. C
Cir. 5
Dk5 94-60499
851FS814
Cir. 7
Dk7 94-1884
44F3d541
Cir. 11
868FS325
§ 12111
et seq.
Cir. 1
826FS586
Cir. 7
Dk7 93-3839
820FS1060
823FS572
859FS1139
859FS1184
864FS803
§§ 12111
to 12213
Cir. 3
868FS735
§§ 12111
to 12117
Cir. 1
868FS384
Cir. 6
861FS617
Cir. 7
835FS460
857FS607
864FS803
Cir. 9
829FS1171
Cir. 10
Dk10 94-1172
Dk10 94-3069
Cir. 11
847FS905
860FS811
864FS1205
§§ 12111
to 12112
Cir. 7
841FS236
§ 12111
Cir. 1
868FS385
Cir. 7
859FS1140
Cir. 9
839FS711
Cir. 10
[illegible]
Cir. 11
855FS374

Subsec. 1
Cir. 7
Dk7 94-1884
Cir. 8
869FS744
Subsec. 2
Cir. 1
Dk1 93-1954
37F3d16
826FS585
859FS602
Cir. 4
835FS891
868FS806
Cir. 6
861FS617
Cir. 7
818FS1277
852FS678
868FS1008
868FS1010
Cir. 9
787FS933
Cir. 11
845FS1529
847FS905
854FS892
864FS1137
Subsec. 3
Cir. 4
50F3d1265
Cir. 7
Dk7 93-3839
Subsec. 4
Cir. 1
819FS137
Subsec. 5
Cir. DC
871FS41
Cir. 4
831FS1306
835FS891
Cir. 7
818FS1277
835FS462
Cir. 8
866FS395
Subd. A
Cir. 1
Dk1 93-1954
37F3d16
859FS602
Cir. 2
828FS1140
869FS112
Cir. 3
864FS422
Cir. 5
838FS1151
Cir. 6
861FS618
Cir. 7
Dk7 93-3839
823FS577
852FS678
857FS607
864FS803

868FS1008
868FS1010
874FS194
Cir. 9
787FS933
829FS1173
Cir. 10
859FS504
Cir. 11
847FS905
854FS892
855FS373
864FS1137
Subd. B
Cir. 11
845FS1529
¶ 1
Cir. 7
4F3d499
Subsec. 6
Cir. 5
869FS449
Subsec. 7
Cir. 2
813FS221
849FS286
Cir. 5
838FS1151
Cir. 7
818FS1277
Cir. 11
847FS905
864FS1138
Subsec. 8
Cir. 2
863FS146
Cir. 3
860FS199
Cir. 4
Dk4 93-2511
Dk4 94-1840
31F3d213
50F3d282
831FS1306
859FS966
868FS807
869FS418
871FS858
Cir. 5
869FS449
Cir. 7
Dk7 94-1860
Dk7 94-2905
47F3d934
820FS1064
Cir. 8
866FS395
869FS744
Cir. 9
864FS996
864FS998
Cir. 10
Dk10 93-6398
Dk10 94-3069
45F3d360
836FS787
859FS504

862FS340
868FS1262
873FS554
874FS343
Cir. 11
849FS778
855FS374
858FS1580
860FS816
860FS1492
864FS1328
866FS1381
866FS1386
Subsec. 9
Cir. 4
Dk4 94-1840
50F3d282
831FS1306
859FS966
Cir. 7
851FS359
Cir. 9
864FS996
Cir. 10
859FS504
Cir. 11
860FS1492
Subd. B
Cir. 4
847FS368
Cir. 7
Dk7 93-3839
Cir. 8
866FS395
Cir. 11
849FS779
858FS1580
860FS1492
Subsec. 10
Cir. 4
Dk4 94-1840
50F3d283
Cir. 11
858FS1580
860FS816
Subd. A
Cir. 7
Dk7 94-1884
44F3d543
Cir. 10
859FS507
Cir.,11
860FS1491
Subd. B
Cir. 10
859FS507
Cir. 11
860FS1491
¶ 2
Cir. 7
44F3d543
¶ 3
Cir. 7
44F3d543

284 • For further information on this citation, see the cited authority in the Citation Summaries section.

the current statute, the correct statute for your research may be found only in the session laws.

The official compilation of federal session laws is called *United States Statutes at Large (Statutes at Large)*. *Statutes at Large* is ordered by public

Illustration 7-11 Abbreviations—Analysis, *Shepard's United States Citations.*

ABBREVIATIONS—ANALYSIS

Form of Statute

Amend.	Amendment	Proc.	Proclamation
App.	Appendix	Pt.	Part
Art.	Article	Res.	Resolution
Ch.	Chapter	§	Section
Cl.	Clause	St.	Statutes at Large
Ex. Ord.	Executive Order	Subch.	Subchapter
H.C.R.	House Concurrent Resolution	Subcl.	Subclause
		Subd.	Subdivision
No.	Number	Sub ¶	Subparagraph
¶	Paragraph	Subsec.	Subsection
P.L.	Public Law	Vet. Reg.	Veterans' Regulations
Pr.L.	Private Law		

Operation of Statute

Legislative

A	(amended)	Statute amended.
Ad	(added)	New section added.
E	(extended)	Provisions of an existing statute extended in their application to a later statute, or allowance of additional time for performance of duties required by a statute within a limited time.
L	(limited)	Provisions of an existing statute declared not to be extended in their application to a later statute.
R	(repealed)	Abrogation of an existing statute.
Re-en	(re-enacted)	Statute re-enacted.
Rn	(renumbered)	Renumbering of existing sections.
Rp	(repealed in part)	Abrogation of part of an existing statute.
Rs	(repealed and superseded)	Abrogation of an existing statute and substitution of new legislation therefor.
Rv	(revised)	Statute revised.
S	(superseded)	Substitution of new legislation for an existing statute not expressly abrogated.
Sd	(suspended)	Statute suspended.
Sdp	(suspended in part)	Statute suspended in part.
Sg	(supplementing)	New matter added to an existing statute.
Sp	(superseded in part)	Substitution of new legislation for part of an existing statute not expressly abrogated.
Va	(validated)	

Judicial

C	Constitutional.	V	Void or invalid.
U	Unconstitutional.	Va	Valid.
Up	Unconstitutional in part.	Vp	Void or invalid in part.

(Continued)

xviii

law numbers. Every *Statutes at Large* volume contains an index that pertains only to the acts contained in that volume. Thus, to use *Statutes at Large,* you must know the public law number of the legislation that affects a pertinent code section or you must find a pertinent subject entry in an index. Each statutory section in U.S.C., U.S.C.A., and U.S.C.S. is followed by a brief statutory history note that provides the public law number, section number, date of enactment, and *Statutes at Large* citations for the original statute, as well as the citation to every subsequent act that has amended it.

Once you have found the applicable session law and section in *Statutes at Large,* skim the marginal notes. See Illustration 7-12 on page 205. The outside margins of the text of a federal session law typically contain notes that further identify the contents of the law. These notes may include, for example, the popular name of the law, words or phrases that highlight the contents of a particular section, references to U.S.C. sections where the law is codified, and cross-references to help you locate other laws that are referred to by the law you are reading. Near the beginning of a law, you will find the original bill number of the law.

For the Canoga case, the end of each codified section contains a reference to the ADA's public law number, Pub. L. No. 101-336, as shown in Illustrations 7-7 (U.S.C.A) and 7-8 (U.S.C.S.) on pages 195-198 This public law was published in the *Statutes at Large* in volume 104, starting at page 327. See Illustration 7-12 on page 205. The ADA had several effective dates—some sections were effective on enactment, some were effective eighteen months after enactment, and the rest were effective twenty-four months after enactment.

d. Using Online Media: LEXIS as an Example

Just as you can research case law online, so too can you research federal and state statutes online through LEXIS and WESTLAW, using similar techniques. This section demonstrates uses of LEXIS and points out the available databases, the differences between statutory and other databases, and the usefulness of online statutory research as compared to research in paper sources.

Your first task in searching statutes online is to select the appropriate database. You may find the statutory databases on LEXIS by selecting its CODES library. The CODES library has (1) group files for all federal and state codes (ALLCDE) and for all advance legislative services (ALLALS); (2) individual state code files, including one for the New Mexico code (NMCODE); and (3) federal files, including a file for the *United States Code* (USCODE) and a file for federal public laws (PUBLAW).

In searching statutory sources online, keep in mind you may have a choice about the amount of material you search. In addition to searching combined files or single code files, you also may choose to search statutory text only, or you may choose to search text plus annotations.

Your next step is to draft your search. You may search the code using either a natural language (Freestyle) search or a Boolean search. When you enter a Freestyle search, LEXIS gives you additional search options that may assist you in improving your search by further narrowing or expanding it.

Illustration 7-12

Americans with Disabilities Act of 1990, Pub. L. No. 101-336, §§ 1-3, 104 Stat. 327, 328-29 (codified at 42 U.S.C. §§ 12101-12102 (Supp. V 1993)).

PUBLIC LAW 101-336—JULY 26, 1990 104 STAT. 327

Public Law 101-336
101st Congress

An Act

To establish a clear and comprehensive prohibition of discrimination on the basis of disability. July 26, 1990 [S. 933]

Be it enacted by the Senate and House of Representatives of the United States of America in Congress assembled, Americans with Disabilities Act of 1990.

SECTION 1. SHORT TITLE; TABLE OF CONTENTS.

(a) SHORT TITLE.—This Act may be cited as the "Americans with Disabilities Act of 1990". 42 USC 12101 note.

(b) TABLE OF CONTENTS.—The table of contents is as follows:

expenses resulting from dependency and nonproductivity.

(b) PURPOSE.—It is the purpose of this Act—

(1) to provide a clear and comprehensive national mandate for the elimination of discrimination against individuals with disabilities;

(2) to provide clear, strong, consistent, enforceable standards addressing discrimination against individuals with disabilities;

(3) to ensure that the Federal Government plays a central role in enforcing the standards established in this Act on behalf of individuals with disabilities; and

(4) to invoke the sweep of congressional authority, including the power to enforce the fourteenth amendment and to regulate commerce, in order to address the major areas of discrimination faced day-to-day by people with disabilities.

SEC. 3. DEFINITIONS. 42 USC 12102.

As used in this Act:

(1) AUXILIARY AIDS AND SERVICES.—The term "auxiliary aids and services" includes—

(A) qualified interpreters or other effective methods of making aurally delivered materials available to individuals with hearing impairments;

(B) qualified readers, taped texts, or other effective methods of making visually delivered materials available to individuals with visual impairments;

(C) acquisition or modification of equipment or devices; and

(D) other similar services and actions.

(2) DISABILITY.—The term "disability" means, with respect to an individual—

The options include (1) designating the "mandatory terms" that LEXIS must find to retrieve a document; (2) adding restrictions to the search, such as date restrictions; (3) selecting alternative terms from a thesaurus; (4) altering the number of documents retrieved—the default is twenty-five documents. After finding the pertinent document, you may browse previous and subsequent sections of the statute to read the entire text.

Keep in mind that many legislative sources use the same terms in varying contexts; for instance, a search regarding the rights of employers to terminate employees for smoking in the workplace raises different concerns than a search regarding the rights of employees to sue for injury they incur from breathing secondary smoke in the workplace—yet both searches would use many of the same search terms. Hence, it often is difficult to use unique terms and to formulate a narrow statutory search. For this reason, it often is more efficient first to use paper sources to gain a good understanding of the subject or to find some unique information about particular legislation, such as its code citation. If you have a code citation, you can find the statute online by using the Lexstat service on LEXIS.

To research the state law issue, you would select NMCODE. This file contains the full text and annotations of the *New Mexico Statutes Annotated*, but not its index. It also includes laws published in the most recent advance legislative service supplements.

An appropriate Freestyle search is [may an employer regulate smoking away from the workplace]. The sample search retrieves section 50-11-3 of the New Mexico Employee Privacy Act; the first page of the screen of this document is shown in Illustration 7-13 on page 207. An appropriate Boolean search is [employ! /p smok!]. This search also retrieves section 50-11-3 of the New Mexico Employee Privacy Act. Hence, for your research situation, both searches were successful and worked efficiently.

You may research the federal issue in the USCODE file. The USCODE file is based on the text of the federal code published in U.S.C.S. It is updated monthly and is current through the most recent issue of the paper advance legislative service published as a supplement to U.S.C.S. You can search the entire file, which includes both text and annotations, or you can use the "text" segment to limit a Boolean search to the text of the statute. To do the latter, use the following search format: [text(employ! /p smok! and disab!)]. Alternatively, if you need a more comprehensive collection of cases than those selected by the publisher to be in the statutory annotations, you should search a case database for references to the statute or specific code sections.

The PUBLAW file includes laws recently enacted by the current Congress and is updated frequently, usually within ten days after the laws are signed. Or you may search one of the separate supplementary files: USTOC, to search the table of contents, or USNAME, to search for an act by popular name.

In the Canoga case, your research focuses on whether an addiction to smoking is a disability protected by federal legislation. An appropriate natural language search is [must an employer accommodate an addiction to smoking as a disability]. An appropriate Boolean search is [employ! /p smok! and disab!]. The natural language search retrieved three ADA sections, but none

Illustration 7-13 New Mexico Statutes § 50-11-3, LEXIS.

```
To be able to browse preceding or succeeding code sections, enter B.  The
first page of the document you are currently viewing will be displayed in FULL.
--------------------------------------------------------------------------------

                          LEVEL 1 - 6 OF 25 DOCUMENTS

                         NEW MEXICO STATUTES ANNOTATED
               Copyright (c) 1978-1995 by The State of New Mexico
                              All rights reserved.

          *** THIS SECTION IS CURRENT To be able to browse preceding or succeeding code sections,
 enter B.  The
first page of the document you are currently viewing will be displayed in FULL.
--------------------------------------------------------------------------------

                          LEVEL 1 - 6 OF 25 DOCUMENTS

                         NEW MEXICO STATUTES ANNOTATED
               Copyright (c) 1978-1995 by The State of New Mexico
                              All rights reserved.

          *** THIS SECTION IS CURRENT THROUGH THE 1995 SUPPLEMENT ***
                *** (FIRST SESSION OF THE 42ND LEGISLATURE) ***

                         CHAPTER 50.  EMPLOYMENT LAW
                         ARTICLE 11.  EMPLOYEE PRIVACY

                        N.M. Stat. Ann. @ 50-11-3 (1995)

@ 50-11-3.   Employers;  unlawful practices

   A. It is unlawful for an  employer  to:

       (1) refuse to hire or to discharge any individual, or otherwise
disadvantage any individual, with respect to compensation, terms, conditions
```

of them were on point. The Boolean search retrieved 164 documents, five of which were ADA sections and one of which (the 127th document) was squarely on point. However, sorting through 164 documents is tedious and not cost-effective. That same section was the only document retrieved in a Boolean search with a segment restricting the search to the text of the statute: [text (employ! /p smok! and disab!)]. The section, 42 U.S.C.S. § 12201, states that the ADA does not preclude the prohibition or restriction of smoking in places of employment.

Another method for locating a statute's citation is to use its popular name to search the USNAME file. To access this file, select the CODES library, find the second screen describing the library, then select the USNAME file. In the file, enter the first three letters of the popular name of the statute and scroll through the list of statutes with those initial letters until you find the correct entry. For each entry, LEXIS displays its popular name and the dates, the public law numbers, and the code citations for the original act and for any subsequent amendment or changes. See Illustration 7-14 on page 208. In the Canoga case, LEXIS would list all popular names that begin with "ame" (the first three letters of "American"). You then must scroll through the list to select the correct entry. As you can imagine, many popular names begin with the word "American," including the ADA.

Illustration 7-14 Americans with Disabilities Act Entry, USNAME File, LEXIS.

```
                    USCS Pop. Name A 1995, *AME

AMERICAN TECHNOLOGY PREEMINENCE ACT OF 1991
   Feb. 14, 1992, P.L. 102-245, 15 USCS § 3701 note.
   Aug. 3, 1992, P.L. 102-329, 15 USCS §§ 1453, 1453 note.

AMERICAN UNIVERSITY INCORPORATION AMENDMENTS ACT OF 1990
   Oct. 31, 1990, P.L. 101-480, 104 Stat. 1160.

AMERICAN WAR MOTHERS INCORPORATION ACT
   Feb. 24, 1925, ch 308, 43 Stat. 966, 36 USCS §§ 91--104.
   Sept. 26, 1942, ch 563, 56 Stat. 758, 36 USCS § 97.
   June 26, 1953, ch 152, 67 Stat. 81, 36 USCS §§ 97, 98.
   April 12, 1974, P.L. 93-267, 88 Stat. 85, 36 USCS § 97.

AMERICANS WITH DISABILITIES ACT OF 1990
   July 26, 1990, P.L. 101-336, 42 USCS 12101 note.
   Nov. 21, 1991, P.L. 102-166, 42 USCS §§ 12111, 12112, 12209.
   Jan. 23, 1995, P.L.  104-1, 42 USCS § 12209.

[*AMN]    Enter p* and up to three letters to jump elsewhere.
          To view a P.L. after 100-242 use LEXSEE  -- e.g.  lexsee 102 pl 166
          To view a USCS section use LXSTAT        -- e.g.  lxstat 42 uscs 5101

AMNESTY ACTS (REMOVAL OF DISABILITIES UNDER FOURTEENTH AMENDMENT)
   May 22, 1872, ch 193, 17 Stat. 142.
   June 6, 1898, ch 389, 30 Stat. 432.
```

To retrieve the text of the statute, you need to enter a Lexstat search. Lexstat is a LEXIS feature that permits you to retrieve a statute by entering its citation. In Lexstat, the federal statutory section you retrieve is contained in the USCODE file; hence, you retrieve the full text of the statute and the accompanying notes and annotations. For example, to use Lexstat to find the definitions section of the ADA, enter its citation: [lexstat 42 uscs 12102]. When you are viewing a statute retrieved in Lexstat, you may use the LINK feature to go directly from that document to other documents cited in the text of the statute or within its annotations without performing another search. You also can return directly to the original document without performing another search and without losing your place in the original document.

Once you have retrieved the text of the statute, note the status line at the beginning of the statute; it tells you the timing of the last update and thereby alerts you to the currency of the database. For an example of this feature in the state code database, see Illustration 7-13 on page 207. Typically, LEXIS integrates recent amendments into the text of a statute. To update beyond that, you will need to search the PUBLAW file to check for recently enacted legislation.

Whether it is more efficient to use an online database or a paper source for statutory research depends on many considerations. Online statutory research generally is more efficient and effective when you need the statute to be fully integrated with all of its updates, when your search needs to be limited with a segment or field search, or when you need the convenience of a linking feature that allows you to go directly from your document to the documents cited in your document. In addition, as in other areas of online research, it is well suited to unique search terms.

On the other hand, paper statutory research is more efficient and effective when the search terms are so generic that you need the benefit of the efforts of a skilled indexer or when you need some of the unique tables or other features of paper sources, such as the tables typically found in the advance legislative services reflecting legislative changes to specific code sections. Some other features, such as the popular names tables, are much easier to use in paper than online.

For the Canoga case, it was equally easy to use the paper source and to develop appropriate online natural language and Boolean searches of the pertinent New Mexico statutes. When researching federal statutes, using the popular names table in the paper index volumes of the codes was faster than searching online.

e. Summary of Canoga Research

For the Canoga case, a state statute addresses whether employers may take disciplinary actions against employees who smoke when away from their place of employment. The General Index of the *New Mexico Statutes Annotated* provided a reference to the state's Employee Privacy Act, which prohibits employers from penalizing employees for smoking when not at work. The annotations did not contain any case law interpreting this statute. There were no amendments or changes to the statute in the annual supplement or the *Advance Legislative Service.*

Another important issue is whether an addiction to smoking is protected as a disability under the federal ADA. Access to the federal codes was gained easily by using the popular name table in any of the federal codes. The statute's definition of disability is so open-ended that it is uncertain whether an addiction to smoking is a protected disability, and no case law digests address that precise question. The advance legislative services showed that recent legislation amended the ADA, but these amendments were unrelated to the Canoga case. *Shepard's United States Citations* yielded an extensive list of cases that cite section 12102 of the ADA; because New Mexico lies within the jurisdiction of the Tenth Circuit, its cases were particularly pertinent. Section 12201(b) does address smoking in providing that the statute permits prohibitions on smoking in the workplace; this provision leaves unanswered whether employers may prohibit employee smoking away from the workplace.

4. What Else?

Additional Features of U.S.C.A. and U.S.C.S. Both annotated federal codes also contain the text and annotations to the United States Constitution, the Federal Rules of Civil and Criminal Procedure, the Federal Rules of Evidence, and various court rules. U.S.C.S. also includes annotations for uncodified federal enactments, such as treaties and uncodified laws and resolutions, while U.S.C.A. does not.

Conversion Tables. If you know the *Statutes at Large* citation or the public law number for the act you are seeking, or if you have a previous section number for a statute that has been renumbered, you may locate the current version of that statute in the code by using a conversion table located in the tables volumes of U.S.C., U.S.C.A., and U.S.C.S. Two tables have particular value: (1) The *Statutes at Large* table lists the acts of Congress in chronological order by public law number and indicates where they appear in the federal code (or why they don't appear); abbreviations explain what legislative changes are embodied in the law. (2) The table of revised titles shows where statutes that have been revised or renumbered appear in the current edition of the code.

Slip Laws. On the federal level, slip laws are published officially by the United States Government Printing Office. They also are commercially available in U.S.C.C.A.N. pamphlets and in the U.S.C.S. *Advance* pamphlets. Some states publish official copies, in slip law form, of each piece of legislation that has been enacted, but many do not. Hence, the advance legislative services, which typically supplement state annotated codes, may be the only source of slip laws.

Authority of State Codes. The authority of state codes varies from jurisdiction to jurisdiction. In some states the original session laws are the final official authority for statutory language if there is a conflict between the language of the code and the language of the session law. You should determine whether your state recognizes the state code or its session laws as the primary source for statutory language. A statute likely governs the matter.

Local Government Law. Your research may include research into legislation enacted by local governmental entities, such as city or county governments. For instance, a municipality may be established under a charter, and its governing body (a city council, for example) may promulgate ordinances or codes. These sources are primary authority to the extent that the governmental body has authority to act. Some jurisdictions publish these sources; some do not. Check with the local library or with the city clerk, the county clerk, or a similar official about how to research the law for a particular local government unit. Although commercially published sources for local government law are rare, Shepard's/McGraw-Hill publishes *Ordinance Law Annotations* for selected city ordinances.

Treaties and Proclamations. Treaties can be found in *Senate Execuive Reports,* which is published in a consecutively numbered series for each Congress. Selected treaties and related presidential proclamations may be found in U.S.C.C.A.N. or in the federal codes.

Other Media. The statutory sources discussed in Part B are available in a variety of media. These are the media available in early 1996:

	Paper	*CD-ROM*	*Computer-Assisted Research*		*Microform*
			LEXIS	*WESTLAW*	
United States Code	√	√			√
United States Code Annotated	√	√		√	√
United States Code Service	√	√	√		
United States Code Congressional and Administrative News	√				√
Statutes at Large	√		*	*	√
State codes	√	√	√	√	√
State session laws	√		*	*	√
Shepard's United States Citations, statute edition	√	√	√	√	

*Similar content is available in the online service's public laws and legislative service databases.

5. How Do You Cite Statutes?

Rule 12 of *The Bluebook* explains how to cite statutes. Rule 12.2.1 dictates the following order of preference for statutory sources (subject to the exceptions in Rule 12.2.2): (1) the current official code, (2) a current unofficial code, (3) official session laws, (4) a looseleaf, (5) a periodical, or (6) a newspaper. Thus, you must cite to the official code, rather than an unofficial code, if the material appears in the official code. You would cite to the current code for statutes currently in force and even those statutes already repealed, if they still appear in the current code. You would not cite an unofficial code unless the section you are citing has been amended so recently that its current text is available only in a more recent unofficial code or its supplement.

A code citation includes the abbreviated name of the code, the (title and) section number(s), and a parenthetical containing the year of publication. Consult *The Bluebook*'s Table T.1 for the specifics of each citation and the abbreviated name of the code. Add the name and section number of the original act if they help to identify the statute. For the year of the code, choose the year on the spine of the volume, the year on the title page, or the latest copyright year—in that order of preference. If the statute or part of the statute that you are citing has been amended since publication of the main volume, the citation must include (in parentheses) both the year of the main volume and the year of the most recent supplement. If the cited material is found only in the supplement, delete the publication date for the bound volume. See Rules 3.2(c) and 12.3.2. Citations to unofficial codes include the name of the publisher in the parenthetical. See Rule 12.3.1(d).

According to Rule 12.2, a session law citation is used (1) when the statutory provision does not appear in a code; (2) when a statute appears in so many scattered locations that no useful citation to the code is possible; (3) when the citation supports the historical fact of enactment, amendment, or repeal; or (4) when the language in the current code differs materially from the language in the session law and the title has not been enacted into "positive law" (as per Rule 12.2.2(c)). Rule 12.4 governs session law citation and requires the name of the act, the chapter or public law number, the session law publication by volume, abbreviated title, the first page of the act, and a parenthetical containing the year of enactment (unless that same year is part of the name of the law). Abbreviations for session law publications appear in Table T.1. If you are citing a specific page, the relevant page number follows the number of the first page of the act. If you are citing to a particular section or subsection, include it after the public law number. If you know the location of a session law in the code, the citation may be included in a parenthetical at the end of the session law citation.

Here are illustrative citations to the state and federal statutes featured and discussed in this chapter:

state code:	N.M. Stat. Ann. § 50-11-3 (Michie 1993).
official federal code:	42 U.S.C. § 12102 (Supp. V 1993).
unofficial federal codes:	42 U.S.C.A. § 12102 (West 1995). 42 U.S.C.S. § 12102 (Law. Co-op. Supp. 1995).
session law:	Americans with Disabilities Act of 1990, Pub. L. No. 101-336, 104 Stat. 327.
session law with § and page nos.:	Americans with Disabilities Act of 1990, Pub. L. No. 101-336, § 2, 104 Stat. 327, 328-29.
session law with code parenthetical:	Americans with Disabilities Act of 1990, Pub. L. No. 101-336, § 2, 104 Stat. 327, 328-29 (codified at 42 U.S.C. § 12102 (Supp. V 1993)).

C. Uniform and Model Acts

1. What Are Uniform and Model Acts?

"Uniform acts" are statutes drafted by public or private organizations to standardize the statutory law of the fifty states, the District of Columbia, and Puerto Rico. Uniform acts are intended as recommendations to legislative bodies for their consideration and enactment. "Model acts" also seek to standardize the law, but the term often is used to designate an act that addresses a topic that may not be of critical concern to all jurisdictions or that likely will not be enacted by a substantial number of jurisdictions.

Uniform and model acts come from a variety of sources: The National Conference of Commissioners on Uniform State Laws (NCCUSL), the American Law Institute, the American Bar Association, the Committee on Suggested State Legislation, and other organizations.

The NCCUSL is by far the most prolific producer of uniform state legislation. The NCCUSL consists of attorneys, judges, legislators, and law professors appointed as commissioners from each state. Only those acts finally approved by a majority of the commissioners are published and sent to state legislatures. The NCCUSL has approved more than 200 model and uniform acts, ranging from highly successful to less successful acts that have yet to be adopted by any state. Areas of coverage are diverse, including child custody, arbitration, taxation, real estate, and anatomical gifts.

The American Law Institute (ALI) also drafts model codes. The ALI's many model laws include the Model Penal Code, the Model Code of Evidence, the Model Land Development Code, and the recent Principles of Corporate Governance.

The ALI also occasionally works in tandem with the NCCUSL on major acts. The Uniform Commercial Code (UCC), a joint NCCUSL-ALI project, has standardized much of commercial practice among forty-nine states, federal jurisdictions, and American territories.

Section committees of the American Bar Association (ABA) also sometimes draft model acts, which are submitted to state legislatures for consideration. ABA section committees, in collaboration with the American Bar Foundation, drafted the Model Business Corporation Act, the Revised Model Business Corporation Act, and the Model Residential Landlord-Tenant Code. Although no jurisdiction has enacted these acts verbatim, these acts have led to important legislative reforms in many jurisdictions.

The Council of State Governments has a Committee on Suggested State Legislation (CSSL), which publishes state legislation that might serve as models for other states to follow. For legislation to be selected, the issue involved must be complex and have national or regional significance; the selected legislation must be innovative, practical, comprehensive, logically consistent, clear, and unambiguous.

Private individuals, most notably law faculty, occasionally propose model legislation. It was the efforts of law professors, for example, that led to the

Model Marketable Record Title Act, which has led to reform in many state title recording acts.

Achieving uniformity in state laws through these efforts benefits the public by facilitating interstate activities and by avoiding conflicts in laws that might prejudice, mislead, or adversely affect the public when parties move from state to state. However, complete uniformity is rarely achieved because few acts are enacted by nearly every jurisdiction and because few uniform or model acts are enacted verbatim. Generally, the act's effect, organization, and underlying policies remain unaltered, so that greater uniformity has been accomplished.

The organization of most uniform or model acts resembles the organization of other statutes, with initial sections on purpose, scope, and definitions, followed by operating provisions, and concluding with consequences and enforcement provisions. The outline of the Model Employment Termination Act (META) on the first page of Illustration 7-15 on page 215 shows the major provisions typically found in a uniform or model act. This act was developed by the NCCUSL.

An important part of uniform or model acts is the commentary that accompanies each act. Comments typically follow the statutory language of most sections. See the second page of Illustration 7-15 on page 216. These comments clarify terms, concepts, or language and explain why the drafters adopted a certain approach or doctrine. In addition, each act is preceded by a Prefatory Note and sometimes an Historical Note. The Historical Note typically gives the date of enactment of an act and notes predecessor acts. The Prefatory Note generally states the pressures that convinced the NCCUSL that a uniform or model act was needed, the details of the act's approval by the NCCUSL, the content of the act, and the major principles behind the act. Finally, a separate note may explain major variations in the act made by the various adopting states.

Uniform and model acts differ significantly from the Restatements of the Law. Restatements are not drafted as proposed legislation and are not intended to be submitted to legislative bodies for enactment (although they occasionally are). Rather, Restatements become law within a certain jurisdiction when a court has embraced a section.

2. Why Are Uniform and Model Acts Useful?

Uniform and model acts are secondary authority. Only when the language contained in the uniform or model act is enacted by a state legislature does the language become primary authority in that jurisdiction.

You are most likely to use a uniform or model act to help you interpret an ambiguous statute that is based on a uniform or model act. If your ambiguous statute and the uniform or model act are sufficiently similar, you can use the comments of the drafters to explain the statute or to discern its policy objectives. In addition, case law interpreting parallel language in other

Illustration 7-15

Model Employment Termination Act, 7A U.L.A. 75-76 (1991).

rights and the remedies available for violations of those rights. Nationwide companies obviously benefit from being able to have standardized personnel policies. But even smaller firms frequently move their workers around the country. Both employers and employees should profit from knowing that their mutual rights and obligations will not turn on the relative accident of where a hiring or firing took place or a job was performed. Interstate competition for "favorable business climates" may also be reduced by establishing uniform standards for employment termination.

Nearly all the comprehensive bills introduced in recent years, including the closely examined bills drafted in California, Illinois, Michigan, and New York, speak in terms of prohibiting discharge except for "just cause." In using the phrase "good cause," the proposed Act intends no substantive difference. The purpose was merely to underscore that an employer's business needs or external economic conditions may be legitimate grounds for a termination, as well as the misconduct or incompetence of a particular employee. "Justice" in the moral sense may have nothing to do with it.

Finally, adoption of a "good cause" standard would not put this country at a disadvantage in global competition by imposing constraints not borne by firms overseas—quite the contrary. The United States is the last major industrial democracy in the world that does not have generalized legal protections for its workers against arbitrary dismissal. All told, sixty countries currently provide these guarantees, including the whole of the European Community, Scandinavia, Japan, Canada, and most of South America.

The changes reflected in this Act, when understood and carefully analyzed by all interested parties, will be found to be a fair and well-balanced solution that eliminates the uncertainty resulting from the continuing shifts in the legal environment. With the decline in the fraction of the work force that is unionized, there is an increased willingness on the part of the state judiciaries to adopt one or more of the wrongful termination doctrines, if the legislatures do not fill the void. There is increasing need for the legislatures to act in this area.

MODEL EMPLOYMENT TERMINATION ACT

1991 ACT

§ 1. Definitions.

In this [Act]:

(1) "Employee" means an individual who works for hire, including an individual employed in a supervisory, managerial, or confidential position, but not an independent contractor.

(2) "Employer" means a person [, excluding this State, a political subdivision, a municipal corporation, or any other governmental subdivision, agency, or instrumentality,] that has employed [five] or more employees for each working day in each of 20 or more calendar weeks in the two-year period next preceding a termination or an employer's filing of a complaint pursuant to Section 5(c), excluding a parent, spouse, child, or other member of the employer's immediate family or of the immediate family of an individual having a controlling interest in the employer.

(3) "Fringe benefit" means vacation leave, sick leave, medical insurance plan, disability insurance plan, life insurance plan, pension benefit plan, or other benefit of economic value, to the extent the leave, plan, or benefit is paid for by the employer.

(4) "Good cause" means (i) a reasonable basis related to an individual employee for termination of the employee's employment in view of relevant factors and circumstances, which may include the employee's duties, responsibilities, conduct on the job or otherwise, job performance, and employment record, or (ii) the exercise of business judgment in good faith by the employer, including setting its economic or institutional goals and determining

Illustration 7-15 *(continued)*

§ 1 **EMPLOYMENT TERMINATION**

methods to achieve those goals, organizing or reorganizing operations, discontinuing, consolidating, or divesting operations or positions or parts of operations or positions, determining the size of its work force and the nature of the positions filled by its work force, and determining and changing standards of performance for positions.

(5) "Good faith" means honesty in fact.

(6) "Pay," as a noun, means hourly wages or periodic salary, including tips, regularly paid and nondiscretionary commissions and bonuses, and regularly paid overtime, but not fringe benefits.

(7) "Person" means an individual, corporation, business trust, estate, trust, partnership, association, joint venture, or any other legal or commercial entity [, excluding government or a governmental subdivision, agency, or instrumentality].

(8) "Termination" means:

(i) a dismissal, including that resulting from the elimination of a position, of an employee by an employer;

(ii) a layoff or suspension of an employee by an employer for more than two consecutive months; or

(iii) a quitting of employment or a retirement by an employee induced by an act or omission of the employer, after notice to the employer of the act or omission without appropriate relief by the employer, so intolerable that under the circumstances a reasonable individual would quit or retire.

Comment

Paragraph (2): The definition of "employer" is based in part on Title VII of the Civil Rights Act of 1964. Since the general view is that state law should apply more broadly than federal law, the suggested minimum number of employees is reduced from 15 to 5, and the 20 qualifying weeks may be spread over a period of 24 months. To enable an early and certain determination of the status of the employer in question, the count should be taken as of the date of the employee's discharge or of the employer's filing for a "declaratory" ruling. Thus, if an employee were terminated on May 31, 1995, the critical period for finding 20 qualifying weeks would run from June 1, 1993, to May 31, 1995. This avoids the problem of the federal approach as reflected in *Slack v. Havens*, 522 F.2d 1091 (9th Cir.1975). In determining whether a person is an employer, employees of that person are counted even though they are not protected by the Act. The language concerning the exclusion of the employer's "immediate family" from the count (but not from the protections of the Act if otherwise covered) is drawn from the Fair Labor Standards Act.

Uniformity is less important with regard to public employees because they are not employees of multi-state employers. In addition, many public employees are members of a civil service system that offers protection against termination. Thus, their coverage is left to local option. A state legislature may wish to consider, however, whether it is sound policy to prescribe differential treatment for such institutions as public and private universities.

Paragraph (3): "Benefit of economic value" includes food, lodging, and tuition reimbursement.

Paragraph (4): Examples of "good cause" for a termination under subparagraph (i) include theft, assault, fighting on the job, destruction of property, use or possession of drugs or alcohol on the job, insubordination, excessive absenteeism or tardiness, incompetence, lack of productivity, and inadequate performance or neglect of duty. Off-duty conduct may be "good cause" if it is relevant to the employee's performance on the job, to the employer's business reputation, or to similar concerns.

In the determination of good cause, principles and considerations generally accepted in arbitration which are to be applied include such factors as the reasonableness of the company rule violated, the employee's knowledge or warning of the rule, the consistency of enforcement of the rule and the penalties assessed, the use of corrective or progressive discipline, the fullness and fairness of the investigation including the opportunity given the employee to present his or her views prior to dismissal, and the appropriateness of the penalty in light of the conduct involved and the employee's employment record. Consideration will also be given to the character of the employee's responsibilities, including the professional, scientific, or technical character of the work, the management level of the employee's position in the enterprise, and its importance to the success of the business. An employer's discrimination in violation of applicable federal, state, or local law, or an employer's violation of established public policy, is inconsistent with the requirement of good cause for termination. Similarly, "whistle-blowers" in various circumstances would be protected against retaliatory discharges.

Under subparagraph (ii), an employer's decision as to the economic goals and methodologies of the enterprise and the size and composition of the work force, as contrasted with decisions as to individual discipline or dismissal, is governed by honest business judgment. In no way is this Act to operate as a plant-closing law; an employer remains entirely free to shut down an operation on economic or institutional grounds. The use of the

76

jurisdictions may be persuasive to a court. Even if your jurisdiction does not have a similar statute, the act may provide persuasive authority about what the law or its public policy should be. If you work with a legislature, you might use uniform or model acts to assist you in drafting new legislation or amendments to existing legislation.

In using uniform or model acts, keep in mind that sometimes a court or legislature may believe that important regional differences justify acting apart from other jurisdictions. In these circumstances, uniform or model acts clearly would not be valuable.

3. How Do You Research Uniform and Model Acts?

a. Using Paper Media

The uniform and model acts of the NCCUSL that have been approved by the commissioners are published by West Publishing Company in *Uniform Laws Annotated* (master ed. 1968-present) (U.L.A.). The *Directory of Uniform Acts and Codes: Tables-Index*, a softbound pamphlet issued as part of the U.L.A. contains many of the finding tools for U.L.A. To locate an act in U.L.A., if you know its name, use the Directory of Uniform Acts, an alphabetical listing of the titles of the acts contained in the U.L.A. along with their U.L.A. volumes and beginning page numbers. If you are seeking to determine which acts your state has adopted, use the Table of Jurisdictions Listing Uniform Acts Adopted. See Illustration 7-16 on page 218. This table lists the uniform or model acts that each jurisdiction has enacted, alphabetically by state and then alphabetically by act within each state. If you are looking for various uniform acts that might address a specific subject, use the topical index entitled Cross Reference Index to Acts.

Once you locate the pertinent model act, you will find several helpful features at the beginning of each uniform act. A table lists, for each enacting state, a citation to the enacting legislation, its effective date, and its code citation. See Illustration 7-17 on page 219. (Because the META has not been enacted in any states yet, this illustration comes from the Uniform Arbitration Act.) The individual sections of the act are followed by explanatory comments drafted by the NCCUSL, notes of variations from the official text in the adopting jurisdictions, citations to legal periodicals, references to West topics and key numbers and C.J.S. sections, references to WESTLAW search techniques, and a digest of cases from all jurisdictions construing this section.

The U.L.A. is updated annually by pocket parts or softbound pamphlets that supplement the text and annotations found in the main volume; they also present the full text of any new uniform or model acts adopted by the NCCUSL.

Illustration 7-16 Jurisdictions and Acts Table, *U.L.A. Directory of Uniform Acts and Codes: Tables-Index.*

JURISDICTIONS AND ACTS ADOPTED

NEW MEXICO

Title of Act	Uniform Laws Annotated Volume	Page
Anatomical Gift Act (1968 Act)	8A	63
Arbitration Act	7	1
Attendance of Witnesses From Without a State in Criminal Proceedings, Act to Secure	11	1
Certification of Questions of Law Act	12	49
Child Custody Jurisdiction Act	9, Pt. I	115
Commercial Code[1]	1 to 3B	
Common Trust Fund Act	7	401
Condominium Act	7	421
Conservation Easement Act	12	Pamphlet
Contribution Among Tortfeasor Act	12	57
Controlled Substances Act (1990)	9, Pt. II	Pamphlet
Controlled Substances Act (1970)	9, Pt. II	1
Criminal Extradition Act	11	51
Custodial Trust Act	7A	Pocket Part
Deceptive Trade Practices Act (1966 Act)	7A	265
Declaratory Judgments Act	12	109
Determination of Death Act	12	Pamphlet
Disclaimer of Property Interests Act	8A	149
Division of Income for Tax Purposes Act	7A	331
Durable Power of Attorney Act	8A	309
Enforcement of Foreign Judgments Act (1964 Act)	13	149
Estate Tax Apportionment Act (1964 Act)	8A	331
Evidence, Rules of (1974)	13A	1
Facsimile Signatures of Public Officials Act	13	249
Federal Lien Registration Act	7A	359
Fiduciaries Act	7A	391
Foreign-Money Claims Act	13	Pocket Part
Foreign Money Judgments Recognition Act	13	261
Fraudulent Transfer Act	7A	639
Guardianship and Protective Proceedings Act	8A	439
Insurers Liquidation Act	13	321
International Wills Act (See Volume 8, Probate Code, Art. II, Part 10)		
Intestacy, Wills and Donative Transfers, Act on	8B	1
Limited Partnership Act (1976 Act)	6	Pamphlet
Military Justice, Code of	11	335
Multiple-Person Accounts Act	8B	165
Nonprobate Transfers on Death Act	8B	191
Notarial Acts, Uniform Law on	14	125
Parentage Act	9B	287
Partnership Act (1914 Act)	6	1
Principal and Income Act (1962 Act)	7B	145
Probate Code[2]	8	1
Reciprocal Enforcement of Support Act (1968 Act)	9B	381
Residential Landlord and Tenant Act	7B	427
Rules of Evidence (1974)	13A	1
Securities Act (1985 Act)	7B	Pocket Part
Simplification of Fiduciary Security Transfers Act	7B	689
Simultaneous Death Act (1993 Act)	8B	Pocket Part
Single Publication Act	14	375

[1] Adopted Article 2A (Leases), 1990 Revision of Article 3, 1990 Amendments to Article 4, Article 4A (Funds Transfers), 1977 Revision of Article 8, and 1972 Revision of Article 9; Repealed Article 6 without adopting 1989 Revision of Article 6.

[2] Adopted 1990 Revision of Article II, and 1989 Revision of Article VI.

48

Illustration 7-17 Uniform Arbitration Act, 7 U.L.A. 1 (1956).

UNIFORM ARBITRATION ACT

Table of Jurisdictions Wherein Act Has Been Adopted

Jurisdiction	Laws	Effective Date	Statutory Citation
Alaska	1968, c. 232	8-6-1968	AS 09.43.010 to 09.43.180.
Arizona	1962, c. 108	6-21-1962	A.R.S. §§ 12-1501 to 12-1518.
Arkansas	1969, No. 260		Ark.Stats. §§ 34-511 to 34-532.
Colorado	1975, p. 573	7-14-1975	C.R.S. 13-22-201 to 13-22-223.
Delaware	1972, c. 382	4-30-1972	10 Del.C. §§ 5701 to 5725.
Dist. of Columbia	D.C.Laws. No. 1-117	4-7-1977	D.C.Code 1981, §§ 16-4301 to 16-4319.
Idaho	1975, c. 117	7-1-1975	I.C. §§ 7-901 to 7-922.
Illinois	1961, p. 3844	8-24-1961	S.H.A. ch. 10, ¶¶ 101 to 123.
Indiana	1969, c. 340	3-15-1969	West's A.I.C. 34-4-2-1 to 34-4-2-22.
Kansas	1973, c. 24	7-1-1973	K.S.A. 5-401 to 5-422.
Maine	1967, c. 430	10-7-1967	14 M.R.S.A. §§ 5927 to 5949.
Maryland	1965, c. 231	6-1-1965	Code, Courts and Judicial Proceedings, §§ 3-201 to 3-234.
Massachusetts ...	1960, c. 374	12-31-1960	M.G.L.A. c. 251, §§ 1 to 19.
Michigan	1961, P.A. 236	1-1-1963	M.C.L.A. §§ 600.5001 to 600.5035.
Minnesota	1957, c. 633	4-25-1957	M.S.A. §§ 572.08 to 572.30.
Missouri	1980, H.B. No. 1203	6-5-1980*	V.A.M.S. §§ 435.350 to 435.470.
Nevada	1969, c. 456	7-1-1969	N.R.S. 38.015 to 38.205.
New Mexico	1971, c. 168	7-1-1971	NMSA 1978, §§ 44-7-1 to 44-7-22.
North Carolina ...	1973, c. 676	8-1-1973	G.S. §§ 1-567.1 to 1-567.20.
Oklahoma	1978, c. 308	10-1-1978	15 Okl.St.Ann. §§ 801 to 818.
Pennsylvania	1980, P.L. 142	12-4-1980	42 Pa.C.S.A. §§ 7301 to 7320.
South Carolina ...	1978, Act 492	5-8-1978	Code 1976, §§ 15-48-10 to 15-48-240.
South Dakota	1971, c. 157	7-1-1971	SDCL 21-25A-1 to 21-25A-38.
Tennessee	1983, c. 462	5-26-1983	T.C.A. §§ 29-5-301 to 29-5-320.
Texas	1965, c. 689	1-1-1966	Vernon's Ann.Texas Civ.St. arts. 224 to 238-6.
Wyoming	1959, c. 116	2-19-1959	W.S.1977, §§ 1-36-101 to 1-36-119.

* Date of approval.

Historical Note

The Uniform Arbitration Act was approved by the National Conference of Commissioners on Uniform State Laws and the American Bar Association, in 1955. An amendment to section 12 was similarly approved in 1956.

The 1955 Act supersedes a prior Act approved in 1925, which had been adopted in Nevada, North Carolina, Pennsylvania, Utah, Wisconsin and Wyoming, and which was withdrawn by the Conference of Commissioners on Uniform State Laws, in 1943.

PREFATORY NOTE

This Act covers voluntary written agreements to arbitrate. Its purpose is to validate arbitration agreements, make the arbitration process

1

For the Canoga case, the Model Employment Termination Act (META) of 1991 appears to be the only uniform or model act on point. As Illustration 7-17 shows, New Mexico has not adopted META. Because no jurisdiction has adopted this model act, it would not have as much persuasive authority as an act that has been widely adopted.

b. Using Online Media: LEXIS and WESTLAW as Examples

It is possible to research uniform and model acts using either WESTLAW or LEXIS. The MODEL library in LEXIS contains the text of selected uniform or model acts. You then must scan the directory for an applicable file. The LEXIS databases contain only selected acts that have been widely adopted by state legislatures; the META is not available on LEXIS.

The databases on WESTLAW are more extensive. In WESTLAW, the ULA database contains the full text of the uniform and model acts, as well as their annotations, as found in U.L.A. in paper media, current to the most recent update to the U.L.A. set. The ULA database provides linkage between the annotations and the full texts of the cases, so you can go directly from a case cited in the annotations to the full text of the case. The text of the META is found in the ULA database.

4. What Else?

NCCUSL *Handbook*. The NCCUSL annually publishes its *Handbook of the National Conference of Commissioners on Uniform State Laws.* The *Handbook* contains several tables listing (1) the approved NCCUSL uniform, model, and other acts; (2) those acts arranged by title, by subject, and by jurisdiction; and (3) acts that have been withdrawn from recommendation because they were superseded or now are considered obsolete. The *Handbook* also discusses the progress of acts currently being drafted and topics that are being considered for referral to a drafting committee.

Shepard's Citations. You can locate sources citing some NCCUSL uniform acts by using the specialized *Shepard's* sets, such as *Shepard's Uniform Commercial Code Citations* (covering the UCC) and *Shepard's Partnership Law Citations.*

Secondary Sources. Sometimes an organization or individual proposing a new uniform or model act first may publish it as part of a legal periodical article if the proponent is not affiliated with an organization that regularly publishes its uniform or model acts. To learn where a NCCUSL uniform or model act is covered in Am. Jur. 2d or A.L.R. annotations, consult each source's table of statutes.

Other Sources of Model Legislation. Organizations other than the NCCUSL often publish their uniform or model acts. To find these acts, use the library catalog and search by author or subject. For instance, ALI model acts are entered in a library catalog under the author heading of "American Law Institute."

Suggested State Legislation. The Council of State Governments annually publishes its model acts in the single-volume publication entitled *Suggested State Legislation.*

Other Media. In 1996, uniform law sources were available in the following media:

			Computer-Assisted Research		
	Paper	*CD-ROM*	*LEXIS*	*WESTLAW*	*Microform*
Uniform Laws Annotated	√			√	
Suggested State Legislation	√				√

5. How Do You Cite Uniform and Model Acts?

Uniform and model acts that have been enacted as a statute are cited to the state statute. See Rule 12 in *The Bluebook.* Other acts are cited to U.L.A. by title, section, volume and page of U.L.A., along with the year in which the act was approved or last amended (not the year of the U.L.A. volume). See Rules 12.8.4 and 12.8.5. For example:

Model Employment Termination Act, § 4, 7A U.L.A. 75, 79 (1991).

D. CONSTITUTIONS

1. What Is a Constitution?

A constitution is primary authority. Indeed, a constitution is the highest law in a constitutional democratic regime. A constitution is a binding document that describes the structure of the government, the inherent powers of the government, and the limits placed on the government's authority to govern with regard to certain matters. A constitution protects the rights of the people governed.

The United States Constitution creates our three branches of government (legislative, judicial, and executive), describes the scope of power of each branch, and maintains the careful balance of powers so critical to our form of democratic governance. The Constitution creates the Congress, empowers it to enact legislation, and describes the procedures by which statutes may be enacted. It also places limits on the power of Congress to legislate in particular subject matters; for example, the First Amendment to the United States Constitution limits the power of Congress to pass statutes that infringe on the freedom of speech, the press, and religion. The United States Constitution also creates the federal court system. It details the process for selecting Supreme Court justices, defines the jurisdiction of the federal courts, and grants Congress the right to establish federal courts. Constitutional provisions pertaining to the executive branch detail the eligibility of a person to stand for election, the election process, the steps to be followed to impeach a president, and succession to the presidency in the event of the president's inability to serve. The Constitution also provides the powers and limitations of the President, such as the right to veto legislation (subject to congressional override), to negotiate international treaties, and to serve as Commander-in-Chief of the military (subject to congressional review and budgetary approval).

Under our federalist system, each state also has a separate constitution. A state constitution likewise details the structure of the state and local governments, grants powers to them to act in certain areas, and protects the right of persons within the state. Typically, the rights protected by a state constitution mirror the rights protected by the federal constitution; however, a state constitution may grant additional rights to its people, as long as those rights do not conflict with the federal constitution. Some state constitutions also govern the conduct of private citizens or organizations. State constitutions are amended more frequently than is the federal constitution. Amendments may be initiated by state legislatures or by public initiative and are then approved by public referendum. The process and votes required are set out in the text of the state constitution.

a. How Is a Constitution Developed?

In the American Revolutionary War era, the thirteen colonial governments sent delegates to participate in a Continental Congress, which served as the first democratic government of the American colonies. By virtue of common consent of the populace, the Continental Congress set out to create a lasting document articulating the fundamental law of the land. The drafting committee appointed by the Second Continental Congress drew up the first Articles of Confederation. This document was submitted to the colonies for ratification, which was accomplished in March 1781, as the war was nearing its end. It was the Articles of Confederation that first created the United States of America. However, certain defects became apparent in the Articles of Confederation; for instance, the document regulated only the states and provided no federal protection to citizens of the United States, it did not authorize

Congress to levy taxes, and it did not grant Congress the power to regulate commerce between the states. Consequently, several state governments lobbied for major revisions in the Articles of Confederation, and, pursuant to this call, a constitutional convention was assembled in Philadelphia in 1787. The major political figures at that time, including Washington, Madison, Jefferson, Franklin, and Hamilton, submitted drafts that were debated and revised many times. Finally, the Constitution was completed and submitted to the states for ratification. With promises that a "bill of rights" spelling out specific protections afforded the governed would soon follow, the Constitution was finally ratified and became effective in 1789. The Bill of Rights, comprised of the first ten amendments to the Constitution, did soon follow.

One of the most important aspects of a constitution is its durable nature. Because it embodies the highest law, a constitution is not easily changed. To amend the United States Constitution, a proposed amendment first must pass two-thirds of both houses of Congress, or the legislatures of two-thirds of the states; it then must be ratified by three-fourths of the states. As testimony to the difficulty in making amendments, in more than 200 years, only 27 amendments have been made to the United States Constitution.

b. What Does a Constitution Look Like?

A constitution looks much like a statute. It is organized by separate parts, such as articles, sections, and clauses.

However, the text of a constitution has characteristics that distinguish it from statutes. The text of a constitution is, comparatively speaking, quite lacking in detail. While a statute often includes definitions that define the terms used in the statute, the text of a constitution instead deals with broader principles stated in terms intended to stand the test of time. The federal bill of rights illustrates this characteristic of a constitution. A bill of rights states the inherent rights of the people and places limits against encroachment of those rights by governmental authorities. The rights of the people are set forth in general terms, such as not being deprived of "life, liberty or property, without due process"; these terms are not defined within the text of the constitution.

Additionally, constitutional amendments sometimes are handled differently than amendments to a statutory section of a code. In a code, any amendments are integrated into the text of the statutory sections; when a constitution is amended, the amendments may appear as separate provisions at the end of the original text. The first ten amendments to the United States Constitution, which serve as our bill of rights, illustrate this principle.

Illustration 7-18 on page 224 shows section 4 of the New Mexico Constitution. This section sets out the inherent rights of the people of New Mexico recognized under the constitution. It is part of New Mexico's bill of rights. As in the federal constitution, note the generality of the language and the absence of defined terms.

Illustration 7-18 N.M. Const. art. II, § 4.

Sec. 4. [Inherent rights.]

All persons are born equally free, and have certain natural, inherent and inalienable rights, among which are the rights of enjoying and defending life and liberty, of acquiring, possessing and protecting property, and of seeking and obtaining safety and happiness.

Rights described in this section are not absolute, but are subject to reasonable regulation. Otero v. Zouhar, 102 N.M. 493, 697 P.2d 493 (Ct. App. 1984), aff'd in part and rev'd in part on other grounds, 102 N.M. 482, 697 P.2d 482 (1985), overruled on other grounds, Grantland v. Lea Regional Hosp., Inc., 110 N.M. 378, 796 P.2d 599 (1990).

Unreasonable interference with others. — This section means that each person may seek his safety and happiness in any way he sees fit so long as he does not unreasonably interfere with the safety and happiness of another. 1966 Op. Att'y Gen. No. 66-15.

Graduated income tax provisions are in no way related to or in conflict with the inherent rights provision in this section. Such income tax provisions do not prevent or deny a person's natural inherent and inalienable rights. 1968 Op. Att'y Gen. No. 68-9.

Economic policy adopted by state. — A state is free to adopt an economic policy that may reasonably be deemed to promote the public welfare and may enforce that policy by appropriate legislation without violation of the due process clause so long as such legislation has a reasonable relation to a proper legislative purpose and is neither arbitrary nor discriminatory. Rocky Mt. Whsle. Co. v. Ponca Whsle. Mercantile Co., 68 N.M. 228, 360 P.2d 643, appeal dismissed, 368 U.S. 31, 82 S. Ct. 145, 7 L. Ed. 2d 90 (1961).

Laws 1937, ch. 44, § 2, Fair Trade Act (49-2-2, 1953 Comp., now repealed), was unconstitutional and void as an arbitrary and unreasonable exercise of the police power without any substantial relation to the public health, safety or general welfare insofar as it concerned persons who were not parties to contracts provided for in Laws 1937, ch. 44, § 1 (49-2-1, 1953 Comp., now repealed). Skaggs Drug Center v. General Elec. Co., 63 N.M. 215, 315 P.2d 967 (1957).

The right of association emanating from the first amendment is not absolute. Its exercise, as is the exercise of express first amendment rights, is subject to some regulation as to time and place. Futrell v. Ahrens, 88 N.M. 284, 540 P.2d 214 (1975).

The right of association has never been held to apply to the right of one individual to associate with another, and certainly it has never been construed as an absolute right of association between a man and woman at any and all places and times. Futrell v. Ahrens, 88 N.M. 284, 540 P.2d 214 (1975).

Constitutional rights of teachers and students. — Neither students nor teachers shed their constitutional rights to freedom of speech or expression at the schoolhouse gate; school officials do not possess absolute authority over their students, and among the activities to which schools are dedicated is personal communication among students, which is an important part of the educational process. Futrell v. Ahrens, 88 N.M. 284, 540 P.2d 214 (1975).

A regulation of the board of regents of the New Mexico state university which prohibited visitation by persons of the opposite sex in residence hall, or dormitory, bedrooms maintained by the regents on the university campus, except when moving into the residence halls and during annual homecoming celebrations, where the regents placed no restrictions on intervisitation between persons of the opposite sex in the lounges or lobbies of the residence halls, the student union building, library or other buildings, or at any other place on or off the campus, and no student was required to live in a residence hall, did not interfere appreciably, if at all, with the intercommunication important to the students of the university, the regulation was reasonable, served legitimate educational purposes and promoted the welfare of the students at the university. Futrell v. Ahrens, 88 N.M. 284, 540 P.2d 214 (1975).

Although personal intercommunication among students at schools, including universities, is an important part of the educational process, it is not the only, or even the most important, part of that process. Futrell v. Ahrens, 88 N.M. 284, 540 P.2d 214 (1975).

Status of resident for divorce purposes. — The New Mexico legislature may constitutionally confer the status of resident for divorce purposes upon those continuously stationed within this state by reason of military assignment. Wilson v. Wilson, 58 N.M. 411, 272 P.2d 319 (1954).

Right to protect property. — The right to protect property being a specifically mentioned right, its presence in this section might provide the basis for additional protection against unreasonable searches and seizures. State v. Sutton, 112 N.M. 449, 816 P.2d 518 (Ct. App. 1991).

Reclamation district contract. — A provision of a reclamation contract allowing a reclamation district to enter into a lawful contract with the United States for the improvement of the district and the increase of its water supply does not violate this section or art. II, § 18. Middle Rio Grande Water Users Ass'n v. Middle Rio Grande Conservancy Dist., 57 N.M. 287, 258 P.2d 391 (1953).

Cause of action as property right. — Cause of action which Indian acquires when tort is committed against him is property which he may acquire or become invested with, particularly if tort is committed outside of reservation by a state citizen who is not an Indian; where Indian is killed as result of such tort, the cause of action survives. Trujillo v. Prince, 42 N.M. 337, 78 P.2d 145 (1938).

Recovery of damages as property right. — A tort victim's interest in full recovery of damages calls for a form of scrutiny somewhere between minimum rationality and strict scrutiny. Therefore, intermediate scrutiny should be applied to determine the constitutionality of the cap on damages in Subsection A(2) of 41-4-19 NMSA 1978 of the Tort Claims Act. Trujillo v. City of Albuquerque, 110 N.M. 621, 798 P.2d 571 (1990).

Ordinance denying right to canvass. — Green River ordinance was held valid despite contention that it deprived photographer who employed solicitors to canvass residential areas of right to acquire and enjoy property. Green v. Town of Gallup, 46 N.M. 71, 120 P.2d 619 (1941).

Comparable provisions. — Idaho Const., art. I, § 1.

Iowa Const., art. I, § 1.

Montana Const., art. II, § 3.

Utah Const., art. I, § 1.

Law reviews. — For survey, "The Statute of Limitations in Medical Malpractice Actions," see 6 N.M. L. Rev. 271 (1976).

Am. Jur. 2d, A.L.R. and C.J.S. references. —

2. Why Are Constitutions Useful?

Constitutions generally regulate only governmental action. They thus are valuable in two circumstances: (1) when a party seeks to assess the validity of an executive or legislative act or (2) when a party seeks to challenge other action taken by a governmental authority for constitutional reasons. The court then looks to the constitution in making its determination regarding the validity of the law or action taken.

On rare occasions, nongovernmental action may be regulated by constitutional law. Some nongovernmental entities may be governed by constitutional law when their actions are quasi-governmental or tightly enmeshed in government functions. In addition, some state constitutional provisions are written broadly enough to apply to private actors as well.

In the Canoga case, the orchestra is a private organization. Hence, a constitution is unlikely to govern its actions. Neither the federal nor the New Mexico constitution apply to this private-sector dispute. A constitutional provision that focused exclusively on governmental actors would apply if the employer were the government or if the employee were challenging a statute on constitutional grounds. Ms. Canoga's private-sector claim could be a constitutional matter under some constitutions that address private sector actions, either expressly or by implication (that is, by court interpretation).

3. How Do You Research Constitutions?

When researching constitutional issues, you really are seeking two primary authorities: (1) the text of the constitution itself and (2) case law interpreting the constitution. Because a constitution typically states general aspirational principles, the courts must interpret the text and apply the concepts in contemporary society. You must read the constitution in conjunction with those judicial decisions to understand the meaning of the constitution as applied by the courts.

a. Using Paper Media

Federal and state statutory codes contain the complete text of the jurisdiction's constitution. The constitution is not part of the code; it is included in the code for convenience. Thus, the text of the United States Constitution can be found in U.S.C., U.S.C.A., or U.S.C.S. Likewise, the state codes contain the text of the state constitutions. Some state codes also contain the text of the United States Constitution.

You can efficiently find case law interpreting a constitutional provision by using an annotated code. Both U.S.C.A. and U.S.C.S. present annotations similar to those that follow statutory sections. These annotations contain digests of cases and citations to various commentary sources, such as legal periodical articles, treatises, and encyclopedias, that refer to and analyze the Constitution. Each of the annotated state codes contains the text of the constitution for that state and similar annotations. To locate the pertinent constitutional provision, you can obtain a citation from a secondary source or use the general index in the annotated code or the outline of the constitution, which typically appears at the beginning of the constitution.

The New Mexico Constitution appears in the annotated code, *New Mexico Statutes Annotated*. You can use either the general index to the annotated code or the outline of the constitution. Section 4 of the New Mexico Constitution enumerates the inherent rights protected under the constitution. See Illustration 7-18 on page 224. Note that privacy is not specifically stated.

Once you have found and read the applicable constitutional provisions and pertinent annotations in the main volume of your code, be sure to update and expand your research. Check the applicable pocket parts and advance legislative services for the annotated code, just as you would in updating a statutory code section. It is rare that an amendment is made to the federal or state constitutions; hence it is more likely that you will find recent cases or citations to commentary sources when you check the updating code services.

To search for the text of any constitutional amendment that a legislative body may have approved for submission to the electorate for vote, you must examine the applicable federal or state session laws. Again, such proposals for constitutional amendments are uncommon, but if the legislature takes such action via legislation, the proposed constitutional amendment will first take the form of a bill. If passed, it will be published with other legislative acts for that year.

Another useful source for updating a constitution is a *Shepard's* statutory citator. *Shepard's United States Citations,* statute edition, contains entries for the federal constitution, and each of the state *Shepard's Citations,* statute edition, contains entries for the state constitution, as well as the federal constitution. The specific section of the constitution is the cited source. Under the heading of the constitutional section is a list of cases and various commentary sources that have cited that particular section of the constitution. The citator also contains information about any constitutional amendments.

b. Using Online Media: LEXIS as an Example

To locate the text of a federal or state constitution online, you can use either LEXIS or WESTLAW. Both systems include constitutions as part of the annotated code databases. Thus, you research constitutions in the same manner that you research federal or state codes.

To use LEXIS as an example, to search the United States Constitution, select the GENFED library. There are two appropriate files: (1) the USCODE file, which contains the text of the United States Constitution and annotations as found in U.S.C.S. (as well as the full text and annotations of the code, of course), or (2) the USCNST file, which contains only the text and annotations of the Constitution as published in U.S.C.S. Because the USCNST file is narrower, it is a more efficient choice. These files are updated monthly when the paper advance legislative service for U.S.C.S. is published.

It is possible to do either a natural language (Freestyle) search or a Boolean search in the USCNST file. An appropriate Freestyle search is: [does an employee have a constitutional right of privacy]. An appropriate Boolean search is: [private or privacy]. For the Canoga case, any search related to privacy would fail to retrieve an applicable constitutional provision because privacy is not an enumerated right in the United States Constitution. Because the database includes annotations, the sample search would retrieve cases that relate to privacy, but none would be relevant to our research situation because the orchestra is not a governmental entity.

To search for the text of a state constitution, you first would select the applicable state code database. For the Canoga case, the NMCODE file contains the full text of the *New Mexico Statutes Annotated,* which includes the text of the New Mexico Constitution and code, plus the related annotations. It also includes the most recent advance legislative service supplements, so this database is updated when the paper copy is updated, which occurs periodically throughout the year.

Neither a natural language nor a Boolean search in this database yielded pertinent documents. As already noted, New Mexico does not recognize privacy as an enumerated constitutional right, and none of the annotations were relevant.

To do more comprehensive research than is possible in a code database with selected case digests, you could search the case law database for your jurisdiction.

Constitutional law research is difficult, whether done in paper or online. Finding case law in paper media typically requires skimming many case annotations on a topic; the index to annotations in the paper code may be a more efficient means of finding relevant annotations. One advantage of the online system is the ability to search by key word; the terms you may be seeking may not be indexed in the paper indexes. The online systems and the paper sources are updated at nearly the same time, so the online system does not provide information that is more current.

c. Summary of Canoga Research

In the Canoga case, it was appropriate to examine the New Mexico Constitution and the federal constitution to determine if there were any constitutional provisions restricting private employers from infringing an employee's right to smoke when away from the workplace. As for federal constitutional law, the orchestra, a private party, is not a public employer and probably does not function as a public or quasi-governmental entity subject to federal constitutional restrictions. Therefore, Ms. Canoga cannot invoke a federal constitutional claim against the orchestra.

Some state constitutions do restrict the actions of private entities as well as the actions of government or quasi-governmental entities. That does not appear to be the case in New Mexico. Furthermore, the New Mexico Constitution does not include privacy as a protected right. Therefore, Ms. Canoga cannot raise a state constitutional action against the orchestra as well.

4. What Else?

Secondary Sources. Numerous secondary sources provide case law information on the United States Constitution. (See Chapter 4.) *The Constitution of the United States of America; Analysis and Interpretation,* published by the Library of Congress, is one of the most comprehensive secondary sources for finding annotations. It is published at approximately ten-year intervals with periodic supplements. It contains the text of the United States Constitution and its amendments, with textual analysis of Supreme Court decisions. You can gain access to this source by using its topical index or by browsing by specific section of the Constitution. Because it is a single volume, it is more convenient to use than the annotated codes. Because it refers only to United States Supreme Court decisions, it is far more limited in scope than the annotated codes and is updated less frequently.

Encyclopedias and Treatises. For an introduction to basic constitutional principles, you may wish to seek out encyclopedias or treatises on constitutional law, such as the following:

Encyclopedia of the American Constitution (Leonard W. Levy, ed., 1986 & Supp. 1992).
John E. Nowak & Ronald D. Rotunda, *Constitutional Law* (4th ed. 1991).
Ronald D. Rotunda & John E. Nowak, *Treatise on Constitutional Law: Substance and Procedure* (2d ed. 1992) (multivolume).
Laurence H. Tribe, *American Constitutional Law* (2d ed. 1988).

Historical Material. If you need to research the historical background of the federal constitution, consult Morris L. Cohen et al., *How to Find the Law* 208-11 (9th ed. 1989).

Periodicals. Legal periodicals are particularly valuable for finding case law and providing commentary on constitutional law. An annual survey of recent Supreme Court decisions, most of which focus on constitutional provisions, is contained in the *Supreme Court Review.* A few specialized law journals, such as *Constitutional Commentary* and *Hastings Constitutional Law Quarterly,* also focus on constitutional questions.

5. How Do You Cite Constitutions?

Constitutional citations are governed by Rule 11 of *The Bluebook.* For provisions currently in force, use the abbreviated name of the jurisdiction, "Const.," and identify the provision. Cite the constitutions discussed above as:

U.S. Const. art. I, § 8.
N.M. Const. art. II, § 4.

E. Concluding Points

Because statutes are primary authority, your research will not be correct, comprehensive, or credible unless you research the statutory law on your topic competently. As you research in statutes, first determine whether your topic is governed by state law, federal law, or both. Begin with a statute from your jurisdiction, read the cases interpreting that statute, and turn to a statute from another jurisdiction only as necessary to find additional cases interpreting the same topic or statutory language.

Paper research in statutory law entails use of an interlocking system of codes, advance legislative services, session laws, and statutory citators. A code provides a topically organized compilation of nearly all of the statutes currently in effect in a particular jurisdiction. An advance legislative service shows the recently enacted changes in the code material. A statutory citator allows you to Shepardize a statute, so that you can learn whether it has been changed and how it has been treated in later cases. Session laws are valuable sources for tracking which version of the statute was in effect as of a particular date.

An alternative to paper research is online research. To research statutes effectively online, you first must select an appropriate code database and write a natural language or Boolean search. Your search can retrieve both the text of the statute and related case annotations, or just the text. Because it is difficult to develop a search using unique terms, it is not always efficient to search statutes online. To search case law interpreting statutes, it may be more efficient to use a case law database for the appropriate jurisdiction. If you already know the citation of a statute and wish to see its text and case annotations, it is easy to perform that search using the Lexstat or FIND function.

Some statutes are drawn from uniform or model acts, which are drafted by public or private organizations to standardize the statutes of the fifty states. These uniform and model acts are actually secondary sources until they are enacted by a jurisdiction, so they are contained in specialized secondary sources. The largest of these sources is available on WESTLAW.

A constitution is the highest law in each American jurisdiction. It is researched by using some statutory sources, as well as some sources particular to constitutional research. Both paper and online sources exist.

8 Locate, Read, and Update Primary Authority: Legislative Process Materials

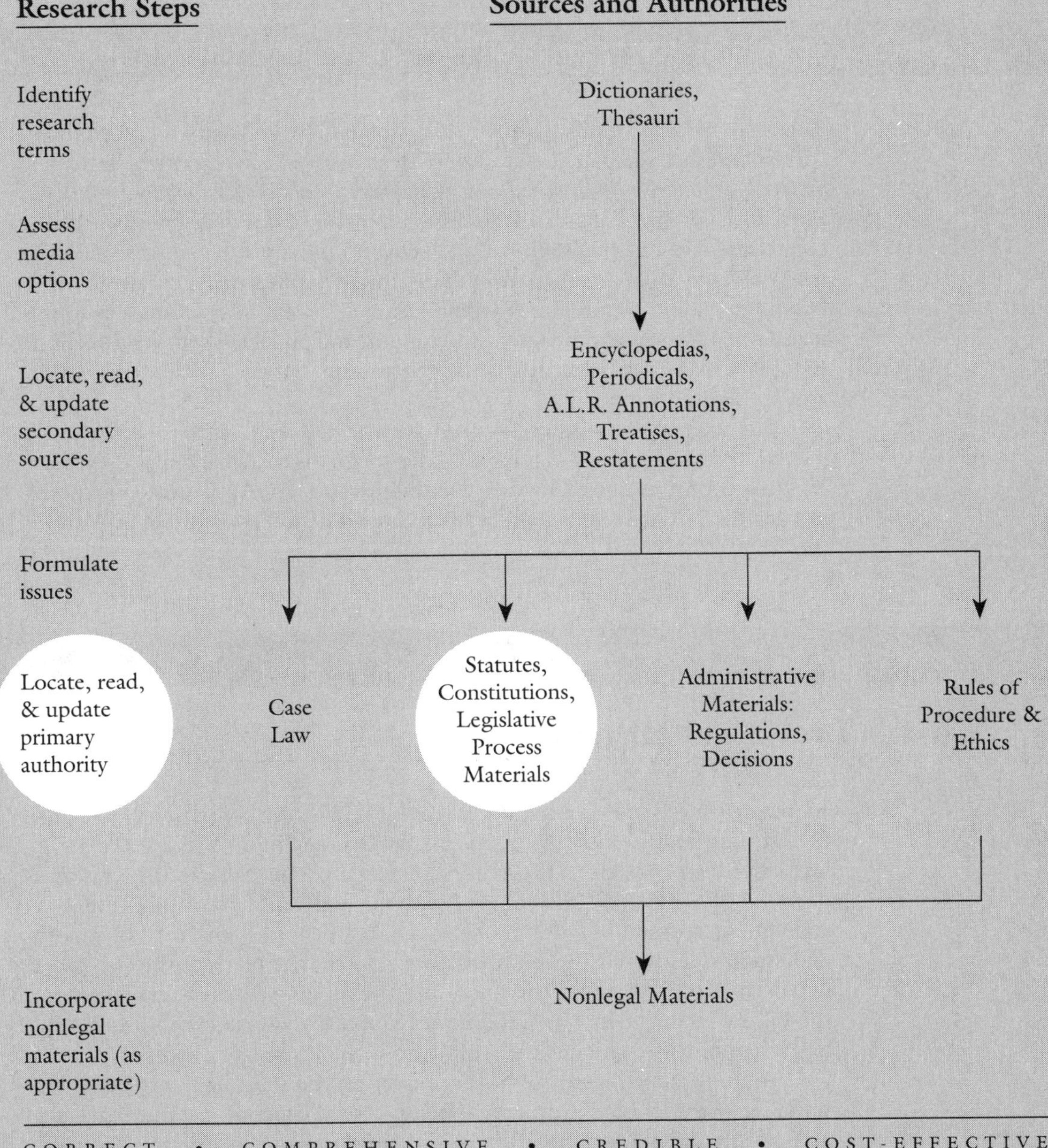

CORRECT • COMPREHENSIVE • CREDIBLE • COST-EFFECTIVE

Summary of Contents

A. Preliminary Points

This chapter covers the legislative process and its relationship with the statutory sources in Chapter 7. Chapter 7 dealt with enacted statutes and their enacted amendments and repeals. Chapter 8 focuses on using legislative process materials to discern legislative intent or research legislative history and to track pending legislation. Part B covers how to locate legislative history materials and evaluate their usefulness in discerning the legislative intent behind a vague or ambiguous statute. Part C covers how to track pending legislation to learn of its progress, its content, and possibly its future direction. Exhibit 8.1 on page 233 depicts the relationship between statutory research and legislative process.

This chapter continues to illustrate the research of the Canoga case (stated at pages 2-3 in Chapter 1). The focus on this chapter is Congress' enactment of the Americans with Disabilities Act (ADA), which is discussed in Chapter 7. The issue is whether nicotine addiction is a "disability" under the ADA.

B. Legislative History

1. What Is Legislative History?

In the broadest sense, a statute's legislative history consists of all of the background and events giving rise to its enactment. In a narrower sense, legislative history refers to the materials created at each stage of the legislative process. These include the initial proposed legislation (the "bill") and its subsequent redrafts, the testimony given by witnesses, any related reports and studies generated by the legislature concerning the bill, the legislative debate that took place on the floor, and the executive's messages following the bill's enactment by the legislature. Exhibit 8.2 on page 233 lists federal legislative history materials that result from the legislative process.

To understand legislative history research, you must have a basic understanding of the legislative process. The process of enacting a statute is similar at both the federal and state levels. For purposes of this example, you will

Exhibit 8.1 Relationship between Statutes and Legislative Process.

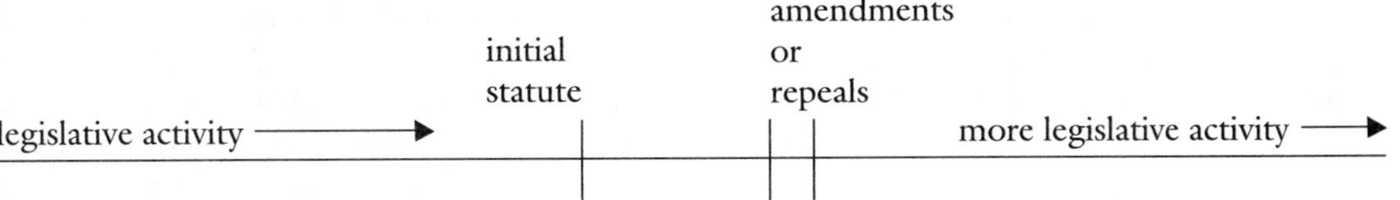

Ch. 8, Part B legislative *history*	Ch. 7, statutory research	Ch. 8, Part C *pending* legislation

Exhibit 8.2 Legislative History Documents.

Document	*Explanation*	*Common Sources (Paper and Microform)*
Bills	Proposed legislation and all versions of the bill	*CIS/Congressional Bills, Resolutions and Laws* on microfiche, U.S. GPO bill collection on microfiche
Hearings	The transcripts of testimony presented to the committee	*CIS/Microfiche Library,* GPO[1]
Prints	Publications that provide information and analysis for the committee	*CIS/Microfiche Library,* GPO[1]
Reports	Committee publications of its findings and recommendations to the parent body on the proposed bill	*CIS/Microfiche Library,* U.S.C.C.A.N., *United States Serial Set,* GPO[1]
House and Senate Documents	Presidential messages and executive agencies' reports to Congress, committee publications not published as prints	*CIS/Microfiche Library, United States Serial Set,* GPO[1]
Legislative debates	Daily transcripts of congressional floor activities	*Congressional Record* (or predecessor title)
Presidential signing statements	General comments concerning the purpose and value of legislation to the public	U.S.C.C.A.N., *Weekly Compilation of Presidential Documents*
Presidential veto messages	Explanation for vetoing legislation	*Congressional Record, U.S.C.C.A.N., Weekly Compilation of Presidential Documents*
Public law	Enacted bill	*Statutes at Large,* U.S.C.C.A.N.

[1]Individual titles are published by the Government Printing Office.

follow a bill through the United States Congress. See Illustration 8-1 on page 235 for a graphic of how a bill becomes law.

Proposed legislation is introduced into a session of Congress by either a member of the House of Representatives or by a Senator. Some bills have multiple sponsors, to reflect broad political support. Each bill is given a unique number, which indicates both the body in which it is introduced and the order in which it is introduced. A Senate bill is identified by a number that begins with "S." for Senate; a House of Representatives bill is identified by "H.R." The same bill (a companion bill) may be introduced into both the House and Senate; in this case it will have two unique bill numbers—one in the House and the other in the Senate.

For example, the Americans with Disabilities Act was originally introduced in several predecessor versions. The enacted version was introduced the Senate as S. 933; it had thirty-five sponsors. See Illustration 8-2 on page 236. The parallel bill in the House was H.R. 2273.

To become enacted as a public law, the bill typically must successfully pass through three legislative stages: consideration by House and Senate committees; debate by both houses of Congress and affirmative votes in both houses; and approval by the President (or congressional override of a presidential veto). At each stage, various kinds of legislative materials are created. See Exhibit 8.2 on page 233.

In the first stage, congressional committees generate hearing transcripts, committee prints, and committee reports. Hearing transcripts are the transcripts of committee proceedings, or hearings, during which witnesses (experts, government officials, or members of the public) testify about proposed legislation. They also may reflect data or documents presented to the committee by these witnesses. See Illustration 8-3 on page 237 for an example of hearing testimony. Committee prints are the "homework" of Congress; they provide the committee with information in the form of statistics, scientific and social studies, historical data, bibliographies, bill comparisons, and other analyses. These prints are written by committee research staffs, the Library of Congress, or independent consultants. Committee reports contain the committee's findings and recommendations to the parent legislative body (House or Senate) concerning its hearings, studies, and deliberations. See Illustration 8-4 on pages 238-239. Of particular importance are conference committee reports, which are the work product of the joint House and Senate committees designed to resolve differences in the text of the bills passed by the two houses. See Illustration 8-5 on page 240. The committees also may use House and Senate Documents and legislative debates. House and Senate Documents include presidential messages, executive agencies' reports to Congress, and some committee publications not published as committee prints.

The second stage involves legislative debates, which generate transcripts of statements made on the floor of both the houses of the legislature, as well as the votes of the legislators. See Illustration 8-6 on page 241.

In the third stage, presidential signing statements and veto messages accompany, respectively, the executive's enactment or veto of a bill. See Illustration 8-7 on page 242.

Once enacted, the bill is assigned a public law number, which reflects

Illustration 8-1

How a Bill Becomes Law, *Congressional Quarterly Guide to Congress* App. 92-A (4th ed. 1991).

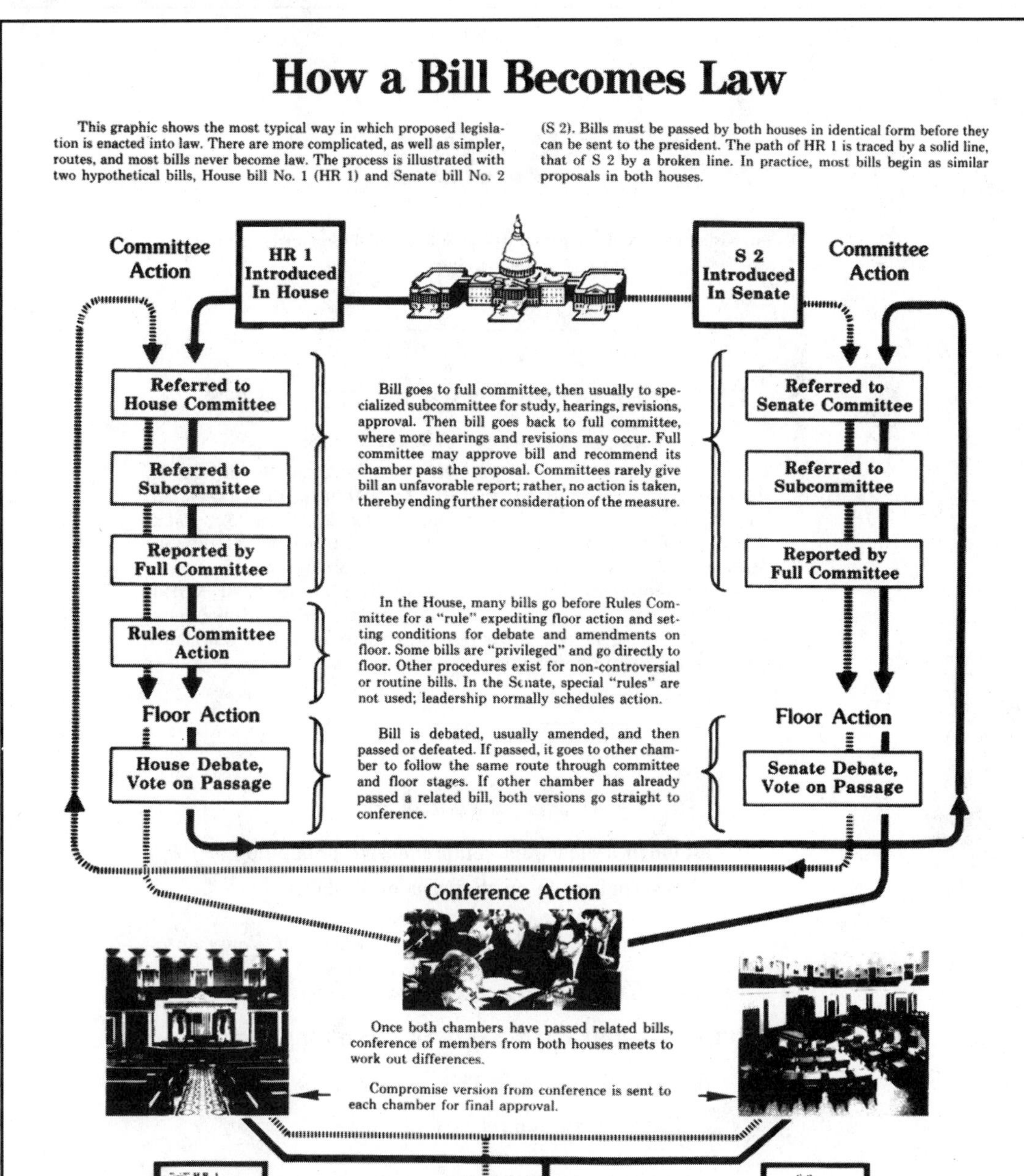

Illustration 8-2 S. 933, 101st Cong., 1st Sess. § 1 (1990).

II

101ST CONGRESS
1ST SESSION

S. 933

To establish a clear and comprehensive prohibition of discrimination on the basis of disability.

IN THE SENATE OF THE UNITED STATES

MAY 9 (legislative day, JANUARY 3), 1989

Mr. HARKIN (for himself, Mr. KENNEDY, Mr. DURENBERGER, Mr. SIMON, Mr. JEFFORDS, Mr. CRANSTON, Mr. MCCAIN, Mr. MITCHELL, Mr. CHAFEE, Mr. LEAHY, Mr. STEVENS, Mr. INOUYE, Mr. COHEN, Mr. GORE, Mr. PACKWOOD, Mr. RIEGLE, Mr. GRAHAM, Mr. PELL, Mr. DODD, Mr. ADAMS, Ms. MIKULSKI, Mr. METZENBAUM, Mr. MATSUNAGA, Mr. WIRTH, Mr. BINGAMAN, Mr. CONRAD, Mr. BURDICK, Mr. LEVIN, Mr. LIEBERMAN, Mr. MOYNIHAN, Mr. KERRY, Mr. SARBANES, Mr. BOSCHWITZ, and Mr. HEINZ) introduced the following bill; which was read twice and referred to the Committee on Labor and Human Resources

---

A BILL

To establish a clear and comprehensive prohibition of discrimination on the basis of disability.

Be it enacted by the Senate and House of Representatives of the United States of America in Congress assembled,

SECTION 1. SHORT TITLE; TABLE OF CONTENTS.

(a) SHORT TITLE.—This Act may be cited as the "Americans with Disabilities Act of 1989".

(b) TABLE OF CONTENTS.—The table of contents is as follows:

Illustration 8-3

Americans with Disabilities Act of 1989, Hearings on H.R. 2273 before the Subcomm. on Employment Opportunities and the Subcomm. on Select Education of the House Comm. on Education and Labor, 101st Cong., 1st Sess. 2 (1990) (statement of Evan J. Kemp, Commissioner, EEOC).

5

TESTIMONY OF
EVAN J. KEMP, JR., COMMISSIONER
U. S. EQUAL EMPLOYMENT OPPORTUNITY COMMISSION
BEFORE THE HOUSE SUBCOMMITTEES ON SELECT
EDUCATION AND EMPLOYMENT OPPORTUNITIES

SEPTEMBER 13, 1989 AT 10:00 A.M.

I am here today not as a Commissioner of the U.S. Equal Employment Opportunity Commission, but as a person with a disability. I am 100% for the Americans With Disabilities Act. But there are those who ask "Does it make economic sense to integrate disabled people into society?" Other people inquire "How many disabled people are there really?" While others ask "Does it really matter? Isn't medical science going to cure most disabling conditions?" Both disabled people and nondisabled and politician and nonpoliticians have all asked these questions many times.

To answer these questions and others, I have found it necessary and helpful to have a philosophical framework to work from. I would like to share it with you.

The disability rights movement addresses the problems of all our citizens who are different in some respect from what society considers to be an acceptable American: the 28 year

the enacting Congress and the order in which the bill became law. See Illustration 8-8 on pages 243-244. For example, Pub. L. No. 101-336 was the 336th act passed by the 101st Congress. If a bill is not passed by the end of a particular Congress in which it was introduced (each Congress has two consecutive one-year sessions), the bill dies. It may be re-introduced with a new bill number in a subsequent Congress. If it passes, it is published first in slip law form, then in compiled session laws.

Legislative history is a unique form of authority. The materials created during the legislative process are primary *sources* in some sense because they

Illustration 8-4

H.R. Rep. No. 485, 101st Cong., 2d Sess. 1, 24 (1990), *reprinted in* 1990 U.S.C.C.A.N. 267-68.

AMERICANS WITH DISABILITIES ACT OF 1990

1 *P.L. 101–336, see page 104 Stat. 327*

2 **DATES OF CONSIDERATION AND PASSAGE**
Senate: September 7, 1989; July 11, 13, 1990
House: May 22, July 12, 1990

4

**Senate Report (Labor and Human Resources Committee)
No. 101–116, Aug. 30, 1989
[To accompany S. 933]**

**House Report (Public Works and Transportation Committee) No.
101–485(I), May 14, 1990
3 [To accompany H.R. 2273]**

**House Report (Education and Labor Committee) No. 101–485(II),
May 15, 1990
[To accompany H.R. 2273]**

**House Report (Judiciary Committee) No. 101–485(III), May 15,
1990
[To accompany H.R. 2273]**

**House Report (Energy and Commerce Committee) No. 101–
485(IV), May 15, 1990
[To accompany H.R. 2273]**

5

**House Conference Report No. 101–558, June 26, 1990
[To accompany S. 933]**

**House Conference Report No. 101–596, July 12, 1990
[To accompany S. 933]**

6

Cong. Record Vol. 135 (1989)

Cong. Record Vol. 136 (1990)

7 *The Senate bill was passed in lieu of the House bill after amending its language to contain much of the text of the House bill. The House Report (Parts I (this page), II (page 303), III (page 445), IV (page 512)) is set out below and the second House Conference Report (page 565) and the President's Signing Statement (page 601) follow.*

HOUSE REPORT NO. 101–485(I)

[page 1]

The Committee on Public Works and Transportation, to whom was referred the bill (H.R. 2273) to establish a clear and comprehensive prohibition of discrimination on the basis of disability, having considered the same, report favorably thereon with an amendment and recommend that the bill as amended do pass.

* * * * *

267

Note:
1. Public law number
2. Dates of consideration and passage by both houses
3. Designation of bill that did not become law
4. Committee reports
5. Conference committee reports
6. *Congressional Record* reprints of debates
7. Cross-references to related U.S.C.C.A.N. reprints

Illustration 8-4 *(continued)*

LEGISLATIVE HISTORY
HOUSE REPORT NO. 101–485(I)

[page 24]

* * * * *

INTRODUCTION

The Americans With Disabilities Act (ADA) will permit the United States to take a long-delayed but very necessary step to welcome individuals with disabilities fully into the mainstream of American society. The specific provisions of the bill which lie within the jurisdiction of the Committee on Public Works and Transportation are primarily within Titles II and III, dealing with publicly and privately provided transportation services.

With regard to pubilicly provided transportation services, the bill requires the purchase of new transit vehicles for use on fixed route systems which are readily accessible to, and usable by, individuals with disabilities, including individuals who use wheelchairs. The bill also requires the provision of paratransit services for those individuals whose disabilities preclude their use of the fixed route system.

Transit agencies across the United States have already made some progress in the provision of accessible transit services—35% of America's transit buses are currently accessible. As more and more transit authorities make the commitment to provide fully accessible bus service, the percentage of new bus purchases which are accessible has grown to more than 50% annually. By the mid-1990's many American cities will have completely accessible fixed route systems. Furthermore, many of the transit systems in America already provide some type of paratransit services to the disabled. So, the passage of the ADA will not break sharply with existing transit policy. It will simply extend past successes to even more cities, so that this country can continue to make progress in providing much needed transit services for individuals with disabilities.

With regard to privately provided transportation services, which do not receive the high levels of federal subsidies that publicly provided services do, the requirements of the bill vary according to the size and type of vehicle, as well as according to the type of system on which the vehicle operates.

Nonetheless, in all cases, the Americans with Disabilities Act provides strong guarantees that individuals with disabilities will be

[page 25]

treated with respect and dignity while using transporatation services. After all, the Americans With Disabilities Act is ultimately a civil rights bill. The history of the United States is rich with examples of diversity triumphing over discrimination, but not so rich that this country can ever afford to exclude, or segregate in any way, the significant number of its citizens who have disabilities.

SECTION 1. SHORT TITLE; TABLE OF CONTENTS

Subsection (a) of this section provides that the Act may be cited as the "Americans with Disabilities Act of 1990".

SECTION 2. FINDINGS AND PURPOSES

This section describes the findings and purposes of the Act.

268

Illustration 8-5

H.R. Conf. Rep. No. 596, 101st Cong., 2d Sess. 57-58 (1990), *reprinted in* 1990 U.S.C.C.A.N. 566.

LEGISLATIVE HISTORY
HOUSE CONF. REP. NO. 101–596

agreed upon by the managers and recommended in the accompanying conference report:

The House amendment struck out all of the Senate bill after the enacting clause and inserted a substitute text.

The Senate recedes from its disagreement to the amendment of the House with an amendment which is a substitute for the Senate bill and the House amendment. The differences between the Senate bill, the House amendment, and the substitute agreed to in conference are noted below, except for clerical corrections, conforming changes made necessary by agreements reached by the conferees, and minor drafting and clarifying changes.

1. Short title

The Senate bill titles the Act the Americans with Disabilities Act of 1989. The House amendment changes the date to 1990.

The Senate recedes.

1A. Findings and purposes

The House amendment, but not the Senate bill, includes the term "color" in its list of factors which have been the basis of discrimination for which there is legal recourse to redress such discrimination.

The Senate recedes.

TITLE I OF THE ADA (EMPLOYMENT)

2. Definition of the term "direct threat"

The House amendment, but not the Senate bill, defines the term "direct threat" to mean a significant risk to the health or safety of others that cannot be eliminated by reasonable accommodation.

The Senate recedes.

3. Definitions of terms "illegal use of drugs" and "drugs"

The Senate bill uses the phrase "illegal drug" and explains that the term means a controlled substance, as defined in schedules I through V of section 202 of the Controlled Substances Act, the possession or distribution of which is unlawful under such Act and does not mean the use of a controlled substance pursuant to a valid

[page 58]

prescription or other uses authorized by the Controlled Substances Act.

The House amendment uses the phrase "illegal use of drugs" and defines the term to mean the use of drugs, the possession or distribution of which is unlawful under the Controlled Substances Act and does not mean the use of controlled substances taken under supervision by a licensed health care professional or other uses authorized by the Controlled Substances Act or other provisions of Federal law. The House amendment defines the term "drugs" to mean a controlled substance, as defined in schedules I through V of section 202 of the Controlled Substances Act.

The Senate recedes.

566

Illustration 8-6

136 Cong. Rec. 13,063 (1990).

June 6, 1990 CONGRESSIONAL RECORD—SENATE 13063

Glenn	Kohl	Pell
Gore	Lautenberg	Riegle
Graham	Leahy	Robb
Harkin	Levin	Rockefeller
Hatfield	Lieberman	Sanford
Hollings	Metzenbaum	Sarbanes
Inouye	Mikulski	Simon
Jeffords	Mitchell	Wirth
Kennedy	Moynihan	
Kerrey	Packwood	

NAYS—53

Armstrong	Garn	Murkowski
Bentsen	Gorton	Nickles
Bond	Gramm	Nunn
Boren	Grassley	Pressler
Breaux	Hatch	Pryor
Bryan	Heflin	Reid
Bumpers	Heinz	Roth
Burns	Helms	Rudman
Byrd	Humphrey	Sasser
Coats	Johnston	Shelby
Cochran	Kassebaum	Simpson
Conrad	Kasten	Specter
D'Amato	Lott	Stevens
Dixon	Lugar	Symms
Dole	Mack	Thurmond
Exon	McCain	Wallop
Ford	McClure	Warner
Fowler	McConnell	

NOT VOTING—7

Baucus	DeConcini	Wilson
Boschwitz	Dodd	
Chafee	Kerry	

So the motion to lay on the table was rejected.

Mr. HELMS. Mr. President, I move to reconsider the vote by which the motion was rejected.

Mr. DOLE. I move to lay that motion on the table.

The motion to lay on the table was agreed to.

● Mr. KERRY. Mr. President, an important family commitment requires that I be in Boston during the time allotted this morning for debate and the subsequent vote on the motion offered by the Senator from North Carolina, to instruct the conferees on the Americans With Disabilities Act [ADA]. I want to make it clear for the record, however, that were I present for the upcoming vote, I would vote against the motion to instruct and in support of the motion to table offered by the majority leader.

The ADA, as passed by the Senate on a vote of 76-8, already excludes coverage of individuals with a contagious disease who pose a threat to the health or safety of others which cannot be eliminated by reasonable accommodation. Further, Mr. President, Dr. Roper, Director of the Center for Disease Control as well as Secretary Louis Sullivan of the Department of Health and Human Services, have stated that people with AIDS do not pose a threat to health or safety in food handling positions, because AIDS is not a foodborne illness.

We should not be in a position where we give rights and protections with one hand as we do with the ADA and then take them away with the other, which is exactly what we would accomplish by approving this motion. The ADA goes to the heart of opening the doors of opportunity and toward eliminating judgments based on fear, prejudice and ignorance and we must protect the integrity of this legislation. As President Bush stated when he urged the Congress to pass the ADA, "I call on the Congress to get on the job of passing a law—embodied in the ADA that prohibits discrimination against those with HIV and AIDS. We won't tolerate discrimination.

Mr. President, we must move forward in helping to eliminate the discrimination faced by the Nation's 43 million disabled individuals. We have made a vitally important step in this regard with passage of the ADA. Let us continue to move forward in our fulfillment of this goal. I reiterate my strong opposition to the Helms motion and my strong support for the majority leader's motion to table.●

The PRESIDING OFFICER. All time having expired, the question is now on agreeing to the motion to instruct the conferees.

The Senator from North Carolina, [Mr. HELMS], is recognized.

Mr. HELMS. Mr. President, I think the Senate has made itself clear on this issue, and I see no point for a further rollcall vote.

I ask unanimous consent that the yeas and nays be vitiated.

The PRESIDING OFFICER. Without objection, the request of the Senator is agreed to.

The question now is on agreeing to the motion to instruct the conferees.

The motion was agreed to.

Mr. HELMS. Mr. President, I move to reconsider the vote by which the motion was agreed to.

Mr. HARKIN. I move to lay that motion on the table.

The motion to lay on the table was agreed to.

The PRESIDING OFFICER. Under the previous order, the Senator from Iowa [Mr. GRASSLEY] is now recognized.

MOTION TO INSTRUCT CONFEREES

Mr. GRASSLEY. Mr. President, I send a motion to the desk and ask for its immediate consideration.

The PRESIDING OFFICER. The clerk will report.

The assistant legislative clerk read as follows:

> The Senator from Iowa, Mr. Grassley, moves that the Senate instruct the Senate conferees on S. 933, the Americans with Disabilities Act, to ensure that the rights, protections, and remedies made available under that Act with regards to employment shall extend to the employees, and prospective employees, of members of Congress or the instrumentalities thereof, and that such employees, or prospective employees, who are aggrieved by a violation of that Act shall have a private cause of action against the individual or entity that has engaged in the violation of such employees rights under the Act in the appropriate district court of the United States.

The PRESIDING OFFICER. The Senator from Iowa.

Mr. GRASSLEY. Under a previous unanimous-consent agreement, that motion is withdrawn.

The PRESIDING OFFICER. The Senator is correct; the motion is withdrawn.

Mr. GRASSLEY. Mr. President, I had planned to offer at this point a motion to instruct the conferees with respect to congressional coverage under S. 933. My motion would have instructed that the conferees provide to aggrieved congressional employees, or prospective employees, among other remedies, a private right of action against Congress, its members, or its instrumentalities.

This right is long overdue, and I am pleased that the Senate is about to turn over a new leaf, when it comes to meaningful congressional coverage of the laws that we apply to all other Americans.

Because of the assurances I have received from my colleagues, Senator HARKIN, on behalf of the conferees, I will not offer that motion. I truly appreciate the commitment of my colleague from Iowa on this point. I know he will be sensitive to the potentially significant constitutional issues involved, and balance them against the rights of victims of discrimination.

I also appreciate the interests of the leadership to move rapidly on this important bill. I agree and am prepared to move.

Mr. President, permitting a right to legal redress of grievances for more than 30,000 employees in and around Capitol Hill—and countless more prospective employees—would help put an end to the shameful practice around here where we say to the American people: "do as we say, not as we do."

Unfortunately Mr. President, the statesman who can best explain this principle can't be here in person. We do, however, have the benefit of his writings on precisely this point, more than 200 years ago.

James Madison, writing in "Federalist 57," explained why it was that Congress would be deterred from passing oppressive laws upon the people. His remedy—that Congress "could make no law which will not have its full operation on themselves and their friends, as well as on the great mass of society."

Madison continued:

> This has always been deemed one of the strongest bonds by which human policy can connect the rulers and the people together. It creates between them a communion of interests and sympathy of sentiments * * * without which every government degenerates into tyranny.

Madison says:

> If it be asked, what is to restrain the Congress from making legal discriminations in favor of themselves, I answer: the genius of the whole system * * * the spirit which activates the people of America, a spirit which

Illustration 8-7

Statement by President George S. Bush upon Signing S. 933, *reprinted in* 1990 U.S.C.C.A.N. 601.

SIGNING STATEMENT
P.L. 101-336

STATEMENT BY PRESIDENT OF THE UNITED STATES

STATEMENT BY PRESIDENT GEORGE BUSH UPON SIGNING S. 933

26 Weekly Compilation of Presidential Documents 1165, July 30, 1990

Today, I am signing S. 933, the "Americans with Disabilities Act of 1990." In this extraordinary year, we have seen our own Declaration of Independence inspire the march of freedom throughout Eastern Europe. It is altogether fitting that the American people have once again given clear expression to our most basic ideals of freedom and equality. The Americans with Disabilities Act represents the full flowering of our democratic principles, and it gives me great pleasure to sign it into law today.

In 1986, on behalf of President Reagan, I personally accepted a report from the National Council on Disability entitled "Toward Independence." In that report, the National Council recommended the enactment of comprehensive legislation to ban discrimination against persons with disabilities. The Americans with Disabilities Act (ADA) is such legislation. It promises to open up all aspects of American life to individuals with disabilities—employment opportunities, government services, public accommodations, transportation, and telecommunications.

This legislation is comprehensive because the barriers faced by individuals with disabilities are wide-ranging. Existing laws and regulations under the Rehabilitation Act of 1973 have been effective with respect to the Federal Government, its contractors, and the recipients of Federal funds. However, they have left broad areas of American life untouched or inadequately addressed. Many of our young people, who have benefited from the equal educational opportunity guaranteed under the Rehabilitation Act and the Education of the Handicapped Act, have found themselves on graduation day still shut out of the mainstream of American life. They have faced persistent discrimination in the workplace and barriers posed by inaccessible public transportation, public accommodations, and telecommunications.

Fears that the ADA is too vague or too costly and will lead to an explosion of litigation are misplaced. The Administration worked closely with the Congress to ensure that, wherever possible, existing language and standards from the Rehabilitation Act were incorporated into the ADA. The Rehabilitation Act standards are already familiar to large segments of the private sector that are either Federal contractors or recipients of Federal funds. Because the Rehabilitation Act was enacted 17 years ago, there is already an extensive body of law interpreting the requirements of that Act. Employers can turn to these interpretations for guidance on how to meet their obligations under the ADA.

The Administration and the Congress have carefully crafted the ADA to give the business community the flexibility to meet the requirements of the Act without incurring undue costs. Cost may be taken into account in determining how an employee is "reasonably accommodated," whether the removal of a barrier is "readily achievable," or whether the provision of a particular auxiliary aid would result in an "undue burden." The ADA's most rigorous access requirements are reserved for new construction where

601

Illustration 8-8

Americans with Disabilities Act of 1990, Pub. L. No. 101-336, §§ 1-3, 104 Stat. 327-29.

❶ **PUBLIC LAW 101-336 [S. 933]; July 26, 1990**

AMERICANS WITH DISABILITIES ACT OF 1990

For Legislative History of Act, see p. 267.

An Act to establish a clear and comprehensive prohibition of discrimination on the basis of disability.

Be it enacted by the Senate and House of Representatives of the United States of America in Congress assembled,

Americans with Disabilities Act of 1990.

SECTION 1. SHORT TITLE; TABLE OF CONTENTS.

42 USC 12101 note.

(a) SHORT TITLE.—This Act may be cited as the "Americans with Disabilities Act of 1990".

(b) TABLE OF CONTENTS.—The table of contents is as follows:

42 USC 12101.

SEC. 2. FINDINGS AND PURPOSES.

(a) FINDINGS.—The Congress finds that—

(1) some 43,000,000 Americans have one or more physical or mental disabilities, and this number is increasing as the population as a whole is growing older;

(2) historically, society has tended to isolate and segregate individuals with disabilities, and, despite some improvements, such forms of discrimination against individuals with disabilities continue to be a serious and pervasive social problem;

(3) discrimination against individuals with disabilities persists in such critical areas as employment, housing, public accommodations, education, transportation, communication, recreation, institutionalization, health services, voting, and access to public services;

(4) unlike individuals who have experienced discrimination on the basis of race, color, sex, national origin, religion, or age, individuals who have experienced discrimination on the basis of disability have often had no legal recourse to redress such discrimination;

(5) individuals with disabilities continually encounter various forms of discrimination, including outright intentional exclusion, the discriminatory effects of architectural, transportation, and communication barriers, overprotective rules and policies,

104 STAT. 328

Note: 1. Public law number and designation of the bill enacted

Illustration 8-8 *(continued)*

failure to make modifications to existing facilities and practices, exclusionary qualification standards and criteria, segregation, and relegation to lesser services, programs, activities, benefits, jobs, or other opportunities;

(6) census data, national polls, and other studies have documented that people with disabilities, as a group, occupy an inferior status in our society, and are severely disadvantaged socially, vocationally, economically, and educationally;

(7) individuals with disabilities are a discrete and insular minority who have been faced with restrictions and limitations, subjected to a history of purposeful unequal treatment, and relegated to a position of political powerlessness in our society, based on characteristics that are beyond the control of such individuals and resulting from stereotypic assumptions not truly indicative of the individual ability of such individuals to participate in, and contribute to, society;

(8) the Nation's proper goals regarding individuals with disabilities are to assure equality of opportunity, full participation, independent living, and economic self-sufficiency for such individuals; and

(9) the continuing existence of unfair and unnecessary discrimination and prejudice denies people with disabilities the opportunity to compete on an equal basis and to pursue those opportunities for which our free society is justifiably famous, and costs the United States billions of dollars in unnecessary expenses resulting from dependency and nonproductivity.

(b) PURPOSE.—It is the purpose of this Act—

(1) to provide a clear and comprehensive national mandate for the elimination of discrimination against individuals with disabilities;

(2) to provide clear, strong, consistent, enforceable standards addressing discrimination against individuals with disabilities;

(3) to ensure that the Federal Government plays a central role in enforcing the standards established in this Act on behalf of individuals with disabilities; and

(4) to invoke the sweep of congressional authority, including the power to enforce the fourteenth amendment and to regulate commerce, in order to address the major areas of discrimination faced day-to-day by people with disabilities.

SEC. 3. DEFINITIONS. 42 USC 12102.

As used in this Act:

(1) AUXILIARY AIDS AND SERVICES.—The term "auxiliary aids and services" includes—

(A) qualified interpreters or other effective methods of making aurally delivered materials available to individuals with hearing impairments;

(B) qualified readers, taped texts, or other effective methods of making visually delivered materials available to individuals with visual impairments;

(C) acquisition or modification of equipment or devices; and

(D) other similar services and actions.

(2) DISABILITY.—The term "disability" means, with respect to an individual—

are generated by a government body while creating primary *authority*—a statute. They are subordinate to the statute itself. However, there is considerable disagreement about whether and to what extent any legislative process materials are themselves primary *authority*.

These materials have differing weights of authority as evidence of legislative intent. The "weightiness" or credibility of the materials depends on how well they represent the actual deliberative process of the legislature, rather than the view of an individual legislator or a witness. Materials generated near the end of the legislative process may be more weighty than materials generated near the beginning of the process. For instance, a conference committee report may be weightier than a committee report. In another example, a floor debate after a presidential veto may be weightier than the presidential veto message. Of course, not all of these materials exist for every bill or statute.

2. Why Is Legislative History Useful?

Rules of statutory construction emphasize the primacy of statutory language as the primary indicator of the legislature's intent. In applying a statute, a court is limited to determining what the legislature intended the words of the statute to mean and whether the legislature was within its constitutional authority in enacting that legislation; a court may not rewrite a statute or create a new one. Therefore, analysis begins with a close reading of the language of the statute. Statutory construction rules forbid the use of other sources, such as legislative history materials, unless a close reading of a statute reveals an ambiguity in the statute. For general principles of statutory construction and the use of legislative history materials, see 2A Norman J. Singer, *Statutes and Statutory Construction* §§ 48.01-.20 (5th ed. 1992 rev.).

Legislative history is one way of understanding a vague or ambiguous statute. This type of analysis hinges on determining the intent of the legislature in enacting the statute. It usually involves answering two questions: First, did the legislature intend the statute to cover the parties or the situation at issue? Second, if the statute does apply, what effect did the legislature intend the statute to have?

As you consider using legislative history materials as an indicator of legislative intent, keep several caveats in mind. First, the legislature may not have had any intent as to your situation. For example, controversies may arise in situations that were not contemplated by those who drafted the legislation, or the law may need to be interpreted in response to changing societal needs.

Second, some courts do not view arguments based on legislative history materials as credible. This skepticism is due in part to the difficulty of discerning from the mass of statements, reports, and procedural maneuvers what the legislature really intended in enacting a statute. Legislative history research rests in part on the premise—or fiction—that some of the statements made by individual legislators and witnesses shed light on the intent of the legislature as a whole. It also rests on the premise (perhaps more believable) that one can tell something about legislative intent by reading committee reports or by studying the various drafts or amendments to the bill as it made its way through the legislative process. None of the material making up a legislative history truly embodies the intent of the entire legislature—except the text of the bill as passed.

Third, in assessing the credibility of a statute's legislative history materials, you should be careful to account for the vagaries of the legislative process. For example, relying heavily on the "extended remarks" of a member of Congress might be imprudent. Extended remarks are not actually made during a congressional debate, but rather are added later to the published transcript of a debate and generally are not read by many members of Congress. In another example, the presidential signing message might contain interpretations of the enacted provisions, but those interpretations are not indicative of Congress' intent.

3. How Do You Research Legislative History?

As you no doubt have surmised, the federal legislative process and the materials it produces can be lengthy and complicated. Your research involves two tasks:

(1) tracing the legislative stages that created, amended, or repealed the statute; and
(2) locating, reading, and analyzing the materials that were produced during those stages.

Some of your work may already have been done for you in a compiled legislative history. However, in other instances, you will have to compile your own legislative history.

Legislative history research can be done in paper media, on CD-ROM, and online. However, unlike sources covered in earlier chapters of this book, many of these media are not alternative ways to research the same material, but rather are used together in a single research process. Accordingly, this part does not separate research in paper and online media.

To use legislative history materials properly, you should acquaint yourself thoroughly with your statute's full legislative history before using selected parts of it. For example, before relying on the testimony of a witness at a legislative hearing, you should assess the expertise of that witness' views and, more important, determine whether the witness was given credence by the legislators in later debates. You also should consider the testimony of opposing witnesses and the weight given to their comments. You may discover that some legislative history materials are no less ambiguous than the statute and that the same material may be used to support both sides of an argument.

If amendments exist, you often should examine the legislative history materials of both the original statute and its amendments. A legislature generally amends a statute to correct a flaw not seen at the time of original enactment, to respond to unforeseen problems, or to accommodate changes in public policy. Thus, the legislative history of an amendment often provides valuable insight into the original statute, along with guidance on what the amendment is intended to accomplish.

In addition, if the legislature considered any related bills on the same subject prior to enacting the statute you are researching, you may find it useful to know what the legislature rejected before it passed the statute you are researching.

a. Locating a Compiled Legislative History or a List of Legislative Materials

Although your goal is to find all of the pertinent primary sources, it often is most efficient to begin with secondary sources. The most efficient approach to legislative history research is to locate a compiled legislative history (a collection of pertinent legislative materials), if one exists. In recent years, commercial publishing companies have been expanding the number and scope of legislative histories that they compile and publish. As a general rule, compiled legislative histories exist only for those statutes of widespread importance; these compilations often will comprise several volumes. Alternatively, you may be able to find a list of the materials that constitute the legislative history of your statute.

To find out whether a compiled legislative history or a list exists for an enacted statute, consult a source such as Nancy P. Johnson, *Sources of Compiled Legislative Histories: A Bibliography of Government Documents, Periodical Articles, and Books* (AALL Publication Series No. 14, 1993), a page of which is shown in Illustration 8-9 on page 248. This publication contains an extensive table that is accessible by public law number or *Statutes at Large* citation. For each compiled legislative history or list, the table gives standard bibliographic information (for example, author, title, publisher, date, and Library of Congress number). The table also notes whether the resource discusses the legislative documents or merely cites them, and which documents (if any) it contains. Another useful source is Bernard Reams, *Federal Legislative Histories: An Annotated Bibliography, and Index to Officially Published Sources* (1994).

In the Canoga case, as Illustration 8-9 on page 248 shows, several publications about the ADA's legislative history exist. These compiled legislative histories and lists appear in a law review article, treatises, and a commercial publication. Illustration 8-2 on page 236 comes from that commercial publication. The compiled sources listed in Illustration 8-9 are probably adequate to complete the Canoga research. The most extensive of the compiled legislative histories is the next-to-last entry, Reams' six-volume set, which contains a chronology of the ADA bills; a bibliography of ADA sources; and the full

Illustration 8-9

Sources of Compiled Legislative Histories.

PUBLIC LAW BILL NUMBER	STATUTE	ACT ENTRY	CONTENTS: ACTUAL DOCS. / CITES TO DOCS.				
			REPORTS	HEARINGS	DEBATES	DISCUSSION	LISTS CITES
101-280 H.J.Res.553	104 Stat. 149	ETHICS REFORM ACT OF 1989: TECHNICAL AMENDMENTS					
		Tax Management Primary Sources, 101st Congress, Wash., D.C.: Bureau of National Affairs, 1989.	X				
101-311 H.R. 4612	104 Stat. 267	BANKRUPTCY: SWAP AGREEMENTS & FORWARD CONTRACTS					
		Collier on Bankruptcy, 15th ed., N.Y.: Matthew Bender, 1993, Legislative History: App. vols.			X		
101-336 S. 933	104 Stat. 327	AMERICANS WITH DISABILITIES ACT OF 1990					
		Americans with Disabilities Act of 1990: Law & Explanation, Chicago, IL: Commerce Clearing House, 1990. L.C.: KF480.A958 1990				X	X
		The Americans with Disabilities Act: A Practical and Legal Guide to Impact, Enforcement, and Compliance, Wash., D.C.: Bureau of National Affairs, 1990. L.C.: KF480.A957 1990				X	X
		Americans with Disabilities Act: A Survey of the Law, Regulations and Legislative History, New York, N.Y.: Practising Law Institute, 1992.				X	X
		BNA's Americans with Disabilities Act Manual, Wash., D.C.: Bureau of National Affairs, 1992. L.C.: KF480.A6B7	X				X
		The Disabled in the Workplace: Analysis of the Americans with Disabilities Act, N.Y.: Research Institute of America, 1990.				X	X
		Arlene Mayerson, The Americans with Disabilities Act—An Historic Overview, 7 **Labor Lawyer** 1 (1991).				X	X
		Henry H. Perritt, Jr., **Americans with Disabilities Act Handbook**, 2d ed., New York: Wiley, 1991. L.C.: KF3469.P47 1991				X	X
		Bernard D. Reams, Jr. et al., **Disability Law in the United States: A Legislative History of the Americans with Disabilities Act of 1990, P.L. 101-336**, 6 vols., Buffalo, N.Y.: Hein, 1992. L.C.: KF480.A32A15 1992	X	X	X		
		John G. Tysse & Edward E. Potter, **The Legislative History of the Americans with Disabilities Act**, Horsham, PA: LRP Publications, 1991. L.C.: KF480.A32A15	X	X			

B210 Rev. 1993

text of bills, hearings, reports, debates, the presidential statement, and other materials. The remainder of this chapter covers the wealth of other research finding tools and sources, under the assumption that no compiled legislative history or list exists.

b. Compiling Your Own Legislative History

Unfortunately, for most statutes, no compiled legislative history or list of legislative documents exists. Or the library you are using may not have the source you need because some of these sources are expensive. Furthermore, if you find a compiled legislative history, you still will need to evaluate whether it is comprehensive and then supplement it if it is not. Thus, you often will need to compile your statute's legislative history yourself.

Exhibit 8.2 on page 233 lists the sources containing legislative process materials. Thus, your legislative history research will include some of the following sources:

(1) the statutory codes;
(2) *United States Code Congressional and Administrative News* (U.S.C.C.A.N);
(3) Congressional Information Service (CIS) system, which includes indexes and abstracts of legislative history sources, and reprints of documents;
(4) various government publications, such as the *Congressional Record,* the *Monthly Catalog,* and bills.

This research process is anything but neat and linear. Rather than use all of these tools, you should tailor your research to the particular setting by choosing a combination of some of these sources. The following discussion presents these sources in order of how easily they assist you in finding credible legislative materials.

(1) The Statutory Codes

Once you have located a statute in one of the federal codes, you can gain a great deal of information about its statutory history simply by reading the notes following the sections. The *United States Code* (U.S.C.), *United States Code Annotated* (U.S.C.A.), and *United States Code Service* (U.S.C.S.) all provide a reference to the original enactment of the statute by listing its public law number, the date the statute was approved, and the *Statutes at Large* citation for the statute. U.S.C.A. is the most helpful of the three codes because it provides an additional item of information—a citation to the legislative history of the statute as published in *United States Code Congressional and Administrative News* (U.S.C.C.A.N.). The three federal codes also provide the same information for amendments. If your statute has been amended, you need to determine from the historical notes in the code when your key language was enacted.

In the Canoga case, Illustrations 7-2, 7-7, and 7-8 on pages 179-180, 195-197, and 198 show that the ADA was Pub. L. No. 101-336, which was approved on July 26, 1990, and published in *Statutes at Large* at 104 Stat. 327. In Illustration 7-7, which is reprinted here as Illustration 8-10 on page 251, U.S.C.A.'s "Historical and Statutory Notes" refer you to a House report, a House conference report, and a signing statement by the President at "1990 U.S. Code Cong. and Adm. News, p. 267."

(2) *United States Code Congressional and Administrative News* (U.S.C.C.A.N.)

United States Code Congressional and Administrative News (U.S.C.C.A.N.), published by West Publishing Company, is a convenient source for finding major legislative history references and reading major legislative materials. Each year's volumes cover a particular session of Congress and contain two sections: (1) a section containing reprints of the *Statutes at Large* session laws and (2) a legislative history section. See Illustrations 8-4 and 8-8 on pages 238 and 243. These sections often appear in different volumes. Both sections are ordered by public law number. The legislative history section contains references to legislative history information, as well as reprints and excerpts of the selected legislative materials that the West editors thought best reflect the legislative history of the bill during the legislative process. U.S.C.C.A.N. is not a comprehensive repository of legislative documents.

The federal codes (along with U.S.C.C.A.N. itself) provide you with four means of access to U.S.C.C.A.N. First, as stated previously, the U.S.C.A. annotations refer directly to the legislative history section of U.S.C.C.A.N. Second, if you know the *Statutes at Large* citation, you can locate the *Statutes at Large* reprint by relying on the spine labels; the reprint refers you to the starting page of the statute's legislative history materials in U.S.C.C.A.N. Third, if you know the statute's public law number, the public law numbers on the spines of the U.S.C.C.A.N. volumes (since 1980) allow you to select the correct volume of legislative history; the legislative history section then is ordered by public law number. Fourth, the annual subject index in the final U.S.C.C.A.N. volume for the year gives page references to both the *Statutes at Large* reprint and the legislative history sections.

The two sections of U.S.C.C.A.N. (*Statutes at Large* reprint and legislative history) typically provide the following information:

- the public law number assigned to the act;
- the designation of the bill that was enacted;
- the date the President approved the act;
- dates of consideration and passage by both houses;
- the designation of a bill that did not become law;
- the committees to which the bills were assigned;
- the numbers and dates of the committee reports;
- the numbers and dates of conference committee reports;

Illustration 8-10 42 U.S.C.A. § 12102 (West 1995).

7. Schools and universities

University's blanket policy prohibiting assignment of roommates to students with disabilities who require personal attendant care unnecessarily separated students with disabilities from those without disabilities and, thus, struck at essence of Americans with Disabilities Act (ADA) and specifically violated statute's stated purpose to provide clear and comprehensive national mandate for elimination of discrimination against individuals with disabilities. Coleman v. Zatechka, D.Neb. 1993, 824 F.Supp. 1360.

§ 12102. Definitions

As used in this chapter:

(1) Auxiliary aids and services

The term "auxiliary aids and services" includes—

(A) qualified interpreters or other effective methods of making aurally delivered materials available to individuals with hearing impairments;

(B) qualified readers, taped texts, or other effective methods of making visually delivered materials available to individuals with visual impairments;

(C) acquisition or modification of equipment or devices; and

(D) other similar services and actions.

(2) Disability

The term "disability" means, with respect to an individual—

(A) a physical or mental impairment that substantially limits one or more of the major life activities of such individual;

(B) a record of such an impairment; or

(C) being regarded as having such an impairment.

(3) State

The term "State" means each of the several States, the District of Columbia, the Commonwealth of Puerto Rico, Guam, American Samoa, the Virgin Islands, the Trust Territory of the Pacific Islands, and the Commonwealth of the Northern Mariana Islands.

(Pub.L. 101-336, § 3, July 26, 1990, 104 Stat. 329.)

HISTORICAL AND STATUTORY NOTES

Revision Notes and Legislative Reports

1990 Acts. House Report No. 101-485(Parts I-IV), House Conference Report No. 101-596, and Statement by President, see 1990 U.S. Code Cong. and Adm. News, p. 267.

CROSS REFERENCES

Auxiliary aids and services as defined in this section for purposes of national service trust fund program, see 42 USCA § 12581.

- the volumes and years of the *Congressional Record* in which the debates appear;
- information about the House bill that was not enacted; and
- a list of documents reproduced in U.S.C.C.A.N.

Typically, the legislative history section for each enactment contains one or more committee reports and perhaps a presidential signing statement. At the end of each edition of U.S.C.C.A.N., Table 4 synopsizes much of the legislative history information listed above in tabular form. See Illustration 8-11 on page 253.

In the Canoga case, the contents of the *Statutes at Large* reprint (Illustration 8-8 on pages 243-244) and the legislative history section (Illustration 8-4 on pages 238-239) show a fairly comprehensive and typical U.S.C.C.A.N. legislative history for the Americans with Disabilities Act (ADA). The two U.S.-C.C.A.N. sections shown in Illustrations 8-4 and 8-8 indicate that the statute was enacted as bill S. 933 on July 26, 1990. The legislation generated two House conference committee reports and two committee reports (one of which was written by four House committees), and the debate spanned two years of Congress; the references and dates for these items are listed in U.S.C.C.A.N. Reprinted in U.S.C.C.A.N. are the House committee report, the later conference committee report, and President Bush's signing statement.

Shown in Illustration 8-4 on pages 238-239, the House committee report was generated by four committees, each of which wrote one part of the report. Among the contents were summaries of the bill, section by section; explanations of specific wording and the committee's intent as to some provisions; reports from the Congressional Budget Office, estimating the cost of the ADA proposed in the House bill; concurring and dissenting views of individual committee members; a list of bill sponsors; lists of hearing witnesses; excerpts of testimony; and findings of the committee. Shown in Illustration 8-5 on page 240, the thirty-five-page House conference committee report cataloged the many differences between the House and Senate bills and noted which version prevailed on each differing provision (usually the House version did). Shown in Illustration 8-7 on page 242, the presidential signing statement explained the origin of the bill, countered arguments against the ADA, and highlighted the need for public education on the ADA.

(3) Congressional Information Service (CIS)

Another research tool for legislative history is the system developed by a private company, the Congressional Information Service (CIS). The CIS system is more complete than U.S.C.C.A.N. This section shows you how it works for legislative documents after 1969; it does not cover in detail the bulkier systems CIS provides for older documents. The CIS system has two major components: finding tools and legislative materials.

(a) CIS Finding Tools

The CIS finding tools provide three means of access to the legislative materials:

Illustration 8-11 Table 4—Legislative History, U.S.C.C.A.N.

TABLE 4—LEGISLATIVE HISTORY

Public Law		104		Report No. 101-		Comm. Reporting		Cong.Rec.Vol.136 (1990) Dates of Consideration and passage	
No.101-	Date App.	Stat. Page	Bill No.	House	Senate	House	Senate	House	Senate
302	May 25	213	HR 4404	434 493	272	App Conf	App	Apr. 3, May 24	May 1, 24
303	May 29	250	HR 1805	327	none	POCS	none	Nov. 6[1] May 8	Apr. 26, May 14
304	May 29	252	HR 3961	453	280	PWT	EPW (S 2068)-	Apr. 24	May 9, 10
305	May 30	253	HR 3910	404	none	EL	none	Feb. 27, May 10	May 7,14
306	June 6	260	HR 644	232	none	IIA	none	Apr. 19	May 22
307	June 6	262	SJR 231	none	none	none	none	May 22	Feb. 26
308	June 6	263	SJR 267	none	none	none	none	May 24	May 8
309	June 18	264	SJR 251	none	none	none	none	June 12	Feb. 26
310	June 18	266	HJR 516	none	none	none	none (SJR 274)	June 7	June 11
311	June 25	267	HR 4612	484	285	J	J (S 396) -	May 15	June 6
312	June 25	271	S 2700	none	none	none	none	June 12	June 6
313	June 27	272	S 286	491	230	IIA	ENR	May 22, June 14	Jan. 24, June 12
314	June 28	281	SJR 245	none	none	none	none	June 12	Feb. 26
315	June 28	282	HJR 575	none	none	none	none	June 19	June 22
316	June 28	284	SJR 264	none	none	none	none	June 19	May 15
317	June 29	285	SJR 246	none	none	none	none	June 18	May 3
318	July 3	287	HR 1622	279	267	J	J (S 1271)-	Oct. 16[1]	June 13
319	July 3	290	HR 3046	329	268	J	J (S 1272)-	Nov. 13[1]	June 13
320	July 3	292	HR 3545	456	312	IIA	ENR	Apr. 24	June 14
321	July 3	293	HR 3834	425	313	IIA	ENR	Mar. 20	June 14
322	July 6	295	HR 5075	none	none	none	none	June 25	June 25
323	July 6	299	HJR 555	none	none	none	none (SJR 330)	May 24	June 18
324	July 6	300	S 1999	517	none	EL	none	June 5	Nov. 22[1] June 22
325	July 6	302	SJR 271	none	none	none	none	June 28	June 18
326	July 6	304	SJR 315	none	none	none	none	June 21	May 15
327	July 6	306	SJR 320	none	none	none	none	June 21	June 18
328	July 8	308	S 2124	none	none	none	none	June 26	Feb. 20
329	July 8	310	SJR 278	none	none	none	none	June 26	June 18
330	July 12	311	HR 5149	none	none	none	none	June 28	June 28
331	July 13	312	HJR 599	none	none	none	none (SJR 338)	June 28	June 28
332	July 16	313	HR 1028	none	none	none	none (S 148) -	May 15	Nov. 3[1] June 29
333	July 16	316	HR 4252	none	none	none	none	May 21	June 28
334	July 16	318	HR 4525	502(I) 502(II) -	none	J POCS	none	June 25	June 28
335	July 17	319	HR 2514	452	none	POCS	none	Apr. 24	June 27
336	July 26	327	S 933	485(I) 485(II) - 485(III)- 485(IV) - 558 596	116	PWT EL J EC Conf Conf	LHR	May 22, July 12	Sept. 7[1] July 11,13

1. 1989 2. Explanation set out in Legislative History section.
3. Became law without the President's signature. 4. List of related reports.

[379]

(1) *CIS/Annual Legislative Histories of U.S. Public Laws* (*CIS/Legislative Histories*);
(2) *CIS/Annual Index to Publications of the United States Congress* (*CIS/Index*) (before 1995, titled *CIS/Annual Index to Congressional Publications and Public Laws*); and
(3) CIS *Congressional Masterfile.*

CIS/Legislative Histories is accessible by means of a statute's public law number. This publication lists all relevant legislative materials for each public law since 1970. It also provides abstracts (brief descriptions) of the public law and major legislative materials. *CIS/Legislative Histories* provide varying amounts of detail on each statute, depending on the significance of the statute. Illustration 8-12 on pages 255-258 shows what is called a "Special Legislative History," including

- the public law number;
- the *Statutes at Large* citation;
- the short title of the act;
- the date of approval;
- the number of the bill that was enacted;
- an abstract of the statute;
- abstracts of reports;
- the designation of bills not enacted;
- the dates of floor debates and references to the *Congressional Record*;
- abstracts and information about committee hearings on the bill;
- references to committee prints;
- notations of presidential documents; and
- CIS accession number.

Note that a CIS Special Legislative History may refer to materials from previous sessions of Congress that are pertinent to the statute. The abstracts describe the bibliographic information and the contents of the legislative materials and thereby assist you in assessing the value of the documents to your research. In addition, the abstracts for hearings sometimes contain specific page numbers on which relevant testimony appears.

For less significant statutes, CIS provides a "Standard Legislative History," which contains abstracts of committee hearings and major reports, but not abstracts of less important reports or testimonies of witnesses appearing before the committee.

To supplement a Standard Legislative History, you could locate additional abstracts in *CIS/Annual Abstracts of Congressional Publications* (*CIS/Abstracts*). This publication is published monthly and cumulated annually. It contains abstracts of legislative materials, including committee hearings, committee prints, House and Senate Documents, and committee reports. These abstracts are arranged by CIS accession numbers, which you would know from a Standard Legislative History. When researching a pre-1984 enactment, check the *CIS/Abstracts* volume for the year following your statute's enactment for the legislative history of the act, as well as for the year of enactment.

Each document listed or abstracted in *CIS/Legislative Histories* has a CIS accession number, as shown in item 13 of Illustration 8-12 on page 257. "CIS90:H341-4" indicates that the abstract of that document appears in the

Illustration 8-12 Special Legislative History, *CIS/Legislative History.*

1 **Public Law 101-336** 2 **104 Stat. 327**

3 **Americans with Disabilities Act of 1990**

4 **July 26, 1990**

Public Law

1.1 Public Law 101-336, approved July 26, 1990. (S. 933) 5

(CIS90:PL101-336 52 p.)

6

"To establish a clear and comprehensive prohibition of discrimination on the basis of disability."

Prohibits discrimination against disabled individuals in employment and public transportation, accommodations, and services.

Establishes a general definition of disability.

TITLE I, EMPLOYMENT.

Includes a provision to restrict use of pre-employment medical examinations and inquiries by employers, labor organizations, and employment agencies. Requires employers to make reasonable accommodations to the limitations of otherwise qualified job applicants or employees with disabilities.

Requires HHS to disseminate a list of infectious and communicable diseases transmissible by handling food.

Provides that the powers and civil and administrative remedies of the EEOC and Department of Justice under the Civil Rights Act of 1964 shall apply to employment discrimination against the disabled.

TITLE II, PUBLIC SERVICES.

Prohibits State and local governments and Amtrak from excluding from programs or services disabled individuals who meet specified eligibility requirements if reasonable modifications of policies or removal of barriers would enable them to participate.

Provides that enforcement for discrimination against the disabled by public entities shall be the remedies in the Rehabilitation Act of 1973.

Requires new vehicles purchased by public entities operating fixed route transportation systems to be readily accessible to and usable by the disabled.

Requires public entities operating fixed route transportation systems to provide paratransit services for individuals whose disabilities preclude the use of the fixed route system.

Requires Amtrak and all commuter rail systems to have at least one car per train readily accessible to and usable by disabled individuals within five years.

Requires Amtrak and key commuter stations to be made readily accessible to disabled individuals within specified time frames.

TITLE III, PUBLIC ACCOMMODATIONS AND SERVICES OPERATED BY PRIVATE ENTITIES.

Prohibits discrimination on the basis of disability by private businesses and other providers of goods, services, or accommodations. Requires businesses to remove barriers and make reasonable modifications of policies in order to provide equal benefits to the disabled, unless such changes are not readily achievable or would result in undue hardship.

Requires OTA to conduct a study to determine transportation access needs of the disabled, and the most cost-effective method of providing disabled individuals with access to buses and bus services.

Requires the Department of Justice to issue regulations regarding prohibition of discrimination in privately owned accommodations and services and DOT to issue regulations on land-based public transportation services.

TITLE IV, TELECOMMUNICATIONS.

Amends the Communications Act of 1934 to require that all telephone common carriers provide relay services for the hearing-impaired and speech-impaired so that they can communicate with persons who are not impaired. Extends FCC regulatory authority to intrastate common carriers for purposes of implementing the relay services requirement.

Requires closed-captioning of all TV public service announcements produced using Federal funds.

TITLE V, MISCELLANEOUS PROVISIONS.

Includes a provision to require the Architectural and Transportation Barriers Compliance Board to issue guidelines for removal of barriers that make goods and services inaccessible to the disabled.

Provides that nothing in the Wilderness Act shall be construed as prohibiting use of wheelchairs in wilderness areas.

Prohibits discrimination on the basis of disability by members of Congress and legislative branch employees.

Amends the Rehabilitation Act of 1973 to revise definitions and make conforming amendments.

6

P.L. 101-336 Reports

101st Congress

7

2.1 S. Rpt. 101-116 on S. 933, "Americans with Disabilities Act of 1989," Aug. 30, 1989.

(CIS89:S543-11 107 p.)
(Y1.1/5:101-116.)

Recommends passage, with an amendment in the nature of a substitute, of S. 933, the Americans with Disabilities Act (ADA) of 1989, to prohibit discrimination against disabled individuals in employment, housing, public accommodations, transportation, or telephone services. Includes provisions to:

a. Establish a comprehensive definition of disability.
b. Clarify ADA applicability to individuals with various diseases and disorders, including individuals infected with the human immunodeficiency virus (HIV).
c. Extend Rehabilitation Act of 1973 nondiscrimination requirements for Federal activities to State and local government entities.
d. Require various Federal departments and agencies to issue regulations and standards for ADA implementation and provide for Department of Justice enforcement procedures.

Includes additional views (p. 96-107).

S. 933 is related to 100th Congress S. 2345.

2.2 H. Rpt. 101-485, pt. 1 on H.R. 2273, "Americans with Disabilities Act of 1990," May 14, 1990.

(CIS90:H643-1 65 p.)
(Y1.1/8:101-485/pt.1.)

Recommends passage, with an amendment in the nature of a substitute, of H.R. 2273, the Americans with Disabilities Act of 1990, to amend the Communications Act of 1934 and the Rehabilitation Act of 1973 to prohibit discrimination against disabled individuals in employment; publicly

68 CIS/INDEX Legislative Histories JANUARY-DECEMBER 1990

Illustration 8-12 *(continued)*

Public Law 101-336 Item 3.5

101st Congress

ENACTED BILL

8

3.5 **S. 933 as introduced May 9, 1989; as reported by the Senate Labor and Human Resources Committee Aug. 30, 1989; as passed by the Senate Sept. 7, 1989; as passed by the House May 22, 1990.**

COMPANION BILL

3.6 **H.R. 2273 as introduced May 9, 1989; as reported by the House Public Works and Transportation Committee, the House Education and Labor Committee, the House Judiciary Committee, and the House Energy and Commerce Committee May 15, 1990.**

OTHER HOUSE BILLS

3.7 **H.R. 3171 as introduced.**

3.8 **H.R. 4807 as introduced.**

OTHER SENATE BILLS

3.9 **S. 1452 as introduced.**

P.L. 101-336 Debate

135 Congressional Record
101st Congress, 1st Session - 1989

9

4.1 **Sept. 7, Senate consideration and passage of S. 933, p. S10701.**

136 Congressional Record
101st Congress, 2nd Session - 1990

4.2 **May 17, House consideration of H.R. 2273, p. H2410.**

4.3 **May 22, House consideration of H.R. 2273, consideration and passage of S. 933 with an amendment, and tabling of H.R. 2273, p. H2599.**

4.4 **May 24, House insistence on its amendments to S. 933, request for a conference, and appointment of conferees, p. H3070.**

4.5 **June 6, Senate disagreement to the House amendments to S. 933, agreement to a conference, and appointment of conferees, p. S7422.**

4.6 **June 26, Submission in the House of the conference report on S. 933, p. H4169.**

4.7 **July 11, Senate passage of motion to recommit the conference report on S. 933, p. S9527.**

4.8 **July 12, Submission in the House of the second conference report on S. 933, and House agreement to the conference report, p. H4582.**

4.9 **July 13, Senate agreement to the conference report on S. 933, p. S9684.**

9

P.L. 101-336 Hearings

100th Congress

5.1 **"Hearing on Discrimination Against Cancer Victims and the Handicapped," hearings before the Subcommittee on Employment Opportunities, House Education and Labor Committee, June 17, 1987.**

(CIS88:H341-4 iii+115 p.)
(Y4.Ed8/1:100-31.)

Committee Serial No. 100-31. Hearing before the *Subcom on Employment Opportunities* to consider the following bills:
H.R. 192, to amend the Civil Rights Act of 1964 to prohibit employment discrimination against handicapped persons.
H.R. 1546, the Cancer Patients' Employment Rights Act, to prohibit employment discrimination against cancer survivors.
Full Committee Member Mario Biaggi (D-NY) presents a statement *(see H341-4.1)* and participates in questioning witnesses.
Includes correspondence (p. 113-115).

June 17, 1987. p. 2-37.
Witnesses: **Moakley, Joe**, (Rep, D-Mass)
Biaggi, Mario, (Rep, D-NY)
Statements and Discussion: Need for H.R. 192; explanation of H.R. 1546.
Insertion:
- Wolfe, M. Ann (CRS), "Survey of State Statutes Concerning Employment Discrimination of Handicapped Persons" May 31, 1987 (p. 16-27).

June 17, 1987. p. 38-86.
Witnesses: **Hoffman, Barbara**, bd member, Natl Coalition for Cancer Survivorship (NCCS).
Monaco, Grace P., atty, representing Candlelighters Childhood Cancer Foundation.
Calonita, Timothy, cancer survivor.
Statements and Discussion: Explanation of H.R. 1546; need for specific legislation to protect cancer patient employment rights; personal experiences with employment discrimination after cancer cure (related materials, p. 68-78).
Insertion:
- NCCS, newsletter, Mar. 1987 (p. 46-53).

June 17, 1987. p. 86-112.
Witnesses: **Rodriguez, Alex**, chm, Mass Commission Against Discrimination.
Kiernan, William E., dir, Training and Research Inst for Adults with Disabilities, Boston Coll.
Davila, Robert R., vp, precollege programs, Gallaudet Univ.

70 CIS/INDEX Legislative Histories JANUARY-DECEMBER 1990

1990 volumes, that the document emanated from the House ("H"), and that the abstract was numbered 341-4.

In the Canoga case, Illustration 8-12 shows a Special Legislative History. Item 10 contains abstracts of the House committee hearings on the ADA;

Illustration 8-12 *(continued)*

Public Law 101-336 Item 5.6

Suarez de Balcazar, Yolanda (et al., Univ of Kansas), "Common Concerns of Disabled Americans: Issues and Options" summary of survey findings, Apr. 1989 (p. 250-290).

Aug. 3, 1989. p. 39-78, 384-415.
Witnesses: **Brady, James S.**, Vice Chairman, National Organization on Disability.
Addesso, Peter, representing Paralyzed Veterans of America.
Feldblum, Chai R., Legislative Counsel, ACLU.
Statements and Discussion: Support for H.R. 2273; need to prohibit all forms of discrimination against the handicapped, citing disabled persons experiences; analysis and clarification of bill provisions, focusing on provisions prohibiting discrimination against the handicapped in employment and public accommodations.

Oct. 11, 1989. p. 80-151.
Witnesses: **Motley, John J., III**, Director, Federal Governmental Relations, National Federation of Independent Business.
Hoey, Christopher J., Assistant Treasurer and Assistant General Counsel, Woolworth Corp.; representing International Mass Retail Association.
DiLuigi, James A., Director, Technical Information, Marriot Corp.; representing American Hotel and Motel Association.
Statements and Discussion: Concerns about H.R. 2273 public accomodations provisions requiring businesses to modify buildings for greater accessibility by handicapped patrons, citing excessive cost of modifications; need to clarify H.R. 2273 provisions regarding public accomodations, with recommendations.

Oct. 11, 1989. p. 151-187.
Witnesses: **Cooper, Laura D.**, Attorney; Chair, Disabled Lawyers Committee, Young Lawyers Division, ABA.
Allen, Scott (Rev.), Commissioner, National Commission on AIDS.
Statements and Discussion: Experiences with discrimination against the handicapped; merits of H.R. 2273; defense of bill anti-discrimination protections for people with acquired immune deficiency syndrome.

Oct. 12, 1989. p. 191-232.
Witness: **Thornburgh, Richard L.**, Attorney General, Department of Justice.
Statement and Discussion: Endorsement of H.R. 2273; examination and clarification of bill provisions prohibiting discrimination against the handicapped, including discrimination in public accommodations.

Oct. 12, 1989. p. 291-318.
Witnesses: **Roth, Paul A.**, President, Roth Cos.; representing National Association of Theatre Owners.
Lynch, Robert D., architect; representing American Institute of Architects.
Statements and Discussion: Problems with H.R. 2273 provisions requiring modification of private buildings and structures for greater accessibility by the handicapped, with recommendations; anticipated difficulties for motion picture theater owners attempting to comply with H.R. 2273 provisions concerning building accessibility.

Oct. 12, 1989. p. 318-382.
Witnesses: **Holzer, Jo**, Executive Director, Council for Disability Rights.
Burgdorf, Robert L., Jr., Associate Professor of Law, School of Law, University of District of Columbia.
Statements and Discussion: Support for H.R. 2273, citing disabled persons experiences; extent of discrimination against the handicapped in public accommodations; explanation of bill provisions requiring modification of private buildings and structures for greater accessibility by the handicapped.
Review of existing standards for building accessibility; perspectives on costs to small businesses of modifying buildings and stuctures for accessibility.

5.7 "Field Hearing on Americans with Disabilities Act," hearings before the Subcommittee on Select Education, House Education and Labor Committee, Aug. 28, 1989.

(CIS90:H341-2 iii+112 p.)
(Y4.Ed8/1:101-56.)

Committee Serial No. 101-56. Hearing in Houston, Tex., before the *Subcom on Select Education* to consider H.R. 2273, the Americans with Disabilities Act of 1989, to prohibit discrimination against the handicapped in employment, housing, public accommodations, transportation, or communications.
Supplementary material (p. 96-112) includes submitted statements, correspondence, and an article.

Witnesses Testimony.
Witnesses: **Whitmire, Kathryn J.**, Mayor, Houston, p. 21-40.
Van Hightower, Nikki R., Treasurer, Harris County, p. 24- 40.
Ellis, Melody G., President, Board of Education, Houston Independent School District, p. 35-40.
Comfort, Judith L., Division Manager, External Affairs, Southwestern Bell Telephone Co.; also representing Southwestern Bell Corp., p. 41-78.
Lanier, Robert C., President, Landar Corp.; representing Metropolitan Transit Authority of Harris County, p. 56-78.
Mosbacher, Robert, Jr., President and Chief Executive Officer, Mosbacher Energy Co., p. 60-78.
Wolf, Howard, Attorney; Board Chairman, Institute for Rehabilitation and Research, Texas Medical Center, p. 62-78.
Smith, Ashley, State Representative, Texas, p. 79-87.
Brooks, Chet, State Senator, Texas, p. 87-95.
Statements and Discussion: Perspectives on H.R. 2273.

5.8 "Hearing on H.R. 2273, the Americans with Disabilities Act of 1989," hearings before the Subcommittee on Employment Opportunities and the Subcommittee on Select Education, House Education and Labor Committee, Sept. 13, 1989.

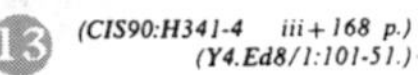
13 *(CIS90:H341-4 iii+168 p.)*
(Y4.Ed8/1:101-51.)

Committee Serial No. 101-51. Hearing before the *Subcom on Employment Opportunities* and the *Subcom on Select Education* to consider H.R. 2273 (text, p. 132-168) and companion S. 933, both the Americans with Disabilities Act (ADA) of 1989, to prohibit discrimination against the handicapped in various areas, including employment.
Supplementary material (p. 125-168) includes submitted statements.

Sept. 13, 1989. p. 2-25.
Witness: **Kemp, Evan J., Jr.**, Commissioner, Equal Employment Opportunity Commission.
Statement and Discussion: Barriers to the employment of disabled individuals, focusing on attitudinal aspects; preference for Senate-passed version of the ADA. 10

Sept. 13, 1989. p. 26-124.
Witnesses: **Rochlin, Jay**, Executive Director, President's Committee on Employment of People with Disabilities.
Donovan, Mark R., Manager, Community Employment and Training Programs, Marriott Corp.
Rasmussen, Duane A., President and Chief Executive Officer, Sell Publishing Co.; representing National Federation of Independent Business, Minnesota Newspaper Association, and Independent Business Association of Minnesota.
Wharen, Paul D., Project Manager, Thomas P. Harkins, Inc.; representing Associated Builders and Contractors.
Mayerson, Arlene B., Directing Attorney, Disability Rights Education and Defense Fund.
Statements and Discussion: Experiences in the development and implementation of programs to facilitate employment of disabled individuals; differing perspectives on H.R. 2273 and companion S. 933, including business concerns regarding employment-related provisions.

74 CIS/INDEX Legislative Histories JANUARY-DECEMBER 1990

these abstracts are verbatim copies of the abstracts in *CIS/Abstracts.* Below item 13 is the abstract of the testimony of Evan J. Kemp, Jr., commissioner of the Equal Employment Opportunity Commission (EEOC), an extremely important witness for this particular legislation. Unfortunately, the abstracts

Illustration 8-12 *(continued)*

Item 8.1 Public Law 101-336

Shishler, Janna, Law Clerk, p. 36-39.
Bowling, Nanette, Staff Liaison to the Mayor's Advisory Council for Handicapped Individuals, Kokomo, p. 40-62.
Turney, John D., Member, Mayor's Advisory Council for Handicapped Individuals, Kokomo; also representing Indiana Commission for the Handicapped, p. 46-62.
Williams, Michael L., Vice President for Ancillary Services, St. Josephs Hospital and Health Center, Kokomo, p. 56-62.
Edwards, Ric, p. 63-81.
Myers, Jeff, p. 68-81.
Hunt, Marchell, Chairperson, Common Concerns, p. 71-81.
Scott, David, representing Indianapolis Resource Center for Individual Living, p. 75-81.
May, Gary E., Commissioner, Indiana Department of Veterans' Affairs, p. 76-81.
Statements and Discussion: Perspectives on H.R. 2273.

5.13 "Americans with Disabilities Act," hearings before the House Small Business Committee, Feb. 22, 1990.

(CIS90:H721-24 iii+213 p.)
(Y4.Sm1:101-45.)

Committee Serial No. 101-45. Hearing to consider the potential effect on business of the Americans with Disabilities Act (ADA), to prohibit discrimination against the handicapped in various areas, including employment and public accomodations.

Supplementary material (p. 62-213) includes witnesses' written statements, and:

- GAO, "Persons with Disabilities: Reports on Costs of Accomodations" Jan. 1990, with tables (p. 186-213).

Feb. 22, 1990. p. 4-10.
Witness: **Hoyer, Steny H.**, (Rep, D-Md)
Statement and Discussion: Endorsement of and need for the ADA.

Feb. 22, 1990. p. 10-56, 76-172.
Witnesses: **Dragonette, Joseph J.**, President, Dragonette, Inc.; representing Chamber of Commerce of the U.S.
Lewis, Kenneth E., certified public accountant; representing National Federation of Independent Business.
Pinkus, David, Owner, North Haven Gardens; representing National Small Business United.
Frieden, Lex, Assistant Professor, Rehabilitation, Baylor College of Medicine; former Executive Director, National Council on the Handicapped.
Mayerson, Arlene B., Professor, Law School, University of California, Berkeley; representing Disability Rights Education and Defense Fund.
Statements and Discussion: Concerns about ADA provisions requiring modification of private buildings and structures for greater accessibility to the handicapped; potential excessive costs for small businesses of complying with ADA public accomodations and employment requirements; need to clarify ADA provisions regarding employment and public accomodations, with suggestions.

Background and importance of the ADA, citing need to prohibit all forms of discrimination against the handicapped; adequacy of ADA provisions protecting small business from excessive costs for modifying facilities; nature and background of discriminatory treatment of the handicapped; assessment of discrimination against the handicapped in employment, with examples and results of various studies on employment discrimination.

Merits of ADA provisions prohibiting employment discrimination; doubted negative impact on business of ADA employment provisions; overview of case law related to discrimination against the handicapped; extent of discrimination against the handicapped in public accomodations; views on discrimination issues and business concerns, with suggestions.

Feb. 22, 1990. p. 57-61, 173-185.
Witness: **Turner, James P.**, Acting Assistant Attorney General, Civil Rights, Department of Justice.

Statement and Discussion: Endorsement of the ADA; refutation of business concerns regarding ADA public accomodations provisions.

P.L. 101-336 Committee Prints

101st Congress

6.1 "Legislative History of Public Law 101-336, the Americans with Disabilities Act, Vol. 1," committee print issued by the House Education and Labor Committee, Dec. 1990. (Not available at time of publication.)

6.2 "Legislative History of Public Law 101-336, the Americans with Disabilities Act, Vol. 2," committee print issued by the House Education and Labor Committee, Dec. 1990. (Not available at time of publication.) 11

6.3 "Legislative History of Public Law 101-336, the Americans with Disabilities Act, Vol. 3," committee print issued by the House Education and Labor Committee, Dec. 1990. (Not available at time of publication.)

P.L. 101-336 Miscellaneous

8.1 Weekly Compilation of Presidential Documents, Vol. 26 (1990): July 26, Presidential remarks and statement. 12

Note: 1. Public law number
2. *Statutes at Large* citation
3. Short title
4. Date of approval
5. Number of bill enacted
6. Abstract of statute
7. Abstracts of reports
8. Designation of bills not enacted
9. References to debates
10. Abstracts of committee hearings
11. References to committee prints
12. Notations of presidential documents
13. CIS accession number

101st Congress, 2nd Session — **CIS/INDEX Legislative Histories 77**

do not mention smoking or nicotine addiction, so your research strategy would be to skim the abstracts to select the most important testimony, like that of the EEOC commissioner.

The second means of finding documents in the CIS system is by using a subject-index approach in *CIS/Index.* You would most likely use the subject-index approach if you had no citation information about a statute (which is uncommon) or if you were researching all legislation concerning a specific subject (which is more plausible) or if you were researching proposed legislation that did not pass. Since 1970, *CIS/Index* has been published in monthly paper pamphlets that are cumulated quarterly and then replaced by an annual bound volume. These bound volumes are later cumulated in volumes covering four- or five-year periods. Each index is organized by subject and by name (for example, authors and witnesses). See Illustration 8-13 below. *CIS/Index* also has several specialized indexes covering titles of acts, bill numbers, report numbers, House and Senate document numbers, Senate hearing numbers, Senate print numbers, and more. The index entry cites the CIS accession number, so you then can locate an abstract of the document in *CIS/Abstracts.*

In the Canoga case, Illustration 8-13 below shows the ADA entries in

Illustration 8-13 Index of Subjects and Names, *CIS/Index.*

Index of Subjects and Names **Americas Watch Committee**

Shipbuilding and ship repair industries
economic problems and ability to support Navy mobilization needs, **89** H561–28.7
State and local taxation of interstate transportation, issues, **89** S261–16.2
Tax laws revision, **88** S361–13.5
Vessels documentation for coastwise trade, **90** H561–12.2, **90** H561–12.6
Vessels operating in coastwise trade, foreign rebuilding and repair work restrictions clarification, **90** H561–11.5
Waste and oil rig transport vessels construction in US, requirements clarification, **88** S261–39.2
Waste transport vessels construction in US, requirements clarification, **88** H561–13.1

American Waterways Shipyard Conference
Fishing vessels operating in US waters, documentation and licensing requirements revision, **88** H561–13.2
Vessels operating in coastwise trade, foreign rebuilding and repair work restrictions clarification, **90** H561–11.2

American West Aircraft Corp.
Indian programs problems, Congressional investigation, **89** S411–29.10

American Whitewater Affiliation
Columbia River segment wild and scenic river designation study, **88** S311–77.2
WVa river conservation programs, **90** H441–10.3

American Wilderness Alliance
Colo wilderness areas estab and boundary revisions, and related water rights issues, **87** H441–20.2
Forest Service administrative appeals regulations revision, **89** H161–43.5
Nebr wilderness areas estab, **87** H441–26.1

American Wildlands
Arctic Natl Wildlife Refuge oil and gas production, Alaska Native-Interior Dept land exchange issues, **90** H441–17.5
Colo wilderness areas estab and expansion, **90** S311–24.2, **90** S311–24.7

American Wind Energy Association
Electric power independent producers, ...

Renewable energy technologies dev programs, **88** H701–49.6
Renewable energy technologies export promotion programs, oversight, **87** H361–72.2

American Wire Producers Association
Steel import restrictions, draft bill text, **87** H781–26, **88** S361–37

American Women in Radio and Television
TV and radio regulation revisions, **88** S261–11.4
TV and radio stations ownership by minorities and women, FCC assistance policies, **90** S261–6.1

American Women's Economic Development Corp.
Women-owned businesses, issues, **89** H721–12.7

American Wood Preservers Institute
Hazardous waste cleanup problems of small business, **89** H721–36.1
Hazardous waste treatment using biodegradation technology, **88** H721–16.2
Hazardous wastes reduction programs, estab, **89** H361–148.4
Pesticide regulatory programs revision, **88** S161–11.7
Pesticides registration with EPA, fees estab, **88** H721–11.4

American Youth Work Center
Missing youth and children location and return efforts, **87** H341–32.3

Americans Against Unfair Airport Fees
Airport anticompetitive user fees and access restrictions on non-tenant businesses, **88** S261–13.1

Americans Disabled for Accessible Public Transportation
Discrimination against the handicapped, prohibition, **89** H341–36.2

Americans Disabled for Accessible Public Transportation of Connecticut
Discrimination against the handicapped, prohibition, **89** H341–36.2

Americans for a Rational Energy Policy
Arctic Natl Wildlife Refuge oil and gas

Cigarette advertising issues and regulation, **90** H361–54.6
Cigarette advertising, safety, and liability issues, **89** H361–107.4
Philip Morris, Inc, Bill of Rights bicentennial promotion, ethical and legal issues, **90** H361–54.4
Smoking ban aboard airliners, **88** H641–22.5, **90** H641–5.3

Americans for Safe and Competitive Trucking
Truck and bus safety regulations revision; Motor Carrier Admin estab, **88** S261–4.4
Trucking industry deregulation issues and proposals, **88** H641–40.14

Americans United for Life
Equal Rights Amendment, policy issues and implications, **90** H521–33.10

Americans United for Life Legal Defense Fund
Equal Rights Amendment, policy issues and implications, **90** H521–33.10

Americans United for Separation of Church and State
Nomination of Antonin G Scalia to be Assoc Justice, Supreme Court, **87** S521–27.8
Nomination of William H Rehnquist to be Chief Justice, Supreme Court, **87** S521–44.6

Americans with Disabilities Act
Discrimination against the handicapped, prohibition, **89** H341–36, **89** H341–81, **89** S541–17, **89** S541–37, **89** S543–11, **90** H341–2, **90** H341–3, **90** H341–4, **90** H343–6, **90** H343–12, **90** H343–20, **90** H361–19, **90** H363–9, **90** H521–37, **90** H523–8, **90** H641–25, **90** H643–1, **90** H721–24, **90** PL101–336
Telephone relay services for the deaf, requirement estab, **90** H361–20

AmericanTours International
Tourism industry status and promotion efforts, **90** S261–1.3

America's Living Standard Act
Trade competitiveness and technology enhancement programs, reorganization, **88** S401–12.7

CIS/Index. The CIS accession numbers listed there include "90 H341-4," which is the testimony of the EEOC Commissioner.

The third means of finding legislative history materials in CIS is to use the CIS *Congressional Masterfile,* a CD-ROM product, which has two parts. *Masterfile 1* covers federal materials through 1969; *Masterfile 2* covers legislative documents published from 1970 to date. Exhibit 8.3 below shows the coverage of the system. This discussion focuses on *Masterfile 2,* which is based on the contents of the paper CIS materials. Like those paper CIS finding tools, *Masterfile* does not contain the full text of any documents.

There are two research approaches in *Masterfile*: (1) using the public law number in a "legislative history search" and (2) using key words or subjects to do a "full search." You most often will use a subject search if you do not know the public law number of the statute you are researching. You will find the directions for an effective subject search on the system itself. The system allows you to use Boolean search operators and truncations, as well as field searches. It also contains both an index and a thesaurus to help you select your search terms.

You may display your search results by Full Record or by Title List. A Full Record Display contains the same information as *CIS/Legislative Histories,* and it includes any available abstracts of the materials. See Illustration 8-14 on page 261. The Title List merely displays a list of CIS's legislative materials with summary bibliographic information: title of the material, the CIS accession number, material type (print, hearing, report, and so forth), and number and session of Congress. See Illustration 8-15 on page 262. In Title List, you may highlight a desired item with the cursor to obtain more complete information.

In the Canoga case, the legislative history search by public law number

Exhibit 8.3

Coverage of the *CIS Congressional Masterfile.*

Masterfile 1	*Masterfile 2*
CIS U.S. Serial Set Index (1789-1969) *CIS U.S. Congressional Committee Hearings Index* (1833-1969) *CIS Index to Unpublished U.S. Senate Committee Hearings* (1823-1968) *CIS Index to Unpublished U.S. House of Representatives Committee Hearings* (1833-1954) *CIS U.S. Congressional Committee Prints Index* (1830-1969) *CIS Index to U.S. Senate Executive Documents and Reports* (1817-1969)	*CIS/Index to Publications of the U.S. Congress* (1970-) *CIS/Legislative Histories* (1969-)

Illustration 8-14 Full Record Display, *CIS Congressional Masterfile.*

CIS NO: 90-PL101-336
TITLE: Americans with Disabilities Act of 1990
LEGISLATIVE HISTORY OF: P.L.101-336
ENACTED BILL: 101 S.933
DOC TYPE: Legislative History COLLATION: 52 p.
DATE: July 26, 1990
CONGRESS-SESSION: 101-2
STAT: 104Stat.327 ITEM NO: 575

"To establish a clear and comprehensive prohibition of discrimination on the basis of disability."
Prohibits discrimination against disabled individuals in employment and public transportation, accommodations, and services.
Establishes a general definition of disability.
TITLE I, EMPLOYMENT.
Restricts use of pre-employment medical examinations and inquiries by employers, labor organizations, and employment agencies. Requires employers to make reasonable accommodations to the limitations of otherwise qualified job applicants or employees with disabilities.
Requires HHS to disseminate a list of infectious and communicable diseases transmissible by handling food.
Provides that the powers and civil and administrative remedies of the EEOC and Department of Justice under the Civil Rights Act of 1964 shall apply to employment discrimination against the disabled.
TITLE II, PUBLIC SERVICES.
Prohibits State and local governments and Amtrak from excluding from programs or services disabled individuals who meet specified eligibility requirements if reasonable modifications of policies or removal of barriers would enable them to participate.
Provides that enforcement for discrimination against the disabled by public entities shall be the remedies in the Rehabilitation Act of 1973.
Requires new vehicles purchased by public entities operating fixed route transportation systems to be readily accessible to and usable by the disabled.
Requires public entities operating fixed route transportation systems to provide paratransit services for individuals whose disabilities preclude the

…TRANSPORTATION BARRIERS COM…
ACT (Wilderness areas access by wheelchairs); WILDERNESS AREAS
(Wheelchairs use in wilderness areas); CONGRESSIONAL.EMPLOYEES
RELATED BILLS: 100 H.R.192; 100 H.R.1546; 100 H.R.4498; 100 S.2345;
101 H.R.2273; 101 H.R.3171; 101 H.R.4807; 101 S.1452

LEGISLATIVE HISTORY REFERENCES:

DEBATE:

135 Congressional Record, 101st Congress, 1st Session - 1989
Sept. 7, Senate consideration and passage of S. 933, p. S10701.

136 Congressional Record, 101st Congress, 2nd Session - 1990
May 17, House consideration of H.R. 2273, p. H2410.
May 22, House consideration of H.R. 2273, consideration and passage of S. 933 with an amendment, and tabling of H.R. 2273, p. H2599.
May 24, House insistence on its amendments to S. 933, request for a conference, and appointment of conferees, p. H3070.
June 6, Senate disagreement to the House amendments to S. 933, agreement to a conference, and appointment of conferees, p. S7422.
June 26, Submission in the House of the conference report on S. 933, p. H4169.
July 11, Senate passage of motion to recommit the conference report on S. 933, p. S9527.
July 12, Submission in the House of the second conference report on S.

Illustration 8-15 Title List, *CIS Congressional Masterfile.*

```
CIS Congressional Masterfile 2
  1990 CIS Publications
    Americans with Disabilities Act of 1990.
        (101-2; Legislative History)
          90-PL101-336
    Field Hearing on Americans with Disabilities Act.
        (101-1; Hearing)
          90-H341-2  [SuDoc Y4.Ed8/1:101-56]
    Hearing on H.R. 2273, Americans with Disabilities Act of 1989.
        (101-1; Hearing)
          90-H341-3  [SuDoc Y4.Ed8/1:101-57]
    Hearing on H.R. 2273, the Americans with Disabilities Act of 1989.
        (101-1; Hearing)
          90-H341-4  [SuDoc Y4.Ed8/1:101-51]
    Americans with Disabilities Act of 1990.
        (101-2; Report)
          90-H343-6  [SuDoc Y1.1/8:101-485/pt.2]
    Americans with Disabilities Act of 1990.
        (101-2; Report)
          90-H343-12  [SuDoc Y1.1/8:101-558]
    Americans with Disabilities Act of 1990.
        (101-2; Report)
          90-H343-20  [SuDoc Y1.1/8:101-596]
    Americans with Disabilities Act.
        (101-1; Hearing)
          90-H361-19  [SuDoc Y4.En2/3:101-95]
    Americans with Disabilities: Telecommunications Relay Services.
        (101-1; Hearing)
          90-H361-20  [SuDoc Y4.En2/3:101-96]
    Americans with Disabilities Act of 1990.
        (101-2; Report)
          90-H363-9  [SuDoc Y1.1/8:101-485/pt.4]
    Americans with Disabilities Act of 1989.
        (101-1; Hearing)
          90-H521-37  [SuDoc Y4.J89/1:101/58]
    Americans with Disabilities Act of 1990.
        (101-2; Report)
          90-H523-8  [SuDoc Y1.1/8:101-485/pt.3]
    Americans with Disabilities Act.
        (101-1; Hearing)
          90-H641-25  [SuDoc Y4.P96/11:101-32]
    Americans with Disabilities Act of 1990.
        (101-2; Report)
          90-H643-1  [SuDoc Y1.1/8:101-485/pt.1]
    Americans with Disabilities Act.
        (101-2; Hearing)
          90-H721-24  [SuDoc Y4.Sm1:101-45]
  1989 CIS Publications
    Oversight Hearing on H.R. 4498, Americans with Disabilities Act
        of 1988. (100-2; Hearing)
          89-H341-36  [SuDoc Y4.Ed8/1:100-109]
    Joint Hearing on H.R. 2273, the Americans with Disabilities Act
        of 1989. (101-1; Hearing)
          89-H341-81  [SuDoc Y4.Ed8/1:101-37]
    Americans with Disabilities Act of 1988.
        (100-2; Hearing)
          89-S541-17  [SuDoc Y4.L11/4:S.hrg.100-926]
    Americans with Disabilities Act of 1989.
        (101-1; Hearing)
          89-S541-37  [SuDoc Y4.L11/4:S.hrg.101-156]
```

yielded the Full Record Display and Title List shown in Illustrations 8-14 and 8-15 on pages 261, 262. The Full Record Display contained the same information as *CIS/Legislative Histories.* The Title List contained references for CIS documents on the ADA. A "full search" using a subject and a key word [discrimination in employment and disab*] yielded 104 items, only a few of which were related to the ADA.

(b) CIS Legislative Materials

Once you have a CIS accession number from one of the finding tools, and once you have read the abstracts to identify which documents are most likely to be useful, you can use that accession number to locate and read legislative documents in the CIS system. The *CIS/Microfiche Library* contains the full text of hearings, committee reports, committee prints, House and Senate documents, and some special publications—but not the bills or debates. These materials are arranged by CIS accession number.

CIS's *Congressional Bills, Resolutions & Laws* is a microfiche copy of the full text of the various versions of the House and Senate bills and resolutions, including any amendments and revisions. These materials are arranged by CIS accession number.

For the full text of debates, CIS offers the permanent edition of the *Congressional Record* on microfiche as a separate set. The *Congressional Record* contains the proceedings of the House, proceedings of the Senate, extension of remarks, and the Daily Digest (calendar, notices and summaries of activities). The proceedings sections are more or less verbatim transcripts of floor debates and actions, including remarks by members of Congress, their votes, proposed amendments, and on occasion the text of the bills under consideration. The text is not a completely accurate account of what transpires in Congress because members of Congress are permitted to revise their remarks. In addition, members are allowed to add to the *Record* comments never made on the floor. This additional information is published as extended remarks. (For some years, revised and extended remarks have been noted by a marginal notation—a black dot.) The *Congressional Record* also contains the text of messages from the President to Congress and some other House and Senate documents.

In the Canoga case, CIS presented a large collection of documents, all of which are on microfiche. The number of documents and their presence on microfiche counsel strongly in favor of using the CIS abstracts as a sorting mechanism before you delve into the CIS microfiche libraries. Illustration 8-3 on page 237 shows the CIS document numbered 90 H341-4, the testimony of the EEOC commissioner, as located in the *CIS/Microfiche Library.* The *Congressional Record* included extensive debates. Unfortunately, none of the CIS legislative materials dealt with the issue of whether nicotine addiction is a disability under the ADA.

(4) Government Publications

The federal government also publishes legislative history materials. This section focuses on the *Congressional Record,* the *Monthly Catalog,* and bills.

The *Congressional Record* is published by the United States Government Printing Office (GPO). It is published daily in softbound pamphlets while Congress is in session. A permanent hardbound edition is published at the end of each session of Congress. In the daily edition, House and Senate proceedings are paginated separately, while the permanent edition uses a continuous numbering system. In the permanent edition, the Daily Digest is cumulated and published as a separate volume.

There are four ways to gain access to the *Congressional Record*. As already noted, one approach is to use U.S.C.C.A.N. to find the number of the volume and the date of the material you are seeking. A second approach is to locate a reference in CIS; a Special Legislative History provides page numbers as well. Third, if you know the date when your bill was debated, you can page through the issue for that date; however, this process is time-consuming.

A fourth approach is to use the *Congressional Record* indexes. Each permanent volume includes an index that cumulates the information for a particular session of Congress, for example, 101st Congress, 2d Session. Each index has two parts: (1) a subject index, which includes entries of topics, legislators, witnesses before Congress, and document titles; and (2) the History of Bills and Resolutions, which is subdivided into one section on House bills and resolutions and one section on Senate bills and resolutions. See Illustrations 8-16 and 8-17 on pages 265 and 266. You always should consult both the House and the Senate history sections to locate all page references to legislative activity pertaining to your bill. The History of Bills and Resolutions provides a synopsis of each bill's progress, as reported in the volume to which the index pertains; it also sometimes includes a list of bill sponsors.

In the time lag between publication of the daily *Congressional Record* and publication of the permanent version, interim indexes are published approximately biweekly; they are useful if you know the dates of debates you are researching. The interim indexes are tricky to use. The History of Bills and Resolutions section refers only to those bills that were acted on during the period covered; if no activity occurred, there is no reference to the bill. If the bill was acted on, the index cumulates all information concerning that bill.

In the Canoga case, Illustration 8-16 on page 265 shows the index entries under "Americans with Disabilities Act," as found in the interim index for June 5 to June 14, 1990. Illustration 8-17 on page 266 shows the S. 933 entry in the History of Bills Section of the index. The bill was passed by the Senate, but the House had strong disagreements over some provisions in that bill. The disagreements were strong enough that the Senate version was not approved, which prompted creation of a conference committee. Illustration 8-6 on page 241 shows a page from the ADA debates, as recorded in the *Congressional Record.*

In addition to the *Congressional Record,* the GPO also publishes various congressional materials as separate publications. These materials include hearing records with exhibits, committee reports, and other congressional documents. The *Monthly Catalog of U.S. Government Publications* lists the legislative, executive, and administrative documents published and sold by

Illustration 8-16

Subject Index, *Congressional Record.*

4

CONGRESSIONAL RECORD INDEX

AKERS, SHERRY

Illustration 8-17

History of Bills Index, *Congressional Record.*

H.B. 2 **CONGRESSIONAL RECORD INDEX**

S. 720—Continued
credit, and for other purposes; to the Committee on Finance.
Cosponsors added, S907, S2487, S3703, S4619, S6531, S8047

S. 798—A bill to amend Title V of the Act of December 19, 1980, designating the Chaco Culture Archaeological Protection Sites, and for other purposes; to the Committee on Energy and Natural Resources.
Cosponsors added, S5922
Reported (S. Rept. 101-307), S7599

S. 865—A bill to amend the Sherman Act regarding retail competition; to the Committee on the Judiciary.
Reported with amendments (S. Rept. 101-251), S2456
Cosponsors added, S6848, S7497

S. 874—A bill to establish national voter registration procedures for Presidential and Congressional elections, and for other purposes; to the Committee on Rules and Administration.
Cosponsors added, S1640, S2487, S2652, S3115, S3416, S4619, S4945, S7148

S. 930—A bill to amend the Occupational Safety and Health Act of 1970 to establish an Office of Construction, Safety, Health and Education within OSHA, to improve inspections investigations, reporting, and recordkeeping in the construction industry, to require certain construction contractors to establish construction safety and health programs and onsite plans and appoint construction safety specialists, and for other purposes; to the Committee on Labor and Human Resources.
Cosponsors added, S7903

S. 933—A bill to establish a clear and comprehensive prohibition of discrimination on the basis of disability; to the Committee on Labor and Human Resources.
Debated, H2639
Amended and passed House (in lieu of H.R. 2273), H2653
House insisted on its amendments and asked for a conference. Conferees appointed, H3070
Senate disagreed to House amendments and agreed to a conference., S7422
Conferees appointed, S7450

S. 980—A bill to amend the Internal Revenue Code of 1986 to improve the effectiveness of the low-income housing credit; to the Committee on Finance.
Cosponsors added, S1982, S4619, S6769, S7603

S. 1067—A bill to provide for a coordinated Federal research program to ensure continued U.S. leadership in high-performance computing; to the Committee on Commerce, Science, and Transportation.
Cosponsors added, S1265, S2652, S3877, S7497

S. 1076—A bill to increase public understanding of the natural environment and to advance and develop environmental education and training; to the Committee on Environment and Public Works.
Cosponsors added, S426, S1030, S5768, S8047
Reported (S. Rept. 101-284), S6067

S. 1178—A bill to improve and expand programs for the protection of marine and coastal waters; to the Committee on Environment and Public Works.
Cosponsors added, S7148

S. 1216—A bill to amend the National Labor Relations Act to give employers and performers in the live performing arts, rights given by section 8(e) of such Act to employers and employees in similarly situated industries, to give to such employers and performers the same rights given by sections 8(f) of such Act to employers and employees in the construction industry, and for other purposes; to the Committee on Labor and Human Resources.
Cosponsors added, S257, S768, S1265, S2948, S4620, S7716

S. 1224—A bill to amend the Motor Vehicle Information and Cost Savings Act to require new standards for corporate average fuel economy, and for other purposes; to the Committee on Commerce, Science, and Transportation.
Cosponsors added, S426
Reported with amendments (S. Rept. 101-329), S7716

S. 1272—A bill to amend chapter 8 of title 17, United States Code, to reduce the number of Commissioners on the Copyright Royalty Tribunal, to provide for lapsed terms of such Commissioners, and for other purposes; to the Committee on the Judiciary.
Reported (S. Rept. 101-268), S4566
Amended and passed Senate, S7913

S. 1273—A bill to amend the Internal Revenue Code of 1986 with respect to treatment by cooperatives of gains or losses from sale of certain assets; to the Committee on Finance.
Cosponsors added, S3115, S3416, S3554, S3703, S4620, S6079, S6848, S8047

S. 1299—A bill to establish a Police Corps program; to the Committee on the Judiciary.
Cosponsors added, S1384, S7644

S. 1331—A bill to amend the Consolidated Farm and Rural Development Act to authorize the Secretary of Agriculture to provide grants to States to establish funds to provide assistance for the construction of water and waste facilities, and for other purposes; to the Committee on Environment and Public Works.
Cosponsors added, S8047

S. 1349—A bill to amend the Internal Revenue Code of 1986 to exclude small transactions and to make certain clarifications relating to broker reporting requirements; to the Committee on Finance.
Cosponsors added, S1524, S2948, S3296, S3703, S4620, S5922, S8047

S. 1384—A bill to amend title XVIII of the Social Security Act to provide direct reimbursement under part B of Medicare for nurse practitioner or clinical nurse specialist services that are provided in rural areas; to the Committee on Finance.
Cosponsors added, S490, S1165, S2122, S3115, S4620, S5839, S6373, S7148, S7497, S7644

S. 1425—A bill entitled the "Nutrition Labeling and Education Act of 1989"; to the Committee on Labor and Human Resources.
Cosponsors added, S8047

S. 1511—A bill to amend the Age Discrimination in Employment Act of 1967 to clarify the protections given to older individuals in regard to employee benefit plans, and for other purposes; to the Committee on Labor and Human Resources.
Cosponsors added, S161, S907, S1265, S1384, S1982, S3115, S3296, S3878, S4285, S4620, S4833, S5021, S5508, S5583, S6155, S6673, S6848, S7053, S7497, S7603, S7644
Reported with amendments (S. Rept. 101-263), S4206

S. 1542—A bill to amend chapter 55 of title 5, United States Code, to include certain employees of the Department of Commerce as forest firefighters; to the Committee on Governmental Affairs.
Cosponsors added, S3209, S4285, S4833, S7148, S7716

S. 1570—A bill to amend the Social Security Act to partially deregulate the collection of fees for the representation of claimant in administrative proceedings; to the Committee on Finance.
Cosponsors added, S7497

S. 1571—A bill to amend the Social Security Act to establish in the Social Security Administration the Office of Chief Administrative Law Judge, and for other purposes; to the Committee on Finance.
Cosponsors added, S7497

S. 1587—A bill to amend the Internal Revenue Code of 1986 to provide for the designation on income tax forms of overpayments of tax and contributions to reward the return of a Vietnam POW/MIA; to the Committee on Finance.
Cosponsors added, S6003, S7644

S. 1630—A bill to amend the Clean Air Act to provide for attainment and maintenance of health protective national ambient air quality standards, and for other purposes; to the Committee on Environment and Public Works.
Debated, S27, S82, S205, S218, S226, S234, S240, S399, S460, S509, S519, S529, S531, S547, S592, S624, S628, S2030, S2142, S2150, S2158, S2160, S2175, S2231, S2238, S2290, S2378, S2380, S2407, S2430, S2562, S2568, S2569, S2584, S2598, S2715, S2724, S2730, S2732, S2762, S2827, S2875, S2975, S3044, S3162, S3191, S3233, S3327, S3353, S3383, S3385, S3386, S3460, S3497, S3504, S3580, S3656, S3667, S3673, S3692, S3717, S3738, S3743, S3748
Reported with amendments (S. Rept. 101-228), S98
Amendments, S463, S491, S580, S624, S630, S642, S1032, S1169, S1170, S1387, S1641, S1858, S1986, S2031, S2071, S2113, S2124, S2169, S2170, S2176, S2177, S2208, S2233, S2235, S2240, S2243, S2250, S2252, S2253, S2284, S2286, S2290, S2291, S2292, S2300, S2301, S2303, S2337, S2338, S2339, S2340, S2342, S2384, S2387, S2399, S2401, S2403, S2404, S2405, S2407, S2416, S2431, S2438, S2453, S2490, S2491, S2492, S2493, S2495, S2569, S2584, S2586, S2591, S2600, S2602, S2609, S2658, S2659, S2722, S2732, S2733, S2734, S2762, S2803, S2807, S2827, S2829, S2830, S2870, S2871, S2872, S2873, S2875, S2891, S2950, S2951, S2952, S2953, S2975, S2976, S2978, S2984, S2985, S2986, S2987, S2988, S2991, S2998, S2999, S3000, S3025, S3026, S3028, S3029, S3030, S3118, S3119, S3120, S3121, S3163, S3191, S3192, S3211, S3219, S3261, S3267, S3268, S3271, S3298, S3299, S3300, S3301, S3302, S3327, S3347, S3348, S3350, S3353, S3354, S3357, S3368, S3369, S3377, S3383, S3386, S3417, S3418, S3419, S3427, S3428, S3429, S3430, S3431, S3460, S3498, S3500, S3502, S3504, S3508, S3509, S3510, S3526, S3561, S3562, S3580, S3633, S3657, S3667, S3668, S3670, S3673, S3682, S3687, S3688, S3689, S3692, S3704, S3705, S3706, S3719, S3730, S3733, S3739, S3743, S3745, S3753, S3754, S3756, S3766, S3768, S3769, S3770, S3771, S3772, S3774, S3778, S3790, S3791, S3792, S3797, S3799, S3801, S3802, S3804, S3881, S3882, S3883, S3885, S3890, S3891, S3892, S3893, S3901, S3906, S3907, S4293
Cosponsors added, S491, S1983, S3878
Unanimous-consent agreement, S3263
Amended and passed Senate, S3833
Debated, H2944
Amended and passed House (in lieu of H.R. 3030), H2945
Title amended, H2945
House insisted on its amendments and asked for a conference, H2945
Conferees appointed, S7541

S. 1651—A bill to require the Secretary of the Treasury to mint coins in commemoration of the 50th anniversary of the United Services Organization; to the Committee on Banking, Housing, and Urban Affairs.
Cosponsors added, S161, S7497, S7716

S. 1664—A bill to establish a congressional commemorative medal for members of the Armed Forces who were present during the attack on Pearl Harbor on December 7, 1941; to the Committee on Banking, Housing, and Urban Affairs.
Cosponsors added, S161, S491, S641, S768, S1030, S1385, S1850, S2331, S2652, S2799, S3115, S4620, S4945, S6531, S6616, S6673, S6848, S7149
Reported (no written report), S7143
Amended and passed Senate, S7723

S. 1703—A bill to amend title 38, United States Code, to permit Department of Veterans Affairs medical centers to retain a portion of the amounts collected from third parties as reimbursement for the cost of health care and services furnished by such medical centers; to the Committee on Veterans' Affairs.
Cosponsors added, S1265, S7497

S. 1719—A bill to designate a segment of the Colorado River in the Westwater Canyon Utah as a component of the National Wild and Scenic Rivers the federal government. You can gain access to *Monthly Catalog* by using its indexes, which are arranged by author, title, subject, or series/report number. The index entry provides a number that refers you to *Monthly Catalog* text. The text, in turn, abstracts the document and provides a SuDoc number, which is a GPO publication number assigned by the Superintendent of Documents. Because the GPO is slow to publish some documents, you may need to consult the issues of *Monthly Catalog* for the year of enactment as well as a year or two thereafter.

Documents can be ordered from the GPO or may be found in federal depository libraries or other libraries. All United States law school libraries are permitted to be federal depositories; however, libraries vary as to which documents they elect to receive. For legislative materials not found elsewhere, you may be able to obtain some printed hearing records, reports, and House or Senate documents directly from the committee.

In addition to the sources mentioned earlier in this chapter, bills also are available from various government sources, most often in microform. To obtain a copy of a bill, you can contact the Clerk of the House or Secretary of the Senate, the bill's sponsor, the committee that considered it, or the Law Library of the Library of Congress.

c. Comparing Legislative History Materials

U.S.C.C.A.N. is the easiest source to use, but its limited content confines its use to only basic legislative history research.

The CIS system is accurate, comprehensive, and well organized; it generally provides the best means of obtaining an extensive legislative history of federal legislation. Its CD-ROM and paper finding tools each offer different features but locate the same content. The CIS *Congressional Masterfile* system on CD-ROM is particularly fast and easy to use, once you have a public law number. However, a search using subjects or key words is difficult because of the number of documents. The actual legislative documents on microfiche are difficult to browse.

Government publications are the least accessible sources because of the time lag preceding publication, the bulkiness of the finding tools, and the lack of a system built around enacted statutes.

d. Summary of Canoga Research

For the Canoga case, the legislative history materials provide little assistance in resolving the question of whether an addiction to smoking is a disability under the ADA. None of the testimony, debates, or reports address this issue directly, although some inferences may be able to be drawn from the disabilities that Congress addressed. On the other hand, this expansive reading of the ADA has not been expressly prohibited by anything in the legislative history.

4. What Else?

Indexes for Earlier Legislative Histories. For legislative materials prior to 1970, CIS has published some separate indexes that you might need to examine to compile a complete legislative history:

- *CIS US Congressional Committee Prints Index* (1830-1969)
- *CIS US Congressional Committee Hearings Index* (1833-1969)
- *CIS Index to Unpublished US Senate Committee Hearings* (1823-1972)
- *CIS Index to Unpublished US House of Representatives Committee Hearings* (1833-1960)
- *CIS US Serial Set Index* (1789-1969)
- *CIS Index to US Senate Executive Documents and Reports* (1817-1969)

These indexes all are accompanied by CIS microfiche sets containing the related documents.

Predecessors to *Congressional Record.* To find debates concerning older legislation, you would need to consult the predecessor titles to the *Congressional Record.* They are the *Annals of Congress* (1789-1824), the *Register Debates* (1824-1837), and the *Congressional Globe* (1833-1873).

United States Serial Set. This source contains House and Senate committee reports, House and Senate Documents (including presidential messages on legislation), and many other materials, such as legislative studies and executive branch publications, internal congressional manuals, and reprints of some nongovernmental publications. It is published by the GPO and is compiled roughly in chronological order, in the order in which the reports and documents are produced.

As you can imagine, the *Serial Set* is a massive source, so access to it is difficult. The best way to access the *Serial Set* between 1789 and 1969 is through the *CIS US Serial Set Index,* which is designed for use with the *CIS US Serial Set on Microfiche.*

State Legislative History. In many states, it is difficult to research state legislative history. Some materials may not be published. Some may be available only on audiotape, without any comprehensive list or index. Many materials may be available only in a single location, often at a state capitol. Before beginning legislative history research in your state, you should seek the advice of your state's legislative reference librarian or consult one of the texts that provide an overview of state legislative history processes and sources, such as Lynn Hellebust, *State Legislative Sourcebook* (1985-present).

Other Media: As of early 1996, these were the media available for legislative materials, sources, and finding tools:

	Paper	CD-ROM	Computer-Assisted Research		Microform
			LEXIS	WESTLAW	
Federal statutory codes	√	√	√	√	√
Statutes at Large	√		*	*	√
U.S.C.C.A.N.	√			**	√
CIS/Legislative Histories	√	√	√	***	√
CIS/Abstracts	√	√			
CIS/Indexes	√	√			
Congressional Record	√		√	√	√
Serial Set	√				√
Monthly Catalog	√	√			√

*Similar content is available in the online service's public laws database.
**Legislative history material appears in the legislative history database.
***Through Dialog.

5. How Do You Cite Legislative Materials?

Rule 13 of *The Bluebook* governs citation to legislative materials. Committee reports are cited by report number, the Congress and session, the page number, and the year. If the report is published in U.S.C.C.A.N., a U.S.C.C.A.N. citation should be added. You also may give the author and title of a report or document. Rule 13.4. For example:

S. Rep. No. 116, 101st Cong., 2d Sess. 1 (1970).
H.R. Rep. No. 485, 101st Cong., 2d Sess. 1 (1990), *reprinted in* 1990 U.S.C.C.A.N. 267.

In citing a hearing transcript, give the subject matter title as it appears on the cover, the bill number, the names of the subcommittee (if any) and the committee, the Congress and session, the page number, the year, and identifying information about the witness. Rule 13.3. For example:

Americans with Disabilities Act of 1989, Hearings on H.R. 2273 before the Subcomm. on Employment Opportunities and the Subcomm. on Select Education of the House Comm. on Education and Labor, 101st Cong., 1st Sess. 2 (1990) (statement of Evan J. Kemp, Commissioner, EEOC).

Unenacted bills are cited with bill number, the Congress and session, and the year. If the unenacted bill can be found in published hearings, that information may be added. Enacted bills are cited as statutes unless they are used to document legislative history, in which case they are cited as unenacted bills. Rule 13.2. For example:

H.R. 2273, 101st Cong., 2d Sess. § 1 (1990).

Congressional debates are cited to the *Congressional Record*; the permanent version must be cited if available. Rule 13.5. For example:

136 Cong. Rec. 13,035-36 (1990).

C. Pending Legislation

Legislative process materials also can be used to track pending legislation. Although statutes generally do not operate retroactively, some clients are concerned enough about future statutes to want to affect the legislation or to adjust their affairs by planning ahead. Research on pending legislation may involve paper or online media.

1. Using Paper Media

A paper source valuable for monitoring the progress of pending legislation is *Congressional Index*, a looseleaf service published by Commerce Clearing House (a commercial publisher). Updated frequently, this service tracks all legislative activities, including the voting record of specific members of Congress. It does not provide the text of bills, only a brief description. *Congressional Index* also lists miscellaneous information concerning the workings of Congress, such as the names of members of Congress, committee members, addresses, and phone numbers.

2. Using Online Media: LEXIS as an Example

Online systems are valuable for tracking pending legislation. The LEXIS databases are comprehensive and current.

To track federal legislation, the files in the LEGIS library are the most helpful. The BILLS file is a combined file that provides the full text of all versions of legislation for the current Congress. It also includes summaries of each bill, its sponsors, committee referrals, and the chronology of the bill's progress from its introduction until its resolution. This file is updated daily while Congress is in session. You may search its two component files, BLTRACK and BLTEXT, separately. The POLSUM file provides summaries of committee hearings. The MARKUP file details the amendments or changes made to a bill in the congressional committee or subcommittee to which the bill has been referred; it is updated daily while Congress is in session. The CMTRPTS file provides the full text of committee reports as soon as they are published. The LEGIS library also contains various files for researching the *Congressional Record* online.

As for state legislation, STTEXT is a group file that contains the full text of pending legislation for all states. The STTRACK file is a group file that contains a summary and legislative chronology of all state legislation for the current legislative session. Additionally, LEXIS has individual TEXT and TRCK files for the individual states. At the time this text was written, no additional information on the Canoga case was available for New Mexico.

3. What Else?

Other popular online updating and legislative tracking systems include WESTLAW's BILLTRK database, Legi-Slate, a commercial vendor, and Washington Alert, published by Congressional Quarterly and available in some WESTLAW systems.

D. Concluding Points

Legislative process materials can be used (1) to locate legislative history materials to discern the legislative intent behind an ambiguous statute or (2) to track pending legislation for an interested client. The legislative materials pertinent to legislative intent have varying "weights," depending on how well they represent the views of the legislature.

As a starting point for your research in legislative history, attempt to find a compiled legislative history or a list of pertinent legislative materials. If none is available or if you need to supplement your findings, the legislative notes following the statutory section provide a starting point for compiling a list of the legislative materials and events. Of most importance is the citation to the *Statutes at Large* because that citation provides access to U.S.C.C.A.N. (In U.S.C.A., you may find a direct citation to the legislative history section of U.S.C.C.A.N.) Then in U.S.C.C.A.N. it is easy to find a list of the major legislative documents and events and the actual text of at least one of the documents.

You instead may use the public law number obtained from a code to search either the paper *CIS/Legislative Histories* or the *CIS Masterfile* CD-ROM system to trace the complete history of legislation. Of particular value are the abstracts because they describe the content of the materials and give specific page references to some materials, which greatly expedites the research. The CIS accession numbers and the detailed bibliographic information for all of the materials are critical for locating the actual text of materials, whether in the CIS system or elsewhere.

The next step is to read the text of the debates and the other materials. The debates and remarks are contained in the CIS and GPO versions of the *Congressional Record*. The other materials (committee prints, hearings, reports, House and Senate Documents, and other special publications) are usually available in a CIS publication or a government publication.

In addition to legislative history research, legislative process materials also can be used to track pending legislation. This research may involve use of *Congressional Index* or various online bill-tracking systems.

9 Locate, Read, and Update Primary Authority: Administrative Materials

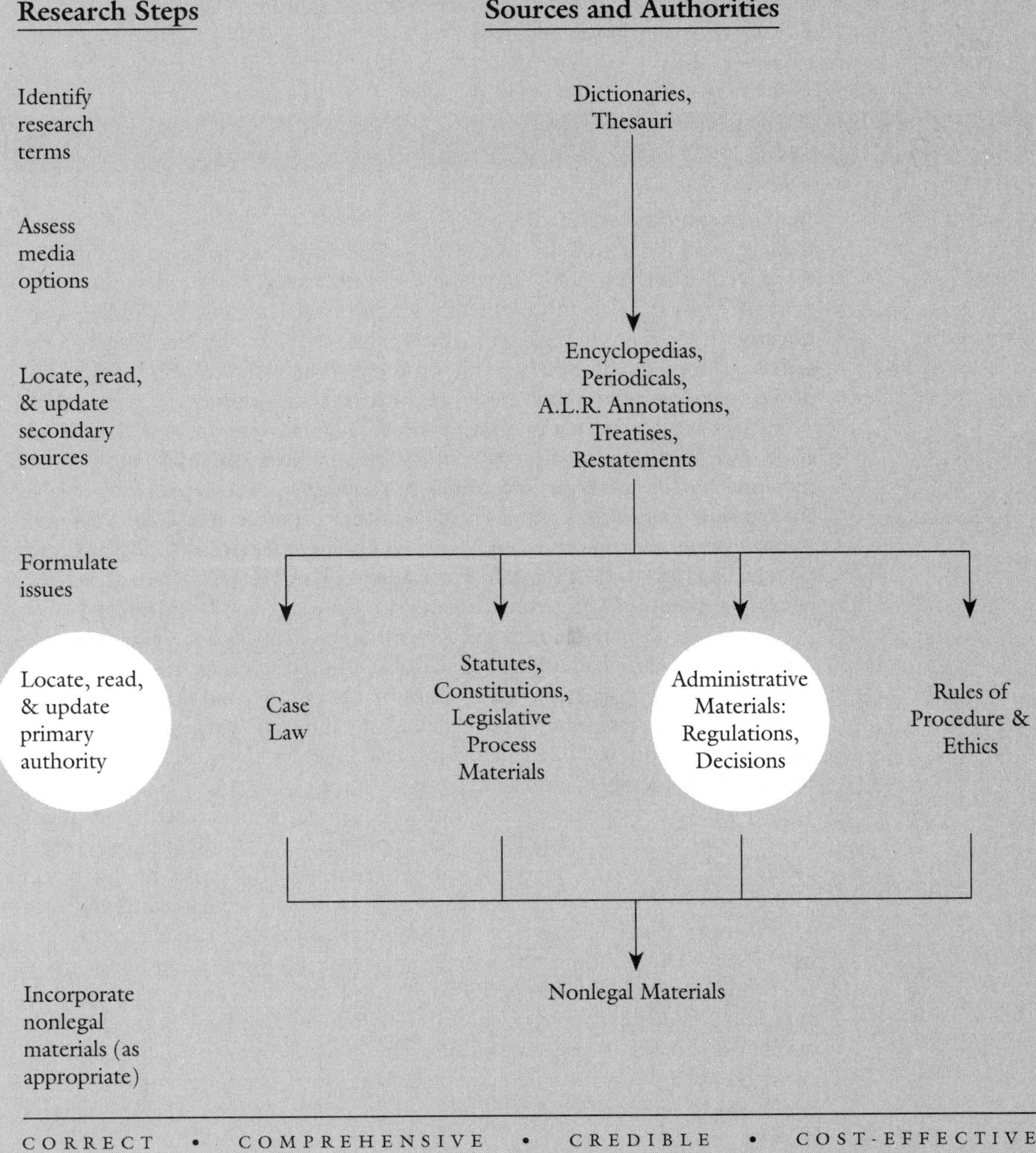

CORRECT • COMPREHENSIVE • CREDIBLE • COST-EFFECTIVE

Summary of Contents

A. Preliminary Points

In the American system of government, the law is made not only by the judiciary and the legislature, but also by administrative agencies. Administrative agencies at the federal, state, and local levels are involved in almost every field of American life and law from agriculture to zoning. Some fields are governed by a single agency; in other fields, there are overlapping federal, state, and local agencies. For some problems that span state boundaries but do not have national implications, regional agencies exist.

In broad terms, many administrative agencies are created to provide close supervision of an industry or set of practices (such as employment relations) or to handle large volumes of cases of a particular sort. They also are created when significant scientific or other expertise in a field is needed. Agencies thus are characterized by a highly structured organization and specialized workforce. They typically are headed by commissioners (or secretaries) who are appointed by the executive and subject to approval by the legislature.

Agencies also are characterized by a range of functions. An agency may have the power to promulgate regulations, adjudicate cases, prosecute violations of the law, inspect private entities or operations, and conduct studies. The first two of these functions—rulemaking and case adjudication—involve lawmaking. As you will see, rulemaking resembles legislative activity, and case adjudication resembles judicial activity.

As an agency exercises these functions, it acts in concert with and under the supervision of the legislature, courts, and executive. The legislature creates the agency through an enabling statute, identifying the goals the agency is to pursue and the functions it may engage in, such as rulemaking and case adjudication. When the agency departs from the course the legislature has set for it, it may be subjected to legislative oversight, loss of funding, or an amendment of the statute. Furthermore, the courts review agency actions, especially rulemaking and case adjudication, for conformity with the enabling statute and constitutional constraints. The links between an agency and the executive vary. Typically agency commissioners are appointed by the executive, and the agency may be highly influenced by the executive on matters of policy.

This chapter explores how to research both rules and decisions rendered by federal agencies, in paper media, in Parts B and C respectively. Part D presents a brief discussion of researching the law of state administrative agencies. Part E discusses the looseleaf service, a source that combines a wide range of authorities within a complex area of law; many looseleafs cover areas of law involving administrative agencies. Part F demonstrates legal research in administrative materials on the Internet.

This chapter explores an issue not yet addressed in our discussion of the Canoga case. Recall that Ms. Canoga's concern over the no-smoking policy was shared to some extent by her co-workers. See the Canoga case in Chapter 1 on pages 2-3. Hence, a possible claim on behalf of Ms. Canoga is that the orchestra violated her right to act in concert with her co-workers, as safeguarded by the National Labor Relations Act (NLRA), also known as the Labor Management Relations Act (LMRA). Thorough research in treatises, for example, would flag this issue for research.

Thus this chapter focuses on the National Labor Relations Board (Board). By way of background, the Board was established in 1935 to protect the rights of employees to form unions and bargain with employers. It also protects employees who engage in "concerted activity," that is, act together to assist each other in their relationship with the employer, even though there is no union on the scene. The statute has been amended over the years as Congress has attempted to balance the rights of employees and employers. The enabling statute gives the Board the authority to promulgate rules (which it has chosen to do only rarely), prosecute and decide cases involving violations of the NLRA (called "unfair labor practices"), and run elections in which employees decide whether to be represented by unions. This chapter touches on the first two functions.

B. Federal Administrative Regulations

1. What Is a Regulation?

a. What Does a Regulation Look Like?

In form, an agency regulation resembles a statute. See Illustration 9-1 on page 276. It consists of general rules applicable to a specified range of actors engaging in specified types of conduct. The regulation may use rather general concepts, although many regulations use quite specific terms because they are intended to give precision to vague statutory language. Regulations generally have prospective effect, that is, they apply to situations arising after their promulgation, and they are applied to specific situations through some other legal process, such as the agency's case adjudication or litigation in the courts.

Illustration 9-1 on page 276 is one of the few regulations promulgated

Illustration 9-1 29 C.F.R. § 103.2 (1994).

Subpart E—[Reserved]

Subpart F—Remedial Orders

103.100 Offers of reinstatement to employees in Armed Forces.

AUTHORITY: 29 U.S.C. 156, in accordance with the procedure set forth in 5 U.S.C. 553.

Subpart A—Jurisdictional Standards

§ 103.1 Colleges and universities.

The Board will assert its jurisdiction in any proceeding arising under sections 8, 9, and 10 of the Act involving any private nonprofit college or university which has a gross annual revenue from all sources (excluding only contributions which, because of limitation by the grantor, are not available for use for operating expenses) of not less than $1 million.

[35 FR 18370, Dec. 3, 1970]

§ 103.2 Symphony orchestras.

The Board will assert its jurisdiction in any proceeding arising under sections 8, 9, and 10 of the Act involving any symphony orchestra which has a gross annual revenue from all sources (excluding only contributions which are because of limitation by the grantor not available for use for operating expenses) of not less than $1 million.

[38 FR 6177, Mar. 7, 1973]

§ 103.3 Horseracing and dogracing industries.

The Board will not assert its jurisdiction in any proceeding under sections 8, 9, and 10 of the Act involving the horseracing and dogracing industries.

[38 FR 9507, Apr. 17, 1973]

Subpart B—Election Procedures

§ 103.20 Posting of election notices.

(a) Employers shall post copies of the Board's official Notice of Election in conspicuous places at least 3 full working days prior to 12:01 a.m. of the day of the election. In elections involving mail ballots, the election shall be deemed to have commenced the day the ballots are deposited by the Regional Office in the mail. In all cases, the notices shall remain posted until the end of the election.

(b) The term *working day* shall mean an entire 24-hour period excluding Saturdays, Sundays, and holidays.

(c) A party shall be estopped from objecting to nonposting of notices if it is responsible for the nonposting. An employer shall be conclusively deemed to have received copies of the election notice for posting unless it notifies the Regional Office at least 5 working days prior to the commencement of the election that it has not received copies of the election notice.

(d) Failure to post the election notices as required herein shall be grounds for setting aside the election whenever proper and timely objections are filed under the provisions of § 102.69(a).

[52 FR 25215, July 6, 1987]

Subpart C—Appropriate Bargaining Units

§ 103.30 Appropriate bargaining units in the health care industry.

(a) This portion of the rule shall be applicable to acute care hospitals, as defined in paragraph (f) of this section: Except in extraordinary circumstances and in circumstances in which there are existing non-conforming units, the following shall be appropriate units, and the only appropriate units, for petitions filed pursuant to section 9(c)(1)(A)(i) or 9(c)(1)(B) of the National Labor Relations Act, as amended, except that, if sought by labor organizations, various combinations of units may also be appropriate:

(1) All registered nurses.

(2) All physicians.

(3) All professionals except for registered nurses and physicians.

(4) All technical employees.

(5) All skilled maintenance employees.

(6) All business office clerical employees.

(7) All guards.

(8) All nonprofessional employees except for technical employees, skilled maintenance employees, business office clerical employees, and guards.

Provided That a unit of five or fewer employees shall constitute an extraordinary circumstance.

by the National Labor Relations Board. It pertains to the Board's exercise of jurisdiction over orchestras as employers.

b. How Is a Regulation Created?

In broad terms, administrative agencies promulgate two categories of regulations: legislative and non-legislative, with the latter including interpretative and procedural regulations. Legislative regulations (also called "substantive" regulations) follow from a specific statutory delegation of power from Congress to the agency to determine what conduct is to be regulated; they are backed by penalties provided in the statute. Interpretative regulations have less force; they are an agency's statement of its interpretation of its enabling statute. While many regulations address substantive matters—that is, what conduct the law permits or prohibits—some regulations address procedural aspects of an agency's operations. The procedures by which the regulation was promulgated indicate which type of regulation it is.

In general, when an administrative agency promulgates legislative regulations, it functions as a quasi-legislature. The agency may decide to address a topic through rulemaking because its enabling statute compels it to, because the public pressures or petitions it to do so, or because its own studies have identified an area of concern. Then the agency may follow one of several processes: notice-and-comment rulemaking, formal rulemaking, or a hybrid process.

In notice-and-comment rulemaking, the agency gives notice to the public of the topic it is about to consider through a notice of proposed rulemaking in the *Federal Register*, described in section 3 below. Thereafter the public may provide pertinent information to the agency through written submissions or, at the agency's discretion, through testimony at agency hearings. The agency considers these comments as it develops the final regulation and issues the regulation with a statement of its basis and purpose.

Formal rulemaking entails a trial-type hearing, in which participants may cross-examine "opposing" witnesses. Furthermore the agency must issue findings and conclusions to support its regulation. Some agencies engage in hybrid rulemaking processes for particular rules.

By contrast, when an agency promulgates interpretative regulations or regulations describing agency procedure or practice, it need not engage in even notice-and-comment rulemaking. The agency may simply issue a final rule based on its own internal deliberations, although it may provide for public participation in its discretion.

2. Why Would You Research Regulations?

Both legislative and interpretative regulations provide insight into what the law is, legislative regulations having more force than interpretative regulations. A legislative regulation constitutes the law so long as the regulation conforms to all applicable legislation, was properly promulgated, is not arbitrary or capricious, and meets constitutional requirements. Somewhat in contrast, an interpretative regulation is a significant statement of the agency's interpretation of the pertinent statute, but it may be disregarded by a court that interprets the statute differently. As you analyze a client's situation, then, you either must or should take the regulation into account, with the weight you afford the regulation depending on its nature.

Regulations pertaining to agency procedures are important for obvious reasons. They set out the steps, time lines, and details of handling a case involving the agency. You must know this information to handle your client's case competently.

3. How Do You Research Regulations in Paper Media (without Looseleafs)?

Comprehensive research into agency regulations entails sources you have seen before: secondary sources, federal statutory materials (particularly the annotated federal codes), and case law sources. Especially when you are researching an unfamiliar area of law, it is wise to begin with secondary sources. They may provide a helpful overview and references to primary authority, and they typically are fairly accessible. The federal statutes are a logical place to begin once you turn to primary authority. Research in case law tends to occur towards the end of your research, after you have located the regulation.

Research in agency regulations also entails several sources not covered in other chapters. Some of these are government publications: the *Code of Federal Regulations* (C.F.R.); the *Federal Register;* and a source that links C.F.R. and the *Federal Register,* the *List of CFR Sections Affected* (L.S.A.). There is no annotated code of federal regulations, however. In addition, you may consult *Shepard's Code of Federal Regulations Citations* once you have located a pertinent regulation.

Exhibit 9.1 on page 279 presents the relationships among these sources in graphic form, and this part follows the sequence presented in the chart. That sequence reflects the development of a regulation as legal authority. It is not, of course, the only sensible sequence; you may start at some other point, depending on your knowledge of the subject.

a. Beginning with the Annotated Statutory Codes

Because an administrative agency is created by statute and its actions must conform to that statute, an important step in regulations research is locating and reading the enabling statute. Chapter 7 covers statutory research.

As you research the enabling statute in *United States Code Annotated*

Exhibit 9.1 Regulations Research in Paper Sources (without looseleafs).

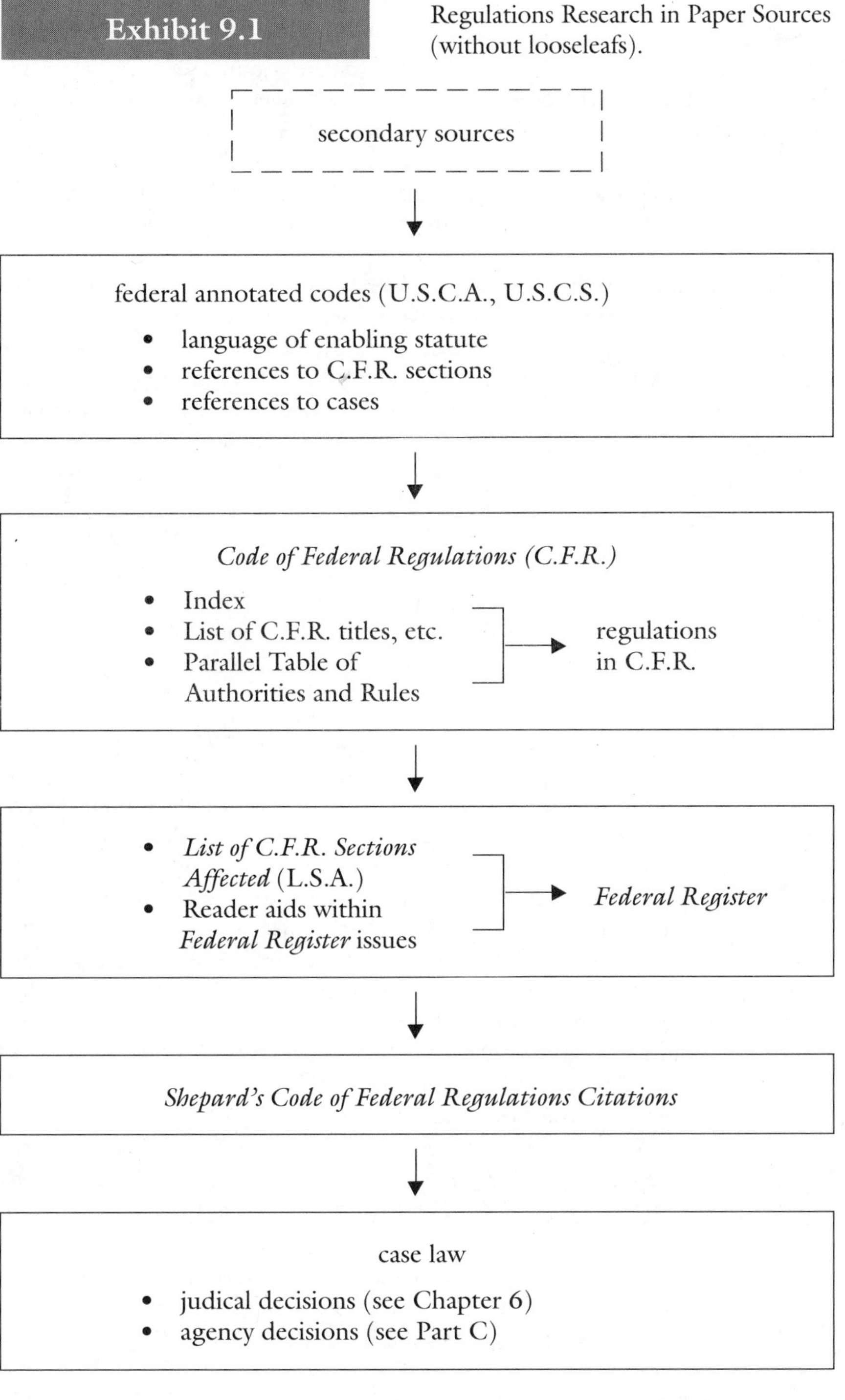

(U.S.C.A.) or *United States Code Service* (U.S.C.S.), you should peruse both the statute and its annotations carefully. As you read the statute, look both for the legal standard that Congress has set for the conduct you are concerned with; also look for indications of the agency's power to promulgate regulations to further develop that statutory standard. As you turn to the annotations, you should look for references to pertinent regulations in C.F.R. and for pertinent cases. Procedural regulations are reprinted in the two annotated codes, in U.S.C.A. near the pertinent statutory material, in U.S.C.S. in separate volumes.

In the Canoga case, you would learn from the enabling statute that the Board's jurisdiction extends to "employers" whose businesses "affect commerce." These terms are defined broadly, and no exclusions apply on these facts. *See* 29 U.S.C. § 152(2), (6), (7) (1994). Congress gave the Board the authority to decline to assert jurisdiction over categories of employers where the impact on commerce is not sufficient to warrant federal involvement, *id.* § 164(c)(1), as well as the general authority to issue regulations, *id.* § 156. If you perused the annotations to the latter provision in U.S.C.S., you would find two potentially helpful references: one to a decision of the Board, the other to a provision of C.F.R., § 103.2 of title 29. While the annotations in U.S.C.A. are not quite as helpful, you would find a general reference to parts 101 and 102 of title 29 of C.F.R. in the annotations to § 156, which generally grants the board rule-making authority.

b. Researching in the *Code of Federal Regulations*

C.F.R. resembles the *United States Code* (U.S.C.); however, it contains federal regulations, not federal statutes. C.F.R. is an official compilation of current federal regulations, with a topical organization that roughly parallels the organization of U.S.C. C.F.R. is divided into titles, and from there into subtitles, chapters, subchapters, parts, and sections.

C.F.R. differs from U.S.C. in an important respect: it is updated virtually continuously. (You can observe the updating pattern by looking at the colors of the many C.F.R. volumes on your shelves; there is a new color each year.) Hence any volume should be within a year, give or take a few months, of being current.

There are several means of locating a pertinent regulation within C.F.R. As noted above, your research in commentary sources or annotated codes may point you to a pertinent regulation. The *CFR Index and Finding Aids,* a separate volume accompanying C.F.R., affords three additional options:

(1) looking up your agency or other research term in the Index;
(2) scanning the List of CFR Titles, Chapters, Subchapters, and Parts for the C.F.R. title corresponding to the U.S.C. title in which the enabling statute appears; and
(3) looking up the enabling statute in the Parallel Table of Authorities and Rules.

See Illustrations 9-2 and 9-3 on pages 282-283. For any particular project, one of these may be more effective than the others, so you should be flexible in your approach. In general, you will be able to discern a pertinent C.F.R. title and part, but probably not a pertinent section, through these methods.

Once you have identified a potentially pertinent part, you should, of course, examine that material in C.F.R. carefully. Because a regulation, like a statute, may consist of several interlocking sections, you should scan, if not carefully examine, all sections within the pertinent part or subpart you have located. Once you have discerned the full range of specific sections pertinent to your client's situation and read them, you should take note of the administrative history material in small print at the end of the regulation. See Illustration 9-1 on page 276. That material provides the *Federal Register* citation and date of final promulgation for your regulation, which can be used to research the administrative history of your regulation.

In the Canoga case, the pertinent regulation is located in Title 29—Labor, Subtitle B—Regulations Relating to Labor, Chapter 1—National Labor Relations Board, Part 103—Other Rules, Subpart A—Jurisdictional Standards. Its section number is 103.2, and it is presented in Illustration 9-1 on page 276. Section 103.2 effectuates the Board's power to limit its jurisdiction to larger employers. Its significance for the Canoga case is that the orchestra must have gross annual revenues from all sources of at least $1 million for the Board to address Ms. Canoga's case. Section 103.2 was promulgated on March 7, 1973, and appears in final form in volume 38 of the *Federal Register* at page 6177.

c. Updating Your Research in the *Federal Register*

As noted above, C.F.R. is generally within about a year of being current. The front cover of each volume indicates how up-to-date it is. Your updating task is to find out what has happened since the date of your C.F.R. volume. The *Federal Register* fills that gap.

The *Federal Register* bears some resemblance to *Statutes at Large*; however, it contains regulations, rather than statutes. The *Federal Register* is a chronological compilation of final as well as proposed regulations. It is published daily, on a very current schedule, and hence is the best paper source of regulations not yet reprinted in C.F.R.

It also is a voluminous source; a daily issue may run hundreds of pages. As a result, even though the material within each daily issue is arranged alphabetically by agency, it would be very burdensome to work your way through all daily issues published since the most current volume of C.F.R., looking for changes in your regulation. You can avoid this burdensome task through use of two tools: *List of CFR Sections Affected* (L.S.A.) (which is a separate set of softcover pamphlets typically shelved at the end of C.F.R.) and the Reader Aids material printed within the *Federal Register.* Thus, researching in the *Federal Register* entails several steps:

Illustration 9-2

List of CFR Titles, Chapters, Subchapters, and Parts, *CFR Index and Finding Aids.*

List of CFR Titles, Chapters, Subchapters, and Parts

TITLE 29—LABOR—Continued

6 Rules of practice for administrative proceedings enforcing labor standards in Federal and federally assisted construction contracts and Federal service contracts.
7 Practice before Wage Appeals Board.
8 Practice before the Board of Service Contract Appeals.
11 Department of Labor National Environmental Policy Act (NEPA) compliance procedures.
12 Uniform relocation assistance and real property acquisition for Federal and federally assisted programs.
14 Security regulations.
15 Administrative claims under the Federal Tort Claims Act and related statutes.
16 Equal Access to Justice Act.
17 Intergovernmental review of Department of Labor programs and activities.
18 Rules of practice and procedure for administrative hearings before the Office of Administrative Law Judges.
19 Right to Financial Privacy Act.
20 Federal claims collection.
22 Program Fraud Civil Remedies Act of 1986.
24 Procedures for the handling of discrimination complaints under Federal employee protection statutes.
25 Rules for the nomination of arbitrators under section 11 of Executive Order 10988.
29 Labor standards for the registration of apprenticeship programs.
30 Equal employment opportunity in apprenticeship and training.
31 Nondiscrimination in federally assisted programs of the Department of Labor—effectuation of Title VI of the Civil Rights Act of 1964.
32 Nondiscrimination on the basis of handicap in programs and activities receiving or benefiting from Federal financial assistance.
33 Enforcement of nondiscrimination on the basis of handicap in programs or activities conducted by the Department of Labor.
34 Implementation of the nondiscrimination and equal opportunity requirements of the Job Training Partnership Act of 1982, as amended (JTPA).
42 Coordinated enforcement.
56 Work incentive programs for AFDC recipients under Title IV of the Social Security Act.
70 Production or disclosure of information or materials.
70a Protection of individual privacy in records.
75 Department of Labor review and certification procedures for rural industrialization loan and grant programs under the Consolidated Farm and Rural Development Act of 1972.
89 Senior community service employment program.
90 Certification of eligibility to apply for worker adjustment assistance.
93 New restrictions on lobbying.
95 Grants and agreements with institutions of higher education, hospitals, and other non-profit organizations, and with commercial organizations, foreign governments, organizations under the jurisdiction of foreign governments, and international organizations.
96 Audit requirements for grants, contracts and other agreements.
97 Uniform administrative requirements for grants and cooperative agreements to State and local governments.
98 Governmentwide debarment and suspension (nonprocurement) and governmentwide requirements for drug-free workplace (grants).

Subtitle B—Regulations Relating to Labor

Chapter I—National Labor Relations Board (Parts 100—199)

100 Administrative regulations.
101 Statements of procedures.
102 Rules and regulations, Series 8.
103 Other rules.

Chapter II—Bureau of Labor-Management Relations and Cooperative Programs, Department of Labor (Parts 200—299)

215 Guidelines, section 13(c), Urban Mass Transportation Act of 1964, as amended.
220 Airline employee protection program.

943

Illustration 9-3

Parallel Table of Authorities and Rules, *CFR Index and Finding Aids.*

Authorities

29 U.S.C.	CFR
9a	29 Part 580
37	45 Parts 95, 204
41a—41b	29 Part 1924
49 et seq	20 Parts 621, 651, 652–656, 658
	29 Parts 42, 507
49k	20 Parts 601, 652, 654
	29 Parts 31, 502
50	29 Parts 29, 30
77a	34 Part 373
141	29 Part 100
146	29 Part 100
151	29 Parts 101–103
156	29 Parts 101–103
158	29 Part 1420
171	29 Part 1420
172—173	29 Parts 1402–1404
172	29 Part 1401
173—174	29 Part 1420
175a	29 Parts 1470, 1471
183	29 Part 1420
201 et seq	29 Parts 42, 510, 516, 517, 536, 548, 775, 782, 790, 1620, 1621
201—219	29 Parts 525, 553, 570, 776, 778–780, 783–786, 788, 789, 791, 793, 794
201	29 Part 526
203	29 Parts 531, 579, 580
204	5 Part 551
204f	5 Part 551
205—206	29 Parts 511, 616, 617, 619, 697, 699, 700, 701, 720, 721, 723–730
206	29 Parts 552, 1614
207	29 Parts 526, 536, 547–550
208	29 Parts 511, 616, 617, 619, 697, 699, 700, 701, 720, 721, 723–730
211—212	29 Parts 575, 579, 580
211	29 Parts 515, 516, 519, 521, 525, 530, 1627
213	29 Parts 536, 541, 551, 552
214	29 Parts 519–523, 527, 528
216	29 Parts 578–580
218	29 Part 575
251 et seq	29 Part 775
259	29 Parts 1, 5
402	29 Parts 401, 451
431	29 Parts 402, 403, 408
432	29 Part 404
433	29 Parts 405, 406
437—438	29 Part 406
437	29 Parts 402–405, 408, 409
438	29 Parts 401, 403–405, 408, 409, 451
441	29 Part 409
461	29 Parts 401, 403, 408
481—482	29 Parts 401, 417, 452
481	29 Part 451
502	29 Part 453
504	28 Part 4
526	28 Part 4

29 U.S.C.—Continued	CFR
551	29 Part 98
557a	30 Parts 56, 57
577a	30 Parts 1, 11, 40–44, 50, 70, 77, 100
621 et seq	32 Part 588
621	29 Part 1625
626	29 Part 1627
628	29 Part 1626
631	29 Parts 1625, 1627
633a	29 Parts 1613, 1614
651 et seq	29 Part 42
651—653	29 Part 1975
651	34 Part 75
653	29 Parts 1911, 1912, 1915, 1917–1919, 1926, 1928, 1975, 1990
655—657	29 Part 1912
655	29 Parts 1905, 1910, 1911, 1915, 1917–1920, 1926, 1928, 1990
	40 Part 311
655 note	29 Part 1910
656—657	29 Part 1912a
656	29 Part 1908
657—658	29 Part 1903
657	29 Parts 1901–1905, 1909–1913, 1915, 1917–1919, 1926, 1928, 1975, 1977, 1978, 1990
	30 Part 11
	42 Parts 85–87
660	29 Parts 1977, 1978
661	29 Parts 2200–2203
665	29 Part 1905
667	29 Parts 1901, 1902, 1952–1956
668	29 Part 1960
670	29 Parts 1908, 1949
	42 Part 86
672	29 Parts 1950, 1951
673	29 Parts 1904, 1960
705—706	34 Part 361
706	10 Part 4
	28 Part 42
	29 Part 32
	32 Part 56
	34 Parts 350, 363, 366, 367, 369, 385
	38 Part 18
	41 Parts 60–1, 60–741
710—711	34 Part 361
711—711a	34 Part 376
711	34 Parts 365, 367, 369, 371–375, 378–380, 385–390
711—712	34 Part 363
717	34 Part 350
721—723	34 Part 361
721—722	34 Part 371
721	34 Parts 350, 365, 367, 369, 372, 385
723	34 Parts 365, 369, 385
730—731	34 Part 361
732	34 Parts 369, 370
740—741	34 Part 361
744	34 Parts 386, 387, 388
750—759	34 Part 351
750	34 Parts 361, 371
759g	34 Part 379

799

(1) consulting L.S.A. to identify where pertinent material might be in fairly recent *Federal Register* issues,
(2) consulting the Reader Aids sections of recent *Federal Register* issues to identify even more recent information, and
(3) reading the material you have located in the *Federal Register.*

(1) *List of CFR Sections Affected*

The first step involves use of L.S.A. L.S.A. lists regulations that have been affected by recent regulatory activity reported in the *Federal Register.* Examples include added, amended, corrected, and removed regulations. See Illustration 9-4 on page 285.

L.S.A. is published monthly, with some issues cumulating material for particular titles. Recall that C.F.R. is republished on a rolling basis. Hence your first task in using L.S.A. is to identify the issues covering the period from the date of your C.F.R. volume to the present.

Your next task in using L.S.A. is to look for listings affecting your regulation. The listings in L.S.A. are ordered by title and section number, indicate what action has been taken, and provide a page number within the *Federal Register.* Where L.S.A. covers a long period, such as a year, the listings may refer to two annual volumes of the *Federal Register*; L.S.A. then uses boldface and standard print to distinguish the two years. Once you have located a page number to check in the *Federal Register*, you may wish to use the Table of Federal Register Issue Pages and Dates within L.S.A.; that table tells you which pages appear in which daily issues of the *Federal Register.*

In the Canoga example, when the research was conducted in early fall of 1995, the most current C.F.R. volume containing section 103.2 of title 29 was current as of July 1, 1994. The June 1995 issue of L.S.A. cumulated material for that C.F.R. volume from July 1, 1994, through June 30, 1995; it served as an annual cumulation. The July 1995 L.S.A. updated the June 1995 issue to the end of July 1995.

Illustration 9-4 on page 285, from the June 1995 issue of L.S.A., indicates that many Board regulations underwent change in 1994 and 1995, including redesignation, amendment, and revision. However, there was no activity involving section 103.2. Note that most of the changes occurred in 1994, as the boldface type indicates. The July 1995 L.S.A. contained no new material regarding Board regulations.

(2) Reader Aids within the *Federal Register*

Your second step is to update the L.S.A information by using the Reader Aids material within the *Federal Register* itself. This material appears near the end of each issue, and it closely resembles L.S.A. See Illustration 9-5 on page 286. Because the Reader Aids material in each *Federal Register* issue for a month cumulates that month's material, you should begin by checking the month-end issues for any months not covered by L.S.A. Then consult the most recent issue for the current month, which cumulates material from the month to date.

Illustration 9-4

LSA—List of CFR Sections Affected.

CHANGES JULY 1, 1994 THROUGH JUNE 30, 1995

TITLE 29 Chapter I—Con.

(d) amended....................................32587
100.570 Redesignated from 100.670 and amended....................................**37159**
100.601—100.670 (Subpart F) Heading redesignated as 100.501—100.570 (Subpart E).......**37159**
100.601 Redesignated as 100.501........**37159**
100.602 Redesignated as 100.502........**37159**
100.603 Redesignated as 100.503........**37159**
100.610 Redesignated as 100.510........**37159**
100.611 Redesignated as 100.511........**37159**
100.630 Redesignated as 100.530........**37159**
100.640 Redesignated as 100.540........**37159**
100.649 Redesignated as 100.549........**37159**
100.650 Redesignated as 100.550........**37159**
100.651 Redesignated as 100.551........**37159**
100.660 Redesignated as 100.560........**37159**
100.670 Redesignated as 100.570........**37159**
102.35 Revised; eff. 2-1-95 through 1-31-96..**65944**
102.42 Revised; eff. 2-1-95 through 1-31-96..**65945**
102.45 (a) revised; eff. 2-1-95 through 1-31-96............................**65945**
102.117 (c)(2)(iii)(a), (b) and (c) redesignated as (c)(2)(iii)(A), (B) and (C); (f), (g) and (i) amended....................................32587

Chapter II—Bureau of Labor-Management Relations and Cooperative Programs, Department of Labor (Parts 200—299)

Chapter II Heading revised.............27860
270 Added...27860

Chapter IV—Office of Labor-Management Standards, Department of Labor (Parts 400—499)

417.16—417.25 (Subpart B) Heading revised....................................**65716**
417.16 Revised.......................................**65716**
417.17 Revised.......................................**65717**

Chapter V—Wage and Hour Division, Department of Labor (Parts 500—899)

500.268 Correctly revised; CFR correction................................15232
506 Authority citation revised.........3977
506.500—506.550 (Subpart F) Revised; interim....................3955, 3977
506.510 OMB number.........................3959
506.520 OMB number.........................3963
506.550 OMB number.........................3968
506.600—506.675 (Subpart G) Revised; interim....................3969, 3977
507.700—507.760 (Subpart H) Revised....................................**65659, 65676**
507.730 OMB number.........................4029
507.760 OMB number.........................4029
507.800—507.855 (Subpart I) Revised....................................**65672, 65676**
508.900 (b)(2)(i) and (d) amended; interim..............................**64776, 64777**
(e) added; interim...........................**64777**
(b)(2)(i) and (d) amended; (e) revised; interim.............34133, 34134
508.910 (b)(2)(i) and (e) amended; interim..**64777**
(b)(2)(i) and (e) amended; interim...............................34133, 34134
508.940 (d)(1)(i)(B), (h)(1) and (3) amended; interim.......................**64777**
(d)(1)(i)(B), (h)(1) and (3) amended; interim............34133, 34134
570.35 (b) revised.............................19339
570.35a (c)(3) revised........................19339
570.41—570.49 (Subpart D) Removed.......................................19339
580 Technical correction................19464
580.6 (a) revised..............................17222
825 Revised..2237
Regulation at 60 FR 2237 eff. date delayed to 4-6-95................6658
825.100 (a) corrected........................16383
825.110 (c) corrected........................16383
825.111 (c) corrected........................16383
825.202 (c) corrected........................16383
825.207 (d)(2) corrected....................16383
825.208 (e)(1) corrected....................16383
825.209 (e) corrected........................16383
825.210 (f) corrected.........................16383
825.214 (a) corrected........................16383
825.301 (b)(1)(v) corrected................16383
825.307 (a)(2) corrected....................16383
825.310 (f) corrected.........................16383
825.312 (b), (c) and (f) corrected 16383
825.500 (c)(4) and (g)(3) corrected; OMB number............................16383
825.702 (d)(2) corrected....................16383
825.800 Corrected.............................16383
825 Appendix A corrected...............16383

Chapter XII—Federal Mediation and Conciliation Service (Parts 1400—1499)

1425 Authority citation revised 2509

NOTE: **Boldface page numbers indicate 1994 changes.**

Illustration 9-5 Reader Aids, *Federal Register.*

26...39236
91...45042
100...43322
202...39236
203...42754
206...42754
291...45331
300...42012
310...42012
320...42012
330...42012
340...42012
350...42012
360...42012
370...42012
380...42012
390...42012
395...42012
586...42972
888...42222, 42230
1710...42436
Proposed Rules:
982...43840
888...42290

25 CFR

151...45528

26 CFR

1...39649, 40075, 40997, 42785, 43531, 44274
20...43531, 43554
25...43531
31...39109
40...40079, 44758
48...40079
301...39652, 40086
602...40079, 40997, 43531, 43554
Proposed Rules:
1...39896, 39902, 40792, 40794, 40796, 42819, 43091
20...43574
40...44788
301...39903, 43091

28 CFR

2...40092, 40094, 40270
49...44279
Proposed Rules:
16...44788

29 CFR

20...41016
1613...43371
1614...43371
1910...40457
1926...39254
1952...43969
2200...41805
2606...39848
2609...39848
2619...42037
2676...42037
Proposed Rules:
1910...39281
1926...45111
2510...39208
2606...44158
2615...41033
2616...44158
2617...44158
2629...44158
Ch. XIV...45388

30 CFR

901...42040
925...43972
946...40271
948...42437
Proposed Rules:
206...40120, 40127, 43735
211...45112
250...41034, 42819
260...43735
256...41034
931...43576
944...43577

31 CFR

0...42042
103...44144
515...39255
Proposed Rules:
1...40797
103...39665, 44146, 44151

32 CFR

92...40277
356...44277
358...44277
372...44277
393...44277
Proposed Rules:
220...39285

33 CFR

100...40096, 43976, 43978, 44424, 44428, 45043, 45044, 45045
110...43372
117...40097, 43373
126...39788
127...39788
137...39849
151...43374
155...43374
156...45006
165...40458, 41017, 41018, 42787, 42788, 42790, 43372, 44428, 44429, 44430, 45046, 45047
322...44760
334...43378
Proposed Rules:
1...39130
117...39287, 40138, 42826, 42827
165...40543
183...40545

34 CFR

76...41286
366...39216
667...41286
668...42408
Proposed Rules:
98...44696
345...40688
371...42490

36 CFR

7...39257
242...40569, 40461
251...45258
261...45258
1220...44634
1222...44634
1228...44634
1234...44634
1253...40416
1405...45335
1410...45338
Proposed Rules:
13...40798
242...42085, 44000
1415...39905

37 CFR

1...41018, 44120
2...41018, 44120
7...41018, 44120
401...41811
Proposed Rules:
1...41035, 42352
3...42352
5...42352

38 CFR

2...40756

39 CFR

111...39111, 43005
Proposed Rules:
111...45298

40 CFR

9...40474, 42791, 43244, 43880
51...40098, 40465, 44762
52...39115, 39258, 39851, 39855, 39857, 40101, 40285, 40286, 40291, 40292, 40465, 40758, 42042, 43008, 43012, 43015, 43017, 43020, 43379, 43383, 43386, 43388, 43394, 43396, 43710, 43713, 43714, 44277, 44431, 45048, 45051, 45054, 45055, 45056
60...43244
61...39263, 43396
63...43244
70...39862, 40101, 42045
75...40295
80...40006
81...39115, 39258, 39857, 40297, 43017, 43020, 45056
82...40420
86...39264, 40474, 43880
93...40098, 44762
300...45343
122...40230
124...40230
131...44120
136...39586, 44670
180...40498, 40500, 40503, 42443, 42446, 42447, 42449, 42450, 42453, 42456, 42458, 43718, 45060, 45062, 45064, 45065, 45067
185...40503, 42453, 42456, 42458, 42460
186...42460, 45067
195...41813
258...40104
261...41817
271...41818, 42046, 43979, 45069, 45071
272...44278
712...39654
721...45072
Proposed Rules:
Ch. I...39668, 44290
9...41870
51...39297, 43092, 44790, 45530
52...39298, 39907, 39910, 39911, 40139, 40338, 40799, 42130, 42491, 43092, 43099, 43100, 43104, 43421, 43423, 43424, 43737, 44452, 45112, 45113
60...41870
61...39299, 43424
70...39911, 40140, 44799, 44805, 45530
71...45530
80...40009, 45580
81...39298, 39911, 40338, 43104, 44452, 45113
85...43092
86...45580
89...45580
93...44790
144...44652
146...44652
148...43654
180...39299, 39302, 40545, 42494, 43738, 45113, 45115
185...39302
194...39131
258...40799
260...41870
262...41870
264...41870
265...41870
268...43654
270...41870
271...41870, 43654
300...41051, 43424, 45117
302...40042
355...40042
372...39132, 44000
433...40145
438...40145
464...40145
721...45119

41 CFR

Ch. 114...39864
101–17...45085

42 CFR

400...45344
409...39122
411...41914, 45344
417...45372
442...45085
484...39122
486...45085
493...45085
Proposed Rules:
412...39304
413...39304
424...39304
485...39304
489...39304

43 CFR

Public Land Orders:
7149...39655
7150...39655
7151...42792
7152...42792
7153...42067
7154...44435
7155...44763
7156...44763
7157...45372
7158...44764

44 CFR

64...39123, 42462

In the Canoga case, researched in the fall of 1995, L.S.A. extended through late July 1995, as noted above. Hence the first Reader Aid material to consult would be in the August 31, 1995, issue. As you can see from Illustration 9-5 on page 286, it has no entries for section 103.2 of title 29. You then would check even more recent issues.

(3) *Federal Register* Text

Once you have learned which portions of recent *Federal Register* issues update your research in C.F.R., the final step, of course, is to read the material you have identified in the *Federal Register.* There you will find whatever changes have been made, along with explanations of them. The explanatory material typically includes a summary, effective date, people to contact within the agency about the regulation, the legal background of the regulation (including its enabling statute), and a discussion of the material received during the rulemaking process and any evolution in the language of the regulation. This information can be invaluable in helping you to understand the regulation.

In the Canoga case, the regulation of interest, section 103.2, has not undergone change since its promulgation in 1973. To learn what a final regulation looks like as it initially appears in the *Federal Register,* see Illustration 9-6 on pages 288-289. Illustration 9-6 is section 103.2 as it appeared in the *Federal Register* in 1973. The first page of Illustration 9-6 is the background and explanatory material; section 103.2 itself appears on the second page. (Both pages have been reproduced from microfilm.)

d. Continuing Your Research in *Shepard's Code of Federal Regulations Citations*

As is true of other forms of primary authority, regulations are cited in cases and commentary. Their citation in case law is the more important, of course. The courts cite regulations when they are asked to apply the regulation to a specific set of facts, assess the regulation's validity in light of the enabling statute and its constitutionality, or both. *Shepard's Code of Federal Regulations Citations* (*Shepard's C.F.R. Citations*) enables you to locate these citations. See Illustration 9-7 on page 290.

In *Shepard's C.F.R. Citations,* the cited sources are sections of C.F.R. The major citing sources are federal court decisions, as reported in various reporters of Supreme Court decisions, *Federal Reporter,* and *Federal Supplement;* state court decisions reported in regional reporters; articles from selected law reviews; and annotations, including *American Law Reports* annotations. *Shepard's C.F.R. Citations* does not, however, include agency decisions as citing sources. (See Part C for a discussion of research into agency decisions.)

As with any use of *Shepard's,* first you must be sure to assemble all volumes needed to cover your regulation from its date of promulgation to the present, which may include hardbound volumes and various paper

Illustration 9-6 38 Fed. Reg. 6,176-77 (1973) (to be codified at 29 C.F.R. § 103.2).

written statements of exceptions and allegations as to applicable fact and law. Upon request of any party made within such 20-day period, a reasonable extension of time for filing such briefs or statements may be granted and upon a showing of good cause such period may be extended, as appropriate.

(b) *By a court.* Where a case has been remanded by a court, the Board may proceed in accordance with the court's mandate to issue a decision or it may in turn remand the case to a deputy commissioner or judge with instructions to take such action as is ordered by the court and any additional necessary action and upon completion thereof to return the case with a recommended decision to the Board for its action.

§ 802.406 **Finality of Board decisions.**

A decision rendered by the Board pursuant to this subpart shall become final 60 days after the issuance of such decision unless an appeal pursuant to section 21(c) of the LHWCA is filed prior to the expiration of the 60-day period herein described, or unless a timely request for reconsideration by the Board has been filed as provided in § 802.407.

RECONSIDERATION

§ 802.407 **Reconsideration of Board decisions—generally.**

(a) Any party in interest may, within no more than 10 days from the filing of a decision pursuant to § 802.403(b) request a reconsideration of such decision.

(b) Failure to file a request for reconsideration shall not be deemed a failure to exhaust administrative remedies.

§ 802.408 **Notice of request for reconsideration.**

(a) In the event that a party in interest requests reconsideration of a final decision and order, he shall do so in writing, stating the supporting rationale for the request and include any material pertinent to the request.

(b) The request shall be sent or delivered in person to the Clerk of the Board, and copies shall be served upon the parties.

§ 802.409 **Grant or denial of request.**

All requests for reconsideration shall be reviewed by the Board and shall be granted or denied in the discretion of the Board.

JUDICIAL REVIEW

§ 802.410 **Judicial review of Board decisions.**

Within 60 days after a decision by the Board has been filed pursuant to § 802.403(b), any party adversely affected or aggrieved by such decision may take an appeal to the U.S. Court of Appeals pursuant to section 21(c) of the LHWCA.

§ 802.411 **Certification of record for judicial review.**

The record of a case including the record of proceedings before the Board shall be transmitted to the appropriate court pursuant to the rules of such court.

Signed at Washington, D.C., this 1st day of March 1973.

PETER J. BRENNAN,
Secretary of Labor.

[FR Doc.73-4262 Filed 3-6-73;8:45 am]

Title 29—Labor

CHAPTER I—NATIONAL LABOR RELATIONS BOARD

PART 103—OTHER RULES

Jurisdictional Standards Applicable to Symphony Orchestras

By virtue of the authority vested in it by the National Labor Relations Act, approved July 5, 1935,[1] the National Labor Relations Board hereby issues the following rule which it finds necessary to carry out the provisions of said Act.

This rule is issued following proceedings conforming to the requirements of 5 U.S.C. 553 in which notice was given that any rule adopted would be immediately applicable. On August 19, 1972, the Board published notice of proposed rule making requesting responses from interested parties with respect to the assertion of jurisdiction over symphony orchestras and the establishment of jurisdictional standards therefor. The Board having considered the responses and its discretion under sections 9 and 10 of the Act has decided to adopt a rule asserting jurisdiction over any symphony orchestra having a gross annual revenue of not less than $1 million. The National Labor Relations Board finds for good cause that this rule shall be effective on March 7, 1973, and shall apply to all proceedings affected thereby which are pending at the time of such publication or which may arise thereafter.

Dated at Washington, D.C., March 2, 1973.

By direction of the Board.

[SEAL] JOHN C. TRUESDALE,
Executive Secretary.

On August 19, 1972, the Board published in the FEDERAL REGISTER, a notice of proposed rule making which invited interested parties to submit to it (1) data relevant to defining the extent to which symphony orchestras are in commerce, as defined in section 2(6) of the National Labor Relations Act, and to assessing the effect upon commerce of a labor dispute in those enterprises, (2) statements of views or arguments as to the desirability of the Board exercising jurisdiction, and (3) data and views concerning the appropriate jurisdictional standards which should be established in the event the Board decides to promulgate a rule exercising jurisdiction over those enterprises. The Board received 26 responses to the notice. After careful consideration of all the responses, the Board has concluded that it will best effectuate the purposes of the Act to assert jurisdiction over symphony orchestras and apply a $1 million annual gross revenue standard, in addition to statutory jurisdiction. A rule establishing that standard has been issued concurrently with the publication of this notice.

It is well settled that the National Labor Relations Act gives to the Board a "jurisdictional authority coextensive with the full reach of the commerce clause.[1] It is equally well settled that the Board in its discretion may set boundaries on the exercise of that authority.[2] In exercising that discretion, the Board has consistently taken the position that it would better effectuate the purposes of the Act, and promote the prompt handling of major cases, not to exercise its jurisdiction to the fullest extent possible under the authority delegated to it by Congress, but to limit that exercise to enterprises whose operations have, or at which labor disputes would have, a pronounced impact upon the flow of interstate commerce.[3] The standard announced above, in our opinion, accommodates this position.

The Board, in arriving at a $1 million gross figure,[4] has considered, inter alia, the impact of symphony orchestras on commerce and the aspects of orchestra operations as criteria for the exercise of jurisdiction. Symphony orchestras in the United States are classified in four categories: college, community, metropolitan, and major.[5] Community orchestras constitute the largest group with over 1,000 in number and, for the most part, are composed of amateur players. The metropolitan orchestras are almost exclusively professional and it is estimated that there are between 75 and 80 orchestras classified as metropolitan. The annual budget for this category ranges approximately from $250,000 to $1 million. The major orchestras are the largest and usually the oldest established musical organizations. All of them are completely professional, and a substantial number

[1] 49 Stat. 449; 29 U.S.C. 151-166, as amended by act of June 23, 1947 (61 Stat. 136; 29 U.S.C. Supp. 151-167), act of Oct. 22, 1951 (65 Stat. 601; 29 U.S.C. 158, 159, 168), and act of Sept. 14, 1959 (73 Stat. 519; 29 U.S.C. 141-168).

[1] See N.L.R.B. v. Fainblatt, 306 U.S. 601.

[2] Office Employees International Union, Local No. 11 [Oregon Teamsters] v. N.L.R.B., 353 U.S. 313; sec. 14(c)(1) of the Act.

[3] Siemons Mailing Service, 122 NLRB 81; Hollow Tree Lumber Company, 91 NLRB 635, 635. See also, e.g., Floridan Hotel of Tampa, Inc., 124 NLRB 261, 264; Butte Medical Properties, d.b.a. Medical Center Hospital, 168 NLRB 266, 268.

[4] As reflected in the rule, this figure includes revenues from all sources, excepting only contributions which, because of limitations placed thereon by the grantor, are not available for operating expenses. These contributions encompassing, for example, contributions to an endowment fund or building fund, are excluded because of their generally nonrecurring nature. (Cf. Magic Mountain, Inc., 123 NLRB 1170.) Income derived from investment of such funds will, however, be counted in determining whether the standard has been satisfied.

[5] The latter three categories are defined by the American Symphony Orchestra League principally on the basis of their annual budgets.

Illustration 9-6 *(continued)*

RULES AND REGULATIONS 6177

operates on a year-round basis. For this category the minimum annual budget is approximately $1 million. Presently, there are approximately 28 major symphony orchestras in the United States. Thus, statistical projections based on data submitted by responding parties, as well as data compiled by the Board, disclose that adoption of such a standard would bring approximately 2 percent of all symphony orchestras, except college, or approximately 28 percent of the professional metropolitan and major orchestras, within reach of the Act. The Board is satisfied that symphony orchestras with gross revenues of $1 million have a substantial impact on commerce and that the figure selected will not result in an unmanageable increase on the Board's workload. The adoption of a $1 million standard, however, does not foreclose the Board from reevaluating and revising that standard should future circumstances deem it appropriate.

In view of the foregoing, the Board is satisfied that the $1 million annual gross revenue standard announced today will result in attaining uniform and effective regulation of labor disputes involving employees in the symphony orchestra industry whose operations have a substantial impact on interstate commerce.

§ 103.2 Symphony Orchestras.

The Board will assert its jurisdiction in any proceeding arising under sections 8, 9, and 10 of the Act involving any symphony orchestra which has a gross annual revenue from all sources (excluding only contributions which are because of limitation by the grantor not available for use for operating expenses) of not less than $1 million.

[FR Doc.73-4374 Filed 3-6-73;8:45 am]

CHAPTER XVII—OCCUPATIONAL SAFETY AND HEALTH ADMINISTRATION, DEPARTMENT OF LABOR

PART 1952—APPROVED STATE PLANS FOR ENFORCEMENT OF STATE STAND-

the protection of employees even though the codes may afford some incidental protection to others. Codes that more directly concern other matters such as the protection of the environment and the public at large are properly not incorporated in the plan, and are dealt with elsewhere by the State of New Jersey and its political subdivisions.

The description of the plan in § 1952.140(b) is accordingly amended to indicate these features of the codes involved by adding a new subparagraph (3) to read as follows:

§ 1952.140 Description of the plan.

* * * * *

(b) * * *

(3) Safety and health codes which are established by the State of New Jersey to protect employees and which incidentally protect others are considered occupational safety and health standards for the purposes of this subpart.

* * * * *

(Sec. 18, Pub. L. 91-596, 84 Stat. 1608 (29 U.S.C. 667))

Signed at Washington, D.C., this 1st day of March 1973.

CHAIN ROBBINS,
Acting Assistant Secretary of Labor.

[FR Doc.73-4355 Filed 3-6-73;8:45 am]

Title 32—National Defense

CHAPTER XVII—OFFICE OF EMERGENCY PREPAREDNESS

PART 1709—REIMBURSEMENT OF OTHER FEDERAL AGENCIES UNDER PUBLIC LAW 91-606.

Eligibility of Certain Expenditures for Reimbursement

1. Section 1709.2 is amended by deleting paragraphs (d), (e), and (f).

Effective date. This amendment shall be effective as of March 1, 1973.

Dated: March 1, 1973

1. The table of contents of Part 3-16 is amended to add Subpart 3-16.8 as follows:

Subpart 3-16.8—Miscellaneous Forms

3-16.804 Report on procurement.
3-16.804-2 Agencies required to report.
3-16.804-3 Standard Form 37, Report on Procurement by Civilian Executive Agencies.
3-16.852 Equal Opportunity Clause (HEW-386).
3-16.853 Request for Equal Opportunity Clearance of Contract Award (HEW-511).
3-16.854 Notice to Prospective Bidders (HEW-512).
3-16.855 Transmittal Letter (HEW-513).
3-16.856 Procurement Activity Report.

AUTHORITY: 5 U.S.C. 301; 40 U.S.C. 486(c).

Subpart 3-16.8—Miscellaneous Forms

2. Subpart 3-16.8 is added to read as follows:

§ 3-16.801 Report on procurement.

§ 3-16.804-2 Agencies required to report.

Each operating agency, the Office of Regional and Community Development, and the Office of Administrative Services, OS-OASAM, shall report its procurement to the Office of Procurement and Materiel Management, OS-OASAM, for the organization as a whole.

§ 3-16.804-3 Standard Form 37, Report on Procurement by Civilian Agencies.

(a)-(e) [Reserved]

(f) *Frequency and due date for submission of Standard Form 37.* Each report shall be submitted in the original and three copies to arrive at OPMM not later than 30 calendar days after the close of each reporting period.

§ 3-16.852 Equal Opportunity Clause (HEW-386).

Use Form HEW-386, Equal Opportunity Clause, if it is prescribed.

§ 3-16.853 Request for Equal Opportunity Clearance of Contract Award.

pamphlets. Then, to locate the *Shepard's* entry for your citation, you would locate the pages covering the title of your regulation and then the material pertaining to your specific section. That material may be spread out because *Shepard's* includes listings not just for specific sections but also for parts or groups of sections, because courts do not always refer to specific sections.

As you decipher the listings, keep in mind that *Shepard's* leads off with citations in case law; commentary citations come at the end. The following abbreviations are used as appropriate:

C	constitutional	V	void and invalid
U	unconstitutional	Va	valid
Up	unconstitutional in part	Vp	void or invalid in part

Illustration 9-7

Shepard's Code of Federal Regulations Citations.

CODE OF FEDERAL REGULATIONS TITLE 29

§ 102.118(b)(2)
Cir. 3
458F2d420*1971
Cir. 5
656F2d82Δ1981

§ 102.118(c)
Cir. 5
563F2d733*1976
Cir. 6
634F2d322*1978
Cir. 9
566F2d1370Δ1978
Cir. 10
424F2d187Δ1970

§ 102.119
Cir. 8
635F2d1383*1979
Cir. 9
727F2d863*1983

§ 102.121
Cir. 3
669F2d135Δ1982
669F2d141Δ1982
Cir. 6
931F2d1096Δ1991
Cir. 9
610F2d569*1978
736F2d1336*1983
Cir. DC
505F2d425*1973
732F2d977*1983

§ 102.124
Cir. 2
708F2d55Δ1983
72NwL96*1976

§ 102.125
Cir. 2
708F2d55Δ1983
72NwL96*1976

§ 102.126
Cir. 2
523F2d527*1966
Cir. 8
596F2d326Δ1979

§ 102.128(e)
Cir. 8
596F2d326Δ1979

§ 102.129(a)
Cir. 8
596F2d326Δ1979

§ 102.130
Cir. 2
669F2d37*1981

§§ 102.143 to 102.155
Cir. 4
695F2d75*1982

§ 102.143
Cir. DC
841F2d1146Δ1987

§ 102.143(b)
Cir. 6
749F2d15Δ1984

§ 102.143(g)
Cir. 9
951F2d1102Δ1991

§ 102.144
Cir. 6
749F2d15Δ1984

§ 102.148
Cir. 9
715F2d1410Δ1983
772F2d1449*1984

§ 102.148(a)
Cir. 6
763F2d231Δ1985
Cir. 8
708F2d1324*1982
Cir. 9
772F2d1449*1984

§ 102.151
Cir. 4
695F2d77*1982

§ 102.444(a)
Cir. 7
756F2d588*1984

§ 102.444(b)
Cir. 7
756F2d588*1984

Part 103
Cir. 7
718FS705Δ1989
Cir. 10
884F2d520Δ1989
137PaL1700*1989
76VaL115*1988

§ 103.1
et seq.
Cir. 5
407FS856*1973

§§ 103.1 to 103.3
72NwL96Δ1977

§ 103.1
440US497*1977
59LE539*1977
99SC1317*1977
Cir. 2
475F2d495Δ1973
Cir. 3
562F2d248Δ1977
Cir. 7
559F2d1114*1970
66MnL432*1980
73NwL464*1977

§ 103.1(d)(4)(ii)
Cir. 1
843F2d623Δ1988

§ 103.2
Cir. 2
514F2d990*1973

§ 103.3
Cir. 1
560F2d490Δ1977
532FS52Δ1982
Cir. 2
708F2d48*1982
973F2d65*1991
Cir. 3
709F2d851*1982
838F2d104*1987
428FS126Δ1977

Cir. 4
529FS420Δ1982
Cir. 5
703F2d915*1982
Cir. 6
745F2d360*1982
Cir. 7
790F2d635*1982
Cir. 9
557F2d695*1976
940F2d538Δ1991
Cir. 11
686F2d1365Δ1982
Calif
197CaR322Δ1983
Minn
403NW887*1986
W Va
364SE259*1987

§ 103.30
Va499US608*1990
Va111SC1541*1990
Cir. 3
991F2d1147*1992
Cir. 4
975F2d1069Δ1992
Cir. 10
884F2d520Δ1989
Cir. DC
884F2d1446Δ1989
90ARF37n
90ARF70n

§ 103.30(a)
Va499US617*1990
Va111SC1545*1990
Cir. 3
991F2d1148Δ1993
Cir. 4
975F2d1072Δ1992

§ 103.30(a)(1)
Cir. 4
975F2d1073Δ1992

§ 103.30(a)(2)
Cir. 4
975F2d1073Δ1992

§ 103.30(b)
Va499US619*1990
111SC1547*1990
Cir. 3
991F2d1148Δ1993

§ 103.100
72NwL96Δ1977

§ 109.18(a)
Cir. 5
577F2d1175Δ1978

§ 110.28
Cir. 2
797FS146Δ1992

§ 110.29
Cir. 2
797FS146Δ1992

§ 120.118(b)(1)
437US241*1977
57LE178*1977
98SC2321*1977

§ 121.383(c)
Cir. 7
614FS1036Δ1985

§ 178.142
Calif
240CaR651*1968
240CaR651*1987

§ 201.3
Cir. 8
46BRW783Δ1984

§ 201.10
et seq.
Cir. 6
327FS302Δ1971

§ 202.4
Cir. 6
188F2d927Δ1951

§ 202.18
Cir. 3
181F2d430*1946

§ 202.32
et seq.
Cir. 1
612F2d604*1943

§ 203.1
et seq.
Cir. DC
181F2d788*1947

§ 203.1
Cir. 3
181F2d430*1945
Cir. 9
563F2d413Δ1977

§ 203.3
Cir. 3
181F2d430*1943

§ 203.14
Cir. 6
188F2d927Δ1951

§ 203.49
Cir. 3
181F2d430*1946
70VaL1190*1985

§ 203.61
Cir. 7
187F2d332Δ1951

§ 203.74
Cir. DC
181F2d788*1947

§ 203.75
Cir. DC
181F2d788*1947

§ 204.2(a)(5)
43ARF13n

§ 204.31
Cir. 3
522F2d491*1974

§ 206.150
Cir. 5
853F2d1163Δ1988

81

Also note that *Shepard's C.F.R. Citations* provides years, in addition to the location of the citation. A date preceded by a triangle is the date of the decision. A date preceded by an asterisk is the date of the regulation as cited in the citing source. The latter date is particularly important when a regulation has evolved over time because it permits you to discern whether the regulation cited in the citing source is the same version of the regulation you are dealing with.

In the Canoga case, as Illustration 9-7 on page 290 shows, section 103.2 has not been cited often. There are no indications that the regulation is unconstitutional, invalid, or void. There is a Tenth Circuit case from 1989 citing part 103 (New Mexico is in the Tenth Circuit). Also of potential note is the Second Circuit case citing the 1973 (and unchanged) version of section 103.2. Several law reviews have discussed part 103. Illustration 9-7 on page 290 is the 1994 main volume *Shepard's* entry for section 103.2; there were no additional updates in the September 1995 supplement.

e. Incorporating Case Law

At several points, this part has referred to case law. Your research in federal regulations is not complete unless you have read case law involving your regulation: applying it to specific situations (also probably interpreting it and possibly reviewing the agency's application of the regulation), assessing its validity under the enabling statute and its constitutionality. You would locate these cases through secondary sources, the statutory annotations, and *Shepard's Code of Federal Regulations Citations.* The tools discussed in Chapter 6, such as digests and *Shepard's Citations* for cases, also are pertinent in this context.

In addition, agencies decide cases involving agency regulations. Part C discusses how to research those decisions.

In the Canoga case, the case law does not contribute much to your understanding of the regulation. The most significant case, the Second Circuit decision in *NLRB v. Rochester Musicians Association,* 514 F.2d 988 (2d Cir. 1975), upholds the Board's assertion of jurisdiction in a case under its then new regulations, but it does not discuss the regulation in detail. The other cases listed in *Shepard's* are not pertinent because they refer to other regulations within part 103.

f. Summary of Canoga Research

The research illustrated in this part has established a simple but crucial point: By legislative regulation, the Canoga case would be within the Board's jurisdiction if the orchestra's gross annual revenues are not less than $1 million. That regulation is currently in force and has not been invalidated by judicial action. Indeed, it has been discussed very little by the courts. While it seems likely that an orchestra would have revenues of more than $1 million, you would need to verify this factual assumption before proceeding very far with a case based on the labor statute.

4. What Else?

Administrative History. If you are seeking the history of a regulation to help you understand its purpose or background or to determine whether it has been promulgated properly, you should consult its publication in the *Federal Register.* As noted already, C.F.R. includes *Federal Register* citations in small print. For thorough research into the background of a regulation, you would consult not only the *Federal Register* materials at the time of final promulgation, but also those appearing when the regulation was proposed.

Proposed Regulations. If you are monitoring an agency's activities for a client concerned about the impact of possible future regulations, you would locate the proposed regulation in the *Federal Register.* When a proposed regulation is published in the *Federal Register,* it typically is accompanied by an explanation of the agency's plans, background on the rule, and the name of a person to contact about it. You can locate information about proposed rules through the L.S.A. and Reader Aids listings of proposed rules, appearing at the end of each title's entries. (Note that in this respect the *Federal Register* is a more comprehensive source than its statutory parallel, *Statutes at Large,* which publishes only enacted statutes.)

Further Information about the *Federal Register.* If you wish to learn more about the *Federal Register,* which has uses beyond those described here, consult the pamphlet entitled *The Federal Register: What It Is and How to Use It.*

Commercial Indexes. If you find the finding tools within C.F.R. and the *Federal Register* difficult to use, you may want to consult *CIS Index to the Code of Federal Regulations* or *CIS Federal Register Index.* Both feature frequent updating and detailed indexing.

Media Options. In addition to the Internet, demonstrated in Part G below, regulations materials appeared in the following media in early 1996:

			Computer-Assisted Research		
	Paper	*CD-ROM*	*LEXIS*	*WESTLAW*	*Microform*
Code of Federal Regulations	√	√	√	√	√
List of CFR Sections Affected	√				√
Federal Register	√	√	√	√	√
Shepard's Code of Federal Regulations Citations	√			√	

5. How Do You Cite Regulations?

Rule 14.2 of *The Bluebook* provides that regulations should be cited to C.F.R. whenever possible. Paralleling statutory citation, the form includes the regulation's name, if it is commonly known by a name; the title of C.F.R.; the abbreviation "C.F.R."; the section number; and the date of the most recent C.F.R. edition. For example:

29 C.F.R. § 103.2 (1994).

The same rule calls for citation to the *Federal Register* for regulations not appearing in C.F.R. The form includes the regulation's commonly used name; the volume of *Federal Register*; the abbreviation "Fed. Reg."; the page number on which the discussion of the regulation or the regulation itself begins, as well as the page number where the portion of the regulation you are citing appears, if you are citing only a portion; the year; and a parenthetical indicating the regulation's eventual codification in C.F.R. For example:

38 Fed. Reg. 6,176, 6,177 (1973) (to be codified at 29 C.F.R. § 103.2).

Rule 14 also covers less commonly used citation forms, such as citation to proposed regulations.

C. Federal Administrative Agency Decisions

1. What Is an Agency Decision?

a. What Does an Agency Decision Look Like?

In form, an agency decision resembles a case decided by a court. It includes a statement of the facts as found by the agency, the agency's decision based on those facts, and the reasoning behind the decision. That reasoning typically includes discussion of the statute, any pertinent regulations, and previous decisions of the agency. As with case law, an agency decision not only resolves the dispute for the litigants, but also operates as precedent for similar situations involving other parties.

Illustration 9-8 on pages 294-295 is an excerpt from a major Board decision pertinent to the Canoga case. It discusses the labor statute's protection of activities not involving unions that are nonetheless protected by the statute because they involve concerted action by employees.

Illustration 9-8

Meyers Industries, Inc., 268 N.L.R.B. 493, 497 (1984).

Meyers Industries, Inc. *and* Kenneth P. Prill. Case 7-CA-17207

6 January 1984

DECISION AND ORDER

On 14 January 1981 Administrative Law Judge Robert A. Giannasi issued the attached decision. The Respondent filed exceptions and a supporting brief. The General Counsel and the Charging Party each filed cross-exceptions with supporting briefs, after which the General Counsel filed a brief in response to the Respondent's exceptions.

The Board has considered the decision and the record in light of the exceptions and briefs and has decided to affirm the judge's rulings,[1] findings,[2] and conclusions only to the extent consistent with this Decision and Order.[3]

[1] On 4 November 1980, after the hearing and before the judge's decision, the General Counsel, with the Charging Party's concurrence, moved to amend the complaint to include an additional allegation that the unlawful nature of Prill's discharge is supported by Sec. 502 of the National Labor Relations Act. The relevant portion of that section states:

> [N]or shall the quitting of labor by an employee or employees in good faith because of abnormally dangerous conditions for work at the place of employment of such employee or employees be deemed a strike under this Act.

The judge, after considering the arguments of all parties, denied the General Counsel's motion by telegram of 11 November 1980. The General Counsel and the Charging Party cross-except. We note that counsel for the General Counsel engaged in lengthy argument at the hearing concerning the theory of her case both before as well as after the presentation of evidence, but gave no indication that Sec. 502 formed the basis for any portion of the General Counsel's case. In addition, although counsel for the Charging Party took the position at the hearing that Sec. 502 was applicable, counsel for the General Counsel thereafter reiterated that the theory of her case rested on *Alleluia Cushion Co.*, 221 NLRB 999 (1975), and at no time adopted the Charging Party's position. Thus, although we agree with the judge that the General Counsel's motion to amend the complaint should be denied, we do so for the reason that the General Counsel neither raised nor litigated the Sec. 502 issue at the hearing. Accordingly, we affirm the judge's ruling and therefore do not reach the issue discussed in fn. 6 of the attached decision of whether Sec. 502 protects an employee in the circumstances of this case.

[2] The Respondent has excepted to some of the judge's credibility findings. The Board's established policy is not to overrule an administrative law judge's credibility resolutions unless the clear preponderance of all the relevant evidence convinces us that they are incorrect. *Standard Dry Wall Products*, 91 NLRB 544 (1950), enfd. 188 F.2d 362 (3d Cir. 1951). We have carefully examined the record and find no basis for reversing the findings.

The Respondent also asserts that the judge's decision is the result of bias. After a careful examination of the entire record, we are satisfied that this allegation is without merit. There is no basis for finding that bias and partiality existed merely because the judge resolved important factual conflicts in favor of the General Counsel's witnesses. As the Supreme Court stated in *NLRB v. Pittsburgh Steamship Co.*, 337 U.S. 656, 659 (1949), "[T]otal rejection of an opposed view cannot of itself impugn the integrity or competence of a trier of fact." See generally *Jack August Enterprises*, 232 NLRB 881 (1977).

[3] The Charging Party urges, as part of its cross-exceptions, that it be awarded a reasonable attorney's fee for this litigation. When a respondent's defense is dependent upon resolutions of credibility and hence is "debatable" rather than "frivolous," the Board has consistently refused to award litigation costs, even if the respondent has "engaged in 'clearly aggravated and pervasive misconduct,' or in the 'flagrant repetition of conduct previously found unlawful.'" *Heck's Inc.*, 215 NLRB 765, 767 (1974); see also *Tiidee Products*, 194 NLRB 1234 (1972). Upon a review of the record, we cannot say that the Respondent's defenses were frivolous.

268 NLRB No. 73

Relying on *Alleluia Cushion Co.*, 221 NLRB 999, the judge concluded that the Respondent violated Section 8(a)(1) of the Act when it discharged employee Kenneth P. Prill because of his safety complaints and his refusal to drive an unsafe truck after reporting its condition to the Tennessee Public Service Commission. Upon careful consideration, and for the reasons set forth below, we reject the principles the Board adopted in *Alleluia*, and do not agree with the view of protected concerted activity which that decision and its progeny advance. We, therefore, find that the Respondent did not violate Section 8(a)(1) by discharging Prill.

I. THE CONCEPT OF PROTECTED CONCERTED ACTIVITY

The concept of concerted action has its basis in Section 7 of the Act, which states in relevant part:

> Employees shall have the right to self-organization, to form, join, or assist labor organizations, to bargain collectively through representatives of their own choosing, and to engage in other concerted activities for the purpose of collective bargaining or other mutual aid or protection . . . .

Although the legislative history of Section 7 does not specifically define "concerted activity," it does reveal that Congress considered the concept in terms of individuals united in pursuit of a common goal. The immediate antecedent of Section 7 was Section 7(a) of the National Industrial Recovery Act of 1933,[4] the purpose of which was, as then Congressman Boland suggested, to "afford [the laboring person] the opportunity to associate freely with his fellow workers for the betterment of working conditions . . . [and it] primarily creates rights in organizations of workers."[5]

A review of the language of Section 7 leads to a similar united-action interpretation of "concerted activity." The wording of that section demon-

Accordingly, we deny the Charging Party's request for reasonable attorney's fees.

[4] 48 Stat. 195, 198.

See also § 2 of the Norris-LaGuardia Act, 47 Stat. 70, 29 U.S.C. § 102. The Supreme Court has stated that "Congress modeled the language of § 7 after that found in § 2 of the Norris-LaGuardia Act . . . which declares that it is the public policy of the United States that 'workers shall be free from the interference, restraint, or coercion of employers of labor, or their agents, in the designation of . . . representatives or in self organization or in other concerted activities for the purpose of collective bargaining or other mutual aid or protection. . . .'" *Eastex, Inc. v. NLRB*, 437 U.S. 556, 565 fn. 14 (1978).

[5] 79 Cong. Rec. H 2332 (daily ed. Feb. 20, 1935) (statement of Rep. Boland), reprinted in 2 Leg. Hist. of the National Labor Relations Act of 1935, at 2431-32 (1935).

Boland's analysis of the "collectivist" antecedents of what became Sec. 7 of the Act was recognized by others. See, e.g., William H. Spencer, *Collective Bargaining Under Section 7(a) of the National Industrial Recovery Act* 3-6 (1935).

Illustration 9-8 *(continued)*

one, we caution that it is by no means exhaustive. We acknowledge the myriad of factual situations that have arisen, and will continue to arise, in this area of the law. In general, to find an employee's activity to be "concerted," we shall require that it be engaged in with or on the authority of other employees, and not solely by and on behalf of the employee himself.[22] Once the activity is found to be concerted, an 8(a)(1) violation will be found if, in addition, the employer knew of the concerted nature of the employee's activity, the concerted activity was protected by the Act, and the adverse employment action at issue (e.g., discharge) was motivated by the employee's protected concerted activity.[23]

We emphasize that our return to a pre-*Alleluia* standard of concerted activity places on the General Counsel the burden of proving the elements of a violation as set forth herein. It will no longer be sufficient for the General Counsel to set out the subject matter that is of alleged concern to a theoretical group and expect to establish concert of action thereby.

We also emphasize that, under the standard we now adopt, the question of whether an employee engaged in concerted activity is, at its heart, a factual one, the fate of a particular case rising or falling on the record evidence. It is, therefore, imperative that the parties present as full and complete a record as possible.

V. APPLICATION OF THE DEFINITION OF CONCERTED ACTIVITY TO THE FACTS OF THE INSTANT CASE

As the judge found, Charging Party Kenneth P. Prill drove trucks for a number of

Although the red Ford truck and trailer were assigned to Prill on what might fairly be described as a permanent basis, during the first 2 weeks of June 1979 Prill's fellow employee, Ben Gove, was assigned that equipment while Prill was absent from work. On a trip to Sudberry, Ontario, Gove experienced steering problems which nearly caused an accident. On Gove's return, he informed Supervisor Dave Faling of difficulties with the truck. Prill, who had by then returned to work, was also in Faling's office to receive paperwork for an upcoming trip. Prill was present when Gove told Faling that he "wouldn't take the truck as far as Clinton and back, until they had done some repair on it. Until someone repaired it. I [Gove] didn't care who done it, but I wasn't going to drive it no farther."

The Respondent's mechanic, Buck Maynard, made an unsuccessful attempt to correct the problems. Thereafter, on a trip to Xenia, Ohio, during which the brakes malfunctioned, Prill voluntarily stopped at an Ohio State roadside inspection station where the trailer was cited for several defects, some relating to the brakes. Prill forwarded the citation to the Respondent's officials.

In July 1979, while driving through Tennessee, Prill was involved in an accident caused by the malfunctioning brakes. Prill telephoned the Respondent's president, Alan Beatty, who instructed Prill to have a mechanic look at the equipment, but to get it home as best he could. The following morning Prill again called Beatty. The Respondent's vice president, Wayne Seagraves, joined the conversation on an extension telephone. Both Beatty and Seagraves were upset with Prill for not

b. How Is an Agency Case Decided?

Agency decisions are the end product of litigation before the agency, just as judicial cases are the end product of litigation in the courts. Agency litigation varies considerably. The parties typically are the government, acting as a quasi-prosecutor or claims administrator, and the private party. While many agency cases are adjudicated informally, some involve formal adjudication that parallels litigation in the courts. The case begins with some form of notice, typically in pleadings that may be construed fairly broadly. There may or may not be discovery (or development of the facts by the lawyers) before the hearing, and preliminary issues may be handled by motion (that is, by written and oral argument rather than presentation of evidence). The hearing resembles a trial with counsel, direct testimony and cross-examination, and exhibits. Evidence may be submitted in writing, and evidentiary rules are relaxed so as to favor admitting evidence that may not be admissible in court during a jury trial. The parties then submit proposed findings to the judge, known as an "administrative law judge" (ALJ), who then renders a decision that may reflect the parties' proposed findings.

The case generally proceeds to higher levels within the agency, ultimately to the commissioners or members of the agency, who then may adopt the ALJ's decision or develop their own decision in response to the arguments of counsel. In some sense, it is fair to think of the commissioners as an appeals court, because they do not hear the evidence themselves. However, the agency decision is not the terminus of the litigation; federal agency decisions are subject to review by the federal court to assure, for example, that there is substantial evidence in the record to support the decision.

If litigation were pursued in the Canoga case under the federal labor statute, it would begin with the filing of a charge against the employer by Ms. Canoga. The Board's staff in the regional office would investigate the facts. If the investigation indicated that the labor statute had been violated, a lawyer in the regional office would file a complaint against the employer and proceed to litigate the case on Ms. Canoga's behalf before an ALJ. The Board would review the ALJ's recommendation and determine whether to adopt the recommendation or write its own decision. The Board's decision would be subject to review in turn by the Courts of Appeals for the Tenth Circuit (which encompasses New Mexico) or the District of Columbia (where the Board's offices are), and thereafter by the United States Supreme Court.

2. Why Would You Research Agency Decisions?

As with agency regulations, the reason for researching agency decisions is that they constitute the law. An agency decision must conform, of course, to the requirements of the enabling statute and Constitution, and the decision also must withstand judicial scrutiny. Thus the agency may properly be seen as subordinate to the legislature and courts. Even so, the decision is law and functions as precedent for other similar situations coming within the agency's jurisdiction. Although stare decisis does not operate as forcefully with agencies as with courts, an agency must explain any deviations from earlier decisions.

3. How Do You Research Agency Decisions in Paper Media (without Looseleafs)?

Comprehensive research into agency decisions, like research in agency regulations, involves secondary sources, annotated codes, several government sources, *Shepard's Citations,* and case law from the courts. As with regulations, because secondary sources may provide a helpful overview as well as references to primary authority, they merit consideration early on. In addition, the annotated codes are an appropriate place to start once you turn to primary authority, and judicial case law tends to come in toward the end of your research.

The government publications vary from agency to agency. The two primary tools typically are a digest of agency decisions and a reporter of agency decisions. Furthermore, which *Shepard's* you will use to update and expand your research depends on the agency.

Exhibit 9.2 below presents the relationships among these sources in graphic form, and this part follows the sequence presented in the chart. That sequence reflects the development of an agency decision as legal authority. It is not, of course, the only sensible sequence; you may start at some other point, depending on your knowledge of the subject.

Exhibit 9.2 Agency Decisions Research in Paper Sources (without Looseleafs).

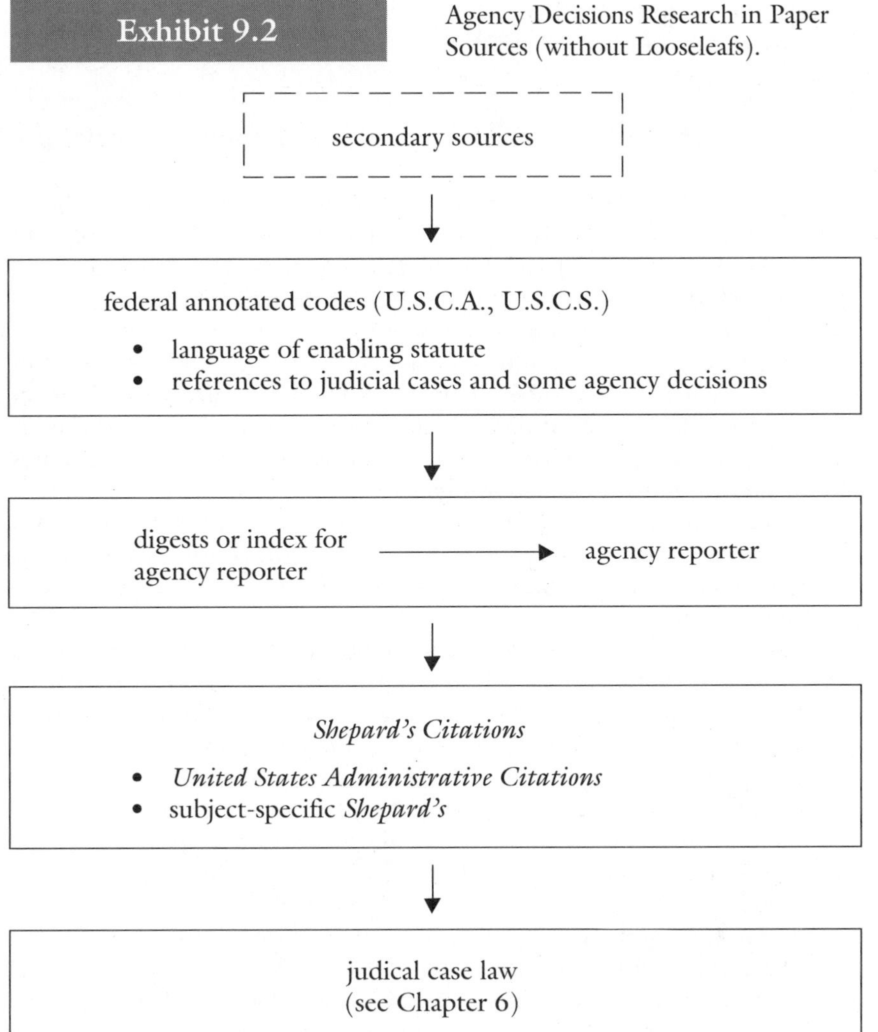

a. Beginning with the Annotated Statutory Codes

When an agency that has the authority to decide cases does so, it implements the language of its enabling statute. Hence you should research that statute early in your research. Chapter 7 covers statutory research.

As you research in the annotated code, you should begin with the statutory language guiding your agency's actions. Furthermore, you also should examine the case annotations for pertinent cases. While most cases noted in the annotations likely will be judicial cases, in U.S.C.S., and U.S.C.A. to a lesser extent, you may find some references to agency decisions as well.

In the Canoga case, for example, the labor statute indicates that it protects not only activities involving unions but also other "concerted activities for the purpose of . . . mutual aid or protection." *See* 29 U.S.C. § 157 (1994). If you read the annotation in *United States Code Service* (U.S.C.S.) under the topic of "activities as concerted activities—generally," you would locate references to various Board and court decisions, including the *Meyers Industries* case featured in this discussion.

b. Researching in Official Reporters of Agency Decisions

The reporting of agency decisions is considerably spottier than the reporting of judicial case law. There is no equivalent of the West National Reporter System. However, the federal government does publish some agency decisions in official reporters. The concluding portion of the federal segment of Table T.1 of *The Bluebook* lists these official reporters.

As is true of reporters of judicial case law, reporters of agency decisions present decisions in chronological order, as they are issued by the agency. Hence a topically organized digest is necessary to research them efficiently. These digests vary somewhat in their organization, detail, and usefulness; indeed they do not exist for some agencies.

In the Canoga case, as *The Bluebook* indicates, you would research in *Decisions and Orders of the National Labor Relations Board* (N.L.R.B.). To locate pertinent Board decisions, you would use two closely related government publications.

The first, *Classification Outline with Topical Index for Decisions of the National Labor Relations Board and Related Court Decisions* (*Classification Outline*), contains the classification system for Board decisions (as well as related court decisions). You could start by looking up your research terms in the Topical Index to identify a pertinent part of the outline. With that guidance, or as a first step, you would scan the Classification Outline until you found the most pertinent topics. See Illustration 9-9 on page 299. These steps would bring you to topic 506, subtopic 2001-5000 (employee rights protected by section 7—nature of activities protected—generally—concerted activity defined). Note how detailed this classification system is.

The second publication, *Classified Index of National Labor Relations Board and Related Court Decisions,* is essentially a digest of Board decisions (as well as related court decisions) organized according to the Classification

Illustration 9-9

Classification Outline, *Classification Outline with Topical Index for Decisions of the National Labor Relations Board and Related Court Decisions.*

506 EMPLOYEE RIGHTS PROTECTED BY SECTION 7

0100 GENERALLY
0114 RIGHT OF SELF-ORGANIZATION
0128 RIGHT TO FORM, JOIN, OR ASSIST LABOR ORGANIZATIONS
0142 RIGHT TO BARGAIN COLLECTIVELY THROUGH REPRESENTATIVE OF OWN CHOOSING
0156 RIGHT TO ENGAGE IN OTHER CONCERTED ACTIVITIES FOR PURPOSE OF COLLECTIVE BARGAINING
0170 RIGHT TO ENGAGE IN OTHER CONCERTED ACTIVITIES FOR MUTUAL AID OR PROTECTION
0180 ATTITUDE TOWARD MANAGEMENT REFLECTING DISSATISFACTION WITH WORKING CONDITIONS AND/OR LACK OF SUCCESS OF UNION CAMPAIGN, ETC.
0184 RIGHT TO REFRAIN FROM EXERCISE OF SECTION 7 RIGHTS
0184-0100 **Generally**
0184-5000 **Subject to membership requirement of valid agreement**
0188 RIGHT TO BE FREE FROM UNFAIR, IRRELEVANT, OR INVIDIOUS TREATMENT BY REPRESENTATIVE
0188-5000 **Differentiation on basis of sex**
0192 RIGHTS DERIVED FROM OTHER FEDERAL LABOR STATUTES
2000 **NATURE OF ACTIVITIES PROTECTED**
2001 GENERALLY
2001-5000 **Concerted activity defined**
2017 NOT ALL CONCERTED ACTIVITIES PROTECTED
2017-0800 **Activity of such character as to render employee unfit for further service**
2017-1700 **Activities tending to disrupt employer's or union's operations**
2017-2500 **Activities relating to intra-union affairs**
2017-3300 **Cessation of work for personal reasons**
2017-4000 **No impact upon terms and conditions of employment**
2017-5000 **Resort to prohibited means**

82

2017-6700 **Activities prohibited by statute**
2017-8300 **Conduct violating valid provisions of contract**
2017-9100 **Conduct in derogation of bargaining representation**
2033 BOARD HAS FUNCTION OF BALANCING CONFLICTING EMPLOYEE AND EMPLOYER INTERESTS
2033-5000 **Exercise of economic pressure not unlawful per se**
2050 EMPLOYER'S MISTAKEN BELIEF AS TO ACTIVITY'S PROTECTED STATUS IMMATERIAL
2060 EMPLOYEES' MISTAKEN BELIEF AS TO VALIDITY OF GRIEVANCE IMMATERIAL
2067 UNION MEMBERSHIP IMMATERIAL
2083 UNION ACTIVITY NEED NOT BE INVOLVED OR COLLECTIVE BARGAINING CONTEMPLATED
3000 **REFUSAL TO CROSS PICKET LINE**
3001 GENERALLY
3001-5000 **Employer may replace non-striking employee refusing to cross line if business reasons so require**
3033 AT PREMISES OF ANOTHER EMPLOYER
3033-0100 **Generally**
3033-2500 **Right protected by 8(b)(4) proviso**
3033-5000 **Primary picket line**
3033-7500 **Secondary picket line**
3033-8700 **Picket line at state subdivision**
3067 AT OWN EMPLOYER'S PREMISES
3067-0100 **Generally**
3067-1700 **Primary line of another union at employee's place of work**
3067-3300 **Primary line of union representing unit of which employee is not member**
3067-5000 **As result of sympathy strike**
3067-6700 **Secondary picket line which is primary line of another union**
4000 **OBJECTIVE AS DETERMINANT OF PROTECTED STATUS OF ACTIVITY**
4001 GENERALLY
4001-5000 **Racial discrimination**
4033 OBJECTIVES WARRANTING PROTECTION OF ACTIVITY
4033-0100 **Generally**

Outline. Each volume of the *Classified Index* covers several volumes of the agency's reporter; unfortunately the *Classified Index* volumes are not cumulative. *Meyers Industries* is listed in the 1984 *Classified Index* under topic 506, subtopic 2001-5000.

The *Meyers Industries* decision is published in volume 268 of N.L.R.B., which is the official reporter of Board decisions. See again Illustration 9-8 on pages 294-295. According to *Meyers Industries,* the act of a lone employee may be "concerted" if it is engaged in with or on the authority of other employees, not solely by the employee acting alone or on her own behalf; furthermore, the employer must know of the act's concerted nature and take the adverse action because of it.

Finally, very recent Board decisions are summarized in a pamphlet, *Weekly Summary of NLRB Cases.* If you identified a potentially pertinent decision in the *Weekly Summary,* you could contact the Board to obtain a slip opinion, that is, a copy of the decision as the Board has rendered it and released it for publication.

c. Updating and Expanding Your Research through *Shepard's Citations*

Just as you must Shepardize a case decided by a court, so must you Shepardize an agency decision to verify that it has not lost its precedential force through adverse subsequent history or adverse treatment in later cases. The later cases may be other Board decisions or judicial cases. Some agency decisions may be updated through *Shepard's United States Administrative Citations* or a specialized *Shepard's.*

Shepard's United States Administrative Citations covers a fairly wide range of agencies. Cited sources include decisions of the Interstate Commerce Commission, Federal Communications Commission, and Securities and Exchange Commission, for example. Citing sources include federal cases from the United States Supreme Court to the federal district courts, state court cases, agency decisions as published in various reporters, selected law reviews, and *American Law Report* annotations.

Labor law cases are covered by *Shepard's Labor Law Citations.* The cited sources include not only Board decisions but also federal court cases involving labor law issues. The citing sources include Board decisions, federal cases from the United States Supreme Court to the federal district court, state court cases, selected law reviews, *American Law Report* annotations, and several treatises.

While the entries in these administrative *Shepard's* resemble those in *Shepard's* covering judicial cases, there are some distinctive features. For example, in *Labor Law Citations,* some citations in citing sources appear in decisions of administrative law judges (rather than the decision of the agency commissioners); these citations are designated "i" (for "interim"). Some citations are to looseleaf services, which are covered in Part E below.

The sample decision for the Canoga case, *Meyers Industries,* is a heavily cited decision. It has an extensive subsequent history, as signified by the following entries: r755F2d941, s281Bd882 No 118, and cc835F2d1481. The F2d entries refer to court of appeals opinions in the case, while the Bd entry refers to another, later Board decision in the same case.

d. Incorporating Judicial Case Law

At several points, this part has referred to the case law of the courts. Your research is not complete until you have located and read this case law. You would locate these cases through secondary sources, the annotated codes, *Shepard's*, and the tools described in Chapter 6 on case law research.

In the Canoga case, if you read the judicial case law in the *Meyers Industries* litigation, you would find that the employee who lost before the Board, Mr. Prill, appealed his case to the District of Columbia Circuit. That court initially ruled in his favor and remanded to the Board for further consideration. When the Board on remand continued to find in the employer's favor on the grounds that the actions of the employee were not "concerted," he again appealed to the District of Columbia Circuit. In a 1987 decision, the court affirmed the Board's holding and approach to the issue of concerted activity. The Supreme Court declined to review the case.

e. Summary of Canoga Research

As this part has demonstrated, the federal labor statute protects employee activities that are concerted and for mutual aid, in quite broad terms. The Board has given meaning to this language not through regulations, but rather through case adjudication. A major case pertinent to the Canoga case is the *Meyers Industries* case, which has been contested on appeal but ultimately affirmed. Under that case, the regional office's lawyer working on behalf of Ms. Canoga would have to establish that her acts were engaged in with or on the authority of other employees, which may be difficult to do on the facts stated in Chapter 1.

4. What Else?

Additional Uses of *Shepard's*. Some administrative *Shepard's* have uses beyond that of updating agency decisions and court cases. For example, *Labor Law Citations* covers statutory provisions as well, but not regulations. It also provides cross-references between official agency reporters and looseleaf services, described in Part E.

Media Options. Administrative agency decisions appeared in the following media in early 1996:

			Computer-Assisted Research		
	Paper	*CD-ROM*	*LEXIS*	*WESTLAW*	*Microform*
Official reporters of agency decisions	√	√	√	√	√
Shepard's United States Administrative Citations	√			√	
Specialized *Shepard's Citations*	√	√	√	√	

5. How Do You Cite Agency Decisions?

Rule 14.3 of *The Bluebook* provides that a citation to an agency decision consists of the case's name, official reporter citation (where available), and date. The case name consists of the full reported name of the first-listed party and does not include procedural phrases. The reporter is abbreviated according to Table T.1. Although Rule 14.3 does not so state explicitly, you must cite the subsequent history of an agency decision, much as you would cite the subsequent history of a judicial case. For example:

No subsequent history:	*Meyers Industries, Inc.*, 268 N.L.R.B. 493 (1984).
Full citation including subsequent history:	*Meyers Industries, Inc.*, 268 N.L.R.B. 493 (1984), *rev'd and remanded sub nom. Prill v. NLRB*, 755 F.2d 941 (D.C. Cir.), *cert. denied*, 474 U.S. 948 (1985), *on remand sub nom. Meyers Industries, Inc.*, 281 N.L.R.B. 882 (1986), *aff'd sub nom. Prill v. NLRB*, 835 F.2d 1481 (D.C. Cir.), *cert. denied*, 487 U.S. 1205 (1987).

If the decision is not published in an official reporter, typically because it is a very new decision, it should be cited to the slip decision along with a citation to a looseleaf service (covered in Part E). For example:

Meyers Industries, Inc., 268 N.L.R.B. No. 73 (Jan. 6, 1984).

D. State Administrative Agency Materials

As noted in Part A, administrative agencies also exist at the state and local levels. Some regulate matters not addressed by federal agencies. Others address matters that are addressed by federal agencies, in which case the state and federal agencies may have work-sharing agreements, or the two agencies may each regulate distinct facets of the broader matter, or there may be overlapping regulation. As you may recall from Chapter 7's discussion of statutory preemption, the relationship between federal and state statutes—and hence federal and state agencies—is a function of Congress' stated intent, the federal interest in uniformity, and the state interest in regulating its own internal affairs.

State administrative agencies make law much as federal agencies do, in the form of regulations and decided cases. It may be somewhat more difficult, however, to research the law of a state administrative agency.

Your state may have a code of regulations, similar to the *Code of Federal Regulations,* accessible by references in the annotated statutory code or an index within the administrative code. It also may have a publication resembling the *Federal Register,* in which new regulatory material appears. Some state agency regulations are available online or on CD-ROM. Or you may need to contact the agency itself.

The decisions of a state agency are likely to be accessible primarily through direct contact with the agency, which may or may not maintain a digest of its decisions. Or your state may have a reporter of agency decisions, or you may be able to locate some agency decisions in a state legal newspaper.

In the Canoga case, if the orchestra's revenues were so small as to fall below the National Labor Relations Board's jurisdictional standards, you would consider whether a parallel state statute might govern the case. Some states have "baby NLRAs" that govern employers falling outside the Board's jurisdiction. Research in the New Mexico statutes would reveal that New Mexico is not one of those states. As a result, there would be no state agency's law to research on this issue.

E. Looseleaf Services

1. What Is a Looseleaf Service?

A looseleaf service is a miniature library of materials within a particular, although not necessarily narrow, subject matter. Most are published by commercial publishers, and many of them cover areas of law involving administrative agencies (hence the discussion of them in this chapter). Although they vary considerably, they share several important characteristics.

First, they bring together in one service a wide range of legal authorities, insofar as these authorities relate to the area of law covered by the looseleaf. The truly comprehensive looseleaf service includes secondary material; digests, cases, and citators; statutes; administrative regulations and agency decisions; indexes and other finding aids. Less comprehensive looseleafs contain some but not all of the preceding items. Comprehensive looseleafs cover not just federal, but also state and even local law. The looseleaf may include cases not reported in official or West reporters. The comprehensive looseleaf also may include such practical materials as forms, reports of pending cases or bills, and summaries of interesting conferences or studies in the particular area of law.

Second, looseleaf services provide this material on a very current schedule. They are updated continuously.

Third, looseleaf services employ a looseleaf format—a binder that can be easily opened for insertion and deletion of pages. The looseleaf format is used to facilitate the continuous updating. As new material arrives, it is slipped into the binder, adding to or replacing older material. The typical looseleaf service consists of more than one binder, each with one or more sections set off by tabs. The more extensive looseleafs also include hardbound volumes for older material, typically cases.

Because some treatises are published in binders, the dividing line between looseleaf services and looseleaf treatises can be blurry. You should think of a looseleaf service as containing more material than a treatise; a looseleaf service contains significant primary authorities as well as commentary. Furthermore, a looseleaf service typically is updated more frequently than a looseleaf treatise.

2. Why Is a Looseleaf Service Useful?

Looseleaf services are useful for several main reasons, all suggested by the preceding description. First, you can cover a range of authorities within a single source; you need not move from an annotated statute to the *Code of Federal Regulations* to a West digest to a West reporter to a *Shepard's Citations* to an agency reporter to another *Shepard's Citations,* for example.

Second, because a looseleaf covers only one area of law, it benefits from a sharp editorial focus on that area. For example, when you look for a statute within a looseleaf, you will not have to bypass statutes on unrelated topics. The digest of cases is much more refined because the classification system needs to cover only one area of law, not all American law. The index is more detailed. Furthermore, because the material is compiled by a single publisher's staff, there are stronger links among the different parts of the looseleaf than exist among separately published sources.

Third, a comprehensive looseleaf service contains material not as easily available elsewhere. Examples include cases not published in other paper reporters and news of pending or current legal developments.

Fourth, the information in a looseleaf service is very current, and the current information may be fully integrated into the older material, thanks to the binder format.

3. How Do You Research in a Looseleaf Service?

If you are researching an area that is new to you, you are unlikely to begin your research in a looseleaf service. Rather you would research first in the secondary sources discussed in Chapter 4, to identify which area of law is pertinent. Your next step may be to consult *Legal Looseleafs in Print,* by Arlene L. Eis, or your library's catalog to determine whether a looseleaf service exists in your subject matter.

Once you have identified a pertinent looseleaf, you would do well to explore it a bit before looking for information on your client's situation. Figure out how many binders there are and what each contains. Look for a section describing how to use the looseleaf (typically located in the first binder) and a table of abbreviations used within the looseleaf. Also locate the overall index and its updates (many looseleafs have more than one index) as well as tables of authorities (such as statutes or regulations). Figure out where the commentary material, statutes, regulations, and cases appear. Locate the most current information (typically in a binder). Also locate any hardbound volumes; these typically contain permanently valuable, but more dated information, such as cases.

Because each looseleaf is unique, your research in looseleafs will vary considerably. The following discussion covers several classic steps you might take in many looseleafs; these steps are presented in graphic form in Exhibit 9.3 below. They entail use of the looseleaf's index, commentary material, statutes and regulations, case digest and reporter, and updating materials.

More specifically, this discussion illustrates these steps using a comprehensive looseleaf service covering employment law, *Labor Relations Reporter* (L.R.R.) published by the Bureau of National Affairs (BNA). While L.R.R. covers various aspects of employment law, including disability discrimination and contract rights of terminated employees, the focus here will be on its coverage of the law of concerted activities under the National Labor Relations Act (NLRA), also known as the Labor Management Relations Act (LMRA).

If you explored L.R.R. with a focus on its discussion of the labor statute, you would note that it consists of several binders and a large collection of bound volumes. As you will see in more detail in the following sections, the main index and other finding aids appear in the *Master Index* binders. The *Labor Relations Expediter* binders contain commentary, statutes, and regula-

Exhibit 9.3 Research in Looseleafs.

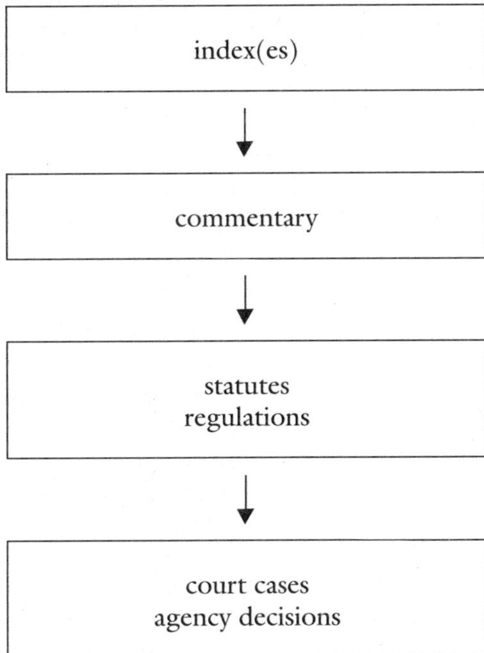

tions, while a *State Laws* binder contains state statutes and regulations. L.R.R. presents case material in a digest and reporter, with the most recent material appearing in binders and the dated material in the bound volumes; there is no citator.

a. Using the Index to Gain Access to the Looseleaf

Many looseleafs are fairly elaborate, with multiple sections each containing different types of authority (for example, commentary, statutes) or covering different topics within the area of law. Thus there may be more than one index: an overall index for the entire looseleaf and subsidiary indexes for parts of the looseleaf. Some of these indexes may have one or more updates, so you should be sure to note their currency. In general, it is wise to consult the broadest index first and then any pertinent subsidiary indexes. As with other types of research, you should pursue various research terms in these indexes.

In the Canoga case, the overall index for L.R.R. is the General Index located in the *Master Index* binder. If you looked up "termination of employment," you would find a long listing, with one useful subheading being "protected activities, discrimination, LMRA." See Illustration 9-10 on page 307. The two references are to the Labor Relations Outline (LR) and to the Labor Relations Expediter (LRX), explained below. (Material at the bottom of the pages of the General Index explains the abbreviations.) If you looked up "orchestra," you would be referred to "entertainment industry." Again see Illustration 9-10 on page 307. That entry in turn would refer you not only to LR and LRX materials but also to a rule: 29 CFR 103.2, at LRX 4159. Small print at the bottom of General Index pages tells you how current this index is (June 1995 when this research was conducted in the fall of 1995). Incidentally, if you scan Illustration 9-10 on page 307, you will see references to other parts of L.R.R., such as FEP (Fair Employment Practices, or discrimination).

As you turn from the index to the text of the looseleaf, take care to discern its numbering scheme. Your looseleaf may be numbered by chapter, section, paragraph, or page—or, most likely, a combination of these. The complex numbering system reflects the need to order material that may be expanding or contracting over time as the law evolves. You must follow the numbering scheme precisely or risk not locating the material you are seeking.

b. Reading Commentary for Background and References

As the sequence of chapters in this text suggests, reading commentary is a sound starting point because it provides an overview of a legal topic and references to primary authority. This observation is applicable to research in looseleafs. Thus you ordinarily will wish to follow up first on the index references to the commentary portion of your looseleaf. That commentary is likely to be current and detailed. See Illustration 9-11 on pages 308-309. To learn when the material you are reading was written,

Illustration 9-10 General Index, *Master Index, Labor Relations Reporter.*

TER
A 756 MASTER INDEX BINDER

TERMINATION OF EMPLOYMENT—Contd.
Procedure—Contd.
—Public employees, LA ▸ 100.5523
Productivity, *see* Incompetence and inefficiency, *this heading;* Loafing, *this heading*
Promotion before, LRX 650:107
Protected activities, discrimination, LMRA
LR ▸ 52.2532 et seq.
LRX 510:207
Protest against, picketing objects, LR ▸ 81.257
Psychological evaluations, LA ▸ 118.655
—Public employees, LA ▸ 100.552565
Public employees
LR ▸ 100.641; LR ▸ 100.647
LA ▸ 100.5501 et seq.
—Mitigation of damages, LA ▸ 100.559525
Quitting jobs distinguished
LR ▸ 118.07
LA ▸ 118.07
—Discrimination, LMRA, LR ▸ 52.257
Racial discrimination, FEP ▸ 108.30251
—Abolition of job, FEP ▸ 108.30263
—Absenteeism, FEP ▸ 108.3

Section 8(a)(1) of LMRA, 8(a)(3) distinguished, discrimination, LMRA, LRX 510:204
Section 8(a)(3) of LMRA, 8(a)(1) distinguished, discrimination, LMRA, LRX 510:204
—Limits, LRX 510:201
Section 8(a)(4) of LMRA, limits, LRX 510:201
Severance pay, *see* SEVERANCE PAY
Sex discrimination, FEP ▸ 108.4112
—Federal employees, FEP ▸ 110.4016
Sexual harassment
LR ▸ 118.640
LA ▸ 118.640
Sleeping on job
LR ▸ 118.654
LA ▸ 118.654
LRX 510:236
—Discrimination, LMRA, LR ▸ 52.2716
—Public employees, LA ▸ 100.552555
Slowdowns
LR ▸ 118.660
LA ▸ 118.6601
Smoking restrictions, public employees, LA

ENT
A 292 MASTER INDEX BINDER

ENTERPRISE COVERAGE STANDARD
See EQUAL PAY ACT; FAIR LABOR STANDARDS ACT (FLSA)

ENTERTAINMENT INDUSTRY
ADA coverage, public accommodations, text, FEPM 401:757
Bargaining units, LR ▸ 65.56
Dog racing, NLRB jurisdiction, LRX 610:208, 211
—Rule (29 CFR 103.3), LRX 4159
Equal Pay Act, exemption chart, FEPM 411:229
FLSA exemption, WH ▸ 113.3201 et seq.
—Child labor, *see* CHILD LABOR, *subheading:* Actors and performers, FLSA exemption
Horse racing
—Bargaining units, LR ▸ 65.29
—NLRB jurisdiction
LR ▸ 43.601
LRX 610:208, 211
——Rule (29 CFR 103.3), LRX 4159
Motion picture industry, *see* MOTION PICTURE INDUSTRY
Musicians, independent contractors, LR ▸ 44.0554
NLRB jurisdiction
LR ▸ 43.601
LRX 610:208
Symphony orchestras, NLRB jurisdiction
LR ▸ 43.601
LRX 610:210
—Rule (29 CFR 103.2), LRX 4159
Theaters
—ADA coverage, public accommodations, text, FEPM 401:757

Coverage, LRX 520:301 et seq.
DOL rules (29 CFR Part 16), LRX 3051 et seq.
—General provisions (29 CFR 16.101 et seq.), LRX 3051 et seq.
—Information required from applicants (29 CFR 16.201 et seq.), LRX 3054 et seq.
—Procedures for considering applications (29 CFR 16.301 et seq.), LRX 3056 et seq.
Eligibility, LRX 520:305
Fair employment practices
FEP ▸ 106.3601
FEPM 431:348
Filing requirements, DOL rules (29 CFR 16.301), LRX 3056
Government's position, substantial justification, LRX 520:303
Homeworker employer certificates, administrative procedures, Equal Access to Justice Act inapplicable (29 CFR 530.414), WHM 97:4014
Judicial review, DOL rules (29 CFR 16.307), LRX 3057
Labor Relations Cases, LR ▸ 71.01
Position of agency, LRX 520:301
Prevailing party, LRX 520:301
Rates of attorneys' fees, LRX 520:305
Recovery of fees, LRX 520:305
—Labor Management Relations Act, LRX 520:306
—NLRB rules, LRX 520:306
Review of awards by Labor Secretary, DOL rules (29 CFR 16.306), LRX 3057
Service Contract Appeals Board, applicability of EAJA to proceedings (29 CFR 8.19)

look at the dates on those pages. To discern how current the discussion is, you generally can look at the date of the most recent new material added to the set (because the portion you are reading may not have undergone recent changes requiring new text).

Illustration 9-11

Labor Relations Expediter, Labor Relations Reporter.

42 LRRM 2620 (CA 2 1958); *NLRB v. Coal Creek Co.*, 204 F2d 579, 32 LRRM 2089 (CA 10 1953); *NLRB v. Mallick & Schwalm Co.*, 198 F2d 477, 30 LRRM 2529 (CA 3 1952).

However, the NLRB's view is that the facts in each case determine whether employees are protected by the act when they take concerted action to protest the selection or termination of a supervisor. Where the identity and capability of a supervisor has a direct impact on employees' own job interests, the board has found that they are legitimately concerned with his identity and have a protected right to protest his termination. *Puerto Kico Foods Products Corp.*, 242 NLRB 899, 101 LRRM 1307 (1979).

Strikes to protest the discharge of supervisors have been found unprotected because the means of protest were not reasonably related to the ends sought. *Dobbs Houses v. NLRB*, 325 F2d 531, 54 LRRM 2726 (CA 5 1963); *Abilities & Goodwill v. NLRB*, 612 F2d 6, 103 LRRM 2029 (CA 1 1979). The NLRB has disagreed, saying that reasonableness is not a test for determining whether a strike is protected. The test, the board says, is whether the discharge of the supervisor had an impact on the strikers in the performance of their jobs. *Plastilite Corp.*, 153 NLRB 180, 59 LRRM 1401 (1965). "The application of Section 7 does not depend on the manner or method by which employees choose to press their dispute, but rather on the matter they are protesting," the court said. *Puerto Rico Food Products*, 242 NLRB 899, 101 LRRM 1307 at 1309 (1979).

The NLRB's order in *Puerto Rico Food Products* was denied enforcement. It was not shown that the work stoppage in fact was a protest over the actual conditions of the strikers' own employment, the court said, adding that the means of protest must also be "reasonable." *Puerto Rico Food Products v. NLRB*, 619 F2d 153, 104 LRRM 2304 (CA 1 1980).

The same court held that an employer lawfully fired 11 supervisors and employees for sending its president a letter requesting the discharge of the general manager at one of the employer's hotels. Reversing the NLRB, the court said the case involved "simply a dispute among managerial employees into which several non-supervisory employees were drawn." *NLRB v. Sheraton Puerto Rico Corp.*, 651 F2d 49, 107 LRRM 2735 (CA 1 1981).

One court has held that a strike seeking the reinstatement of supervisors may be protected if the individuals involved are not employer representatives for the purpose of adjusting grievances or collective bargaining. *NLRB v. Puerto Rico Rayon Mills*, 293 F2d 941, 48 LRRM 2947 (CA 1 1961).

Discharge of 'managerial' employee (LR ▶ 52.041, 52.05) — Reversing the NLRB, the Eighth Circuit upheld the discharge of a managerial employee for failing to remain neutral during an organizing campaign. The purpose of the act, the court said, is to protect "workers," not individuals who are not members of any bargaining unit and who are more closely aligned with management than with the bargaining unit. *NLRB v. North Arkansas Electric Co-op*, 446 F2d 602, 77 LRRM 3114 (CA 8 1971)

§ 7. Concerted employee activities under LMRA. (LR ▶ 52.2532 et seq.) LMRA Sec. 7. declares the employees' right "to engage in other concerted activities for the purpose of collective bargaining or other mutual aid or protection." The obvious forms of concerted activities are joining a union, soliciting other employees to join, attending union meetings, going on strike, etc. But the area of "concerted activities" protected by the LMRA is broader.

To be "concerted," an employee's activity must be engaged in with or on the authority of others, not solely by and on behalf of the employee himself. To establish the illegality of discipline based on such activity, the NLRB's general counsel must show not only that the activity was "concerted," but that the employer knew of its concerted nature, that it was

Illustration 9-11 *(continued)*

LRX 510:208 DISCHARGE No. 660

"protected" by the LMRA, and that the discipline in fact was motivated by this protected concerted activity. *Meyers Industries*, 268 NLRB 493, 115 LRRM 1025 (1984), overruling *Alleluia Cushion Co.*, 221 NLRB 999, 91 LRRM 1131 (1975); see also *Walls Mfg. Co.*, 128 NLRB 487, 46 LRRM 1329 (1960) and *Myers Products Corp.*, 84 NLRB 32, 24 LRRM 1216 (1949).

The District of Columbia Circuit ordered the board to reconsider its *Meyers* ruling. *Prill v. NLRB* (Meyers Industries), 755 F2d 941, 118 LRRM 2649 (1985).

On reconsideration, the board adhered to its definition of concerted activities. It also stressed that its *Meyers I* definition encompasses those circumstances where individual employees seek to initiate, induce, or prepare for group action, as well as individual employees bringing truly group complaints to the attention of management. *Meyers Industries*, 281 NLRB No. 118, 123 LRRM 1137 (1986).

The District of Columbia Circuit affirmed. The board's definition under which an employee's conduct is not "concerted" unless it is engaged in with or on the authority of other employees, is a reasonable interpretation of Section 7 of the act, the court said. *Prill v. NLRB* (Meyers Industries), 835 F2d 1481, 127 LRRM 2415 (1987).

An individual employee who reasonably and honestly invokes a right set forth in his collective-bargaining

definition of concerted activities was not inconsistent with the *Interboro* doctrine.

Concerted activity may take place where only "one person is seeking to induce action from a group." *Salt River Valley Assn. v. NLRB*, 206 F2d 325, 32 LRRM 2598 (CA 9 1953). Thus, it is illegal to discharge one employee for seeking overtime for company workers. *NLRB v. Lion Brand Mfg. Co.*, 146 F2d 773, 15 LRRM 870 (CA 5 1945). Where "one employee discusses with another the need for union organization, their action is 'concerted' . . . for it involves more than one employee, even though one be in the role of speaker and the other of listener." *Root-Carlin*, 92 NLRB 1313, 27 LRRM 1235 (1951). Two employees' informal protest against the elimination of overtime work was held protected although the employees had no authorization from other employees. *Ohio Oil Co.*, 92 NLRB 1597, 27 LRRM 1282 (1951).

Employees have the right to engage in concerted activities "even though no union activity be involved," and even though no collective bargaining is "contemplated" by the employees involved. *NLRB v. Phoenix Mutual Life Insurance Co.*, 167 F2d 983, 22 LRRM 2089 (CA 7 1948), cert. denied, 335 US 845, 22 LRRM 2590 (1948). A meeting of dissident union members to seek a change in the union's bargaining policy is protected. *NLRB v. NuCar Carriers*, 189 F2d 756, 28 LRRM 2160 (CA 3 1951), cert. denied, 342 US ... LRRM 2384 (1952).

In the Canoga case, the commentary within L.R.R. is known as the Labor Relations Expediter (LRX) and is located within the *Labor Relations Expediter* binder. If you pursued the "protected activities" LRX reference from the General Index noted above, you would locate Illustration 9-11. Illustration 9-11 on pages 308-309 is a portion of the LRX discussion of the law of discharge; it focuses on "concerted employee activities under LMRA." Illustration 9-11 sets out the main legal principles on this topic as well as references to primary authorities and citations within L.R.R. where those authorities appear; in particular it refers to the *Meyers Industries* case. Note that Illustration 9-11 dates to October 1988; this date alerts you to the date of the most recent important legal developments on the topic.

If you did not have a cite to LRX from the General Index, you could scan the list of chapters at the outset of LRX for possibilities. See Illustration

9-12 below. That list of chapters reveals a bit of how the publisher has created a flexible numbering system. The page numbers do not run consecutively from the beginning of LRX to the end; rather they start over with each chapter.

Illustration 9-12 List of Major Expediter Chapters, *Labor Relations Expediter, Labor Relations Reporter.*

No. 730 LRX 300:i

MAJOR EXPEDITER CHAPTERS

5-23-94

7

c. Using the Looseleaf as a Source of Statutes and Regulations

Looseleaf services in areas governed by administrative agencies typically contain statutes and agency regulations, both in their current form. Both federal and state materials may be available. Hence one advantage of a looseleaf is that you can locate these materials without having to use a statutory index, the C.F.R. index, L.S.A., and the *Federal Register* on the federal side and without having to use comparable state sources.

Most looseleafs afford several means of locating statutes and regulations: through the overall index, through a subsidiary index to the section containing the statutes and regulations, through a table of contents at the beginning of a set of statutes or regulations, and through references in the commentary section. The federal and state materials typically appear in separate sections or binders.

In the Canoga case, you could locate both the federal statute and the federal regulation in the Text of Laws and Regulations section in the *Labor Relations Expediter* binder. As to the regulation, you already have seen a reference to section 103.2 in the General Index. Illustration 9-13 on page 312 is the regulation as it appears in the Text of Laws and Regulations section. Note that the publisher has provided references to the enabling statute (under Authority) and the citation to the *Federal Register* where the regulation was promulgated in final form.

To locate New Mexico state materials, you would look in the *State Laws* binder covering Minnesota to Wyoming. Illustration 9-14 on page 313 is the beginning of the material appearing under "Labor Relations Acts." As you can see, although New Mexico does not have a baby NLRA for the private sector, it does have a labor statute governing public employment. The looseleaf contains that statute, its regulations, and case annotation material.

d. Using the Looseleaf as a Source of Cases and Decisions

Many looseleaf services covering areas governed by administrative agencies contain agency decisions and cases from the courts on subjects within that area of law. The most comprehensive looseleafs contain not only the cases, but also digests and citators. Others may contain only the cases and indexes.

As a means of researching case law, looseleaf services offer several advantages over other case reporters and official reporters of agency decisions. The looseleaf may well encompass judicial cases unreported in general case reporters. The looseleaf service typically is more up-to-date than a government reporter of agency decisions. And the digest will be more focused and hence more detailed.

Your first step in conducting case law research is to discern where the cases are digested and reported. The newest digest material typically appears in the binders. Older material is removed from the binders and republished in softcover or hardbound books, or it may be moved into another looseleaf binder called a "transfer binder." Thus you typically must work through

Illustration 9-13

29 C.F.R. § 103.2 as reprinted in Text of Laws and Regulations, *Labor Relations Expediter, Labor Relations Reporter.*

National Labor Relations Board Other Rules

Text of 29 CFR Part 103, other rules of the National Labor Relations Board. The text below appears as last amended at 54 FR 16347, April 21, 1989.

Part 103—Other Rules

Authority: 29 U.S.C. 156, in accordance with the procedures set forth in 5 U.S.C. 553.

Source: see information contained in brackets following each section.

Subpart A—Jurisdictional Standards

§103.1 Colleges and universities.

The Board will assert its jurisdiction in any proceeding arising under sections 8, 9, and 10 of the Act involving any private nonprofit college or university which has a gross annual revenue from all sources (excluding only contributions which, because of limitation by the grantor, are not available for use for operating expenses) of not less than $1 million.

[35 FR 18370, Dec. 3, 1970]

§103.2 Symphony orchestras.

The Board will assert its jurisdiction in any proceeding arising under sections 8, 9, and 10 of the Act involving any symphony orchestra which has a gross annual revenue from all sources (excluding only contributions which are because of limitation by the grantor not available for use for operating expenses) of not less than $1 million.

[38 FR 6177, Mar. 7, 1973]

§103.3 Horseracing and dogracing industries.

The Board will not assert its jurisdiction in any proceeding under sections 8, 9, and 10 of the Act involving the horseracing and dogracing industries.

[38 FR 9507, Apr. 17, 1973]

Subpart B—Election Procedures

§103.20 Posting of election notices.

(a) Employers shall post copies of the Board's official Notice of Election in conspicuous places at least 3 full working days prior to 12:01 am of the day of the election. In elections involving mail ballots, the election shall be deemed to have commenced the day the ballots are deposited by the Regional Office in the mail. In all cases, the notices shall remain posted until the end of the election.

(b) The term "working day" shall mean an entire 24-hour period excluding Saturdays, Sundays, and holidays.

(c) A party shall be estopped from objecting to nonposting of notices if it is responsible for the nonposting. An employer shall be conclusively deemed to have received copies of the election notice for posting unless it notifies the Regional Office at least 5 working days prior to the commencement of the election that it has not received copies of the election notice.

(d) Failure to post the election notices as required herein shall be grounds for setting aside the election whenever proper and timely objections are filed under the provisions of §102.69(a).

[52 FR 25215, July 6, 1987]

Illustration 9-14

New Mexico Statutory Materials, *State Laws* (*Minnesota to Wyoming*), *Labor Relations Reporter.*

Labor Relations Acts—

ED. NOTE: New Mexico has no labor relations act comparable to the federal Labor Management Relations Act or similar laws enacted in some of the states. However, Sec. 50-1-5 of the act establishing the state labor and industrial commission, above, makes it unlawful for the commission's director or agents to advocate organization or disorganization of a labor union.

Public Employees: Bargaining Rights

Full text of Ch. 10, Article 7D, Secs. 10-7D-1 to 10-7D-26 of the New Mexico Statutes Annotated, comprising the state collective bargaining statute providing rights, responsibilities, and procedures in the employment relationship between public employees and public employers, as enacted by Ch. 9, L. 1992. Secs. 10-7D-8 and 10-7D-9 are effective July 1, 1992; all other sections are effective April 1, 1993 and expire on July 1, 1999.

Sec. 10-7D-1. Short title. —Secs. 10-7D-1 through 10-7D-26 of this Act may be cited as the "Public Employee Bargaining Act."

Sec. 10-7D-2. Purpose of Act. —The purpose of the Public Employee Bargaining Act is to guarantee public employees the right to organize and bargain collectively with their employers, to promote harmonious and cooperative relationships between public employers and public employees, and to protect the public interest by assuring, at all times, the orderly operation and functioning of the state and its political subdivisions.

Sec. 10-7D-3. Conflicts. —In the event of conflict with other laws, the provisions of the Public Employee Bargaining Act shall supersede other previously enacted legislation; provided, that the Public Employee Bargaining Act shall not supersede the provisions of the Bateman Act, the State Personnel Act, Secs. 10-7-1 through 10-7-19 NMSA 1978, the Group Benefits Act, the Per Diem and Mileage Act, the Retiree Health Care Act, public employee retirement laws, or the Tort Claims Act.

Sec. 10-7D-4. Definitions. —As used in the Public Employee Bargaining Act:

A. "Appropriate bargaining unit" means a group of public employees designated by the board for the purpose of collective bargaining;

B. "Appropriate governing board" means the policymaking body or individual representing a public employer as defined in Sec. 10-7D-7 of the Public Employee Bargaining Act;

C. "Board" means the public employee labor relations board;

D. "Certification" means the designation by the board of a labor organization as the exclusive representative for all public employees in an appropriate bargaining unit;

E. "Collective bargaining" means the act of negotiating between a public employer and an exclusive representative for the purpose of entering into a written agreement regarding wages, hours, and other terms and conditions of employment;

F. "Confidential employee" means a person who assists and acts in a confidential capacity with respect to a person who formulates, determines, and effectuates management policies;

G. "Exclusive representative" means a labor organization that, as a result of certification, has the right to represent all public employees in an appropriate bargaining unit for the purposes of collective bargaining;

recent material in the binders and then back in time through transfer binders or bound volumes.

Your second step is to determine which topics and subtopics within the digest to read. You may well have a helpful citation to a digest topic from the overall index or commentary. You also may find it useful to scan the outline of the digest to identify additional possibilities. Your third step is then to read the digest material under those topics and subtopics to identify potentially pertinent cases.

The final steps are to locate your cases in the case reporter and to update them through a citator.

In the Canoga case, to research backwards from the present in L.R.R. would entail reviewing the very recent materials filed under the Cumulative Digest and Index (CDI) tab in the *Master Index* binder, then older softcover volumes, and then even older hardbound volumes. For example, two issues of the CDI in the *Master Index* binder covered 1995 when this problem was researched in the fall of 1995, a softcover pamphlet covered 1994, and hardbound volumes extended back farther in time. The most recent cases appear in the *Labor Management Relations: Decisions of Boards and Courts* binder, while older ones appear in hardbound volumes called *Labor Relations Reference Manual.*

On the issue of concerted activity, you would turn to case law research with a good lead if you pursued the research path suggested above. Both the General Index and the discussion of concerted activity in LRX point to LR ▶ 52.2532 et seq. See Illustrations 9-10 and 9-11 on pages 307-309. LR refers to the Labor Relations Outline of Classifications, which appears in the *Master Index* binder. Topic 52 is Employer Discrimination in Regard to Employment, and subtopic .2532 covers concerted activities in general terms. See Illustration 9-15 on page 315. Illustration 9-16 on page 316 is the material from the hardbound CDI covering 1986-1990; it includes one of the several decisions in the *Meyers Industries* case. As you can see, the L.R.R. digest covers court cases as well as Board decisions. Illustration 9-17 on page 317 is the first page of one of the updates to the CDI as filed in the *Master Index* binder.

Thus, your research in the L.R.R. digest would point you to the *Meyers Industries* case. The digest provides not only a citation to an official or West reporter where available, but also a citation to L.R.R.M., the looseleaf's case reporter. You then would read the case in one of the cited reporters. Illustration 9-18 on page 318 is the later of the two Board decisions in *Meyers Industries* as it appears in L.R.R.M. Note that the publisher has reprinted the material from the digest at the outset of the case (just as West reprints the headnotes at the outset of a case in a West reporter).

The illustrations in this section pertain to federal cases because of the predominance of federal law in this area.

e. Updating Your Research

The chief means by which looseleafs provide updated information has already been described: the use of binders with pages that are easily inserted and

Illustration 9-15

Labor Relations Outline of Classifications, *Master Index, Labor Relations Reporter.*

▸ **51.—Contd.**

.74 Union elections

Organization, meetings, etc., on company time and property

.761 —In general

.763 —Favoritism; ban on solicitation; unequal treatment of unions

.769 —Bulletin board use and notice of meetings

.781 —Solicitation and dues collection

.80 Special facilities and services

Financial aid, gifts, etc.

.841 —In general

.853 —Loans; dues payments, etc.

.857 —Payment for time spent in union activities

.861 —Concessions, vending machines, etc.

.863 —Union expenses paid

.88 Wage increases or employee benefits

.96 Re-formed and successor organizations

▸ **52. Employer Discrimination in Regard to Employment**

.01 In general

.02 Preliminary injunction against violation of LMRA

Persons entitled to protection

.041 —In general

.042 —Race, sex, etc., discrimination based on

.044 —Relatives of union members

.046 —Mistake as to employee's activities or status

.047 —Persons outside bargaining unit

.048 —Temporary, extra, part-time, or probationary employees

.05 Supervisors and other management personnel, treatment of; coercive effect on others

.06 Management rights generally

.12 Encouragement or discouragement of union membership generally

.14 Individual contracts, employment applications, and waiver of rights; change to contractor status

.16 Burden of proof; weight of evidence

Refusal to hire, or discouraging hire of union members or sympathizers

.221 —In general

.225 —Blacklisting or refusal to recommend

.227 —Former employees; seasonal workers

.229 —Strikers, refusal to hire

Discharge and layoffs

.241 —Discharge generally

.242 —What constitutes a discharge; layoff distinguished; forced retirement

▸ **52.—Contd.**

.243 —Layoffs in general; permanent or temporary layoffs; disciplinary layoff

.247 —Successive layoffs or discharges; discharge following reinstatement

.251 —Contracts with unions, violation of; termination of contract

—Concerted activities; protected activities

.2532 ——In general

.2533 ——Abstention from concerted activity

.2534 ——Activities in advance of or apart from organization; individual activities

.2535 ——Boycotts; "disloyalty" to employer

.2536 ——Grievances generally; bypassing contract procedure; union officers and agents, protection in performance of union duties

.2537 ——Meetings, conferences, and hearings

.2538 ——Wage demands

.2539 ——Strikes, picketing, and slowdowns as protected

.2541 ——Minority demands; dissident groups; intraunion disputes

.2542 ——False or abusive statements or threats

.2543 ——Racial, national origin, or sex discrimination, protest against

.2544 ——Work jurisdiction disputes

.257 —Quit or discharge; constructive discharge; retraction of resignation

.259 —Discharge following transfer or refusal to accept transfer; attempt to discredit employee; entrapment

—Reasons for discharge, discipline, layoff or refusal to reinstate

.2672 ——In general

.2678 ——Demand by union or fellow employees; intraunion disputes and rival unions

.2682 ——Absence or tardiness; leave of absence; overstaying leave; leaving plant or work place

.2683 ——Accident record, driving rules, law violations, criminal record

.2684 ——Altercations with others; fighting; violence

.2690 ——Communist activities; refusal to testify

.2692 ——Damage to or loss of machines, materials, etc.

.2695 ——Discourtesy toward or complaints by customers

Illustration 9-16

Labor Relations Cumulative Digest and Index Labor Relations Reporter.

LR CDI (1986-90) EMPLOYER DISCRIMINATION ▶52.2532

▶ **52.2532** (Contd.)

fered" is protected by LMRA Sec. 7, and therefore newspaper violated Sec. 8(a)(1) by discharging authors, despite claim that letter violated confidentiality.—*Id.*

U.S. District Courts

NLRB properly claimed that employer's discharge of workforce within days after they began organizing activities was motivated by protected activities; discharges were consequence of union president's phone call to employer and employer's claim that adverse economic conditions caused discharges is pretext. —*NLRB v. Ehrlich Beer Corp.* (DC SNY, 3/4/87) 125 LRRM 2399

NLRB

Employer unlawfully told employees they were laid off for trying to obtain union representation and engaging in protected activities. —*Pete O'Dell & Sons Steel Erectors* (277 NLRB 1358, 12/31/85) 121 LRRM 1115

Employer unlawfully discharged employee who complained about its tip system; employee's conduct was continuation of protected activity. —*Loft (Showcase Inc.)* (277 NLRB 1444, 1/7/86) 121 LRRM 1177

Employer unlawfully pulled employee's timecard, told him he would be serving as union observer at election that day and would be paid by union, and told union agent that employee could stay out for day. —*Reeves Bros. Inc.* (277 NLRB 1568, 1/13/86) 121 LRRM 1201

Employer unlawfully refused to reinstate employee who, out of fear for her safety, had not crossed picket line, since reason was her signing of union card; other employees who had stayed away from work for same reasons had been recalled. —*Zartic Inc.* (277 NLRB 1478, 1/10/86) 121 LRRM 1231

Employer lawfully discharged employee who it believed was responsible for obscene graffiti on its property; defacement as means of propagating slogans is not protected activity. —*United Artists Theatre Circuit Inc.* (277 NLRB 115, 10/31/85) 121 LRRM 1283

Employer unlawfully maintained rule forbidding discussion of salaries and discharged employees pursuant to rule; discussions were protected activities. —*American Lebanese Syrian Associated Charities Inc. d/b/a A.L.S.A.C.* (277 NLRB 1532, 1/10/86) 121 LRRM 1286

On remand, NLRB reviews discharged employee's entire work record and concludes that while GenCoun has established prima facie case of discriminatory discharge, employer has shown that it would have discharged employee even in absence of protected activity. —*McLean Trucking Co.* (279 NLRB 342, 4/21/86) 122 LRRM 1092

Employer unlawfully discharged group leader for her protected activity of discussing with employee wage rates paid to other workers who had been promoted. —*Scientific-Atlanta Inc.* (278 NLRB 622, 2/19/86) 122 LRRM 1263

Employer unlawfully issued written warning to employee; reason was her protected activity of stating at employee meeting, in response to employer's complaint of loud playing of radios, that stereo headphones used by workers were not too loud and that wire cutting machine was noisier than radios. —*Rockwell International Corp.* (278 NLRB 55, 1/16/86) 122 LRRM 1285

Employer unlawfully discharged employees, even though employees' work stoppage is not protected activity. —*Electronic Data Systems International Corp.* (278 NLRB 125, 1/22/86) 122 LRRM 1333

Employer unlawfully discharged truck driver; discharge was motivated by his protected activity of lobbying for truck air conditioners. —*Woodline Motor Freight Inc.* (278 NLRB 1141, 3/25/86) 122 LRRM 1355

Protection for joint employee action lies at heart of LMRA, and definition of concerted activity under *Meyers Industries I* proceeds logically from such analysis insofar as it requires some linkage to group action in order for conduct to be deemed "concerted." —*Meyers Industries Inc.* (281 NLRB 882, 9/30/86) 123 LRRM 1137

On remand from court that directed NLRB to reexamine its *Meyers Industries I* rule in light of Supreme Court's decision in *NLRB v. City Disposal Systems*, NLRB finds that definition of concerted activity under *Meyers I* strikes reasonable balance between concept of "concerted activities" and concept of "mutual aid or protection" that underlie Sec. 7.—*Id.*

Invocation of contractual employee rights is continuation of ongoing process of "concerted" activity, whereas invocation of

For Guidance see Introduction 1141

Illustration 9-17 Update Pamphlet, *Cumulative Digest and Index, Master Index, Labor Relations Reporter.*

FILE in Master Index Binder under Cumulative Digest & Index —LR tab and before Final CDI (148 LRRM) beginning with page C-II A401. **DISCARD** previous Supp. CDI and Master CDI (149 LRRM) beginning with pages C-II A201 and C-II A301.

LABOR RELATIONS REPORTER®

September 11, 1995

Final CUMULATIVE DIGEST and INDEX (CDI) Labor Relations (149 LRRM)

May 1—August 28, 1995

(See also CDI beginning with page C-II A401, and bound CDI volumes.)

Classification numbers identified by the symbol "▸" in this CDI represent specific points of labor relations law. They are located by topic in General Index under tab (A). The Outline of Classifications under tab (C-I) provides the description of each number.

Each descriptive entry below provides the particulars in a given case relating to the classification number. See LRRM Binder 2 for latest cases.

▸ **4.01** RLA does not pre-empt former employee's state-law claim that railroad's decision to discipline him, allegedly for unsafe work practices, and to discharge him, allegedly for conduct unbecoming an employee, was racially motivated in violation of Mich. Elliott-Larsen CRA. —*McGinnis v. Norfolk & Western Railway Co.* (DC EMich) 2164

▸ **4.05** Discharged town constable was not required to exhaust her state administrative remedies before filing claim under CRA of 1871 alleging that town violated her First Amendment rights by discharging her for attempting to affiliate with other constables in labor union. —*Wilbur v. Harris* (CA 2) 2201

Ill. appellate court's presiding justice, who allegedly discharged court's research attorney in retaliation for union-organizing efforts to effectuate change in court's leave policy, is entitled to qualified immunity from personal liability in action under CRA of 1871 alleging violation of attorney's right of free association guaranteed by First and Fourteenth Amendments. —*Gregorich v. Lund* (CA 7) 2278

Discharged black employee, who alleges that employer terminated him in violation of CRAs of 1866 and 1964 and that union breached its fair-representation duty by refusing to arbitrate his grievance, need not prove that employer breached labor contract. —*Grooms v. Wiregrass Electric Cooperative Inc.* (DC MAla) 2157

Probation officers and their association failed to state claim under Civil Rights Act of 1871 by alleging that Chief Justice of N.J. SupCt and Associate Justices acted under color of state law to deprive probation officers of

Vol. 150, No. 2
1043-5506/95/$0+$1.00

Illustration 9-18 *Meyers Industries, Inc.*, 123 L.R.R.M. (BNA) 1137 (Sept. 30, 1987).

MEYERS INDUSTRIES 123 LRRM 1137

MEYERS INDUSTRIES —

MEYERS INDUSTRIES, INC., Tecumseh, Mich. and KENNETH P. PRILL, an Individual, Case No. 7-CA-17207, September 30, 1986, 281 NLRB No. 118 [supplementing 268 NLRB 493, 115 LRRM 1025]

Before NLRB: Dotson, Chairman; Babson and Stephens, Members.

INTERFERENCE Sec. 8(a)(1)

— Concerted activity ▸50.06 ▸52.2532

Protection for joint employee action lies at heart of LMRA, and definition of concerted activity under Meyers Industries I (115 LRRM 1025) proceeds logically from such analysis insofar as it requires some linkage to group action in order for conduct to be deemed "concerted" within meaning of Act.

— Concerted activity ▸50.06 ▸52.2532 ▸36.97

On remand from federal appeals court that directed NLRB to reexamine its Meyers Industries I (115 LRRM 1025) rule in light of U.S. Supreme Court's decision in NLRB v. City Disposal Systems (115 LRRM 3193), NLRB finds that definition of concerted activity under Meyers I strikes reasonable balance between concept of "concerted activities" and concept of "mutual aid or protection" that underlie Section 7 of LMRA. Meyers I definition is not so broad as to create redundancy in Section 7 of Act, but expansive enough to include individual activity which is connected to collective activity, which lies at core of Section 7.

— Concerted activity ▸50.06 ▸52.2534

There is nothing in Meyers Industries I (115 LRRM 1025) definition of concerted activity which states that conduct engaged in by single employee at one point in time can never constitute concerted activity within meaning of Section 7 of LMRA; on the contrary, that definition in part attempts to define when act of single employee is or is not "concerted."

— Concerted activity ▸50.06 ▸52.2534 ▸36.97

On remand from federal appeals court that directed NLRB to reexamine its Meyers Industries I (115 LRRM 1025) rule in light of U.S. Supreme Court's decision in NLRB v. City Disposal Systems (115 LRRM 3193), Board reiterates that definition of concerted activity in Meyers I encompasses those circumstances where individual employees seek to initiate, induce, or prepare for group action, as well as individual employees bringing truly group complaints to attention of management.

— Concerted activity ▸50.06 ▸52.2532

Invocation of employee rights under collective bargaining contracts is continuation of ongoing process of employee "concerted" activity within meaning of LMRA, whereas employee invocation of rights under other statutes that benefit employees is not. Although it is NLRB's duty to construe labor laws so as to accommodate purposes of other Federal laws, this is quite different matter from Board's taking it upon itself to assist in enforcement of other statutes.

— Concerted activity — Discharge ▸36.97 ▸52.2731 ▸52.2534

On remand from federal appeals court that directed NLRB to reexamine its Meyers Industries I (115 LRRM 1025) rule in light of U.S. Supreme Court's decision in NLRB v. City Disposal Systems (115 LRRM 3193), Board affirms finding that employer did not violate LMRA when it discharged driver who refused to drive allegedly unsafe vehicle and reported vehicle to state authorities, since his conduct does not constitute protected concerted activity. (1) Driver acted alone and without intent to enlist support of other employees; (2) his purely individual activities were not related to other employees' concerted activities in any demonstrable manner; (3) even assuming that otherwise lawful discharge may have some remote incidental effect on other employees, such incidental effect does not render discharge unlawful.

— Concerted activity — Meyers Industries I rule ▸52.2532 ▸36.97 ▸38.73 ▸50.06

On remand from federal appeals court that directed NLRB to reexamine its Meyers Industries I (115 LRRM 1025) rule in light of U.S. Supreme Court's decision in NLRB v. City Disposal Systems (115 LRRM 3193), NLRB adheres to definition of concerted activity set forth in Meyers I as reasonable construction of LMRA.

[*Text*] On 6 January 1984 the National Labor Relations Board[1] issued its Decision and Order in this proceeding (Meyers I)[2] in which it overruled Alleluia Cushion Co.[3] and its progeny; defined the concept of concerted activity for purposes of Section 7 of the National Labor Relations Act; and reversed the judge's finding that the Re-

[1] Member Johansen did not participate in this decision.
[2] 268 NLRB 493, 115 LRRM 1025 (1984)
[3] 221 NLRB 999, 91 LRRM 1131 (1975).

replaced. Thus, when you read commentary in a looseleaf binder, it likely reflects any recent changes in the law. When you read a statute or regulation in a looseleaf, you likely are reading the current version. When you consult the most recent digest material and accompanying cases, you update the cases in the older volumes or transfer binders. In some looseleafs, the newest information appears in a separate section, which obviously should be consulted.

In addition, some looseleafs include citators, a useful means of verifying the currency of primary authority as well as expanding your research. Other looseleafs do not include citators, so that you would consult the pertinent *Shepard's Citations* for this purpose. Indeed, *Shepard's* may well use the looseleaf reporter as a cited source. Or it may provide cross-references between the looseleaf citation and other reporters containing the case, so that you then can Shepardize the case by the other reporter.

In the Canoga case, the featured looseleaf does not include a citator. It is possible, however, to derive cross-references between the L.R.R.M. and other reporters and then to use that cross-reference to Shepardize the case in *Shepard's Labor Law Citations.* For example, to Shepardize the second decision of the Board in *Meyers Industries,* you first would consult the BNA to NLRB cross-reference table to obtain the official N.L.R.B. citation. (Recall that Bureau of National Affairs is the publisher of L.R.R.M.) See Illustration 9-19 on page 320. You then could Shepardize the decision by its official N.L.R.B. citation (as illustrated above in Part C).

4. What Else?

Tables of Authorities. Many looseleafs contain tables of cases, statutes, or regulations. These are useful tools when you approach the looseleaf with an idea of a pertinent authority or when you come to that information midway in your looseleaf research.

Current Awareness Publications. Comprehensive looseleafs have current awareness publications, frequently published pamphlets that permit a regular reader to keep abreast of recent developments. The pamphlet may contain synopses of recent legal authorities, analyze significant new laws, recount the results of recent studies, report on important conferences, and list upcoming events. In addition, some legal authorities, especially new statutes and regulations, often are first available in paper media in update publications issued by looseleaf publishers. Current awareness publications may be filed in their own binder and covered by a periodic index.

Other Media. Some looseleafs services appear in CD-ROM, and some appear online.

Illustration 9-19 *Shepard's Labor Law Citations.*

Vol. 123 **CROSS REFERENCES BNA TO NLRB**

—1058— (280Bd1317)	—1105— (280Bd922)	—1134— Case 2 (279Bd998)	—1160— (281Bd1178)	—1200— (281Bd546)	—1222— Case 3 (279Bd160)
—1061— (279Bd1064)	—1106— (281Bd309)	—1135— Case 1 (279Bd222)	—1163— (281Bd1108)	—1204— (281Bd1006)	—1223— Case 7 (280Bd1114)
—1063— (279Bd693)	—1107— (280Bd698)	—1135— Case 2 (279Bd874)	—1165— (281Bd508)	—1205— Case 1 (281Bd338)	—1225— (281Bd986)
—1064— (280Bd937)	—1112— (281Bd458)	—1136— Case 1 (279Bd22)	—1167— (280Bd19)	—1205— Case 2 (281Bd927)	—1227— (279Bd1320)
—1070— (281Bd203)	—1113— (281Bd542)	—1136— Case 2 (279Bd84)	—1171— (281Bd709)	—1207— Case 3 (280Bd75)	—1228— Case 1 (279Bd412)
—1071— (280Bd696)	—1116— (281Bd226)	—1136— Case 3 (279Bd45)	—1173— (281Bd861)	—1207— Case 6 (280Bd354)	—1228— Case 2 (281Bd1232)
—1073— (281Bd336)	—1123— (279Bd858)	—1137— (281Bd882)	—1174— (281Bd1160)	—1209— (281Bd1013)	—1230— (279Bd777)
—1074— (280Bd818)	—1124— (279Bd883)	—1144— (281Bd798)	—1175— (281Bd588)	—1213— (281Bd1029)	—1231— (281Bd789)
—1078— (280Bd113)	—1125— (279Bd601)	—1145— (279Bd6)	—1177— Case 1 (281Bd577)	—1215— (281Bd1191)	—1233— (281Bd903)
—1080— (280Bd85)	—1127— (279Bd1051)	—1146— (281Bd468)	—1177— Case 2 (281Bd728)	—1217— (279Bd877)	—1235— (279Bd791)
—1084— (281Bd294)	—1128— (279Bd1170)	—1140	—1179— (281Bd1034)	—1218— (281Bd742)	—1237— (282Bd21)
—1085— (279Bd538)	—1129— Case 1 (279Bd198)				

5. How Do You Cite to a Looseleaf Service?

While many authorities located in a looseleaf appear elsewhere in a source preferred by *The Bluebook,* you may cite to a looseleaf on occasion under Rule 18 of *The Bluebook.* The most common instance is when you are citing to a very recent agency decision not yet available in the agency's official reporter. The citation form then includes the slip opinion citation with the looseleaf volume, abbreviation as stated in Table T.16, and page number or other subdivision inserted. For example:

> *Meyers Industries, Inc.,* 281 N.L.R.B. No. 118, 123 L.R.R.M. (BNA) 1137 (Sept. 30, 1986).

This example assumes that the 1986 decision is so new that it does not yet appear in the official reporter and has not yet been reviewed by the court of appeals.

F. Administrative Agency Research on the Internet

Among the many items available on the Internet are publications of government agencies. Changes in what is available and how it can be searched are frequent; hence you should explore the system for new and better options often. This part demonstrates a search for federal regulations conducted in the fall of 1995.

Searching for federal regulations on the Internet entails several discrete steps: signing on and selecting your search engine (which enables you to gain access to various servers), identifying possible servers (databases with programs permitting you to search them) and selecting one or more to use, devising and running your search within that server, and retrieving your results. Each system has its own unique features and modes of operation; hence you would do well to take advantage of the assistance programs within each system you use. You cannot, for example, assume that the Boolean search strategies used on WESTLAW or LEXIS operate in the same way within a different system on the Internet.

One way to locate servers containing federal regulations would be through Netscape, a World Wide Web browser; its Net Search web page directory leads you to the Infoseek Net Search search engine (as well as other search engines). You could also get to Infoseek directly if you knew its Internet address and typed it in: in this case, [http://www2.infoseek.com/]. If you entered [code federal regulations] in Infoseek, you would obtain a list of one hundred servers containing federal regulations. Some are government servers, some commercial. Some purport to be exhaustive, while others are confined to specific legal topics.

One of the comprehensive government servers is U.S. House of Representatives—Internet Law Library, which includes the *Code of Federal Regulations,* developed by the House of Representatives Information Systems. If you perused the assistance available to the user, you would learn, for example, that this server permits you to conduct both Boolean and natural language searches, includes a thesaurus accessible through a "concept" search, and searches multi-word terms if they are identified by single quotation marks. It has a default search limit of sixty documents.

The citation list for the C.F.R. database presents the citations from the most statistically to the least statistically relevant (rating the most relevant as ninety-nine and working down from there) and includes a one-line description alongside the citation. See Illustration 9-20 on page 322. Once you have a citation list, you can retrieve any document on the citation list; the document is essentially identical to the paper version, including the cite, text (with the

Illustration 9-20 Citation List, U.S. House of Representatives—Internet Law Library (Code of Federal Regulations).

48 documents returned for Query : "'title 29' and jurisdiction and board"

DB	SCORE	DOCUMENT
cfr	99	32 CFR Sec. 588.79
cfr	96	29 CFR PART 101 PART 101 - STATEMENTS OF PROCEDURES SUBPART A - GENERAL STATEME
cfr	95	29 CFR Sec. 2706.170 Sec. 2706.170 Compliance procedures.
cfr	95	29 CFR PART 102 PART 102 - RULES AND REGULATIONS, SERIES 8 SUBPART A - DEFINITI
cfr	95	29 CFR Sec. 102.98 Sec. 102.98 Petition for advisory opinion; who may file; whe
cfr	95	29 CFR Sec. 1952.170 Sec. 1952.170 Description of the plan.
cfr	94	29 CFR Sec. 1910.120 Sec. 1910.120 Hazardous waste operations and emergency res
cfr	94	29 CFR Sec. 1910.110 Sec. 1910.110 Storage and handling of liquefied petroleum
cfr	94	29 CFR Sec. 101.42 Sec. 101.42 Procedures for obtaining declaratory orders of t
cfr	94	29 CFR Sec. 101.41 Sec. 101.41 Informal procedures for obtaining opinions on
cfr	94	29 CFR Sec. 100.670 Sec. 100.670 Compliance procedures.
cfr	94	20 CFR Sec. 655.100 Sec. 655.100 Overview of this subpart and definition of ter
cfr	94	29 CFR Sec. 2608.170 Sec. 2608.170 Compliance procedures.
cfr	94	29 CFR Sec. 2205.170 Sec. 2205.170 Compliance procedures.
cfr	94	29 CFR Sec. 1952.210 Sec. 1952.210 Description of the plan as initially approve
cfr	94	29 CFR Sec. 1207.1 Sec. 1207.1 Establishment of special adjustment boards (PL E
cfr	94	29 CFR Sec. 100.102 Sec. 100.102 Responsibilities.
cfr	94	29 CFR Sec. 1613.806 Sec. 1613.806 Petition to EEOC; finality of decisions.
cfr	94	29 CFR Sec. 101.40 Sec. 101.40 Proceedings following the filing of the petitior
cfr	94	29 CFR Sec. 101.39 Sec. 101.39 Initiation of advisory opinion case.
cfr	94	29 CFR Sec. 1615.170 Sec. 1615.170 Compliance procedures.
cfr	94	29 CFR Sec. 1600.735-204 Sec. 1600.735-204 Outside interests, employment, busir
cfr	94	29 CFR Sec. 102.110 Sec. 102.110 Proceedings before the Board; briefs; declarat
cfr	94	29 CFR Sec. 102.105 Sec. 102.105 Petitions for declaratory orders; who may file
cfr	93	29 CFR Sec. 1910.109 Sec. 1910.109 Explosives and blasting agents.
cfr	93	29 CFR Sec. 1207.3 Sec. 1207.3 Compensation of neutrals.
cfr	93	29 CFR Sec. 783.29 Sec. 783.29 Adoption of the exemption in the original 1938 A
cfr	93	32 CFR Sec. 591.5102
cfr	93	29 CFR Sec. 1918.106 Sec. 1918.106 Protection against drowning.
cfr	93	29 CFR Sec. 102.135 Sec. 102.135 Employment-management agreements.
cfr	93	29 CFR Sec. 102.99 Sec. 102.99 Contents of petition for advisory opinion; conte
cfr	93	29 CFR Sec. 101.43 Sec. 101.43 Proceedings following the filing of the petitior
cfr	93	29 CFR Sec. 1978.112 Sec. 1978.112 Arbitration or other proceedings.
cfr	93	29 CFR Sec. 1977.18 Sec. 1977.18 Arbitration or other agency proceedings.
cfr	93	29 CFR Sec. 102.103 Sec. 102.103 Proceedings before the Board; briefs; advisory
cfr	92	29 CFR Sec. 1952.240 Sec. 1952.240 Description of the plan as initially approve
cfr	92	29 CFR Sec. 1952.124 Sec. 1952.124 Completion of developmental steps and certif
cfr	92	29 CFR Sec. 1918.3 Sec. 1918.3 Definitions.
cfr	92	29 CFR Sec. 102.15 Sec. 102.15 When and by whom issued; contents; service.
cfr	92	29 CFR Sec. 1952.290 Sec. 1952.290 Description of the plan as initially approve
cfr	92	29 CFR Sec. 1910.141 Sec. 1910.141 Sanitation.
cfr	92	29 CFR Sec. 103.3 Sec. 103.3 Horseracing and dogracing industries.
cfr	92	29 CFR Sec. 103.2 Sec. 103.2 Symphony orchestras.
cfr	92	29 CFR Sec. 103.1 Sec. 103.1 Colleges and universities.
cfr	92	29 CFR Sec. 102.100 Sec. 102.100 Notice of petition; service of petition.
cfr	92	29 CFR Subpart H Subpart H - Declaratory Orders and Advisory Opinions Regardinc
cfr	92	29 CFR Subpart H Subpart H - Advisory Opinions and Declaratory Orders Regardinc
cfr	92	29 CFR Sec. 101.33 Sec. 101.33 Initiation of formal action; settlement.

search terms highlighted), and *Federal Register* information following the text.

As for the Canoga case, if you were to use this server to research the jurisdiction issue discussed in Part B, you might approach it in two different ways. You might focus on legal concepts and enter ['title 29' and jurisdiction and board], if you assumed (properly so) that regulations under the labor statute would appear in title 29 of C.F.R. because the statute appears in title 29 of U.S.C. (While you could use National Labor Relations Board as a search term, it may be that the Board's regulations would not use the entire term.) Another option would be to focus on factual concepts; a simple fact-oriented search would be [orchestra].

Illustration 9-20 above is the citation list for the first search; note that it yielded forty-eight citations, including section 103.2 of title 29. The [orchestra] search yielded thirteen citations, again including section 103.2 Illustration 9-21 below is section 103.2 as it appears in the U.S. House server.

Of course, you would be interested in knowing whether there is more up-to-date regulatory material in the *Federal Register.* Using the same steps as described above, you could locate the *Federal Register* in the U.S. House of Representatives—Internet Law Library server. The default setting provides for a citation list of forty documents. The database encompassed only 1994 and 1995 *Federal Registers* (as of late 1995); of course, your primary interest in the *Federal Register* in most situations will be in the recent volumes.

Your search in the *Federal Register* should be focused on updating material. Hence you would want to confine your search to the recent volumes not incorporated into the current C.F.R. Your search could be quite narrow, such as the citation of the regulation, or somewhat broader, such as the name of your agency.

If you were researching the Canoga case in the fall of 1995, you would search in the 1995 *Federal Register* (volume 60). Because section 103.2 is from title 29 part 103, the narrow search would read ["29 cfr part 103"]; it yielded one document, a proposed regulation not pertinent to orchestras. The broader search might read ["national labor relations"]; it yielded forty documents. Illustration 9-22 on page 324 is a page from the second document (which amends the Board's administrative regulations).

Illustration 9-21

29 C.F.R. § 103.2, in U.S. House of Representatives—Internet Law Library (Code of Federal Regulations).

```
-CITE-

    29 CFR Sec. 103.2

-EXPCITE-

    Title 29
    Subtitle B
    CHAPTER I
    PART 103
    Subpart A

-HEAD-

    Sec. 103.2 Symphony orchestras.

-TEXT-

      The Board will assert its jurisdiction in any proceeding arising
    under sections 8, 9, and 10 of the Act involving any symphony
    orchestra which has a gross annual revenue from all sources
    (excluding only contributions which are because of limitation by
    the grantor not available for use for operating expenses) of not
    less than $1 million.
    (38 FR 6177, Mar. 7, 1973)
```

Illustration 9-22

Amendments to 29 C.F.R. Parts 100 and 102, in U.S. House of Representatives—Internet Law Library (Federal Register).

[Federal Register: June 23, 1995 (Volume 60, Number 121)]
[Rules and Regulations]
[Page 32587]
From the Federal Register Online via GPO Access [wais.access.gpo.gov]

===

NATIONAL LABOR RELATIONS BOARD

29 CFR Parts 100 and 102

Miscellaneous Amendments

AGENCY: National Labor Relations Board (NLRB).

ACTION: Miscellaneous amendment rule.

SUMMARY: The National Labor Relations Board is issuing a miscellaneous amendments rule to its administrative regulations to update cross-references and to change the NLRB's headquarters address.

EFFECTIVE DATE: The miscellaneous amendments are effective June 23, 1995.

FOR FURTHER INFORMATION CONTACT: Gloria Joseph, Director of Administration, National Labor Relations Board, Room 7108, 1099 14th Street NW, Washington, DC 20570-0001. (202-273-3890).

SUPPLEMENTARY INFORMATION: On July 21, 1994, the National Labor Relations Board amended its administrative regulations (59 FR 37157) governing the standards of conduct and financial disclosure requirements of its employees of the Agency. Most of those regulations had been superseded by the Standards of Ethical Conduct for Employees of the Executive Branch issued by the Office of Government (OGE). The NLRB published the rule to repeal those portions of the provisions that were superseded by the executive branch-wide standards and to update cross-references in the current regulations that continued to be applicable. Again, on May 5, 1995, the NLRB published a rule to correct amendatory instructions 4, and 5, and amendatory instruction 10. (59 FR 37158) of the July 21, 1994 amending rule (60 FR 22269). This miscellaneous amendments rule is being published to update cross-references, and change the NLRB's headquarters address in some sections from its former address of 1717 Pennsylvania Avenue NW to its current address of 1099 14th Street NW.

List of Subjects in 29 CFR Parts 100 and 102

Administrative practice and procedure; Civil rights; Claims; Equal employment opportunity; Individuals with disabilities.

Parts 100 and 102 of Title 29 CFR are amended as follows:

PART 100--ADMINISTRATIVE REGULATIONS

1. The authority citation for part 100 is revised to read as follows:

Authority: Sec. 6, National Labor Relations Act, as amended (29 U.S.C. 141, 146).

Subpart A is also issued under 5 U.S.C. 7301; 5 U.S.C. app. (Ethics in Government Act of 1978); E.O. 12674, 3 CFR 1989 Comp., 215, as modified by E.O. 12731, 3 CFR 1990 Comp., p. 306; 5 CFR 2635.105, 2635.403, 2635.802(a), 2635.803; 18 U.S.C. 201 et seq.; 18

As is true of other technological media, the Internet can be a valuable research tool in certain situations. It is a viable research option, of course, only if the information you seek is available through the Internet. As with online research in WESTLAW and LEXIS, some topics are more researchable than others through Boolean and natural language search strategies. Furthermore, you must work within the limits and possibilities afforded by the specific server, which you must learn as you move from one server to the other. As for cost, there often is no search fee, as there is with WESTLAW and LEXIS, although you must, of course, have Internet service.

G. Concluding Points

To conduct comprehensive research into an area governed by an administrative agency, you must research not only the law created by the agency, but also the statute creating the agency and judicial cases reviewing the agency's actions. The law created by the agency may consist of regulations or decisions or both. This complex body of law may be researched in paper media without looseleaf services, in paper media through looseleaf services, online (in LEXIS, WESTLAW, as well as the Internet), or through a combination of these options.

Researching the law generated by a federal agency in paper media other than looseleaf services entails combinations of government and private publications. The major sources for research in federal regulations are the statutory codes, the *Code of Federal Regulations,* the *Federal Register, Shepard's Code of Federal Regulations Citations,* and case law sources. The major sources for research in federal agency decisions are the statutory codes, official reporters (along with their indexes or digests), an appropriate *Shepard's Citations,* and case law sources. Obviously these research processes can be very time-consuming, although they should yield correct results if performed carefully.

Looseleaf services offer a cost-efficient alternative to these processes. As miniature libraries, looseleafs contain commentary, statutes, regulations, cases from the courts, and agency decisions. These materials are thorough and updated frequently, so that research in looseleaf services is likely to yield correct results.

This chapter has demonstrated one online alternative to research in paper media: use of the Internet to research agency regulations. Other media options include use of WESTLAW and LEXIS and CD-ROMs (described in Chapter 3).

10 Locate, Read, and Update Primary Authority: Rules of Procedure and Ethics

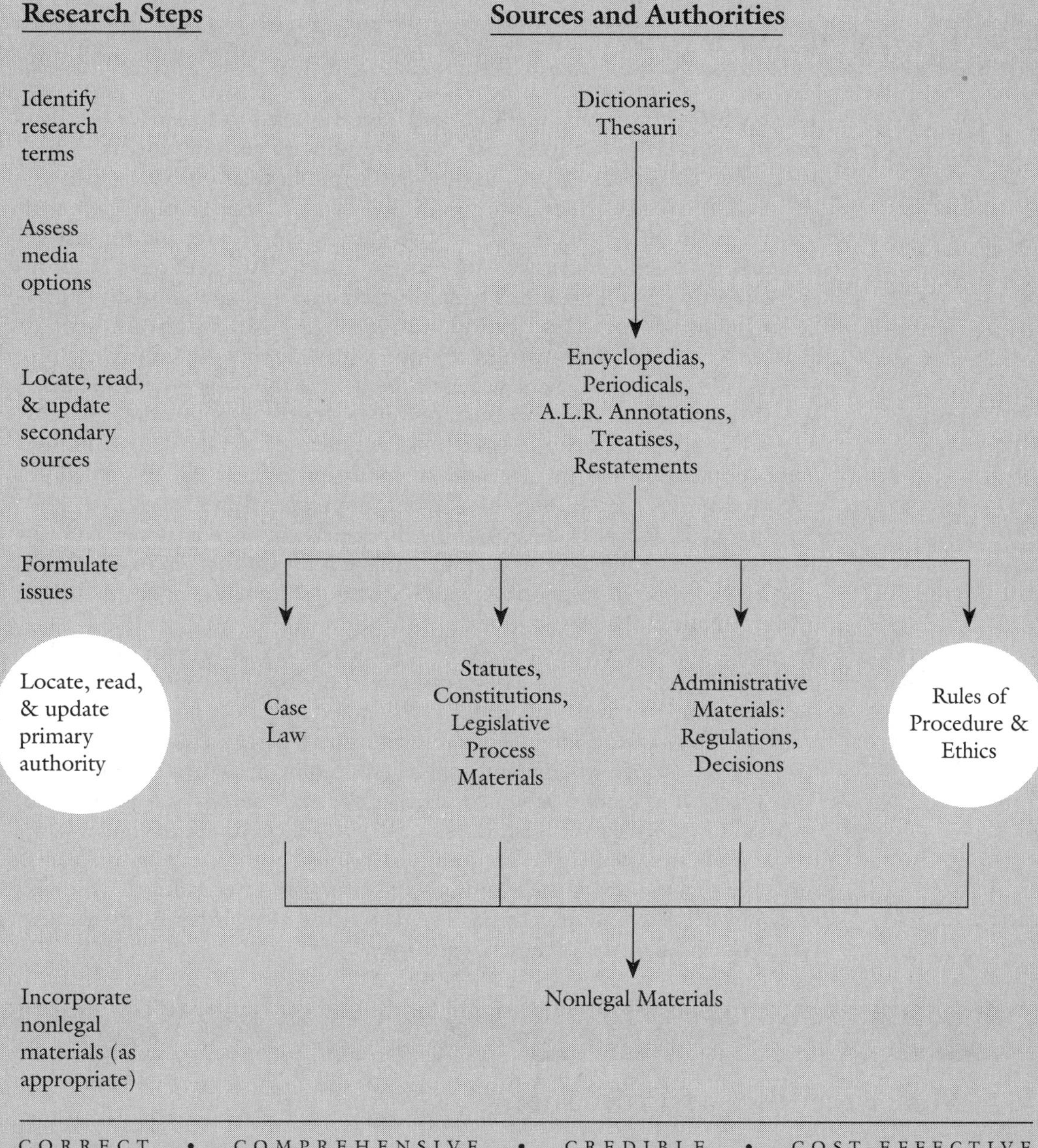

Summary of Contents

A. Preliminary Points

This chapter explores the methods and materials used to research rules that govern the practice of law. These rules are primary authority because they are created by various government bodies acting in their official capacity.

Part B discusses rules governing the procedural aspects of litigation in the courts. Each jurisdiction has its own rules of procedure, and most have several sets for different phases (such as trial or appellate) and types (such as civil or criminal) of litigation. These overarching rules for a jurisdiction may be supplemented by rules developed by a single court or district. Part B covers both federal and state rules of procedure, which are parallel in structure and research method. (There also are rules governing many other legal matters, such as administrative proceedings, international disputes, and proceedings before specialized tribunals such as family court or arbitration. Although these specialized rules may bear some similarity to the rules of procedure discussed in this chapter, they are beyond the scope of this text.)

Part C discusses the law governing the ethical conduct of lawyers, known as rules of professional responsibility. This discussion focuses on the state rules of professional responsibility and the model rules and codes prepared by the American Bar Association.

For examples, this chapter turns again to the Canoga case, stated on pages 2-3. Assume that you have unsuccessfully sought a settlement from the orchestra, that you have decided to pursue litigation on behalf of Ms. Canoga, that you have identified viable state and federal claims, and that you have not yet decided whether you will be proceeding in state or federal court. Two practical matters that would arise in the early stages of litigation are addressed in this chapter: First, how would you deliver notice of your lawsuit to the orchestra, which is a corporation, or put another way, how do you serve the orchestra with the summons and complaint? Second, may you talk directly with Ms. Canoga's co-workers about the facts of her case, or must you work through the orchestra's attorney?

B. Rules of Procedure

1. What Are Rules of Procedure?

Although the distinction is not always clear, most lawyers distinguish "substantive law" from "procedural law." Substantive law governs the rights, duties, and powers of people and entities as they carry out their personal and business affairs. By contrast, procedural law consists of procedural rules and case law interpreting the rules. Procedural law governs litigation, that is, the processing of disputes within the legal system, most typically the courts. Procedural law regulates how a case is brought before a particular court and how the case proceeds from its inception until a final outcome is reached. It provides guidelines that the parties must observe in carrying out the litigation and assist the court, as well as the lawyers, in administering justice fairly and efficiently.

Most jurisdictions have several sets of rules of procedure, each addressing certain phases and types of litigation. For example, a jurisdiction may have rules of civil procedure, criminal procedure, evidence, and appellate procedure. Exhibit 10.1 below diagrams the typical arrangement. Furthermore, a particular court or district may have local rules outlining the details of its practice.

In most jurisdictions, some procedural law appears not in the rules of procedure, as this chapter uses that term, but in the statutes of the jurisdiction. For example, the rules on how quickly you must bring a claim (statutes of limitation) and which court has the power to adjudicate a claim (jurisdiction) typically are found in statutes, rather than in rules of procedure. In a few jurisdictions, all of the rules of procedure are enacted as part of the state statutes, rather than as separate rules. Chapter 7 on statutory research describes how to research statutory materials.

a. How Are Rules of Procedure Developed?

Procedural rules are created either by the legislature, by the court, or by interaction of both branches of government.

At the federal level, it is not clear in the United States Constitution whether Congress or the federal courts have primary rulemaking authority. Most commentators believe that Congress has the right to prescribe rules of

Exhibit 10.1 Rules of Procedure.

	Civil Cases	*Criminal Cases*
Pre-trial pleadings discovery motions	Civil procedure	Criminal procedure
Trial	Evidence, civil procedure	Evidence, criminal procedure
Post-trial motions	Civil procedure	Criminal procedure
Appeals	Appellate procedure	Appellate (or criminal appellate) procedure

procedure for the federal courts, while the individual federal courts are free to issue local rules on matters not covered by Congress' rules. As a practical matter, Congress has delegated a great deal of rulemaking authority to the United States Supreme Court.

The enactment of the Federal Rules of Civil Procedure (FRCP) is an example of this delegation. Under the Rules Enabling Act of 1934, ch. 651, 48 Stat. 1064 (1934), Congress gave the Supreme Court the power to prescribe rules of procedure for the federal district courts and the District of Columbia, as well as the obligation to report to Congress. In 1935, the Supreme Court appointed an Advisory Committee on Civil Rules to prepare a draft. After making some changes, the Supreme Court adopted the rules in 1937 and submitted them to Congress via the Attorney General. Although these rules were never formally adopted by both houses of Congress, the rules became effective in 1938. The FRCP have been amended by the Supreme Court several times since then.

Most states have delegated rulemaking authority to the highest state court or a special governmental body; some state legislatures then review and adopt the rules. In other states, the legislature or other advisory body drafts a bill containing the needed procedural rules, and the legislature enacts the bill according to its usual process of statutory enactment. In many states, the procedural rules are modeled after the FRCP, attesting to the success of the federal rules.

The development of the law of evidence—which governs the presentation of testimony and other evidence during trial—is similar, yet also different. The Federal Rules of Evidence (FRE) were drafted by a committee appointed by the Supreme Court and then adopted jointly by Congress and the Court in 1975. Over two-thirds of the states have evidence rules based on the FRE. A few have adopted rules based on the Model Code of Evidence, a model law prepared by the American Law Institute (see Chapter 7 for a discussion of model laws). In jurisdictions with rules of evidence, cases interpret the rules. In other jurisdictions, the law of evidence is governed purely by case law.

b. What Do Rules of Procedure Look Like?

A typical set of procedural rules looks much like a statute or, more precisely, a uniform or model act. Each rule describes in general terms the litigation practice it covers, stating what is or is not permissible. Each rule is separately numbered, often with subdivisions. Advisory comments and historical notes, prepared by the advisory committee or by the law book editors, generally accompany the rules. The comments prepared by the rules' drafters explain or illustrate their intent; such comments typically address the purpose of the rule, previous rules that have been superseded, and perhaps proposed amendments that were rejected. Although the comments of the advisory committee do not carry mandatory authority, they are highly persuasive.

Each set of rules is organized topically, generally with a chronological organization. The FRCP, for example, are arranged roughly in the sequence in which litigation usually proceeds in the trial court, from initiation of the lawsuit until judgment. The introductory rules indicate that the FRCP pertain to civil matters brought before the federal district courts. The next few rules address commencement of a lawsuit, covering such matters as service of process, filing of pleadings, the form of pleadings and motions, and designation of parties to the suit. The next two parts of the rules regulate discovery, such as depositions and interrogatories, and the trial itself. Rules concerning judgments and remedies follow. The last several rules cover specialized and miscellaneous matters.

Illustration 10-1 on page 332 is Rule 4(h) of the Federal Rules of Civil Procedure, which governs service of process on corporations and other business entities. Illustration 10-2 on page 333 is an excerpt of the accompanying notes prepared by the Advisory Committee on Civil Procedure to accompany the 1993 amendments to Rule 4.

2. Why Would You Research Particular Rules of Procedure?

If your client's case is being or likely will be litigated, you would research procedural rules to learn the proper steps for carrying out litigation. Procedural rules are binding on the litigants and their lawyers. Failure to follow the applicable procedural rules impedes the efficient resolution of the case and may be grounds for dismissal of the suit or for sanctions against the client or the lawyer.

As already noted, rules of procedure exist at both the federal and state levels, reflecting our federalist system. Assessing which set of rules applies depends largely on considerations of federal and state jurisdiction, as discussed in Chapter 6 on cases. The key is to determine whether your claim will be pursued in federal or state court. The federal courts apply federal rules, and each state court applies its state's rules. For example, federal rules apply even when a federal court is adjudicating a claim based on the substantive law of a state, as occurs in diversity jurisdiction cases.

In the Canoga case, to initiate suit against the orchestra, one of the first questions you must consider is how to deliver the summons and complaint to the orchestra. This initial step, known as "service of process," provides notice to the defendant that a lawsuit has been brought and tells the defendant the reasons for the suit. Because the defendant orchestra is a corporate entity, you must know how to serve a corporation. Rules governing service of process on corporations are contained in both the federal and New Mexico rules of civil procedure. Because you have not yet decided which court you will proceed in, this part explores both the federal and state rules.

3. How Do You Research Rules of Procedure?

a. Researching Federal Rules of Procedure Using Paper Media

The focus of research in procedural rules is, of course, the text of the rule, but the rule is rarely the endpoint of your research. Often the language of

Illustration 10-1 Fed. R. Civ. P. 4(h).

fecting service on the defendant unless good cause for the failure be shown.

(3) A defendant that, before being served with process, timely returns a waiver so requested is not required to serve an answer to the complaint until 60 days after the date on which the request for waiver of service was sent, or 90 days after that date if the defendant was addressed outside any judicial district of the United States.

(4) When the plaintiff files a waiver of service with the court, the action shall proceed, except as provided in paragraph (3), as if a summons and complaint had been served at the time of filing the waiver, and no proof of service shall be required.

(5) The costs to be imposed on a defendant under paragraph (2) for failure to comply with a request to waive service of a summons shall include the costs subsequently incurred in effecting service under subdivision (e), (f), or (h), together with the costs, including a reasonable attorney's fee, of any motion required to collect the costs of service.

(e) Service Upon Individuals Within a Judicial District of the United States. Unless otherwise provided by federal law, service upon an individual from whom a waiver has not been obtained and filed, other than an infant or an incompetent person, may be effected in any judicial district of the United States:

(1) pursuant to the law of the state in which the district court is located, or in which service is effected, for the service of a summons upon the defendant in an action brought in the courts of general jurisdiction of the State; or

(2) by delivering a copy of the summons and of the complaint to the individual personally or by leaving copies thereof at the individual's dwelling house or usual place of abode with some person of suitable age and discretion then residing therein or by delivering a copy of the summons and of the complaint to an agent authorized by appointment or by law to receive service of process.

(f) Service Upon Individuals in a Foreign Country. Unless otherwise provided by federal law, service upon an individual from whom a waiver has not been obtained and filed, other than an infant or an incompetent person, may be effected in a place not within any judicial district of the United States:

(1) by any internationally agreed means reasonably calculated to give notice, such as those means authorized by the Hague Convention on the Service Abroad of Judicial and Extrajudicial Documents; or

(2) if there is no internationally agreed means of service or the applicable international agreement allows other means of service, provided that service is reasonably calculated to give notice:

(A) in the manner prescribed by the law of the foreign country for service in that country in an action in any of its courts of general jurisdiction; or

(B) as directed by the foreign authority in response to a letter rogatory or letter of request; or

(C) unless prohibited by the law of the foreign country, by

(i) delivery to the individual personally of a copy of the summons and the complaint; or

(ii) any form of mail requiring a signed receipt, to be addressed and dispatched by the clerk of the court to the party to be served; or

(3) by other means not prohibited by international agreement as may be directed by the court.

(g) Service Upon Infants and Incompetent Persons. Service upon an infant or an incompetent person in a judicial district of the United States shall be effected in the manner prescribed by the law of the state in which the service is made for the service of summons or other like process upon any such defendant in an action brought in the courts of general jurisdiction of that state. Service upon an infant or an incompetent person in a place not within any judicial district of the United States shall be effected in the manner prescribed by paragraph (2)(A) or (2)(B) of subdivision (f) or by such means as the court may direct.

(h) Service Upon Corporations and Associations. Unless otherwise provided by federal law, service upon a domestic or foreign corporation or upon a partnership or other unincorporated association that is subject to suit under a common name, and from which a waiver of service has not been obtained and filed, shall be effected:

(1) in a judicial district of the United States in the manner prescribed for individuals by subdivision (e)(1), or by delivering a copy of the summons and of the complaint to an officer, a managing or general agent, or to any other agent authorized by appointment or by law to receive service of process and, if the agent is one authorized by statute to receive service and the statute so requires, by also mailing a copy to the defendant, or

(2) in a place not within any judicial district of the United States in any manner prescribed for individuals by subdivision (f) except personal delivery as provided in paragraph (2)(C)(i) thereof.

(i) Service Upon the United States, and Its Agencies, Corporations, or Officers.

(1) Service upon the United States shall be effected

(A) by delivering a copy of the summons and of the complaint to the United States attorney for the

Illustration 10-2

Fed. R. Civ. P. 4(h) Comments of Advisory Committee (1993).

Rule 4 **RULES OF CIVIL PROCEDURE**

Two minor changes in the text reflect the Hague Convention. First, the term "letter of request" has been added. Although these words are synonymous with "letter rogatory," "letter of request" is preferred in modern usage. The provision should not be interpreted to authorize use of a letter of request when there is in fact no treaty obligation on the receiving country to honor such a request from this country or when the United States does not extend diplomatic recognition to the foreign nation. Second, the passage formerly found in subdivision (i)(1)(B), "when service in either case is reasonably calculated to give actual notice," has been relocated.

Paragraph (2) provides alternative methods for use when internationally agreed methods are not intended to be exclusive, or where there is no international agreement applicable. It contains most of the language formerly set forth in subdivision (i) of the rule. Service by methods that would violate foreign law is not generally authorized. Subparagraphs (A) and (B) prescribe the more appropriate methods for conforming to local practice or using a local authority. Subparagraph (C) prescribes other methods authorized by the former rule.

Paragraph (3) authorizes the court to approve other methods of service not prohibited by international agreements. The Hague Convention, for example, authorizes special forms of service in cases of urgency if convention methods will not permit service within the time required by the circumstances. Other circumstances that might justify the use of additional methods include the failure of the foreign country's Central Authority to effect service within the six-month period provided by the Convention, or the refusal of the Central Authority to serve a complaint seeking punitive damages or to enforce the antitrust laws of the United States. In such cases, the court may direct a special method of service not explicitly authorized by international agreement if not prohibited by the agreement. Inasmuch as our Constitution requires that reasonable notice be given, an earnest effort should be made to devise a method of communication that is consistent with due process and minimizes offense to foreign law. A court may in some instances specially authorize use of ordinary mail. *Cf. Levin v. Ruby Trading Corp.*, 248 F.Supp. 537 (S.D.N.Y.1965).

Subdivision (g). This subdivision retains the text of former subdivision (d)(2). Provision is made for service upon an infant or incompetent person in a foreign country.

Subdivision (h). This subdivision retains the text of former subdivision (d)(3), with changes reflecting those made in subdivision (e). It also contains the provisions for service on a corporation or association in a foreign country, as formerly found in subdivision (i).

Frequent use should be made of the Notice and Request procedure set forth in subdivision (d) in actions against corporations. Care must be taken, however, to address the request to an individual officer or authorized agent of the corporation. It is not effective use of the Notice and Request procedure if the mail is sent undirected to the mail room of the organization.

Subdivision (i). This subdivision retains much of the text of former subdivisions (d)(4) and (d)(5). Paragraph (1) provides for service of a summons on the United States; it amends former subdivision (d)(4) to permit the United States attorney to be served by registered or certified mail. The rule does not authorize the use of the Notice and Request procedure of revised subdivision (d) when the United States is the defendant. To assure proper handling of mail in the United States attorney's office, the authorized mail service must be specifically addressed to the civil process clerk of the office of the United States attorney.

Paragraph (2) replaces former subdivision (d)(5). Paragraph (3) saves the plaintiff from the hazard of losing a substantive right because of failure to comply with the complex requirements of multiple service under this subdivision. That risk has proved to be more than nominal. *E.g., Whale v. United States*, 792 F.2d 951 (9th Cir.1986). This provision should be read in connection with the provisions of subdivision (c) of Rule 15 to preclude the loss of substantive rights against the United States or its agencies, corporations, or officers resulting from a plaintiff's failure to correctly identify and serve all the persons who should be named or served.

Subdivision (j). This subdivision retains the text of former subdivision (d)(6) without material change. The waiver-of-service provision is also inapplicable to actions against governments subject to service pursuant to this subdivision.

The revision adds a new paragraph (1) referring to the statute governing service of a summons on a foreign state and its political subdivisions, agencies, and instrumentalities, the Foreign Sovereign Immunities Act of 1976, 28 U.S.C. § 1608. The caption of the subdivision reflects that change.

Subdivision (k). This subdivision replaces the former subdivision (f), with no change in the title. Paragraph (1) retains the substance of the former rule in explicitly authorizing the exercise of personal jurisdiction over persons who can be reached under state long-arm law, the "100-mile bulge" provision added in 1963, or the federal interpleader act. Paragraph (1)(D) is new, but merely calls attention to federal legislation that may provide for nationwide or even world-wide service of process in cases arising under particular federal laws. Congress has provided for nationwide service of process and full exercise of territorial jurisdiction by all district courts with respect to specified federal actions. *See* 1 R. Casad, *Jurisdiction in Civil Actions* (2d Ed.) chap. 5 (1991).

Paragraph (2) is new. It authorizes the exercise of territorial jurisdiction over the person of any defendant against whom is made a claim arising under any federal law if that person is subject to personal jurisdiction in no state. This addition is a companion to the amendments made in revised subdivisions (e) and (f).

This paragraph corrects a gap in the enforcement of federal law. Under the former rule, a problem was presented when the defendant was a non-resident of the United States having contacts with the United States sufficient to justify the application of United States law and to satisfy federal standards of forum selection, but having insufficient contact with any single state to support jurisdiction under state long-arm legislation or meet the requirements of the Fourteenth Amendment limitation on state court territorial jurisdiction. In such cases, the defendant was shielded from the enforcement of federal law by the fortuity of a favorable limitation on the power of state courts, which was incorporated into the federal practice by the former rule. In this respect, the revision responds to the suggestion of the Supreme Court made in *Omni Capital Int'l v. Rudolf Wolff & Co., Ltd.*, 484 U.S. 97, 111 (1987).

Complete Annotation Materials, see Title 28 U.S.C.A.

30

the rule will be less than perfectly clear in its application to your client's situation. You then will use commentary to help you understand the rule. You generally will look to case law for additional authority. The courts assess the constitutionality of and apply procedural rules in specific cases, just as they do with statutes. To obtain this combination of rule, commentary, and case law, you will use sources used in other forms of research (and hence covered in more detail in other chapters): treatises, annotated codes, case reporters, and *Shepard's Citations.* You also will use sources unique to research in procedural rules: deskbooks and specialized reporters. Exhibit 10.2 below presents a flowchart of a generally useful sequence of sources.

(1) Deskbooks

Procedural rules are published in their most compact form in a "deskbook," a single volume that usually contains the text of a jurisdiction's various sets of rules of procedure, comments or notes of the advisory committee on those rules, and some model forms. However, deskbooks do not contain case annotations or extensive commentary. Illustration 10-3 on page 335 shows the table of contents of a representative federal deskbook. Most deskbooks are published annually and are not updated until the next edition is published. Thus deskbooks are fairly current, but not necessarily up-to-date.

There are several means of locating a pertinent rule within a deskbook. If you are not sure which set of rules covers your topic, you may use a general index for the deskbook. If you know which set of rules is pertinent, you may prefer to use the index to that set of rules. (Some deskbooks have a general index or specific indexes, but not both.) Or you can scan the table of contents at the beginning of a set of rules.

Researching Rules of Procedure.

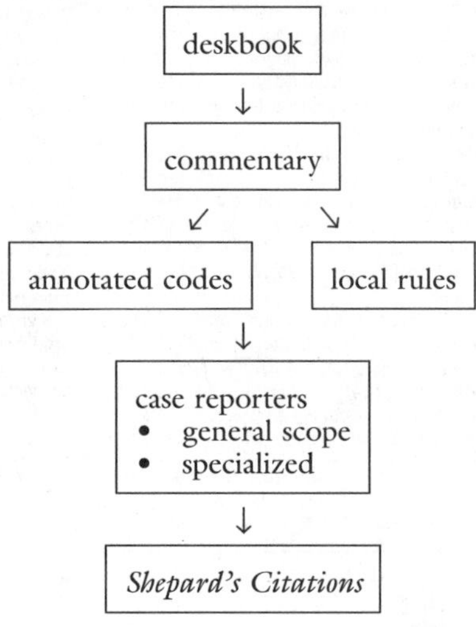

Illustration 10-3

Table of Contents, *Federal Civil Judicial Procedure and Rules.*

TABLE OF CONTENTS

*

Once you have located the pertinent rule, you should read it much as you would read a statute. For example, you should read or scan the entire rule, not just a section that seems to be on point. Indeed, it often is wise to scan nearby and related rules as well. You should read any other rules to which your rule refers. In addition, you should read the historical notes or advisory comments to learn about the drafters' intent and any amendments to the rule (so that your research in case law will be focused on cases arising under the current language). Finally, you should check for forms that accompany your rule; these forms may be printed in an appendix to the set of rules. The forms are intended only to illustrate an appropriate format of pleadings. Illustration 10-4 on page 337 is an example of a form accompanying the rules.

In the Canoga case, your focal rule in federal district court is Rule 4(h) of the Federal Rules of Civil Procedure. See Illustration 10-1 on page 332. In general terms, it provides for service upon an officer, managing or general agent, or agent authorized to receive service. Or service may be accomplished according to the law of the state, as the cross-reference to Rule 4(e)(1) indicates. Among other points, you would learn from the comments in Illustration 10-2 on page 333 that Rule 4(h) carries over key language from the former Rule 4(d)(3). The appendix includes a form for a summons issued pursuant to Rule 4, which requires the defendant to serve an answer upon the plaintiff within twenty days following receipt of the summons, so as to avoid default judgment. See Illustration 10-4 on page 337.

(2) Treatises and Other Commentary

As with any area of law, commentary can help you understand a procedural rule; your options include periodicals, *American Law Reports* annotations, encyclopedias, and treatises. The following major treatises are highly persuasive commentary on federal procedural research:

Fleming James, Jr., et al., *Civil Procedure* (4th ed. 1992) (single-volume treatise).

James W. Moore et al., *Moore's Federal Practice* (2d ed. 1948-present) (multivolume looseleaf treatise covers civil, criminal, appellate, and admiralty rules).

Charles A. Wright, *The Law of Federal Courts* (1994) (single-volume treatise).

Charles A. Wright & Arthur R. Miller, *Federal Practice and Procedure* (1969-present) (multivolume treatise covers civil, criminal, appellate, and evidentiary rules).

Some procedural treatises are organized by rule, while others are organized by topic. You would use the index, the table of contents, or the rule number to locate applicable sections of the treatise. These treatises analyze the rules, comments, and accompanying case law, as well as discuss historical and drafting considerations. As with any treatise, they provide references to the leading cases (but not necessarily all pertinent cases). Some treatises are updated by pocket parts or replacement volumes. Illustration 10-5 on pages 338-339 is

Illustration 10-4

Form 1—Summons, Appendix of Forms, *Federal Civil Judicial Procedure and Rules.*

APPENDIX OF FORMS

(See Rule 84)

Introductory Statement

1937 ADOPTION

1. The following forms are intended for illustration only. They are limited in number. No attempt is made to furnish a manual of forms. Each form assumes the action to be brought in the Southern District of New York. If the district in which an action is brought has divisions, the division should be indicated in the caption.

2. Except where otherwise indicated each pleading, motion, and other paper should have a caption similar to that of the summons, with the designation of the particular paper substituted for the word "Summons". In the caption of the summons and in the caption of the complaint all parties must be named but in other pleadings and papers, it is sufficient to state the name of the first party on either side, with an appropriate indication of other parties. See Rules 4(b), 7(b)(2), and 10(a).

3. In Form 3 and the forms following, the words, "Allegation of jurisdiction," are used to indicate the appropriate allegation in Form 2.

4. Each pleading, motion, and other paper is to be signed in his individual name by at least one attorney of record (Rule 11). The attorney's name is to be followed by his address as indicated in Form 3. In forms following Form 3 the signature and address are not indicated.

5. If a party is not represented by an attorney, the signature and address of the party are required in place of those of the attorney.

Form 1.

SUMMONS

UNITED STATES DISTRICT COURT FOR THE SOUTHERN DISTRICT OF NEW YORK

Civil Action, File Number ____

A. B., Plaintiff

v. *Summons*

C. D., Defendant

To the above-named Defendant:

You are hereby summoned and required to serve upon ____, plaintiff's attorney, whose address is ____________, an answer to the complaint which is herewith served upon you, within 20 [1] days after service of this summons upon you, exclusive of the day of service. If you fail to do so, judgment by default will be taken against you for the relief demanded in the complaint.

____
Clerk of Court.

[Seal of the U. S. District Court]
Dated ____________

(This summons is issued pursuant to Rule 4 of the Federal Rules of Civil Procedure).

(As amended Dec. 29, 1948, eff. Oct. 20, 1949.)

1 If the United States or an officer or agency thereof is a defendant, the time to be inserted as to it is 60 days.

Form 1A.

NOTICE OF LAWSUIT AND REQUEST FOR WAIVER OF SERVICE OF SUMMONS

TO: ___(A)___ [as ___(B)___ of (C)___]

A lawsuit has been commenced against you (or the entity on whose behalf you are addressed). A copy of the complaint is attached to this notice. It has been filed in the United States District Court for the ___(D)___ and has been assigned docket number ___(E)___.

This is not a formal summons or notification from the court, but rather my request that you sign and return the enclosed waiver of service in order to save the cost of serving you with a judicial summons and an additional copy of the complaint. The cost of service will be avoided if I receive a signed copy of the waiver within ___(F)___ days after the date designated below as the date on which this Notice and Request is sent. I enclose a stamped and addressed envelope (or other means of cost-free return) for your use. An extra copy of the waiver is also attached for your records.

If you comply with this request and return the signed waiver, it will be filed with the court and no summons will be served on you. The action will then proceed as if you had been served on the date the waiver is filed, except that you will not be obligated to answer the complaint before 60 days from the date designated below as the date on which this notice is sent (or before 90 days from that date if your address is not in any judicial district of the United States).

If you do not return the signed waiver within the time indicated, I will take appropriate steps to effect formal service in a manner authorized by the Federal Rules of Civil Procedure and will then, to the extent authorized by those Rules, ask the court to require you (or the party on whose behalf you are addressed) to pay the full costs of such service. In that connection, please read the statement concerning the duty of parties to waive the service of the summons, which is set forth on the reverse side (or at the foot) of the waiver form.

I affirm that this request is being sent to you on behalf of the plaintiff, this ___ day of ______, ___.

____
Signature of Plaintiff's Attorney or Unrepresented Plaintiff

Complete Annotation Materials, see Title 28 U.S.C.A.

240

Illustration 10-5

4A Charles A. Wright & Arthur R. Miller, *Federal Practice and Procedure* §§ 1100-1101 (2d ed. Supp. 1995).

negotiated. Atlantic Financial Fed. v. Bruno, D.C.Pa.1988, 698 F.Supp. 568.

§ 1099. Service on Infants and Incompetents

Subdivision (g) of amended Rule 4 retains the text of former subdivision (d)(2). Provision is made for service upon an infant or incompetent person in a foreign country.

Infants and incompetent persons are not subject to the new subdivision (d) regarding waiver of service because their presumed inability to understand the request for waiver mandates service through fiduciaries.

Supplement to Notes in Main Volume

1. State law

U.S. v. O'Gilvie, D.C.Kan.1993, 149 F.R.D. 645.

6. Rule 4(c)(2)(C)(ii)

Waters v. Farmers Texas County Mut. Ins. Co., C.A.5th, 1993, 9 F.3d 397 (government's mailing of cross-claim directly to person whom government knew to be a minor did not provide effective service under Rule 4(c)(2)(C)(ii)).

G. SERVICE ON CORPORATIONS AND OTHER ASSOCIATIONS

§ 1100. Service on Organizational Defendants—In General

Rule 4(h), as amended in 1993, retains the text of former subdivision (d)(3), with changes reflecting those made in subdivision (e). It also contains the provisions for service on a corporation or association in a foreign country formerly found in subdivision (i).

§ 1101. Service on Organizational Defendants—Scope and Application of Rule 4(d)(3)

In view of the broad provision in Rule 4(d)(3) for service on officers, managing agents, and general agents and the ability to serve organizations under Rule 4(c)(2)(C)(i),[8.1] the precise scope of the "authorized * * * by law" language probably is of little practical moment.

8.1 Authorized by law

Woodbury v. Sears, Roebuck & Co., D.C.Fla.1993, 152 F.R.D. 229 (applying both Florida statute and Federal Rule 4(d)(3) to find that corporation file maintenance leader was not agent authorized by law to receive service of process).

Supplement to Notes in Main Volume

5. Express appointment

Select Creations, Inc. v. Paliafito America, Inc., D.C.Wis.1993, 830 F.Supp. 1223.

Service upon the state attorney general did not constitute effective service upon state officials in their individual capacities because the plaintiff failed to show that the attorney general was

Illustration 10-5 *(continued)*

§ 1101 **PROCESS** Ch. 3
Rule 4

authorized to accept service of process. Love v. Hayden, D.C.Kan.1991, 757 F.Supp. 1209.

8. State statutes

See also

Printed Media Servs. v. Solna Web, Inc., C.A.8th, 1993, 11 F.3d 838 (Minnesota federal district court applied Minnesota statute authorizing extraterritorial service on foreign corporations in certain situations, under aegis of Rule 4(d)(3), which permits service on agents designated by appointment or by law; since entity receiving process meant to be served upon defendant was not appropriate agent within meaning of state statute, service was improper).

9. Service at place of abode insufficient

But see

Apollo Technologies Corp. v. Centrosphere Industrial Corp., D.C.N.J.1992, 805 F.Supp. 1157 (allowing service of process at president's home).

11. Delivery to receptionist

Direct Mail Specialists, Inc. v. Eclat Computerized Technologies, Inc., C.A.9th, 1988, 840 F.2d 685 (delivery to receptionist sufficient even though not an employee of defendant).

In the absence of proof that a defendant's secretary was duly appointed to receive process as his agent, service

1988 WL 121585, **citing Wright & Miller.**

Receptionist at corporate offices who stated that she could accept summons was an implied agent authorized by appointment and capable of accepting service. Kuhlik v. Atlantic Corp., D.C.N.Y.1986, 112 F.R.D. 146.

But compare

Grand Entertainment Group, Ltd. v. Star Media Sales, Inc., C.A.3d, 1993, 988 F.2d 476 (service on receptionist for building who was not directly employed by defendants was invalid).

12. Importance of notice

District court did not abuse its discretion in denying corporate defendant's motion to set aside a default judgment based on a filing or clerical error which resulted in failure of in-house counsel to discover plaintiff's service of process and ensure that an appearance was entered on behalf of defendant; district court could reasonably view the error as careless and within the meaningful control of defendant. North Cent. Illinois Laborers' Dist. Council v. S.J. Groves, & Sons Co., C.A.7th, 1988, 842 F.2d 164.

Inter-City Prods. Corp. v. Willey, D.C.Tenn.1993, 149 F.R.D. 563, **citing Wright & Miller.**

Spann v. Colonial Village, Inc., D.C.D.C. 1988, 124 F.R.D. 1, 2, **citing Wright & Miller.**

an excerpt from the Wright and Miller multivolume treatise. The illustration is taken from the supplement because the rule was recently revised.

For the Canoga case, the commentary in *Federal Practice and Procedure* is helpful in understanding the relationship between Rule 4(d)(3) and its 1993 amendment, Rule 4(h). Because Rule 4(h) retained most of the language of the previous rule, the previous cases on former Rule 4(d)(3) will still be valuable for construing the revised Rule 4(h).

(3) Annotated Codes

Even though rules of procedure may not be enacted through the same process as statutes, they typically can be found in statutory codes. At the federal level, *United States Code* (U.S.C.) contains unannotated versions of all of the federal rules, including the FRCP, as a part of title 28 (which addresses issues of jurisdiction, the judiciary, and judicial procedure). In *United States Code*

Annotated (U.S.C.A.) and in *United States Code Service* (U.S.C.S.), the annotated rules either are appended to title 28 or can be found in volumes located at the end of the set.

If you do not already have a reference to the pertinent rule, you may locate it through the general index for the entire code, the index for a particular set of rules (except in U.S.C.), or the table of contents for a particular set of rules. The U.S.C.A. general index uses "Rules of Civil Procedure" as a heading, and U.S.C.S. uses "Federal Rules of Civil Procedure." If you know which set of rules likely addresses your topic, it is more efficient to use the index for that set of rules rather than the general index; these specific indexes appear immediately after the rules to which they apply. Or you can scan the table of contents if you already have some familiarity with the litigation process and its specialized jargon, because the order of rules roughly parallels the sequence of litigation.

Once you have found an applicable rule, you should read it and the accompanying notes or comments (unless you already have done so in a deskbook). Then scan the annotations—the major reason to research in annotated codes. Their main contribution is the digests of cases that discuss the rules. The annotations also include references to form books, law reviews, treatises, and legal encyclopedias.

Changes in the federal procedural rules are not made frequently. Any rule changes adopted after publication of the main volume of the code—as well as any recent annotations—can be found in the code's updating materials.

For the Canoga case, the general indexes in U.S.C.A. and U.S.C.S. contain entries for Rule 4(h) under the subheading of "corporations—summons, service." If you read the cases digested in the annotations, you would learn that a complaint served upon a domestic corporation can be made upon an officer or upon any person affiliated with the corporation who would appear to have the authority to receive service or would know the significance of the legal papers. The updating materials for the federal codes revealed no recent changes to Rule 4(h), but a few recent cases were digested.

(4) Researching Case Law Interpreting Procedural Rules

(a) General Federal Reporters and *Federal Rules Decisions*

Regardless of whether the rules originated with the legislature or the court or both, the courts interpret and apply rules of procedure. Just as with other legal issues, procedural case law can be mandatory or persuasive precedent (depending on the jurisdiction of the court and the case).

Federal procedural case law is extensive because there are many federal district (trial) and appellate courts, and virtually every case has some procedural dimension. Many of the decisions are published. Federal district court cases in which procedural issues appear along with other substantive issues are reported in *Federal Supplement* (F. Supp.); appellate decisions are reported in *Federal Reporter* (F., F.2d, and F.3d) and in the various reporters of United States Supreme Court decisions (*United States Reports, Supreme Court Reporter,* and *United States Supreme Court Reports, Lawyers' Edition*).

Additionally, a specialized case reporter, *Federal Rules Decisions* (F.R.D.), is devoted to district court cases involving the Federal Rules of Civil Procedure and the Federal Rules of Criminal Procedure; other rules are discussed tangentially. F.R.D. also contains proposed rule changes, reports of studies, and articles written by judges, practitioners, and law professors addressing the rules.

Commentary sources and the case digests in annotated statutes are effective starting points for finding cases in these reporters. In addition, a West digest often is a fertile source of references to cases interpreting procedural rules. You may use *Federal Practice Digest 4th* or its predecessor titles to research procedural topics. Some procedural topics are grouped under the name of the rules, such as "Federal Civil Procedure"; other procedural topics appear under other digest topics.

For the Canoga case, one relevant case reported in F.R.D. is *McCarthy v. Langston,* 23 F.R.D. 249 (N.D. Fla. 1959); the court held that process was validly served upon a corporate officer when the summons and complaint were served upon the corporate president's wife, in that she recognized the significance of the legal papers.

(b) *Federal Rules Service*

An additional source containing federal procedural case law is the *Federal Rules Service,* published by Lawyers Cooperative Publishing. The *Federal Rules Service* contains cases construing the Federal Rules of Civil Procedure and the Federal Rules of Appellate Procedure. Cases often appear in the *Federal Rules Service* sooner than in other publications, and some of the cases are not published elsewhere.

Using the *Federal Rules Service* to find case law related to a particular rule involves several steps. The first step is to find an applicable Findex number. The Findex is a detailed topical index published in two parts: one for the Federal Rules of Civil Procedure and the other for the Federal Rules of Appellate Procedure. The Findex numerical scheme roughly parallels the numbering of the rules; the Findex uses whole numbers and decimal numbers to divide the rules and their subdivisions into subtopics. See Illustration 10-6 on page 342. You usually will find it helpful to consult the Findex to understand subtopics represented by the decimal numbers. The Findex number does not always parallel the current rule number if the rule has been amended recently. If you do not know which federal rule applies, you can use the Word Index to find a pertinent Findex number. The Findex and the Word Index are located in the Finding Aids volume of the *Federal Rules Service.*

The second step is to locate digests of pertinent cases. The *Federal Rules Digest* contains digests of the cases reported in the *Federal Rules Service* and is organized by Findex number. See Illustration 10-7 on page 343. The *Digest* groups the case synopses by court—appellate court cases first, followed by district court cases, and then cases from specialized courts; each group of cases is reported in chronological order. Case digests contain references to the *Federal Rules Service* reporters and to other reporters, such as West

Illustration 10-6 Findex, *Federal Rules Service.*

RULE 4

PROCESS

4a. Summons—Issuance
- .1 When issued; responsibility for service
- .2 Separate or additional summons
- .3 Effect of delay in issuance (see also Findex 4d.81)

4b. Summons—Form (see also Form 1)
- .1 In general
- .2 Effect of informality

4c. Service
- .1 Subpoena: see Findex 45c.
- .2 Other process
  - .21 Service by marshal
  - .22 Special appointment of other persons
  - .23 Service under state law (see also Findex 4d.7)
  - .24 Service by nonparty adult
  - .25 Service by first class mail
  - .26 Notice and acknowledgement
    - .261 Time for return
    - .262 Award of costs of personal service
    - .263 Oath or affirmation
  - .27 Special appointments for service: see Findex 4c.22

4d. Summons and Complaint: Person To Be Served
- .1 Upon competent adult
  - .11 Personal service
  - .12 Service on member of household (see also Findex 5b.23)
    - .121 "Dwelling house"
    - .122 "Usual place of abode"
    - .123 "Person of suitable age and discretion"
  - .13 Service on agent of individual for receiving process
    - .131 Authorized by appointment
    - .132 Authorized by law
- .2 Upon infant or incompetent
  - .21 Service according to state law
- .3 Upon corporation, partnership, or association
  - .31 Foreign corporation
  - .32 Domestic corporation
  - .33 Partnership (see also Findex 17b.3)
  - .34 Association (see also Findex 17b.3)
  - .35 On whom served
    - .351 Officer

204

Illustration 10-7

Federal Rules Digest, Federal Rules Service.

general agent" of the former. Grantham v. Challenge-Cook Bros., Inc., 13 Fed Rules Serv 2d 16, 420 F2d 1182 (CA7 1969).

Service of process on the wife of the president of defendant corporation in a derivative suit did not constitute effective service on the corporation. Therefore, in view of the fact that the corporation was an indispensable party, an order dismissing the action after the representative shareholders sold their stock was necessarily without prejudice to the rights of the corporation. Tryforos v. Icarian Development Co., S. A., 21 Fed Rules Serv 2d 560, 518 F2d 1258 (CA7 1975).

Service of process in a debt action against a corporation was properly effected by leaving the summons and complaint with the only person present in defendant's office, a receptionist, since an uncontroverted affidavit from an employee of plaintiff stated that defendant's president complained in a telephone call the next day about being served with process. Despite the language of Rule 4(d)(3), service is not limited solely to officially designated officers, managing agents, or agents appointed by law for the receipt of process, since the Rules are to be applied in a manner that will best effectuate their purpose of giving defendant adequate notice. Defendant was a small one and the role played by the receptionist was presumably commensurately large. Her sole presence in the office demonstrated that she had more than minimal responsibilities. Further, defendant's president, a lawyer, should have been well aware of the danger of ignoring process and permitting a default judgment to be taken. Direct Mail Specialists, Inc. v. Eclat Computerized Technologies, Inc., 10 Fed Rules Serv 3d 802, 841 F2d 685 (CA9, 1988).

DISTRICT COURTS

Service of process on an agent of a local union is not service upon the international union where the local and the international are separate and autonomous and the person served is not otherwise an agent of the international or authorized to accept service in its behalf. Farnsworth & Chambers Co., Inc. v. Sheet Metal Workers International Ass'n, Local 49, 20 Fed Rules Serv 15, 125 F Supp 830 (D NM, 1954).

Service of process may not be made by serving a corporation authorized to sell steamship tickets for defendant where such corporation was not appointed as agent for service of process nor was it made an agent by federal or state law. Impoco v. Lauro, 21 Fed Rules Serv 10, 16 FRD 522 (D Mass 1955).

The Canadian Government may not be made a defendant in an action in a federal court by service of process on a consul. Oster v. Dominion of Canada, 23 Fed Rules Serv 10, 144 F Supp 746 (ND NY 1956).

Service of process on a domestic corporation was valid where the summons and complaint were left at the corporate office for service of process with the wife of the president of the corporation and the president personally acknowledged receipt of the papers within a day thereafter. The acts of the marshal were sufficient to apprise the corporation with notice of the suit. McCarthy v. Langston, 2 Fed Rules Serv 2d 6, 23 FRD 249 (ND Fla, 1959).

Absent state law to the contrary, valid service is not made on a foreign corporation by leaving the summons and complaint at the home of an agent of reporters, if the cases are published in them. Some of the cases carry a blank parallel citation (for example,—F.2d—), which means that the editors believe that the case will be published later in the indicated reporter. Hence, if you encounter a blank parallel citation, you should use the table of cases in an appropriate digest or an online database to determine whether the case has been subsequently published elsewhere.

The third step is to read any pertinent cases. The full texts of the cases digested in the *Federal Rules Digest* are printed in the *Federal Rules Service* reporters, and some are printed in other reporters.

To update your research in the *Federal Rules Service,* you can use the paper advance sheets called "releases," which are published monthly. Each release contains the full text of recent cases and a Findex case table containing a cumulative listing of Findex numbers, related case names, and references to where each case can be located in one of the releases. Because the table is cumulative, you must scan only the Findex case table in the most recent release. See Illustration 10-8 on page 345.

For example, in the Canoga case, you can gain access to the *Federal Rules Service* by searching the Findex by FRCP rule number or by using the Word Index. See Illustration 10-6 on page 342. You would learn that subdivision (h) of Rule 4 is covered by Findex number 4d.35, reflecting the old subdivision designation (4d) for the rule on serving corporations. The digests published under Findex number 4d.35 address service of process on a corporation. None of the appellate cases referred to are from the Tenth Circuit, which encompasses New Mexico. However, the digest of a Ninth Circuit case, *Direct Mail Specialists, Inc. v. Eclat Computerized Technologies, Inc.,* suggests that the rule should be applied pragmatically, so as to reflect the situation of the defendant and the rule's purpose of assuring the defendant adequate notice. It is then necessary to read the full text of the case in one of the reporters, whether *Federal Rules Service* or F.2d. In the most recent *Federal Rules Service* release, there is no entry under the pertinent Findex number, which means that no pertinent case has been published recently. See Illustration 10-8 on page 345.

(5) *Shepard's Citations*

As with cases, statutes, and administrative materials, procedural rules can be Shepardized so that you can be certain that the rule is current, as well as find additional sources that cite the rule. Both *Shepard's United States Citations, Statute Edition* and *Shepard's Federal Rules Citations* cover all of the federal rules, including FRCP, as cited sources. The citing sources in *Shepard's Citations, Statute Edition* include selected official and unofficial federal reporters, A.L.R. annotations, and the *A.B.A. Journal. Shepard's Federal Rules Citations* includes these citing sources as well as regional reporters and several selected law reviews.

In both of these *Shepard's,* each set of rules is presented separately, and each list may be further divided by the rule's subdivisions. The list of citing cases is segmented by federal circuits (and in *Shepard's Federal Rules Citations,* by state). Abbreviations precede some citing sources. These abbreviations

Illustration 10-8 Findex Case Table, Monthly Release, *Federal Rules Service.*

Federal Rules Service 3d

Findex™ Case Table

Volume 31

HOW TO USE THIS TABLE

Step 1. Check to see if the FINDEX™ number you are using is listed in the "FINDEX™ " column below.

Step 2. If it is listed, there will be a direct reference to the page number where cases are reported in this Volume.

FINDEX™	Title	Page
1.317	North River Insurance Co. v. Greater New York Mutual Insurance Co. (ED Pa)	1127
4c.21	Graham v. Satkoski (CA7)	12
	Jones-Bey v. Wright (ND Ind)	1367
4d.11	Lowe v. Hart (MD Fla)	142
4d.12	Churchill v. Barach (D Nev)	474
4d.122	Jaffe & Asher v. Van Brunt (SD NY)	155
4d.123	Churchill v. Barach (D Nev)	474
4d.131	Lowe v. Hart (MD Fla)	142
4d.51	Lowe v. Hart (MD Fla)	142
4d.54	Henderson v. United States (CA5)	1098
4d.8121	Henderson v. United States (CA5)	1098
4j.1	Henderson v. United States (CA5)	1098
4j.21	In re Van Meter (BAP 9)	313
	Tyson v. City of Sunnyvale (ND Cal)	742
	Espinoza v. United States (CA10)	1229
	Mendez v. Elliot (CA4)	1449
4j.23	Lowe v. Hart (MD Fla)	142
	Braithwaite v. Johns Hopkins Hospital (D Md)	387
	Espinoza v. United States (CA10)	1229
	Fultz v. Rittlemeyer (WD Va)	1334
	Jones-Bey v. Wright (ND Ind)	1367
4j.24	Graham v. Satkoski (CA7)	12
4j.26	Jones-Bey v. Wright (ND Ind)	1367
4j.27	Graham v. Satkoski (CA7)	12
	Braithwaite v. Johns Hopkins Hospital (D Md)	387
	Lambert v. United States (CA5)	653

xiii

may refer to legislative action—for example, "A" (amended) or "Rn" (renumbered)—or to judicial action—for example, "V" (void) or "U" (unconstitutional). You should pay particular attention to these citations because they may indicate the validity of the rule you are researching.

For the Canoga case, *Shepard's* indicates that Rule 4(h) has not been invalidated, nor has it been cited often (probably because it is fairly recent). To be cautious and to seek additional citations, you also could Shepardize the predecessor Rule 4(d) in earlier editions of *Shepard's.*

(6) Local Rules

You have not finished your research into procedural rules until you have reviewed the local rules (also called "court rules") for the court in which you are litigating your case. Local rules govern practice before a particular court, such as a circuit court of appeals or a district (trial) court. The scope of local rules differs from court to court. Some local rules cover such mundane matters as filing procedures and fees, paper size, and the color of brief covers. Other rules address more substantial matters, such as pre-trial conferences and the allocation of responsibility between judges and magistrates (lower-level judges). In most instances, local rules supplement the procedural rules discussed thus far. Thus you must be aware of both sets of rules. Illustration 10-9 on page 347 shows Rule 10 of the United States District Court for the District of New Mexico.

Local rules for the federal courts of appeals, including the Supreme Court, appear in U.S.C.A. and U.S.C.S. The local rules of the many federal district courts are not available in the codes. These rules can be found most readily in *Federal Local Court Rules,* a set of looseleaf binders that are published by Lawyers Cooperative Publishing and are part of the *Federal Rules Service.* This set is updated regularly. To find pertinent rules, first locate the set of rules for the appropriate court, and then use the index or table of contents for that set.

Shepard's United States Citations, Statute Edition and *Shepard's Federal Rules Citations* cover the local rules of the federal courts.

For the Canoga case, if you were to litigate in the United States District Court for the District of New Mexico, you would peruse the rules of that court in *Federal Local Court Rules.* Illustration 10-9 on page 347 shows Rule 10, which governs the form of pleadings. It requires 8 1/2 × 11″ white paper, double-spacing, and the case file number on the first page.

b. Researching Procedural Rules in CD-ROM Media

Commercial publishing companies increasingly are using the CD-ROM medium for handling multivolume treatises, looseleafs, and other materials. One example of a treatise on CD-ROM is *Federal Practice and Procedure,* written by Wright and Miller, discussed earlier. The text of the paper version is reproduced in the CD-ROM medium. Just as with the paper treatise, the CD-ROM medium does not integrate the textual material contained in the supplements with the textual material of main volumes; thus, the main text

Illustration 10-9 U.S. Dist. Ct. N.M. R. 10.

henceforth submit, in the case of responsive pleadings, a separate pleading addressing each motion or other pleading to which a response is made;

IT IS FURTHERED ORDERED that all pleadings filed with the Clerk of the Court shall include in the caption title a clear identification of the matter raised and, in the case of responsive pleadings, a clear identification of the pleading, including the filing date thereof, to which a response is made.

Rule 8. General rules of pleading

8.1. Affirmative defenses. If an answer or other pleading raises or contains any of the seven enumerated defenses provided in Rule 12(b) of the Federal Rules of Civil Procedure, the party filing such pleading shall request in writing that such portion of the answer or other pleading be treated as a motion and, thereafter, it shall be considered as a motion filed under D.N.M.LR-Cv 7 of these Rules. Should a party fail to make such written request, such a defense may be treated as having been waived, except for jurisdictional defenses.

Rule 10. Form of pleadings

10.1. Form. All pleadings, motions, affidavits, briefs, points and authorities, and other documents, including all exhibits presented for filing shall be on white, opaque, unglazed paper of good quality and shall be legibly typewritten or printed without interlineations defacing them. The size of the paper shall be $8^1/_2 \times 11$ inches. The body of all documents shall be double spaced, except citations, footnotes and quotations, which may be single spaced. The case file number, including the initials of the assigned district judge and magistrate judge, shall be included on the first page of each document filed.

10.2. Pleadings and papers tendered for filing. The Clerk shall not refuse to accept for filing any paper presented for that purpose solely because it is not in proper form. If a pleading or other paper is filed without signature, it shall be stricken unless it is signed promptly after the omission is called to the attention of the pleader or movant.

a. *Non-conforming pleadings filed by pro se litigants.* A non-conforming pleading or paper tendered for filing by any pro se party shall be accepted by the Clerk pursuant to D.N.M.LR-Cv 10.2, except as otherwise ordered by the Court. The Clerk shall promptly thereafter notify the pro se party, in writing, of the deficiency in the pleadings or papers so filed, and shall provide the pro se party with such forms and instructions as may be available and applicable to the particular instance. Notice of non-conforming pleadings sent by the Clerk shall inform the pro se party that failure to remedy pleading deficiencies within forty-five days from the date of the notice may result in dismissal of the party's claims pursuant to D.N.M.LR-Cv 41.1. Upon the failure of any pro se party to comply with notice pursuant to this rule by remedying pleading deficiencies, or otherwise showing good cause for non-compliance, the Clerk may dismiss the party's claims as otherwise provided pursuant to D.N.M.LR-Cv 41.1 and subject to review by the Court.

10.3. Exhibits; attachments to pleadings. Exhibits shall not be attached to complaints, answers, counterclaims, crossclaims, third party complaints, and any updating supplements must be searched separately. To update the materials, a new replacement disk is issued two or three times each year, shortly after new supplements are printed in paper.

Once you have selected Wright and Miller's *Federal Practice and Procedure,* you must choose how you wish to gain access to the textual information. If you have only a limited knowledge of the procedural rules, the most useful search choices are the Document List and Search Book options.

The Document List command permits you to scan the table of contents for each of the sets of federal rules covered by *Federal Practice and Procedure.* When using the Document List, you first must select the title of the set of federal rules you wish to search; the abbreviation "CV" means Civil Rules. You then can scroll the table of contents for that set of rules. The table of contents is segmented topically by section (just as in the paper treatise), and each section, which contains either the text of a rule or commentary, is treated as a separate document that can be retrieved. The tables of contents of the main volume and the supplements are listed separately; only after you have scrolled through the entire tables of contents of the main volumes will you come to the table of contents of the supplement. See Illustration 10-10 below.

The Search Book option provides a template permitting you to perform a Boolean search of the entire set of *Federal Practice and Procedure,* not specific sets of federal rules within the treatise. The Boolean search capability works just like any other Boolean search on WESTLAW; thus, you may use

Illustration 10-10

Document List Screen, CD-ROM, *Federal Practice and Procedure.*

```
                        PREMISE Research Software 2.11
  File  Edit  Search  Browse  Services  Help               |Press F1 for Help
FED PRACT & PROC-WRIGHT/MILLER                       CV Contents -- Civil Sections
7                                                          Document pg 1 of 2
13.   ▸Supplemental Rules for Certain Admiralty and Maritime                  ↑
         Claims.......................................... 3201-3256

1994 Supplement--Civil Rules

▸Time Table for Lawyers in Federal Civil Cases (Supp.)

Chapter                                                    Sections
 1.   ▸History of Procedure in the Federal Courts (Supp.).....  1001-1007
 2.   ▸Scope and Effect of Rules; One Form of Action (Supp.)..  1008-1045
 3.   ▸Commencement of Action; Service of Process and Other
         Papers; Time (Supp.).............................  1051-1171
 4.   ▸Pleadings and Motions (Supp.)......................  1181-1531
 5.   ▸Parties (Supp.)....................................  1541-1961
 8.   ▸Judgment (Supp.)...................................  2651-2922
 9.   ▸Provisional and Final Remedies and Special Proceedings         ↓
Press ALT for Menu.            | ALL DOCS     |          |          |
```

F2	F3	F4	F5	F6	F7	F8	F9	F10
View Library	Document List	Search Book	Go Back	Next Term	Next Document	Retrieve Document	Print	Download

truncated words, root expanders, connectors, and fields to expand or narrow your search.

CD-ROMs published by West Publishing Company can be linked to WESTLAW. Once a document is retrieved on CD-ROM, you can use the LINK feature to obtain the full text of cases and other materials contained in WESTLAW databases if the CD-ROM refers to them. Other WESTLAW services, such as *Shepard's,* Insta-Cite, and QuickCite, also are available.

For the Canoga case, to search for a rule regulating service of process upon a corporation, both the Document List and Search Book command options were effective. The Document List provided access to the table of contents of the volumes containing the federal civil rules of procedure. It was possible to retrieve a list of treatise sections that appeared relevant, including sections 1051-1171, which cover "Commencement of Action; Service of Process and Other Papers; Time." See Illustration 10-10 on page 348.

A second option was to use the Search Book command to perform a Boolean search. An effective search was [service w/2 process w/5 corporat!]. This search retrieved forty-one documents (treatise sections), including sections beginning at 1100.

Both searches retrieved treatise sections that discussed Rule 4 of the FRCP. See Illustration 10-11 below, which shows a screen from the CD-ROM search. The next step was to scan these sections to find the text of the rule itself, relevant commentary, and references to cases and other sources.

Illustration 10-11 Text Screen, CD-ROM, *Federal Practice and Procedure.*

```
                    PREMISE Research Software 2.11
  File  Edit  Search  Browse  Services  Help            |Press F1 for Help
FED PRACT & PROC-WRIGHT/MILLER     CV Sec. 1100. Service on Organizational De...
6593                       Result 7 of 41                   Document pg 1 of 2
------------------------------ Page 6593 follows -----------------------------↑
                                 CHAPTER 3
     COMMENCEMENT OF ACTION;  SERVICE OF PROCESS AND OTHER PAPERS;  TIME
                              RULE 4. PROCESS
              G. SERVICE ON CORPORATIONS AND OTHER ASSOCIATIONS

Sec. 1100. Service on Organizational Defendants--In General


   Prior to the advent of the federal rules, state procedures for serving
process on organizational defendants, such as corporations, partnerships, and
similar associations, had to be followed in the federal courts under the
Conformity Act. ▸(FN1)  In instances in which state practice was relatively
archaic or inflexible, this led to a highly unsatisfactory result in the federal
courts. ▸(FN2)  In addition, geographic limitations on service of process
prevented federal courts from exercising the full measure of jurisdictional   ↓
Press ALT for Menu.               | RESULTS ONLY | SEE ALSO |           |
```

F2	F3	F4	F5	F6	F7	F8	F9	F10
View Library	Document List	Search Book	Go Back	Next Term	Next Document	Retrieve Document	Print	Download

These cases, including *Direct Mail Specialists, Inc. v. Eclat Computerized Technologies, Inc.*, are the same cases referred to in the paper treatise, of course. You can retrieve the full text of the cases using the LINK feature. And you can Shepardize the cases using WESTLAW's online *Shepard's* service, which is tied to the CD-ROM. According to *Shepard's,* the cases are still good law.

c. Researching State Rules of Procedure

Research in state rules of procedure in many ways parallels research in federal rules of procedure. First, the sources at the state level generally are similar to those at the federal level. Second, the rules themselves may parallel the federal rules in organization, numbering, and wording. Hence interpretations of the federal rules, whether in comments by the drafters or commentary or case law, may be helpful to your understanding of the state rules.

State procedural rules either are incorporated into the state's statutory code or stand as a separate set of rules. To locate either kind of rule, you could use a deskbook paralleling the federal deskbooks discussed above, or you could use an annotated state code. See Illustration 10-12 on page 351. In the state code, you typically can find pertinent rules by using the general index for the entire code, the index for a specific set of rules, or the table of contents for a particular set of rules. The annotations to the rules generally contain the advisory comments of the body that promulgated the rules, as well as digests of cases, references to secondary sources, and forms. See Illustration 10-12 on page 351. As in the federal annotated codes, the material in the main volume can be updated and expanded with the usual statutory supplements already covered in Chapter 7.

Only a small percentage of state procedural decisions are ever published because disputes involving rules of procedure often are resolved in trial court opinions. In most states, the only reported cases are those decided by the state high court and intermediate appellate court; in a few states, some trial court decisions also are published. Generally state court decisions on issues arising under procedural rules appear in the general reporters for cases from that state (the West regional reporter and any official reporter), although a few states also have separate reporters for cases involving procedural rules. To locate state cases, you would use the annotations in the annotated codes or the digests linked to the state's case reporter (such as the regional or state digest published by West).

To update and expand this research, you would Shepardize your state rule and case law. All state procedural rules can be Shepardized in the statute edition of the state *Shepard's Citations.*

In the Canoga case, Illustration 10-12 on page 351 is Rule 1-004(F) of New Mexico's Rules of Civil Procedure for the District Courts, which governs the service of summons in actions brought before the New Mexico state trial courts. The New Mexico Rules of Civil Procedure for the District Courts, enacted by the New Mexico legislature, are contained in a separate part of the *New Mexico Statutes Annotated.* The rule regulating service of

Illustration 10-12 N.M. R. Civ. P. 1-004(F).

....

Date of Signature

F. **Summons; how served.** Service shall be made as follows:

(1) upon an individual other than a minor or an incapacitated person by delivering a copy of the summons and of the complaint to him personally; or if the defendant refuses to receive such, by leaving same at the location where he has been found; and if the defendant refuses to receive such copies or permit them to be left, such action shall constitute valid service. If the defendant be absent, service may be made by delivering a copy of the process or other papers to be served to some person residing at the usual place of abode of the defendant who is over the age of fifteen (15) years; and if there be no such person available or willing to accept delivery, then service may be made by posting such copies in the most public part of the defendant's premises, and by mailing to the defendant at his last known mailing address copies of the process;

(2) upon domestic or foreign corporation by delivering a copy of the summons and of the complaint to an officer, a managing or a general agent, or to any other agent authorized

6

by appointment or by law to receive service of process and, if the agent is one authorized by statute to receive service and the statute so requires, by also mailing a copy to the defendant; upon a partnership by delivering a copy of the summons and of the complaint to any general partner; and upon other unincorporated association which is subject to suit under a common name, by delivering a copy of the summons and of the complaint to an officer, a managing or general agent, or to any other agent authorized by appointment or by law to receive service of process and, if the agent is one authorized by law to receive service and the statute so requires, by also mailing a copy to the unincorporated association. If the person refuses to receive such copies, such action shall constitute valid service. If none of the persons mentioned is available, service may be made by delivering a copy of the process or other papers to be served at the principal office or place of business during regular business hours to the person in charge thereof;

(3) upon the State of New Mexico:

(a) in any action in which the State of New Mexico is named a party defendant, by delivering a copy of the summons and of the complaint to the governor and to the attorney general;

(b) in any action in which a branch, agency, bureau, department, commission or institution of the state is named a party defendant, by delivering a copy of the summons and of the complaint to the [illegible] department, commission or

E. On Corporations, Partnerships and Associations.

This rule and 38-4-5 NMSA 1978 are not inconsistent, they are complementary. Section 38-4-5 NMSA 1978 appoints a partner an agent with authority to receive service of process which is plainly contemplated by Subdivision (o) (see now Paragraph F(2)) of this rule, which speaks of an agent authorized "by law" or "by statute" to receive service of process. United Nuclear Corp. v. General Atomic Co., 90 N.M. 97, 560 P.2d 161 (1976).

Suits may be brought by or against a partnership as such. A partnership is a distinct legal entity to the extent it may sue or be sued in the partnership name. Loucks v. Albuquerque Nat'l Bank, 76 N.M. 735, 418 P.2d 191 (1966).

Service must be on officer or agent. — Subdivision (o) (see now Paragraph F(2)) provides that service may be had upon either domestic or foreign corporations by delivering a copy of the summons and complaint to an officer, the managing or general agent, or to any other agent authorized to receive service. Crawford v. Refiners Coop. Ass'n, 71 N.M. 1, 375 P.2d 212 (1962).

Of such rank and character that communication to defendant is reasonably certain. — Where the form of service is reasonably calculated to give the foreign defendant actual notice of the pending suit, the provision for such service is valid, and every object of the rule is satisfied where the agent is of such rank and character so that communication to the defendant is reasonably certain. United Nuclear Corp. v. General Atomic Co., 90 N.M. 97, 560 P.2d 161 (1976).

Such as director of dissolved corporation. — Service upon a director of a dissolved corporation in Arizona is sufficient under the New Mexico nonresident motorist statute, and it is not necessary that service be made in the state of incorporation. Crawford v. Refiners Coop. Ass'n, 71 N.M. 1, 375 P.2d 212 (1962).

Or general partner. — The federal rule, which is identical insofar as pertinent to this rule, has been construed to mean that service of process on a general partner is effective service on the partnership. United Nuclear Corp. v. General Atomic Co., 90 N.M. 97, 560 P.2d 161 (1976).

But not member. — The trial court did not err in vacating a default judgment under Rule 60(b)(4) (see now Rule 1-060) where the motion for default judgment filed by plaintiff was not consistent with the return of service and the affidavit of the deputy sheriff that service of process was made on a member, not an officer or as otherwise provided in Subdivision (o) (see now Paragraph F(2)) since the court could have found the judgment void although it did not make this ruling explicit. Gengler v. Phelps, 89 N.M. 793, 558 P.2d 62 (Ct. App. 1976).

Secretary of state's failure to serve. — Paragraph F(2) requires that service be made to an authorized agent or to the principal office or place of business of the corporation in question; where, through the secretary of state's inadvertence, this was not done, a party ought not profit from the secretary of state's failure. Abarca v. Hanson, 106 N.M. 25, 738 P.2d 519 (Ct. App. 1987).

process upon a corporation can be found using the index to the rules or the table of contents to the rules, which refer you to Rule 1-004. As you can see from Illustration 10-12 on page 351, that rule strongly parallels federal Rule 4(h), although it is not identical. The annotations to the rule indicate that the rule has been cited in a handful of reported New Mexico appellate cases. To Shepardize the state rule, you would need to consult the *Shepard's New Mexico Citations.*

As is true at the federal level, your research is not complete until you have reviewed any pertinent local rules. Local rules for state courts may be published as part of the jurisdiction's statutory code or in a state deskbook. (Some state deskbooks also contain the local rules of the federal courts for that state.) Some local rules may be available only from the clerk of the court in question.

The local rules for New Mexico state courts are published as part of *New Mexico Statutes Annotated.* In the Eighth Judicial District Court of New Mexico, which is the district covering Taos, there is no local rule regulating the format of pleadings. In this case, it is advisable to contact the clerk of the court to ascertain the common practices for that court.

d. Researching Rules of Evidence

For the most part, evidence research parallels the process described above. For example, the rules and their comments appear in deskbooks and annotated codes, and you could find references to pertinent cases in digests. Several noteworthy sources dedicated to evidence are

Jack B. Weinstein & Margaret A. Berger, *Weinstein's Evidence: Commentary on Rules of Evidence for the United States Courts and State Court* (1975-present) (multivolume treatise).

John H. Wigmore, *Evidence in Trials at Common Law* (rev. ed. Peter Tillers) (1983-present) (multivolume treatise).

Gregory P. Joseph, Jr., et al., *Evidence in America: The Federal Rules in the States* (1987-present) (four-volume looseleaf service that compiles the evidentiary rules and analyzes case law of states that have adopted rules based on the FRE).

McCormick on Evidence (John W. Strong ed.) (4th ed. 1992) (single-volume treatise).

Federal Rules of Evidence Service (case reporter and digest paralleling *Federal Rules Service,* published by Lawyers Cooperative Publishing).

4. What Else?

Form Books. Many practitioners rely on form books, which publish sample forms and pleadings that can assist them in drafting documents. These sample forms can be useful, but they must be used with care. Major difficulties can result from selection of the wrong form, an outdated form, or a standard form that does not precisely fit the needs of a particular case. Sources of forms drafted for use in federal courts include *Bender's Federal Practice Forms, West's Federal Forms, Federal Local Court Forms,* and *Federal Procedural Forms, Lawyers Edition*. State forms may be available in local practice publications, such as continuing legal education materials. General-purpose forms that cover substantive as well as procedural issues appear in *American Jurisprudence Pleading and Practice Forms Annotated* and other similar sources.

Specialized Courts. For some specialized courts, such as the Bankruptcy Court, the court rules, along with commentary, forms, case law, and related annotations, can be found in comprehensive looseleafs. Likewise, rules for some specialty courts are Shepardized in specialized citators; for example, the bankruptcy rules are Shepardized in *Shepard's Bankruptcy Citations.*

Other Media. As of early 1996, these were the available media for the following sources:

			Computer-Assisted Research		
	Paper	*CD-ROM*	*LEXIS*	*WESTLAW*	*Microform*
Federal Practice and Procedure	√	√		√	
Federal Rules Decisions	√	√	√	√	√
Federal Rules Service and *Digest*	√				
Shepard's Federal Rules Citations	√				
Federal Rules of Evidence Service	√				

5. How Do You Cite Rules of Procedure?

Rule 12.8.3 of *The Bluebook* dictates the form for citation to procedural rules. A proper citation includes the appropriate abbreviation for the title of the rules and the number of the rule being cited. For example:

Fed. R. Civ. P. 4(h).

Practitioners' Note P.4(b) and Rule 12.9 of *The Bluebook* govern in-text references to a federal rule and call for a less abbreviated presentation. For example:

Rule 4 of the Federal Rules of Civil Procedure
Rule 4 (if it is clear that you are discussing Rule 4 of the Federal Rules of Civil Procedure)

If state rules of procedure are numbered as part of the statutory codification, they are cited as statutes. If the rules are not numbered as part of a code (even though they may appear in the annotated statute volumes), they are cited in much the same manner as the federal rules under Rule 12.8.3, but you should use an abbreviation that reflects the official name of the state rules. For example:

N.M. R. Civ. P. 1-004(F).

If a case in *Federal Rules Service* also has been published in an official or a West case reporter, use the official or West citation, to the exclusion of the *Federal Rules Service* citation. *See* Table T.1. The correct citation form for cases reported only in *Federal Rules Service* is governed by Rule 18.1 on services (looseleaf and bound). This rule requires any citation to a bound volume of a service to contain the case name, the volume number, the name of the service (abbreviated per Table T.16), the abbreviated name of the publisher placed within parentheses, the page number where the case begins, and a final parenthetical containing the name of the court and the year. For example:

Direct Mail Specialists, Inc. v. Eclat Computerized Technologies, Inc., 10 Fed. R. Serv. 3d (Law. Co-op.) 802 (9th Cir. 1988).

C. Lawyering Rules: "Rules" of Professional Responsibility

1. What Are Rules of Professional Responsibility?

Lawyers have a unique role in our society. Because of licensing requirements, lawyers have a monopoly on providing legal services. Lawyers have the ability to affect the decisions of their clients and the outcomes of matters that often are confidential and personal. Because of their expertise and training, lawyers often serve in decisionmaking positions as judges, legislators, executive officers, or administrators. Lawyers also are frequently catalysts for law reform. Thus, lawyers often are in positions to exert enormous power over the affairs of their clients and over the public at large.

Because of this power, the legal profession has recognized its responsibility to regulate the practice of law. Early on, the profession policed itself. Over time, that tradition has given way to modified self-regulation, which is usually performed by the state bar association, a board, a commission, or a committee under the auspices of the court or legislature. Currently, the legal profession in each state is governed by rules of professional responsibility, also called codes of conduct, canons of ethics, or similar nomenclature.

a. How Are Rules of Professional Responsibility Developed?

The entity authorized to promulgate professional rules varies from state to state. Either the state supreme court or the state legislature is authorized to promulgate rules of professional responsibility. Typically, an advisory committee recommends and drafts new rules and changes to existing rules, which are then published, before adoption, for review and comment by the legal community and the public. Additionally, a bar association, board, committee, or commission may be authorized to license lawyers, oversee compliance with the state's rules of professional responsibility, and discipline attorneys or judges who violate the rules.

The American Bar Association (ABA) has been a major source for the development of rules of professional responsibility. The ABA adopted its first rules in the 1908 Canons of Professional Ethics, which it recommended to state and local bar associations for adoption. These canons were not mandatory, but bar associations and courts did look to them for guidance in establishing standards of conduct and in disciplining lawyers. The ABA later adopted a more comprehensive set of rules, the 1970 Model Code of Professional Responsibility (Model Code). This code subsequently was widely adopted by many state and local bar associations. It had a three-part structure: the "Canons" served as broad "axiomatic" principles; "Ethical Considerations" (ECs) provided aspirational and explanatory provisions; and "Disciplinary Rules" (DRs) set minimum, mandatory standards.

In response to criticism of the 1970 Model Code, the ABA appointed a Special Commission on Evaluation of Professional Standards (the Kutak Commission) to study and revise the rules. After wide debate within the legal community, the ABA finally adopted the Model Rules of Professional Conduct (Model Rules) in 1983. The Model Rules, which have a simpler structure, have been adopted by many states, often with some modifications. However, some states have retained rules patterned after the 1970 Model Code of Professional Responsibility.

More recently, in 1992, the ABA adopted several changes to the Model Rules as recommended by the ABA's Commission on Evaluation of Disciplinary Enforcement (the McKay Commission), which focused predominantly on disciplinary procedures. Minor amendments were made in 1994.

Throughout the late 1970s and the 1980s, the ABA continued to make recommendations regarding organizational structure and procedural systems to govern attorney discipline. These recommendations are called Model Rules for Lawyer Disciplinary Enforcement.

The ABA and most state regulatory entities occasionally issue ethics opinions that are intended to explain or clarify the rules. An ethics opinion may be written as a general statement of policy concerning application of a rule, or it may be issued in response to a specific question about a rule. Ethics opinions are merely advisory and carry no binding force of law.

b. What Do Rules of Professional Responsibility Look Like?

Most rules of professional responsibility look much like a statute, a set of rules of procedure, or a uniform or model act. The 1983 Model Rules of Professional Conduct begin with a preamble on a lawyer's responsibilities, a scope note, and a terminology section. Thereafter, the rules are divided into eight parts: parts 1 through 4 address a lawyer's role in the practice of law (such as attorney-client relationships and the attorney as counselor and advocate), and parts 5 through 8 address related matters (such as the structure and responsibilities of law firms and the provision of pro bono legal service). Some rules set mandatory standards of conduct (for example, a lawyer shall not commingle client funds), and some set aspirational guidelines (for example, a lawyer may serve as guardian of a client if the client cannot adequately protect his or her own interests).

The format of a rule and its related materials varies. Each rule from the 1983 Model Rules is followed by comments, which are written by the ABA advisory committee and explain the application of the rules. See Illustration 10-13 on page 357. Although most of the governing principles are similar in both the 1970 Model Code and in the 1983 Model Rules, the 1970 Code used a different three-part format (Canons, Ethical Considerations, and Disciplinary Rules). Illustration 10-14 on pages 358-359 shows Canon 7 and DR 7-104 of the 1970 ABA Model Code. State and local rules may follow the format of the 1983 ABA Model Rules or the 1970 ABA Model Code, or they may have yet another organizational scheme. See Exhibit 10.3 on page 360.

For the Canoga case, an important ethical issue is whether Ms. Canoga's attorney is permitted to contact other employees of the orchestra or whether her attorney must deal only with the attorney representing the orchestra. Illustration 10-15 on page 361 shows Rule 16-402 of the New Mexico Rules of Professional Conduct, which addresses this issue.

2. Why Would You Research a Particular Rule of Professional Responsibility?

Because the ABA is a voluntary association to which only a portion of all lawyers belong, the standards set by the ABA are not binding by themselves on any attorney. However, the rules adopted by the regulatory state entity

Illustration 10-13

Model Rules of Professional Conduct Rule 4.2 cmt. (1994).

RULE 4.2 COMMUNICATION WITH PERSON REPRESENTED BY COUNSEL

In representing a client, a lawyer shall not communicate about the subject of the representation with a party the lawyer knows to be represented by another lawyer in the matter, unless the lawyer has the consent of the other lawyer or is authorized by law to do so.

Comment

[1] This Rule does not prohibit communication with a party, or an employee or agent of a party, concerning matters outside the representation. For example, the existence of a controversy between a government agency and a private party, or between two organizations, does not prohibit a lawyer for either from communicating with nonlawyer representatives of the other regarding a separate matter. Also, parties to a matter may communicate directly with each other and a lawyer having independent justification for communicating with the other party is permitted to do so. Communications authorized by law include, for example, the right of a party to a controversy with a government agency to speak with government officials about the matter.

[2] In the case of an organization, this Rule prohibits communications by a lawyer for one party concerning the matter in representation with persons having a managerial responsibility on behalf of the organization, and with any other person whose act or omission in connection with that matter may be imputed to the orga-

77

Rules 4.3 & 4.4 **ABA MODEL RULES**

nization for purposes of civil or criminal liability or whose statement may constitute an admission on the part of the organization. If an agent or employee of the organization is represented in the matter by his or her own counsel, the consent by that counsel to a communication will be sufficient for purposes of this Rule. Compare Rule 3.4(f).

[3] This rule also covers any person, whether or not a party to a formal proceeding, who is represented by counsel concerning the matter in question.

Model Code Comparison

This Rule is substantially identical to DR 7-104(A)(1).

Illustration 10-14 Model Code of Professional Responsibility Canon 7, EC 7-18, DR 7-104 (1980).

CANON 7

A Lawyer Should Represent a Client Zealously Within the Bounds of the Law

SERVING AS THE CLIENT'S ADVOCATE

EC 7-1 The duty of a lawyer, both to his client[1] and to the legal system, is to represent his client zealously[2] within the bounds of the law,[3] which includes Disciplinary Rules and enforceable professional

1. "The right to be heard would be, in many cases, of little avail if it did not comprehend the right to be heard by counsel. Even the intelligent and educated layman has small and sometimes no skill in the science of law." Powell v. Alabama, 287 U.S. 45, 68-69, 77 L. Ed. 158, 170, 53 S. Ct. 55, 64 (1932).

2. *Cf.* ABA CANON 4.

"At times . . . [the tax lawyer] will be wise to discard some arguments and he should exercise discretion to emphasize the arguments which in his judgment are most likely to be persuasive. But this process involves legal judgment rather than moral attitudes. The tax lawyer should put aside private disagreements with Congressional and Treasury policies. His own notions of policy, and his personal view of what the law should be, are irrelevant. The job entrusted to him by his client is to use all his learning and ability to protect his client's rights, not to help in the process of promoting a better tax system. The tax lawyer need not accept his client's economic and social opinions, but the client is paying for technical attention and undivided concentration upon his affairs. He is equally entitled to performance unfettered by his attorney's economic and social predilections." Paul, *The Lawyer as a Tax Adviser,* 25 ROCKY MT. L. REV. 412, 418 (1953).

3. *See* ABA CANONS 15 and 32.

ABA Canon 5, although only speaking of one accused of crime, imposes a similar obligation on the lawyer: "[T]he lawyer is bound, by all fair and honorable means, to present every defense that the law of the land permits, to the end that no person may be deprived of life or liberty, but by due process of law."

"Any persuasion or pressure on the advocate which deters him from planning and carrying out the litigation on the basis of 'what, within the framework of the law, is best for my client's interest?' interferes with the obligation to represent the client fully within the law.

"This obligation, in its fullest sense, is the heart of the adversary process. Each attorney, as an advocate, acts for and seeks that which in his judgment is best for his client, within the bounds authoritatively established. The advocate does not *decide* what is just in this case—he would be usurping the function of the judge and jury—he acts for and seeks for his client that which he is entitled to under the law. He can do no less and properly represent the client." Thode, *The Ethical Standard for the Advocate,* 39 TEXAS L. REV. 575, 584 (1961).

"The [Texas public opinion] survey indicates that distrust of the lawyer can be traced directly to certain factors. Foremost of these is a basic misunderstanding of the function of the lawyer as an advocate in an adversary system.

"Lawyers are accused of taking advantage of 'loopholes' and 'technicalities' to win. Persons who make this charge are unaware, or do not understand, that the lawyer is hired to win, and if he does not exercise every legitimate effort in his client's behalf, then he is betraying a sacred trust." Rochelle & Payne, *The Struggle for Public Understanding,* 25 TEXAS B.J. 109, 159 (1962).

"The importance of the attorney's undivided allegiance and faithful service to one accused of crime, irrespective of the attorney's personal opinion as to the guilt of his client, lies in Canon 5 of the American Bar Association Canon of Ethics.

"The difficulty lies, of course, in ascertaining whether the attorney has been guilty of an error of judgment, such as an election with respect to trial tactics, or has otherwise been actuated by his conscience or belief that his client should be convicted in any event. All too frequently courts are called upon to review actions of defense counsel which are, at the most, errors of judgment, not properly reviewable on habeas corpus unless the trial is a farce and a mockery of justice which requires the court to intervene. . . . But when defense counsel, in a truly adverse proceeding, admits that his conscience would not permit him to adopt certain customary trial procedures, this extends beyond the realm of judgment and strongly suggests an invasion of constitutional rights." Johns v. Smyth, 176 F. Supp. 949, 952 (E.D. Va. 1959), *modified,* United States ex rel. Wilkins v. Banmiller, 205 F. Supp. 123, 128, n. 5 (E.D. Pa. 1962), *aff'd,* 325 F. 2d 514 (3d Cir. 1963), *cert. denied,* 379 U.S. 847, 13 L. Ed. 2d 51, 85 S. Ct. 87 (1964).

"The adversary system in law administration bears a striking resemblance to the competitive economic system. In each we assume that the individual through partisanship or through self-interest will strive mightily for his side, and that kind of striv-

277

Illustration 10-14 *(continued)*

tional standards set forth in *Brady* and *Agurs* and still be in violation of DR 7-103(B). See *State v. Harwood,* 94 Idaho 615, 495 P. 2d 160, 162 (1972), in which the court stated that DR 7-103 and EC 7-13 imposed a duty on the prosecution "to make available all evidence which tends to aid in ascertaining the truth."

COMMUNICATING WITH ONE OF ADVERSE INTEREST

EC 7-18 The legal system in its broadest sense functions best when persons in need of legal advice or assistance are represented by their own counsel. For this reason a lawyer should not communicate on the subject matter of the representation of his client with a person he knows to be represented in the matter by a lawyer, unless pursuant to law or rule of court or unless he has the consent of the lawyer for that person.[30] If one is not represented by counsel, a lawyer representing another may have to deal directly with the unrepresented person; in such an instance, a lawyer should not undertake to give advice to the person who is attempting to represent himself,[31] except that he may advise him to obtain a lawyer.

DR 7-104 Communicating With One of Adverse Interest.[74]

(A) During the course of his representation of a client a lawyer shall not:

(1) Communicate or cause another to communicate on the subject of the representation with a party he knows to be represented by a lawyer in that matter unless he has the prior consent of the lawyer representing such other party[75] or is authorized by law to do so.

(2) Give advice to a person who is not represented by a lawyer other than the advice to secure counsel,[76] if the interests of such person are or have a reasonable possibility of being in conflict with the interests of his client.[77]

TEXTUAL AND HISTORICAL NOTES

In the tentative draft (October 1968) and the preliminary draft (January 1969), EC VII-18 and EC 7-18, respectively, read as

30. *See* ABA CANON 9.

31. *Id.*

74. "*Rule 12*. . . . A member of the State Bar shall not communicate with a party represented by counsel upon a subject of controversy, in the absence and without the consent of such counsel. This rule shall not apply to communications with a public officer, board, committee or body." CAL. BUSINESS AND PROFESSIONS CODE §6076 (West 1962).

75. *See* ABA CANON 9; *cf. ABA Opinions* 124 (1934), 108 (1934), 95 (1933), and 75 (1932); *also see* In re Schwabe, 242 Or. 169, 174–75, 408 P.2d 922, 924 (1965).

"It is clear from the earlier opinions of this committee that *Canon 9* is to be construed literally and does not allow a communication with an opposing party, without the consent of his counsel, though the purpose merely be to investigate the facts. *Opinions 117, 55, 66,*" *ABA Opinion* 187 (1938).

76. *Cf. ABA Opinion* 102 (1933).

77. *Cf.* ABA CANON 9 and *ABA Opinion* 58 (1931).

Exhibit 10.3 States Adopting Codes of Professional Responsibility Based on the ABA Model Rules or the ABA Model Code.

Modeled on the ABA Model Rules

Alabama	Kentucky	Oklahoma
Alaska	Louisiana	Pennsylvania
Arizona	Maryland	Rhode Island
Arkansas	Michigan	South Carolina
Colorado	Minnesota	South Dakota
Connecticut	Mississippi	Texas
Delaware	Missouri	Utah
District of Columbia	Montana	Washington
Florida	Nevada	West Virginia
Hawaii	New Hampshire	Wisconsin
Idaho	New Jersey	Wyoming
Indiana	New Mexico	Puerto Rico
Kansas	North Dakota	

Incorporating parts of the ABA Model Code and parts of the ABA Model Rules

Illinois
New York
North Carolina
Oregon
Virginia

NOTE: Other states may have codified rules that are not based on either of the ABA model codes.

(that is, the regulatory commission, ethics board, committee, bar association, or other entity authorized to do so) are mandatory for lawyers licensed in that state.

The regulatory state entity establishes an enforcement mechanism that usually involves a disciplinary committee or similar body that licenses lawyers and enforces the rules of professional responsibility. This body hears complaints regarding allegations of professional misconduct, issues decisions, and disciplines noncomplying lawyers. In addition to the regulatory state entity, local bar associations also may have ethics committees that hear complaints about attorney misconduct and make findings and recommendations to the state authorities. Sanctions for violations of ethical or professional standards include public or private censure, suspension of one's license to practice law, or disbarment.

Violations of ethical or professional standards also may expose an attorney to liability to the client for malpractice. In assessing the seriousness of the misconduct and in determining liability, the courts often look to the rules of professional responsibility enforced by the state regulatory entity. In some circumstances, professional misconduct also can result in criminal penalties. In short, failure to meet professional standards not only harms the client and

Illustration 10-15 N.M. Rules of Professional Conduct Rule 16-402 cmt. (1994).

16-402. Communication with person represented by counsel.

In representing a client, a lawyer shall not communicate about the subject of the representation with a party the lawyer knows to be represented by another lawyer in the matter, unless the lawyer has the consent of the other lawyer or is authorized by law to do so. Except for persons having a managerial responsibility on behalf of the organization, an attorney is not prohibited from communicating directly with employees of a corporation, partnership or other entity about the subject matter of the representation even though the corporation, partnership or entity itself is represented by counsel.

COMMENT TO MODEL RULES

Compiler's notes. — The New Mexico rule differs from the ABA model rule in that the New Mexico version adds the second sentence.

ABA COMMENT:

This Rule does not prohibit communication with a party, or an employee or agent of a party, concerning matters outside the representation. For example, the existence of a controversy between a government agency and a private party, or between two organizations, does not prohibit a lawyer for either from communicating with nonlawyer representatives of the other regarding a separate matter. Also, parties to a matter may communicate directly with each other and a lawyer having independent justification for communicating with the other party is permitted to do so. Communications authorized by law include, for example, the right of a party to a controversy with a government agency to speak with government officials about the matter.

In the case of an organization, this Rule prohibits communications by a lawyer for one party concerning the matter in representation with persons having a managerial responsibility on behalf of the organization, and with any other person whose act or omission in connection with that matter may be imputed to the organization for purposes of civil or criminal liability or whose statement may constitute an admission on the part of the organization. If an agent or employee of the organization is represented in the matter by his or her own counsel, the consent by that counsel to a communication will be sufficient for purposes of this Rule. Compare Rule 3.4(f) [16-304F].

This Rule also covers any person, whether or not a party to a formal proceeding, who is represented by counsel concerning the matter in question.

COMPILER'S ANNOTATIONS

Taking statement from defendant without notice to attorney. — Obtainment by the prosecuting attorney of defendant's statement without informing his attorney of the impending interview and thus giving the attorney a reasonable opportunity to be present at the interview is unethical conduct by the prosecution. United States v. Thomas, 474 F.2d 110 (10th Cir.), cert. denied, 412 U.S. 932, 93 S. Ct. 2758, 37 L. Ed. 2d 160 (1973).

Rule applies even if other party initiates contact. — The proscriptions of this rule apply equally to situations when the party represented by another attorney may initiate the contact with opposing counsel. In re Herkenhoff, 116 N.M. 622, 866 P.2d 350 (1993).

Cannot be offered into evidence. — Once a criminal defendant has either retained an attorney or had an attorney appointed for him by the court, any statement obtained by interview from the defendant may not be offered in evidence for any purpose unless the accused's attorney was notified of the interview which produced the statement and was given a reasonable opportunity to be present. United States v. Thomas, 474 F.2d 110 (10th Cir.), cert. denied, 412 U.S. 932, 93 S. Ct. 2758, 37 L. Ed. 2d 160 (1973).

Jurisdiction over assistant U.S. attorney. — The New Mexico Disciplinary Board, and not the United States District Court, was the appropriate forum for adjudicating a claim against an assistant United States attorney permitted to practice solely by virtue of his New Mexico license. In re Doe, 801 F. Supp. 478 (D.N.M. 1992).

Federal removal not proper. — Assistant United States attorney could not properly remove disciplinary proceeding under this rule to federal court under 28 U.S.C. § 1442, and case was remanded accordingly to the New Mexico disciplinary board. In re Gorence, 810 F. Supp. 1234 (D.N.M. 1992).

Am. Jur. 2d, A.L.R. and C.J.S. references. — 7 Am. Jur. 2d Attorneys at Law § 60.

Communication with party represented by counsel as ground for disciplining attorney, 26 A.L.R.4th 102.

Right of attorney to conduct ex parte interviews with corporate party's nonmanagement employees, 50 A.L.R.4th 652.

Attorney's liability for nondisclosure or misrepresentation to third-party nonclients in private civil actions under federal securities laws, 112 A.L.R. Fed. 141.

7 C.J.S. Attorney and Client §§ 77 to 87.

16-403. Dealing with unrepresented person.

In dealing on behalf of a client with a person who is not represented by counsel, a lawyer shall not state or imply that the lawyer is disinterested. When the lawyer knows or the reputation of the profession, but also can carry grave personal consequences for the attorney.

3. How Do You Research Rules of Professional Responsibility?

In the hierarchy of sources regarding professional responsibility, the following sources carry mandatory authority: (1) the text of the state rules of professional responsibility and (2) state court cases interpreting the rules. The following sources carry persuasive authority: (1) comments of the advisory committee, (2) ethics opinions and disciplinary decisions issued by state agencies, (3) cases decided by courts from other jurisdictions regarding an identical or similar rule, (4) the ABA model rules or code of professional responsibility, and (5) ABA ethics opinions. Additionally, you should search secondary sources, such as treatises and legal periodicals, for commentary.

Exhibit 10.4 below shows the important sources for researching professional rules.

Exhibit 10.4 Sources for Researching Professional Rules.

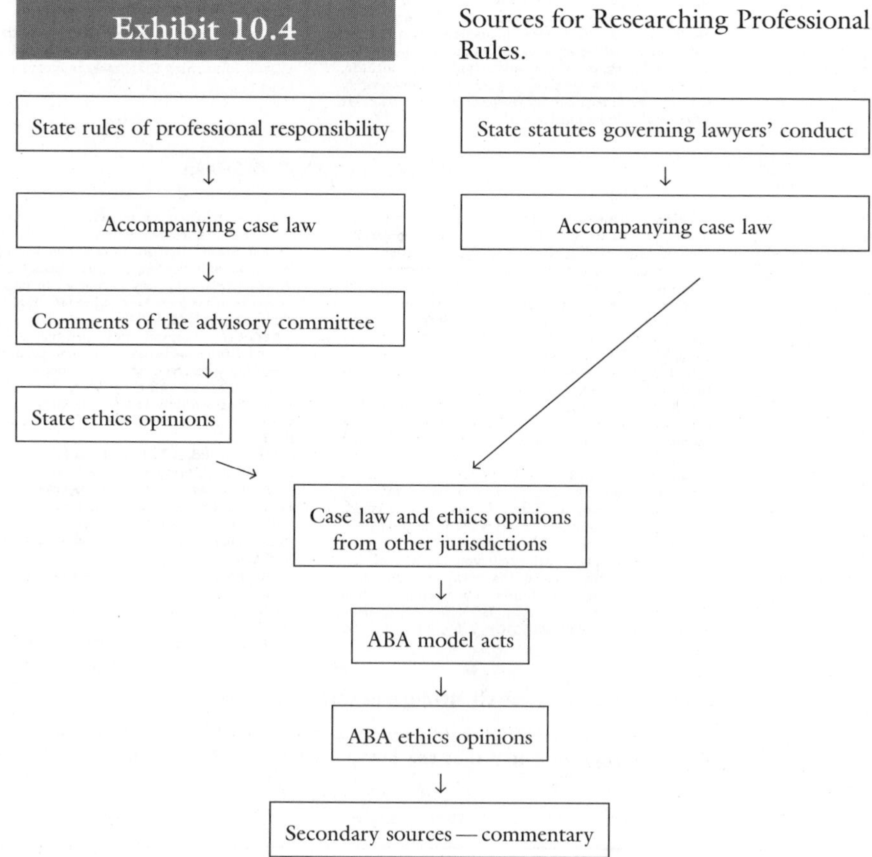

a. Researching State Rules of Professional Responsibility

For the majority of states that have adopted a comprehensive set of professional rules, the text of the rules is published in a state deskbook or other separately published official publication. A state deskbook typically contains the text of the rules and comments of the advisory committee or adopting authority, but not cases or references to other sources. Deskbooks are issued annually. Thus, very recent amendments and new rules will not be included.

Additionally, the annotated state code typically includes the rules, generally in a separate volume. You can find professional responsibility rules in annotated codes by searching the general index for the entire code, searching the separate index for the rules, and scanning the table of contents for the rules. Because the rules are not lengthy, it often is efficient to scan the table of contents. The rules are annotated in a manner similar to statutory sections, including any comments of the state advisory committee, the state statute's compiler's notes (which often indicate which ABA model, if any, that the state rule is based on), case annotations, historical notes of previous rules, and references to secondary sources. See Illustration 10-15 on page 361. The rules are updated using the same updating materials and advance legislative services that update the statutory sections of the code.

Proposed amendments and recently adopted rules of professional responsibility generally are published in legal newspapers or state bar journals. These publications also may contain comments explaining the new rules.

For the Canoga case, the New Mexico Rules of Professional Conduct are published in a separate section of the *New Mexico Statutes Annotated.* To research the issue of whether an attorney may contact an employee of a defendant, you can use either the index for the Rules of Professional Conduct or scan the table of contents. (The general index of the code directs you to the index for the professional rules.) Both searches are effective and lead you to Rule 16-402 of the Rules of Professional Conduct, "Communication with person represented by counsel." After reading the text of the rule itself, you should read the annotations, particularly the compiler's notes. The compiler's notes state that the New Mexico rule was modeled after the ABA Model Rule, but that the second sentence of Rule 16-402 differs from the Model Rule. In New Mexico, an attorney may communicate with an employee of an opposing party, unless the employee is an officer or manager.

To update your research of New Mexico Rule 16-402, you should check the looseleaf supplement and the *Advance Annotations and Rules Service* pamphlets of the *New Mexico Statutes Annotated.* Neither contained any changes to the rule or any additional cases that address this issue.

b. Researching State Cases Interpreting Rules of Professional Responsibility

Courts construe and apply rules of professional responsibility, just as they construe statutes. Some cases arise in the context of a disciplinary action brought against an attorney for violation of a rule of professional responsibility. Others arise from a civil claim brought by a client based on attorney malpractice. Still others arise from state or federal prosecution for criminal activities that also violate rules of professional responsibility. Only the decisions from your jurisdiction are mandatory primary authority.

In those states that include the rules of professional responsibility as part of their annotated code, the code annotations contain digests of cases. You also can use the sources discussed in Chapter 6, including West's key number digests (usually under the heading "attorney and client") and online research tools.

For the Canoga case, there is one pertinent New Mexico case digested under Rule 16-402 in the annotations, *In re Herkenhoff,* 116 N.M. 622, 866 P.2d 350 (1993). It discusses when an attorney may communicate with a party represented by counsel, but does not specifically address whether an attorney may communicate with an employee of an opposing party. See Illustration 10-15 on page 361.

c. Researching State Ethics Opinions and Disciplinary Decisions

The regulatory state entity may issue ethics opinions and disciplinary decisions on questions arising under the state's rule of professional responsibility. Ethics opinions are statements made by the regulatory body to clarify or explain a rule. Opinions are not binding. Disciplinary decisions are rendered by the state regulatory body to resolve complaints of unprofessional conduct brought against an attorney. If the attorney is found in breach of a professional rule, the state regulatory body may impose sanctions. The decisions are binding. These decisions and ethics opinions may help you interpret a professional rule.

State codes sometimes contain references in the annotations to state board disciplinary decisions or ethics opinions. However, the text of the opinions and decisions is not easy to find. Ethics opinions and disciplinary decisions may be published in state bar association journals or in legal newspapers. For example, the New York State Bar Association publishes *Opinions of the Committees on Professional Ethics of the Association of the Bar of the City of New York and the New York County Lawyers' Association,* which collects the ethics opinions and disciplinary decisions construing the New York state, city, and county codes of professional conduct; this set includes some materials selected from other states.

For the Canoga case, no state ethics opinions and disciplinary decisions appear in the annotations for Rule 16-402, nor do any appear in other available sources.

d. The ABA Model Rules: Researching Persuasive Authority

If the state rules are based on ABA model rules or code, several sources related to the ABA model serve as persuasive authority: the text of the ABA model and the comments of the advisory committee, ABA ethics opinions, case law from other states that have adopted an identical or similar ABA rule, and commentary provided by respected scholars. The next section explains what these persuasive materials are, while the second section explains how to research them.

(1) Understanding the ABA Materials

The ABA model rules and code have no authority unless they have been adopted by your state. Therefore, you first need to know whether your state rule is based on an ABA model, and if so, which version—the 1970 Model Code or the 1983 Model Rules. You also need to know whether the specific state professional rule you are researching was adopted verbatim or differs significantly. This information typically is found in the state compiler's notes of the state rules.

For example, the compiler's notes shown in Illustration 10-15 on page 361 indicate that Rule 16-402 of the New Mexico Rules of Professional Conduct was modeled after the 1983 Model Rule. Compare the text of Rule 16-402 as shown in Illustration 10-15 with ABA Model Rule 4.2 as shown in Illustration 10-13 on page 357. You can see that the New Mexico rule differs significantly from the ABA version—the second sentence was added by the New Mexico Supreme Court before it adopted the state rule. In this case, the ABA Model Rules (and related interpretative materials to be discussed below) may serve as persuasive authority for resolving controversies involving the first sentence of Rule 16-402, but not the second sentence.

If your state's rule does track an ABA model provision and your jurisdiction has no pertinent case law, you may be able to find case law from other states that have adopted a rule that is identical or similar to the rule in your jurisdiction. If so, that case law will carry persuasive authority.

For the Canoga case, because New Mexico Rule 16-402 mirrors only part of Rule 4.2 of the ABA Model Rules, cases from other jurisdictions that have adopted Rule 4.2 first would provide persuasive authority only as to the first portion of the New Mexico rule.

To assist lawyers and courts in interpreting the rules, the ABA's Standing Committee on Ethics and Professional Responsibility issues formal and informal ethics opinions interpreting the Model Rules and, in the past, the Model Code. The ABA's formal opinions are statements of the committee that are intended to clarify a rule or to address subjects of general interest to the practicing bar. Informal opinions are responses to specific questions regarding particular factual situations. Although these opinions neither have the force of law nor carry enforceable professional sanctions, they often are used by state regulatory bodies and even by courts as persuasive authority in resolving questions involving attorney conduct.

Illustration 10-16 on page 366 is an excerpt of ABA Formal Opinion 359, issued in 1991. This opinion addresses whether "a lawyer representing a client in a matter adverse to a corporate party that is represented by another lawyer may, without the consent of the corporation's lawyer" contact a former employee. The focus here on a former employee is narrower than the issue

Illustration 10-16 ABA Comm. on Ethics and Professional Responsibility, Formal Op. 359 (1991).

AMERICAN BAR ASSOCIATION

STANDING COMMITTEE ON ETHICS AND PROFESSIONAL RESPONSIBILITY

Formal Opinion 91-359 **March 22, 1991**
Contact with Former Employee of Adverse Corporate Party

The prohibition of Rule 4.2 with respect to contacts by a lawyer with employees of an opposing corporate party does not extend to former employees of that party.

The Committee has been asked for its opinion whether a lawyer representing a client in a matter adverse to a corporate party that is represented by another lawyer may, without the consent of the corporation's lawyer, communicate about the subject of the representation with an unrepresented former employee of the corporate party.

The starting point of our inquiry is Model Rule of Professional Conduct 4.2, which states:

> In representing a client, a lawyer shall not communicate about the subject of the representation with a party the lawyer knows to be represented by another lawyer in the matter, unless the lawyer has the consent of the other lawyer or is authorized by law to do so.

The rule is, for purposes of the issue under discussion, substantially identical to DR 7-104(A)(1), which states as follows:

> (A) During the course of his representation of a client a lawyer shall not:
>
> (1) Communicate or cause another to communicate on the subject of the representation with a party he knows to be represented by a lawyer in that matter unless he has the prior consent of the lawyer representing such other party or is authorized by law to do so.

This opinion is based on the Model Rules of Professional Conduct and, to the extent indicated, the predecessor Model Code of Professional Responsibility of the American Bar Association. The laws, court rules, regulations, codes of professional responsibility and opinions promulgated in the individual jurisdictions are controlling.

posed in the Canoga case, yet the discussion provides some insight regarding the meaning and application of Rule 4.2 and its earlier counterpart, DR 7-104(A)(1). In addition to the committee's opinion concerning application of the ABA rule, the opinion cites cases that have construed the rule.

(2) Researching the ABA Materials and Secondary Sources

Various deskbooks contain the current version of the ABA's Model Rules (or the earlier Model Code) and the comments of the advisory committee. An example is *Selected Standards on Professional Responsibility* (1996), edited by Thomas D. Morgan and Ronald D. Rotunda. As with other deskbooks, the text is current only as of the date the manuscript was submitted for publication; it does not reflect recent changes or amendments. To find an applicable rule, you can either scan the table of contents of the rules or use the index. Some deskbooks include tables of cross-references between the Model Rules and the Model Code. See Illustration 10-17 on page 368. Deskbooks do not carry annotations of cases or other sources.

Treatises provide more comprehensive coverage of state and ABA materials. Most treatises are organized by rule or canon number. To find the pertinent rule or canon, you can either scan the table of contents or use the index. Many of these sources also contain cross-reference tables.

An example is *The Law of Lawyering: A Handbook on the Model Rules of Professional Conduct,* by Geoffrey C. Hazard, Jr. and W. William Hodes (2d ed. 1990-present). This two-volume looseleaf treatise contains the full text of the Model Rules and the Model Code, as well as the comments of the advisory committees. It also contains the author's commentary on the rules, including references to case law and ethics opinions. A special feature of this treatise is the "illustrative case" sections, which present hypothetical issues and explanations concerning application of the rules. See Illustration 10-18 on page 369. For some rules, a "supplemental authorities" section contains a listing of other secondary sources, including references to legal periodicals and treatises. *The Law of Lawyering* is organized by the 1983 Model Rules; you also can use the index or scan the table of contents to locate pertinent material.

ABA ethics opinions regarding the 1970 Model Code and the 1983 Model Rules are reported in *Recent Ethics Opinions,* which is published by the ABA Standing Committee on Ethics and Professional Responsibility. This source includes formal and informal ethics opinions, commentary on various ethical problems and their historical development, and references to court decisions and opinions of state and local disciplinary agencies. Recent opinions, indexes, and cross-reference tables are contained in the *Recent Ethics Opinions* looseleaf binder. Older ethics opinions are compiled in separate volumes; these predecessor titles are *Informal Opinions, Formal and Informal Opinions,* and *Opinions of the Committee on Professional Ethics with the Canons of Professional Ethics Annotated and Canons of Judicial Ethics Annotated.*

Additional commentary sources on the rules of professional responsibility include the following:

Illustration 10-17 Cross-Reference Table, *ABA Model Rules of Professional Conduct.*

ABA MODEL RULES

TABLE A
(Continued)

ABA MODEL RULES	ABA MODEL CODE
Rule 3.8(c)	EC 7-11, EC 7-13, EC 7-18
Rule 3.8(d)	EC 7-11, EC 7-13, DR 7-103(B)
Rule 3.8(e)	None
Rule 3.8(f)	None
Rule 3.8(g)	EC 7-14120
Advocate in Nonadjudicative Proceedings	
Rule 3.9	EC 7-11, EC 7-15, EC 7-16, EC 8-4, EC 8-5, DR 7-106(B)(2), DR 9-101(C)
Truthfulness to Others	
Rule 4.1	EC 7-5, DR 7-102(A)(3), (4), (5) & (7), DR 7-102(B)
Communication with Represented Persons	
Rule 4.2	EC 2-30, EC 7-18, DR 7-104(A)(1)
Dealing with Unrepresented Persons	
Rule 4.3	EC 2-3, EC 7-18, DR 7-104(A)(2)
Respect for Rights of Third Persons	
Rule 4.4	EC 7-10, EC 7-14, EC 7-21, EC 7-25, EC 7-29,

American Bar Association, Center for Professional Responsibility, *Annotated Model Rules of Professional Conduct* (1995) (organized by ABA Model Rules; contains text of Model Rules, commentary, and references to case law).

American Bar Foundation, *Annotated Code of Professional Responsibility* (1979) (organized by Canons of the ABA Model Code; contains text of Model Code, commentary, and references to case law).

ABA/BNA Lawyers' Manual on Professional Conduct (1983-present) (organized by topic based on the Model Rules; contains text of Model Rules, Model Code, commentary on the Model Rules and state professional rules based on the ABA model codes, case digests, digests of recent ABA and state ethics opinions, text of ethics opinions).

Illustration 10-18

2 Geoffrey C. Hazard, Jr. & W. William Hodes, *The Law of Lawyering: A Handbook on the Model Rules of Professional Conduct* § 4.2:106 (Supp. 1993).

Thus, when Rules 4.2 and 3.4(f) are read together, it appears that a lawyer *opposing* an organization is prohibited from contacting the control group or those present employees who were direct actors in the underlying transaction or who could "bind" the organization with their statements. Correspondingly, a lawyer appearing *for* the organization is permitted to "request" all employees to refuse to discuss the matter except in formal depositions or in the lawyer's presence. See Illustrative Case 4.2:106.

§4.2:106 Illustrative Case: Interviewing an Employee of an Opposing Party in Litigation

> Lawyer L is litigating a products liability action against a major producer of home appliances. After considerable discovery has been taken, L sends an investigator to the home of J, one of the company's janitors, to learn information about certain plastic parts the company has claimed were discarded.

As in Illustrative Case 4.2:102, it makes no difference that L has not gone to interview the janitor himself. If the contact is improper, L will have violated Rule 8.4(a) by procuring a violation of Rule 4.2 through the acts of another.[0.1] Furthermore, since the investigator is in his employ, L will also have violated Rule 5.3 regarding nonlawyer assistants. Whether the contact *is* improper is difficult to say, however.

0.1. It goes without saying that if *ex parte* communication with an employee is improper, *a fortiori* it would be improper to invite the employee surreptitiously to provide copies of the employer's documents. See *In re Shell Oil Refinery*, 144 F.R.D. 75 (E.D.La. 1992), where the court avoided deciding whether the particular employee was "off limits" under Rule 4.2 (the issue discussed in §4.2:105), holding instead that clandestine "discovery" was incompatible with the formal and adversary discovery regime operative in the federal courts. Compare Illustrative Case 3.4:402.

National Reporter on Legal Ethics and Professional Responsibility (1982-present) (organized by state; contains text of state professional rules, text of state ethics opinions, and some case law).

Encyclopedias and law review articles also contain discussions of professional rules, and they typically contain references to case law concerning the rules.

e. Summary of the Canoga Case

For the Canoga case, the attorney representing Ms. Canoga may need to question the officers and manager of the orchestra, as well as other employees. To determine whether it is permissible to do so, you would study Rule 16-402, one of the Rules of Professional Conduct as promulgated by the New Mexico Supreme Court and published in the *New Mexico Statutes Annotated*. See Illustration 10-15 on page 361. As explained by the state compiler's notes, although Rule 16-402 was based on ABA Model Rule 4.2, a second sentence was added to the New Mexico rule; it provides that an attorney is not prohibited from contacting nonmanagerial employees, even if the corporation is represented by counsel.

Because the ABA Model Rule and the New Mexico professional rule differ as to the second sentence, the ABA Model Rule and its related comments and annotations, case law from other states, and ABA ethics opinions provided no assistance in interpreting the second sentence of the state rule.

f. *Shepard's Professional and Judicial Conduct Citations*

Shepard's Professional and Judicial Conduct Citations cites cases or opinions interpreting the professional rules. The cited sources include the ABA Model Rules, the ABA Model Code, the Formal and Informal Opinions, and the Code of Judicial Conduct. Citing sources include cases, state rules of professional conduct, and selected secondary sources. You may search *Shepard's Professional and Judicial Conduct Citations* by using either the rule or opinion number.

In the listings of ethics opinions, there are abbreviations unique to this *Shepard's*, "F" (formal opinion) or "I" (informal opinion). The entries include citations to recent ethics opinions and cases.

Illustration 10-19 on page 371 shows recent entries for Model Rule 4.2. Note the reference to New Mexico Rule 16-402 and a few cases.

g. Researching Rules of Professional Responsibility Online Using LEXIS as an Example

The ABA Model Rules and the Model Code can be researched using either WESTLAW or LEXIS. However, not all state rules of professional responsibility and only a few ethics opinions are included online. Cases interpreting

Illustration 10-19

Shepard's Professional and Judicial Conduct Citations.

MODEL RULES OF PROFESSIONAL CONDUCT **Rule 4.4**

618A2d384
622A2d237
633A2d960
640A2d349
656A2d434

New Mexico

Rule 16-402
847FS966
116NM624
866P2d352

North Dakota

Rule 4.2
484NW508

Oklahoma

Rule 4.2
940F2d1341
829P2d960
61OBJ3428
46OkLR28

Pennsylvania

Rule 4.2
769FS902
848FS1202
134FRD120
157FRD340
160FRD495
138PaL767
53PitL292
53PitL335
53PitL356
53PitL459
53PitL515
54PitL471
36VR1343

Rhode Island

Rule 4.2
183BRW33

Texas

Rule 4.02
956F2d103
967F2d1023
880FS498
880SW33
891SW763
Subd. a
956F2d103
983F2d618
875SW787
Subd. d
956F2d103

Utah

Rule 4.2
139FRD414
1991UtLR [647

Washington

Rule 4.2
117Wsh2d [886
64WAp396
822P2d210
824P2d1243

Wisconsin

Rule 20:4.2
165Wis2d [729
171Wis2d54
171Wis2d68
478NW590
489NW922
490NW16
530NW388
531NW464
1991WLR [1150

Wyoming

Rule 4.2
809P2d268
843P2d614
880P2d108

Rule 4.3

Rule 4.3
843F2d657
885FS1480
141FRD562
149FRD109
32CA4th99
37CaR2d [845
29GSB105
79VaL1904

Alabama

Rule 4.3
53Law312

Connecticut

Rule 4.3
65CBJ88
66CBJ219

Delaware

Rule 4.3
593A2d [1015

Florida

Rule 4-4.3
42FLR453

Illinois

Rule 4.3
8F3d606

Indiana

Rule 4.3
67ILJ554

Kansas

Rule 226
Subd. 4.3
248Kan194
255Kan800
877P2d425

Louisiana

Rule 4.3
585So2d516

Maryland

Rule 4.3
51MdL289

Michigan

Rule 4.3
768FS1212
72MBJ657
72MBJ1304
74MBJ166
74MBJ177

Mississippi

Rule 4.3
587So2d232
60MLJ578

Missouri

Rule 4.3
34StLJ41

New Hampshire

Rule 4.3
136NH665
622A2d [1214

New Jersey

Rule 4.3
766FS264
134FRD94
145FRD356
134NJ303
247NJS321
252NJS514
254NJS244
257NJS160
261NJS204
589A2d183
600A2d167
603A2d165
607A2d [1389
618A2d385
633A2d964

Pennsylvania

Rule 4.3
781FS344
160FRD494
138PaL767
53PitL340
Subd. a
160FRD494
Subd. c
160FRD494

Texas

Rule 4.03
880SW46

Utah

Rule 4.3
139FRD418

Wisconsin

Rule 20:4.3
165Wis2d [733
478NW592

Wyoming

Rule 4.3
843P2d622

Rule 4.4

Rule 4.4
141FRD562
105HLR815
106HLR [1247
66SCL1005

Alabama

Rule 4.4
53Law312

Arizona

ER 4.4
174Az149
178Az549
847P2d1096
875P2d782

Connecticut

Rule 4.4
234Ct543
65CBJ90
66CBJ235

Delaware

Rule 4.4
583A2d [1345

District of Columbia

Rule 4.4
81Geo2497

Florida

Rule 4-4.4
618So2d203
641So2d400
644So2d506
42FLR452

Illinois

Rule 4.4
8F3d606
218IlA880
161IlD491
578NE1137

Indiana

Rule 4.4
148FRD255
613NE846
640NE1056
649NE1026
66NDL729
69NDL234

Kentucky

Rule 4.4
78KLJ787

Louisiana

Rule 4.4
585So2d516
597So2d445
634So2d330

Maryland

Rule 4.4
329Md258
619A2d103
51MdL77

Michigan

Rule 4.4
143FRD124
71MBJ423
72MBJ68

Minnesota

Rule 4.4
529NW685

Mississippi

Rule 4.4
605So2d36
618So2d [1295
621So2d222
625So2d420

Missouri

Rule 4.4
808SW357
34StLJ41

New Hampshire

Rule 4.4
137NH115
137NH574
626A2d397
630A2d777

New Jersey

Rule 4.4
145FRD356

New Mexico

Rule 16-404
112NM133
116NM624
812P2d787
866P2d352
866P2d353

North Dakota

Rule 4.4
524NW105

Oklahoma

Rule 4.4
796FS1456

Pennsylvania

Rule 4.4
98DLR674
136PaL [1815

Texas

Rule 4.04
880SW46
Subd. a
6F3d339
Subd. b
887SW936
887SW946
¶ 1
832SW107

Utah

Rule 4.4
139FRD418

Washington

Rule 4.4
26Goz436

Wyoming

Rule 4.4
805P2d863

125

professional rules and related civil or criminal issues may be searched in case law databases using standard search methods. This section focuses on the LEXIS professional rules databases.

There are three points of entry for researching ethics materials on LEXIS. The ABA library contains several pertinent files, including files for formal ethics opinions (FOPIN), informal opinions (INFOP), and the Codes of Professional Responsibility and Judicial Conduct (CODES). The ETHICS file combines all of the above documents.

There also is an ETHICS library, which is even more comprehensive. It contains files that cover the rules of professional responsibility for states that publish their rules of professional responsibility as part of their code (ALLCDE); it also contains case law concerning rules of professional responsibility for each of the fifty states. These files contain the same information found in the statutory code files and the state case law files. In the ETHICS library, the individual state files are designated by applicable state abbreviation, (for example, NM for New Mexico). Additionally, the ETHICS library contains separate files for materials published by the American Bar Association, including the ABA Codes of Professional and Judicial Conduct (CODES), the ABA's formal opinions (FOPIN) and informal opinions (INFOP), as well as the ethics opinions of selected bar associations—California (CABAR), New York (NYBAR), and New York City (NYCBAR). Additionally, the ABAJNL file contains articles and feature materials published in the *ABA Journal,* such as the ABA's ethics opinions and proposed rules changes. Finally, the OMNI file combines all states' case law concerning rules of professional responsibility.

An additional approach is to use individual state code and case files. For example, to research the New Mexico Rules of Professional Conduct, the best starting point is the STATES library and the NMCODE file, because New Mexico publishes its rules of professional responsibility as part of the state code. This file is updated shortly after new statutory or rule provisions are published. Because the code file is based on the state annotated code, the rules of professional responsibility are accompanied by the same annotations found in the code: state compiler's notes, historical notes, case digests, digests of ethics opinions, and references to other sources. LEXIS includes the LINK feature, which permits you to jump from a cited source, or one referred to in the annotations, to its full text.

Once you have selected a pertinent database, you can enter either a natural language (Freestyle) or Boolean search. An effective Freestyle search is [can an employee's attorney contact other employees]. This search in NMCODE yielded several statutory sections and rules that addressed employee communication with attorneys, including Rule 16-402 in the New Mexico Rules of Professional Conduct. See Illustration 10-20 on page 373. An effective Boolean search would be: [attorney or lawyer w/25 communicat! or talk! or contact! w/25 employ!]. In this circumstance, the Freestyle search is easier to develop because an exact word match is not required; it is hard to anticipate what terms would be used in this issue.

Once you have read the rule, you should search relevant case law and perhaps ethics opinions, both of which may assist you in interpreting and

Illustration 10-20 New Mexico Rule 16-402, LEXIS.

```
                    LEVEL 1 - 11 OF 25 DOCUMENTS

                    NEW MEXICO RULES ANNOTATED
              Copyright (c) 1995 by The Michie Company
                        All rights reserved

 *THIS DOCUMENT IS CURRENT THROUGH ALL AMENDMENTS RECEIVED AS OF JAN. 1, 1995*

                    RULES OF PROFESSIONAL CONDUCT
                     ARTICLE 4.  OTHER THAN CLIENTS

                    R. Prof. Conduct Rule 16-402

Rule 16-402. Communication with person represented by counsel.

In representing a client, a lawyer shall not communicate about the subject of
the representation with a party the lawyer knows to be represented by another
lawyer in the matter, unless the lawyer has the consent of the other lawyer or
is authorized by law to do so. Except for persons having a managerial
responsibility on behalf of the organization, an attorney is not prohibited from
communicating directly with employees of a corporation, partnership or other
entity about the subject matter of the representation even though the
corporation, partnership or entity itself is represented by counsel.
```

applying the rule. To search for other cases, you also can search the case law databases, using the same techniques and databases studied earlier. It often is effective to use the rule number as a search.

4. What Else?

Specialized Rules of Professional Conduct. In 1971, the ABA adopted Standards Relating to the Administration of Criminal Justice, which regulate the role and conduct of prosecuting and defense attorneys involved in a criminal matter. These standards cover matters related to the function and roles of the prosecutor and defense counsel.

In 1972, the ABA first adopted the Model Code of Judicial Conduct, which regulates the conduct of judges; its most recent major amendments were adopted in 1990. These canons address such diverse matters as judicial decorum, independence of judgment, membership in organizations, and financial issues.

Additional *Shepard's Citations*. *Shepard's United States Citations, Statute Edition* also covers the Model Rules, the Model Code, and the Code of Judicial Conduct. The rules are Shepardized using the rule number as the "cited source." Only federal court decisions construing these professional rules are included. The decisions are listed under each rule number and are subdivided by the federal circuit in which the rendering court is located.

Proposed Rules. Drafts of new rules and the reports of studies that the ABA undertakes concerning new rules often are published as separate publications to permit the ABA membership to make comments about the proposed changes. Proposed amendments to the rules, recently adopted rules, and comments concerning the rule are published in the *ABA Journal.*

Drafting History. The ABA has published the *Legislative History of the Model Rules of Professional Conduct: Their Development in the ABA House of Delegates,* which provides additional insight into the meaning of the rules.

Other Media. As of early 1996, the sources discussed in this section appeared in the following media:

			Computer-Assisted Research		
	Paper	*CD-ROM*	*LEXIS*	*WESTLAW*	*Microform*
ABA Model Rules And Model Code	√	√	√	√	√
State professional rules	√	√	√	√	√
Shepard's Professional and Judicial Conduct Citations	√				

5. How Do You Cite Rules of Professional Responsibility?

Rules for citing the ABA acts of professional responsibility are governed by Rule 12.8.6 in *The Bluebook.* To cite a particular rule, first give the complete name of the act followed by the designation or type of rule (canon, rule, or standard), the rule number, and the year that the act was adopted, unless the act has incorporated subsequent amendments, in which case you would give the year of the last amendment. To cite a single rule, you would cite as follows:

for current state rule and comment:	N.M. Rules of Professional Conduct Rule 16-402 cmt. (1994).
for current ABA rule:	Model Rules of Professional Conduct Rule 4.2 (1994).
for 1970 Model Code, before amendments:	Model Code of Professional Responsibility DR 7-104(A)(1) (1970).

Citations to formal and informal opinions also are governed by Rule 12.8.6. They should include the name of the issuing body, the opinion number, and the year. For example:

ABA Comm. on Ethics and Professional Responsibility, Formal Op. 359 (1991).

D. CONCLUDING POINTS

Researching federal and state rules of procedure typically involves several sources. Deskbooks contain the text of the rules and comments of the drafting committee. Treatises contain the text of the rules with explanatory commentary and references to relevant case law and other secondary sources. To further research cases interpreting the federal rules, you can search the annotations found in the annotated codes, use the West reporters and digests, or use a specialty case reporter and digest system, such as the *Federal Rules Service* and the *Federal Rules Digest.* The research in any of these sources can be updated and expanded using the statute edition of the *Shepard's* for your jurisdiction. Local court rules may be found in the annotated codes, deskbooks, or specialty looseleafs, such as *Federal Local Court Rules.* Rules of procedure also can be searched online using the code databases of either LEXIS or WESTLAW.

Issues concerning the professional obligations of an attorney are governed by state rules of professional responsibility. These rules typically are published as part of the state codes and also may be published in state law deskbooks. To understand these rules, you should research case law, advisory committee comments, and state ethics opinions. Because state rules of professional responsibility often are based on the ABA model rules or code, the comments of the advisory committee, ABA ethics opinions, and case law from other jurisdictions that have adopted language based on the same ABA model may serve as persuasive authority or assist in interpreting state rules. These materials can be found in various paper sources. State rules of professional responsibility and the ABA materials also can be found online using WESTLAW or LEXIS.

11 Incorporate Nonlegal Materials

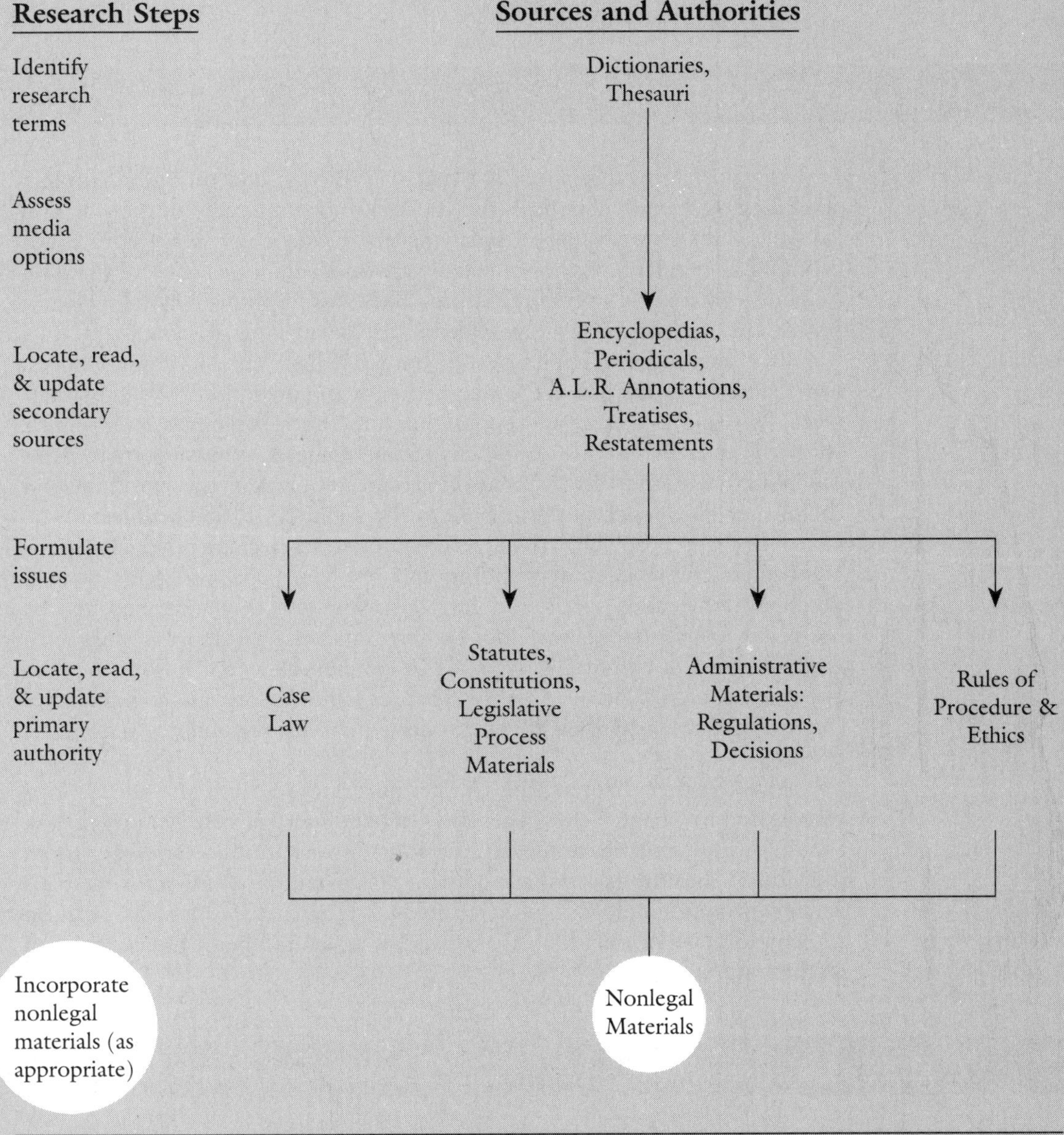

CORRECT • COMPREHENSIVE • CREDIBLE • COST-EFFECTIVE

Summary of Contents

A. Preliminary Points

Law is a normative discipline. Lawmakers prescribe and proscribe conduct according to the public policies they believe to be implicated in the situation (as well as their own values). As lawmakers decide cases, enact statutes, or promulgate regulations, they inevitably act on assumptions of fact regarding human behavior and events in nature. These assumptions generally go unstated, and they are only rarely tested in the lawmaking process.

Of course, other disciplines study human behavior and its consequences. For example, economists are concerned with the operations of the marketplace. Psychologists study why people commit crimes. Biologists and chemists study the effects of toxins on the environment. Because researchers in these disciplines state and test assumptions about people and the world around them, they have much to contribute to the solution of legal problems.

This chapter provides a basic introduction to researching nonlegal materials that are useful in understanding and resolving legal problems. Part B describes nonlegal materials, and Part C explains why these materials may be useful in client representation. Part D then examines several tools for nonlegal research that are commonly available in law libraries. Part E notes how to cite these sources. The goal of this chapter is not to provide an exhaustive treatment of nonlegal research, but to alert you to the possibilities of nonlegal research.

As with other chapters, this chapter illustrates research into the Canoga case, stated in Chapter 1 at pages 2-3. In handling that case, you might ask the following primarily nonlegal questions: How harmful is smoking to an individual's health? Is smoking addictive? Do employer no-smoking bans actually prompt employees to quit smoking? How intrusive is such a ban on the employee's personal life? The materials illustrated here suggest answers to these questions.

B. What Are Nonlegal Materials?

Every discipline has its own research methodology. Many disciplines rely on the scientific method or on observation, both of which differ from the legal methods discussed elsewhere in this text.

The scientific method is used not only by natural scientists, such as chemists and biologists, but also by social scientists, such as psychologists. The scientific method seeks to describe what occurs in human behavior or nature, explain why it occurs, and predict future events accordingly. The researcher begins with an observation about an unexplained behavior or event, formulates an explanation through inductive reasoning, predicts future behavior through deductive reasoning, and then verifies that prediction and the explanation through experimentation. If the prediction plays out consistently, the researcher concludes that the prediction is true. The results typically are presented in statistical or visual form.

An alternative (and often complementary) method is observation. Historians, anthropologists, and sociologists, among others, rely on careful observation of past or present events. This observation may be first- or second-hand, through the records created by others or machines. Results of this type of research may be statistical or narrative, depending on the nature of the observation.

Whatever the research methodology, the results of nonlegal research typically are published in journals, books, or (in some circumstances) online sources. In this respect, legal and nonlegal research resemble each other.

As examples of nonlegal materials, consider the following materials pertinent to the Canoga case: Illustration 11-1 on page 380 is the first page of a two-part article summarizing medical research on the adverse health effects of smoking, drawn from the *New England Journal of Medicine,* regarded as a leading journal in medicine. Illustration 11-2 on page 381 is a short pamphlet by the American Heart Association on the addictive effects of nicotine; it in turn refers to a report by the federal Surgeon General. Illustration 11-3 on page 382 is the beginning of a study on the impact of employer smoking bans on employee smoking practices, from *Public Health Reports,* a publication of the federal Department of Health and Human Services. Finally, Illustration 11-4 on page 383 reports the results of a poll on the issue of whether it is fair for an employer to fire an employee for smoking off-duty. Note that Illustrations 11-1 and 11-2 are both summaries of natural science research of various types, while Illustration 11-3 is a report of social science research reflecting the scientific method, and Illustration 11-4 reports data from a form of observation (polling).

C. Why Would You Research Nonlegal Materials?

While your primary expertise as a lawyer will be legal research, few problems are purely legal in nature. It will be in your client's best interest for you to understand any nonlegal dimensions of the situation. Whether you are advising a client, litigating a case on a client's behalf, or lobbying a legislature or agency for laws favoring your client's interest, nonlegal materials may provide important insights.

First, in advising a client about appropriate actions to take in light of legal rules, you may well conclude that the client has several options that are

Illustration 11-1

Jonathan E. Fielding, *Smoking: Health Effects and Control*, 313 New Eng. J. Med. 491 (1985).

MEDICAL PROGRESS

SMOKING: HEALTH EFFECTS AND CONTROL

(First of Two Parts)

JONATHAN E. FIELDING, M.D., M.P.H.

CIGARETTE smoking has been identified as the single most important source of preventable morbidity and premature mortality in each of the reports of the U.S. Surgeon General produced since 1964. The estimated annual excess mortality from cigarette smoking in the United States exceeds 350,000, more than the total number of American lives lost in World War I, Korea, and Vietnam combined and almost as many as were lost during World War II.[1] It is estimated that among the 565,000 annual deaths from coronary heart disease, 30 per cent, or 170,000 deaths, are attributable to smoking.[2] Furthermore, 30 per cent of the 412,000 annual cancer deaths — about 125,000 — are attributable to smoking, with 80 per cent resulting from carcinoma of the lung.[3] Chronic obstructive lung diseases such as chronic bronchitis and emphysema account annually for another 62,000 smoking-related deaths.[4] It has been estimated that an average of 5½ minutes of life is lost for each cigarette smoked, on the basis of an average reduction in life expectancy for cigarette smokers of five to eight years. For a 25-year-old man who smokes one pack per day (20 cigarettes), the reduction averages 4.6 years, whereas for a man of the same age who smokes two packs per day (40 cigarettes), 8.3 years of expected longevity are lost.[5] One recent analysis of mortality suggests that differences in the rates of cigarette smoking between men and women over the age of 30 are the overwhelming cause of male–female longevity differences and that increases in the difference in life expectancy between the sexes since 1930 are largely attributable to cigarette smoking.[6] Although the appraisal probably overstates the contribution of smoking to sex-based differences in longevity, smoking is probably responsible for some of the more than seven years' discrepancy in life expectancy between the sexes in the United States.

ECONOMIC COSTS

It is estimated that the total direct health care costs associated with smoking are in excess of $16 billion annually (these figures have been updated to represent 1985 dollars). Indirect losses attributable to smoking for lost productivity and earnings from excess morbidity, disability, and premature death are estimated at $37 billion annually.[7] These figures translate into an annual per capita social cost directly attributable to smoking of approximately $200; the economic burden on each nonsmoker for providing medical care for smoking-induced illness exceeds $100, paid primarily through taxes and health insurance premiums.[1] Smoking is responsible for one quarter of all the mortality caused by fire and accounts for close to $500 million in other losses.[8] Smoking-related fires claim over 1500 lives and injure another 4000 people annually, making smoking the nation's leading cause of fire deaths in apartments (38 per cent), hotels and motels (32 per cent), mobile homes (23 per cent), residential buildings (21 per cent), and private dwellings (17 per cent).[9]

From the University of California, Los Angeles, Schools of Public Health and Medicine. Reprint requests should be addressed to Dr. Fielding at the University of California, Los Angeles, School of Public Health, Los Angeles, CA 90024.

CORONARY HEART DISEASE

According to reasonable estimates from several investigators, 30 to 40 per cent of the 565,000 deaths from coronary heart disease each year can be attributed to cigarette smoking.[2] Some portion of the other cardiovascular mortality from diseases such as stroke, peripheral vascular disease, atherosclerosis at other sites, and other vascular problems is also attributable to smoking. Evidence from both cohort and case–control studies supports the statement in the 1983 Surgeon General's report that "cigarette smoking should be considered the most important of the known modifiable risk factors for coronary heart disease in the United States."[2] Ten major cohort studies, accounting for over 20 million person-years of observation in several countries, each revealed a higher incidence of myocardial infarction and death from coronary heart disease — averaging 70 per cent — in cigarette smokers than in nonsmokers. This set of studies also demonstrated that, whether in the United States, Canada, the United Kingdom, Scandinavia, or Japan, smokers as a group have excess mortality from coronary heart disease that is approximately 70 per cent above that of nonsmokers. The pooled data from five large studies showed that men 40 to 59 years of age who were smoking a pack or more per day at the time of initial examination had a risk for a first major coronary event that was 2.5 times as great as that of nonsmokers, with a strong dose–response relation.[10]

Studies both in the United States and abroad have demonstrated consistently that women whose smoking patterns are similar to those of men have a similar increased risk of death from coronary heart disease and for common morbidity from the disease, such as angina pectoris, as compared with nonsmokers.[2,11] The risk of death from coronary heart disease among both male and female smokers is increased by early

Illustration 11-2

American Heart Association, *Nicotine Addiction* (date unknown).

NICOTINE ADDICTION

When a person smokes a cigarette, the body responds immediately to the chemical nicotine in the smoke. Nicotine causes a short-term increase in blood pressure, heart rate, and the flow of blood from the heart. It also causes the arteries to narrow. Carbon monoxide reduces the amount of oxygen the blood can carry. This, combined with the effects produced by nicotine, creates an imbalance in the demand for oxygen by the cells and the amount of oxygen the blood is able to supply. Smoking further increases the amount of fatty acids, glucose, and various hormones in the blood.

There are several ways that cigarette smoking may increase the risk of developing hardening of the arteries and heart attacks. First, carbon monoxide may damage the inner walls of the arteries that encourages the buildup of fat on these walls. Over time, this causes the vessels to narrow and harden. Nicotine may also contribute to this process. Smoking also causes several changes in the blood. They include increased adhesiveness and clustering of platelets in the blood, shortened platelet survival, decreased clotting time, and increased thickness of the blood. These effects can lead to a heart attack.

The 1988 Surgeon General's Report, "Nicotine Addiction," concluded that:

* Cigarette and other forms of tobacco are addicting.

* Nicotine is the drug that causes addiction.

* Pharmacologic and behavioral characteristics that determine tobacco addiction are similar to those that determine addiction to drugs such as heroin and cocaine.

For additional information on this subject, contact your local American Heart Association office or call 1-800-242-8721.

tenable from a legal standpoint. Which of these should be chosen may well depend on their advisability from a nonlegal perspective. Rules of professional conduct encourage lawyers to advise clients about the economic, moral, social, and political dimensions of the representation. Model Rules of Professional Conduct Rule 2.1 (1995). The better informed you are on these dimensions, the stronger your advice will be. (Of course, if the situation requires extensive knowledge of a nonlegal field, you should involve an expert from that field.)

In the Canoga situation, for example, assume that you had been hired by the orchestra before it drafted its policy. Had you determined that the law gave the employer the option of restricting smoking at work, you still would want to consider whether the health risks were substantial enough to warrant the ban. Illustration 11-1 on page 380 would provide helpful background. In addition, Illustration 11-3 on page 382 would help you advise the orchestra as to whether a ban would be productive in reducing smoking by employees.

Second, in litigating a case for a client, you almost certainly will discover that the law raises certain issues of fact. Some factual issues are unique to your client's case, while others may be general matters of fact that researchers in other disciplines may have explored. In some cases, it will be worthwhile to verify the law's assumptions against the nonlegal research and to challenge or prove the law's assumptions as appropriate. You may choose to offer

Illustration 11-3

Lyle R. Petersen et al., *Employee Smoking Behavior and Attitudes Following a Restrictive Policy on Worksite Smoking in a Large Company,* 103 Pub. Health Rep. 115 (1988).

PAGE 2

15TH ARTICLE of Level 1 printed in FULL format.

1988 U.S. Department of Health and Human Services;
Public Health Reports

Public Health Rep 1988; 103:115-120

March, 1988 / April, 1988

SECTION: ARTICLES; General

LENGTH: 2750 words

TITLE: Employee Smoking Behavior Changes and Attitudes Following a Restrictive Policy on Worksite Smoking in a Large Company

AUTHOR: LYLE R. PETERSEN, MD, STEVEN D. HELGERSON, MD, MPH, CAROL M. GIBBONS, MS, CHANELLE R. CALHOUN, MPH, KATHERINE H. CIACCO, MPH, KAREN C. PITCHFORD, MPH

SYNOPSIS: A Connecticut insurance company adopted a policy prohibiting smoking in all work areas. Three months later, the authors assessed smoking behavior changes and attitudes of a sample of 1,210 employees, 56.6 percent of the total.

The survey showed that the policy of no smoking in the work areas did not markedly affect smoking cessation, that it reduced cigarette consumption for those who continued to smoke, that those who previously smoked most were most likely to reduce consumption, and that despite negative feelings about the policy by smokers, only 29 percent of smokers and 4 percent of nonsmokers wanted a worksite smoking policy eliminated.

During the 1-year prepolicy period, smoking prevalence decreased from 25.2 percent to 23.6 percent of the sample. During the 3-month postpolicy period, smoking prevalence decreased to 22.0 percent. During the prepolicy period, consumption did not change significantly (from 0.99 to 0.95 packs per day) and few smokers increased (11 percent) or decreased (13 percent) consumption. During the postpolicy period, consumption decreased by 32 percent to 0.67 packs per day, and 12 times as many smokers decreased (44 percent) as increased (3.5 percent) consumption. Of those who smoked at least two packs per day, 93 percent smoked less after the policy. Among nonsmokers, 70 percent thought the policy had a positive overall effect on the work environment, compared with 19 percent of smokers.

TEXT:
CIGARETTE SMOKING is considered the largest cause of preventable premature death and disability in our society. It is 1 of the 15 health priority areas spotlighted by the Public Health Service's Objectives for the Nation initiative[n1,n2]. The increasing awareness of the health consequences of smoking, particularly the possible danger of passively inhaled smoke by nonsmokers, has focused attention on smoking in the workplace[n3,n4].

Legislation regulates smoking in the workplace in 22 or more States. Three recent surveys indicate that 32 to 36 percent of business have enacted smoking policies[n5-n7]. Smoking policies within the private sector differ considerably in the extent to which they limit worksite smoking. Only a few large companies have banned smoking entirely from the workplace[n3].

testimony by an expert from the nonlegal discipline. Or you may incorporate nonlegal materials into your briefs to the tribunal hearing the case; such a brief is called a "Brandeis brief," after Justice Louis Brandeis of the United States Supreme Court, who pioneered its use while a practicing lawyer.

Illustration 11-4

Roper Center for Public Opinion, Survey re Employee Smoking, May 1992, *available in* DIALOG, POLL Database, File no. 013.

```
                                                                PAGE    1

                  Rank(R)                  Page(P)       Database    Mode
                  R 2 OF 5                 P 1 OF 2      POLL        Page

013   Some  companies  are trying to keep health care costs down by setting
rules  for  employee   behavior,  both  on  and  off  the job. At one such
company,  a  woman signed an agreement not to smoke  on or off the job and
she  was fired when it was discovered she was smoking at home. Do you think
it was fair or unfair to fire her?

Right/fair                                             29%
Wrong/unfair                                           68
It depends (vol.)                                       2
Don't know/refused                                      1

ORGANIZATION CONDUCTING SURVEY: PRINCETON SURVEY RESEARCH ASSOCIATES (PSRA)
SPONSOR:                        Family Circle Magazine
SOURCE:                         FAMILY CIRCLE MAGAZINE ETHICS POLL #2

SURVEY BEGINNING DATE: 05/01/92
                    (C) 1995 ROPER CTR FOR PUB OPINION RES  ALL RTS. RESERV.

                  R 2 OF 5                 P 2 OF 2      POLL        Page

SURVEY ENDING DATE:     05/07/92
SURVEY RELEASE DATE:    05/00/92

INTERVIEW METHOD:       Telephone
NO. OF RESPONDENTS:     750
SURVEY POPULATION:      National adult

DESCRIPTORS:            BUSINESS; RIGHTS; HEALTH; WORK; VALUES
                    (C) 1995 ROPER CTR FOR PUB OPINION RES  ALL RTS. RESERV.
```

In the Canoga case, for example, one of the issues raised is whether smoking, or more precisely nicotine addiction, is a disability under nondiscrimination statutes. Effectively analyzing this issue requires reliance on medical research into the phenomenon of nicotine addiction. The report referred to in Illustration 11-2 on page 381 would be one starting point.

Third, in lobbying for a favorable statute or administrative regulation on behalf of a client, you may find nonlegal materials useful. So that the law will achieve the desired results, legislatures and administrative agencies typically seek to understand the realm of behavior they are seeking to govern. Nonlegal materials may give you insights that may form a foundation for developing arguments or testimony to present.

In the Canoga situation, for example, if you represented a group of workers fearful of excessive employer interference with their smoking and no state statute addressed their concern, the poll presented in Illustration 11-4 above would provide support for the argument that the public disfavors employer regulation of off-duty smoking and that legislators should act accordingly.

D. How Do You Research Nonlegal Materials?

It is well beyond the scope of this text to discuss fully how to conduct research in such fields as medicine, public health, and sociology. Rather, this part shows you how to use the tools available in most law libraries to begin such research. As is true of legal research, useful tools appear in various media. And the research skills, such as development of research vocabulary and selection of useful media, parallel those used in legal research.

1. Researching in Paper Media

A good starting point is a text about research in various disciplines: *Guide to Reference Books* (11th ed. 1996), edited by Robert Balay with the assistance of librarians from various disciplines. *Guide to Reference Books* lists and describes research tools; it is organized by field and then by category, such as guides and periodicals.

Your library may have standard reference sources or major journals in the nonlegal discipline of interest to you. The books should be accessible via the library's catalog. The journals may be accessible through such indexes as *Index to Periodical Articles Related to Law* or *Social Sciences Index* or through the journal's own index.

2. Researching Online

Given the rapid growth in research materials in many nonlegal fields, online technologies are important research tools in nonlegal research, as they are in legal research. This section briefly notes how the following services could be used: NEXIS, DIALOG, and the Internet.

NEXIS is an online service affiliated with LEXIS. It provides access to a wide collection of newspapers, magazines, wire services, and newsletters, primarily on general, financial, and medical topics. You may focus your search on a subject matter (such as accounting or medicine), region of the country, type of publication (such as newspapers or wire services), or time period (the past two or three years, earlier than that, or both).

DIALOG is a service similar to NEXIS that is affiliated with WESTLAW. It provides a wide range of databases pertinent to such broad topics as business, social science and humanities, and medicine. Some databases contain documents in full text, while others contain only indexes or abstracts.

The Internet provides a constantly expanding range of information in many nonlegal disciplines. It is a potentially useful source for information on many topics and may become a leading inexpensive source of information from government agencies.

In the Canoga case, all of the illustrations were located online. Illustration 11-1 (the *New England Journal of Medicine* article) was located through the NE-JNLMED database in DIALOG; the search was [smoke & "lung capacity"]. Illustration 11-2 (the American Heart Association pamphlet on nicotine addiction) was located through the Internet, using the MetaCrawler Multi-Threaded Web Search Service, with the address http://metacrawler.cs-.washington.edu:8080:/, and the search [nicotine addiction]. That search also yielded a direct reference to the Surgeon General's report and information about how to obtain it by phone. Illustration 11-3 (the study of an employer's no-smoking policy) was located through the HLTJNL file within the HEALTH library on LEXIS; the search was [smoking w/p employer or workplace]. And Illustration 11-4 (the poll results) was located through DIALOG's Public Opinion Online database; the search was [smok! cigarette / p employee discharg! terminat!].

E. How Do You Cite Nonlegal Materials?

Most nonlegal materials you might wish to cite will be covered by Rule 15 (books and pamphlets), Rule 16 (periodicals), or Rule 17 (unpublished and nonprinted sources) of *The Bluebook*. The citation forms are the same for nonlegal and legal materials. Here are citations for the materials featured in this chapter:

Jonathan E. Fielding, *Smoking: Health Effects and Control*, 313 New Eng. J. Med. 491 (1985).

American Heart Association, *Nicotine Addiction* (date unknown).

Lyle R. Petersen et al., *Employee Smoking Behavior and Attitudes Following a Restrictive Policy on Worksite Smoking in a Large Company*, 103 Pub. Health Rep. 115 (1988).

Roper Center for Public Opinion, Survey re Employee Smoking, May 1992, *available in* DIALOG, POLL database, File no. 013.

F. Concluding Points

Few legal problems are purely legal problems; most have nonlegal dimensions as well. Whether in advisory, litigation, or lobbying contexts, to serve your clients well, you may need nonlegal information. You can obtain some such information with relative ease in a law library in paper media, such as journals or books, or through online sources, such as DIALOG, NEXIS, and the Internet. The basic skills involved in this research are the same as those taught in other chapters on legal research.

12 Developing an Integrated Research Strategy

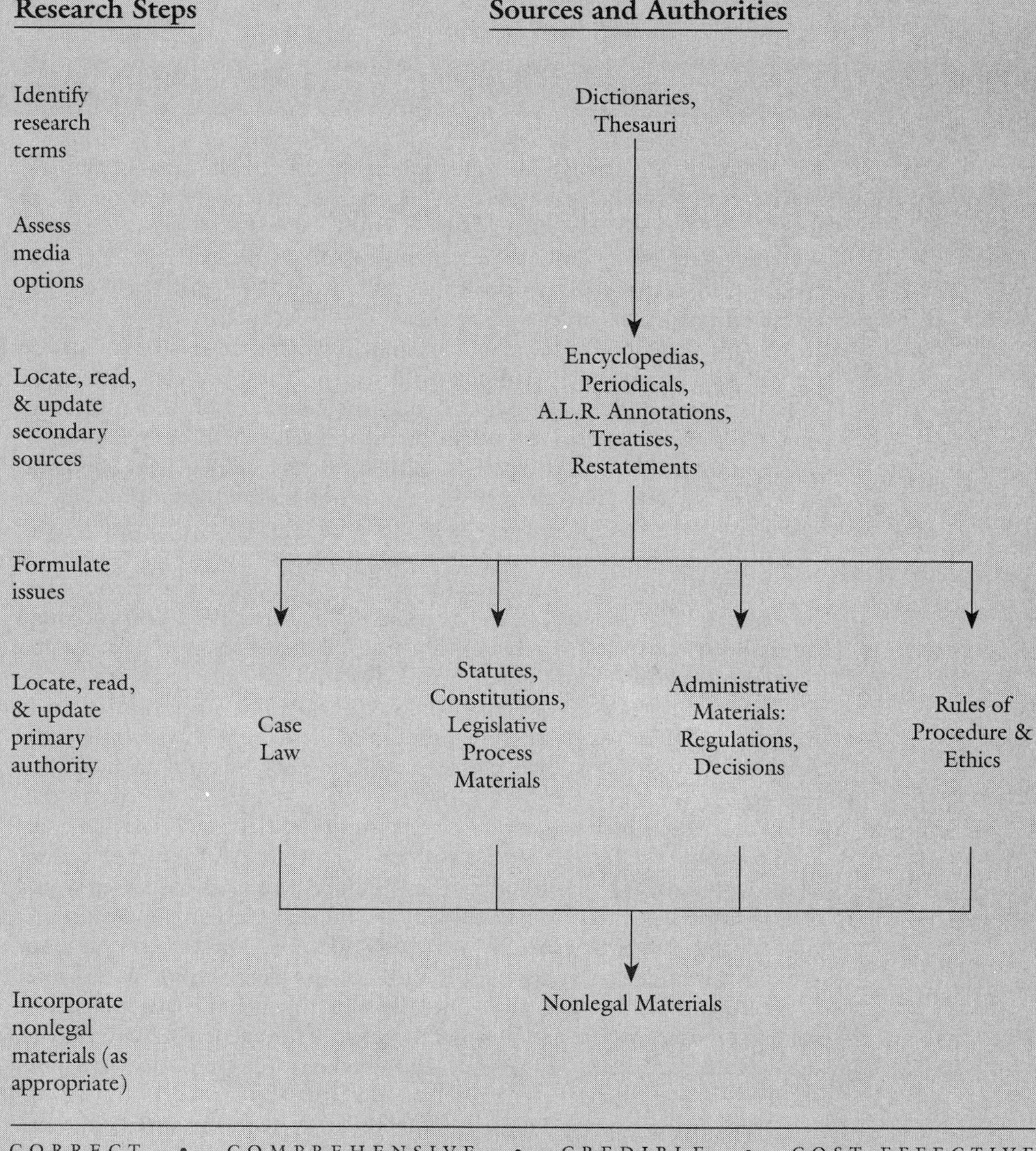

CORRECT • COMPREHENSIVE • CREDIBLE • COST-EFFECTIVE

Summary of Contents

A. Introduction

Now that you have worked with a range of legal research sources, you have begun to realize that each person's research strategies depend on his or her familiarity with the general subject matter and specific topic, acquired preferences regarding various research sources and media, and research expertise, as well as the materials available to the researcher. Nonetheless, there are certain constants in legal research.

To prove our point, one of us, Christina Kunz, drafted a research situation for three of our research assistants to research. The researchers were Tim Stocking, Renee Michalow, and Courtney Candalino, all of whom were second- or third-year law students. This chapter presents their research journals, followed by analysis and comparison of their research strategies and findings.

First, a caveat: This chapter is derived from research conducted in the spring of 1995. You could test your updating skills by researching more recent developments in this new area of the law.

Second, another caveat: Each researcher stopped when he or she determined that the substantive claim (or claims) of the clients met the procedural threshold specified in the research situation. Should the dispute persist and the stakes increase, all of the researchers would do further research.

Third, a note: The researchers did not include full *Bluebook* citations in their research journals because the purpose of these journals was to show the research process, not to write the final office memorandum describing their results.

Fourth, an observation: You may be surprised that the researchers pursued somewhat different theories and have somewhat different perceptions of the helpfulness of the authorities they found. An experienced lawyer would not be surprised at this. In many situations, there are several—indeed sometimes many—ways to arrive at a research solution. Furthermore, the law requires interpretation and application to concrete facts. It is up to the lawyer to ascertain the possible legal theories, develop them, and choose those best suited to the facts of the situation and the goals of the client. It takes creativity, intelligence, judgment—and highly developed research skills—to accomplish this task.

What follows in Part B is the research situation that our research assistants researched.

B. The Frequent Flyer Case

The corporate headquarters of Federal Airlines is in Minnesota, and Minnesota is Federal's principal place of business and one of its three hubs of operation, the other two being Dallas-Ft. Worth and Seattle. Like many corporations, Federal is incorporated in Delaware.

Federal initiated a frequent flyer program in 1981. It was the first airline to do so. Its early program gave mileage credit for Federal flights; the program was expanded in 1986 to include mileage credits for hotels, rental cars, long-distance telephone services, and restaurants. A person wishing to join the program had to fill out an application from a brochure (see Illustration 12-1 on pages 390-391) describing the rules of the program and send it to the airline. Each brochure contained a unique tracking number that could be placed on the applicant's (now enrollee's) Federal tickets. The terms in Illustration 12-1 appeared in brochures from 1981 to this month. Federal's monthly statements occasionally contained notices of special promotional programs, such as extra mileage credit for miles flown on new routes or routes on which Federal wanted to boost ridership. As detailed in Illustration 12-1, an enrollee received a FreeFlight certificate from Federal after the enrollee compiled the specified number of mileage credits. These certificates could be redeemed for a free flight on Federal.

This month, Federal announced that, effective immediately, it will restrict the manner in which program credits can be used. The changes prohibit the use of certificates for flights during "blackout periods," namely five popular holiday and vacation travel periods. These blackout dates also are stated on each certificate issued this month or later. In addition, new "capacity controls" limit the number of certificate-holders who can fly on each flight to 5% of tourist class and 5% of first class. Until now, the number of persons actually using FreeFlight certificates has ranged between 0% and 20% per flight. Enrollees can "buy their way past" a blackout date or a capacity control by turning in one additional certificate per roundtrip. An enrollee must use two additional certificates to fly during a blackout date in spite of a capacity control for a particular flight. These changes are motivated by rising costs and shrinking revenues at Federal Airlines. They apply to mileage credits accumulated either before or after the announcement.

A group of enrollees has approached your law firm about suing Federal for changing the rules of the program. These enrollees have mileage credits for miles flown before these changes, as well as certificates earned (but not yet used). They accumulated credits from Federal flights, even if doing so was more costly and less convenient than doing business with other airlines. Do they have any basis for suing Federal?

Proceed with your research until you can ascertain whether plaintiffs have a breach-of-contract claim that will survive a motion to dismiss for failure to state a claim in a Minnesota state court. (Do not address issues concerning jurisdiction, venue, or class actions. Also do not address any quasi-contract claims.)

Illustration 12-1 Federal Airlines Brochure.

Federal Airlines FreeFlight Program

Join the Federal FreeFlight Program and make your airline travel pay off! Federal, the first airline to give its customers a "pay back" on their airline dollars, offers its customers the chance to earn mileage credit that can be redeemed for free flights on Federal. Depending on the number of miles flown, you can earn a ticket to travel within the continental United States, or to Europe or even Asia. Here are the trips you can earn with your Federal mileage credits:

20,000 miles	1 roundtrip ticket within continental U.S.
40,000 miles	2 roundtrip tickets within continental U.S. OR 1 roundtrip ticket between U.S. and Europe
60,000 miles	3 roundtrip tickets within continental U.S. OR 1 roundtrip ticket between U.S. and Asia

FreeFlight mileage credit is determined on the basis of nonstop distances between the airports where your flight originates and terminates. On connecting flights, you receive mileage credit for each segment of your trip; on single-plane flights, you receive the nonstop origin-destination mileage.

Once you fly the requisite number of miles, Federal will issue FreeFlight certificate(s), which you can exchange for the ticket(s) listed above anytime within two years of the issuance of the certificate. This program allows you to earn Federal FreeFlight certificates for yourself or anyone else traveling with you on the same flight.[1] A great idea for a holiday with a loved one or a family vacation.

Just fill out the application on the back of this brochure and return it. You can even start earning mileage credit today—just note your flight number and date on your application and give the Federal ticket agent the application number before you receive your boarding pass. That application number will serve as your FreeFlight number.[2]

Federal's Automated Mileage Tracking System Works for You

When you fly Federal Airlines, just give your FreeFlight number to your travel agent, a reservations agent, or to the airport ticket agent at time of check-in. Federal Airlines' computerized mileage tracking and reporting system then automatically records all your FreeFlight transactions.

1. Otherwise, Federal FreeFlight certificates are not transferable to other people.
2. Federal reserves the right to restrict, suspend, or otherwise alter aspects of the Program.

Illustration 12-1 (*continued*)

Active members regularly receive a mileage summary that details the total credit for each FreeFlight transaction and their total accumulated mileage in the program.

Claiming Your FreeFlight Awards

- Full terms and conditions for certificate usage and award travel are enclosed with your award certificates.
- FreeFlight certificates are nontransferable, but they can be used to pay for a ticket of someone traveling with you.
- Certificates will be mailed only to the FreeFlight member claiming the award and only to the member address on file.
- Travel awards are only good for designated award destinations served at the time of certificate issuance and also at the time the ticket is used.

FreeFlight Reminders

- Only travel taken after you receive your FreeFlight number in this brochure is credited toward FreeFlight awards. No retroactive credit will be given.
- Mileage will be credited only to the account of the FreeFlight member who actually flies. Mileage credit is not transferable and may not be combined among FreeFlight members.
- Your mileage summary recaps your account activity through the Summary Date indicated at the top of the form. Federal Airlines flights are normally posted to your account within a few days of the actual flight date. If credit for current flights does not appear on your summary, please contact the FreeFlight department in writing and include copies of your ticket receipt and boarding pass.
- Free transportation awarded from FreeFlight certificates cannot be used to accrue mileage credit.
- At no time may FreeFlight mileage credit or certificates be purchased, sold, or bartered. Any such mileage or awards are void if transferred for cash or other consideration.

FreeFlight program rules, regulations, travel awards, and special offers are subject to change without notice. Federal Airlines reserves the right to terminate the FreeFlight program at any time.

C. Three Research Approaches on the Frequent Flyer Case

All three researchers began their research by formulating research terms, according to the categories in Chapter 2. Exhibit 12.1 on page 392 shows

Exhibit 12.1 Research Terms for Factual Categories.

	Who	*What*	*When*	*Where*	*Why*
Tim	airline, company, purchaser, consumer, offeror/ offeree, seller/ buyer, vendor/ purchaser, frequent flyer	frequent flyer program, promotional scheme, bonuses, credits, incentives, coupon, voucher, frequent flyer miles	timing of passengers' receipt of brochure from airline, passengers' flights on airline, program changes made by airline	Minnesota company, nationwide market	airline sought to increase market share by attracting customers who fly enough to benefit from frequent flyer program
Renee	airlines, corporation; enrollee, frequent flyers, customers, riders, passengers	frequent flyer program, contract, promotional brochure; mileage credits, travel certificates, award certificates; capacity controls, blackout dates, program credit restrictions	mileage credits received for miles flown before changes to program, certificates earned (but not yet used)	Minnesota	enrollees joined program even though doing so was sometimes more costly & less convenient than doing business with other airlines; Federal motivated by rising costs & shrinking revenues
Courtney	flyers, frequent flyers, enrollees; airlines, Federal Airlines, FreeFlight administrators	incentive program, program brochure, tracking number, frequent flyer miles, travel certificates, free flights, altering terms	program developed in 1981, changed in 1986, sign up, return brochure, get tracking number, get monthly statements, acquire miles, change in policy, this month	Federal Airlines, corporation based in Minnesota (corporation, principal place of business, 1 of 3 hubs), 2 hubs in Dallas & Seattle, incorporated in Delaware, national participants	enrollees get credit for Federal flight miles, then certificates for free flights; Federal's rising costs & shrinking revenue led to program changes; enrollees suing because they can't use certificates during specified periods or must use more

Exhibit 12.2 Research Terms for Legal Categories.

	Legal Theory	*Relief*	*Procedural Posture*
Tim	contracts, sales of services, breach, failure to perform, estoppel, alteration, modification of existing contract	recover damages for decreased value of certificates and mileage credits	will claim survive a motion to dismiss?
Renee	breach of contract	reinstate old terms for mileage credit earned prior to program changes	motion to dismiss for failure to state a claim
Courtney	breach of contract —agreement, promise, deal, bargain, consideration, terms, offer, acceptance —bilateral/unilateral —express/implied contract (law/fact) —change of terms, notice	money/damages; change back to old terms; exception for miles previously earned	motion to dismiss

their research terms for the five factual categories. Exhibit 12.2 above shows their research terms for the three legal categories. What follow are their research journals, as they located, read, and analyzed the various sources. As you read these journals, focus on the reasoning steps behind the research process, rather than the final conclusions, which were fairly similar.

1. Tim's Journal

I decided to begin with secondary sources because I was unfamiliar with this area of the law and did not know if it is regulated by statute or only common law. I planned to start with the term, "frequent flyer." I thought that national encyclopedias (C.J.S. and Am. Jur.) and Restatements were not likely to be helpful because the issue is so new and because the indexes and tables of contents for these sources seem to use older legal terms more frequently than other commentary sources do. The term most likely could be found in recent legal periodical articles or perhaps an A.L.R. annotation (if there had been enough cases in this area of the law to collect and analyze as a group). I considered using a treatise on aviation law but then concluded that frequent flyer programs are more likely to be covered by a treatise on contract law. My strategy was to use *LegalTrac* to search for a secondary source on this issue. If there was nothing there, I would consult the *Index to Legal Periodicals and Books* (I.L.P.B.). After that, I would look in A.L.R., then treatises, and finally a state encyclopedia.

In *LegalTrac*, the term "frequent flyer" led to several relevant articles. One newspaper article sounded particularly on point—"Class Action OKd Against Retroactive Limits on Frequent-flier Benefits" in the *Chicago Daily Law Bulletin*. I read it to see if it led to primary sources. This article reported on *American Airlines v. Wolens* (U.S. 1995). The case involved an airline doing exactly the same thing as in our hypothetical: changing a frequent flyer program so that credits earned in the past will be less valuable to the enrollees in the future. I did not expect to find a federalism aspect to this problem, but the *Wolens* Court held that Congress' passing of the Airline Deregulation Act of 1978 (a different ADA from the one in the previous chapters) to deregulate the airline industry has pre-empted states from applying state consumer fraud statutes or deceptive advertising practices statutes against the airline industry. More importantly for my assignment, the Court ruled that the ADA did not pre-empt common law contractual claims against airlines from being heard in state courts. The lower courts in *Wolens* did not reach the merits of the contract law issues because American Airlines appealed a pre-trial ruling. However, I noted that the lower courts did not dismiss the common law contract claim altogether, which might support an argument against a motion for failure to state a claim in Minnesota.

I read *Wolens* to verify the report of the case, and then I Shepardized it and found nothing (although I didn't expect to find much because it was decided just a few months prior to this writing).

A.L.R. turned out to be a dead end as far as frequent flyer programs are concerned.

The contract treatises that I checked, Williston and Corbin, clarified the contractual aspect of the problem quite a bit. (I prefer the multivolume to the abridged single editions because the indexes are more complete and because they usually are updated.) I looked in Corbin's index under "revocation, power reserved in offer," and read the pertinent text. It led me to conclude that Federal made an offer to anyone who heard of its promotion, signed up for the program, and purchased Federal's airline tickets; the reward was that Federal would give each participant credits for a later FreeFlight certificate. Federal had control over its offer and could limit it. Federal limited it with the following clause in the second footnote of the brochure: "Federal reserves the right to restrict, suspend, or otherwise alter aspects of the Program."

I next looked up "rewards, unilateral contract," and learned that contests have been held to be offers for unilateral contracts that become binding once the requested act has been performed. The discussion did not specify whether "performed" means that the offeree must have begun or finished the requested act. Thus, it was not clear whether acceptance occurred when customers began their performance (that is, enrolling in the program and purchasing tickets) or when they finished (sent in their certificates for free tickets). If the acceptance was the later event, Federal might be able to change the terms of the offer until the moment of acceptance.

I decided to research the procedural standard for failure to state a claim in Minnesota before looking further for the applicable substantive law, so I would know when a motion for failure to state a claim fails. Because I already knew the key legal phrases, computer-assisted legal research (CALR) seemed the quickest way to do that. Using LEXIS, I entered the Minnesota case law file and did a Boolean search: [motion to dismiss and failure to state a claim]. The result was 111 cases. I read the most recent cases until I found the standard set out in *Federated Mutual Insurance Co. v. Litchfield Precision Components, Inc.* (Minn. 1990). That case cited *Elzie v. Commissioner of Public Safety* (Minn. 1980) as stating the rule to be "whether the complaint sets forth a legally sufficient claim for relief." Using Lexsee to pull up *Elzie,* I read the following standard: "A claim is sufficient against a motion to dismiss based on Rule 12.02(5) if it is possible on any evidence which might be produced, consistent with the pleader's theory, to grant the relief demanded." Therefore, I had to find at least one legal theory that supports the plaintiffs' claim for damages or specific performance. Shepardizing *Elzie* showed that it is still good law.

I next planned to use *Dunnell Minnesota Digest,* a state encyclopedia, to search for primary authority. I was not yet ready to use a West digest. Under the forest and trees analogy, *Dunnell* provides a view of the whole forest, while a West digest shows the law one tree at a time. I was still unfamiliar enough with the law that I needed a good view of the forest. Researching in *Dunnell* turned out to be a dead end. The most helpful material was on modification of contracts, but it analyzed the law from the perspective of mutually agreed-upon modifications of an existing agreement. It did not cover unilateral contract situations in which an offeror reserves the right to change the offer at any time prior to full performance of the requested act. The section on rescission dealt with contracts formed in fraudulent circumstances, which was not relevant. Surprisingly, the index did not have anything useful under revocation. I skimmed the sections on offer and acceptance, but did not find anything there either, nor could I find anything helpful by looking under the most general topics I could find in the index—"contracts" and "vendor and purchaser." I exhausted my research terms, but did not find anything directly on point.

I switched to *West's Minnesota Digest 2d* and found a tree to latch onto in the midst of this forest after all. Using the outline for the topic of Contracts, I found a key number on "contracts—modification." It contained a reference to "alteration or addition of terms." This section referred to a case that is directly analogous to our client's situation, although it does not involve airlines or frequent flyer programs. I read the case. In *Mooney v. Daily News Co.* (Minn. 1911), the supreme court held that a newspaper offering a prize to the person who could produce the highest number of newspaper subscriptions could not alter the terms of the offer, without the consent of the offeree, after an offeree had begun to amass subscriptions and send the proceeds to the newspaper. It also ruled that the offeror could not give the rules an interpretation contrary to their true meaning. A contest is analogous to a frequent flyer program—both involve advertised promotions that amount to unilateral contract offers to the participants. Therefore, there is a good argument that the certificates already earned (as well as the miles collected but not yet turned into certificates) cannot be devalued by Federal imposing blackout restrictions or other modifications without the consent of the plaintiffs.

Shepardizing *Mooney* led to eight other cases, as well as three A.L.R. annotations on contests. One annotation on contests analyzed a contest as a unilateral contract offer to participate in a contest that benefits the offeror through increased sales or interest in its product. The offer is accepted by the anonymous offerees performing the requested acts laid out in the contest. One annotation listed three Minnesota cases, the most relevant being *Holt v. Rural Weekly Co.* (Minn. 1928), but those cases did not add anything to *Mooney,* except to show that Minnesota courts have not dismissed cases brought by contestants who did not receive what they were promised after they did the requested act. Shepardizing the Minnesota cases from A.L.R. showed that they are still good law but did not lead to any more primary authority.

Again using the digest, I looked up other research terms developed during my initial brainstorming. Cases on "vendor and purchaser" dealt mainly with cases involving real estate transactions. Several other terms were of no use either. But "revocation—offer of contract" led to two recent cases that solidified the earlier analysis of the problem, *Sylvestre v. State* (Minn. 1973) and *Peters v. Mutual Beneficial Life Insurance Co.* (Minn. Ct. App. 1988). They both held that a change in the terms of the offer amounts to a revocation of the offer, but that once performance by the offeree under a unilateral contract has begun, the offer may no longer be revoked. In our case, the plaintiffs partially performed Federal's offer when they began performing the requested acts by the airline—purchasing tickets from Federal and refraining from using other airlines, even when riding on Federal was more expensive. Thus, Federal's changes in the terms of the program applied only to the new members of the program and to old members who had completed one certificate and were beginning to earn another one.

Sylvestre included discussion of consideration. This discussion reminded me that I also needed to ascertain whether the alleged contract was supported by consideration. I returned to Williston's and Corbin's contracts treatises. They set out the requirements of consideration as including bargained-for exchange and the benefit-detriment test. I realized that the alleged unilateral contract met the requirements because Federal's promise induced the plaintiffs' performance and that performance was both a detriment to plaintiffs and a benefit to Federal. Federal's right to terminate or modify did not create an illusory promise or a "free way out" because the rule from *Sylvestre* and *Peters* prevented Federal from terminating or modifying the promise once a particular plaintiff had begun to perform in response to that promise.

I located several representative cases referred to in the treatises and used the cases' key numbers to locate similar Minnesota cases in *West's Minnesota Digest 2d.* I read those cases, Shepardized the remaining cases, and thereby confirmed that my assessment on consideration was correct.

Therefore, I am convinced that the plaintiffs can bring suit against Federal for breach of a unilateral contract. The enrollees have a case that should survive a motion to dismiss for failure to state a claim in Minnesota.

2. Renee's Journal

My first step was to consider the facts carefully in light of the assigned issue: whether the enrollees had entered into a contract with Federal, which Federal then breached. I questioned whether Federal's note in the brochure that program rules "are subject to change without notice" was relevant to this potential contract. I also wondered whether the enrollees' relief in the alternative might be that they could be governed by the old rules for mileage credits/certificates earned prior to the changes, while new mileage credits earned would fall under the new rules containing capacity controls.

I usually begin my research by reading commentary when I am researching in areas I don't know much about or that seem broad and undifferentiated to me. Here, I needed to establish a general understanding of the legal status of frequent flyer programs. I usually begin with law reviews. I find law review searches on the JLR or LRI database (JLR is a full-text database; LRI is a periodical index) on WESTLAW to be helpful. I then attempt to locate any A.L.R. annotations that might be helpful. An annotation may focus on frequent flyer programs because they are a relatively recent controversy. The breadth of an A.L.R. annotation will be about the same as the breadth of a law review article.

My WESTLAW strategy is first to write a number of searches in advance, generally going from a broad to narrow search. This process allows me to determine whether my broad search is not as broad as initially expected or is much too broad; if the latter is true, I quickly edit my query to obtain a progressively more focused result. Then, by printing a cite list, I can use paper sources.

In WESTLAW's JLR database, a query for ["frequent flyer"] generated well over 100 law review articles, so I quickly narrowed the search. A second search for [breach & contract & "frequent flyer"] produced eleven articles. In order to save costs on WESTLAW, I glanced at the citation list and printed the list, so I could do more research in paper sources. The WESTLAW search also alerted me to an airline-specific journal of which I had never heard. Another cite directed me to a potentially useful CLE publication. A third and narrower search for ["frequent flyer" & airline & corporation & "mileage credit"] resulted in two law review articles, the titles of which referred to the possible tax implications of frequent flyer bonus programs. I felt that this search was too narrow and decided to follow up on the results of the second search.

In WESTLAW's LRI database, using the second, successful search from above, I obtained citations to three articles. The LRI results seemed right on point. The LRI abstracts said that an American Airlines case from Illinois on frequent flyer programs would be going to the U.S. Supreme Court in the fall of 1994. I made a note to search for the case when I was ready to locate primary authority. Also, LRI pointed me to some journals I had never heard of, such as *Travel Weekly*. One trick I use when I discover an industry-specific journal is to skim through the tables of contents of more recent issues to see if any new relevant articles have been published that did not show up in my WESTLAW search. In this case, nothing relevant was listed.

From the citation list, I chose several recent articles that appeared relevant. One of the articles summarized *American Airlines v. Wolens* (U.S. 1995), in which a group of frequent flyer program members sued the airline, alleging that the airline had violated a contract that was part of the frequent flyer program. I learned that the case was returned to state court on the basis that the complaint set forth causes of action cognizable under state law for breach of contract.

My next step, after researching commentary for a background, is to go to case law by using either the case cites that I found in the commentary sources or through the relevant digests. At this point, I felt that I should research primary authority, beginning with *Wolens.* To find the United States Supreme Court cite, I did a title search on WESTLAW; then I used WESTLAW's Insta-Cite, which gave me all of the direct and indirect history, including negative indirect history, of this case. This listing included the citation to the most recent decision from the United States Supreme Court on January 18, 1995, as well as a decision by the Illinois Supreme Court on March 16, 1995. The Supreme Court held that federal law pre-empted the statutory consumer fraud action for injunctive relief, but not the breach-of-contract claim under state law. The Illinois decision remanded the case to the trial court for proceedings on the breach-of-contract claim.

My next step was to research Minnesota state law on what a plaintiff must allege to survive a motion to dismiss for failure to state a claim. Because I already knew some pertinent terms and concepts, I moved directly to digests. I used *West's Minnesota Digest 2d* Descriptive Word Index and looked under "motions." I found helpful material under "involuntary dismissal, pleading, defects in, in general." The digests for several cases suggested that a motion to dismiss for failure to state a claim would be granted only if it appeared beyond a reasonable doubt that plaintiff could prove no set of facts that would entitle him or her to relief. I read those cases and Shepardized them without any additional insights or leads.

To determine what is required for a contract to exist, I looked under "Contracts" in *West's Minnesota Digest 2d* and skimmed the topic outlines at the beginning of the topic. I located the West key numbers on contract formation. The cases under those key numbers discussed the making and communication of an offer, acceptance as assent to that offer, and consideration. At first glance, the frequent flyer clients could arguably claim that the program brochure was an offer to enter into a contract with a particular frequent flyer customer, especially because each brochure contained a unique tracking number that could be placed on the applicant's Federal tickets.

My next step was to research whether the offer was accepted and whether the parties' assent was supported by valid consideration. Again I turned to *West's Minnesota Digest 2d* and found relevant case law. Consideration requires a promise that induces some benefit accruing to the promisor or some detriment suffered by the promisee. In this case, there needs to be some benefit to Federal or some detriment to the passengers. It is possible that the detriment to the enrollees resulted from their purchase of Federal flight tickets when doing so was more costly and less convenient for them than doing business with other airlines. If so, the contract in this case was a unilateral contract because it was created when a promise was accepted by performance of a particular act or forbearance. Then the promise of free tickets was accepted by the enrollees in exchange for their performance of purchasing Federal airline tickets. A leading case appeared to be *Hartung v. Billmeier* (Minn. 1954). The unresolved question is how many tickets each enrollee needed to purchase to accept the offer.

Not finding any case law in the digest to resolve this point, I decided to run a quick WESTLAW search. I searched for [award or prize] in the MN-CS database. Only two cases, neither on point, showed up. I searched for the same terms in ALL-CASES and of the fifty-four cases I retrieved, one Eighth Circuit case from Missouri seemed helpful. In that case, a woman sought prize money offered by McDonald's Corporation during a promotion. *Waible v. McDonald's Corp.* (8th Cir. 1991). The court stated that the token received by the plaintiff allegedly at the McDonald's restaurant was an offer for a unilateral contract that could be accepted only by performing all of the terms and conditions of the promotion. I believe we can analogize to the Federal FreeFlight brochure. The brochure offered a free ticket only when an enrollee had paid for a certain number of flights and had accumulated the requisite number of miles. Thus, an enrollee would have performed completely only when he or she had accumulated 20,000 paid miles.

I became more certain that the enrollees who had received FreeFlight tickets for mileage accumulated prior to the rule change had accepted the contract offer through performance and thus would be subject to the old rules. However, Federal's brochure reserved to Federal the right to make any contract changes. I did another WESTLAW search in MN-CS for [performance and "unilateral contract"] to see what additional information I could gather. Generally, I found that once a party to a unilateral contract begins the required performance, the offer for the unilateral contract may not be changed or revoked. *Peters v. Mutual Beneficial Life Insurance Co.* (Minn. Ct. App. 1988). When Federal unilaterally changed its program, it created an argument for the enrollees that the contract was breached. Nothing new showed up in Shepardizing or updates. At this point, I think that the enrollees have enough of a claim to survive a motion to dismiss for failure to state a claim in a Minnesota court.

3. Courtney's Journal

Under my research plan, the first step was to research the procedural standard (how to survive a motion to dismiss for failure to state a claim). Motions to dismiss are governed by court rule, so I planned to use *Minnesota Statutes Annotated* to find the rule and then to read the pertinent cases listed in the annotations. My second step was to research the substantive claims. The issue seemed discrete enough that there could be law review articles specifically discussing legal issues relating to airlines and frequent flyers. I also planned to use *Dunnell Minnesota Digest* (a state encyclopedia) to get basic background and possibly cases. I then planned to use *West's Minnesota Digest 2d* to find Minnesota cases, read the cases, see what works, and use those key numbers to go back to the digest.

I remembered studying motions to dismiss for failure to state a claim but could not remember the specific rule. In *Minnesota Statutes Annotated,* I looked in the index under "failure to state a claim." There was nothing, so I looked under a related motion, summary judgment, and found references to Rules of Civil Procedure 56.01, 56.02, 12.02, and 56.03. Rule 12.02 allows a defendant to bring a motion to dismiss for failure to state a claim upon which relief can be granted. After scanning the annotations, I selected three cases to read. These cases set out various standards for denying a motion to dismiss for failure to state a claim: whether the complaint sets forth a legally sufficient claim for relief; whether it is possible, on any evidence that might be produced, consistent with the pleader's theory, to grant the relief demanded.

Having finished my procedural research, I moved on to research the substantive claims. I first did a *LegalTrac* search on the subject of airlines and then narrowed the search to contract and frequent fliers. I read a 1993 case note that I thought might give me a start: *Constitutional Law—Federal Pre-emption—The Federal Aviation Act Does Not Prevent State Claim Against an Airline for Breach of the Covenant of Good Faith and Fair Dealing Arising from Overbooking.* According to the article, as part of the Airline Deregulation Act of 1978 (ADA), a federal pre-emption provision was added to the Federal Aviation Act (FAA) barring any state from enacting or enforcing "any law, rule, regulation, standard or other provision having the force and effect of law relating to rates, routes or services of any air carrier." However, the FAA does not prevent a state law claim against an airline for breach of covenant of good faith and fair dealing arising from overbooking. While this article is not directly applicable to the situation, issues of good faith and fair dealing sometimes come up in contract claims. The article discussed a leading case: *Morales v. Trans World Airlines* (U.S. 1992).

I read *Morales,* then did a *LegalTrac* search for "Morales" to find law review articles. I found an article entitled *Morales v. TWA, Inc.: Federal Pre-emption Provision Clips States' Wings on Regulation of Air Fare Advertising.* The *Morales* court held that the ADA pre-empts state statutory claims developed to control content and format of airline ads, as well as state consumer protection statutes.

I Shepardized *Morales* on WESTLAW and printed out the cases listed there. I found *American Airlines v. Wolens* (U.S. 1995), originally an Illinois case, reviewed by the United States Supreme Court on the pre-emption issue. The facts of the case are almost identical to the claims of the Federal Airlines frequent fliers. The Supreme Court held that the ADA pre-empted plaintiffs' claims based on the Illinois Consumer Fraud and Deceptive Business Practices Act, but did not pre-empt a common law breach-of-contract action alleging the airline had violated an agreement that it entered into with its passengers. *Wolens* established that our clients' state common law claims are not pre-empted. However, the Supreme Court's decision did not give much guidance beyond that; it left open the contract issue for adjudication on remand.

I Shepardized *Wolens* on WESTLAW. I was not able to find anything about what happened to the case on remand because the case was decided only a few months earlier.

Because the case was decided recently, I figured there probably would not be any Minnesota cases based on the decision. But I decided to check *West's Minnesota Digest 2d* under the applicable key numbers anyway. Although there were not any pertinent cases under those key numbers, I decided to browse the aviation and contracts topics. I found one case that seemed pertinent, *Mooney v. Daily News Co.* (Minn. 1911). I read the case. The court held that a newspaper's offer of a prize to the person obtaining the highest number of paid subscriptions to the newspaper became an executory contract after each contestant partially performed the terms of the offer and communicated the fact of that performance to the newspaper. By analogy, Federal Airlines, by the published terms and conditions of the frequent flyer program, may have created a contract with the flyers when the flyers joined the program and began to take flights on Federal. This case seemed applicable, so I Shepardized it and came up with five similar cases.

I knew then that I would have to formulate the contract claim without the benefit of a Minnesota case dealing specifically with contracts between airlines and frequent flyers, so I should think more about basic contract principles. First, the flyers could argue that the brochure with the terms and conditions of the program constituted an express offer. The terms of an offer may be changed at any time before acceptance, but once accepted the terms are fixed and may not be changed unilaterally. The flyers did not give Federal a promise to fly Federal, because they were not obligated to fly Federal once they joined the program. But perhaps the flyers accepted the offer by their performance, which also was consideration for the contract; thus, the contract would be unilateral. What was sufficient performance by the flyers to constitute acceptance and consideration?

By filling out the brochure and mailing it back, the flyers indicated their acceptance, but it is hard to see what consideration they had furnished at that point—they were not promising anything, they had not given up anything, nor had they given Federal any benefit. However, arguably, their part performance may be sufficient—that is, joining the program and flying the airline. The consideration would be that the members flew Federal when they were not obligated to do so, even when doing so was at a higher cost and less convenient (and therefore a detriment), in exchange for the mileage credit; in addition, Federal was benefited by those flights.

Was there consideration from Federal? The airline specifically reserved the right to change the terms of the program. However, the flyers could argue that the airline reserved the right only to change the terms for the future, not to alter the terms for the miles previously acquired. If Federal could change the terms at any time, then it really would not be offering much.

The flyers also may be able to claim that an implied contract was created by Federal and the program members. That is, looking at the circumstances as a whole, a contract may be inferred from the conduct of the parties. It seems the flyers would have a clearer argument by claiming an express contract was created by the terms of the brochure, but I need to do more research.

I decided to look through *Dunnell Minnesota Digest* (a state encyclopedia) to make sure my thoughts about basic contract law were accurate and to find cases. According to *Dunnell,* the requirements of a unilateral contract are offer, communication to and acceptance by offeree, and consideration. An offer must be sufficiently definite to form the basis of a contract. In *Lefkowitz v. Great Minneapolis Surplus Store, Inc.* (Minn. 1957), the defendant placed a newspaper advertisement stating that the first person to the store could buy a fur coat for only $1; the plaintiff, a male, was the first to reach the store with one dollar, but the defendant refused to give the plaintiff the coat claiming that the offer was subject to a store rule that only a female could claim the coat in the ad. The court held that an ad addressed to the public is an offer if the facts show some performance was promised in positive terms in return for something requested. An offer may be revoked before acceptance, but after acceptance the offeror does not have the right to impose new or arbitrary conditions not contained in the published offer. The plaintiff was awarded the coat.

Lefkowitz seems very helpful to the Federal flyers' claims. Arguably, the airline's brochure was specifically clear, definite, and explicit and left nothing open for negotiation, so it was an offer. The Federal members responded to an ad—they joined the program and flew the airline, the action requested in the ad. Now that the plaintiffs seek the benefit promised, the airline, like the defendant in *Lefkowitz,* is trying to change the rules. However, unlike the defendant in *Lefkowitz,* the airline reserved the right to change the rules. I noted that I need to research this distinction.

Dunnell led me to several additional helpful cases: *Hartung v. Billmeier* (Minn. 1954), involving an employee's suit for a bonus; *Mooney,* described above; *Holt v. Rural Weekly Co.* (Minn. 1928), a similar case; and *Sylvestre v. State* (Minn. 1973), involving retirement pay for judges. All of these cases support the Federal frequent flyers' argument that their complying with the rules by joining the program and flying Federal created either a binding contract that obligated Federal to award the prizes as promised or an irrevocable offer that prevented Federal from changing the terms. The cases all Shepardized as good authority.

Dunnell also indicated that consideration, an essential element of contract formation, requires the voluntary assumption of an obligation by one party on the condition of an act or forbearance by the other. Consideration may consist of either a benefit accruing to a party or a detriment suffered by another party. The point at which the members suffered detriment was when they restricted their freedom of motion by flying Federal, which likely was the moment of acceptance or part performance.

Still feeling a little uneasy about the express reservation of Federal to change the terms at any time, I continued to research that topic. *Dunnell* and *West's Minnesota Digest 2d* did not seem to have anything directly on point, nor did A.L.R. However, on WESTLAW, I found an Eighth Circuit

Court of Appeals case from Illinois, *Weiss v. Duro Chrome Corp.* (8th Cir. 1953). The case upheld a contract clause in which the employer explicitly reserved the right to change the commission without giving advance notice to the employee. The contract also specified the employee had the option of terminating his relationship with the employer if he did not like the modifications. The court refused to give a remedy to the employee when he had accepted the changed terms by cashing monthly checks for a year. Shepardizing showed that this case has not been overruled nor has it been cited in a Minnesota case, so it is merely persuasive primary authority.

The Federal flyers, too, could take their business elsewhere if they did not like the modified terms. However, Federal changed the terms and gave notice only after the flyers had accumulated years' worth of mileage credits. The flyers can now choose not to accumulate more miles on Federal based on the new award levels. However, at the time they flew, before the changes, they were acting under the belief that the terms were what Federal said they were. It seems reasonable that Federal would not have to be forever bound by the terms it originally set out. However, it does not seem reasonable that the reservation to change terms would apply to previously acquired miles so as to retroactively diminish the value of the miles the flyers signed up to acquire.

D. Analysis of the Research Approaches

At first glance, it may seem that the three researchers' approaches are more different than similar. Although there are many differences, the differences are matters of detail. The fundamental similarities in the three approaches are much more important. Each researcher had some sense of the tasks he or she needed to accomplish at each step and chose research tools to accomplish those tasks. In other words, each researcher's process was driven by tasks, not by tools.

Each researcher carefully considered the facts and figured out what he or she already knew about the law. Each researcher then chose words to express the factual and legal concepts he or she perceived in the problem. (See Exhibits 12.1 and 12.2 on pages 392 and 393.) Words are one of the chief tools you use in legal research; be aware of how you choose your terms and be deliberate in your choices. All three researchers listed the following indexing terms in some form: airline, frequent flyer, program, mileage or miles, contract, breach, and motion to dismiss. Most of these terms were useful in some setting, be it an index, a topic outline, or a CALR search. In addition, the following helpful terms appeared on only one list: offer, promise, consideration, acceptance, bilateral/unilateral, alteration, and modification. The researchers who initially did not list these terms encountered them later in their research and pursued them at that time. Remember to be alert for additional terms as you research.

Each researcher took note of the jurisdiction of the problem before beginning to research. Events occurring in Minnesota could be covered by federal, Minnesota, and local law. The writers focused on federal and state law because local law was unimportant in this situation. Furthermore, while all researchers focused on mandatory law, they remained open to the possibility of broadening their research—that is, using law from sister jurisdictions to aid in interpreting the mandatory authorities. This sense of jurisdictional priorities makes it possible to perform cost-effective, yet comprehensive research.

All of the researchers split their research into discrete research tasks, so as to make it more manageable. They split off the procedural issue (motion to dismiss for failure to state a claim) from the substantive issue. Then they split the substantive issue into discrete research topics such as unilateral contract, consideration, termination, modification, and revocation. This separation into sub-issues allowed the researchers to complete one portion of the research before moving on to the next portion.

It is interesting that the researchers tackled the procedural issue at different points in their process. Courtney tackled it first, while Tim and Renee tackled it at or near the end of their research in secondary sources. Everyone completed the procedural research before the major portion of the research for primary authority because the procedural posture determined the stopping place in the substantive research.

Although each researcher knew that he or she was looking for primary authority (such as statutes, cases, and court rules), each researcher started with secondary sources. As the researchers explain and their research scenarios demonstrate, secondary sources typically allow you to do cost-effective research by obtaining an overview of an area of law, insight into the pertinent legal theories, and references to primary authority. Each researcher thus perceived that his or her first research task was to obtain the information provided through commentary.

Each researcher, in making his or her specific choices among secondary sources, implicitly or explicitly assessed the strengths and weaknesses of the sources, as well as his or her general preferences. All of the researchers elected not to use the Restatements, all of them found A.L.R. not to contain any annotations on the frequent flyer topic, and all of them found legal periodicals to be very helpful. It makes sense that legal periodicals contained material on this relatively new and narrow legal problem because legal periodicals excel in covering emerging legal topics that are narrow in scope. Tim and Courtney used *LegalTrac* to locate pertinent articles, while Renee instead used WESTLAW. The researchers used research terms like "frequent flyer" and "contract"; they then relied on the article's titles and abstracts to inform them of the contents of the articles. These articles led all three of the researchers more or less directly to *Wolens,* the United States Supreme Court's pronouncement that narrowed frequent flyer lawsuits to the common law claims by pre-empting the state statutory claims.

In addition to legal periodicals, Tim used two contracts treatises to expand his knowledge about revocation of offers, unilateral contracts, and consideration. The other two researchers did not use treatises. Both Tim and Courtney turned to *Dunnell Minnesota Digest,* a misleadingly named state encyclopedia, while no one used the general-scope encyclopedias. Courtney had considerably better luck in *Dunnell* than Tim did. This difference in the researchers' perception of how helpful a particular source pivoted on the research terms used by the researchers; it also may have depended on whether the researcher used the table of contents as well as the index.

Although all of the researchers looked for commentary in the initial research on each sub-issue, recall that commentary can be useful at later stages of research as well. Furthermore, the relationship between primary and secondary authorities is a two-way street. While a researcher typically uses secondary authority to locate primary authority, the reverse also can be done.

The ultimate focus of the research process for all researchers was, of course, mandatory primary authority. All three researchers found that federal law, in the form of the Airline Deregulation Act and *Wolens,* re-focused their research toward contract law under Minnesota common law. The Minnesota case law does not address frequent flyer programs specifically, so the researchers drew analogies to related fact situations, like the newspaper subscription contest in *Mooney* and the fur coat advertisement in *Lefkowitz.* Aside from those analogies, the state common law research largely involved the task of locating pertinent rules of law and applying them to the facts. All researchers found these rules of law—as indeed they must to accomplish this project successfully. Unlike secondary authority, primary authority is not optional. Furthermore, having found one rule, you may not stop until you know that you have found all of the pertinent rules.

The depth of the contract law research was determined by the procedural law governing the situation. Here, the Minnesota Rules of Civil Procedure and interpretive case law set the standards for the scope of the assignment—to determine whether the contract claim could withstand a motion to dismiss.

Although finding and reading primary authority are necessary steps, the researchers made different choices among finding tools and media. Renee, for instance, began her procedural research in *West's Minnesota Digest 2d,* which led her to the pertinent cases. Courtney began her procedural research in the court rules in *Minnesota Statutes Annotated*; the annotations to the rules led her to the pertinent cases. Tim did his procedural research on LEXIS, using a Boolean search in the Minnesota case law library; he then read recent cases until he found the pertinent standard. Again, the task to be accomplished was fixed, but the researchers chose different tools to accomplish the task.

Furthermore, all three researchers blended computer-assisted research with paper sources. Renee used WESTLAW to perform her initial search for legal periodical articles on frequent flyer programs; she later returned to WESTLAW to search for Minnesota cases on performance in unilateral contracts. In both instances, she chose computer-assisted research because she thought it would be faster than paper sources for that particular search and because she was searching for terms that would be used consistently and without much variation. Tim chose LEXIS for his procedural research for the same reasons. Courtney turned to WESTLAW toward the end of her research when all of the paper sources she had been using came up dry on how to interpret Federal's express reservation of the right to change the terms of the program. Note that each researcher was able to articulate when and why he or she used computer-assisted research instead of the paper sources. These deliberate choices among media resulted in efficient and cost-effective research by all of the researchers.

Finally, note that all researchers updated their research results regularly, sometimes near the end of the research on each sub-issue and sometimes as each source was used. The classic means of updating cases is through *Shepard's*; the use of electronic citators is newer and perhaps more expedient. The classic means of updating statutes is through pocket parts and update pamphlets. Again, the task must be accomplished, but there are various ways to perform it.

We hope that working through this book has provided you with information about and insights into legal research, so that you understand the research tasks you need to accomplish, as well as the tools that will enable you to accomplish those tasks.

Research Situations and Problem Sets

The following materials constitute research exercises, each consisting of two parts. First, we have provided realistic research situations to research; you have ten options to choose from for each exercise. Second, for each set of sources or steps in the research process, we have provided problem sets, consisting of questions that will guide you through the sources in a structured way. As you will see, some research situations will be used in several problem sets, so you can see how the different sources combine into a research process. As you also will see, some chapters in the text are covered in only one problem set, while the more complex chapters are covered in several problem sets. (There are no problem sets for Chapters 1 and 3.)

All pages in this part of the book are perforated, so you can tear out the problem sets to submit to your teacher. Do not tear out the research situations, however, as many of them are used for several problem sets.

CHAPTERS 2, 4, 5 RESEARCH SITUATIONS

RESEARCH TERMS SECONDARY SOURCES ISSUE FORMULATION

You will be selecting one of the research situations stated below for the following problem sets for Chapters 2, 4, and 5:

Problem Set for Chapter 2.	Research Terms
Problem Set for Chapter 4 Part B.	Encyclopedias
Problem Set for Chapter 4 Part C.	Legal Periodicals
Problem Set for Chapter 4 Part D.	*American Law Reports* (A.L.R.)
Problem Set for Chapter 4 Part E.	Treatises
Problem Set for Chapter 4 Part F.	Restatements
Problem Set for Chapter 5.	Issue Formulation

Unless otherwise instructed by your professor, you should select one research situation to work for all of these problem sets. We suggest that you leave pages 409-412 in your book (or at least do not turn them in to your professor), so you will have ready access to the texts of the research situations as you work through each problem set.

Research Situation A:

Ms. Rebecca Burgman has become concerned about her elderly mother, Mrs. Prudence Recht. Mrs. Recht has become increasingly disoriented and confused in recent years, but continues to live alone on the family homestead in Elizabethtown, Pennsylvania. Because her mother's mental and physical capacities have been steadily declining, Ms. Burgman has tried to visit her mother more frequently. Recently Mrs. Recht told her daughter that her "spiritual leader" had told her to place all of her trust and faith in the church and, as evidence of her faith, to give all of her material possessions to the church. Ms. Burgman has contacted you for legal advice because she is concerned about the amount of control that the spiritual leader seems to have over her mother. She specifically wants to know if a gift to a religious group under these circumstances is valid.

Research Situation B:

In 1990, Mr. Tony L. Sutheerawata, owner of a chain of tanning salons, signed a ten-year lease with Salas-Engels Realty for commercial space located in Missoula, Montana. Ms.

Marta Salas signed the lease as landlord. The tanning salon was profitable for a few years, but then business declined. Ms. Salas refused to let Mr. Sutheerawata out of the remaining five years of the original lease, so Mr. Sutheerawata advertised to re-let the space. Fortunately he was able to find an interested party. Mr. Sutheerawata transferred the remaining five years to Ms. Jacqueline Navarro, who planned to open an aerobics studio. Ms. Salas objected to this transfer and pointed to language in the original lease signed by Mr. Sutheerawata that read, "Tenant may not assign or sublet the lease to any other party without Landlord's prior consent." Mr. Sutheerawata wants to know whether Ms. Salas can refuse to consent to the assignment.

Research Situation C:

The Beanery, Inc., is a very successful enterprise that specializes in marketing European blends of coffee. The Beanery wishes to buy a shop in a trendy area of Washington, D.C., but it is concerned that the seller would expect a premium if it became aware that the purchaser was so profitable. Hence, the Beanery has asked Lucille Drew to serve as its agent. Ms. Drew agreed to sign the agreement to buy the shop in her own name and then assign the purchase agreement to The Beanery. When negotiating with the seller, Ms. Drew did not disclose that she was serving as an agent for The Beanery, and she was able to negotiate a favorable sale price. Ms. Drew signed the purchase agreement, but when she later attempted to assign the purchase agreement to The Beanery, the seller refused to honor the agreement. The seller invoked a provision in the purchase agreement that prohibited an assignment of the agreement; instead, the seller offered to renegotiate the agreement with The Beanery, but for a much higher price. The Beanery does not want to renegotiate the purchase agreement. The Beanery wants to know if, under agency law, it can enforce the terms of the agreement as negotiated by Ms. Drew, its agent.

Research Situation D:

Mr. Max Burnham, a resident of Tucker, Georgia, is the owner of a late-model sports car. When he awoke one morning and did not find his car where he thought he had parked it, he reported it stolen. Within a week, Mr. Burnham's insurer settled his claim under the theft provision of the insurance policy. Later, the insurer learned that Mr. Burnham had been given a citation for drunk and disorderly conduct the night before the alleged theft and that, in fact, the car had been towed away and impounded. The insurer wants to know whether it has a right to restitution of the payment made to Mr. Burnham because of a mistake about the facts related to the loss.

Research Situation E:

Ms. Karen Selleck is an artist who specializes in realistic paintings of cats, primarily used for greeting cards and calendars. Of course, she has several pedigree cats herself, which she shows occasionally in cat shows near her home in Albany, New York. Apparently, she and one of her cats were photographed at a show, unbeknownst to her. The picture, which is lovely, is now appearing in advertising circulars for a local cat food company. Ms. Selleck wants to maintain her privacy and is incensed that her picture is being used for a commercial purpose without her consent. She wonders whether she has a good case against the cat food company.

Research Situation F:

Dr. Karen Ihito is a pediatric ophthalmologist at a pediatric partnership located in Berring, Texas, a small town with only one clinic and no hospital. The nearest clinic is twenty miles away; the nearest hospital is seventy-five miles away. When Dr. Ihito began this job two years ago, she signed a non-competition clause as a part of her partnership. The clause stated, "If Dr. Ihito leaves the partnership for any reason, she promises not to work as a pediatric ophthalmologist within three years anywhere within a forty-mile radius from the courthouse in Berring, Texas." Dr. Ihito now wishes to leave the partnership to work at the clinic located twenty miles away. There are no other ophthalmologists within that same area. Before she makes her decision about whether to change employers, she wishes to know whether the non-competition clause is valid.

Research Situation G:

Tim and Bette Terra are first cousins, are married to each other, and live in New York. Mr. and Mrs. Terra were married in Arizona. This type of marriage is valid in New York, but is not valid in Arizona. Mr. and Mrs. Terra want to know whether their marriage will be treated as legal in New York, despite the conflict between the states' laws.

Research Situation H:

Ms. Jane DePaul, your client and a resident of Cincinnati, Ohio, owns a pit bull terrier. She has owned it for nine years, since he was a puppy. Ms. DePaul monitors the dog quite carefully, given the breed's propensity toward biting. When she lets it out in the evening, she has him on a six-foot leash in her fenced yard. To her knowledge, the dog has never bitten or attacked anyone, until last night. Last night, after letting the dog out, Ms. De Paul heard loud screams from her backyard. Upon investigating, she found a man lurking under a window. She did not know him; he clearly was trespassing in her yard. The dog had bitten the man on the arm and was growling at him. When the dog heard Ms. DePaul's voice, he backed off, and the man fled. Although Ms. DePaul is relieved that the man left without harming her, she is concerned about any liability she may have toward him as a result of the bite.

Research Situation I:

Three years ago Robert and Rachel Boyd of Tucson, Arizona, adopted Roberta, when she was one month old. Only one of Roberta's natural parents, her unmarried mother, was a party to the adoption proceedings. Recently Roberta's putative biological father contacted the Boyds, telling them that he had not been informed of the adoption proceedings and had not consented to the adoption. He wants custody of his daughter. The Boyds want to know if he is likely to be able to get the judgment determining the child's status reversed.

Research Situation J:

Mr. Jeff Zhu owns a small vineyard and winery located near Eugene, Washington. Over the years, Mr. Zhu discovered that the grapes grown on Ms. Shelly Kerner's sandy land, when mixed with his own grapes, produced a superior red wine. Hence, he entered into a contract with Ms. Kerner to buy a large quantity of next season's grapes. The contract stated that the grapes were to be grown on Ms. Kerner's sandy land. Ms. Kerner planted and cultivated the grapes in sufficient quantity to perform the contract, but an extraordinarily severe rain storm resulted in a flood that destroyed Ms. Kerner's vineyards. Ms. Kerner advised Mr. Zhu that it would then be impossible for her to perform the contract, and she thereafter delivered no grapes to him. Mr. Zhu claims that Ms. Kerner has breached the contract. Ms. Kerner wishes to know if she will be liable to Mr. Zhu or if delivery is excused under these circumstances.

Problem Set for Chapter 2. Research Terms

Your Name ______________________________

Professor ______________________________

Circle the letter of the research situation you selected (see pages 409-412):

A B C D E F G H I J

1. Read through the research situation carefully. List the main concepts in each of the eight categories below. In some cases you may not be able to identify concepts for a category.

factual "who"

____

____

factual "what"

____

____

factual "when"

____

____

factual "where"

____

____

factual "why"

____

____

legal theory

____

____

relief

____

____

procedure

____

____

2. Select two or three factual concepts and two or three legal concepts you have listed. For each, think of related terms, such as synonyms, antonyms, broader terms, and narrower terms. Present them here, whether in ladder, wheel, or list form, or a combination of these.

3. Look up one or two of your legal terms in a legal thesaurus, such as Burton's *Legal Thesaurus* or Statsky's *West's Legal Thesaurus.* List your initial term and up to five related terms that could be pertinent to your research situation.

____

____

____

4. Look up one or two of your legal terms in a legal dictionary, such as *Ballentine's*, *Black's*, or the dictionaries written by Gifis, Gilmer, Oran, Radin, Redden and Veron, or Rothenberg. Write out or paraphrase the definition(s); you need not include references to other sources.

____

____

____

____

____

____

5. Provide the proper *Bluebook* citation for a definition you chose for Question 4.

____

____

Problem Set for Chapter 4 Part B. Encyclopedias

Your Name ______________________ Professor ______________________

Circle the letter of the research situation you selected (see pages 409-412):

A B C D E F G H I J

Note: If you have not yet developed research terms for the research situation you selected, do so before you begin this problem set, using the methods suggested in Chapter 2. See the problem set for Chapter 2 for assistance.

American Jurisprudence, Second Edition

1. Use your research terms in the index or the topic list to locate pertinent material in *American Jurisprudence, Second Edition.* List the research terms you used along with the pertinent topics and section numbers within those topics that you found.

Research Terms Used:	Corresponding Topic(s) and Section(s) Found:
____________	______________________
____________	______________________
____________	______________________
____________	______________________

2. Select a topic to explore. Examine the introductory material to that topic, including the topic outline, at the beginning of the topic you selected. List the topic you have selected, as well as at least three sections that appear to be pertinent to your research situation. Include the section numbers and the subject headings for those sections.

Topic Selected: ______________________

Section Numbers:	Corresponding Subject Headings for Those Sections:
________	______________________
________	______________________
________	______________________
________	______________________

3. Read at least three pertinent sections. Note here legal rule(s), definition(s), and principle(s) that are pertinent to your research situation.

4. Review the footnotes to those sections for references to primary authority. List two or three references that could be pertinent to your research situation. If possible, find primary authority from the jurisdiction in your research situation.

5. To update and expand your research, consult the supplement. Did you find any additional information that is pertinent to your research situation? If so, record it here. If not, write "none."

6. Provide the proper *Bluebook* citation to the material you just reviewed, including any additional material in the supplement.

Corpus Juris Secundum

7. Use your research terms in the index or the topic list to locate pertinent material in *Corpus Juris Secundum*. List the research terms you used along with the pertinent topics and the section numbers within those topics that you found.

Research Terms Used: Corresponding Topic(s) and Section(s) Found:

______________________ ____

______________________ ____

______________________ ____

______________________ ____

8. Select a topic to explore. Examine the introductory material to that topic, including the topic outline, at the beginning of the topic you selected. List the topic you have selected, as well as at least three sections that appear to be pertinent to your research situation. Include the section numbers and the subject headings for those sections.

Topic Selected: ____

Section Numbers: Corresponding Subject Headings for Those Sections:

______________________ ____

______________________ ____

______________________ ____

______________________ ____

9. Read at least three pertinent sections. Note here legal rule(s), definition(s), and principle(s) that are pertinent to your research situation.

____

____

____

____

____

____

____

10. Review the footnotes for references to primary authority. List two or three references that could be pertinent to your research situation. If possible, find primary authority from the jurisdiction in your research situation.

____

____

____

____

____

11. To update and expand your research, consult the supplement. Did you find any additional information that is pertinent to your research situation? If so, record it here. If not, write "none."

12. Provide the proper *Bluebook* citation to the material you just reviewed, including any additional material in the supplement.

Concluding Question

13. Has your research in encyclopedias brought forth any legal or factual concepts that you had not yet identified? If so, state them here.

PROBLEM SET FOR CHAPTER 4 PART C. LEGAL PERIODICALS

Your Name ____________________ Professor ____________________

Circle the letter of the research situation you selected (see pages 409-412):

A B C D E F G H I J

Note: If you have not yet developed research terms for the research situation you selected, do so before you begin this problem set, using the methods suggested in Chapter 2. See the problem set for Chapter 2 for assistance.

1. Select one of the following legal periodical indexes and circle its title:

LegalTrac *Current Law Index* (C.L.I.) *Index to Legal Periodicals and Books* (I.L.P.B.)

2. Although you sometimes would do a comprehensive search using indexes that span many years, for this assignment, use indexes for the years designated:

Research Situation A:	1991-94
Research Situation B:	1988-89, 1995-96
Research Situation C:	1982-84
Research Situation D:	1984-85, 1989-90
Research Situation E:	1983-86
Research Situation F:	1992-94
Research Situation G:	1980-82
Research Situation H:	1988-90
Research Situation I:	1993-95
Research Situation J:	1987-90

Using the research terms you have developed, find two or three subject headings or subheadings in your index that appear to be pertinent to your research situation. List the research terms you used and the corresponding subject headings you found.

Research Terms Used:	Corresponding Subject (Sub)Heading(s) Found:
__________	__________
__________	__________
__________	__________
__________	__________

3. Select one of the subject headings and subheadings you found in the index, and list it below. Scan the articles listed under that heading and subheading. Select one or two articles that seem pertinent to your research situation. For each of the articles you select, give the title and citation information found in the index. (You need not use proper *Bluebook* citation.)

Subject Heading and Subheading: ______________________________

Article Selected and Corresponding Citation Information:

____

____

____

4. Move to the legal periodical collection, and locate one of the volumes listed below for your research situation. Circle your choice:

Research Situation	*Legal Periodical and Volume*	*Segment*
A	The Catholic Lawyer, vol. 35	Part B
	Duquesne Law Review, vol. 30	Last half of article
B	DePaul Law Review, vol. 36	Part II
	Willamette Law Review, vol. 31	Parts II, III
C	Commercial Law Journal, vol. 88	Part III
	Detroit College of Law Review, 1984 vol.	Part II
D	Texas Law Review, vol. 67	Parts I B, II A
	Virginia Law Review, vol. 71	Part II B
E	Albany Law Review, vol. 48	Part II B
	Annual Survey of American Law, 1985 vol.	Part II
F	American Business Law Journal, vol. 31	Material under Physicians and Dentists: The Public Interest
	Baylor Law Review, vol. 44	Part II C
G	Family Advocate, vol. 3	Entire article
	Loyola Law Review, vol. 26	Part I A (1)
H	Cleveland State Law Review, vol. 37	Part IV
	University of Dayton Law Review, vol. 13	Part III E
I	Catholic University Law Review, vol. 42	Part III
	Texas Law Review, vol. 72	Part III C
J	Mercer Law Review, vol. 40	Part II
	St. Louis University Law Journal, vol. 31	Part II B

Find a pertinent article in that volume by checking the table(s) of contents or index for that volume. What type of article does it appear to be—a student case comment, a lead article, an essay, or something else?

____

5. Skim the introduction and conclusion of your article, if any, to get a sense of the article. Then read the segment of the article indicated in Question 4.

Note here legal rule(s), definition(s), and principle(s) that are pertinent to your research situation.

6. Examine the footnotes for the segment listed above. List two or three primary authorities referred to in those footnotes that could be pertinent to your research situation. If possible, find primary authorities from the jurisdiction in your research situation.

7. Using the factors discussed in Chapter 4, evaluate the article as a source of background, analysis, and references.

8. Provide the proper *Bluebook* citation to this article.

9. What steps might you take to expand or update the information found in this article?

10. **Optional Question:** Use *Shepard's Law Review Citations* to expand your research.

(a) Remember that *Shepard's* does not cover all periodical titles. Is your journal covered by this *Shepard's* title?

(b) If so, the article you read is the cited source. Look it up by journal name, volume, and page numbers. If any entries appear in *Shepard's,* record the first two entries listed. (Use the table of abbreviations at the front of the volume to decipher the entries.)

11. Has your research in periodicals brought forth any legal or factual concepts that you had not yet identified? If so, state them here.

PROBLEM SET FOR CHAPTER 4 PART D. *AMERICAN LAW REPORTS* (A.L.R.)

Your Name ____________________ Professor ____________________

Circle the letter of the research situation you selected (see pages 409-412):

A B C D E F G H I J

Note: If you have not yet developed research terms for the research situation you selected, do so before you begin this problem set, using the methods suggested in Chapter 2. See the problem set for Chapter 2 for assistance.

1. Locate the *ALR Index.* Using the research terms you have developed, find one or two subject headings that appear to be pertinent to your research situation. List the research terms you used and the corresponding subject headings you found.

Research Terms Used:	Corresponding Subject Heading(s) Found:
__________	__________
__________	__________
__________	__________
__________	__________

2. Scan the listing of annotations under the subject headings and select two or more annotations that appear to be pertinent. For each annotation you select, give the full title and other citation information found in the index. (You need not use proper *Bluebook* citation.)

____

____

____

____

____

____

3. Locate one of the annotations you listed in your answer to Question 2. Examine the introduction and the special features, such as the index or the Table of Jurisdictions Represented. Explain how these features helped you to locate material pertinent to your research situation.

____

____

____

____

4. Read the pertinent sections of that annotation. Note here legal rule(s), definition(s), and principle(s) that are pertinent to your research situation.

____

____

____

____

____

____

____

5. List some of the primary authorities referred to in the annotation that could be pertinent to your research situation. If possible, find primary authorities from the jurisdiction in your research situation.

____

____

____

____

____

6. To update and expand the information in the main volume, consult the supplement.

(a) Has your annotation been superseded? If so, what is the citation for the new annotation?

____

(b) Is there any supplemental information pertinent to your research situation? If so, record it here. If not, write "none."

____

____

____

____

7. Provide the proper *Bluebook* citation to your annotation, including any additional material in the supplement.

8. **Optional Question:** Use *Shepard's Citations for Annotations* to expand your research. The annotation is the cited source. Look it up by series, volume, and page number. If any entries appear in *Shepard's,* record the first two entries here. (Use the table of abbreviations at the front of the volume to decipher the entries.)

9. Has your research in A.L.R. brought forth any legal or factual concepts that you had not yet identified? If so, state them here.

PROBLEM SET FOR CHAPTER 4 PART E. TREATISES

Your Name ______________________ Professor ______________________

Circle the letter of the research situation you selected (see pages 409-412):

A B C D E F G H I J

Note: If you have not yet developed research terms for the research situation you selected, do so before you begin this problem set, using the methods suggested in Chapter 2. See the problem set for Chapter 2 for assistance.

1. Circle the area(s) of the law involved in your research situation. There may be more than one.

Agency Conflicts of Laws Contracts Family Law (Domestic Relations)
Insurance Judgments Property Restitution Torts

2. Locate two treatises covering the area of law in your research situation, by using the library catalog, browsing the shelves, getting an expert's recommendation, or looking for a reference in a textbook. List the title and author(s) of each treatise below. (You need not use proper *Bluebook* citation.)

____

____

____

____

3. What approach did you use for finding these treatises, and why?

____

____

____

____

4. Examine both treatises briefly. Using the factors discussed in Chapter 4, evaluate these treatises as a source of background, analysis, and references.

____

____

____

5. Using the index or the table of contents of one of the treatises you selected, locate parts of the treatise that are pertinent to your research situation. Read those parts. (If you find that the treatise is not very helpful, feel free to find a better treatise.) Note here legal rule(s), definition(s), and principle(s) that are pertinent to your research situation.

6. List two or three references to primary authority that could be pertinent to your research situation. If possible, find primary authority from the jurisdiction in your research situation.

7. Update the information covered by your treatise by consulting a pocket part or other supplement, if any.

(a) Was there a supplement for your treatise?

(b) If so, did you find any new information that is pertinent to your research situation? If so, record it here. If not, write "none."

8. Provide the proper *Bluebook* citation to your treatise, including any additional material in the supplement.

____

____

____

9. Has your research in treatises brought forth any legal or factual concepts that you had not yet identified? If so, state them here.

____

____

____

____

____

PROBLEM SET FOR CHAPTER 4 PART F. RESTATEMENTS

Your Name ______________________ Professor ______________________

Circle the letter of the research situation you selected (see pages 409-412):

A B C D E F G H I J

Note: If you have not yet developed research terms for the research situation you selected, do so before you begin this problem set, using the methods suggested in Chapter 2. See the problem set for Chapter 2 for assistance.

1. Circle the area of the law involved in your research situation.

Agency Conflict of Laws Contracts Judgments

Property (Donative Transfers) Property (Landlord and Tenant)

Restitution Torts

Although you sometimes would do a comprehensive search of more than one Restatement series, for this assignment, use the second series if there is more than one.

2. Locate the Restatement index(es) or table of contents for the topic and series indicated above. Using the research terms you have developed, find one or more Restatement sections that appear to be pertinent to your research situation. List the research terms you used and the corresponding Restatement sections you found (number and subject matter).

Research Terms Used:	Corresponding Sections and Subject Matter Found:
______________	______________________________
______________	______________________________
______________	______________________________
______________	______________________________

3. Locate and read the rules in the sections listed above (but not yet the comments, illustrations, Reporter's Notes, and Statutory Notes). Note here legal rule(s) that are pertinent to your research situation.

4. Select one section that is pertinent to your research situation. Read the material following that rule (comments, illustrations, Reporter's Notes, and Statutory Notes, if any). Also skim any cross-referenced sections and the sections in the vicinity of your section. Note here additional legal concepts that are pertinent to your research situation.

5. Provide the proper *Bluebook* citation to the Restatement material you used to answer Question 4, including specific comments and illustrations, if applicable.

6. Locate and review the case digests for the Restatement section you cited in your answer to Question 5. List one or two cases that could be pertinent to your research situation. If possible, find cases from the jurisdiction in your research situation.

7. **Optional Question:** Use *Shepard's Restatement of the Law Citations* to expand your research. The Restatement section from your answer to Question 5 is the cited source. Look it up by topic, series, and section number. If any entries appear in *Shepard's,* record the first two entries here. (Use the table of abbreviations at the front of the volume to decipher the entries.)

____

____

____

8. Has your research in Restatements brought forth any legal or factual concepts that you had not yet identified? If so, state them here.

____

____

____

____

____

PROBLEM SET FOR CHAPTER 5. ISSUE FORMULATION

Your Name ______________________ Professor ______________________

This problem set builds on the Chapter 2 and Chapter 4 problem sets. You should review your work before beginning this problem set.

Circle the letter of the research situation you selected (see pages 409-412):

A B C D E F G H I J

1. List the major legal topics pertinent to your research situation that you read about in your secondary source research.

____

____

____

2. On this and the next page, in outline, flowchart, or other form of your own making, present the legal framework suggested by your commentary research. Include legal principles, rules, and definitions. In a parallel design, note the facts from your research situation that are pertinent to each of the legal concepts you have presented. (See Exhibit 5.2 on page 122 for one example.)

3. Now write issues to research in primary authority. Each issue should combine legal concepts and facts in question form. You may have one or more issues, and your issue(s) may or may not have sub-issues.

____

____

____

____

4. Finally, note any additional facts you would wish to know as you continue to work on your research situation.

Chapters 6, 7 Research Situations

Cases State Statutes

You will be researching the research situation stated below in various states for the following problem sets for Chapters 6 and 7:

First Problem Set for Chapter 6.	Cases in Paper
Second Problem Set for Chapter 6.	Online Citators for Cases
Third Problem Set for Chapter 6.	Online Full-Text Searching for Cases
First Problem Set for Chapter 7.	State Statutes in Paper
Second Problem Set for Chapter 7.	State Statutes Online

Research Situation

Your client, James Forester, owns a large tract of land in a developing suburb. On two sides, it already is bordered by housing developments, and soon there will be developments on the remaining two sides. These neighborhoods house many children.

As Mr. Forester is well aware, children from these neighborhoods come onto his property, although he has not invited them. Mr. Forester believes that the children are drawn primarily to an old barn on the property. The barn was built nearly a century ago, when the property was first used as a farm. Because no one has farmed the property for about a decade, the barn has slowly deteriorated. Nonetheless, children enjoy playing in and around it. The rusty fence and "no trespassing" signs around the perimeter of the property do not seem to deter the children.

Mr. Forester is concerned about the safety of these children, as well as his own liability should any of them be injured on the property.

First Problem Set for Chapter 6. Cases in Paper

Your Name ______________________ Professor ______________________

Your research situation is stated at page 441. Your research in secondary sources has suggested the following issue to pursue in case law: *Is the owner of an old and dilapidated barn liable in negligence to children trespassing on the property?* Assume that this topic is governed by state case law.

Select one of the following states in which to perform your research. Circle your choice.

Arkansas	Illinois	Pennsylvania
Connecticut	Kansas	West Virginia
Georgia	Nebraska	Wisconsin
Idaho		

1. Which reporter(s) contain cases decided by the appellate court(s) of the state you selected? (Remember that Table T.1 in *The Bluebook* provides information about state reporters.)

____

____

____

2. (a) Which West digests cover cases decided by the appellate court(s) in the state you selected? (See Exhibit 6.2 on pages 144-145.)

____

(b) If there is more than one, which is the most efficient to start with, and why?

____

____

____

3. Select an appropriate digest to work with, and collect the volumes of the digest (main volumes and supplements) needed to research your topic back to 1950. For this research problem, cases decided since 1950 suffice. **Note:** You need not collect the advance sheets of your reporter yet.

(a) List the series and dates of the volumes you have collected.

____

(b) As to your selected jurisdiction, note the most recent volume(s) covered by the most recent digest supplement.

____

4. (a) Use the outline of West topics (located near the front of digest volumes) to identify potentially useful topics. List up to three possibilities.

____

____

(b) Now use the Descriptive Word Index to identify potentially useful topics and key numbers. The topics you find may or may not be the same as those you found in Question 4(a). (The Descriptive Word Index is in separate volume(s) typically shelved at the end of the digest.) List at least three key numbers—along with their topics—to pursue.

____

____

5. Select a potentially useful topic; note it here. Locate and scan the topic outline in the main volume of your digest. Did you discover any other potentially useful key numbers? If so, record the new key number(s) here.

____

6. Scan the headnotes reprinted under two or three of the most promising topic/key numbers you developed in your answers to Questions 4 and 5.

(a) List several cases that could be pertinent to your research situation; for each case list the name of the first party, the court, the date of the case, and its citation (proper *Bluebook* form is not required).

____

____

____

____

____

(b) To facilitate your professor's evaluation of your work on the following questions, from this point on, please focus on a pertinent case from the following year in the jurisdiction you originally selected.

Arkansas	1957
Connecticut	1961
Georgia	1982
Idaho	1985
Illinois	1955
Kansas	1976

Nebraska	1976
Pennsylvania	1966
West Virginia	1967
Wisconsin	1953

Locate a headnote describing that case in the digest (if you have not already done so). Record the name and citation of that case (proper *Bluebook* form is not required).

____

____

____

7. Locate that case in a reporter, read it, and provide the following information about the case:

(a) the name of the case, court, and date, as they appear in the opening block

____

____

____

(b) the key facts of the case

____

____

____

____

____

(c) the name of the prevailing party

____

(d) the legal rule(s), definition(s), and principle(s) that are pertinent to your research situation

____

____

____

____

____

____

____

(e) the numbers of the headnotes corresponding to the rule(s) pertinent to your research situation (for use in Shepardizing your case)

(f) whether there is a concurrence or dissent and, if so, the main point made in that opinion

---

---

8. (a) Locate an advance sheet for your reporter that is not covered by the hardbound digest and its supplements. (Review your answer to Question 3.) Record the volume(s) and page numbers of the reporter contained in that advance sheet. **Note:** If this were a real research project, you would review the digest material in all advance sheets and hardbound volumes not covered by the hardbound digest and its supplements.

(b) Locate the digest material in that advance sheet. Are there any entries for your state under the topic/key numbers you have been researching? If so, note the name(s) of the case(s). If not, write "none."

---

9. To update and expand your research, which *Shepard's Citations* could you use?

---

10. Select an appropriate *Shepard's Citations* to use, and collect the volumes and supplements you need to Shepardize the case you used in Question 7. List the title and the dates of the volumes and supplements..

---

11. Peruse the entries for your case in the *Shepard's* volumes and supplements covering your case. Record the information requested below, to the extent it exists:
(a) the case's parallel citation(s)

(b) citations to the history of the case (for example, citations carrying the notations a [affirm], m [modify], r [reverse], v [vacate]) (see Illustration 6-8 on page 158)

(c) citations indicating that the case has been overruled or criticized or questioned by a court within your selected state

---

(d) three cases from courts within your selected state that explain, follow, or distinguish your case

---

(e) three cases from courts within your selected state referring to the headnotes you identified in your answer to Question 7(e) as pertinent to your research situation

---

(f) the first citation to the case by a federal court

(g) the first citation to the case by a court of a different state and the name of the state

---

(h) any citation in a commentary source

---

12. As needed, follow up on any citations in your answer to Question 11 that affect the status of your case as good law, by locating the citing case in the reporter and scanning it. Is your original (cited) case still good law? Why, or why not?

---

13. Provide proper *Bluebook* citations for your case:
(a) if you were writing to the court that decided the case

(b) if you were writing to a court in a different state

Note: In some situations your answers to (a) and (b) will be the same.

14. If you were to continue your research—as indeed you should if this were a real research project—which two or three cases would you be sure to pursue? Explain why you would pursue each of them. Select those cases from your answers to Questions 6(a) and 11.

____

____

____

____

____

____

____

SECOND PROBLEM SET FOR CHAPTER 6. ONLINE CITATORS FOR CASES

Your Name ______________________ Professor ______________________

Although Chapter 6 has demonstrated online citators on WESTLAW, you may do comparable research on LEXIS. Select one of the online legal research systems for this problem set. Read the vendor's materials on that system's citators. Circle the system you selected:

LEXIS WESTLAW

Then complete this problem set using the *Chase v. Luce* case, reproduced at pages 453-455.

1. Circle the citators available on the system you selected.

Shepard's	*Shepard's* PreView	QuickCite
LexCite	Insta-Cite	Auto-Cite

2. Using *Shepard's* online, Shepardize *Chase v. Luce*. What search did you enter?

____

3. What *Shepard's* paper titles are included in the online *Shepard's* display for your case? If your search retrieved more than one online document, note the corresponding paper *Shepard's* series and division for each.

____

____

4. Review the *Shepard's* display for your case, using both documents if there is more than one. List the parallel citation(s) for *Chase,* if any.

____

5. Does the *Shepard's* display provide any subsequent history for *Chase*? Explain your answer.

____

____

6. Retrieve the first case noted as distinguishing *Chase* by typing the number that corresponds to its citation. (Review pages 157-158 for the meaning of *Shepard's* codes.)

(a) Record the name of the case you retrieved.

____

(b) Page through the case until you reach the page that cites *Chase v. Luce*. How does the court distinguish the citing case from *Chase v. Luce*?

____

____

____

____

____

7. Return to your *Shepard's* display for *Chase v. Luce*. What did you enter to return?

____

8. The online *Shepard's* allows you to limit your display to any headnote number of your choice. From the copy of the *Chase* case on pages 453-455, select the headnote number pertinent to the legal standard governing when a possessor of land is liable for injuries to trespassing children, and limit your display to sources citing that headnote.

(a) Record your search.

____

(b) How many cases did you retrieve?

____

(c) Browse the first case. How does it affect the authority of *Chase v. Luce*?

____

____

____

____

(d) State the name of that citing case.

____

9. Return to the full *Shepard's* display for *Chase*. Circle yes or no to indicate which documents appear in the *Shepard's* displays for the case. When you have finished, print your *Shepard's* results.

Decisions from courts of other states	Yes	No
Decisions from federal courts	Yes	No

A.L.R. annotations	Yes	No
Law reviews other than the *ABA Journal*	Yes	No
Treatises	Yes	No

10. Update *Shepard's* using *Shepard's* PreView and QuickCite on WESTLAW or LexCite on LEXIS, as applicable.

(a) If you are using WESTLAW, record the following:

(1) the *Shepard's* PreView search command

____

(2) the first new citation you retrieved by entering that command, if any

____

(3) the QuickCite command

____

(4) the search performed by the system after you entered that command

____

(b) If you are using LexCite, record the following:

(1) the library and file you searched

____

(2) your reason(s) for picking that library and file

____

____

(3) the first citation you retrieved

____

11. Using the same online system, Insta-Cite or Auto-Cite your case, as appropriate.

(a) Record your search.

____

____

(b) What information does the display provide as to *Chase*?

____

____

____

12. Based on your research in *Shepard's*, do you consider *Chase* to be a strong case to cite? Explain your reasoning.

13. Evaluate the paper and online research methods for using citators. Explain the advantages and disadvantages of the two research methods.

1950, when plaintiff became bedridden, until her 71st birthday. The only other item of damage proved is an $82 doctor bill. These items in the aggregate total $20,829.06, and thus the verdict for $26,544.50 includes an award for pain and suffering of $5,715.44. The evidence is that plaintiff has had a great deal of pain and suffering since the accident and that such pain and suffering will continue. Under the circumstances the evidence is more than sufficient to sustain the verdict.

[5–8] In view of defendant's admitted liability and in view of our conclusion that the verdict is not excessive, the contention that the verdict was motivated by passion and prejudice is moot. Clearly the trial court did not abuse its discretion in denying a new trial on the grounds of passion and prejudice engendered by the arguments of plaintiff's counsel. It is to be borne in mind that a new trial for the misconduct of counsel is never granted as a disciplinary measure but only to prevent a miscarriage of justice.[2] We do not, however, condone the use of arguments which are not justified by the evidence. Illustrations to illuminate a jury argument may be drawn from everyday life or from the Bible as was done in this case, but such illustrations must not be so used that they themselves, separate and apart from the actual evidence, become vehicles for casting opprobrium upon the opposing party and his witnesses.

The order of the trial court is affirmed.

Affirmed.

CHASE et al. v. LUCE.

No. 36062.

Supreme Court of Minnesota.

May 22, 1953.

Actions, consolidated for trial, for injuries sustained by five-year-old girl in fall through second floor of house, which was being constructed by defendant, and for her father's medical expenses. The District Court, Hennepin County, Paul J. Jaroscak, J., entered judgment on verdict for girl and father, and defendant appealed. The Supreme Court, Loring, C. J., held that evidence was sufficient to sustain verdict.

Affirmed.

1. Negligence ⚷33(3)

Possessor of land is liable for injuries to trespassing children where possessor knows, or should know, that children are likely to trespass upon place where condition is maintained and that condition is one which involves an unreasonable risk of death or injury to children, and children do not discover condition or realize risk involved, and utility to possessor of maintaining condition is slight as compared to risk to children.

2. Negligence ⚷134(5)

Parent and Child ⚷7(12)

In actions, consolidated for trial, for injuries sustained by five-year-old girl in fall through second floor of house which was being constructed by defendant, and for her father's medical expenses, evidence was sufficient to sustain verdict for girl and father.

Syllabus by the Court.

In action for injuries to a seven-year-old girl incurred in an unfinished house, evidence is sufficient to sustain a verdict for plaintiffs.

Freeman, Larson & Peterson, and Robert L. Hoppe, Minneapolis, for appellant.

Vennum, Newhall & Ackman, Minneapolis, for respondents.

LORING, Chief Justice.

This appeal involves an action by a seven-year-old girl to recover damages for injuries sustained on the premises of defendant and alleged to be the result of the negligence of defendant's agents, servants, and

2. Harris v. Breezy Point Lodge, Inc., 238 Minn. —, 56 N.W.2d 655; Moose v. Vesey, 225 Minn. 64, 29 N.W.2d 649.

employees.[1] The jury returned a verdict for plaintiffs, and the trial court denied defendant's motion for judgment notwithstanding the verdict. Judgment was entered for plaintiffs, and defendant appeals from this judgment.

Resolving all conflicts and doubts in favor of the prevailing parties below, the following appear to be the facts. Defendant was building several houses in south Minneapolis. Plaintiff Judith Chase, who was five years old at the time, entered one of these houses. Although there is considerable conflict as to whether there was a latch on the door, there is sufficient evidence to support a finding that there was no latch on the door at the time of the child's entrance. In view of the verdict, we must assume this to be the fact. See, 1 Dunnell, Dig., 3d Ed., § 415. b. While there were no steps up to the door, it appears that there were blocks placed there to afford access to the door. Judith apparently went up a flight of rough stairs to the second floor. There were no floor boards laid on the second floor, and the joists were about 16 inches apart. Nailed to the bottom of these were some rock lath strips. Judith apparently stepped in between the joists onto the rock lath strips and fell through to the first floor, sustaining the injuries involved here. The joists were about eight inches high, and there was evidence to show that these rock lath strips would not support Judith's weight when dropped from a height of four inches. The issue of contributory negligence was specifically excluded. The jury returned verdicts for Judith and her father for $3,000 and $622.29 respectively.

The only question involved in this appeal is whether or not there is sufficient evidence to justify a finding that defendant was guilty of negligence and that such negligence was a proximate cause of plaintiff's injuries. The instructions are unchallenged.

[1] As correctly set forth in the instructions, a possessor of land is liable for injuries to trespassing children where:

(1) The place where the condition is maintained is one upon which the possessor knows, or should know, that such children are likely to trespass; and

(2) The condition is one of which the possessor knows, or should know, and which he realizes, or should realize, as involving an unreaonable risk of death or serious bodily harm to such children; and

(3) The children, because of their youth, do not discover the condition or realize the risk involved in intermeddling in it or in coming within the area made dangerous by it; and

(4) The utility to the possessor of maintaining the condition is slight, as compared to the risk to young children involved therein.

These rules are found in Restatement, Torts, § 339; Gimmestad v. Rose Brothers Co., Inc., 194 Minn. 531, 261 N.W. 194; Weber v. St. Anthony Falls Water Power Co., 214 Minn. 1, 7 N.W.2d 339.

[2] Applying each of these rules to the facts of the case at bar, we reach the following conclusions:

Inasmuch as defendant admitted that he knew there were numerous small children in the area; defendant's employees had chased children away on several occasions; and defendant was in the business of building houses and could be readily charged with the knowledge that children might enter an unfinished house through an unlatched door, a jury is justified in finding that defendant or his agents knew or should have known that children would be likely to trespass in the manner of plaintiff here. See, Heitman v. City of Lake City, 225 Minn. 117, 30 N.W.2d 18; Schmit v. Village of Cold Spring, 216 Minn. 465, 13 N.W.2d 382, 154 A.L.R. 1325; Gimmestad v. Rose Brothers Co., Inc., 194 Minn. 531, 261 N.W. 194; Weber v. St. Anthony Falls Water Power Co., 214 Minn. 1, 7 N.W.2d 339.

1. Her father brought a separate action for medical expenses. The two cases were consolidated for trial and are submitted as a single case on this appeal pursuant to a stipulation that a decision in one action shall be considered applicable to both.

Inasmuch as the rock lath strips might easily appear to a five-year-old child to be capable of supporting her weight, a jury is well warranted in finding that this condition, when coupled with the ease of access afforded by the unlatched door and unobstructed passage to the second floor, involved an unreasonable risk of injury to children. See Weber v. St. Anthony Falls Water Power Co., 214 Minn. 1, 7 N.W.2d 339.

In view of the age of the child, a jury is warranted in finding that she did not discover or realize the generally dangerous condition of a house under construction and the particular danger involved in stepping between the joists onto the rock lath strips.

Inasmuch as there was evidence introduced showing the feasibility and ease of latching the door, nailing the door shut, barricading the stairway, or covering the second-floor stair well—all with no damage to the property—a jury might well find that any "utility" to defendant in failing to take one of these precautions was negligible in comparison with the risk involved.

The satisfaction of each of these elements was a proper question for a jury, and there is ample evidence to sustain their verdict.

Affirmed.

ROGER L. DELL, J., not having been a member of the court at the time of the argument and submission, took no part in the consideration or decision of this case.

BORAK v. H. E. WESTERMAN LUMBER CO. et al.

No. 35994.

Supreme Court of Minnesota.

May 15, 1953.

Proceedings for workmen's compensation. To review order of Industrial Commission denying compensation for death of claimant's husband from carbon monoxide poisoning sustained while decedent was attempting to start his automobile preparatory to going to his work as manager of lumber company, claimant brought certiorari. The Supreme Court, Frank T. Gallagher, J., held that where decedent customarily used or was expected to use his automobile at his place of business, and his employer knew, or should have known, of such customary use, accidental death of decedent arose out of and in course of his employment.

Reversed.

1. Workmen's Compensation ⚷1939

Although conclusions of Industrial Commission as a trier of facts must stand, where commission has choice between conflicting evidence or where diverse inferences may be drawn from evidence, conclusions which are manifestly and clearly contrary to the evidence cannot stand.

2. Workmen's Compensation ⚷1412

Industrial Commission, in determining facts from competent evidence, must accept as true the positive, unimpeached testimony of credible witnesses, unless such testimony is inherently improbable or rendered so by facts and circumstances disclosed at the hearing.

3. Workmen's Compensation ⚷1581

In proceeding to obtain compensation for death of claimant's husband from carbon monoxide poisoning sustained while decedent was attempting to start his automobile preparatory to going to his work as manager of lumber company, evidence established that decedent customarily used or was expected to use his automobile at his place of business, that his employer knew, or should have known, of such customary use.

4. Workmen's Compensation ⚷635

Where manager of lumber company customarily used or was expected to use his automobile at his place of business, and his employer knew, or should have known, of such customary use, accidental death of manager from carbon monoxide poisoning, while manager was attempting to start his automobile preparatory to going to his work, arose out of and in course of his employment. M.S.A. § 176.01, subd. 11.

THIRD PROBLEM SET FOR CHAPTER 6. ONLINE FULL-TEXT SEARCHING FOR CASES

Your Name ______________________ Professor ______________________

Although Chapter 6 has demonstrated full-text searching on WESTLAW, you may do comparable research online using LEXIS. Select one of the online legal research systems for this problem set. Read the vendor's materials for full-text and natural language searching.

Circle the system you selected:

LEXIS WESTLAW

Your research situation is stated at page 441. Your research in secondary sources has suggested the following issue to pursue in case law: *Is the owner of an old and dilapidated barn liable in negligence to children trespassing on the property?* Assume that this topic is governed by state case law.

Select one of the following jurisdictions in which to perform your research. Unless otherwise instructed, select a different jurisdiction from the jurisdiction you selected for the first problem set for Chapter 6. Circle your choice:

Arkansas	Illinois	Pennsylvania
Connecticut	Kansas	West Virginia
Georgia	Nebraska	Wisconsin
Idaho		

1. The first step is to select an appropriate database for your search.

   (a) List all databases containing the case law from your state.

   ____

   (b) Pick the most appropriate database. Which database did you select?

   ____

   (c) Why did you pick that database?

   ____

   ____

(d) What is the scope of coverage of the database you selected? Give both the content of the database and the dates of coverage.

2. Write a Boolean search for your research situation.
   (a) Record your search.

   (b) Run that search. How many cases did you retrieve?

   (c) Browse some of the retrieved cases. If the number of cases you retrieved seems too large or too small, revise your search until you retrieve a reasonable number of pertinent cases. What is your revised search, if any?

   (d) Record the name and year of the most recent pertinent published case retrieved by your search.

   (e) Print the citation list for your Boolean search. Attach it to your problem set.

3. Read the case you referred to in your answer to Question 2(d).
   (a) What method did you choose for browsing, and why?

   (b) Note here the legal rule(s), definition(s), and principle(s) from the case that is pertinent to your research situation.

4. Write a natural language search for the same research situation.
   (a) Record your search.

____

____

(b) Run that search. Record the name and year of the most recent pertinent case retrieved by your search.

____

(c) Clear the screen for a new search. What did you enter?

____

(d) Key the same search you recorded in (a). Now modify that search as permitted by the online choices offered on your search screen. Record your new search.

____

____

(e) Enter that search and skim your search results. Was your first or second natural language search more effective? Why?

____

____

____

(f) Print your citation list for your last natural language search. Attach your citation list to your problem set.

5. Which search seemed more effective, your best Boolean search or your best natural language search? Why?

____

____

____

____

____

6. Evaluate the paper and online research methods for researching case law. Explain the advantages and disadvantages of the two research methods.

____

____

____

First Problem Set for Chapter 7. State Statutes in Paper

Your Name ______________________ Professor ______________________

Your research situation is stated at page 441. Your research in secondary sources has suggested the following issue to research in state statutes: *If an owner of land dedicates his property to the public for recreational use, is he liable for injuries to visitors on the land due to the condition of the land?*

Unless otherwise instructed, select the same jurisdiction you selected for the first problem set in Chapter 6. Circle your choice:

Arkansas	Illinois	Pennsylvania
Connecticut	Kansas	West Virginia
Georgia	Nebraska	Wisconsin
Idaho		

1. Name the statutory code(s) for your jurisdiction. Place an asterisk after the title of any that is annotated.

____

____

2. In an index to the annotated code, locate and list up to three potentially useful subject headings and subheadings, along with the code section(s) referred to under each.

Headings and Subheadings:	Code Section Numbers:
______________________	____________
______________________	____________
______________________	____________

3. Locate and read the code section(s) pertinent to your research situation. Remember to read all related sections.

(a) Give the date of the main volume and pocket part (or annual supplement) you must check to be sure your statutory research is correct and current.

____

____

____

(b) Based on the material in the publications you referred to in your answer to Question 3(a), note here the statutory purpose, scope, definitions, rules, and exceptions pertinent to your research situation.

(c) Provide the proper *Bluebook* citation for the pertinent code section(s), as found in the code you are using. Remember to cite a pocket part (or annual supplement), if appropriate.

4. Examine the statutory history notes following the code section containing the language that most directly addresses your research situation, and provide the following information.

(a) Identify which section you selected.

(b) State the year that code section was originally enacted.

(c) Give the session law reference for the original act. You need not use *Bluebook* form.

(d) If the code section has been amended since it was first enacted, note the reference to the most recent amendment by its session law citation. You need not use *Bluebook* form. If there has been no amendment, write "none."

(e) Assume your research situation occurred on April 1, 1990. Would the language of the current statute have been in effect then? Explain your answer.

(f) If a different, earlier version of the statute was in effect on April 1, 1990, what source would you examine to find the statutory language that was in effect then?

5. Examine the annotation(s) for the code section you cited in Question 4(a).

(a) List up to three cases (not necessarily in proper *Bluebook* form) that could be pertinent to your research situation. (If you were doing actual research, you would, of course, read the cases.)

(b) List one or two secondary sources (not necessarily in *Bluebook* form) that could be pertinent to your research situation. If none, write "none."

6. You next need to update your code research beyond the most recent pocket part (or annual supplement) to see if any recent legislative activity has affected your research situation.

(a) Note the source you used.

(b) Provide a citation to any new public law that is pertinent to your research situation, and explain its effect.

7. **Optional Question:** If your library has the state *Shepard's Citations* for your jurisdiction, collect the volumes and supplements you need to Shepardize your code section. List their dates.

8. **Optional Question:** Peruse the entries for the code section you listed in Question 4(a) in the *Shepard's* volumes and supplements covering that section. Record the information requested below to the extent it exists:

(a) a citation to legislative activity involving your code section, e.g., amendment

___

(b) a citation to a case that adjudicates the constitutionality of your code section

___

(c) the most recent state case listed in *Shepard's* that has cited your code section

___

SECOND PROBLEM SET FOR CHAPTER 7. STATE STATUTES ONLINE

Your Name ______________________ Professor ______________________

Although Chapter 7 has demonstrated full-text searching on LEXIS, you may do comparable research online using WESTLAW. Select one of the online legal research systems for this problem set. If you have not already done so, read the vendor's materials for full-text and natural language searching. Circle the system you selected:

LEXIS WESTLAW

Your research situation is stated at page 441. Your research in secondary sources has suggested the following issue to research in state statutes: *If an owner of land dedicates his property to the public for recreational use, is he liable for injuries to visitors on the land due to the condition of the land?*

Unless otherwise instructed, select a different jurisdiction than the one you selected for the first problem set in Chapter 7. Circle your choice:

Arkansas	Illinois	Pennsylvania
Connecticut	Kansas	West Virginia
Georgia	Nebraska	Wisconsin
Idaho		

1. The first step is to select an appropriate database for your search.

(a) List all databases containing the text of the code for the state you selected.

____

(b) Select the database containing the code and its annotations. Which database did you select?

____

2. Run a natural language search for your research situation.

(a) Record your search.

____

____

____

(b) Enter that search. How many documents did you retrieve?

____

(c) How current are the documents you retrieved?

____

(d) Scan the documents you retrieved. If your original search did not work well, i.e., it did not yield pertinent statutory material, revise your search. What is your revised search, if any?

____

____

____

(e) Note the section number(s) of pertinent statute(s) you retrieved. Include a title number or name as appropriate.

____

(f) Print the citation list for your natural language search. Attach it to your problem set.

3. Now run a Boolean search for your research situation.
(a) Record your search.

____

____

____

(b) Enter that search. How many documents did you retrieve?

____

(c) Scan the documents you retrieved. If your search did not work well, i.e., did not yield pertinent statutory material, revise your search. What is your revised search, if any?

____

____

____

(d) Note the section number(s) of the pertinent statute(s) you retrieved. Include a title number or name as appropriate.

____

(e) Print the citation list for your Boolean search. Attach it to your problem set.

4. Which search seemed more effective, your best Boolean search or your best natural language search? Why?

5. Synopsize the rule of law from the statute that is pertinent to Mr. Forester's situation. Be sure to include any pertinent definitions, scope provisions, rules, and exceptions.

6. Review the annotations for your statute.

(a) List the name and year of a case that appears pertinent, and briefly explain why you think it may be pertinent.

(b) List one or two secondary sources referred to in the annotation, if any.

7. Update your statutory research online (without using *Shepard's*).

(a) Explain the steps you took.

(b) Note recent changes that are pertinent to Mr. Forester's situation, if any.

8. Shepardize your statute online.
(a) Record your search.

(b) Provide the reference to a case (not necessarily in *Bluebook* form) that adjudicates the constitutionality of your statute. If none, write "none."

9. To locate very recent case law interpreting your statute, search for your statute within the case law database for your state.
(a) Note the name of that database.

(b) Write a search using your statute's number. Include a date restrictor to confine your search to cases decided within the past year.

(c) Note the name and year of the most recent case retrieved by your search, if any.

10. Evaluate the paper and online research methods for researching statutes. Explain the advantages and disadvantages of the two research methods.

CHAPTERS 7, 8 RESEARCH SITUATIONS

FEDERAL STATUTES LEGISLATIVE MATERIALS

You will be selecting from the research situations stated below for the following problem sets for Chapters 7 and 8:

Third Problem Set for Chapter 7.	Federal Statutes in Paper
Fourth Problem Set for Chapter 7.	Federal Statutes Online
Problem Set for Chapter 8.	Legislative Materials

Research Situation A:

Your client, Ms. Maria Dobbins, owns a chain of pet stores. She imports wildlife from Peru. Recently, Ms. Dobbins has learned that Peruvian law prohibits exporting wildlife that dwell in its jungles. She has relied on the representations of her Peruvian shipper that her importation was legal. Now Ms. Dobbins is concerned that she may have violated United States law by illegally taking the wildlife. Your research in secondary sources has suggested the following issue to research in federal statutes: *Is Ms. Dobbins violating United States law by importing wildlife from a country that prohibits their export, and if so, might she have an "innocent owner" defense against forfeiture of the wildlife?* (Do not use related statutes 16 U.S.C. §§ 4901-4916 or 19 U.S.C. § 1527.)

Research Situation B:

Your clients, Mr. and Mrs. Neil, are a self-employed couple who own a small construction company. They have received food stamps since a recession sharply reduced the volume of their business and their household income fell to federal eligibility levels. Lately their business has improved, but they are having problems maintaining their rapidly deteriorating equipment. Your research in secondary sources has suggested the following issue to research in federal statutes: *May a self-employed couple deduct depreciation on their business equipment when calculating their income to determine their continued eligibility for food stamps?*

Research Situation C:

Your client, Mr. Luke Grant, operates a precious metals reclamation facility. This facility takes old computer parts, shreds them, and then through various processes extracts the valuable metals. A dangerous toxic substance, polychlorinated biphenyl (PCB), is used in this process. Recently the Environmental Protection Agency (EPA) obtained an ex parte administrative warrant to inspect the facility. During the inspection, the EPA administrator photocopied records and photographed the premises. Now he has subpoenaed several employees' testimony. Your research in secondary sources has suggested the following issue to research in federal statutes: *Does the EPA have the authority under the Toxic Substances Control Act to obtain an ex parte warrant to inspect a facility that produces toxic substances and to photocopy records and photograph the facility?*

Research Situation D:

Your client, Mr. Andrew Unger, paid $10,500 cash to a local bank so it could wire $10,000 to his daughter, Lillian, in California. The bank asserts that it wired the money, but Lillian claims that she never received it. Your research in secondary sources has suggested the following issue to research in federal statutes: *Is Mr. Unger's cash payment and the subsequent transfer of the money an "electronic fund transfer" that is protected by federal statute?*

Research Situation E:

A Mississippi court awarded custody of an Indian child who was born to an unmarried mother from the Choctaw Tribe to a non-Indian couple. The mother was domiciled on the reservation, but the child was not born on the reservation and never lived there. You represent the Mississippi Band of Choctaw, which argues that the adoption is invalid because the tribal court has exclusive jurisdiction over the custody proceeding. Your research in secondary sources has suggested the following issue for research in federal statutes: *Does an Indian tribe have exclusive jurisdiction over the custody proceeding of an Indian child whose mother was domiciled on the reservation if the child was not born on the reservation and never lived there?*

Research Situation F:

Your client, Meg Harrington, purchased a vehicle for her family's personal use and holds title to the car in her name. The purchase was financed by Second Bank and secured by a lien on the car. Shortly after the purchase, Ms. Harrington, who owns a meat packing company, consolidated the car loan and some business loans so she would have one monthly payment to make to the bank. Recently Ms. Harrington has had to file bankruptcy to handle her personal debts. The bank has repossessed the car and is planning to liquidate her debt by auctioning the car. Ms. Harrington has heard that she has a right of "redemption," that is, that the law makes it possible for her to reclaim the car by paying the bank the amount of its secured claim. However, when she called the bank about this, an employee told her that redemption is possible only for consumer debts, and that because she consolidated some of her business debts with her consumer debt, the consumer debt is now a non-consumer debt. Your research in secondary sources has suggested the following issue to research in federal statutes: *Does bankruptcy law permit a party to redeem personal property intended primarily for family use from a lien securing a consumer debt, and if so, is a consumer debt that has been consolidated with a non-consumer debt still a consumer debt for purposes of redemption?*

Research Situation G:

Your client, Julia Davidson, has been charged with being "about to transport" more than $10,000 outside the United States without filing the customs report required of those who import or export large amounts of currency. She was arrested at a hotel in Manhattan about 10 hours before she was to leave Kennedy Airport for Madrid. Your research in secondary sources has suggested the following issue to research in federal statutes: *Is it a federal crime to attempt not to file the customs report required of those who import or export large amounts of currency?*

Research Situation H:

Attorney Jack Chisholm represents a bank that sued Shirley DeMars to recover the balance due on her defaulted car loan. In an attempt to settle the suit, Mr. Chisholm wrote Ms. DeMars a letter listing the amount she owed under the loan agreement, plus an amount owed for insurance purchased by the bank when Ms. DeMars did not keep the car insured as she had promised. Ms. DeMars claims that the attorney's representation of the amount of her debt was false and constituted an attempt to collect an amount not authorized by the loan agreement. She wants to sue him. Your research in secondary sources has suggested the following issue to research in federal statutes: *Is an attorney who regularly, through litigation, tries to collect consumer debts a "debt collector" within the meaning of federal statutes that regulate fair debt collection practices for consumer debts?*

Research Situation I:

Your client, Mr. Jasbir Sandhu, has been charged in federal court with attempted murder of the Chief Minister of one of India's states. The Minister had come to this country for eye surgery. The State Department failed to complete the paperwork to designate the Minister an official guest, but it did initiate security procedures to protect him. Your research in secondary sources has suggested the following issue to research in federal statutes: *Is attempted murder of a foreign "official guest" a federal crime, and if so, may one be an "official guest" if the government has not formally designated one an "official guest"?*

Research Situation J:

Your client, attorney Andrea Newby, handled a bankruptcy proceeding for a corporate client. Because corporations seeking bankruptcy protection lack the funds to pay all their debts, the court must authorize payment for any legal work on the case. Your client submitted her bill to the court, but the court refused to authorize payment for some of the work done by her paralegal. Your research in secondary sources has suggested the following issue to research in federal statutes: *Is an attorney entitled to separate compensation for all the work done by a paralegal on a bankruptcy case, and if so, what is the standard for the compensation?*

Third Problem Set for Chapter 7. Federal Statutes in Paper

Your Name ______________________ Professor ______________________

Circle the letter of the research situation you selected (see pages 469-471):

A B C D E F G H I J

1. Locate in U.S.C.A. or U.S.C.S. the statute that pertains to your research situation. Which code did you select to use? Circle your choice.

U.S.C.A. U.S.C.S.

2. In an index to the annotated code, locate and list up to three potentially useful subject headings and subheadings, along with the title and code section(s) referred to under each. If you have trouble locating an entry in one of the indexes, try the index to the other code.

Headings and Subheadings:	Title and Section Numbers:
______________________	______________________
______________________	______________________
______________________	______________________

3. Locate and read the code section(s) pertinent to your research situation. Remember to read all related sections.

(a) Identify the main volume and pocket part (or annual supplement) you must check to be sure your statutory research is correct and current.

____

____

____

(b) Based on the material in the publications you referred to in your answer to Question 3(a), note here the statutory definition(s), purpose, scope, rule(s), and exceptions pertinent to your research situation.

____

____

(c) Provide the proper *Bluebook* citation for the pertinent code section(s) as found in the annotated code you are using. Remember to cite the pocket part (or annual supplement), if appropriate.

4. Examine the statutory history notes following the code section containing the language that most directly addresses your research situation, and provide the following information.

(a) Identify which section you selected.

(b) State the year that code section was originally enacted.

(c) Give the public law number and section of the act that originally created your code section, and give the session law citation for the original act. You need not use *Bluebook* form.

(d) If the code section has been amended since it was first enacted, note the reference to the most recent amendment by its session law citation. You need not use *Bluebook* form. If there has been no amendment, write "none."

(e) Assume your research situation occurred on April 1, 1990. Would the language of the current statute have been in effect then? Explain your answer.

(f) If a different, earlier version of the statute was in effect on April 1, 1990, what source would you examine to find the statutory language that was in effect then?

5. Scan the case annotations for the code section you cited in Question 4(a), and locate a case that appears pertinent to your research situation. For purposes of this exercise, find and cite the case identified below. You should remember that your research often will not lead to a case directly on point.

Research Situation A:	a 1988 Southern District of Florida case
Research Situation B:	a 1994 District of Maine case
Research Situation C:	a 1988 District of Rhode Island case
Research Situation D:	a 1990 District of Colorado case
Research Situation E:	a 1989 United States Supreme Court case
Research Situation F:	a 1980 Western District of Virginia *Bankruptcy Reporter* case
Research Situation G:	a 1988 Southern District of New York case
Research Situation H:	a 1995 United States Supreme Court case
Research Situation I:	a 1986 Fifth Circuit case
Research Situation J:	a 1994 Third Circuit case

(a) Provide the citation to the case as given in the annotation. (You need not use proper *Bluebook* form.)

____

(b) Read the case annotation. Note here the summary of the case provided in the annotation. (If you were doing actual research, you would, of course, read the case itself.)

____

____

____

____

____

6. Scan the additional references following the code section you identified in Question 4(a). Indicate which of the following types of information are referred to. Be sure also to check all applicable supplementary materials.

_______ A cross-reference to a related statute
_______ A citation to a legal periodical article
_______ A citation to a legal encyclopedia
_______ A citation to a West topic and Key Number
_______ A citation to an A.L.R. annotation
_______ A citation to a treatise

7. You next need to update your code research beyond the most recent pocket part (or annual supplement). You may do so by using either additional supplementary pamphlets that are part of the annotated code sets (see Exhibit 7.2 on page 193) or by using *United States Code Congressional and Administrative News.* For this exercise, use one of the recent softbound pamphlets of U.S.C.C.A.N. to update your research. (If you were actually doing

research, you would use the most recent pamphlet, but to avoid congestion in using this source, you may use any softbound pamphlet published within the last year.) Examine Table 3 to locate any recent legislation that affects your code section(s), if any.

(a) Give the month and year of the U.S.C.C.A.N. you are using.

(b) Note the public law number(s) and section(s) of the act(s) affecting your code section(s), if any. If none, write "none."

(c) Read each public law number and section that you noted in Question 7(b) and note its impact on your research situation.

---

8. Update and expand your research by using *Shepard's Citations.*

(a) Give the title and edition of the *Shepard's Citations* you are using to update and expand your research and list the dates of the volumes and supplements you need to Shepardize the code section you cited in Question 4(a).

(b) Examine *Shepard's* to determine whether there has been any legislative activity that has affected your code section, such as amendments, changes, or repeals. Record here the most recent activity listed. If none, write "none."

(c) Next, determine whether the constitutionality of your code section has been adjudicated. Record here the most recent such citation. If none, write "none."

---

9. Since the *Bluebook* requires that you cite to the official code, examine U.S.C. to determine the date of the volume containing your code section. Give the proper *Bluebook* citation for your code section.

Fourth Problem Set for Chapter 7. Federal Statutes Online

Your Name ______________________ Professor ______________________

Although Chapter 7 has demonstrated full-text searching on LEXIS, you may do comparable research online using WESTLAW. Select one of the online legal research systems for this problem set. If you have not already done so, read the vendor's materials for full-text and natural language searching. Circle the system you selected:

LEXIS WESTLAW

Complete this problem set using one of the research situations on pages 469-471. Unless otherwise instructed, select a different research situation from the one you selected for the third problem set for Chapter 7. Circle your choice:

A B C D E F G H I J

1. The first step is to select an appropriate database for your search. If the system you selected has both an annotated and an unannotated code database, select the unannotated database. Record the name of the database.

____

2. Run a natural language search for your research situation.
(a) Record your search.

____

____

____

(b) Enter your natural language search. **Note:** LEXIS automatically searches the full text of the statutes and the annotations unless you limit your search to the text segment. Do so here by using the editing restrictions as prompted by the online screen. How many documents did you retrieve?

____

(c) How current are the documents you retrieved?

____

____

(d) Scan the documents you retrieved. If your original search did not work well, i.e., did not yield pertinent statutory material, revise your search. What is your revised search, if any?

(e) Note the section number(s) of pertinent statute(s) you retrieved. Include a title number or name as appropriate.

(f) Print the citation list for your natural language search. Attach it to your problem set.

3. Now run a Boolean search for your research situation.
(a) Record your search.

(b) Enter that search. How many documents did you retrieve?

(c) Scan the documents you retrieved. If your search did not work well, i.e. did not yield pertinent statutory material, revise your search. What is your revised search, if any?

(d) Note the section number(s) of the pertinent statutes(s) you retrieved. Include a title number or name as appropriate.

(e) Print the citation list for your Boolean search. Attach it to your problem set.

4. Which search seemed more effective, your best Boolean search or your best natural language search? Why?

5. Synopsize the rule of law from the statute that is pertinent to your research situation. Be sure to include any pertinent definitions, scope provisions, rules, and exceptions.

6. Update your statutory research online (without using *Shepard's*).

(a) Explain the steps you took.

(b) Record any recent changes that affect your research situation. If none, write "none."

7. Shepardize a pertinent code section online. Use a section you identified in Question 3(e).

(a) Identify the code section you selected.

(b) Record your search.

(c) Provide the reference to a case (not necessarily in *Bluebook* format) that adjudicates the constitutionality of your statute. If none, write "none."

8. Now search the statutory annotations for federal case law that applies to your research situation. If you need to move to the annotated code database, do so. List one of the most recent cases that appears pertinent to your research situation, and explain why it seems pertinent.

___

___

___

___

9. Now select a federal case law database that includes district court, courts of appeals, and United States Supreme Court cases. Find the most recent case citing your statute.

(a) Note the name of the database.

___

(b) Write a search using your statute's title and section number. Include a date restrictor to confine your search to cases decided within the past year.

___

___

(c) Note the name and year of the most recent pertinent case retrieved by your search, if any.

___

___

10. Evaluate the effectiveness of paper and online research methods for researching statutes. Explain the advantages and disadvantages of the two research methods.

___

___

___

___

___

PROBLEM SET FOR CHAPTER 8. LEGISLATIVE MATERIALS

Your Name ______________________ Professor ______________________

Complete this problem set using one of the research situations stated at pages 469-471. Unless otherwise instructed, select the same research situation you selected for the third problem set for Chapter 7. Circle your choice:

A B C D E F G H I J

Legislative History

1. If you have not already done so, locate and read in U.S.C.A. or U.S.C.S. the statute(s) that pertain(s) to your research situation.

(a) Circle the annotated code you selected.

U.S.C.A. U.S.C.S.

(b) Locate the statutory section containing the language that most directly addresses your research situation. Note the title and section number here.

____

2. Locate the statutory history notes for the statutory section you identified in Question 1(b). That material typically is located immediately following the statute. Research the public law enacted in the following year:

Research Situation A:	1981
Research Situation B:	1977
Research Situation C:	1976
Research Situation D:	1978
Research Situation E:	1978
Research Situation F:	1978
Research Situation G:	1986
Research Situation H:	1986
Research Situation I:	1972
Research Situation J:	1978

Record the following legislative history information for that public law. (Your answers need not be in proper *Bluebook* form.)

(a) public law number

____

(b) date of bill's approval by President

(c) *Statutes at Large* citation

---

3. Locate the legislative history section of U.S.C.C.A.N. pertaining to the public law number specified in Question 2(a). Record the following information found there, if any. If the information is not present, write "none." You need not use proper *Bluebook* form.

(a) House bill number

House committee

House report number

---

date of House report

(b) Senate bill number

Senate committee

Senate report number

---

date of Senate report

(c) conference committee report number

---

conference committee report date

(d) number of bill enacted (House or Senate)

(e) date(s) of consideration by the House

(f) date(s) of consideration by the Senate

(g) volume(s) of the *Congressional Record* containing that consideration in (e) and (f)

(h) number and session of Congress that passed your bill (indicated on the spine of the U.S.C.C.A.N. volume)

---

4. Using U.S.C.C.A.N., scan the pertinent portions of the following legislative history document (the page numbers given are U.S.C.C.A.N. page numbers, not the page numbers of the legislative document):

Research Situation A:	S. Rep. No. 123, page 1760
Research Situation B:	H.R. Rep. No. 464, pages 2014–15
Research Situation C:	S. Rep. No. 698, page 4514
Research Situation D:	S. Rep. No. 915, pages 9405–06
Research Situation E:	H.R. Rep. No. 1386, pages 7543–44
Research Situation F:	S. Rep. No. 989, page 5881
Research Situation G:	Signing Statement by the President, page 5394
Research Situation H:	H.R. Rep. No. 405, pages 1752–54
Research Situation I:	S. Rep. No. 1105, pages 4316–19
Research Situation J:	H.R. Rep. No. 595, page 6286

(a) Note here any guidance that is pertinent to your research situation.

(b) Provide the proper *Bluebook* citation to the first page of this document.

---

5. Locate and read the CIS legislative history of your statute in the appropriate abstract volume of *CIS/Annual* (for statutes that predate 1984), or in the *CIS/Legislative Histories* volume (for statutes that date 1984 or later), or in the CIS *Congressional Masterfile* in CD-ROM.

(a) Compare the information found in CIS to your answers in Questions 2 and 3. If you found any significant new information in CIS, note here its content.

(b) Note the CIS accession number for the document you cited in your answer to Question 4(b).

---

6. Locate and read the following CIS document:

Research Situation A:	H563-17 (1981), pages 10–11
Research Situation B:	H161-3 (1976), pages 84–92
Research Situation C:	H503-55 (1976), pages 87–88
Research Situation D:	H243-10 (1978), pages 4, 19–20
Research Situation E:	S963-20 (1977), pages 43–45, 52
Research Situation F:	H523-14 (1977), pages 127–28, 380–81
Research Situation G:	H523-40 (1986), page 19
Research Situation H:	S243-2 (1984), page 86
Research Situation I:	H523-31 (1972), pages 1–3
Research Situation J:	S523-29 (1978), pages 40–41

(a) What type of legislative history document does the abstract describe?

(b) Note here any guidance that is pertinent to your research situation.

(c) Provide the proper *Bluebook* citation to the text you just read.

____

____

____

7. Locate the volume(s) of the *Congressional Record* that you listed in your answer to Question 3(g).

(a) Locate the entry for the bill that was enacted using either the House or Senate bill and resolutions sections of the index to that volume. List the pages containing the presentation of the bill to the President and approval of the bill.

____

(b) Locate the pages where the following floor debate is reported, again by using the House and Senate bills and resolutions sections of the index.

Research Situation A:	S. 736: Amendments (the third page reference in a group of three)
Research Situation B:	S. 275: Debated (last page reference; when you find it, skip forward 70 pages)
Research Situation C:	S. 3149: Conference report submitted in House (second reference)
Research Situation D:	H.R. 13007: Debated
Research Situation E:	H.R. 12533: Amended and passed the House
Research Situation F:	H.R. 8200: House concurred in Senate amendments
Research Situation G:	H.R. 5217: Reported with amendments
Research Situation H:	H.R. 237: Rules suspended. Passed House
Research Situation I:	H.R. 15883: Amended and passed Senate (skim first 6 pages)
Research Situation J:	H.R. 8200: Senate concurred in House amendment (first reference; skim 6 pages)

Note here any guidance that is pertinent to your research situation.

____

____

____

____

____

____

____

(c) Provide the proper *Bluebook* citation to the text.

____

____

8. If all of the documents you have found provided the same guidance on your research situation, which would you rely on as the most authoritative? Why?

9. Using secondary sources, determine whether a compiled legislative history exists for your statute. If you find one, cite it here in proper *Bluebook* form. If none, write "none." (You usually would take this research step early in your research.)

Pending Legislation

10. Select a source to assist you in locating pending legislation that could be pertinent to your research situation.

(a) Name here the source you have chosen to search.

(b) Describe your search method in that source.

(c) Note pending legislation, if any, you have discovered by bill number and title.

(d) Note the most recent action taken on the bill.

Chapter 9 Research Situations: Administrative Materials

You will be selecting from the research situations stated below for the following problem sets for Chapter 9:

First Problem Set for Chapter 9.	Administrative Materials in Paper (without Looseleafs)
Second Problem Set for Chapter 9.	Administrative Materials in Looseleafs
Third Problem Set for Chapter 9.	Administrative Materials on the Internet

The facts of each research situation are followed by references to the governing agency and two statutes pertinent to the administrative materials you are seeking; you could have obtained these references by research in secondary sources. (The statute references do not contain dates, because the years of the code volumes will change over time.) Use the specified looseleaf service in the second problem set unless your professor instructs otherwise.

Research Situation A:

Your client is the professional basketball team, the Midtown Marvels. The general manager of the team would like to hire a few teenagers to serve as ball boys and ball girls at home games. Research the federal standards on employing fourteen- and fifteen-year-olds in these positions.

Substantive Statute: Fair Labor Standards Act, 29 U.S.C. § 212(c)
Enabling Statute: 29 U.S.C. §§ 203(*l*), 211, 212(c)
Agency: Wage & Hour Division of the Department of Labor
Looseleaf Service: *Labor Relations Reporter* (BNA)

Research Situation B:

Matt and Toni Adams recently bought a house. They financed the mortgage through Rainbow Bank. The Adamses are concerned because the bank failed to include in the finance charge the cost of mortgage insurance (also known as credit life and disability insurance) required by the bank. Research whether Rainbow Bank has violated the truth-in-lending standards regarding computation of finance charges.

Substantive Statute: Consumer Credit Protection Act, 15 U.S.C. § 1605(a)(5)
Enabling Statute: 15 U.S.C. § 1604
Agency: Federal Trade Commission
Looseleaf Service: *Consumer Credit Guide* (CCH)

Research Situation C:

Mike Johnson owns a factory that processes corrosive chemicals (which do not qualify as toxic or hazardous chemicals). All employees are required to follow strict safety procedures; however, accidents still may occur with chemicals coming into contact with an employee's skin or eyes. Mr. Johnson is concerned with the adequacy of the on-site medical services and first aid facilities. Research the federally required safeguards, including quick-drenching facilities, for employees working with corrosive chemicals.

Substantive Statute: Occupational Safety & Health Act, 29 U.S.C. § 654
Enabling Statute: 29 U.S.C. § 655
Agency: Occupational Safety and Health Commission (within the Labor Department)
Looseleaf Service: *Employment Safety & Health Guide* (CCH)

Research Situation D:

Linda and Carlos Zamera have been married for one year. The Zameras live in the United States; Linda is a citizen, and Carlos is applying for citizenship. Recently, Carlos learned that he fathered a son six years ago when he was living in Colombia. The Zameras would like to bring the boy to the United States to live permanently and wish to know whether Linda could successfully petition to have her stepson admitted to the United States as an immediate relative. Research what evidence Linda must produce to support her petition.

Substantive Statute: Immigration & Nationality Act, 8 U.S.C. §§ 1101(b)(1)(B), 1151(b), 1154(a), (b)
Enabling Statute: 8 U.S.C. § 1103
Agency: Immigration & Naturalization Service
Looseleaf Service: *Immigration Law & Procedure* (Bender)

Research Situation E:

Your client, George Stevens, owns a clothing manufacturing company. Mr. Stevens is concerned with some foreign companies that are exporting large quantities of sweaters to the United States at less than fair value. Mr. Stevens' company manufactures sweaters that are very similar to the imported sweaters. Mr. Stevens feels his business may be adversely affected by the imports. Research the standard for determining whether an industry has been materially injured by the dumping of foreign merchandise.

Substantive Statute: Tariff Act, 19 U.S.C. § 1673
Enabling Statute: 19 U.S.C. §§ 66, 1500, 1624
Agency: International Trade Commission (in the Commerce Department)
Looseleaf Service: *International Trade Reporter* (BNA)

Research Situation F:

Your client, Mark Jenkins, is a registered broker-dealer who does not belong to a securities association registered under section 78o-3. Mr. Jenkins deals in unexempted securities and would like to know if he is required to join a securities association. Research the standards on registration of brokers and dealers, and any exemptions from those standards.

Substantive Statute: Securities & Exchange Act of 1934, 15 U.S.C. § 78o(b)(8), (9)
Enabling Statute: 15 U.S.C. § 78o(b)(9)
Agency: Securities & Exchange Commission
Looseleaf Service: *Federal Securities Law Reports* (CCH)

Research Situation G:

Richard Boydon is opening a small retail electronics store. He would like to know what rules he must adhere to regarding the display and availability of warranties on his products as to customers. Research the standards governing availability and display of warranties of consumer products.

Substantive Statute: Magnuson-Moss Warranty Act, 15 U.S.C. §§ 2301-2302
Enabling Statute: 15 U.S.C. § 2302(b)
Agency: Federal Trade Commission
Looseleaf Service: *Trade Regulation Reporter* (CCH)

Research Situation H:

Stephanie Cairn is the president of Willow Valley Bank. The bank is a member of the Federal Reserve System. Ms. Cairn is a passive investor in Gotti, Inc., a corporation managed by Mr. Gotti. Gotti, Inc., has received loans from Willow Valley Bank. Mr. Gotti recently asked Ms. Cairn to submit a request to the bank board to extend the credit on the loans to Gotti, Inc. Research whether Willow Valley Bank can extend its credit to Gotti, Inc. Ignore issues relating to dollar-amount limits.

Substantive Statute: Federal Deposit Insurance Act, 12 U.S.C. § 375b(1), (2), (9)
Enabling Statute: 12 U.S.C. § 375b(10)
Agency: Federal Reserve System
Looseleaf Service: *Federal Banking Law Reports* (CCH)

Research Situation I:

Lynn Traynor heads the human resources department at a juvenile correction facility that employs forty persons. The facility houses both male and female juveniles; however, the living areas are strictly segregated by sex. Recently, a female employee requested a transfer from being a female group leader to a male group leader. Ms. Traynor denied the request. She is concerned about privacy considerations for the young male juveniles. The position of group leader requires the employee to conduct body searches and supervise bathroom areas. Research whether this situation would qualify for an exception to the prohibition against sex discrimination in employment.

Substantive Statute: Equal Employment Opportunity Act, 42 U.S.C. §§ 2000e(b), 2000e-2(a), (e)
Enabling Statute: 42 U.S.C. § 2000e-12
Agency: Equal Employment Opportunity Commission
Looseleaf Service: *EEOC Compliance Manual* (CCH)

Research Situation J:

Your client, Waste Recyclers, Inc., laid off Mary Collins in March of last year. The National Labor Relations Board (NLRB) recently ruled under section 10(a) (29 U.S.C. § 160(a)) that Ms. Collins was laid off because of unfair labor practices and has ordered Waste Recyclers to pay Ms. Collins backpay. The parties have not been able to come to any agreement about backpay, so the NLRB has issued and served on Waste Recyclers a notice of hearing without backpay specification. Research whether Waste Recyclers must file an answer to the NLRB prior to the hearing.

Substantive Statute: Labor Management Relations Act, 29 U.S.C. §§ 158(a), 160
Enabling Statute: 29 U.S.C. § 156
Agency: National Labor Relations Board
Looseleaf Service: *Labor Relations Reporter* (BNA)

First Problem Set for Chapter 9. Administrative Materials in Paper (without Looseleafs)

Your Name ______________________ Professor ______________________

Circle the letter of the research situation you selected (see pages 487-490):

A B C D E F G H I J

1. In U.S.C.A. or U.S.C.S., locate, read, and update the substantive statute section(s) specified in your research situation. Summarize the statute's contents, and note its probable effect on your client.

2. Scan the annotations following the text of the substantive statute section(s), including material in the supplements, if any. Look for references to pertinent agency decisions and regulations. (The material may not contain references to both types of authority.) List the references that appear to be pertinent to your research situation.

(a) Agency decisions

(b) Agency regulations

____

____

____

____

3. In U.S.C.A. or U.S.C.S., locate, read, and update the enabling statute section(s) specified in your research situation.

(a) List some of the agency's powers and duties stated in this statute.

____

____

____

(b) Using the annotations, list references to agency regulations that appear to be pertinent to your research situation.

____

____

____

4. Supplement your answers to Questions 2(b) and 3(b) by locating the most current *CFR Index and Finding Aids* volume and looking for a C.F.R. part. You may use the subject-matter index; the Parallel Table of Authorities and Rules; or the CFR Titles, Chapters, Subchapters, and Parts. Remember that possible indexing terms include your agency's name and terms from the substantive and enabling statutes.

(a) Subject-matter index

Index Heading and Subheading(s):	C.F.R. Part(s):
________________	________________
________________	________________
________________	________________
________________	________________

(b) Parallel Table of Authorities and Rules

U.S.C. Section:	C.F.R. Section(s):
________________	________________
________________	________________
________________	________________
________________	________________

(c) CFR Titles, Chapters, Subchapters, and Parts.

5. Scan the portions of C.F.R. that you listed in your answers to Questions 2(b), 3(b), and 4. If the C.F.R. part you are scanning is very lengthy, check the end of the pamphlet to see if it has its own index. Select the C.F.R. section most pertinent to your research situation. (Although you often would use more than one C.F.R. section, for the remainder of this problem set, you will focus on only this C.F.R. section referred to as the "regulation" in subsequent questions.) Read the regulation carefully.

(a) Note the C.F.R. title and section that you selected.

(b) Note the rule(s) of law that are pertinent to your research situation. Include definitions and exceptions from other sections where pertinent.

(c) Note how this C.F.R. section further develops the rule(s) in the substantive statute section.

(d) Record the first date after the regulation (usually the date of final promulgation for the regulation) and the accompanying reference to the *Federal Register*. If no date appears there, look instead at the source note following the table of contents for that C.F.R. part. If no source note appears, look for the source note in the preceding year's C.F.R. pamphlet.

(e) List the date of effectiveness for the C.F.R. pamphlet you are using.

(f) Provide the proper *Bluebook* citation to this regulation.

---

6. Your next research step would be to use one or more L.S.A. pamphlets to update your C.F.R. research completely. However, to enable you and your classmates to use the L.S.A. pamphlets at the same time, we want you to select any one of the L.S.A. pamphlets that update your answer to Question 5(e).

(a) Note the L.S.A. pamphlet's dates of coverage for the C.F.R. title you are researching.

(b) Locate the listing for the regulation you selected in Question 5. Record here any information L.S.A. contains on this regulation. If no information is present, write "none." However, even if no information is present, you still need L.S.A. information to answer the next sequence of questions, so select a nearby C.F.R. section for which L.S.A. does contain information, and record this new C.F.R. section number and its L.S.A. information here.

(c) Check the L.S.A. Table of *Federal Register* Issue Pages and Dates to determine the date of the *Federal Register* in which the information in Question 6(b) appears, and note that date here.

---

7. The usual next research step would be to check the Reader Aids charts in very recent *Federal Register* issues that have not been covered by the most recent L.S.A. pamphlets. However, you instead should move directly to the issue of the *Federal Register* referred to in your answer to Question 6(c), and read the material noted.

(a) If that material pertains to your research situation, summarize its effect on your research situation. If it does not pertain to your situation, write "not applicable" and then describe the agency's action.

(b) Provide the proper *Bluebook* citation to the *Federal Register* material you just read.

---

8. Using paper or online *Shepard's,* Shepardize the regulation you read in Question 5.
(a) Note the title or database you used.

(b) Record the entries to any decisions declaring your regulation constitutional or unconstitutional, valid or void or invalid. If there are no such entries, write "none."

---

9. **Optional Question:** Use Table T.1 in the *Bluebook* to determine whether the decisions of the agency specified in your research situation currently are published in an official reporter. If so, list the title of the reporter. If no such reporter currently exists, write "none" and skip to Question 11.

---

10. **Optional Question:** Determine whether your library has a paper or online *Shepard's* that covers the decisions of the agency specified in your research situation. If so, list the title or database. If neither is available, write "none."

---

11. Based on your research thus far, summarize your conclusions and your remaining questions about your research situation.

Second Problem Set for Chapter 9. Administrative Materials in Looseleafs

Your Name ______________________ Professor ______________________

Complete this problem set using one of the research situations on pages 487-490. Unless otherwise instructed, select a different research situation than the one you selected for the first problem set for Chapter 9. Circle your choice:

A B C D E F G H I J

1. Locate the looseleaf service specified in your research situation. Read its instructions on how to use the looseleaf, and then explore the looseleaf. If these instructions are not adequate, ask your librarian for any pamphlets describing how to use the looseleafs published by that publisher.

(a) List the number of looseleaf binders and the general contents of each.

____

____

____

____

____

(b) List the finding tools (indexes, digests, tables, etc.) contained in the looseleaf.

____

____

____

(c) Note whether there are any associated hardbound volumes and looseleaf transfer binders and, if so, their contents.

____

____

____

2. Use the looseleaf's finding tools to locate the looseleaf's commentary on the legal issue in your research situation. Read that commentary.

(a) Note how you located the commentary.

(b) Note here any legal rule(s), definition(s), and principle(s) that are pertinent to your research situation.

(c) Indicate how current this commentary is.

(d) List references in the commentary to pertinent portions of the same looseleaf.

3. Locate (in the looseleaf) the most current version of the substantive statute and the enabling statute specified in your research situation. Read them.

(a) Summarize the substantive statute and note its probable effect on your research situation.

(b) List some of the agency's powers and duties under the enabling statute.

(c) Indicate how current these versions of the statutes are.

4. Use the looseleaf's finding tools or references to locate (in the looseleaf) a regulation that appears to be pertinent to your research situation. If you locate more than one pertinent regulation, scan them and select the one that is most pertinent. Read it carefully.

(a) Note how you located the regulation.

(b) List the references to the regulation, including both its location in the looseleaf and its location in C.F.R. or *Federal Register.* (You need not use proper *Bluebook* form.)

(c) Note the rules of law that are pertinent to your research situation. Include definitions and exceptions where pertinent.

(d) Indicate how current this regulation is.

5. In the looseleaf, use the digests to locate citations to judicial and agency decisions pertinent to your research situation.

(a) Select the decision that seems to be most pertinent to your research situation. Record the reference to that decision. (You need not use proper *Bluebook* form.)

(b) Read that decision in the looseleaf or its accompanying hardbound volumes. Note the rule(s) of law that are pertinent to your research situation. Include definitions and exceptions where pertinent.

6. List how you would update all of your looseleaf research, using both the looseleaf and other means. (You need not do so.)

(a) Commentary

(b) Statutes

(c) Regulation

(d) Judicial and agency decisions

Third Problem Set for Chapter 9. Administrative Materials on the Internet

Your Name ______________________ Professor ______________________

Complete this problem set using one of the research situations on pages 487-490. Unless otherwise instructed, select a different research situation than the research situations you selected for the first and second problem sets for Chapter 9. Circle your choice:

A B C D E F G H I J

1. Sign onto the Internet and select a search engine. List it here.

____

2. Identify the available servers containing federal regulations in your subject matter and select a server with pertinent coverage and useful search capabilities.
   (a) Which server did you choose?

____

   (b) Why?

____

____

____

____

3. Browse the assistance program for the server to learn of its search conventions. Then write a search for your research situation.
   (a) Record your search.

____

____

   (b) Run that search. Note the number of regulations that your search retrieved.

____

(c) Browse some of the retrieved regulations. If the number of regulations seems too large or too small, revise your search until you retrieve a reasonable number of pertinent regulations. Record your revised search, if any.

___

___

(d) Print the citation list for your final search. Attach it to your problem set.

(e) Record the reference for the most pertinent regulation retrieved by your search. (You need not use proper *Bluebook* form.)

___

___

(f) Read that regulation. Note the rule(s) of law that are pertinent to your research situation. Include definitions and exceptions where pertinent.

___

___

___

___

___

___

___

CHAPTER 10
RESEARCH
SITUATIONS

RULES OF PROCEDURE

For the single problem set for Chapter 10, select one of the following research situations, which you will research—once in federal materials and a second time in state materials. Thus you will see the parallels between those materials. To enable your teacher to check your work more precisely, select a federal case from the specified federal court and year of decision. When you research in state law, you may select any pertinent case from the courts of the specified state.

Research Situation A:

You are representing Ms. Biggert who is seeking to establish the paternity of her child (and thus to obtain child support payments). She has sued a man she believes is the father, and he has asserted that his brother is the real father. Based on your experience in such cases, you would like to obtain blood tests from both men to compare to the child's blood. Under the rules permitting medical examinations, is the court likely to order these tests?

Federal:	Select a 1955 case from the Eastern District of New York
State:	Massachusetts

Research Situation B:

You have brought suit on behalf of Ms. Ginny Simons, who was injured in a two-car traffic accident. Your complaint asserts negligence on the part of the other driver and details the factual grounds for your claim. The answer, however, simply asserts as a defense that "Plaintiff's negligent acts are the sole cause of her injuries." Is this vague assertion sufficient to raise the defense of contributory negligence?

Federal:	Select a 1948 Fifth Circuit (Louisiana) case
State:	District of Columbia

Research Situation C:

Your client, Ms. Teddy Kurz, owns substantial grazing acreage. She has discovered that livestock from a neighboring farm has seriously depleted her crop of grass; the neighbor,

Mr. Timothy George, asserts that the area where the grazing took place is his property. You wish to join the action to resolve the title issues with an action for damages. Can you join the equitable and the legal claims in one suit?

Federal: Select a 1942 Tenth Circuit (New Mexico) case
State: Kentucky

Research Situation D:

Your client, Mr. Aaron Johnson, purchased a tract of land, believing it to be unspoiled. Mr. Johnson has now learned that the former owner disposed of waste on the land some years ago. Mr. Johnson is certain that his impression of the land's condition was based on false statements made by the owner during the negotiations for the sale of the land, but he is not sure exactly when the false statements were made, whether they were oral or in writing, or where they were made. The negotiations lasted several months and took place in several cities. Can you bring a complaint for fraud without more factual detail?

Federal: Select a 1991 First Circuit (Massachusetts) case
State: Alabama

Research Situation E:

Your client, Ms. Nora Gray, is an actress. She was injured when a light fell on her and struck her during rehearsals, and she has sued the studio. The studio has sought admissions from Ms. Gray, one of which pertains to her doctors' prognoses for her. Ms. Gray does not know what each doctor who has treated her would state as her prognosis. Must you inquire of the doctors in order to respond to the request for admission, or can you indicate that you are unable to admit or deny the statement?

Federal: Select a 1950 case from the Southern District of Iowa
State: West Virginia

Research Situation F:

Your client, Lauren Hudacek, suffered various physical and mental injuries in a serious accident while mountain-climbing. The jury awarded her substantial damages. The trial court entered judgment on the verdict but did not include pre-judgment interest. You believe that your state's law requires pre-judgment interest. Can you depict this omission as a mere clerical mistake (even though the sum is substantial) and obtain an amendment of the judgment on that ground?

Federal: Select a 1972 Third Circuit (Pennsylvania) case
State: Colorado

Research Situation G:

You unsuccessfully defended a products liability and negligence case on behalf of your client, Min's Sport Shop. The plaintiff, Sjur Anderson, alleged that he was injured because the running track purchased from Min's was improperly assembled, but Mr. Min asserts that Mr. Anderson improperly modified it. During the jury trial, the plaintiff's girlfriend, Jennifer Kozar, testified that the plaintiff had told her that he had not modified the running track. You had objected to the admission of this statement into evidence on the basis that it constituted hearsay, but the judge erroneously admitted it. Later in the trial the plaintiff testified that he had not modified the running track; this testimony was properly admitted into evidence without objection. The jury's verdict in favor of plaintiff suggests that this evidence was weighty. You are now considering whether to move for a new trial and wonder whether the evidentiary ruling was harmless error since Ms. Kozar's testimony was merely cumulative. (Research civil procedural rules, not rules of evidence.)

Federal: Select a 1970 Seventh Circuit (Illinois) case
State: North Carolina

Research Situation H:

As an attorney for the Department of the Interior, you recently became aware of litigation between private landowners concerning the hunting of squirrels. One of the landowners had set aside a private woodland preserve that had become home to a colony of squirrels and other woodland creatures. The abutting landowner, who operated a tree farm and greenhouse, complained that the squirrels harmed his young trees; he had begun to set traps and poison to kill the squirrels. The trial judge has already entered judgment and held that the squirrels were a nuisance and could be hunted when they entered onto the land of the abutting tree farmer. You believe this case is important to the Department of the Interior because it concerns the hunting, trapping, and removal of a unique species of squirrels. You are certain that the Department has sufficient interest to intervene in the case. But, because the judge has already entered judgment, is it still timely for the Department to intervene?

Federal: Select a 1977 Fifth Circuit (Alabama) case
State: Wisconsin

Research Situation I:

You are clerking for a judge who has been asked by the plaintiff to dismiss a case. The defendant has already filed an answer and incurred some litigation expenses. You believe the plaintiff is planning to pursue a case in a different court. Must or should the court require the plaintiff to pay the defendant's costs as a condition of granting the plaintiff's request for voluntary dismissal?

Federal: Select a 1992 Sixth Circuit case
State: Arizona

Research Situation J:

In late 1985, your client, Dr. Key Alonso, hired Haber Construction (HC) to add a bedroom and bath onto his home. After a few years of use, cracks developed in the walls of the addition. An architect who inspected the addition discovered serious structural defects in the addition that were a result of poor workmanship and the use of inferior products. You filed suit on behalf of Dr. Alonso. At first, you named only Mr. Mark Haber as defendant in the complaint because you thought that HC was a sole proprietorship. You have just learned that HC is actually a partnership and that Mr. Steve Szymanski is also a partner. Unfortunately, the statute of limitations on this action lapsed since the time the pleadings were served and filed and now. You now wish to amend the complaint to include the partnership and Mr. Szymanski. Will the amended pleading relate back to the date of the original complaint?

Federal: Select a 1975 case from the Third Circuit (Indiana)
State: North Dakota

Problem Set for Chapter 10. Rules of Procedure

Your Name ______________________ Professor ______________________

Circle the letter of the research situation you selected (see pages 503-506):

A B C D E F G H I J

Federal Rules of Procedure

1. Using a deskbook, locate the federal rule pertinent to your research situation.
(a) State the rule insofar as it applies to your research situation.

____

____

____

____

____

____

(b) Read the advisory committee notes. State any pertinent explanation of the rule.

____

____

____

____

(c) Provide the proper *Bluebook* citation to the rule.

____

____

(d) Based on your answers to (a) and (b), can you resolve your issue, or is there ambiguity in the rule's application to your research situation? Explain.

____

____

____

____

2. Select a civil procedure treatise (whether in paper or CD-ROM) and locate a discussion concerning the same rule.

(a) What further explanation (if any) does the treatise provide concerning the application of the rule to your research situation?

(b) List several cases referred to in the treatise that could be pertinent to your research situation.

(c) Provide the proper *Bluebook* citation to this treatise, including any additional material in the supplement.

3. Locate the federal rule that governs your research situation in either *United States Code Annotated* or *United States Code Service.*

(a) Scan the headings for the case annotations. List one or more headings that appear to be pertinent to your research situation.

(b) To facilitate grading by your instructor, use the annotations to locate a pertinent federal case with the characteristics described in your research situation. Read the case. What information does the case provide concerning the application of the procedural rule to your research situation?

(c) Provide the proper *Bluebook* citation to this case.

4. Before you rely on any case, what must you do to determine that the case is still good law? (You need not actually take this step to complete this problem set.)

State Rules of Procedure

5. Using the annotated state code for the jurisdiction stated in your research situation, locate the state rule of procedure that governs your research situation.

(a) State the rule insofar as it applies to your research situation.

(b) Read the advisory or drafting committee notes, if any. Note any pertinent explanation of the rule.

(c) Provide the proper *Bluebook* citation to the rule.

(d) Based on your answers to (a) and (b), can you resolve your issue, or is there ambiguity in the rule's application to your research situation? Explain.

6. (a) Scan the headings for the case annotations. List one or more headings that appear pertinent to your research situation.

(b) Locate a pertinent state case; if there is more than one, select the most recent. Read the case. What information does the case provide concerning the application of the procedural rule to your research situation?

(c) Provide the proper *Bluebook* citation to your case.

7. Before you rely on any case, what must you do to determine that the case is still good law? (You need not actually take this step to complete this problem set.)

CHAPTER 11
RESEARCH
SITUATIONS

NONLEGAL MATERIALS

For the single problem set for Chapter 11, select one of the following research situations. You should feel free to research whatever nonlegal issue of fact strikes you as important and interesting; we have suggested one possibility in parenthesis. (Research Situations A and D through J are drawn from the exercises for Chapters 2, 4, and 5. Research Situation B is drawn from the exercises for Chapters 6 and 7. Research Situation C is drawn from the exercises for Chapters 7 and 8.)

Research Situation A:

Ms. Rebecca Burgman has become concerned about her elderly mother, Mrs. Prudence Recht. Mrs. Recht has become increasingly disoriented and confused in recent years, but continues to live alone on the family homestead in Elizabethtown, Pennsylvania. Because her mother's mental and physical capacities have been steadily declining, Ms. Burgman has tried to visit her mother more frequently. Recently Mrs. Recht told her daughter that her "spiritual leader" had told her to place all of her trust and faith in the church and, as evidence of her faith, to give all of her material possessions to the church. Ms. Burgman has contacted you for legal advice because she is concerned about the amount of control that the spiritual leader seems to have over her mother. She specifically wants to know if a gift to a religious group under these circumstances is valid. (A possible issue is how religious advisors influence elderly persons.)

Research Situation B:

Your client, James Forester, owns a large tract of land in a developing suburb. On two sides, it is already bordered by housing developments, and soon there will be developments on the remaining two sides. These neighborhoods house many children.

As Mr. Forester is well aware, children from these neighborhoods come onto his property, although he has not invited them. Mr. Forester believes that the children are drawn primarily to an old barn on the property. The barn was built nearly a century ago, when the property was first used as a farm. Because no one has farmed the property for about a decade, the barn has slowly deteriorated. Nonetheless, children enjoy playing in and around it. The rusty fence and "no trespassing" signs around the perimeter of the property do not seem to deter the children.

Mr. Forester is concerned about the safety of these children, as well as his own liability should any of them be injured on the property. (A possible issue is what kind of dangers and accidents unsupervised children encounter on others' land.)

Research Situation C:

Your client operates a precious metals reclamation facility. This facility takes old computer parts and shreds them, and then through various processes extracts the valuable metals from the rest of the materials. A dangerous toxic substance, polychlorinated biphenyl (PCB), is used in this process, and the Environmental Protection Agency (EPA), fearing that some of it is escaping into a nearby river, obtained an *ex parte* ("on one side only") warrant to enter the premises and make an inspection. During the inspection, the EPA administrator photocopied records and photographed the premises. Your client wants to know if the EPA has the authority to obtain the warrant for the inspection and make the photographs. (A possible issue is how PCB affects people's health)

Research Situation D:

Mr. Max Burnham, a resident of Tucker, Georgia, is the owner of a late-model sports car. When he awoke one morning and did not find his car where he thought he had parked it, he reported it stolen. Within a week, Mr. Burnham's insurer settled his claim under the theft provision of the insurance policy. Later, the insurer learned that Mr. Burnham had been given a citation for drunk and disorderly conduct the night before the alleged theft, and that, in fact, the car had been towed away and impounded. The insurer wants to know whether it has a right to restitution of the payment made to Mr. Burnham because of a mistake about the facts related to the loss. (A possible issue is how insurance companies are reacting to increased claims of stolen cars.)

Research Situation E:

Ms. Karen Selleck is an artist who specializes in realistic paintings of cats, primarily used for greeting cards and calendars. Of course, she has several pedigree cats herself, which she shows occasionally in cat shows near her home in Albany, New York. Apparently, she and one of her cats were photographed at a show, unbeknownst to her. The picture, which is lovely, is now appearing in advertising circulars for a local cat food company. Ms. Selleck wants to maintain her privacy and is incensed that her picture is being used for a commercial purpose without her consent. She wonders whether she has a good case against the cat food company. (A possible issue is how effective it is to use cats and other pets in pet food advertising.)

Research Situation F:

Dr. Karen Ihito is a pediatric ophthalmologist at a pediatric partnership located in Berring, Texas, a small town with only one clinic and no hospital. The nearest clinic is twenty miles away; the nearest hospital is seventy-five miles away. When Dr. Ihito began this job two years ago, she signed a non-competition clause as a part of her partnership. The clause stated, "If Dr. Ihito leaves the partnership for any reason, she promises not to work as a pediatric ophthalmologist within three years anywhere within a forty-mile radius from the courthouse in Berring, Texas." Dr. Ihito now wishes to leave the partnership to work at the clinic located twenty miles away. There are no other ophthalmologists within that same area. She wishes to know whether the non-competition clause is valid. Then she will make her decision about whether to change employers. (A possible issue is how a rural medical practice differs from an urban practice.)

Research Situation G:

Tim and Bette Terra are first cousins, are married to each other, and live in New York. Mr. and Mrs. Terra were married in Arizona. This type of marriage is valid in New York, but is not valid in Arizona. Mr. and Mrs. Terra want to know whether their marriage will be treated as legal in New York, despite the conflict between the states' laws. (A possible issue is how common genetic defects are in children born to first cousins.)

Research Situation H:

Ms. Jane DePaul, your client and a resident of Cincinnati, Ohio, owns a pit bull terrier. She has owned him for nine years, since he was a puppy. Ms. DePaul monitors the dog quite carefully, given the breed's propensity toward biting. When she lets him out in the evening, she has him on a six-foot leash in her fenced yard. To her knowledge, the dog has never bitten or attacked anyone, until last night. Last night, after letting the dog out, Ms. De Paul heard loud screams from her backyard. Upon investigating, she found a man lurking under a window. She did not know him; he clearly was trespassing in her yard. The dog had bitten the man on the arm and was growling at him. When the dog heard Ms. DePaul's voice, he backed off, and the man fled. Although Ms. DePaul is relieved that the man left without harming her, she is concerned about any liability she may have toward him as a result of the bite. (A possible issue is whether pit bulls as a breed are inherently dangerous.)

Research Situation I:

Three years ago Robert and Rachel Boyd of Tucson, Arizona, adopted Roberta, when she was one month old. Only one of Roberta's natural parents, her unmarried mother, was a party to the adoption proceedings. Recently Roberta's putative biological father contacted the Boyds, telling them that he had not been informed of the adoption proceedings and had not consented to the adoption. He wants custody of his daughter. The Boyds want to know if he is likely to be able to get the judgment determining the child's status reversed. (A possible issue is how children are affected by custody fights between biological and adoptive parents.)

Research Situation J:

Mr. Jeff Zhu owns a small vineyard and winery located near Eugene, Washington. Over the years, Mr. Zhu discovered that the grapes grown on Ms. Shelly Kerner's sandy land, when mixed with his own grapes, produced a superior red wine. Hence, he entered into a contract with Ms. Kerner to buy a large quantity of next season's grapes. The contract stated that the grapes were to be grown on Ms. Kerner's sandy land. Ms. Kerner planted and cultivated the grapes in sufficient quantity to perform the contract, but an extraordinarily severe rain storm resulted in a flood that destroyed Ms. Kerner's vineyards. Ms. Kerner advised Mr. Zhu that it would then be impossible for her to perform the contract, and she thereafter delivered no grapes to him. Mr. Zhu claims that Ms. Kerner has breached the contract. Ms. Kerner wishes to know if she will be liable to Mr. Zhu or if delivery is excused under these circumstances. (A possible issue is how factors such as climate and soil conditions affect grape production by vineyards.)

Problem Set for Chapter 11. Nonlegal Materials

Your Name ______________________ Professor ______________________

Circle the letter of the research situation you selected (see pages 511-514):

A B C D E F G H I J

1. State one or more matters of general fact that you would like to be able to determine in order to analyze your research situation fully. By "matter of general fact," we do not mean a fact about your client's specific situation, but rather an observation about human behavior or events in nature.

____

____

____

2. **Optional Question:** Consult the *Guide to Reference Books* to learn about major research sources in the discipline that might study your factual issue. List here the discipline you looked up and the titles of the first two sources listed for that discipline.

____

____

____

3. You may research in whatever medium and source you find most appropriate and accessible for your factual question, such as paper indexes and journals, DIALOG, NEXIS, or the Internet. Describe your research process here:

(a) the medium and source you used (e.g., the DIALOG database)

____

____

(b) in general terms, the information that source made available to you (e.g., the types of journals and their dates)

____

____

(c) your research terms

____

____

(d) your use of those research terms (e.g., how you used an index, the successful search you entered in NEXIS)

____

____

____

4. Append to this problem set a print-out or photocopy of the first page of the most pertinent material you located. State here what you learned that might be useful in analyzing the research situation.

____

____

____

____

____

5. Provide the proper *Bluebook* citation to that material.

____

____

____

CHAPTER 12
RESEARCH
SITUATION

DEVELOPING AN INTEGRATED RESEARCH STRATEGY

Research Situation:

You represent Linh Hoang, who owns a real estate development company. Mr. Hoang is planning to build a new 120-unit apartment complex, Forest Glen, which will be located on the outskirts of the city near a beautiful forest preserve. The plans are not yet finalized, but the initial concept is to build the apartment complex in two phases of development. Each development phase will employ a different architectural scheme, and the units in each phase will be marketed somewhat differently. Phase 1 will contain one- and two-bedroom luxury apartments intended for occupancy by senior citizens. Phase 2 will contain efficiency and one-bedroom apartments marketed at a slightly lower rent, also intended for older adults. None of the apartments will be used for federal or state subsidized housing. As now planned, neither phase would be appropriate for families with children. Before the development plans are finalized, Mr. Hoang wants to be sure that he may legally develop a senior citizens complex that would exclude children.

Unless your professor instructs you otherwise, assume that the facts arise in your own state.

Problem Set for Chapter 12. Developing an Integrated Research Strategy

Your Name

____

Professor

____

Your research situation is stated at page 517.

Legal research in a practice setting requires you to integrate the skills discussed in this text: developing research terminology, using secondary sources for background and references, formulating issues to research in primary authority, researching those issues in various forms of primary authority, and incorporating nonlegal materials where appropriate. This problem set gives you the opportunity to combine these skills.

Unless your professor instructs you otherwise, prepare a "research log" for this situation by following the outline and instructions below. Append to your log the first page of each source you feature in your log.

I. Research Terms

Remember that there are five factual categories and three legal categories. Some of these may be more significant than others. Be sure to generate related terms (synonyms, antonyms, broader and narrower terms). Note the definitions of any terms you looked up in legal dictionaries, and include proper citations.

II. Secondary Sources

Locate and read three secondary sources on this topic. Examine a variety of sources, e.g., include a periodical article, encyclopedia, and treatise. As to each, present the following information:

A. its proper citation
B. the legal principle(s), rule(s), and definition(s) it presents
C. several references to pertinent primary authority it provides
D. the process you used to locate the source
E. ways you could or did update and expand the research in the source (if any)

III. Issue Formulation

State the issue(s) to be researched in primary authority. Be sure to link factual and legal concepts. If appropriate, use more than one issue or sub-issue to identify related points.

IV. Primary Authority

First, draw the following matrix, and check the boxes for the types of authority that address the research situation. **Note:** Given the nature and posture of the research situation, there is no need to explore rules of procedure or ethics.

	Federal	*State*
Case law		
Statutory law		
Agency regulations		
Agency decisions		

Second, for each major primary authority you locate through your research, present the following information:

A. its proper citation
B. the law stated in the authority, e.g., a case brief, an outline of a statute or regulation
C. references to other sources provided within the authority itself or the source in which you located the authority
D. the process you used to locate the authority
E. the process you used to verify that the authority is good law

Present as many authorities as you most likely would cite in a legal memorandum on this topic. In particular, you should include all pertinent statutes. You need not include every pertinent case because some cases duplicate others in terms of legal principles. Unless you are otherwise instructed, it is sufficient to present five important cases.

Third, if you locate a pertinent federal statute and discern an ambiguity in its language or application to the research situation, explore up to three documents of federal legislative history. For each, present the following information:

A. its proper citation
B. the guidance it provides
C. references to other sources provided within the document itself or the source in which you located the document
D. the process you used to locate the authority

V. Nonlegal Materials

It may be helpful to know nonlegal information about the availability of rental housing for families with children. Research that topic, and present the following information regarding your research:

A. the proper citation of a useful source
B. a synopsis of the information it provides
C. the process you used to locate that source

VI. Further Analysis

First, state any additional facts you need to learn from your client before you can complete your analysis of the situation (if any).

Second, state your legal analysis of the research situation based on the facts you now know.

Third, state the recommendations you would make to your client based on what you now know.

INDEX